**Steven Erikson** is a qualified archaeologist and anthropologist. His debut fantasy novel, *Gardens of the Moon*, was shortlisted for the World Fantasy Award and introduced readers to his epic, ten-book 'Malazan Book of the Fallen' sequence, which has been hailed 'a masterwork of the imagination'. He has also written a number of novellas set in the same fantasy world and *Willful Child*, an affectionate parody of a long-running science-fiction television series. He followed this with *Forge of Darkness*, the first volume in a new epic fantasy trilogy which takes readers back to the origins of the Malazan world. *Fall of Light* continues this epic tale. Steven Erikson lives in Victoria, Canada.

To find out more, visit www.malazanempire.com and www.steven-erikson.com

## Acclaim for Steven Erikson

'Erikson is an extraordinary writer . . . my advice to anyone who might listen to me is: treat yourself' STEPHEN R. DONALDSON

'A master of lost and forgotten epochs, a weaver of ancient epics' SALON.COM

'Brilliant . . . we all wondered how Erikson could possibly follow up arguably the best fantasy series of all time. *Forge of Darkness* will dispel any and all doubters (if any do indeed still exist out there) that Steven Erikson is the best writer on the planet' SF SITE

'This masterwork of the imagination may be the high watermark of epic fantasy' GLEN COOK

'Arguably the best fantasy series ever written . . . the quality and ambition of the ten books that make up *The Malazan Book of the Fallen* are unmatched within the genre' FANTASYBOOKREVIEW

'Nobody does it better than Erikson . . . the best fantasy series around' SFFWORLD

'Erikson's strengths are his grown-up characters and his ability to create a world every bit as intricate and messy as our own' J. V. JONES

'Erikson's magnum opus, *The Malazan Book of the Fallen*, sits in pole position as the very best and most ambitious epic fantasy saga ever written' FANTASYHOTLIST

'Erikson is almost in a league of his own in genre fiction terms – by turns lyrical, bawdy, introspective, poetical and blood-soaked . . . incredible'  BOOKGEEKS

'Erikson is able to create a world that is both absorbing on a human level and full of magical sublimity . . . A wonderfully grand conception . . . splendidly written . . . fiendishly readable'  ADAM ROBERTS

'It's not just the vast imaginative sweep but the quality of prose that lifts the Malazan sequence above the usual run of heroic fantasy'  *SFX*

'One of the most original and engrossing fantasy series of recent times'  *INTERZONE*

*Also by Steven Erikson*

WILLFUL CHILD
THIS RIVER AWAKENS

*The Malazan Book of the Fallen*
GARDENS OF THE MOON
DEADHOUSE GATES
MEMORIES OF ICE
HOUSE OF CHAINS
MIDNIGHT TIDES
THE BONEHUNTERS
REAPER'S GALE
TOLL THE HOUNDS
DUST OF DREAMS
THE CRIPPLED GOD

THE FIRST COLLECTED TALES OF
BAUCHELAIN AND KORBAL BROACH

*The Kharkanas Trilogy*
FORGE OF DARKNESS
FALL OF LIGHT

*and published by Bantam Books*

# FALL OF LIGHT

## The second book in the Kharkanas Trilogy

Steven Erikson

**BANTAM BOOKS**

LONDON • TORONTO • SYDNEY • AUCKLAND • JOHANNESBURG

TRANSWORLD PUBLISHERS
61–63 Uxbridge Road, London W5 5SA
www.penguin.co.uk

Transworld is part of the Penguin Random House group of companies
whose addresses can be found at global.penguinrandomhouse.com

First published in Great Britain in 2016 by Bantam Press
an imprint of Transworld Publishers
Bantam edition published 2017

A CIP catalogue record for this book
is available from the British Library.

ISBN
9780553820133 (B format)
9780857503381 (A format)

Typeset in 10.5/12pt Sabon by Falcon Oast Graphic Art Ltd.
Printed and bound by Clays Ltd, Bungay, Suffolk.

Penguin Random House is committed to a sustainable
future for our business, our readers and our planet. This book is made from
Forest Stewardship Council® certified paper.

1 3 5 7 9 10 8 6 4 2

To Howard Morhaim

# Contents

# Acknowledgements

Thanks to advance readers: A. P. Canavan, Steve Diamond, Baria Ahmed, Judith Collins and Sharon Sasaki. This one took awhile and your patience is much appreciated. Thanks, as ever, to Clare Thomas, Simon Taylor, and Howard Morhaim.

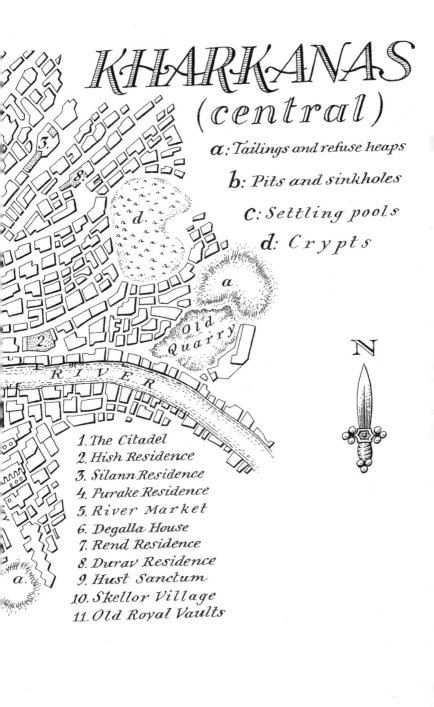

# KHARKANAS
## (central)

*a*: Tailings and refuse heaps

*b*: Pits and sinkholes

*c*: Settling pools

*d*: Crypts

N

1. The Citadel
2. Hish Residence
3. Silann Residence
4. Purake Residence
5. River Market
6. Degalla House
7. Rend Residence
8. Durav Residence
9. Hust Sanctum
10. Skellor Village
11. Old Royal Vaults

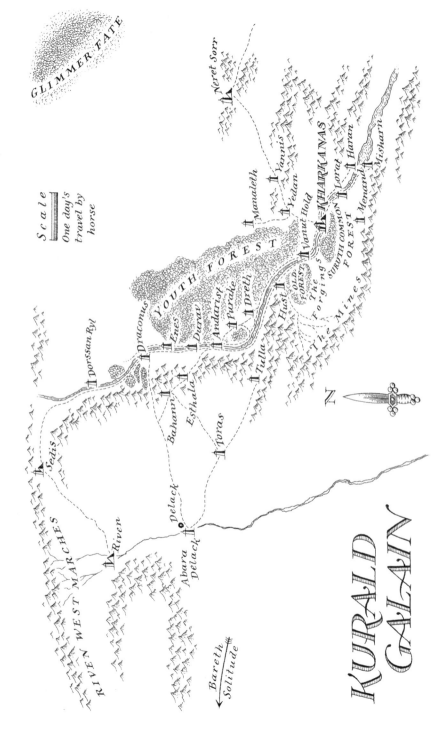

GLIMMER FATE

Neret Sorr

Scale

One day's travel by horse

Dorssan Ryl

YOUTH FOREST

Manaleth

Yannis

Yedan

KHARKANAS

Vanut Hold

Lorat

Haran

Dracones

Enes

Dirav

Andarist

Thurake

Preth

OLD FOREST

The

Forgings

SURETH COMMON

FOREST

Menanl

Mishar'n

Sedis

Bahann

Hust

Esthala

Tulla

The Mines

N

Toras

River

RIVEN WEST MARCHES

Delack

Abara
Delack

Bareth
Solitude

KURALD
GALAIN

# THEL AKAI, JAGHUT, TISTE REALMS

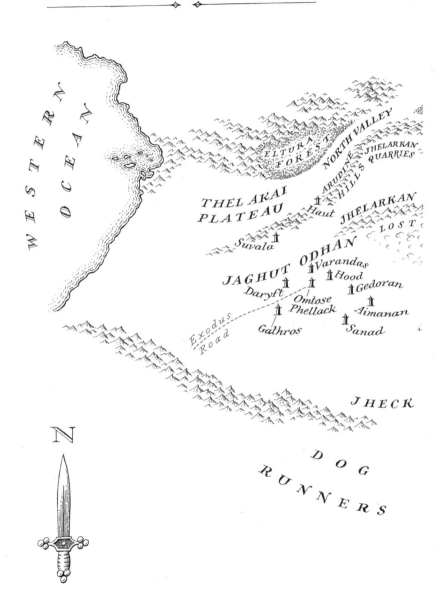

# DRAMATIS PERSONAE

*PURAKE HOLD*

Anomander
Andarist
Silchas Ruin
Kellaras
Prazek
Dathenar

*TULLA HOLD*

Hish Tulla
Venes Turayd
Rancept
Sukul Ankhadu (hostage)
Gripp Galas

*DRETH HOLD*

Drethdenan
Horult Chiv
Sekarrow

## DRACONS HOLD

Draconus
Spite
Envy
Ivis
Yalad
Sandalath Drukorlat (hostage)

## HOUSE DURAV

Spinnock Durav
Faror Hend

## VANUT HOLD

Lady Degalla
Jureg Thaw
Lord Vanut Degalla
Syl Lebanas

## THE CITADEL AND PRIESTHOOD

Mother Dark
Emral Lanear
Endest Silann
Cedorpul Ahras
Rise Herat
Orfantal
Ribs

## HUST

*The Forge Works*
Hust Henarald

*The Hust Legion*
Toras Redone
Galar Baras
Seltin Ryggandas

## THE SHAKE

*The Yannis Monastery*
Sheccanto Derran
Warlock Resh
Caplo Dreem

*The Yedan Monastery*
Higher Grace Skelenal
Witch Ruvera

## URUSANDER'S LEGION

Scara Bandaris
Ilgast Rend
Esthala
Kagamandra Tulas (Shorn)
Tathe Lorat
Sheltatha Lore
Infayen Menand
Sharenas Ankhadu
Hallyd Bahann
Sagander

## THE BORDERSWORDS

Lahanis

## THE DENIERS

Wreneck
Narad
Glyph

## THE PRISONERS

Wareth
Listar
Rebble
Rance

## THE WARDENS

Calat Hustain
Faror Hend
Spinnock Durav
Bursa
Finarra Stone

## NERET SORR (TOWN OF)

Vatha Urusander
Hunn Raal
Serap
Sevegg
Renarr
Syntara

# The Tiste: Holds, Greater and Lesser Houses, Priesthood and Court

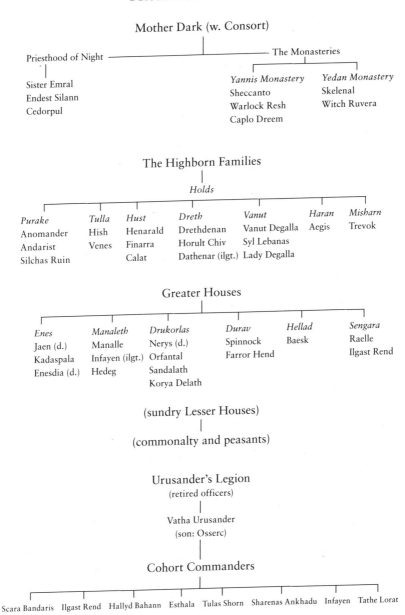

Mother Dark (w. Consort)

Priesthood of Night — The Monasteries

Sister Emral
Endest Silann
Cedorpul

*Yannis Monastery*
Sheccanto
Warlock Resh
Caplo Dreem

*Yedan Monastery*
Skelenal
Witch Ruvera

## The Highborn Families

*Holds*

*Purake*
Anomander
Andarist
Silchas Ruin

*Tulla*
Hish
Venes

*Hust*
Henarald
Finarra
Calat

*Dreth*
Drethdenan
Horult Chiv
Dathenar (ilgt.)

*Vanut*
Vanut Degalla
Syl Lebanas
Lady Degalla

*Haran*
Aegis

*Misharn*
Trevok

## Greater Houses

*Enes*
Jaen (d.)
Kadaspala
Enesdia (d.)

*Manaleth*
Manalle
Infayen (ilgt.)
Hedeg

*Drukorlas*
Nerys (d.)
Orfantal
Sandalath
Korya Delath

*Durav*
Spinnock
Farror Hend

*Hellad*
Baesk

*Sengara*
Raelle
Ilgast Rend

(sundry Lesser Houses)

(commonalty and peasants)

## Urusander's Legion
### (retired officers)

Vatha Urusander
(son: Osserc)

## Cohort Commanders

Scara Bandaris   Ilgast Rend   Hallyd Bahann   Esthala   Tulas Shorn   Sharenas Ankhadu   Infayen   Tathe Lorat

# BOOK ONE

---

*The Seduction of Tragedy*

*S*O THEY LUST FOR BLOOD. POETS KNOW ITS TASTE, BUT SOME *know it better than others. A few are known to choke on it. Stand at a distance, then, and make violence into a dance. Glory in its sounds, in the mayhem and those stern expressions that seem better suited to an unpleasant task completed with reluctant forbearance. There is for the audience that glee of admiration in the well-swung sword, the perfect thrust, the cold, professional face with the flat eyes. Revel, then, in the strut, and see something enticing in the grim camaraderie of failed men and women—*

*Failed? You say many do not see that? Oh dear.*

*Shall I then offer up the reek of shit and piss? The cries for loved ones far away? The hopeless longing for a mother's embrace to ease the pain and the terror, to bless the gentle slowing of the hammering heart? Shall I describe the true faces of violence? The twist of fear, the heaviness of dread, the panic that rushes in a surge of blood, a surge that drains the visage and bulges the eyes? But what value any of this, when to feel is to acknowledge the frailty of one's own soul, and such frailty must ever be denied in the public swagger that so many find essential, lest they lose grip.*

*Indeed, I would think armour itself whispers of weakness. Tug free the helm's strap, let your scalp prickle in the cool air. Strip down until you stand naked, and let's see again that swagger.*

There are poets who glory in their recounts of battle, of all those struggles so deftly ritualized. And they tend lovingly their garden of words, heaping high the harvest of glory, duty, courage and honour. But each of those luscious, stirring words is plucked from the same vine, and alas, it is a poisonous one. Name it necessity, and look well upon its spun strands, its fibrous belligerence.

Necessity. The soldiers attack, but they attack in order to defend. Those they face stand firm, and they stand firm to defend as well. The foes are waging war in self-defence. Consider this, I beg you. Consider this well and consider this long. Choose a cool dusk, with the air motionless, with dampness upon the ground. Draw away from all company and stand alone, watching the dying sun, watching the night sky awaken above you, and give your thoughts to necessity.

The hunter knows it. The prey knows it. But on a field of battle, when every life totters in the balance, where childhoods, begun long ago, and youthful days suddenly past, have all, impossibly, insanely, led to this day. This fight. This wretched span of killing and dying. Was this the cause your father and mother dreamed of, for you? Was this the reason for raising you, protecting you, feeding you, loving you?

What, in the name of all the gods above and below, are you doing here?

Necessity, when spoken of in the forum of human endeavour, is more often a lie than not. Those who have laid claim to your life will use it often, and yet hold you at a distance, refusing you that time of contemplation, or, indeed, recognition. If you come to see the falseness of their claim, all is lost. Necessity: the lie hiding behind the true virtues of courage and honour – they make you drunk on those words, and would keep you that way, until comes the time for you to bleed for them.

The poet who glories in war is a spinner of lies. The poet who delights in visceral detail, for the sole purpose of feeding that lust for blood, has all the depth of a puddle of piss on the ground.

Oh, have done with it, then.

# ONE

STEPPING OUT FROM THE TENT, RENARR FACED THE bright morning light, and did not blink. Behind her, on the other side of the canvas wall, the men and women were rising from their furs, voicing bitter complaints at the damp chill, snapping at the children to hurry with the hot, spiced wine. Within the tent, the air had been thick with the fug of lovemaking, the rank sweat of the soldiers now gone, the metallic bite of the oils with which the soldiers honed weapons and worked to keep leather supple, the breaths of drunkards and the faint undercurrent of vomit. But out here those smells were quickly swept away, clearing her head as she watched the camp stir awake.

She took coin no different from the other whores, although she did not need it. She made her false moans and moved beneath a man like a woman both eager and hungry, and when they shuddered, emptying their hoards into her and becoming weak and childlike, she held them as would a mother. In every way, then, she was the same as the others. Yet they kept her apart, forever pushed away from their close company. She was the adopted daughter of Lord Urusander, after all, Legion Commander and reluctant holder of the title of Father Light, and this was a privilege worthy of dreams, and if flower petals were scattered in her wake, they were the colour of blood. She had no friends. She had no followers.

The company she kept had all the warmth of a murder of crows.

There was frost silvering the tufts of grass between the tents and the ground was frozen hard underfoot. The smoke rising from the cookfires did not rise far, drifting like confusion about the heads of the soldiers as they readied their gear.

She could see, in their agitated gestures, in the nerves betrayed by fumbling at buckles and the like, and could hear, in the surly tones of their conversations, that many now believed that this would be the day. A battle was coming, marking the beginning of the civil war. If she turned to her left, and could make her vision cut through the hillside to the northeast, through the unlit tumble of stone and earth and root and then out again into the morning light, she would see the camp of the Wardens, a camp little different from this one, barring these snow-burnished skins and hair now the hue of spun gold. And in that other camp's centre, on a standard rising from the command tent, she would make out the heraldry of Lord Ilgast Rend.

The day felt reluctant, but in an ironic way, like a woman feigning resistance on her first night, with rough hands pushing her thighs apart, the air then filling with its share of harsh breaths, ecstatic moans and clumsy grunts. And when it was all done with, amidst deep pools of satisfied heat, there would be blood on the grass.

*Just so. And as Hunn Raal would say, had he the wits, justice is a sharp-edged thing and today it will be unsheathed, and wielded with a firm hand. The reluctance is an illusion, and as only Osserc knows, my resistance was indeed feigned, the day Urusander's son took me to rough bed. We are awash in lies.*

Of course, it was equally likely that Lord Urusander would defy this seemingly inevitable destiny. Bind the woman's legs together, securing a chastity belt with thorns on both sides, to refuse satisfaction from either direction. He might well ruin things for everyone.

So, in its more prosaic details – the frost, the faint but icy wind, the plumes of breath and smoke, the distant neighing of horses and the occasional bray of a pack-mule; all the sounds of a day's dawning in the company of men, women, children and beasts – she could, if unmindful, believe the stream of life to be unbroken, with all its promise arrayed before it, bright as the morning sun.

She drew her cloak about her rounded shoulders, and set out through the camp. She passed between tent rows, stepping carefully to avoid the ropes and stakes, taking caution on the furrows that cut diagonally across her path, and the stubble left behind by the harvesting only a week past. She skirted the trenches carved deep into the soil where wastes floated on the sluggish surface of murky water, along with the bloated carcasses of rats. By mid-afternoon, when the sun warmed the air enough, mosquitoes would arrive in thick, spinning clouds, thirsty for blood. If soldiers stood arrayed in ranks, facing the enemy, there would be little comfort preceding the clash of weapons.

Though her mother had been a captain in the Legion, Renarr had little sense of the makings and leavings of war. For her, it was a force that had, until now, been locked in her past: a realm of sudden absences, hollow with losses and ill luck, where even sorrow felt cool to the touch. It was a place somewhere else, and to give it any thought was to feel as if she was stealing a stranger's memories. The veterans she took to her furs had known that realm, and each night, as the prospect of battle drew closer, she sensed in them a vague weariness, a kind of fatalism, dulling their eyes and stealing away what few words they were inclined to utter. And when they made love, it seemed an act of shame.

*My mother died on a field of battle. She woke to a morning like this one, settling bleak eyes upon what the day would bring. Did she taste her death on the air? Did she see a vision of her rotting corpse, there in her own shadow? And would she have known, by sight, the weapon that would cut her down – a blinding flash drawing closer through the press? Did she look into the glaring eyes of her slayer, and see in them her death writ plain?*

*Or was she no different, on that morning, from every other fool in her company?*

The questions seemed banal, like things covered in dust, the dust shaken free, blown into the air by a heavy but meaningless sigh. Renarr was not born to take sword in hand. The knife in its thin leather sheath at her hip was modest in its pragmatic necessity. She was not yet ready to imagine drawing it. As she walked, unburnished, her skin as yet unblessed by whiteness, soldiers surrounded her, and in the bright light, which rose like another world, a world unlike the night before, she was deftly ignored, seen but not seen, and the sight of her, if it yielded anything at all, raised surely little more than a pang of regret – the soft feel of her flesh, the weight she carried that surprised every man she straddled in the dark. None of these things were relevant now.

But there was power to be found nonetheless: the cheap woman as harbinger of regret, making faces turn away, making strong men bend to some task, frowns cascading on their bared brows. The pleasures of flesh made but a sharp fold in the sensations of life, and upon its opposite side that flesh knew pain and terrible damage. In a careless moment, one could mistake the stains of one for the other.

She was the reminder they did not want, not here and not now, and so she walked unaccosted, too solid to be a ghost, but shunned all the same. Of course, this could perhaps be said of all ghosts – the living ones at least – and if so, then the world was full of them, solid but not quite solid enough, and each day they wandered unseen, dreaming of a future moment, imagining their one perfect gesture that would yield in everyone the delicious shock of recognition.

The banner of the command tent, the golden sun in its blue field, was directly ahead now, and as she drew nearer she noted the gap surrounding that tent, as if some invisible barrier occupied the space. No soldiers edged closer and those that she could see, there on the periphery, were all turned away. Moments later, she could make out shouting from within, the harsh bark of anger, bridling: the voice of Vatha Urusander, commander of the Legion and her adoptive father.

Those who might have replied to Urusander spoke in low tones, with murmurs that failed in passing through canvas walls, and so it seemed as if their lord was arguing with himself, like a madman at war with the voices in his head. For a brief instant, Renarr imagined him alone in the command tent. And in she would stride, to witness his decrepit ignominy. She saw herself observing, strangely unaffected, as he swung to her a confused, baffled face. Then the moment passed and she approached the entrance, where the stained flap hung down like a beggar's blanket.

She was still a half-dozen strides from the tent when she saw that flap stir and then buckle to one side. Captain Hunn Raal emerged, drawing on his leather gauntlets as he straightened. His face was red beneath the bleached mask of his miraculous transformation, but then, it was always red. Pausing, he glanced around, gaze momentarily fixing on Renarr, who had slowed her steps. One of his cousins appeared behind him, Sevegg, and upon her round, chalky face there was a subtle flash of expression, which might have been pleasure, that then curled into a sneer when she saw Renarr.

Nudging her cousin, Sevegg stepped to one side and sketched a mocking bow. 'If you ache on this chill morning, dear girl,' she said, 'winter is not to blame.'

'I am well beyond aching,' Renarr replied, moving past.

But Hunn Raal reached out and touched her shoulder.

She halted, faced him.

'I think he would not delight in seeing you, Renarr,' the captain said, studying her with his bloodshot eyes. 'How many cloaks of defeat can one man wear?'

'You smell of wine,' Renarr replied.

She drew aside the flap and strode into the tent.

Their lord was not alone. Looking tired, Lieutenant Serap – two years older than her sister, Sevegg, and a stone heavier – sat to the man's left, in a battered camp-chair little different from the one bearing Urusander's weight. The map table was set up in the centre of the chamber, but it stood askew, as if it had been shoved or kicked. On its battered surface, the vellum map denoting the immediate area had pulled loose from its anchor stones on one end and the corners had curled up and around, as if eager to hide what it revealed.

With skin so white as to be almost glowing, Renarr's adoptive father was staring at the muddy canvas floor beyond his equally muddy boots. There was gold in his long hair now, streaking the silver. Virtually all among the Legion were now white-skinned.

Serap, her expression grave, cleared her throat and said, 'Good morning, Renarr.'

As soon as she began speaking, Urusander stood, grunting under his breath. 'Too many aches,' he muttered. 'Memories awaken in the bones first, and send pain to every muscle, and all this serves to remind a man of the years behind him.' Ignoring his adopted daughter, the lord faced Serap and seemed to study her quizzically for a moment. 'You've not seen my portrait yet, have you?'

Renarr saw the lieutenant blink, as if in surprise. 'No, milord, although I am told Kadaspala's talent was—'

'His talent?' Urusander bared his teeth in a humourless smile. 'Oh indeed, let us speak of his talent, shall we? Eye wedded to hand. Deft strokes of genius. And in this, my likeness is well captured in thinnest paint. You can look upon my face, on that canvas, Serap, and tell yourself how perfectly it renders depth, as if I stood in a world you could step into. And yet draw close, if you dare, and you'll find my face is naught but paint, thin as skin, with nothing behind it.' His smile was strained now. 'Nothing at all.'

'Milord, no painting can do other than that.'

'No. In any case, the portrait awaits a washing of white now, yes? Perhaps a sculpture, then? Some Azathanai artisan with the usual immeasurable talent. Dust on his hands and a chisel that shouts. But then, whenever has pure marble revealed the truth beneath the surface? The aches, the strains, the twinges springing from nowhere, as if every thread of nerve within has forgotten its own health.' Sighing, he faced the entrance. 'Even marble pits with time. Lieutenant, I am done with Hunn Raal on this day, and all matters of campaign. Do not seek me out and send no messenger in search – I am going for a walk.'

'Very well, milord.'

He strode from the tent.

Renarr walked over to the chair Urusander had vacated and settled in it. The heat of him remained on the leather saddle.

'He'll not acknowledge you in this state,' Serap said. 'You have fallen far and fast, Renarr.'

'I am a ghost.'

'The ghost of regret for Lord Urusander. You appear as the underside of your mother, like a turned stone, and where all we saw of her was in sunlight, you are nothing but darkness.'

Renarr held out her right arm and studied the not quite pearlescent skin. 'Stained marble, not yet gnawed by age. Naked, you are like snow. But I am not.'

'It comes to you,' Serap said. 'But slowly, to mark the reluctance of your faith.'

'Is that it? I but wear my hesitation?'

'At least our enemies wear their blight for all to see.'

Renarr dropped her arm. 'Take him to your furs,' she said. 'His aches, his twinges – drive away his thoughts of mortality.'

Serap made a disgusted sound, and then asked, 'Is that what you glimpse each night, Renarr? In that uncaring face hovering above your own? Some faint flush of immortality, like a rose in a desert?'

Renarr shrugged. 'He's made his flesh a sack of faults. Untie the knot, lieutenant.'

'For the good of the Legion?'

'If your conscience needs a salve.'

'Conscience. That's a word I'd not thought to hear from you.' Serap waved a hand in dismissal. 'Today, it will be Hunn Raal leading the Legion. Out to parley with Lord Ilgast Rend. This madness needs to end.'

'Oh yes, and he's a man of constraint, is our Hunn Raal.'

'Raal is given his orders, and we were witness to them.

31

Urusander fears arriving at the head of his legion will prove too provocative on this day. He will not invite public argument between himself and Lord Ilgast Rend.'

Renarr shot the woman a quick glance, then looked away again. 'Trust Hunn Raal to make this argument public, if we are to descend into euphemisms for battle.'

Shaking her head, Serap said, 'If weapons are drawn this day, they will come first from Ilgast Rend and his misfit Wardens.'

'Jabbed by insult and driven to a corner by Hunn Raal's smirking visage, I would say what you describe is inevitable.'

The woman's fine brows lifted. 'A whore and seer both. Well done. You have achieved what Mother Dark's priestesses yearn for as they thrash through the night. Shall I send you to Daughter Light, then, as her first acolyte in kind?'

'Yes, that is indeed the name Syntara has chosen for herself. Daughter Light. I always thought it a presumption. Oh, and now of you, too, in assuming you have the right to send me anywhere.'

'Forgive my transgression, Renarr. There is a tutor in the camp – have you seen him? The man lacks a leg. Perhaps he would take you under his care. I shall suggest it to Urusander when next I see him.'

'You mean Sagander, fled from House Dracons,' Renarr replied, indifferent to the threat. 'The whores speak of him. But he already has a child he deems to teach. The daughter of Tathe Lorat, or so I am told. Sheltatha Lore, upon whom he leans, like a man crippled by self-pity.'

Serap's eyes hardened. 'Sheltatha? That's a rumour I have not yet heard.'

'You do not consort with camp-followers and whores. Well, not regularly,' she added with a small smile. 'In any case, I have had my fill of tutors. Too many years of that, and oh how delicately they treated the daughter of a dead hero.'

'They did not fail in honing your wit, Renarr, although I doubt any would take pride in the woman they created.'

'More than a few come to mind who would happily

share my furs and consider sweet their belated reward.'

Snorting, Serap arose. 'What did you come here to witness, Renarr? This is your first time to your father's command tent since we left Neret Sorr.'

'I needed to remind him,' Renarr replied. 'While I remain unseen to his eyes, still he steps around me.'

'You are his anguish.'

'I have plenty of company in that, lieutenant.'

'And now?'

'Now, I will join my giggling companions, atop a hill from which to watch the battle. We'll fix corbie eyes on the field below, and talk of bloodied rings and brooches.'

She felt the woman's eyes upon her for some time, a full four or five breaths, and then Serap exited the tent, leaving Renarr alone.

Rising, she approached the map table, replacing the anchor stones to force down the curled edges of the map. Then she leaned over it and studied the thin inked lines denoting the terrain. 'Ah, that hill there, then, should do us well on this day.' *Conversations of greed with glinting eyes. Sharp laughter and cackling, crude jests, and if the men and women we took last night soon lie cold and still in the mud of the valley below, well, there will always be others to take their place.*

*Avarice makes whores of us all.*

\*     \*     \*

Captain Havaral rode at a canter down the slope, the wind skirling dead leaves across his path. The broad basin of the valley ahead was not quite as level as he would have liked, with a slight climb favouring the enemy. From the crest of the rise behind him, where Ilgast Rend had arrayed his army of Wardens, the lie of the land here had seemed more or less ideal, but now he found himself picking his way around sink-holes hidden by knots of leafless brush and small, twisted trees, and here and there thin but deep run-off tracks crooked their way downward, inviting a horse's ankle and then the sickening *snap* of bones. The Wardens were a mounted force,

33

relying upon speed and mobility. What he was seeing of this slope troubled him.

He had been a Warden all his adult life, and had in Calat Hustain's absence often taken overall command as senior officer. It was not easy to simply shrug off his sense of betrayal in learning that Lord Ilgast Rend had supplanted him in this responsibility, but he would follow orders nonetheless, without a word of complaint, nor an instant's resentment in his expression. Personal slights were the least of his worries this morning, in any case. That the Wardens had marched on Urusander; that he and his companions were now preparing for battle, all for the sake of a few hundred slaughtered peasants in the forests, was, to his mind, utter madness.

To make matters worse, they had no reliable intelligence on the Legion's complement. Was it fully assembled? Or was it, as Rend clearly believed, yet to achieve that? Pragmatic concerns, these. On this day they could find themselves facing the full might of Urusander's Legion.

*Civil war. I refused to think on it. I stripped the hides off my Wardens whenever they even so much as hinted at it. Now here I am, an old fool, laid siege to by knowing looks. Best hope, then, that I've not burned the last vestiges of respect among my soldiers. Nothing fashions a fool quicker than a hollow tirade.*

But even fools could possess courage. They would follow his orders. To think otherwise was inconceivable.

For the moment he rode alone, watched by fifteen hundred of his kin, carrying to Lord Urusander an invitation to private parley with Ilgast Rend. This battle could still be prevented. Peace could be carved out of this misshapen mess, and to yearn for that was not a failing of courage. It was, in truth, a desperate grasp for the last vestiges of wisdom.

How would Urusander fare in the face of Lord Rend's fury? That would be a scene worth witnessing, if only through a pinprick hole in the tent's back wall. Not that such a thing was even possible. The two men would meet alone, and it was unlikely that their voices would carry enough to be heard by anyone outside.

He was halfway across the basin when he saw a troop of riders appear on the opposite crest.

Havaral frowned, his mount momentarily losing its way as he unconsciously slackened the reins.

The banner did not belong to Vatha Urusander. Instead, the standard-bearer was displaying the colours of the Legion's First Cohort.

*Hunn Raal. Have we not had enough of that man?*

The insult was plain, and Havaral found himself hesitating. Then he silently berated himself. *No, not for me. I am neither Calat Hustain nor Ilgast Rend. I have no right to wear this affront. Besides, Urusander might be awaiting word, and but sends his captain just as Rend has sent me.* The notion sounded convincing in his head, provided he did not direct too much scrutiny its way. Kicking his mount forward, with renewed assurance, he continued on, heading directly for the delegation.

Sevegg rode beside her cousin, and the others in Raal's company were the same lackeys who had accompanied him on their visit to the camp of the Wardens. The truth of the rumours was plain to Havaral's eyes. They were transformed, their skins like alabaster. Still, seeing this miraculous blessing of Light was a shock. They rode with arrogance, with the air of believing themselves privy to dangerous secrets and so worthy of both fear and respect. Like so many soldiers, they were worse than children.

The air tasted bitter, and Havaral struggled not to spit.

In crass announcement of discourtesy or bold contempt, they reined in first, to await his arrival.

The wind was building, cutting down the length of the basin, spinning leaves around the ankles of the horses and making them skittish, and already clouds of mosquitoes lifted up from the grasses to swarm in the shelter of soldier and mount.

As Havaral drew up before them, Sevegg was the first to speak. 'Ilgast sends an old man to greet us? We can hardly call you a veteran, can we? Wardens are not soldiers. Never were, as you shall soon discover.'

Hunn Raal held up a hand to forestall any further commentary from his cousin. 'Captain Havaral, isn't it? Welcome. The morning is chilly, is it not? The kind that settles into your bones.'

*And that was meant to soften my resolve? Vitr take me, man, you are not even sober.* 'I bring word from Lord Ilgast Rend,' Havaral said, fixing his gaze on Raal's reddened eyes made ghastly against the white skin. 'He seeks private parley with Lord Vatha Urusander.'

'I am sorry, then, my friend,' said Hunn Raal, the secret smile of drunks playing about his thin lips. 'That is not possible. My commander has instructed me to speak in his stead. That said, I am happy to parley with Lord Rend. Although, I think, not in private. Advisers are useful in such circumstances.'

'Bodyguards, you mean? Or assassins?'

'Neither, I am sure,' Hunn Raal said, with a short easy laugh. 'It seems your commander esteems his life of greater import than is warranted. Nor am I inclined to feel in any way threatened by his close proximity.'

'The pride of the highborn,' Sevegg said, shaking her head as if in disbelief. 'Wave him down here, captain, and let's get on with it. Since he would play the soldier again, remind him of our plain ways.'

'Enough of that, cousin,' Hunn Raal said. 'See how this man pales.'

Havaral collected the reins. 'What you invite upon yourselves on this day, sirs, is a stain of infamy that even *your* skins cannot hide. May you ever wear it in shame.' Swinging his mount around, he set off back across the basin.

As they watched him ride away, Sevegg said, 'Dear cousin, do let me cut him down, I beg you.'

Hunn Raal shook his head. 'Save the bloodlust, dear. We leave Rend to unleash his rage, thus provoking the battle to come. By this means, cousin, we are absolved of the consequences.'

'Then I will find that old man on the field, and take his life.'

'He was no more than a messenger,' Hunn Raal said.

'I saw hate in his eyes.'

'You stung it awake, cousin.'

'The slur in sending him to us belongs to Lord Ilgast Rend, I'll grant you. But I see nothing to respect among the Wardens. If only it was Calat Hustain leading them.'

Her cousin snorted. 'Dear fool, Calat would never have brought them to us in the first place.'

She said nothing for a moment, and then managed a dismissive shrug. 'We're saved the march, then.'

'Yes.'

At Hunn Raal's lead, they pulled their horses round and set off, back the way they had come. The mosquitoes swept in pursuit, but were soon outdistanced.

*　　*　　*

The morning lengthened, gathering its own violence with a sharp, buffeting wind that flattened the grasses on the hill where Renarr stood, a short distance from the other men and women. Behind them, on this island of ill desires, the orphaned children who had, in no official manner, adopted the score or so whores who shared this particular tent ran and laughed and cursed the frenzied insects. Some were building a fire from a few ragged dung-chips, in the hope that the smoke would send the bugs away, but such fuel offered up little in the way of relief. Others lit pipes if they could beg the rustleaf from a favoured whore. Those who could not simply stuffed grass into the bowls. Their wretched coughing triggered gales of piping laughter.

Whores from other tents were appearing along the hilltop, a few shouting insults across the gaps. The rival groups of children began throwing stones at one another. The day's first blood was drawn when a sharp rock caught a girl on the temple, adding to her facial scars. In fury she charged the boy who had thrown the rock and he fled squealing.

Renarr watched with all the others as boy and girl ran down the slope.

To the right, Hunn Raal had drawn up his own cohort,

although the ancient title was misplaced, as each cohort of Urusander's Legion now comprised a full thousand soldiers. This was the force Raal offered up to the measure of Ilgast Rend and his Wardens, who were arrayed on the valley's opposite ridgeline. Unseen by the Wardens and their lord, two flanking cohorts waited on the back-slope, with units of lightly armoured cavalry among the foot soldiers.

Along the crest, she could see, pikes were being readied in the six-deep line behind Hunn Raal and his officers, and she understood such weapons to be the best suited when facing cavalry. A few hundred skirmishers were moving down the slope, armed with javelins. Some of these shouted now at the two children, warning them off, but neither reacted, and the girl's long legs were closing the gap between her and the smaller boy, whose laughter was gone, and who ran in earnest.

Renarr could see how the blood now covered one half of the girl's face.

The boy made a sharp turn moments before she reached him, rushing out towards the distant enemy.

Catching up again, the girl pushed with both arms, sending the boy tumbling. He rolled and sought to regain his feet but she was quicker, driving him down with her knees, and only now did Renarr see the large rock in her right hand.

The shouts from the skirmishers fell away, as the girl brought the stone down on the boy's head, again and again. The waving arms and kicking legs of the boy flopped out to the sides and did not move as the girl continued driving the rock down.

'Pay up, Srilla!' cried one of the whores. 'I took your wager, so pay up!'

Renarr pulled her robe tighter about herself. She saw a skirmisher move nearer the girl, and say something to her. When it was clear that she was not hearing his words, he edged closer and cuffed the side of her head. Dropping his javelin, he grasped the girl's arms and forced the bloodied stone from her small hands. Then he shoved her away.

She stumbled off, looking up and seeing, as if for the first time, where her hunt had taken her. Once again her long legs flashed as she ran back towards her hill, but she ran as one drunk on wine.

The body of the boy was small and bedraggled, spread-eagled like the remnant of some grisly sacrifice, and the skirmishers gave it a wide berth as they advanced.

'Now that's the way to start a war!' the whore cried, holding up a fist clutching her winnings.

*　　*　　*

The captains and their messengers clustered around Lord Ilgast Rend. For all that the nobleborn commander looked solid, heavy in his well-worn armour and bearing a visage betraying nothing but confidence as he sat astride his war-horse, Havaral fought against a cold dread. There was a hollow pit in his gut that no bravado could fill.

He remained at the outer edge of this cluster of officers, with Sergeant Kullis at his side, to act as a rider and flag-crier once the orders were given.

Flat-faced and dour, Kullis was a man of few words, so when he spoke Havaral was startled. 'It is said every army is like a body, a thing of flesh, bone and blood. And of course, the one who commands can be said to be its head, its brain.' The sergeant's voice was pitched low. It was unlikely that anyone else could make out his words.

'This is not the time, sergeant,' Havaral said in a soft growl, 'to raise matters of faith.'

As if unwilling to be dissuaded, Kullis continued, 'But an army also possesses a heart, a slow-beating drum in the very centre of its chest. A true commander knows that he or she must command that first, before all else.'

'Kullis, that will be enough.'

'Today, sir, the heart commands the head.'

The sergeant's methodical thinking had made slow and measured steps, arriving at a truth Havaral had understood with the man's first words. Lord Ilgast Rend was too angry, and the drumbeat's ever quickening pace had brought them headlong to this ridge, beneath this cold morning sky. The enemy facing them here were, one and all, heroes of Kurald Galain. Worse, they had not marched on the Wardens, and so had offered no direct provocation.

*It will be simple, then, to set the charge of this civil war's beginning at the feet of Lord Ilgast Rend. And us Wardens.*

'We wonder, sir,' Kullis then said, turning to look upon his captain, 'when you will speak.'

'Speak? What do you mean?'

'Who better knows the mind of Calat—'

'Calat Hustain is not here.'

'Lord Ilgast—'

'Was given command of the Wardens. Sergeant, who is this "we" you speak of?'

Kullis snorted. 'Your kin, sir. All of whom are now looking to you. This moment, sir. They are looking to you.'

'I conveyed Hunn Raal's words,' Havaral said, 'and the lord chooses to answer them.'

'Yes sir, I see the knife in his hand. But we sacks of blood now bear beads of sweat.'

Havaral looked away. The sickness pooling in his stomach churned. His eyes travelled down the length of the Wardens waiting on their wood-armoured horses, the breaths of the beasts softly pluming, the occasional head tossing amidst the mosquitoes. His kin were motionless in their saddles, their lacquered, banded-wood breastplates gleaming in the bright sunlight. Beneath the rims of their helmets he saw, one after another, faces too young for this.

*My blessed misfits, who could never in comfort wear the soldier's garb. Who forever stood outside the company of others. Could face down a dozen scaled wolves, and not blink. Ride to the Vitr and voice no complaint at the poison air. Wait here now, for the call to advance, and then to charge. My children.*

*My sacks of blood.*

'Sir.'

'Urusander's Legion is eager for this,' Havaral said. 'Once at strength, it would have had to march on the Wardens, before closing on Kharkanas. The Legion could not

40

countenance us at its back. We meet it today, on dead grasses and in a bitter wind, and dream of a gentle spring to come.'

'Sir—'

Havaral turned on the man, his face twisting. 'Do you think the captains have all remained mute?' he hissed. 'Did you fools actually imagine we swallowed down our bile, and did nothing but bow meekly before our commander?'

Kullis flinched slightly at his captain's words.

'Hear me,' Havaral said, 'I do not command here. What shame would you have me suffer? Do you think I will not be riding down there with you? With my lance drawn and hard at your side? Abyss take you, Kullis – you have unmanned me!'

'Sir, I did not mean such a thing. Forgive me my words.'

'Did I not warn you against matters of faith?'

'You did, sir. I am sorry.'

Voices rose then, drawing their attention to the valley floor, where two small figures had appeared, one pursuing the other.

They then, in silence, witnessed a murder.

Skirmishers arrived to chase away the child, and continued on in their advance.

A moment later, Ilgast Rend's voice carried clear in the cold air. 'The Legion ill keeps its tent, it seems. Think well on that misery, Wardens, and the cruelty of childhood. Hunn Raal commands the field of play in the manner of the thug. The bully. And dreams of a place for himself in the Citadel.' The words did not echo, as the wind was quick to sweep them away. After a brief pause, the lord continued, 'But you are children no longer. Awaken what memories you need, and make answer!'

Clever words, Havaral conceded, to so probe old wounds.

'Ready lances and prepare to advance. Captains Havaral and Shalath, flanks will rise to canter and then swing inward at the blue flags. We'll trap those skirmishers and be done with them.'

Havaral gathered his reins. 'To our troop now, sergeant. Trust this will be well timed, as I see the pikes now on the move.'

'They yield the crest,' Kullis said, as they set off for the flank units.

'The slope suffices.'

'And less winded our mounts upon reaching them!'

Nodding, Havaral said, 'They see the wooden cladding and imagine our horses lacking in endurance. They are in for a surprise, sergeant.'

'That they are, sir!'

'Ilgast Rend was a soldier,' Havaral said. 'Remember that – battle is no stranger to him.'

'I'll watch for the blue flags, sir.'

'You do that, sergeant.'

They arrived opposite their troop, wheeling forward just as the command to advance was sounded. ''Ware your steps, Wardens!' Havaral shouted, recalling the pitfalls on the slope.

Taking the lead, the captain began the descent. His mount wanted to canter rather than trot, but he held the reins tight and leaned back in the saddle, forcing the animal to take its time.

The skirmishers, each one bearing three or four lances, were spreading out. They seemed reluctant now, their pace slowing upon seeing the cavalry drawing closer.

From a troop to Havaral's left, a horse screamed, tumbling its rider as it broke a foreleg in a burrow or rut.

'Eyes ahead!' Havaral snapped. 'Gauge every step!'

Drawn by sweat and harsh breaths, the mosquitoes massed ever thicker as the Wardens made their way towards the valley floor. The captain heard comrades cough as they inhaled bugs. Curses sounded, but mostly the sound was of creaking armour, the thump of horse hoofs, and the gusting wind that slid beneath iron helms and moaned as if trapped.

Havaral left the slope and rode out on to the basin, at last giving the horse freedom to quicken its trot. His troop drew up behind him, keeping pace.

He had loved a man once, long ago now, and the memory of that face had been years buried. It appeared suddenly in his mind's eye, as if emerging from shadows, as lively and enticing as it had ever been. Others crowded behind it, all the confused desires that had marked his adolescence, and with them came a dull pain, an ache of the spirit.

It was no crime to turn from the common path, yet it came at a cost nonetheless. No matter. The young man had gone away, unwilling to stay with any one lover, and his name had vanished from the living world after the burning of his village by Forulkan raiders. Whether he died or took for himself another life, Havaral knew not.

*But now your knowing smile is before me. I only regret the end, my love, only the end.*

Confusion filled his head, and sent down into his soul a sorrowful song that brought the blur of tears to his eyes. *An old man's song, this one. A song of all the deaths in a normal life, how they come up and then go past like verses, and this chorus that bridges each one, oh, it voices nothing but questions none can answer.*

Beside him, Sergeant Kullis leaned over and, with a hard smile, said, 'How clear the mind is at this moment, sir! The world is almost too sharp to behold!'

Havaral nodded. 'Damn this wind,' he then growled, blinking.

The first shade of blue appearing among the flag-stations lifted them into a canter, and they swung out, away from the skirmishers. As the horseshoe formation took shape, the foot soldiers suddenly recoiled in comprehension. The flags spun to show the deeper blue side, announcing the inward wheel and the charge.

The skirmishers had drawn out too far – Havaral could see that plain – and the pike line was still trudging at its turgid pace, only halfway down the far slope.

Havaral brought his lance down and slid its butt into the arm's length leather sheath affixed to the saddle. He heard and felt the solid impact the end made with the bronze socket.

'They're all caught!' Kullis shouted. 'We're too fast!'

The captain said nothing. He saw javelins launched from arms, saw lances dip to knock most of them away before they could strike the chests of horses. A few animals screamed, but now the voices of the Wardens filled the air, rising above the thunder of horse hoofs.

*Borrowed anger this might be, but it will do.*

Skirmishers scattered like jackrabbits.

A few hundred Legion soldiers were about to die, and the tears streamed from Havaral's eyes, making cold tracks down his cheeks.

*It begins. Oh, blessed Mother Dark, it begins.*

*        *        *

Sevegg cursed and then turned to Hunn Raal. 'They went too far, the fools. Who commands them?'

'Lieutenant Altras.'

'Altras! Cousin, he's a quartermaster's aide!'

'And so very eager, like a pup off its leash.'

She looked at the captain at her side. His profile was sharp, almost majestic if one did not look too closely. If witnessing the imminent slaughter of three hundred Legion soldiers affected him, there was no discernible sign. *A different flavour of command, then. Lord Urusander would never have done it this way. And yet, there is no value in questioning this.* She studied her cousin's face, remembering how that expression crumpled in lovemaking, achieving nothing so much childlike as dissolute.

On the field below, the wings of the Warden cavalry tightened their deadly noose about the skirmishers. Lances dipped, caught hold of bodies and lifted them into the air, or drove them into the ground. Most weapons took soldiers from behind.

From the corner of her eye she caught Hunn Raal's gesture, an almost lazy wave of one gauntleted hand.

Behind them, the outer units of Legion cavalry on the back-slope lurched into motion, quickly surging into a canter. Then, pivoting as if one end was fixed to the ground, the troops wheeled to face the slope. The riders leaned forward as their mounts climbed.

*He should have ordered this earlier. A hundred heartbeats. Five hundred. Not a single skirmisher will be left.*

As if reading her mind, Hunn Raal said, 'I had a list of malcontents. Soldiers too inclined to question what is necessary to bring peace to the realm. They argued at the campfires. They muttered about desertion.'

Sevegg said nothing. There was no crime in asking questions. The last accusation was absurd. Deserters never talked about it beforehand. Instead, it was the opposite. They went quiet in the days before disappearing. Every soldier knew the signs.

The foremost ranks of the Legion cavalry crested the slope, swept over and then flowed down in a solid mass, arriving on the field of battle beyond the Warden flanks. She saw the first of the enemy riders discover the threat, and confusion take hold, lances lifting to allow the quick about-face. The centre formation, where the bulk of Rend's force still advanced at the trot, began to bulge.

'See that,' Hunn Raal suddenly said. 'He abandons his flanks to a mauling, and sets eyes only for our pikes.'

'Those armoured mounts of theirs are surprisingly agile,' Sevegg said, seeing how the outside ranks were already settling, lances dipping as they rode out to meet the Legion cavalry.

'Outnumbered,' Raal said, 'and on weary beasts.'

The way ahead for Rend's centre was now clear, with only motion-less bodies to ride over as they approached the slope. Three-quarters of the way down the hillside, Raal's pikes now halted, setting their weapons and anchoring the heels against the unyielding, frozen ground.

In the past war against the Jheleck, the pike had proved its efficacy. But the giant wolves charged without discipline, and proved too foolish and too brave and too stubborn to change their ways. Even so, Sevegg could not see how the Wardens could answer that bristling line of barbed iron points. 'Rend has lost his mind,' she said, 'if he hopes to break our centre.'

Hunn Raal grunted. 'I admit to some curiosity about that. We'll see soon enough what he has in mind.'

The Legion cavalry had turned inward, rising to the charge.

The Wardens answered. Moments later, the leading edges collided.

*       *       *

On the crest of her hilltop, Renarr flinched at the distant impact. She saw bodies silently rising as if invisible hands had reached down from the empty sky, snatching them from their saddles. Their limbs flailed, and blooms of red snapped sudden as flags in the midst of the crush. Horses went down, thrashing and kicking. An instant later, the thunder of that collision reached her.

The whores were shouting, while the children now crowded between the men and women along the ridge, silent and watching with wide eyes, some with thumbs in their mouths, others pulling on pipes.

Renarr could see how, in the initial impact, many more Legion horses staggered and fell than did those of the Wardens. She suspected that this was unanticipated. An advantage of the wooden armour of the enemy's mounts, she supposed, which while providing surprising defence did little to slow the swiftness and agility of the beasts. Even so, the Legion's superior numbers checked that counterattack, absorbing the blow, and now, as riders fought in the crowded, churning maelstrom, the Wardens began giving ground.

She looked to the centre, and saw the foremost Wardens reach the base of the slope. Flags rippled, changing colour in a wave leading out from the stations upon the opposite hill-side, and all at once the Wardens charged up the slope.

The pikes awaiting them glinted in the sun like the thread of a mountain stream.

Sensing someone at her side, Renarr glanced down and saw the girl with the bloodied face. Tears had cleaned her cheeks in narrow, crooked trails, but her pale eyes, fixed upon the battle below, were dry.

*       *       *

His lover's face was everywhere now, upon all sides. Beneath the rims of helms, among his kin and among the enemy

46

surging around him. He sobbed as he fought, howled as he cut down that dear man again and again, and screamed each time one of his comrades fell. He had left his lance buried halfway through a horse, the point driving into its chest and reaching all the way to its gut. Disbelief had flashed through Havaral then: he'd felt little resistance along the weapon's shaft. The point had slipped past every possible obstacle. The horse's rider had attempted to swing his heavy longsword at the captain, but the beast collapsing under him had tugged him away, and moments later a Warden's lance cut clean through his neck, sending the head spinning.

His troop was falling back, collapsing inward. Lord Rend had done nothing to prevent it, and Havaral understood the role his flank now inherited, as a sacrificial bulwark protecting the centre. They would fight on, without hope of victory or even escape, and in this forlorn fate their only task was to take a long time in dying.

He knew nothing of the rest of the battle. The few flags he caught sight of, barely glimpsed and distant on the far slope, were all black.

He swung his sword, hacking at Legion soldiers. The multitude of his lover's face showed twisted, enraged expressions, filled with hate and fury, with terror. Others showed him that face in grey, clouded confusion, as they sank back, or slid from their saddles. The surprise of death was one no actor on a stage could capture, because its truth cast an inhuman shade upon the eyes, and that shade spread out to claim the skin of the face, rushing down to bleach the throat. It was silent and it was, horribly, irrefutable.

*Beloved, why are you doing this to me? Why are you here? What have I done to you, to so earn this?*

He had lost sight of Kullis, and yet longed for the man, desperate to see a visage other than those that now surrounded him. He imagined holding the man tightly in his arms, burying his face in the crook of neck and shoulder, and weeping as only an old man could.

Was not love its own shock? A match to that of death? Did it not take the eyes first? Such reverberations as to weaken the bravest man or woman – its trembling echoes never left a mortal soul. He had fooled himself. There was no music in this, no song, no chorus of longing and regret. There was only chaos, and a lover's face that never, ever went away.

He killed his beloved without pause. Again and again, and again.

*　　*　　*

With a gap of only a few horse-lengths separating the two centres, Sevegg saw the lances of the enemy riders angle to one side, and only at that instant did she note that one entire half of the Wardens in the front line had anchored their weapons on their left sides – and that line was to her right.

As the forces collided, the foremost line of riders peeled out to the sides in staggered timing, and a roar of clashing announced the rippling collision of their lance shafts with those of the pikes facing them as they swept those weapons outward, as if folding to one side blades of grass.

Immediately behind them, and matching the staggered cadence of those before them, the second line hammered into the exposed front line of the centre, the impact rippling out to the sides.

Sevegg shouted her astonishment. The precision of the manoeuvre was appalling, the effect devastating.

The Legion centre buckled, as dying bodies were plucked from the ground and driven into the ranks behind them. Pikes caught on fellow soldiers, dragging weapons or snapping the shafts. Moments later swords flashed down, hacking at heads, necks and shoulders.

Against the slope, the soldiers struggled to back up, many driven to the ground instead, and still the fist of the enemy drove deeper, churning up the slope.

'Shit of the Abyss!' Hunn Raal hissed, suddenly galvanized. 'Commit our foot flanks!' he shouted, rising on his stirrups. 'Hurry, damn you all!' He sawed his mount around. 'Second rank centre, down the slope at the double! Form a second line and hold to save your lives!'

*And ours.* Sevegg's mouth was suddenly dry, and she felt her insides contract, as if every organ fought to retreat, to flee, only to be trapped by the cage of her bones. She closed a hand about the grip of her sword. The leather wrapping the handle was too smooth – not yet worn or roughened by sweat – and the weapon seemed to resist her grasp.

'Keep it sheathed, you fool!' her cousin snapped. 'If you panic my soldiers I'll see you skinned alive.'

Below, the Wardens chopped, slashed and hacked their way ever closer. Of the six-deep line of pikes, only two remained, and the lead one was fast fragmenting.

Then soldiers seethed over the crest to both sides of Sevegg and Hunn Raal, closing up once past and levelling their pikes.

'We'll grind them down now,' Hunn Raal said. 'But damn, that was well played.'

'He did not imagine he was facing three entire cohorts,' Sevegg said, her voice sounding thin to her own ears, even as relief flooded through her.

'I could have done with two more.'

*Thus emptying Urusander's camp. But that would have made Raal's intent too clear.*

'Ah, see the left flank! Our cavalry is through!'

She looked, and relief gave way to elation. 'I beg you, cousin, let me join them!'

'Go on, then. No, wait. Hold together your troop, Sevegg. Wet your swords by all means, but only on the edges – I want you riding for Ilgast Rend. He does not escape. Chase him down if necessary. He will face me in chains today, do you understand me?'

'Alive then?'

'Alive. Now, go, have your fun.'

*Too quick to call me the fool, cousin. I won't forget these public humiliations, and when I next have you in my arms, I'll remind you of pleasure's other side.* Waving to her troop, she set off along the crest.

\*   \*   \*

49

Kicking, Havaral tried pushing his way out from under his dead horse. The beast's weight was immense, trapping one leg, and yet still he struggled. When the pinned knee succumbed to the relentless pull, and the bone popped from its joint, he shouted in pain.

Blackness washed through him, and, gasping, he fought to remain conscious.

*Well, that is that. I go nowhere.*

Somewhere behind him, beyond sight, the Legion cavalry was savaging the centre. The captain had failed to hold them back, and now, he knew, the battle was lost.

Bodies and carcasses lay in heaps around him. Blood and spilled entrails made a glistening carpet on the ground, and he was covered in the same. The mosquitoes swarmed so thick around his face they filled his mouth like soft cornmeal, choking him as he swallowed them down again and again. The insects seemed both frenzied and baffled by this unflinching bounty, and though they clustered in such numbers as to blacken nearby corpses in their hunger, it appeared to be futile, as though they could not draw blood without the pressure of their prey's pumping heart.

Havaral assembled these observations, holding on to his musings as if the rest of the world, with all its drama, and all its wretched desperation, was now beneath notice. Even his lover was gone from the field, and those faces that he could see, whether Warden or Legion, were one and all made strangers by death. He knew none of them.

He heard voices nearby, and then a guttural shout, and moments later a rider appeared, reining in and suddenly looming above him. The sun was high, casting the figure in silhouette, but he knew the voice when she spoke. 'Old man, such fortune in finding you.'

Havaral said nothing. Mosquitoes kept drowning in the corners of his eyes, making them water all the more. He thought he had wept himself dry long ago. The high sun disturbed him. Surely they had fought longer than that?

'Your Wardens are broken,' Sevegg said. 'We slaughter them. They thought we would permit a retreat, as if honour still lived in this day and age. Had any of you possessed a soldier's mind, you wouldn't have been so naïve.'

Blinking, he studied the dark shadow where her face should be.

'Will you say nothing now?' she asked. 'Not even a curse or two?'

'How fits shame, lieutenant?'

To that query she made no reply, but quickly dismounted, and then moved to crouch beside him. At last he could see her face.

She was studying him curiously. 'We captured Lord Rend. My troop now delivers him to Hunn Raal. I will grant Ilgast this – he did not flee us, and looks to accept his fate as just punishment for failing on this day.'

'Today,' agreed Havaral, 'marks a day of failures.'

'Well, let me give you this. You'll not scorn my pity, I hope. I see you at last. Old and useless, with every pleasure long behind you now. This hardly seems a fitting end, does it? Alone, with only me to caress your eyes. So, at the very least, I choose to offer you a gift. But first, I see you covered in blood and guts – where is your wound? Do you feel much pain, or has that faded?'

'I feel nothing, lieutenant.'

'That's good then.' She laughed. 'Here I was going on and on, too unmindful by far.'

'I'll take the sharp point of your gift now, Sevegg, and deem it the sweetest kiss.'

Sevegg frowned briefly, as if struggling to understand the meaning of his invitation. Then she shook her head. 'No, I cannot do that. I'll let you bleed out instead.'

'This is your first field of battle, isn't it?' he asked.

Her frown deepened. 'Everyone has a first.'

'Yes, I suppose that's true. I will concede your innocence here, then.'

The furrows of her brow beneath the helm's rim faded, and, smiling, she said, 'That's generous of you. I think now we could have been friends. I could well have looked on you as a father.'

51

'A father to you, Sevegg Issgin? Now you curse me in earnest.'

She bore that well and nodded, looking off to one side for a moment before returning her attention to him. 'So there's still some fire in you. Not a daughter, then. We'll imagine the lover instead. More blessed then my gift.' She reached down and grasped the wrist of his left hand, tugging off the gauntlet. 'Here, old man, one last time, a soft pleasure.' And she moved his hand up under her leather breastplate. 'You can squeeze if you've the strength.'

He met her eyes, feeling the swell of her tit cupped by his calloused palm. And then he laughed.

Confusion clouded her face, and at that moment, as he brought up his other hand and drove the knife it held up under her rib cage, using all his strength to pierce the leather, and felt it slide home to take her heart – at that moment, he looked hard at her face, seeing no one but a stranger. And this pleased him even more than the surprise he saw in that visage.

'I bear no wounds,' he said to her. 'A veteran would have checked, woman.'

The weapon sobbed as she slipped back from him and fell awkwardly on to her heels.

Someone shouted in dismay. There was hurried motion. A sword flashed in Havaral's eyes, like a lick of blinding sunlight, and at the same instant something slammed into his forehead, delivering a new, unexpected surprise.

Peace.

*     *     *

Soldiers had brought camp-stools to the summit overlooking the valley of the slain, with one to take Hunn Raal, as he contended with the grief of his cousin's treacherous murder. The captain sat with a jug of wine balanced on one thigh, the other leg flung out, the foot resting on its outer ankle. He was indifferent to the activity around him, and the wine in his gut felt heavy and sour, yet comforting all the same.

He had ill news to deliver to Serap, who had become the

52

last survivor among his kin. There was greater need now in keeping her close by Urusander's side, as a valued officer in the commander's staff. On the day that Urusander took the throne beside Mother Dark's, she would be well placed in the new court. But he was running out of pawns.

Some hurts were not worth looking at, and if his display here before his soldiers – that of a captain reduced to a man, and a man reduced to a grieving child in a family twice broken – if all that yielded pity he could use, well, he would.

Drunks were well known as master tacticians. Seductively familiar with strategies of all sorts. The hurting thirst of his habit had honed him well, and he would not refuse his own tempered nature. Drunks were dangerous, in every way imaginable. Especially in matters of faith, trust and loyalty.

Hunn Raal knew himself, down to the core – to that dark, gleeful place where he invented new rules for old games, and made small excuses kneel in servitude to their father and master, their mother and mistress, all of whom were one and the same. *Where the me within me sits. My very own throne, my very own slippery seat of imagined power.*

*Urusander, you will take what we give you. What I give you, and what our new High Priestess gives you. I see now the fantasy of your elevation, your return to glory. But you will suffice, and I will empty the libraries of every scholar across Kurald Galain to keep you buried to your neck in mouldy scrolls, and so content in what little world you would live in. This is a kindness beyond imagining, milord, beyond imagining.*

He could weather any amount of berating from his commander, and anticipated a tirade to end this triumphant day. It would not sour Hunn Raal. Not for a moment. If anything, he would struggle to keep a smile from his face. Now was not yet the time for contempt.

Eventually, he looked up, to the nobleborn commander who had been bound in chains and made to kneel on the cold, hard ground opposite him. The distance between them was modest, and yet impossibly vast, and this notion made Hunn Raal drunker than any jug of wine could achieve. 'Do you recall,' he now said, 'how we rode together out to the Wardens' summer camp?'

'I should have cut you down then.'

'In conversation with my friends,' Hunn Raal said, ignoring Rend's pointless, redundant assertion, 'with you lagging out of earshot, I made a comment about you. There was laughter. Do you, perchance, recall that moment?'

'No.'

Hunn Raal said nothing as he slowly leaned forward, and then he smiled and whispered, 'I think you lie, friend.'

'Think what you like. Deliver me to Urusander now. This scene grows tired.'

'What words, like rotten fruit, have you collected up, Ilgast, to deliver to my commander, I wonder?'

'I leave you to tend that garden alone.'

Hunn Raal waved his free hand. 'You know, you impressed me today. Not the whole day, mind you. Your desire to seek this battle, for example, was ill conceived. But I saw your genius in that clash against my pikes – I would think only the Wardens could have managed that. The finest riders this realm has ever known. And see what you've done – you've thrown them away. If in the name of justice I would deliver you to someone, surely it would be Calat Hustain.'

At that, he was pleased to see, Ilgast Rend flinched.

The pleasure did not last, and he felt a sudden regret. 'Oh, Ilgast, look what you've done this day!' The words came out in pain, in honest anguish. 'Why did you not bring the Wardens to our cause? Why did you not come here to embrace our desire for what's right? How differently this day would have played out.'

'Calat Hustain refused your invitation,' Ilgast said, trembling. 'I could not in honour betray that.'

Hunn Raal scowled in exasperated disbelief. 'My friend!' he whispered, leaning still closer. 'By your honour you could not *betray* him? Ilgast – look upon the field behind you! Yet you would fling those words at me? Honour? Betrayal? Abyss below, man, what am I to make of this?'

'Not even you can deepen my shame, Hunn Raal. I am here, clear-eyed—'

'You are nothing of the sort!'

'Deliver me to Urusander!'

'You've taken your last step, my friend,' Hunn Raal said, leaning back. Closing his eyes, he raised his voice and said, in a weary tone, 'Have done with it, then. This man is a criminal, a traitor to the realm. We've already seen how the nobleborn can bleed like any other mortal. Go on, I beg you, execute him now, and show me no corpse when I next open my eyes.'

He heard the solid chop of the sword blade, a moment's worth of choked sob, and then the man's body falling along with his head. Fingers playing on the ear of the wine jug, he listened as both offending objects were dragged away.

A soldier then spoke. 'It is done, sir.'

Hunn Raal opened his eyes, blinking in the bright glare, and saw that it was so. He waved his soldiers away. 'Leave me now, to my grief, and make a list of heroes. It has been a dark day, but I will see light born of it nonetheless.'

Overhead, the winter sun offered little heat. The cold air invited sobriety, but he was having none of that. He'd earned his right to grieve.

*       *       *

Renarr watched the other whores moving among the corpses below, and the children running this way and that, their thin cries drifting up as they found a precious ring or torc, or a small bag full of coins or polished river pebbles. The light was fading as the short day hurried to its close.

She was chilled to the bone, and not yet ready to think of the boldness of the men who would find her in the evening to come, but her imagination defied such aversion. They would taste different – she was sure – but not on the tongue. This would be a deeper change, something to absorb from sweat and from what they leaked in their passion. It was a taste she would glean wherever their flesh met. She could not yet know, of course, but she did not think it would be bitter, or sour.

55

There would be relief, and perhaps something of the despondent, in that intimate flavour. If it burned, it would burn with life.

She caught sight of the girl whose killing had started the day. She walked with followers now, regal as a queen among the dead.

Renarr studied her, and did not blink.

\* \* \*

*You could find a kind of justice in Urusander's fate, although I will grant you, his ascension to the title of Father of Light made justice a mockery. So yes, indulge me now and give this blind old man a moment or two to catch his breath. This tale has far to go, after all. Free me to muse on the notions of righteous consequence, since they lie scattered before us like stepping stones across history's torrent.*

*I have no doubt Urusander was no different from you or me, or rather, no different from most thinking creatures. For myself, I make no common claim. The poet's view of justice is a secret one, and you and I need not discuss its rules. A few deft twitches on the fingers of one hand bind us in hidden kinship, with strangers none the wiser. So I am certain that you too will hold back when I speak of Urusander's similitude.*

*To be plain, he saw justice as a clear thing, and from that raging river of progress, which ever tugs us along, he longed to dip a hand in at any point and raise to the heavens a pool of clean water, sparkling in the cup of his palm.*

*We look upon this same torrent and see the silts of flood waters, of banks breached, and islands of detritus crowded with shivering refugees. To steal a palm's worth is to look down upon a cloudy, impenetrable world, a microcosm of history's messy truth. And in the anguish and despair with which we contend, upon observing our dubious prize, we can hardly call our vision a virtue.*

*Virtue. Surely, of all words that might belong to Lord Vatha Urusander, it is that one. Such clear justice, in hand as it were, must indeed be a worthy virtue. So, Urusander was a man who longed to cleanse the waters of history, through the sluice of hard judgement. Must we fault him in that noble desire?*

*There is that old saying, couched as a truism, and to utter it is to assert its primacy: justice, we say, is blind. By this we mean that its rules defy all the seeming privileges of the wealthy and the highborn. Laudable, without question, if from the rules of justice we are to fashion a civilization worthy of being deemed decent and righteous. Even children can be stung in the face of what they perceive to be unfair. Unless, of course, they are the ones profiting from it. And in that moment of comprehension, of unfairness to the other also being a reward to oneself, that child faces – for the first but not the last time – the inner war we all know so well, between selfish desire and the common good. Between injustice, clutched so possessively deep in the soul, and a justice that now, suddenly, stands outside that child, like a stern foe.*

*With luck, the regard of others will force submission upon the child, in the name of fairness, but make no mistake, it is indeed forced. Wrenched from small hands, and then indifferent to the child's raging impotence. Thus in our childhoods we learn the lessons of strength and weakness, and violence delivered in the name of justice. We deem this maturity.*

*Father Light. Such a bold title. Sire to the Tiste Liosan, observing all of his children from a place of clear, unopposed light. A place of purity, then, eternal bane to darkness. A father to lead us into history. The god of justice.*

*Of course he adored the Forulkan, barring those hundreds who slid lifeless down the blade of his sword. After all, their worship of justice was intransigent in the virtue of its purity. As unassailable, whispers this poet, as a blind man's darkness. But then, we poets suffer our imperfections, do we not? We are seen, in our seeming equivocations and indecision, as weak of spirit. Gods help a kingdom ruled by a poet!*

*What? No, I do not know King Tehol the Only. Will you interrupt me again?*

*So. I sense you manning still the ramparts of your admiration for the Son of Darkness. Will I never scour that romance from your vision? Must I beat you about the head with his flaws, his errors in judgement, his obstinacy?*

*You are eager for the tale. No patience left for an old man trying to make a point.*

*Kadaspala etched his god, in the end. Did you know that? He etched that god into life, and then, appalled at the long-awaited perfection of his talent, he killed them both.*

*What are we to make of that?*

*No matter. We have already seen Kadaspala find the promise of peace, delivered by his own hands, in a time of unbearable grief. The visionary is the first to be blinded, if a civilization is to fall. Set him aside. He is no longer relevant. Leave him to his small chamber in the Citadel, muttering his madness. His work is done. No, another artist must be dragged to the fore. Another sacrifice necessary to advance a people's suicide.*

*In this tale, then, look to the sculptor's hands . . .*

*. . . as he carves his monument. I leave the choosing of its title to you, my friend. But not yet. Hear the tale first. There is only so much we can indulge, before the chorus grows restless, and gives voice to its displeasure.*

*I am known to flirt with impatience? Now, surely, that is an unjust accusation.*

# TWO

---

BARELY A SMUDGE AGAINST THE GLOOM, THE SUN WAS fading in the sky over the city of Kharkanas. The two lieutenants from the Houseblades of Lord Anomander, Prazek and Dathenar, met on the outer bridge and stood leaning on one of its walls, forearms on the stone. Like children, their upper bodies were tilted forward as they looked down upon the waters of the Dorssan Ryl. To their right, the Citadel stood like a fortress of night, defying the day. To the left, the city's jumbled buildings crowded up against the flood wall as if caught in the act of marching over the edge.

Below the two men, the river's surface was black, twisting with thick currents. Even now, the occasional charred tree trunk slid past, like the swollen limb of a dismembered giant. Ash-grey mud crusted the sheer walls that made up the banks. The boats moored to iron rings in the walls, near the stone steps that reached down into the water at intervals, looked neglected, home to dead leaves and murky pools of rainwater.

'There is discipline lacking,' murmured Prazek, 'in our sordid post upon this bridge.'

'We are looked down upon,' Dathenar replied. 'See us from atop the tower. We are small things upon this frail span. Witness as we betray errant curiosity, not suited to sentries at

59

all, and in our pose you will find, with dismay, civilization's slouching departure from the world.'

'I too saw the historian at his lofty perch,' Prazek said, nodding. 'Or rather, his hooded regard. Did it track us out here? Does it fix still upon us?'

'I would think so, as I feel a weight upon me. At least an executioner's shroud offers mercy in hiding the face above the axe. We might splinter here under Rise Herat's judgement, bearing as it does no less sharp an edge.'

Prazek was of no mind to argue the point. History was a cold arbiter. He studied the black water below, and found himself distrusting its depth. 'A force to splinter us into dust and fragile slivers,' he said, hunching slightly at the thought of the historian looking down upon them.

'The river below would welcome our sorry fragments.'

The currents swirled their invitation, but there was nothing friendly in the sly gestures. Prazek shook his head. 'Indifference is a bitter welcome, my friend.'

'I see no other promise,' Dathenar said with a shrug. 'Let us list the causes of our present fate. I will begin. Our lord wanders lost under winter's bleak cloak, and makes no bold bulge in his struggle – look out from any tower, Prazek, and you see the season unrelieved, settled flat by the weight of snow, where even the shadows lie weak and pale upon the ground.'

Prazek grunted, his eyes still fixed on the black waters below, half his mind contemplating that mocking invitation. 'And the Consort lies swallowed in a holy embrace. So holy is that embrace, that there is nothing to see. Lord Draconus, you too have abandoned us.'

'Surely, there is ecstasy in blindness.'

Prazek considered that, and then shook his head again. 'You've not dared the company of Kadaspala, friend, else you would say otherwise.'

'No, some pilgrimages I avoid by habit. I am told his self-made cell is a gallery of madness.'

Prazek snorted. 'Never ask an artist to paint his or her own room. You invite a spilling out of landscapes one would not wish to see, for any cause.'

Dathenar sighed. 'I cannot agree, friend. Every canvas reveals that hidden landscape.'

'Manageable,' said Prazek. 'It is when the paint bleeds past the edges that we recoil. The wooden frame offers bars to a prison, and this comforts the eye.'

'How can a blind man paint?'

'Without encumbrance, I should say.' Prazek waved one hand dismissively, as if to fling the subject into the dark water below. 'So,' he continued, 'to the list again. The Son of Darkness walks winter's road seeking a brother who chooses not to be found, and the Suzerain confides in the night for days on end, forgetting even the purpose of dawn, while we stand guard on a bridge none would cross. Where, then, the shoreline of this civil war?'

'Far away still,' Dathenar answered. 'Its jagged edge describes our horizons. For myself, I cannot cleanse my mind of the Hust camp, where the dead slept in such untroubled peace, and, I confess, nor can I scour away the envy that took hold of my soul on that day.'

Prazek rubbed at his face, fingers tracking down from his eyes to rake through his beard. The water flowing beneath the bridge tugged at his bones. 'It is said that no one can swim in the Dorssan Ryl now. It takes every child of Mother Dark down to her bosom. No corpse is retrieved, and the surface curls on in its ever-twisting smiles. If envy of the fallen Hust so plagues you, friend, I'll offer no staying hand. But I will grieve your passing as I would my dearest brother.'

'As I would your leaving *my* company, Prazek.'

'Very well, then,' Prazek decided. 'If we cannot guard this bridge, let us at least guard each other.'

'A modest responsibility. I see the horizons draw closer.'

'But never to divide us, I pray.' Prazek straightened, turning his back to the river and leaning against the wall. 'I curse the poet! I curse every word and each bargain it wins! To so profit from beleaguered reality!'

Dathenar snorted. 'An unseemly procession, this row of words you describe. This rut we stumble along. But think on the peasant's language – as it wallows in its simplicity, off among the fields of fallow converse. Will the day begin in rain or snow? Does your knee ache, my love? I cannot say, dear wife! Oh and why not, husband? Beloved, the ache that you describe can have but one meaning, and on this morning lo! among the handful of words I possess, I cannot find it!'

'Reduce me to grunts, then,' said Prazek, scowling. 'I beg you.'

'We should so descend, Prazek. Each of us like a boar rooting in the forest.'

'There is no forest.'

'There is no boar, either,' Dathenar retorted. 'No, we hold to this bridge, and turn eyes upon the Citadel. The historian looks on, after all. Let us discuss the nature of language and say this: that power thrives in complexity, and makes of language a secret harbour. And in this complexity the divide is asserted. We have important matters to discuss! No grunting boar is welcome!'

'I understand what you say,' Prazek said, with a wry smile. 'And so reveal my privilege.'

'Just so!' Dathenar pounded a fist on the stone ledge. 'But listen! Two languages are born from one, and as they grow, ever greater the divide, ever greater the lesson of power delivered, until the highborn who are surely highbred are able to give proof of this, in language solely their own, and the lowborn who can but grunt in the vernacular are daily reminded of their irrelevance.'

'Swine are hardly fools, Dathenar. The hog knows the slaughter awaiting it.'

'And squeals to no avail. But consider these two languages and ask yourself, which more resists change? Which clings so fiercely to its precious complexity?'

'Troop in the lawmakers and the scribes—'

Dathenar's nod was sharp, a flush deepening to midnight on his broad face. 'The educated and the trained—'

'The enlightened.'

'This is the warring tug of language, friend! The clay of ignorance against the rock of exclusion and privilege.'

'Privilege – I see the root of that word, in *privacy*.'

'A fine point you make, Prazek. Kinship among words can indeed reveal hints of the secret code. But here, in this war, it is the conservative and the reactionary that stand under perpetual siege.'

'As the ignorant are legion?'

'They breed like vermin.'

Prazek straightened and spread wide his arms. 'Yet see us here, on this bridge, with swords at our belts, and bolstered in spirit by the eagerness of honour and duty. See how it wins us the privilege of giving our lives in defence of complexity!'

'To the ramparts, friend!' Dathenar cried, laughing.

'No,' his companion said in a growl. 'I'm for the nearest tavern, and bedamned this wretched privilege. Run the wine down my throat until I slur like a swineherd!'

'Simplicity is a powerful thirst. Words softened to wet clay, like paste squeezed out between our fingers.' Dathenar's nod was eager. 'This is mud we can swim in.'

'Abandon the poet then?'

'Abandon him!'

'And the dread historian?' Prazek asked, smiling.

'He'll show no shock at our faithlessness. We are but guards huddled beneath the millstone of the world. This post will see us crushed and spat out like chaff, and you know it.'

'Have we had our moment, then?'

'I see our future, friend, and it is black and depthless.'

The two men set out, quitting their posts. Unguarded behind them stretched the bridge, making its sloped shoulder an embrace of the river's rushing water – with its impenetrable surface of curling smiles.

The war, after all, was elsewhere.

\*     \*     \*

'It can be said in no other way,' Grizzin Farl sighed, as he ran a massive, blunt fingertip through the puddle of ale on the tabletop: 'she was profoundly attractive in a plain sort of way.'

The tavern's denizens were quiet at their tables, and the air in the room was thick as water, gloomy despite the candles, the oil lamps, and the fiercely burning fire in the hearth. Conversations rose on occasion, cautious as minnows beneath an overhanging branch, only to quickly sink back down.

Hearing his companion's faint snort, the Azathanai straightened in his seat, in the pose of a man taking affront. The wooden legs beneath him groaned and creaked. 'What do I mean by that, you ask?'

'If I—'

'Well, my pallid friend, I will tell you. Her beauty only arrived at second, or even third, glance. Was a poet to set eyes upon her, that poet's talent could be measured, as if on a scale, by the nature of his or her declamation. Would frenzied birdsong not sound mocking? And so impugn that poet as shallow and stupid. But heed the other's song, at the scale's weighty end, and hear the music and verse of a soul's moaning sigh.' Grizzin reached for his tankard, found it empty. Scowling, he thumped it sharply on the table and then held it out.

'You are drunk, Azathanai,' observed his companion as a server rushed over with a new, foam-crowned tankard.

'And for such women,' Grizzin resumed, 'it is no shock that they do not consider themselves beautiful, and would take the mocking chirps as deserved, while disbelieving the other's anguished cry. So, they carry none of the vanity that rides haughty as a naked whore on a white horse, the woman who knows her own beauty as immediate, as stunning and breathtaking. But do not think me unappreciative, I assure you! Even if my admiration bears a touch of pity.'

'A naked whore on a white horse? No, friend, I would never query your admiration.'

'Good.' Grizzin Farl nodded, drinking down a mouthful of ale.

His companion continued. 'But if you tell a woman her beauty emerges only after considerable contemplation, why, I think she would not sweetly meet the lips of your compliment.'

The Azathanai frowned. 'You highborn have a way with

words. In any case, do you take me for a fool? No, I will tell her the truth as I see it. I will tell her that her beauty entrances me, as it surely does.'

'And so she wonders at your sanity.'

'To begin with,' the Azathanai said, belching and nodding. Then he raised a finger. 'Until, at last, my words deliver to her the greatest gift I can hope to give her – that she comes to believe in her own beauty.'

'What happens then? Seduced, swallowed in your embrace, another mysterious maiden conquered?'

The huge Azathanai waved a hand. 'Why, no. She leaves me, of course. Knowing she can do much better.'

'If you deem this worthy advice on the ways of love, friend, you will forgive the renewal of my search for wisdom . . . elsewhere.'

Grizzin Farl shrugged. 'Bleed to your own lessons, then.'

'Why do you linger in Kharkanas, Azathanai?'

'Truth, Silchas Ruin?'

'Truth.'

Grizzin closed his eyes briefly, as if mustering thoughts. He was silent for another moment, and then, eyes opening and fixing upon Silchas Ruin, he sighed and said, 'I hold trapped in place those who would come to this contest. I push away, by my presence alone, the wolves among my kin, who would sink fangs into this panting flesh, if only to savour the sweat and blood and fear.' The Azathanai watched his companion studying him, and then nodded. 'I hold the gates, friend, and in drunken obstinacy I foul the lock like a bent key.'

Finally, Silchas Ruin looked away, squinting into the gloom. 'The city has gone deathly quiet. Look at these others, cowed by all that is as yet unknown, and indeed unknowable.'

'The future is a woman,' said Grizzin Farl, 'deserving a second, or third, glance.'

'Beauty awaits such contemplation?'

'In a manner of speaking.'

'And when we find it?'

'Why, she leaves you, of course.'

'You are not as drunk as you seem, Azathanai.'

'I never am, Silchas. But then, who can see the future?'

'You, it appears. Or is this all a matter of faith?'

'A faith that entrances,' Grizzin Farl replied, looking down at his empty tankard.

'I have a thought,' Silchas Ruin said, 'that what you protect is that future.'

'I am my woman's favourite eunuch, friend. While I am no poet, I pray she is content with the love she sees in my eyes. Utterly devoid of song is hapless Grizzin Farl, and this music you hear? It is no more than my purr beneath her pity.' He gestured with the empty tankard. 'Men such as I will take what we can get.'

'You have talked yourself out of a night with that serving woman you so admired.'

'You think so?'

'I do,' said Silchas. 'Your last request for more ale surely obliterated this evening's worth of flirtation.'

'Oh dear. I must make amends.'

'If not the common subjects of Mother Dark, there are always her priestesses.'

'And wiggle the bent key? I think not.'

After a moment, Silchas Ruin frowned and leaned forward. 'One of these barred gates is *hers*?'

Grizzin Farl raised a finger to his lips. 'Tell no one,' he whispered. 'They've not yet tried the door, of course.'

'I don't believe you.'

'My flavour hides in the darkness, whispering the disinclination.'

'Do you think this white skin announces my disloyalty, Azathanai?'

'Does it not?'

'No!'

Grizzin Farl scratched at his bearded jaw as he contemplated the young nobleborn. 'Well, curse my miscalculation. Will you dislodge me now? I am as weighty as stone, as obstinate as a pillar beneath a roof.'

'What is your purpose, Azathanai? What is your goal?'

'A friend has promised peace,' Grizzin Farl replied. 'I seek to honour that.'

'What friend? Another Azathanai? And what manner this peace?'

'You think the Son of Darkness walks alone through the ruined forest. He does not. At his side is Caladan Brood. Summoned by the blood of a vow.'

Silchas Ruin's brows lifted in astonishment.

'I do not know how peace will be won,' Grizzin continued. 'But for this moment, friend, I judge it wise to keep Lord Draconus from the High Mason's path.'

'A moment, please. The Consort remains with Mother Dark, seduced unto lethargy by your influence? Do you tell me that Draconus – that even Mother Dark – is unaware of what goes on outside their Chamber of Night?'

Grizzin Farl shrugged. 'Perhaps they have eyes only for each other. What do I know? It is dark in there!'

'Spare me the jests, Azathanai!'

'I do not jest. Well, not so much. The Terondai – so lovingly etched on to the Citadel floor by Draconus himself – blazes with power. The Gate of Darkness is manifest now in the Citadel. Such force buffets any who would seek to pierce it.'

'What threat does Caladan Brood pose to Lord Draconus? This makes no sense!'

'No, I see that it does not, but I have already said too much. Perhaps Mother Dark will face the outer world, and see what is to be seen. Even I cannot predict what she might do, or what she might say to her lover. We Azathanai are intruders here, after all.'

'Draconus has had more congress with Azathanai than any other Tiste.'

'He surely knows us well,' Grizzin Farl agreed.

'Is this some old argument, then? Between Draconus and the High Mason?'

'They generally avoid one another's company.'

'Why?'

'That is not for me to comment on, my friend. I am sorry.'

Silchas Ruin threw up his hands and leaned back. 'I begin to question this friendship.'

'I am aggrieved by your words.'

'Then we have evened this exchange.' He rose from his chair. 'I may join you again. I may not.'

Grizzin watched the nobleborn leave the tavern. He saw how others looked up at the white-skinned brother of Lord Anomander, as if in hope, but if they sought confidence or certainty in Silchas Ruin's mien, the gloom no doubt defeated that desire. Twisting in his chair, Grizzin caught the eye of the serving woman, and with a broad smile he beckoned her over.

\* \* \*

High Priestess Emral Lanear stepped up on to the platform and looked across to see the historian near the far wall, as if contemplating a leap to the stones far below. She looked round, and then spoke. 'So this is your refuge.'

He glanced at her, briefly, from over a shoulder, and then said, 'Not all posts have been abandoned, High Priestess.'

She approached. 'What is it you guard, Rise Herat, demanding such vigilance?'

Shrugging, he said, 'Perspective, I suppose.'

'And what does that win you?'

'I see a bridge,' he replied. 'Undefended, and yet . . . none dare cross it.'

'I think,' she mused, 'simple patience will see a resolution. This lack of opposition is but temporary.'

His expression betrayed doubt. He said, 'You assume a resolve among the highborn that I have yet to see. If they stand with hands upon the swords at their sides, they are turned against the man who now shares her dark heart. Their hatred and perhaps envy of Draconus consumes them. Meanwhile, Vatha Urusander methodically eliminates all opposition, and I do not sense much outrage among the nobility.'

'They will muster under Lord Anomander's call, historian. When he returns.'

He looked her way once more, but again only for a moment before his gaze skittered away. 'Anomander's Houseblades will not be enough.'

'Lord Silchas Ruin, acting in his brother's place, is already assembling allies.'

'Yes, the gratitude of chains.'

She flinched, and then sighed. 'Rise Herat, lighten my mood, I beg you.'

At that he swung round, leaned his back against the wall and propped his elbows atop it. 'Seven of your young priestesses trapped Cedorpul in a room. It seems that in boredom they had fallen to comparing experiences at their initiations.'

'Oh dear. What lure does he offer, do you think?'

'He is soft, one supposes, like a pillow.'

'Hmm, yes, that might be it. And the pillow invites, too, a certain angle of repose.'

The historian smiled. 'If you say so. In any case, he sought to flee, and then, when he found his path to the door barred, he pleaded his weakness for beauty.'

'Ah, compliments.'

'But spread out among all seven women, why, their worth was not much.'

'Does he still live?'

'It was close, High Priestess, especially when he suggested they continue the conversation with all clothing divested.'

Smiling, she walked to the wall beside the man. 'Bless Cedorpul. He holds fast to his youth.'

The historian's amusement fell away. 'While Endest Silann seems to age with each night that passes. I wonder, indeed, if he is not somehow afflicted.'

'In some,' she said, 'the soul is a hoarder of years, and makes a wealth of burdens unearned.'

'A flow of blood from Endest Silann's hands is yet another kind of blessing,' Rise observed, twisting round to join her in looking out upon the city. 'At least that is done with, now, but I wonder if some life-force left him through those holy wounds.'

She thought of the mirror in her chamber, that so obsessed her, and there came to her then, following the historian's words, a sudden fear. *Does it steal from me, too? Thief of my youth? Or is time alone my stalker? Mirror, you show me nothing I would want to see, and like a tale of old you curse me with my own regard.* She shrugged the notion off. 'The birth of the sacred in spilled blood – I fear this precedent, Rise. I fear it deeply.'

He nodded. 'She did not deny it, then.'

'By that blood,' said Emral Lanear, 'Mother Dark was able to see through Endest's eyes, and from it all manner of power flowed – so much that she fled its touch. This at least she confessed to me, before she sealed the Chamber of Night from all but her Consort.'

'That is a precious confession,' Rise said. 'I note your burgeoning privilege, High Priestess, in the eyes of Mother Dark. What will you do with it?'

She looked away. At last they had come to the reason for her seeking out the historian. She did not welcome it. 'I see only one path to peace.'

'I would hear it.'

'The Consort must be pushed aside,' she said. 'There must be a wedding.'

'Pushed aside? Is that even possible?'

She nodded. 'In creating the Terondai upon the Citadel floor, he manifested the Gate of Darkness. Whatever arcane powers he had, he surely surrendered them to that gift.' After a moment she shook her head. 'There are mysteries to Lord Draconus. The Azathanai name him Suzerain of Night. What consort is worth such an honorific? Even being a highborn among the Tiste is insufficient elevation, and since when did the Azathanai treat our nobility with anything but amused indifference? No. Perhaps, we might conclude, the title is a measure of respect for his proximity to Mother Dark.'

'But you are not convinced.'

She shrugged. 'She must set him aside. Oh, give him a secret room that they might share—'

'High Priestess, you cannot be serious! Do you imagine

Urusander will bow to that indulgence? And what of Mother Dark herself? Is she to divide her fidelity? Choosing and denying her favour as suits her whim? Neither man would accept that!'

Emral sighed. 'Forgive me. You are right. For peace to return to our realm, someone has to lose. It must be Lord Draconus.'

'Thus, one man is to sacrifice everything, but gain nothing by it.'

'Untrue. He wins peace, and for a man obsessed with gifts, is that one not worthwhile?'

Rise Herat shook his head. 'His gifts are meant to be shared. He would look out upon it as if from the wrong side of a prison's bars. Peace? Not for him, that gift. Not in his heart. Not in his soul. A sacrifice? What man would willingly destroy himself, for *any* cause?'

'If she asks him.'

'A bartering of love, High Priestess? Pity is too weak a word for the fate of Draconus.'

She knew all of this. She had been at war with these thoughts for days and nights, until each became a wheel turning in an ever-deepening rut. The brutality of it exhausted her, as in her mind she set Mother Dark's love for a man against the fate of the realm. It was one thing to announce the necessity for the only path she saw through this civil war, measuring the mollification of the highborn upon the carcass, figurative or literal, of the Consort, in exchange for a broadening of privilege among the officers of Urusander's Legion, but none of this yet bore the weight of Mother Dark's will. And as to that will, the goddess was silent.

*She will not choose. She but indulges her lover and his clumsy expressions of love. She is as good as turned away from all of us, while Kurald Galain descends into ruin.*

*Will it take Urusander's mailed fist pounding upon the door to awaken her?*

'You will have to kill him,' Rise Herat said.

She could not argue that observation.

'The balance of success, however,' the historian went on,

'will be found in choosing whose hand wields the knife. That assassin, High Priestess, cannot but earn eternal condemnation from Mother Dark.'

'A child of this newborn Light, then,' she replied, 'for whom such condemnation means little.'

'Urusander is to arrive to the wedding bed awash in the blood of his new wife's slain lover? No, it cannot be a child of Lios.' His gaze fixed on hers. 'Assure me that you see that, I beg you.'

'Then who among her beloved worshippers would choose such a fate?'

'I think, on this stage you describe, choice has nowhere to dance.'

She caught her breath. 'Whose hand do we force?'

'We? High Priestess, I am not—'

'No,' she snapped. 'You just play with words. A chewer of ideas too frightened to swallow the bone. Is not the flavour woefully short-lived, historian? Or is the habit of chewing sufficient reward for one such as you?'

He looked away, and she saw that he was trembling. 'My thoughts but spiral to a single place,' he slowly said, 'where stands a single man. He is his own fortress, this man that I see before me. But behind his walls he paces in fury. That anger must give us the breach. Our way in to him.'

'How does it sit with you?' Emral asked.

'Like a stone in my gut, High Priestess.'

'The scholar steps into the world, and for all the soldiers that comprise your myriad ideas, you finally comprehend the price of living as they do, as they must. A host of faces – you now wear them all, historian.'

He said nothing, turning to stare out to the distant north horizon.

'One man, then,' she said. 'A most honourable man, whom I love as a son.' She sighed, even as tears stung her eyes. 'He is all but turned away already, and she from him. Poor Anomander.'

'The son slays the lover, in the name of the man who would

be his father. Necessity delivers its own madness, High Priestess.'

'We face difficulties,' Emral said. 'Anomander is fond of Draconus, and this sentiment is mutual. It is measured in great respect and more: it possesses true affection. How do we sunder all of that?'

'Honour,' he replied.

'How so?'

'They are two men who hold honour above all else. It is the proof of integrity, after all, and they choose to live that proof in all that they do.' He faced her again. 'A battle is coming. Facing Urusander, Anomander will command all the Houseblades of the Greater and Lesser Houses. And, perhaps, a resurrected Hust Legion. Paint this picture I offer, High Priestess. The field of battle, the forces arrayed opposite one another. Where, then, do you see Lord Draconus? At the head of his formidable Houseblades – who so efficiently annihilated the Borderswords? He will stand on his honour, yes?'

'Anomander will not deny him,' she whispered.

'And then?' Rise asked. 'When the highborn see who would stand with them in the battle to come? Will they not in rage – in fury – step to one side?'

'But wait, historian. Surely Anomander will blame his highborn allies for abandoning the field?'

'Perhaps at first. Anomander will see that defeat is inevitable. Thus, there will be the humiliation of the surrender to Urusander, and he cannot but see the Consort's gesture as the cause of that. A surrender forced by Draconus's pride, and when the Consort remains unrepentant – he can do no other, as he will see the surrender as a betrayal, as he must; indeed, he will understand it as his own death sentence – then, Lanear, we see them set upon one another.'

'The highborn will acclaim Anomander's disavowal of that friendship,' she said, nodding. 'Draconus will end up isolated. He cannot hope to defeat such united opposition. That battle, historian, will be the last of the civil war.'

'I love this civilization too much,' Rise said, as if tasting the words for himself, 'to see it destroyed. Mother Dark must never know any of this.'

'She will never forgive her First Son.'

'No.'

'Honour,' she said, 'is a terrible thing.'

'All the more egregious our crime, High Priestess, in forging a weapon in the flames of integrity, a fire we will feed until it burns itself out. You see him as a son. I do not envy you, Lanear.'

A voice screamed in her mind, rising up from her wounded soul. The pain that birthed that scream was unbearable. Love and betrayal on a single blade. She felt the edge turn and twist. *But I see no other way! Must Kharkanas die in flames? Will Urusander's soldiers be made into crass thugs, and as thugs take power unopposed, unchecked? Are we doomed to make lovers of war into our rulers? How soon, then, before Mother Dark reveals a raptor's eyes, with talons gripping the arms of the throne? Oh, Anomander, I am sorry.* Roughly, she wiped at her eyes and cheeks. 'I will trap the crime in my mirror,' she said in a broken voice, 'where it can howl unheard.'

'And to think how Syntara underestimates you.'

She shook her head. 'No longer, perhaps. I have written to her.'

'You have? Then it begins in earnest.'

'We will see. She is yet to reply.'

'Did you address her as an equal, High Priestess?'

She nodded.

'Then you make your language *familiar*, in the ancient sense of the word. She will preen in that plumage.'

'Yes. Vanity was ever the breach in her walls.'

'We assemble a sordid list here, Lanear. When fortresses abound, we make sieges life's daily habit. In such a world, we each stand alone at day's end, and face in fear our barred door.' The strain deepened the lines on his face. 'A most sordid list.'

'Each one a single step upon the path, historian. No longer can you hold to this post, high above the world. Now, Rise Herat, you must walk among the rest of us.'

'I will write none of this. The privilege is gone from my heart.'

'It is just the blood on your hands,' she replied, without much sympathy. 'When it is all said and done, you can wash them clean in the river below. And in time, as that river flows on and on, the truth will be dispersed, until none could hope to discern your crimes. Or mine.'

'Then I will see you kneeling at my side on that day, High Priestess.'

She nodded. 'If there can be whores of history, Rise, then we are surely in their company.'

He was studying her, with the face of a condemned man. *See now, woman? The mirrors are everywhere.*

\*    \*    \*

Step by step, pilgrims made a path. Seeking a place of tragedy deemed holy, or a site sanctified by nothing more than a truth or two scraped down to the bone, the ones who sought out such places transformed them into shrines. Endest Silann understood this now: that the sacred was not found, but delivered. Memory spun the thread, each pilgrim a single strand, stretched and twisted, spun, spun into life. It did not matter that he had been the first. Others among his priestly kin were setting out, into the face of winter, to arrive at the ruined estate of Andarist. They walked in his footsteps, but left no blood on the trail. They arrived and they stood, looking upon the site of past slaughter, but did so without comprehension.

Their journey, he knew, was a search. For something, for a state of being, perhaps. And in that contemplation, that silent yearning, they found . . . nothing. He imagined them stepping forward into the clearing before the house, walking around, eyes scanning the worthless ground, the crooked stones and the withered grasses that would grow thick and green in patches come the spring. Finally, they crossed the threshold, walking over the flagstones hiding the mouldering corpses of the slain, and before them, in the chill gloom, waited the hearthstone, now a sunken altar, with its indecipherable words carved upon its stone face. He saw them looking around, imaginations conjuring up ghosts, placing one here, another there. They sought, in the silence, for faint echoes, the trapped cries of loss and anguish. They took note, without question, of the black droplets of blood everywhere, not understanding their meandering way, not understanding Endest's own senseless wandering – no, they would seek some vast meaning in that trail on the stones.

Imagination was a terrible thing, a scavenger that could grow fat on the smallest morsels. Hook-beaked, talons scraping and clacking, it lumbered about casting a greedy eye.

But in the end, it all meant nothing.

His fellow acolytes then returned to the Citadel. They looked on him with envy, with something like awe. They looked to him, and that alone was like the reopening of wounds, because there were no worthy secrets hiding in Endest's memories. Every detail, already blurring and blending, was meaningless.

*I am the priest of the pointless, seneschal to the hapless. You see my silence as humility. You see the wear in my face as some burden willingly taken on, and so give me a gravity of countenance I hardly deserve. And in your debates, you ever turn to me, seeking validation, revelation, a pageant of wise words behind which you can dance and sing and bless the darkness.*

He could not tell them the source of his weariness. He could not confess the truth, much as he longed to. He could not say, *You fools, she looked through my eyes and made them weep. She bled through my hands and saw in horror that it sanctified, dripping tears of power. She took hold of me only to then flee, leaving behind nothing but despair.*

*I will age as hope dies. I will bend to the weight of failure. My bones will creak to the crumbling of Kurald Galain. Do not look to my memories, my brothers and sisters. Already they twist with doubt. Already they take on the shape of my flaws.*

*No. Do not follow me. I but walk to the grave.*

A short time earlier, while he sat on the bench of the inner garden, huddled against the bitter cold, beneath a thick cloak of bear fur, he had seen the young hostage, Orfantal, run alongside the fountain with its black frozen pool. The boy held a practice sword in one hand, and the dog, Ribs, ran beside him as if it had rediscovered its youth. Now free of worms, it had gained weight, that beast, and showed the sleek muscles of its hunting origins. Together, they played out imaginary battles, and more than once Endest had come upon Orfantal in his death-throes, with Ribs drawing close beside the boy as he lay on the ground, spoiling the gravitas of the scene with a cold wet nose snuffling against Orfantal's face. He'd yelp and then curse the dog, but it was difficult to find malice in the love the animal displayed, and before long they would be wrestling on the thin carpet of snow.

Endest Silann was no indulgent witness to all of this. In the dull, half-formed shadows cast by child and dog, he saw only nightmares in waiting.

Lord Anomander had left the wretched house of his brother – scene of recent slaughter – in the company of the Azathanai High Mason, Caladan Brood. They had struck north, into the burned forest. Endest had watched them from the blood-stained threshold.

'*I will hold you to your promise of peace,*' Anomander had said to Brood, just before they left, when they all still stood in the house.

Caladan had regarded him. '*Understand this, Son of Darkness, I build with my hands. I am a maker of monuments to lost causes. If you travel west of here, you will find my works. They adorn ruins and other forgotten places. They stand, as eternal as I could make them, to reveal the virtues to which every age aspires. They are lost now but will be rediscovered. In the days of a wounded, dying people, these monuments are raised again. And again. Not to worship, not to idolize – only the cynics find pleasure in that, to justify the suicide of their own faith. No, they raise them in hope. They raise them to plead for sanity. They raise them to fight against futility.*'

Anomander had gestured back to the hearthstone. '*Is that now another one of your monuments?*'

'*Intentions precede our deeds, and then are left lying in the wake of those deeds. I am not the voice of posterity, Anomander Rake. Nor are you.*'

'*Rake?*'

'*Purake is an Azathanai word,*' Brood said. '*You did not know? It was an honorific granted to your family, to your father in his youth.*'

'*Why? How did he earn it?*'

The Azathanai shrugged. '*K'rul gave it. He did not share his reasons. Or, rather, "she", as K'rul is wont to change his mind's way of thinking, and so assumes a woman's guise every few centuries. He is now a man, but back then he was a woman.*'

'*Do you know its meaning, Caladan?*'

'*Pur Rakess Calas ne A'nom. Roughly, Strength in Standing Still.*'

'*A'nom,*' said the Son of Darkness, frowning.

'*Perhaps,*' the Azathanai said, '*as a babe, you were quick to stand.*'

'*And Rakess? Or Rake, as you would call me?*'

'*Only what I see in you, and what all others see in you. Strength.*'

'*I feel no such thing.*'

'*No one who is strong does.*'

They had conversed as if Endest was not there, as if he was deaf to their words. The two men, Tiste and Azathanai, had begun forging something between them, and whatever it was, it was unafraid of truths.

'*My father died because he would not retreat from battle.*'

'*Your father was bound in the chains of his family name.*'

'*As I will be, Caladan? You give me hope.*'

'*Forgive me, Rake, but strength is not always a virtue. I will raise no monument to you.*'

The Son of Darkness had smiled, then. '*At last, you say something that wholly pleases me.*'

'Yet still you are worshipped. Many by nature would hide in strength's shadow.'

'I will defy them.'

'Such principles are rarely appreciated,' Caladan said. 'Expect excoriation. Condemnation. Those who are not your equals will claim for their own that equality, and yet will meet your eyes with expectation, with profound presumption. Every kindness you yield they will take as deserved, but such appetites are unending, and your denial is the crime they but await. Commit it and witness their subsequent vilification.'

Anomander shrugged at that, as if the expectations of others meant nothing to him, and whatever would come from his standing upon the principles he espoused, he would bear it. 'You promised peace, Caladan. I vowed to hold you to that, and nothing we have said now has changed my mind.'

'Yes, I said I would guide you, and I will. And in so doing, I will rely upon your strength, and hope it robust enough to bear each and every burden I place upon it. So I remind myself, and you, with the new name I give you. Will you accept it, Anomander Rake? Will you stand in strength?'

'My father's name proved a curse. Indeed, it proved the death of him.'

'Yes.'

'Very well, Caladan Brood, I will take this first burden.'

Of course. The Son of Darkness could do no less.

They had departed then, leaving Endest alone in the desecrated house. Alone, with the blood drying on his hands. Alone, and hollowed out by the departing of Mother Dark's presence.

She had heard every word.

And had, once more, fled.

He shivered in the garden, despite the furs. As if he had never regained the blood lost all that time past, there at the pilgrims' shrine, he could no longer fight off the cold. *Do not look to me. Your regard ages me. Your hope weakens me. I am no prophet. My only purpose is to deliver the sanctity of blood.*

Yet a battle was coming, a battle in the heart of winter, upending the proper season of war. And, along with all the other priests, and many of the priestesses, Endest would be there, ready to dress wounds and to comfort the dying. Ready to bless the day before the first weapon was drawn. But, alone among all the anointed, he would possess another task, another responsibility.

*By my hands, I will let flow the sanctity of blood. And make of the place of battle another grisly shrine.*

He thought of Orfantal dying, in the moment before Ribs pounced, and saw the spatters of blood on the snow around the boy.

She had begun returning now, faint and silent, and with his eyes, the goddess etched the future.

That was bad enough by itself, but something he could withstand.

*If not for her growing thirst.*

*Do not look at me. Do not seek to know me. You'll not like my truths.*

*Step by step, this pilgrim makes a path.*

\* \* \*

Bedecked in his heavy armour, Kellaras stood hesitating in the corridor when Silchas Ruin appeared. The commander stepped to one side to let the lord past. Instead, Silchas halted.

'Kellaras, have you sought entry into the Chamber of Night?'

'No, milord. My courage fails me.'

'What news do you bring that so unmans you?'

'None but truths I regret knowing, milord. I have word from Captain Galar Baras. He has done as you commanded, but in the observation of his new recruits, he reiterates his doubt.'

Silchas turned to study the blackwood door at the corridor's end. 'No counsel will be found there, commander.'

*I fear you are right.* Kellaras shrugged. 'My apologies, milord. I sought but could not find you.'

'Yet you stepped aside and voiced no greeting.'

'Forgive me, milord. All courage fails me. I believe what I sought in the Chamber of Night was a gift of faith from my goddess.'

'Alas,' said Silchas Ruin in a growl, 'she makes faith into water, and pleasures in its feel as it drains from the hand. Even our thirst is denied us. Very well, Kellaras, I have your news, but it changes nothing. The Hust armour must be worn, the swords held in living hands. Perhaps this will be enough to give Urusander pause.'

'He will know the measure of those in that armour, milord, and the fragility of the grasp upon those swords.'

'You would spread the sand beneath your feet out and under my own, Kellaras, but I need to remain sure of each stride I take.'

'Milord, any word of your brothers?'

Silchas frowned. 'You think us eager to share such privacies, commander? Your lord will find you in good time, and yield no sympathy should your courage fail in his eyes. Now, divest yourself of that armour – its display whispers of panic.'

Bowing, Kellaras backed away.

Facing the Chamber of Night, Silchas Ruin seemed to hesitate, as if about to march towards it, and then he wheeled round. 'A moment, commander. Send Dathenar and Prazek to the Hust, and charge them take command of the new cohorts, and so give answer to Galar Baras's needs, as best we can.'

Startled, Kellaras asked, 'Milord, are they to don Hust armour? Take up a Hust sword?'

Silchas Ruin's face hardened. 'Has courage failed everyone in our House? Leave my sight, commander!'

'Milord.' Kellaras quickly set off. As he marched up the corridor, he could feel Ruin's baleful glare upon his back. *Panic's bite is indeed a fever. And here I am, the flea upon a thousand hides.* He would return to his chamber and remove his armour, setting aside the girdle of war, but retain his sword as befitted his rank. Silchas was right. A soldier makes of his garb a statement, and an invitation. It was the swagger of violence, but inside that armour there could be diffidence and, indeed, great fear.

He would then set out and find Dathenar and Prazek where he had left them, upon the Citadel's bridge.

*Harbinger blades for those two, and a chorus of scales. Oh, my friends, I see you shrivel before my eyes at this news. Forgive me.*

The Citadel's darkness was suffocating. Again and again he found the need to pause and draw a deep, settling breath. In the corridors and colonnaded hallways, he walked virtually alone, and it was all too easy to imagine this place abandoned, haunted by a host of failures – no different, then, from any ruin he had visited out in the lands to the south, where the Forulkan left only their bones amidst the rubble. The sense of things still unfinished was like a curse riding an endless breath. It moaned on the wind and made stones tick in the heat. It whispered in the sifting of sand and voiced low laughter in the slip of pebbles between the fingers.

He could see this fortress devoid of life, a scorched shell that made Dark's temple a bitter jest. Worshipped by spiders in their dusty webs, and beetles crawling through bat guano – a man wandering through such a place would find nothing worth remembering. The failings of the past cut like a sharp knife through any hope of nostalgia, or sweet reminiscence. He could not help but wonder at the impermanence of such places as temples and other holy sites. If nothing more than symbols of lost faith, then they stood as mortal failings. But if gods died in such ruins – if they felt a blade sink into their hearts, or slide smooth across their soft throats, then the crime was beyond any surrendering of faith.

Still, perhaps holiness was nothing more than an eye's gift – upon these stones, or that tree, or the spring bubbling beneath it. Perhaps the only murder possible in such places was the one that left hope lying lifeless upon the ground.

Leaving his chamber and making his way towards the outer ward and the gate, beyond which waited the bridge, Kellaras was forced to cross the Terondai's glittering pattern cut into the flagstones. He could feel the power beneath him, emanating in slow exudations, like the breath of a sleeping god. The sensation crawled across his skin.

He emerged into the chill night, where frost glistened on the stone walls and the lone Houseblade positioned at the gate stood huddled beneath a heavy cloak, dozing as she leaned against the barrier. Hearing his approach, she straightened.

'Sir.'

'You have closed the gate.'

She nodded. 'I saw, sir, that the bridge was unguarded.'

'Unguarded? Where, then, are Dathenar and Prazek?'

'I do not know, sir.'

Kellaras gestured and she hurried to unbar the gate. The hinges squealed as she pushed on the portal. The captain passed through, on to the bridge. The bitter chill in this almost perpetual night was made all the more fierce by the black waters of the Dorssan Ryl. His boots cracked on ice as he hurried across the span.

He could well guess the refuge Dathenar and Prazek had found. Dereliction by officers was a grievous offence, and worse, the example it set could deliver a mortal wound to morale. Yet, in his heart, Kellaras could not blame his two friends. Their lord had abandoned them, and the one brother who remained to command the Citadel's Houseblades often mistook birthright for wisdom: with this last command, written in the spinning of a heel, half the officers remaining to the Houseblades were divested of their colours.

Without question, Galar Baras and the Hust would welcome this gift, although Kellaras suspected that even his friend would be startled at the largesse, and perhaps wonder at Silchas Ruin's unleavened generosity with respect to Anomander's soldiers.

Attachment to any other force might be cause for envy, under the circumstances, but Kellaras was under no illusions, and he well knew the effect delivering this command would have upon Dathenar and Prazek. *As good as banishment. And so it will seem, given their abandoning their post, and to be honest, I am loath to deny the connection. Officers, by the Abyss! No, it's serendipitous punishment, enough to sober them to the quick.*

The Gillswan was a tavern that made a virtue of its obscure location, down a curling slope to a loading dock and sunk into the foundations of a lesser bridge. The cobbles were uneven due to frost-heaving, all the more treacherous with the addition of frozen puddles filling the gaps left by missing stones. Despite this, the gloom failed in disguising the pitfalls, and Kellaras made his way to the low door without mishap. He pushed it open and felt smoky heat gust into his face.

Prazek's voice crossed the cramped, crowded room. 'Kellaras! Here, join us hogs in the swill! We are drunk in defeat, my friend, but see us welcome the woe and wallow of our fate!'

Kellaras saw his friends, leaning against one another on a bench backed by a wall. Ignoring the crowd of off-duty Houseblades, even those that called out in greeting, he made his way over to Dathenar and Prazek, pulled out a chair and sat down opposite them. Faces flushed, they smiled. Then Dathenar pushed a flagon towards the commander, and said, 'It's the beastly tongue that wags us this night, my friend.'

'There is pomp to this circumstance nonetheless,' Prazek said, lurching forward to rest his thick forearms on the table. 'No highborn can truly sink into the hole of ignorance's cloying mud. We poke our faces free again and again, gasping for air.'

'If this fug be air,' Dathenar said in a growl. 'Besides, I am too drunk to swim, too bloated to drown, and too confused to tell the difference. We left the bridge – this much I know – and that is a crime in the eyes of our lord.'

'Fortunate, then,' said Prazek, 'that our lord's eyes are elsewhere.'

'Unfortunate,' corrected Kellaras, 'since I must see in his stead.'

'That will make any man's eyes sting,' Dathenar said.

'I'll not deny that,' Kellaras replied, pointedly.

But neither man was in any condition for subtlety. With a

broad, sloppy smile, Prazek waved one hand. 'Must we take our posts again? Will you berate us with cold promises? At the very least, friend, build us a fine argument, an intricaspy – intrica*cy* – of purpose. Hook fingers into the nostrils and drag out the noble horse, so we may see its fine trappings. Honour's bridle—'

'Pride's stirrups!' shouted Dathenar, raising his flagon.

'Duty's bit between the teeth!'

'Loyalty's over-worn saddle, so sweet under the cheeks!'

'To take belch's foul cousin—'

'Friends,' said Kellaras in a warning hiss, 'that is enough of that. Your words are unfit for officers of Lord Anomander's Houseblades. You try my indulgence. Now, be on your feet, and pray the cold night air yields you sobriety.'

Prazek's brows lifted and he looked to Dathenar. 'He dares it, brother! To the bridge, then! Torches approach from some dire quarter. 'Tis revelation's light, to make every sinner cower!'

'Not the bridge,' Kellaras said, sighing. 'You have been reassigned. Both of you. By command of Silchas Ruin. You are to join the Hust Legion.'

This silenced them. Looking upon their shocked expressions offered Kellaras no satisfaction.

'F-for abandoning our posts?' Prazek asked in disbelief.

'No. That crime stays between us. The matter is more prosaic. Galar Baras has terrible need for officers. This is Ruin's answer.'

'Oh,' muttered Dathenar, 'it is indeed. Ruin, ruinous answer, ruin of all privilege, ruin of life. A command voiced with distinction – alas, we hear it all too well.'

'Our privilege to do so,' nodded Prazek, 'in language less than obscure.'

'More than plain, brother.'

'Just so, Dathenar. See me long for sudden complexity. Wish me swathed in obfuscation and euphoric euphemism. I would flee to the nearest lofty tower, worthy of my hauteur. I would sniff and decry the state's sordid . . . state, and then frown and announce: the wine is too tart. Too . . . too, far too . . . tart.'

'I'll whip the servant, brother, if that pleases you.'

'Pleasing is dead, Dathenar, and dead . . . pleasing.'

Dathenar groaned and rubbed at his face. 'Prazek, we should never have left unguarded the bridge. See what fate we let cross, when a mere switch would have sent the hog running. So be it. I yield to simple fate and name her just.'

Prazek pushed himself upright. 'Commander Kellaras, we are, as ever, at your call.'

Grunting, Dathenar stood as well. 'Perchance the sword has a bawdy tale, to amuse us in our perfidy. And the armour – well, it is said to be loquacious to a fault, but I'll not begrudge the warning voice, even should we fail in heeding it.'

Standing, Kellaras gestured to the door. 'Step carefully once outside, friends. The way back is uncertain.'

Both men nodded at that.

# THREE

---

'*THERE WILL BE JUSTICE!*'

When that call came, echoing down the long, foul tunnels, Wareth thought it a sour joke. Belatedly, he comprehended the earnestness in that cry. And when he dropped the heavy pick in his hands, the sudden absence of that familiar weight almost made him stagger back a step.

He was alone, at the far end of a deep vein. The words whispered their echoes as if the iron ore itself was speaking to him in the darkness. He remained motionless, drawing in the chill air, as the ache in his hands slowly faded. The past was a cruel and remorseless pursuer, and in this place – for Wareth and for all the others down these shafts – it muttered of justice more often than not.

Again the call sounded. Close around him, the rock wept its unceasing tears, making glittering runnels around patches of luminescence, pooling at his feet. If those words iterated a promise, it was far too late. If a summons, then far past time. He had yet to turn round. The way ahead, just visible in the gloom, was a blunted, battered wall. He had been beating at it for weeks now. It had served him well, as a place where he could, with his back to the world, live out his wakeful existence. He had grown to admire the vein's stubborn defiance, had come to grieve its shattering surrender, piece by piece.

The pick Wareth had wielded was a fine tool. Iron tamed and given shape. Iron domesticated, subjugated, forged into a slayer of its wild kin. This was the only battle he fought, and he and the pick fought it well, and so the wild ore retreated, shard by shard. Of course, the truth was, the vein did not retreat. It simply died, in buckets of rubble. This was the only war he knew how to win.

The cry sounded a third time, but fainter now, as the other miners worked their way to the surface, rising sunward. He thought to retrieve his pick, to resume his assault. The wild stood no chance. It never did. Instead, he swung round, to make his way back to the surface.

More often than not, justice was a word written in blood. The curiosity that tugged him onward, and upward, made him no different from anyone else. That righteous claim needed a victim. It depended on there being one, and this fed a kind of lust.

Hunched over, he made his way up the shaft, his boots splashing through the pools made by the weeping rock. The trek took some time.

Eventually, he stood at the mine's ragged entrance, blinking in the harsh sunlight. Sharp pains stabbed at his lower back as he straightened to his full height for the first time since rising from his cot that morning. Sweat streamed from him despite the air's wintry bite, mixing with dust and grime as it ran down his bared torso. He could feel his muscles slowly contracting to the cold and it seemed as if simple light and clean, bitter air could cleanse him, scouring skin, flesh, bone and down into his very soul, and so yield the miracle of restitution, of redemption. In the wake of that notion came mocking derision.

Other miners were shouting, some singing, running like children across the snow-dusted ground. He heard the word *freedom* and listened to laughter that would make a sane man cringe. But Wareth looked to the prison guards for the truth of this day. They still ringed the vast pit that housed the mining camp's compound. Many of them now ebon-skinned, they leaned on their spears and made grim silhouettes against the skyline on all sides. At the south edge, at the end of the ramp that climbed to a barricaded gatehouse and barracks, the iron gates remained shut.

He was not alone in remaining silent, and watchful. He was not alone in his growing scepticism.

No one freed prisoners, unless indeed the civil war had seen an overthrow of all authority; or, with a new ruler upon the Throne of Darkness, an amnesty had been announced. But the cries of freedom lacked specific details. *'We are to be freed! On this day! Prisoners no longer!'*

*'There will be justice at last!'*

That last proclamation was absurd. Every miner in this camp belonged here. They had committed crimes, terrible crimes. They had, in the words of the magistrate, abrogated their compact with civil society. In more common diction, they were one and all murderers, or worse.

The guards remained. Society, it seemed, was not yet ready to welcome them. The hysteria of the moment was fast fading, as others at last took notice of the guards in their usual positions, and the barred gate with its barbed fangs. Elation collapsed. Voices growled, and then cursed.

Wareth looked over to the women's camp. The night-shifters were stumbling from their cells, dishevelled and drawing together in knots. No guards stood between them and the men. He could sense their burgeoning fear.

*All the animals loose in the corral. Even this cold air cannot stifle a beast's passions. Trouble is moments away.*

Regretting leaving his pick behind, he looked round, and saw a shovel on the ground beside an ore cart, a breach of rules more shocking than anything else this day. He walked over and collected it, and then, as if unable to stop what he had begun, he slowly made his way towards the women.

Wareth was tall, and his nine years in the shafts as lead rock-biter had broadened his shoulders and thickened his neck. His body now bore unnatural proportions, his arms and torso too large for his hips and legs. The curl and pull of overworked muscles had spread wide his shoulder blades while drawing him inward at his upper chest, giving him a hunched-over appearance. The bones of his legs had bowed, but not as much as he could see in many other miners. At shift's end, after his meal, he took to his cot, where he had bound belts to the iron frame, and these he fastened about himself, forcing his legs straight. And the one man he trusted, Rebble, would come to him then and tighten the straps across his chest and shoulders, forcing them flat. The agony of these efforts lived with him every night, yet exhaustion proved its master, and he slept despite the pain.

With something cold gripping his insides, he wended his way through the crowd, pushing aside those who had not seen him approaching. Others simply stepped back to clear his path. Faces frowned at him, uncomprehending, eyes narrowing as they saw the shovel in his hands.

He was through most of the press when a man ahead suddenly laughed and shouted, 'The kittens are awake, my friends! See the way unopposed – I think this is the freedom we've won!'

Wareth reached the man even as he began moving towards the women.

With all his strength, he swung the shovel into the man's head, crushing one side of the skull and snapping the neck. The sound it made was a shock that silenced those nearby. The body fell, twitched, blood and something like water leaking out around its broken head. Wareth stared down at the corpse, filled with the usual revulsion and fascination. The shovel was almost weightless in his hands.

Then something pulled him away, made him continue on, to take his place in the gap between the men and the women. As he turned to face his brothers of the pit, resting the shovel on one shoulder, he saw Rebble emerging, carrying a bulker's pick. The third man to appear, also armed with a shovel, was Listar. Quiet and shy, his crime was a lifelong abuse of his wife that ended in her strangulation. But questions remained whether the cord had been in his hands. Questions, too, on that charge of abuse. But Listar would say nothing, not even to plead innocence. Wareth could never be sure of the man, yet here he was, ready to give his life in defence of unarmed women.

Rebble was tall and wiry. He had not cut the hair on his head and face since arriving at the mine, seven years past. His dark eyes glittered amidst a black, snarled nest, showing everyone that his temper was close. Once unleashed, the man knew not how to stop that rage. He had killed four men, one of whom had possibly insulted him. The other three had tried to intervene.

No others joined Wareth, and he saw men finding their own picks and shovels, and then making their way forward. One of them pointed a shovel at Wareth. 'Ganz never even saw you coming. The coward strikes again. Rebble, Listar, look to this man who holds your centre, and when I go to him, watch him run!'

Wareth said nothing, but even he could feel how their moment of bold chivalry was fast fading. Neither Rebble nor Listar could count on him, and they had just realized it. He turned to Rebble and spoke under his breath. 'Break open the women's shed. Let them arm themselves.'

Rebble's smile was hard and cold. 'And you'll do what, Wareth? Hold them here?'

'He may not, but I will,' said Listar. 'This is a day of justice. Let me face it and be done with.' He glanced over at Wareth. 'I know you hated Ganz. His mouth always got him in trouble. But this stand here, Wareth? It's not like you.'

Listar spoke the truth, and Wareth had no answer to give.

Ganz's friend was edging closer, with his companions drawing up behind him.

Wareth had hoped that some old feuds would erupt among the men. Explosions of violence to distract them – acts of vengeance such as his attack on Ganz. Instead, he had caught their collective attention. A mistake, and one likely to see him killed. *A pick between my shoulder blades.*

*As I run.*

With a curious glance at Listar, Rebble moved off.

Ganz's friend laughed. 'The bold line collapses!'

The heat was building in Wareth despite the chill, an old familiar fire. It pooled and dissolved his insides. He could feel it burning his face and knew that for shame. His heart pounded fast and a weakness took his legs.

A loud crack startled everyone, and then the squeal of the shed door sounded behind Wareth.

'Shit,' someone swore. 'We're too fucking late now. Wareth, you'll pay for this. Cut him down, Merrec. The chase will make it a fine game, hey?'

Men laughed.

Wareth turned to Listar. 'Not today, then, your justice.'

Listar shrugged, stepping back. 'Then another. So, best you start running.'

Merrec advanced on Wareth. 'You've killed enough people from behind. All these years. Stand still now, rabbit.' He raised the shovel.

Wareth tensed, terror rising up from his stomach to grip his throat. He prepared to throw the shovel, before bolting.

There was a solid thud and Merrec halted suddenly, looked down at the arrow buried deep in his chest.

Someone shouted.

Merrec sank to the ground, disbelief giving way to agony on his face.

The guards were now descending from the rim of the bowl, and on the gatehouse ramp there stood a dozen soldiers, and from them came a thin moaning sound.

Wareth knew that sound. He knew it well. He flinched back, dropping his shovel.

\*     \*     \*

'That was dishonourable,' said Seltin Ryggandas, glaring at Galar Baras. 'By this craven murder, with a hunter's arrow at that, we are to see the rebirth of Hust Legion?'

*Dishonour. Now there's a word. Dry as tinder, needing only the hint of a spark to flare up, burn bright, rage incandescent. Dishonour. The stake pinning us all to the ground, and see us now. You, Hunn Raal, with your poisoned wine, and me, here, both of us writhing in place.* Galar Baras drew off his gauntlets and carefully folded them, before tucking them behind his sword-belt. 'Quartermaster,

92

even honour must, on occasion, surrender to timing.'

Seltin's expression of disgust was unchanged. 'Timing? You waited too long to intervene.'

Ignoring the Legion's quartermaster, Galar Baras glanced skyward. The chill winter blue was unbroken by cloud, making the vault seem all the more remote. *As we see the heavens constrained, by all that we do here. No matter – these are smaller dramas than they feel.* He turned to the pit's overseer. 'Sir, tell me about those three.'

The elderly man shook his head. 'If you sought to single them out in the name of decency, your desire was misplaced. No, it was doomed from the start, as I could have told you, captain. Not one down there is worthy of Lord Henarald's largesse. They ended up here for a reason, every one of them.'

Galar Baras sighed. He had weathered the same complaints, the same bleak observations, from the overseers of the last two prison mines. 'Indulge me then, and speak of the three men who chose to defend the women.'

The overseer was long in replying, warring with something like reluctance, as if in the details he would offer, hope would die many deaths. Galar felt a moment of sympathy for the man, but insufficient to dissuade him from his task here. He was about to set iron in the command when the overseer finally spoke. 'The lanky one, who showed the wit to break open the shed and so give leave to the women to arm themselves, he is named Rebble.'

'Go on.'

'Brave enough, I suppose. But captain, Rebble is slave to a mad rage. He skirts a pit, and is known to leap into it at the slightest hint of disrespect.'

*Dishonour, again. It is the only language left us, it seems, here in Kurald Galain.* 'Rebble, then. The next man?'

'Listar, upon the other side, was a bully to the weak, and down there the weak are all long dead. His stand surprised me, I admit. He was accused following charges laid by the family of his murdered wife. Accused, tried, and then sentenced. None refuted the evidence, least of all Listar.'

'He confessed his guilt?'

'He said nothing at all, and upon that matter remains silent to this day.' The overseer hesitated, and then added, 'Guilt binds his tongue, I should think. Captain, do not imagine some secret virtue in Listar's silence. Do not look for anything worthy of redemption – not here, not among those men and women below.'

'Now, the big-shouldered one.'

'The worst of the lot,' the overseer said, frowning at Galar. He paused, and then added, 'A Legion soldier, but witnessed to be a coward in battle.'

'Legion?' Galar Baras asked. 'Which legion?'

The overseer scowled. 'You do not recognize him? I thought you but played with me. That is Wareth, once of the Hust.'

Galar Baras looked back down in the pit. For a moment, he could not see Wareth. Then he caught sight of him, sitting on the side of an ox-trough, forearms resting on his thighs as he looked out on the compound, where the guards were forcing the men to one side and the women to the other. For all the comfort of picks and shovels in the hands of the prisoners, none was foolish enough to face armoured guards wielding spears. 'He has changed,' the captain said.

'No,' the overseer replied. 'He hasn't.'

*Redemption – ah, but overseer, what else can I offer? What other currency, beyond vile freedom, for these fools who so ruined their lives? That word should not taste so bitter. That desire should not make such grisly paths, bridging what was and what is to come.*

The notion hovered in his mind, as if a standard raised high, to face an enemy upon the other side of the valley. *Yet dishonour has its own banner, its stained flag of recrimination. Are they even enemies? But look at any civil war, and see two foes marching in parallel, stubborn on their chosen tracks to their chosen future. To clash upon battle's field, they must first clash in their respective minds. Arguments of righteousness will lead us all, in the end, to the anguished need for redemption.*

*All for day's end. And yet, for these prisoners, these crimi-*
*nals, I can only offer them a walk back along the path they*
*each left behind, an uncurling of deeds, an unravelling of*
*fates.*

This purpose, here, made for solitary thoughts. But not a single doubt could be exercised, he knew. The time was not now. The company was all wrong. 'Sergeant Bavras, take two with you and go down and collect Listar, Rebble and Wareth.'

'Wareth, sir?'

'Wareth,' Galar Baras said. 'Overseer, if you'd be so kind, I would make use of your office in the gatehouse.'

The man shrugged. 'My office. Both title and place are dead to me now. Or so I now understand. At my age, captain, the future narrows to a single road, fading into the unseen. One walks, eyeing the closing mists, but no mortal power of will, or desire, can halt these plodding steps.'

'Lord Henarald will not abandon you, sir.'

'Shall I, too, don a dead soldier's weeping armour? Take up a howling sword? Not my road, captain.'

'I'm sure that you will be free to choose from a number of appointments, overseer.'

'They would kill me, you know,' the man said, nodding down at the prisoners. 'A thousand times over. For so long, I have been the face of their guilt, which they will despise until death takes them.'

'I imagine so. I am not so foolish as to think otherwise. But sir, there is more to being a soldier of the Hust than just the weapons and armour.'

'They'll not fight for the realm.'

'To that, I must agree,' said Seltin Ryggandas, crossing his arms.

'If you two are correct,' Galar said, 'then, overseer, you will soon be back here. And so will those men and women below. And you, quartermaster, can return to your store-rooms of materiel, with none to claim it.'

Seltin's laugh was low and only mildly harsh. 'You describe a clerk's paradise, captain.'

After a moment, the overseer snorted. 'There is such joy in this appointment.'

Galar Baras managed a smile, and he settled a hand on the man's shoulder. 'For what is to come, which would you prefer, your task or mine?'

The overseer shook his head. 'Captain, I yield my office.'

*     *     *

Wareth stood as the three Hust soldiers approached. He saw that they had already rounded up Listar and Rebble, and neither man looked pleased. Proof to the rumours, the Hust soldiers now wore banded armour of the same black-smeared iron as the weapons in their scabbards, and as they drew nearer the moaning sounds shifted into a kind of chatter, as if a crowd was gathering. Wareth thought he heard laughter.

'Come with us,' the sergeant said.

'I prefer the shafts below,' Wareth said. 'Ask your captain to make this day like any other. For me. There is still ore to be won from the rock.'

The sergeant was working hard at keeping the disgust from his expression. He was young, but not too young for contempt. 'This pit is now closed. Save your words for the captain.' He gestured and then set off. The two soldiers moved to push Wareth forward. He fell in alongside Rebble and Listar.

'What manner of game is this?' Rebble asked. 'If they were coming for you, that I can see. It's a wonder they didn't execute you in the field. But what do they want with us?'

Wareth had his ideas about that. If those ideas circled the truth, he surely did not belong in the company of these two prisoners. 'My sword defied them,' he said.

'What?'

'On the field,' Wareth said. 'When they sought to disarm me, before executing me. My sword tried to kill them all.'

'Then it's true,' said Listar. 'The weapons live.'

'In the end,' Wareth said, 'I agreed to surrender it. By then, the commander had arrived, and I was sent to her tent in chains. She was drunk . . . with victory,' he added.

'She deemed the mines a mercy?' Rebble asked, in astonishment.

'No. Perhaps. I could not guess her mind.'

He knew the soldiers were listening to this conversation, but none offered a comment.

They reached the ramp and began the ascent. The captain had left the small company of Hust soldiers positioned there, and the overseer stood to one side, like a man forgotten. Wareth met his eyes and the overseer shook his head.

*Am I to be executed then? We three are collected up, but for two purposes. Theirs, I think I understand. Mine? Well, nine years is a long reprieve, by any sane standards.*

He could feel his terror returning, familiar as a treacherous friend. It muttered its belated warnings, fuelling his imagination. It mocked his stupidity.

*I should have ignored the unarmed women. I should have let this damned Hust captain see what we all really were. But Ganz used to spit down from the top of the shaft, aiming for me beside the water station. I don't forget such things.*

They passed through the gate. On one side of the gatehouse, beyond the razor-studded bars, was a door that had been left open. The sergeant halted the group just outside the doorway. 'The captain wishes to speak to each of you, but one at a time.' The man pointed at Listar. 'You first.'

'Any reason for that?' Rebble asked in a growl.

'No,' the sergeant replied, before escorting Listar into the corridor beyond the door.

The remaining pair of soldiers moved off to one side, and began a muted conversation that was marked, on occasion, by a glance back at Wareth. Now he took note that one of them – the woman – had a hunter's bow strapped to her back. *Merrec's last kiss.*

'You've too many friends,' Rebble muttered, pulling at the joints of his fingers, making each one pop. He did this in a particular order, the part of the habit that defied Wareth's attempts at making sense of it, and once again he bit back on his curiosity. For all he knew, it was the secret code of his friend's forbearance, and a fragile one at that.

'Before you,' he now replied, 'I had but one.'

Rebble glanced at him with his dark, half-mad eyes. 'That sword?'

'You have the truth of it.'

'Yet you never saw me as metal for your confessions.'

'I would say, perhaps, I learned my lesson.'

Rebble grunted, nodding. 'I have many friends. Of course I do. Better my friend than my enemy, hey?'

'The regret of the broken bodies strewn in the wake of your temper, Rebble. But when that rage is chained, you are an honourable man.'

'You think? I doubt the worth of that honour, Wareth. Maybe this is why we're friends.'

'I will take that wound,' Wareth said after a moment. 'It was your temper, after all, that warded me when I was bound to the cot.'

'If you'd been bound face-down, even that would not have sufficed.'

'Rapists don't live long in the pit.'

'Nor do the raped.'

'So,' Wareth said, and he ground the word out. 'We have a code.'

'Of honour? Maybe so, when you put it that way. Tell me, does it take cleverness to be a coward?'

'I think so.'

'I think so, too.'

The sergeant reappeared with Listar. The miner looked confused and would not meet the eyes of his companions, and there was something in the set of his body that whispered defeat.

The sergeant gestured to one of the waiting soldiers and said, 'Take him to the wagons.' Then he pointed at Rebble. 'Now you.'

'If any of you asks me to cut my hair,' Rebble said, straightening from the wall against which he had been leaning, 'I'll kill you.'

'Come with me.'

Wareth was left alone. He glanced over to see the last

remaining soldier studying him. After a moment the woman turned away. *That's right. You saved my life. How does it feel?*

*No matter. Merrec got what he deserved. A bully. Full of talk. All the women he had, all the husbands he cuckolded, until the one who got in his face and made trouble. But a knife in the back took care of that one. And you dared to call me a coward, Merrec?*

*But you would have done for me today, knowing I'd run.* He studied the Hust soldier, the slantwise curve of her back as she settled most of her weight on one leg, hip cocked. Her attention was fixed southward, out across the broken landscape pockmarked by pulled tree trunks. Her armour seemed to ripple of its own accord. On occasion, the scabbarded sword at her side jolted as if knocked by her knee – but she had made no move.

The Hust. Few were left. The story had come in hushed tones – even for the savage killers in the pit, there was something foul in the poisoning of almost three thousand men and women. But it seemed that civil war precluded all notions of criminality, and who among the victors – standing beside Hunn Raal – would even contemplate a redressing of justice? Blows were struck, the cause sure and true, a rushing sluice to wash away what lingered on the hands, what stained the boots. The first words of the triumphant were always about looking to the future, restoring whatever nostalgic illusion of order they'd fought for. The future, for such creatures, was a backhanded game of revising the past. It was a place, Wareth well knew, where lies could thrive.

He was chilled now, having left his shirt in the shaft far below the earth's surface. He used the wall behind him to keep his back straight, although the effort made his spine ache, but the cold of the stone quickly sank into his muscles, offering some relief.

A coward saw regret as if regarding a lost lover, as a thing used hard and fast only to quickly pall, pulling apart in mutual disgust. Those regrets then died of starvation. But their carcasses littered his world, all within easy reach.

Occasionally, when driven by need, he would pick one up and seek to force life into it once again. But any carcass could be prodded this way and that, given gestures that resembled those of the living. A child would understand this easily enough, and deem it play. The games adults played, however, existed in a realm of ever-shifting rules. Regrets were the pieces, escape the coward's prize, and each time, the prize turned out to be failure.

He lived in a world of confusion, and neither the world nor the confusion ever went away. *I am slave to living, and nothing is to be done for that. He will see that. The captain is not a fool. Wise enough to survive the Poisoning. One of the very few, if the rumours are true.*

Had he stayed, hidden among them, he would now be dead.

*But the coward ever finds ways to live. It is our one gift.*

The sound of footsteps, and then Rebble reappeared. He looked over at Wareth. 'Half the game, us,' he said. 'I pity the other half.'

'The women?'

Rebble nodded.

The sergeant detailed the last soldier to escort Rebble to the wagons beyond the camp. Before they drew out of earshot, Rebble turned and shouted, 'The captain has lost his mind, Wareth! Just so you know!'

Scowling, the sergeant waved Wareth into the corridor.

'You do not argue his opinion,' Wareth said as they approached the office.

Saying nothing, the man opened the door and gestured.

'Alone?' Wareth asked.

'The captain elects privacy in this,' the sergeant said, 'as is his privilege. Go in now, Wareth.'

But the miner hesitated, eyes narrowing on the man. 'Did we once know each other?'

'No, but your name is known to us all. The Hust Legion's lone blot of shame.'

From within the office, the captain spoke. 'That's enough, sergeant. Wait outside.'

'Sir,' the man replied.

*And if shame was the only blot, we could do away with swords. And war. And punishment, for that matter. We would guard ourselves against the crime of failing oneself, and feel only pity – like Rebble – for those who fell.*

Wareth walked into the overseer's office. Looking round for a moment, he saw a clerk's abode, which made somewhat pathetic the hatred the prisoners had heaped on the overseer. Then he looked down at the man seated behind the desk. It was a moment before he could pierce the ebon skin and see the features. Galar Baras.

The captain looked distracted, perhaps even irritated. He moved a hand, encompassing the room. 'Not much different from my own. Well, the one I had in Kharkanas. Needless to say, the similarity has soured my mood.'

Wareth remained silent.

Sighing, Galar Baras went on, 'Rebble claimed it was his idea. Breaking open the shed. But I saw you speak to him in the moment before. I think it was your idea, Wareth.'

'And this is an important distinction, sir?'

'It is. So, tell me the truth of it.'

'The idea was Rebble's, sir. As he told you.'

The captain slowly leaned back in the chair. 'I understand you want to return to the pit. Will you work alone, then?'

'You cannot take these men and women for the Hust, sir. You cannot.'

'So everyone keeps telling me.'

'Is this by Commander Toras Redone's order, sir? You've seen us. Go back and tell her it's a mistake.'

'The disposition of the commander is not your concern, Wareth. Right now, I am your only concern.'

'Do not execute me, sir. It's been nine years, damn you!'

Galar Baras blinked. 'That notion had not even occurred to me, Wareth. All right, you turned and fled. You probably had your reasons, but that was long ago.'

'Nothing has changed, sir.'

'You stood between the men and the women down there.

You were the first to do so. I was looking for leaders. Natural leaders. Ones with honour.'

Wareth laughed. It was a hard, bitter laugh. 'And I stepped to the fore! Oh, you poor man.'

'At least we can share the chagrin,' Galar Baras said, smiling.

'It's impossible, sir. And not just with me. Rebble's temper—'

'Yes, I know all about that. And Listar strangled his wife.'

'Even if he didn't, sir, he is guilty of something, and whatever it is, he would walk into death at the first chance.'

'Then help me.'

'Sir?'

Galar Baras leaned forward. 'We are in a civil war! Mother Dark's most powerful army lies buried beneath mounds a league south of here! And now we've had word of a battle – the shattering of the Wardens. As of this moment, the only forces standing between Kharkanas and Urusander are the Houseblades of the Great Houses.'

'Then surrender, sir.'

The captain shook his head. 'Not my call, Wareth. I have been commanded to replenish the Hust. I need bodies.'

'And you are desperate,' Wareth said. 'I see.'

'I doubt you do.'

'I see well enough, sir. Go back to the commander—'

'This order comes from the Lord Silchas Ruin.'

'Not his to make!' Wareth snapped. 'Toras Redone—'

'Lies disarmed and in a drunken stupor in a locked room.'

After a moment, Wareth said, 'She was drunk when she spared me.'

'I know.'

'You do? How? She was alone in the command tent.'

'She told me.'

Wareth fell silent.

'I need officers,' Galar Baras said.

'Promote every Hust soldier you have left, sir.'

'I will, but they're not enough.'

'You will forge a nightmare. The Hust swords will twist in the hands of this pit's murderers.'

Galar Baras's eyes were level. 'I would think it the other way round, Wareth.'

'This is your faith in all of this? Abyss below! Captain, I know the limits of those weapons – perhaps more than any of you, and I tell you, it is not enough.'

'Your sword failed in making you brave.'

'It begged in my hand, damn you! And still I ran!'

'I see only one way through this, Wareth. I am attaching you to my staff.'

'You are indeed mad. Sir.'

'Then I well suit the times, lieutenant.'

'Lieutenant? You would *promote* a coward? Sir, the sergeants will turn their backs to you. As for my fellow lieutenants, and your fellow captains, they will—'

'I am the last captain bar one,' Galar Baras said. 'And that one is in no condition to assume command. There were two others, after the Poisoning. Both took their own lives.'

'You'll need more.'

'I'll worry about that time when it comes. As for your fellow lieutenants, they will take their orders from me, as expected. Oh, I am not so foolish as to think you face anything but a lonely future, but, Wareth, you will be my bridge to these prisoners. From you, to Rebble and Listar, and to whatever women I can lift through the ranks – and as to that, can you give me a few names?'

'Only by reputation,' Wareth said, and in his mind he could well see the future the captain offered him. *In his staff, hovering around the command tent. Away from the battle.* The image rose like an island from the seas of his confusion and fear. *I can weather the scorn. I've lived with my own long enough.* 'We were kept entirely separate, and hardly saw one another. They were the cats, the night-shift in the shafts.'

'I know, Wareth. This isn't the first pit I've emptied. I'll take those names, lieutenant.'

'When I said "reputation", I did not mean it in a good way.'

'Right now, that distinction is irrelevant.'

Wareth looked down at the man. 'I think, sir, that we will lose this civil war.'

'Keep that opinion to yourself.'

'As you wish.'

'Now, the names, lieutenant.'

*       *       *

The stench of a burned forest slipped in through every pore. Its stink soaked skin and the flesh beneath. It lurked in a man's hair, his beard, like a promise of fire. It fouled clothes and the taste of food and water. Glyph walked through heaps of ash, around blackened stumps and the bones of tree-falls with their charred roots stark in the still air. His face was covered by a rag, leaving exposed only his red-rimmed eyes. He wore the hide of a deer, turned inside out in a feeble effort at disguise, as the deerskin's underside was pale grey. He had rubbed handfuls of gritty ash into his black hair.

He could see too far in this forest, now. In past winters, there had been enough evergreen to offer up places to hide, blocking lines of sight, to allow a hunter to move unseen if care was taken.

Among the Deniers, it was the men who hunted. This tradition was older than the forest itself. And the great hunts, in the spring and again at summer's end, when all the men set out, bearing bows and javelins, making their way through the forest to where the last herds still walked in their seasonal migration, far to the north now – these things too were old beyond memory.

Traditions died. And those who held fast to them, cursing and filled with hate as their precious ways of living were torn from their hands, they dwelt in a world of dreams where nothing changed. A predictable world that knew nothing of the fears that every mortal must face. He recalled the tale of the lake, and the families that lived on its shore. In all of their memories, reaching back to the very beginning, they fished that lake. They used spears in the shallows during the spawning season. They used nets and weirs at the streams that fed the lake. And for the creatures that crawled upon the lake bottom, they built traps. It was their tradition, this way of living, and they were known to all as the people who fished the lake.

There came a spring when no women walked out from that place, seeking husbands among the other peoples. And those women of the other peoples, who thought to travel to the homes of the people who fished the lake, they arrived to find empty camps and cold hearths, with huts fallen in under the weight of the past winter snows. They found nets, rotting on the scaffolds where they'd been hung to dry. They found unused fish spears amidst the high heaps of fishbone and broken mussel shells. They found all this, but nowhere could they find the people who fished the lake.

One young woman looked out to the lake's lone island, a hump of moss and rock on which the last tree had been cut down long ago. Taking a canoe, she set out for that island.

There, she found the people who fished the lake. Crow-picked and withered by the winter. Their skin was sun-blackened in the manner of fish strips hung over a smoking fire. The children that she found had been eaten, every bone picked clean, and the bones then boiled so they were now light as twigs.

And in the lake, no fish remained. No mussels and no freshwater crabs or lobsters. The waters were clear and empty. When she paddled back across it, she could look down to a lifeless bottom of grey silts.

Tradition was not a thing to be worshipped. Tradition was the last bastion of fools. Did the fisherfolk see their final fate? Did they comprehend their doom? Glyph believed the answer to both questions, among those who still worked the waters, was *yes*. But the elders on the shore droned on about vast harvests in times past, when the gutted fish hung in their tens of thousands and the smoke of the fires drifted low and thick on the water, hiding the lake's distant shores. Hiding this island, even. And oh, how they all grew fat and lazy in the weeks that followed, their bellies soft and bulging. There are fish in the lake, the elders said. There have always been fish in the lake. There always will be fish in the lake.

And the witch flung fish spines on to level beds of ash, reading in their patterns the secret hiding places of those fish. But she had done the same the last season, and the one before that, and now no hiding places remained.

The elders stopped telling their stories. They sat silent, their bellies hollowing out, the bones of their wizened faces growing sharp and jutting. They spat out useless teeth. They bled at their fingertips, and made foul stench over the shit-pits. They grew ever weaker, and then slept, rushing into the distant dreams of the old days, from which they never returned.

One cannot eat tradition. One cannot grow fat on it.

The witch was cast out for her failure. The nets were all bound together, into one that could sweep through half the lake, from the muddy bottom to the surface. There was talk that some otters might be snared, or fishing birds. But those creatures had long since left. Or died. Every canoe was pushed out into the water, to draw that net through the waters. They circled the island, a slow spin around its treeless mound, and when at last they returned to their camp, everyone joined in the task of drawing in that net.

It was easier than it should have been.

Tradition is the great slayer. It clings to its proof and it drowns in its own net, from which nothing ever escapes.

Glyph and the other men had left their camps when the leaves turned brown. They trekked into the north, out on to the barrenlands, seeking the last, dwindling herds that had summered in the forest. Bearing bows and javelins, they gathered into hunting parties, seeking hoof-sign, and at night they told tales of past hunts, of hundreds of beasts slain where the herds crossed the cold rivers. They spoke of the wolves that joined them, and became comrades in the slaughter. Wolves they all came to know by sight – and surely, it was the same for the wolves – and like old friends they were given names. Odd-eye. Silvermane. Broketooth.

And, as the fires died down and darkness closed in with

the moaning wind, the hunters sought to find the names the wolves had for each of them.

Fartwind. Sackscratch. Prickpump. Nubhide.

Laughter bit the cold from the air on those nights.

The layering of memories built tradition's high walls, until the place made by those walls became a prison.

Glyph now saw how the very last tradition, when all the others had done their grisly work, was just this: a prison. The tales told, the memories gathered up like clay and then made into something hard as stone. It was what the elders of the lake had clung to, with their bleeding fingers. It was what Glyph and his fellow hunters had clung to, on those empty nights so filled with empty words.

He walked through the scorched bones of the forest, and the bitter ash on his tongue had become a kind of mortar, and he felt himself beginning the building of his own wall. A modest two or three stones. A meagre wall. But he would find more to work with, he was certain of that. Constructed from new memories. These memories . . .

The failed hunt just past. The cruel pathos of the stories told at night out in the barrens. The hopeless search for hoof-sign. The wolves that did not come and did not howl with the fall of dusk.

The long return to the forest, hungry and silent with shame. The smoke to the south, above the treeline. The sudden scattering of the parties, as family members drew together and then split away, rushing to the camps of their kin. The wandering among the slain. The dead wife, the dead sister who had made it halfway out of her burning hut before a sword slid into her back. The dead son whose neck had been snapped.

The desperate journey to the monasteries of Yedan and Yannis. The beseeching of the priests and priestesses within. The bitter bargain offered.

*Bring us your children.*

The hunters wailed. They cried, *What children?*

On that day, Glyph took for himself that vicious title the people of the towns and the city had given them. He was now a Denier.

107

The name had become his promise. His destiny, in fact. *Denier. Denier of life. Denier of truth. Denier of faith.*

Dusk had arrived when he finally found the camp of the Legion soldiers whom he had been tracking. There were three of Urusander's ilk, travelling east, making for Neret Sorr as had so many others before them. Glyph crept his way closer in the darkness, safe beyond the dung-chip fire's pool of light. He still possessed all his arrows, a half-dozen of them bearing iron barbs. The others were flint-tipped.

When he was in place, beside a stump and behind the tree that had toppled from it, he silently removed three arrows, the first two iron-headed, the last one bearing his best flint – long-bladed and sharp-edged under the single strand of gut binding it to the end of the shaft. Each arrow he set point-down into the ground beside him, making a neat row.

Two men and a woman. They were talking. The two men were arguing over who would lie with the woman this night. She was laughing as she set one against the other. They sat round the fire, under the cold night's bright stars. Glyph concluded, as he waited, that she wanted neither of them.

He selected the first iron-barbed arrow and set it to his bow's gut string. Lifted the weapon clear of the black trunk and drew on the string as he did so, pulling until it pressed against his lower lip.

Then he released the arrow.

The man directly opposite Glyph made a choking sound, toppling backward.

His friend on his right barked a laugh, as if the dead man was jesting. But then the woman spied the fletching jutting from the dying man's throat, and she cried out.

Glyph was already drawing the bow. The second iron arrow sank deep under her left breast. With a small gasp, she fell on to her side.

The last man unsheathed his sword, wheeling round, but blinded still by the firelight.

The flint-tipped arrow buried itself in his stomach. He shrieked, doubling over. The arrow's shaft tilted and then, at his frantic scrabbling, it fell to the ground. The long flint head remained in his gut.

Glyph settled back, watching.

The man sank to his knees, moaning.

Shaking his head, Glyph spoke. 'You will run.'

The head snapped up, revealing a face pinched with fierce pain. 'Come here, you fucking turd, so I can cut you down before my last breath!'

'You will run,' Glyph repeated. 'Or I will put another arrow in you, and you'll not be able to hold up your sword. Then I will come to you and with my knife I will slice off your cock. Then your sac, and throw them on to your pretty fire. I will drag you half across that fire, and add the remaining chips over your legs, and we'll watch you roast down there.'

'Fuck!' The man groaned to his feet, still doubled over, and then he staggered out from the firelight.

He was slow, his flight aimless. Glyph stayed fifteen paces behind him, moving quietly.

In his mind he saw the flint arrow-head, buried deep in the man's body, slicing this way and that with each stride the soldier took. And he imagined the pain, the raging fire.

After a disappointingly short time, the man fell to the ground, curling up around his wound.

Glyph approached.

The soldier had dropped his sword early on in his flight, not that he could have done anything with it now. Moving to stand beside the prone form, Glyph sighed. 'It is tradition,' he said, 'to use the arrow for beasts. An ignoble weapon. That is how we are to think of it. To down a fellow man or a woman from a distance is the coward's way. But we Deniers are making a new tradition now.'

'Go to the Abyss,' the man gasped, eyes squeezed shut.

'You made a few new ones of your own,' Glyph said. 'So really, you have no cause to complain. What new traditions, you ask? I will remind you. The hunting and killing of women and children. Of elders. Rape, and whipping little boys through the air. Watching a beautiful young woman burned in half, before one of you showed a last vestige of mercy and stabbed her through the heart. A sister, that one, always laughing, always teasing. I loved her more than my life. As I did my wife. And my son. I loved them all more than my life.'

He continued looking down, and saw that the soldier was dead.

Drawing his iron knife, he knelt and pushed the body on to its back. He cut into the blood-smeared gut, making the arrow-wound big enough to fit his hand, and then, carefully, he worked his hand into that hot fissure. The flint edges were sharp and he did not want to cut himself. Finally, the tips of his fingers found the blade. It had worked down into the man's liver, slicing it almost in half. Gingerly, he drew it out, praying that it had not broken against a bone.

But no, the arrow-head was whole, not even chipped anywhere along its edges. Glyph wiped it clean on the man's cape.

Then he straightened and began making his way back to the camp. There would be food there, and he'd not eaten in a week. This hunt had taken all of his strength and he was feeling light-headed.

He wanted to retrieve his arrows from the other bodies, check the iron points, and then find the shaft that had fallen out from the last man.

*Here is my new story. Before the end, some fish had left the lake. They went upstream. When they returned, they found all their kin gone. In rage, one walked out from the water, leaving for ever his world, and blessed by the lake's grieving spirit he was given legs and arms, and his scales fell away to be replaced by skin. He was given eyes that could see in this new, dry world. He was given lungs that did not drown when filled with air. He was given hands with which to collect weapons.*

*Then he set out.*

*The people who fished the lake had distant kin, out on the drylands.*

*He would cast wide his net.*

*And begin the tradition of slaughter.*

*He realized that he would need a name. So he named himself Glyph, so that others could read the truth of his deeds, and so that the other fish that walked out on to the land and were given arms, legs and hands would join him.*

He saw before him a modest wall, there on the shore, between water and land. The birth of a tradition, in a place between two worlds. *I came from the water, but now I walk the shore. And from the land beyond there will be streams of blood and they will bless this shore, and make of it a sacred thing.*

*　　*　　*

Wreneck's mother told him that he was now eleven years of age. That seemed a long time to be alive, since most of it had been hard. Always working, always worrying. Whippings and kicked shins from his mistress, and all the other little things she did that hurt him: it seemed that those things made up all the millions of days in which he had been alive.

The burns from the fire had left smooth, shiny weals on his hands, his forearms, his shoulders, and on his left cheek just under the eye. He might have more on his head, but his hair had mostly grown back. Those scars were like places where the roughness had been rubbed away, and only when the sunlight was on them did they begin hurting again. The scar where he had been stabbed was bigger and took a lot longer to heal.

He had not returned to the ruins of the Great House. He had heard from his mother that ghosts had been seen there. But one day, ghosts or not, he knew he would make his way back. He would walk in the burned-out ruins. He would remember how everything had looked before the coming of the soldiers. There was a reason for having to go back, but he did not yet know what it was. The idea of it, of standing on the blackened stones of the Great House's threshold, seemed like the end of something, and that end felt right, somehow.

It was worth reminding himself, he decided, that whole worlds could die. No different from people. People who died left bones. Worlds left ruins.

He had saved a girl at that estate, a girl he had loved, but she was gone now. Returned, he supposed, to her family, but as that family was not from round here no one knew who they were, or even where they lived. His ma wouldn't tell him anything about any of that. It was just a truth he had to live with, an unhappy one like all the other unhappy ones: Jinia was gone.

There were lots of burned places now. Black ruins on the skyline on all sides of Abara Delack. Looted farmhouses made blackened smears across the fields. He couldn't see much of the monastery from where he lived with his mother, and yet, above all the others, it drew his eye the most: a distant hill toothed by a ragged black wall. He was curious about it. He wondered if he would feel the same about it as he did about the Great House, as a place deserving at least one visit.

Ma wanted him close by these days. She wanted him going nowhere out of her sight. But he was eleven now. And he looked even older, especially with the burn scars. And this morning, when at last he slipped out from her grasp, and set off down the track that led to the road that led through the town and then back up again on the other side, to the old monastery, she had wailed behind him, reaching out with her hands as if to drag him back.

Her tears made him feel bad, and he vowed to fix everything when he returned home. The soldiers were finally gone from Abara Delack. They had marched east, into the forest that had been burned down first, to make the going easier. But people were hungry in the town. They were leaving because there was not enough food there. When they left, pulling carts, they took with them whatever the soldiers hadn't stolen from them. Wreneck had seen them on the road, all going somewhere else, but it seemed no one could decide where that was, as the families went off in different directions from each other. And every now and then one of them came back, only to leave again a few days later, heading out another way.

So the town Wreneck walked into was almost empty of

people, and those who remained were mostly staying in their houses. The livery had burned down, he saw. So had the land office. A few men and women stood outside the tavern, not doing much or saying anything, and they watched Wreneck walk past.

Pausing, he looked into the narrow alley beside the tavern, thinking to see the one-armed man who had been Orfantal's mother's secret friend, since the alley was where the man lived. But he wasn't at his usual place on the steps to the cellar. Then he caught a faint motion deeper in the alley's shadows, something small and huddled, trying to keep warm beneath a thin blanket.

Wreneck headed over, stepping quietly, as if sneaking up on a nesting bird. He couldn't remember the man's name, so he said nothing.

When the figure started and looked up, Wreneck halted. He saw, shining out from a grimy face, eyes that he knew well.

'Jinia?'

At the name the girl shrank back, pushing up against the stone wall and turning her face away. Her bare feet pushed out from under the thin blanket, and their soles were black and cracked.

'But why didn't you go to your family? Ma said you did. She said you went off in the night, when I was asleep. When I was still getting better.'

She said nothing.

'Jinia?' Wreneck edged closer. 'You need to come back home with me.'

Finally, she spoke, her voice thin and sounding tired. 'She didn't want me.'

'Who?'

Still she kept herself turned away, her face hidden. 'Your mother, Wreneck. Listen. You're a fool. Go away. Leave me alone.'

'Why didn't she want you? I saved you!'

'Oh, Wreneck, you don't know anything.'

Confused, he looked around, but no one was in sight. The

people in front of the tavern had not come to help, or even look. He didn't understand grown-ups at all.

'I'm broken inside,' she said, in a dull voice. 'I won't have babies. Everything down there will hurt, always. This is my last winter, Wreneck, and it's how I want it. There's no point. No point to any of this.'

'But,' said Wreneck, 'I'm broken inside, too.'

She was so quiet he thought she hadn't heard him, and then she sobbed.

He went to her. Knelt at her side and put a hand on her shoulder. She smelled bad. She smelled like what the old men had begun distilling in their sheds, and only now did Wreneck see the rotting heap of potato skins nearby, that she had been eating. 'Look,' he said. 'You don't want to die. If you did you wouldn't be eating that. And you wouldn't be trying to stay warm. I love you, Jinia. And that brokenness. That hurt. It's just what lives inside. That's all it is. On the outside, you're always the same. That's what we'll give each other – everything that's on the outside, do you see?'

She wiped at her face and then looked up at him, the eye that wasn't wandering meeting his gaze. 'That's not how it is, Wreneck. That's not love at all. You're too young. You don't understand.'

'That's not true. I'm eleven now. I've made a spear, and I'm going to hunt them down and I'm going to kill them. Telra and Farab and Pryll. I'm going to stick my spear in them until they're dead. And you're going to watch me do it.'

'Wreneck—'

'Come with me. Let's go explore the monastery.'

'I'm too drunk to walk.'

'It's just what you've been eating.'

'It kills the pain.'

'So you can walk and it won't hurt.' He reached down and helped her stand. 'I'm going to take care of you,' he said. 'From now on.'

'Your mother—'

'And after the monastery, we're going away. I told you. We're going hunting, for the people who did that to you.'

114

'You'll never find them.'

'I will.'

'They'll kill you.'

'They tried that already. It didn't work.'

She let him take her weight and when he felt it there was a stab of dull pain from the sword-scar. They tottered for a moment, and then hobbled out of the alley.

As they turned to make their way up the street, one of the men in front of the tavern called out, 'You're wasting your time, son. All you'll get is a lot of blood.'

The others laughed.

Wreneck swung round. 'You grown-ups make me ashamed!'

They were silent then, as he and Jinia slowly walked up the main street. She leaned hard against him, but he was still big, still strong, and where the soldier had stabbed him it only hurt a little bit now, not like the first time, when he thought that maybe something had ripped.

Everyone was broken inside. It was just that some were more broken than others, and when they were broken bad inside, it was all they could do to keep the outside looking normal. That took all the work and that's what living was – work. He had years of practice.

'You're sweating,' Jinia said when at last they reached the outskirts of town and looked up to the hill and its summit where huddled the scorched ruins of the monastery, showing them a gap-toothed wall and a gateway with no gate.

'It's hot.'

'No, it's cold, Wreneck.'

'I'm just working hard, Jinia. I'm used to that, and it's good and you know why?'

'Why?'

He thought about how he would say what he felt, and then nodded. 'It reminds me that I'm alive.'

'I'm sorry, Wreneck,' she said. 'For your burns, from when you carried me through the burning rooms. I should have said that before. But I was mad at you.'

'Mad at me? But I saved your life!'

115

'That's why, Wreneck.'

'They weren't much,' he said after a moment. 'Those rooms, I mean. There was hardly anything in them. So the places where rich people live, why, they're still just rooms.'

They had begun the ascent, much slower now. At his words, Jinia snorted. 'They would tell you otherwise.'

'I saw them. Those rooms. They can try telling me anything they like. I saw them.'

'You were friends with Orfantal.'

Wreneck shook his head. 'I was a bad friend. He hates me now. Anyway, I won't be that again. The nobleborn grownups don't scare me any more. Orfantal wasn't like them, but I'm sorry that he hates me.'

'Nobleborn,' she mused, and he smelled her sweet breath. 'It seems I've found one of my own.'

He didn't understand what she meant. She was still a little drunk.

Then they ran out of breath with which to talk, as the hill was steep and the track slippery under its thin coat of snow. The monks were all dead for sure, since they would have swept this clear. There was nothing living in sight. Even the crows had long gone.

At last, they reached the summit, and Jinia stepped away from him, to stand on her own, but she reached across and took his hand.

Suddenly cowed by her gesture, and the feel of her thin fingers and her pinched palm, so easily swallowed up by his too-big hand, Wreneck said nothing. But he felt very grown up.

'I'm not so cold any more,' she said. 'Not so drunk, either. But the pain's back.'

He nodded. Yes, it was back, and not just where the soldier had stabbed him. It was back in other places, too, all through his insides. Aches. Deep, deep aches. When he could stand them no longer and he had to move, he stepped forward, and she fell in at his side, and they walked towards the shell of the tumbled wall's gate.

'They used to bring food into town and give it away to the

poor,' Jinia said. 'But only once or twice a year. The years they didn't, everyone hated them. But it was just bad harvests. When they only had enough to feed themselves. Still, everyone hated them.'

They passed beneath the arch and strode into the littered compound, and were halted by the sight of all the snow-covered corpses.

Jinia pulled sideways at his hand, stretching out his arm.

But all the pain he'd been fighting against inside was suddenly too much, and blood had leaked out from his sword-wound, and once it leaked out, the battle was over. Darkness took him, and he sank into it, although in the instant before he knew nothing, he heard Jinia cry out as his hand tugged loose from her grasp.

When he next opened his eyes, the ground under his back was wet where the snow had melted. Jinia was kneeling beside him, and she had taken off her blanket and draped it over him, and he saw tears on her cheeks. 'What's wrong?' he asked her.

'You fainted. There was blood. I thought – I thought you died!'

'No,' he said. 'I didn't. It was just that the wound remembered the sword.'

'You should never have helped me.'

'I can't help helping you,' he said, pushing the brokenness back inside and sitting up.

She wiped at her cheeks. 'I thought I was alone. All over again. Wreneck, I can't do this with you. I lost everything and I have nothing and it has to stay that way.'

He watched her stand, watched her brush the crusted snow from her bared, bony knees, revealing cracked red skin and scabs. 'You can't make me hope,' she said. 'It's not fair.'

'You're leaving me?'

'I told you! I can't stay with you!'

'Don't die in that alley, Jinia.'

'Stop crying. I won't. I'll survive. I'm like you. They can't kill us. I get food left for me. Not every grown-up is bad, Wreneck. Don't think that, or you will be a very lonely man.'

She looked around. 'There're cloaks I can find here, maybe even real blankets – horse-blankets, maybe. There're some sheds that didn't burn. I'll search in those and find something. I won't freeze to death.'

'You promise?'

'I promise, Wreneck. Now, when you go back home, go round the town. Don't go down the main street. Some people there are mad at you, for what you said. It's a longer walk, but go across the fields. Say you'll do that. Say it.'

He wiped at his eyes and nose. 'I'll cross the fields.'

'And don't tell your mother about any of this.'

'I won't. But I won't be there long anyway.'

'Stay with her, Wreneck. If you leave, you'll break her heart.'

'I'll make it better.'

'Good. That's good.' She nodded towards the gateway. 'Go on, then.'

The sadness in him was a worse pain than any other he'd ever felt, but he stood up. The cold bit at his wet shirt against his back. 'Goodbye, Jinia.'

'Goodbye, Wreneck.'

Then, remembering his regrets after he saw Orfantal off, he lunged to her and hugged her tight, and all the pain he felt when he did that, from the sword-wound, from everything else, seemed right.

She seemed to shrink in his arms, and then she was pushing him away, taking hold of his shoulders to turn him round and then giving him a little push.

He walked through the gateway.

Wreneck would cross the fields, as he had promised. But he wasn't going home. He was going off to make things right, because even in this world some things just had to be made right. His ma would still be there when he finally went home, after he'd done everything he needed to do. He could fix things with her then.

But now, he would wait for dusk, hidden from sight, and then go and collect the spear he had buried under the snow near the old stone trough.

He was eleven, and it felt as if the year before it had been the longest one in his life. As if he'd been ten for ever. But that was the thing about growing older. He'd never be ten again.

The soldiers went east, into the burned forest.

He would find them there. And do what was right.

\*     \*     \*

'What are you doing?' Glyph quietly asked.

Startled, the dishevelled man looked up. He was crouched beside a heap of stones that had been pulled from the frozen ground along the edge of the marsh. His hands were filthy and spotted with blood from scrapes and broken fingernails. He was wearing a scorched wolf hide, but it didn't belong to him. Nearby, left on the snow-smeared ground, was a Legion sword and scabbard and belt.

The stranger said nothing, eyes on the bow in Glyph's hand, the arrow notched in the string, and the tension of the grip.

'You are in my family's camp,' Glyph said. 'You have buried them under stones.'

'Yes,' the man whispered. 'I found them here. The bodies. I – I could not bear to see them. I am sorry if I have done wrong.' He slowly straightened. 'You can kill me if you like. I won't regret leaving this world. I won't.'

'It is not our way,' Glyph said, nodding down at the stones.

'I'm sorry. I didn't know.'

'When the soul leaves, the flesh is nothing. We carry our dead kin into the marsh. Or the forest where it is deep and thick and unlit.' He waved slightly with the bow. 'But here, there was no point. You take the bodies away to keep your home clean, but no one lives here any more.'

'It seems,' said the man, 'that you do.'

'They had rotted down by the time I returned. No more than bones. They were,' Glyph added, 'easy to live with.'

'I would not have had the courage for that,' the stranger said.

'Are you a Legion soldier?'

The man glanced across at his sword. 'I killed one. I cut him down. He was in Scara Bandaris's troop – the ones who deserted and rode away with the captain. I went with them for a time. But then I killed a man, and for the murder I committed Scara Bandaris banished me from his company.'

'Why did he not take your life?'

'When he discovered the truth of me,' the man said, 'he deemed life the greater punishment. He was right.'

'The man you killed – what did he do to you? Your face is twisted. Scarred and bent. He did that?'

'No. This face you see has been mine now for some time. Well, it's always been mine. No.' He hesitated, and then shrugged. 'He spoke cruel words. He cut me with them, again and again. Even the others took pity on me. Anyway, he was not well liked, and none regretted his death. None but me, that is. Those words, while cruel, were all true.'

'In your eyes, I can see,' Glyph said, 'you yearn for my arrow.'

'Yes,' the man whispered.

Slipping the arrow's notch from the string, Glyph lowered his bow. 'I have been hunting Legion soldiers,' he said, stepping forward.

'You have reason,' the man said.

'Yes. We have reasons. You have yours, and I have mine. They wield your sword. They guide my arrows. They make souls leave bodies and leave bodies to lie rotting on the ground.' He brushed the cloth hiding the lower half of his face. 'They are the masks we hide behind.'

The man started, as if he had been struck, and then he turned away. 'I wear no mask,' he said.

'Will you kill more soldiers?' Glyph asked.

'A few, yes,' said the man, collecting up his sword-belt and strapping it on. 'I have a list.'

'A list, and good reasons.'

He glanced across at Glyph. 'Yes.'

'I name myself Glyph.'

'Narad.'

'I have some food, from the soldiers. I will share it with

you, for the kindness you meant when burying my beloved family. And then I will tell you a story.'

'A story?'

'And when I am done with my story, you can decide.'

'Decide what, Glyph?'

'If you will hunt with me.'

Narad hesitated. 'I am not good with friends.'

Shrugging, Glyph went over to the hearth. He saw that Narad had taken away the stones that had ringed the ashes and cinders, adding them to the cairn. He set about finding some smaller stones, to build up around the hearth and so block the wind while he set to lighting a fire.

'The people who fished the lake,' he said as he drew out his fire-making kit and a small bag of dried tinder.

'This is your story?'

'Not theirs. But of the Last Fish. The story is his, but it begins with the people who fished the lake.'

Narad removed his sword again and let it drop. 'There's little wood left to burn,' he said.

'I have what I need. Please, sit.'

'Last Fish, is it? I think this will be a sad story.'

'No, it is an angry story.' Glyph looked up, met the man's misaligned eyes. 'I am that Last Fish. I have come from the shore. This story I will tell, it has far to go. I cannot yet see its end. But I am that Last Fish.'

'Then you are far from home.'

Glyph looked around, at the camp of his family, and the scraped ground where there had been bones. He looked to the fringe of brush and the thin ring of trees that still survived. Then he looked up at the empty, silvered sky. The blue was going away, as the Witch on the Throne devoured the roots of light. Finally, he returned his gaze to the man now seated opposite him. 'Yes,' he said. 'I am far from home.'

Narad grunted. 'I have never before heard a fish speak.'

'If you did,' Glyph asked, looking across at him, 'what would he say?'

The murderer was silent for a moment, his gaze falling from Glyph's, and then moving slowly over the ground to settle on the sword lying in the dirty snow. 'I think . . . he might say . . . *There will be justice.*'

'My friend,' Glyph said, 'on this night, and in this place, you and me. We meet each other's eyes.'

The struggle that came in answer to Glyph's words revealed itself on Narad's twisted face. But then, finally, he looked up, and between these two men the bond of friendship was forged. And Glyph understood something new. *Each of us comes to the shore. In our own time and in our own place.*

*When we are done with one life, and must begin another. Each of us will come to the shore.*

# FOUR

'LEAD UNTO ME EACH AND EVERY CHILD.'

A statement so benign, and yet in the mind of the Shake assassin Caplo Dreem it dripped still, steady as the blood from a small but deep wound, a heavy tap upon his thoughts, not quite rhythmic, like the leakage of unsavoury notions best left hidden, or denied outright. There were places into which an imagination could wander, and if he could but bar these places, and stand guard with weapons unsheathed, he would frighten off any who might venture near. And should one persist and draw still closer, he would kill without compunction.

But the old man's thin lips, wetted by the words, haunted the lieutenant. He would as soon welcome a dying man's kiss as see, once again, Higher Grace Skelenal grind out that invitation, in that wretched chamber of shadows, with winter creeping in under the doors and through the window joins, making dirty frost on floor and sill. Breath riding the chill air like smoke, the old man's hands trembling where they feebly gripped the arms of the chair, and the avid thing in the deep pits of his eyes belonging in no temple, in no place proclaimed holy, in no realm of propriety or decency.

'Lead unto me each and every child.'

He could remind himself that the old were useless in most ways. Their limbs were weak, their hearts frail, and their minds slipped and wallowed, or drifted along sordid streams few would call thought. Yet, for all of that, they could tend, severally, fecund gardens of desire.

Caplo would yield no pity in such places. He recoiled from plucking the luscious fruit, knowing well the poison juices each one harboured. Growth was no proof of health, and a garden made verdant with lust mocked every notion of virtue.

'Your expression, friend,' ventured Warlock Resh, 'could turn a winter's storm. I see a sky filling with fear as you bend your countenance upon the way before us, and that is not like you. Not like you at all.'

Caplo Dreem shook his head. They walked the rough, stony track side by side. The day was dull, the weather unobtrusive. The low hills to either side had lost all colour. 'Winter,' he said, 'is the season that drains the life from the world, and the world from my eyes. There is something foul, Resh, in this denuded framework. I am not inclined to welcome the sight of shrivelled skin and raw bones.'

'You shape only what you see, assassin, and see only what you would first shape. We cannot settle what it is that is inside with what it is that lies outside, and so toss them between our hands, as might a juggler with hot stones. Either way, our flesh burns.'

'I would bless the blisters,' said Caplo in a low growl, 'and note the pain as real enough.'

'What haunts you, my friend? Am I not the dour one between us? Tell me the source of your troubles.'

'The hungers of old men,' the assassin replied, shaking his head again.

'We bend holy accord to profane need,' Resh said. 'Raw numbers. The Higher Grace spoke only what is written.'

'And in so speaking, flayed the skin from pernicious appetites all his own. Is this the secret lure of holy words, warlock? Their precious *pliability*? I see them curl and twist like ropes. And all of this, no less, in the name of a god. Indeed, performed as ritual appeasement. How then to imagine that god's regard as pleased, or approving? I confess to you on this road: my faith withers with the season.'

'Faith I did not know you possessed.' The warlock ran a hand through his heavy beard. 'We are eager, it's true, to confuse salvation with rebirth, and imagine a soul revived in its husk. But such flares are brief and easily ignored, Caplo. Skelenal and his appetites squirm in solitude – we have all made certain of that. Not a single child will come within his reach.'

Caplo shook his head. 'Push on, then, through the centuries, and look once more upon our faith.' He waved a hand, although the gesture faltered as his fingers made claws in the air. 'Pliable words for the child's pliable mind, which by prescription we knead and prod, and so make new shapes from old. And by this mishmash we cry out improvement!' The breath gusted from him. 'Nature yields its familiar patterns – those enfolding convolutions hiding under every skull, be it the cup of man, woman, child or beast. See our descendants, Resh, heavy in robes and brocaded wealth. See the solemn processions in flickering torchlight. I hear chants that have lost all meaning. I hear yearning in every inarticulate, guttural moan.

'Heed me! I have found a truth. From the moment of revelation, of religion's stunning birth, each generation to follow but moves farther away, step by passing step, and this journey down the centuries marks a pathetic transgression. From sacred to secular, from holy to profane, from glory to mummery. We end – our faith ends – in pastiche, the guffaw barely held in check, and among the parishioners a chorus of arrayed faces look on, helpless and bereft. While in the shadows behind the altar, foul-fingered men grope children.' He paused to spit on the ground. 'Beneath the eyes of a god? Truly, who will forgive them? And truer still, my friend, how sweet is the nectar of their abasement! I suspect, indeed, that this thirst lies at the core of their weakness. To revel in unforgivable guilt is their soul's own reward.'

Resh was silent for a long while after that. Ten strides, and then fifteen. Twenty. Finally, he nodded. 'Sheccanto lies as one already dead. Skelenal shakes his palsied limbs loose in anticipation. And the assassin of the Shake contemplates patricide.'

'I would cut the shrivelled cock at its root,' Caplo said. 'Blunt the precedent in a welling of blood.'

'Your confession is not for my ears, friend.'

'Then stop them with blessed ignorance.'

'Too late. But many who mourn a graveside in silence will harbour condign thoughts of the departed, with none to know the difference.'

Caplo grunted. 'We wear grief like a shroud, and pray the weave is close enough to hide our satisfied expressions.'

'Just so, friend.'

'Then you will not oppose me?'

'Caplo Dreem, should such need arrive, I will guard your back on the night itself.'

'In faith's name?'

'In faith's name.'

The monastery and Skelenal were behind the two men now, shuttered away from the day's steel light. Ahead, waiting on a low rise that seemed to bridge a pair of weathered hillocks, was Witch Ruvera. Ritually bound to Warlock Resh, assuming the role of wife to her husband, she wore a visage of cold stone, and its lines grew even more severe when she fixed her gaze on Caplo Dreem. As the two men drew nearer, she spoke. 'Name me the company that welcomes an assassin.'

Sighing, Resh said, 'Dear wife, Mother Sheccanto may be reduced to frail whispers, but we hear her desires nonetheless.'

'Does the hag fear me now?'

The breath hissed from Caplo. 'It seems you need no assassin to wield blades here, witch. Mother feared the risk you will take on this day, and charged me to protect you.'

Ruvera snorted. 'She would know more of the power I have found. The company you will not name is one where trust lies strangled upon the threshold, and the gathering rustles like snakes in the straw.'

'You invite unwelcome friends,' said Caplo with a faint

smile, 'sleeping in barns. Rest your imagination, witch. I am but a guardian this day.'

'With lies to protect,' Ruvera said in a half-snarl, before turning away. 'Follow, then. It is not far.'

Resh shrugged when Caplo cast him a bemused glance. 'Some marriages aren't worth consummating,' the warlock said.

Ruvera barked a laugh at that, but did not look back at the two men.

'By contemplation alone,' said Caplo, 'even I would flee into a man's arms. I see at last the turn of your motivations, and indeed desires, friend Resh. Are we forever trapped in mockeries of family? Husband, wife, son, daughter – the titles assert, bold as spit in the face of the wind.'

'I mistook them for tears,' Resh said, grimacing. 'Once upon a time.'

'When you were no more than a child, yes?'

'I will grant Ruvera this: she gave me confusion's face, and every line made sharp its denial.'

The witch ahead of them laughed again. 'A face, and a groping hand that awakened nothing. But that was my revelation, not his. Now,' she added, drawing up on the edge of the rise, 'observe this new consecrated ground.'

Resh and Caplo joined her and stood, silent, looking down.

The depression was oval-shaped, five paces across at its widest point, and eight in length. Its sides were undercut beneath the flowing curl of long-bladed grasses, making the lone step down uncertain, but the basin itself was level and free of stones.

The strange feature was situated on a flat stretch, part of which had been broken and planted by the nuns a few decades past – without much success – and beyond which rose low hummocks, many of which bore springs near the fissured rocks of their summits. The endless leak of water cut deep channels into the sides of those hills, converging into a single stream that only broke up again among the furrows of withered weeds. But the depression remained dry, and it was this peculiarity that made Caplo frown. 'Consecrated? That blessing is not yours to make.'

Ruvera shrugged. 'The river god is dead. Lost to the curse of Dark. Betrayed, in fact, but no matter. The woman on her throne in Kharkanas has no regard for us, and we would do well to shrink from her attention. Husband, seek out and tell me what answers you.'

'Did you make this pit by your own hand?' Resh asked.

'Of course not.'

Caplo grunted and spoke before Resh could answer his wife. 'Then let us ponder its creation, with cogent reason. See the drainage channels from the hills beyond. They reach a level to match the land around the basin, and if not for the irrigation scars would plunge into the ground and course onward, unseen. Yet here, below the crust of the surface, there was buried a lens of wind-blown sand and silts. So. The springs fed their water and the water found its hidden path, cutting through that lens, sweeping it away, thus yielding a depression of the crust.' He turned to Ruvera. 'Nothing sacred in its making. Nothing holy in its manifestation. It was the same hidden seepage that defeated the nuns who sought to grow crops here.'

'I await you, husband,' said the witch, her face set as if denying Caplo's presence, and any words he might utter.

'I am . . . uncertain,' admitted Resh after a moment. 'Caplo's reason is sound, but it remains mundane, if not shallow. Something else thrives beneath the surface. No gift of the river god. Perhaps not holy at all.'

'But powerful, husband! Tell me you can feel it!'

'I wonder . . . is this Denul?'

'If the sorcery here heals,' Ruvera said in a low voice, 'it is the cold kind. The hardening of scars, the marring of skin. It refutes sympathy.'

'I sense nothing,' said Caplo.

'Husband?'

Resh shook his head. 'Very well, Ruvera. Awaken it. Demonstrate.'

She drew a deep breath. 'Let us take this expression of

power, and make it into a god. We need only the will to do so, to choose to shape what waits in promise. We perch on a precipice here, but a ledge remains, enough to walk on, enough to stand upon. And from this narrow strand, we can reach out to both sides, both worlds.'

'You invent from shadows,' Caplo said. 'I have never trusted imagination – or if I once did, no longer. Make your idol, then, witch, and show me it is worthy of a bow and scrape. Or palsied genuflection. Make me kneel abject and humbled. But if I see the impress of your palms and fingertips in the clay, woman, I will refuse worship and call you a charlatan.'

'The hag you still call Mother shows her teeth at last.'

To that, Caplo simply shrugged.

'Ruvera,' said Resh, eyeing her, 'I see you hesitate.'

'I have reached down before,' she replied, 'and brushed . . . something. Enough to feel its strength. Enough to know its promise.'

'Then why decry the assassin's presence, wife?'

'It may be,' she said, eyes on the depression, 'that the power requires a sacrifice. Blood. My blood.' She swung to Caplo. 'Do not defend my life. We have lost our god. We possess nothing, and yet our need is vast. I am willing.'

'Kurald Galain's squall descends to a secular war,' Caplo said. 'A civil war. We can stand outside it, now. No sacrifice is necessary, Ruvera. I may not like you, but I will not see you cast away your life.'

'Even to stand apart, assassin, will need strength.' She waved vaguely northward. 'They will demand we choose sides, sooner or later. Captain Finarra Stone remains as guest to Father Skelenal, and asks that we commit ourselves in Mother Dark's name. But our family remains unruly. Our patriarch dithers. He has no strength. Sheccanto fares even worse. We must choose another god. Another power.'

Resh clawed at his beard, and then nodded. 'It falls to us, yes. Caplo—'

'I will decide in the moment,' the assassin said. 'A knife commits but once.'

Ruvera hissed in frustration, and then dismissed him with

a chopping hand. Facing the depression again, she closed her eyes.

Caplo stood waiting, unsure whether to fix his attention upon the witch, or the innocuous depression before them. Beneath his heavy woollen cloak he closed gloved hands around the grips of his knives.

Resh's sharply drawn breath drew the assassin's attention upon the shallow basin, where he saw the withered grasses lining it stir, then flatten away from the edge, as if they were the spiky petals of a vast flower. The cracked soil in the centre of the pit now blurred strangely, forcing Caplo to blink and struggle to focus – but his efforts failed, and the blurring deepened, the mottled colours melting, smearing. And now something was rising from below. A body of some sort, lying supine. In the instant of its first appearance, it seemed but bones, peat-stained and burnished; in the next the skeleton vanished beneath the meat of muscles and the stretched strings of tendons and ligaments. Then skin slipped on to the form, rising from below like mud, and its hue was dark. Hair grew from that skin, covering the entire body, thickest beneath the arms and at the groin.

If standing, the creature would have been only slightly shorter than the average Tiste.

Caplo edged forward, tugged by curiosity. He studied the manifestation's peculiar, bestial face – how the mouth and jaw projected, drawing out and flattening the broad nose. The closed eyes were nestled deep in their sockets, the brow half enclosing them thick and jutting. The forehead sloped back beneath the black, dense hair of the scalp. The creature's ears were small and flat against the sides of the head.

He noted the rise and fall of its narrow but powerful chest the moment before the creature opened its eyes.

Lips stretched back, revealing thick, stained teeth, and from its throat droned a dull, broken sound. The apparition then shivered, blurred and suddenly broke apart.

Ruvera cried out, and Caplo heard Resh's curse. The assassin's knives were out, but the weapons were no answer to his confusion, as in the place where a body had been lying moments before there now appeared a dozen creatures, sleek and black, weasel-like but larger, heavier. Fangs glistened and eyes flashed.

And then a full score of the beasts swarmed out from the pit.

Caplo heard the witch shriek, but he could do nothing for her as three of the creatures lunged towards him. He leapt back, slashing out with his knives. One edge sliced hide, but then the hilt snagged in fur and savage jaws closed around his hand. They crunched down through the bones, and heavy molars began grinding and tearing through. Screaming, Caplo tore his hand from the creature's mouth.

Another beast hammered into his midriff, claws ripping to get through his clothing. He staggered back, disbelieving. The third apparition's canines punched through flesh as its jaws closed on his left thigh. The weight pulled him down to the ground. He still held one knife, and twisting round, he drove the blade into the base of the beast's skull, tore the weapon free and slammed it into the side of the animal clinging to his chest. The creature's jaws, which had been striving to reach his throat, snapped shut, just missing the assassin's neck. A wet cough sprayed blood out from its mouth. Rolling on to his side, Caplo stabbed again and felt death take his attacker.

The first apparition returned to bite into his upper arm, above the mangled hand. The pressure of those jaws crushed bones as if they were dry sticks. Caplo dragged it close with his arm and cut open its throat, down to the vertebrae.

He rolled again, pulling his arm loose from the now slack jaws. He staggered to his feet in a half-crouch, and, glaring, readied himself to meet the next assault. But the scene before him was motionless. He heard the barks of the creatures, but some distance away and fast dwindling. Warlock Resh knelt on the ground a few paces away, the carcasses of two beasts before him. His cloak had been shredded, revealing the heavy chain beneath it. Here and there, massive claws were snagged in the links, dangling like fetish charms.

Just beyond the warlock, Caplo saw a woman's severed

arm. The air reeked of shit, and, twisting slightly, he saw a long sprawl of lumpy intestines, stretching out as if they had been dragged. The nearest end plunged into a small huddled body, the legs of which had been chewed off at the knees.

'Resh—'

The warlock reached out and tugged loose one of his short-handled axes from the nearest carcass.

'Resh. Your wife—'

His friend shook his head, climbed drunkenly upright. 'I will bury her here,' he said. 'Go back. Make your report.'

'My report? Beloved friend—'

'Leave us, Caplo. Just . . . leave us now, will you?'

The assassin straightened. He did not know if he would make it all the way back. His right arm streamed blood down through the torn flesh and shattered bones of his hand, making wavering strings between the ground and his finger-tips. His left thigh felt swollen and hard, as if the muscle was turning to stone. Unlike Resh, he had not been wearing armour, and claws had torn across his ribs under his arms. Still, he turned away from his friend, raised his head, and slowly made for the trail.

*My report. Blessed Mother and Father, Witch Ruvera is dead. A creature awakened, became many creatures. They were . . . they were uninterested in negotiation.*

*It seems, Mother and Father, that upon this land we would call our own, we are all but children. And this is the lesson here. The past waits, but does not invite. And to walk into its room yields only the death of innocence.*

*See me, Mother and Father. See your child, and heed the knowing in his eyes.*

His blood was leaving him. He felt lightheaded, and the world around him was changing. The path vanished, the grasses growing higher – he fought them as he walked, struggling to pull his legs through the tangled blades. The winter had vanished and he could feel the weight of the sun's heat upon his back. All around him, animals were walking the plain – animals such as he had never seen before. Tall, gracile, some banded, some striped or spotted in dun hues.

He saw creatures little different from horses, while others bore impossibly long necks. He saw apes that looked like dogs, travelling on all fours, with thin tails standing high behind them. This was a dream world, an invented world that had never existed.

*Imagination returns to haunt my soul. It arrives in a curse, ragged of edge and painfully sharp. Reason drip-drip-drips to spatter the grass. And what remains? Nothing but cruel, vicious imagination. A realm of delusion and fancy, a realm of deceit.*

*There is no paradise – do not mock me with this scene! The world is unchanging – admit to it, you fool! Raise up the hard truths of what truly surrounds you – the barren hills, the bitter cold, the undeniable heartlessness of it all! We know these truths, we know them: the viciousness, the cruelty, the indifference, the pointlessness. The stupid pathos of existence. For this, no reason to battle, to fight on. Empty my soul of causes, and then – only then – shall I know peace.*

Cursing, he fought against the mirage, but still the grasses pulled at him, and he heard their roots ripping free to the tug of his shins.

Now he was in shadows, entering a forest. Tangles of brush clogged the clearings at its edge, and then he was among straggly pines and spruce, the air cooler, and in the gloom beneath thick stands he saw bhederin, hulking and heavy, small ears flicking and red-rimmed eyes fixing on him, watching as he stumbled past.

Somewhere nearby a beast was ripping apart the bole of a fallen tree. He could hear the claws gouging and splintering the rotted wood.

A moment later he came upon the creature, and it was identical to those from the basin. It lifted its broad head, tilted a wood-flecked snout in his direction, and then bared its fangs in a snarl, before bounding away, running in the manner of an otter. Caplo stared after it, noted the blood on its hindquarters.

*You show me this? I will remember you. I swear it. We are not finished, you and I.*

The ground underfoot grew hard, and then he was crossing a flat stretch of bedrock, its surface scraped and denuded. The blood draining from his hand made dull sounds as each drop struck the stone. *Do I carry a brush? Does the paint drip? No. No brush – this flayed, heavy thing is what remains of my hand. No matter. The next rain will wash it all away.*

*It's awake now. This thing of the past, this stranger who can become many. Pulled loose from the earth, reborn. And so very hungry.*

*Ruvera. You felt its slumbering power. You touched it with trembling hands, and thought to make it your own. But the past cannot be tamed, cannot be changed to your whim. The only slavery possible is found in the now, and its promise lurks among the ambitious – the fools so crowding the present and forever jostling, as if by will alone they could displace the undefended children, the children not yet born . . . They'll put the rest of us in our place, to be sure, and if I am not among them, then I will stumble in shackles, just another slave. Another defenceless child.*

Imagination was the enemy, but the bludgeon of will could defeat it, the stolid stupidity of every self-avowed realist incapable of dreaming could stifle it, like a pillow over a face. *Chained to your desires, you would pull the world down to your pathetic level. Come then, make it barren and lifeless, colourless and unrelieved. I am with you. I see reason's bloody underside. I see the value in this emasculation. The past is where imagination dwells – and we will have none of that. I surrender nothing, and by dispiriting the world, I become its master. I become the god – it is plain now, plain to me – the path awaiting us . . .*

He shook his head, and the scene around him cavorted wildly. Stumbling, he fell to the hard ground, felt the brittle stubble of winter grasses stabbing the side of his face, the icy bite of frozen soil sinking into his cheek.

*Reality's kiss.*

Someone was shouting. He heard the thump of footsteps fast approaching.

'Revelation,' Caplo whispered. 'I hear the past calling. Calling.'

*And it mutters, with a lick of withered lips, 'Lead unto me each and every child.'*

*Revelation.*

And then the women were all around him, and he felt soft hands. Smiling, he let himself drift away into darkness.

But not all the way.

\* \* \*

Finarra Stone, captain in the Wardens, looked down upon the recumbent form of Caplo Dreem. The shutters, thrown back, offered up the uncertain light of the day's dull overcast, filling the cell and settling a grey patina upon the man's face. The sweat of fever gave that face the look of stained porcelain. After a long moment she turned away.

They had cut off the ruined right hand and forearm, sealing the stump with heat and some kind of pitch the colour of honey. The smell filling the room was that of burned hair and the suppurations of infection in the other wounds covering the assassin's body.

She remembered her own battle against the same pernicious killer, not so long ago. But then Lord Ilgast Rend had been there, with the gift of Denul.

No one expected Caplo to live out the day.

She looked across to Warlock Resh, who sat red-eyed and haggard in a chair facing the cot. 'I saw the bite marks,' she said to him. 'Similar to Jhelarkan, but smaller.'

He grunted. 'Hardly. A wolf's canines in the mouth of a weasel. Even a bear would run from such a beast.'

'Yet they were the ones that fled, warlock.'

He licked chapped lips. 'We'd killed five of them.'

She shrugged, glancing back to Caplo. 'He would not have accounted for even one more. Leaving just you, surrounded, beleaguered on all sides. Armour or no, warlock, they would have taken you down.'

'I know.'

When he said nothing more, she sighed. 'Forgive me. I intrude upon your grief with my questions.'

'You intrude with your presence, captain, but give no cause for the bitter taste in my mouth.'

'It is said the Jheck of the south are a smaller breed.'

'Not Jheck,' Resh replied. 'They were as I described them. Some animal long since vanished from the world.'

'Why do you say that?'

He leaned forward and rubbed at his face, knuckling hard at his eyes. 'Dispense with the scene itself, if you would understand its significance. Ruvera, my wife, discovered something ancient, buried. It slept in the manner of the dead. We believe that sleep to be eternal, do we not?' And he looked up at the captain, his small eyes squinting.

'Who can say?' she replied. 'Who can know? I have heard tales of ghosts, warlock, and spirits that once were flesh.'

'This is a world of many veils,' Resh said, 'only one of which our eyes are meant to pierce. Our vision strikes through to what seems a sure place, solid and real and, above all, wholly predictable – once the mystery is expunged, and be sure: no mystery is beyond expunging.'

'Those are not a warlock's words,' Finarra observed, studying him.

'Aren't they? By my arts do I not seek order, captain? The rules of what lies beyond the visible, the tactile? Find me answers to all things, and at last my mind will sit still.'

'I would not think that journey outward,' she said.

He shrugged. 'Yes. There is symmetry. Outward, inward, the distances travelled matched and so doubled, yet, strangely, both seeking the same destination. It is a curious thing, is it not? This invitation to the impossible, and the faith that even the impossible has rules.'

She frowned.

Resh continued, 'My wife spoke of the need for blood, for a price to be paid. I believe that she only half understood the meaning of that. To draw something back, from deep in death, into the living world, must – perhaps – demand the same among the living. If a warlock seeks to journey both outward and inward, in search of the one place where they meet, then the corollary is one of contraction, to collide in the same place, the same existence. For the dead to walk back into life, the living must walk into death.'

'Then Ruvera's life was the coin for this spirit's resurrection?'

He sighed. 'It is possible. Captain, the veils are . . . agitated.' After a moment, he cocked his head, his gaze still fixed upon her. 'Coin? I wonder. It may be . . . not coin, but food. Power, consumed, offering the strength to tear the veil between the living and the dead, and so defy the laws of time.'

'Time, warlock? Not place?'

'They may be one and the same. The dead dwell in the past. The living crowd the present. And the future waits for those yet to be born, yet in birth they are flung into the present, and so the future ever remains a promise. These too are veils. With our thoughts we seek to pry our way into the future, but those thoughts arrive as dead things – it is a matter of perspective, you see. To the future, both present and past are dead things. We push through, and would make the as yet unknown world a better version of our own. But with nothing but lifeless weapons to hand, we make lifeless victims of those yet to be born.'

She shook her head, feeling a strange, disquieting blend of denial and uncertainty. For all she could tell, Resh's mind had broken, battered by shock and grief. She saw no clarity of purpose in his musings. 'Return, if you will,' she said, 'to this notion of power.'

The man sighed, wearily. 'Captain, there has been a flooding of potentialities. I know of no other way to describe sorcery – the magic now emerging. I spoke of three veils, the ones through time. And I spoke of the veil between life and death, which may indeed be but a variation, or a particularity, of the veils of time. But I now believe there are many, many veils, and the more we shred them, in our plucking of such powers, in our clumsy explorations, the less substantial they become, and the weaker the barriers between us and the unknown. And I fear what may come of it.'

Finarra looked away. 'Forgive me, warlock. I am a Warden and nothing more—'

'Yes, I see. You do not comprehend my warning here, captain. The newborn sorcery is all raw power, and no obvious rules.'

She thought of this man's wife, Ruvera. It was said that the beasts had torn her limb from limb. There was shock in this, and for the Shake, terrible loss. 'Have you spoken to the other warlocks and witches among your people?'

'Now you begin to glean the crisis among us,' Resh replied. He slowly lifted his hands and seemed to study them. 'We dare not reach, now. No thoughts can truly pierce this new future.'

'What of Mother Dark?'

He frowned, gaze still fixed on his hands – not an artist's hands, but a soldier's, scarred and blunt. 'Darkness, light, nothing but veils? What manner the gifts given to her by Lord Draconus? What is the meaning of that etching upon the floor in the Citadel? This *Terondai*, that now so commands the Citadel?'

'Perhaps,' she ventured, 'Lord Draconus seeks to impose rules.'

His frown deepened. 'Darkness, devoid of light. Light, burned clean of darkness. Simple rules. Rules that distinguish and define. Yes, Warden, well done indeed.' Resh pushed himself upright. He glanced at the unconscious form of his lifelong friend. 'I must see this Terondai for myself. It holds a secret.' Yet he did not move.

'You have not long to wait,' Finarra said quietly.

'I have been contemplating,' Resh said, 'a journey of another sort. Into the ways of healing.'

She glanced at Caplo Dreem. 'I imagine, warlock, the temptation is overwhelming, but did you not just speak of the dangers involved?'

'I did.'

'What will you do, then?'

'I will do what a friend would do, captain.'

'This is sanctioned?'

138

'Nothing is sanctioned,' he said in a growl.

Finarra studied the warlock, and then sighed. 'I will assist in any way I can.'

Resh frowned at her. 'The Shake refuse your petition. You are blocked again and again. You find us obdurate and evasive in turn, and yet here you remain. And now, captain, you offer to help me save the life of Caplo Dreem.'

She drew off her leather gloves. 'Your walls are too high, warlock. The Shake understand little of what lies beyond.'

'We see slaughter. We see bigotry and persecution. We see the birth of a pointless civil war. We see, as well, the slayers of our god.'

'If these things are all that you see, warlock, then indeed you will never understand my offer.'

'How can I trust it?'

She shrugged. 'Consider my purpose as most crass, warlock. I seek your support. I seek to win your favour, that you might add your weight when I next speak to Higher Grace Skelenal.'

He slowly leaned back. 'Of no value, that,' he replied. 'The matter is already decided. We will do nothing.'

'Then I will leave as soon as I am able. But for now, tell me what I can do to help you heal your friend.'

'No god looks down, captain, to add to your ledger of good deeds.'

'I will measure my own deeds, warlock, good and bad.'

'And how weighs the balance?'

'I am a harsh judge of myself,' she said. 'Harsher than any god would dare match. I look to no priest to dissemble on my behalf.'

'Is that a priest's task?'

'If not, then I would hear more.'

But he shook his head, rising with a soft groan. 'My own dissemblers have grown quiet of late, captain. I look for no sanction now, in what I do. And for the Shake, no god observes, no god judges, and in that absence – forgive us all – we are relieved.'

She walked to the cell door and dropped the latch, and then faced the warlock. 'And now?'

'Draw your blade, captain.'

'Against what?'

He managed a strained smile. 'I have no idea.'

*     *     *

Caplo was being dragged across rough ground, a stony slope. Though his eyes were open, he could make out very little. A flare of light blurred his vision, perhaps from a fire, and the grimy hand gripping his ankle pulled him along as if he weighed nothing. He could see the strange splaying of his toes, and feel hairs being pulled by the stranger's calloused hand, and the sharp stones gouged his bare back, tugging at still more hair.

Into a cave, then, rank with animal smells, rotting meat, and woodsmoke. The stone floor was greasy beneath him. There was no strength left in his body, and he felt his arms like thick, bristly ropes against the sides of his face as the limbs trailed up past his head. The cold, damp stone formed a crevasse into which his body slipped easily, as if it had gone this way a thousand times before. From somewhere deeper in the cave there was a dull, droning sound.

The passage narrowed, dipped and then climbed. His captor's breath sounded harsh, whistling. The slap of its feet on the floor echoed ahead, like a drumbeat.

Everything drifted away, and when it returned the motion had ceased, and the space on all sides was filled with shifting bodies, barely seen in the light of embers filling skull-cups set on ledges on the walls. There was paint on those walls, he now saw. Beasts and hatchwork, handprints and upright stick figures, all rendered in red, yellow and black.

He tried sitting up, only to find that he was bound at the wrists and ankles. The thick ropes snapped taut then, raising him from the stone floor. He felt his head fall back, bouncing once, but then hands closed around the back of his skull, lifting until he could see down the length of his own body.

But the body was not his. Wiry hair covered it. His chest bulged like a bird's. The strain on his joints burned, lancing

140

pain down the length of his limbs to where the knotted ropes dug tight. He could not feel his hands and feet.

*Dog-Runners hunting. I was asleep in a tree, my belly full. Above the scrubland, beyond the flats with their thin courses of trickling water slicking the clay. Animals licked the ground there with swollen tongues. They died in the heat, and there was food for all.*

*Dog-Runners hunting. No glory in driving a spear into a bloated carcass. They wanted a leopard, for its fur, its fangs and claws. Nothing to eat on a leopard. The liver kills. The heart is bitter. Leopards hate dying. They die in rage. They die filled with spite. Dog-Runners hunting leopard, eyes on the trees, shapes sprawled on thick branches. Blood-trails, streaks up the dusty boles, the prancing clashes of vultures and kites in a dance around the tree. The leopard looks down, interested but sleepy. Flies feed on its stained muzzle, tickling the whiskers.*

*All of this timeless, the ticking of the day's heat, the night to come. No change comes to this scene. It could as easily be painted on a cave wall.*

*Dog-Runners hunting. I was asleep in a tree. One of me only. They saw me and thought, ah, the last of the Eresal in the hills, in the woodland, in the scrubland they now claimed. A young male, doomed to wander in search of a mate, a troop, but he was alone now. No other Eresal, not here, and how the others screamed when they died! They screamed, while the huge beasts they ran with fled the Dog-Runner spears, or died their own deaths in thrashing fury.*

*The very young had their skulls broken, their flesh cooked, their livers eaten raw.*

*Dog-Runners hunting.*

*Slingstones brought me down. Stunned by the fall. They rushed upon me, beat me senseless.*

*Leopard spirit. Claws marked the tree. They paid no heed.*

*We who lived fell away. We who lived returned to the tall grasses, the dark nights echoing with the yelps of hyena and the coughs of lion. We slunk back into the unseen rivers, when the world was timeless. We reached out to the spirits. We touched their hearts, and those hearts opened to us.*

The ropes pulled with savage tugs, a panicky motion to mark sudden consternation. From the outer chambers of the cave there were screams now, echoing horribly closer and closer still.

*Touch the leopard, run with the leopard, live the ways of the leopard.*

*They hunt alone.*

*Until the night the Eresal came to them. In the shifting grasses, the eye is easily deceived. But this is no flaw of the beholder, no weakness of the witness. This is the blurring of magic. Who brought us this gift? This escape from extinction? There was talk of a mother who would rut everything in sight. A hoarder of seeds, a living vessel of hope.*

*A Mahybe.*

In the cave, his kin were coming, committing terrible slaughter in the blood-splashed chambers.

He was one, bound here. He was many, and the many now came.

Hoarse cries rising around him, the ember light bursting as a skull was knocked to the floor. Rushing, jostling bodies, the clatter of weapons, and then his kin were among them.

The ropes fell slack, dropping him to the floor.

A body fell hard against him, one hand closing to make a fist in the hair of his head. In the crazed half-light, something gleamed. The Dog-Runner straddled him and he looked up into its face. The pale blue eyes were lit with terror. Then the hunter lifted into view a flint knife and drove it into his chest.

In his dying breath, he laughed.

Because it was too late.

\*       \*       \*

The cell had grown unnaturally hot. Finarra Stone sweated in her armour, her grip on the leather-bound handle of the sword slick and uncertain. Warlock Resh had knelt beside Caplo Dreem's cot, head bowed, his hands resting palm-up

142

on his thighs. She had not seen him move in some time.

Her stay in this monastery had gone from days to weeks. News from beyond the walls was virtually non-existent. And yet she found something almost comforting in this imposed ignorance, as if by remaining here, witness to the small lives bound up in all their small gestures of priestly custom, she could hold back the world beyond – as if, indeed, she could halt history in its tracks. She now believed she understood something of what drew men and women to places such as this one. A deliberate blindness to invoke the lure of simplicity seemed the gentlest of rituals, with only a drop or two of blood spilled.

If gods could truly offer up a simple world, would not every mortal soul fall to its knees? As buildings crumbled, as fields fell fallow, as injustices thrived in blessed indifference. She had seen temples and sacred monuments as gestures of diffidence, stone promises to permanence, but even stone cracked. There was nothing simple in the passing of lives, in the passing of entire ages. And yet, for all her convictions – that verged on the worship of complexity – something deep in her heart still cried for a child's equanimity.

But the Shake places of worship were now lifeless. They had become tombs to their slain god. The faith of these people here was blunted, like fists pounding a sealed door. The simplicity they had found, she realized, was no virtue, and if a child's face could be conjured from this, it was dark and obstinate.

They would stand to one side, Resh said. But she believed that position was suspect. They would find themselves not to one side at all, but in the middle.

This warlock here, risking his life for his friend, was the last soldier available to Skelenal and Sheccanto, although 'soldier' was perhaps the wrong word. These men and women were trained in the ways of battle. But of leaders they had but one, now. A grieving man, a man consumed with doubts.

It was difficult to gauge the passage of time, but she was growing weary of standing, and the strain of staying alert clawed down the length of her nerves. She let the tip of her sword rest against the wooden boards of the floor.

'Abyss below!'

Resh's bellow startled her and she staggered back a step. Before her, the warlock had lurched upright, flinging himself on to the body of Caplo Dreem, as if seeking to hold the unconscious man down.

Wondering, frightened, she dropped her sword and lunged forward.

Caplo Dreem was not resisting Resh – he was not struggling at all – and yet she saw his form *blur*, as if it was moments from vanishing. The warlock grasped the assassin's right arm and leaned down on Caplo's chest. 'Take the other arm!' he shouted. 'Do not let him leave!'

*Leave?* Baffled, she moved round to the left side of the cot and grasped Caplo's left arm with both hands. The stump, she saw, had bled through the heavy knot of bandages. Horrified, she saw the talons pierce the gauze. 'Warlock! What is happening?'

'Admixture of blood,' Resh said in a rough hiss. 'The old one within him mocks the child still – he drags it along. No abandonment. No murder. They will dwell together – I hear it laughing.'

'Warlock, what has your magic unleashed here?'

The talons had sliced through the bandages, fingers splaying as they grew. On Caplo's sweat-lathered arm, Finarra saw a mottled pattern forming on the skin, darkening to form a map of dun spots that seemed to float on a shimmering surface of gold and yellow. The flesh under her grip felt as if it was melting away.

'Not my doing,' Resh said in something like a snarl. 'I couldn't get in. Even with the sorcery I awakened, I couldn't get in!'

A guttural growl emerged from Caplo, and she saw that he had bared his teeth, although his eyes remained shut.

'He must not veer,' said Resh.

'Veer? Then indeed they were Jheck—'

'No! Jheck are as children in the face of this – this *thing*. It is old, captain – gods, it is *old*! Ah, Ruvera . . .'

The spots were fading. She saw the talons retracting into fingers. His forearm and hand had grown back, slick with blood and the torn fragments of scorched flesh. The wounds of the thigh were but faint scars now, all signs of infection gone.

'He retreats,' Resh said in a frail gasp. He looked across at her, his eyes wide and frightened. 'Understand me, captain, none of this was my doing. They but wait, now.'

'They?'

'I spoke of the revenant awakened by my wife – how one became many.'

'And this now afflicts Caplo Dreem?'

'Yes.'

'Is it an illness? A fever?'

'I think . . . no. It is—' He shook his head. 'I cannot be certain. It is . . . an escape.'

'From what?' She leaned back, released Caplo's arm, and studied the warlock. 'From death itself? He was going to die—'

'No longer. But I can say nothing more, captain.'

'And when he awakens? Your friend – will he be as he once was?'

'No.'

The fear in his eyes would not fade. Looking into them, she thought of caged beasts.

'Remain with me,' he then said. 'Until he awakens.'

Straightening, she searched the floor until she spied her abandoned sword. She strode over, crouched and closed her hand about the damp, cold grip.

Someone pounded on the door, startling them both.

'Go away!' Resh roared.

＊　　＊　　＊

The line of hills ended in a series of ridgebacks, steep-sided and bare of all growth. The soil was stony, the hue of rust, forming fans at the base that spread out over the edge of the plain. Sharp-edged rocks studded these fans, glinting like gems in the pale, wintry light.

145

Kagamandra Tulas stood facing east, looking out over the flats to the distant line of black grasses. Below him the red fans of silt had the look of draining wounds, bleeding out across the dull grey clays of the plain. He had made his camp just behind this last serrated line of the hills, sheltered against the bitter winds that swept down from the northeast. In the midst of tumbled, fractured boulders, near a massive nest of withered branches and trunks from some seasonal flood, he had built a small wooden shelter, tucked against an overhang. The opening faced on to a small firepit, where he cooked his meals, slowly working through the serendipitous cache of fuel. A dozen paces along the crevasse was a cut to one side that led to a cul-de-sac where he had hobbled his horse.

Somewhere between his departure from Neret Sorr and here, the tide of determination and will had died away. A better man would have pushed on in defiance of his own sordid failings. At the very least, he would have completed his journey to the winter fort of the Wardens, or perhaps onward from there, to the Shake denizens of Yannis Monastery or Yedan. And from such places Kharkanas was not far, not far at all. Each step offered its own momentum, something even a mule understood.

Heroic journeys, as sung by poets, never stumbled against a lack of fortitude in the hero. The inner landscape of such men and women was something strange and foreign to the audience, and so it was ever intended, as a poet's purpose was neither simple nor innocent.

No mortal could set himself against such a hero. Perhaps that was the secret lesson in such tales. But Kagamandra had long since abandoned the romance of heroism, as if life could be lived only from a distance, with oneself that figure, forever remote on the horizon, crossing an arid landscape with every step a battle won, where every war was a war worth fighting. In this scene, there was no promise to draw closer. Details surrendered to the necessity of purpose.

He had once believed that such tales would be spun of his own life, of his exploits on the field of battle. He had once yearned for the attention of poets – in the days when songs

146

showed no bitter underside, before the world grew jaded with itself.

Sharenas – cousin to Hunn Raal and the woman who had quite possibly stolen his heart – had urged him to ride to his betrothed. Was that not a heroic quest? Did that not invite a song or a poem? Would not such a journey win for him Faror Hend's undying love? But as he rode out from Neret Sorr, leaving behind that wretched, reborn army, did he truly believe any of that? Should he find her, should he come at last face to face with Faror Hend, what would she see? A desperate, pathetic old man, who would grasp hold of her in the way of all old men: as if she embodied his long-lost youth. How could she not flinch from his approach? How could she not distrust anything he had to say?

Vows of freedom were like a dog clamping jaws on its own tail. With the promise between its teeth, it could run for ever.

The sky to the east was heavy with clouds, polished iron and promising snow. He was running low on food and these hills were mostly barren, barring a few rabbits that still eluded the snares he'd set. The forage he'd brought with him for his horse was almost all gone and the animal was weakening by the day. The exigencies of survival should have already forced him to resume his journey, but even this impetus had yet to drive him from his lair.

His father had known him for a self-indulgent child, and, should the man's spirit still linger, it would yield no surprise when looking now upon its only surviving son. The privilege of dying while still filled with promise had belonged to Kagamandra's brothers. Somewhere leagues to the south, three cairns made islands on the plain, and around each of them the grasses grew verdant, and come the spring flowers would blossom in colourful profusion about the stones.

He had spent years telling himself to not begrudge the liberation his brothers had found: that blessed release from expectation and the sordid disappointments that followed.

*I do not love her. That much is clear. Nor do I wish her love. I am a ghost. I linger on through lack of will.*

147

In the distance, riders had emerged from the wall of black grasses. Some led horses bearing what looked like bodies. He had been watching the troop for some time as they walked their mounts alongside the sharp edge of Glimmer Fate. They were now directly opposite him and would soon pass as they continued south.

There was an ancient saying his father had been wont to use, wielding the words like weapons to batter down his children. *A hero's name will live for ever. Die forgotten, and you have not lived at all.* When Kagamandra had returned home from the wars, the lone survivor among his father's children, he had been a hero of renown, a warrior raised high on the shield of nobility – gifted with title and honour. His father had stared at him with lifeless eyes and said nothing.

In the following year, the old man elected to waste away to nothing, behaving as if all his sons had died. He never again spoke Kagamandra's name. *You'd forgotten it, perhaps. And so I, who lived, never lived at all. Your favourite saying, Father, proved a lie, when at last it settled at your feet. Or was it you who failed it?*

*No matter. Not a single reward did not taste bitter once I returned home. I did not return to find my bride awaiting me. I did not return to my father, for the news had preceded my arrival, and when at last I came, he was already standing in the shadow of death.*

He did not love Faror Hend. He'd not even wanted her. When he huddled under the furs at night, hearing the distant cries of the lizard wolves of Glimmer Fate, he thought not of that young woman. He thought, instead, of Sharenas.

How many fatal choices could a man make? *Many, because even death need not be sudden. It can be measured out like sips of poison. Each day can be greeted as if it too had died, and but awaited your arrival.* How many deaths could a man endure? *I still walk a field of corpses, and not one of them has anything good to say, but I have learned to look them in the eye and not flinch. I thank my father for that.*

He stepped away from the ledge, worked his way down the narrow, crooked path to his camp.

He fed the last of the forage to his horse and then gathered and bound his bed furs, strapped on his sword and checked over the rest of his gear before saddling his scrawny mount.

A short time later, astride his horse, he emerged from the defile, swung the animal over the crest and rode down a red slope of silts to the hard, frozen plain. Snowflakes spun down from the sky. He set out at a slow canter, to work some heat into the beast's legs.

∗     ∗     ∗

Bursa re-joined them. 'It is Kagamandra Tulas, commander.'

Calat Hustain rode on for a moment longer, and then reined in. The rest of the troop drew up around their leader.

The veteran sergeant settled in the saddle, gloved hands resting on the horn. Since the day on the Vitr shore, Bursa had not slept well. Each night pulled him into a fevered world where dragons wheeled overhead whilst he ran across a vast, featureless plain. His arms were burdened with strange objects: a silver chalice, a crown, a sceptre, a small chest from which gold coins spilled.

In this nightmare, he was the lone protector of these treasures, but the dragons were not hunting him. They but circled overhead like carrion birds. They waited for him to fall, and onward he ran, flinching from their vast shadows that played over the ground ahead. The coins kept falling, bouncing and scattering in his wake – there seemed to be no end to them. And when the sceptre slipped through his grasp and fell, he found another one, identical to the last, still in his arms.

The crown, he saw, was broken. Mangled. The chalice was dented.

The Eleint were patient overhead. He could not run for ever, and there was no place in which to hide. Even the ground under his feet was too hard for him to make a hole, to bury his precious hoard.

Awakening in the dawn, he was red-eyed with exhaustion, and he found himself repeatedly searching the sky during the course of each day's travel.

They had seen no further sign of the terrible creatures. The Eleint had plunged into this world through a gaping rent in the air above the Vitr, only to then vanish. Somehow, this was worse – and during the day Bursa almost longed to see one, a minute talon-slash of black off in the distance. But this desire never lasted the journey into sleep.

At Calat Hustain's command he had ridden back to discern the identity of the lone rider following them. It seemed now that they would await the man. Bursa glanced across at Spinnock Durav, and felt a stab of something close to resentment. The young could weather anything, and among them there were those who stood out even among their peers, and Spinnock Durav was such a man. Was it his perfect features that made certain the founding stones of his confidence, or did some residue of untrammelled self-worth seep out to settle into his face, creating the illusion of balance and open equanimity?

Bursa was tasked with protecting the young Warden by none other than Captain Finarra Stone. But it had been Spinnock's warning cry that had saved everyone, down at the shoreline. Or perhaps Bursa misremembered – it had been a fraught time. But when he revisited that shout in his memory, it came in Spinnock's voice.

*I begin to obsess. Again. All my life, this same game. I but move from one to another. No peace, no hope of rest. I run like the fool of my dreams, carrying the last treasures of Wise Kharkanas.*

*Eleint.*

*Spinnock Durav. She should never have charged me with this task. Should never have invited me to fix my attention upon him. Did she guess nothing of the envy hiding within me, and how it would find Durav? Obsession runs down the same path, again and again. Each time, the same stony trail. Envy is a sharp emotion. It has purpose and it has power. It needs someone to hate, and it seems I have found him.*

Spinnock Durav caught his eye and smiled. 'Another two days of this, sergeant, and then we're home.'

Bursa nodded, tugging at the strap on his helm, where it had begun rubbing his throat raw. The air was cold and it was dry, and his skin never did well in this miserable season. He leaned back and scanned the dull sky. The snow spinning in the air seemed to fail in reaching the ground.

'Cold up there, I'd think,' said Spinnock, edging his mount up alongside Bursa. 'Even for a dragon.'

Bursa scowled. Of course the man had noted his habit, and now teased him for it. 'My bones ache,' he said to Durav. 'Tells me a storm is coming. I but seek its measure.'

Spinnock offered another quick smile and nodded. 'I thought we might outrun it, sergeant.' He twisted to watch the approach of Kagamandra Tulas. 'But it seems not.'

Only then, in following the young man's gaze, did Bursa see the swollen bank of the storm front, spread across the north horizon. Grunting, he shook his head. His thoughts stumbled with weariness, building reckless bridges in his mind.

Calat Hustain tapped heels against his horse's flanks and worked his way free of his troop, reining in just beyond the last horses with their bound corpses as Kagamandra Tulas finally arrived.

'Captain,' said Calat in greeting. 'You are far from the track between Neret Sorr and our winter camp – have you been looking for me? What dire Legion pronouncement must I face now?'

The grey-bearded warrior was unkempt, his heavy cloak filthy. The horse he rode was gaunt. He held up a gauntleted hand as if to forestall Calat's questions. 'No word from Urusander accompanies me, commander. I travel upon my own purpose, not that of the Legion.'

'Then you have no news?'

Bursa saw Kagamandra hesitate, and then shrug. 'Winter is a yoke upon all ambitions. But I would say beware the spring, Calat Hustain.'

'Must every soldier of the Legion threaten me?'

'I am a captain no longer, sir. My old allegiances are done.'

Calat Hustain was silent for a moment, and then he said, 'Cut off the limb. Still it bleeds.'

Kagamandra squinted across at Calat, and then growled something under his breath. He shook his head, and his anger was evident. 'If my warning of a coming war stings you like a thorn, then, commander, I wonder what wilderness grows riot in your skull. For the sake of your Wardens, I advise you hack your way free. The threat of war greets all of us, or would you claim special privilege in the face of its tragic promise?'

'Yet you would seek the Wardens,' said Calat. 'Kagamandra, Faror Hend will not be found at our winter camp.'

'Then tell me where I will find her.'

'I cannot, beyond what I have already said. She does not await you at this trail's end.'

Bursa knew that his commander could have been more forthcoming. He could not decide if Calat's pettiness shamed him or left him satisfied. There had been nothing inviting in Calat's initial greeting, and now it seemed as if, in understanding the reason for Kagamandra's journey, Bursa's commander stood before a caged dog, jabbing between the bars with a sharp stick.

*We are all tired. Battered by circumstance. Pity grows sparse in this season.*

With a nod, Kagamandra collected his reins. He set out towards the hills to the west.

'Wise enough to find shelter,' Spinnock murmured. 'I wonder if we should do the same.'

'And follow Tulas?' Bursa asked in a hoarse whisper. 'I invite you to offer our commander that suggestion.'

Although Spinnock answered that with a smile, at last Bursa saw a hint of frailty in it, and as the young Warden remained silent when Calat gestured and the troop resumed its southward trek, skirting the edge of Glimmer Fate, the sergeant found himself chewing a certain pleasure in this modest victory.

*That was worthy guarding, was it not? Do not make a fool of yourself to your commander, Spinnock Durav. Best speak*

*to me first, believing as you do an ease between us, and in me
a secure home for your foolish words. And if I should hoard
them, well, that is my business.*

He was thinking, again, of the vast empty plain, on which
shadows raced as dragons sailed the sky overhead, his arms
burdened, and the breath ragged in his throat, when the
winter storm reached them in a gust of bitter cold wind, and
a flurry of icy sleet.

\*　　\*　　\*

Narad crouched close to the fire, watching the others who
had come in answer to Glyph's summons, though he knew
not the nature of that invitation. It seemed as if there were
voices in this ruined forest that he could not hear. Blunted
and dulled by his sordid self, all sensitivity was lost to him.
With his eyes, he was reduced to indifferent observation; the
few sounds he heard were nothing more than mundane camp
sounds of hunters gathering; the taste in his mouth was bitter
with stale scraps of food and brackish water. With this prison
that was his body, he could feel frozen ground underfoot, and
the brittle fragility of the twigs and branches that he fed
into the flames. This, then, was all that he was. No different
from the half-dozen scrawny dogs that had joined their makeshift tribe.

The Deniers surrounding him were strangers, in ways
Narad could barely fathom. They moved in near silence,
spoke rarely, and seemed obsessed with their weapons – the
hunting bows, and the bewildering array of arrows, each one
somehow distinct in its purpose, each made unique in the
twist of the fletching, or the barb, the length of shaft or
the wood used, or the material from which the point was
fashioned. With matching meticulousness, these men and
women, and even the youths among them, worked also on
their long-bladed knives, with oil, with spit, with various
sands and gritty clay. They unwrapped and wrapped again
the antler or bone handles, using leather, or stringy grasses,
or gut. A number carried throwing spears, and made use of
weighted atlatls made of soapstone, or greenstone – these

artfully carved in sinewy, serpentine patterns that made Narad think of water in streams, or rivers.

The obsessions invoked patterns, ways of moving that were repeated without variation. The rote dispensed with the need for words, and no paths were crossed, no task interrupted, nothing to change one day from the next. From this, Narad had begun sensing the way of living among these people of the forest. Circular in its seeming mindlessness, no different from the seasons, no different from life's own cycle.

And yet, in purpose, Glyph's tribe was bending itself to the task of murder. All this was preparation, offering up a deceiving rhythm that could lull a man unaccustomed to patience.

*A man such as me. Too clumsy to dance.* He had looked over the Legion sword he now carried. It seemed serviceable. Someone had taken care of the honed edge, smoothing out burrs and softening nicks. The scabbard required no repairs. The belt's leather was burnished and worn, but nowhere overstretched. The rivets were firmly in place, the buckle and rings sound. His examination had taken but a score of breaths.

And now he waited, watchful but emptied of feeling, and found for his self a greater affinity with the wandering dogs than with these hunters, these avowed killers.

Patterns were something he understood. All that he was, and had been, or would be, ever circled around some thing, some force – he imagined it as an iron stake driven deep into the ground, and affixed to it was a solid, thick ring. Whatever he did, whatever he planned to do, was bound to that ring, in knots no mortal could break. Sometimes the rope felt long, looping, eager to unfurl and let him run and run far, but never as far as he had imagined, or dreamed that he could. And so he would be pulled round, to the right or the left, and though he kept running, he but tracked a circle. The stake stood in a glade, with all the earth around it beaten down, the grasses worn away, the trails circling and circling.

He had killed and would kill again. He had found himself plucked loose from the company of others, singled out, scorned and belittled and mocked. Every promise of brotherhood proved an illusion. There had been no women strong enough to cut the rope, or work loose the stake itself. Instead, he but dragged them into his coils, pinned them down, took what he needed but never found – *never, never that way. Our bodies close in seeming intimacy, but the truth is a savage thing. What I long for . . . what I longed for, was something tender.*

*But that language was never given me. Give shape to my frustration, then, in brutal rape, in the empty triumph of power. I could take a thousand women this way, into my embrace, where the grasses are worn down and dust stings the eye, and never find what I seek.*

*Patterns. Round and round I go, nailed in place, trapped, doing again what I did before, and again, and again.*

He but waited for the falling out, the first cruel comment, the birth of barbed words flung his way. Wasn't it enough that he was not of this forest? That the hunters only tolerated him because Glyph had told them to? How soon would the resentment of that eat through this thin civility?

Better had Glyph sent an arrow into his chest, with point of flint, iron, bone or antler, in spinning flight, the length of shaft perfectly suited, the wood elegant in its supple answer to the bow's string.

There were thirty or so Deniers in this camp now. If they each had a tale to tell, it was whispered in that voice Narad could not hear, the mouths moving behind masks, and all the while the quiet, maddening preparations continued. *Round and round and—*

Glyph moved to settle into a crouch beside him. 'I name you the Watch. In our old language: Yedan.'

Narad grunted. 'I do little else.'

'No. For the time of night, when you wake. When you rise and walk the camp. The time of night when your haunts return to you. Your nerves tremble. A restless thing takes you, a thing you cannot name, unless you clothe it in your deepest fears. You wake and stand, when others would fight back into sleep, into losing themselves again. This is a terrible vigil, a solitary vigil. It is the vigil of one who stands alone.'

With the toe of one boot, Narad pushed the end of a branch deeper into the fire. He could think of nothing to say. The other names he had earned had stung. But not this one. He wondered why.

'My hunters honour you,' said Glyph.

'What? No, they ignore me.'

'Yes, just so.'

'You call that honouring? You Deniers – I don't understand you.'

'The Watch is always alone. Their story makes them so. We see in your eyes, friend, that you have never known love. Perhaps this is necessary, for the task awaiting you.'

Narad thought about Glyph's words. He had set for himself a task. That much was true. But he had doubt as to the purity of his purpose: after all, that Legion troop was witness to his shame, and the faces he saw, at night – the ones that started him awake with the sky black overhead – were ones he wanted to cut away, cut down, crush under his heel. *My shame. Each of them. All of them.* He could raise high his vow, voice her name like a prayer, and announce himself the weapon of her vengeance. And even then, he would hear his own whispered hunger, heart-wounded and pathetic, for something like redemption.

There were mines where worked the fallen and the failed, the unforgivable fools who carried with them their unforgivable deeds. They crawled into the earth, burrowed under heavy stone and layers of rock. They dug their way through their unforgiving world, and deemed that a kind of penance. He should have gone to such a place. *If only to shatter the bedrock holding that iron stake, shatter it, see me burst free, to run a straight path – straight as an arrow, straight over the nearest cliff.*

To Glyph he now said, 'My task is vengeance. Against my own shame. Others took . . . bits of it. I need to hunt them down and take it back. If I can do that . . . if I can reach that, that place . . .'

'You will then be redeemed,' said Glyph, nodding.

'Which must not be, Glyph. Must never be allowed to

happen. For what I did . . . no redemption is possible. Do you understand?'

'The Watch, then, must guard a bridge destined to fall. The Watch who stands, and stands fast, is our harbinger of failure.'

'No. What are you saying? This – this crime of mine – it has nothing to do with you Deniers. Your cause is just. Mine isn't.'

'The two must recognize each other, friend, and then together look upon the deed between them. See how it is, in the end, one and the same.'

Narad studied the warrior. 'It seems you have already invented me, Glyph. Found a way to, well, hammer me into your way of seeing the world. I am an awkward fit, don't you think? Best find another, someone else, someone with less . . . less history.'

But Glyph shook his head. 'We do not fear this . . . your awkward fit. Why fear such a thing? A world made smooth allows no purchase. Neither a way into it nor a way out from it. It is closed on itself. It makes its own answer, and so lies undisturbed by doubt.'

Narad scowled at the fire. 'What are we waiting for, Glyph? There are soldiers I need to find and kill.'

Glyph waved a hand, and then straightened. 'Visitors are coming. They will soon be here.'

'All right. Coming from where?'

'From a holy shrine. From an altar black with old blood.'

'Priests? What need have we for priests?'

'They walk the forest. For days now. We have been following their progress, and it seems that it will bring them here, to this camp. So we wait, to see what comes of it.'

Narad rubbed at his face. The ways of the Deniers remained a mystery. 'When do they arrive, then?'

Glyph set a hand on Narad's shoulder. 'Tonight, I think. In your time of waking.'

In his dream Narad walked a shoreline of fire. He held a sword in his hand, but trailed its tip through the sand, and

157

the sand was spitting sparks and flaring as embers were pushed to the sides of the wavering furrow left by the weapon's point. The blood on the blade had burned, curled black. He was exhausted, and he knew that somewhere behind him he had left behind a much larger wake, one made up of corpses piled to either side.

Flames surrounded him, rising high as burning trees. Ash rained down.

There was a woman beside him. Perhaps she had always been there, but he had no sense of time. He felt as if he had been walking this shoreline for ever.

'You'll find no love here,' the woman said.

He did not turn to her. It was not yet time to see her, to meet her eyes. She walked like a sister, not a lover, or perhaps just a companion, but not a friend. When he answered, a tremble of shock followed his own words. 'Yet here I will stand, my queen.'

'Why? This is not your war.'

'I have been thinking on that, highness. On war. I have been thinking that it does not matter where the war is, or who fights it. Or whether we hold blood ties to the slayers, or not. It could well be on the other side of the world, fought by strangers, for reasons we cannot even understand. None of that matters, highness. It is our war nonetheless.'

'How so, Yedan Narad?'

'Because, in the end, nothing divides us. Nothing distinguishes us. We commit the same crimes, taking lives, holding ground, yielding ground, crossing blood-drenched borders – lines in the sand no different from this one here. With fires at our backs, and fires ahead – I thought I understood this sea, highness, but now I see that I did not understand it at all.' He raised his sword and pointed its tip at the shimmering, flame-wrought surface beyond the shore. The weapon bucked and trembled in his hand, as if bound to its very own will. 'That, my queen, is the realm of peace. We dream of swimming it, but when at last we do, we but drown.'

'Then, O brother, you give us no hope, if war defines our existence, and peace our death.'

'We all commit violence on ourselves, highness. It is more than just brother against brother, sister against sister, or any other combination you care to imagine. Our thoughts wage savage mayhem in our skulls, with no respite. We fight desires, wave banners of hope, tear down the standards of every promise we have dared utter. In our heads, my queen, is a world that is without peace, and by that description we define life itself.'

'You question your purpose, brother,' she said. 'After all this. It is no surprise.'

'I was a lover of men, Twilight—'

'No. That is not you.'

Confusion took him and he almost stumbled. Drunkenly righting himself, he let the sword drop again, the point sending up a burst of sparks as it struck the sands. They walked on. He shook his head. 'Forgive me, it nears the time.'

'Yes. I understand, brother. The night crawls; even should we lie in sleep and so see nothing of it, still, it crawls.'

'I would have you, my queen, uproot the spike.'

'I know,' she replied in a soft voice.

'Their faces were my shame.'

'Yes.'

'So I cut them all down.'

'White faces,' she murmured. 'Not sharing our ... indecision. We are their only shadow, brother, and in that, we can never lie to them. You did what you had to do. You did what they demanded of you.'

'I died in my sister's arms.'

'Not you.'

'Are you sure, my queen?'

'Yes.'

He halted, shoulders hunching, head bowing. 'Highness, I must ask you – who set this world afire?'

She reached out to him, one soft gore-smeared hand touching the line of his jaw, lifting his gaze to her own. The rapists had done their work. There was no forgetting that. He remembered the feel of her broken body beneath him, and the ragged mess that had been her wedding dress. With dead eyes, she looked upon him, and her dead lips parted, to utter the dead words, 'You did.'

Narad's eyes blinked open. It was night. The few fires had burned down, and the scorched stumps of trees stood thin and black on all sides of the camp. The others were asleep. He sat up, tugged aside the ratty furs of his bedding.

He welcomed her haunting, but not the illusions it delivered. He was not her brother. She was not his queen – although perhaps, in some ways, he had made her so – but that honour, as he felt it in that place, on that fiery shoreline, was not his alone. It was an earned thing. She led her people, and her people were an army.

*Wars inside make wars outside. It has always been this way. There is nothing left, but everything to fight for. Still, who dares imagine this a virtue?*

He lifted hands to his scarred, mangled face. The aches never quite faded away. He could still feel her grimed fingers along the line of his jaw.

Motion caught his eye. He quickly stood and faced it. Two figures were walking into the camp.

The heavier of the two reached out to stay his companion, and then strode towards Narad.

*He is not Tiste. He wears the guise of a savage.*

*But the one who waits behind him, he is Tiste. Andii.*

The huge stranger halted before Narad. 'Forgive me this,' he said in a low, rumbling voice. 'There is heat in the earth beneath us. It burns fiercest beneath your feet.' He paused and tilted his head. 'If it eases you, consider my friend and me as . . . moths.'

The others in the camp had awakened, were sitting up, but otherwise not moving. All eyes were fixed upon Glyph, who had risen and was joining Narad.

The stranger bowed to Glyph. 'Denier, will you welcome us to your camp?'

'It is not for me,' Glyph replied. 'I am the bow bent to the arrow. In this matter, Azathanai, Yedan Narad speaks for us.'

Narad started. 'I've not earned any such privilege, Glyph!'

'This time of night belongs to you,' Glyph replied. 'This is not where you stand, but when.'

Narad returned his attention to the stranger. *Azathanai!* 'You are not our enemy,' he said slowly, flinching at the faint question in his tone. 'But the one behind you – is he a Legion soldier?'

'No,' the Azathanai replied. 'He is Lord Anomander Rake, First Son of Darkness.'

*Oh.*

The lord then stepped forward, his attention fixed, not on Narad, but on Glyph. 'We need not linger, if welcome is not offered. Denier, my brother haunts this forest. I would find him.'

Narad staggered back, his knees suddenly weak. A moment later he sank down on to his knees as the words of the evening just past returned to him.

*'Coming from where?'*

*'From a holy shrine. From an altar black with old blood.'*

He felt a hand upon his shoulder, a grip both soft and yet solid. With his own hands he had been clawing at his face, but now all strength left him, and they fell away, leaving him nowhere to hide. Shivering, eyes bleakly fixed on the ground before him, he listened to the storm in his skull, but it was a roar without words.

'We know him,' Glyph replied. 'Look north.'

But the Azathanai spoke then. 'Anomander, we're not done yet here.'

'We are,' the Son of Darkness replied. 'We walk north, Caladan. Unless this Denier lies.'

'Oh, I doubt that,' Caladan replied. 'Still, we are not done yet. Bent Bow, your Watch suffers some unknown anguish. Does he refuse us welcome? If he does, then we must quit this forest—'

'No!' snapped Lord Anomander. 'That we shall not do, Caladan. Look at this . . . this Yedan. He is not one of the forest dwellers. He bears a Legion sword, for Abyss's sake. More likely we have stumbled into one of Urusander's famous

161

bandits – his very reason for invading the forest. I can now imagine them as godless as Urusander's own, and a pact forged between the two.'

Narad closed his eyes.

'A fine theory,' Caladan said, 'but, alas, utter nonsense. My lord, understand me – we walk lightly here, or not at all. We will await the word of the Watch, no matter how long it takes.'

'Your advice confounds,' Anomander said in a growl. 'It is of a kind with all that now crowds me.'

'Not the advice that confounds, lord, but the will that resists it.'

The hand on Narad's shoulder was not a man's hand. For this reason alone, he dared not open his eyes. *Welcome to these two? How can I, without uttering the confession that now struggles to win free? Brother of the husband to be, I was the last to rape your brother's would-be wife. I alone saw the light leave her eyes. Will you give me leave, good sir, to seek redress?*

When Glyph spoke, his voice came from a few strides away, 'His torment is not for you, Azathanai. Nor for you, Lord Anomander. Dreams make the path to waking, for the time of the Watch. We know nothing of that world. Only that its shaping is given form by anguished hands. And one of you, Azathanai or lord, now rattles that thing in his soul.'

'Then name our crimes,' Anomander said. 'For myself, I will face them, and deny nothing that I have done.'

Narad lifted his head, but refused to open his eyes. *Ah, this.* 'Azathanai,' he said. 'You are welcome here.'

Hunters now stirred, rising on all sides, taking hold of weapons.

Anomander said, 'So I am denied, then.'

Narad shook his head. 'First Son of Darkness. The time is not yet for . . . for our welcome. But I will promise this. When we are needed, call upon us.'

At last, Narad heard the voices of his fellow hunters, their murmurs, their curses. Even Glyph seemed to hiss in sudden shock, or frustration.

But Anomander was the first to reply. 'Yedan Narad, this

civil war does not belong to you. Though I can see how your companions might like to witness what vengeance I may deliver, in the name of the slain people of this forest.'

'No,' said Narad, and his shuttered eyes offered him nothing but a silvered realm, mercurial and flaring as if with unseen fires. That seemed fitting enough. 'That is not our battle, you are right. Not . . . how we will fight our . . . our enemies. I speak of something else.'

'You stumble—'

Caladan cut off the Son of Darkness with a harshly rasped, 'Stifle your mouth, you fool!'

'When the fires take the sea,' Narad said, seeing once again that terrible shoreline where he had walked. The hand on his shoulder held him with a savagely tight grip now, sending pain lancing through him. 'Upon the shoreline,' he said. 'There, when you ask it of us, we will stand.'

'In whose name?' Caladan asked.

'Hers,' Narad replied.

The Deniers shouted, in fury, in outrage.

But Narad opened his eyes and met Lord Anomander's startled gaze. And said, a second time, 'Hers.'

He watched as Caladan reached out, grasped hold of Lord Anomander's left arm, and dragged the Son of Darkness out from the camp. As if a single additional word might shatter everything. In moments both were gone, vanishing among the burned boles.

Glyph stepped in front of Narad, his face contorted. 'You pledge us to Mother Dark?'

'No,' Narad said.

'But – I heard you! We all heard you! Your words to the First Son of Darkness!'

Narad studied Glyph, and something in his expression swept the rage from Glyph's face. 'She was not in my dream, Glyph,' he said, attempting a smile that made the hunter recoil before him.

'Then—' Glyph paused and looked away, as if seeking one last sight of the two who had come among them, but they were gone. 'Then, brother, he misunderstood you.'

'But the other one did not.'

'The Azathanai? How can you know?'

Narad smiled again, although it was a hard thing to manage. 'Because of what he did, Glyph. How fast . . . how fast he took Anomander away. No explanations, you see? No chance for . . . for clarification.'

'The Azathanai chose to deceive the Son of Darkness?'

*Yes. But that, well, that is between them.* 'Not our concern,' he said, turning on his knees to find his bedroll.

'When Lord Anomander calls, will we answer?'

Narad looked across at Glyph. 'He won't have to, Glyph. That place I described? I fear we will already be there.'

*Standing fast, upon the shores of peace. In her name.*

'Glyph?'

'Yedan Narad?'

'Your old language. Have you a name for a shoreline?'

The hunter nodded. 'Yes.'

'What is it, then?'

'Emurlahn.'

*Yes. There.*

# FIVE

---

AND HERE THE TALE'S TONE MUST CHANGE.
A war upon death? The wayward adventures of the Azathanai? Foolish youth and bitter ancients – raise a sceptical brow, then, and let us plunge into the absurdity of the unimaginable and the impossible.

I'll not gainsay the prowess of the Azathanai, nor seek to diminish the significance of their meddling. Draconus was not alone in his headlong careering into disaster. The question, for which there remains no answer, is this: are they gods? If so, then childish ones. Stumbling with their power, careless with their charges. Worthy of worship? You would well guess my answer.

You are curious, I gather, and indeed led into bemusement, by my fashioning this tale. In your mind, I am sure, the place of beginnings lacked the formality of territories, shorelines, the hinting of a discrete and singular world, upon which myths and legendary entities abound. Dare I suggest that what clashes is within you, not me? The deep past is a realm of the imagination, but one made hazy and indistinct with mystery. Yet is it not the mystery that so ignites the fire of wonder? But the unformed realm is a sparse setting, and little of substance can be built upon the unknown.

I give you places, the hard rocks and dusty earth, the withered grasses and besieged forests. The cities and

165

*encampments, the ruins and modest abodes, the keeps and monasteries – enough to yield comforting footfalls, enough to frame the drama, and in so doing, alas, mystery drifts away.*

*If I was to speak to you now of countless realms, jostling in the ether, and perhaps setting each one as an island in the mists of oblivion, might the imagination spark anew? Draw close, then. The island that is Kurald Galain and Wise Kharkanas abuts realms half seen, rarely sensed, within which mystery thrives. Let us unfold the world, my friend, and see what wonders are revealed.*

*A war upon death. The wayward adventures of the Azathanai. Foolish youth and bitter ancients ...*

\*  \*  \*

In a place where the gloom never eased, there stretched a plain of windblown silts. Lying half buried in beds of the dun, fine-grained material, the detritus of countless civilizations cluttered every possible view, reaching out to the horizons. Godly idols crouched with their backs to the incessant wind, shouldering high dunes that curled round to make empty bowls in their laps. The statues of kings and queens stood tilted, hip-deep, with arms upraised or one hand reaching out as if to grant benediction. The tall backs of thrones thrust like tombstones from the flats. Here and there, foundation walls from crumbled palaces and temples made ridges and lines; rooms sculpted hollows, and cracked domes rose in polished humps.

Wings folded, the Azathanai Skillen Droe followed the set of tracks wending its way across this eerie, despondent landscape. Flight was out of the question, as the air was caustic above the plain, and riding the high, grit-laden winds was too excoriating, even for one such as he.

Instead, the tall, arched figure plodded shin-deep through the desiccated, lifeless silts, his reptilian eyes fixed on the ragged trench made by the one who had walked ahead of him. His mysterious predecessor was dragging something that did little more than glide over the deep furrows carved by its thick, bandy legs.

It had been a long time since Skillen Droe last visited this realm. Since then, the wreckage and ruins had proliferated. Most of the idols he did not recognize. Many of the statues portraying emperors, kings, queens and child-gods revealed features that were alien and, at times, disturbing to Skillen's sensibility. And he could feel the push and tug of the wayward currents of invisible energy that he knew as the Sideways, although he was not the Azathanai who had coined that name.

Forgotten monuments rode the Sideways, inward from other realms. Like flotsam, fragments washed up here, as if this plain served a singular purpose as the repository of failed faiths, abandoned dreams and broken promises. Perhaps it was, as some of his kin believed, the corner of the mind, and the mind in question was the universe itself.

It was difficult to decide if the notion pleased or irritated him. If indeed the universe possessed a mind, it was a cluttered one. And if corners such as these thrived in that mind, then the custodian was asleep, or, perhaps, drunk. This river of semi-consciousness abounded in musing eddies and swirls, in spirals of relentless notions, spinning and spinning until they devoured themselves. Ideas rushed forward only to recoil from boulders in the stream, curling off to the sides and dissolving in the churning tumult. No, this was a mind in hibernation, where only vague memories and flashes of inspiration made the waters restless.

*But mine is not the mind to impose rhythms upon the cosmic storm. This flesh does not yield itself to a surrendering, to what waits beyond it. I only play with the words of others, my throat tickled by some imagined instinct, spitting up the dregs of the countless poets I have devoured.*

*This plain is silent, mostly. These statues, once painted, now lean weathered and weary. The gods squat and pray for a prayer, yearn for a whisper of worship, and, failing all that, would be content enough with a pigeon settling to rest atop the head – but even that modest blessing is denied them here, in this corner of the mind, this vault of the Sideways.*

Through the wrack, he could make out something ahead.

A structure of what looked like stone rose from the general ruination, enclosed by a low wall. The silts surrounding all of this seemed preternaturally level. Skillen could see what looked like a gatehouse to the right, an ornate arch of elegant, panelled stone. But he was approaching from one side, following the tracks that led to the stone wall directly before him.

Spreading his leathery wings, Skillen beat at the air for a moment, raising clouds. The Azathanai slipped forward, lifting higher with sharp, hard flaps, and then swiftly gliding closer. He saw the tracks resume in the yard of the house, wending round in a haphazard pattern to eventually intercept the stone-lined path from the gatehouse – and there, huddled upon the raised steps of the building's entrance, was a lone figure that appeared to be brushing itself off, puffs of dust surrounding it.

Skillen glided over the wall and settled lightly on the pathway. At his arrival, the seated figure looked up, but its face remained hidden beneath a heavy hood of coarse wool.

'Skillen Droe, I did not think you would come.'

Not yet choosing to reply, Skillen turned to face the gatehouse. A Sideways current was pouring through it, although the torrent of energy stirred not a grain of dust or silt. After a moment feeling its power burnishing the scales of his brow, cheeks and needle-fanged snout, Skillen faced the house once more. The stream swept round him and flowed into and through the huge wooden door behind the figure seated on the steps.

The hooded man might have nodded then, as the hood shifted slightly. 'I know. It is an answer, of sorts.' One pale hand gestured back to the house behind him. 'Drains. Repositories. Bottomless, it seems. Possibilities, forever rushing in. Vanishing? Who can say? Some thoughts,' he continued, in a musing tone, 'escape the peculiar. Evade the particular. They tear free and so cease their private ways. And the river swells, and swells yet more. Skillen, old friend, what have you been up to?'

'*It is risky*,' Skillen ventured, in a wave of scents and flavours.

168

The seated, hooded man sighed. 'I imagine so. All that you offer, while in that dread stream . . . will it simply fill the house, do you think? Your manner of speaking here, flowing past me and through this absurd wooden door – your words: do you fear their immortality as they seep into mortar and stone?'

'*K'rul. Why here?*'

'No reason,' K'rul replied. 'Rather, no reason of mine. You saw the tracks? A Builder found me. I was . . . exploring.' He paused for a moment, and when he resumed his tone changed, seeking something more conversational. 'Mostly, I am ignored. But not this time, and not with this one.' K'rul waved at himself. 'It dragged me here. Well, at first it dragged me about the yard, as if wanting to leave me there, or there, or perhaps there. No place seemed to satisfy it. In the end, it left me on the doorstep, as it were, and then? Why, it vanished.' K'rul rose and brushed more dust from his robes. 'Skillen, you might find an easier converse if you stood not on the path. This Sideways is particularly potent, is it not?'

Skillen glanced about the yard, noting those smudged places where the Builder had deposited K'rul. There was no discernible pattern in that map. After a moment, he edged off the stone pathway. '*What waits inside?*'

K'rul shook his head, the motion making the hood fall back, revealing a drawn, bloodless face. 'Like the others, I would imagine. The rooms . . . upside down. One walks upon an uneven ceiling, a confusion of buttresses and steep ramps leading down . . . or is it up? To wander within is to know inverted thoughts. The displacement of perspective may well hold a message, but it is lost on me.'

But Skillen barely heard the words, so appalled was he by K'rul's condition. '*What afflicts you?*'

'Ah, you have travelled far, then. Is isolation such a comfort? Forgive me that question, Droe. Of course, there is peace to be found in not knowing, in not being, in not hearing, and not finding. Peace, in the way of becoming forgetful, while to others, mostly forgotten.' K'rul managed a wan smile. 'But still, I would know: if you have been, then where? And if not, then, why?'

'*I found a world in argument with itself. The delusion of intelligence, K'rul, is a sordid thing.*'

'And this towering form you now present to me? Do you wear the guise of these . . . creatures?'

'*One of their breeds, yes. I played the assassin,*' Skillen replied. '*Subtlety is lost on them. They raise a civilization of function, mechanical purpose. They are driven to explain all, and so understand nothing. They refuse artistry. But artistry hides in the many shades of one colour. They have rejected the value of the common spirit in all things. They cleave to one colour, and heed but one shade. The rational mind can play only rational games: this is the trap. But I did take note, K'rul, of the arrogance and irony implicit in their worship of demonstrable truths.*' He paused, and then added, '*They are coming.*'

K'rul barked a laugh, harsh enough to cut the air. 'Do you recall, I once spoke of possibilities? Well, I have made a gift of them. Or, rather, *gifts*. Magic, requiring no bargaining with the likes of you or me. And already, those gifts are being abused.'

Skillen waited, withholding every scent, every flavour. There was sorcery in the spilled blood of Azathanai. K'rul had very nearly bled himself dry. The gesture was that of an unbalanced mind.

The man before him made an ambiguous wave of one hand, and said, 'Errastas seeks to usurp command of these gifts.' He cocked his head and studied Skillen, and then added, 'No. Command is not, I now think, the right word. Allow me to offer you one that you, in your present state, might better comprehend. He seeks to impose his *flavour* upon my gifts, and from that, a sort of influence. Skillen, I do not think I can stop him.'

'*What else?*'

'Starvald Demelain,' K'rul said. 'The dragons are returning.'

Skillen Droe continued to stare at K'rul, until the man

looked away. The loss of blood, so vast, so profound, had broken something inside this man. The notion made Skillen Droe curious, in a morbid way. *'I heard your call, K'rul, and so here I am. I preferred you as a woman.'*

'My days of birthing are done, for a time.'

*'But not, it seems, your bleeding.'*

K'rul nodded. 'The question is: who will find me first? Errastas, or – should she emerge from Starvald Demelain – Tiam? Skillen Droe, I need a guardian. You see me at my most vulnerable. I could think of none other than you – none other so determined to remain apart from our worldly concerns. And yet, what do you offer me? Only a confession. Where have you been? Elsewhere. What have you been doing? Setting traps. Still . . . I do ask, Skillen.'

*'I am to blame for the dragons—'*

'Hardly!'

*'—and I do not fear Errastas, or any other Azathanai.'*

K'rul answered that mockingly. 'Of course you don't.'

Skillen Droe made no reply.

K'rul shook his head. 'Please excuse that, Skillen. At the very least, I must tell you what he has done.'

Skillen Droe released a sigh heavy with indifference. *'As you will.'*

'Will you protect me?'

*'Yes. But know this, K'rul. I still preferred you as a woman.'*

\*     \*     \*

It had begun with a conversation, in the way that the uttering of words, on easy breath, lodged like seeds, grew and then ripened in the minds of all who would later claim to be present. A conversation, Hanako reflected, to elucidate the absurdity of everything that followed. This was the curse among the Thel Akai, where only silence could stop the onrushing flood of those things, countless in number, upon which the battered survivors might look back, nodding at the signs, the precious omens, and all those casual words slipping back and forth.

But silence was a rare beast among the Thel Akai, and from this tragic truth, the lifeline of an entire people trembled to a thousand cuts. Surely, before too long, it would snap. Even as he and his kin tumbled down in helpless mirth.

Too often among his kind, laughter – unamused and disabusing – was the only response to pain, and this notion twisted Hanako round, once again, to the clear-eyed affirmation of the absurd.

He sat upon the sloped side of a boulder, streaming blood from more wounds than he dared contemplate. His heaving chest had slowed its frantic gasps. The blood he had swallowed – his own – was heavy in his stomach, boiling like bad ale. From the huge boulder's other side and so out of sight, Erelan Kreed was working his knife through tough hide, humming under his breath that same monotonous and tuneless scale of notes, like a cliff-singer slapping awake his vocal cords, making the sounds of stretching and tightening, bunching and tickling. Kreed was known to drive village dogs mad whenever the fool was busy at something.

The hand with the knife had a voice. The other hand, pulling away that rank skin of fur, answered with its own. The sob of sagging muscle and folds of fat made a wet chorus. Of all creatures known to Hanako, only flies could dance to this song, were any bold or desperate enough to brave this chill, mountain air.

Before Hanako, on the roughly level terrace that had marked their camp, Lasa Rook was only now gaining her hands and knees, her fit of laughter finally relenting. When she lifted her head to look at him, he saw the thick glitter of tears in her eyes, the wet streaks that ran down through the dust on her rounded cheeks, and the now dirty mucus tracking down from her nostrils. 'What,' she asked brightly, 'still nothing to say? A pronouncement, if you please! The moment begs for a word, if not two! I beseech you, Hanako! 'Twas but a slap or two from the Lord of Temper, and still you bridle!'

'I could but wince,' he said, sighing, 'at seeing the stitch in your side.'

'It was your seeming impatience that so struck me,' she replied, drawing a muscled forearm across her mouth to sweep up the mucus and dirt, leaving it to glisten in the fine, almost white, hairs of her wrist. She then lifted and swept back her mass of wavy, golden hair. 'But that is the curse of youth, after all. Berate me for my insensitivity, Hanako, and we can shudder down into our familiar roles.'

From behind the boulder, Erelan Kreed's perfidious song ended abruptly. Stones grated underfoot, and then the warrior emerged, dragging the cave-bear's skin behind him. 'You complained of the night's chill, Hanako,' he said. 'But now, in the months and perhaps years to come, you will be able to keep warm at night . . . as you chew the lord's hide into suppleness.'

Lasa snorted, and so was forced to clean her nose yet again. 'A suppleness the lord knew well. As well as his own skin. But years, Erelan? More like decades. The lord's manifestation here, Hanako, is unmatched in my memory. It's a wonder he managed to find a cavern big enough to home him.'

'More the wonder that we did not even see it,' said Erelan, 'since it lies not twenty paces above us.'

'And so the boulder that would so hide Hanako's morning toilet did proffer the lord a most squalid gift, upon the very threshold of his abode.' Even as she said this, she offered Hanako the breathtaking smile that had already ensnared three husbands.

'I proffered no such gift,' Hanako replied. 'That unleavened loaf now resides in my left boot.'

This comment made Lasa Rook fold over once again, her laughter so intense that she struggled to breathe.

Stepping past Hanako, Erelan slapped a bloody hand down on the young warrior's shoulder. 'Next time you decide to wander off, pup, at the very least carry a weapon. You've not the claws or fangs to equal a bear. Still, the rolling embrace was a fine mummery to start this day.' He then thrust something in front of Hanako's face, making him flinch back. 'Here, the lord's lower jaw – it pretty much fell away. You came as close to tearing it off as to make a cutter hesitate to take coin.'

Sighing, Hanako accepted the trophy. He stared down at the jutting canines, remembering how they felt as they scored across his scalp. The thin white rings of the tongue-nest, lined up in parallel rows, were delicate as seashells.

'As for the tongue,' Erelan continued, 'why, we have us breakfast.' With that, the warrior continued on, stepping round the prostrate form that was Lasa Rook, and crouched down before the hearth. He had tucked the thick severed tongue through his belt, and now he drew it out to settle it atop a stone of the hearth, where it began sizzling. 'The Lord of Temper's run out of things to say, ha ha.'

There were many misfortunes to take and give shape to a Thel Akai's life, but Erelan Kreed's feeble witticisms were among the cruellest of curses. They were enough to dampen Lasa's ground-kicking mirth, and once more she sat up, her reddened eyes fixing upon the slab of meat now sizzling on the rock, her expression settling somewhat.

Stifling a groan, Hanako pushed himself upright. 'I am for the stream,' he said.

'Then we'll see what needs threading,' Lasa said, nodding.

*Impatient youth? Yes, I see that, Lasa Rook. Given our purpose, and that joyous decision that so started us on this march, the bear might well have saved me the journey.* Sighing yet again, Hanako skirted his way along the terrace until he came to the tumbling fall of water and its momentary pool that filled the bowl it had worn in the stone shelf. His few clothes were sodden rags now and he left them on the ground as he stripped down.

The water was clear, clean and stunningly cold. The shock against the lacerations covering most of his body quickly gave way to blessed numbness as he stood beneath the falls. *Hanako, who so hates the cold these days. So quickly chilled by an unseasonal breath of wind. Hanako, who once crawled across a frozen lake, what has become of you?* There was an old saying among the Thel Akai. *'Born in the mountains, she longs for the valleys. Born against the sea, she longs for the plain. Born in the valley, she sets eyes upon the snow-clad*

174

*peaks . . .' And so on, as if the point already made could never be made to perfection, and the axe swings eternal against the tree, until the leaves raining down bury us. There we stand, senseless to the tremble in our hands, blind to the mulch against our eyes.*

*Thel Akai, you are brutes among flowers.*

The cold water washed away the blood, slowed the ooze from the wounds. Naked and chilled down to his aching, bruised bones, Hanako returned to the camp.

He found both Erelan and Lasa crouched at the fire, slicing greasy strips from the charred meat. Lasa's brows lifted upon seeing him. 'So this was tongue after all,' she said as she licked her fingertips, and then she cocked her head, 'leaving me to wonder at my ambivalence.'

Erelan frowned up at him. 'Have you no other clothes?'

'I have . . . some few scraps,' replied Hanako. 'But I need sewing up.'

Lasa rose and drew close. She set to examining his wounds, touching here and there, standing all too close – close enough to have something brush her thigh. Glancing down, Lasa hummed under her breath. She lifted her gaze and arched one brow. 'Not a mountain's mantle of bitter snow can shrivel bold Hanako. I pronounce you fit and in no need of awl and gut.'

'Do you mock me?' he asked.

'If one scar entices,' she said, stepping back, 'then your thousand will win you a launching of lust such as the world has never before seen. See how I struggle to constrain myself, young warrior? And I, a woman with three husbands!'

'You would keep me at your knee, Lasa Rook.'

Her eyes widened. 'Ah, now! You are right to chastise me. You have indeed grown – why, from thigh to knee, I should say, and more.'

Erelan Kreed laughed, but it was an uncertain laugh.

With a bright, sidelong glance, Lasa turned away. 'We should be going. I will make a play of purpose to this wayward impulse, and shake the reins of my two work-horses.'

Frowning, Hanako knelt at his pack and drew out what

little spare clothing he'd thought to bring with him. Overhead, the morning sun was already warm upon his torn back, making each gash sting. Yes, she was right to call them hers, although thus far neither he nor Erelan advanced any claim to an inviting caress. Three husbands left behind and Lasa Rook was yet to betray any greed to add others to her night beneath the furs. Work-horses indeed.

Gingerly, he drew on a worn hemp-woven shirt, and then leggings of the same coarse material.

'Be sure to bring that fur,' Erelan Kreed said as Hanako gathered up his gear. 'It is a warrior's way to wear their conquests, and to accept gifts from the Lord and Ladies of the Wild. By that cloak, Hanako, you honour the slain.'

Lasa kicked her way through the coals of the hearth, stamping each one underfoot. 'Your way, Kreed, and none other's. You'll wear honour as if it fits, even as it stretches and tears to the swell of pride. The slain crowd your wake, and their realm is no more and no less than resentment. That you breathe in their stead. That your hearts still pound in your chest. That you move in flesh and bone and make nothing of the ghosts that haunt you. All of this gnaws their souls without resolution.'

But Erelan was humming again, as he tied up his bedroll.

Drawing close to Hanako once more, Lasa Rook dropped her voice. 'Oh, do take the fur, Hanako. You wrestled it off the lord, after all. And all for want of a decent night's sleep.'

'I would have yielded,' said Hanako, 'had he given me the choice.'

'It's said that fear eats at a soul, but I would say it differently. Fear eats away at the choices before you, Hanako, until but one remains. The Lord of Temper knew that fear.'

'He emerged to find me blocking his escape from the cave, Lasa Rook.'

She nodded. 'And in nature he is no different from us. We do not understand the notion of retreat.' She turned then to study the way ahead and below. The mountainside tumbled away in ridges, down into a forested valley. A glittering lake was awakening to the rising sun in the valley's deep basin.

'Even this march,' she continued, 'is ridiculous.' The thought brought a bright smile to her as she swung back to grin at Hanako. 'What direction? Where lies death, brave young warrior? To the east, where the sun is reborn each dawn? To the west, where it falls away each dusk? What of the south, where fruit rots on the branch and insects swarm without rest upon the ground, in daily tasks of dismemberment? Or perhaps the bitter north, where a sleeping woman awakens to find the corpse-serpent has stolen half her body? Or awakens not at all, and lies unchanging for all time? In each direction, death stands triumphant. We seek to join the Jaghut-with-ashes-in-his-heart. We march here to join his march there – but where is there?'

Hanako shrugged. 'This I would know, too, Lasa Rook. I would see how this Jaghut answers.'

'Is it a worthy war?'

He glanced away, down into the verdant valley, down to that silver blade of a lake, remembering the conversation that had begun this journey. The tale, arriving on unseen wings, of a grieving Jaghut, railing against the death that took his wife, and the terrible vow that came of that. Was it not the fate of the living to struggle with the feeling of impotence that came in the witnessing of death? Was there not, in truth, nothing to be done, nothing but weathering the weight, the clawing anguish, the fierce anger? How bold could this Jaghut be, in declaring war upon death itself?

There had been mocking laughter, as if all present would test each other, would beat as if with swords on the mettle of the Thel Akai and their perverse appreciation of delicious, maddening absurdity. And yet. How quickly the derision gave way to that dark current in their souls, as remembered grief rose like ghosts in the night, as each and every instance of impotence bled anew. And so the conversation curled in on itself, all humour lost, and in its place emerged a blackened, scorched gleefulness. A delight sweeter than any other. A burgeoning astonishment at the Jaghut's glorious audacity.

Many dreams were offered up, beckoning, inviting a soul to follow. Few were mundane. Fewer still were even possible.

But in each, Hanako knew, there was a taste of something like hope, sufficient to lure one on to that path, if only in the realm of the wishful. Dreams were to be tolerated, year after year the flavour dulling with pity and diminished by bitter experience, until they burned holes in the gut. He knew that all too well, even when he was mocked for his youth – since when, after all, did dreams belong only to the old and wise, who knew them solely by the disappointment left behind? Was it not the realm of *children* that still beckoned, crowded, as it was, to the heavens with dreams – dreams not yet slashed to ribbons, not yet torn down, or rotted from within?

Death was the reaper of ambition, the devourer of hope. So muttered the ancients in every village, around the night's hearth-fires, with the flames animating the death-masks of their faces. Only memories could live in such faces, when the nights ahead promised so little.

Still . . . born with ambition and knowing only hope, children knew nothing of death.

Conversations such as the one Hanako had witnessed in his village had no doubt burst up like wildfires among all the Thel Akai settlements, from mountain to coast and in all the valley settlements that huddled between the two. The Jaghut had called for an army, in the name of a war that could not be won.

The Thel Akai gave their answer with the drumbeat of heavy, bitter laughter, and said, *That is a war we can wage.*

The pathos of such a claim was enough to make one drunk. He felt that loose, wild surge rising up again in his chest as he pondered Lasa Rook's question. Its taste was a fool's triumph. 'A worthy war? It is, I think, the *only* worthy war.'

Her laughter was low, with a kind of intimacy that made Hanako's skin prickle with sweat beneath his clothes. 'You will speak for me, then,' she said, 'in my defence.'

He frowned. 'I do not understand. Your defence against whom?'

'Why, my husbands, of course, once they figure out where I went.' She turned then and squinted expectantly back up the mountain trail, before once again flashing him that smile.

'But let us lead them a fair chase! What say you, bold slayer of the Lord of Temper?'

Hanako looked across to Erelan Kreed. The huge warrior appeared to have been stricken by Lasa Rook's revelation. 'Damn you, Lasa Rook!' he growled.

Her brows lifted. 'What have I done now?'

'Leave it to you,' Erelan said, 'to make even *this* war a complicated one.'

In a sudden surge of appreciation, Hanako smiled across at Erelan Kreed, and then he burst out his laughter. Upon seeing the flare of pride in the warrior's eyes, Hanako's laughter redoubled.

A war upon death? Why, what could be complicated about that?

'Follow me, my brave guardians!' cried Lasa Rook. 'I will swim in that lake by noon!'

*    *    *

Even after centuries, in which the chaos of the love between them coruscated in wild ebbs and flows, the fever of desire could take them in an instant. In hissing savagery, talons scored deep, tearing loose scales that spun earthward. Jaws snapped and sank fangs into the thick muscles of the nape. The wings hammered in confusion, and Dalk Tennes, gripping tight, would feel her terrible weight dragging them both to the mountain peaks far below.

*Beloved wife, I felt you twist away – once the fury was spent in us both. I saw you slide along a strong current, finding at last an updraught that sped you away. Moments later, Iskari Mockras, you were little more than a speck, but still I trembled to your heat, and knew that you did the same to mine, as it lingered on within you.*

*We are fragments of Tiam. Something like children, but too wise for that title. We preen with the air of ancients, but remain too foolish to hold that pose. The winds we ride – this sea of endless sky – hold us aloft, neither too high nor too low. We are in the middle of our lives, in the age of walking backwards.*

Since the opening of the gate, since that sudden torrent that was either escape or a summons that could not be denied, Dalk had flown a wild cavort, striving to distance himself from his dragon kin. There had been clashes, mindless as ever, as each dragon raged against its own splintered nature. The histories and bloodlines that bound them all, heavier than any chain, tighter than any skin, made a fever of companionship.

Yet he had taken his lover anyway, high above these mountains, and after weeks of stalking. And he had then left her to fall away, satiated and wounded, wanting only to sleep in some solitary place. Where she could heal, and muse on the snarling spawn to come.

Was this instinct, this need to so claim a new world? So the rocks and earth would tremble to the sharp cries of the new-born, to make a home of the unknown. Or was every desire no less than the caged soul deafened by its own cacophony? Instincts could make for a host of regrets, and Dalk was still undecided on what flavour this deed would take. The voice within the mind that spoke to some *other*, and that other none but itself. In spiralling dialogue of endless persuasion, entire realms could be swallowed up, encompassed, mapped with delusions, and so claimed for one's own. *And yet, for all this, the cage door does not open.*

*And so, we rule what we have always ruled, and every border beyond the limits of our skull is but an illusion. Now watch us fight for them. Watch us die for them. This is not majesty that fills graveyards, but sophistry.*

*We are new in this world, and yet have nothing new to offer it.*

*My eyes guide me, from one unfamiliar place to the next, but I cannot escape the place behind my eyes, this cage of self, and these words – these endless words!*

Escape, or summons. The matter was yet to be determined. Magic burned bright in this strange realm, but flowed untethered. Currents charged nowhere, clashed without purpose.

*In hissing savagery, talons scored deep, tearing loose scales*

180

*that spun earthward. Jaws snapped and sank fangs into the thick muscles of the nape. The wings hammered in confusion, and I, gripping tight, felt her weight . . .*

He would hunt anew.

*I shall make this sorcery mine.*

Moments later, as he sailed the high winds rising from the walls of mountains that faced the western sea, Dalk Tennes caught the scent of freshly spilled blood. Turning, he banked, and then began a lazy spiral earthward. Desire's spending made for fierce hunger.

*    *    *

'There is some witchery in a wife's silence,' said Garelko.

'It was the lure of a few more moments in bed,' Ravast replied, nodding. 'Had she forgotten us? Did she tend the garden, unmindful of how the morning lengthened? Why charge this sleep – so gleefully snatched – with her curse that is our guilt? I was restless in my somnolence.'

Tathenal laughed behind Ravast. 'But not enough to prise open an eye! To look about, wondering, flinching at the cold hearth, hearing – with burgeoning consternation – the snores of Garelko.'

'Ah, but those I am used to,' Ravast said. 'No more jarring than your beastly grunts. Still, what you say is true enough. We rejected the signs of amiss.'

'Husbands live under that cloud with unceasing trepidation,' Garelko said, as he led the small troop down the steep, rocky trail. 'As upon a frozen lake, the ice beneath us is of unknown thickness. As in a forested trail, with the scent of cat all about, where every tautberry glows feline eyes to our overwrought imaginations. As upon a cliff's edge, with the dread shadow of some winged monster sliding over us.'

At that last observation, Ravast snorted heavily. 'So you go on about that, an event neither I nor Tathenal did witness. The sky was clear, the morning fresh, and if there was indeed a shadow, then some condor mistook the top of your head for a rival's nest. But, upon closer inspection – the shadow that made you start – the wise bird saw no eggs worth mentioning.'

'We are men,' grunted Garelko. 'Eggs are for breaking.'

'We are husbands,' corrected Tathenal. 'Eggs are for juggling.'

Ravast sighed. 'Amen to that.'

'I was speaking of the witchery of a wife's silence, my beleaguered brothers. Have you not seen her standing at the door, her back to you? Did your knees not tremble, as your mind scampered like a stoat back through the day, or was it last week? When you might have with blind bliss committed some slight?'

Ravast shrugged. 'The heart that questions its own love will stew in the mildest season. Our bellies have been on fire for months now.'

'Back to that again, Ravast?' Tathenal drew closer and slapped Ravast on one shoulder – the one that did not bear the weight and show the edge of the slung battleaxe. 'Her love for us is gone! Your moans will make felt from handfuls of wool, and so suffocate the very virtue whose death you fear.'

'I wish you'd not mentioned wool,' Ravast said in a growl. 'Stapp was too eager to promise taking our flocks into his care. I do not trust that man.'

'And when she stands beside you,' Garelko resumed, 'yet says nothing? Is that the warmth and comfort of companionship? Shall we bathe in her moment of sentimental foolery? That roaringly impossible instant when she's forgotten all our past crimes? In saying nothing, she wields a menagerie of power. For me, why, I'd rather the whip of her words, the tirade of her temper, the crash of crockery against the side of my skull.'

'You are a beaten dog,' Tathenal said, laughing again. 'Garelko, first of her husbands, first to her bedding. First to flutter and fold to the slightest wind of her displeasure.'

'Let us not speak of her displeasing winds,' said Ravast.

'Why not?' Tathenal asked. 'A subject we three can share in a welter of mutual sympathy! The true curse of our union is her love of cooking, so dispiritingly mismatched to her talent. Have we not eaten better these three nights upon the trail? Is this not why not one of us has suggested we hasten our pace and so catch up to her? Are we not, in fact, revelling in the glory of well-made repast? My stomach is too dumb to lie, and my how easy it sits right now!'

'Women,' said Garelko, 'should be barred from every kitchen. Our wife's enthusiasm keeps her slim, when better she wallow in fat with grease painting flabby lips.'

'Hah,' growled Tathenal. 'Even Lasa cannot bear too much of Lasa's cooking. This is none other than her conspiracy that ensures her svelte demeanour. You have the truth there, Garelko. Should we ever catch her, we'll turn this table. We'll truss her up and chain her well away from the kitchen. We'll give her a taste of decent food, and watch how she billows to our ministrations.'

'This seems a worthy vengeance,' said Ravast. 'Shall we vote on this course of action?'

Garelko halted on the trail, forcing the other two to do the same. He swung round to face them, offering up an expression of disdain. 'Listen to you bold whelps! A vote, no less! A course of action! Why, with such resolve we three could throw back a thousand charging Jhelarkan. But see her regard slide over us, and all resolve crumbles like a well-made pie!' He wheeled round again, shaking his head as he resumed the march. 'The courage of husbands is directly proportionate to the proximity of the wife.'

'It need not be that way, Garelko!'

'Ah, Ravast, you are a fool. How things need to be weigh as nothing to how they are. Hence, our bowed dispositions, our harried reflections, the flighty birds of our eyes.'

'Not to mention your nestly hair.'

'Assuredly that, too, Tathenal. And it's a wonder I have any left.'

'Less a wonder than a nightmare. Were you prettier in your youth, Garelko? It must have been so, since I am still waiting to witness a single moment of pity in our wife.'

'Before marriage,' Garelko said, 'I was desired far and wide. I caught the eyes of mothers and daughters alike. Even our man-lover of a king could not keep his hands from me –

and who among us could deny his eye for beautiful men?'

'He's the lucky one,' muttered Ravast. 'Or, was. Famous lovers should never grow too old. Better they die of burst hearts in a thrash of supple limbs and leaking oils. Such swans creep into the sordid.'

'And still he preens,' said Tathenal, 'and so embarrasses us all.'

Garelko threw up a dismissive hand. 'The fate of every ageing king. Or queen, for that matter. Or, to be fair, every hero.'

'Bah!' retorted Tathenal. 'It is the fate of the young who cease being young. And so it is all our fates.'

'And this is what now haunts our wife?' Ravast asked. 'Does she so fear the loss of her wild beauty that she would make death stand in the place of ageing?'

'Suicidal defiance?' mused Tathenal behind Ravast. 'There is a certain charm to that.'

'Charm and Lasa Rook do not sit well together,' said Garelko. 'Slovenly lust? Yes. Seduction and the promise of manly dissolution? Of course. Manipulation and sudden vengeance? Absolutely. That smile and those eyes that could make even a man-loving king tremble? Oh, we've seen it ourselves, have we not? Why, I do not imagine—'

Garelko stepped round a sharp bend in the trail at that moment, and the scene before him cut the words from his tongue. Following a step behind, Ravast looked up and halted.

Before them, on a broad ledge, a reptilian monstrosity had been feeding on a massive, skinned carcass, and now it lifted its gore-smeared head to face them. The beast's hiss sprayed all three Thel Akai with a fine mist of blood.

As the creature's long neck curled, raising the head high, Garelko brought round his iron-shod staff from where it had been slung across his back, and leapt forward.

Reptilian jaws stretched wide and the head lunged down.

Garelko slipped to one side and drove the heel of his staff into the beast's right eye.

Roaring, it pulled its head back.

Battleaxe in his hands, Ravast ran up on to the sloped side of a boulder, gaining height as he did so. Seeing the creature lashing out with an enormous taloned hand, Ravast launched himself from the boulder. Axe blade met that sweeping hand, the edge driving between two fingers, slicing through the webbing and then deep between the bones.

Recoiling, the beast stumbled back – tearing the axe from Ravast's grip – and then rolled on to the carcass on which it had been dining. The stripped cage of the carcass's ribs splintered and collapsed like brittle sticks, carrying the creature over on to its folded wings.

Tathenal raced past, between Ravast and Garelko, swinging his blunt-tipped, two-handed broadsword, chopping deep into the thrashing beast's left thigh.

The creature continued rolling until it slammed into a massive boulder. The impact lifted the rock and sent it tumbling off the ledge beyond. A moment later the beast followed, vanishing – with trailing tail – from sight. Concussions shook the ground as the boulder made its wild descent to the treeline far below.

Then there was a thundering, snapping sound, and they saw the monster sailing out on its broad wings, skimming over the forest's canopy. Its flight was erratic, as the head was strangely tilted. Ravast's axe gleamed bright in the sunlight, firmly wedged between the talon-clad fingers of one hand.

Tathenal lifted up his sword to show the others the three scales still clinging to the blade's edge.

'Very well, Garelko,' said Ravast, 'not just shadows.'

'Lasa camped here,' Garelko pronounced, scanning the ledge. 'Look, see how she kicked out the hearth's coals, same as she does at home. Our wife's habits make a trail we need no hound to follow.' He slung the staff over on to his back once more and set off down the trail. The others followed.

'Oh no,' Garelko continued, 'as I was saying, there is little charm in our dear wife. Deadly allure? Oh, indeed. That whimper-enticing heft of her thigh when sitting with folded legs, so smug an invitation for a man's hand? How could we deny that? And what of the . . .'

The conversation continued, as the three husbands made their way down towards the forest.

It was nearing midday.

*     *     *

'My husbands are in no hurry, it seems,' said Lasa Rook, 'and for that they will pay dearly. Am I not enticing enough? Desirable enough?' She edged close to Hanako, until their shoulders were pressing. 'Well?'

'You are these things, Lasa, and more,' said Hanako, struggling to keep his eyes on the trail.

'Of course,' she went on, 'they are angry with me, and rightly so.'

Behind them, Erelan said, 'You did not even leave them a note.'

'Ah! Not what I was thinking about, to be honest. Thrice, now, I've almost burned down the house. There is a careless imp in me – oh, do not look so shocked, Hanako! I will admit to my flaws, no matter how attractive and endearing they might be! In any case, the imp has a temper, too, as each night it and I must witness – yet again – my three husbandly oafs shovelling down the wretched fare I set before them. Have they no taste?'

'They must have,' objected Erelan, 'since they married you!'

'Ha ha! I am ambushed. Then I shall say it so: in the years since their lucid moments of appreciation, they have let themselves descend into dullardly obtuseness, into vapid venality. Their palates belong to dogs, their grunts are those of pigs – is it any wonder the imp snarls and kicks at coals until the rugs smoulder on all sides?'

'What cause this vengeance of yours?' Hanako asked.

Her shoulder pushed him hard enough to make him stumble. 'So spake the virgin to marriage!'

Erelan laughed his uncertain laugh, and Lasa rounded on him. 'And you! O warrior who wears everything he conquers! Where is your wife? What? None ever waved an inviting hand? How is it we supple reflections have not swooned in

186

answer to your stolid prowess? Your pride of glory and the rotting trophies you hang from your person?'

Hanako dared not glance behind him to see the effect of her tirade on Erelan Kreed. He was thankful enough that she'd already dismissed him.

'Your wit is a song to my ears, Lasa,' Erelan said, 'and so I laughed.'

'You've not met my wit,' Lasa warned in a low tone. 'And you should thank the hoary rock-gods for that.' She swung round again. 'Bah, I need a bath. Hanako, dear youngling, when we reach the lake – unless it was ever a mirage, designed solely to haunt a woman's need for a decent toilet – will you indulge my body with soap and oils?'

'What of your husbands?'

'Well, they're not here, are they? No! The fools are probably well off the trail I set them. Picking berries, perhaps, with lips of blue as they natter endlessly about everything and nothing. Or they have found slabs on which to lie in the sun – as they often do when guarding the flocks. To think, they imagine that I can't see them up in the hills! I have the sharpest eyes, Hanako. The sharpest! No, they are indolent and smug, slovenly and lazy.'

'I will attend to you at the lake, then,' said Hanako.

She pushed up against him once more. 'Will you now?'

'You tease me unduly, Lasa Rook.'

'I but tease out what hides in you.'

'Is it any wonder I remain wary?'

She waved a hand. 'I will brush aside your temerity, Hanako of the Scars, Slayer of the Lord of Temper. My husbands can rot. I will take a lover, to spite them all. I might choose you, Hanako, what do you think of that?'

'I see three deaths awaiting me, since surely my dying once will not be enough.'

'What? Oh, them. Think on that some more, youngling. They already know I travel with company – oh, Erelan would give them no cause for jealousy, as his only love is the warrior's vanity. But you, Hanako. Young, handsome, and are you not the tallest brave in the village? The strongest? Did you not just this morning tear the lower jaw off the Lord of Temper? And then break his neck? No, dear lover to be, it seems even you cannot light a fire to their heels. But look – is that a glimmer ahead, through those branches? Is the sun not directly above us?'

'There is no way to—'

'Hush! It is my blessing to experience synchronicity in life. Perfections meet wherever I make my island. Smile sweetly, and show sure hands in the spreading of soap and oil, Hanako, and I might let you walk upon my shore.'

*There to fetch up like a half-drowned man.* 'I fear that lake will be as cold as was the stream.'

'A challenge to your manhood, then.' A moment later she halted and raised a hand.

*Company ahead? Well, it seemed a decent lake. Perhaps the Dog-Runners have made a camp upon its shoreline.*

Erelan edged up to join them, and then, drawing his long-handled mace, moved ahead in a low crouch.

Glancing across at Lasa Rook, Hanako saw her meet his gaze in the same instant, and she rolled her eyes. They set out after Erelan Kreed, stepping carefully.

The treed trail ended a dozen paces ahead, pushed up against a scree of low boulders crowded with the leavings of high floods in the past. Erelan had crept up against this bulwark and was peering through a skeletal skein of branches. From the shoreline just past him, something was thrashing in the shallows, and it sounded big.

Hanako reached for his father's sword – which he had foolishly left near his bedding as he ventured off for his dawn meeting with the Lord of Temper – which now formed the spine to his bedroll. Sliding it from its scabbard, he studied its dull, pocked length. The single edge was ragged, notched. There was a distinct leftward curve visible along its backed reach. The history of this blade was one of successive failures. It was no wonder he hesitated unsheathing it.

Lasa Rook settled a hand on his scabbed, slashed and swollen forearm. 'Leave this for Erelan,' she whispered. 'See how he charges himself with delight?'

188

They drew closer, until they fetched up alongside their warrior companion. Through the latticework of tangled brush, Hanako looked out upon a winged, scaled monstrosity. It favoured one forelimb and bled from a haunch as it staggered clumsily in the shallows. The massive head at the end of its long, sinewy neck was pitching wildly, tilting to one side.

Erelan's eager words came in a hiss. 'Blinded in the right eye. I but wait until it makes itself blind to the shore.'

'Why not leave it be?' Hanako asked.

Erelan grunted. 'See that axe – there upon the strand? Torn out from that forefoot?'

Lasa gasped. 'Oh dear, that weapon belongs to my beloved Ravast!'

'Look then,' Erelan continued in a rough growl, 'to the blood on its maw – the gore slung between fangs!'

'My husbands have been devoured, and not by me!'

Erelan straightened suddenly. 'This warrior avenges you, Lasa Rook!' Leaping up on to a boulder, he readied his mace, and then jumped down on to the pebbled wrack and raced forward.

The monster heard nothing as it slapped at the water. Its blinded eye was turned to the shoreline, and so it saw nothing of Erelan's furious charge.

The heavy mace struck the beast's head, just behind the blinded eye. The impact was sufficient to crush its orbital, its flared cheekbone, and one side of the creature's skull.

Blood sprayed from its nostrils and it lurched away with a drunken stagger.

Erelan struck again, this time with a blow coming from high above, straight down on to the flat of the creature's head. The mace buried its striking end in the skull, halted only by the weapon's bronze-sheathed shaft. Pitching suddenly on to its side, the dying beast coughed out a heavy gush of blood. Legs kicked fitfully as Erelan wrenched free his mace. He clambered on to the monster's back, perching atop one shoulder, and swung a third time. The snap of the bones of the neck was sharp, echoing out across the lake's waters.

The creature slumped in twitching death.

Hanako set out, Lasa following, arriving on the pebble-strewn beach in time to see Erelan draw out his gutting knife and begin carving into the carcass's chest.

'He seeks the hearts,' said Hanako, 'in keeping with his warrior's—'

'Host to every manly fever,' Lasa Rook said in a bitter tone, 'his antics leave us cold. My husbands!' She fell to her knees at the axe lying on the stones. 'Ravast, so young, so fresh to my bed! I see the fury of your battle! The bravery of your stand! Who was first to dive down the fiend's maw? Garelko, too slow as always, too old, in all his creaking ways! Tathenal! Did the beast toss its head in swallowing you down? Like a sliver of flesh? Like a fish down a heron's gullet? Did you complain all the way? Oh, my heart grieves! Ravast!'

Having carved a gaping hole in the creature's steaming chest, Erelan barked triumphantly as he struggled to pull free an enormous, blood-drenched mass of muscle that still trembled. 'See, I have the first one! Hah!' He fell back on to the gravel, knees crunching in the polished stones. Raising the heart high above his head, he leaned back, letting the draining blood wash down over his face, and filling his mouth.

The visage he swung over to Lasa Rook was ghastly. 'I am your champion, Lasa—'

Then Erelan's eyes widened amidst the sea of red. 'Iskari Mockras! Arak Rashanas, my foul brother, lusts after you! I pursue him! Too many insults, too many betrayals! There were crushed eggs making a path to your high perch! He leaves you to yearn and doubt my seed's power! I will kill him!' Rearing upright, the beast's heart tumbling out from his grip, Erelan staggered a step, and then clutched the sides of his head. 'I took her again, Arak Rashanas! She will yield my spawn in this new world! They are born with the hate of you in their hearts – this I swear!'

He stumbled into the water. 'This fire! This pain! Latal! Mother! Heal me!'

Erelan fell, as if in a swoon, and the waters closed around him in a bloom of blood.

Hanako rushed into the icy shallows. Reaching Erelan, he lifted the warrior under the arms – saw with horror the pink water draining from Kreed's slack mouth. Wounds reopened across Hanako's body as he dragged Erelan back on to the shore.

Lasa had not moved from where she knelt before Ravast's axe, but her face was ashen as she looked across at Hanako's struggles. 'Is he dead?' she asked.

Hanako did not yet know the answer to that, so he said nothing as he rolled Erelan on to his side. He pressed a hand against the warrior's neck, and felt in the veins there the thundering, panicked beat of the man's hearts. 'He lives but I fear his chest may burst, Lasa!'

Then Erelan spasmed. His boots kicked gouges through the pebbles. His hands waved blindly but still managed to push Hanako away. Erelan fell over on to his back, his eyes wide as they stared skyward. 'She sings my name – in the ache within her – my love sings my name!'

'What do you mean?' Hanako asked. 'Erelan?'

'Dalk!'

'Erelan!'

Something flashed to life in Erelan's eyes, and they fixed suddenly on Hanako. Horror and terror warred in that wild stare. 'Hanako!' he whispered. 'I – I am not alone!'

      *      *      *

His belly filled with berries, Ravast dozed in the sun. They occupied a clearing they had spied off to one side of the trail, in which huge slabs of stone lay strewn about, marking some fallen temple, perhaps, or the gutted remnants of a looted barrow. No matter. The midday sun bathed the glade with sweet warmth, and the travails of the world seemed far away.

Tathenal was pottering among the menhirs, while Garelko snored loudly from his own bed of stone.

'Ravast, I proclaim these Azathanai.'

'Fascinating.'

'You are still too young,' Tathenal said. 'Nothing of the

profundity that accompanies antiquity is to be found in your squealing pup of a soul. While I, who have known a host of wretched decades – not as many as Garelko, let us be sure – I, then, am grown into the appreciation of our brief flit of life in the midst of this grinding, shambling, plodding march of pointless time. Did I say pointless? I did, and heed that well, Ravast.'

'Your words are as a song to lull this child into sleep,' Ravast said.

'Like birds my wisdom flaps about your skull, despairing of ever finding a way in. The Azathanai are most ancient folk, Ravast. Mysterious, too. Like an uncle who dresses strangely and has nothing to say, but offers you a knowing wink every now and then. Yes, they can be maddening in their obscurity, and such knowing regard would wordlessly tell us of outlandish adventures and sights seen to steal the breath of lesser folk.'

Blinking against the glare, Ravast half sat up and peered across at Tathenal. The man was seated on one dolmen, the index finger of his right hand tracking the unknown words carved into the stone's facing. 'You speak of Kanyn Thrall—'

'Who then wandered off again! Years, now, since last we have seen him, or known of his whereabouts. But now, at last, I am beyond caring. He but served as an irritating example. I was speaking of the Azathanai, and their obsession with stone. Statues, monuments, ringed circles, chambered tombs – always empty! – and their madness reaches yet further, Ravast! Stone swords! Stone armour! Stone helms, which will serve only stone heads! I imagine they shit stone, too—'

'Well, we've seen enough suspicious pebbles on this trail—'

'You mock me, but I tell you, there is no place in all the world which they have not seen, have not explored, have not interfered with. The Jaghut were right to oust the one they found hiding in their midst. You might think us Thel Akai immune, but there is no telling if an Azathanai hides among us – they choose the flesh they wear, you know—'

'Well, that is nonsense, Tathenal,' said Ravast, leaning back again and closing his eyes. 'Were they as you say, they would not be mortal – they would be gods.'

'Gods? Well, why not? We worship the rock-gods—'

'No we don't. We just blame them when things go wrong.'

'And when we are blessed we thank them.'

'No. When things go right, we congratulate ourselves.'

'Oh, cynical child, does this fresh world so weary you? Are you left exhausted after uncovering all the world's truths? Will you slouch and slide your jaded eye upon all the fools whose company you are cursed to endure?'

'You mock my tolerance. It is only my youthful vigour that sustains me.'

'The Azathanai built this, only to knock it down – not even a Thel Akai could so push these stones, uprooting them like this. I see about us the echoes of old rage. For all we know, our very own rock-gods were Azathanai.'

'Then it is well that we lost faith.'

'*She* hasn't.'

Ravast frowned at that, and then sat up. 'I would venture the opposite! It is no faith that makes anyone face death and only death. It is, if anything, surrender. Abjection. There is not a fool to be found who would worship death.'

'Ah, but she marches not to kneel before the Lord of Rock-Piles, but to war against him.'

'Might as well beat against a mountainside.'

'Just so,' Tathenal said, looking at the rubble around them.

'There will be no Azathanai among the Jaghut's company,' Ravast said. 'I suspect no more than a handful of fools. Other Jaghut, bound only by some kind of loyalty to the grieving brother. Perhaps a few Dog-Runners, eager to find a song in the deed. And we Thel Akai, of course, for whom such a summons is too outrageous to refuse.'

'We refused it.'

'In the name of flocks to keep, gardens to tend, nets to weave. And yet, Tathenal, look at us, here on this trail.'

'We pursue her to bring her back. With weapons of reason, we will convince her—'

'Hah! Idiot! She's but extended our leashes, and knows the patience of the mistress. Look at us here, playing at freedom! But soon we will resume this trek, and she will take up the slack.'

There was a loud grunt from Garelko and they turned to see the man bolt upright, eyes wide. 'Ah!' he cried. 'I dreamed a dragon!'

'Was no dream, you fool,' Tathenal said. 'We met the beast this morning, and saw it off.'

Garelko squinted across at Tathenal. 'We did? Then it was all real?'

Ravast stared at Tathenal. 'That was a dragon?'

'What else could it have been?'

'I – I don't know. A giant lizard. Winged. With a long neck. Snaking tail. And scales . . .'

The other two husbands were now studying him, with little expression. Ravast scowled. 'By description,' he muttered, 'I suppose the comparison is apt.'

Groaning, Garelko stretched. 'This fusion of dreams and truth has left me out of sorts. For all I know, I've not yet wakened, and it is my curse to see both of you haunting me even in my slumber. Pray there comes a day when there are as many girls born among the Thel Akai as boys. Then, a husband can stand alone, face to face with his wife, and there will be peace and everlasting joy in the world.'

Tathenal laughed. 'You dodder, Garelko. The Tiste make such marriages and are no happier than us. The curse of your dreams has you yearning for the madness they espouse.'

'Then wake me, I beg you.'

Sighing, Ravast slipped down from the slab. 'I feel the leash grow taut, and would not welcome a whipping.'

'You are long since whipped well and truly,' said Tathenal.

'Oh, roll over, will you?'

The three Thel Akai readied their gear once more, and in so doing Ravast was reminded again of his lost weapon. To a dragon, no less. Few would ever believe him, and the exhortations of his fellow husbands held little veracity. It was, in any case, an unpleasant notion, this proof of legends and old, half-forgotten tales.

Words momentarily exhausted, they made the trail in silence, and resumed their descent.

*     *     *

'Beyond you, I am in need of allies.'

Skillen Droe glanced over at the cloaked figure trudging alongside him. *'You will find few.'*

'There is a caustic sea, the essence of which is chaos.'

*'I know it.'*

'Mael does not claim it,' K'rul said. 'Indeed, none of us does. Ardata has ventured there, to its shoreline, and contemplates a journey into its depths. There is some risk.'

*'Is she alone?'*

K'rul hesitated, and then said, 'I cannot be certain. Ardata guards her realm jealously. It is my thought that we could appeal to that possessiveness.'

*'I will defend you, K'rul. But we are not allies. You have foolishly made yourself vulnerable.'*

'Very well.'

*'I will make this plain to her.'*

'Understood, Droe.'

They walked now along the edge of a vast pit. Its sheer walls were cracked, shattered as if from the blows of some giant hammer. The dusty floor of the crater showed crystalline outcrops that glittered with blue light. A steep ramp had been carved into the opposite cliff-side, curling round until it was out of sight, somewhere against the edge they skirted. Thus far, Skillen Droe could not see where the ramp debouched. There was something strangely protean about the dimensions of this pit, and the landscape surrounding it. They had been edging along it for some time now.

*'This is a quarry, K'rul?'*

'The Builders, I would think. They have, they tell me, reduced entire worlds to rubble, leaving them to float in

195

clouds that ever circle the sun – a sun not our own, one must assume.'

*'The pit is devoid of Sidleways. Its air is still. There is no energy left in it. To descend, K'rul, is to die.'*

'I have no answers to their endeavours, Droe, or the means by which they wield their power. The houses they build here disappear shortly after their completion.'

*'Only to reappear elsewhere, as if grown from seeds.'*

'Something drives them to do what they do,' K'rul said, pausing to cough for a moment. 'Or indeed, someone. We share that at least with the Builders – the mystery of our origins. Even the force that cast us down upon the realm, to find flesh and bone, seems beyond our ken. Have we always been? Will we always be? If so, for what purpose?'

Skillen Droe considered K'rul's words for a time.

Beneath the gloomy sky, they walked on. Their pace was slow, as K'rul seemed to have little strength. If he still dripped blood from his sacrifice, the crimson drops did not touch these dusty silts. No, they bled elsewhere.

*'It is our lack of purpose, K'rul, which drives us onward. Sensing absence, we seek to fill it. Lacking meaning, we seek to find it. Uncertain of love, we confess it. But what is it that we confess? Even a cloud of rubble will one day accrete, making something like a world.'*

'Then, Skillen, if I understand you, beliefs are all we have?'

*'The Builders make houses. From broken stone they build houses, as if to gift the disordered world with order. But, K'rul, unlike you, I am not convinced. Who, after all, broke the stones? It is my thought that the Builders are our enemy. They are not assemblers of reason, or even purpose. Their houses are built to contain. They are prisons – the Builder who dragged you to that house sought to chain you to it, in its yard so perfectly enclosed by that stone wall.'*

K'rul halted, drawing Skillen around. A pale hand reached up into the shadow of the hood, as if K'rul was setting fingers to his brow. 'And yet, it failed.'

*'Perhaps you were still too powerful. Perhaps, the house was not yet ready for you.'*

'We have kin who worship such houses.'

*'Lacking meaning and purpose, they seek to find it. In the ordering of stone – does that surprise you, K'rul? Are the Builders our children, or are we theirs? If we are but gener-ations, one preceding the other, then which of us has fallen from our purpose?*

*'The Builders are building worlds of denial, K'rul. The question you must ask is this: for whom are they meant? And, it follows, is it our task to oppose them? Or simply watch, decrying the entropy that is their monument?*

*'Worship? Only a fool worships what is already inevitable. If I cared – if I thought it would prove efficacious, I would tell our kin this. Your obeisance is pointless. Your adoration kisses a skull, and where you kneel, there is only dust. Your faith is in a god with no face.'*

Once again, K'rul passed a hand over his hidden visage. 'Skillen Droe, you name me a fool, and rightly so.'

*'What inspired your gift, K'rul?'*

'Does it matter?'

Skillen shrugged his sharp, protruding shoulders. *'I cannot yet say.'*

Sighing, K'rul resumed walking, and a moment later they strode side by side again, skirting the endless crater. 'I sought a breaking of the rules, Skillen. Oh, I know, *what* rules? Well, it seemed – seems – to me that they exist. More to the point, they do not answer to us. Look well on each of us. We Azathanai. On our habits, our proclivities and predilections, and how they serve our need to distinguish each of us from the others. But rules precede us, as cause precedes effect.

'Some things we do share. For one, the habit that is our possessiveness, when it comes to our power. I admit, I found inspiration in the Suzerain of Night, when from love he gave a mortal woman so much of his own power. And, once it was done – well, he could not take it back.'

*'I was unaware of this. I am shocked by this news. I did not think Draconus so . . . careless. Tell me of his regrets.'*

'I do not know that he has any, Skillen. There is, I have found, something almost addictive in surrendering power. To

197

become drunk on helplessness – well, it has ceased being so strange a notion. I heeded the Suzerain's gift, and deemed it, in the end, too modest. That has since changed, as Draconus has gone yet further, but of that I will tell you later.'

'*I fear tragedy in that tale.*'

'Again, a modest one. If not for what I was driven to do. So, together now, Draconus and K'rul, we come to threaten the realm with devastation. By our gifts. By the helplessness we so coveted. Understand, it did not seem that way, not to begin with. The acts were . . . generous. Was this, in fact, our purpose? The mystery of our existence, solved by simple sacrifice? By yielding so much of ourselves?'

'*You have given to mortals the gift of sorcery. But it is not mortals who now threaten you, is it? You spoke of Errastas, and the flavour of influence he seeks to impose upon your gifts. You say that you cannot stop him. If that is true, what do you now hope to achieve?*'

'Ah. And this, old friend, is why I sought you out. I admit, I considered your remorse. The burden of regret you carry, so fierce as to drive you from our company.'

'*You would use me so?*'

'I would rather you did not see it that way, Skillen. Consider this, instead, yet one more gift. From me to you. Nothing substantial, as we might measure it, but sufficient to give purpose.'

'*You offer me purpose? Born of old crimes? Name me this gift, then. And consider well before you speak, since I am contemplating rending you limb from limb for your temerity.*'

'Redemption.'

Skillen Droe was silent – even in his thoughts – as his soul seemed to recoil from that word. Rejection and disbelief, denial and refusal. Such impulses needed no language.

K'rul seemed to comprehend at least some of that, for he sighed and said, 'Errastas seeks to impose a kind of order upon my gifts, and make of chance a secret assassin to hope and desire. Droe, there are gates, now. They await guardians. Suzerain powers. But I cannot look to the Azathanai.

198

Draconus would seek them among the Tiste, but I deem that dubious and, indeed, fraught. No, I knew I must look elsewhere.' He hesitated, and then said, 'Old friend, Starvald Demelain has opened on to this realm, twice now. There are dragons among us – the boldest of the kin, no doubt. Ambitious, acquisitive.'

'*You would bargain with them? K'rul, you are a fool! To think they would welcome my presence! I am the last they would yearn to see!*'

'I disagree, Droe,' K'rul replied, with anger in his tone now. 'I told you. I am not done with my gifts. This yielding rises from a tide to a flood. We need no other treasure to dangle in the bargain. In all instances but one, Skillen, the dragons will fight for what we offer.'

'*You would unleash such battles? Will you see Tiam herself manifest on this realm?*'

'No, we will find them as they are – singly, dispersed and eager to keep it that way. As for Tiam, again I have an answer, a means of preventing her. I believe it will work, but once more, in this I will truly need your help. Indeed, our powers must be combined.'

'*I see now. Your gift of redemption to me, and from this, my gratitude to you, and from that, my power conjoined to yours. You have thought far, K'rul, with me like a loyal hound at your heel every step of the way.*'

'I considered only the means by which I could win your allegiance.'

'*And have you contrived similar manipulations for those others whose alliance you seek? What of Ardata, then? Ah, of course, the chaos of the Vitr, so close in substance to the lifeblood of dragons.*'

'Chaos is necessary,' K'rul said, 'to balance what Errastas seeks.'

'*Who else waits unknowing in the wings? Mael? Grizzin Farl? No, not him, unless it is to send him among your enemies. Kilmandaros? Nightchill? Farander Tarag? What of Caladan Brood – I would have thought that the High Mason, above any of us, would have been your first choice in this. With Brood at your side, not even Errastas could—'*

'Caladan Brood is, for the time being, lost to us.'

Skillen Droe studied K'rul – they had, at some point in the past few moments, halted once again. *'In what manner is he lost, K'rul? Does he play High King somewhere? Then I will fly to him and drag him from his pathetic throne. What of Mael? Does he hide still beneath the waves, building his castles of sand?'*

'Caladan Brood yields not to earthly ambitions, Droe. But he is bound to another cause. It may walk in step with our own, but no more in the manner that Draconus does, with his own singular efforts. As for Mael, well, we are not on speaking terms for the moment.'

Skillen's laugh was a hiss, harsh and almost painfully dry. *'So I am third among your choices.'*

'No. Without you, Skillen Droe, I have no hope of achieving what I seek.'

*'That much I do comprehend, K'rul. Very well, you have made me curious. Tell me, what scheme have you concocted to keep each and every dragon from charging into battle with me, upon first sight?'*

'None.'

*'What?'*

'Abyss take us, Skillen! Name me one dragon that could defeat you in single battle?'

*'Then you see me fighting each and every one?'*

'Not necessarily. And if so, be sure not to kill them. No, Skillen, you still don't understand why I so need you. When we step on to the mortal realm, they will know that you are among them once again. Skillen Droe, I need you, as bait.'

Skillen reached out, and down, closing a massive, scaled hand around the front of K'rul's cloak. He lifted K'rul up until his companion's face was close to his own. The hood fell back, and Skillen was pleased to see the faintest flush fill K'rul's thin cheeks.

'I'd rather you not drop me from this height,' K'rul said in a tight, strained voice.

'*You said Starvald Demelain has opened twice. How many dragons are we talking about?*'

'Oh, the first time yielded but one dragon, and it is already dead.'

'*Dead?*'

'Well, as dead as dragons are able to get.'

'*Who killed it?*'

'I'm not sure. Its carcass rots on the shore of the Vitr.'

'*Which dragon? Name it!*'

'Korabas Otar Tantaral.'

'*Korabas!*'

'But don't worry,' said K'rul. 'I'm not done with her just yet.'

# SIX

THE NAILS ON GOTHOS'S HAND, WHERE IT RESTED ON
the stained tabletop, were amber-hued and long, more
like talons, and as they tapped a slow syncopation, one
falling after the other, Arathan was reminded of stones in the
heat. The vast table had been dragged in from some other
now abandoned abode. Devoid of accoutrements, it stretched
out like a weathered plain, with the sunlight that played out
across its surface making a slow crawl to day's end.

Arathan stood near the entrance, leaning against the doorway's warped frame, to gather as much of the courtyard's
chill air as he could. Within the chamber, braziers had been
laid out, four in all, emanating a dry heat, caustic and
enervating. Against one side of his body, he could feel winter's
breath, while upon the other, the brittle heat of a forge.

Gothos had said nothing. Beyond the clicking of his nails,
and the almost mechanical rise and fall of his fingers as they
tapped, he yielded nothing. Arathan was certain that Gothos
was aware of his arrival, and by indifference alone offered
invitation to join the Jaghut at one of the misshapen chairs
crowding the table. But Arathan knew that no conversation
would be forthcoming; this was not so much a mood afflicting
Gothos, as yet another of those times characterized by
obstinate silence, a belligerent refusal to engage with
anyone.

One could, unfettering the imagination, conjure up a chorus of bridling emotions to fill such silences. Condescension, arrogance, contempt. In its company, it was easy to wince to the bloom of shame, with the sting of irrelevance at its heart. Arathan suspected that the Jaghut's bitter title – Lord of Hate – was derived from these spells, as in frustration fellow Jaghut threw up walls of indignation, pocked with murder-holes from which they might let loose their own missiles, and make of the whole thing a clattering war, a feud raised up against a multiplying nest of imagined insults.

But whatever barriers the silence posed, there was nothing personal to them. They stood not in answer to any particular threat. They faced out upon every imaginable quarter, standing fast against both presence and absence. This was, Arathan had come to believe, not the silence of an embittered man. It accused no one, acknowledged not a single enemy, and because of this, it infuriated all.

A month had passed since Lord Draconus, his father, had left Arathan in the keeping of the Lord of Hate. A month spent struggling with the endless, impossible nuances in the Jaghut language – its written form, at least. A month spent in the strange, baffling dance he'd found himself in, with the hostage Korya Delath.

And what of this army camped beyond the ruined city, the gadflies to Hood, as Gothos called them? Each night, it seemed, another few figures marched in – Thel Akai from the north, Dog-Runners and Jheck from the south. Upon the strand of desolate beach two days to the west, long wooden boats had pulled up, disgorging blue-skinned strangers from some offshore strew of islands. There was a war among those islands, and the ships – Arathan had been told – were battered, fire-scarred, the wooden decks stained black with old blood. The men and women wading ashore were, many of them, wounded, flat-eyed and too exhausted to be wary. Their leather armour showed damage; their weapons were notched and blunted, and they walked like people who had forgotten the stolid certainty of unmoving earth beneath their feet.

A dozen Forulkan numbered among the thousand or so now crowding the camp, and here and there – startling to Arathan's eyes – could be found Tiste. He had made no effort towards any of them and so knew nothing of their tale. Only one among them bore the inky stains of a Sworn Child to Mother Dark. The rest, he surmised, were Deniers, dwellers from the forests, or the hills bordering the realm.

Sorcery seethed through that sprawling camp. Foodstuffs were conjured from earth and clay. Boulders leaked sweet water without surcease. Fires burned without fuel. In the cold night, voices rose in song, bone pipes made hollow music and taut skins were drummed to raise up a surly chorus beneath the glittering stars. From atop the lord's tower, in the lee of the looming Tower of Hate, Arathan could look out upon that glittering, red-hazed camp. *An island of life, its inhabitants eager to sail out from its safe shore. Dead is the sea they seek, its depth beyond comprehension.*

The songs were dirges, the drumbeats the last thumps of a dying heart. The bone pipes gave voice to skulls and hollow ribcages.

'*They attend their own funeral,*' Korya had said, venting her frustration at Hood's benighted gesture. '*They whet their swords and spear-points. Make new straps and stitches in armour. They game in their tents and take lovers to their furs, or just use one another as a herder his sheep. Look on them, Arathan, and divest yourself of all admiration. If this is all that life can offer in defiance of death, then we deserve the brevity of our fates.*'

It was clear that she did not see what Arathan saw. All deeds could be seen as sordid, in the flipping of a stone, or the stripping away of hides. The proudest candle vanishes unseen into a raging house-fire, with none to recount the beauty of its delicate glow, or the dignity of its desire. This was nothing but one's own bitter cast of mind, the well-set frown with every muscle bent to its will, to make a face eternal in its disapproval. Arathan wondered if he would one day see that twisted pattern upon Korya's visage – when youth surrendered to decades of sour misery.

She saw nothing of the glory that, in the contemplation of Hood and his heartbreaking vow, so easily took away Arathan's breath, and left him feeling humbled with wonder.

*'Madness. Pointless. The railing of a fool. The myths are not literal. There is no river to cross, no whirlpool to make a hole in a lake, or the sea. There are no thrones to mark the threshold of imaginary realms. It is all ignorance, Arathan! The superstitions of the Deniers, the dirt-eating of the Dog-Runners, the grinning rock-faces of the Thel Akai. Even the Jaghut – with all their talk of thrones, sceptres, crowns and orbs – allegory! Metaphor! The poet speaks what the imagination paints, but the language belongs to dreams, and every scene conjured up is but a chimera. You cannot declare war upon death!'*

And yet he did. With hand made into fist, Hood hammered words from stone. Mountains were pounded into rubble. Dreams burned like cordwood in the forge, each one cast in like an offering. Warriors and soldiers collected up their gear, left behind their petty squabbles and the fools who would order them about, and set off on what all knew would be their final march.

*Sacrifice, Korya. Dismantle the word, and see the sacred in giving. The blessing that is surrender. Hood's army assembles. One after another, the warriors arrive, and pledge allegiance not in the name of victory, but in the name of surrender. Sacrifice. To win its war, this army must begin defeated.*

He would not speak his thoughts on this, not to anyone. The details of his life thus far were his own to keep, and the scars they left in him were written in a secret language. His life was accidental, a discarded tailing to a few moments of desire. Unwanted, he'd been left to obsess over an endless and growing list of wants.

*He met my eye and called me son. A want appeased, yes, only to be answered with abandonment. You gain by losing everything. Family, the love of a woman, the fathering of a child. The fashioning of a home, the mapping of private rooms in measured pace. The understanding of love itself, here with the Lord of Hate.*

*There is nothing confusing about Hood and his vow. Or this grim army yielding up songs every night. Loss is a gift. Surrender is victory. You will see, Korya, if you stay with me in this. You will see and at last, perhaps, you will understand.*

The scuff of boots from across the square – Arathan glanced over to see Haut, Varandas, and another Jaghut approaching. They were heavy in their arcane armour, iron painted with frost. It was unusual to not see Korya at her master's side, but something in Haut's demeanour spoke of a bitter argument just left behind, and Arathan felt a pang of sympathy for the old warrior the others named captain.

Shifting round, Arathan fixed his gaze on Gothos, but nothing had changed there. The clawed fingers tapped, the sun's light crawled, and the dull gleam of the lord's eyes remained motionless, like dusted glass.

'For Abyss's sake, boy,' Haut said as they drew nearer, 'hunt her down, throw her into the hay, and put us all out of our misery.'

Arathan smiled. 'I have seen her future, Haut, and surrender does not dwell there.'

'He's within?' asked the huge Jaghut whom Arathan did not know. This warrior's visage was flat, seamed with scars. He wore his dark hair in long, knotted braids, his tusks silver-tipped but otherwise stained deep amber.

Arathan shrugged. 'For all the good it will do you.'

'He calls us to join him,' the stranger continued, scowling. 'I see us freezing in chilled company . . . again.'

'Now now, Burrugast,' said Varandas, 'he unmanned me long ago, so I will suffer no more in the frigidity of his obstinacy. Indeed, I find myself looking forward to the fury to come.'

'Varandas claims a woman's forbearance,' said Haut, 'so let us yield a moment of pity for the fool who tweaks his nipples.' He raised a jug into view. 'I have wine to thaw the lord's surly repose.'

'Beware the drunkard's wisdom,' Burrugast said in a growl.

Arathan edged back into the room to allow the three Jaghut ingress. The heat swirled against them all, eliciting a grunt from Varandas. At once, their armour glistened as if with sweat. Haut moved forward to set the clay jug on the table-top, and then dragged out a chair and sat. Varandas walked to a shelf and collected a host of pewter cups.

Gothos gave no indication of recognition that company had arrived. Arathan found a chair and pulled it back to a wall close to the entrance, hopeful for a cooling draught.

With the three guests now seated, Haut rubbed at his narrow face and then began pouring out the wine. 'The great tome that is the Folly goes poorly, I assume. Even reasons for suicide can grow long in the tusk at times, one concludes. Meanwhile, death waits on the Throne of Ice.'

'Ice,' snorted Burrugast. 'It has the patience of winter, and in our host's bleak soul, that is a season without end.'

'We are called here,' said Varandas as he examined his ragged nails, 'so that we might be disavowed of Hood's mad-ness. The arguments will be assembled, every blade honed sharp by wit and whatnot. Steel your shoulders to the weight of contempt, my friends. To the assault of derision, the salvos of ridicule. We invite the siege, like fools atop our hoard.'

'The hoard means nothing to Gothos,' said Burrugast, drink-ing deep from his tankard. 'The Lord of Hate is known to shit coins and gems, and piss rivers of gold. There is no honest blood coursing through his veins. We are in the liar's lair . . .'

Haut leaned forward, one hairless brow lifting to arch a mass of wrinkles on his forehead. 'Oh dear,' he muttered. 'Leave off the allusions, Burrugast. Of all accusations one can level upon Gothos, and there are many to be sure, dis-honesty is not one of them.'

Burrugast shook his head. 'I'll not divest myself of this chain, buckle and greaves. There are two armies assembled here. The one we have just left, and the one lounging at this table's head. I am girded for war and will remain so.'

'And will it serve you well on this day?' Varandas asked. 'Already you drip, Burrugast, to the drumming of his ink-stained fingers. We have locked our shields and await his reason, knowing well how it cut through us the day he slew civilization. With wine I assemble myself – praying that the grape serves me better today than armour and shield did yesterday.'

'The drunk answers every assault with smirking equanimity,' observed Haut, pouring his cup full again. 'All reasoned words thud like pebbles in the sand. Made immune, I imbibe the nectar of the gods.'

'Death is at the heart of this scene,' Varandas said, punctuating his assertion with a belch. 'There is no road to its border, he will tell us. No high walls to hammer against. The raids are always done by the time we arrive, the looters long gone, the rapists' gift of pain and horror fled the sightless eyes of every victim. We pursue a wake we can never hope to catch, much less breach, the echo of riders leaving only dust, fires only charcoal and ash.'

'Hood seeks a direction,' Burrugast said, 'but none offers itself with a righteous claim. Might as well war against the night sky, Gothos will tell us. Or the rising sun.'

'We are chained to time,' added Haut, 'and yet, death lies beyond time. The running sands are all stopped in that unknown place. Nothing moves, neither to advance nor retreat, and the absence shows us no face, no enemy arrayed before us. Are we to carve blades through indifferent waves? Cursing the seas so deftly defying our pretensions? He will say this to us, knowing we have no answer.'

'It is cause for fury!' Burrugast shouted, a fist thumping the tabletop. 'We have faced reason, and have stared it down! We have withstood every argument and seen it off! This lord here spoke against all progress, all hope, all ambition – I now accuse him as death's own agent! Seeking to turn us away, fugged by defeat, despondent and bemused and thoroughly disarmed before we march a single step! He is Hood's sworn enemy! Love's scarred foe! The face of misery cursing every claim to delight! I will not yield to this despiser!' And with that, he thrust out his cup and Haut refilled it from the jug that never seemed to empty.

Arathan leaned his chair back, tilted against the beaded stone wall. His eyes were half closed as he regarded Gothos, who sat as if still alone, still waiting – or not waiting at all, despite those tapping talons on the old wood. Tension made the hot air brittle.

A sound to his right made him twist round slightly, to see a blue-skinned woman standing in the threshold. She was squatter than a Tiste, her limbs solid, her face round, with eyes of brown so deep as to be almost black. A curved knife was tucked into her thin leather belt, over which bulged a belly that had known plenty of ale. Her accent strange, she said, 'There was word of a gathering. Hood's officers, I am told.'

'His officers?' Haut looked around, frowning. 'Why, of course. Here we sit, chosen and select, if only in our own minds. Yet observe this master of his own demise – and ours, too, if his will prevails. Friend from the sea, allow me to introduce the Lord of Hate, Gothos, who defies Hood in all things, and sets before us a fierce challenge against our solemn vow. Come in, friend; we fools will grasp with desperation your alliance in the face of this withering flood.'

Uncertainly, she ventured inside, and took a chair on the other side of the table, almost directly opposite Arathan. Her dark eyes fixed on him and she nodded a faint greeting.

'Yes,' said Varandas, as he offered the woman a cup of wine, 'he is the child who will march with us. So young to challenge death. So bold and so careless with the long life promised him – the promise that belongs only to the young, of course. The rest of us, naturally, have since choked on its dregs and done our share of spitting out. Should we not talk him out of this? Well, if Gothos himself has failed in achieving that, what hope have we?'

'If we tremble here,' said Burrugast to the woman, 'do add your shield to our line, but tell us your name and what of your story you would offer strangers.'

She looked down at her cup as she drank, and then said, 'I

see no value in my name, as I am already surrendered to my fate. I ask not to be remembered.' Her eyes shifted to the Jaghut at the table's head. 'I never thought I would find myself in the company of the Lord of Hate. I am honoured, and more to the point, I welcome his indifference.' She paused and looked round at the others, ending once more on Arathan. 'You have already lost this battle against Gothos, and every reason he flings at you, to give proof to your madness. This sentiment is one you would do well getting used to, don't you think? After all, death will answer us likewise.'

Haut sighed. 'Pray someone step outside and intercept the Seregahl, and what agents of the Dog-Runners might be on their way to this assembly. Snare the Forulkan's speaker, too, with knotted cords about her ankles, and leave her lying on the cold stones. Whip the Jheck into yelping retreat. I for one do not know how much more I can take. Here, Varandas, I will have the jug back.'

They drank. They said nothing, the silence stretching. The clawed fingers made notches in the time that passed.

'He exhausts me,' Varandas finally muttered. 'Defeat has made me stupid, too stupid to heed his wisdom.'

'It is the same for all of us here,' said Haut. 'Gothos has failed. Everyone, rejoice.' He looked down at the tabletop, and added, 'As you will.'

Burrugast was the first to rise, wobbling slightly. 'I will return to Hood,' he said, 'and report his rival's surrender. We have, my friends, withstood our first assault.' He raised his empty cup. 'See. I collect a trophy, this war's spoil.'

Weaving, he made his way outside, clutching the pewter cup as if it was gold and studded with gems. A moment later, Varandas stood and followed him out.

Rubbing at his lined face, Haut nodded, as if to some unspoken thought, and then stood. 'Gothos, once again you are too formidable to withstand. And so I retreat. No doubt Korya waits in ambush – is it any wonder I would run to death?'

As Haut strode from the chamber, the blue-skinned woman – who had been staring at Arathan with disconcerting intensity – now rose. She bowed towards Gothos, and then said to Arathan, 'This last war should not be your first, boy. You miss the point.'

He shook his head, but said nothing. The surrender in his soul would remain private. Of all the vows breeding in this place, it was to his mind the only one worth keeping.

Scowling, she departed.

Alone with Gothos again, Arathan finally spoke. 'I expected at least one Azathanai,' he said. 'They are in the camp, I'm told. A few. Keeping to themselves.'

The fingers drummed.

'I thought I would hear your final arguments,' Arathan said, squinting across at the Lord of Hate.

Abruptly, Gothos stood and turned back to face his desk close to the lead-paned window with its burst webs of frost. 'Let it not be said,' he muttered, 'that I did not try my best. Now, Arathan, I need more ink, and another stack awaits you.'

Arathan bowed his head in seeming acknowledgement, but mostly to hide his smile.

＊     ＊     ＊

The three blue-skinned warriors flung their gear to the ground close to the natural wall made by the huge boulder atop which Korya was perched. Peering down, wondering if they knew of her presence, she studied their long shadows in sinewy play over the frozen ground, flowing from and following the two women and one man as they set about preparing their camp.

*The shadows betray will. Ignore the flesh and see only how the will flows like water, like ink. Enough to fill a thousand empty vessels. A thousand Mahybes. But no shadow can push a pebble, bend a twig or flutter a leaf. And a vessel thus filled remains empty. This then is the lesson of will.*

The man below had been carrying a small open stove of iron with four splayed legs, which he set down close to the wall. He now spilled coals from a lidded cup into its basin, and then began feeding in chunks of stone that looked like pumice. Green flames lifted into view, edges flickering yellow and blue. The rising heat startled Korya with its intensity.

The rhythm of their speech was odd but the words were understandable. This was a detail that had lodged in her mind, as something unusual, and perhaps worthy of examination. For the moment, however, she was content to slip through the army's encampment, to perch and listen in, to make of herself something less than a shadow.

One of the women now said, 'A mob to make a city.'

The other woman, younger, smaller, was laying out the makings of a meal – mostly dried fish and seaweed. She shrugged and said, 'Does it matter where we washed up? I saw Hyras floating in the bilge with an eel in his mouth. Fat like a black tongue. Hyras had no eyes to see, but that tongue never stopped wiggling.'

'Someone said there were officers,' the first woman said. 'Command tent, or even a building.' She shook her head. 'Our self-proclaimed captain's not saying anything, but that was a short briefing up at that tower.'

'Makes no matter,' said the man, as he moved back from the heavy heat cast off by the pumice stones. 'Defeat rides a failing wind, once you get far enough away from the red waters. I saw nothing of what happened to us on the strand we found.' He paused, and then added, 'We're safe.'

'Left the ships to roll,' said the younger woman.

'The tide'll take them out,' the man said. 'The sands reach out a league or more, not a reef in sight, not a killer stone to mark.' He seemed to glare across at both women. 'Fit for tombs and nothing else now, anyway.'

The younger woman snorted. 'You were quick to take the flame away, Cred, and with it the Living Claim.'

'Quick and clear-eyed, Stark,' Cred replied, with an easy nod.

The older woman dragged a cask close. She twisted the dowel loose and tapped her finger against the water that splashed free. Stoppering it again, she sighed and said, 'Salt needs sucking out. It's a problem.'

'Why?' Stark demanded. 'Make blood and be done with it.'

'We're inland,' the older woman replied. 'There are faces to the magic here, more even than what's out at sea. Most of them I don't know.' She looked around, spread her hands and said, 'We're poor offerings to make us a bargain.'

'Stop being so afraid,' Stark retorted. 'We need fresh water.'

The older woman twisted to regard Cred. 'What do you think?'

Cred shrugged. 'We need the water, and a handful of salt wouldn't hurt us, neither. Something to trade. Dog-Runners from inland will take it, for good red meat in exchange. Me, Brella, I kept the coals alive – I've not had to face any of these strange spirits yet.'

'But if you needed to?'

'Can't argue with need, Brella. Drip some blood, see who comes.'

This was the magic now roiling through this camp. A thousand paths, countless arcane rituals. It seemed rules grew up fast, making intricate patterns, proscriptions, and not one warlock or witch seemed to agree on any of them. Korya suspected that none of those rituals mattered in the least. The power was a dark promise, and the darkness promised mystery. *It's all writing in the sand.*

*Until that sand turns to stone.*

Haut had explained about the blood, the unseen torrents that now flowed through all the realms. The madness of a lone Azathanai named K'rul. The sacrifice of a foolish god. Hood's grief and torment was nothing compared to what K'rul had unleashed upon the world, and yet here in this absurd camp, with its thousands of strangers now crowding close, Korya had begun to sense the collision now under way.

*Death is the world's back turned on the wonder of living. No magic flows into that realm. And yet, sorcery gathers here, and readies to march on the place where it cannot dwell. The enemy is absence, but this means nothing to Hood.*

*Haut is right. No war is impossible. No victory is unattainable. No enemy is invincible. Name your foe, and your foe can fall. Call it out, and it must answer. There is sorcery here, too much, too wild, too undefined. What might it yield, when guided by Hood? By a Jaghut poisoned by grief?*

She watched Brella take a knife-tip to the thumb-pad of her left hand. A trickle of black. Peculiar draughts slipped past where Korya crouched, sweeping down to crowd invisibly around the sea-witch. Something farther away, huge and ancient, groaned awake.

*Oh, that's not good.*

Korya straightened, standing tall atop the boulder. She faced in the direction of the awakener. What was it? Barely sentient, remembering some ancient sensation, an itch, a thirst. Heaving itself into motion, it approached.

*       *       *

Using one of the braziers, Arathan brewed tea. Gothos sat at his desk, but had turned the chair to one side in order to stretch out his legs. His hands rested now on his thighs. The tapping was done, and the fingers were curled as if waiting for something to grasp. His face was a clash of shadows. The sun outside was sinking, the light withdrawing as if inhaled, to mark the fiery orb's dying gasp, and shadows flowed out from between abandoned buildings, spilling in through the doorway.

Readying two cups, Arathan rose and brought one over to the Lord of Hate.

'On the desk, if you will,' Gothos said in a low rumble.

'You eschewed the wine,' Arathan said, setting the cup down and returning to his place beside the brazier. He thought to add something more, but nothing came to mind. Instead, he said, 'I feel filled with words, lord, and still, I can think only of my father. And the Azathanai blood within me.'

Gothos made a gesture of dismissal. 'Blood is not an honorific. You cannot choose your family, Arathan. When

214

the moment comes, and by honour and by love you must face the choice, meet his eye and call him friend.'

'Friend?' Arathan considered that for a moment, and then shook his head. 'I see nothing between us to suggest friendship.'

'Because you are incomplete, Arathan. Oh, very well, a lesson then, long overdue. I am rarely loquacious, so pay attention. I do not challenge the acuity of your observations, or your thoughts, such as you reveal to any of us. Among kin, we are one in a most familiar crowd, defined by how each family member sees us, and the manner in which they see us was carved out long ago, in childhood. Theirs, yours. These are strictures, confining, resisting change. True, you may find friends among siblings, or even think of an aunt, or an uncle, in such a manner. But they are all simulacra. A family is a gathering of blood-kin wielding fists. Attacking, defending, or simply determined to make space amidst the tumult.'

Arathan thought back on what little he knew of his own kin. The half-sisters who seemed chained to childhood, who had flitted through his life like vicious afterthoughts. The father who had ignored him for most of Arathan's existence, only to drag him to the forefront of a journey undertaken in the name of gifts, and who in the end made of Arathan himself a gift.

Had Raskan been a friend? Rind? Feren?

After a time, he grunted and said, 'My horses proved loyal.'

Gothos snorted a laugh, and then reached for the cup. He sniffed at it, sipped, and then said, 'This, then, is friendship. A family you choose. What you give to it, you give freely. What you withhold from it, measures its depth. There are those who know only distant relations – associates, if you will. Then there are those who would embrace even a stranger, should that stranger venture a smile or nod. In each instance described, we see facets of fear. The dog that growls should anyone come near. The dog that lies on its back and exposes its throat, surrendering to anyone, with begging eyes and a demeanour made helpless.'

'You describe extremes, lord. There must be other kinds, healthier kinds.'

'I would first describe the ones that damage, Arathan, so that you may begin to eliminate past experiences, insofar as friendship is concerned.'

Sighing, Arathan said, 'I have but few experiences as it stands, lord, and would rather not see them savaged.'

'Better to defend your delusions, then?'

'Comforts are rare enough.'

'You will come upon those who exude life, who burn bright. In their company, how are you to be? Proud to name them friend? Pleased to bask in their fire? Or, in the name of need, will you simply devour all that they offer, like a force of darkness swallowing light, warmth, life itself? Will you make yourself a rocky island, black and gnarled, a place of cold caves and littered bones? The bright waves do not soothe your shores, but crash instead, explode in a fury of foam and spray. And you drink in every swirl, sucked down into your caves, your bottomless caverns.

'I do not describe a transitory mood. Not a temporary disposition, brought on by external woes. What I describe, in fashioning this island soul, so bleak and forbidding, is a place made too precious to be surrendered, too stolid to be dismantled. This island I give you, this soul in particular, is a fortress of need, a maw that knows only how to ease its eternal hunger. Within its twisted self, no true friend is acknowledged and no love is honest in its exchange. The self stands alone, inviolate as a god, but a besieged god . . . forever besieged.' Gothos leaned forward, studied Arathan with glittering eyes. 'Oddly, those who burn bright are often drawn to such islands, such souls. As friends. As lovers. They imagine they can offer salvation, a sharing of warmth, of love, even. And in contrast, they see in themselves something to offer their forlorn companion, who huddles and hides, who gives occasion to rail and loose venom. The life within them feels so vast! So welcoming! Surely there is enough to share! And so, by giving – and giving – they are themselves appeased, and made to feel worthwhile. For a time.

'But this is no healthy exchange, though it might at first seem so – after all, the act of giving will itself yield a kind of euphoria, a drunkenness of generosity, not to mention the salve of protectiveness, of paternal regard.' Gothos leaned back again, drank more from the cup in his hands, and closed his eyes. 'The island is unchanging. Bones and corpses lie upon its wrack on all sides.'

Arathan licked dry lips. 'She was not like that,' he whispered.

Shrugging, Gothos turned his head, to study the dull frozen fog on the window above the desk. 'I do not know whom you mean, Arathan. When you find a true friend, you will know it. There may be challenges in that relationship, but for all that, it thrives on mutual respect, and honours the virtues exchanged. You need no fists to make a space for yourself. No one clings to your shadow – even as they grow to despise that shadow, and the one who so boldly casts it. Your feelings are not objects to be manipulated, with cold intent or emotion's blind, unreasoning heat. You are heard. You are heeded. You are challenged, and so made better. This is not a tie that exhausts, nor one that forces your senses to unnatural extremes of acuity. You are not to be tugged or prodded, and your gifts – of wit and charm – are not to be denigrated for the attentions they earn. Arathan, one day you may come to call your father a friend. But I tell you this, I believe he already sees you as one.'

'What gives you reason to so defend him, lord?'

'I do not defend Draconus, Arathan. I speak in defence of his son's future. As does a friend, when the necessity arises.'

The admission silenced Arathan. *And yet, is he not the Lord of Hate? From where, then, this loving gift?*

Gothos reached out and ran his fingers, splayed out, down the ice-rimed glass of the window. 'The notion of hatred,' he said as if catching Arathan's thoughts, 'is easily misapplied. One must ask: what is it that this man hates? Is it joy? Hope? Love? Or is it, perhaps, the cruelty by which so many of us live, the unworthy thoughts, the revel of base emotions, the sheer stupidity that sends a civilization lurching onward, step by step into self-destruction? Arathan, you are here, far away from the Tiste civil war, and I am glad for that. So too, I suspect, is your father.'

The shadows stole into the chamber, barring the strange bars of the sun's last light, streaming in through the streaks the lord's fingers had left behind on the glass.

Arathan drank the tea and found it surprisingly sweet.

✻   ✻   ✻

'It's done,' Brella said dully.

'But the bleeding does not stop,' Cred observed, edging closer.

'I know,' she mumbled, head dipping. 'Too many here. Too many . . . drinking deep.'

'See the boulder!' Stark hissed. 'It bleeds water!'

The stove's heat made the rock's face sizzle as the streams whispered down. 'Brella!' cried Cred, pulling her close in a rough embrace. 'Stark, tear some cloth – make bandages! It pours from her!'

Korya stared down upon them. She could feel the spirits, swirling round the three figures below. They flowed into the water trickling down the stone, raced to sudden death in the fierce heat of the stove. Their death-cries were childlike. Others crowded about Brella, an eager mob. Twisting round, Korya glanced back across the fire-studded encampment. The monstrous emanation was drawing closer – she saw small fires dim in a broad swath marking its passing. She heard distant shouts as the sensitive among the army – the adepts – recoiled from its passage.

Brella was doomed. So too the fire-spirits bound to the pumice stones in the stove, and possibly Cred himself. The spirit reaching for them held the memory of global floods, of cold, unlit depths and crushing pressure. Of seas that boiled, and ice that cracked and shattered. Mountains reduced to rubble filled its throat. It crawled. It heaved itself forward, desperate for the taste of mortal blood.

*K'rul. You damned fool. We stumble into this sorcery in ignorance. We imagine a world for the taking, filled with*

218

*small powers eager to answer our needs. We are drunk on wonder, seeking satiation with no thought of the founts we find – or who guards them.*

The camp seethed with motion now. A panic seemingly without source tightened throats, constricted chests, bringing pain to every breath drawn, every gasp loosed. She saw figures fall to their knees, hands at their faces. Fires winked out, snuffed by the growing pressure that it seemed only she could see.

'Oh, enough.' Korya spread out her arms. *See this vessel, old one! Come to me, as a crab finds its perfect shell! I can hold you. I am your Mahybe, your home. Refuge. Lair. Whatever.*

She saw a shape taking form, ghostly, ethereal. Wormlike, and yet shouldered behind the blunt, eyeless head. The arms were gnarled and thick, planted on the ground like forelegs, and they were the only limbs visible, as the body snaked out, its distant end vanishing into the earth. The emanation towered over the entire camp, big enough to make a modest meal of the thousand souls cowering there.

*Shelter first. And then you can feed.*

The head lifted, questing blind, and then somehow Korya felt the old one's attention fix on her. It surged forward.

*Mahybe. A vessel to be filled.* Was this to be her task in life? Deadly trap for every ambitious power, every hungry fool?

*I will hold you inside. It's the curse of every woman, after all—*

Someone scrabbled up the boulder's broken side, but she had no time to see who would join her in this fraught moment. The leviathan was coming, and she felt something inside her open up, gaping, widening—

'Stupid girl,' a voice beside her said.

Startled, she turned to see Haut. He stretched out one hand, as if to push away the ancient power. Instead, he twisted the hand until it was palm-up, uncurling his fingers.

With a piercing shriek, the leviathan lunged forward, swept down upon them like a toppling tower.

Winds roared in Korya's skull. She felt the hard, wet stone slam against her knees, but she was blind now, deafened, and whatever had yawned wide inside her was now stoppered shut, ringing like a bell.

Moments later, in a sudden, disorienting shift, she heard the trickling of water, the faint hiss from the heat still bathing the boulder's opposite side. She opened her eyes, feeling impossibly weak. The roaring was gone, leaving only echoes that drifted through the emptiness within. The leviathan had vanished. 'W-what?'

Reaching down one-handed, Haut helped her upright. 'I prepared you for this? Hardly. Here.' He grasped her right hand and brought it up to set something small, polished and hard into its grip. 'Don't break it.'

Then Haut moved away, clambering back down the rocky slope, muttering under his breath and waving both hands, as if fighting off a chorus of unspoken questions.

Korya opened her hand and looked down at what she held.

*An acorn? A fucking acorn?*

From below, Brella was coughing, but with vigour. And then Stark said, in a faintly wild tone, 'Can we drink that water now?'

\*     \*     \*

Varandas stepped in alongside Haut when the captain returned from the outcrop, and they continued on, with Burrugast trailing, towards Hood's tent.

'She's ambitious, this Tiste girl of yours,' Varandas said.

'Youth is a thirst that will drink any old thing, once,' Haut replied. 'It is that fearlessness we observe with bemusement, and not a little envy. She has grown sensitive, too – I believe she saw the thing, saw the truth of it.'

'And yet,' muttered Burrugast behind them, 'she invited it nonetheless. Foolish. Precipitous. Dangerous. I trust, captain, she'll not be accompanying us on this march.'

'I await an Azathanai to take charge of her,' Haut replied.

'They care nothing for hostages,' Varandas said. 'Nor

prodigies. I can think of not one Azathanai who will accede to your wish.'

They were passing among the warriors and their small camps. The sudden, debilitating force that had descended upon everyone had left them shaken, confused, angry. Voices rose in argument, bitter with accusations, as men and women turned on the warlocks and witches in their company. Flushed with firelight, faces swung towards the three Jaghut striding past, but none called out. Overhead, winter's stars glittered, the sky-spanning band assembled like a belligerent host.

At Varandas's assertion, Haut shrugged. 'Then a Dog-Runner, if the Azathanai will not have her.'

'Send her home,' said Burrugast. 'You never did well with pets, Haut. Especially other people's pets.'

Haut scowled. 'I warned Raest. Besides, in the end, he could not find dishonour in the tomb I raised for that idiot cat. In any case, this Tiste is not a pet.'

Burrugast grunted. 'What is she then?'

'A weapon.'

Varandas sighed. 'You leave it on the field, and invite anyone to come and collect it. This seems . . . irresponsible.'

'Yes,' Haut agreed, 'it does, doesn't it?'

Hood's tent was small, of a size to suit a single occupant, with that occupant doing little more than sleeping. It had been raised on the floor of what had once been a tower, the walls of which had collapsed long ago. The low foundation stones roughly encircled the camp, with a few scattered blocks drawn up to provide seats around a desultory hearth. Cowled against the chill, Hood sat alone.

'Hood!' barked Burrugast as the three arrived. 'Your self-proclaimed officers are here! Iron of spine and steeled with resolve, our hands twitch in anticipation of sharp salutes and whatnot. What say you to that?'

'Ah now, Burrugast,' Varandas pointed out, 'an unseemly challenge rides your greeting. Beloved Hood, Lord of Grief, pray do not let him sting you to life. The drama alone might kill us all.'

'They but followed me here,' said Haut, sitting down

opposite Hood. 'Worse than dogs, these two. Why, just yesterday I found them both upon the western shore, rolling in rotten fish. To hide the scent, no doubt.'

'Ha,' said Varandas, 'and what scent would that be?'

'A complex odour, to be sure,' Haut allowed, adjusting himself atop the blockish stone. 'Hints of derision, mockery. Smudges of contempt. The flavour of rooks on a leafless branch, looking down upon a raving fool. The glitter of sordid patience. Flavours of sorrow, but already turned bitter, as if grief deserves not a face, nor a purpose. And, at the last, wisps of envy—'

'Envy!' snorted Burrugast. 'This fool would elevate his personal pain, and make it a plague to take us all!'

'This fool would stand for us, in our stead, against a most implacable enemy. That we now join him marks the honesty we have each faced, the thing in our souls that cries out against the void. Envy, I say, in seeing courage not found in ourselves. This is a wake I will walk, and so too will you, Burrugast. And you, Varandas. The same for Gathras, and Sanad. Suvalas and Bolirium, too. We defiant, miserable Jaghut, alone in the futures awaiting us – and yet, here we are.'

Making a vaguely helpless gesture with one hand, Varandas lowered himself into a crouch, close to the fire. 'Bah, there's no heat from these flames. Hood, you would have done better with a mundane lantern. Or one of those Fire-Keepers who tend their charge. These flames are cold.'

'Illusion,' said Haut. 'Light has its rival, and so too heat. We fend off darkness as a matter of course, and since when did an icy breath bother us?'

'They seek a commander for this enterprise,' said Varandas. 'Hood offers nothing.'

Haut nodded. 'Just my point. This hearth and the light it yields – not real. Nor is the station of command – neither real, nor relevant. Hood pronounced his vow. Was it meant to be answered? Do we all gather as if summoned? Not by our Lord of Grief, surely. Rather, by the nature of the enterprise itself. One Jaghut gave voice, but the sentiment was heard by all – well, all of us here.'

Burrugast growled under his breath. 'How then to command this army? By what means are we to be organized?'

In answer, Haut shrugged. 'Do you need a banner? An order of march? What discipline, Burrugast, do you imagine necessary, given the nature of our enemy? Shall we send out scouts, seeking the dread border – when in truth it is only found in our minds, between self and oblivion?'

'Then are we to sit here, rotting, befouling the land around us, until age itself creeps over us, stealing souls one by one? You call this a war?'

'Call it *all* a war,' Haut said.

'Captain,' Varandas said, 'you have led armies, seen fields of battle. In your past, you knew the privations, the brutal games of necessity. You won a throne, only to flee it. Stood triumphant on a mound of the slain, only to kneel in surrender the following dawn. In victory you lost everything, and in defeat you won your freedom. Of all who would join Hood, I did not expect you.'

'Ah, you old woman, Varandas. It is in that very curse – my most martial past – where hides the answer. To a warrior, war is the drunkard's drink. We yearn unending, seeking the numbness of past horrors, but each time, the way ahead whispers of paradise. But no soldier is so blind as to believe that. It is the unfeeling that we seek, the immunity to all depravity, all cruelty. The only purity in the paradise into which we would march is the timelessness it promises.' He shook his head. 'Beware the lustful ambitions of old warriors – it is our thirst that makes politics, and we will drink of mayhem again and again.'

Burrugast thumped his thigh in frustration and faced Hood. 'Yield us a single word, I beg you. How long must we wait? I will see this enemy of yours!'

Hood lifted his gaze, studied Burrugast for a long moment, and then Varandas who still crouched, and finally Haut who sat opposite him. 'If you have come here,' he said. 'If you would follow.'

'I cannot decide,' said Burrugast. 'Perhaps none of us can.

A war is already being waged, in our minds. Should reason win, you will find yourself alone.'

Hood smiled then, without much humour. 'If so, Burrugast, then I will still tend to this fire here.'

'The illusion of fire – the illusion of life itself!'

'Just so.'

'Then' – Burrugast looked to the others – 'what is it you mean to say? That you are already dead?'

Hood spread his hands out, held them motionless in the flickering flames.

'Then what is it you await?'

Haut grunted. 'An end to the battles within us, Burrugast, is what Hood waits for – if indeed he waits for anything. Look inward, my friends, and take up weapons. Begin this night your war on reason. In ashes we will find our triumph. In desolation we will find the place where the march can begin.'

Varandas sat down on the cold ground, leaning back on his hands with legs outstretched, boots at the very edge of the hearthstones. He sighed. 'I foresee little challenge in the war you describe, Haut. A thousand times a night, I slay reason – but yes, I see it now. We Jaghut must take the lead in this, veterans as we all are. Girded obstinate, armed stubborn, arrayed in bloody-mindedness, we are unmatched.'

In the brief silence that followed, they all heard the sounds of heavy boots, drawing closer. Haut twisted round to see a score or more Thel Akai approaching. 'Now then, Hood, see what the night brings. It's the wretched Seregahl.'

Warriors, forsworn of all family ties, defiant of peace, blades unleashed in countless foreign wars, these Thel Akai were, to Haut's mind, a curse to their people's name. But the fiercest contempt held for the Seregahl belonged to other Thel Akai. *'They have slain their own humour, the fools – and see what misery remains!'*

The lead Seregahl – none knew their names, and for all Haut knew, those too had been surrendered to whatever secret purpose they held – now halted at the stone wall encircling Hood's camp. Huge, heavy in battered armour, and taking a pose that involved leaning on the long handle of a massive double-bladed axe, the Seregahl commander scowled through a tangled nest of hair and beard. 'Hood! The Seregahl will command the van – it is not for us to chew the dust of lesser folk. We shall raise a worthy banner to this noble cause. To slay death! In victory, we shall return all to the realm of the living, and be done with dying for ever more!'

Varandas, squinting up at the Thel Akai, frowned and said, 'An impressive if well-rehearsed speech, sir. Even so, you describe a crowded world.'

The warrior blinked at Varandas. 'A welcome future, then, Jaghut! Think of the wars that will be fought, as all battle to claim land, wealth, security!'

'Fruitless battles, I should think, since no enemy will ever die.'

'Pointless wealth, too,' Haut added, 'as by the accumulation of weight alone, it will surely lose all lustre.'

'Security naught but an illusion,' Burrugast added, 'held but briefly, until the next wave of raging foes.'

'As for the land,' Varandas noted, 'I see an ocean of crimson mud, banners tottering, tilting, sinking. None to die, no room for the living – why, this future life you describe, Seregahl, makes of death a heaven. Who, in that time, will rise up to pronounce a war upon life?'

'This is strife's own circle,' Haut noted, giving Varandas a nod. 'And that surely deserves a bold van.' He looked up at the Seregahl and said, 'Be assured that you will lead the army, sir, come the day we march. With the blessing of not only Hood, but also his chosen officers, such as you see here.'

The lead Seregahl fixed dark eyes upon Haut, and then he said, 'Captain. I had heard that you were here. We have fought one another, have we not?'

'A time or two.'

'We have defeated one another.'

'A more astute observation, sir, would be to say that we have shared opposing victories.'

The Thel Akai grunted, and then, gesturing, about-faced

his troop, and off they marched into the gloom, weapons clanking.

'You did well to see them off, Hood,' said Varandas. 'I now long to witness one more face to face meeting, between you and Gothos. Why, the railing might tear down the stars themselves.'

Haut shook his head. 'Then you long for nothing, friend. What think you the Lord of Hate need say to the Lord of Grief, or, indeed, the latter to the former? If they do not know each other now, in places beyond crude words, then neither deserves his title.'

Hood surprised them all by rising to his feet. Drawing the cowl more tightly about his worn features, he waved lazily at the hearth. 'Mind the fire, will you?'

'Is it time, then?' Burrugast asked.

Hood paused. 'Your query is not for me.'

They watched him walk away, southward, towards the ruins of Omtose Phellack.

'I see no value in minding these flames,' muttered Varandas.

A moment later, all three started laughing. The sound rang out through the dark camp, and was long in dying.

*       *       *

While there were in the camp Thel Akai, Forulkan, Jheck and Jhelarkan, blue-skinned peoples from the sea, and even Tiste, by far the most numerous group was that of the Dog-Runners. Korya wandered between their small fires, the low, humped huts that covered pits dug into the hard clays, the flat stones where women worked flint during the day. Not everyone slept beneath the furs. Many were awake to the watch, this time in the night when restlessness opened eyes, when thoughts stirred from the embers of half-forgotten dreams.

She felt their regard as she walked past, but believed that they gave little thought to her. They but observed her, in the manner of animals. The night was a private world, the watch its most hidden refuge. She thought of Kharkanas, and imagined it now as a city transformed. Unrelieved by light, it must hold to some kind of eternal contemplation, each denizen remote, drifting away from mundane concerns.

The poets would stumble on to new questions, unimagined questions. To utter them was to shatter the world, and so none spoke, none challenged the darkness. She thought of musicians, sitting alone, fingers light upon the strings, calloused tips shivering along the taut gut, searching their way forward, seeking a song for the absence all around them. Each note, plucked or sung, would stand alone, inviting no comforting answer, no birth of melody. Asking, forever asking, *What next?*

In her mind, Kharkanas was a monument to the night's watch: pensive and withdrawn. She saw towers and estates, terraced dwellings and bridges, all thrown up in miniature, made into a place for the dolls of her youth. Clothes drab, colours washed out, in tired poses; she could look down upon them, and offer each one – all of them – not a moment's thought.

*See the circlet of their mouths, their unblinking eyes. Standing motionless, arranged by an unseen hand. Some drama waits.*

*If I was their god, I'd leave them that way. For ever.*

*Oh, this is a cruel span of night, to imagine an uncaring god, an indifferent god. Suffer a father's dismissal, a mother's, a brother's or a sister's, or even a child's, but suffer not the same dismissal from a god. A better fate, to be sure, standing frozen, for ever and timeless, with all the modest ambitions a doll might possess. Frozen, like a memory, isolated and going nowhere. A scene to make playwrights tremble. Poses to make sculptors shy away. A breath drawn, forever awaiting the song.*

*Some questions must never be asked. Lest the moment freeze in eternity, on the edge of an answer that never comes.*

Kharkanas the Wise City belonged to the night, now; to darkness. Its poets stumbled on unseen words. Its sculptors collided with shapeless forms. Its singers pursued down every corridor some dwindling voice, and the dancers longed for one last sure step. Its common denizens, then, waited for a dawn that would never come, even as the artists fell away, curled black like rotting leaves.

She realized that someone was padding softly at her side – lost in her thoughts, she had no idea how long she had been accompanied by this stranger. Glancing across, she saw a young Dog-Runner, yellow-haired, wearing a cloak of hides – narrow, vertically sewn strips, multihued and glistening, that left tails dragging in his wake. Red-ochre rimmed his light blue or grey eyes, with a single tear tracking down each cheek, ending in the wisps of golden whiskers on his jaw.

He was handsome enough, in that savage, Dog-Runner way. But it was the soft smile playing across his full mouth that caught her attention. 'What so amuses you?' she asked.

In answer, he made a series of gestures.

She shrugged. 'I do not know that manner of Dog-Runner communication – your silent talk. And please, do not start singing to me either. That, too, means nothing to me, and when two voices come from a single throat, why, it's unnerving.'

'I smile at you,' the youth said, 'with admiration.'

'Oh,' she replied. They continued walking, silent. *Damn you, Korya, think of something to say!* 'Why are you here? I mean, why did you come? Are those tears painted on your cheeks? Do you hope to find someone? Someone dead? You long to bring him, or her, back?'

Tentatively, he reached up and ventured a touch upon one of the red-painted tears. 'Back? There is no "back". She never left.'

'Who? Your mate? You seem young for that, even for a Dog-Runner. Did she die in childbirth? So many do. I'm sorry. But Hood is not your salvation here. This army is going nowhere. It's all pointless.'

'I have made you nervous,' he said, edging away.

'You wouldn't if you answered a single cursed question!'

His forearms were freckled, a detail that fascinated her, and they moved as if to hold up the words he spoke. 'Too many questions. I wear my mother's grief, for a sister she lost.

A twin. I follow to take care of her on this journey. Mother's dead twin speaks to her – even I have heard her, shouting in my ear, waking me in the night.'

'The dead woman talks, does she? Well, what does she have to say?'

'The Jaghut and his vow. They must be heeded.'

'It's not enough that the living want their dead back – now the dead want to come back, too. How is it souls can get lonely, when their entire existence is alone? Is mortal flesh so precious? Wouldn't you rather fly free of it, sail off into the sky? Dance around stars, feeling no cold, no pain – is that not a perfect freedom? Who would want to return from that?'

'Now I have made you angry.'

'It's not you. Well, it is, but don't take it personally. I just can't make sense of any of you.'

'You are Tiste.'

Korya nodded. They'd walked to the camp's very edge, and before them was a plain of scattered stones, shaped but broken or eroded, the city's dwindling demise. 'A hostage to the Jaghut, Haut. The Captain. The Old Misery. The Lord of Riddles. Crier of Aches and Imagined Illnesses. He has made me a Mahybe – knock me and I'll ring hollow.'

The youth's eyes were wide now, studying her avidly. 'Lie with me,' he said.

'What? No. I didn't mean – what is your name, by the way?'

'Ifayle. In our language, it means "falling sky".'

She frowned at him. 'Something falling from the sky?'

He nodded. 'Like that, yes.'

'On the night you were born, something fell from the sky.'

'No. I fell from the sky.'

'No you didn't. You fell out between your mother's legs.'

'Yes, that too.'

She pulled her eyes away from his intense, unambiguous gaze, and studied the plain. Silvered by frost and starlight, it stretched away into the southeast for as far as she could see. 'You shouldn't follow the Jaghut,' she said. 'They're not gods. They're not even wise.'

'We do not worship Hood,' Ifayle said. 'But we kneel to his promise.'

'He can't fulfil it,' Korya said harshly. 'Death is not something you can close hands around. You can't . . . strangle it, much as you'd like to. Hood's promise was . . . well, it was metaphorical. Not meant to be taken literally. Oh, listen to me, trying to explain poetic nuances to a Dog-Runner. How long were you following me, anyway?'

He smiled. 'I did not follow you, Korya.'

'So, you just popped up from the ground?'

'No, I fell from the sky.'

When she set about, marching back into the abandoned city of Omtose Phellack, Ifayle did not follow her. Not that she wanted him to – although seeing the look on Arathan's face would have been a delight – but his abandonment seemed sudden, as if she'd done something to make him lose interest in her. The notion irritated her, fouling her mood.

She drew out the acorn and studied it, seeking to sense the power hidden inside. There was nothing. It was, as far as she could tell, just an acorn. Conjured up on a treeless plain. *Don't break it,* he said.

She drew nearer the Tower of Hate. Arathan would be asleep. Even the thought of that frustrated her. *This is still the watch . . . almost. He should be awake. At the window, looking out on Hood's sea of burning stars, wondering where I've gone to. Whom I might be with.*

*Rutting some Dog-Runner with snowy eyes and freckles on his arms. If Ifayle really wanted me, as he said, he would've followed. Empty chambers abound in this city. He didn't even smell bad, all things considered.*

*The invitation was a tease. Lucky I saw through it and made plain my shock. My disgust. That smile was amused, not admiring. That's why I bridled. And Arathan's no better. Gift to Gothos, only now he says he's leaving. Joining Hood, and why? Nothing but sentiment, the rush of the impossible to take hold of every romantic, deluded soul.*

*Look at them all!*

*Death will have to chase me down. Hunt me across, I*

*don't know, centuries. And even then, I vow to leave it . . .*
*dissatisfied.*
   *You fell from the sky, did you? With flecks of golden sun-*
*light on your arms, I saw. How quaint.*

\*     \*     \*

Restless but reluctant to leave Gothos's company and make
his way back to the abode he and Korya shared, Arathan sat
close to the ebbing heat from one of the braziers, at last
thankful for its warmth. She would be lying in wait, he
suspected, to assail him once again, to scoff at his foolish
romanticism. And he had little with which to fend off her
arguments.

Dawn was not too far away, in any case. Winter was a
pernicious beast, he decided, to make caves, holes and gloomy
chambers so inviting, where musings could huddle and stretch
hands out over softly glowing embers. The outer world was
bleak enough without the sleeping season's reminder of what
was lost, and what still remained months away. And yet, he
thought to walk the camp in the day to come, or perhaps
wander once more through the ruins of abandoned Omtose
Phellack, to let the musings unfurl in winter's cold, unyielding light.

The chill and the flat light would give hue to his memories
of loss, to the surrendering of his heart that, it had since
turned out, was no surrender at all. He could rattle the chains
he dragged in his wake, marvelling at the blue of their iron
links, or the snaking trails they made through dustings of
snow and frost.

He had come, forlornly, to the belief that love was given
but once. No doubt, as Gothos had suggested, there was a
plethora of feelings that sought the guise of love, but in truth
proved to be lesser promises, guarded commitments, alliances
of sympathy, and so, when exposed, revealed their fragile
illusions. It was likely, in fact, that Feren had held him in such
a state, with her love for him nothing more than a thinly disguised need, and in his giving her the child she wanted, she
dispensed with the child whose furs she shared. It was a hard

admission, to accept his inability to understand what had happened, to know that he had indeed been too young, too naïve. And none of that recognition, in his misguided self, did much to ease his resentment of his father.

It was no surprise that Draconus knew Gothos, or that they shared something like friendship. The old would give account to a wisdom mutually shared, like some tattered blanket against the long night's chill, and offer up a thread-bare corner for the young to grasp – if only they would. But that was but one more burden on a young spirit, but one more thing to slip from the grasp, or see torn loose by an unexpected tug. He could not hold on to what he had not yet earned.

These notions did nothing to ease the loss that haunted him. His love for Feren was the only real emotion within him, the chains wrapped tight. It was the only truth he had earned, and every fragment of wisdom, crumbled loose, shedding like rust from the creaking links, was bitter in his heart.

A pewter cup struck his left knee, sharp enough to make him start, and as the cup chimed like a muted bell while it rolled on the floor at his feet, Arathan looked across to glare at Gothos.

'More tea,' said the Lord of Hate from his chair at the desk.

Arathan rose.

'And less angst,' Gothos added. 'Make hasty your flight from certainty, Arathan, so you can stumble the sooner into our aged, witless unknowing. I am tempted to curse you as in a child's tale, giving you a sleep centuries long, during which you gather like dust useful revelations.'

Arathan set the pot back on to the embers. 'Such as, lord?'

'The young have little in their satchel, and so would make of each possession something vast. Bulky, heavy, awkward. They end up with a crowded bag indeed – or so they believe, when we look upon it and see little more than a slim purse dangling jauntily from your belt.'

'You belittle my wounds.'

'Cherish the sting of my dismissal, won't you? I'll see it

fiery and swollen, inflamed and then black with rot, until all your limbs fall off. Oh, summon the Abyss, and dare it be vast enough to hold your thousand angry suns. But if mockery wounds so readily—'

'Forgive me, lord,' Arathan interrupted, 'I fear the old leaves in this pot may prove bitter. Shall I sweeten what I serve you?'

'You imagine your silence does not groan like a host of drunk bards lifting heads to the dawn?' Gothos waved a hand. 'The older the leaves the more subtle the flavour. But a nugget of honey wouldn't hurt.'

'Was it Haut who said the tusk sweetens with age, lord?'

'Sounds more like Varandas,' muttered Gothos. 'The fool shits coddled babies at the sight of a lone flower sprung from between stones. On his behalf I do invite you to his company on the next maudlin night, which would be any night you choose. But I should warn you, what begins as a gentle passing between you of your sore, broken hearts will soon turn into a hoary contest of tragedies. Gird yourself to the battle of whose past wounds have cut deepest. Come morning, I'll send someone to clean up the mess.'

Arathan collected up the cup and poured tea. He dropped a nugget of honey into it. 'There was a stabler, on my father's estate, who made and ate rock candy. His teeth had all rotted away.' He strode over to set the cup down on the desktop.

Gothos grunted. 'An affliction when the child is taken too soon from the mother's tit. Spend the rest of your days sucking on something, anything, everything. There are Dog-Runners who slip in among the herds they hunt, to suckle animal teats in the season. They too have no teeth.'

'And none of these Dog-Runners are trampled?'

'Obsession incurs risk, Arathan.'

Arathan stood studying the Lord of Hate. 'I imagine something like your Folly must incur many risks, lord. How is it you have avoided such dread pitfalls?'

'In itself, a suicide note involves no particular obsession,' Gothos replied, collecting up the cup. 'My haunting is both singular and modest, in that I mean to get it right.'

'And when you do, lord? When you finally get it right?'

'Proof against the accusation of obsession,' the lord answered, 'since what drives me is simple curiosity. Indeed, what will happen when I finally get it right? Be sure I will find a means of letting you know the day that occurs.'

'I hesitate to say that I look forward to it, lord, lest you mistake my meaning.'

'Ah,' said Gothos after sipping, 'did I not warn you that old leaves hold a most subtle flavour? You have over-sweetened your offering, Arathan, as the young are wont to do.'

Arathan turned at a sound from the doorway, to see Hood standing in the threshold. The cowled Jaghut studied Arathan for a moment, and then stepped inside. 'I smell that foul tea you so adore, Gothos.'

'Properly aged as is appropriate,' Gothos responded. 'Arathan, fill him a cup, in which he may drown his sorrows, sweetly.'

'I despaired,' Hood said, collecting up a chair.

'This is your story, yes.'

'Not that, you gas-bloated goat. Day and night I am assailed. The questions alone invite my hunger for death. Imagine, the fools clamour for organization! Pragmatic necessities! Supply equipage, cooks and meals!'

'Is it not said that an army travels on its stomach?'

'An army travels on its griping, Gothos, which surely sustains it beyond all fodder.'

'I too have been besieged, Hood,' said the Lord of Hate, 'for which you are to blame. This day, it was your officers who made a mess of my afternoon, as Arathan is my witness. So, as I feared, you are the cause of sorrows not just your own—'

'That cause for sorrow not my own,' Hood growled.

'No,' Gothos said. 'But your answer to tragedy surely is. As for me' – he paused to hold up his cup, as if he could some-how see through the pewter to admire the hue of the tea – 'I would have set out hunting Azathanai, the ones with blood on their hands. Tragedy sits still as a frozen pond, upon which no firm footing is possible. Vengeance, on the other hand, can silence any army, in that grim, teeth-grinding way we both know all too well.'

Hood grunted. 'The offence taken by innocent Azathanai will serve what need there may be for vengeance.'

'Hardly. They're almost as useless as we are, Hood. Expect nothing concerted, not even a proclamation of . . . oh, what would it be? Censure? Decided disapproval? Disagreeable frown?'

'I am scoured of vengeance,' Hood said. 'Made hollow as a bronze urn.'

'And so I shall think of you from now on, Hood. As a bronze urn.'

'And when I think of you, Gothos, I shall imagine a book without resolution, a tale without end, an endeavour without purpose. I shall think of pointlessness, in a pointed fashion.'

'Perhaps,' Gothos said, leaning back. 'Of course, that all depends on who outlives the other.'

'Does it?'

'Possibly. It was a thought, presumably relevant.'

Hood's cold eyes fixed on Arathan – who sat once more beside the last surviving brazier – and the Jaghut said, 'This one, Gothos, I will send back to you. Before we cross a threshold where no return is possible.'

'I thought as much,' Gothos said, sighing.

'Unless you'd rather I didn't.'

'No. That is, I'd rather you did. Send him back, if not here, then somewhere else. Just not there.'

Arathan cleared his throat. 'And I see that neither of you imagines that I might have a say in all this?'

Hood looked to Gothos. 'Did the pup speak?'

'Some semblance of speech, yes,' Gothos said. 'It does not mark his more admirable trait.'

Arathan said, 'I will speak my piece, to you, Lord Hood, when the time comes – when we reach that threshold you describe. And you will hear me, sir, and make no argument against my continuing on, in your company.'

'I will not?'

'Not, sir, when you hear what I will say.'

'He knows our minds, you see,' said Gothos to Hood. 'Being young and all.'

'Ah, that. Yes, of course. Forgive me for forgetting.' With that, Hood leaned back and stretched out his legs, his pose matching that of Gothos.

Arathan stared at them both.

A moment later, Gothos started tapping on the arm of his chair. Glancing over, Arathan saw Hood nodding off to sleep.

# SEVEN

A MAN WITHOUT DAUGHTERS, SHARENAS ANKHADU reflected as she studied her commander, knew little of subtlety. Vatha Urusander faced south, his back to the keep's outer wall, the detritus from the chute leading from the kitchen heaped behind him, at the base of a wedge-shaped stain on the stone wall. He stood with his boots in scraps of rubbish. Knucklebones blushed pink, tubers black with rot, broken pottery, peels and lumps of fat too rancid to burn. Despite the late afternoon's bitter cold, steam rose from that mound like the smoke from some hidden peat fire. There was, she decided, fecundity in what rotted, but hardly the appetizing kind.

In her absence, the list of the slain had grown. Curious, for a war as yet undeclared. She eyed her commander, wondering if she knew him at all. Aching from the long ride, she waited at a distance, her clothes spattered with mud, her hands quickly growing numb with cold beneath the soaked-through leather riding gloves.

Winter was the season of isolation. Worlds closed in, crowded up one against another. Trapped in such confines, surrounded by forbidding cold and frozen land, one could obsess on what was still to come, speaking heated words, making the season of spring into a promise of fire. She had ridden far in her exploration of the realm, through bleak wastelands, scorched forests, winding through hills silvered by snow and frost. And like anything coming in from the cold, she was rarely made a welcome guest. It did not take an ice-locked keep to forge solitude. Winter's isolation belonged as much to the mind as to the world outside it.

A painter of portraits would grin at the image before her now, in that cruel, superior way of artists who saw all that they needed to see. Complexity was confusion more often than not, while clarity could gift one with simplicity. In any case, the backside of a fortress was sordid enough in its mundane truths. Gatehouses, formal lanes and a bold façade all served what was required of them, elevating the titled few and their claims of privilege and wealth, and of course such edifices fronted the building, like a tapestry hiding a crumbling wall.

*No different from men and women, then: buildings shit out a hole in their backside.*

The notion made her think of Hunn Raal and his smile, the one he saved for the people he despised. Knowledge assembled secret hoards, and the man now leading the Legion in all but name was greed's own tyrant these days. Worse, there was now something else about him, an emanation of sorts, beyond the usual rank wine staining his breath and souring his sweat. Sharenas wondered if she was alone in sensing that change – perhaps, simply, she had been gone too long.

*Too long, and ill timed this departure. We went our separate ways, Kagamandra Tulas. You and I, so long ago now, it seems. Have you found your betrothed yet? Did you flinch, or did you stand in the manner of the man you would be? Kagamandra, I have come back to Neret Sorr, and I miss you.*

When at last Urusander shifted his gaze and saw her, she noted his surprise. 'Captain! I did not know you had returned to us.'

'I have but just arrived, sir,' she said.

She studied him as he approached. Like an apparition, he wore winter's skin, white and vaguely translucent, as if clad in ice. The lines of his face were etched deep in the fading light. This transformation still startled her. *The High Priestess Syntara names it purity. But I see a season of thought, the details of belief and conviction, all frozen in place. We are invited into sleep, drawn ever deeper into a world of extremes, where our hearts are locked.*

*Light yields no empathy. This is not the man I once knew.*

Urusander said, 'Tell me, I beg you, that Toras Redone has seen reason. I will not see a repeat of Lord Rend's mad attack upon us, when we remain here, at peace.'

He hesitated then, and she could guess at the reason. He had ever been a reluctant commander, too severe for court politics, uncomfortable in the presence of the nobles of the Great Houses and their subtle, ambivalent ways. Nor was he a man known for being loquacious. But now, and here, there was little choice.

'This is not how it was meant to be,' he said. 'If I did not move, it was with reason. If I chose to suspend judgement, I had good cause. Sharenas, we are not as we once were.' He gestured, indicating his face, and then studied his hand, as it hovered before him. 'Not this. The High Priestess sees far too much in such mundane attire. No, what has come to us – to us all – is a kind of ambiguity, as if our spirit has stumbled, suddenly lost.' His gaze narrowed as he studied his bleached hand. 'And yet, does this not invite the very opposite? The marks of faith?' He glanced at her. 'I am unchanged in that. She would call me Father Light, but that title is like a blow to the chest.' Shaking his head, he looked away, letting his hand drop.

*Father Light. High Priestess, have you no sense of irony? This father here has done poorly with his charges, true-born and adopted. Worse still, his soldiers run wild, like a family torn loose. He is father to thousands.*

*Commander, what will you do about your children?*

'Sir, Syntara would set you opposite, but equal, to Mother Dark. It is, I know, somewhat . . . simplistic. But perhaps that offers its own appeal.'

'You cannot hold it in,' he muttered, as if suddenly distracted. 'Not for ever. No mortal has that capacity.'

'Sir?'

His voice hardened. 'Anger, Sharenas, is an unruly beast. We chain it daily, seeking the civil mien. Witness to injustices on all sides, appalled at the brazen abuse of that most basic notion of fairness, so arrogantly abrogated. And then, there is the effrontery. Indeed, humiliation. I would have walked away from it. You know that, Sharenas, don't you?'

She nodded.

He went on. 'But the beast broke free and now runs hard – but to where? Seeking what? Reparation or vengeance?' He shifted to face south, as if he could somehow look upon the Citadel itself. 'He painted what he saw, and now ... now, Abyss take me, he sees nothing. By this terrible act of self-mutilation' – he turned his head to meet her gaze – 'did he make vow to the triumph of Dark? This is what I ask myself, again and again.'

*Before me stands a man with too many thoughts and too few feelings.* 'Sir, Kadaspala was driven mad, by what he found, by what had been done to his sister and his father. There was no intent in what he did to himself, unless it was to claw out the anguish filling his head.'

After a moment, Urusander grunted, and his tone turned wry. 'I lost grip on the chain and that beast is well beyond my reach now. I understand how it must seem, to Anomander, and to all the other highborn. Vatha Urusander waits in Neret Sorr, eager to begin the season of war.'

To that, she said nothing.

'Sharenas, what word do you bring?'

What word? Well, an expected question, under the circum-stances. *Still ... blessed Abyss, what island have I stumbled upon? What forbidding seas surround it? Was I alone in rid-ing into the face of winter, looking upon freshly made barrows? Here you stand, seeking word of the outside world. Your island, sir, is lost on every map. Kadaspala? Forget that fool! We now gather with all swords drawn! Urusander, how do I venture close?* 'Sir, Commander Toras Redone is presently indisposed. Broken, I am told, by grief.'

The bleached visage before her revealed no hint of

subterfuge as he frowned. 'I do not understand. Has she lost a dear one, then?'

Sharenas hesitated. This was not a challenge to her courage – she would speak the truth here, as befitted Urusander's most loyal captain. But this man's innocence frightened her – *an innocence, it seems, won in the slipping free of a chain. I see less a father and more a child. Reborn, Syntara? Indeed, and it's a cold, cold cradle.* 'Sir, it seems that Hunn Raal has told you little of his various missions across Kurald Galain. I but rode into his wake, sir, and made of it all I could glean, although, it must be said, I was rarely welcome.'

At the mention of Hunn Raal's name, Urusander's expression twisted. 'He is censured, I assure you, captain. This war against the Deniers is an absurd dissembling of our cause. It has done more harm than good. The man does not comprehend justice, nor even propriety, it seems.' He half turned, to gaze southward again, and set a hand to his face, but cautiously, as if uncertain what his touch would find. 'What is it, Sharenas, which you must speak? And why this hesitation?'

'In a moment, sir, if you will forgive me. Since I last departed here, there have been changes.'

He shot her a look. 'You doubt your footing?'

*You fool. I doubt yours.* 'The High Priestess holds to a lofty station now. Is it Hunn Raal who sits cupped in her hand? What of Captain Serap? Sir, I must know – who advises you on affairs of the state?'

Urusander scowled. 'I have accepted the responsibility for my legion,' he said, his voice trembling with suppressed emotion – if not anger, then, perhaps, it was shame. 'I will reassert the justice of our cause.' He paused, and then said, 'Captain, I am offered no advice, nor do I ask it. It may be that this may change, since now you have returned. But the others, they come to me inside clouds of confusion, and leave me bemused, and then made to feel foolish for being so blind.'

'They tell you nothing?'

'The pending wedding is all they will speak of. As if that was for them to decide upon!'

*Ah, you see their contempt, then. Is this how it is, now? Righteous fury lost on the horizon, amidst white winds. And here before me, Vatha Urusander, the greying wolf with its fangs pulled.* 'Sir, what you might call marriage, they name machination. In a joining of hands, as you might see it, they grasp for leverage. Not a union of love, then. Nor one of respectful regard, you with her, her with you. Rather, they set you both upon the same anvil, and from two blades they would hammer and twist the pair of you into one single weapon.'

'For them to wield?'

She almost stepped back at the sudden fire in his eyes, a flame of light unnatural in its fierceness. *The fangs remain, but still I sense his . . . helplessness.* Was this the mark of Syntara's blessing? Skin of white and the blinding fires of Liosan . . . *all pointless?* Did she curse as well as bless? What reach this newfound power of hers, and was that what Sharenas saw in Hunn Raal? 'It is my thought, sir, that they would take hold of such a weapon, even knowing the threat of uncertain edges, a sliding grip, an unexpected unbalancing, and swing hard, unmindful of innocent victims.'

'As you say,' he said sharply, 'an uncertain weapon, no matter what they might desire, or expect. To think that we are seen this way, a Legion commander and a goddess. As mere tools for their ambitions. I will speak to her!'

He meant Mother Dark, she presumed. 'They must line the steps of that path first, and so they urge you to remain here. Sir, was it truly your desire to . . . do nothing?'

'And yield trust to any messenger? Were you, captain, not enough?'

'Day by day, sir, my reiteration of your avowed loyalty, in the name of peace, rang more and ever more hollow.' *Pray that stings you, Urusander. Words scud like clouds over the blood-soaked landscape. High and noble they might be, but their shadows prove weak.*

He squinted southward for a time, and then seemed to deflate. 'I am filled with promises,' he said. 'None worth the weight of the breath that utters them.'

The wealth of light, it seemed, invited extremity. There would indeed be little balance left to this newly forged weapon. In sudden clarity, she saw the marriage, this union that would bring peace upon the realm. *A bloody peace. Light and Dark will war, one against the other. I see the spitting out of children, a family brood both venal and vicious. A marriage of two bedrooms, two keeps, two worlds.* 'Commander Toras Redone's grief, sir, is for the soldiers of the Hust Legion, almost all of whom are now dead.'

The face he swung to her was such a cascade of expressions that she could make no sense of it. 'That cannot be. Have the Forulkan returned? Does the war begin again? I'll not yield this time! I will pursue them down to the very sea, and see the crest ride red for years upon that cursed shore!'

She blinked. 'No. The Forulkan have not come. They renew no war. Did their own queen not acknowledge the justice of their defeat? Lord Urusander, you broke them, and they shall not return.'

'Then what has befallen the Hust?'

'Treachery,' she replied, once more searching his face, and once more baffled by what she saw. *A warlord in search of an enemy. But surely, this is the season for it, as the chambers you pace grow smaller and smaller still.* 'They were poisoned,' she said. 'In a single night, following a gift of wine and ale. A gift, sir, from Captain Hunn Raal.'

When he said nothing, when he but stared at her, his face like cracked ice, Sharenas looked away – almost desperately. 'This is why,' she said, 'they speak only of the wedding.'

Urusander finally spoke, his tone viciously cold. 'How does the First Son give answer? Does he now march upon us?'

'With what?' Sharenas snapped. 'The Houseblades of the nobles? None are summoned to Kharkanas. Lord Anomander is not even there. Instead, he searches for Andarist. Lord Silchas commands in his place, and seeks to restore the Hust Legion.'

'But – how?'

'He raids the mining pits, sir.'

Urusander raised a hand between them, as if to push her

away. She fell silent. With her words she had battered at him, wielding them as would a madwoman. No shield thrown up against them survived their relentless frenzy. She thought she saw in him, now, at last, signs of shock. *But balance is not a game. Have I pushed too far, even when I spoke nothing but the truth? Is this, perhaps, the reason for keeping Urusander ignorant?*

'They think me a puppet,' Urusander said. 'I was told that Ilgast Rend defied every effort at conciliation. He threw away the lives of the Wardens, and killed many of my own soldiers. Was it courage or cowardice that he chose to die in battle?' He waved a hand. 'When Calat Hustain learns of this, of what Rend did with his people . . . ah, even I do not know how I would survive that. Such betrayal, and by a noble-born . . .' His voice trailed away. He stared south again. 'It is curious, is it not, how the horrors climb the walls of our right-eous indignation? Up and out, spilling over the battlements with howls, in a night of lit torches and wind-whipped flames. I see their grim forms, spreading out, and out, over Kurald Galain. Hunn Raal? May the spirits forgive me, but it was my hands that shaped him. My blessed, poisoned portrait.'

'Sir, it is not enough to harden yourself to such atrocities.'

'You misjudge me, Sharenas,' Urusander replied. 'It seems that you have forgotten the campaigns against the Forulkan and the Jhelarkan. No battle shall be unveiled until it is already won. I must think like a commander. Again, after all this time. Gift me with your patience, and consider my words a promise.'

Sharenas shook her head. 'The time for patience has passed, sir. Your camp is in need of cleansing.'

Urusander glanced at her again. 'Is it so hard to under-stand?' he asked her. 'I keep looking for justice.'

Sharenas looked down at the castle leavings that crowded the lord's ankles. *You'll not find it here, Vatha Urusander.* 'Sir, Hunn Raal cannot be trusted.'

His mouth twisted into a faint smile. 'And you can?'

She had no reply to that question. Any exhortation would demean her.

After a moment he shook his head. 'Forgive me, captain. As you say, there have been changes since you were last here. Thus, you remain, for the moment at least, outside all of that. Your clay is still wet, awaiting impress, and I but wonder at who would claim such an unmarred surface.'

'Sir, I cannot but doubt Hunn Raal's version of that battle. I have known Lord Ilgast Rend all my life. I fought at his side. We knew fear upon the field, in the clash of weapons and the roar of the press. True, he possessed a fierce temper—'

'Captain, he chose to march upon us. He arrayed the Wardens and sought battle. None of that can be questioned.'

'Perhaps not. And if he came with his own Houseblades, and not Calat Hustain's Wardens, I could be made to believe Hunn Raal's tale – although even then, I would expect an exchange of insults, and indeed a grievous offence committed, to which Ilgast had no choice but to give answer. But the charge set upon Lord Rend – the safe keeping of the Wardens – he would have taken most seriously.'

'It seems not,' Urusander retorted.

'There was the matter of the pogrom—'

Urusander grunted dismissively. 'For which Rend chose not to accept my own promise of justice, to be attended upon every criminal in my ranks, every slayer of innocents.'

'Did you give him that promise, sir? Face to face?'

He drew his cloak tighter about him, and then turned to the narrow trail that led back to the gatehouse. 'I was indisposed on that day,' he muttered. He set out.

Rattled by that admission, Sharenas followed. 'And then, sir,' she persisted, 'there is the murder of the Hust.'

'Your point?'

'The attending of justice, sir.'

He halted abruptly and faced her. 'Civil war, captain. This is what is now upon us. Though I held to peace – though here I chose to remain, holding fast upon my legion. Though I summoned every wayward veteran back into my fold, under my responsibility. Yet still they elected to march upon me. How can I know if Ilgast Rend was not following Anomander's orders? How can I not contemplate the purpose of striking at my legion before it was fully assembled, the tactical value, the strategic purpose of such a thing? After all, captain, it is what I would do.'

He resumed walking.

'I doubt that, sir.'

Her words brought him back. 'Explain, captain.'

'If at Anomander's behest, sir, Ilgast Rend would surely have come with more than just the Wardens. His own Houseblades, for one, and perhaps even those of Anomander. Or what of the Shake? Who more bears the wounds of that pogrom than the warrior monks of Yannis? And what of the other Great Houses? To crush you now would be the proper tactic. Sir, Ilgast Rend brought to us a show of force, a symbol of his disapproval. Something happened, in that meeting between him and Hunn Raal. If Raal can poison three thousand men and women of the Hust, would he shy from provoking Rend to a foolish decision?'

Urusander studied her. The day was failing around them, the wind picking up, bitter with cold. 'I cannot say,' he finally said. 'Let us ask him, shall we?'

'Best wait on that,' Sharenas said. 'Forgive me, sir. But we do not know the strength of your camp. I would speak to Lieutenant Serap first. She has suffered the loss of two sisters, after all, and this might well have cleared her vision of Hunn Raal. More, I would know the High Priestess's place in all of this. And what of Infayen Menand, and Esthala, and Hallyd Bahann? Commander, these officers I have just mentioned – your favoured in the Legion – each one has been named in the pogrom and its grisly list of terrible crimes. Each one, I would say, has acted upon Hunn Raal's orders.'

'You think,' Urusander said, 'that you and I will stand alone, against an array already bound in conspiracy.'

'A conspiracy in your name, sir, although that cause floats before them as but the thinnest veil. When the last flames of this war die down, I envisage a sudden end to the illusions, and ambition will stand naked before us.'

'Who commands the Legion, captain?'

She shook her head. 'The last commander to lead it into

246

battle, sir, the last to lead it into victory, was Hunn Raal.'

'I have made a mistake,' Urusander said.

'Nothing that cannot be remedied,' Sharenas replied.

'Sharenas Ankhadu, are we now at war?' He looked away. 'I called it such, only a few moments ago.'

'Even from this, sir, peace can be won without any more blood-shed.'

'Barring those who have committed crimes in my name.'

*Indeed? And will you now do our enemy's work for them? Execute the majority of your officers? Whether Ilgast Rend heard your promise or not, he would have been sceptical. Your justice, Urusander, thrives best in imagination. It remains an ideal, unsullied by any real world.*

*Scud over us if you will. I chose the land below you, and choose it still.*

They continued on, skirting the edge of the high ground as they made their way to the front gatehouse. The setting sun on their left was a red smear on a horizon made dark by the burned grimace of the forest. Above that smear, the sky was streaked in gold.

She thought again about Urusander's last promise. Justice shone fierce and blazing in the man walking at her side. Should he seek to impose it, however . . . *in the face of this man's justice, mortal flesh will simply melt away.* No, he would be blunted at every turn. What had begun with the slaying of Enesdia – the slaughter at the wedding site – was a cascade of retribution. Too many aggrieved agencies to see anything like proper justice in what was to come. She was not even certain that Urusander could regain control of his own Legion. *Not while Hunn Raal lives.*

The Issgin line lived under its own curse, and Hunn Raal was but the latest in its filial list of fools. But such stains had a way of spreading outward.

Urusander's justice was without subtlety. There was not just one war being waged here. Surely he must comprehend that. *And what of me? Have I now committed myself to Vatha Urusander? Am I not nobleborn? What harsh choice awaits me, should this all unravel?*

No, now was not the time to decide. For this moment, she would hold to honour, and her duty to her commander. For as long as he seemed fit to command. If there came a time when she must cut herself loose, she would be ready.

'Sharenas,' Urusander said, 'I am pleased that you are back.'

*       *       *

There was value in keeping close those who dwelt in all company, mostly unseen, always beneath regard, who served the single purpose of cleaning up whatever mess had been left behind. This notion lingered in the mind of High Priestess Syntara as she idly watched the maid gathering up the meal's leavings. She knew, as well, how a man's thoughts would set off down entirely different paths, gauging and perhaps even reflective, as eyes fixed on the swell of the girl's behind, the thinness of her skirt.

Base impulses rode wine-heavy fumes, and there was no need to glance across at her guest to glean his musings. A drunk's appetites were blind to every edge. Plates could crash, the young woman could cry out, as in his mind he flung her to the floor, and made blurred the boundaries of his desire.

It was no easy thing, to spar with a man like Hunn Raal. While her sober cleverness could slip in and around, past and through, a drunk was prone to sudden, unexpected moves. The dance was always uncertain.

For the moment, however, in this satiated silence following food and too much wine, she could ignore Hunn Raal and contemplate the necessity of people beneath notice. Only a deluded fool had the audacity to assert the notion that all were equal – no matter the arbiter, the final judge of such things; the sheer idiocy of such a claim earned no serious contemplation. Judgement was no crime in itself, and hardly a thing to shy away from, if the alternative was a levelling of all things to some idyllic, but impossible, ideal.

She had heard Urusander drone on about justice, as if by proscription and delineation law could be made to stand in place of what was both undeniable and wholly natural. *If in earning privilege, in attaining mastery over others, we find ourselves waging perpetual war to keep all things in their proper place – lesser people included – is it any wonder that we select few come to live a life under siege? And who can be surprised when desperation drives us to despicable acts of cruelty?*

*Such laws as Urusander would impose fashion for us the enemy's face. It can be no other way. Things are not equal. People are not equal. There are those few who will rule, while the rest must follow.*

*Hunn Raal can have this woman, this maid, should he so choose. Her life is in his hands. In mine, too, for that matter. But we need no laws to force upon us the ethics of our comportment. Virtue never stands outside awaiting invitation like a stranger at a gathering. It is born of the light within us.*

*In any case, see how bright it burns in some, but not others.*

The maid departed.

'She is new?' Hunn Raal asked.

Syntara sighed. 'Many young women now come to me. It is my task to interview them, and find their place in things, be it household or temple.'

'Ah,' Hunn Raal said, slowly nodding. 'She did not pass muster then, as a priestess in waiting.'

'Lowborn and ignorant,' Syntara said, settling back on the cushions. 'Wholly lacking in any spark.'

Hunn Raal reached for his cup. 'Most of the soldiers in my legion would share that assessment, should you make it of *them*. Lowborn. Not knowing much. And yet, are they not valuable? Are they not worth fighting for? Their lives, High Priestess, should not be a waste.'

'Oh, spare me,' she replied. 'You fling them into the teeth of battle and think only of the outcome, the groaning shift of vast unseen scales. Does it nudge you a step closer to what you seek? That is your only concern, captain.'

Beneath heavy lids, he studied her for a moment, and then shook his head. 'You are wrong. We seek recognition. For the sacrifices we made.'

'Oh? And did the Houseblades of the Great Houses not make the same sacrifices? Why then do they not rate in your esteem?'

'But they do. Soldiers, little different from us. It is their masters with whom we have a disagreement. In fact, High Priestess, it would not surprise me to find, on the day of battle, many of those Houseblades refusing to draw weapons, refusing indeed what their lords and ladies would demand of them.'

'Is this your dream, Hunn Raal? A true uprising of the commoner, the lowborn, the ignorant and the witless? If so, then High House Light is not for you.'

Smiling, he held up a pallid hand and studied it. 'The gift made no such distinctions, Syntara, and certainly not those you would now impose. How quickly a faith is corrupted.'

Anger flashed through her, but she bit it back. 'Consider this, then. If there are none to serve, if, in the elevation of everyone, litter fills the streets, meals remain uncooked, crops lie unharvested, clothes unmended, the dust left to choke us all in our repasts, how fares this new paradise of yours, Hunn Raal?'

He scowled across at her.

She continued. 'You wear a sword, captain, hinting at the threat behind your every request. But not just requests – after all, we need not mince words' meaning here – no, behind your *expectations*. Of obedience. Of compliance. Of the continuation of the way things are, provided that the way things are sets you above those others, and makes solid your claim to rule over them.

'As for your soldiers, why, I would think each dreams an identical dream – no different from your own. A retinue of servants for each soldier, slaves even, as proof of that "recognition" you so desire. Every ploughed field will sprout some new estate, as your beloved soldiers scramble to carve out their rightful place in the new scheme. As for the peasants, why, their lives will not change. They were never meant to change, not by your reckoning, in any case. You would shake the order, but not so much as to send the framework

250

down into crashing ruin. This war of yours, Hunn Raal, is but a shuffling of the pieces. That and no more.'

'And what is it that you seek, High Priestess, if not the same, as you elbow your way to the table?' He snorted behind his cup. 'You dance well, but it is in the same fire as the rest of us.'

'No,' she replied. 'You can have that table, Hunn Raal, and all the new but grubby faces around it. What I seek is a new place, a new realm, in fact. One where Light rules, and Dark has no claim. I will make it here, in Neret Sorr.'

'That wins us nothing, Syntara. They will marry. There will be unification through balance, Dark upon one side, Light upon the other.' His expression grew ugly. 'Now you sit here, seeking to change what we agreed upon, and I like it not.'

She narrowed her gaze on him. 'I sense how the power of my gift now infuses you,' she said. 'Who would have thought that Hunn Raal, this rough, rarely sober captain of the Legion, should find in himself a burgeoning sorcery? By title you should name yourself warlock and be done with it.'

He laughed, collecting up the wine jug and leaning back on the cushions. He poured his cup full once more. 'I'd wondered if you knew. It is . . . interesting. I explore it, but cautiously, of course. Risky to be headlong in such matters, as I am sure you have discovered.'

'My comprehension is absolute,' Syntara replied. 'So much so that I advise you to be most careful in that exploration, Hunn Raal. You may in ignorance unleash something you cannot hope to control.'

'Abyss take me, Syntara, but you have grown arrogant. Young women come to you, shining with dreams of a better future for themselves, for their wretched lives, and you set most of them to scullery, to waiting on you and your guests. Your High House Light looks suspiciously similar to every other noble household, and yet here you sit, spouting bland pretensions to justify your – apparently – near universal contempt for everyone else.' He paused, drank deep, and then said, 'I see now what Lanear saw in you. The beauty of your flesh belies an ugly soul, Syntara.'

'No longer,' she snapped. 'I am purged. Reborn.'

'Repeated, more like,' he said, smirking.

There would come a time, possibly soon, when she would no longer need this man. The notion calmed her down. 'You have not yet asked, Hunn Raal.'

'Asked what?'

'The maid. Do you want her tonight? If so, she's yours.'

He set the jug and cup down, and then rose, carefully. 'A man has needs,' he muttered.

She nodded. 'I'll send her to your chambers, then. You may have her, for a day or two. But no longer, lest the dishes pile up.'

He stared down at her with his red-rimmed eyes. 'You say I should name myself warlock, Syntara. I would offer some advice of my own, to you. You are not alone in this newfound power. Best, I think, we work together. Urusander weds Mother Dark. He is given the title of Father Light. The civil war ends on that day. As for you and Emral Lanear, well, fight with your temples all you want, just keep it civil.'

She said nothing as he made his way out. Drunks made dangerous adversaries indeed. No matter. Warlock or no, he would never be her match.

In her mind, she unleashed a momentary spasm of power. A side door was pushed open almost immediately thereafter, and the serving girl stumbled into the chamber, her eyes wide and frightened.

'Yes,' murmured Syntara, 'that was me. Now, come closer. I need to look at your soul.'

Even terror could not win out against Syntara's will. She found the girl's soul, and crushed the life from it. In its place, she planted the seed of herself, a small thing, that would control its newfound body, and lead it into untold horrors. Through the girl's eyes now, Syntara could look out, whenever she chose to, and not even Hunn Raal would be the wiser.

'Now then, warlock,' she said in a low whisper, 'let's see the depths of your appetites, shall we? Things to use, things to abuse, things to twist my way.'

Syntara sent the girl to the captain's quarters.

There was value in keeping such creatures close at hand.

*Lowborn, ignorant. Such a pathetic soul, so easily snuffed out. No great loss.*

She would raise a temple, here in Neret Sorr. And set into its floor a Terondai, artfully recreating the sun and its torrid gift of fire. An emblem of gold and silver, a symbol of such wealth as to make kings ill. A temple to house a thousand priestesses, two thousand servants. And in the central chamber, she would raise a throne.

The marriage was doomed. There was not enough left in Vatha Urusander to assure a proper balance. Perhaps, she reflected, he had never been what others believed him to be. There was little of value in commanding an army: the talents required seemed few, and the measure of respect accorded it woefully out of proportion.

One need only look at Hunn Raal to see the truth of that. His talent, such as it was, served to feed the ambitions of others, clothed in the trappings of an acceptable violence. When she looked upon soldiers, she saw them as children, still trapped in their games of heroism, triumph, and great causes. But so much of that was delusion. Heroes fell into their heroism, mostly by accident. The triumphs were short-lived and, ultimately, changed nothing, which made those triumphs hollow. As for great causes, well, how often were they revealed to be little more than personal aggrandizement? The elevation of stature, the tidal swell of adoration, the penile gush of glory.

*Pray the servants tiptoe in to clean away the sordid stains, once that blazing light was past.*

The young woman would please him, she knew. Every hero of the male frame needed his compliant beauty, a creature excited by the stench of old blood on his hands, thrilled to see his wake where bodies lay piled in heaps. Why, she all but drooled at the prospect of his strong arms about her.

The heroes marched back and forth in the courtyard below, day after day, clanking and boisterous in this serious posturing. They each stood, in ranks or alone, with blades within easy reach. This announced to all their dangerous selves. No, she understood them well enough. And like the fate awaiting Vatha Urusander, all would soon come to comprehend their own irrelevance.

*There has never been an age of heroes, or not one of which the poets sing in their epic tales. Rather, we but witness one age upon another, and another, each one identical in every detail but for the faces – and even those faces blur into sameness after a time. In recognizing that, is it any wonder Kadaspala went mad?*

*Oh, they might point to the slaughter, the murder of his sister. But I believe it to be another kind of death that has broken our age's greatest painter of portraits. When at last he realized that every face was the same. And it looked out at him, ox-dull, belligerent and unchanging. And what were once virtues were suddenly revealed for what they truly were: pride and pomp, preening and pretence.*

*The age of heroes comes as a belief, and leaves unseen, as a conviction. Not even witnessed, it then finds resurrection in the past, the only realm that it can call home.*

There was nothing to weep for, no true loss to bemoan.

She would raise a temple to Light, and by that Light she would reveal unwelcome truths, and by that Light, there would be no place to hide. *And then, my friends, in that new age where heroes cannot be found, let us see what glory you might win.*

*But fear not. I will give you a thousand mindless virgins to use. Of them, there is an inexhaustible supply.*

*With my temple and the new age it will birth, I can offer this promise – a world where no lies can thrive, not even the ones you whisper to yourself. Only truth.*

*Urusander wants pure justice? Well then, in the name of Light, I shall deliver it.*

\*　　\*　　\*

With sufficient pressure, even the most pastoral of communities could crack. Too many strangers, too many new and unpleasant currents of power, or threat, and neighbours came to acquire cruel habits. Suspicion and resentment thrived, and the unseen torrent that rushed deep, stirring up sediments, held all the violence waiting to happen.

The town beneath Urusander's keep had suffered too long. It had reeled to unexpected deaths, buckled to sudden losses, and the crowds of unfamiliar faces, most of them arrogant and contemptuous, turned moods dark and foul.

Captain Serap avoided the Legion camps surrounding the town. Outwardly, she was contending with the grief of two dead sisters, and so her fellow soldiers remained at a distance, and this well suited her. If indeed she was suffering the loss of loved ones, it felt vague, almost formless. She had found a tavern on the high street, which, while it occasionally played host to off-duty soldiers, was more often than not crowded with villagers, whose brooding resentment hung thick and bitter in the smoky air.

It was an atmosphere she welcomed; the heavy swirl of ill humour was now something she could wear, like a winter cloak, and beneath its suffocating weight she was muffled, muted inside and out.

There was no desire to get drunk. No particular need for numb oblivion, and the wild flare of a night's worth of lust, desire, and thrashing limbs in one of the upstairs rooms ranked low in her list of needs.

The only gift she sought – the one she had found in this place – was solitude. It had always struck her as odd, how so many of her fellow soldiers feared isolation, as if stranded upon a tiny island with only their own self for company. Moments existed to be rushed through, filled to the brim with . . . with whatever. Anything within reach, in fact. Conversations crowded with nothing of worth; games where knucklebones rolled and bounced and wagers were made in bold gesture or wild shout; the hard muscle pulled close, or soft flesh depending on one's tastes. A few might sit alone, working on knife edges or whatnot, while still others muttered a lifetime's worth of confessions into their ale tankards, nodding as they gauged the worth of every returning echo. But all that this did was mark the time passed

255

and make it nothing more than something to be filled.

Lest the silence begin speaking.

It was astonishing, Serap reminded herself, just how much the silence had to say, when given the chance.

Sisters made a community, tightly bound and conspiratorial. That community mocked every need for solitude, if only to fend off the threat it posed. She should have missed it more than she did. Instead, she felt cut loose, set adrift, and now she floated on fog-bound water, where barely a ripple marred the blank surface.

It was a strange realm, this muttering silence, this reflective pool that seemed so dismissive of pity, grief, and commiseration. She had no desire to reach down to break the mirrored perfection of the calm surrounding her. It was enough, she felt, to simply listen.

Risp died in battle, far off to the west. Her first battle. Sevegg had died just outside Neret Sorr, slain by a wounded officer of the Wardens. That, too, had been her first battle. There were details, in the skein of war, which rarely earned mention – the truth of so many who died doing so in their first ever battle. It hinted too much of something unpleasant, something cruel lying in wait beyond the limits of civil contemplation. The silence whispered it to those who dared listen. *'It is to do, darling, with the sending of innocents to war.'*

Well, of course. Who would do such a thing?

*'They do. Over and over again. Training is but the thinnest patina. The innocence remains. Even as each young soldier's imagination builds proper scenes for what is to come, the innocence remains. Now then, sweet children, draw that blade and march into the press.*

*'Here arrives the first shock. Faces twisted with intent. Others arrayed before you, each one seeking to end your life. Your life! What has happened here? How can this be?'*

Oh, it could be. It was. None of the trappings, girded and stout, could truly hide the white, unstained banners carried by so many into battle.

But to think on it was to feel one's own heart breaking,

breaking and breaking. '*Never mind those young faces striving to look fierce, or dangerous. Never mind the mimicry they attempt, to appear wizened, wearied, unaffected. All of that, darling, is a mask turned both inward and out, convincing neither. Focus with purpose here, upon those white, pristine banners.*

'*And think, if you dare, of those who sent them into battle. Think, Serap, as I cannot. Must not. But if we draw too close, you and me, if we press on with this silent conversation, one of us will flinch in the end. And flee.*

'*To silence's end, closed out with empty conversations, or tankards of ale, or men into whose lap you will slide with laughter and promise. Into company, then, and the filling of this moment. Filling unto bursting, eager to flow over into the next moment, and the next . . .*'

Solitude demanded courage. She knew that now. The crazed revellers displayed their cowardice in that wild and insistent commune with anything and everything: that incessant need to blend in, and among, and keep forever at bay the howling silence of being alone. But she would not yield to contempt, for she could see in their need something she knew well.

*Despair.*

*Despair is the secret language of every generation in waiting. And you find it in the face of every innocent soul, as it marches into its embattled future. While the rest of us, innocent no longer, look on with blank, indifferent eyes.*

She sat alone at her table, in the gloom and smoke, and on all sides, white banners waved in the silence.

A short while later, two soldiers entered the tavern. There had been a time, not long ago, when Urusander's discipline was like a fist closed about his legion. Propriety and courtesy ruled the behaviour of his charges, when on duty or not.

But Hunn Raal was no Vatha Urusander. The lessons the captain had learned from his battles in the past fell upon the wrong side of propriety, and made mockery of courtesy. Of course, he was far from alone in this sour aftermath, where cynicism and contempt stalked the veteran soldier, and if she gave it some thought, Serap found herself skirting dangerous notions about the worth of things, and the true cost of war.

The newcomers swaggered in, inviting challenge. They were not entirely sober, but neither were they as drunk as they let on.

Settled back in her chair, in shadows, Serap remained undetected by the two men as they strode to the bar.

'I smell Deniers,' one of the soldiers said, gesturing at the barkeep. 'Ale, and none of that watered-down piss you're offering everyone else in here.'

'There's but one keg,' the barkeep said, shrugging. 'If you don't like what I serve, you can always leave.'

The other soldier grunted a laugh. 'Aye, we could. Not saying we will, though.'

Farmhands at a nearby table were pushing back their chairs. Brothers, Serap decided, four in all. Burly, too poor to drink enough to get drunk, they now stirred, disgruntled as bears.

The barkeep set two tankards down and asked for payment, but neither soldier offered up any coins. They collected their tankards and drank.

The four brothers now stood, and the scrape of chairs brought the two soldiers around. Both men were smiling as they reached for their swords.

'Want to play, then?' the first soldier asked, drawing his blade.

On seeing the weapon, the brothers hesitated at their table. None carried weapons of any sort.

Serap rose, stepped out from the gloom. When the soldiers saw her, their expressions went flat. She approached them.

'Sir,' the second soldier said. 'It wasn't going anywhere.'

'Oh but it was,' Serap replied. 'It was going right where you wanted it to go. How many are waiting outside?'

The man started, and then offered her a lopsided grin. 'There's been rumours, sir, of Deniers, hanging out in the town. Spies.'

The first soldier added, 'Had a squad-mate get stabbed

258

nearby, sir, just the other night. He never saw who jumped him. We're fishing for knives, that's all.'

'Hebla got himself stuck by a fellow soldier,' Serap said. 'The man cheats at knuckles, a game none of the locals can afford to play with Legion soldiers. What company are you two in?'

'Ninth, sir, in Hallyd Bahann's Silvers.'

'His Silvers.' Serap smiled. 'How Hallyd likes his pompous nick-names.'

The second soldier said, 'We'll be sure to let our captain know how you feel about them nicknames, sir.'

'Is that a prick of the blade, soldier? Well then, when you do tell Hallyd, be sure to hang around, in case your mention reminds him of when I laughed outright in his face. Silvers, Golds! Why not shave your heads and call yourself Pearls? Or, for the more useless ones in your company, the Shiny Rocks? Well, I'm afraid my laughter snapped his temper, the poor man. Easily done, of course, as you will find.'

She watched them, noting how both men struggled to work out how they might respond to her. The prospect of violence was not far away. After all, if this officer had insulted their commander, might they not earn Hallyd's backing should that officer's blood be spilled? Indeed, had she not just provoked them, calling into question their company's honour?

When the first soldier adjusted the grip of his sword, Serap smiled and stepped close to him, one hand reaching up as if to caress the side of his face. Seeing his confusion, her smile broadened, even as she drove her knee up and into his crotch.

Whatever crunched there sent the man to the filthy floor like a dropped sack of turnips.

Serap was already turning, sending her left elbow into the face of the second soldier, breaking his nose. The rush of pleasure she felt as the man's head snapped back was almost alarming. In a flash, she realized that her own fury had been building for some time, seeking an outlet – any outlet.

She was now moving back, to acquire the proper distance. A kick with the side of her boot, at a downward angle, to strike the broken-nosed soldier's left leg, just below the knee, yielded another satisfying pop. Howling, the man collapsed.

The tavern door was shoved open and three more soldiers rushed in. Serap faced them.

'Stand down!' She pointed to the foremost soldier, a woman she thought she recognized, although the name escaped her. 'Collect up your squad-mates, corporal. Drawing a sword on an officer of the Legion is a capital offence – disarm this one here and place him under arrest. I am off to have a word with your captain, as it seems he is losing control of his Silvers.'

The corporal's eyes were wide, and then she said, 'Yes sir. Our apologies, sir. There was word of insurgents in this tavern—'

'A reason to pick a fight with the locals, you mean. I have not yet decided how many of you will end up charged. I suppose it depends on what you do next, corporal, doesn't it?'

The three newcomers were quick in carrying off their fallen comrades.

When they were gone, Serap selected a coin from her purse and set it on the bartop. 'For their ales,' she said, before striding over to where stood the four young brothers. 'Listen to me, you fools. When two soldiers come in wearing swords, you leave them be. Understand? First off, they're not on their own. Second, they're thirsty for blood. Am I making myself clear?'

Nods answered her.

'Good, now sit down and order a round – the tab is mine.' She then returned to her table.

Settled into the shadows once more, Serap waited for her bloodlust to pass. The silence had things to say about that, but she was in no mood to pay attention to it, right now. Alas, it was persistent. *It is afflicting us all, this growing anger, and how it so easily answers all that ails us, all that haunts us, and all that frightens us.*

*I wanted a fight as much as they did.*

*Oh, banner of white, you came in with such a swagger, I wanted to see it stained red. If only to make a point.*

*Now, if only I could work out what that point was, we
could close out the night and be done with it.*

\*　　\*　　\*

'It was awful,' the man said. 'I – I can't get it out of my skull,
that's all.' And he leaned forward where he sat on her cot,
hiding his face in his hands.

Renarr studied him for a moment, and then moved to her
trunk. 'I have some wine here,' she said, flipping back the lid
and reaching inside.

'Gives me a headache,' the man said behind his hands.

'Then remove your clothing, and we can forget this world
for a time.'

'No.'

'Soldier, what do you want from me?'

His hands dropped away from his face, but he refused to
meet her eyes. 'Around the campfire, with people you fight
beside – people you fight *for*, in fact – well, you'd think we
could talk about anything. But it's not so.'

Renarr poured herself a goblet of wine, settled the trunk's
lid back down and sat upon it. 'Even words aren't free,' she
said.

'I know. I'll pay you ... for your time. If that's
acceptable.'

She considered his offer. 'I'm not your mother,' she said.
'Nor your wife. When I spoke of escaping this world for a
time, I meant it as much for me as for you. But I suppose my
side of the bargain rarely occurs to any of you, does it? After
all, you pay to answer your needs, not the whore's.' She waved
a hand as he made to rise from the cot. 'You need not go.
What your coin buys from me is mostly up to you. That is the
point I was trying to make. But I was also warning you – I
have no special wisdom, no worthy advice. I cannot light
your path, soldier.'

'Then what can you do?'

'I can listen. For the coin. As I said, you are paying for
what you need.'

He shot her a look, and she could not but see his youth, his

261

child's eyes so terribly trapped in a man's body and a soldier's armour. 'You're a cold one, aren't you?'

'Yes,' she replied. 'I suppose I am.'

'It may be what I need,' he said, looking upon the floor of the tent, his hands now clasped together but restless. 'Hard judgement. Righteous condemnation.'

She sipped the wine. It was on the turn. 'High words,' she said, 'for a soldier.'

'There were three boys in the forest camp. Young, not one taller than my hip. We were three squads. Fourth, Seventh, Second. Well, when we were done with the mother, some of the men – they went for the boys, too. Those boys . . . it wasn't me who cut their throats, when it was done, but I wish it had been. I wish the mercy had been mine to offer them.' He was trembling now, his entire body, making the cot creak. The words had rushed out, and she could see in his eyes that there was no going back. 'I didn't touch them, those boys. I could never have done anything like that. But now, all the time, they're with me. The looks on their faces when we . . . when we did what we did to the mother. And then, the shock when we turned on them, too. Blank faces, like dolls . . .'

He wept.

Renarr remained sitting on the trunk, confused. Did this soldier want comfort? Or did he indeed seek condemnation? It was clear that crimes had been committed. Urusander would see those men hanged. In fact, it was possible that all three squads would dance on the rope. Her adoptive father was famous for his righteous outrage. 'Have you reported this to your captain?' she asked.

The blunt, toneless question met the man's grief and swept it aside. She might as well have struck him across the face. Wiping at his eyes, straightening where he sat, he glared across at her. 'Is that a joke? The bitch sent us into that camp! She could hear that mother's screams from where she lounged in the next glade! Oh, and what was she doing while we murdered that family?'

'Never mind,' Renarr cut in, before the soldier could tell her what his captain had been up to. Renarr already knew enough to guess who the woman was. 'And,' she added, 'obviously, Hunn Raal is not, strictly speaking, next on the chain of command. Is he? No, it's the captains made equal, with only Urusander above them.'

The man abruptly stood, began pacing. 'You can't know,' he said. 'Hiding out here. Can you?'

She felt herself grow cold, and struggled to still her shaking hand as she drank again from the goblet. 'You know who I am,' she said. 'You sought me out, thinking . . . what? That I would take this to Urusander? It was in your head – why, I have no idea – that my father and I still acknowledge each other. How did you work this out? Oh, he sends her down to the whore camps because she's bored, the dear lass. Is it not what a father would do?'

He stopped pacing, and sat again, looking away. 'Then deliver his justice yourself, Renarr. With your own hand! This heart wants to still its infernal beat! My bones close around it – I can barely breathe. I swear, those raped children – they've found me. Haunting me day and night now. It's not what I signed up for, don't you see? Not in my vow of service to the realm!'

'It would seem that by far the most righteous punishment for you, soldier, is to leave you alive. Haunted by guilt for the rest of your years. You flee the ghosts of three raped boys, do you? Even when you did not take part? Well, how sad for you.'

He glared at her now, visage darkening. 'I'm not paying for contempt.'

'Oh, I am sorry. I was trying to make a point. It was clearly fine, then, that you raped the mother. Her ghost wanders elsewhere, one presumes. But those poor boys, with you watching on! Like botflies they're now under your skin, gnawing their way into your heart. Of course, they were the ones watching you, at least at first, while you fucked their screaming mother.'

He stood, reaching for his weapon-belt. 'For this, I'll pay you nothing.'

'For this,' she retorted, 'I will not be a coward's path. You know the way to the keep, soldier. I am sure Urusander is there even now. And yes, he will accept an audience with a soldier of his legion.'

'My squad-mates—'

'Oh yes, them. Why, they'll know, of course, once the charges are brought down. I see now why you thought it best to go through me. In that instance, you all stand accused, and all face the same punishment. You stand with your brothers and sisters, and not once do they question you or your loyalty.' Renarr finished her wine.

'It's not cowardice,' the young soldier said.

'Isn't it? Your entire tale is one of cowardly acts, from the moment you rode into the forest, hunting Deniers. Slaughtering women and children? Setting their homes ablaze? Entire companies, so brave in how you outnumbered your every opponent, and set swords to their flimsy spears and whatnot. Your armour against their thin hides. Your iron helms and their oh-so-fragile skulls.'

He drew his gutting knife.

She met his gaze, unafraid, understanding what this night had brought to her. 'So be it,' she said quietly. 'Give me, then, your one moment of courage.'

With a savage slash – beneath eyes suddenly triumphant – the soldier cut his own throat. Blood poured out, rushing from the severed jugular.

He toppled and she stepped back.

*He made of this whore's tent a temple, and me his priestess. Or, at least, someone to stand in for his god – as priestesses are purported to do. He uttered his crimes . . .* But the body lying on the floor beside her cot, so motionless now when an instant earlier it had been bursting with life – she could not tear her gaze from it.

*There are ways of leaving. The worst of these is also the most final. You see, the bastard left, yet left his body behind. Why does the thought make me want to laugh? Guests will leave a mess, won't they just? It falls to the host to see it cleaned up.*

*I am no priestess. This is no temple. But the confessions*

*spill out night after night – none as bleak as this one, to be sure. But it was coming. I should have seen that. The fools have blood on their hands, guilt in their souls. The High Priestess of High House Light isn't much interested in all that, alas. And their mothers are far away.*

*It is, I see now, an issue of faith. Faith and faiths, the natural ones and the other kinds, the imposed kinds.*

She recalled the aftermath of the battle against the Wardens, and all the cries from the soldiers left dying on the field, while the whores and looters walked among them. So many had called out, like children, for their mothers. Their god, or goddess, was too remote for them, in that drawn-out journey into death. It was a faith they'd dropped away from, abandoned. What was left, if not the purest, the sweetest of all faiths? *'Mother! Please! Help me! Hold me!'*

Renarr had been witness to all that, there amidst the heaped bodies and the stench. But her memories of her own mother offered nothing. Too vague, too formless, making that ethereal, half-imagined figure almost godlike.

*Wrong faith, then. Not one for me to call upon, not now, not later. Not even at the very end, I should think.*

But these soldiers, they were far from their mothers, and few were able to reach their wives or husbands, assuming they had any. Failed by the High Priestess and that remote and strangely sinister temple they were even now building, and its god so bright as to blind all who might gaze upon it. Failed, too, that faith in the mother always close, always a short tear-filled run away, her arms opening wide to collect up the wayward child. Faiths, then, failed and failed again. What was left?

*The whore, of course. Confused and confusing idol. Priestess and mother, lover and goddess, and all faith reduced to the basest of needs, one simple game to play out all the infernal wars of power. Astonishing, isn't it, what a few coins can purchase?*

Renarr collected up her heaviest cloak, and strode out from her tent. She set out from the whores' camp where it clung to one side of the Legion's outermost earthworks, and made her way along the embankment. Ahead, the dull, muted lights of Neret Sorr, and beyond that, the high hill of Urusander's fortress.

Men had a way of filling her up, it seemed. He had sought her out, to make her his hand of justice. She had refused him to his face, and in answer to that he had taken his own life. She recalled the triumph in his eyes at that final moment, at the gift his own knife gave to him. There was something in those young eyes that fascinated her.

*What did he see, I wonder? What avenue opened before him? A sudden way through, an escape from all the torment? Or was it just the venal act of a selfish child, wanting to somehow punish the woman standing before him . . . just passing the guilt along, as cowards will do.*

*Well, in that he failed. The poor, misguided fool.*

But there was some irony, she decided, in that she now found herself walking into Neret Sorr, and that fell keep looming above it.

*Dear Father. I bring word of hidden temples where your soldiers confess their crimes. I stand before you, a much-used priestess, carrying in me a soldier's plaintive cry for absolution . . . well, a few hundred soldiers and a few thousand plaintive cries. They have lost their faiths, you see. All of them, barring the renting of my flesh, thus relieving us all with assurance that, in coin, at least, one kind of faith remains secure.*

*This is how the power of the bargain wins out against all other powers. Tell the High Priestess to pay heed. Invite confessions amidst handfuls of coin, to ensure that the believers understand how this deal gets made. They'll grasp the notion quickly enough, until every temple is sheathed in gold.*

*But tell her, also, to do nothing with such confessions. Mouth the proper words of absolution, if she must, but set out no course of hard justice, or proper retribution. Dead sinners are no longer generous, after all, and no longer impelled to rent for a time the easement of their guilt. Take it from a whore, dear Syntara, it's about renting, not purchasing.*

She walked through the town. Frost limned the muddy

ground, the walls of buildings. Overhead, the stars ever in their place, forever silent, eternally witnessing. She had grown to appreciate their remoteness. *Whore as goddess and goddess as whore. Oh, how confused your worship, yes? Never mind. It all works out in the end – I saw as much in that soldier's eyes.*

*   *   *

There had been a smithy below the keep's hill, but its owner had died. The house, sheds and outbuildings had been torn down, along with flanking houses, to make room for the new Temple of Light. Hunn Raal was amused when he thought of the scorched earth awaiting the foundation stones, the heaps of ash, clinkers and cinders; the ragged tailings and sand-studded droplets now hard and brittle as glass.

Few understood the manifold expressions of the sacred that so cluttered the world on all sides. Few had the wits to see them. Kurald Galain, after all, was born of fires, of forges and vast forests of fuel awaiting the heat and smoke of industry. Pits in the ground, veins of ore, streams of sweat and dripping blood, the straining struggles of so many men and women to make of life something better, if not for themselves, then for their children.

Fitting, then, to raise a temple upon such holy ground. Not that Syntara would ever comprehend that. She was intent, he now understood, upon a narrowing of the sacred, threateningly surrounded by a wild, chaotic proliferation of the profane. Once all such potential threats were eliminated – indeed, desecrated – then, why, she would hold within her embrace all that was sacred.

Religion, Hunn Raal decided, was the marriage of holiness with base acquisitiveness, self-defined and purposefully delineated to eliminate natural worship – worship lying beyond the temple walls, beyond the rules, the prohibitions. Lying beyond – more to the point – the self-pronounced authority of whatever priesthood arose to manage, with grubby hands, the sacredness of things. *And, incidentally, getting rich on the proceeds.*

Well, he understood High Priestess Syntara. It wasn't difficult. He even understood the Deniers, and the threat they posed, with their open faith – with the way they made all things in their lives holy, from whittling down a tent stake to singing and dancing under the light of full moons. Even the Shake temples saw those forest-dwelling savages as a threat to whatever privileges the monks and nuns claimed as their own. Which was, if one considered it, ridiculous, since those savages of the wood were, in fact, the Shake's congregation, their blessed children.

*Oh, that's right. Their blessed children. Real children, that is, the ones they could steal, I mean. Never mind the mothers and fathers. Just the children, please, for our blessed ranks.*

He took another mouthful of wine, swirled it through the gaps in his teeth, then pulling it back to flow over his tongue one more time, before swallowing. Thus. He understood Syntara and her pious High House of Light. He understood the Deniers, too, and the Shake.

*But not Mother Dark. Not this empty darkness and its unlit temple, its unseen altar and invisible throne. Not this worship of absence. Dear Emral Lanear, I do sympathize. Really. Your task is nigh impossible, isn't it, whilst your goddess says nothing. In that despairing silence, why, I too might decide to take to my bed as many lovers as I could. To fill up all those empty spaces, the ones inside and out.*

*Well, Urusander old friend, you can have her. If you can find her, that is.*

*Rest assured, Syntara will bring light to the scene. Enough to expose the conjugal bed, at least. She'll wave a hand and deem it a blessing. As if you two were children who would only fumble helplessly in the dark.*

*Wed the two, then. Urusander's fiery bright cock. Into her unlit cunt. Maybe that union was always holy, now that I think on it. A man's raging light, a woman's purest dark. We men, we do have a thing for caves, and other comforting places. Our womb, from which we were so ignominiously thrown out. To then spend a lifetime trying to crawl back – but what is it that we truly seek? Sanctuary, or oblivion?*

Glancing down, he pushed the maid's head away from his crotch. 'Oh, give it up, will you? I've drunk too much tonight.'

She glanced up at him, just a flicker's worth of eye contact, and then she rolled on to her side.

'Amuse yourself,' Hunn Raal said.

*Now, dear Syntara, let's discuss the notion of murder, shall we? Shall we paint your temple blood red? Or should we wait a few generations first? At the very least, set the engineers to fashion ingenious gutters to channel a flow you would wish endless.*

*And yet, you decried my seeming thirst. Border guards, Wardens, Deniers. The Hust. I am indeed soaked with blood. All necessary, alas. We'll save the Shake for later. The nobles need humiliating first. Anomander and his brothers brought to their knees. Draconus sent packing – although, between you and me, Syntara, I admit to some admiration for the Consort. Now there's a man unafraid of darkness! So unafraid as to climb back into the womb and make of it the finest palace of delight!*

*It's no wonder his nobleborn kin so envy him, enough to foment abiding hatred. Yes, of course we'll make use of that, given the chance. Still . . . poor Draconus. No man deserves your fate, to be twice cast out of the womb.*

Lying beside him, back arching, the maid made moaning noises, and gasps. But the ecstasy sounded forced. *This lass would have done fine as a priestess, I think. Too bad.*

*Oh, Syntara, we were speaking of murder, weren't we? And all the paths to and from its grisly gate. And here is my promise: when we're done with our task; when at last Lord Urusander stands beside Mother Dark, the two wedded . . . do not expect a third throne, Syntara – not for you and not for your church. If we can scour out the wretched Deniers and the Shake – if we can burn them into ash and cinders – do you imagine we could not do the same to you?*

*By fire, this gift of light, no?*

He had explored the newfound sorcery within him, with far greater alacrity than he had led Syntara to believe. Enough to know that the woman pleasuring herself beside him in this bed was nothing but a husk. And this in turn amused him greatly, as the secret spark within the maid – Syntara herself – now struggled to bring life back into that body's benumbed carcass.

*Go screw yourself, Syntara. Or, rather, go on screwing yourself. We have all night, after all.*

He recalled that flicker – the meeting of his gaze with hers – and the faint unease in the maid's once pretty eyes. *I imagine you first crowed at my seeming impotence. But now, do you begin to wonder?*

*I may be base. A drunk. A man standing in the middle of a river of blood. But I won't fuck a corpse, woman. Take your voyeur games elsewhere.*

*When next we meet, over fine wine and decent food, we'll talk of . . . oh, I don't know . . . how about this as a worthy topic? Yes, why not? We'll speak of desecration. A topic on which, I'm sure, you'll have plenty to say, High Priestess.*

*Tell me again, won't you, of those artful gutters beneath the floors of the temple?*

*And I might speak to you, perhaps, of sorcery beyond the reach of any god or goddess, beyond the reach of every temple, every church, every priesthood with all its strident rules and lust for the butchery of the blasphemous.*

*A magic unfettered. Natural worship, if you will.*

*Of what, you ask?*

*Why, the same as yours, High Priestess. The worship of power.*

*This power – and I dare you to take it from my hand.*

He drank down another mouthful of wine, sluicing it as was his habit, while beside him – making the bed creak – the maid went on and on, and on.

\*     \*     \*

Sharenas strode into the tavern. After a moment, she could make out a figure seated at the back, shrouded in gloom. She crossed the chamber, threading between tables where townsfolk were seated, welcoming both the sour heat and the furtive glances. Even the faces of strangers offered a kind of comfort – too long riding alone, camping in wild places, abandoned places. And other nights, as guest in a household, she had felt the pressure of her hosts' unease, their mistrust. Urusander's Legion, once elevated so high, honoured and respected by all, had stumbled fast.

The truth, which in better times was happily ignored, was that the sword always cut both ways. Valiant defence, brutal attack, it was all down to the wielder's stance, the direction chosen. The saved could become the victim in an instant.

Sharenas disliked the notion: that she, too, was dangerous, unpredictable, with the weapon at her belt ever ready to be unsheathed. But the world made its demands, and she too must answer them.

Reaching the table, she met Captain Serap's eyes, seeing in them a cold, glittering regard. Sharenas sat opposite, her back to the room. 'Captain. I am sorry for your losses.'

'We were all there,' Serap said. 'Do you remember? Riding out to meet Calat Hustain. You chose Kagamandra's side for most of that journey, as I recall. Happy enough to flirt with a promised man.'

Sharenas nodded. 'Whilst you and your sisters giggled and whispered, so pleased with your new ranks. Lieutenants, back then, as I recall. Unblooded officers, crowded under Hunn Raal's soggy wing.'

Serap studied her with a tilted head, and then smiled wistfully. 'We were young then. The world seemed fresh. Alive with possibilities.'

'Oh, he was happy enough to lead us, wasn't he?' Sharenas started as someone stepped close – a boy, likely the barkeep's son, setting down a tankard before her. The youth quickly retreated. 'Do you still look upon him with admiration, Serap? Cousin Hunn Raal. Murderer, poisoner. He's gathered every betrayal imaginable into a single knot, hasn't he?'

Serap shook her head, and then shrugged. 'It may seem to be clumsy on his part, Sharenas. But it isn't. Every crime he commits ensures that Urusander remains unstained. My cousin doesn't hide, does he? He chooses to wear his culpability, and knows that he can bear its terrible weight. It is, in fact, a family trait.'

'Hmm. I'd wondered about that. The seeming clumsiness, that is. It would be easy to assume the drunkard's natural carelessness, the sloppiness that comes with dissolution. Even so, Serap – the slaughter of a wedding party?'

Serap waved a hand, and then frowned. 'Not the Hust? You surprise me. Or perhaps not, as the noble blood in you must howl loudest when the lives of kin are sacrificed. Mundane soldiers, even ones bearing demon-haunted weapons, are beneath notice – well, maybe a mutter or two, if only at the crassness of the deed.'

Sharenas allowed herself a slow smile. 'I always judged you the sharpest. So, is this how it is, then? You stand with Hunn Raal.'

'Blood of kin, Sharenas. But you should understand this. In so many ways I still have the eyes of the innocent. I will care for my soldiers. I will, if necessary, give my life for theirs.'

'Bold words,' Sharenas replied, nodding. 'I'm curious. Do you believe Hunn Raal would do the same?'

Something fluttered in Serap's eyes, and the woman glanced away. 'Have you reported to the commander?'

'I have spoken to Urusander, yes.'

'Does he remain . . . disinterested?'

A curious question. Sharenas collected up her tankard, drank down a mouthful of the weak ale, and grimaced. 'You do not come here for this, do you?'

'Supplies are low. Everyone has to make do.'

'How would you react, I wonder, if I now told you that Vatha Urusander intends to arrest Hunn Raal, and a good many other captains of the Legion? And that I bear with me the evidence of their many crimes – crimes that can only be answered by the gallows.'

Serap laughed.

Settling back in her chair, Sharenas nodded. 'And this was a man we once followed, unquestioningly. A man we would give up our lives for. Back when the enemy was foreign. Well, as you say, Serap, we were all young once, and that was long ago.'

'Best you choose your side, Sharenas, with great care. He is not the man he once was. In many ways,' she added, 'we'd do better with Osserc.'

'He has not returned, then.'

'No. And no word of where he has gone.'

Sharenas glanced away. 'I have advised against confronting Hunn Raal. For the moment.'

'Wise.'

'Things need cleaning up first.'

Serap's brows lifted. 'Oh? And how will you manage that?'

Sharenas rose in one fluid motion, the blade leaving the scabbard with a hiss, and then lashing out across the table, taking Serap by the neck. The keen edge cut through, separating the woman's head from her shoulders. As the head pitched forward to thump hard on the tabletop, blood shot from the stump of Serap's neck, like a fountain in a courtyard. But the pulsing torrent was shortlived.

Sharenas stepped around the table and gathered up a corner of Serap's cloak. She carefully wiped down her blade. Behind her, in the tavern, there was absolute silence.

'Like this,' she answered quietly. She studied the head lying on the table, the look of surprise fast fading as all life left the eyes, as the nerves of the face surrendered, slowly sagging. It was, she decided, a rather innocent face.

Sharenas sheathed her sword, and then drained the tankard and set it down beside the head. She drew out a coin and snapped it down, and then swung about and strode from the tavern.

It was a start. She had a long night ahead of her.

Outside once more, shivering in the bitter cold night air, she set out for the Legion camp.

\*       \*       \*

'Shit.' Hunn Raal sat up on the bed. The wine was heavy and acrid in his gut, but the sickness suddenly roaring in his skull had little to do with that.

Beside him, the nameless maid stirred, and said in a slurred voice, 'What is it?'

He twisted round, reached out and took hold of the young woman's neck. It felt flimsy in his grip. 'Look at me, High Priestess. Are you there?' He then grunted. 'Yes, I see that you are. Blood has been spilled. Blood of my family. Someone has murdered Serap. Down in the town.'

The maid's childlike face, round and soft, was darkening above Hunn Raal's grip. Voice now rasping, she said, 'Best awaken the guards, then.'

Face twisting with disgust, Hunn Raal pushed the woman away, hard enough to send her over the far side of the bed. He quickly threw on his clothes, and strapped on his sword-belt. He paused then, weaving slightly. 'No, enough of this.' A pulse of sorcerous power, held inside, made him suddenly sober.

The maid had climbed to her feet on the other side of the bed, her naked body ghostly pale. 'How did you do that?'

Snarling, he spun to face her. 'Get out.' Another surge of sorcery, reaching into the body facing him, grasping hold of that secretive sliver of Syntara, and then tearing it loose, flinging it away like a torn rag. The maid collapsed.

*Oh, a fine new rumour for Hunn Raal now – he kills the women he fucks. Strangles them, by the marks round the poor girl's neck. Well, yet another sordid cloak to wear. These burdens are enough to make a man drink.*

He gathered up a fur-lined cape, and then strode from the bed-chamber.

Two guards stood at the far end of the corridor. Hunn Raal marched towards them. 'Pult, rouse a squad to guard Vatha Urusander's private chambers. If he wakes to the noise, inform him that we have an assassin in the town below, but that I have begun the hunt. Mirril, you're with me.'

As Pult set off towards the troop hall, Mirril fell in a step behind Hunn Raal as he made his way to the keep's central staircase.

'There's a dead woman in my bedroom,' he told her. 'Never mind the rumours that'll come of that. The High Priestess of

Light has a growing thirst for corpses – not that you can easily tell who's dead and who isn't, once she's done with them. Look for the eyes, Mirril – they don't match the face around them.'

The soldier made an obscure warding gesture.

'Just get rid of it,' Hunn Raal ordered. 'No family to inform, I should think. Bury her in the refuse heap below the kitchen chute.'

'And if, uh, she comes back to life again, sir?'

He grunted. 'I doubt that – I wasn't fooled, you see. But still . . . oh, take off its legs, then. Arms, too.'

'Sir, I would advise the hog pens, rather than the heap.'

He glanced back at her as they reached the top of the stairs. 'And the next slice of ham you eat, Mirril? How will it sit? No, the notion doesn't appeal to me. Perhaps a shallow grave, then. Pick people you trust in this.'

'Of course, sir.'

'And let the soldiers know – no one from the High Priestess's household can be trusted.'

'That's past saying, sir.'

They reached the main floor opposite the front doors. 'Good,' said Hunn Raal. 'Off you go, then.'

'Yes sir.'

He left her to take care of the maid and set out across the compound towards the barracks. By rota, a company of Hallyd Bahann's Golds were quartered there, five squads in all. Two guards stood at post outside the barracks entrance, both coming to attention upon seeing Hunn Raal approach.

'Wake the lieutenant,' Hunn Raal said to one of them, and then he beckoned the other closer. 'Saddle up, soldier, and take this word down to the Legion camp. We're on the hunt for an assassin – someone has just murdered my cousin, Serap. In the town proper. I want two companies to enter Neret Sorr and begin looking for the body. We can pick up the trail from there, if need be. Though,' he added, 'I doubt it will be necessary.' Seeing the questioning look on the man's face, Hunn Raal said, 'I doubt she's the only intended target this night, soldier.' Pausing, hands on his hips, he faced the gatehouse. 'Civil wars are dirty, but we need to hold fast to our cause.'

Led by the lieutenant – a young man Hunn Raal did not know – the Golds emerged from the barracks, still buckling on their gear, a few of them swearing at the bitter chill.

'Lieutenant,' Hunn Raal said, 'shape up your soldiers, and be smart about it. One squad remains on station here. The rest of you, we're marching down into Neret Sorr.' He gestured at the lieutenant to join him, and then set out, at a brisk pace, towards the gatehouse, and the switchback track that led down into the town.

*　　*　　*

Renarr had time to step into a shadow-thick alcove at the gatehouse before the gates swung wide and a rider emerged, pushing his horse into a careless gallop as soon as he was clear of the gate. An instant later a company of soldiers, led by Hunn Raal, appeared, moving at a quick pace. When the last soldiers in the column were past, she waited a few moments longer, and then walked back on to the track, just as the gatehouse guards were pushing at the squealing gate. One cursed upon seeing her, clearly frightened by her sudden appearance. She moved forward.

'Who's that, then?' the other guard asked, holding up a staying hand.

'Renarr. Summoned by my father.'

She saw, as lanterns were drawn close, both recognition and suspicion. They would have known, after all, if Urusander had dispatched any messenger down into Neret Sorr. But then one grunted and said to the other, 'Captain Sharenas left earlier.'

This man looked enquiringly at Renarr, who solemnly nodded.

They waved her through. 'Not a good night,' the first guard said as she passed. 'Killings in town below, we heard. Black-skinned assassins, agents of Lord Anomander. Officers of the Legion getting backstabbed. It's what it's come to.'

'Best stay here at the keep tonight,' called out the other guard.

She continued on.

There were lights in the tower, where Urusander kept his private abode. She thought she saw a dark shape move past a window, but could not be sure. The courtyard was slippery underfoot, slick with frost. She glanced over at the squad mustered up near the barracks, and saw some of them watching her as she crossed to the keep's main entrance.

She'd probably taken a few of them to her bed, but at this distance, and in the uneven light, there was no way to tell.

*Father, I should tell you. I have intimate knowledge of your legion, its soldiers, with their myriad faces, their singular needs. I know them better than you. It's how certain things blur together, you see. The heat of sex and the heat of battle. Death entwined with love, or something like love, if we are generous enough to gauge the motions, there beneath the furs.*

*Tents and temples, beds and altars, the propitiations and rituals, all the forms of confession, weakness and desire. The conceits and pride's fragile temerity. All the appetites, Father, flow together in those times, those places. I could list for you the cowards, and the ones who would stand fast. I could speak to you about conscience and grief, and above all, about what a soldier needs.*

*Alas, that need no mortal can answer, though I can see you, Father, I can see you trying. When few others would dare.*

*Shall we give it a name, that need? Dare we venture inward, to face that sorrowful child?*

*Tent and temple, we raise them to disguise all that haunts our soul. Between lover and priest, I think, it is the lover who can reach closest to that shivering, wide-eyed child. The priest, ah, well, the priest killed his inner child long ago, and now but plays at wonder, dancing joy's steps with shuffling, self-conscious feet.*

*Consider this, Father. No whore has ever sexually abused a child. I know this – I watch them, my hard women and*

*men of the stained cloth. Some are harsh bitches and bastards,
no doubt about that. Hardened beyond pain. For all that,
they know innocence when they see it.*

*But priests? Most are fine, I'm sure. Honest, diligent,
trustworthy. But what of those few others who took on the
robes and vestments for unholy reasons? What do they see
– the ones so eager to ruin a child?*

*Best ask the High Priestess, Father, because I have no
answer to that question. All I know, and I know this with
certainty, is that inside that abusing bastard priest there is
the corpse of a child. Wanting company.*

She was in the house now, upon the stairs, reaching the
landing and making her way towards Urusander's wing of
the keep.

Soldiers stood at guard in the corridor. They eyed her
warily as she approached.

'My father is awake,' she said. 'Captain Sharenas summoned
me to him, at his request.'

They moved aside.

One spoke as she passed. 'Taking the night off, Renarr?'

Low laughter, dying away when she opened the door and
strode into the first chamber.

A desk buried beneath scrolls and the strange seashell cases
the Forulkan used to store their sacred writing. Behind this
misshapen monument, her adoptive father. He had half risen
at her appearance, and now, upon his weary face, there was
the look of a cornered man.

She recognized that expression: she had seen it on occasion
in her tent. Indeed, she had seen it this very night.

Renarr unclasped her cloak and folded it carefully against
the back of a chair. Then she walked over to a side table. 'The
last wine I had this evening,' she said, taking up a decanter
and sniffing at the mouth, 'was sour.' She poured herself a
glass. 'Father,' she said, turning to face him, 'I have so many
things to say to you.'

He would not meet her gaze, intent instead on a scroll laid
out before him. 'It's rather late for a conversation,' he said.

'If you mean the time of night, then, yes, perhaps.'

'I did not mean the time of night.'

'Oh, that bulwark,' she said, sighing. 'I know why you threw it up, of course. Your love for my mother, and what did I do? I went into the camps, into the taverns, to learn a trade. Was I punishing you? Perhaps I was simply bored. Or at that age where rebellion seems a good idea, an idea full of . . . ideals. So many of us, at around my age, will flare bright, with the vague, despondent understanding that it will all fade. Our fire. Our nerve. The belief that it all means something.'

He studied her at last, with the heaped desk between them.

'Osserc is out there,' Renarr continued, 'flaring bright. Somewhere. Me, I didn't walk that far.'

'Then, Renarr, is your . . . rebellion . . . at an end?'

Was that hope she saw in his eyes? She couldn't be sure. 'Father, I can't give you my reasons. But I know what my choices yielded, beyond this much-used body. My mother was an officer in your company. I was her daughter, held apart from her beloved legion. So, I knew nothing of it, nothing of a soldier's ways, nothing of my mother's ways.' She sipped the wine. 'What she did to me, and what you did to Osserc . . . well, of your children, one of us at last understands your reasons.'

She did not think there was enough in her words to make his eyes glisten, and the sudden emotion, so exposed and raw in Urusander, shocked her.

Looking away, Renarr set down the goblet. 'A young soldier of the Legion came to me tonight. He came, not for my cheap gifts of love, but to confess his crimes. Slaughter of innocents. Terrible rapes. A mother, her young boys. He named the squads and the company. Then he stood before me, and cut his own throat.'

Urusander rose from behind the desk. Then he was directly before her. He moved as if to reach out, to take her into something like an embrace, but something held him back.

'Father,' she said, 'you have troubled children.'

'I will make amends, Renarr. I promise you. I will make amends!'

She would not yield her heart to him, lest it sting with pity. In any case, such feelings within her had sunk into the depths. She did not think she would see them again. 'Your High Priestess, Father, needs to understand – her temple, the faith she offers, it needs to be more than it is. Speak to her, Father, speak to her of hope. It's not all there simply to serve her. She needs to give something back.'

She stepped away, retrieving her goblet. She drained it, and then went to her cloak. 'My bed is not the place for confessions, especially the bloody kind. As for absolution,' she turned and offered him a faint smile, 'well, that will have to wait. There are things remaining, Father, that I still need to learn.'

The man looked wretched, but then he slowly straightened and met her eye, and nodded. 'I will wait, Renarr.'

She felt that promise like a blow to her chest, and quickly angled away, to struggle with her cloak and fumble at the clasps.

Behind her, Urusander said, 'Take your old room tonight, Renarr. Just this night. There are dire events in the town below.'

She hesitated, and then nodded. 'This night, then. Very well.'

'And Renarr, tomorrow morning, I would hear from you the details of that young soldier.'

'Of course.' But he would not. She would be gone with the dawn.

*Bedrooms of girls and boys. All the way to tents and temples. Whoever could have imagined the distance possible between them, all in the span of a handful of years?*

\*     \*     \*

Silann walked through the camp, hunched over against the cold. His wife's new habit of sending him on errands, delivering messages, along with a host of other demeaning tasks, was growing stale. He understood the nature of this punishment, and to begin with he had almost welcomed the escape from her company. Better than weathering the contempt in

280

her eyes, the myriad ways of dismissal she had perfected in his presence.

Command was a talent, and he was not foolish enough to believe that he possessed it in abundance. Mistakes had been made, but thus far there had been no obvious, or direct, repercussions. That was fortunate and Silann had sensed a rebirth of possibilities, the way ahead opening up. He would do better next time. He would show Esthala that she had not married the wrong man.

Still, an angry woman carved deep trenches, and pulling her from them would not be an easy task. But he would make her see him in a new way, no matter what it took.

There had been that boy, that escape. And Gripp Galas. Back then, there was pressure, with choices that needed making, the kind of pressure that could stagger anyone in the same situation. Blood to be spilled, and then quickly buried. Moments of panic could take the surest officer.

Well, they were past that now. She was holding this grudge far too long. No one deserved the disgust she seemed so determined to level upon him, not after all these years of marriage. *Uneventful marriage. No crises, and a son – true, he's rejected the soldier's path, but surely we can forgive him that, if only to accept, finally, that his is a weak soul, a soft soul, too tender for most professions, and we well know the harshness of an army's culture. Its cruelties.*

*No, it's all for the better, Esthala, and all this contempt – for me, for our son, for so many others – it offers no useful salve to your life. You must see that.*

*To reveal tenderness, darling, is not a confession of weakness. And even if it is, then we must all know that weakness, with someone.*

*You seek to be strong, at all times, in all company. It makes you impatient. It makes you cruel.*

Still, he was done with delivering mundane messages. He would face her down, this night. There were different kinds of strength, after all. He would show her his, and name it love.

He started as a figure joined him, matching his stride. A

glance across revealed a hooded, cloaked form and little else. 'What is it you wish with me, soldier?'

'Ah, forgive me, Silann. It is Captain Sharenas, fighting the cold however I can.'

Though she did not draw back the hood, Silann knew the voice. 'Welcome back, Sharenas. Have you just returned, then?'

'Yes. I was on my way to speak to your wife, in fact.'

*Ah, then . . . well, Esthala and I will need to find another night, I suppose. Tomorrow night, to work things through, to make it better again.* 'She is awake,' Silann said. 'I too am on my way back to her.'

'I assumed as much,' Sharenas said.

The camp was relatively quiet, as the cold bit ever deeper. A few fires were still lit, making lurid islands of orange, yellow and red light. But most tents they passed were dark, tied up, as soldiers slept beneath blankets and, if they were lucky, furs.

'Have you reported to Lord Urusander?' Silann asked.

'I have,' she replied. 'It was . . . extensive. The countryside, Silann, has become a troubled place. Many have died, and few of those were deserving of the violence delivered upon them.'

'That is always the way, in civil war.'

'Worse, of course, when the victims knew nothing of any civil war. When, alas, they were the first ones to fall to it. Knowledge and intention, Silann. In these circumstances, we can name them crimes.'

A faint tremor slipped through Silann. 'Have you . . . have you compiled details, then?'

'As best I could,' Sharenas replied. 'It was difficult, as not everyone was willing to speak to me.' She paused, and they turned down a side avenue, approaching the command tent of Esthala's cohort; then she said, 'But I was fortunate to find some who would.'

'Indeed.'

'Yes. Gripp Galas, for one. And, of course, young Orfantal.'

Silann's steps slowed and he half turned to the woman walking beside him. 'An old man, I'm told, prone to baseless accusations and pointless feuds.'

'Galas? I think not.'

'What then do you wish with my wife?'

'Only what needs doing, Silann. A conversation, just like the one I'm having with you right now.'

When he halted, Sharenas turned back to face him. The hood still hid her features, but he saw the glitter of her eyes. 'This is an unpleasant conversation, Sharenas,' he said. 'I don't think my wife will welcome your presence, not tonight, in any case.'

'No, I suspect you're right in that, Silann. A moment—' She reached for something under her cloak. 'I have something for you.'

He caught a flash of blue iron, felt a sharp sting under his chin, and then it seemed that everything simply drained away.

Blinking, he found himself lying on the ground, with Sharenas bent over him.

It was all . . . strange. Disturbing. He felt a hilt pressed up against the underside of his chin, and something was pouring out from his mouth, sliding thick and hot down his cheeks.

*No. I don't like this. I'm leaving now.* He closed his eyes.

Sharenas pulled the dagger free. She collected Silann by the collar and dragged him between two equipment tents. Then she cleaned her blade on his cloak and sheathed it again.

It was only twenty or so paces to Esthala's tent. Straightening, Sharenas resumed her journey. She reached the front and tapped at the ridge-pole, and then drew back the flap and stepped inside.

There was a brazier on the floor, emanating dry heat and a soft glow. Beyond that, Esthala was on a cot, settled back but still dressed. She looked over and frowned. Sharenas drew back her hood before the woman could speak, and saw a swift change of expression accompany recognition, but not one she could easily read.

'Sharenas! I see you've not yet shed the leagues of travel behind you. But still,' she sat up, 'welcome back. There's mulled wine near that brazier.'

'Your husband will be late, I'm afraid,' Sharenas said, drawing off her cloak. 'I ran into him, on his way up to the keep.'

'The keep? That idiot. I told him to send a rider if he did not find one of her acolytes. He gets nothing right.'

Sharenas collected the pewter jug and poured out two cups of the steaming wine. The sharp smell of almonds wafted up into her face. Leaving one cup where it was, she brought Esthala the other one.

The captain stood to receive it. 'So, what brings you to me, then? And couldn't it wait until the morning?'

Sharenas smiled. 'You are legendary, Esthala, for working through the night. I myself recall, when we arrayed for battle on a clear morning, seeing you heavy with sleep. Quite the harridan, in fact.'

Snorting, Esthala drank.

From the camp outside, distant alarms rang out.

'What now?' Esthala asked, turning to set her cup down on the edge of the cot and reaching, at the same time, for her sword-belt.

'Probably me,' Sharenas replied, drawing her sword.

Esthala caught the faint rasp and whirled.

The sword's blade sliced through the front half of her throat. Sharenas quickly stepped back to avoid most of the blood that sprayed out from the wound.

Esthala stumbled back, both hands grasping at her neck, and fell awkwardly across the cot, snapping one of its legs. As the cot sagged, the woman rolled off it to settle face-down on the tent floor. Her legs twitched for a few moments, and then fell still.

Sharenas quickly sheathed her weapon, cursing under her breath. She had been anticipating most of the night, for the work that needed doing. Instead, the Legion camp was now wide awake. And, in moments, one of Esthala's lieutenants would come to the tent.

Still, there was time – at least for her to make her way to where the horses were kept. *My apologies, Urusander. This hasn't quite worked out as I had planned. And now I must ride away, with a bounty on my head.*

*Not all the nobles are hiding in their keeps, doing nothing. I will defend my blood first, Urusander. Surely you'll understand that. Civil war is a messy business, isn't it? Just ask Gripp Galas.*

The rage within her remained bright and hot. It yielded a fierce, demanding thirst. She had wanted to stalk the night, moving through the camp, from one command tent to the next. *For you, Vatha Urusander. And for Kurald Galain.*

*And another. But he rides far from here now, seeking the woman he would marry. I am relieved, Kagamandra, that you do not see me on this night, nor the trail of blood I have left behind me. And now, alas, I must flee, my work unfinished. And that, my friend, galls.*

With her dagger, she cut through the back wall of the tent, and then slipped out into the night.

*   *   *

Humiliation bred a kind of hunger. Dreams of vengeance and acts of malice. Corporal Parlyn of the Ninth Company in the Silvers stood near the tavern door, leaning against the frame, and eyed Bortan and Skrael as they stood over the headless corpse of Captain Serap, their expressions difficult to read in the wavering light.

Neither man was displeased, she was certain, at Serap's sudden demise. And if not for the beating they'd taken at her hands, incapacitating both of them for most of this night, they would have been among the first suspects in the murder.

The four brothers who had been sitting near the captain, however, were consistent in their retelling of events, and their tale matched that of the barkeep and his pale, shivering son. A travel-stained officer of the Legion had sat with Serap, engaging in quiet conversation that was brought to an abrupt end with the slash of a sword. Serap's head was still lying on the table, stuck there, cheek and hair, by the thick pool of blood beneath it.

Serap's lips were parted, caught in an instant of surprise. Her eyes, half-lidded, stared out with the chilling disinterest of the dead. Earlier that evening, Corporal Parlyn had stood opposite her, facing a sharp dressing down in front of her squad. The wake of that had curdled Parlyn's insides, stung bitter and dark with vague hatred. But even that was not enough to leave her satisfied at the captain's death.

Hunn Raal had come and gone. A few words ventured by the corporal, relating the story told by the witnesses, and then he was off, but not before countermanding his initial order to scour the town. It was, perhaps, the reason for her squad's present disgruntlement. Bortan and Skrael had both drawn closer to the four brothers, who stood in a nervous clump behind their table. The stench of blood was heavy in the air, and, like wolves, her two soldiers were ready to bare fangs.

Humiliation. The denizens of the tavern had witnessed it, delivered by Serap herself, and Bortan and Skrael were hungry to pass it on.

Parlyn was tired. They'd been given the task of removing what was left of Serap, but it seemed that her energy – what little remained – was trickling away, drip by drip. Even her soldiers stood as if uncertain where to start.

*But a vicious fight with the locals would answer their need quickly enough.* Sighing, she stirred into motion, stepping into the room. 'Skrael, find us a sack, for the head. Bortan, take Feled there and go hunt us down a stretcher.' She paused, glancing across to the last three soldiers in the squad. 'The rest of you, take station outside, eyes on the street.'

That last command was not well received. It was cold out there. Parlyn scowled until the three soldiers shuffled towards the door. She glanced back to see the barkeep appear from the kitchen with a burlap sack, which he pushed into Skrael's hands.

Bortan, with a final glare back at the brothers, joined Feled at the door. They exited.

One of the brothers stepped forward, eyes on Parlyn, who raised her brows. The man hesitated, and then said, 'She did good by us, sir. We'd like to be the ones to carry that stretcher . . . to wherever it needs going.'

Parlyn frowned. She glanced across at Skrael, who stood near the table, staring down at the severed head. There was no question that he'd heard. The corporal moved close to the farmer and said in a low voice, 'I appreciate the sentiment, but by the time Bortan gets back, I expect you four to be gone. Our blood's up, you see. Someone's murdered a Legion officer. It's our business now.'

The man looked back at his brothers, and then faced her again. 'To show our respect, you see.'

'I understand. If her ghost lingers, she'll know how you feel. Go home, now.'

'Well, I hope you catch that murderer, that's all.'

'We will.'

The four made their way out of the tavern. Parlyn watched them leave and then turned to see Skrael glaring at her.

'Yes,' she snapped, 'it'd be easier, wouldn't it?'

'Sir?'

'If they were the shits you wanted them to be.'

'Not just me, sir. You called us out this night, to do some hunting.'

'I did. Turns out, we were hunting the wrong enemy. I'll accept that, with humility. You might try the same. Now, is that a coin there in the blood?'

He looked down at the table. 'It is.'

'Slip it into her mouth and close up that jaw, if you can. Silver eases the ghost.'

Skrael nodded. 'So they say.'

He collected up the coin and studied it for a moment. 'Barkeep says this one was Sharenas's. Paying for the drink, I suppose.'

Parlyn had heard the same. It seemed an odd thing to do. She wondered about the conversation between those two officers, and how it could have led to what had happened here. She wondered, too, how Hunn Raal had known.

The sound the head made when Skrael pulled it free triggered in Parlyn an old memory from her childhood. *Out behind the house where the wagon ruts ran down into that dip in the road. Mud that could pull your boot right off if you weren't careful.*

*We used to think it was bottomless, that mud, enough to suck you right down, swallow you whole.*

*Yes, that's the sound.*

Left behind on the tabletop, blood and strands of hair. An empty tankard.

*Well, I guess we're not all going up on report after all. There's a bright side to everything. And when Raal catches up to Sharenas, why, we'll see her swing.*

Skrael moved past her, the sack clutched in both hands. He grimaced. 'Heavier than I expected, sir. Where to?'

'Put it down by the door. We'll wait for Bortan and Feled with the stretcher.'

She heard him cross the room, but did not turn. He'd pocketed the silver coin, she had seen. But the night was nearly done, and she was past caring.

# EIGHT

---

THE TWO HORSEMEN RODE OUT THROUGH THE thinning forest. The day was cold, the sky clear but dull, as if hidden behind a veil of soot. They were slumped in their saddles, the horses walking, and, as ever, the two men were engaged in conversation.

'A most high court, a most select education, and see what it brings us, Dathenar.'

Dathenar rolled his broad shoulders beneath the heavy cloak. 'Every bridge is but an interlude, Prazek,' he said. 'The arc and the span held more worth than we imagined on that dread night of our faltering. We should have stood fast at our station, scowling in each direction. Back to back, and so facing all manner of dire threat.'

'Dire threat indeed,' Prazek said, nodding. 'The treacherous wind, gusting so foul and portentous.'

'The unleavened night, bitter as black bread.'

'Fend us, too, Dathenar, from wretched imagination all our own, and the venal thoughts of irate commanders, prone to dancing on our bones. And if we still be clothed around our precious sticks, muscle and gristle bound to honourable purpose, well, that is faint distinction.'

'You speak ill of Silchas Ruin?'

Prazek worked with his tongue at something stuck between his teeth, somewhere near the back, and then said, 'I've seen white crows with softer regard, and indeed am known to fashion a pleasant disposition from their glittering beads.'

Dathenar reached up and rubbed at his bearded jaw. 'You liken us to carrion, and our lord's brother to the winged arbiter of every battlefield. But bleached of hue, you say? In war, I wager, every field is aflutter with black and white. Foe and friend, all those hostile comments and unpleasant looks, and laughter the kind to make you shiver. In all, a misanthropic place, ill suited to civil debate.'

'I've heard tell,' Prazek said, 'of a time when we were gentle. Fresh upon the land, behind us some sordid path spewing us out from some forbidden tale of misadventure. But see these majestic trees, we said! Such clear streams! A river like bold sinew to bind the world. Why, here were pits studded with ore, bitumen for the fires, soft hills to welcome sheep and goats.'

'Even then, I suggest,' said Dathenar, 'there were crows of white and crows of black, to keep things simple.'

Prazek shrugged, still trying to dislodge whatever was jammed between two molars. 'Simple enough for the flames and the forge, the night sky filled with sparks and embers. Simple, too, for the columns of smoke and the sludge to foul every pool, every lake and every stream. Why, we were avatars of Dark even then, though we knew it not. But still, let's look back on those gentle times, and take note of their myriad instances of gentlest murder.'

'Destruction is known to thrive in indifference,' Dathenar said. 'We are in sleep, calmly, and indeed comely, committed to our placid repose. As you say, these are instances of gentle mayhem, ruckled and ruined, and blissfully innocent the hands gripping the axe.'

'Weapons needed forging, of course,' Prazek said, nodding and then spitting. 'Civilization's demands are simple ones, after all. Unambiguous, you might say. It is only in the boredom of Kurald Galain's advanced age, such as we find here, that we tangle the threads, nestle in agitation, and upend our civil simplicity, our simple civility, and like so many turtles on our backs, we flinch at crazed scenes on all sides.'

'And so you long for simpler times.'

290

'Just so. White crows upon one flank, black crows upon the other, and every field a battlefield, and every enemy a foe and every comrade a friend. Decide upon the handshake and dispense with mangling complexity. I long for the rural.'

'And thus the rural finds you, brother.'

Leaving behind the last of the tree stumps and spindly saplings, they rode out upon the track leading into the hills. Ahead, denuded rock outcroppings and sweeps of winter-dead grass made a rough jumble.

'It finds me with cruel vigour,' Prazek said in a growl. 'Chased by chills and stiffened leather, chafed of thigh and carbuncled of joint.' He then pulled off his worn glove and reached into his mouth. A moment's effort and he pulled free a shred of old meat. 'This, too.'

'Simple maladies,' Dathenar easily replied. 'The complaints of peasants.'

Prazek pulled the glove back on. 'Well, peasantry defines itself in that miserable self-regard, and now I find myself a purveyor of mud and unheralding skies, no different from said peasant in my squinty eye and cheeky tic, and were my feet upon the ground, why, I'd shuffle one or both, to nudge along my slow thoughts.'

'Simpler times,' Dathenar agreed. 'Musings on the weather can fill a skull with clouds, enough to reduce every horizon. It's well you shuffle a foot or two, if only to lay claim to the ground upon which you stand.'

'The threadbare fool knows well that stony soil beneath him,' Prazek retorted. 'And so too observes the passing of armies in column, the tidings of smoke above the trees and flotsam in the stream. He raises a damp finger to gauge every new wayward sigh of the wind, too. Then bends once again to shoulder the wrapped bundle of firewood, and sniffs at the smell of plain cooking adrift on the breeze. His wife has paced her cage all day, wearing ruts in the cabin's floor.'

'No certainty that pacing,' Dathenar said. 'Why, she might be sharpening stakes or, deadlier still, whittling. She might be tending a babe in a crib and humming country hymns to pastoral idyll.'

'Ha! In tending that babe, Dathenar, she notes the wooden bars of the tiny cage, and then perchance glances up to see the same writ large about her. Yes, she might indeed be sharpening stakes.'

'But her husband's an honest man. See his battered hands and blunted finger nubs, the old scars of youthful zeal and the limp from when he miscalculatedly addressed one knee with a hatchet. Oh, those were wild times back then, hi ho! And in such demeanour, why, his idle thoughts hum a somnolent buzz, kept in beat by his plodding boots on the muddy track.'

'You paint a generous picture, Dathenar. But come the summer a company rides up to gather in the wretched fool. They shove a spear into his hands and wave flags, be they dark or light, crowned or crown-hungry. They take the wife, too, if no crib proffers necessity.'

'Out marching in column, Prazek.'

'Reduced to simple thoughts pertaining to weather, aches, and the season's gentle turn. At least until arrives the moment of terror-strewn mayhem, spears all a-clatter.'

Dathenar grunted, frowning. 'But wait! Where are the glittering heroes waving their swords in the air? What of the stirring speeches such as to awaken the zeal of mind-wandering farmers and herders? See them stand in that ragged row—'

'Feet shuffling.'

'One or two, as befits the moment. Forget not the squint and tic.'

'And the limp, too,' Prazek added. 'They tilt heads as the windbag rides back and forth on a confused horse—'

'This way? Yes! No! That way! What madness afflicts my gouty master so eager to straddle me?'

'Dathenar! Enough of the horse thoughts, all right?'

'They were brought to mind by our chargers, with their ears flickering to catch every word we utter. My humblest pardon, brother, I beg you. The horse, back and forth. You were saying?'

'The king's speech!'

'What king? Whereof comes this king of yours?'

Prazek cleared his throat. 'Well, let me amend that, by saying this. A king in his own mind, or indeed a queen in her own mind. It's a crowded skull, to be sure, lofty with minarets and teetering with towers, sparkling with spires, all so grandiose as to beggar any . . . beggar. And see the selfsame monarch, marching this way and that up and down the echoing halls with their rustling tapestries. Why, a scion of self-importance! He wears the headdress of a high priest this moment, and a jewelled crown the next. The robes of the judge, the clasped hands of the humble penitent. The bared head of the husband and the godly penumbra of the father. Is it any wonder that he casts coy glances at his reflection in every mirror, so inviting to worship and adoration this man—'

'Or woman,' Dathenar interjected.

'No, he is not a woman. She would be a woman, but not him.'

'Pray get him and us out of his skull, Prazek, and attend to his stirring speech to the peasant soldiers.'

'Easier said than done,' Prazek replied. 'Very well. Since we two are so busy, so thoroughly distracted by all the noble thoughts implicit in our noble bearing and whatnot, taking little note of peasants by the wayside—'

'We've seen none.'

'No matter. They exist in principle, I'm sure.'

'Let's hear this call to war!'

'Yes, why not, Dathenar? A moment, while I compose myself.'

'I see a week at least.'

'My dearest soldiers! My beloved citizens! My wretched minions!'

Dathenar tilted his head back and yelled, 'We're here, sire! Summoned—'

'Press-ganged.'

'Your pardon, press-ganged into your service, as if tithes weren't enough—'

'You, peasant, what was that you mumbled?'

'Nothing, sire, I but await your speech!'

'Dearest instruments of my will, howsoever I will it – and I will—'

'Now there's a chilling promise.'

'We are gathered here upon the eve of battle—'

'Best make it dawn, Prazek, we're nearing the hills.'

'Upon the dawn of a day promising glorious battle! Permit me to elaborate. The battle is yours and the glory is mine. There will be no confusion regarding this matter, I trust. Excellent! You are here, and you will fight in my name, for one perfectly reasonable reason – to wit, because you are not over there, upon the valley's other side, fighting in the name of him, or her. In other words, you are here and not there. Is that clear, then?'

'Sire! Sire!'

'What is it?'

'I have a brother who fights for him or her, over there!'

'That man is no brother of yours, fool.'

'But our mother—'

'Your mother was a whore and a liar! Now, where was I?'

Dathenar sighed. 'We were being stirred unto inspiration.'

Prazek waved a hand. 'I hold high this sword, my kin, my comrades, and with it do point *that* way, towards the enemy. And where my sword points, you follow. You will march, yes, and when close enough, why, you will charge, and if you prevail, I will be pleased, and further pleased to send those of you left alive back to your shacks and barns, if you please. But if you fail, I'll not be pleased. No, not at all. In fact, your failure will mean that I'm likely to get my skull cracked open—'

'Spilling into the ditch minarets and towers and spires all tumbling every which way. Crowns askew, robes besmudged, bared head laid bare through and through, and, alas, godliness snuffed out like a guttered candle.'

'Just so. Was that succinct enough, then? Now, we march to war!'

With this strident challenge ringing in the air, the two men fell silent, both slumping a bit further into their saddles. Until

Dathenar sighed and said, 'Never mind the peasants, Prazek, and let's speak instead of prisoners.'

'A touchy subject,' Prazek replied. 'Of crime or duty?'

'Your distinction reeks of the disingenuous.'

'In this mud, no distinction is possible.'

'And we not yet upon battle's field.'

Prazek stood on his stirrups and looked about, eyes narrowed.

'What now, brother?'

'Somewhere, lying in the grasses about us, is a pillager of prose, a looter of language.'

Dathenar snorted. 'Nonsense, we but ape the noble cause, my friend. With hairy discourse.'

Settling back down in the saddle, Prazek scowled. 'Let us defy the ghost, then, and ride on in silence. I must prepare, in my mind, my stirring speech to my prisoners.'

'You'll win their hearts, I am sure.'

'I need only their swords to cheer.'

'Yes,' Dathenar grunted, 'there is that.'

A short time later, a score of crows winged out from the hills, and made their way overhead, seeking the distant trees. The two officers exchanged a look, but, for a change, neither spoke.

\* \* \*

Flakes of snow drifted down from laden branches, carpeting the stone-lined track ahead, like the petals of fallen blossoms. Spring, however, seemed far away. The sound of his horse's hoofs was sharp and solid, and yet Captain Kellaras heard little echo, as the snow-shrouded forest made for a muted world. This was one of the few remaining stretches of true wilderness left in the realm, spared the axe only by an ancient royal mandate, granted to an ancestor of House Tulla.

The night before, he had heard wolves, and their voices, rising so mournfully into the night, had stirred something primal within the captain, something he had not known existed. He pondered that experience now, as he let his horse choose its own pace on the slippery cobbles, and it seemed that his thoughts well matched his surroundings. Cloaked in strange isolation, where the only sounds he heard belonged to himself, his mount, and their journey.

Wilderness offered a curious solitude. The comforts of society were gone, and in their place, indifferent nature – but that indifference set forth a challenge to the spirit. It would be easy to choose to see it as cruel, and to then fear it, flee it, or destroy it. Even easier, perhaps, to surrender to animal instincts, to live or die by its own rules.

Long before villages, or towns, or cities, the wild forests were home to modest huddles of makeshift huts, to clans of family. Each camp no doubt commanded a vast range, since such forests were miserly in what they yielded. But by the hearth-fires alone, the wild was kept at bay, and in those flames, a war had begun.

It was not difficult to see the path of devastation made by that still ongoing war, and from the perspective of where he now rode, in this silent forest, it was a challenge to find virtue in the many monuments to victory with which his kind now surrounded itself. Keeps of stone and timber laid claim to the simplest needs, of shelter and warmth and security. Villages, towns and indeed cities gave purpose and protection to the gathered denizens, and the pursuit of convenience was a powerful motivator in all things. All of these creations were fashioned from the bones of nature, the slain corpses in this eternal war. In this manner, the victors did enclose themselves in what they had killed, be it tree or wild stone.

Surrounded by death, it was little wonder that they would sense virtually nothing of what lay beyond it. And yet, from nature's bones the artists among the people would find and make things of great beauty, things that pleased the eye, with poetry of form and the peace of those forms rearranged in seeming balance. More to the point, Kellaras realized, so much of what was deemed pleasing, or satisfying, or indeed edifying, was but a simulacrum, a reinventing of what nature already possessed, far beyond the lifeless walls and tamed fields.

Was art, then, nothing more than a stumbling, half-blind

journey back into the wilderness, with each path selected in groping isolation, endlessly rediscovering what should have been already known, reinventing what already existed, recreating the beauty of what had already been slain?

It would be a shock indeed, should an artist reach this revelation: comprehending the relationship of their art with murder, with generations of destruction, and with this long, long journey away from those first hearth-fires, in that first forest, when the enemy at hand was first glimpsed, like a spark in the mind, and from it was born the first fear. The first unknown.

If imagination's birth had come from something as ignoble as fear, then, at last, Kellaras understood this eternal war. By a wilful twist of the mind, he could of course choose to be selective in what he saw, and what he felt, and, from those two forces in combination, in what he believed. A brightly gaze, then, to paint the world with the bliss of optimism, and every wonder crafted by the hand, whether mundane tool or glorious edifice, as symbols of the triumphant spirit. But each such pronouncement, no matter how bold the assertion, or how adamant the claim to virtue, was but a cry in the face of a deeper silence, a silence in which lurked a vague unease, a yearning for something else, something more.

*Lift high gods and goddesses, if you will. Dream of exaltation, in what the altar bleeds, in what the fires burn, in what art we raise, in what industry we occupy our lives. Each is lifted into view from an ineffable need, a yearning, a hunger to fill some empty space inside.*

*Our spirits are not whole. Some crucial piece has been carved from them. If we go back, and back, to a forest such as this one, and make for ourselves an entire world of the same, we come to the silence, and the isolation, and the seed-ground of our every thought, beaten down, unlit and awaiting the season's turn. We come to our beginning, before the walls, before the keeps and towers, with nothing but living wood encircling our precious glade.*

*In such a place, the gods and goddesses must step down from the high heavens, and kneel, with us, in humility.*

But Kellaras was not so naïve as to imagine such a return. The rush and the conflagration of progress were demonic in their intensity. *And we stake our lives in this fight for our place in things we ourselves invented. And in our new world, nature is indeed very far away.*

Rounding a slow wend in the road, he caught his first glimpse of the outer wall of the Tulla estate. The past summer's vines made a stark, chaotic latticework upon those walls, like withered veins and arteries drained of all life. The track straightened before a gateway, and beyond, centred amidst expansive grounds, rose the estate itself, built upon massive Azathanai foundation stones. Various outbuildings clustered to either side of the structure, including stables and a mill. Riding through the gateway, Kellaras saw the frozen sweep of a fishpond on his left, and three rows of leafless fruit-bearing trees on his right.

Even here, almost three days away from Kharkanas, the power of Mother Dark was visible, with shadows that belonged to an eclipse, and a pervasive glower to the day's fractured light. Kellaras glanced again at the orchard, wondering at the fate of those trees. *Perhaps in darkness, new trees will come, bearing fruit of another kind.*

*Or perhaps those trees, and the forest beyond, will simply die.*

Still, it was curious that no such die-back had yet occurred, even within Kharkanas itself. As if plants sensed nothing of light's loss; as if they held to an older, brighter world. Was that yet another front of the selfsame war? Or was Mother Dark's sorcery a gift given solely to the Tiste? He wondered if the Azathanai perceived the dying light. He would have to ask Grizzin Farl. *And if not? Will it mean that we are all subject to an illusion, our very minds under manipulation by Mother Dark?*

*More and more, this faith tastes sour. Mother, is this your darkness upon my mind, stealing away what others can rightly see? And, in surrendering thus to your will, what else must we yield? It is said believers are selective in what they see of the world – do you announce this with blatant metaphor made real? And if so, what is your point?*

Two figures appeared from near the stables. Kellaras angled his mount and rode towards them.

Gripp Galas wore but the thinnest hide, and steam rose from his shoulders, his thinning hair stringy with sweat. Beside him, Lady Hish Tulla stood with furs wrapped about her form.

Kellaras reined in before them. 'Have the servants all fled, then, milady?'

'The house staff remain,' she replied, eyeing him levelly. 'In winter's season, there is little to do here, captain. In any case,' she added, 'we prefer the solitude.'

Kellaras remained in the saddle, still awaiting their invitation. He had expected some difficulty here, and well understood Hish Tulla's reluctance. 'This forest surely invites it, milady. Wilderness has indeed become a refuge.'

'And yet,' she replied harshly, 'you come to bring word of the war beyond. If I could make the trees iron, captain, and each branch a blade, I would raise every wilderness into an impregnable fortress. Ringed in the blood of unwelcome visitors, it would surely grow vast.'

In her bold words, he heard the echoes of his own earlier thoughts, and was in no way inclined to challenge her sentiment. And still, he found himself shaking his head. 'Milady, it is by unnatural privilege that you find yourself in this refuge, and herein, you face no daily struggle to survive. You would arm your imagined defenders of that privilege, as if the war they are to fight is for you alone, rather than, indeed, their own survival.'

A grunt from Gripp Galas. 'He has you there, my love. The arrow flew true and sharp, pinning the leaf to the trunk.' The old man waved. 'Do dismount, captain, and be welcome in this house.'

Hish Tulla's shoulders seemed to slump beneath the furs, and she stepped towards Kellaras. 'The reins, then, captain. My husband has been cleaning the stables, with something like manic zeal. Winter has him pacing. He will hear your tales, as will I, if I must.'

As Kellaras dismounted and Hish led his horse into the stables, Gripp stepped closer and said, 'Come into the house, captain. The guest rooms are presently closed up, but we've plenty of wood, and some heat will take the damp from the chamber. I will send you a servant and see that a bath is drawn. We will dine at the seventh bell.' He turned to lead the way to the house.

'Thank you, Gripp,' said Kellaras, following. 'The promise of warmth already loosens my bones.'

The old man, once Lord Anomander's most revered servant, cast a glance back at Kellaras. 'Simple promises,' he said, 'of no consequence. Pray we spend this evening in such easy company.'

To that, Kellaras said nothing, and yet the silence found its own timbre, and the captain was not so benumbed with cold to fail in sensing the sudden tension from Gripp Galas, as the man preceded him towards the estate's front door.

As they stepped into the antechamber, Kellaras could hold to his silence no longer. 'Forgive me, Gripp. I am not here of my own accord.'

Gripp nodded but made no other reply. They swung left from the main hall and strode down a chilly corridor, dark for most of its length, until they reached a T-intersection where a small lantern glowed on a niche set in the wall. To the right and six paces in, the aisle ended at a door. Gripp pulled on the handle and the portal swung open with a loud squeal. 'Guests,' he muttered, 'have been few and far between.'

Kellaras followed him into the chamber. Although unlit, he could see it well enough. Sumptuous and welcoming, with two additional rooms just beyond the main one. Gripp set about lighting lanterns.

'It is a measure, perhaps,' ventured Kellaras, 'of our wayward notions, that the celebration of a marriage must have a specified duration. A ceremony, a wedding night, a few days allowed beyond that. And then, why, the return to an uncelebrated life.'

Gripp snorted as he scraped cinders from the hearth. 'Our

commander once made a similar observation, I recall.'

'That he did,' Kellaras said. 'Anomander so dislikes the notion of an uncelebrated life. In marriage or otherwise.'

'No wonder, then,' Gripp said, glancing over, 'that he left us an entire season.'

Kellaras shook his head. 'He did not send me, Gripp.'

'No? And yet, did you not say, you have been ordered here?'

'I have. Forgive me. Perhaps following supper, and in the company of your wife.'

Gripp's gaze flattened. 'That's not a temper you should test, captain.'

'I know. But to speak to you here, alone, would be a dishonour.'

Gripp straightened, dusting his hands. 'I'll have the servant bring wood and get this started. Oh, and the bath. I'll send Pelk – she could scrub the stripes off a hyldra, and make you beg for more.'

Kellaras's brows lifted. 'Gripp, I have no—'

'Abyss take us, captain, the woman's bored half out of her mind. Be a mindful guest, will you? I'd be most obliged.' Gripp strode to the door.

'This Pelk – is she—'

'Indulge me, Kellaras, I beg you. You'd thought this house quiet, here in winter's hoary hold. But I tell you, as a man surrounded by women, I'll appreciate even a night's inattention, barring that from my wife.'

'Ah. Very well, Gripp. We will see what comes of that.'

From the door, Gripp eyed him uncertainly. 'The bath or my wife's attention?'

Kellaras smiled. 'The bath. In the other matter, I shall bear your shield.'

Gripp Galas nodded, in the manner of a man whose deepest fear has just been confirmed. A moment later the door closed behind him.

Freeing himself of his heavy woollen cloak, Kellaras walked to the lead-paned windows. The chamber overlooked the courtyard behind the house, where the snow was smeared with dirt on the cobbles, and woodchips made a path from a storehouse up to the servants' entrance of the main building. He watched small dun-coloured birds hopping about on a heap of kitchen leavings.

A moment later he saw Gripp Galas appear, still in his thin, sodden shirt. Wood-splitting axe over one shoulder, he crossed the courtyard, heading for the timber shed.

A short while later there was a scratching at the door, and Kellaras turned away from the window in time to see a woman enter the chamber. She was in her middle years, short-haired, solid of build, and stood upright, straight-backed, as she studied the room.

Kellaras cleared his throat. 'You must be Pelk.'

Flat eyes shifted to him and she nodded. 'Apologies, sir. There's some dust. The fire will do for the damp, but the bed needs airing, and drying heat. Gripp's bringing some wood.'

'Yes,' he replied. 'If you listen carefully, you can hear the axe.'

Pelk snorted. 'He'd fell a hundred trees and rebuild this house from scratch, just to keep himself occupied. I'd wager he wears a smile right now, as the splinters fly.'

Kellaras cocked his head. 'You are a veteran of the wars, Pelk.'

She had set about wiping down surfaces with a grey rag. 'Those times are done,' she said, shaking her head.

'Were you a Houseblade in Lady Hish Tulla's company?'

'For a time. Mostly, though, I trained her. Sword, spear, knife, and horse.'

'I am sure I am not alone,' ventured Kellaras, 'in admiring your lady's . . . comportment. The pride in her stance, I mean to say.'

She was now studying him in turn, revealing nothing.

He cleared his throat. 'Forgive me, Pelk. My point is, I can now see from whom she took her guidance.'

After a moment, Pelk grunted and resumed cleaning.

'There was mention of a bath.'

'Water's on the coals, sir.'

'I take it that you will lead me to the chamber.'

'We have to go outside and then back in, I'm afraid. A wing's been closed off, you see. Locked up and sealed.'

Kellaras collected up his cloak again. 'Tell me, Pelk, are there any other guests here at the moment?'

She paused near the hearth, but did not turn to face him. 'No. Just you.'

Kellaras hesitated, and then returned to the window. 'It is just the season,' he said.

'Sir?'

'Gripp Galas. He has led a busy life. He's not used to having little to do. But the season wears on all of us.'

'I'm sure,' she muttered, leaving Kellaras to wonder what she had meant by that, given that her tone was utterly devoid of sympathy. Then she swung to face him. 'It's time. Will you require my attentions in the bath?'

'Not necessary, but I would welcome them.'

At last, something enlivened her gaze, and she was deliberate as she assayed the man before her. 'Aye,' she said, 'it's the season. Follow me, then.'

They set out, and Pelk led him straight down the corridor rather than returning the way Gripp and Kellaras had first come. Reaching a narrow passage of stairs, lit only by a lantern with a wick burned down to a bare nub, they descended to a servants' run that extended parallel to the back wall. Here the dust was thick underfoot, undisturbed except for their own steps. Every ten or so paces, there was a small door on the left side. Only one, two-thirds of the way down, revealed thin slivers of light from the room beyond.

They continued on until reaching the end, where a heavy door upon the right opened out into the back courtyard of the house. Pelk led him alongside the outer wall to the corner, and then round to halfway up the side of the house, where another door awaited them. Here, she produced a key and fought for a time with the lock, before managing to push the door open. A cloud of steam billowed out past her.

'Quickly now,' she said, beckoning him inside, and then closing the door behind him.

A half-dozen lanterns had been lit. An iron tub dominated the centre of the room, while off to one side was a huge hearth over which sat a grille. A cauldron steamed above the glowing embers, sweat trickling down its flared sides to hiss in the flames below.

'Strip down, then,' Pelk said, collecting up a bucket to dip into the cauldron.

Kellaras found pegs to take his clothes, close enough to the hearth to warm them while he bathed. Behind him, he heard water splashing into the tub. He sat on a chair to pull off his mud-crusted boots. There were sensations in the world, in the life's span, that could only be treasured, and surely one was the anticipation of blessed warmth, after days of chill and damp. It occurred to him, alas, how quickly the memory of such times drifted away, amidst the crush of immediate necessities that seemed so eager to impose themselves. The mind had a way of leaping from comfort into unease, with far greater alacrity than the other way round.

Musing on these disquieting notions, he pulled off the last boot, and then the filthy gauze strappings that padded and insulated his foot, and stood once more, naked. Turning, he saw Pelk standing beside the tub, similarly disrobed.

She had a soldier's build, barely softened by age or inactivity. There was a faint roll of fat encircling her belly, just above the hips, and protruding slightly at the front. Her breasts were full but not disproportionately so. Beneath the left one there was an old scar, a finger's length, stitching a line between her ribs. Kellaras stared at it. 'Abyss take me, Pelk, that looks right above the heart. How you survived—'

'I ask myself that often enough,' she interrupted, a harshness coming to her tone. 'A cutter told me my heart's in the wrong place. If it'd been in the right place, I'd have died before I hit the ground. Now, as you can see, the tub's too big for me to be standing outside it and scrubbing your back – not without putting a vile ache in my spine. So, we get in together.'

'Ah, yes, of course.'

'There're advantages,' she said.

'Excuse me?'

'My heart being in the wrong place. Makes it hard to find, and I prefer it that way. If you understand me.'

He was not sure that he did, but he nodded anyway.

Man or woman, few could claim a life lived without regrets. As a child Kellaras had listened, eager as any boy wearing a wooden sword, to tales of great heroes, all of whom – he saw now – strode through a miasma of violence, stern-faced and righteous. The virtues set forth, step by step, were of the basest sort, and vengeance was the answer to everything. It slashed, it carved, it marched monstrously through a welter of blood. The hero killed for love lost, for love denied, for love misunderstood. The delivery of pain to others, in answer to a pain within – a soul wounded and lashing out – ran like a dark current through every tale.

Still, through it all, the hero remained resolute, or so Kellaras saw it, when looking through his child eyes. As if some aspect of intransigence had made of itself the purest virtue. For such a figure, the notion of feeling – feeling anything but cold satisfaction – in the midst of terrible deeds, and seemingly endless murder, was anathema.

Few heroes wept, unless the tale was a rarity: one tangled in tragedy, and those stories fought a losing battle against the pathological mayhem of the grand heroes, for whom the world of legend was home, and every victim, deserving or not, served as nothing more than a grand staircase of bones leading to the hero's own exaltation.

A child with a wooden sword could find in such tales an outlet for every injustice and outrage perpetrated upon him, or her. This was not so surprising, given the secret concord between immaturity and cold malice. It was only decades later that Kellaras began to comprehend every hero's child-like thoughts, that bridling rage, that hunger for revenge, and see for himself what they appeased in so many of his companions. Pure vengeance was nostalgic. It winged back like the voice of a god into childhood, home to the first betrayals and injustices, the first instances of blind fury and impotence, and it spoke of restitution in chilling tones.

Witnessing a tale of heroes, told, written or sung, was like a whispered promise. The betrayers must die, cut down by an implacable iron blade swung by an implacable iron hand. And though betrayal could be found in many guises, including mere indifference, or disregard, or impatience, or a treat denied the grasping hand and its unreasoning demand, yet the incipient storm of violence must be vast. There are times in a child's life when he or she would happily kill every adult in sight, and this then was the hero's secret, and the true meaning of his tale of triumph: *what I hold inside is the master of all that I survey. Against all that the world flings at me, I shall prevail. In my mind, I never stumble, stagger, or fall. In my mind, I am supreme, and by this sword, I deliver the truth of that, blow upon blow.*

*Inside me is the thing that would kill you all.*

Such a world was not one where feelings counted for much. Indeed, they could be deemed enemies to purpose and desire, to need and the pure pleasure of satisfying that need. *The heroes, oh, my heroes of childhood, in their shining, blood-spattered worlds of legend – they were, one and all, insane.*

Kellaras had stood in a line, had faced an enemy. He had seen the ruinous disorder of battle. He had witnessed breathtaking deeds of heroic self-sacrifice, tragedies played out before his eyes, and nowhere in such recollections could he find a hero of legend. *Because true wars are fought amidst feelings. Be they fear or dread, pity or mercy. And each act, driven by answering hatred and spite, explodes in the mind with horrified wonder. At the self, brought so low. At the other, whose eyes match one's own.*

*In the field of battle, our bodies fight with frenzy, but in every face can be seen that appalling tearing loose, disconnecting soul from body, self from flesh. In war, the terrible wonder cries out from a thousand voices. That we are brought to this. That we should lose all that we hold dearest – our compassion, our love, our respect.*

If he thought, now, of those heroic tales, he looked upon the heroes and could find, nowhere within himself, a single shred of respect. *Misguided children, every one of you.*

*Slayers of innocents, in the slaying of whom you feel nothing but the cold fire of satisfaction. You play out the vengeance game and with every victory you lose everything.*

*And you poets, with the timbre of the awe-filled in your voices, look well to the crimes you commit, with every stirring tale you sing. Look well to the overgrown child you lift high and name hero, and consider, if you dare, the tyranny of their triumph.*

*Then, set your eyes upon your audience, to see for yourself the shining rapture in their faces, the glittering delight in their eyes. These are the awakened remnants of the child's cruel mind, enlivened by your heedless words.*

*So tell me, dear poet, at evening's end, the story told, the ashes drifting from the cold hearth, does the blood still drip from your hands? More to the point, does it ever stop?*

Her hands, upon his flesh, were hard with calluses. The harsh soap scraped him with grit, and he could feel the weight of her, and her heat, and when she moved round to settle over him, guiding him inside, he pushed from his mind the memory of heroes, and reached instead for the reality of this moment shared, between two veterans of too many battles.

Here, then, were feelings. Beyond the tactile, beyond the sensual. Here, then, was the language that spoke against tyranny in all its guises. But the world he found, in her arms, was a world for adults, not children.

Though she had spoken of her hidden heart, he found his own easily enough, and gave it to her that night. Unexpectedly, wrapped in his own sense of wonder. He knew not what she would do with it, or even that she understood what he had done. There was the risk, so very real, that she would cast it aside, mocking him with harsh laughter, as a child lacking understanding discards the important things which, when offered, so often prove troubling.

He whispered no words, as the gift he gave seemed, for that moment, beyond language. And yet, in his mind, he reached out to close his hand about the throat of the nearest poet. Dragged the fool close, and hissed, '*This, you bastard, is where you grow up. Now, sing to me of love, like one who knows it, and at last I will hear from you a true tale of heroes.'*

Love lost, love denied, love misunderstood. Woman or man, few could claim a life lived without regrets. But such regrets dwelt in the realm of the adult, not the child. They were, in truth, the essential difference between the two.

*Sing to us of true heroes, so that we may weep, for something no child will ever understand.*

\*　　\*　　\*

'My uncle, Venes,' said Hish Tulla, 'commands my Houseblades. They wait in Kharkanas.' Her eyes, so startling in their beauty, were now cold as coins. 'But no word comes from the Citadel.'

Kellaras nodded, reaching for his wine. He paused when Pelk, leaning in to collect up his plate, brushed close. He could smell the soap on her still, sweet and soft as a kiss. Momentarily discomfited, he sipped the wine, and then said, 'Silchas readies the Hust Legion, milady.'

'He is with them, then?'

'No. Following Commander Toras Redone's incapacitation, Galar Baras now conducts the assembling and training of the new recruits.' He glanced briefly at Gripp Galas, who was still picking at his meal. 'I have made acquaintance with Galar Baras. We travelled together on a journey out to Henarald's forge. Should Toras remain . . . sheltered, he will serve in her place, with honour and distinction.'

Hish Tulla leaned back slightly, her gaze remaining fixed and predatory as she studied Kellaras. 'A messenger from Venes brought the tale. Prisoners from the mines? What manner of army does Silchas imagine from such a dubious harvest? Loyalty to Mother Dark? Filial duty towards those who happily and righteously imprisoned them? What of the victims of their crimes, those who mourn the ones lost?' She collected a jug from the table and poured herself another goblet's worth of the strong, tart wine. 'Captain, Hust weapons in the hands of such men and women invites a third front to this wretched war.'

308

'Prazek and Dathenar have been sent to assist Galar Baras,' Kellaras said.

Gripp Galas pushed his plate aside, the food upon it barely touched. 'He had no right, captain. Anomander's Houseblades! What was so wrong with the officers of his own Houseblades?'

Hish Tulla set the goblet down and rubbed at her eyes, then looked up, blinking, and said, 'I was there, upon the Estellian Field.'

Kellaras slowly nodded. 'Would that I had seen it, milady—'

'Oh, Gallan made decent shape of it, and to hear him tell the tale you would swear he was there, in the midst of that battle. And saw what I saw, what Kagamandra saw, and Scara Bandaris, too. Those two chattering fools, Prazek and Dathenar—' She shook her head. 'If ever legend's heroes walked among us, then we can name them here and now.'

'Silchas had no right,' Gripp said again, and Kellaras saw the fists the man had made of his hands, heavy as stones on the table.

'One hopes,' Hish added, 'Galar Baras sees to their proper use. Sees past their prattle, that is. When I think on them, captain, an image comes to my mind. The Dorssan Ryl in winter, so heavily sheathed in ice, and upon the ice the blandest snow from nights of gentle falling. Where, in this scene I describe, will we find Prazek and Dathenar? Why, they are the black current beneath, strong as iron, that courses on, hidden away from all our eyes. But listen well and you will hear . . .' she suddenly smiled, 'that prattle.'

'By my order,' Kellaras said, 'did I send them from Kharkanas.'

'You?' Gripp demanded.

'My order, but Silchas Ruin's command. Lord Anomander is gone, Gripp, and if his shadow alone remains, it is white, not black.'

'What of Draconus?' Hish demanded. 'If any should assume overall command in Anomander's absence, it is the Consort.'

Kellaras eyed her, bemused. 'Milady, he attends Mother Dark, and makes no appearance.'

'Still? What madness indulgence has become! Upon your return, captain, pray pound upon that door. Awaken the warrior and, if need be, physically drag him from Mother Dark's arms! He is needed!'

Now Gripp too was looking at Hish, as if in wonder.

Kellaras cleared his throat. 'Milady, it seems your confidence in Lord Draconus arises from deeds of which I am not aware. Certainly, he fought well in the wars, and even turned a battle's tide—'

'Lisken Draw, that was,' Gripp cut in. 'The Jhelarkan's second season. With my own eyes, I saw him meet the charge of a wolf that was as big as a pony. Bare-handed, he took hold of its neck, lifted it high – I was close enough to hear the bones of the beast's throat crunch, like a sparrow's wing. It was dead long before he drove it into the ground.' He glanced up at Kellaras. 'A clan's war-master, that wolf. Broke the enemy's will there and then. The rest of the season was one long pursuit into the north.'

None spoke for a time. Kellaras replayed in his mind the scene Gripp Galas had just described. He barely fought off a shiver. And then, once again, he looked across to Hish Tulla. 'Few would welcome Lord Draconus as commander, milady. Indeed, I cannot think of a single highborn who would acknowledge his authority.'

'I would,' she snapped. 'And not hesitate.'

'Then you see beyond his advantage, milady, which the others cannot.'

'Base envy – such fools! The choice was Mother Dark's! Think any of them the better suitor? Then by all means present the case to her, and dare her mockery. But no, this desire of theirs paces behind the curtain – we but witness the shuffling feet and bulges in the fabric.'

'What they cannot hope to possess, milady, makes all the more savage their jealousy. Resentment is an acid upon every blade, but as you say, they dare not confront the woman for the choice she made. So who remains for their ire? Why,

310

Draconus, of course. And now, with the battle against the Borderswords—'

'Oh indeed,' Hish snarled, 'such a paltry deceit!'

'Some remain unconvinced.'

'So they choose to, feeding an already fatted pig.' She then waved a hand, as if to push away the subject, and collected her goblet again. 'We were host to Captain Sharenas, a week or so ago. The word she brought to us from Neret Sorr, and Vatha Urusander, made no sense. He asserts his innocence in all things – the pogrom, the slaughter of House Enes, even the annihilation of the Wardens – none by his doing!'

Kellaras sighed. 'This baffles me, milady. It is difficult to imagine Hunn Raal given so free a rein. Vatha Urusander—'

'Is a broken and bowed man, captain. There is no other explanation. Even Sharenas was at a loss to explain . . . well, much of anything. Still, she sought assurances, none of which I would give.'

Kellaras glanced away. 'This holding of yours, milady, proves not as isolated as I had imagined.'

'You are not alone in that,' she answered bitterly. 'Still, I have issued an order to my western estate. That fortress is to hold, if only to protect young Sukul Ankhadu. I have faith in Rancept and will keep him where he is. Still, tell me, how fares young Orfantal?'

'He remains a child finding his place, milady. It is unfortunate that Silchas is now his lone guardian among the Purake. Still, I have from Orfantal this message: he misses you terribly.'

There was a soft grunt from Gripp. 'He saw too much of me upon that escape from the hills. It was a foul thing that he witnessed the blood on my hands. I expect him to hold me at a distance from now on, and perhaps that is just as well.'

'His words and sentiment, Gripp, were for you and Lady Hish Tulla both.'

'A fair effort, captain, but beware that your generosity here may risk impugning him.'

Kellaras fell silent. He well recalled the flash of fear in Orfantal's face upon mention of Gripp Galas.

'Abyss take us, Pelk,' said Gripp in a low growl, 'do find a cup and join us, will you?'

'Only because I am done,' the veteran replied, coming forward to drag out the chair beside Kellaras's own. Sitting down, she accepted from Hish a goblet.

'Tell us your thoughts, Pelk,' Hish said.

'Not much worth the telling, milady. Vatha fights clouds of confusion, and half of them have been stirred up by those surrounding him. On the field, you'll recall, he ever demanded the high ground, to give him a clear sight of things. Mayhap,' she added, 'he imagined that his keep over Neret Sorr would give him the same. Of course, it couldn't, not when the battlefield is all of Kurald Galain.' She drank, and then shrugged. 'Anyway, it's Silchas who's the problem, and that's why Kellaras is here, I'd wager.' And she turned to him. 'Time, I'd say, to spit it out, captain.'

'I suppose it is,' he replied. 'Very well. Lest the tone here harden in casting Silchas Ruin in the poorest light, he well recognizes his . . . extremity. More, he alone remains of the brothers, and so must weather the fear, the currents of accusation, and the general sense of malaise that now fills not just the Citadel, but all of Kharkanas. Much of the anger rightly belongs not upon Silchas, but upon Anomander.'

Gripp hissed and thumped the table, rattling what remained of cutlery. 'Would he be anywhere but in the Citadel, if not for Andarist?'

'You judge too harshly a grieving man, husband,' said Hish.

'There are many flavours to grief,' he replied.

Pelk said, 'Do go on, Captain Kellaras.'

Though he had known her but one day, he already comprehended her relentless streak. 'Silchas pleads for Anomander's return. He seeks only to step to one side. Accordingly, he asks that his brother be found, and returned to Kharkanas. He understands, of course, that such a task will be difficult, for Anomander is not a man easily swayed. He may well need convincing.'

Gripp said, 'I shall set out tomorrow.'

'No!' Hish Tulla shouted. 'He promised! Husband! You are free of him! Deny Kellaras – oh, forgive me, captain, I know it is not you – Gripp, listen! Deny Silchas. He has no right! Have you not already said so?'

'I do this, wife, not for Silchas, but for Anomander.'

'Don't you understand?' she demanded, leaning towards him. 'He freed you. By solemn vow! Gripp, if you hunt him down, if you do what Silchas asks of you, he will be furious. He is no longer your master, and you no more his servant. The word given was Anomander's – and that is the only one that will matter to him. Husband, please, I beg you. He is a man of honour—'

'Who else can hope to find him and, more to the point, bring him back?' Gripp asked her.

'Husband, he freed you – he freed us – because that was what he wanted. It was his gift, to me and to you. Will you set it aside? Will you return it to his hands?'

'Hish, you don't understand—'

'What is it that I do not understand, husband? I know these men—'

'In many ways, yes, and better than any of us. I do not deny any of that, beloved. But it is also now clear to me that you don't understand them in the ways that I do.'

She leaned back, expression tight, arms crossing. 'Explain, then.'

'Anomander will understand, Hish. Why I came, why I found him. He'll understand, too, the words that I bring, and the necessity behind them.'

'Why? He has no reason to!'

'He has. Beloved, listen to me. Anomander . . .' Gripp hesitated, his gaze faltering. A moment later, he seemed to tremble, and then, with a deep breath, he continued. 'Beloved, Anomander does not trust Silchas.'

There was silence at the table. Kellaras slowly closed his eyes. *Yes. Of course. And yet . . .*

'Then why,' Hish asked, her voice rasping, 'did he ever leave?'

'For Andarist,' Gripp replied without hesitation. 'They are

313

three, yes, with Anomander upon one point, Silchas the other. But the one who binds them, who maintains the balance – that one is Andarist. Anomander is facing more than one schism.'

'Then,' said Hish Tulla, suddenly rising, 'you will bring him here first.'

'I will,' Gripp said.

'Your pardons,' Kellaras said, looking to them both, and ignoring Pelk's sudden hand upon his left arm, 'but no. He must return to the Citadel—'

'Captain,' said Hish in something like a snarl, 'we have another guest.'

'Andarist,' said Gripp, slumping back in his chair.

'Then . . . then, Abyss below, summon him! Here!'

'No point,' said Gripp. 'He would refuse you. He has claimed a wing here in the house, barricaded, the doors locked. His flight into the wilderness, away from the scene of slaughter, brought him, eventually, to us. Well,' he amended, 'to Hish Tulla. Who, in his moment of greatest need, had taken him into her arms, when none other dared.' After a moment, the old man shrugged. 'We sent him our servants. None returned to us. Presumably, they feed him, keep the chambers clean . . .'

Kellaras slowly sat back, dumbfounded, appalled.

'That is why,' said Gripp, 'when I find Anomander, it will be here that we come. Before Kharkanas.'

Kellaras nodded. 'Yes, Gripp Galas. Yes. Of course.'

Pelk pulled at his arm, angled him on to his feet. Confused, he swung to her.

'He leaves tomorrow, does Gripp,' she said, trying to hold him with her eyes.

Kellaras glanced across at Hish Tulla, and saw in her face such desolation as to blur his vision. *See me now, Oh Prazek and Dathenar? You are not alone in grieving over the discord I bring. This task of mine . . . I did not choose it. It finds me. Alas, it finds me.*

\*       \*       \*

Flanked by Rebble and Listar, Wareth made his way towards the small crowd that had gathered at an intersection between the rows of tents. Peatsmoke hung in wreaths over the enormous encampment, motionless in the still, bitter cold air. Just to the south, the makeshift army's refuse heap and cesspits were marked by a thicker, darker column of smoke, towering high and tilted like a spear driven into the ground. Ravens wheeled around that column, as if eager to roost. Their distant cries held the timbre of frustration.

'Step aside, all of you,' Rebble said in a growl as they reached the score or so recruits, and Wareth saw faces turn towards them, and belligerent scowls quickly vanish behind masks of studied caution when they saw who had challenged them. Men and women backed away to clear a path.

The body sprawled face-down on the frozen ground was naked from the waist up. A dozen or more knife wounds spotted the pallid back. A few had bled freely, crusting the incision made by the blade, but many others were virtually bloodless.

'Give us room,' Rebble ordered, and then, frowning down at the corpse, he sighed, his breath pluming. 'Who's this one, then?'

Crouching and wincing as his misshapen spine creaked, Wareth pulled the body on to its back. The night's cold made the corpse stiff, with the arms extended up beyond the man's head. Fingerprints, painted in smudged blood, encircled both wrists, from when the killer had dragged his or her victim into the intersection. While Wareth studied the unfamiliar face before him, Listar moved away, seeking heel-tracks on the thin, smeared layer of snow still covering the narrow passages between tents.

It didn't seem likely that he would find any. This murderer was in the habit of dropping the bodies far away from the tent in which each killing had taken place, though how that was managed without anyone's taking note remained a mystery. In any case, it was now part of the pattern, as were the successive knife wounds driven into a body from which life had fled.

'Anyone know him?' Wareth asked, straightening to scan the circle of faces.

There was no immediate reply. Wareth studied the expressions surrounding him, seeing, not for the first time, the ill-disguised contempt and disdain in which he was generally held. Officers had to earn respect, but the labours required lay somewhere in the future, if at all. And in this miserable company of reluctant recruits, rank alone was a flimsy framework, weakened still further by an almost institutional hatred for authority. When it came to Wareth, his reputation made the entire conceit totter, moments from violent collapse. He had warned Galar Baras often enough, to no avail.

But these were his own thoughts, his own internal pacing to and fro, upon which attended every fear, real and imagined. The voices of those fears ran the gamut of whisper to frenzied roar, and in all cacophony, they made a chorus of terror. *Most urgent music, the kind to fill the skull of a running man, a fleeing man. But all these frantic steps take me nowhere.*

'From which pit?' Rebble demanded. 'Anyone?'

A woman spoke. 'He was named Ginial, I think. From White Crag Pit, same as me.'

'Hated or liked?'

The woman snorted. 'I was a cat. Never paid much attention to what the dogs were up to.'

Wareth eyed her. 'But you knew his name.'

She refused to meet his gaze. Instead, she answered Rebble as if he had been the one to ask the question. 'A killer of women, was Ginial.' She shrugged. 'We knew about those ones.'

At that, Rebble shot Wareth a look.

Listar returned. 'Nothing, sir. Like the others.'

*Sir.* How that word struck him, like a muddy stone to the chest. Wareth glanced away, past the blank faces with their eager animal eyes. He squinted at the towering column of smoke.

Rebble said, 'Well, looks like we got us some volunteers. Right here, just waiting for us. Four of you, pick him up and take him to the fires – now now, soldiers, no need to fight for the privilege.'

As the woman moved to collect up one outstretched arm, Wareth said, 'No, not you.'

Scowling, she stepped back a step.

Rebble edged close to her. 'When the lieutenant talks to you, recruit, give 'im your cat's stare, and when he asks you something, hiss your words loud and clear. It don't matter that he's all bent and ugly. Understand?'

'Yes sir.'

'There,' and Rebble smiled out through his snarl of beard, revealing startlingly white teeth, 'now that didn't pinch too much, did it? Just keep playing at soldier and who knows, you might climb up to become one. Maybe.'

Wareth's new corporal, and personal strong-arm to the new lieutenant, was certainly enjoying his newly won privileges. With each day that passed, Rebble was sounding more and more like a veteran of many battlefields. *Every army has a temper. Abyss save us if it's Rebble's.*

With the body gone, the remaining onlookers wandered off. The woman alone remained, shifting weight from one foot to the other, not looking at anyone in particular.

'Your name, recruit?' Wareth asked her.

'Rance . . . sir.' She lifted her head then and fixed defiant eyes upon him. 'Drowned my own baby. Or so I'm told and why would anybody lie? I don't remember any of it, but I did it. Wet hands, wet sleeves, wet face.'

Wareth held her gaze until she broke it. That regard of his was something he had learned to perfect long ago, discovering how easily it could be mistaken for resolve and inner strength. *Games of disguise. Wareth knows them all. Yet here he stands, his deepest secret known to us. So should he not feel free? Unencumbered? At last able to dispense with what so hungrily devoured all his energy, year after year, step after step in this useless life? The hiding, the deceptions, the endless pretence?*

*But no, a man such as Wareth, well, he but finds new hauntings, new instruments of torture.*

317

*Still, a rampant murderer stalking the camp will serve as a worthy distraction.*

*If only it did.*

Still grinning, Rebble said to Rance, 'Yes, it's a dangerous thing, that speaking up.'

She grimaced. 'You're short on opinions, sir? Camp with the cats.'

'Is that an invitation?'

'Even you might not survive the night . . . sir.'

Wareth said, 'Rance. We need squad leaders.'

'No.'

Rebble laughed, clapping her hard on the shoulder, enough to make her stumble. 'You passed the first test, woman. We don't want them as are hungry for the rank. You got to say no at least five times, and then you're in.'

'Once will do, then.'

'No good. You already said it twenty times in that pretty round skull of yours. You'd be amazed at what old Rebble can hear.'

'They won't follow me.'

'They won't follow anyone,' Wareth said, still eyeing her. 'That's what makes it an adventure.'

Her sharp glare found him again. 'Is it true, sir? Did you run?'

Rebble growled under his breath, but Wareth gestured the man to silence, and then said, 'I did. Ran like an arse-poked hare, with the sword in my hand screaming its outrage.'

Something settled in her face, and whatever it was, Wareth had not expected it. *No disgust. No contempt. Then what is it I'm seeing?* Rance shrugged. 'A sword that screams. Next time, I'll be right there beside you, sir.'

The weapons and armour of the Hust were yet to be distributed. They remained in heavily guarded wagons, the iron moaning day and night. Every now and then one wailed through its burlap mummery, like a child trapped in the jaws of a wolf.

In her eyes he saw recognition.

*Killed your baby, did you? Not knowing what to do with*

318

*the damned thing, as it screamed and screamed. Not knowing how you could cope – not just that day, but for the rest of your life. So you took the easy way out. End the screams, in a tub of soapy water.*

*But the screams don't end, do they? Unless, of course, your mind snaps, and it all vanishes inside. As if you weren't even there. But for all that not-knowing, there remains a bone-deep terror – the terror of one day remembering.*

'Your killer's killing men who hurt women,' Rance said. 'It's what they all share, these victims. Isn't it?' She hesitated and then said, 'Could be a woman.'

*Yes. We think so, too.*

'I think you just joined the investigation,' Rebble said.

'What makes you think I want her caught?' Rance snapped in reply.

'That's fine, too,' Rebble answered, nodding. 'We're not much interested either. But the commander wants it all settled.'

'When the last woman-killer is dead,' she replied. 'Then it will settle.'

'Could be a few hundred men, maybe more,' said Wareth, studying her, noting the redness of her hands, as if she had recently scalded them, and the guardedness that clenched her face. 'Too many to lose.'

Rance shook her head. 'Then tell him how it is, sir.' Her eyes found his again, and indeed he thought of a cat. 'Tell him how it's the men who are cowards who hurt and kill women. Tell him about their small minds, full of dark knots and darting fears. Tell him how they can't think past that first rush of blind rage, and how satisfying it is to just give up thinking altogether.' Colour had risen to her face with her words. 'Tell the commander, sir, that these dead bastards are worthless in any army. They'll run. They'll make trouble with us cats, looking for more women to bully and threaten. Better to see them all dead. Sir.'

Wareth glanced across at Rebble, and saw the man grinning, but it was a cold grin that could go in any direction.

Listar stood silent, a few paces away. *Wife slayer.*

Did she know? *Of course she knows. Crimes are the meat of our conversations, and we'll chew the gristle over and over again, in the belief that, with enough jawing, the flavour will change and the bitterness will go away. The sour misery of it all . . . listen! Just fade into nothing, will you? Oh, we're a stubborn lot, especially with those faiths promising escape.*

'They ain't all cowards,' Rebble said, still grinning, but something was lit in his eyes.

She was sharp enough to notice and stepped back. 'If you say so, sir.'

'I do. More to the point, some killings, well, they just happen. In a red haze.'

'Yes, I suppose so.'

'That's how forgetting and remembering becomes the worst part of it.'

Now, at last, Wareth saw the woman pale. 'You have the truth of that,' she said in a low, frail voice.

Then Rebble's grin spread into a smile. 'But me, I don't have that problem. I remember every poor bastard I went and killed. The ones I meant to, the ones I didn't. If I gave you all their names, would you know which was which? No. Nobody would. Because it really makes no difference to anybody, not even me. That's my problem, you see. What I can't remember, no matter how hard I try, are my reasons for killing anybody. The arguments, I mean, the ones that broke out and turned bad.' He shook his head, showing an exaggerated expression of bafflement. 'Not a single reason, not one.'

Sighing, Wareth looked away. Rebble's new habit was making speeches, but none of them left a listener feeling at ease. *Is there anything beneath all that, Rebble? Something you're trying to tell us? Something you need to confess? What's stopping you?*

Rance simply nodded in answer to Rebble's words.

The tall, wiry man then turned and walked over to Listar. 'Let's go find the dead man's tent, Listar, and see what's to be seen.' He glanced over at Wareth. 'It's almost tenth bell, sir.'

'I know,' Wareth replied. 'Go on then, the two of you.'

He watched the two men head off towards the White Crag block.

'Can I go now, sir?'

'No. Come with me.'

She surprised him by offering no objection, and fell in at his side when he set out for the command centre. 'Better you than him, sir.'

'Just smile and nod, no matter what he says.'

'I'd forgotten about Listar,' she said.

'Rebble figured you were looking to wound, I think. He didn't like it.' Wareth hesitated, and then said, 'Listar isn't a coward. He wants to die. He won't take a guard at his tent at night, despite these murders. Every time we find ourselves standing over another body, he's disappointed that it's not him lying there at our feet.'

Rance grunted, but said nothing.

'Not much longer now, I think.'

'What?'

'We've got a problem with desertions, Rance. And not enough old Legion soldiers to ring the camp. Besides which, the deal was freedom, only to win it we'd have to serve, but given the chance we'll take the freedom and Abyss take the serving part. I think it will all fall apart.'

'So why make me do anything? Just let me go back to my tent—'

'You weren't anywhere near your tent when looking at that body,' Wareth observed as they drew closer to the larger cluster of tents at the camp's centre. 'Not if you're in the White Crag block.'

'I was just wandering, sir. They won't accept me, you know.'

'Who's the worst of your lot, Rance, for making trouble with you?'

'There's one. Velkatal. She dropped six babies, then left them to run wild. Four were dead before coming of age, and the other two ended up in the mines and died in them. But to hear her tell it, she was the world's best mother.'

'Fine. Make her your Rebble.'

Rance snorted. 'She'd be the first to mutiny under my command.'

'Not after I inform her that whatever your fate, she will share it.'

'So that is how you make squad leaders. And that's why Rebble keeps you alive.'

'It's how we're making squad leaders,' Wareth agreed. 'But as for Rebble, he started keeping me alive back in the pit. So, I don't know his reasons, but there was no deal made that's changed anything. At least, not that he's told me.'

'You never killed a woman, did you?'

'No. Rance, there're all kinds of cowards out there.'

She grunted again, her only response.

*　　*　　*

Fleeing the future seemed the most sordid of acts, and yet Faror Hend felt that she was making a habit of it. Two men haunted her wake, and the one pursuing her was, to her mind, the wrong man. At night, lying sleepless on her cot, with the tent walls slumping with the weight of the ice left by her breath, she could, upon closing her eyes, see a figure, tall and spectral, emerging from a vast, lifeless plain. He was walking towards her, hunting her down, and for all the monstrosity of the image, she knew that there was no evil in him. He was simply her fate, bound in promise, inescapable.

Yet in her dreams, when at last sleep found her, she saw Spinnock Durav, a cousin too close for propriety. She saw his youth, nearly a match to her own. She saw his smile, and basked in the wit of his sly words. He offered her an image, a possibility, that burned with mockery – the cruel, sneering kind. Though he stood close, she could not reach for him. Though she longed to take him, he was like a man armoured against her every charm. She would then wake, her soul heavy and cringing with the hopelessness of her desire. He had, after all, pushed her away, confessing instead his love for Finarra Stone, and the bitter irony of that revelation still tasted like ashes in Faror's mouth.

With dawn streaking the east horizon, she would leave her

tent, and set out in the direction of that growing light, drawn to its red slash, the fires of a new day's birth. With each and every night a realm of ashes and despair, she fled into the light. An army encamped was a creature of routine, mechanical and obstinate in its witless, dull-brained way. It offered nothing new, no change in its surly, trudging mood.

Out past the pickets, facing on to a snow-smeared plain, she would stand, wrapped in her heavy cloak, and look for a figure, walking on foot, coming out of dawn's blazing fire. *New day, new life. Those who play at soldiers stir behind me, and before me, somewhere out there, a man striding out from a soldier's end.*

*Mechanical things will break. Dirt and rust to bind the gears, millstones worn down, ratchets and brackets weakened by strain unto snapping. But some, no matter how carefully fitted the assembled parts, are destined to not work at all. And even then, look into the east, out on to this empty plain. There he walks, a broken cog, seeking a new routine. Husband. Wife.*

*I flee, but in truth, there is nowhere to run to. The future chases me, hunts me.*

On this day, Commander Galar Baras had summoned her to join him in his staff meeting. She saw no reason for that. She was a Warden, not an officer of the Hust. More to the point, she needed to leave, to ride for her own company – back to Commander Calat Hustain, and Spinnock Durav.

Would Kagamandra be there as well? Hunched over some table, his vein-roped hand curled round a tankard, enwreathed in the smoke from the hearth, a grey figure with hooded eyes? Or was he in fact somewhere between here and the fort of the Wardens? And if so, which path would she take upon her return? *Do I meet him? Or do I leave the tracks, journey at night and hide well during the day?*

*Such shame in these childish thoughts!*

After some time, she turned about and made her way back into the Hust encampment. It was not the army she had expected to find. The machine might well rattle on, like the vast bellows of Henarald's forge, all iron arms, wheels and cogs, but it was a sickly assemblage now.

The horror of Hunn Raal's poisoning dwelt in Faror Hend's mind like some vast fortress, isolated, rising from an island surrounded by forbidding seas. Every current pushed her away, and she was reluctant to fight that tide. Ambition was one thing. The desire for restitution held at its core a righteous cause. Sufficient for a civil war? She could not see that. But then, had not Hunn Raal sought to prevent such a war? With no legions to stand against Urusander's, that civil war was as good as done.

Instead, the Hust Legion sought a rebirth. Walking into the camp, where men and women sat in clumps around morning cookfires, she could feel nothing of the surety that belonged to a military gathering. Instead, the atmosphere swirled with resentment, defiance, fear and dread.

These new soldiers were killing each other. Those that didn't desert. They spoke of freedom as if it meant unfettered anarchy. It was a wonder to Faror that this camp had not already burst apart. She did not understand what held it together. *Or, perhaps, I choose not to understand. How that, beyond all the resentment and fear, there can be heard a soft whisper, a voice filled with promises, yet strident with need.*

*The weapons of the Hust never shut up. Bound and wrapped tight, still they sing. Faint as a breath upon this chill wind.*

*If the prisoners fear, they also desire. And few, I wager, understand that this desire came not from them, but from the guarded wagons, from the stacks of blades and bundles of chain armour. From the greaves and vambraces, from the helms and their rustling camails. Voices whispering without end.*

She fought against that terrible music. She did not belong here.

The command tent was directly ahead. Two Hust soldiers flanked the entrance. Muttering and something like soft laughter rained from them although they stood mute, faces impassive, and as Faror passed between them she fought off a shiver.

Within, the quartermaster, Seltin Ryggandas, was crouched before a free-standing woodstove in the centre of the chamber, feeding it dung-chips. Captain Castegan – the last of the surviving officers of that rank, apart from Galar Baras himself – was standing near a portable table. He had been near retirement, a man whose weak bladder had saved his life the night of Hunn Raal's visit, as he would not drink alcohol. It was clear, from his bent form and sunken expression, that he cursed his caution, although Faror suspected that Castegan's deepest hatred belonged to all those in Kharkanas who had refused to let the Hust Legion follow its soldiers into extinction.

Galar Baras was sitting on a travel chest, half turned away from everyone else, and nothing in his demeanour invited conversation. To Faror's eyes the man had aged beyond his years in the past few weeks.

Moments later, the officers drawn from the prisoners began arriving. The first man, Curl, had been a pit blacksmith, pocked by half a lifetime's worth of burns from embers and spatters of molten metal. He was hairless, his skin black as Galar's, with soft, blunt features that looked vaguely melted. Bland, empty eyes, pale as tin, slid across the others in the tent, hesitating only an instant upon Faror Hend.

Despite the brevity of that pause, Faror felt herself grow cold. Curl had killed his partner in the smithy in the small village where he lived and worked. He had then broken the man's bones, battering the body through most of a night, until what he had left would fit easily into the forge's brick-lined belly. For all the calculation in removing the evidence of his crime, he had not considered the black columns of smoke that poured from the chimney to settle heavy and rank upon the village, delivering the stench of burned clothing, hair, bones and flesh.

None knew what had motivated Curl to murder his partner, and he was not forthcoming on the matter.

Behind him came the one woman promoted thus far, from Slate Pit to the northwest. Aral was gaunt, her black hair streaked with grey, with a pinched, pale face and eyes that seemed capable of holding a world's fill of malice and spite. She had, one fine evening, fed a dozen select guests her husband for supper. That her guests were one and all related to her husband made the deed all the sweeter, as far as she was concerned, and she would have happily included any or all of them as dessert. When Faror had heard the tale, from Rebble one night over a cask of ale, his telling had dragged her past horror into humour. But upon meeting Aral, all amusement vanished into the depthless darkness of her gaze.

'*It's the husband you need to think about, Warden,*' Rebble had added later. '*I mean, one look into those eyes . . . no, not a thing to marry, not in there. Not a thing to love, or cherish, or – gods forbid – worship. That woman – I near piss myself every time we chance to meet gazes. So you can't help but wonder at the man who took her hand. But one thing's for certain. She'll be a fine commander, since no man or woman, if they got eyes to see, would ever go against her.*'

'*That's a dubious justification,*' Wareth had replied. '*It's not just giving orders, Rebble. Being an officer's a lot more than that. It's down to who you'll follow.*'

'*Well, lieutenant, if you know anything about that, it'd be from the backside.*'

'*True enough, Rebble, but that don't make my vision any less clear.*'

Of these new officers, selected from the prisoners, only Rebble and Wareth had caught Faror Hend's interest. Rebble was a victim of his own temper, and that was far from a rare thing. Nothing in Rebble baffled her. As for Wareth . . . well, monstrous he might appear to be after years of wielding a pick, but there was something gentle in the man. Gentle and, she had to admit, weak. It may well have been his cowardice that made him as clever as he was. She would not trust Wareth in any setting that threatened violence, but she did not anticipate ever finding herself in such a situation when she might have to: accordingly, she accepted him as he was, and perhaps the real reason for that was, just as with Rebble, she understood him.

Her aversion to joining the military had guided her into the company of the Wardens. She saw nothing inviting or glorious in battle, and had no desire to seek it out.

Accompanying Aral were Denar and Kalakan, a pair of thieves who had broken into an estate in Kharkanas, only to stumble into what they swore was a father raping all four of his children, with the wife lying dead on the floor in the room's centre. By their tale, which they still maintained as the truth, the man in question was highborn enough to sell his innocence to the magistrate, and, indeed, to twist the scene around, accusing the thieves of the murder and the rapes. As the four children were, one and all, driven too deep into shock to be capable of responding to anyone or anything, it was the noble's word against two common thieves.

Denar and Kalakan had been sent to separate pits, only to reunite here in the Hust Legion. Their promotions were earned by the sharpness of their minds, and the cutting precision of their wit. Their sheer popularity made the charges against them seem profoundly unlikely, and, as it turned out, the two men had been partners in love as well as thievery.

A few moments later, Wareth arrived, and with him was a young woman who seemed far from pleased to be in his company, or anyone's company for that matter. She immediately moved off to stand with her back against canvas, arms crossed and eyes upon the muddy floor.

*You have my sympathy. This is a bag full of knives, and here you all are, with your hands plunged into it.*

She saw Galar Baras studying the newcomer with a frown, and then he looked away, scanning the others for a moment before nodding and rising. 'Today,' he said, 'we begin issuing weapons and armour.'

Castegan seemed to choke, but it was the quartermaster who said, 'Commander, you cannot do that!'

'It's time, Seltin.'

'The blades are eager for blood,' Castegan said. 'They are stung, each and every one of them. You can hear it, Galar Baras. The betrayal burns them.'

Sighing, Galar said, 'Enough of that nonsense, Castegan. Yes, the iron has a voice, but you would make those weapons out to be more than what they are. Henarald himself explained how the Hust iron reacts to changes in temperature, and how each blade talks to those nearest it, as would a tuning fork. What we hear is pressure, and tension. These weapons, Castegan, are not alive.'

Castegan scowled. 'It may be that they weren't, Galar, but they are now. And I tell you this' – he rapped the scabbard at his belt – 'my blade slides into my dreams every night now. Begging for blood. Beseeching me to be the hand of its vengeance.' He jabbed a finger at his commander. 'Tell me, does your sword sleep at night?'

Galar met Castegan's gaze for a long moment, and then he turned away. 'Wareth, do you have anything to report?'

'No sir. Just another murder. Another woman-killer now stumbles through the everlasting Abyss. The mystery of how the bodies are moved continues to perplex us. We've gone nowhere in our investigation.'

'And who is this woman you have brought to us?'

'Rance, sir. From White Crag Pit. She has the makings of an officer, sir.'

Galar Baras grunted, and then faced her. 'Rance. What think you? Shall I distribute the weapons and armour of the Hust to you and your fellow recruits?'

Her eyes narrowed on the commander. 'It's a conversation we cannot but overhear, sir,' she said. 'Those . . . things. What you suggest . . . I don't know if any of us want to be part of that conversation.'

'Not a conversation,' Castegan said. 'An argument. They'll pluck at the worst in you. Think on that, Galar Baras! Think on these wretched murderers you would now arm! There will be chaos. Bloody chaos.'

Denar cleared his throat, glancing briefly at Kalakan, and then said, 'Sir, it's chaos already, and that's building. We all spent years working, stumbling exhausted back to our bunks. Now we just march this way and that – at least, those willing to listen to us. Most of them, sir, just lie around bickering.'

Kalakan added, 'We need more than just weapons, maybe. We need to be doing something. Anyway.'

Galar Baras nodded. 'Well, consider this, then. It seems that Urusander is not interested in doing things the traditional way. He will not wait for spring. He will probably begin his march on Kharkanas before the month's out.'

Faror Hend wondered at that, and then she said, 'Forgive me, commander. But that would be foolish of him. The Wardens—'

Castegan cut her off with a harsh bark of laughter. 'Then you've not heard. Ilgast Rend was given command by Calat Hustain and took your Wardens to Neret Sorr. There was a battle with Urusander's Legion. Rend's dead, the Wardens shattered.'

She stared at the man, unable to comprehend his news. Galar Baras stepped close and set a hand upon her shoulder. 'Damn Castegan for his insensitivity, Faror. I would have spoken of it to you, once this meeting was done. I am sorry. The tale but just arrived, from a courier out of Kharkanas.'

'This is the season of sordid ends,' Castegan said, now pacing. 'No time for sentimentality. I make my words hard and cruel, not out of malice, but to impress upon everyone here that niceties are an indulgence we can no longer afford. Galar – send that rider back to Kharkanas, with a message for Silchas Ruin. The effort here has failed. There is no Hust Legion. It's dead. Gone. Exhort him to sue for peace.'

Faror backed away from Galar's grip, until she felt the cold, wet tent wall at her back. *Ilgast Rend . . . no! My friends—* 'Commander, what is the fate of Calat Hustain? He rode out to the Vitr with a company—' *Spinnock! You still live. Oh, feel my relief – woman, are you truly this shallow?* 'Captain Finarra Stone was sent to the Shake. Does she – has she learned of this?' *What, what am I to do now?*

A camp-stool nudged her left leg, and she looked down, uncomprehendingly, until Wareth's voice said, 'Sit, Faror.'

Numb, she sank down.

Galar Baras was speaking. '. . . mission is now imperative. He wants us ready to march in two weeks. The matter is made simple. We have no choice, now.'

'Untrue!' Castegan said in a snarl. 'We cannot hope to

command these savages! The only choice left us is to surrender!'

'Wareth.'

'Commander?'

'Gather the sergeants and corporals drawn from the prisoners. Add more to make the complement complete. I will want that list before noon today. Bring them to the training ground. We will do this in two phases. They are the first to be armed and armoured.'

'Long overdue,' said Curl, making fists with his battered hands. 'I would feel that iron. Taste it. Listen to its song.'

'Wareth, take your fellows out to the wagons. Oh, by the way, your old blade awaits you.'

At those words, Wareth flinched. 'Sir, I beg you, not that one.'

'You are bound to it,' Galar Baras replied. 'Until death takes you. Really, Wareth, you already knew that.'

'Then, sir, I humbly request that I remain unarmed.'

'Denied. Seltin, join Wareth and see to the proper issuing to my lieutenants here. Thereafter, remain at your post, and double the guard over the wagons. We will see what happens when the sergeants and corporals return to their squads – this afternoon and tonight. Then, if all goes well, we will equip the regulars tomorrow.'

As the quartermaster led the prisoners out of the tent, Galar turned to Castegan. 'Get out. I will speak in private with Faror Hend now.'

'Consider well,' said Castegan in a growl, 'the honour of the Hust Legion.'

'See to your own, Castegan!' Galar snapped, eyes holding on Faror where she sat.

The man straightened. 'When it is all I have left to defend, Galar Baras, I require no admonition from you.'

Galar turned on him. 'Is it honour you now fight for? I would think guilt a more apt word for what gnaws at your soul. Swallow it down whole, Castegan, and muse long on its weight. At the very least, it will keep your feet on the ground.'

'Commander Toras Redone defied my seniority here—'

'Defied? No. She *questioned* it. You may have me in years, but not years in service to the Hust. I will, if you ask it, release you to return to your original legion. I am sure you will have plenty of intelligence to sell to Urusander.'

Castegan was trembling as he faced his commander. 'You make a dangerous offer, Galar Baras.'

'Why? This is not a gale you need face. Leave it to push you round, and, like a hand at your back, send you running home.'

Saying nothing more, Castegan strode from the tent.

After a long moment, Galar Baras faced Faror Hend once again. 'What Lord Ilgast Rend did was unforgivable.'

She snorted. 'He need not beg for forgiveness any longer, sir, now that he lies dead.'

'Faror, Lord Silchas Ruin has given me command of all forces but the Houseblades of the highborn Houses. For all that, I expect it to be temporary. When Lord Anomander returns, it will be Silchas taking my place.'

She blinked up at him. 'Toras Redone will return to command the Hust, sir.'

'I think not.'

'Her husband will see to it.'

Galar Baras studied her briefly, and then shrugged. 'Perhaps. But we cannot rely upon that. The Wardens are no more. I am attaching you to my staff, elevating your rank to captain. You will command a company, Faror Hend.'

'Sir, I cannot. Calat Hustain is my commander still.'

'He has lost his command. Faror, I have word – there are survivors from the battle. Not many, but some. Seen on the south tracks. They are fleeing here, captain.'

*Oh, gods below.* 'Sir, send a rider to Yedan Monastery. Captain Finarra Stone is there. She will be the ranking officer, not me.'

'Until then, it will have to be you, Faror Hend.'

'Sir, I do not want a Hust sword.'

Galar strode to the woodstove. He kicked the latch so that the grilled door opened, and then crouched to fling in handfuls of dung-chips. 'There was a time,' he said, 'when the Hust Legion was a name spoken of with pride. For all the tales of cursed weapons and such, we stood against the Forulkan. We saved not just Kharkanas, but all of Kurald Galain.'

'I am not a soldier, Galar Baras.'

His shoulders shook in silent laughter. 'Oh, have I not heard that said enough yet?'

'How can you hope to resurrect the Hust Legion?' she asked. 'To what it once was? Where, sir, will you find glory in these men and women?'

He straightened, but kept his face averted. 'I can but try.'

*　　*　　*

'Nothing downtrodden in yonder peasants,' Prazek observed.

'Nothing peasantry in them either, brother,' Dathenar replied.

Ahead upon the track stood a score or more figures. They had been hurrying from the west, bundled under gear wrapped in blankets and furs. Upon spying the two approaching riders, they had drawn up in a clump, barring the way.

Clearing his throat, Dathenar said, 'Lacking a king, they merely await your first and, one hopes, most stirring speech, Prazek.'

'I have speech to stir indeed.'

'Emotions to churn, thoughts to swirl, but save your last handful of spice, Prazek, for the final turn.'

'You invite a burning hand, Dathenar, to give bridling sting to my slap.'

'Shall a slap suffice? I see not the yoke of drudgery before me, but loot collected in the dark, and in haste. And see how they are armed, with cudgels, spears and brush-hooks.'

'Forest bandits, perchance? But then, why, their zeal with said brush-hooks is unequalled in the annals of wayfarers, for not a tree stands to hide their hidey-hole.'

'Zealotry has its downside,' Dathenar added, nodding.

Three over-muscled men had stepped out from the crowd.

Two wielded spears made of knives bound to shafts, while the one in the centre carried a pair of brush-hooks, one of which appeared to be splashed with frozen blood. This man was smiling.

'Well met, sirs!' he cried.

The two riders reined in, but a dozen or so paces distant from the three men.

'Met well indeed,' Prazek called back, 'since by cogent meditation I conclude you to be recruits of the Hust Legion, but it seems you travel without an officer, and perhaps have found yourselves lost so far from the camp. Fortunate for you, then, that we find you here.'

'For this day,' Dathenar added, 'you will see our lenient side, and rather than tangle your mob's many legs with something as mentally challenging as a proper march in cadence, you can scurry back to the camp like a gaggle of sheep.'

'Sheep, Dathenar?' Prazek asked. 'Surely, by the belligerence arrayed before us, we must consider the simile as inaccurate. Better we deem them goats.'

'Listen to these shits!' one of the men said, and the others laughed. 'You sweat perfume too, do you?'

'Goatly humour,' Prazek explained to Dathenar. 'Forever barking up ill-chosen trees. Sweat, good sir, belongs to the unwashed multitudes, such as are lacking the civil hygiene of panic well hidden. If perfume you seek, why, set nose to your own arse and breathe deep.'

'Prazek!' exclaimed Dathenar. 'You bend low to crass regard.'

'No more than but to match said gentleman's anticipated posture.'

'Shut your mouths,' snapped the man with the two brush-hooks, no longer smiling. 'We'll take your horses. Oh, and your weapons and armour. And if we're feeling . . . what was that word? Lenient? . . . we might let you keep your silk sac-bags, so whatever shrivelled stuff's inside 'em don't disappear entirely.'

'That stretched a breath, Dathenar, did it not?'

'I myself hearkened more to the stretching of his thoughts,

333

not to mention grammar, Prazek – nigh unto breaking, I'd swear.'

'Let us dispense with leniency, Dathenar. Surely the Hust Legion can indulge our spat of discipline as might be needed here.'

Someone in the crowd now said, 'Leave 'em be, Biskin. They's feckin' armoured and feck.'

'Now there are wise words,' said Dathenar, brightening.

'Indeed?' Prazek asked. 'How could you tell?'

No answer was possible, as the first three men charged them, with a dozen or so others following.

Weapons leapt from scabbards. The mounts surged forward, eager to close.

Hoofs lashed out, blades slashed, stabbed and twisted. Figures flew away to the sides of the track, while others vanished beneath the stamping horses. Blades flickered. Voices shrieked.

Moments later, both Houseblades rode clear and then reined in to wheel round. In their wake, a dozen deserters were still standing. Half that number writhed on the ground, while the remaining bodies did not move at all. There was blood on the track, blood bright upon the thin drifts of snow to either side.

Dathenar whipped his sword blade downward, shedding gore from its length. 'Wise words, Prazek, are rarely understood.'

Their horses stamped and snorted, eager for another charge into the press, but both men were quick to quiet them.

Prazek eyed the deserters. 'Few enough now, I think, to see them march in proper cadence.'

'The cadence of the limp, yes.'

'The limp, the shuffle, the stagger and the reel.'

'You describe the gait of the defeated and the cowed, the battered and the bruised.'

'I but describe what I see before me, Dathenar. Which of us, then, shall round up and make them proper?'

''Twas your stirring speech, was it not?'

'Was it? Why, I thought it yours!'

334

'Shall we ask Biskin?'

Prazek sighed. 'Alas, Biskin tried to swallow my horse's left fore-hoof. What remains of his brain bears the imprint of a horseshoe, decidedly unlucky.'

'Ah, and do we see the other two from the front? One I know flung his head out of the path of my sword.'

'Careless of you.'

'No, just his head. His body went the other way.'

'Ah, well. This is poor showing on our part, as the other man lost his hat.'

'He wore no hat.'

'Well, the cap bearing most of his hair, then.'

Dathenar sighed. 'When leaders wrongly lead, why, best that others step in to take their place. You and I, perhaps? See, they recover – those that can – and look to us with the broken regard of the broken.'

'Ah, so I see. Not goats then after all.'

'No. Sheep.'

'Shall we dog them, brother?'

'Why not? They've seen our bite.'

'Enough to heed our bark?'

'I should think so.'

'I should, too.'

Side by side, the two officers rode back to the deserters. Overhead, crows had already gathered, wheeling and crying out their impatience.

# BOOK TWO

*In One Fleeting Breath*

# NINE

BENEATH THE FLOOR OF THEIR FATHER'S PRIVATE ROOM there was a hypocaust, through which lead pipes ran, the hot water in them serving to heat the chamber above. There was height enough to crawl, and to kneel, if one was careful to avoid the scalding pipes.

Envy and Spite sat cross-legged, facing each other. They were rank and scrawny, their clothes and skin smeared with soot, grease and dust. Of late, their meals had consisted of rats, mice and spiders, and the occasional pigeon that lingered too long on a ledge within reach. Both girls had become adept at hunting since the new kitchen staff had arrived, and with them a host of other strangers, replenishing the household. Raiding the pantry was no longer possible, and guards now paced the corridors at night.

The taste of misery could be sweeter with company, but the two daughters of Lord Draconus looked upon one another with venom rather than camaraderie. For all that, circumstances were what they were, and both understood the necessity of their continued alliance. For now.

When they spoke, it was in hushed whispers, despite the gurgle of the pipes.

'Again,' hissed Spite, her eyes wide and glittering.

Envy nodded. Heavy footsteps paced above them, from a sealed chamber forbidden to all but Draconus himself. Each time Spite and Envy had ventured into this heady passage, seeking warmth as the winter bit deeper into the stones of the estate, they had heard these same muffled strides, pacing as would a prisoner, circling the confines, spiralling inward to the room's centre, only to begin again, reversing the pattern.

Their father was still in Kharkanas. Had he returned, freedom would have quickly come to a messy and most final end for Envy and Spite. In the wake of murder, the loyalty of blood was a thread that could snap.

'I miss Malice,' Spite said, in a near whimper.

Envy snorted. 'Yes, dear, we should have kept her around, flesh rotting off, hair falling out, and those horrible dead eyes that never blinked. Worse, she stank. That's what happens when you break her neck and she comes back anyway.'

'It was an accident. Father would see that. He'd understand that, Envy. Power, he told us, has its limits, and they need testing.'

'He also told us that we were probably insane,' Envy retorted. 'Our mother's curse.'

'His curse, you mean, in falling for mad women.'

Envy settled on to her back and stretched out on the hot tiles. She was sick of staring at her sister's ugly face. 'Their fault, the both of them. For us. We didn't ask to be like this, did we? They never gave us a chance to be innocent. We've been . . . neglected. Abused by indifference. It was watching the maids playing with themselves at night that twisted our minds. Blame the maids.'

Spite slipped on to her side and pulled herself alongside her sister. They stared up at the raw underside of the floor tiles and the black wood that held them in place. 'He won't kill us for Malice. He'll kill us for all the rest of them. For Atran and Hilith and Hidast, and Dirty Rilt and the other maids.'

Envy sighed. 'That was the best night ever, wasn't it? Maybe we should do it again.'

'They know we're here.'

'No they don't. They suspect, but that's all.'

'They know it, Envy.'

'Maybe, since you ruined that hound's brain, the one they

brought in to sniff us out. It howled all night before they had to cut its throat. They can't find us, and we've never been seen. They're just guessing. It was you ruining that dog that got them suspicious.'

Spite laughed, but softly, making the sound a dry rattle. 'The sorcery – it's everywhere. You feel it, don't you? All those wild energies, all within reach. You know,' she rolled to face Envy, 'we probably could do it again, like you said. Only not with knives this time, but with magic. Just kill them all, with fire and acid, with melting bones and rotting faces, and blood black as ink. Why, we could redecorate, in time for our father's return – won't he be surprised!'

Her voice had grown a little too loud, and the footsteps above them stopped suddenly.

The girls looked at each other in terror.

Something was up there, something demonic. A guardian, perhaps, conjured into being by Draconus.

After a moment, the steps resumed.

Envy reached out and dug her fingernails into Spite's left cheek, hard enough to start tears in her sister's eyes. She edged close and hissed, 'Don't ever do that again!'

Glaring, Spite clawed and gouged the back of Envy's hand, until Envy let go.

They pushed away from each other, feet lashing out in savage kicks until beyond range. The effort left them breathless.

'I want a bottle of wine,' Envy said, after a time. 'I want to get drunk, the way the new surgeon does. What is it with surgeons, anyway? Staring at walls for half a day. Hands shaking and all the rest. Clearly, dealing with sick people is bad for the health.' She turned over on to her belly and began inscribing patterns with a fingernail in the rough stone beneath her. 'Drunk, all my words slurring. Staggering around, pissing on the floor. Then, I'll turn myself into a demon of fire, and anyone who comes near me will burn to ashes, even you. And if you run, I'll track you down. I'll make you kneel and beg for mercy.'

Spite scratched at a flea-bite under her tunic. 'I'll be a

demon of ice. Your fires will wink out, making you useless. Then I'll freeze you solid, and break pieces off whenever I get bored. And I won't kill everybody here. I'll make them my slaves, and make them do things to each other that they'd never do, but they'd have no choice.'

The pattern Envy had scratched into the stone was giving off a faint, amber glow. She cut a nail's line across it and the light flickered and then died. 'Ooh, I like that. The slaves thing, I mean. I want the maids – you can have the rest, but I want the new maids. They don't believe any of the stories. They laugh and squeal and try to frighten each other. They're all fat and soft. After I'm done with them, they'll never laugh again.'

A faint blue penumbra now rose from Spite. 'You can have them. I want the rest. Setyl and Venth and Ivis and Yalad. And especially Sandalath – oh, I want her more than any of the others. That's how we do it, Envy. With magic. Ice and fire.'

Envy crawled close to her sister. 'Let's plan, then.'

Above them, the footsteps paused once more. An instant later the hot air filling the crawlspace seemed to flinch, as bitter cold poured down from between the tiles. Fiercer than winter's breath, the air burned what it touched.

Whimpering, Envy scrabbled for the chute in the wall, Spite clambering behind her.

They did not know what hid in their father's secret chamber. But they knew enough to fear it.

\*      \*      \*

Master-at-arms Ivis walked out beyond the gate, drawing his cloak tighter about him as the north wind cut across the clearing. If he swung left, he would come to the killing ground, where it was impossible to not see the signs of the battle that had taken place there, only a season past. In his previous visits, wandering over the chewed-up ground with its spear-points darkening with rust, its stained shafts of splintered wood, its rotting cloth and leather straps curled like burned fingers, he could hear the echoes still. Faint shouts hanging in the dead air, weapons clashing, horse hoofs thundering and the cries of beast and Tiste.

Only a fool could feel nothing in such a place, no matter how ancient the actual battle. A fool whose spirit was deadened, or just plain dead. Brutality was a stain upon the world, and it seeped deep into the earth. It tainted the air and made each breath lifeless and stale. It clung to time, entwined in the tatters and shreds trailing in its wake. *Time . . .* Standing in that place, Ivis believed he could almost see that ethereal, haunted figure, a lord of grisly progression. The strides devoured the ground, and yet the Lord of Time never left. Perhaps it too was made a prisoner, chained with shock. Or, just as likely, that wretched lord but wandered lost, blinded by something like sorrow. Upon a field of battle, no path led out. None that a mortal could see, at any rate.

It was behind him now, that tragic battle, and yet still he walked through its bitter cloud. *In step with the lost Lord of Time. It is not only the dead who return as ghosts. Sometimes, the living make ghosts of their own, and leave them in places where they have been. Will I turn left here on this trail, then, to meet my own gaze, with but a span of ruined earth between us?*

He had done it often enough. But not, he decided, today. Instead, he struck out straight ahead, towards the ragged fringe of the forest on the other side of the wagon track.

*Into the realm of skewered goddesses. Sharpened stakes.* The forest was now a place to be feared – when had that loss come upon Ivis and his kind? The first village? The first city? That first stretch of torn, cleared ground? There would have been a moment, a cusp, when the Tiste changed, when they left behind their sense of being prey, and in its place became the hunter. Forests were refuges for quarry. They offered camouflage, hidden trails and secret escape routes. Trees to climb, branches to venture out upon. They beguiled with ceaseless motion, or deep shadows. In a single flash, they could confound lines of sight. '*Into the deep wood the prey flee, and into the deep wood we follow/and in the knowledge of our seeing, we make it shallow.*' Even in his youth, the poet Gallan had seen clearly enough. He had grown up in an age of trophies, of antlered skulls, fanged jaws, and dappled, tanned skins that mocked the pretence of the unseen.

*We both saw the forests emptied, made shallow with our knowing. And yet, for all that, the slaughter could not defeat our abiding fear.*

Fighting the chill, he strode into the forest, boots silent upon the thick, wet leaves.

Another battlefield, this one, with the scars of slaughter upon all sides.

He yearned for the return of Lord Draconus. Or even a simple word – a missive sent from the Citadel. He had fashioned a report of the battle with the Borderswords, dispatching it to Kharkanas. It had elicited no response. He had reported in detail the murders within the house. Even this was met with silence.

*Milord, what would you have me do? Two daughters are left to you, their hands red. We found the charred remains of the third – Malice, we think – in an oven. Envy and Spite, milord, hide in the bones of the house. But it's a flimsy refuge. With a word the walls can be breached. With a word, Lord Draconus, I can have the horrid creatures in chains.*

But this led Ivis into a realm in which he did not belong, and responsibilities he would rather do without. Was this cowardice? Was there not the necessity of justice in the matter of slain men and women? *But milord, they are your daughters. Your charge. For you to deal with, not me, not a master-at-arms, who by every law imaginable would see the two of them skinned alive.*

*Return to us, I beg you, and make right this crime. Their blood protects them from me. But not from you.*

*More to the point, milord, what if they seek to strike again? We have our hostage to think of, the sanctity of her life – Abyss take me, the sanctity of what remains of her innocence!*

*I will defend her, milord, even against your daughters.*

He was among black spruce now, passing between boles

that had bled sap now frozen into obsidian-hued beads, as if the trees were bleeding black glass. It was said that in the far north, such trees could explode in the depth of winter. When the air grew cold enough to pain the lungs with each breath drawn. It would not surprise him: this wood made for a foul fire, and its habit of growing up from sunken and rotted ground gave the trees a deathly feel.

At least they reared straight, and seemed to know a youthful span before their sudden death, when all life fled them in a seeming instant. Then, straight or not, they would become skeletal, home to spiders and not much else.

He paused at a faint smell upon the cold wind. Woodsmoke. *Shallow, and shallow again. Even you, smoke, now taint my memory. It is fire's light that is brittle, not its heat. Quench one and still flinch from the other. I'll take the glow as a promise and leave it be. Deniers, if indeed you have returned to this forest, play out your rituals in private, and know well my aversion. The stench suffices.*

He swung about, set off back to the keep. It seemed that no matter which direction he chose, it was not a day for wandering.

Winter had cooled Kurald Galain's rage, surely. The civil war slept restless as a hungry bear in its cave, but he would with relief call it sleep nonetheless. Swords sipped the oil in their scabbards, whilst other weapons were plied, to keep banked what the season's turn promised.

He would lead the Houseblades out then, Ivis believed. Into the new warmth and lengthening days. Even in the absence of his lord, he would fight on behalf of the Great Houses. As the beast shook itself awake, lumbering into the bright spring air, he would wield Draconus's soldiers like a sharp talon in the First Son's reach. *We'll take to the blood as well as any other, and make of Urusander's Legion a field of meat. Lord Anomander, do set us where you will, but pray it is in the heart of the fight. I have deceits to answer, in the name of the Borderswords.*

The stolid, grey walls of the keep stretched out before him, beyond the track's single ditch. He carried with him that tendril of woodsmoke. *No, Ivis, say it plain. Stay where you are, Draconus. Leave it to me to fold us into Anomander's army. By this single act, your enemies are plucked. If instead you take the vanguard . . . ah, forgive me, I see us standing alone on that fell day. At our backs, not the host of noble allies, but bared teeth and rank indignation.*

*Stay, milord, and make your Houseblades a gift to the Son of Darkness. In the name of the woman you love, make us a gift.*

A few paces clear of the trees, as he crossed the wagon trail, a sound behind him made him turn, to see three figures at the edge of the treeline. They wore skins, two of them wearing the ragged heads of ektral. For an instant, riding a thrill of fear, Ivis had thought them demonic – some blend of Tiste and beast – but of course, he then realized, the antlered ektral were but headdresses.

*Deniers. Torturers of goddesses. The night before the summoning, you sat together, sharpening stakes at the edge of the glade. You invented a ritual, and filled it with power, and then you did something terrible.*

Teeth bared, Ivis drew out his sword.

The three drew back, beneath the shadows.

Ivis saw that they were unarmed. Even so, the gloom of the forest behind them could be hiding any number of warriors. *I'll not take a step. If you would speak to me, come forward.* But such boldness belonged to his mind, the words left unspoken. The truth was, fear gripped his throat. The thought of sorcery had unmanned him.

After a moment, one of the shamans stepped forward. As the figure drew closer, he saw that it was a woman, her face ritually scarred to make ragged streaks running down her cheeks. Unlike the two who wore ektral headdresses, the hood covering her head was furred, the fur black but silver-tipped. It hung down to cover her shoulders and was drawn together at the front by a single toggle. Her pale eyes were bleak as they fixed upon his face, and then the sword he held in his hand.

Ivis hesitated, and after a moment he slowly returned the weapon to its scabbard.

She drew nearer.

At last he found his voice. 'What do you want? I saw her. The goddess in the glade. Nothing you can say will wash the blood from your hands.'

She received his harsh words without expression, and when she spoke her tone was flat. 'We have come to tell you, Keep-Soldier, what has birthed this war.'

Ivis scowled. 'You would not bow before Mother Dark—'

'She never asked us to.'

'And if she had?'

After a moment, the woman shrugged. 'When the animals are gone. When hunting ends, and the ways of living change. When one must look to tamed animals, and the planting of crops. When all the old ways of bravery and prowess are done away with, the hunters will turn upon one another. Honour becomes a weapon, but it pursues no wild beast. Instead, it pursues your neighbour.' She pointed to the keep behind him. 'The birth of walls.'

Ivis shook his head. 'There was war, with the Forulkan. We were forced to create an army. When the war was done, witch, only then did that army turn upon us. Honour was well served in the instant, but its flavour quickly fades, and now the taste is bitter.'

'What drove the Forulkan into our lands? For them, too, the old ways were dead.'

'Is this all you wanted to say? Why bother? We could argue causes until the last sunset; it avails us nothing.'

'The Shake will leave their fortresses,' the woman said. 'They will come to us, in the forests. You will try to find us, but we will not be found. Not by you, not by Father Light. We are no longer in your war.'

Ivis snorted. 'You think to usurp Higher Grace Skelenal?'

The witch was silent for a long moment, and then she said, 'The goddess you saw chose the manner in which she manifested. When we found her . . . we fled. If others set upon her, they belonged to the forest. Spirits of wood. Spirits of old bones and blood-hungry earth and roots. For us, there was no need to hear her words. We well knew what she would say to us.' The witch raised both hands, out from under the skins she was wearing, and Ivis recoiled upon seeing the stakes driven through both. 'It is our fate to slay the old ways of living. We take too much joy in the slaughter, in the proof of our skills with spear and arrow. Longing gave power to our summoning. We must now suffer the proof of our regret.'

'Then . . . send her back.'

'Seen or unseen, flesh or ghost, she suffers still. You and I, we have murdered the old ways, and all that we will come to, it is of our own making.' She hesitated, and then cocked her head. 'You can always blame your neighbour.'

She bowed before him, and turned away.

Ivis watched her re-join the others, and the three shamans slipped back into the forest. In moments they vanished from sight.

*Blame the neighbours. Yes, we'll do that. When we can, if only to make living easier.*

He resumed walking, his scowl deepening as he looked upon the wall before him. The Deniers would do as they must. If indeed they chose to disappear, rejecting the vengeance they had every right to seek, well, regrets had a way of breeding, and the swarming spawn could drown a soul in an instant.

Passing through the gate, his steps slowed as he studied the keep before him. *Ah, milord. Your daughters? Well now, there was a fire in the house . . . we saw naught the telltale flickers of light, and all too late felt its murderous heat.*

*Come the spring, milord, I see a sky made grey with smoke.*

＊  ＊  ＊

Sandalath Drukorlat sat near the fire in the common room, away from the others. The new surgeon, Prok, was singing a ballad, words slurring and the brightness of his gaze an alcoholic sheen through which he blinked regretfully at the world. Whatever sorrow existed in the song lost its truths in the maudlin self-pity of the man's voice.

Seated near the surgeon, in poses of faint attention or

outright uninterest, were arranged the other newcomers to the household, as well as Armourer Setyl and Horse Master Venth Direll. The new keeper of records, a woman named Sorca, hid her face behind the bowl of a pipe. Her complexion, oddly smooth and unlined, was the same hue as the smoke she sent out in long, tumbling streams from her somewhat overly generous mouth. Her hair was cut short as if to undermine her femininity, but her broad features were soft and peculiarly welcoming. For all that, the woman rarely spoke, and when she did, it was in a low mutter, as if all conversation was in truth a private one, she with herself. Sandalath had yet to see her smile.

Sitting close to the new keeper was the woman who had replaced Hilith as head of the house-servants. Bidishan was wiry, nervous, carrying herself with an air of impatience, as if some vital task yet awaited her for which she needed all her energy, but, Sandalath had come to realize, there was no such task, and each day and evening was consumed by the same headlong rush. Perhaps it was sleep that Bidishan hurried towards, as if oblivion was the only island to take her exhausted self, flung insensate upon the strand at day's end, and in the realm of dreams the woman unleashed all that was in her soul.

Musing on the notion, Sandalath felt a pang of sympathy for Bidishan. Within the mind, after all, was a world of unchecked dramas, where loves were unveiled and made so bright, so fierce, as to sting the eyes, and every gesture could make the earth groan, and every glance could awaken unfettered flames of passion.

In that world, Bidishan was beautiful, young, filled with vivacity. And others who came upon her, why, they saw her truly, and in the face of such encounters they avowed their hearts, and made every labour bent to her service an act of worship.

Sandalath knew her own such world, also clothed in sleep. And often, she found herself longing for its embrace, for in this cold, wintry place, with its stone walls hiding secret passageways, her waking moments were filled with anxiety, fear and longing. In her thoughts and in her body, she lived with nervous fires flickering without end. When she could, she fled them all, huddling beneath furs in her bed, and, as sleep took her, slipping back to the life that existed before House Dracons, before the murderous spawn of Draconus and the blood splashing floor and walls, before the bodies carried out into the bleak light of the courtyard and the small white bones in the bread oven. Before the terrible battle that had been fought outside the keep's walls.

A secret lover, the pleasure of his touch, his weight upon her in the high grasses far beyond the sight of her mother. A son, free to play out his games of war amidst the scorched embers of the old stables. Children were visible shouts of life, a crowing delight in possibility and promise.

*He was taken from me, taken from my sight. Where he once lived, in my life, there is nothing. An emptiness, empty of life and love. Empty, I fear, of hope.*

Was that child not the mother's gift? Children were where things could start over, be made different, where wounds could be avoided, evaded. Where dreams could live again, passed on in the clasp of her hand to his. Youth sent echoes into the world, echoes that could rush over a mother and sweep her back into her own past, and the swirling sorrow of such moments, so bittersweet, could become a kind of strength, a protectiveness both savage and undying. As if, in protecting the child, the mother was also protecting what remained of the child she had once been.

Bridges such as these should never be dismantled.

And yet, when Sandalath thought of her own mother, she felt nothing. *No bridge there. She sold off the stones, one by one, until she had us all perched upon a single block, a tottering foundation stone, the height of which she held to be more vital than anything else, even love.*

*Nerys Drukorlat, was it Father who stole everything from you? His war? His wounding? His death? But Orfantal wasn't your child with which to begin again, to make right.*

*He was mine.*

Prok's song stuttered and then fell away as the surgeon lost his memory of the words. From near the kitchen door, Yalad – now the gate sergeant – rose to collect wood for the fire. She watched him approach and answered his weary smile with one of her own.

Houseblades were stationed in every common room now, and at the doors to the private ones. It was, in some ways, absurd. The girls hid in their hidden places. Ivis himself had said they could root them out at any time. Instead, such a moment would have to await the return of Lord Draconus. *And in the meantime, we live in terror of two wretched children.*

After stoking the fire, Yalad drew a chair close to Sandalath and sat, leaning back and stretching out his legs. 'This is welcome warmth, yes?'

Prok found another ballad, beginning the song loud and stentorian, rocking in his chair to some unheard musical accompaniment, the hand holding its tankard of wine lifting up and down to set the beat.

Wincing, Yalad sighed. 'Do you ever wonder, milady, why so many of our songs do little more than moan over things lost or never owned in the first place?'

*No. Not really.* 'Our good surgeon, sir, knows better than to choose the more raucous ones, lest Commander Ivis arrive again at the most inopportune instant, with us witness to the rise of startling colour to his face.'

'He was mordant on your behalf, milady. Surely you understand that.'

'Of course, and by such willingness he charms me, gate sergeant.'

Yalad smiled. 'That admission would see him crimson.' He slowly shook his head. 'And Ivis as old as he is, I'd never thought to see him on such uncertain footing. The charm, milady, is yours, and makes him young again . . . but in a most unsettling way for us who serve under him.'

'I would not see his authority undermined, sir,' Sandalath said, frowning. 'Advise me, if you will, on how best to blunt what charms I may possess.'

'I cannot, milady,' Yalad said, 'as no man here would even think of withering such gifts, natural as they are.'

She regarded him beneath veiled lids. 'Sir, you learn well the language of the court. Or is there more of the courting in it than is seemly?'

'No,' he replied. 'I know well my station, milady, and more to the point, yours. It is an otherwise grim season we suffer here, and so we take such pleasures as we can find.'

She continued studying him. 'I envy the cleverness in you, gate sergeant. If I possess charms, they are sadly childlike. A sheltered life shrinks the world for the one who suffers in it. All too often, innocence yields naivety, and when pushed from the small world into the vaster one beyond, the creature finds herself both unknowing and lost.'

'Your confession humbles me, milady.'

She waved a hand. 'It is nothing. I stood atop a tower, witnessing the death of too many men and women. I never thought that war would come so close, no longer a thing in the distance, beyond some border. Now, it strides across familiar ground, and makes that ground newly estranged.' She started as a log abruptly shifted in the hearth, sending up a flurry of sparks. 'It does little good,' she added, 'when the walls breathe, and, I fear, blink.'

'You are safe, milady,' Yalad said. 'Failing any other option, we'll starve them out.'

Further conversation between the two was interrupted by the arrival of Surgeon Prok, his song done. Clumsily, he dragged a third chair up, and then slumped down in it with a heavy sigh. 'You can strip the bark from a tree and think nothing of it,' he said, nodding to himself. 'But peel back a man's skin and, ah, entire worlds are jarred askew. We shiver and are made vulnerable.' He smiled across at Yalad. 'I make my war with ruined flesh, gate sergeant. To make it right again. But you, with that blade at your side, you make the trees bleed.'

Yalad frowned. 'It's said the priests have found a sorcery that heals, Prok. They name it Denul. Perhaps what ails you is your impending obsolescence.'

Prok's florid face broadened in a smile. 'No risk of that to the soldier, though. Obsolescence.' He stretched the word out, tasted it, and seemed to find it foul. After a moment, he leaned back, raising the tankard before him. 'I have imbibed of that sorcery, Yalad. You wonder at with whom you bargain, with such sudden power in your hands. Imagine, if you will, a future in which healing is possible for everything, every ailment, every wound. Should a remnant of life linger in the flesh, why, we can save the fool. The question then is: should we?'

Sandalath glanced at Yalad, and then said, 'But why would you not, surgeon? I would think, in such a future, you would find an answer to your desire – to make things right again, to mend the broken, to heal the diseased, or the wounded.'

He tilted the tankard in her direction. 'To the crowded future, then.'

She watched him drink, and then said, 'Even magic cannot refuse death.'

'True enough,' he allowed. 'We but prolong the moment of its arrival. Denul becomes a cheat, milady, to delight in the instant but dismay in the distance. It is more than life that is extended, it is also the agony of failure, for fail we will, and fail we must. Yalad's war has its victories and its losses. It surges ahead, and then yields ground. It can even end, for a time. But the healer knows only retreat, and each step yielded is bitter, the ground soaked in blood.'

'Then the sorcery is a boon,' she replied. 'Indeed, it is a godly gift.'

He met her eyes, and she saw through their reddened gleam to a sudden, raw pain. 'Then why, milady, does it taste so sour?'

'That would be the wine, Prok,' Yalad said, with a faint smile.

He shifted his gaze to the gate sergeant. 'Yes, of course.'

A few moments later, Commander Ivis entered the chamber, pulling off his heavy cloak. He paused for a moment to study the occupants of the room, and then, with the briefest of glances at Sandalath, made his way across to the kitchen.

Ivis was a rare presence at the dinner table these evenings. His habit of walking the grounds beyond the keep walls often devoured half the night. Once, in her room and readying for sleep, Sandalath had paused at the window, and, looking down, saw the commander standing at the graves of those household staff who had been murdered by the daughters of Draconus. She could not be sure, but she thought that the mound he faced belonged to the old surgeon, Atran. When she was alive, he had affected distracted ignorance of her desire, as if taking pleasure was a notion he had no business entertaining, given his duties. Sandalath suspected that he now regretted his aloofness.

'I wonder,' mused Prok once Ivis had gone, 'if it takes a surgeon's eye to see what ails a man, or woman, when that person has made disguise a profession.'

'Keep such thoughts to yourself,' Yalad snapped.

'Forgive me, gate sergeant. You are most correct. But understand: I describe no blessing on my part. This gift pains the recipient, who would rather return it than accept the burden. But then, into whose hands?'

'Is Denul truly godless?' Sandalath asked.

Prok seemed to flinch. 'Imagine that: the power of life and death in my hands arrives as a godless thing. How eager we are to turn about miracles, and make them as mundane as, oh, binding the laces on your moccasin. Yet with each wonder we tread underfoot, the world gets just a little more . . . pale.'

'Why not brighter, surgeon?' Sandalath suggested. 'What need for gods, should the future bring us all such powers?'

He blinked at her. 'You think gods offer nothing more than the delusion of bargaining, milady? With every moment, we speak with the world, and in its own way it speaks back – should we choose to hear it. But now, cut out its tongue. Excise its participation in this dialogue. Indeed, do that and to continue speaking will feel most foolish, yes? The prayer unanswered makes for a bleak echo.' He leaned forward and carefully set the tankard down on the stone dais surrounding the hearth. 'Or worse, the returning whisper will arrive filled with utter nonsense. It is my belief, milady, that cults and religions often find their shape out of the necessity to fill the silence of a world made godless, and it was made godless precisely because we stopped listening. In place of honest humility, then, are set rules and prohibitions, inquisitions and the violent silencing of a host of avowed or imagined enemies. Do this and not that. Why? Because the god said so, that's why. But was that really the god speaking, or just some twisted echo of mortal flaws and frailties, each one adding to the list of holy pronouncements?'

'Dangerous words this night,' Yalad said. 'Best you go to your room, Prok, and sleep.'

'With the dinner bell not yet sounded, gate sergeant? Would you have me starve?'

'Mother Dark is not—'

'Ah, Mother Dark, yes, who hides unseen and has nothing to say, so the priestesses open wide their legs seeking mundane ecstasy, or at the very least, satiation.' Prok waved a hand to cut off Yalad's retort. 'Yes, yes, I understand, and in her absence and in her silence she in truth informs us of something profound. But truly, Yalad, how many are capable of appreciating that level of subtlety? The cult that makes its rules simple will thrive. Reduced to a phrase or two should suffice. It will be interesting to see what the followers of Father Light will make of their faith – but whatever it is, no matter how simple or complex, you can be sure that Mother Dark will issue faint reply.'

Sandalath chanced to glance towards the kitchen door, and saw Ivis standing there. There was no doubt that he had heard the surgeon's words, but she could read nothing from his expression. An instant later the bell sounded.

Sighing, Prok worked himself upright. 'A chair to take me, a table to lean against – what more does a man need? Come, Yalad, join me in fighting off starvation's dogs one more night, yes?'

The gate sergeant rose and faced Sandalath. 'Milady?'

She took the hand he offered her, but let his grip slip away once she was on her feet. Turning, she met the eyes of Ivis, and smiled.

He bowed slightly in her direction.

Accompanied by Keeper Sorca, Matron Bidishan, Setyl and Venth, they set off for the dining room. For this evening at least, Ivis would join them.

*    *    *

Wreneck's long hunt for the soldiers who had hurt Jinia had not begun well. Winter was a world made gaunt with starvation. But, it now seemed, even endings didn't quite end.

The warmth of the palm resting upon his brow seemed to hover at a vast distance from the place in which Wreneck had found himself. And where he had found himself, he was not alone. A figure sat beside him, not close enough to reach out and touch – meaning the hand upon Wreneck's forehead did not belong to this stranger. But the figure was speaking, often in a language he could not understand, and at times the voice was a woman's, while at other times it belonged to a man. The times when the stranger spoke in Wreneck's own language, the words were confusing, as if Wreneck was nothing more than a witness, as if the words were not meant for him at all.

But the hand upon his brow was different, because it felt real. Still, it was far away. What lay between was dark, but the darkness roiled, like soot-filled water, and that water was icy cold. He had no desire to set out across it, and so come closer to the warmth, though he understood that such feelings seemed wrong.

'Besides,' muttered the stranger at his side in a man's voice, 'desire itself is a cruel parent, when the child knows no strength.'

There was some comfort here, anyway, in the midst of his companion's grown-up words, even when they weren't meant for him.

'Men,' said the stranger, 'suffer many things. Some they give voice to, all too often, and make of them a dirge that drains the interest from any within hearing. But other sufferings are quiet things, held tight with a hand clamped over the mouth. That hand can silence or suffocate, or both; and there

356

is no proof that the man sought one but not the other. But the idea of choice is unimportant. These kinds of suffering are reluctant to die, and if murder is the desire, strength is the betrayer.'

Wreneck nodded, thinking he understood. It was part of being a man, he told himself, that made the secret suffering so powerful.

As if the stranger had heard his thoughts, he said, 'Hidden deep inside, it grows fat on what morsels of sweet, deadly imagination the man offers it, and this is a butcher's tally of fears and dreads.'

Still, the hand upon Wreneck's brow felt dry, not blood-soaked. Despite the comfort of this unknown companion, it might be worth the journey back, to where lived winter's pale light. He had been so cold, on those nights, with the forest yielding him little. The world, he now knew, promised nothing.

His friend spoke again, this time in a woman's voice. 'If the world was a parent – to all that lived upon it – then love died long ago, after too many ages of mutual cruelty. Burning forests. Dying trees. A child trapped by the flames. The shaking of earth and rock-falls, or houses falling down killing everyone inside. A beautiful baby, dying for no good reason. No, we have lots of reasons to hate the world, and the world has lots of reasons to hate us. It goes on and on, now, and still we keep being cruel to each other.

'And we pretend we're winning. Until we lose again. This is how things rise and fall, and how things once strong can end up burned out and in ruin, with weeds growing up from the cracked flagging. This is how proud old women end up dying in the dirt, or just burning up like a straw doll. Things rise and fall, the way the chest does when you're breathing. And, dear child, you're still breathing. Shall we count this a victory?'

*There were gravestones, and crypts. I walked over mounds. It was cold, everything was cold. The stones, the sky. I found a pit and sank into it. Like a dead man. Until the cold went away.*

357

*It is as my friend says. Men twist to what they suffer inside. Jinia, I will find them and kill them. They won't be able to hide, because what they did will be right there, on their faces.*

'The life of a child finds strength,' said his friend, now a man again, 'in its potential. That potential is stubborn. It doesn't understand surrender . . . until it does, and with that understanding, the child withers and dies. You, Wreneck, don't comprehend the notion of surrender. This is what draws us to you. You have the will of tender shoots, as they emerge from cracks in stone, or between the flagstones. Victory is far away, but inevitable. In this manner, the child is closest to nature, when the adult has long since fled the cost of ambition, and must live, day upon day, with the price of an entire language built around notions of surrender.'

*Who are you?* Wreneck asked.

'We are dying gods.'

*Why are you dying?*

'To make way for our children.'

*But they need you!*

'They think not. Lessons, Wreneck, are not easily won. We see a future filled with blood. But you, child, we were drawn to you. Even so near death, you shine bright. We will leave you now. Do not ask our blessing. It has become a curse. Nature is an eternal child. Thus we, the eternal children of the world, now understand the notion of surrender. It is time, alas, to go away.'

Some memories returned to Wreneck, and with them, his friend vanished.

He had felt them lift his body from the grave. He was light in their hands, almost floating, and the rags he wore were stiff with frost. He thought he heard them speaking and there were two voices thus far. Just the two, and then the smell of woodsmoke and maybe heat, and now he was swaddled in furs. Beneath his back was a thick, tanned hide, and beneath that there were hot stones lifted out from the fire. Still, the hand upon his brow was the warmest thing he felt, and yet it remained impossibly far away.

*Dying gods, I miss you.*

The world beyond the farm and the town of Abara Delack was bigger than he had imagined. It just went on and on, like someone repeating the words of creation over and over again. *Trees, hills, rocks, river, ditch, trees, trees, track and trail, road and ditch, hills, trees, stream, trees. Sky and sky and sky and sky . . .* and the further it sprawled, the colder it got, as if the words had lost their love of themselves, as if the creator of the world was just getting tired of the whole thing, the over-and-over-again of it. *Trees and sky and trees and glade and graves and pit and down here, yes, just down here, is what you need. See how small it is? Perfect.*

'Some never awaken,' said a voice, and this one was real.

'He will,' replied the other, closer, belonging to the one whose hand was upon his brow. 'You ever underestimate the strength of the Tiste.'

'Perhaps I do at that.'

'And he's young, but not too young. A tough boy, I should say. See the burn scars and whip marks? And that one I'd wager was a sword-thrust. Should have killed him. It is difficult to claim that this child knows nothing of survival.'

'What will you do with him?'

'Dracons Keep is nearest us.'

'Ah, I see. But Lord Draconus is not in residence, is he?'

'Probably not, as you say, Azathanai.'

'Mother Dark still holds him close.'

'It may be that, yes.'

'What else?'

There was a pause, and then came the reply, 'He steps away from things. He chooses to remain in darkness, unseeing and unseen. By deliberate absence from all affairs, he wishes to be forgotten.' The voice sighed and then continued. 'Hopeless, yes. Events will drag him out before too long.'

'As they will drag you back. To Kharkanas.'

'Will you accompany me, then?'

'To the Citadel? I think not. Walls and stone overhead makes me uncomfortable. No, I will simply await you, nearby.'

The hand slipped away, and Wreneck felt its sudden absence with a pang. But he heard the soft laugh, and then, 'The High Mason cringes from walls and stone roof.'

A few moments passed, and then the other man said, 'Every monument I raise from the earth is a prison, First Son. In being made, it is contained. In its shape, it displaces emptiness. In its conceit, it seeks to defy time.'

'Well tended, such a monument can withstand ages, Caladan.'

'Even as its meaning weathers away. Tend to the stone or bronze, yes, and keep it pristine. But, I wonder, who tends to the truth of it? It would be better, I sometimes think, if I simply sank my works into bogs, to dwell in darkness and mud.'

'An altogether different kind of monument,' said the nearer man, as he brought his hand once again to rest upon Wreneck's brow. 'A different meaning, too.'

'Intention, First Son, yields no echoes. All who come afterwards, to gaze upon my art, can only wonder at my mind, even as they note every chisel scar, and ponder the sure hand that dealt it. They will, of course, make a feast of the morsels, and assert their pronouncements to be a certain truth.'

The hand slipped away again and Wreneck heard the man beside him rise to stand, and his voice now drifted down as if coming from a cave, or the ledge of some tower or cliff. 'Your angst is not unfamiliar, Caladan Brood. I've heard the poet Gallan snarling when in his cups. Still, there is little artistry in my life. My mind works in plain ways, my meaning plainer still.'

The one named Caladan Brood, whose voice was strangely heavy, now made a sound that might have been laughter. 'And your swordplay knows no subtlety, Rake? The machinations of court? You fail to convince me with your claims.'

'The issue is simple enough,' Rake replied. 'Urusander and his legion will quit Neret Sorr before the break of winter's hold. Together, they will march upon Kharkanas, with the intention of setting Urusander upon a throne, at Mother Dark's side.'

'And what in such a scenario so offends you, First Son? Tell me, if you will, what sets the common soldier so far beneath those of noble blood? By what means do you measure worth?'

'Ask the common soldier, Caladan, and the words are direct enough. Coin and land, standing and prestige. A freedom with indulgences, a certain pomp. The very things they curse in their enemies are what they seek for themselves. The argument, friend, is held low, and in that modesty, iron will shout in the manner of bullies. It is a pathetic language, this argument, with mutual stupidity setting the limits of the exchange.'

'Yet you must march to meet him, with swords and spears to speak for you.'

The First Son – Wreneck knew that title, as he had heard Lady Nerys utter it often enough, in tones of awe – was slow in replying, and when he did, his voice was cold. 'The pretensions of the nobles are little better, Caladan. They see their perch as crowded enough. I have an angry child to either side of me, and I like it not – is this my sole task? My singular service to Mother Dark? To stand between two self-serving brats? No. If I am to march against Urusander, I need better reason than that.'

'And have you one?'

'I take offence at the presumption.'

'Whose?'

'Well, all of them. But mostly Urusander's – or perhaps it is Hunn Raal's, but I have doubts as to the importance of the distinction.'

'Do you know, then, Mother Dark's mind?'

The First Son's laugh was bitter, and then he said, 'She has her Consort. Is this not plain enough? But then a kinswoman of yours, Azathanai, flung a burning brand into the haystack. Andii and now Liosan – we are a people divided, and I cannot but believe that was your Azathanai's intent, to see us weakened. And I must wonder, why?'

'Look to Draconus for an answer to that, First Son.'

'Draconus? Why him?'

'He has brought Dark to the Tiste.'

'The Terondai on the Citadel's floor? No. The Azathanai named T'riss had already done her damage by then.'

'The Gate, which I suppose we must now call Kurald Galain, is an iteration of control,' Caladan replied, 'over a force that was and remains pervasive, existing as it does in opposition to Chaos.'

'To Chaos? Not Light?'

'Light, if you would consider this, is an absolution of Chaos. In its purity it finds order, with substance and hue. This is how Chaos seeks, in its own fashion, its own obliteration.'

'I do not understand you, Caladan. You speak of these elemental forces as if they possessed will.'

'No, only proclivity. Name any force and, with sufficient contemplation, you will discern that it cannot exist alone. Other forces act upon it, make demands of it, and even alter the edges of its own nature. This is Creation's dialogue, but even then, what seems but opposition, of two forces set against one another, is in truth a multitude of interactions, of voices. Perhaps dialogue is the wrong word. Think more of a tumult, a cacophony. Each force seeks to impose its own rhythm upon all of Creation, and what results may well seem disordered, but I assure you, First Son, this chorus makes music. For those willing or able to hear.'

'Caladan, return this discussion to Draconus, and T'riss.'

'A lover's gift – well, too many gifts, and too generous their span. In his blessing of the woman he loves with the power of Elemental Dark, Draconus imposed an impossible imbalance upon Creation. The world, First Son – any world – can hold only its necessary forces, and these in delicate balance. The Azathanai you have named T'riss had no choice, although in the boldness of her act she displayed nothing of the subtlety of our kind. It may be that the Vitr has damaged her in some way.'

'I would track her down, Caladan, to learn more of all this.'

'She may well return,' Caladan said. 'But for now, it is unlikely you can find her trail. She walks unseen paths. You

362

must understand, First Son: the Azathanai are skilled at not being found.'

'Then, you say, the blame is with Draconus.'

'With the weakness in his heart, but is it right to blame such a thing? In the prelude to war, compassion is the first victim, slain like a child upon the threshold.'

'Lord Draconus is my friend.'

'Then sustain it.'

'But . . . remaining at her side as he does, he disappoints me.'

'You have set your expectation against the compassion you claim to possess, and now the child bleeds anew.'

'Very well, I will seek to withhold judgement on Draconus.'

'Then, I fear, you will stand alone in the war to come.'

'The thought,' the First Son said, 'of a highborn victory tastes as sour as does the thought of Urusander's ascension. I am of a mind to see them both humbled.'

'Ascension is a curious word in this context.'

'Why?'

'Mother Dark . . . Father Light. The titles are not empty, and if you think the powers behind them are but illusions, then you are a fool.'

Wreneck heard a gasp, but it was a moment before he realized that it had come from him. He was back, in a place of warmth. He had crossed the icy river all unknowing. He opened his eyes.

A tall warrior stood above him, studying him with calm eyes. Off to one side, seated on a scorched stump, was a huge figure wearing silver fur upon his broad shoulders, with something bestial in his broad, flat face that made Wreneck shiver.

'The chill remains deep in your bones,' the First Son said to Wreneck. 'But you have returned to us, and that is well.'

Wreneck glared across at Caladan Brood. 'First Son, why do you not kill him?' he asked.

'For what reason would I do that, even if I could?' Lord Anomander asked.

'He called you a fool.'

The First Son smiled. 'He but reminds me of the risk in careless words. Well now, we found you in a grave, yet here you are, resurrected. But this winter has been hard on you – when did you last eat?'

Unable to recall, Wreneck said nothing.

'I will prepare some broth,' said Caladan Brood, reaching across to his pack. 'If you will make this child your conscience, best he know the bliss of a full stomach.'

The First Son grunted. 'My conscience, Caladan? He just urged vengeance against you.'

'After riding the back of our conversation, yes.'

'I doubt he understood much of it.'

The Azathanai shrugged as he withdrew items from the pack.

'Why,' Anomander persisted, 'would I make this foundling my conscience?'

'Perhaps only to awaken it within you, First Son, given his impulsive bloodlust.'

Lord Anomander looked back down at Wreneck. 'Are you a Denier orphan, then?' he asked.

Wreneck shook his head. 'I was a stabler for House Drukorlat. But she was murdered and everything was burned down. They tried to kill me and Jinia, too, but we lived, only she's hurt inside. I remember their names. I am going to kill them. The ones who did that to Jinia. I have a spear . . .'

'Yes,' the First Son said, his expression grave, 'we found that. The shaft seems sound, lovingly tended, I would judge. But it could do with a better-weighted blade. You have their names, you say. What else do you recall of these murderers?'

'Legion soldiers, sir. They were drunk, but they took orders and things. There was a sergeant. They thought I was dead, but I wasn't. They were going to burn us all in the house, but I got me and Jinia out.'

'Lady Nerys is dead, then.'

Wreneck nodded. 'But Orfantal had already been sent away, and Sandalath, too. There was just the three of us left, but I wasn't let in the house, and the barn burned down and she didn't really want me any more anyway.'

Lord Anomander continued studying him. 'And Sandalath . . . if I recall, she is now a hostage in Dracons Keep.'

Wreneck couldn't remember if that was true, but he nodded. 'And that's where you're taking me, isn't it?'

'A quiet listener, this one,' said Caladan as he set a battered pot upon the embers.

'Good men are,' said Wreneck. 'It's only little boys who are too loud, getting whipped for it as is proper.'

Neither the First Son nor the Azathanai replied to this.

After a time, Wreneck sat up, and Caladan Brood brought to him a bowl of broth. Wreneck held it in both hands and felt how the heat seeped through to his fingers. The sensation was painful, but he welcomed it nonetheless.

Then Lord Anomander spoke. 'It may comfort you to know that Orfantal is safe, in the Citadel.'

Wreneck glanced over, and then frowned down at the bowl and its steaming broth. 'She said I sullied him. We had to stop being friends.'

'Sandalath?'

'No. Lady Nerys.'

'Who was free with her cane.'

'Me and Jinia had to know our place.'

'Would you rather,' Lord Anomander said, 'that I did not deliver you to Dracons Keep? I recall Sandalath, from her time in the Citadel. She was clever, and seemed kindly enough, but time will change people.'

'She liked it that Orfantal had someone to play with, but it was wrong. Lady Nerys explained it.' Wreneck sipped at the broth. He had never tasted anything better. 'I can't stay long at Dracons Keep, even if Sandalath wants me there. I have bad men to kill.'

'This,' said Caladan Brood, 'proves a most cruel conscience.'

'Go slowly with that broth,' Lord Anomander said. 'Tell me your name.'

'Wreneck.'

'Have you brothers or sisters?'

'No.'

'Your parents?'

'Just my ma. The man who made me with her was with the army. He also made horseshoes and other stuff, but he died to a horse-kick. I don't remember him, but Ma says I'm going to be big, like he was. She sees it in my bones.'

'You'll not return to her?'

'Not until I kill the ones who hurt Jinia. Then I'll come back. I'll find Jinia in the village and we'll get married. She says she can't have children, not any more, after what they did, but that doesn't matter, and it doesn't matter if Ma doesn't like her either, because of how she's been used and all. I'll marry Jinia, and protect her for ever.'

Lord Anomander was no longer looking down at Wreneck. He was instead looking across at Caladan Brood. He said, 'And so I now raise my standard, Azathanai, to a deserved future, and a conscience scrubbed clean. If not in the name of love, then what cause suffices?'

'Draconus would stand with you, First Son, beneath such a standard. And thus the nobles are lost.'

Lord Anomander turned away, studied the barren trees with their scorched trunks that surrounded the glade. 'Are we then past the age of shame, Caladan? No sting should I ridicule my fellow highborn?'

'Its power has diminished. Shame, my friend, is but a ghost now, haunting every city, every town and village. It has less substance than woodsmoke, and but rubs the throat with little more than an itch.'

'I shall make it a wildfire.'

'In such a conflagration, First Son, guard your standard well.'

'Wreneck.'

'Milord?'

'When your time comes . . . for vengeance. Find me.'

'I don't need any help. They stuck a sword in me and I didn't die. They can try it again and I still won't die. My promise keeps me alive. When you become a man, you learn to do what you say you will do. That's what makes you a man.'

'Alas, there are far fewer men in the world than you might think, Wreneck.'

'But I'm one.'

'I believe you,' Lord Anomander replied. 'But understand my offer before you reject it. When you find those rapists and murderers, they will be in a cohort, in Urusander's Legion. There may well be a thousand soldiers between you and them. I will clear your path, Wreneck.'

Wreneck stared at the First Son. 'But, milord, I am going to do it at night, when they're sleeping.'

Caladan Brood grunted a laugh, and then spat into the fire. 'It is a clever man who thinks hard on how to achieve his promise.'

'I am loath to risk you, Wreneck. Find me in any case, and we can discuss the necessary tactics.'

'You have no time for me, milord.'

'You are a citizen of Kurald Galain. Of course I have time for you.'

Wreneck didn't understand that; he was not sure what the word 'citizen' meant. The bowl was empty. He set it down and pulled the furs closer about him again.

'It nears dusk,' said Lord Anomander. 'Sleep, Wreneck. Tomorrow, we take you to Dracons Keep.'

'And I will see again my promise to Draconus,' Caladan Brood said.

'Your meaning?'

'Oh, nothing of import, First Son.'

Wreneck settled back, warm inside and out, with only the occasional cramp from his stomach. He thought about Dark, and Light, and Creation, and Chaos. They struck him as big things, ideas that men such as Lord Anomander and Caladan Brood would speak of when they thought no one else was listening. He tried to imagine himself talking about such matters, when he was older, when the life he had lived had been set aside and a new life had taken its place. In that new life, he would think about serious things, but not, he suspected, things like Dark and Light and Creation and Chaos, because with those things, it sounded too easy to push them away, far enough away to keep them from hurting. No, the serious things he would think about, he decided as he closed his eyes, would be ones that mattered. Ones that worked to make him a better man, a man not afraid of feelings.

He remembered his wail for his ma, after all the killing was over with and he was still alive and Jinia was hurt. That cry seemed to have come from a child, from Wreneck the child, but it hadn't. Instead, it had been the birth-cry of a man, the man that Wreneck had become, and the man that he now was.

The notion sent a shiver through him, though he wasn't sure why. But it didn't feel made up. It felt true, even if he wasn't sure what made it true. *But one thing I now know. I made it through all of childhood, and not once did I learn about surrendering.*

*I swam across the icy stream without even knowing it, and now I am safe again, for a time. Here with Lord Anomander, who is the First Son of Mother Dark. And with the Azathanai, who even if he's not good for anything else can at least make a fine bowl of broth.*

He closed his eyes, and moments later was fast asleep.

In his dreams, the dying gods awaited him. They seemed without number. He stood in their midst, confused and wondering. They were, one and all, kneeling to him.

*　　*　　*

There was an old memory, but it was the kind that never went away, and ever seemed closer than one would expect, given the span of years that had passed since. There had been a column, filled with families, their livestock, and wagons heaped with everything that would be needed to break land and build homes. Ivis was young, just one more dust-covered child with more energy than sense. They had been journeying into the north, beyond the forest, and the horizon was far away. Ivis remembered his wonder at that, as if the world had simply unfolded.

They had passed old cairns and tracks worn into battered swaths by wild herds. There had been stones and boulders in rows, not parallel as might line a road, but converging, often on the southern slope of a rise. Some of the cairns had sprouted dead saplings, many of them toppled after the past winter, when the winds had been fierce. These saplings had no roots. They had been hacked at the base into rough points, and driven into the heaps of stone. The mystery of such a thing was more enticing to Ivis than whatever truth he might have discovered, with a few questions to any of the adults – in particular the hunters. Instead of runs and blinds and kill-sites, he had chosen reasons more ethereal for all the strange formations they had found on the vast plain.

Gods stood tall, and with hands spread could command the sky. At night, the gleam of their eyes burned through the darkness with a cold light. And in looking down, they made clear their message: they were far away, and from that distance was born indifference. Still, once, long ago, these gods had not been far away. Indeed, they had sat with their mortal children, sharing the same fires. This was the age before the gods left the world, Ivis had told himself, before mortals had broken their hearts.

The lines of boulders, the cairns upon the summits, the huge wheels – all of these had come in the wake of the gods' leaving. The desperate mortals had looked up at the sky, witness to the dwindling fires of all that was now lost.

It well suited a child's mind to believe that the ones left behind, abandoned, would seek a new language, written in stone upon the plain, with which to call upon the gods. And, at least in the beginning of these notions, there had been little recognition of the desperation behind such efforts. The stars were far away, but not so far as to lose sight of the world below.

The day had been bright, clear, when the Jhelarkan attacked the column. Invisible borders had been crossed by the home-steaders, although, as Ivis later understood, the Tiste were hardly ignorant of their transgression. Sometimes, among a people, there existed a certain arrogance. It had been built up, that arrogance, in a multitude of layers, making it strangely impregnable to the weaker virtues of fairness and respect. It spoke with deceit, and when that failed, with slaughter.

But arrogance had a way of misunderstanding things. If the first Jhelarkan had seemed confused by notions of ownership; if they had not quite understood what it was that the Tiste expeditions were demanding, nor the claims they subsequently made – none of this was synonymous with weakness. In retrospect, Ivis now understood, the Jhelarkan had proved rather adept in grasping the new language thrust upon them, with its forts and outposts, its timber harvests and slaughtered beasts.

A few shouts upon the other side of the column, and then screams, and Ivis, running back to the wagon where sat his mother and grandmother, his much younger cousins huddled in the protective clutch of arms that had, until that moment, done such a good job of holding off the cruelties of the world . . . Ivis, confused, frightened, seeing a horrifying shape lunge into the midst of his family, making the wagon rock, and another one, its huge jaws closing round the head of the ox in its traces, dragging the bellowing beast down on to its fetlocks.

The blood that erupted from Ivis's kin was like a sheet thrown out on the wind. The enormous wolf – *soletaken* – slaughtered everyone in the wagon. Then it was scrambling down, snarling and flinching at a spear-thrust from a hunter Ivis could not see, and the refuge towards which the young boy had been running was but a heap of torn bodies.

In his terror, he had run under the wagon, where he huddled. From above, the blood of his family drained down like rain between the slats, covering him.

His memories of the rest of that attack were blurred, too vague to parse. The Jhelarkan had been a hunting pack turned war-band. They could easily have butchered everyone in the column. Instead, they had struck once, and then retreated. They had sought to deliver a message, in language most plain. Only years later, when the war had begun in earnest, did the Jhelarkan come to understand that warnings never worked. Arrogance, after all, met such warnings with words like *infamy*. Arrogance responded with *indignation*. And this was the fuel for vengeance and retribution, the birth-cries of war, and the Tiste made it so, in ways wholly predictable and, he now understood, utterly contemptible.

*In the mind, death plays with the dead, to breed more death. The stronger death's hold, the more foolish the mind. Why, I wonder, does history seem to be little more than a list of belligerent stupidities?*

How rare was it, he asked himself, that virtues changed the world? How brief and flitting such bright moments? *But then, since when did love bend to reason? And how much vengeance is fed by the loss of someone dearly loved?*

The Jhelarkan lost the war. They lost their land. Righteousness was demonstrated with blood and battle. Justice was won with triumph, making a lie of both.

In all of this was proved the indifference of the gods, and the language of stone boulders upon the plain was a language too simple to manage the complexities of the new world. His memory of that day, beyond even the murder of his family, belonged to the futility of the old ways. Those boulders no doubt still remained, serving now as monuments to failure. The Tiste claimed the land, and in a few short years the wild herds were all gone, and with the ground too poor for crops and too cold for livestock, the settlers eventually left their winnings, returning south.

The servants had cleared the last of the plates and bowls from the table and jugs were brought to fill tankards with heady, steaming mulled wine. Ivis had said little during the meal, rebuffing efforts directed his way. His concentration had wavered from the conversations until his sense of them was lost, and in the fugue that followed, he let lassitude take hold. Some nights, words proved too much of an effort.

He was, nevertheless, all too aware of Sandalath, seated upon his right. Impropriety was seductive. Unease and the notion of the forbidden proved spices to his desire. Still, he knew that he would do nothing, break no covenant. *Barring the slaying of my lord's daughters.* The notion startled him, the truth of it shocking enough to sweep aside his lassitude.

371

Yalad was speaking. '. . . and so a chilly week ahead is likely. The outer walls will be bitter cold, and that makes the timing propitious. It will force them closer to the heart of the house.'

Ivis surprised everyone by speaking. 'Your point, gate sergeant?'

'Ah. Well, I was suggesting, sir, the closing off of the outer passages at that time, further reducing their avenues of escape.'

'And why would that be a good thing?'

Yalad's brow clouded. 'To better effect their capture, sir.'

'They may be children, Yalad,' said Ivis, 'but they are also witches. What manner of chains do you think will hold them?'

Surgeon Prok cleared his throat and said, 'Falt, the herb-woman from the forest, could not stay long her last visit to me. The power of those two hellions proved too inimical. It infests the entire house. Sorcery abounds these days, gate sergeant, and it is as unruly as the season.' He tilted his tankard towards Ivis. 'The commander has the right of it. We have no means of containing them, barring immediate execution, which the commander will not sanction.'

Leaning back, Yalad held up both hands. 'Very well. It was but an idea.'

'The situation is indeed trying,' Prok offered by way of mollification. 'At times, in my station, I catch a scuffle or drawn breath, and find myself fixing gaze upon this wall or that. I believe I have found a secret door, and have chocked it secure. But magic . . . well, it is difficult feeling entirely safe.'

Ivis gestured to a servant. 'Build up that fire again, will you?'

Although unsettled by the discussion thus far, with its ponderings on witchery and murder, Sandalath was unaccountably relieved when Ivis stirred awake enough to engage in the conversation. He had been a distant, remote presence during the meal, seemingly unmindful of the company.

There were ghosts in this house now, and no doubt in the courtyard and beyond, out upon the battlefield. There was a restlessness to the air that had little to do with the chill draughts as the winter wind fought its way through cracks and beneath doors.

Upon her left, Sorca was refilling her pipe. The rustleaf was mixed with something, perhaps sage, that made for a pungent but not un-pleasant scent.

Sandalath noted, across from them, Surgeon Prok eyeing the woman. 'Sweet Sorca,' he said, 'it is held by some of my profession that rustleaf is an inimical habit.'

For a time it did not seem that Sorca thought the comment worthy of a response, but then she stirred slightly, reaching out to collect her tankard. 'Surgeon Prok,' she said, her voice so quiet as to make the man opposite her lean closer to hear, 'it is a scribe's fate to end the day with a blackened tongue.'

Prok tilted his head to regard her, with a loose smile upon his features. 'Often noted, yes.'

'Is ink inimical?'

'Drink down a bottle and you will surely die.'

'Just so,' she replied.

They waited, until Prok's smile broadened. He leaned back. 'Let us imagine, if you will indulge me, that future where healing is at hand for all things, or, to be more accurate, most things, for as Lady Sandalath noted earlier, death remains hungry and none can halt its feeding, but merely delay it for a time. Why, amidst such curative boon, should we not expect a society at ease with itself?' He tipped his tankard towards Sorca. 'She thinks not.'

'I heard no such opinion from our keeper of records,' Yalad said.

'You didn't? Then allow me to make it plain. Are we to live our lives in constant fear – present circumstances notwithstanding? Are we to flinch from all that we might touch, or ingest? From that cloud we must pass through should we cross, say, Sorca's wake down a corridor? Or, in her instance, the ink with which she plies her trade? To what extent, one wonders, does equanimity confer health and well-being? A soul at ease with itself is surely healthier than one stressed with worry and dread. What of the overly judgemental among us? What ill humours are secreted internally by embittered comparisons of moral standing? What poisons attend to self-righteousness?'

'Perhaps,' ventured Yalad, 'with sorcery making redundant the need for gods – with all their necessary configurations of sin and judgement – we will indeed turn to the mundane truths – or seeming truths – of health and well-being, upon which one might rest such notions as justice, blame and righteous punishment. In a way, is it not a simpler way of thinking?'

Prok stared at Yalad with undisguised delight. 'Gate sergeant, I applaud you. After all, the mind of a god and the manner in which it assays judgement and punishment is by nature beyond our understanding, and in such a wayward world as ours, why yes, that surely serves as perversely comforting. But in contrast, as you say, we in a godless world are invited to judge one another, and by harsh rules indeed. Cast down your judgement! And if Sorca does not kneel to your reasoned distemper, why, pronounce banishment, and by this wetted cloth wash thy hands of her!'

'In such a world,' murmured Yalad, 'I see the powers of healing withheld from those deemed undeserving.'

Prok's eyes were suddenly keen. 'Just so. The future, my friend, offers no respite for the unwell, the impure, the flawed and the peculiar. By its habits a society may well be judged, but more sure our assessment, I wager, when we judge its treatment of the habituated and the wilfully non-conforming.' The surgeon refilled his tankard. 'You are witness to my vow, then, by what powers Denul invests in me, and by what skills and learning I may possess, that I will heal without judgement. Until my dying day.'

'Bless you,' said Sorca, behind a cloud of smoke.

Nodding in acknowledgement, Prok continued. 'On the field of battle, the surgeon has no regard for the allegiance of the soldier in dire need. It is, in fact, a point of pride among my ilk to dismiss the political world and its ambitions, and seek to heal all who can be healed, and, failing that, to mourn only the tragedy of the argument's harvest. Few, after all, would appreciate a surgeon's history of the world, wherein each successive chapter recounts ever the same litany of broken bodies and shallow triumphs.' He waved dismissively, and then added, 'But history teaches us nothing new. And should I choose to look ahead, to what is yet to come, why, I see a future made most toxic, born on the day society sets the value of wealth above that of lives.'

Sandalath started. 'Surely, surgeon, that could never come to pass!'

'Cruel judgement – the poor deserve to be poor, and in the failing of their spirit, why, illness is only just. Besides, who would want to invite a burgeoning of these un-worthies, who in their poverty fall to endless breeding? As for the mis-fits, so stubborn in their refusal to conform, let them suffer the consequences of their own misdeeds!'

'If that awaits us,' Sandalath said, 'I'd rather be quit of it than witness such corruption. What you describe, surgeon, is simply horrible.'

'Yes, it is. While I am content for payment of my services little more than the meeting of my needs, I do fear a time when we measure all services against a stack of coins.'

'Prok,' interjected Ivis, 'do you know the tale of the Lord of Hate?'

The surgeon simply smiled. 'Commander, tell us, please, for can we not but wonder at the naming of such a lord?'

'I have it from Lord Draconus himself,' Ivis began. 'Told to me when we were on campaign. There was a Jaghut, named Gothos. Cursed with preternatural intelligence and a relent-less nature, his eye was too sharp, his wit too keen. In this, Prok, he was perhaps much like you.'

The surgeon smiled and raised his tankard in salute.

Ivis eyed Prok with an expression of faint distaste. After a moment, he continued. 'Gothos began an argument, and found himself unable to halt his pursuit of it. He spiralled down, and down. Was he seeking truth? Or did he desire something else? A gift of hope, or even redemption? Did he dream of finding, at the very end, a world unfolding with the natural beauty of a rose?'

'What was the argument?' Sandalath asked.

Ivis nodded. 'In a moment, milady. For now, let us examine a more common need, perhaps even a counter-argument, and that is one of balance. In the act of observing, should one not seek its measure, if only to ease the soul? The good with the bad, the glorious with the craven? If only to even the weights upon each scale?'

Prok spoke in a heavy tone. 'The weights, Ivis, are not equal.'

'Gothos would agree with you, surgeon. Civilization is a war against injustice. In its steps it might stutter on occasion, or even at times bow to exhaustion, but it holds nevertheless to a certain purpose, and that is, most simply put, a desire to defend the helpless against those who would prey upon them. Rules breed more rules, laws abound. Comfort and safety, lives lived out in peace.'

Prok grunted and Ivis responded with a pointed finger, silencing him. The commander then resumed. 'Complexity grows ever more complex, but there is a belief that civilization is a natural force, and, by extension, that justice itself is a natural force.' He paused, and then half smiled, as if at a memory. 'My lord Draconus was most explicit on this point. That night, he argued as if defending himself, so stern was his regard.' Then he shook his head. 'But at some point, civilization forgot its primary purpose: that of protection. The rules and laws twisted round to fashion constraints to dignity, to equality and liberty, and then to the primal needs of security and comfort. The task of living was hard, but civilization was intended to make the task easier, and in many ways it did – and does. But at what cost?'

'Forgive me, commander,' said Prok, 'but you return us to the notion of dignity, yes?'

'What value this "civilization", surgeon, if it dispenses with the virtue of being *civil*?'

Prok grunted. 'There is nothing more savage than a savage civilization. No single man or woman, no band or tribe,

376

could ever aspire to what a civilization is capable of committing, not just upon its enemies, but upon its own people.'

Ivis nodded. 'Gothos plunged to the nadir and found those very truths in that dreadful place. How was it possible, he wondered, that justice made for an unjust world? How was it possible that love could breed such hatred? The weights, he saw, were as you said, Prok. No match to the other, not by any conceivable measure. We look to humanity in the face of inhumanity, our only armour frail hope, and how often – in a civilized setting or a barbaric one – does hope fail in protecting the helpless?'

'The pits are filled with corpses,' Prok muttered, reaching again for the wine, though it had long since gone cold. 'Prisoners put to the sword, a conquered city put to the torch, and those who are to die are made to dig their own graves. 'Tis an orderly thing.'

Ivis was studying the surgeon. 'You attended the sacking of Asatyl, in the far south, didn't you?'

Prok would meet no one's eye. 'I walked away from the Legion on that day, commander.'

There was a long silence that was, perhaps, not as long as it felt for Sandalath, who had seen something pass between Ivis and Prok. She did not know the name of Asatyl, nor the event of its conquest, but the surgeon's response left her chilled.

Ivis slowly pushed his own tankard away, the gesture strangely deliberate. 'Gothos walked into the heart of his city, to where the Jaghut who ruled collectively were all gathered. Among them, to be sure, there were great minds, and many who still held to the ideal of civilization. But then Gothos ascended the central speaker's dais. He began his oration, and when, at last, he was done, he was met with silence. On that day, the Jaghut civilization ended. And in the days that followed, Gothos was named the Lord of Hate.'

'Then well named,' commented Yalad.

But Ivis shook his head. 'Clearly you misunderstand, gate sergeant. The hate was for the truth of Gothos's words. The title was most bitter, but held no spite for Gothos himself. And even then, Lord Draconus was adamant in insisting that even for Gothos there was no hatred of civilization. It was, instead, a recognition of its doom – the inevitable loss of its original purpose.'

'"Name it a prison / if only to see the bars,"' quoted Prok.

Sorca cleared her throat and said, '"Then name each bar / and gather them round."'

'"In the name of friendship,"' Prok finished, now meeting Sorca's gaze.

'Civilization will grow until it dies,' Ivis said. 'Even without purpose, or corrupted from the same, still it grows. And from its burgeoning complexity, Chaos is born, and in Chaos lies the seed of its own destruction.' He shifted, as if suddenly embarrassed, and then said, 'So Lord Draconus concluded. Then we stood, to walk the rows of tents, and gaze into the north, the sky of which glowed from the fires of the Jhelarkan horde.'

Shivering, Sandalath rose. 'It is past late,' she said apologetically. 'I am afraid my mind has grown too weary to wrestle with such nuances as this conversation yields.'

Yalad rose and bowed to her. 'Milady, I will escort you to your room, and check on the guards stationed there.'

'Thank you, gate sergeant.'

As the others rose to bow to her, Sandalath caught the eyes of Ivis, and saw in them – unaccountably it seemed – nothing but pain. Dismayed, she left the chamber with Yalad at her side. He'd begun talking, but she barely heard a word.

*You loved her that much? It is hopeless, then.*

She thought of the bed awaiting her, and the dreams she would seek on this night. *I'll have you find me there, commander. And must take some comfort in that.*

Outside, the wind moaned like some beast pinned under stone.

*     *     *

As the forest opened out, revealing rough hills pocked with the caves of old mine shafts, Wreneck saw two ravens by the side of the track, picking at the carcass of a third one. Their heads tilted round to fix gazes on the new arrivals, and one voiced a screeching caw.

Caladan Brood made a gesture. 'We are invited to an unholy feast,' he said.

'The burning of the forests has left many creatures to starve,' Lord Anomander replied.

'Shall we stay the night at Dracons Keep, First Son?'

'Perhaps. In my few visits, as the lord's guest, I found it amenable enough ... with the exception of the three daughters. Beware meeting their eyes, Caladan. Engage in the regard of a snake and you will find a warmer welcome.'

Caladan Brood glanced back at Wreneck, who trailed behind, already exhausted although barely half the day was done. 'Children seek their own. Is this a wise choice?' Then, to Wreneck, he said, 'Not much further. We are almost there.'

'They keep to themselves, I recall, holding in contempt even their half-brother, Arathan. In any case, I will be placing Wreneck in the care of Sandalath. And Ivis is a man I would trust with my life.'

'I have never seen that before,' Wreneck said as they walked, leaving behind the ravens. 'Eating their own, I mean.'

'Nor I,' the Azathanai replied. 'They are inclined to grief when one of their kin dies. There is something unpleasant in this air, and its power grows the nearer we get to Dracons Keep. It is possible,' he continued, but now to Anomander, 'that something has afflicted our destination.'

The First Son shrugged. 'All your talk of sorcery reaches me as would words of a storm whose wind I cannot feel, nor hear. What you name mystery I receive with ignorance. You could well be speaking another language.'

'And yet, First Son, you witnessed its work, when I first came among you, to set the hearthstone for your brother. And on that day, we made vows that bound together our souls.'

'Ah, I wondered when the chains between us would begin to chafe you, Azathanai.'

'I feel no strain, I assure you, Anomander Rake. But this journey, in search of Andarist, well, to my sense of things, I see a circle closing. But only for me. If I am to speak here as your shadow, I say we have strayed far from the necessary path.'

'You counsel my hasty return to Kharkanas.'

'If Kharkanas will sharpen your focus, First Son, upon your realm's most pressing needs, then yes.'

Lord Anomander halted and turned to Caladan. 'She has turned from me, the one she would call her First Son. She has made darkness her wall, her unrelieved keep. Where, then, is *her* focus? Upon her children? Evidently not. Let her indulge as she will in her lover's arms – I will not step between them. But when she dares ask me to bring this conflict to an end, yet refuses the call to arms, what is a warrior to do with that charge?' He swung round, resumed marching. 'For now, I will serve my own needs, if only to match her reflection.'

'And will she make note of your gesture, First Son?'

'When the notion of interest finds her,' Anomander said in a growl, 'she might blink to the meaning. It is said,' he added in a bitter tone, 'that the darkness does not blind, yet she has made me as blind as Kadaspala.'

'She speaks the truth,' said Caladan. 'The darkness does not blind. And Kadaspala, I fear, is a poor comparison, since he is made blind by his own hands. In the name of grief, he sacrificed beauty. And here you walk, Anomander, in the name of vengeance. If not beauty your sacrifice, then some other thing. In each instance, the wound is self-inflicted.'

'As you said,' Anomander snapped, 'Kadaspala was a poor comparison.'

'What would you have of Mother Dark?'

'If she is to be our goddess. If, indeed, she is to be my mother, inasmuch as the station is well-nigh vacant. Must I list the expectations? Set aside worship – I know her too well. I fear even the role of the mother struggles in me – she is not too many years older, after all. Thus, what is left to me to consider?'

'The throne.'

'Yes. The throne. The mundane perch upon which we paint prestige and authority like gilt. And from that vantage all faith in order must descend like gentle rain. Knock it askew and the realm totters. Bathe it in blood, and the lands burn. Should one take that seat, the hands must grip tight the arms.'

They were among the hills now, with the raw stone on either side silvered in frost. Wreneck walked in their wake, listening, understanding little. The sky overhead was the hue of sword blades.

'Assemble for me, then,' said Caladan Brood, 'the necessities of proper rule.'

'You invite this game?'

'Indulge me.'

Lord Anomander sighed. 'Virtues cannot be plucked from position, Azathanai. Nor worn like gem-studded robes. Justice does not live in the length of a sceptre, and the mere wood, nails and cloth of a throne invests nothing but the illusion of comfort. Pomp and ritual belabour the argument, and far from stirring a soul can more easily be scorned and given the drip of irony.'

'You speak, thus far, as preamble. I will hear your list, First Son.'

'I but voice my dislike of the very notion of rule, Caladan. She has made it too easy to confuse the worship that comes with a god or goddess with that of the honourable choice to serve one who rules, if that rule is worthy of respect.' Anomander shook his head. 'Very well. Live as if you believe in the virtues of your people, but rule without delusions, neither of them nor of yourself. Where stands the throne? In a field of poppies, with the boldest and brightest flowers crowding close, eager to numb your every sense. Their whispers will weave about you a poisonous cloud, through which you must strain to pierce the haze, if you can. Ambition has its own nature, and in every measure it proves simple enough to discern. The ruler's goal is wisdom, but wisdom is as fodder for the ambitious, and given the chance they will pick its bones clean long ere the serving reaches the throne. By such scraps one must raise up a righteous rule. Is it any wonder so many fail?'

Caladan was silent for a moment, and then he grunted and said, 'You set an impossible table, upon which no mortal can hope to attend.'

'You think I do not know it?'

'Describe for me, if you can, the nature of this wisdom.'

Anomander snorted impatiently. 'Wisdom is surrender.'

'To what?'

'Complexity.'

'To what end?'

'Swallow it down, spit it out in small measures, to make palatable what many may not otherwise comprehend.'

'An arrogant pose, First Son.'

'I do not claim it, Azathanai, just as I refuse for myself the notion of rule. And, in the name of worship, I am lost in doubt, if not outright disbelief.'

'And why is that?'

'Power does not confer wisdom, nor rightful authority, nor faith in either of the two. If it offers a caress, so too can it by force make one kneel. The former is by nature suspect, while the latter – well, it can at least be said that it does not disguise its truth.'

'You yearn for liberty.'

'If I do, then I am the greater fool, because liberty is not in itself a virtue. It wins nothing but the false belief in one's own utterly unassailable independence. Even the beasts will not plunge to that depth. No, if I yearn for anything, it is for responsibility. An end to the evasions, the lies spoken in the mind and the lies spoken to others, the endless game of deeds without blame, and all the causes of seeming justice behind which hide venal desires. I yearn for the coward's confession, and understand me well here, Caladan: we are all cowards.'

For reasons Wreneck could not grasp, Lord Anomander's reply silenced Caladan Brood. They trudged on, and no further words came from any of them. With the sun a pale white orb high to the southwest and the afternoon on the turn towards dusk, they came within sight of Dracons Keep.

Wreneck studied the high wall and the gate, and then the freshly mounded earth rising here and there in the land surrounding the fortress. Here there were ravens aplenty. With the day's end, they would rise from those strange hills and make for the forest branches.

Caladan Brood spoke then. 'Lord Anomander, what will you do if one day you find yourself in the role of a king, or, indeed, a god?'

'Should such a day ever arrive,' the First Son replied, 'I will weep for the world.'

The gates opened upon their approach. One man emerged, old and worn but wearing the garb of a soldier, and Wreneck saw his pleasure and surprise when Anomander embraced him.

As they moved beneath the gate, Wreneck also saw how Caladan Brood hesitated, his eyes raised and fixed upon the unknown words carved into the lintel stone.

Then, a moment later, they were in the courtyard, and he saw Sandalath, who came to him with a cry, as would a mother for her son.

From a slit in the tower, in the room their brother Arathan had once claimed as his own, Envy and Spite stared down on the newcomers in the courtyard.

'That's Lord Anomander,' said Spite.

Envy nodded. 'I do not know the other. He has the manner of a beast.'

'The First Son's found a pet.'

'One day,' said Envy, 'I will marry Lord Anomander. And I will make him kneel before me.'

Spite snorted. 'If you make him kneel, you will have broken him.'

'Yes,' Envy replied. 'I will.'

'That's an ugly boy,' Spite observed, through her now end-less shivering.

Envy studied the scene below. 'He will be staying here. With Sandalath – he must be from Abara Delack.'

'I don't like him. He makes my eyes sting.'

*Yes. He shines bright, does that one.* After a moment, Envy gasped, even as Spite flinched back from the window.

For an instant, both girls had seen, in the sudden brightening of the aura surrounding Wreneck, a multitude of figures, ghostly, all blending and flowing through one another, and they had then stilled, suddenly, to lift their gazes to the tower.

*Gods! He's brought gods with him! That boy! A thousand gods!*

*They see us! They know us!*

Unwelcome guests had come to House Dracons. The two girls fled for the cracks.

# TEN

THE COURT POET OF KHARKANAS DEPARTED THE chamber, and in the silence that followed, it seemed to Rise Herat that Gallan had taken with him every possible word, every conceivable thought. Sorcery still roiled about in the room, heavy and sinuous as smoke from a brazier. Cedorpul, seated on a bench that lined one wall, had leaned his back against the worn tapestry behind him, closing his eyes. Endest Silann, sallow despite the ebon hue of his skin, sat on the edge of the old dais, his hands cupped in his lap and his eyes fixed upon them with peculiar expectancy.

Standing opposite the doorway through which Gallan had departed, Lord Silchas studied the swirls of magic that still drifted above the tiled floor. His arms were crossed, his features fixed and without expression.

'The Court of Mages,' said Cedorpul, his eyes still closed. 'Well, it was a bold ambition.'

Rise Herat rubbed at his face, but everything seemed strangely numb to his touch, as if he was no more than an actor upon some stage, truths hidden behind thick makeup, while he stumbled through a play constructed of lies and penned by a fool.

'Why does it still linger?' Silchas asked.

'Slipped the tether,' Endest Silann replied after a moment,

squinting down at his hands. 'He left it to wander like a lost child.'

Silchas turned to the young priest. 'His reason?'

'To prove the conceit,' Cedorpul answered when it became obvious that Endest would not. 'That we can control this power. That we can shape it to our will. It is as elusive as darkness itself, a thing that cannot be grasped. The Terondai bleeds this ... stuff. It fills every room in the Citadel. It commands the courtyard and stalks the streets beyond.' He finally opened his eyes, revealing their red-shot exhaustion, and met Silchas's stare. 'Have you seen where it gathers, milord? About statuary, the monuments of the city's squares, the caryatids shouldering the lintel stones of our proud public edifices. Around tapestries. In the taverns where bards sing and pluck their instruments.' He waved a plump hand. 'As if it possessed eyes and ears, and the ability to touch, or, perhaps, taste.'

'The one you would make seneschal to this Court of Mages,' said Silchas, baring his teeth, 'simply flings it all back into your face, Cedorpul.'

'It is his manner to mock our aspirations. A poet who ran out of words. An awakener of sorcery with nothing to say.'

'How did he come by this power? To awaken the darkness?'

Endest snorted, and then said, 'Forgive me, milord. He found the power in his words. In the rhythms, the cadences. Unmindful, he discovered that he was capable of uttering ... holiness. Needless to say,' Endest added, attention returning once more to his cupped hands, 'the discovery offended him.'

'Offended?' Silchas prepared to say more, but then, with a helpless gesture, he swung round and walked to a sideboard where stood a large clay jar of wine. He poured full a goblet, and, without turning to face the others, he said, 'And you, Cedorpul? How did you come by it?'

'Could I answer you thus, I would be a relieved man.'

'Thus?'

'By prayer, milord, as befits a priest serving a goddess.'

Silchas drank down a mouthful, and then said, 'If not born of the sacred, Cedorpul, then describe to me what mundane gesture enlivened the magic?'

'Curiosity, milord, but not mine. The sorcery itself.'

Silchas spun round. 'Then it lives? It possesses a will of its own? Darkness as sorcery, now manifest in our realm. What does it want of us?'

'Milord,' said Cedorpul, 'none can say. There is no precedent.'

Silchas faced Rise Herat. 'Historian? Have you perused the most ancient tomes, the mouldy scrolls and clay tablets and whatnot? Is there or is there not, here in the Citadel, the gathered literature of our people? Are we indeed in a time without precedent?'

*A time without precedent? Oh, surely we are in such a time.* 'Milord, there are many myths recorded in our library, mostly musing on origins of various things. They seek to map an unknown realm, and where memory does not survive, then imagination serves.' He shook his head. 'I would not put much trust in the veracity of such efforts.'

'Use what you will of them nonetheless,' Silchas commanded, 'and speculate.'

Rise Herat hesitated. 'Imagine a world without sorcery—'

'Historian, we are in the midst of its burgeoning, not its extinction.'

'Then, in principle, magic is not in question. It exists. It has, perhaps, always existed. What, then, has changed? A burgeoning, you say. But consider our own creation myths, our tales of the Eleint, the dragons born of sorcery, and indeed the guardians of the same. In the distant past, if we give such tales any credence at all, there was magic in the world, beyond even what we see now. As a force of creation, perhaps, an ordering of chaotic powers and, possibly, emerging with the necessity of a *will* behind that ordering. Shall we call this a faceless god?'

'And there,' interjected Cedorpul in a weary tone, 'is where you stumble, historian. Who created the creator? Whence the divine will that engendered divine will? The argument devours its own tail.'

'And in that myth,' Rise Herat said, ignoring Cedorpul, 'many are made as one, and one as many. Tiamatha, the dragon of a thousand eyes, a thousand fanged jaws. Tiamatha, who makes from her subjects her own flesh.' He paused, and then shrugged. 'Too many of these oldest of stories invoke the same notions. The Dog-Runners will sing of the Witch of Fires, from whose womb every child is delivered, even as she dwells in each flicker of flame. Again, one who is many.'

Cedorpul made a disgusted sound. 'Dog-Runners. Abyss take us, historian. They also tell of a sleeping world, earth as flesh, water as blood, and every creature but a conjuration of the sleeper's dreaming.'

'Troubled dreaming,' Endest muttered.

'What remains without precedent,' Cedorpul insisted, 'and what must therefore be examined as the source of this new-found sorcery in our realm, is the Terondai carved upon the floor of the Citadel. The gift given by Lord Draconus to Mother Dark.'

Rise Herat studied the rotund priest, noting the sheen of sweat upon the man's brow and cheeks. If magic was indeed a gift, it did not sit well with Cedorpul. 'The High Priestess believes that the gift was both unexpected and unwelcome.'

Shrugging, Cedorpul looked away.

After a moment, the historian turned back to Silchas. 'Milord. For answers, we must look to Draconus.'

Silchas scowled. 'Then send her back in there.'

'The High Priestess has not been granted leave to enter the chamber, and her entreaties yield only silence.'

'This avails us nothing!'

At Silchas's shout, the others flinched. Barring Endest Silann, who simply looked up, frowning at the lord. 'Faith and magic,' he said, 'are easily conflated. It comes from our need for belief, and for the efficacy of that belief. But so too is it a failure of imagination to, in turning to face one, set the back to the other.'

Silchas seemed to snarl without sound before saying, 'Elaborate ... with clarity, priest.'

'There is an Azathanai statue,' Endest said, 'found at the north end of Suruth Common. Do you know it, milord?'

Struggling with his temper, Silchas managed a sharp nod.

'A figure made up of faces. Upon the entire body, a multitude of faces, all staring outward with stubborn, fierce expressions. Gallan has told me the name of that work.'

'Gallan cannot read Azathanai,' growled Cedorpul. 'He but invents his own knowledge, to better stroke his sense of superiority.'

'What is the name of that sculpture, historian?'

'Milord, it is named Denial.'

'Very well. Continue.'

To Rise Herat, Endest Silann looked already ancient beyond his years, as if ill and nearing death. But when he spoke, his voice was soft, calm, preternaturally sure. 'Faith is the state of not knowing, and yet, by choice, *knowing*. Every construct of reason propping it up plays a game, but the rules of that game are left, quite deliberately, incomplete. Thus, the argument has, to be crass, *holes*. But those "holes" are not synonymous with failure. If anything, they become a source of strength, as they are the places of knowing what cannot be known. To know what cannot be known is to find yourself in an unassailable position, proof against all argument, all dissuasion.'

'And sorcery?'

Endest smiled. 'Does it require faith to see magic? Well, perhaps, the faith that one can believe what one sees with one's own eyes. If, however, one chooses not to believe what one can oneself see, or feel, or taste, then in that direction waits madness.'

'This sorcery,' said Cedorpul, leaning forward, 'comes from *darkness*. From the Terondai. From the power of our goddess!'

'Power she now uses, yes,' said Endest Silann, 'but it did not come from her. It is not derived from her.'

'How can you know that?' Cedorpul demanded.

Endest raised his hands, revealing the blood now dripping from them, from deep wounds piercing through the palm of each. 'She is using it now,' he said, 'to attend this gathering, in spirit, if not in flesh.'

At that, Silchas moved to kneel before Endest Silann. 'Mother,' he said, head bowed, 'help us.'

Endest shook his head. 'She'll not speak through me, Silchas. She but watches. It is,' he added with sudden bitterness, 'what she does.'

Straightening, Silchas made fists with both hands, as if about to strike the young priest seated before him. He struggled to keep his voice under control. 'Then what does she want of us?'

'I have no answer, milord, because I feel nothing from her. I am but her eyes and ears, whilst the blood flows, whilst the power bleeds.' He twisted round to smile across at Cedorpul. 'My friend, this power simply exists now. It is among us, for good or ill. Gallan, our would-be seneschal, rejects it, and for that I am relieved.'

'Relieved? Why?'

'Because, once tasted, it seduces.'

'Endest,' asked Rise Herat, with a sudden chill rippling through him, 'does she taste it now, then?'

The priest looked down, as if faltering upon the cusp of his reply, but then nodded.

'And . . . has it . . . seduced her?'

He needed no other answer, the historian realized, than the blood draining down from Endest's hands.

*   *   *

There had been a desire, possessed of value, to assemble a cadre of mages. A court, to be more specific, of Tiste Andii practitioners. Whether it was talent or something else, many hands were now able to reach into that power, and to shape it, although the notion of control was, it turned out, dubious. There was something wayward, untamable, in this sorcery. Rise Herat understood Gallan's warning, its bitter nuances, and, like the poet, the historian feared the magic now among them.

'*Name it for the realm,*' Gallan had said, earlier, when he stood in the centre of the chamber and the sorcery rose up to entwine his form, its serpent tendrils questing and probing like blunt-headed worms. '*We become synonymous with this flavour, and the darkness from which it emerges.*'

'It is not the name that interests me,' Cedorpul had retorted. 'We would proclaim you seneschal. If words are your power in this new art, then lead us. We will all find our own paths, Gallan. The point is, there is need. You must see that. Neret Sorr now blazes with light. Syntara organizes against us, and would see a path burned into the heart of Kharkanas.' He had stepped closer to Gallan then, his eyes fierce. 'I have dreamed it, that golden road of fire.'

'*Dreamed it, did you?*' Gallan had laughed. '*Oh, I do not doubt you, priest. Against the waking world, the mind finds its own realm, and fills it with myriad fears and dreads. Where else would one play so freely with dire possibility?*' He had raised a hand, and the tongues of smoky darkness had wreathed his arm. '*But this? It has no answer to Liosan. Light is revelation. Dark is mystery. What marches upon us cannot be defeated. We – and the world – must ever yield. Imagine, my friends, what we are about to witness. The death of mystery, and such a bright world will come, blinding us with truths, humbling us with answers, scouring us clean of that which we cannot know.*'

In some ways, the new world Gallan described well suited Rise Herat, who was by nature frustrated with things he could not know, with meanings at which he could only guess, and where his every effort to surmise trembled at the roots with doubt. Was this new future not an historian's paradise? Everything explicable, everything understandable.

A world made mundane.

And yet, a part of him recoiled at the notion, for when he looked closely, he saw a future made stale, lifeless. The death of mystery, he realized, was the death of life itself.

Gallan had dropped his arm, watched as the magic drained away from his body. '*Revelation shall surely bless us. Doubt lies bloody upon the altar. Into the channels it drains, drip by drip, and then ebbs. We shall make a thousand thrones. Ten thousand. One for every fool. But the altar remains singular. It will take any and every sacrifice, and thirst yet for more.'* He had then smiled at the historian. *'Prepare to recount the future, Herat, and describe well the long lines, the glint of row on row of knives in waiting hands. And upon the other hand – why, I shall tell this to Kadaspala, so that he may paint it – place a tether, and upon the end of its modest length, name some private beast.*

*'Praise the light! We march to slaughter!'* He grinned mockingly at Cedorpul. *'Name it for the realm. The sorcery of Kurald Galain.'*

And so, laughing, he had stridden from the chamber.

*       *       *

Rise Herat made his way to the private chambers of High Priestess Emral Lanear. He was thinking on the nature of conspiracy, which, among those who both feared and named it, seemed to always possess at its core a misguided belief in the competence of others, as weighed against the incapacities – real or imagined – of the believer. Therefore, he concluded, the belief in conspiracy was in truth an announcement of the believer's own sense of utter helplessness, in the face of forces both mysterious and fatally efficient.

If he looked to his own role, now, as a conspirator against both Anomander and Draconus, he felt nothing of the competence and confidence that should have come to him, settling upon his shoulders like a vestment in some secret ceremony of the capable. The world might move to hidden players, to well-disguised schemes and venal cabals, but it did not move smoothly. Rather, in the confused and raucous clash of muddled plans and desires, the world but lurched, and often in the wrong direction.

History mocked the pretensions of those who believed themselves in charge – of anything, least of all themselves. There was no doubt, in Herat's mind, that conspiracies arose, like poisonous flowers, in every age, snaring those moments of terrible consequence that, more often than not, ended in violence and chaos. If civilization was a garden, it was poorly tended, with every hand at odds with the next. Private desires fed the wrong plants, and made for all a bitter harvest.

At the very least, the paranoid were well fed, though by nature their ability to discriminate between diabolical genius and woeful incompetence was non-existent. It was grist, after all, offering sweet sustenance to a soul panicked by its own helplessness.

He shared with the High Priestess an assembly of sound justifications. They sought to save the realm, and to end the civil war. They sought, beyond the singular moment of violent betrayal, a peaceful future. Kurald Galain must survive, they told each other, and lives would have to be sacrificed in order to assure that survival.

*But not mine. And not yours, Emral Lanear. Where, then, is our sacrifice? Nothing but the carcasses of our honour. Conspiracy will devour its own truths, and even should we succeed, we are left as nothing but husks, mortal forms to house ruined souls. Is that not a sacrifice? Will we not find victory a bleak realm of sour satisfaction, with ourselves haunted by the truth behind every lie?*

*Crowd me in the comforts of what we win . . . I see a man drunk upon the divan, eager to waste the years left to him.*

*And you, my dear? How will faith taste to your bloodied tongue?*

The corridors of the Citadel held a kind of promise, in that there was light in the darkness. His eyes could see, although now even the torches had been dispensed with. Cedorpul asserted that the talent with which the Mother's children could pierce the darkness was her gift to them for their faith in her. The notion pleased Herat in too many ways, and should he list them he would see plain his own desperation, as a man making a banquet of a morsel.

He paused in one passageway as a trio of young priestesses hurried past him, their hoods over their heads and eyes down. They swirled in their silks, almost shapeless, but the scents of their perfumes made for a heady wake as the historian continued on. A goddess of love would be welcome in these times, but the pleasures of sex could not be her only gift. Lust spoke a base language, and its role in the course of history, Herat well knew, was fraught with tragedy and war.

*But we are cold in our desires, the High Priestess and I. There is no heat in our plans, and the poses we will create invite no caress. She takes no men to her bed, not any more. The gate, as Cedorpul might say, has closed.*

*Yet her priestesses still swim the deep carnal seas, and call it worship.*

*But Mother Dark is no goddess of love. We were mistaken in that, and now lust boils unabated. We rush forward, with no time to temper our deeds with thought. The reins have been plucked from our hands, and this road we descend is steep.*

*Let us hold on a while longer, to this delusion of control.*

Reaching the door to Emral Lanear's chamber, Herat gave a single tug on the silk cord hanging in its vertical niche in the wall. Hearing her muffled invitation, he opened the heavy door and stepped into the room beyond.

Until recently, there had been a full-length mirror of polished silver set against the wall opposite the door that had commanded the entire chamber with its play of motion and seemingly sourceless light. Rise Herat had found it disquieting, as the polish was far from perfect, and indeed there were strange dips and exaggerations in the reflection the mirror offered, making it an enemy to vanity. Of late, however, a thick tapestry had covered the mirror, as it did now. Initially, Herat had wondered at the gesture, but not for long. This was not the time, he understood, for catching glimpses of oneself, like flitting thoughts or hints of something that might be guilt.

The tapestry covering the mirror was an old one, depicting a scene from an unfamiliar court, a crowded throne room in which figures bedecked in barbaric furs were arrayed in a half-circle, their backs to the viewer, all facing a vaguely female form seated on a throne. This woman was either asleep or dead. The splendour of the throne room offered a stark contrast to the savages gathered there, displaying such riches as to make the chamber more like a royal vault than a court. For all Rise Herat's knowledge of history, he could place neither the artist nor the scene.

But nothing of the past held any relevance, not any more. It had become a realm made perfect by virtue of being unreachable. For all that, its lure remained, as seductive as ever. Entire revolutions, he knew, could be unleashed in the name of some impossible, mostly imagined past. A creation fashioned as much from ignorance as from knowledge. Such dreamers invariably ended up wallowing in blood, and should they ever win their desire, their world proved to be one filled with repression and terror. There was too much anger, when the dream was revealed as being impossible, and when others failed to match the ideal, and before long many were made to kneel, broken by either fear or despair, while the bodies of those who refused to kneel made heaps in hastily dug pits.

*Simple observations, my friends. I am not one for judgement, but one might whisper, now and then, to those dreamers, and say: dream not of the impossible past, but of the possible future. They are not one and the same. They cannot ever be the same. Know this. Understand this. Make peace with this. Else you fight a war you can never win.*

Emral Lanear emerged from her bedroom beyond the reception chamber. She wore plain silks, of a hue of deep grey, its sheen like dull pewter. Her hair was drawn up, but roughly so – by her own hand rather than that of a hand-maid. There were shadows under her eyes, the smudge of exhaustion that was as much spiritual as physical.

'Historian. It's late. Is it late?'

'No, High Priestess, we are upon the sixth bell.'

'Ah,' she said in a vague murmur, and then gestured. 'Will you sit? I sent them all away. Too much chattering. One day, I fear, our world will be inundated with a multitude of people with little to say, but all the time in the world in which to say it. The cacophony will deafen us all, until we are insensate, drunk on the trivial. Upon that day, civilization will die with little fanfare, much less anyone's noticing.'

Herat smiled as he took a seat in the chair she had

indicated. 'They will but step over the cracks in the street, the rubbish upon their doorsteps, and make displeased faces at the foulness in the air they breathe and in the water they drink. Still, their prattle will prattle on.'

She wavered slightly where she stood, and Herat wondered if she was drunk, or in the fumes of d'bayang, the faint scent of which now reached him from the bedroom.

'High Priestess, are you not well?'

'Oh, dispense with the pleasantries – or will we make our own prattle? What have you gleaned of him? How solid does he stand?'

Herat glanced away, blinked at the tapestry scene. 'If he could,' he ventured, 'he would straddle the gap. A warrior Silchas may be, but he has no stomach for crossing blades with those who were once his friends. Honour holds him to his brother's side, but in his heart he shares a deep detestation for the Great Houses, and all the pretensions of the highborn.'

When he looked back to her, he found her studying him from beneath half-lowered lids. 'Then he will serve, won't he?'

'To make the insult sting? Yes. His temper undermines him.'

'What else?'

For a moment, he was not sure what she meant, but then he sighed. 'The Court of Mages. There was a scene, High Priestess. Sorcery, yes, but Gallan discarded its value. He did not linger. Silchas made plain his frustration.'

'And Endest Silann?'

'He bled.'

'I felt that,' Emral Lanear said, turning away, as if moments from dismissing him and retreating once more to her bedroom. Then she halted and brought a hand to her face. 'She rushes to him, to the wounds. For all that she seems to hide, Herat, she betrays a needful thirst.'

'Then ignorance is not her flaw.'

The High Priestess flinched, and shot him a glower. 'I would it were,' she snapped. 'To stand as a valid excuse. No, it is the alternative that wounds like a knife, against which we have no defence.'

'None,' said Herat, 'but to ever raise the stakes.' He well knew the alternative to which she alluded, as it was a flavour to sour every historian and every scholar, artist and philosopher. *This dread fear, this welter of despair. The guiding forces of the world, not awkward in ignorance, but turned away, in indifference.*

*By this we name the Abyss, and see in our souls a place devoid of hope.*

*Mother Dark, are you indifferent to us?*

*If so, then our goddess has by nature become cold, and rules with a careless hand. By this, she reduces our beliefs to conceits, and mocks all that is longing within us.* 'Emral,' said Herat, 'if this is so' – *our indifferent mother* – 'then what point in saving Kurald Galain?'

'I have had swift reply from Syntara.'

He frowned. 'This proves a weak winter.'

'It does,' she agreed. 'My overture is well received. Neither unrelieved darkness nor light will serve us. There must be a proper union, a balance of powers. That there be light in darkness, and darkness in light.'

'Ah. I see.'

Her sudden smile was brittle. 'I think not. By "darkness" she means all that is base – vices, in truth. Fear and evil, the malign essence of mortal nature. In "light" and "light" alone dwell the virtues of our nature. She swallows us with difficulty, and sees the balance as a war of wills, upon the field of each and every soul. Fear blinds, after all, as befits darkness made absolute, while purest light reveals courage, fortitude, and the gift of seeing both truthfully and clearly.'

'Purest light will blind as surely as absolute darkness,' Herat pointed out, scowling.

'And so the admixture is invited.'

Herat grunted. 'An alchemy of impurity.'

'And thus the fate of all mortal beings, historian, shall be one of unending struggle.'

The historian shrugged, looking away. 'She but articulates

every age past, and every age to come. Still, to cast us into such a venal role . . .'

'There is this thing,' Emral Lanear said, 'with betrayal. It becomes easier to stomach the second time around.'

'You will turn upon her?'

'Entice her with seeming victory, yes. But I will fight for the virtue of darkness, by striking from it, unseen.'

Rise Herat nearly choked on the statement, wondering if she even grasped its appalling hypocrisy. He squinted at the tapestry scene. 'So, what is this, then? I know not the artist, nor the court and its players.'

Frowning, the High Priestess turned to the hanging. 'Woven by an Azathanai, I was told.'

'Whence came it?'

'A gift, from Grizzin Farl.'

'He arrived without much upon his back, High Priestess.'

She shrugged. 'It is their way, I suppose, to present gifts from unknown places.'

'And the scene?'

'Muddled, apparently. The weaver sought to elevate a momentous event among savages. Dog-Runners, in fact.'

'Ah, then the woman on the throne must be the Sleeping Goddess.'

'I imagine so, historian.'

Rise Herat rose and approached the tapestry. 'She grasps something in her right hand – can you make it out?'

'A serpent aflame,' Emral replied, joining him. 'Or so Grizzin described it.'

'That is fire? It seems more like blood. What does it signify?'

'The gift of knowing.'

He grunted. 'The gift of knowing that which cannot be known, I presume. But, I think, it is but half a serpent. There is the head, but no tail.'

'The snake emerges from her palm,' said Emral Lanear, before turning away once more.

Rise Herat swung to her, but could not catch her eye, nor, as she moved away, her expression. *Fire . . . blood. Eyes that see, but reveal nothing. No different from what afflicts Endest Silann. Dog-Runners, you have a sister goddess in your midst.* A moment later the breath hissed through his teeth. 'High Priestess? Is Grizzin Farl still a guest of the Citadel?'

'He is.' She was standing near her bedroom door now, as if impatient to see him depart her company.

'Where?'

'The south tower, I believe. Historian—' she added as he moved to leave.

'Yes?'

'Give some thought, if you will, on the matter of High Priestess Syntara.'

'Why not?' he muttered in reply. 'As you say, Emral, it gets easier.'

She was through and into her bedroom before Herat closed the chamber door.

*    *    *

Lady Hish Tulla had announced her intentions shortly before their departure, and so now Kellaras and Gripp Galas waited beside their saddled horses. The chill of the early morning was burning away to a bright, stubborn sun, as an unseasonal warm spell loosened winter's hold upon the forest. Kellaras watched the ex-soldier, Pelk, preparing two additional mounts.

A man with a crueller mind might well conclude that Hish was reluctant to let her husband go; that she had sought in desperation for a reason to accompany Gripp and Kellaras, for at least part of their journey. But the stifling sorrow that was now wrapped about Kellaras would not yield to such crass thoughts. Hish Tulla's impatience with her fellow highborn was a sound reason for her decision. She and Pelk would ride to Tulla Keep, west of Kharkanas, returning to the company of hostage Sukul Ankhadu and Castellan Rancept, and there await a gathering of representatives from each of the Greater Houses. Such a meeting was long overdue, and already two riders had departed, bearing missives announcing the summons.

It seemed unlikely that any House would refuse the request. If the present need was not pressing then indeed nothing would move them. And yet, Kellaras wondered, who in the eyes of the highborn would prove the subject of their complaint, Urusander or Draconus? *Or, for that matter, the House of Purake, and my lord, Anomander, who could well be seen to have abandoned his responsibilities?* He understood, from Lady Hish Tulla's words over the past two nights, at the dinner table, that her loyalty to Anomander was beyond question, but even she could not but struggle to defend his decision.

Gripp Galas's assertion that Anomander did not trust his own brother, Silchas, still reverberated in Kellaras, like a hammer upon a shield, jarring his bones, weakening his faith. With this lever, Gripp would bend Anomander back to his proper role, as defender of Kharkanas and Mother Dark. *Upon filial distrust, then, we are to awaken in Anomander the sting of honour. Is it any wonder that it does not sit well?*

Lady Hish Tulla at last emerged from the house, wearing a heavy cloak over her armour. Striding to her horse, she swung up into the saddle and gathered the reins. She eyed her husband, and something in that regard seemed to pierce him, as he quickly turned away, attending to his mount's tack one last time before setting his boot in the stirrup and pulling himself astride the beast.

Kellaras and Pelk followed suit. The captain sought to meet Pelk's eye, seeking a flicker of something, anything, that might whisper of the two nights they had shared, but once mounted, the ex-soldier's attention fixed upon the track awaiting them. After a moment, she loosened the sword in its scabbard at her hip.

The gesture startled Kellaras, and he turned to Hish Tulla. 'Milady, do we ride into battle?'

Hish glanced across at him, but said nothing.

Clearing his throat, Gripp said, 'Captain. There's been movement in the stand outside the grounds. Wolves, perhaps, driven south by hunger. Or we have unannounced guests.'

'Man or beast,' Kellaras said, scowling, 'I now fear I have brought them here.' He hesitated, and then said, 'Perhaps we are unwise to leave the keep—'

'These are my lands,' Hish Tulla said in a harsh tone. 'Wolves will not try us, but if there are men and women hiding in this forest, I will face them. If they mean ill, their impudence will cost them dearly. No, Kellaras, I am not one to be bearded in my own den. See to your weapons, sir.'

After a moment, Kellaras dismounted again and reached for his surcoat of chain, which he had rolled and bound behind the saddle's seat. 'Forgive me,' he said. 'I will be but a moment.'

A short time later, bedecked and already sweating beneath his felt and chain, he swung back on to his horse, anchoring his lance in its seat. Even as he readied the reins, Pelk set out to take point, and they rode from the clearing, through the vine-tangled gateway, and on to the track that wended its way into the forest.

The sunlight was blinding where it struck patches of snow on the ground and the ice upon branches and twigs. Where such bright fires did not flare, all was in shadow, dull and devoid of colour. There was no sound nor, as far as Kellaras could see, any motion among the trees. They rode on, no one speaking.

Kellaras found himself welcoming the thought of battle. He would delight if given leave to unleash violence. There was a certain tension of the spirit that knew no other answer, and yearned for the sound of blades clashing, the heavy gasp of a body yielding to a sword or lance, the cries of the dying and wounded. It was easy, he reminded himself, to fall into a kind of lassitude, as often struck warriors when finding themselves in civil settings, constrained by the rules of peace.

The poets named it a melancholia, a hero's affliction. Bards sang of the hollowness within, and the echoes that haunted the warrior whose deeds were long past, with weapons gathering dust and the nights growing ever longer.

*In Kharkanas, I walked the corridors, fed the needs of flesh, saw and was seen. And yet, I may as well have been a ghost, a man half there, half somewhere else. And when, on rare occasions, I caught the stare of a fellow soldier, I saw the same in the hollow eyes before me. We but ape these civil pretensions, as we wait for the loosening of our leashes.*

*When the future promises that terrible freedom, we learn to abide. But when at last we are done with such things, when the promise dies and it comes to us that now, finally, no such freedom awaits us, then we are struck deep. We are done and it is done. The melancholia will take us and drag us down into its deathly mire.*

*Gripp Galas, how did you stand it?*

*Ah, well, no need to answer. I listened to your war with wood, the bite of your axe.* Gripp was at the moment riding behind Lady Hish Tulla, taking up the rearmost position as they rode the trail. Kellaras did not turn to glance back, but he imagined a new life in the old man now, a sharpness to his eyes. Some things, he understood, could not be put away.

*You know this, Hish Tulla, and you resent its truth. Even now, you feel him pulling away from you. I am sorry, and yet, it may be that I have just saved your husband. Still, I doubt you will thank me. Perhaps love blinded you to the warrior's curse, or you came to believe your love could smother it. But in this winter you saw his pacing, his restlessness and agitation . . . or perhaps it was nothing more than his sudden age, his nights by the fire, the faint flickers of flames seeming to die over and over again in his sunken eyes.*

*Or are these fears mine and mine alone? Dare I turn to see for myself? Is this a truth I need to confirm . . . to what end?*

*Should I survive this time, and come to some unknown future, will I too, chilled in the bone, stare into the fire, remembering its heat?*

He was startled when Pelk twisted in her saddle, and nodded at him, even as she drew her sword.

Kellaras lifted the lance from its socket, half rose in the stirrups – still he could see nothing.

Then there were figures on the path twenty paces ahead, a

furtive line of movement. Pelk reined in, and Kellaras moved up alongside her on the left, to guard her flank.

Faces mostly hidden in rough-woven scarves glanced their way, but the procession continued on, from left to right, northward into the forest. Kellaras saw hunting weapons – strung bows, spears.

'Deniers,' said Gripp Galas from behind him. 'A hunting party.'

'I gave no leave,' Hish Tulla snapped. She raised her voice. 'I give no leave! You walk upon Tulla's Hold!'

The figures halted on the trail, and then, a moment later, one emerged from the south edge of the treeline, stepping on to the track, and then taking a half-dozen strides towards the riders. Drawing away the scarves, he showed a young, thin face. Behind him, hunters were fitting arrows to the strings of their bows.

Hish Tulla snarled under her breath, and then said in a low voice, 'They would not dare. Are we a hunter's prey?'

Kellaras edged his mount forward, lowering the tip of his lance. At the gesture the youth halted. 'Clear the path,' the captain commanded. 'There is no reason for death on this day.'

The young man pointed at Hish Tulla. 'She claims to own what cannot be owned.'

'You are in a preserve, Denier, and yes, she does indeed own it.'

But the youth shook his head. 'Then I claim the air she breathes, as it has flowed down from the north – from my homeland. I claim the water in the streams, for they journeyed past my camp.'

'Enough of this nonsense!' said Hish Tulla. 'By your argument, whelp, you can make no claim to any beast dwelling in this forest. Nor to the wood for your fires at night. For they owned this long before you or I ever ventured here.' She gestured with one mail-clad hand. 'I hold to one simple rule. You may hunt here, but you will do me the courtesy of announcing your desire first.'

The youth scowled. 'You would refuse us.'

'And if I did?'

He said nothing.

'You are a fool,' Hish Tulla said to him. 'You ask, so that I may say yes. Do you believe you are the first hunters to visit my land? I see none but strangers behind you. Where are my old neighbours, with whom I shared gifts, and with whom I exchanged words of respect and honour?'

The youth tilted his head to one side. 'If you so desire,' he said, 'I will take you to them. They are not far. We came upon their bones this morning.'

Hish Tulla was silent for a long moment, and then she said, 'Not by my hand.'

The hunter shrugged. 'This, I think, would ease their grief.'

'Have you found a trail?' Gripp Galas suddenly asked. 'The slayers – do you now track them?'

'Too long past,' replied the youth. He shifted his attention back to Hish Tulla. 'We shall not be long here,' he said. 'This forest you call yours is of no interest to us.'

'Then where do you go?' Gripp asked.

'We seek the Glyph, who walks beside Emurlahn.' He pointed at Hish Tulla. 'Tell the soldiers, the innocents of the forest are all dead. Only we remain. Their deaths did not break us. When the soldiers come again into the forest, we will kill them all.'

The young hunter returned to his troop, and moments later the last of them had filed across the track, vanishing into the trees.

'What is this Glyph he speaks of?' Hish asked.

Shrugging, Gripp said, 'They are organized now.'

'They cannot hope to cross blades with Legion soldiers.'

'No, my love, they cannot. But,' he added, 'arrows will suffice.'

The breath hissed from his wife. 'Then indeed we have descended into savagery. And yet,' she continued after a moment, 'the first acts of barbarity did not come from the Deniers, did they?'

'No, milady,' Kellaras replied. 'In Kharkanas, I spent some

time tallying reports of the slaughter. That young man was correct. The innocents are all dead, and their bones litter the forests of Kurald Galain.'

'Yet Urusander claims to represent the commoners of the realm? How does he not choke on his own hypocrisy?'

'He chose, my love, not to include the Deniers in his generous embrace.' Gripp Galas leaned to one side and spat. 'But to be fair, I would wager Hunn Raal was the one to set the Legion wolves upon these fawns.'

'The distinction is moot,' his wife retorted. She gathered up her reins. 'Ride on, then. We but build upon our charge of outrage, and must hold to the faith that a day will come when we can unleash it. Captain Kellaras.'

'Milady?'

'Be certain that Lord Anomander understands. I will unite the highborn to this cause. I will see the matter of the Consort set aside, to wait for a later time. Now, we must unmask our enemy, and see the way before us clear and without compromise. Tell him, captain, that I swear to this: no political machination will stifle my distemper. There will be retribution and it will be just.'

They set out once again. Behind Kellaras, Hish Tulla continued. 'Hunn Raal will hang. As for Urusander, let him plead his innocence before knowing eyes, beneath public regard. Upon that stage, he will fail to dissemble. Captain, was it not your lord who said that justice must be seen?'

'He did, milady.'

'Just so. Let it be seen.'

Kellaras remained alongside Pelk, even as she quickened her pace to draw some distance from Hish and Gripp Galas, as husband and wife had fallen to a low exchange of words. The captain glanced across at her. 'They were tempted,' he said.

She nodded. 'Stone-tipped, the arrows they chose for us.'

'Meaning?'

'Uncommon pain, I'm told, when there is a sharp stone lodged deep in your body, cutting this way and that with your every breath. I would think,' she added in dry tones, 'that even a soldier could not fight on, through such pain. As weapons of war, it's my thought, captain, that arrows will make warfare a thing not of honour, but of dishonour.'

He grunted sourly, thinking back to his own hunger for violence. 'Perhaps, then, war's true horror will be revealed for all to see, and make us one and all recoil.'

Her answering smile was guarded. 'Shocking us into eternal peace? Captain Kellaras, you have the dreams of a child.'

Stung, he said nothing.

She shot him a look, her eyes widening. 'Abyss take me, Kellaras – you thought that an insult?'

'I – well—'

'Discount the gifts in your heart if you must,' she said, 'but leave them free for me to hold, and hold I will, tighter than you could ever imagine.'

Her words set an ache in his chest. Blinking against the glare of sunlight on snow and ice, he rode on in silence.

Behind them, husband and wife bickered.

\* \* \*

There was a time, long before Grizzin Farl had taken for himself the title of Protector, when he had made the blade of his war-axe the voice of his temper. He had been like a drunkard, with fury his wine. Youth had a way of carving everything into sharp relief, making divisive every world and every moment within it. Anger was his only answer to the revelation of injustice, and injustice was everywhere. In those times when exhaustion took him – when the ongoing battle against authority, tradition, and the churning cycles of habit made him stumble, stagger into some emptiness – he fostered for himself a façade of cynicism. The zeal of the axe-blade was quickly blunted, and the weapon proved heavy in his aching arms. With that cynical regard, he saw awaiting him a future of unrelenting failure.

Youth made rage and world-weariness into lovers, with all the passion and private heat that one would expect, when the blood was still fresh. Desire fed lust, and lust promised satiation, but it whispered clumsy words. Vengeance, a matching in kind between crime and punishment, as if justice could bring down the hands of a god, to make clear and certain every divide, and, by so doing, reduce the complexities of the mortal world into something simpler, easier to stomach.

He had soon found himself among the Forulkan, to see with his own eyes how such justice was meted, and in this time he began to awaken in unexpected ways. Perhaps it was nothing more than nostalgia that could lead one to yearn for some imagined simplicity, a world shaped in childhood, and then reshaped by remembrance into something idyllic. It was, indeed, all too easy to forget the confusion of a child's world, where what was known was minimal, and therefore seemed but a simple and possibly more truthful representation of reality. Sufficient to serve that child and so give comfort to the child's mind. But nostalgia was a dubious foundation to something as vital as a culture's system of justice. Grizzin had seen quickly the flaws in this nostalgic genesis, as it proved to be the core of the Forulkan court.

Still young, he had revelled in the theme of vengeance within the Forulkan system. But before long his cynical regard saw too clearly the abuses, the subtle ways of undermining the very notion that the blade of justice hung over everyone. Instead, he saw how, among the privileged, escaping that shadow of retribution and responsibility had become a game. He had seen the evasions, the semantic twisting of truth, the deliberate obscuring of meaning, and the endless proclamations of innocence, each and all delivered with the same knowing glint in the eye.

The lovers of his youth grew strained.

One day, in the Great Court where sat the Seven Magistrates and the Seven Governors, and all the assemblies of guild and craft, and the commanders among the Deliverers, and the Company of Deliberators, Grizzin Farl had drawn his double-bladed axe, shaking it free of its blade-sheath.

The wine flowed sweet on that day, in torrents upon the tiled floor, gushing round the artfully carved legs of the benches and pews. It splashed high against precious tapestries, and into the niches housing the marble busts of famous adjudicators and philosophers. The Great Court was transformed into a drunkard's paradise.

Rivers of wine, as red and deep as the throats slashed open, as the stumps of severed limbs, as flesh sliced away. Rage itself had recoiled from its lover's sudden, inexplicable fury, as if in an instant a mirror had been thrown up between them, and rage saw itself truly for the first time. Whilst, behind the barrier, the cynic stalked the halls, wielding a dripping axe, and with a dry laugh announced a terrible freedom.

The Azathanai who would years later become the Protector, Defender of Nothing, was born in the wake of that slaughter. He had stepped out from the Great Court as a child from a bloodied womb, painted in all the hues of justice, gasping at the shock of cold air as it swept in from shattered windows, with stained glass crunching under his feet and distant cries from the streets below.

*Play me with words, my friends, and see what comes of it. Mock my ideals, whisper of the fool before you, who came with such hopes. Behold this summoned tantrum, this child's incandescence. Surely, by your wilful arts, your clever dismemberment of once lofty ideals, and by your own brand of cynicism, so filled with contempt, you gave birth to me, your new child, your Innocent. And should I bring flame to your world, be not surprised.*

*I walk as a lover spurned.*

*Until the moment of this vow, which I hold still. Never again will my heart arrive in innocence. Never again will I make the foolish loves of youth into a man's ideal, and so suffer a longing for something that never was. Speak not to me of the balance of possessions, the imperatives of restitution, the lie of retribution and the hollow lust of vengeance.*

*In this denial, I pose no imposition. Do what you will. Ashes await us all. This lover of the world has set aside his love, for now and for ever more. See me as your protector, but one who values nothing, who yields with this eternal smile, and leaves you to glory in everything but justice. For justice you do not own.*

*When you brought down the hands of a god, I drenched them in mortal blood.*

*Pray the god found the wine bitter.*

He had heard that in the decades since that time a cult had risen among the Forulkan, worshipping Grizzin Farl as a vengeful god. Indeed, as a god of justice. There would always be, he now understood, those for whom violence was righteous.

Sudden motion before him made the Azathanai lift up his head, though it seemed to weigh too heavy for this world. He saw Lord Silchas, sinking down into a chair the Tiste had drawn close. The pallid face seemed thin as paper, the red eyes like ebbing coals. 'Are you drunk, Azathanai?'

'Naught but memories, lord, to set a man's mind afire.'

'I imagine,' said Silchas as he poured a tankard full from the pitcher on the table, 'you have a surfeit of those. Memories.'

Grizzin Farl leaned back, only now hearing the muddy noise of the tavern crowd surrounding them. 'My humour is plucked on this night, lord,' he said. 'A flower's bud, wingless and without colour.'

'Then you suit my demeanour well enough, Azathanai. The historian, Rise Herat, is looking for you.'

'To the past I have nothing to say.'

'Then you should find him equitable company. He awaits you in your quarters, I believe.'

Grizzin Farl studied the highborn. 'There is a fever in this city.'

'Kharkanas was never easy with winter,' Silchas replied. 'Even in the time before the darkness, the air would feel harsh, making our bones seem brittle. Alas,' he added, pausing to drink, 'I fared worse than most. I still do. Each winter I spend yearning for summer's heat.'

'Not all welcome the season of contemplation,' Grizzin agreed.

Silchas snorted. 'Contemplation? It gives rise, as you say, to

409

fevered thoughts.' Then he shook his head. 'Azathanai, there is more to it. I would shake loose my limbs, and take hold of sword or lance. A lightness to come to my steps. Pale I may be, but my soul is drenched in summer's flame.'

Grizzin glanced across, catching the blood-gleam in the warrior's eyes. 'It is said that Lord Urusander is expected to march before the thaw.'

'Then I will raise my own heat, Azathanai.' After a moment, in which he seemed to contemplate the prospect with avid anticipation, Silchas shrugged, as if dismissing the notion. 'But I come here to you,' he said, 'with more purpose than just announcing the historian's desire to speak to you. On this day I have witnessed sorcery, an unfurling of magical power. It seemed . . . unearned.'

Grizzin Farl collected up the jug and refilled his tankard. 'Unearned?'

'Need I explain that? Power too easily come by.'

'Sir,' said Grizzin, 'you are a highborn. Noble in title, within an aristocracy of privilege in which the premise of what is earned or unearned matters not. Chosen by birth is no choice at all. Yet your kind cleave the child, by rules unquestioned, to cast one into privilege and the other deprivation. This civil war of yours, Silchas Ruin, poses a challenge to all of that. And now . . . sorcery, at the hands of anyone, provided they apply discipline and a diligence in its mastery . . . why, I see Urusander's cause bolstered, at the expense of your own.'

Baring his teeth, Silchas said, 'I am not blind to the imbalance! This magic will undermine us, perhaps fatally so. There is order in hierarchy, after all, and it is a necessary order, lest all fall into chaos.'

'Agreed, chaos is most unwelcome,' said Grizzin Farl. 'Surely a new hierarchy will emerge, but by its own rules. You will see your old aristocracy shattered, sir. Will Lord Urusander take the magic into his own embrace, or simply seek out those adepts most likely to become masters? Will the new age see the rule of sorcerer kings and queens? If so, then any commoner can take the throne. Kurald Galain, my friend, totters upon a precipitous brink, yes?'

'I still await words that comfort, Azathanai.' Silchas drank from his tankard, and then, as a server arrived with a new pitcher, the lord reached across to drag it near. 'You perturb the waters for your own amusement, I suspect.'

Grizzin Farl let his gaze slide away from the warrior opposite him, out into the tavern's sullen crowd, the layers of pipe- and woodsmoke. Conversations were rarely worth listening to, when people were in the habit of repeating themselves, as if by each utterance they sought a different response. *Find a truth and make it into a chant. Find a falsehood and do the same. Assemble truths and lies and name it faith. Taverns and temples, see the libations flow, and all the sacrifices made. Here is a truth. Wherever mortals gather, ritual will rise, and in each place of ritual, habit and gesture invoke a hidden comfort. In these patterns, we would map our world.*

'You do not deny it, then?'

Grizzin started, and then sighed. 'My friend, forgive me for mocking your noble pretensions. I see them too clearly to do otherwise.'

'Why do you call me friend? Why, more to the point, do I consider you the same?'

'My words anger you, Silchas, and yet you indulge that anger for but a moment before you see through the red haze, and must accept the truth of what I say, no matter how bleak or uncomplimentary it proves. I do admire this in you, sir.'

'When we converse, I feel the strain of my temper.'

'It will not snap,' Grizzin said.

'If it did? You clearly do not fear it.'

'I gave up on fear long ago.'

At that, Silchas leaned forward, eyes narrow. 'Now that is an admission! Tell me, pray, how you managed it?'

A brief flash clouded Grizzin's mind as he saw himself reflected in broken glass, staggering from a place of slaughter. 'When we lash out,' he said, 'we do so from fear. Recall, if you will, your every breaking of temper, the shock of it once you have struck, once you have done damage. In a sane mind, the act makes one recoil, dousing the fires inside. And with it, the first fear dies, only to have a new one take its place – the fear of the consequences of your violence. Two arguments, but only one voice. Two causes, but only one response. When you at last understand this, my friend, then the voice that is fear grows most tiresome. It repeats itself and so proves its own stupidity, and if by its stupid words you are led into violence, a relinquishing of all control, then you can only be a fool. A fool,' Grizzin Farl repeated, 'gullible and not very bright. When you match the stupidity of your fear, you insult your own intelligence, and with it all belief in yourself.'

Silchas was studying him. 'Azathanai, you must understand, an entire people can be consumed by such fear.'

'And so it lashes out, often against itself – against kin, against neighbour. Fear, in such a time, becomes a wild fever, burning all that it touches. And yes, it is utterly stupid.'

'Imagine, Azathanai, that fear when given the power possible in magic. You invite a world in flames.'

'Where you will, perhaps, thrive?'

With a troubled expression now on his pale face, Silchas sat back once more. 'You have swung me about, Azathanai, to winter's worship. May the season never end.'

'When will you summon the Hust Legion?'

Silchas blinked, and then shrugged. 'Soon, I think. It is absurd. We assemble a rabble armed with insane iron, to fling against the realm's finest army.'

'And the Houseblades of the Great Houses?'

'I am surprised this interests you.'

'The Houseblades do not, to be honest,' admitted Grizzin Farl. 'But I see something awaiting the Hust Legion – too vague to be certain. Only a sense of foreboding, as if a fate is taking shape, a future as yet unimaginable.'

'They may well be cursed now,' Silchas said. 'A legion made into our realm's madness. There is no glory to be found walking from graves, Grizzin Farl. Nor from mining pits, or freshly dug barrows. Whatever spirit Hust Henarald imbued into the iron from his forges, the murder of three thousand men and women now taints it. So, you wonder why I still hesitate in summoning such an army?'

412

'The fate awaiting them is beyond you, Lord Silchas.'

'Indeed? Then who will deliver it?'

'I am poor at prophecy,' Grizzin Farl said. 'Still, though I see nothing but a blur, I hear a voice, and words spoken in the tone of command.'

'But not mine.'

'No. The voice I hear belongs to Anomander.'

Silchas let out a sudden sigh. 'Then he returns. Good. I am truly done with this. Tell me, Azathanai, are there any quicker paths to sorcery?'

The question ran like ice through Grizzin Farl. He dropped his gaze to the tankard in his hands, seeing the lurid play of lamplight upon the surface of the ale within. 'None,' he said, 'you would welcome.'

'I would hear them nonetheless.'

Grizzin Farl shook his head, and rose. 'I have kept the historian waiting too long. My friend, discount my last words. They were ill advised. The days ahead will prove desperate enough, I wager, without the lure of such recourse.' Bowing to the lord, the Azathanai left the table.

*Protector of nothing, not this path, not any path. When next you find me, Silchas Ruin, I will of course yield to your demands, seeing in you the ambition which you will name necessity. The easier path is not one to welcome – I said as much – but in the slaying of fear, my warning will not stop you, will it?*

*Draconus. Caladan Brood. Unknown sister T'riss. See what we begin here. The wolves are awake, and we drip words in a trail of blood.*

*Let them find their own hunger, as they must.*

*But oh, see what we begin here.*

Outside the tavern, in the street surrounded by the brittle city, the sky above looked strangely shattered, with dark and light and colours splaying out like shards, as if made of stained glass cast awry. Grizzin Farl studied it with watery eyes.

Cynicism and rage, both drunk upon the other. *It's enough to make one feel young again.*

He set off for the Citadel. It was time to speak to the historian.

*       *       *

Orfantal halted in the doorway. He saw the historian, Rise Herat, seated in a chair that had been positioned near the hearth, which was only now flickering into life. The room was chilly, unlit except for the lapping flames rising around the wood.

'He's here,' said the historian, gesturing to the floor beyond his boots. 'Do come in, Orfantal. Ribs arrived in such a pant I believe you have worn the beast out.'

Still clutching his wooden sword, Orfantal walked over. The dog lying before the hearthstone was fast asleep.

'Too many battles for one day, Orfantal. He's not as young as he once was.'

'When I'm a warrior, I will have pet wolves at my side. Two of them. Trained for war.'

'Ah, you see a long war ahead of us, then.'

Orfantal sat down on the edge of the hearthstone, with the heat against his left side. 'Cedorpul says these things never go away. If not one reason, then another. Because we love fighting.'

'It wasn't always so. There was a time, Orfantal, when we loved hunting. But even then, I will grant you, there was a lust for blood. When the time came that we tamed those beasts we would eat, still the hunters went out. They were like children who refuse to grow up – there is a power there, in that ability to decide life and death. The innocence of the prey is irrelevant to such children. Their need is too selfish to consider the victims of their indulgence.'

Orfantal reached down to scratch behind Ribs's ragged ear. The dog sighed in its sleep. 'Gripp Galas cut a man's throat open. From ear to ear. Then he hacked the head off, and carved something on the brow.'

Rise Herat said nothing for a long moment, and then he grunted. 'Well. We are indeed in a war, Orfantal. Gripp Galas saved your life, did he not?'

414

'He killed that man for his horse.'

'He saw the need, one must assume. Gripp Galas is an honourable man. You were his responsibility. I would wager what you saw there was Gripp's anger. We're in a time when to be upon the other side is itself a crime, with death the punishment.'

'Heroes don't get angry.'

'Oh but they do, Orfantal. They most certainly do. Often, it's anger that drives them to heroic acts.'

'What makes them so angry?'

'The unfairness of the world. When it's made personal, the hero becomes indignant, and filled with refusal. The hero will not abide what it seems must be. These are not thoughts. They are acts. Deeds. Something unutterable made manifest, and in witnessing, our breaths are taken away. We cannot but admire audacity, and the way in which it defies the rules.'

'I don't think Gripp Galas is a hero,' said Orfantal. The fire on his left was building, flames wrapping round the cluttered shafts of wood. Soon it would grow too hot for him to sit where he was, but not yet.

'Perhaps not,' the historian said. 'He is, I fear, too pragmatic a man for heroism.'

'What are you doing in Grizzin Farl's chamber?'

'Awaiting his return. And you?'

'Looking for Ribs. He comes here a lot. They're friends, Ribs and Grizzin Farl.'

'I recall hearing that the Azathanai plucked the beast from the Dorssan Ryl. Saved the dog's life, in fact. This will forge a bond, I'm sure.'

'Lord Silchas is Grizzin's friend, too.'

'Is he now?'

Orfantal nodded. 'It's the helplessness they share.'

'Excuse me?'

'That's what Grizzin says. The white shadow to a brother's dark power. That skin, he says, will undo Silchas, even though it's unfair. People are driven to do things, says Grizzin, by what they think is lacking in them.'

'The Azathanai has many things to say to you, it seems.'

'It's because I'm young,' Orfantal explained. 'He talks to me because I don't understand what he's talking about. That's what he says. But I understand him better than he thinks. I dreamed once there was a giant hole in the ground behind me, and it kept growing, and I kept running to keep from falling in, and I ran through walls of stone, and mountains, and across the bottom of deep lakes, and then ice and snow. I ran and ran, to keep from falling into the hole. If it wasn't for that hole, I could never have run through a stone wall, or all the rest.'

'And so people are driven to do by what's lacking in them.'

Orfantal nodded. He edged away from the growing flames, but the room beyond was still cold.

'How proceed your studies?'

Shrugging, Orfantal reached down to stroke Ribs's flank. 'Cedorpul's busy, with all that magic and stuff. I miss my mother.'

'Your aunt, you mean.'

'Yes. My aunt.'

'Orfantal, have you met the other hostage in the Citadel?'

He nodded. 'She's young. And shy. She runs away from me, up into the safe room. Then she locks the door so I can't get in.'

'You're chasing her?'

'No, I'm trying to be nice.'

'I suggest trying to be somewhat less . . . direct. Let her come to you, Orfantal.'

'I miss Sukul Ankhadu, too. She drinks wine and everything. It's as if she's already grown up. She knows about all the Great Houses, and the nobles, and who can be trusted and who can't.'

'She is not aligned, then, with sister Sharenas.'

'I don't know.' Finally, the heat was too much. Orfantal rose and walked a few paces from the hearth. 'Cedorpul told me about the sorcery. The Terondai's gift to all of the Tiste Andii.'

'Oh? And have you explored the magic for yourself, Orfantal? I should warn you of the risks—'

416

'I can do this,' Orfantal cut in, raising his arms out to the sides. Darkness suddenly billowed, coalesced, making forms that made the historian recoil in his chair. 'These are my wolves,' Orfantal said.

From before the hearthstone, Ribs bolted, claws clattering and skidding on the flagstones as he pelted for the doorway.

The conjurations had indeed assumed wolf-like shapes, but tall enough at the shoulder to surpass Orfantal's own height. Eyes glowed amber.

'I can go into them,' Orfantal continued. 'I can jump right out of my body and go into them, both of them, at the same time – but they have to stay together when I do that. If I go into just one of them, I can still make the other one follow me, or do whatever I tell it to do. It feels strange, historian, to walk on four legs. Is this the same as what the Jheleck can do?'

'Orfantal, if you would, send them away again.'

Shrugging, Orfantal dropped his arms. The blackness swirled, then dispersed like ink in water.

'No,' Rise Herat said, 'that was nothing like what the Jheleck do. Theirs is an ancient magic, more . . . bestial, and wild. To witness it, I'm told, burns the eyes. Your . . . conjurations . . . they were subtler. Orfantal, have you shown anyone else this power of yours?'

'Not yet.'

'Best you do not.'

'Why?'

'You said that your soul can travel into them, yes? Then, consider them a last recourse. Should you find your life in danger. Should a mortal wound take you, in the body you now own, then, Orfantal, flee to your . . . friends. Do you understand me?'

'Can I even do that?'

The historian shook his head. 'I don't know for certain, but it seems to be an option – from what you have just described. This secret, Orfantal – hold to it, for, should it become known, then your wolf-friends will be vulnerable. Tell me, must they be close when conjured into being?'

417

'I don't know. I could try to raise them in a different room, maybe, and see if that works.'

'Experiment, but privately. Let none see. Let none know.'

Orfantal shrugged again, and then turned to the door. 'Ribs ran away again.'

'I begin to comprehend why.'

At that moment, heavy footsteps announced the return of Grizzin Farl. As the Azathanai entered the chamber, he tilted his head and sniffed the air. 'Ah, well,' he murmured, gaze settling on Orfantal. 'My silent foil – will you join the historian and me in conversation?'

'No sir. I'm going to look for Ribs.'

'Yes, he blurred past me in yonder corridor. Look for him in the furthest corner of the Citadel, or indeed in the stables outside.'

Nodding, Orfantal left the two and set out. He recalled Rise Herat's words about hunters, and hunting, and the child mind that got trapped in all of that. But he wasn't interested in using his wolves to hunt, and he wasn't interested in hunting, either. There were no heroes among hunters, because killing was easy. *Unless, of course, the prey decides it's not innocent any more. And then stops being afraid. And decides that running is useless, because some appetites you can't run away from, and a big hole behind you can be a mouth, too, getting bigger and bigger.*

*Wolves like mine . . . they aren't afraid. They can turn. They can hunt the hunters.*

*What, I wonder, will that feel like?*

\*　　\*　　\*

'She sees through the wounds in his hands,' Rise Herat said. 'That tapestry gift to Emral Lanear, it's meant to show us that none of this is new. It's happened before. The power in blood. What else, Azathanai, should we know?'

'You fill me with sorrow, historian, with such anger.'

'The gifts of the Azathanai are never what they seem.'

Belching, Grizzin Farl drew up another chair, and sat. 'I have drunk too much ale.'

The historian studied the Azathanai, who was staring into the flames of the hearth. 'Then indulge in loquaciousness.'

'Indulgence is the sweet drink, yes. There is an Azathanai, a woman of flesh. Her name is Olar Ethil. Have you heard of her? No. Ah, well. Perhaps not by name, but recall your dreams, historian, those troubling ones, when a woman you know and yet do not know comes to you, often from behind. She presses herself against you, and offers a carnal invitation. You would think,' he said, sighing, 'that she is but the harbinger of base desires, a play of lust and, indeed, indulgence, particularly of the forbidden – however you might imagine it.'

'Grizzin Farl, you know nothing of my dreams.'

'Historian, I know what all men share. But, very well. Look instead into this fire. There are faces in the flames, or rather one face, offering myriad expressions. The Dog-Runners learned to worship that face, that womanly thing. Olar Ethil was wise. She knew the manner in which she would make herself known to them. Goddess of flames, awakener of heat. Lust, desire, bloodlust. She'll warm your flesh, but burn your soul.'

'A serpent grows from her hand, yes? She is the one in the tapestry.'

But the Azathanai shook his head. 'Yes, and no. The Dog-Runners will speak of their goddess of the earth. They name her Burn, and they hold that she sleeps an eternal sleep. In her dreams, she makes the world of men. But Olar Ethil stands near, sometimes beside the Sleeping Goddess, sometimes barring the way to her. She is jealous of Burn, and steals the heat from her. Every hearth, every lick of flame, is stolen. The serpent is fire, and blood. Life, if you choose. And yet, at its core, it is a force of destruction.'

'You Azathanai play at being gods.'

'Yes. Some of us do. Power is seductive.'

'Even the Dog-Runners deserve better. Is Burn too an Azathanai?'

'I cannot even say if Burn exists, historian. The belief in her does, and that suffices. It will guide the believers, and give shape to their world. You must lean towards the pragmatic, Rise Herat. Motivations are mere ghosts, and if meaning rides in the wake of every deed, indulge it at your leisure.' Grizzin Farl looked up, met the historian's eyes. 'What you choose to do can, without effort, be seen as a betrayal. Though you might name it the purest act of integrity imaginable.'

Rise Herat felt the blood pool in his gut, chilling his limbs. 'Do you accuse me of something, Azathanai?'

Grizzin Farl's brows lifted. 'Not at all. I but question the validity of your role in life. The historian will dissect events, counting the ledger's list of deeds, and seek meaning from invented motives. When you invite indulgence, I see how familiar to you its flavour.'

'Mother Dark is as much a goddess as is this Olar Ethil,' Rise Herat said. 'Sorcery in the blood. There, on the throne, her eyes are closed. She might be sleeping. She might be dead. Still, through serpent eyes she sees the world. And, I am told, the blood's taste is seductive. What has Draconus done?'

'To your liege? Why, he has made her into a goddess. Do you name this love? Between lovers, worship is all sharp edges. Every embrace, no matter how heated, bleeds something. That woman behind you in your dreams, she means you ill. Or, in the next breath, blessing and revelation. The possibilities are endless, until you turn round.'

It was a wonder, Rise Herat reflected, that no one had as yet killed this Azathanai, so frustrating and infuriating was his conversation. He imagined that facing a sword-master would feel much the same, with every attack anticipated, every move effortlessly countered, and like the sword-master, Grizzin Farl was in no hurry to deliver the fatal wound. He scowled at the Azathanai. 'Mother Dark is the absence at the centre of our worship. Is this by her choice, Grizzin Farl? Or does the blood – and her thirst – drive her farther and farther from mortal concerns? You say that Burn sleeps – did she choose to, or has she succumbed to some curse? You say that Olar Ethil inhabits the flames of the hearth – is this all that gods do? Simply *watch*?'

'It may indeed seem that way, yes. But I already warned you against imagining motivations, inventing meanings.'

'But she does nothing! No acts, no deeds! There is nothing to imagine or invent!'

'And so the historian starves. But, soon to grow sated, yes? The enemy to order stirs in a distant camp. An army will march on Kharkanas. What, you wonder, will she do then? Where, you wonder, are those who will fight in her name? And, as for that name . . . what is the cause it represents? Assemble the beliefs, and paint in gold their many virtues. But that you cannot do, because *she does not speak*.'

Rise Herat glared at the Azathanai, who stared back with calm, sorrow-filled eyes.

After a moment, the historian looked away. 'The High Priestess has not been given leave to visit the Chamber of Night.'

'Nonsense,' Grizzin Farl replied. 'She chooses not to, because she has something she wishes to keep hidden from Mother Dark. But now the goddess makes use of poor Endest Silann, and deception grows harder to hide. You, sir, are doubtless in league with the High Priestess. You intend something, in Mother Dark's name, but whatever it is, she must never know what you have done. Now,' the Azathanai's gaze suddenly hardened, 'bend your deeds into worship.'

Rise Herat felt sick inside, as if he had fostered an illness of his own invention, to now lodge in his flesh, sour his blood, and bruise his organs. 'Very well,' he said in a dry, rasping voice. 'Join me, Grizzin Farl. Let us go to the Chamber of Night. Let us speak to her.'

'She remains with Draconus.'

'Then we will speak to them both!'

The Azathanai pushed himself upright. 'As you wish. Shall we collect up the High Priestess along the way?'

Rise Herat grimaced. 'We can at least ask her.'

They departed the room. Behind them, the flames in the hearth devoured the last of the wood, and knew a time of hunger.

Emral Lanear, High Priestess of Dark, sat lost in a world of smoke. A vision blurred saw few cracks, and the future, laid out so smooth and perfect, proved no different from the present. This was the lure of d'bayang. There had been a time when ritual had surrounded its indulgence, and the dreamscape the smoke offered whispered messages both profound and quickly forgotten. The intent, she supposed, had to do with stepping aside, out of the flesh, outside the strictures of reality. Couched in ritual or not, it was an escape. The distinction, between then and now, belonged to intention.

*Escape as ritual promises a return to the present, when the ritual is done. Escape as ritual is meant to seed the ground between the dreamscape and the real world. But here and now, I seek no return to any present, and I will make of the ground between a wasteland of despair. Mine is not an escape seeking discovery, but one born of flight.*

She had once valued her own sobriety, the keen mind delighting in its wakefulness, its precious acuity. She had been unable to imagine wilfully surrendering such gifts, and had seen enough fools in her life to know, with dismay, the minds of company grown dull on alcohol or smoke. *Fleeing without moving. Drowning in one's chair. The bleary gaze, the comfort with confusion, the slow disintegration of time, and the slow losing of one's place in its eternal stream.*

*But look at me now. With a future crowded with crimes, I make an island and clothe it in fog. Let time stream past; I yield no harbour.*

*It is delusion. Rise Herat saw well the desire in my eyes, which should have shamed me. But I am past shame, and that too proves an alluring escape.*

Alas, a kind of crystal clarity remained in her mind, something immune to all her efforts at flight and evasion. Its light was guilt, painting her entire inner world. *Not the d'bayang. That is too paltry a reason.*

*I am High Priestess to Mother Dark. And yet, in place of obeisance, vespers and rituals, I weave a web of spies, each one conducting subterfuge with her legs spread wide. Her* mind was trapped in a cage of her own making, wherein every thought was cast into a construct of potential alliances, possible weaknesses, spilled secrets, and the option of coercion into a host of deceptions and machinations. By these efforts – this wretched course she had taken – she was seeing her world remade. She now weighed in terms of cold economy the value of each and every citizen of the realm. Collusion against opposition, strength against weakness, deceit against trust.

Like the d'bayang, this newly born way of thinking was in truth an inward spiral, with her own needs at the core. It was a world view that she now realized was far from unique, and, personal as it seemed, she but reflected the mien of countless others.

*How many wealthy nobles, I wonder, see the world in the same way? Was it not, indeed, the means by which they acquired their riches, and with them their unshakable belief in their own superiority?*

*But, Mother forgive me, it is a cold realm I find.*

The smoke warred against it, but feebly. With slurred words, it whispered lazy invitations into a refuge of ennui, to the sodden bliss of the insensate. Floppy limbs half beckoned in her mind, barely seen amidst the grey cloud. *Over here . . . come . . . here waits oblivion.*

Hardly a worthy goal for a spymaster. *I lust for knowledge, yet refuse to taste it. I gather news and facts and secrets, and do nothing with them. I am like the Protector, Grizzin Farl, who claims to protect nothing. Just as the historian refuses to record history, and the goddess refuses the comforts of worship.*

*While arrayed against us, a general who would rather not lead, a commander who follows only his own drunken whims, and a high priestess still awaiting her god.*

*We are, all of us, nothing but impostors to our cause, because the cause we espouse is nothing more than the blind we raise to hide our own ambitions. This, I now believe, is the secret behind every war, every clash that sees blood spill to the ground.*

The ritual of smoke could, on occasion, offer cruel insights.

Faintly, she heard the chime of the bell cord. *Again? Am I to be afforded no rest, no luxury of escape?* Senses blunted, her body leaden, she forced herself from the divan, found a cloak to hide all that felt exposed, and made her way from the bedroom into the outer chamber.

'Enter.'

The historian's appearance was no surprise, but the presence of Grizzin Farl was. Searching his expression, she found little given away. The Azathanai made a profession of secrets. Even so, she did not detect his usual façade of bluff amusement.

'What brings you here?' she asked them.

Rise Herat cleared his throat. 'High Priestess. The Protector has agreed to guide us into the presence of Mother Dark.'

*To what end?* These words almost spilled from her, but she managed to hold them back. She would not give them the raw extremity of her own despair, or that of her fears. 'I see. Are we to fling ourselves against her indifference one more time? Very well. Lead us, Grizzin Farl.'

The Azathanai bowed and then retreated into the corridor. Emral and Rise followed.

After a moment, as they walked, the historian spoke to her with atypical formality. 'High Priestess, it is time to inform Mother Dark of the events occurring in her realm – yes, I well understand her usage of Endest Silann, but even there, we cannot know the fullest reach of her knowledge, or her awareness. More to the point, Endest resides here in the Citadel, and concerns himself little with what goes on beyond its walls. Is it not time for a full accounting?'

The question was doubly edged, and Emral understood that the historian was not unaware of this. He was, after all, one who chose his words carefully. 'Your desires are ambitious, historian. But we will see. As you say, the effort is timely.'

Before long, they reached the ancient corridor that led to the Chamber of Night. The damage left behind by the Azathanai T'riss was still visible, in cracks and fissures latticing the stonework, in the slumped, uneven flooring. The passage was unoccupied, in itself a bleak statement of affairs. Approaching the door, Grizzin Farl hesitated, glancing back to his companions.

'There has been a burgeoning within,' he said. 'A deeper and more profound manifestation of Dark. No doubt the effects of the Terondai, the Gate's proximity.' He shrugged. 'I sense the changes, but can discern little else. Nevertheless, I hereby warn you both: what lies beyond this door is changed.'

'Then,' answered Emral Lanear, 'it behoves the High Priestess to comprehend such a transformation, don't you think?'

The Azathanai studied her, and something in his expression hinted of irony. 'High Priestess, as it turns out, that which cloaks your mind may prove a benison.'

She frowned, but was given no chance to reply, as Grizzin Farl turned to the door, reached out to the latch, and swung wide the portal to the Chamber of Night.

The cold that flowed out was redolent with fecundity, and this alone shocked Emral Lanear.

She heard a grunt from Grizzin Farl, as if in acknowledgement of her own shock, as the darkness within was, from where they stood upon the threshold, absolute.

'What awaits us?' Rise Herat asked. 'My eyes, though gift-given, cannot pierce this shroud. Grizzin Farl, what can you discern?'

'Nothing,' the Azathanai replied. 'We must enter in order to see.'

'Even the floor is lost to us,' the historian retorted. 'We could find ourselves plunging into an abyss. This chamber is negation, a realm devoid of all substance.' He faced Emral Lanear, his eyes wide with alarm. 'I now counsel against this.'

But Emral Lanear found herself shrugging, and then she stepped past the historian and, without giving Grizzin Farl a glance, continued on into the Chamber of Night.

She felt compacted earth beneath her feet, damp and cool

through the thin soles of her slippers. The smell of deep decay and verdant life swarmed around her, as if the air itself was alive. *We are no longer within the Citadel.*

Grizzin Farl joined her, standing close upon her left, a presence more felt than seen. 'He has taken this too far,' the Azathanai said in a low rumble. 'Gates possess two sides. By presence alone they divide worlds. The Terondai, High Priestess, issues into this place.'

'And what place is this?' Rise Herat asked from directly behind Emral.

'Eternal Night, historian. Elemental Night. Name it as you will, but know that it is pure. It is *essence*.'

Emral could hear something like wind soughing through trees in the distance, but she felt no breath upon her chilled face. A moment later the Azathanai's huge hand closed about her upper arm, and Grizzin whispered, 'With me, then. I sense a presence ahead.'

They began walking, with Rise close behind them – he might have been gripping the Azathanai by belt or clothing. 'How far?' Emral asked.

'Uncertain.'

'Where sits Mother Dark's throne?' the historian demanded, his voice taut. 'Have we lost her utterly now?'

'Such questions will have to await answers,' Grizzin Farl replied. 'This realm sets itself against me. I do not belong, and now, more than ever before, I feel unwelcome.'

'Can we return?' Emral asked the Azathanai.

'Unknown,' came his disturbing response.

The feel of the earth beneath her was unchanging. There was not a single stone or pebble, nor a plant or any other protuberance rising from the level clay. Yet the redolence was cloying and thick, as if they walked a rain-drenched forest.

'We have made an error,' said Rise Herat, 'entering this place. High Priestess, forgive me.'

Still they could see nothing, not even the ground upon which they walked. Yet, when the heavy sound of footsteps approached from directly ahead, it was but moments before Emral Lanear could distinguish the figure in growing detail.

It was monstrous, hunched and towering over even Grizzin Farl. Its hands hung down past its knees, the arms massive in their musculature. Its head was disproportionately small, the pate hairless, the eyes sunken deep.

Striding closer, and closer still. Moments before reaching them, it said, 'Food.'

One heavy hand swung up, struck Grizzin Farl in the chest. The Azathanai was flung back, spinning in the air.

Another hand then reached out for Emral Lanear.

But Rise Herat was quicker, dragging her back by the cloak she wore, out beyond the demon's grasping fingers.

She stumbled as the historian continued pulling her, tugging until she was turned round, and then they were running, blind, lost.

Behind them, the demon gave chase, each step a thump of thunder upon the ground. Distinctly, it said again, 'Food.'

Warring against her benumbed senses, terror clawed its way free, making a hammer of her heart. She ran as she had not run since she was a child – but those memories were not ones of fear. Now, she felt herself overwhelmed, too vulnerable to comprehend. The way ahead was emptiness, and in that absence there was only the desolation that came with the realization that there was nowhere to hide.

Beside her, Rise Herat's breaths were harsh and straining. For a moment, Emral Lanear almost laughed. The indolence of their lives in the Citadel had ill prepared them for this. *Lying languid. Lungs full of smoke. Dreaming of chants and solemn processions. The poisons in betrayal's gilded cup.* Already, the muscles of her legs were losing strength, and it seemed the weight of her own body was growing too burdensome to bear.

*Lithe child, where have you gone? Do you hide there still, beneath layers of adulthood?*

Rise Herat stumbled, and suddenly he was gone from her side. Crying out, Emral Lanear slowed, twisting round—

She saw the demon lumber to where the historian had fallen. Its hands reached down to take hold of him.

Then there was blurred motion, a succession of meaty

427

thuds, and it seemed that the darkness itself had coalesced into something solid, immensely powerful. It swarmed over the demon, and with each blow blood spurted. The demon reeled back from the assault, voicing a child's bawl of frustration, shock and pain. Then it wheeled round and ran away.

Rise Herat remained on the ground, as if broken by some unseen wound, and when he propped himself up on one elbow, the effort clearly cost him dearly. Emral stumbled towards him, and then halted as their saviour lost the swirling darkness enwreathing it, and she found herself facing Lord Draconus.

'High Priestess,' the Consort said, 'have you not yet understood how unwise it is to accept Grizzin Farl's protection?'

Rise Herat coughed from where he now sat. 'Milord, you saved our lives.'

Draconus glanced down to study the historian. 'If you will wander strange realms, Rise Herat, you must first understand that your own has been made uncommonly sparse of predators – beyond your own kind, that is. Most realms are much . . . wilder.' He lifted his gaze and met Emral's eyes. 'There are dangers. Tell me, would you as blithely enter a cave mouth in some mountainside?'

Grunting, Rise Herat managed to regain his feet, though he still struggled to find his breath. 'Tales of old, told to children,' he said. 'The heroes plunge into caves and caverns again and again, and each time find peril.'

'Just so,' Draconus replied. 'Yet this is no child's tale, historian. And there is no story master to twist the fates and deliver unlikely succour. Leave the exploits of heroes upon the breath, where they can do little harm.'

Rise coughed and then said, 'Hardly, milord. On occasion, fools like us are inspired by their deeds, only to find our own breaths lost.'

'Lord Draconus,' said Emral. 'Can you lead us back to the Citadel?'

'I can.'

Rise Herat finally straightened. 'Milord, Grizzin Farl

named this place Elemental Night, or Eternal Night. How has this realm come to be, upon the very threshold of the temple's nave? What has happened to the Chamber of Night and its throne? Where is Mother Dark?'

'Fraught questions,' came a voice from one side, and a moment later Grizzin Farl appeared. 'Draconus, old friend, must you make a map of mystery? By what you have scribed, powers will root to the place of their containment. These gates. You invite vulnerability. Chaos wanders in its hunt. Name me the gate able to flee?'

Seeming to ignore the Protector's questions, the Consort said, 'Mother Dark discovers the breadth of her realm—'

To which the Azathanai cut in sharply, 'You give her this, and expect her to be unchallenged?'

'Her challengers are no more,' Draconus replied, finally facing the Azathanai. 'Do you think I would be so careless in my preparations?'

Something in the Consort's words clearly appalled Grizzin Farl, but he said nothing.

Draconus turned back to Emral Lanear. 'She attends her places of faith, High Priestess. But in substance, she is stretched . . . thin. Thin as, you might say, Night's own blanket.'

'Can she be summoned?' Emral asked. *Or are we forsaken?*

Draconus hesitated, and then said, 'Perhaps.'

Rise Herat seemed to choke, and then said, '*Perhaps?* Milord! Her High Priestess asks – no, *prays* – for the presence of her goddess! Is Mother Dark now indifferent to her chosen children?'

'I would think not,' Draconus snapped.

'Kurald Galain descends into bloody civil war,' the historian retorted in a half-snarl. 'Lord Draconus, your very station finds you upon a crumbling pedestal. Urusander means to make himself her husband, and has taken the title of Father Light. And where is Lord Anomander, her First Son? Why, off in the wilderness, tracking a brother who would not be found!' Rise then whirled to face Grizzin Farl. 'And you

Azathanai! Now in our midst! A deceiver to guide us into this realm, and what of the one accompanying Lord Anomander? T'riss was but the beginning, but now your kind creep into our business. State it plain, Grizzin Farl, what do you here?'

The Protector was slow in responding. Watching the Azathanai, Emral waited to see where his eyes might take his gaze, and a part of her anticipated – with peculiar certainty – that he would find Lord Draconus before answering the historian. But he did not. Instead, Grizzin Farl lowered his head, choosing to study the ground. 'It is my task, historian, to attend.'

'Attend? Attend what?'

'Why,' the Azathanai looked up, 'the end of things.'

In the silence that followed, it fell to Lord Draconus to finally speak. 'High Priestess, historian, I will guide you now to the portal that leads back to the Citadel.' He then faced Grizzin Farl. 'You, however, will remain. We will have words.'

'Of course, old friend.'

'And I would know of this other Azathanai, who accompanies Lord Anomander.'

The answer to that would be easy enough, but neither Emral nor Rise Herat spoke, and after a moment it was clear that Grizzin Farl had said all he intended to say, at least in their presence.

*'Old friend.' This Consort bears unseemly gifts, and reveals powers uncanny. How thin, I now wonder, does the Tiste blood run in you, Draconus?*

*Your 'old friend' gives nothing away. I should have expected as much.*

*So, the Azathanai gather to witness the end of us, and this leads me to a truth. Forgive me, Lord Anomander, for what is to come. Nothing here is your fault, and if we crowd round to take strength from your honour, it is because we lack it in ourselves. We will feed and may well grow mighty, even as we cut you down.* She met the depthless eyes of Lord Draconus. 'Please, then,' she said. 'Take us home.'

*And Grizzin Farl, you have my thanks. For revealing what you could not reveal.*

*The highborn are right, though they understand it not. Still, they are right.*

She studied Lord Draconus, as if seeing him for the first time. *The enemy among us now guides us here in this Eternal Night.*

*If I can, Consort, I will see Lord Anomander turn against you, by every measure. If it lies within my power, I will see the First Son kill you, Draconus.*

*For what you have done.*

The end of things. In this realm, the notion felt all too real.

# ELEVEN

HUNCHED AND GAUNT, THE OLD MAN WITH ONE LEG worked his crutches with jarring intensity, as if, at any moment, what held him up could pull loose from his grip, twisting to make a cruciform upon which the fates would nail him. The lines of his face made for hard angles, matching the harsh resentment in his eyes. His thin, pale lips moved to a voiceless litany of curses as his eyes tracked the floor ahead of him. And yet, for all of that, he trailed High Priestess Syntara as if he was her shadow, bound to her by laws that could not be sundered by any mortal hand.

Renarr watched their approach with detached amusement. For her, religion was a wasteland, a place only the broken would choose to stumble on to, their hands outstretched to grasp whatever came within reach. She recalled her own thoughts from some weeks past: the conflation in her mind of whore's tent and temple, and the squalid surrender that fused into one these seemingly disparate settings. The need was the same, and for many the satiation achieved by both proved shortlived and ephemeral.

The High Priestess was bedecked in flavours of white and gold. An ethereal illumination clung to her like smoke. Her heart-shaped face glistened as if brushed with pearl-dust, and the colour of her eyes seemed to shift hues in a soft stream of blues, magenta and lilac. She was indeed a creature of stunning beauty.

'Blessings upon you,' said Syntara when at last she halted a few paces away from Lord Urusander, who had turned to face the new arrivals from his position by the tall, narrow window overlooking the courtyard.

Eyeing her adoptive father, Renarr sought to gauge his mood, seeking some hint as to the stance he would take with the High Priestess, but as ever, Urusander was closed to her. There was, she supposed, something to admire, and perhaps even emulate, in her lord's ability to contain his emotions. If, however, she might have expected the man to be affected by Syntara's radiance, his first words dispelled the notion utterly.

'This light hurts my eyes,' Urusander said. 'I would rather the very stones of this keep not glow day and night. Your blessing,' he continued, 'has made me raw with exhaustion. Now, since you have sought me out, dispense with the incidentals and speak your mind.'

Smiling in answer, Syntara said, 'You are witness to a power born to deny darkness, Lord Urusander. Here, we find ourselves in a holy sanctum, the very heart of that power. Light exists to be answered, and that answer will soon come. Mother Dark but awaits you.'

Urusander studied the High Priestess for a moment, and then said, 'I am told that Hunn Raal proclaims himself an *archmage*. He has invented for himself the title of Mortal Sword to Light. He has, for all I know, a dozen more titles beyond those, to add to that of captain in my legion. Like you, he delights in inventing appellations, as if they would add legitimacy to his ambitions.'

It was, these days, almost impossible to discern a paling of visage among the Children of Light, but Renarr imagined she detected it nonetheless in the lovely, perfect face of Syntara. But the insult's sting did not last long, for Syntara then resumed her smile and added a sigh. 'Hunn Raal invents titles to affirm his place in this new religion, milord. "Mortal Sword" marks him as the first and foremost servant to Father Light.'

'He would claim for himself a martial role in this cult, then.'

If anything, this cut deeper, and again it was a moment before Syntara recovered. 'Milord, this is no mere cult, I assure you.' She gestured, almost helplessly. 'See this burnish of Holy Light? See how the air itself is suffused with Light's essence?'

'With eyes closed and yearning for sleep,' Urusander growled, 'I see it still.'

'Milord, you are named Father Light.'

'Syntara, I am named Vatha Urusander, and the only title I hold is that of commander to my legion. What makes you believe I desire a union with Mother Dark? What,' he continued, his tone growing harsher, 'in my history, invites you – and Hunn Raal – into the belief that I desire her as my wife?'

'Nothing,' Syntara replied, 'except your legacy of honouring duty.'

'Duty? And who proclaims it so? Not Mother Dark. Nor the highborn, for that matter. You crowd me with your expectations, High Priestess, but the voices that roar through my skull deafen but one ear. From the other, why, blessed silence.'

'No longer,' Syntara replied, and at last Renarr noted a glimmer of something like triumph in her mien. 'I am now engaged in conversation with High Priestess Emral Lanear, and no, it was not I who initiated the contact. Milord, she acknowledges the necessity of balance, a redress in the name of justice. She recognizes, indeed, that there must be a union between Father Light and Mother Dark. Milord, if she does not speak on behalf of her goddess, then she can hardly lay claim to her title of High Priestess, can she? This,' she said, taking a step closer, 'is the overture we were seeking.'

'By marriage arranged,' Urusander said with a bitter smile, 'the state wins peace. By choices removed, we are to be content with one path.'

'Mother Dark concedes,' Syntara said. 'Is this not victory?'

'And yet the Hust Legion readies for war.'

The High Priestess made a dismissive gesture. 'It but restores itself, milord. How could it do otherwise?'

'Better to bury those cursed weapons,' Urusander said. 'Or melt them down. Hust Henarald took his arts too far, into mysteries better left untouched. I decry Hunn Raal's treachery, while a part of me understands his reason. But do inform this Mortal Sword, Syntara, that holy title or not, he will be made to answer for his crimes.'

Her brows lifted. 'Milord, he does not acknowledge my authority over him, despite my overtures. When I first heard of the title he had invented for himself I sought out the Old Language, seeking an alternative that would properly belong within the temple hierarchy. I found the title of "Destriant", signifying the position of Chosen Priest – yet a priest belonging to no temple. Rather, a destriant's demesne is all that lies *beyond* sacred ground.' She paused, and then shrugged. 'He refused it. If Hunn Raal is to answer for his crimes, it must be Father Light who will stand in judgement.'

'Not his commander?'

There was a sardonic hint to Syntara's reply. 'I await your endeavour's account, milord. I believe he has since dispensed with the rank of captain.'

'Where is he now?'

'Returned to the Legion camp, I understand. There is the matter of the companies out tracking Sharenas Ankhadu.'

The mention of Sharenas's name elicited a frown from Urusander, and he turned away to face the window again, and this was to Renarr the only sign of his dismay.

Syntara stood as if awaiting his regard once more. He had, after all, voiced no dismissal. After a moment, her gaze slipped to Renarr, who was seated on a chair near the lord's desk. The High Priestess cleared her throat. 'Blessings upon you, Renarr – I apologize for not taking note of your presence earlier. Are you well?'

Inconsequential enough to escape notice? Hardly. 'Discomfited, to be honest,' Renarr replied, 'as I ponder just how your pet historian will alter the portents of this meeting in whatever account he records for posterity. I assume his presence is deemed necessary, given the need for a Holy Writ of some sort, a recounting of Light's glorious birth, or some such thing.' She smiled. 'If I could be bothered, I might match him with a scroll or two. How odd the birth of a new religion if it does not quickly fracture into sects. Is it not a proper task to plant the seeds of schism as early on as possible? The Book of Sagander, and the contrary Book of Renarr, Adopted Daughter to Father Light. Imagine the holy wars to come of that, with the tree so eagerly shaken before its roots even set.'

Syntara's blink was languid. 'Cynicism, Renarr, is a stain upon a soul. Its reflection is bitter, even to you, I imagine. Come to the Chamber of Light. With prayer and service, you can be cleansed of what troubles you.'

*My troubles? Oh, woman, what you call a stain is my coat of arms. It lies emblazoned upon my soul, and the promise of redress belongs not to you, nor Light, nor any temple of your making.* 'Thank you for the offer, High Priestess, and do not doubt that I appreciate the sentiment behind your desire.'

Sagander pointed at Renarr and said, in a half-snarl, 'You are no daughter by blood, whore. Beware your presumption!'

At that, Urusander swung round. 'Get that wretched scholar from my chamber, Syntara. As for recording this meeting, why, my hand does not tremble at the prospect. Sagander, your writings are well known to me, inasmuch as they mangle every notion of justice imaginable. Your mind was never equal to the task of your heart's desire, and clearly nothing has accrued to you in the years since, barring layers of spite. Both of you, get out.'

Bridling, Syntara drew herself taller. 'Milord, Mother Dark expects a formal reply from us.'

'Mother Dark, or Emral Lanear?'

'Would you have Mother Dark address you in person? She speaks through her High Priestess. No other interpretation is possible.'

'Truly? None? And do you speak for me? Or is it Hunn

436

Raal who claims that right? How many voices shall I possess? How many faces in my visage can this precious Light behold?'

'Hunn Raal is indeed an *archmage*,' Syntara snapped, making the title one of derision. 'He makes mockery of the sorcery he now explores. Even so, it is born of Light. The power we now possess cannot be denied, milord.'

'I argued against our irrelevance,' Urusander retorted. 'That and nothing more.' Now there was anger visible in the commander, reverberating through his entire body. 'An utterance of bitterness, a plea for something like a just reward for all that we sacrificed for our realm. I voiced it to the highborn, seeking the release of land as recompense, and was rebuffed. This, High Priestess, was the seed of my complaint. And now, as you and countless others ride the back of my dismay, we find ourselves charging into death and destruction. *Where, in all of this, is my justice?*'

Renarr had to credit Syntara's self-possession, in that she neither stepped back nor flinched from Urusander's anger. 'You will find it meted out, milord, by your hand, from a position of equality – from the Throne of Light, which will stand beside the Throne of Dark. This is why the highborn will gather against you. It is why they will fight your ascension. But you, Urusander, and Mother Dark – only the two of you, bound together, can stop this. From that throne, you will force from the highborn every concession you desire—'

'It is not for me that I desire anything!'

'For your soldiers, then. Your loyal soldiers who, as you have said, deserve to be rewarded.'

A few moments passed, in which no one spoke or moved. Then Urusander waved dismissively. 'Bring to me this note from High Priestess Emral Lanear. I will read it for myself.'

'Milord, I can recount it for you word for word—'

'My reading skills will suffice, Syntara, unless you also desire the title of my secretary?'

Renarr snorted.

'Very well, then,' Syntara said. 'As you wish, milord.'

Their departure was marked by the hollow thumps of the

historian's crutches. As the doors closed, Renarr said, 'You'll never see it, you know.'

He shot her a searching look.

'It will have been transcribed,' Renarr went on. 'There will be a notation from Syntara attached, explaining that the original was in High Script, or some arcane temple code. They are not done with playing you, Father. But now, after today, there will be a new diligence to their scheming.'

'Why?'

'Because it seems that you have awakened to this moment, and your place in it.'

He sighed. 'I miss Sharenas Ankhadu.'

'The one who set about murdering your captains?'

'I gave her cause. No. They gave her cause. Slayers of innocents, leaders of a misguided pogrom. She was the sword in my hand.'

'The true instigator of that pogrom still lives,' Renarr said. 'He bears the new title of Mortal Sword. And now he wields sorcery. Would that Sharenas had begun with him.'

He was now studying her. 'Will you now stand in her place, Renarr? Are you to be my confidante?'

The question arrived somewhere between hope and a plea. 'Father, when I last departed this keep, you sent a squad to escort me back. Now, here I am, no longer a plaything for your soldiers. Required to remain in your presence or, by your leave, in an adjoining room. Will you now make me your reluctant conscience? If so, best not chain me.'

'I need no conscience but my own, Renarr. But . . . you saw through the subterfuge of this meeting. You swiftly and truly gleaned the purpose of that miserable scholar. You grasp – instinctively, I believe – the needs of this new religion, its raw hunger and brutal pragmatism. And she accused *you* of cynicism! In any case, Syntara had not planned for you. She left her flank exposed, and Sagander served as a poor excuse in its defence.'

Renarr rose from the chair. 'Forgive me, Father. Best not rely upon me to ward your flank. I am far too capricious in my own amusements. Sagander's well-known disgust for the common-born and the fallen was the only invitation I required. I baited him out of boredom.'

He said nothing as she made her way from the chamber.

*Oh, Sagander. Old man, mediocre scholar, an historian rocking on crutches from one scene to the next. Even the blessing of Light but underscores your flaws. Such clarity of vision, as promised by this burgeoning faith, yields no shades to truth, or justice.*

*Do you grasp that, Urusander?*

*Your High Priestess fears your Mortal Sword. Your historian is maimed by his own bigotry, and feeds fires of hatred behind his eyes. Your first captain dreams of his bloodline restored. And your adopted daughter must turn away from this dance no matter how honest its meaning, or how honourable its desire.*

*I see this light, Father, in all that comes. But I will not blink.*

Still, the echo of those crutches lingered in Renarr, reminder of woundings that took away more than limbs or flesh. Scaffolds assembled to take the nails of pain and torment need not be visible to any mortal eye, and if the figure writhing upon the frame remained unseen, still the blood dripped.

*Coat of arms. My banner. My perfect, perfected stain.*

*       *       *

Captain Hallyd Bahann slid a hand down from Tathe Lorat's bared shoulder, brushing the length of her upper arm, and then smiled across at Hunn Raal. 'I know the risks in leading my company upon her trail, Mortal Sword.'

Hunn Raal tilted his head to one side. 'Indeed? Are three hundred soldiers insufficient to guard you from the wrath of Sharenas Ankhadu?'

The man's smile broadened. 'The risk lies not in what I hunt, but in what I leave behind me, here in Neret Sorr.' He flicked a glance at the woman beside him, but if she took note she showed no sign, content instead with playing with the unsheathed dagger she held in her hands.

Hunn Raal pondered the man for a moment, bemused by

the fragility of his arrogance and narcissism. Then he shrugged. 'You suggest a most frail union, captain, if in the moment of your absence you imagine Tathe Lorat quickened to infidelity.'

At that, Tathe Lorat managed a languid smile, though her gaze did not lift. She said, 'Appetites sing their own song, Mortal Sword, against which I often prove helpless.'

Grunting, Hunn Raal reached for his goblet of wine. 'Weakness is a common indulgence. Control, on the other hand, requires strength.' He studied her as he drank, and then said, 'But you'll walk no knife's edge, will you, Tathe Lorat, with pleasures at hand upon either side?'

'Just my point,' Hallyd said, struggling to pull the conversation back to him, and only now could Hunn Raal see the brittle need in the man for Raal's attention, especially at this moment. It would not do, after all, to be dismissed before he even departed the tent. But his next words belied Raal's suppositions. 'And so I must ask you, Mortal Sword, will you keep her occupied? Too many young soldiers will catch her eye, weakening the authority of command, but if she shares the furs of the Mortal Sword's bed, well . . .'

Disgust was too kind a word for the antics of these two captains. It was a wonder Urusander had indulged them for as long as he had. But of course the matter was more complex, now. Hunn Raal had lost some vital allies among the captains of the Legion. 'As you wish. But captain, what of Tathe Lorat's own desires?'

'You are challenged,' Tathe Lorat murmured to her husband, still playing with her knife.

In response to Raal's question, Hallyd Bahann shrugged.

Sighing, Hunn Raal looked away. 'Very well. Tell me, Hallyd, what have your scouts determined?'

'She somehow acquired an extra horse. Avoiding all settlements, she rode westward, into the forest.'

'Where, presumably, she intends to hide.'

'She has little choice. We have all routes south blockaded or patrolled. If Kharkanas was her intent, we will deny it to her. Thus, where else might she seek sanctuary?'

'Dracons Keep.'

'Across the Dorssan Ryl? The ice is notoriously treacherous. We might well drive her to such desperation. Once we reach the forest edge, I intend to advance my company in a pronged formation. We will sweep her up and force her ever westward, until her back is to the river. Mayhap she attempts it, and drowns.'

'Not good enough,' Hunn Raal snapped. 'I want her captured. Brought back to Neret Sorr. If she drowns in the Dorssan Ryl, she will have won a victory over me. Unacceptable, captain. More to the point, what if she manages to cross?'

'Then I will besiege Dracons Keep.'

'You will do nothing of the sort.'

'We are not Borderswords, sir. We are Legion soldiers.'

Hunn Raal rubbed at his eyes, and then levelled a hard look upon the man before him. 'You will not offer up to Ivis the prospect of wiping out one of my companies, Hallyd. Are we clear on this? If Sharenas makes it to Dracons Keep, you are to withdraw. Return here. Her accounting will have to wait.'

For an instant it seemed that Hallyd would challenge him, but then he shrugged and said, 'Very well, sir. In any case, I intend to run her down long before she reaches the road, much less the river.'

'That would be preferable, captain.'

After a moment, Hallyd Bahann cleared his throat and then rose from his seat, adjusting his armour and winter cloak. 'We depart now, Mortal Sword.'

'Do not take too long,' Hunn Raal said. 'I intend to see us on the march in a month's time.'

'Understood.'

The captain exited the tent. Leaning back, Hunn Raal studied Tathe Lorat. Eventually, she sheathed her knife and looked up to meet his gaze. 'Does the challenge in keeping me satisfied excite you, Mortal Sword?'

'Stand up.'

'If you insist.'

'Tell me. Do you wish to remain a captain in Urusander's Legion, Tathe Lorat?'

She blinked. 'Of course.'

'Excellent. Now hearken well, captain. You are not among my indulgences. Not now, and at no time in the future.'

'I see.'

'Not quite, as I am not yet finished. In your mate's absence, fuck whom you will. I will of course know about it, no matter how carefully you arrange your trysts. And when the news reaches me, and should your lover be found within the Legion ranks, I will see you stripped and thrown to the dogs. If Hallyd chooses to retrieve you upon his return, well, that is his business. Am I understood, captain?'

Tathe Lorat stared down at Hunn Raal, expressionless. Then she smiled. 'Oh dear. The Mortal Sword defines a new opprobrium against which we must now contend, does he? If Mother Dark's temple whores make a virtue of carnal indulgences, are we to seek the opposite? Abstinence, sir, will yield your faith few followers.'

'You misunderstand, Tathe Lorat. The Legion is frail enough since Captain Sharenas's betrayal. It will not do to have you invite favours, jealousy, and unbound lust among my soldiers. It is bad enough you pimp out your own daughter – and speaking of which, that must end as well. Immediately. Win your alliances by less despicable means.'

'The ways of my kin are not for you to determine, Mortal Sword.'

He'd finally stung her awake, he observed, and this led him to consider the hidden fires of Tathe Lorat's hatred for her own child. The simple fact was, together, Tathe Lorat and Hallyd Bahann posed a potential problem that could present to him, at some future point, an outright rivalry to his ambitions. Although they were for the moment sworn to him, he would be a fool to believe that things wouldn't change once Kharkanas was in the Legion's hands.

'You are a Child of Light now, Tathe Lorat,' he said. 'But it appears that the significance of that transformation still eludes you. Very well. Consider this.'

The sorcery that erupted from him flung her from her feet. She struck the tent wall, bowing the canvas and bending the poles on that side. She slid down amidst broken stools and a crumpled cot. From outside came a shout and the rattle of weapons being drawn. In answer to that, Hunn Raal extended his power, creating an impenetrable dome of light around his command tent. Even the soldiers' cries of alarm could not pierce the barrier.

Imagining Syntara, in her temple, struck so suddenly by this distant conflagration of power made Hunn Raal smile as he watched Tathe Lorat climb weakly to her knees, her hair hanging in disarray and drifting to unseen currents of energy. 'Now,' he said. 'In matters of kin, why, you are mine. We are all Children of Light now, after all. Our family has grown, but your protector remains one man – the man you see before you. Thus, Tathe Lorat, the title of Mortal Sword. And a sword, as you know, cuts both ways.'

She staggered to her feet, fear undisguised in her expression now as she regarded him.

Hunn Raal nodded. 'Send Sheltatha Lore to the keep. Assuming we get past Syntara and her temple cronies, we shall make this a poignant charge, in setting the child's care at the feet of Lord Urusander's adopted daughter.'

'As you command, Mortal Sword.'

'Now,' he continued as he relented his magic, the dome of light beyond the tent immediately vanishing, 'be on your way. Inform the guards beyond that all is well, but that my tent is in need of repair.'

Saluting, Tathe Lorat departed.

A short time later, Hunn Raal drained his goblet of wine and rose, pleased at the grace that accompanied the effort. The sorcery within him flowed easily through the alcohol, lending an acuity that defied his habit. There were times, of course, when the clarity frustrated him. Particularly in the depths of night, when the longing for oblivion commanded his soul. But like the Holy Light's refusal of night's gift of darkness, Hunn Raal was denied his escape.

It was folly to expect that such blessings of magic would not come with a toll. He was already learning to hide his sobriety when it suited him. He was well served by the assumptions of others, as they watched him dip into his cups and believed his wits dulled.

Hunn Raal departed the command tent.

Outside, he saw a work crew approaching with new poles, guides, and a mallet to aid any new placement of stakes that might be required. To the ruined furniture within the tent, Hunn Raal was indifferent. Better, in some ways, if the reminders of his power remained. If fear added to his authority, bolstering his new title, then it was all to the good.

He walked through the camp, unmindful of the soldiers, their cookfires and their muted conversations. The bitter cold of the air barely reached him. There was enough power within him, at this moment, to thaw the ground beneath the entire camp. Yielding to a kind of laziness, he let the sorcery bleed into his vision, altering the landscape around him. Refulgent light devoured details on all sides, while the cookfires seethed like knotted fists of flame. Figures in the avenues between tents revealed a preternatural ambience, sometimes flickering, sometimes fiercely bright. Nearby, a soldier sat with his sword bared in his lap, working a stone along its edge. Seeing the iron blade feeding upon the ethereal light made Hunn Raal pause, frowning.

The iron's thirst seemed unquenchable. Bemused, but insufficiently so to pursue his own unease, Hunn Raal continued on.

A few moments later he was drawn to a cookfire, sensing from its virulent flames something like defiance. As he approached, the soldiers who had been gathered round the firepit rose and then backed away. Ignoring them, the Mortal Sword stared down into the hearth.

*There is something . . . something there. I . . .*

He could not pull his gaze from the flames as that unknown force reached out, plucking at his will, mocking the sorcery within him.

*What is that? A face? A woman's face?*

He heard laughter not his own, rustling in his skull like autumn leaves. And then a woman's voice spoke in his mind, and its power was such that he felt like a newborn pup, helpless on the ground as something vast reached out to prod and poke it. The realization further weakened him, and he felt his soul suddenly cowering.

*'Thyrllan itha setarallan. New child, born to the flames, I see your helplessness. Bethok t'ralan Draconus, does he even comprehend? See these measures of love, every span meted in desperation. She strides the Eternal Expanse of Essential Night, seeking what? Power is not born of love, except among the wise, for whom surrender is strength. Alas, wisdom is the rarest wine, and even among those who partake of it, there are few who will know its flavour. But you, O Mortal Sword of Light, walking preened with pride and drunk on nothing but self-satisfaction – your ignorance makes your power deadly, untempered. I felt you, was drawn to you.*

*'Discipline your subjects as you will, but understand this: power draws power, extremity invites extremity. Indulge in foolish displays, and there are those, more than your equal in strength, but wiser in its use, who will crush you into dust. Dislike of temerity is commonplace. Affront at misuse rarer, but potent nonetheless.'*

'Who – who speaks? Name yourself!'

*'Petty demands from a petty mind. Listen well, as I do not often offer advice unbidden, unpaid for. His first gift to her was a sceptre. Bloodwood and Hust iron. You must forge an answer. Find your most trusted blacksmith, an artisan of metals. The crowns can wait, while the orbs . . . destined for another place, another time. This night, build for me a fire, out beyond your civil strictures. Make it large, and feed it well. I will return to the flames then, and guide you and your blacksmith to the First Forge.*

*'Balance, Mortal Sword. Each gesture answered. Each deed matched.'*

'If no payment is asked,' Hunn Raal said, 'then why do this for me?'

'*You? Do you think arrogance charms? I am a woman, not a half-grown girl with fresh blood on the grass. I do nothing for you, Hunn Raal. But you will learn temperance. That cannot be helped and so I make no claim to its gift. Light must face Dark as an equal—*'

'It is no equal,' Hunn Raal snapped. 'Darkness kneels to Light. It falters, fails, retreats.'

Her rattling laughter returned. '*You heed too few of my words. Kneels? Falters? Look to the night sky, foolish man, and gauge the victor in the contest between Dark and Light. Drink yourself insensate, and discover whether oblivion greets you with light or darkness. In eternity's span, Light must ever fail. Waning, flickering, dying. But Dark abides, upon either side of life.*

'*Tell all this to your High Priestess. Puncture her bloated presumption, Mortal Sword. If you seek domination in your absurd war, you will fail.*'

'Mother Dark has already yielded to our demands. If a battle awaits us, our enemy will fall, and there will be no one to oppose our march into Kharkanas. In that, woman, I care nothing for Light or Dark. I will win for the Legion the justice they have earned, and if this makes the highborn kneel, then I will attend their humiliation with pleasure.'

'*Build me a fire.*'

Scowling, Hunn Raal said, 'I will think on it.'

'*Build me a fire.*'

'Did you not hear me? I will think on it.'

'*Thyrllan itha setarallan.*' She seemed to reach into him then, grasping not his heart, nor his throat, but his cock. Sudden heat engorged it, and an instant later he spurted savagely, saw his seed devoured by flames. She laughed. '*Build me a fire.*'

She released him. He staggered back, blinking awake to the mundane surroundings of the camp, the abandoned hearth before him, the dozen or so soldiers gathered round to witness.

Hunn Raal looked down. He had been standing amidst the flames during his conversation with the demon. His boots had burned away, his leather riding trousers were blackened and curled, revealing his burnished white, now hairless, legs. His cock hung out from what remained of his breeches, still dripping.

*Ah, Abyss take me . . .*

Still. Her grip had been sure. He wanted to feel it again.

\* \* \*

Infayen Menand sat up on her cot, pushing hair from her eyes, and squinted across at her lieutenant. 'He did what?'

'Masturbated, sir. As his clothes burned away.'

'And the flames did not harm him?'

'No sir.'

'Hmm. I want some of that magic, I think.' Glancing up, she noted a glint of hilarity in the soldier standing before her, and scowled. 'Against the flames, fool, not the rest. Get out.'

When the man was gone, Infayen remained sitting for a time, and then she rose, collected her cloak, and left her tent.

She walked through the encampment, and then took the high track that skirted Neret Sorr's main street, remaining on the back-slope of the ridge as she traversed the length of the village until the trail intersected the cobbled ascent to the keep, whereupon she began the climb to the inner gatehouse.

A short time later she reached the courtyard, crossed it and entered the estate itself. The emanation from the stones washed walls and floors, streamed down from vaulted ceilings, until every high window appeared, not as a portal of sunlight, but as a dulled stain marring the refulgence. The intensity of the ethereal aura deepened as she approached the now sanctified east wing of the keep, the newly named Temple of Light.

The architecture ill suited the name's implied glory, as most of the rooms were cramped, with low ceilings, and the tiled floors bore scrapes and gouges from careless shifting of heavy furniture. The central Chamber of Light, now home to its

447

eponymous throne, was the ground floor of the tower. The floors above had been removed, permitting the golden light to rise skyward with such vehemence at the top that the conical roof was no longer visible – instead, it seemed that a newborn sun commanded the tower's loftiest reach.

None of this impressed Infayen much, and in that regard it was in keeping with her life's experiences thus far. She understood the paucity of her own imagination, and the absence of wonder that accompanied it, but considered neither to be egregious flaws. In place of such dubious virtues, she held to an unassailable capacity for severity, and this trait made her the most respected and feared captain in Urusander's Legion. She knew this and felt no pride, nor sense of accomplishment. It was, after all, the legacy of the Menand bloodline, the last remnant of a heroic family that had seen its prestige battered, stained and finally dragged down into disrepute – all through no particular fault of kin, present or past. Rather, the qualities of command which Infayen had inherited had, time and again during the wars, driven her ancestors to the forefront of every battle, every dire extremity, every desperate and forlorn last stand. The implacable rules of attrition did the rest. The Menand name was now synonymous with failure.

Infayen possessed a bastard daughter, Menandore, fostered with another family in some pallid mockery of the tradition of hostages among the highborn, but it was an arrangement yielding no gain, supplying the simple expediency of keeping the wretched child out of Infayen's way, which further served to drive the unwanted daughter from her thoughts as well.

Imagination was necessary in contemplating an offspring's future, and with it all the presentiments and potentials revealed by that child. Infayen saw Menandore, in those rare times that she considered the question, as serving as nothing more than a flawed replacement to herself, come the day when Infayen fell in her own battle, her own forlorn stand. As such, the bastard daughter marked a natural step in her family line's inevitable descent.

New blood stood no chance against the House of Menand's fate. Necessity, after all, possessed a bloodless quality, for all the blood it might have spilled, or would spill in the days to come. Families rarely fell in sudden collapse. More common, she knew, was the slow decrepitude of generation following generation, like the turgid swirling of a muddy pond as the season dried, and dried.

In such straits, imagination was useless, and she saw herself as well adapted to her diminishing world. Leave it to the others, with their emboldened ambitions and awkward avarice, to reap the glories of this civil war. Infayen expected to die in the victory. Her lifeblood, draining away, would fill a bowl, to be delivered to her daughter, and from that coagulated failure Menandore was welcome to sip, as her mother had done before her.

*Welcome*, the taste would say, *to the family.*

Once she announced herself, she did not have to wait long before being granted an audience with the High Priestess.

The Chamber of Light was bright enough to blind her to its details, barring that of Syntara who stood awaiting her. This was satisfactory. She had no interest in the trappings of this new faith.

'Hunn Raal fucked a cookfire,' she said.

Syntara's perfect brows lifted.

In a monotone, Infayen explained what had been witnessed.

✻   ✻   ✻

Betrayal was not something Sharenas Ankhadu had contemplated when mapping out the course of her life. Perhaps, on occasion, she might find herself a victim to it. But the blood on her own hands was unexpected, and the righteous cause driving those who now pursued her gnawed at her resolve. Her list of reasons for doing what she had done held a taint of selfishness. Indignation and affront were all very well, sufficient to justify harsh words or, in extremity, a slap. Modest answers, in other words, to match the personal scale of the moment. *But a sword through the neck, at a tavern table, with the head rolling, bouncing upon the ale-spilled wood . . . when did I begin this new habit of losing control?*

Vatha Urusander was a man with blunted needs. She had supped on his frustration, and had walked down into Neret Sorr, and then into the Legion camp, bloated by its fury. Each face she had confronted had seemed transformed, its every detail born anew in her searing focus. *These are the enemies of peace. The face of Serap. The faces of Esthala and her husband. Of Hallyd Bahann, Tathe Lorat, Infayen. Hunn Raal.*

*Some of those faces are now still, enlivened no more. Frozen in their moments of culpability. The others . . . they bear lively masks of rage, and yearn for my death.*

*If betrayal has a known visage in this, it is mine.*

Flakes of snow drifted down silent as ash. The sky above was bright but colourless, as white as the layers of snow now clinging to leafless branches and carpeting the forest floor. Winter's gift was stillness, the muting of life into something like somnolence. The blinding shock of blood did not belong. Disquieted by what felt to her like an act of iniquity, if not desecration, Sharenas crouched and ran the length of her sword blade across the wool of the soldier's tunic, wiping clean the gore from one side. She reversed the flat of the weapon and repeated the task, and then, with a final regretful glance at the pallid, lifeless face of the man who had been tracking her – seeing how the snowflakes still melted as they alighted upon his brow, cheeks, and beard, and swam like shallow tears upon his staring but sightless eyes – she straightened and slid the sword back into its scabbard.

Flames had devoured the forest here and there, leaving scorched patches and elongated runs of blackened ruin. The stench remained, making acrid the cold air. She had found tracks nonetheless: the spalled punctures of deer hoofs, the clawed punches of hunting creatures, and here and there, already vanishing beneath the new snowfall, the pattered prints of small birds and scampering mice.

She had abandoned the horses, stripping them of saddle, bridle and bit, knowing that the animals would find habitation when the needs for food and shelter overwhelmed whatever elation attended their sudden freedom. It was in the

450

nature of domesticated beasts to welcome the company of their masters, or so she had always believed. Generation upon generation of dependency could transform familiarity into need.

*And so it may be for us Tiste as well. I have known too much solitude of late. And yet, when I found myself among my own kind, what did I do? How often are we compelled to destroy what we need, as if driven towards misery as a stream finds a sea?*

Dismayed by her thoughts, she set out, plunging deeper into the forest. She had passed through burned-out camps, walked among bones still bearing remnants of gristle. She had found, beneath a thin tatter of blanket, the corpse of an orphaned child.

Outrage was a powerful emotion, but all too often it drowned in helplessness, and all its flailing amounted to little. Still, Sharenas found she could feed upon it, when need arose to demand from her the necessary violence. Such virtues remained hollow, however, when she found herself simply fighting for her own survival.

*Kagamandra, where are you now? Why do I long to feel your arms around me, hard as bent branches, with loss written in your every caress? As if you offer nothing more than winter's embrace, while my own season wallows in indecision. Still I hunger for you.*

*I know I cannot have you. No point in imagining impossible scenarios. Your path is plain, and holds still to its honour. By that alone we are driven apart. I must and will ever remain a stranger to your destiny, and you cannot but answer mine in kind.*

Sound carried in this forest. She was not alone, and the shouts in the distance were harsh, eager and deliberate. They would herd her now, drive her to some place of their choosing, where her fate would stumble into their hands – within the reach of their weapons. Already they had refused her way southward. For the moment, however, her hunters were mere scouts, and the advantage remained hers. They were too few in number, and the cordon they sought to impose could be broken through, particularly behind her, back towards the open eastlands.

But the scouts represented the leading elements. Half a company of regular Legion soldiers might well have already set out from Neret Sorr, under the command of a lieutenant, if not a captain. The scouts were intended to harry and force her to keep moving. The regulars were there to take her down. She would find no safety to the east.

*Kagamandra, see what I have done. See where it has taken me. I have begun my own war against Urusander's Legion. Will I find allies among the Legion's enemies? I cannot say. Why would they welcome a betrayer, a murderer, into their camp? How fragile this banner of righteous retribution, and dare I raise it before me to defend what I have done?*

She worked her way westward, keeping to the deer trails, praying for the snowfall to thicken. But the sky slumbered still, and the flakes drifted down like the unmindful shedding of remnant dreams. *I know. You frown at this mention of outrage – you know enough to distrust it, in yourself, in others. Is that disapproval in your eyes? Dispense with this hunger for judgement. When you are married, it will ill suit you, inviting as it does rightful retort.*

*I will keep you here, for the company. Stay silent. This is the season you wear best, Kagamandra.*

She caught the snap of branches ahead and to her right. Drawing her sword, she hunched down and continued forward, her moccasins making little sound upon the snow-softened trail.

The woman had sought a place of hiding, perhaps intending ambush, but the skein of dogwood she had crawled into was more dead than alive, partially caught by the past season's fire. Twigs that should have bent broke instead. Even so, if Sharenas had not been relatively near by, and had the timing been otherwise, she might well have stumbled into the trap.

Instead, she approached the crouching scout from a flank, keeping what she could between her and the woman, until one footfall made a thin creaking sound. As the scout turned,

Sharenas was already rushing forward, thrusting her sword through the lattice of twigs and branches.

With a faint squeal, the woman lunged back, seeking to avoid the thrust. But the branches behind her caught her motion, bowed, and then propelled her forward again, and the sword's point punched into her chest.

The tip sliced through wool, and then leather and skin, but rebounded off the scout's sternum. The blow was enough to knock the woman off her feet, and she flailed in the thicket as she fell.

Sharenas advanced, slashing against the outside of the woman's right thigh, cutting flesh down to the bone. Blood sprayed and the scout screamed.

*Now they will converge in earnest.* Sharenas shifted her sword's angle and chopped down again. This blow severed a major artery in the woman's right leg, and cut deep enough to nearly sever the limb, although the thigh bone remained in place to grip the meat. Yanking her blade free, she met the frightened, shocked eyes of the young woman, and then, shaking blood from her sword, retreated into the forest once more.

*I should have killed her – but her death is assured, too much and too quick her loss of blood. Still, she might have strength remaining to point her friends after me.*

*Oh, Sharenas, think it through! My tracks are now plain enough!*

Behind her, voices converged, and the forest awakened to discordant sounds, and once again Sharenas fled the loss of control, cursing the place in which she found herself. *I succumb to the criminal's mind, stumble from one wrong to the next, and the stupidities mount higher. This fool's legacy is now mine.*

Swearing under her breath, she quickened her pace.

＊　　＊　　＊

'Nothing must impugn the glory of the faith,' Syntara told the scholar who now sat at the desk. 'Father Light has revealed his worthiness by the reluctance he displays. He speaks only for his soldiers, his followers, and thinks naught of himself. This is the proper manner of both a god and a king.'

Sagander's hand, gripping the stylus, was yet to move from where it hovered over the parchment. His eyes were in the habit of watering profusely in this preternatural light, and often he would reach down as if to adjust or knead the leg that was not there. On occasion, she had heard the words hidden by his muttering, as he spoke to demons of pain, begging an end to their torment. At times, she believed he prayed to those demons. The man's usefulness, she considered as she studied him from her chair upon the dais, might well be coming to an end.

'Do my instructions confuse you?'

Scowling, Sagander half turned away. 'She mocked the very thing you would now have me do. This is the flaw among our people against which I have battled for most of my life. The lowborn must not be raised above their capacity.' He shot her a dark glance. 'Urusander's common soldiers. Even the officers. They all seek to uproot rightful order—'

Syntara felt a smirk come to her lips. 'You elected the wrong side, scholar. Reveal such thoughts unwisely and your head will roll.'

'Draconus is the enemy, High Priestess!'

'So you keep telling me. But he will stand alone when we are done. There will be no Consort at the court of Father Light and Mother Dark.'

'You do not yet grasp the danger he presents, High Priestess. It is my fate to go unheeded. He journeyed to the lands of the Azathanai. He spoke with the Lord of Hate. He holds congress with unknown powers. Consider his gifts to Mother Dark! Whence came such things? A sceptre to command darkness. A mere pattern carved by sorcery upon a floor – that opens a gate into a nether realm!'

'Cease your shouting, old man. I am not blind to the threat posed by Lord Draconus. Yes, there is mystery about him. I believe he has indeed conspired with the Azathanai, and we as yet know nothing of the bargain's cost. But consider the one named T'riss, and the gift she in turn gave to me. Without her, there would be no Light.'

'Then,' muttered Sagander, 'the Azathanai but play both sides, seeking discord. Seeking the ruin of Kurald Galain.'

'Too bad,' Syntara murmured, 'that you were unable to accompany Draconus into the west.'

'He sought no witness to his deeds there. They all worked against me. In all innocence, I fell into their trap.'

Syntara affected a bemused frown. 'I thought it was a falling horse that broke your leg.'

'Yes,' he hissed. 'A broken leg. What of it? When do such minor injuries demand a severing of the limb? But I was unconscious. I could not assay the damage for myself. I was deprived of choosing my treatment. They were ... opportunistic.'

'Have you no words left for the book?'

He flung the stylus down. 'Not now, High Priestess. The pain has grown worse again. I must seek my draughts.'

*Yes, your draughts. Your potions of forgetting. In this way, you pledge fealty to your gods of pain. You kneel to them. You offer up a drunken smile to their dulled retreat. As upon an altar, you wet your throat with libations, and sicken the temple of your flesh.* 'Of course. Be gone, then, scholar. Take your rest.'

'Renarr needs to be removed,' Sagander said, reaching for his crutches. 'She stands too close to Father Light. She whispers words of poison.'

'Perhaps you are right. I will think on the matter.'

She watched the scholar hobble from the chamber. Her thoughts of Renarr quickly fell away, as she turned her mind to Lord Urusander. *At his heart a common soldier. He knows well the artifice of his noble title, the puerile claim of an invented ancestry. In that at least, Sagander has the truth of it. The lowborn suffer the inadequacies of their impure blood, and we see it clearly in Urusander.*

*Still, I must make him Father Light.*

*Duty, Urusander. Even the ox knows its demand.*

There was something there, then, that indeed echoed

Sagander's assertions. When musing on the notion of duty, it was undeniable that the virtue's strength waned the higher one climbed through the classes. And yet, was it not the high-born who spoke most often of duty, when demanding the service of the commonalty, upon farms and among the ranks of soldiery? In the building of cobbled roads and the raising of estates and keeps? Duty, they cried, in the name of the realm.

*But usurpers do not come from the common folk. No, they are the rivals standing too close to the throne. They are the pledged allies, the advisers, the commanders.*

*Think on this, Syntara. How will you tread this narrow path ahead? The closer we get to the throne room of the Citadel, the greater the risk of betrayal.*

*Urusander, you must learn again the meaning of duty. In the name of peace, recall your low origins, and be assured that I will blunt the fawners who would stoke your fires of personal ambition, of unnatural elevation.*

*I must reconsider my conversation with Emral Lanear. Let our aspects achieve a proper balance, to make the queen temper the king and the king temper the queen. To make the god and goddess exchange fealty, and in time come to need the weaknesses of the other. For should they lock gazes and feed mutual strengths, both faiths will be lost, and Kurald Galain with them.*

*Emral. We need to work in concert. Mother Dark was a Tiste once, a mortal woman, a widow. Urusander was a commander in a legion. These are their ignoble legacies. It falls to you and me, Lanear, to invest them both with proper humility.*

*And to watch, with a multitude of spies and assassins, those who would crowd too close to either of them.*

*Perhaps, in fomenting aloofness, Mother Dark has the right of it. None shall draw too close. In the distance of their station, we can ensure their sanctity. This will need to be perfectly played. We shall be as sisters, you and I, Lanear.*

*And yet again, Sagander spoke truly. Draconus stands too close to Mother Dark. He holds too many of her secrets. It will not be enough to banish him. A knife in the back, or poison in the cup, or, if luck holds, a pathetic end in the mud of a battlefield.*

*We High Priestesses, we shall stand between our rulers and everyone else. We must be the raised dais, the guardians of the portal, and the veil through which every word must pass, from below to above, from above to below.*

Syntara gestured with her mind, a flare of power, and a moment later a priestess entered the chamber.

'Analle, attend my words.'

'High Priestess,' the young woman said, gaze averted as she ducked her head.

'Bring to me the missive sent by Emral Lanear. And then summon a messenger. I must write to my sister. Quickly!"

Analle dipped her head again and rushed from the room.

Fingers tapping on the arm of the chair, Syntara sighed. She would need to devise a new version of the note sent to her by Lanear. Emral was too blunt in her style, too revelatory of the necessary manipulations, even when peace was the ultimate aim. Details might well offend Urusander. No, she would have to indulge what editorial talents she possessed.

*Forgive me, Urusander. The note was in a temple cursive form, requiring transcription. I assure you of its accuracy, as I have done the translation myself. You will note the temple seal upon the document, signifying its official recognition.*

In a displeasing flash, dark in her mind, she saw Renarr sitting in that infernal chair of hers, and the derisive amusement plain upon her face. *Always an error to invite a whore to ascend to a new station. People will settle upon the level that comforts them, and abide by natural laws, as Sagander says, which dictate the limits of their capacity.*

*And yes, it is this new flexibility, as desired by Hunn Raal and his commoners, which does indeed pose a threat. We risk the anarchy of the undeserving, who must remain forever discontented with their elevation, knowing all too well how it hides their paucity of talent and ability – the lies behind their every claim of worth.*

*I see bloody days ahead.*

*Emral Lanear, we must make assassins of our best priestesses. Let lust be the lure, with soft pillows to stifle the cry.*

From beyond her room, the slapping of bared feet. The day ahead promised to be a long one.

*        *        *

As befitting his new station, Sagander now had the use of a cart, and a page to manage the mule, making the journey down into the encampment beyond Neret Sorr far less of an ordeal. His aches dulled by the bitter oils of d'bayang, he lolled in the padded seat he'd had installed in the cart, his lone leg stretched out to match the ghost of the other, and watched the track wend its way behind him.

Atop the hill, the keep was now strangely imbalanced, as its eastern wing blazed blindingly bright, as if the sun had shed a precious tear that still burned upon the stones. The purity of that light stung his eyes, left them reddened and weak. This seemed unfair. Looking upon his hands, he saw their alabaster perfection, inasmuch as one could call such twisted, wrinkled appendages perfect. And when divested of all clothing, the bleached hue of Light's blessing commanded all of him.

*Except, of course, for the leg that no one else sees. That, my friends, remains black as onyx. And so it shall be, until the day my vengeance is satisfied. Draconus, hide your bastard son – one day he will return and I will be waiting for him. As for you, why, I hold to my vow. I will stand over your corpse.*

The boy's quirt snapped upon the rump of the mule, startling Sagander.

*That would have served me better than my hand, the day I punished Arathan for his disrespect. A sting upon the cheek, a red welt to remind him, perhaps even a scar. Draconus would not have begrudged me that. A tutor must have discipline. By rule of law, if my hand did not touch him . . . but no, he's a bastard whose own father refused him! No meeting of eyes between them! I remained within my rights!*

There was a court in his mind, with tiers crowded with scholars – rivals, enemies, backstabbers – and judges arrayed behind a long bench. And in a ring outside all of them, he saw a crowd, packed shoulder to shoulder, and faces he knew well. Many belonged to his childhood, a gathering of tormentors and bullies and friends who had betrayed his trust. He saw the sour visages of bitter tutors still gripping their canes. Before this hate-filled, contemptuous mob, Sagander stood upon the speaker's platform, and in the realm of his imagination he spoke with stunning eloquence, with the orator's natural gift. He arrayed his defence of his actions, assembled the damning details of the abuse that then befell him.

And as he neared his final statement, he saw how the faces of the multitude, on all sides, were transformed by his words, their owners made to feel shamed by their past crimes, their cruel dismissals, and the vast catalogue of hurts to which they had each contributed. He saw, too, how the stern regard of the judges slowly, inexorably, swung to Draconus and Arathan, who stood in the cage of the accused.

Their condemnation would prove sweet, but sweeter still would be the judges' words of awe with which they finally addressed Sagander.

'*You shall be elevated, great scholar, to the highest post in Kurald Galain. Upon a dais one step higher than that of the twin thrones, there to offer your blessed, brilliant insights – to give, in short, proper guidance to our god and goddess . . .*'

The court never left his mind, and so too did it eternally echo with Sagander's impassioned genius. Innocence could be won from the truth, compensation wrung by the same implacable power. Justice could be carved from a perfection of words, sentences, thoughts made concrete. In such a world, let the bullies and betrayers and tormentors beware.

In that court, upon that platform, Sagander stood upon two hale legs. There was new magic in the realm, after all. Who could say what was possible?

They skirted Neret Sorr upon the high track, and then

clumped and rolled and rocked down into the Legion camp, the young page straining as the way grew rougher with frozen ruts and greasy stones. A short time later they drew up before the scholar's tent.

While he had a room in the keep, Sagander maintained this more modest abode, not out of any love of soldiery or the mess cook's fare, but for reasons of the private company he entertained within. Batting at the helping hands of the boy, he set his crutches down and worked his way off the cart's edge. 'Return at dawn.'

'Yes sir.'

'But first, open the tent flap.'

'Sir.'

Sagander ducked his way within, feeling a gust of heat from the brazier that he'd ordered maintained at all times. One of Syntara's failed acolytes was seated nearby, and she looked up with a startled expression.

'Is this all you do?' he demanded. 'Staring at the coals until they burn down? Have you no clothes to mend, no stitchwork or knitting? What of bandages? There's always the need for weaving those in an army, yes? Keep your hands busy, child, lest your mind rot more than it already has. Now, go. And remember to set the lamp upon the pole at the entrance. Yes, just so, now out with you.'

When she was gone, he hobbled over to the ornate chair he'd had brought down from the keep and settled into it, stretching out the leg none other could see. Glowering down at it, he squinted at the ebon hue. It was a younger man's leg, well muscled, filled with strength and life. Only rarely, when he'd imbibed too much d'bayang, did the bone break, one splintered end pushing up through the flesh, and the leg then twisted and shrank to proportions to match its companion, before the black hue shifted into shades of green, and the stench of gangrene rose from the limb like smoke.

At times, deep in sleep, he saw his severed leg lying upon bloodied grasses. He saw it nudged by a boot into a latrine trench. He saw it befouled.

*I will answer in kind, this I swear, upon your corpses.*

*Upon your faces, I will answer in kind. No act is final. Another inevitably awaits.* In his mind, he uttered this promise to every face in the crowd. They were asides, too faint to be heard by the judges, but the face of each enemy who heard his promise, why, how it blanched! How the lip quivered!

*Now, my friends, which among you will be the first to beg for mercy?*

After a time, the tent flap rustled, and then slipped aside to permit the entrance of Sheltatha Lore.

Sagander smiled. 'Ah, the lantern was noted. Excellent, my child.'

'Are you in pain again, tutor?'

At times, there was something in her tone that reminded Sagander of Arathan. A hint of . . . no, he could not quite grasp it. He could see no insolence in her eyes, only respect and deference. And such an eagerness to serve! There was no sound reason for doubt, and yet . . . 'Ah, the pain. If it must be the answer to my good deeds, well, whoever said the world was fair, yes?'

She moved further into the tent, and once again Sagander marvelled at the natural grace that came with the young. 'But things will be made fair, tutor, and soon. And perhaps, among the new practitioners of Denul, you will find an unexpected salvation.'

He eyed her, silent as she settled herself upon a heap of cushions beside his cot, and then he said, 'In the meantime, dear innocence, I have need of you.'

The smile she offered him looked genuine enough, but something in it – in the eyes, possibly, which seemed to softly fulminate, as if the surface was slowly melting in the heat – troubled Sagander. *Too much like Arathan, this child. But unlike my failures with that bastard, I will make this creature pure again. For all the abuses her mother has inflicted upon her, I have her salvation to achieve, and achieve it I shall.* 'Can you sense it, child? This ghost of mine?'

'I can,' she replied. 'Always. And still I wonder, tutor . . .'

He tilted his head. 'You wonder what, beloved?'

461

'Why its skin remains so black.'

Sagander held his smile, but with difficulty. It was one thing to indulge her wilful imaginings, to invite from her those strange, but hopeless, efforts at comforting his invisible pain, but this! *This is the sorcery at work. It seethes through us all, a plague's breath of unnatural power.*

'Tutor? Is something wrong? Come, lie here upon your cot, and invite again my caress. Your ghost limb desires it still, yes?'

*But I feel nothing. It was a game. It brought you close, within reach of my hand. And I could touch what I dare not desire. It was enough, my own small need, and each night you spend here, with me, is another night away from your whore of a mother, from her endless vengeance upon her own daughter. Nothing cruel in this bargain – but now . . .* 'It is difficult this night,' he said, his voice thin and weak, sounding piteous even to his own ears. 'The ghost is insensate to all but its own pain.'

'We shall see,' Sheltatha said.

After a moment, Sagander brought his lone leg under him and used a single crutch to push himself upright. He hobbled the two steps over to his cot, twisted and slumped down upon the canvas, making the legs creak. 'Well then,' he gasped. 'Here I am—'

The tent flap was suddenly yanked aside, and an armoured figure ducked in, straightening with a harsh sigh.

Infayen Menand. Heavy and indolent where Sheltatha was supple and sweet; harsh and cold where Tathe's daughter was kind and warm.

Sagander scowled. 'What are you doing here, unannounced, uninvited? Leave us, captain, unless Tathe now owns you as well—'

'Tathe doesn't even own herself,' Infayen said, her eyes flat as they fixed upon Sheltatha Lore, who returned the stare with a closed expression belonging to a much older woman. 'I have come at the command of Mortal Sword Hunn Raal. The child Sheltatha Lore is to be escorted to the keep. Her care is now the responsibility of the Temple of Light. Get off those cushions, girl.'

'I am her tutor—'

'As you please,' Infayen cut in. 'If the temple deems lessons proper, they will undertake them from now on. Of course,' she added, finally levelling her gaze on Sagander, 'you may well find for yourself a role in that, but you will teach your lessons at the temple, not here in your tent.'

After a moment, Sagander nodded sharply. 'Yes, of course. In fact, I believe that I approve.'

'Well, that relieves us all. On your feet, Sheltatha.'

Sagander set a hand upon the girl's shoulder and said, 'Go on. It is indeed for the best.'

In silence, Sheltatha Lore stood. At a gesture from Infayen, the girl strode from the tent. As Infayen moved to follow, she paused at the tent entrance and glanced back at Sagander. 'It may be,' she said, 'that you do not number among those who have damaged her. I saw not enough here to decide either way. But I will nonetheless insist upon an end to privacy when it comes to your tutoring the girl.'

'You impugn my honour!'

'How often that proclamation from those who have none.'

'Said the woman who has slaughtered children in the forest!'

She said nothing for a long moment, her flat eyes fixed upon him, and for an instant Sagander believed he saw what those children and elders must have seen, even as the sword swung down to take their lives. Suddenly chilled by terror, he stared up at the captain.

'In the name of duty,' Infayen said, 'one must, at times, set honour aside. Were you not once tutor to a bastard whelp?'

'The duty of which saw my honour betrayed,' Sagander replied shakily. He shook his head. 'I never abused her trust, captain. Ask her. I sought to save her from her mother.'

'You would have failed.'

'Perhaps.'

'Even the temple will fail,' Infayen said.

'Then you deem this pointless?'

'It is not the coin in hand that makes the whore, tutor. It is making a commodity of one's own body that makes a woman

463

a whore. The flaw lies in the spirit. Sheltatha and her mother are the same in this regard, no different from Renarr. If you believe salvation is possible, then why in the next breath speak against the elevation of us soldiers?'

'By your argument, captain, you oppose Hunn Raal's desire, and indeed that of Urusander himself.' Sagander leaned forward. 'Is that a wise admission?'

'In the name of duty one must at times set aside honour,' Infayen repeated.

A moment later she was gone, the flap settling back down. Much of the brazier's heat had been lost, and Sagander shivered, reaching for his furs. He settled on to the bed. The ghost moaned out its ache. These soldiers, he was coming to understand, were not all alike. Their uniforms deceived with the illusion of conformity, and as time stretched on – as this miserable winter persisted – the inherent weaknesses of the military system began to show.

*Put a sword in every person's hand, and they discover an edge to their opinions, but such opinions, no matter how inane and ignorant, twist to ambition, until each wielder draws blood upon every side. There can be no congress among the witless and the avaricious. Betrayal waits in the wings, and all that is won must then be carved into pieces, and should inequity appear, the slaying begins anew.*

*The creation of an army invites poison into the realm. I am well placed to observe this, and I will make it central to the thesis of my last great work. The stations of society are natural creations, governed by natural laws. This civil war, it is nothing but hubris.*

*Only from the temples will we find salvation. Syntara must be made to understand this. The balance of faiths she espouses must give guidance to the balance of classes in Kurald Galain. A few to rule, and many to follow.*

*Urusander is useless. But perhaps he will serve as a figure-head. No, we who possess the necessary intelligence, and talents, we shall be the true rulers of this realm. Let the god and goddess drift away into their private worlds. One step down from the dais is where real power is worked, and there is where you will find me.*

*I must write to Rise Herat. An overture would not be amiss. He surely understands the necessity of our respective roles in what is to come. But I will address him as an equal, to make certain that he understands our new relationship. Meted in wisdom, we shall conspire to save Kurald Galain.*

*An end to soldiers. The rise of scholars. I see a renaissance in the offing.*

The plain woman who fed the brazier now returned, eyes averted, a bucket of dung in each hand.

He watched as she knelt at the iron brazier and began feeding chips into it. An all too modest skill, maintaining such a fire, requiring little more than small measures of brawn, discipline, and a few sparks of wit. It was well that she possessed a task to suit her, he reflected. *This is civilization's gift. Finding a task to match the capability of each and every citizen of the realm. But make it plain that limits exist, for the good of all. And, if necessary, a mailed fist to prove the point.*

*The highborn have it right. Houseblades to police their holdings. A city constabulary. An army? Disband it, and put an end to its unruly nest, lest the vermin breed discontent.*

'When you're done there,' Sagander croaked to the servant, 'attend me here. The night is cold, and I have need of your warmth.'

'Yes sir,' the woman replied, dusting her hands.

Syntara was generous, and generosity among the powerful was truly a virtue.

*       *       *

'She would gather the whores into a single room,' Renarr said, smiling, 'and name it a temple of disrepute, no doubt.'

Sheltatha Lore stood before her, still heavily cloaked from her march up from the camp. She seemed neither discomfited nor confused by the new arrangements.

'So, it was Syntara who sent you to me?'

Shrugging, Sheltatha said, 'Hunn Raal decided this. Infayen

465

delivered me. Syntara thought to interpose her will, but in the end she rejected me for the temple, noting my misused flesh and so on.' She paused and looked around. 'Have you the use of an adjoining room? My needs are modest. Presumably, my clothes and the rest will be sent up from the camp, eventually. I assume the food is better here, to make up for the duller company.'

Renarr held her smile. 'First, you will need to cultivate your contempt, Sheltatha Lore. If your words would cut, sharpen your guile, and above all be selective in choosing your target. I am not one you can wound.'

Sheltatha shrugged off her cloak, leaving it to fall to the floor. 'The soldiers talked about you,' she said. 'You are missed, or, rather, were. A soldier killing himself in your tent has somewhat stained your reputation.'

'I have high expectations,' Renarr replied, still seated, still studying the daughter of Tathe Lorat.

Sheltatha's brows lifted, and then she laughed. 'This – I know what this is, you know.'

'Do you?'

'Yes. This is an attack upon my mother. They tell me it's for my own good, but they never really understood any of it. When she realizes she can no longer abuse me, she will find comfort in my absence. You see, I was better at it than her.'

'Better at what?'

'I learned the sensual arts at a very young age. I have not begun to sag, or waste with drink or smoke. My youth was her enemy and she well knew it. She made her own habits her instruments of abuse, and having given them to me, she desired to watch them deliver to me their ruin.'

'You are perceptive. Do you deem this wisdom? It is not.'

Smiling, Sheltatha Lore raised her hands, and from both white fire suddenly flared into life. 'The flame purges, as required. My flesh knows no taint. My habits deliver no stain. Well, not for long, anyway.'

'Clever,' Renarr said. 'So, you are now separated from your mother. Tell me, what do you seek for yourself?'

Sheltatha lowered her hands, and the fires dwindled and

then vanished. Her eyes scanned the chamber. 'Nothing.'

'Nothing?'

'I am surrounded by ambition. It makes every visage ugly to behold.'

'Ah. Then what of my visage?'

Sheltatha glanced over at Renarr, and after a moment she frowned. 'No, you remain pretty enough.'

'And is that something to admire, even aspire to? Shall I teach you the art of my own immunity? You see, I have no need to purge anything from me.'

'I doubt the fires would find you in any case.'

'I agree. I therefore elect more mundane means, which might serve you should the sorcery one day fail.'

'Fail? Why should it fail?'

'Everything,' Renarr said, 'comes with a cost. A debt is already begun, although you do not yet know it, or feel its weight upon you. Be assured, it exists.'

'How do you know?'

'You see ugliness in the faces of the ambitious. That is their debt, writ plain enough to your eyes. When I look upon you, here, now, I too see what the magic demands of you.'

Sheltatha cocked her head. 'What, then? What do you see?'

'The wasteland in your eyes.'

After a moment, Sheltatha blinked, and then turned away. 'Which room will be mine, then?'

'Do you invite my instruction?'

'Do you name yourself wise?'

'No. Just more experienced.'

Sheltatha sighed. 'I had a tutor already. He touched me for pleasure – oh, nothing crass or bold. The very opposite, in fact. A hand upon mine, briefly. A brush of a shoulder, or a tap upon my knee. It was charming in its pathos, to be honest. He too wanted to steal me away from my mother and her ways. But his lessons were worthless. Why should yours be any better?'

'What did he try to teach you?'

'I have no idea. Perhaps he was working up to it. Oh, and

he had me massage the leg he lost. The ghost, he calls it. But I could see it plain enough. Remnant energy would best describe the emanation. The body sees itself as whole, no matter the reality of its state. That's curious, is it not?'

'Do you see this energy upon hale limbs and bodies, Sheltatha?'

'Yes. It shows strong among some, weak in others. It comes in many hues. Yours, at this moment, is the colour of a clear sky, close to dawn. Blue, with something hinting at slate beneath it. Dawn, or on the edge of dusk. This tells me, Renarr, that you hide a secret.'

'We can then make this your study, to begin with,' said Renarr.

'How so, when you reveal no such talent?'

'Never mind the sorcery itself. Indulge in your own explorations with that. Rather, work with me upon the proper reading of those emanations. Let's discover what you can glean from those you meet, or are able to see.'

'High Priestess Syntara was proof against my abilities.'

'I'm not surprised. What of Infayen?'

'She can kill without feeling. But that numbness makes her dull and insensitive. She cannot grasp subtlety and so fears it. When sensing its proximity, her energy darkens with suspicion, hate, and the desire to destroy all that she cannot understand.'

Grunting, Renarr stood. 'Good. Useful. So long as no one else knows about your hidden talents.'

'None but you.'

'Then why reveal yourself to me? We hardly know each other.'

'Your energy did not change in my presence,' Sheltatha replied. 'That means you want nothing from me, and mean me no harm. You're just curious. And,' she added, 'my magic didn't change anything in you. No fear, no wonder, no envy. The secret you hold, Renarr, has nothing to do with me, but it's the strongest thing I've ever seen.'

'Come, then, and I will show you your room.'

Nodding, Sheltatha followed Renarr.

468

*'The strongest thing I've ever seen.'* Beneath it, the colour of slate.

The High Priestess had been too quick in her dismissal of this girl, and that was fortunate, as far as Renarr was concerned. *Secrets are what they are. Is it fear that makes one keep them? Not always. No, for me, there is no fear. For me, there is only patience.*

*The sky at dusk. Waiting for the night to come.*

# TWELVE

'YOU FEAR DESIRE,' SAID LASA ROOK, HER EYES LURID in the fire's light. 'Hanako of the Scars, I fold back my furs for you, that we may partake in senseless rutting, followed by tender cuddles. Which one pays for the other, I wonder? No matter, choose one as the oyster and the other as the shell, and should I paint in gold its opposite, well, such are the risks of love.'

Hanako pulled his gaze from hers with an effort and glared into the flames. 'Is this your flimsy veil of grief, Lasa Rook, so quickly flung away at the first heat?'

'My husbands are no more! What am I to do?' She swept her hair back with both hands, a gesture that thrust out her chest and, as Hanako mused on the curse of anatomy, the breasts upon it. 'A vast emptiness has devoured my soul, dear boy, and it is in need of filling.'

'More husbands?'

'No! I am done with that! Do you not see me running light as a butterfly through the meadows of my liberated mind? Look well into my eyes, Hanako, slayer of the Lord of Temper. In these pools awaits all manner of lascivious curiosity, forward and back, sideways and upside down. You need only find the courage to look.'

But that he would not do. Instead, he twisted slightly upon the fallen tree trunk where he sat, and frowned at the wrapped

470

form of Erelan Kreed. The warrior was muttering in his sleep, an endless litany of strange names, punctuated by vile hissing and bone-chilling curses. The madness had not abated, and it had been three days now. Even the mosquitoes and biting flies avoided him.

The valley and the dread lake where Kreed had slain the dragon was far behind them, and yet it seemed that the world was reluctant to yield the pattern, as they now sat beside yet another lake, at the base of yet another thickly forested valley. For two days Hanako had carried the warrior, his armour and his weapons, and on both nights, with dusk's sudden arrival, he had sunk down to the ground on trembling legs, too weary to even eat.

Lasa Rook had taken to cooking their meals, although Hanako was the one to force food into the mouth of Erelan Kreed, fighting the warrior's delirium and wild, batting hands, his fierce eyes and teeth bared like fangs.

In consideration of that, Hanako wondered, tenuously, if Erelan was perhaps saner than he appeared. *Lasa Rook cooks food to make even the dead fast. I must warn this Jaghut lord. Lead her to no kitchen beneath the rock-piles, lest you unleash the undead in frenzy and madness, spill them fleeing into the mortal realms!*

'Oh, bless me, Hanako,' Lasa sighed, 'do reach out a pawing hand at the very least? Here, I yield you these lobes, my oft-plucked fruit, so well handled and tender, whose very nipples cry out with the memory of tweaks and twists. They have the taste of honey, I'm told, and the scent of flowers.'

'I've seen you dab them every morning,' Hanako said.

'A secret revealed! And yet you still speak of marriage? Hanako, this journey of ours is almost as bad, with all the shattered privacy of making toilet and other things. Imagine this intimacy, young sir, with no end in sight! Shall I pluck importunate hairs from alarming locales upon your person, while you squeeze blackheads upon mine? Shall we take turns wiping the drool from our chins with every dawn, for years on end? Tell me, what other details of marriage can I offer you, to disavow all your notions of romantic bliss?'

'Please, Lasa. My thoughts are for Erelan Kreed. He does not improve. There was madness in that dragon's blood.'

'It's said that there are celibate monks among the south-dwellers. Pray rush to their cold company, Hanako.'

'Lasa Rook, I beg you, we must discuss what to do with our friend here!'

'We bring him down to the Jaghut, of course. And whatever Azathanai might be lounging about. They can examine our blathering warrior here, and decide if he is fit to live or die. This matter, you must see, Hanako, lies beyond us. Now, where was I? Ah, these protrudinous fruit, so swollen and inviting—'

With a low growl, Hanako rose to his feet. He stepped away from the fire, moving past Lasa, and made his way down to the pebbled shoreline.

The stars were strewn upon the still surface of the lake. Cool air rose from the water, lifting to Hanako the faintly pungent smell of decay where detritus made a cluttered rim of the shoreline. He walked along that verge, his steps slow. Rock and water . . . the world had a way of making border-lands the repository of the discarded, as if in the collision of smaller worlds things did not merge, only break.

The Thel Akai, such lovers of tales from distant lands, were nonetheless a people content with their own isolation. There were things to protect, after all, and pre-eminent among them a host of precious but flimsy beliefs. There was little defence, however, against the invasion of ideas, beyond whatever strength was offered by collective prejudices. And even among an isolated people such as the Thel Akai, factions arose, jostling for dominance, always eager to impose distinctions.

The only weapon of any worth against such idiocy was laughter, and it cut sharper and deeper than any blade.

A war upon death. That was worth a bold guffaw. *Now watch us laugh all the way to the feet of the Lord of Rock-Piles himself. Some ideas will turn the blade, wounding the wielder with unexpected suddenness.*

He turned at the sound of splashing from the lake, caught the glimmer of churning water as a figure clambered into

472

view. Hanako saw a flash of tusks, and then heard muttered cursing as the stranger struggled with a bulky, sodden pack. He dragged it ashore, and then straightened, turning to face Hanako. 'Is this the crude self-obsession of youth, Thel Akai, or has mercy simply died along with everything else?'

Hanako stepped forward, in time for the Jaghut to thrust the heavy sack into his hands.

'It's time to give thanks to that fire of yours,' the Jaghut said, stepping past. 'A beacon, a promising pyre, a rack to dry flesh and bone. It was all these things, and more.'

Hanako grunted under the weight of the sack, which was still draining water. He hurried to catch up to the Jaghut. 'But – where did you come from?'

'A boat, Thel Akai. By this means, one can journey across lakes. Unless,' he added, 'the boat changes its mind, and longs instead to explore the bottom.'

As they drew nearer the fire, Lasa Rook's voice drifted out to them. 'Another wastrel, Hanako? But not the grunts and growls of a bear, nor the hiss of a dragon. Why, this venture offers everything but the sweaty squeeze beneath the furs. Tell me, oh please, the tale of a shipwrecked prince flung so callously upon my lap, as it were . . .'

She was standing, awaiting them, and her words trailed away when the Jaghut stepped into the light, already stripping off his soaked clothing.

'Unless you're in the habit of devouring small children with your sweet trap, woman, best look back upon your companion, if satisfaction is what you seek.'

Lasa Rook snorted, and then moved to sit once more. 'Wastrels indeed. Do charge these flames, Hanako, and with luck, such heat will dry our guest to a frail wisp, lifting him high into the night and gone.'

Now naked, the Jaghut moved closer to the hearth and began laying out his clothes. 'Thel Akai,' he said, making the words sound like a mild irritation, 'you've been tumbling down out of the mountains for weeks now. All through the nights, as I communed with the walls of my cave, and paced the rough floor in search of quietude, I have been subjected to echoing braying I assumed to be laughter.' Finished with his clothing, he moved closer to the flames and held out his hands to the heat. 'But let it not be said that a Jaghut worth his salt would call but one cave his refuge. I set out, then, seeking a more remote cache.'

'His boat sank,' Hanako explained.

Lasa Rook lifted a bright gaze to him. 'At last, brevity! Heed well this deplorable youth, Jaghut, and consider – in your own time, to be sure – the value of being succinct. After all, we do not all live for ages untold, inviting such preambles as to witness the greying of hair and bending of bones.'

After a moment, the Jaghut rose and retrieved the pack that Hanako had dragged into the firelight. He pulled free the straps and drew out a bundled chain surcoat, followed by a helm, a belt and twin scabbarded shortswords.

Hanako stared. 'You swam carrying all that? I think even I could not manage such a thing, sir.'

'When swimming fails, one walks.'

'Listen to him, Hanako. Before this night is done, he will tell you of the stars he gathered from the sky.' She rose. 'I'm for sleep, yielding to you snores rather than moans. But do lean an ear to this pallid Jaghut, and partake in his dirge of exhausted wisdom. No finer music could more quickly put me to sleep.'

Hanako moved to check on Erelan Kreed, but the warrior remained unconscious, his brow hot with fever. Troubled, Hanako returned to sit opposite the Jaghut.

'What ails your friend?'

'He slew a dragon, and then drank its blood.'

The Jaghut grunted. 'I expect he eats his own lice, too.'

'I am named Hanako.'

'I know.'

Hanako waited, and then shrugged before dragging close a branch torn from a tree they had pulled up from the high-water line. He flung it on to the fire. Sparks scattered and then died.

'Names,' said the Jaghut, 'become their own curses. They are seared upon your soul, destined to follow your every deed. Such flimsy frames to bear inordinate burdens. It is my thought that we should all dispense with our old names, perhaps once every ten or so years. Imagine the wonder of beginning anew, Hanako, cleansed of all history.'

'I would see a world, sir, where every crime was escaped.'

'Hmm, you have a point there, but I wonder, what is it, precisely?'

'With our names comes responsibility, for all that we have done, and all that we promise to do. But also, sir, how would we keep track of our companions? Our friends? Family?'

'Yes, but your point?'

Hanako frowned. 'You are Jaghut. You are unlike the rest of us. It is the very continuity that we yearn for, which you would reject. Well, which you *have* rejected.'

For a time neither spoke, and the only sound beyond the crackling flames was the drone of Lasa Rook's snoring.

Then the Jaghut said, 'Hanako, I am named Raest.'

'Then welcome, Raest, to our fire.'

'Voice a single jibe, Hanako, and I might have to chop off your head. Just so you understand how this night will play.'

'I am too worried for Erelan Kreed, to be honest.'

'He will live. Or die.'

'Ah. Thank you.'

'If he lives, he will not be the man you once knew. If you trusted this Erelan Kreed, trust him no longer. If you thought you knew him, you know him no more. And, should he instead die, why, honour who he once was. Raise a decent cairn and sing his praises.'

Hanako stared into the flames. 'We journey, Raest,' he said, 'in answer to the call of one of your kin.'

'Hood. Now that is a name worthy of being a curse.'

'You will not answer his need?'

'Of course not.'

'You say that other Thel Akai have passed through this valley, and past your cave. It seems, then, that there will be many more in Hood's army than I had first imagined.'

'Thel Akai, who like a good joke,' Raest said, nodding. 'Dog-Runners, who have made sorrow a goddess of endless tears. Ilnap, who flee a usurper among their island kingdom. Forulkan, seeking the final arbiter. Jheck and Jhelarkan, ever eager for blood, even should it ooze from carrion. Petty tyrants from across the ocean, fleeing the High King's incorruptible justice. Tiste, Azathanai, Halacahi, Thelomen—'

'Thelomen!'

'Word travels swift and far, Hanako, when even the waves carry the tale.'

'Then,' whispered Hanako, 'this shall be a most formidable army.'

'I would almost yield my isolation to see Hood's ugly face, once he realizes the true tragedy that is the answer to his ill-considered summons.'

'I should have realized,' Hanako said. 'Grief will make a vast legion. How could it not?'

'It is not the grief, young Thel Akai, but the questions for which there are no answers. Against such silence, frustration and fury will see every sword drawn. Hood longs to face an enemy, and will, I fear, refashion death into a god. A being worthy of cursing, a face to be carved from senseless stone, offering up a blank, stony gaze, a grimace of granite.' Raest snorted. 'I see dolmens in the offing, and sacred wells from which the stench of rotting meat rises, to greet dancing flies. There will be sacrifices made, in the delusion of fair bargain.'

'The Thel Akai,' said Hanako, 'hold to a faith in balance. When there is death, life will answer it. All things in this world, and in every other, ride upon a fulcrum.'

'A fulcrum? And who then fashioned this cosmic construct, Hanako?'

'It is simply how things are made, Raest. Mountains will crack and tumble, making the ground level where once stood cliffs. Rivers will flood and then subside when the waters drain away. For every dune raised up by the winds, there is an answering hollow.'

'For every cry, there follows a silence. For every laugh, there is weeping. Yes, yes, Hanako.' Raest waved a long-fingered, almost skeletal hand. 'But alas, what you describe to me is the mind's game with itself, haunted by the need to make sense of senseless things. To be certain, there are vague rules at work, which observation can detect. Crumbling mountains and flooding rivers and the like. The grinding wheel of the stars at night. But such predictability can deceive, Hanako. Worse, it can lead to complacency. Better to heed the unlikely, and assemble such rules only after disaster's dust settles. After all, the heart of that need is comfort.'

Hanako glanced away, and then scowled down into the flames of the fire. 'You mock our beliefs.'

'But gently, I assure you.'

'As you would a child, you mean.'

'Such is our curse,' Raest replied. 'In fact,' he added, 'one cannot help but detest the Jaghut in general. Permit me, if you will, to explain.'

Hanako pushed more of the branch into the fire. He considered the Jaghut's offer. There would indeed be value in learning more of these strange people. After a moment, he nodded. 'Very well.'

Raest reached out to collect a stick, one end of which he thrust into the embers. 'Some dread failure overtook us, one in which the intellect, knowing only itself, rose to dominate our proud selves, and by the seduction of language then set about denigrating all that was not rational, all that hovered tantalizingly out of reach, beyond its power to comprehend, much less explain away. Although it works hard at doing precisely that: explaining away, dismissing, impugning, mocking. The cynical eye is cast, and the cleverness of the mind ascends to assume the pose of the haughty. What results, sadly, is an intellect that won't be denied its own sense of superiority.' He held up the stick with which he had been stirring the embers, studied the small flames flickering from its blackened tip. 'Is there anything more obnoxious than that?'

Hanako found himself matching Raest's examination of the small tongues of fire writhing about the stick's tip.

Raest continued. 'So Gothos gave to us this wretched truth, and in so doing, he showed us the paucity of our lives. The intellect delights in standing triumphant within us, even as the ashes rise past our knees, as the skies darken and grow foul with smoke; even as children starve or are flung into the face of war and strife. Because the mind that has convinced itself of its own superiority is incapable of humility, and in the absence of humility, it is incapable of growth.' He waved the stick before him to make the tip glow, inscribing patterns that seemed to linger in the air. 'To all this, Caladan Brood but nodded, and built for us a monument to our own stupidity. The Tower of Hate. Oh, how we laughed at the wonder of it, the blatant skyward stab of our obdurate natures. A monument, in truth, to announce the fall of our civilization . . . now that was a night of celebration!'

'But surely,' objected Hanako, 'the rational state proffers many gifts to a civilization!'

Raest shrugged, and then set one hand over one of his eyes, blinking with the other. 'Why yes, I see them now! These gifts!' He withdrew his hand and frowned. 'Oh dear, is that the cost? What my second eye observes – all those poor fools made to kneel in the dirt! And the well-meaning but utterly self-deceiving leaders – living in such splendour – who hold in their hands the life and death and liberty of those abject minions! And there, ever ready with their salutes, the soldiers who would impose the will of said leaders, in the subjugation of their fellows. Why, reason rules this world! The necessities of organization are such *rational* constructs – who could deny their worth?' He snorted. 'Hmm, shall we ask the slaves, in the few moments they win each day in which to pause and draw breath from their labours? Or shall we ask the leaders, who in the luxury of privilege are granted time to contemplate the system in which they thrive? Or, perhaps, the soldiers? But then, they are told not to think, only to obey. Where, then, among these myriad participants, are we to look for judgement?'

'The bards, the poets, the sculptors and painters.'

'Bah, who ever listens to them?'

'You heeded Caladan Brood.'

'He drove the spear into our civilization, yes, but that

civilization was already a corpse, already cold and lifeless upon the ground. No, the role of artists is to attend the funerals. They are the pall-bearers of failure, and every wonder they raise high in celebration harks back to a time already dead.'

'Some would dance, and give to us joy and hope.'

'The gift of momentary forgetfulness,' Raest said, nodding. 'This we name entertainment.'

'Does that not have value?'

'It does, except when pursued to excess. At that point, it becomes denial.'

'What, then, is your answer, Raest?'

The Jaghut's tusks flashed dully as Raest grinned. 'I shall endeavour to create a new civilization, one heeding the inherent flaws of its organization. I shall, indeed, attempt the impossible. Alas, I can already foresee the outcome, as I am driven by frustration and, ultimately, despair. The possibility must be acknowledged – which we dare not do – that we, being imperfect creatures, are ever doomed to fail in achieving the perfection of a just society, a society of liberation, balanced and compassionate, reasonable and spiritual, devoid of tyrannies of thought and deed, absent wanton malice, the cruelty of natural vices, be they greed, envy, or the desire to dominate.'

Hanako studied the flames, considering the Jaghut's chilling words. 'But, Raest, can we not try?'

'To try implies a willingness to accept our flaws, and to serve the cause of mitigating them. To try, Hanako, begins with acknowledging those flaws, and that requires humility, and so we return, once again, to an intellect convinced of its own superiority – not just superiority over others of its own kind, but superiority over nature itself. The Tiste poet Gallan said it well when he wrote "The shore does not dream of you". Do you know that poem?'

Hanako shook his head.

'Do you grasp the meaning of that line?'

'Nature will prove itself superior to our every conceit.'

Raest nodded, his eyes shining in the firelight. 'Humility.

Seek it within yourself, be as sceptical of your own superiority as your intellect is sceptical of the superiority of things other than itself. Turn your critical faculties inward, with ruthless diligence, and by that you will understand the true meaning of courage. It is the kind of courage that sees you end up on your knees, but with the will to rise once more, to begin it all over again.'

'You describe an unending journey, Raest, of a nature which would test a soul to its very core.'

'I describe a life lived well, Hanako. I describe a life of worth.' Then he flung the stick on to the flames. 'But my words are not for the young, alas. Even so, they may echo into future years, and rebound when the time is propitious. Thus, I offer them to you, Hanako.'

'For your gift this night,' Hanako said, 'I thank you.'

'A gift you barely comprehend.'

The Thel Akai heard the wryness in the Jaghut's tone, stealing the sting from the words. 'Just so, Raest.'

'The Dog-Runners speak with rare vision,' Raest said, 'when they say that in the flames of the hearth, we can see both our rise and our fall.'

'And the ashes in the morning to come?'

The Jaghut's twisted mouth fashioned a bitter grin. 'Those ashes . . . yes, well. There are none to see them, just as none of us can do aught but remember heat yet remain doomed to feel no warmth from the memory, so we know but cannot know what it was like to be born, nor what it will be like to die. Ashes . . . they will tell you that something has burned, but what is the shape of that thing? For those who burned but faintly, some form remains, enough with which to guess. But for those who burned fiercely, ah, as you say, nothing but a heap of ashes, swiftly scattered on the wind.'

'Is there no hope for legacy, Raest?'

'By all means hope, Hanako. Indeed, aspire. But what the future will read from what you leave behind is beyond your power to control. And if that is not humbling, then nothing is.'

'And yet,' said Hanako, 'I travel to find an army that seeks death, to wage a war that cannot be won. In my heart, I yearn for failure, and dream of glory.'

'And no doubt you will find it,' Raest replied.

'Tell me of the Azathanai.'

'Squalid wretches every one of them. Look not to the Azathanai for guidance.'

'How did you walk across the bottom of the lake, carrying your armour?'

'How? A few steps, amidst clouds of silt, and then back to the surface, and then down again, for a few more strides. It was dull work, I tell you. There is a forest down there, making a tangle of everything. And hearthstones in rings, like pocks, making treacherous holes. Tree stumps and overly curious fish. Biting eels. I've had better days.' With that, Raest rose. 'Sleep beckons.'

But Hanako was not yet finished with this unexpected guest. 'Raest, can you heal Erelan Kreed?'

The Jaghut paused, and then said, 'No. As I said, the blood will either kill him or it won't. But what I can offer is a warning. The kin of the slain dragon will know your friend by the scent of that Draconic blood. Some will seek to resume old arguments.'

Hanako stared at Raest. 'They will hunt us?'

The Jaghut shrugged. 'You have lively days ahead of you, Thel Akai.'

*       *       *

With dawn's light creeping around the sides of the mountain to the east, Garelko, the eldest of Lasa Rook's husbands, walked up to the side of the dragon's carcass and gave it a kick. Rank gases hissed out from somewhere below. Coughing, he staggered back.

From the makeshift hut the three Thel Akai had built for the night just past, up beyond the high-water mark, Ravast laughed. Crouched in the entranceway, he watched as Garelko then waded into the water to approach the carcass from that side.

'Aai!' Garelko cried as he looked down. 'The water seethes with ravenous crayfish!'

Tathenal appeared from further up the strand, dragging another uprooted tree. Upon hearing Garelko's cry, he paused and looked up. 'You haunt that poor beast like a wolf its kill. Leave off that which you cannot claim, unless by stink alone you would assert kinship.'

'Wait!' said Garelko, peering down. 'What glimmer is this I see? Ah, nothing but the picked bones of Tathenal's curiosity. 'Twas but the tiniest bird, if one can judge said bones. Do you still hear the snicker of pincers in your ears, O brother of fate? Why, they must have set upon you in the night.'

'What truths then does the dead beast yield?' Tathenal asked.

'Many truths, Tathenal.' Garelko waded back on to the shore. 'By gleaning examination of myriad details, I conclude, for example, that the dragon did not make that cairn of stones in which was entombed Ravast's battleaxe.'

'Indeed? Then did it not crush its own skull either?'

'I wager that gift belonged to Erelan Kreed.'

'Why, such perception in old Garelko! But can you be certain that it was not the ravenous crayfish that scuttled in sudden ambush, whilst the wounded beast wallowed in the shallows?'

'Your mocking words, Tathenal, well match your ignorance. I felt the snip of pincers and can tell you, only a fool would underestimate their vicious efficacy.'

'A foolish dragon, at the very least,' Ravast suggested as he emerged from the hut and made his way down on to the shoreline. 'Tathenal, I see you have collected for us another tree. Will you add it to the seven others and make for us a neat pile?'

Tathenal scowled up at him. 'The dream felt very real, pup. I tell you, we all came close to drowning, and if not for the ship I built, blessed as I was by premonition, we would all be dead now.'

'Dead in your dream realm, you mean.'

'And who is to say that such realms are lacking in verisimilitude, Ravast? Indeed, that realm may well be the repository of our precious souls, and should we die in it, we would awaken with lifeless eyes and an insatiable predilection for funereal attire. Dour and solemn may well describe your tastes in fashion, but not mine!'

'But Tathenal,' said Ravast, 'by all means build your timbered salvation, only do it in your sleep, in the realm where it will be needed.' He gestured at the uprooted trees now lining their camp. 'These will avail you not, unless you envision a ship able to ply waters both real and imagined.'

'Wise observation,' observed Garelko, now studying Tathenal with some scepticism. 'And one which had already occurred to me, since it is the eldest who know wisdom. Perhaps, in reconsidering Ravast's words, it would be better to conclude not wisdom, but the youthful quickness of the youthful mind, that so swiftly rushes to the place of obvious absurdity, particularly when contemplating someone else's efforts.'

'A rush to ill-considered judgement, you mean,' retorted Tathenal. 'Near children such as Ravast are incapable of understanding nuance in matters of the metaphysical. Lost on him, as well, is my gracious generosity in offering him a berth upon my vessel.'

'I see no vessel,' said Ravast. 'I see trees, branches, leaves and roots.'

'It is the superior mind that can observe this meanest material, and yet see in it a sharp-prowed monument to maritime majesty.'

'They buried my axe,' Ravast said, 'fearing that it was all that remained of us. We came too late, alas, to see the wet stains of our wife's tears, as she flung herself atop the rock-pile, tearing hair from her scalp in reams of grief and whatnot.'

'I looked for but found no clumps of hair,' Garelko said. 'No, it's far more likely that she has already taken young, all-too-handsome Hanako to her furs, and if her mighty will reveals the power she imagines it to possess, why, already she swells with illegitimate child. I see her, here in my mind's eye, already sated and, curse that Hanako, satiated as well! The smugness of her glinting regard haunts me! The faint smile of womanly victory over us, in all those battles we never recognize, even as our blood drips. I see it, hovering like a knife above my heart, to make sudden blur towards my beleaguered manhood!'

'That cut is years old, Garelko,' Tathenal said. 'An eel made lifeless by age, flopping no more.'

'Ravast, come to my aid. Young and old must ally, and by stinging rebuke savage the one who possesses not enough of either. Tathenal, by all means build your boat, but we must leave you behind, and rush to the moment when we stumble upon our disloyal wife, as she thrashes in the arms of Hanako the adulterer. You and I, Ravast, we shall unveil the cuckold's razor beak, and see in our wife's wide eyes that first flowering of fear and dread! And then, with her dignity squirming beneath our heel, we shall grind her into misery and remorse, and so win a cornucopia of favours!'

'Bright fruit and venomous nectar, more like,' said Tathenal, sneering. 'When I see you both flounder in deep waves, and hear your piteous cries, why, I will blithely sail past you both, and offer up the meanest flutter of fingers.'

'When next you see me in your dreams,' Ravast said, 'observe as I rush to the flood, inviting every lungful of sweet water. Welcome my carcass, Tathenal, as it rolls to and fro, and be at ease, knowing I died happy.'

Garelko grunted. 'Ravast, you've not been married long enough to have lifeless eyes. In perusing my reflection this morning, in the lake's mirrored surface, I was shocked at the dullness of my own gaze.'

'Our shock is long past,' said Tathenal. 'Yours is a gaze, Garelko, that can blunt a sword's edge, and by wit you bludgeon us all. My poor humour reels bruised and struck senseless. So by all means, take the pup and be off, both of you!'

Ravast turned back to the hut. 'We'd best dismantle our abode, Garelko, since it was by our own hands that it was thus raised.'

'A moment there! Where will I sleep?'

'Why, Tathenal,' said Ravast, 'you can sleep in your boat.'

Garelko laughed. 'Sweet dreams, Tathenal! Hahahaha!'

'Very well,' sighed Tathenal after a moment's consideration, 'I will accompany you, to ensure that you are safe, as I alone among the three of us happen to be in my fighting prime. The pup is too wild and wayward and still thinks himself a hero, whilst the ancient man of creaking bones can scarcely lift his weapon.'

'Ah,' said Ravast, 'we can leave the hut then, for the next party of fools.'

'You confess your spite!'

'I confess nothing, except, perhaps, a sudden laziness. Now, have we not lingered here long enough? We have a treacherous wife to hunt down!'

'I shall shake my fist at her most stentoriously,' said Garelko as he collected his gear. 'As a bear awakened from its cave, my lips shall writhe and my fangs gnash with eerie clicking sounds. Like a wolf in the deep snows, I shall shake my hide and free the hackles to rise. With all the remorselessness of an advancing crayfish, my pincers shall open wide in waving threat and snippery danger.'

'Finally,' said Tathenal, 'in simile he finds the proper scale.'

A short time later, the three husbands of Lasa Rook set out, once again upon the trail of their wife.

Perhaps it was the dragon's carcass, but Ravast's thoughts were soon mired in memories of battle. He had been new to his weapons when Thelomen raiders struck their village. He could remember their blunt-prowed ships driving up upon the pebbled strand, and how armoured figures swarmed over the sides and began running up the slope. The village dogs were in a frenzy, rushing down to challenge them. Most of the beasts were wise enough to harry rather than close, but a few went down to spears, dying loudly, in a mess of blood and entrails. Ravast, rushing to join a line of men and women who'd collected up weapons and, here and there, some pieces of armour or a helm or a shield, had fallen into a gap between two kin. Readying his axe and shield, he only then realized that he was in the first line, the one made up of the most ancient members of the clan. They stood for the sole purpose of slowing the Thelomen advance, thus earning the village's younger warriors the time to fully arm and armour themselves, whilst youths corralled the children to guide them into the forested crags inland.

The only defender not in his proper place was Ravast.

But it was too late, as the first wave of Thelomen reached them.

Widows and widowers, the lame and the bent, Ravast's companions fought hard and in silence, long past all thoughts of complaint or fear. When they fell, they made no cries, and not one begged for mercy. It was only much later that Ravast understood how that battle, that savage defence of the village, marked for his companions a purpose to their deaths – a moment they had all been waiting for. When faced with the choice of sudden death or the lingering wasting away of old age, not one had hesitated in taking up a weapon.

Ravast alone survived, and fought with such desperation that he held the attackers back, until the now caparisoned warriors who had finally gathered behind him elected to advance to join him rather than waiting in their shield-wall.

The Thelomen had been driven back that day, without ever reaching the village. Ravast had been proclaimed both a hero and a fool, and on that day he had caught the eye of Lasa Rook.

Thereafter, Ravast fought that battle many times, in the tales told at the hearth, and in his dreams, where the fear took hold of him in ways he had not known on the day itself. He did well to disguise it, of course, as befitted the young hero of that day. But the truth of it was, he carried more scars from the dreams of the battle than from the battle itself.

Lasa Rook had won him with little effort, not knowing, he suspected, the lame, shivering creature that hid inside his hale young body. Fear had made a life of farming and herding most welcome, and if others noted how strange it was that such a natural warrior should choose to set aside his weapons and armour, it was easy enough to then consider the lure of Lasa Rook, the village's most desired woman.

He had learned to hide that fear, and had raised high walls around his dreams. Tathenal could well dream of floods and devastation, and gather uprooted trees with which to build his salvation. But no such gesture existed for Ravast. Neither a ship built by any Thel Akai, nor one built by a god, could ride above the waves of fear.

*Upon such seas, every vessel will sink, vanishing beneath the roiling tumult. Upon such seas, a man such as I can only drown.*

And yet, here he walked, at seeming ease alongside his fellow husbands.

*She will not risk the Jaghut's unreasoning path. She will know when to turn back. Long before any battle. If not, then I will confess to her. I will tell her about the widows and widowers, the too old and the crippled, who rushed to their place in that first line. And the silence that took them, bittersweet with anticipation, and how they all gathered up their own fears, and sent them into the one man who did not belong among them.*

*I will tell her of my fears, and if I must fall in esteem in her eyes, then still I shall not hesitate.*

*Wife. You buried my axe.*

*But I buried it long ago.*

*You think me now dead. But I died in that line. I, Ravast, widower to them all.*

*We will laugh then, in our breaking of souls, and set our vision back upon the trail, to our distant, peaceful farm, which lies upon the heel of the Lower Rise, just above the veil of morning smoke from the village below.*

*The dogs are barking, I hear, but not in alarm. They are just keeping their throats ready.*

*Because the Thelomen will come again, in their ships, and I will take my place in that first line. Where I will stand in silence. And in blessed anticipation.*

He thought back to the dragon's carcass, and the frantic swing of his axe, that only by chance struck the beast's taloned paw. The walls had held on that day, if only because the battle proved so brief in duration. The walls had held, but barely.

'Another slope and another mountain and another high pass!' Garelko groaned as they climbed up from the lake's edge. 'Ravast, I beg you, carry this old man!'

*No, I already carry too many.*

Tathenal said, 'The saddle pass is high enough, I should think. That will see us safe from the flood. When next we camp, I have in mind a new idea. Ravast, consider this when you build our hut for the night. Hull-shaped, and sound of flank . . .'

Tathenal's dreams of flood the night just past were not the first. For years, he had been haunted by visions of disaster, against which his will proved, time and again, utterly helpless. Behind the veil of sleep, the mind had a way of wandering into strange places, as if the soul knew that it was, in truth, lost. Landscapes arrived twisted, known and yet unknown, and he would see faces that he recognized, yet did not, and in walking through his dreams, in turning to him and speaking in garbled tongues, they proved little more than harbingers of confusion.

For all that, the sense of dread persisted, like the scent of a storm upon the air. The roots of a mountain grown corrupted and rotten – he alone could feel its tremors, its promise of imminent collapse. A tendril of smoke upon the breeze – none other noticed the glow of the raging flames deep in the forest, the growing roar of conflagration. Diseases among the livestock, birds falling from the sky, the village cats poisoned and dying beneath wagons. Each time, Tathenal was alone in seeing the signs, unheeded in his cries of warning, and the last to fall to whatever calamity – fleeing exhausted, whimpering, and yet burning with validation.

Prophets thrived on being ignored. They delighted in being proved right, and delighted yet more in seeing misery and suffering afflict every fool who dared to mock. Tathenal had long since learned to keep his fears to himself, barring the occasional confession to his closest companions – his fellow husbands. Their chiding and amusement comforted him, when he chose to not think about it too much. Familiar voices took the sting from dismissive words. Habits and patterns could be worn like old clothes.

There was little challenge in assembling each scene of destruction, plucking free the specific details, and then recognizing the singular fear hidden behind them all. Worse, he was hardly unique in his terror of death. Warriors marched into its face at every battle, and their courage was but the visible side of the mask, when the unseen side, flush against the skin of their faces, was cold and clammy with fear. Wives who commanded the hearth, as mistresses of the farm and its myriad denizens, wove blankets, or pushed the dust from the rooms; they dragged husbands or lovers to their furs and blazed like fires against the darkness. Herders counted their flocks and sought signs of wolves on the mountain paths. Wood-carvers gathered dead trees and fought their own kind of war, seeking resurrection in what they made. Poets and hearth-singers pulled threads from tattered souls, eliciting emotions which, in the end, were proofs against death.

The enemy forced every act, every deed. The enemy pursued, or stalked, or waited in ambush. It could not be defeated, and it never lost.

Tathenal understood the Jaghut, Hood. He understood this summoning, and the outrage that gave it such appeal. He understood, as well, the futility of it.

Middle among the husbands, he found himself upon an ever-moving bridge, with the youth, Ravast, carrying one end, and the elder, Garelko, the other. Their positions were fixed, but the march through time could not pause, not for an instant. Until death came to take one of them. Then, the journey would stagger, stumble and slide. In a predictable world, Garelko would fall first, and Tathenal would find himself taking the old man's place, as the new eldest, and if Lasa Rook was as unchanging as she seemed, then Ravast would find himself upon that bridge, trapped in the middle, with a new youth upon the other end.

It was an awkward construct in Tathenal's mind, and yet it held, stubborn and persistent. He did not particularly like it, sensing its lack of artistry, and, indeed, its lack of purpose. *It*

*is simply how we are. A stupid thing to consider. A bridge?
Why a bridge? What unknown torrent does it span? And
why am I alone in finding my feet not upon solid ground, but
upon an uncertain purchase? When I at last find myself the
eldest, will I step with relief upon some future shore, some
river's verge or chasm's blessed ledge? And, should I arrive
there, what will I see ahead of me?*

*We carry our bridges, from birth until death. If I name it
the soul, then it is no wonder I ever fear the flood, the fire,
the avalanche. Or the gnawing waste of disease, and every
hidden, unseen place of neglect. But these two companions,
holding me up at either end, ah, I set too vast a weight upon
them.*

He understood the nature of love, such as he felt for his
fellow husbands. They stood aligned and together, with Lasa
Rook opposite them. The specifics were not relevant. No soul
deserved to stand alone, and families both found and made
served the same purpose. In his dreams, it was this that he
saw swept away, time and again. In his dreams, he ever ended
up alone.

There would be an army, clustered around Hood and his
vow. Tathenal was certain of it. An army such as no world
had ever seen before. Its enemy was impossible, but that did
not matter – no, in truth, it was that impossibility that would
give the army its strength. He could not explain his certainty;
could make little sense of his faith. But he would see that
army, and, perhaps, join it.

*I will step off the edge of this bridge. Knowing what will
come of that. And it may be that, when the end comes, I will
understand. Death will defeat time, when nothing else can.
Lasa Rook, beloved wife, will you see the glory of that?*

He did not believe any of the others would follow him,
especially not Lasa Rook, and he was settled with that final
departure.

It would be better, he decided, if he dreamed of that army.
He knew, when at last he joined the ranks, his dreams of
disaster would leave him. *An end to my fear of being alone.
An end to a soul's solitude, when death at last arrives.*

*There is something in that, something in there, that comforts.*

*Hood, your army will be vast.*

Garelko made his way along the trail, taking the lead and so setting the pace. He deemed this the proper thing, since he was the eldest. He imagined himself the silver-muzzled wolf, the noble king, the wizened veteran of a thousand hunts. *Our quarry is elusive, to be sure. But my mind's eye is sharp. I see her swaying hips, and those buttocks, smooth as damp clay, as giant pots, two fused into one, rolling as she walks. A behind to bury your face in, with breath held, of course. But still, I will lunge without hesitation.*

*Not a wolf, but a sea lion, fierce and weighty, yet elegant in the water. In the midst of a surging wave, rushing for the crevice, the niche in the stone wall of her coy indifference. The echoes of her yelp will be as music to my soul.*

*And the swell of her belly! See these hands? They are made to cup such wonder, to stroke and gather in the folds that proffer wealth, like bolts of the softest cloth. Are we not sensual creatures? And do not the rough edges of age, these calluses and brittle nails, bely the tenderness of a loving touch? Or eager lust, for that matter?*

*The pup sneers, as only pups can, but such haughtiness is flimsy disguise over inexperience. I see through him, indeed, and think nothing of his airs. Youth has that swollen self to contend with, while I am past such conceits. Like an animal I will roll in my pleasures, and make of her a sack of moans.*

*She thinks us dead. She gasps in the arms of Hanako, no doubt, even at this very moment! Well, what's another husband to add to the milling herd? It is experience she will long for, before too long, and by the time we find her, well, I see her eyes light up like torches in a cave.*

*Behind and belly, and now her breasts.*

*Weight and heft, sweet as bladders of wine, and my hands such a perfect fit beneath each fleshy pronouncement! Why, she could smother a horse with those twin tomes of sensuality! I see the animal dead with a smile on its face – no, a moment, such an image alarms my sensitive self. We shall send the horse back into the field; she can smother something else . . . think on it later.*

*We are hunters, and she the quarry. That much is plain. Unencumbered, as far as notions go.*

*I didn't even believe in dragons. Slithering myth, seductive legend, scales and forked tongue, wings and whipping tail! An outrageous interruption to our conversation. Eating a skinned bear, no less! Was it so dainty of sensibility as to peel the beast before devouring? How curious! How ignoble for the Lord of Temper!*

*Dragons! Whence came the wretched thing?*

*But in rank decay, how mundane. Yet, was it not noble in form? No, it was not. A vile thing, this hoary beast of legend. We shall have to kill every one we come across, if only to appease the symmetry of sweet nature. Such insults must not go unchallenged.*

*I will take her from behind, and then from the front, fighting her breasts as if wrestling two bags of ale with stuck stoppers. Pull, you fool! Twist and pull!*

*The wizened wolf knows well its prey. A thousand hunts, a thousand conquests, and this trail is older than you might think, and yet, old man or not, I find it fresh as strawberries!*

*The pup knows nothing of this. Even Tathenal barely comprehends. The sweetness of life is anticipation. This, then, is our real moment of glory, yet listen to them, grunting and gasping as we climb yet another mountain's backside, about to plunge into the crack of the pass, and crawl our way down its length – be tempted not by any caves you might spy, my fellow husbands! They are but distractions! She runs in order to be caught!*

*Ah, Lasa Rook, beloved, your sweat should taste sweet as wine. Which we can achieve, once I pour wine all over you.*

*Is not the mind a wondrous world? That thoughts and aspirations can cavort with such glee? That desires can spool out into such wild mess as to tangle every sense, and confound the spirit in a welter of delicious indulgence!*

*Reality stands no chance against such inner creations.*
*Dragons notwithstanding.*

'Ease up the pace, Garelko! You will rush us to our deaths!'

Garelko's whiskered lips stretched into a grin . . . that just as quickly faded. *Oh, such ill-chosen words!*

&ast; &ast; &ast;

'I would have preferred a simpler path,' muttered K'rul. 'A modest step on to the withered plain, flanked by hills, and before us the tall poles surmounted with skulls, to mark the Jhelarkan claim to the territory. A week's journey north of that, and we find ourselves in the place we sought.'

Skillen Droe shifted slightly, his neck twisting as he looked back upon K'rul. *'The Jheleck would not welcome me.'*

'Oh, them too? What have you done to earn their enmity? In fact, is there anyone who would actually welcome you, Skillen Droe?'

The giant winged reptile tilted his head, considering, and then said, *'None come to mind, but I will give it more thought.'*

K'rul rubbed at his neck, where the bruises remained from when his companion had lifted him into the air. He studied the scene before them, and then sighed. 'I wonder, is it your imagination, or mine, that conjures up worlds such as this one? Or do I reveal the flaw of conceit?'

*'If such landscapes are the products of your mind, or mine, K'rul, then conceit is the least of our worries.'*

In the basin before them sprawled a city, so vast it climbed every slope, with a heavy cloud of dust shrouding the entire valley. Spires towered above angular tenements and what seemed to be public buildings, monumental in a solid, belligerent style. There were causeways spanning the gaps between the spires, and a vast gridwork of canals in which clear water flowed, with ornate bridges precisely placed at intervals, linking each district.

What jarred the eye were the city's scale and the seething press of denizens crawling upon every available surface. Not a single spire was taller than K'rul himself, and the denizens were insects. Ants, perhaps, or termites, or some other such hive-dwelling creature.

'I foresee difficulties crossing it,' K'rul said. 'Without, that is, leaving ruin in our wake. I think,' he added, 'we'll need the use of your wings.'

'*It is the way of such insects,*' said Droe, '*to ignore anything and everything, until that thing in some way disturbs them. Occupied as they are with more immediate endeavours, scurrying about on their rounds. The exigencies of survival, status, cooperation and such consume their entire existence.*'

K'rul considered Droe's observations, and then grunted and said, 'But are there malcontents among them, I wonder? Plotters seeking freedom from their daily travail: that miserable crawl from birth to death? With heavy boots and careless steps, we could be the scourge of gods down there, and from our passage cults will rise in the years to follow, as memories blur and twist. Vengeful or indifferent? All a matter of interpretation.'

'*You imagine this as more than a simple illusion of civilization, K'rul? Are these insects in possession of written records? Histories and compilations? Literature?*'

'Droe, I see sculptures, there in the central plaza. There are artisans among them. Surely, there must be poets, too? And philosophers and inventors. Historians and politicians – all the natural pairings of professionals who, in the end, prove to be sworn enemies of one another.'

'*A curious notion, K'rul,*' said Droe. '*Philosophers and inventors as enemies of one another? I beg you, explain this.*'

K'rul shrugged. 'The inventor possesses a lust for creation, but rarely if ever thinks of unintended consequences to whatever is invented. In answering a dilemma of functionality, or pursuing the dubious reward of efficiency, changes arrive to a society, and often they prove overwhelming. And surely, Skillen, you need not an explanation of the hatred politicians hold for historians – which by hard experience is rightly reciprocated. The Lord of Hate had much to say on the matter, which I found it difficult to refute. Civilization is an argument between thinkers and doers, just as invention is an argument against nature.'

'*Among these insects, then, in this city, you believe there is true civilization. But my eyes, K'rul, are perhaps keener than yours. I see how they march to and fro, and each one identical to the next, barring the ones we might deem soldiers, or constabulary. If there be a queen or empress, she hides, perhaps, in the cellar of that central palace, and speaks in scents and flavours.*'

'As do you, Skillen Droe. Yet does your chosen manner of communication lack subtlety? Does it fail in the necessary intricacy to express complex thought? Someone indeed rules below, and is served by an inner court. The soldiers maintain order and enforce cooperation. The sculptures are raised, to gods, perhaps, or even heroes of the past. What leads you to doubt?'

'*It is not doubt that I feel, K'rul.*'

'Then what?'

'*I feel . . . belittled.*'

'Well.' After a moment, K'rul sighed. 'Hard to argue against that. Still, we skirt the most intriguing issue here. These realms, which we stumble upon, when our only intent is to reach a destination. At times,' he admitted, 'I feel as if nature sets against us obstacles, each one intended to obscure.'

'*Obscure what, precisely?*'

K'rul shrugged. 'Some banal truth, no doubt.'

'*Each and every journey I have undertaken, K'rul, insists upon a passage of time, manifest in the gradual alteration, or development, of the landscape. The eye measures the step, the step spans the distance, and the mind conjures for itself a place for it, and gives it a name. But we sentient beings, we are ones to clutter time, to crowd it or stretch it out, when in truth it is unchanging.*'

K'rul eyed the winged reptile. 'Is this how your most recent hosts deem things? Have we not also the will to bend time, as it suits us?'

'*I cannot say. Have we?*'

'In the absence of confusion, we find easy synchronicity with time's natural passing, with its fixed pace. Alas, Skillen, confusion walks with us, stubborn as a shadow.' He paused, and then waved at the city before them. 'An insect sets out, there to the west, and begins its march to the easternmost end of the scape. In its modest scale, the journey is long, arduous even. Yet you, Skillen, with your wings spread, could paint your shadow upon the gap in mere moments. Time, it seems, possesses a varying scale.'

'*No. It is only perception that varies.*'

'We have little else.'

'*The K'Chain Che'Malle, K'rul, are makers of instruments and machines. They contrive clocks that divide time itself. Thus, it is fixed in place. The procession of the gears never varies.*'

'But would a citizen of the city below sense the same intervals as those K'Chain Che'Malle?'

'*Perception suggests not . . . and yet, as I said, the gears are precise and the intervals consistent.*'

'And so, once again,' mused K'rul, 'we must look upon scale, and deem it relevant.'

'*It may be,*' said Skillen Droe as he unfolded his wings, '*that in creating their clocks, the K'Chain Che'Malle have imposed an order, and a focal point, upon a force of nature that heretofore knew no rules. And by this creation, we are now trapped.*'

The notion disturbed K'rul, and he had no response to make.

'*I see a sea beyond the valley.*'

'A sea! Now I begin to suspect who imposed this world upon us!'

'*Too bad, since he too will not welcome me.*'

Skillen Droe collected up K'rul with one long-fingered, taloned hand, and unceremoniously took to the air, wings snapping. As they rose higher, K'rul could see that the land they had walked upon was in fact an island, although there had been no sense of that when striding through the mists earlier in the day. The realm of detritus and dust, of abandoned thrones and monuments, had dwindled into the fog that seemed to mark the boundaries between worlds.

Such distinctions seemed arbitrary, and the uncanny proliferation of realms, to which the Azathanai had access, had led K'rul into the belief that, by some strange synthesis of creation, he and his kind were the makers of such places. It was a difficult notion to shake, particularly when it seemed – as it did now – that two wills could war with creation itself.

This island was a manifestation of Mael's whimsy, and Mael was in the habit of mocking the pretences of solid ground that rose like raised welts upon the perfect surface of his seas and oceans. He was also in the habit of peopling such lands with irritatingly poignant absurdities.

*Insects! A city of spires and statues, bridges and canals! You deem this humour, Mael?*

They swept over the city in the valley, shadow trailing, and a short time later reached the sandy strip of the shoreline. Out of courtesy, Skillen brought them down upon the white beach. The air here was sharp but warm.

His feet settling into the sand, K'rul straightened his clothing. 'Your talons have put holes in my robe,' he said.

Mael appeared, walking out from the lazy waves that whispered over the strand. Momentarily tangled in seaweed, the Azathanai paused to pluck it free, and then continued on. The man was naked, pale, his eyes a bland, washed-out blue. His black hair was long, hanging limp over his broad shoulders. Reaching the shore, he pointed a finger at Skillen Droe. 'You owe me an apology.'

*'My life is measured in debts,'* Skillen Droe replied.

'I see an easy solution to that,' Mael said, and then his gaze shifted to K'rul. 'At the very least, you should have elected to bleed out into the sea. Instead, we are witness to a crude proliferation of untempered power. Did no one advise you against such an act?'

'I chose not to table the decision for discussion, Mael,' K'rul replied. 'Not that any of us ever discuss anything before doing whatever it is we end up doing. In any case,' he added, 'we are not all insects.'

Mael smiled. 'An exercise,' he said, 'that amuses me.'

'To what end?'

The Azathanai who ruled the seas simply shrugged. 'What do you two want? Where are you going?'

'To the Vitr,' K'rul replied.

Mael grunted and looked away. 'Ardata. And the Queen of Dreams.'

'Well, to be more precise, the bay known as Starvald Demelain, where, it seems, the Gate once more resides.'

'Open? Unguarded?'

'We cannot be sure,' K'rul admitted. 'Hence, our journey. Now, if you'll kindly get this damned sea out of our way . . .'

Mael frowned. 'I didn't make this. Or, rather, I didn't deliberately put it in your way. Indeed, I assumed that you came here to speak to me. Are you saying that you didn't?'

'No,' K'rul answered. 'We didn't.'

They were all silent for a moment, and then Mael grunted. 'Oh. Well, right then. I suppose we're done here.'

Skillen Droe said, *'I apologize, Mael. It did not occur to me that you laid claim to everything beneath the waves, even submerged mountains.'*

'It wasn't the mountain as such, Droe, it was you breaking it, and then lifting it into the damned sky. You left a damned hole, you fool, a raw wound in the seabed, and now fires burn down in the depths, and strange creatures gather round the edges, living and dying with every flare. If that's not enough, I almost scalded myself when I went to look.'

*'It did not occur to me to think—'*

'Yes,' cut in Mael, 'and you need not add anything to that confession.'

K'rul glanced at Skillen Droe. 'What mountain? Lifted, where, precisely?'

*'Into the sky, as Mael explained, K'rul. Hollowed out, a city resides within. I made use of K'Chain Che'Malle technology, testing its limits, as it were. As it is, it has proved a noble residence.'*

'Residence?' K'rul asked. 'Who dwells within it?'

498

'Well, no one yet. The matter is rather confused at the moment, since I have lost track of it.'

Mael snorted. 'You lost your floating mountain?'

'Momentarily. I am sure it will turn up somewhere. Now, Mael, if you permit, I will carry K'rul across your sea, and we shall endeavour to make no disturbance.'

Turning back to the sea, Mael dismissively waved a hand.

They watched him walk back beneath the surface. Then Skillen pointed, and they saw a small sailing ship plying the shallows of the bay, a tiny craft no longer than K'rul's foot.

'Oh, really, now.'

* * *

The repast of lunch was now done. Tathenal set hands on hips and considered for a time, even as his fellow husbands stamped out the embers of the cookfire, and then he shrugged. 'Sordid demands upon our lives. We must abandon our well-earned rest, bowing once more to our hasty pursuit of grief, joy and subtle vengeance. In my mind I do indeed see her, and at her shoulder, face stricken, young Hanako, Lord of Betrayals. He but deserves the meanest glance, for now she strides forth in red outrage. "You made me think you were all dead!" she cries and all at once we are the accused, cringing to her timorous tirade, and before a single breath's passed, hear us blubber our wet-lipped apologies, words tumbling in haste.' He shook his head. 'No, my dreams were in error. No vessel of wood and dreams shall save us from this maelstrom of malaise.'

'Your wallowing ways are a chore to us all, Tathenal,' said Garelko.

'And yet each dusk, old man, I shall still gather driftwood, lest the nightmares of my unsettled sleep awaken truthfully to a night of terrible flood.'

'In the meantime,' ventured Ravast as he shouldered his pack, 'she draws another step distant, our beloved, grieving widow. Do neither of you find it odd that she marches to the death we presumably have already found? Perhaps indeed a certain new purpose has enlivened her stride—'

'Aye, anticipation of the forthcoming night in which her cave stretches to swollen meat,' muttered Garelko, though he smiled. 'The Lord of Cuckolding has taken her hand, so sweetly to match the pup's incorrigible youth, too smug for any other man to stomach—'

'No, you doddering fool,' Ravast retorted. 'Think on it! She journeys in search of us! Into that hoary realm of spiders and webs, the cold sand upon which serpents lie curled in slumber as they await the night. The cramped confines, Garelko, of the rock-pile!'

As Garelko paused to scratch his jaw, Tathenal joined him and peered curiously at Ravast. 'Garelko, you old goat, listen to the boy. He may have a point. In all misapprehension, our widow now rushes to her fierce battle with death itself! Not, alas, with amused mien, but with terrible purpose! She wishes us back!'

'Then it behoves us,' Garelko said in a musing tone, 'to reach her before she takes that fatal step.'

'The chasm crossed,' Tathenal added with a nod. 'The river forded, the pit leapt into, the veil parted, the chalice sipped, the—'

'Oh, enough, Tathenal!' Ravast snapped, turning from them both, and then wheeling back round. 'Your slow wit will ever stumble in the dust of my wake, and that goes for you too, Garelko. No, the time has come for me to take to the fore, to ascend to predominance. It was,' he added, 'long in coming.'

He watched as the two older men exchanged a glance, and then Garelko smiled at Ravast. 'Why, of course, by all means to the fore, young wolf. Do lead us doddering discards. We shall grip hard the gilded hem of your trailing genius, and consider ourselves blessed.'

Tathenal cleared his throat. 'I see the way ahead, bold Ravast, a descent from these mountains. Be assured we shall follow your hasty plunge, and leave to you that first leap into her delighted embrace, and should Hanako's smooth expression darken, why, we are reunited with our weapons, are we not? We shall lay out his cold body in a pool of hot blood! Hoary as Thelomen we shall cleave in half his skull to make the greenest cup for her bedside!'

Sighing, Ravast turned away. 'Follow then, and never doubt for a moment: this throne has a new master.'

'But I've yet to make toilet!' cried Garelko in sudden dismay.

Ravast scowled. 'Best make it a deferential one, old goat. Then catch us up in the instant past the shudder.'

Tathenal hissed in sympathy. 'Oh, how I hate that shudder.'

Setting out, Ravast led the way, skirting the lake, and it was not long before Garelko caught up. The trail angled away from the shoreline and began its wending descent. The verdant canopy below was dark, yet lit gold here and there when the sunlight broke through the gathering clouds.

A storm was coming, blighting the day, and this lent zeal to their haste. Revelling in his youth, Ravast smiled at hearing the panting breaths of the two men behind him. While Garelko could set a matching pace for the morning, at last the creaky ancient was failing. This was a worthy pace, proof that this day had seen the world change, utterly and irrevocably. The chest could swell to such largesse, and he counselled upon himself a few moments of sober intro-spection. Myriad were the responsibilities of leading the pack, and it would be well to exercise some humility in his new-found power.

But there was too much pleasure, for now, to contemplate tendering mercy unto his older comrades, with their wobbly legs and watery eyes. He quickened his pace.

'The tyrant unleashed!' gasped Garelko somewhere behind him.

'A storm draws upon us,' Ravast called out over a shoulder. 'The air is edged. Know you well this stillness. We must soon find shelter—'

'Rain!' shouted Tathenal. 'Rain and flood! Rain and flood and mudslides! Rain and flood and mudslides and—'

'Cease wailing!' Ravast hissed. 'Your caterwaul is a summons to the Lady of Thunder!'

'I but remind her of our mortal selves, pup!'

'I am pup no longer!'

'Hear him snarl,' Garelko said. 'Woof woof!'

Ravast spun round. Seeing their open grins, fury filled him with sudden, searing realization. 'You but mocked me!'

'You're all tuft and paws,' Garelko said with a sneer. 'Thought to knock the pair of us, did you? But who will guard you in the night? Perch there indeed, upon that lonely throne! I see your eyes shot through, hands trembling, limbs leaping, starting at every shadow!'

'He ages before us,' Tathenal added. 'Beneath the burden of universal spite and, before long, disdain. Palpitating shell of a man, once young, once so bold! Wisdom cannot be wrested, pup!'

Ravast made fists and raised them threateningly. 'Shall I break you both in half? Did I not defend the entire village against a Thelomen raiding party?'

'Oh dear,' laughed Garelko. 'Not that again!'

Shaking his head, Tathenal said, 'He'll crawl to us soon enough, belly to the dust, a whimper and curled tail—'

Ravast turned on him. 'You but await your ascent, Tathenal? Is that how it is? What have you promised Garelko here? A new mattress? What vows have you two exchanged, to keep me under your heels?'

'It will be a fine mattress,' Garelko said, and Tathenal nodded.

'Now, pup,' Garelko continued, 'I see a clearing below and to the right, if my useless eyes are not so useless, and is that not a glimpse of slated roof, pitched just so? A beckoning abode, a serendipitous shelter, but perhaps already occupied? Must we roust some hapless denizen? Three Thel Akai need plenty of room, after all.'

'This mockery will not be forgotten,' Ravast promised. 'But still, out with the weapons, in case indeed we need to shoo away some other. Garelko, take up that oafish mace and lead us on, as befits your claim of continued rule.'

Teeth bared, Garelko unslung the weapon and edged past Ravast. 'Ah, pup, take note and see how it's done.'

'Just don't bash down the door,' Tathenal advised.

Garelko frowned. 'Why not?'

'We must keep out the weather, of course. This is the purpose of doors and walls and so on.'

The eldest husband paused. 'You have a point. Suggestions?'

'You could knock,' said Tathenal.

'Knuckles to wood, aye, sound notion.' He shouldered his mace and glanced at Ravast. 'See, pup? A wise leader must learn the art of assuaging his underlings. Of course, such recourse had already occurred to me, being eldest and so on. Yet I remained silent, to give Tathenal leave to feel clever. This is the art of command.'

Tathenal stepped close to Garelko and grabbed the man's left ear. 'This is big – does it come off?'

'Aaii! That hurts!'

Releasing him, Tathenal gave Garelko a hard push. 'Get on with you, goat. I already hear the wind riding the treetops.'

Grumbling, Garelko set off down the trail. After a moment, Ravast and Tathenal followed.

There was a flavour, to be sure, that came with such a longstanding companionship, and although Ravast was the youngest and newest to the cause – that cause being the mutual loyalty necessary to survive marriage to Lasa Rook – he had little choice in acknowledging its value. This, of course, did not obviate the pleasures of one-upmanship. For the moment he had been bested, but in the very next instant Garelko had failed in pressing his newfound alliance with Tathenal, and this was pleasing.

He crept, now, alongside Tathenal, in the wake of bold Garelko. *Bold? The codger has never been bold in his over-long life! No, he is shamed to the fore, by none other than me! This is something to savour indeed, petty as it is! Oh, Lasa, do return with us and yield a lifetime of the inconsequential, I beg you!*

They reached the edge of the small clearing in time to see Garelko arrive at the door. Using the butt of his mace he hammered on the frame, as even a light tap from the Thel

Akai was likely to punch a hole through the door's flimsy planks. After a moment, Garelko turned. 'No one home—'

The door swung open and stepping into the gap was a Jaghut.

Rare was the Jaghut face that betrayed emotion, much less frustration, and yet even in the gathering gloom this man made his frustration woefully evident. 'Why,' he said in a half-snarl, 'a lone cabin in the deep forest, high upon a wild mountain, well off the trail – now in there lives a denizen inviting company! Worse yet, more Thel Akai! A night in which I anticipated sober study now lies in ruin, as I must weather the grunts, sighs and farts of three oversized guests, not to mention their likely appetites!' Then he stepped back and swept an arm in invitation. 'But do come in, you and your two huddled shadows in the thicket beyond. Welcome to the last refuge of Raest, and heed well in your manners the misery your arrival brings.'

Garelko glanced back and waved Ravast and Tathenal forward. He then sheathed his mace once more, ducked, and made his way into the cabin.

Tathenal made a faint snickering sound and Ravast jabbed the man in the ribs. 'None of that!' he hissed.

'Jaghut!' muttered Tathenal, still grinning. 'We shall pluck his strings the whole night, and leave such discord as to confound the man for years to come!' He clutched at Ravast's arm and pulled him close. 'This is just what we require!' he whispered. 'A sorry victim upon whom to gang up, and so further consolidate our solidarity! Pity this fool, Ravast, pity him!'

'I have pity for everyone in your company, Tathenal. Indeed, upon this journey I have cried myself to sleep every night.'

They continued on, reaching the doorway and then jostling a moment before Ravast stepped back to give his fellow husband leave to enter first.

The low rafters forced them all to the solid but narrow chairs Raest now pulled up around a modest table upon which the leavings of a meal still remained. The air was slightly sour with woodsmoke as the chimney was not drawing well, and there was the faint tang of something acrid, reminding Ravast of snake piss.

'A sup or two remains in the cauldron,' Raest said wearily. 'Sit, lest you bring down the roof and worse with your solid skulls wagging this way and that.'

'Kind sir,' Garelko said with a nod as he eased himself down in the chair. 'Ah, a perch for a single ham, better than none!'

'A body part that grows larger in the telling,' Raest said, moving over to a softer chair set up near the hearth. 'Come the night you three will have to cosy up here on the floor. It's dirt but at least it's dry.'

Tathenal rummaged in his pack, pulling out three tin bowls, and then, bent over, made his way to the cauldron, nodding to Raest as he drew near. 'Most generous, Raest of the Jaghut. The foulness of the weather and all that.'

His host did little more than grunt, reaching for a steaming tankard on the flagstone at his side.

'Do forgive us,' Tathenal continued as he ladled stew into the cups, 'for ruining your sober study. Still, I have heard you Jaghut are known to indulge in such things, perhaps, to excess? Consider this night, then, a moment of relief in your otherwise unleavened existence.'

'Relief? Oh yes, come the dawn and my seeing the last of you.'

Smiling, Tathenal collected up the three bowls and crabbed his way over to the table.

Ravast, already seated beside Garelko, spoke. 'Good Raest, we thank you for this. Hear that wind's howl – how it builds to rank fury. Mountain storms are the worst, are they not? Mmm, this stew smells wonderful, and this meat . . . what alpine ruminant fell to your snare or arrow, might I ask?'

'There is a lizard that lives in the scree, venomous and ill spirited. Some can grow as long as you are tall. Indeed, they have been known to eat goats, sheep and Jaghut children we don't like.'

Ravast paused with his spoon hovering over the bowl. 'This is a venomous lizard?'

'No of course not. You're eating mutton, you fool.'

'Ah, then, about that lizard?'

'Oh, only that I found one has made a home of my cottage. It now regards us from the rafters, directly above you, in fact.'

Ravast slowly looked up, to see cold, glittering, unblinking eyes fixed upon him.

'Hence my warning about you three taking your seats as quickly as possible,' Raest added. 'Such are the responsibilities of a host, trying as they might be.'

'I never much liked mutton,' confessed Garelko as he slurped.

'Which is insane,' snapped Tathenal, 'since we are sheep herders.'

'Yes, well, that's just it, isn't it? Two belly-bulging meals a day for how many decades? Each one knobby with mutton. That said, this meat here's gamey, suggesting a wild sheep rather than our gentled breeds of the north. Thus, both overly sweet and roiling pungent. My bowels shall be busy tonight.'

At the groans of both Ravast and Tathenal, Raest cursed under his breath and took another mouthful of his mulled wine.

'I remain curious, Raest,' Tathenal said after a moment or two, 'about this sober study of yours. Have you Jaghut not surrendered the future? What more remains to be contemplated?'

'Why, the past, of course. Of the present, best we say nothing.'

'But, kind sir, the past is dead.'

'That's rich, from you fools so eager to hasten through Hood's gate.'

Ravast interjected, 'Oh, sir, we do nothing of the sort! Indeed, we pursue our wife, with the very aim of bringing her back home before she strides through that sordid portal!'

'The pathetic moan of disappointing husbands the world over, no doubt. And is your wife buxom, sensuous in an indolent if slightly randy way? Golden-locked, blossom-cheeked, full-lipped and inclined to snoring?'

506

'Yes! All those things!'

'In the company of a Thel Akai brave, big enough to break you all into pieces? A true warrior of a man, wearing nothing but rags and yet freshly scarred and scabbed from head to toe?'

Garelko choked on his stew. Ravast realized that his jaw now hung, leaving his mouth gaping. He managed a dry swallow and then looked to both Garelko and Tathenal. 'Did you hear that? She's had her way with him! Torn his clothes to shreds! Clawed and bitten and scratched in her lustful frenzy! She's never done all that to any of us, damn her!'

'We are undone,' groaned Tathenal, lowering his head into his hands. 'Cuckolded, cast aside, flung away, dismissed! No match to young Hanako, Thief of Love! Hanako the Ravished, the Pawed and Clawed, the Smarting yet Smug!'

Raest observed them all, now sipping gently from his tankard. 'And the other one, dragon-fevered. Met them a few nights past, on my way here. We shared a fire. For this reason and only this reason, I do return the favour.'

It was a moment before Ravast frowned. 'Dragon-fevered? Is this some new southern plague, then?'

'Oh, a plague to come, I'm sure. He'll live or he won't. Mayhap you'll find a cairn beside the trail below. Or not. Or, just as likely, the stiff corpse of this Hanako, his throat lustfully gnawed right down to the vertebrae. All skin rent from his flesh, and a smile upon his ashen face.'

'You shatter our resolve,' moaned Garelko, pulling at what remained of his hair. 'Husbands? Should we perhaps consider returning home? Leaving her to . . . to him? I admit, I am defeated. Left behind, indeed. She's used us up, worn us out, and now blithely moves on – even you, Ravast, young as you are, not warrior enough for Lasa Rook! Aaii! We have lost the battleground between our wife's ample legs!'

Ravast found that he was trembling. Outside, the rain had begun, lashing down amidst trees that thrashed in the gale. Lightning flickered through cracks and joins; thunder followed. 'No, Garelko. We shall confront her! We shall bear witness to her face, to her confession, to that cruel triumphant glint in her eye.'

'A knife in my heart would be kinder!'

'A flood—'

'Enough about the flooding, Tathenal!' snapped Ravast. He thumped the tabletop, rattling the bowls. 'She would stride merrily into the realm of the rock-piles? Fine then, and three boots to her plush backside to send her on her way!'

'Ladies of Fury,' sighed Garelko, 'her plush backside!'

'This is all rather pathetic,' Raest said from his chair. 'But highly entertaining.'

At that moment thunder hammered the ground, so close as to seem to have come from just outside the cabin's door. Everything shook and with an alarmed hiss the venomous lizard fell from the rafters and landed heavily on the tabletop, where it writhed briefly before righting itself and glaring about, head snapping from one side to the other.

Garelko's hand shot out, grasping the creature by the snout. He stood and lifted the lizard, walking over to the door. 'Duck for this damned thing? Not likely.' Opening the door he flung the lizard out into the night. And then paused, staring out into the gloom.

'Close that door, please,' Raest said. 'You're scattering the embers here and these boots are almost new. Well, before they got soaked through.'

Garelko eased the door shut with a curiously gentle motion, and then, hunched over, made his way back to his chair. 'Alas, Raest,' he said, sighing as he sat. 'It seems you have another guest.'

'Is the lizard preparing to insist? No? Then who? I heard no knock.'

'Good thing, too,' Garelko said. 'Sir, there is a dragon in your yard.'

Raest set his tankard down. 'Only the wicked know peace.' With a grunt he arose, gathering up a dusty, stained leather cloak that hung on a peg to one side of the door. That it had been hanging there for a long time was evinced by the stretched nipple that remained when he shrugged it on, riding his left shoulder. Tathenal turned away, hand covering the lower half of his face as he fought against an unseemly guffaw.

Garelko dared but a single glance at his fellow husband, lest he too burst loose in unholy mirth. Instead, he pushed his chair back and half stood. 'Good sir, I will accompany you. Accosting a dragon seems perhaps dangerous. See how I am armoured and armed—'

Ravast added, 'Do join dear Raest, then. We've seen off one dragon already, although that was mostly me and my axe in its foot. I leave this one to you, old goat. Tathenal is welcome to the next one.' He reached for Garelko's unwanted bowl of unwelcome mutton stew.

'I require no armed escort,' Raest said, now collecting a leather cap, such as might be worn beneath a helm, which he pulled on with some effort, only to remove it immediately, reaching into the cap and withdrawing what looked like a mouse's nest of dry grasses. Emptied, the cap proved a better fit. Thus attired, the Jaghut opened the door once more and strode outside.

Garelko followed. 'Good sir,' he began, 'about that other dragon—'

'Kilmandaros has much to answer for,' Raest cut in.

Before them, filling most of the clearing, the dragon stood upon its four squat limbs in a weary crouch, its tattered wings half cocked in the manner of an exhausted bird. Its massive head was turned and glittering eyes regarded them.

Frowning, Garelko said to Raest, 'Sir, you take in vain the name of our sweet if fictional goddess mother.'

'Oh, she's real enough, Thel Akai. She's never liked dragons, you see, and it seems some of her prejudice now infuses her wayward children. You may well be in the habit of attacking them, but not here and not now. So listen well. Draw not that weapon. Make no threat. Be gentle in your regard – well, as gentle as that face of yours can manage. As for the conversation, leave that to me.'

'Conversation? Sir, with this wind I can barely hear you as it is.'

'Not with you, idiot. With the dragon.'

'I will delight in being the first Thel Akai to hear the slithery speech of a dragon, then!'

'You will hear her or not. The choice belongs to her, not you.'

'A female then! How can you tell?'

'Simple. She's bigger.' With that, Raest strode forward, Garelko falling in a step behind the Jaghut. They halted no more than five or six paces from the creature's snout. The dragon had lowered her head to bring it level with Raest. Rain streamed down the scales, the occasional flash of lightning sending reflected light shimmering across the pebbled hide.

When the dragon spoke, her voice filled Garelko's skull, cool and sweet. *A Jaghut and a Thel Akai. Yet not at each other's throats, from which I conclude that you have but just met, with the night still young.*

'You are of course welcome,' said Raest out loud, 'to wait out this storm in the faint shelter of my glade. Once the storm is past, however, I expect you to continue on to wherever it is you're going. It's not that I don't like dragons, you understand. Rather, I prefer solitude.'

*'Of course you do, Jaghut. What then of this Thel Akai?'*

'Gone in the morning as well. This one and his fellows still in the cabin.'

*'I found a slain brother, higher upon the trail.'*

Garelko cleared his throat. 'Alas, he surprised us.'

In that instant, the dragon's gaze acquired sharp intensity, fixing solely upon Garelko. *'Do you fear me vengeful, Thel Akai?'*

Garelko blinked water from his eyes. 'Fear?'

Raest said, 'Thel Akai haven't the wits to be frightened. That said, I'll have no fighting in my damned yard, is that understood?'

*'You are Jaghut. I am of no mind to challenge your temper. I am Sorrit, sister to Dalk, who now lies dead beside a lake, slain by Thel Akai. This realm proves dangerous.'*

'In this realm, Sorrit, resides Kilmandaros.'

510

'*Perhaps then I shall gather my kin, so that we may contemplate vengeance.*'

Raest shrugged. 'You will find her to the east, on the Azathanai Plain. She no longer guides her children, at least not with deliberation. The curse of being a god is how quickly one becomes bored. Not to mention frustrated, exasperated and, eventually, spiteful. But, to ease you somewhat, I have heard no word of Skillen Droe.'

'*Your news is welcome, Jaghut. Once this storm eases, I will indeed be on my way. As for you, Thel Akai, Dalk lusted for my blood. It is well that he is dead.*'

Garelko grunted in surprise, and then said, 'It is sad when siblings fall out. Families should be bastions of well-being, kindness and love.'

'*Is yours, Thel Akai?*'

'Well, it shall be, perhaps, once we hunt down our wayward wife, kill her lover, and drag the damned woman back home.'

Raest slapped Garelko on the upper arm. 'Let us go back inside. I'm getting wet.'

As they turned about, Garelko took the opportunity to pat the Jaghut on the left shoulder, not out of affection, but to flatten the stretched nipple in the leather, which had been driving him mad.

\*       \*       \*

There was little comfort to be found in being carried by Skillen Droe. K'rul hung like carrion in the taloned grip of his companion, with the choppy waves of the sea far below. Droe's leathery wings sent the chill air beating down, and the only relief came when they slipped into a thermal of rising warm air and the wings could stretch out motionless as they scythed forward.

Above them the sky remained cloudless and cerulean, the sun hanging directly overhead as the morning gave way to afternoon. As there didn't seem to be much to say, and speaking would require shouting, K'rul held his peace, while Skillen Droe self-evidently kept his thoughts to himself.

511

K'rul had begun dozing when he was jolted awake by a sudden rush of air. Skillen Droe had begun a sharp descent, and K'rul twisted round to look down.

A boat. It sat grounded upon a shoal, perhaps a hundred spans from a narrow sliver of coral-sand that could barely be called an island. There was nothing else in sight out to every horizon, only the endless swell of heaving waves.

There were two occupants in the craft. Only one was visible as the other was mostly hidden beneath a tattered grey parasol. K'rul looked down to see flaming red hair, artfully if loosely curled and piled high above a face turned up to the sun. That face was impossibly white, as if no rays could bronze it. The woman wore what looked like an evening gown, the silk a bright emerald green and the frills a deeper shade. Though the gown was intended to reach down to her ankles, she had drawn it up to expose her white thighs.

The boat had two benches, one fore and one aft. In between these was a broad-bellied gap that had once held a step-mast, but the step, sail and mast were nowhere to be seen. The woman sat at the bow, while her companion with the parasol occupied the stern.

Skillen Droe elected to land in the gap between them, his wings beating fiercely for a moment before catching an updraught that allowed him to hover briefly, sufficient to set K'rul down before he settled his own weight amidst a crunch and groan of wood, and then Skillen folded his wings and hunched down.

The boat was well and truly aground. K'rul straightened his clothes before facing the woman and bowing slightly. 'Cera Planto, it has been too long since I last looked upon your lovely self.' Glancing at the huge, iron-skinned, tusked man in the shade of the parasol, K'rul nodded. 'Vix, I trust you are well.'

Vix replied with a single grunt, his one eye glittering.

Cera Planto fanned herself, 'Always the sweetest compliments from you, K'rul, but do tell me, what on earth has happened to Skillen Droe?'

'A new guise for an old self,' K'rul replied. 'Should he

choose to speak, his words will come in scents and flavours in the mind. Peculiar, but affecting.'

'Oh, I doubt he'll have words for us, since that last unfortunate incident.' Her broad, flaring cheekbones bore an unnatural flush amidst powdered white, and the kohl surrounding her deep blue eyes and fading up to her eyebrows glistened metallic green. 'Are there not those among us, no matter what cast or credence, for whom mishap circles with persistent perfidy? So I see Skillen Droe, forever abuzz with ill chance.'

As if in reply, Skillen Droe settled lower in the craft, hooking his wings to offer himself shade, and then tilted his snouted head forward, opaque lids rising up to cover his eyes.

K'rul sighed. 'Well, he has been flying us for some time.'

'Then you have satisfied his need to feel useful,' Cera replied. 'Always the considerate one, you.'

'I am sure,' said K'rul, 'once he has rested, he will be happy to dislodge your craft.'

'Oh, Vix can do that any time. He's just being stubborn.'

'Not half as stubborn as you,' Vix growled.

'We shall see about that, won't we?'

'You have left spawn among the mortals,' K'rul said to Vix. 'They name themselves Trell, and make war with the Thelomen.'

Vix reached up to straighten his thin, wispy moustache, ensuring that the long black braids properly flanked his broad, tusked mouth. 'I am profligate, to be sure. As for war, well, of course, why ever not?'

'But you claim the Thelomen as your spawn as well,' K'rul pointed out.

'Just so. They actually share the same god. Me. And yet in my name they unleash hate and venom upon each other. Is that not amusing? Mortals are petty and vicious, unthinking and spiteful, inclined to stupidity and wilfully ignorant. I do so love them.' He then made the habitual gesture K'rul had seen countless times before: reaching up to lightly brush the stitches sealing shut the lids of his left eye. 'I contemplate a third breed, an admixture of Thelomen, Trell and Dog-Runner, whom I shall name Barghast. I expect they will war against everyone.'

'Dog-Runner? I would think Olar Ethil might object to that, Vix.'

'I piss in her fire. See how she objects to that.'

Sighing again, K'rul settled into a cross-legged position, facing Cera Planto once more. 'And what have you been up to, my dear?'

'We thought to explore an Azath House.'

'In a boat?'

'Unsuccessfully. But no matter. Eventually, Vix will lose this war of obstinacy and send us on our way once more. I foresee innumerable adventures in the offing.' She collected up a small wooden carrying case, setting it on her lap before unclasping the lid and opening it. 'In the meantime, I found a most iridescent breed of beetle on a tropical island, and had Vix collect as many of them as possible.' She drew out a mortar and pestle, and then a bronze jar. 'The wings, when finely ground and mixed with a drop of beeswax and olive oil, make for a most delightful kohl, don't you think?'

'Very enticing,' K'rul said.

'But you look pale. Decidedly too masculine, too, but never mind that. Almost bloodless, one might say. Have you been up to no good again?'

'I have given freely of my power, Cera, not to any breed of mortal, but to all breeds of mortal. My blood swirls in the cosmos, swims to unmindful currents.'

Her deep blue eyes had narrowed and she now regarded him with vague disappointment. 'Did you hear that, Vix? And you boasted of profligacy.'

Behind K'rul, Vix said, 'Beware the Thelomen finding potent magic. Hmm. I shall have to pay them a visit, assuming once more the role of vengeful god.'

'Do not wait too long,' K'rul said to the tusked Azathanai behind him, 'lest they do the swatting down.'

'What a mess you've made,' Vix said.

Shrugging, K'rul said, 'It's done. But now, with Skillen

514

at my side, we set out to force some order upon the maelstrom.'

'How?' Cera Planto asked.

'Dragons.'

'Oh,' said Cera. 'Poor Skillen Droe!'

*     *     *

At last the mountains were behind Hanako and Lasa Rook, and ahead lay a level plain where even the forest dwindled, giving way to tufts of wiry grasses that looked sickly clinging to the salty clay. Hanako staggered woodenly beneath Erelan Kreed's slack weight, while at his side Lasa Rook hummed a children's song the words of which Hanako barely remembered, only that it was a tale of some orphan – and how many of those were there, anyway? – stealing fruit from some orchard, and some old witch who lived in an apple tree. One night the lad reached up and plucked the wrong fruit. *Don't mess with witches!* ran the refrain, *They're rotten to the core!*

Lasa Rook stopped humming abruptly, and then said, 'Hanako of the Scars, your burden is exhausting you, leaving you little energy or attention to lavish upon me, and you well know how I enjoy being lavished. The situation, darling, is unsupportable.'

'Perhaps,' said Hanako, 'if you could carry your own bedroll, and this cooking gear—'

'Really? You would ask that of me? Why, if you were one of my husbands . . . but no, this time, in your ignorance, I shall forgive you. There is a force in the world – in all worlds, no doubt – like invisible fingers, ever plucking and pulling us down. Thus, as the years draw on, the face sags, the breasts too, and the belly and all places where the flesh bulges. It follows, sweet boy, that one must endeavour to diminish such burdens as best as one can. See this youthful visage? It remains so precisely because I have husbands to carry everything. Now, here you are, in their stead. If misery attends you, it is because you are yet to claim your reward. I am not to blame if you flatly refuse my appreciation!'

515

Hanako mumbled a mostly inarticulate apology.

They continued on, in uncomfortable silence, until they almost stumbled upon a lone figure before them. The man was seated cross-legged on the hard-packed clay, his back to them. An empty wooden bowl was at his side. He was gaunt, wizened and mostly hairless, and as Hanako and Lasa drew up to either side of him, he spoke without opening his eyes or shifting his head. 'I believe the universe is expanding.'

The two Thel Akai halted, Hanako groaning as he let the body of Erelan Kreed slip down from his shoulder and into his arms, and then, as he crouched, on to the ground.

'There is a manner,' the stranger continued, 'in which the soul can free itself of the flesh, and so wing swift as thought into the reaches of space. I have been contemplating this, as I dined. As one does. And it has occurred to me that the expanding universe is nothing more and nothing less than mortal souls in eternal flight. And that, should you somehow appear at the very edge of this ever-expanding creation, you would find the very first soul, impossibly ancient, so far along on its journey from its mortal flesh that not even dust remains of that body. We must be grateful to that soul, don't you think? For . . . all of this.'

A moment later, the old man tilted slightly for a brief moment of flatulence, and then settled back once more. 'Beans, but no rice.'

Hanako and Lasa exchanged a look, and then Hanako bent down and collected up Erelan Kreed once more. They walked past the old man, leaving him to his contemplation.

Some time later, Lasa Rook hissed and shook her head. 'Azathanai.'

# THIRTEEN

'HE HAS FRECKLES,' KORYA SAID. 'ON HIS ARMS.' Arathan looked up from the vellum. 'Do you see this? What I'm scribing on, Korya Delath? It's vellum. I don't know where he gets it from, but it must be rare. And expensive, and should I be startled into making an error—'

She stepped inside, letting the old goat-skin curtain fall back to fill the doorway. 'Why aren't you in the Tower of Hate?'

Sighing, Arathan set down the stylus. 'I needed somewhere without interruptions. Gothos was getting too many visitors. Everyone's com-plaining. Though it has nothing to do with Gothos, they all seem to think he has some influence with Hood. But he doesn't. Who has freckles?'

She strolled closer, eyeing the decrepit furnishings, the arcane symbols scratched into the plastered walls. 'Young, sweet Ifayle. A Dog-Runner. He wants to sleep with me.'

Arathan returned to his transcribing. 'That's nice. I hear they have lice and ticks and fleas. Maybe those weren't freckles at all, just welts from all the bites and things.'

'They were freckles. And he's clean enough. They use oils on their bodies. Drowns everything, and highlights the red in the hairs on his arms – they glisten like gold.'

'You really like his arms, don't you?'

'They're strong, too.'

'So go roll in the grass with him, then!'

'Maybe I will!'

'Better do it now, since presumably this Ifayle's here to march with Hood.'

'March? Where? When? There's a reason Hood's not packed up his tent – he can't figure out where to go!'

Arathan scowled down at the vellum, resumed his work. 'Don't be absurd. He's just waiting.'

'For what?'

'More people are still coming in—'

'A mere trickle, and most of them are undecided. More curious than anything else. People like spectacle, and that's all this is. Vapid, useless, pointless spectacle! Hood's joke, and it's on all of you.' She walked over to the etched wall. 'What's all this about?'

Arathan shrugged. 'It's not Jaghut script. Gothos said something about a mad Builder.'

'Builder?'

'The ones who make Azath Houses.'

'No one makes Azath Houses, you fool. That's the whole point, the whole mystery of them. They just appear.'

'What's that in your hand?'

'This? An acorn. Why? Do you have a problem with it?'

'Well, there are no oaks here.'

'So? Anyway, the Azath Houses just grow up out of the ground.'

He leaned back. 'Have you seen this happen?' he asked.

'Haut explained it. And their yards are hungry.'

'What does that mean?'

'Just what I said. Their yards are hungry. Haut's own words. I have a good memory, you know. Better than most people.'

'So you don't know what it means either. Hungry yards. Sounds . . . ominous.' Abruptly he began cleaning his stylus, and then he stoppered the bottle of ink.

'What are you doing? I thought you were busy.'

'There is an Azath House at the western edge of the ruins. When Omtose Phellack was a thousand years old, it sprang up one night, upsetting the Jaghut no end. But as none could get inside, and it was proof against all magic, they decided to ignore it.' He collected up his cloak. 'I think I'll go take a look.'

'I'm coming with you.'

'Ifayle's freckles won't like that.'

'You do know that they won't let you go, Arathan. The Jaghut. You're hiding, anyway. From what? Probably a woman. It was a woman, wasn't it? People have said things.'

'Who? Never mind. No one here knows anything about it. You're just making all this up.'

'Who was she? What did she do to you?'

'I'm going now,' he said, stepping past her and yanking the curtain aside.

Korya followed, feeling unaccountably pleased with herself. They emerged from the small hovel that had once been some sort of store. The breeze was cool but not cold, and an unseasonal thaw softened the air. As they set out, she saw how many of the long-abandoned buildings were now occupied once more. Blue-skinned Ilnap had formed enclaves, although there was nothing festive in their efforts to establish some sort of community, and more often than not they found themselves glowering across at bands of Dog-Runners encamped on the other side of the street, who were in the habit of treating abodes as if they were caves, the rubbish piling up in front of the gaping doorways.

Before long, however, she and Arathan left the inhabited reaches of the dead city behind, making their way down barren, silent streets. Here and there a squat tower had tumbled and the broken stone spilled out into passageways, blocking their progress and forcing them to seek out the narrower alleys threading through overgrown gardens.

'Imagine,' said Arathan, 'just abandoning all of this. Imagine, a simple argument from one Jaghut, from Gothos, bringing down an entire civilization. One wouldn't think such things possible. Could the same happen to us Tiste? Could someone just step forward and argue us out of existence?'

'Of course not,' Korya replied. 'We prefer our arguments messy, ugly, with plenty of spilled blood.'

He glanced sharply across at her. 'More news of the civil war?'

'Deniers came into the camp yesterday. Hunters who'd come home to their forest camps to find their mates slaughtered. The children too. Those hunters have lost their black skin. They're now grey, as grey as the Dog-Runners when they smear themselves in ash.' She shrugged. 'Rituals of mourning, only with the Deniers, it's permanent.'

Arathan fell silent, as if considering her words, as they worked their way through the ruins. They had moved past the squatters now, and the solemnity of a discarded city hung heavy in the still air.

'I have to go back,' Korya said.

'Back? To what? You were made a hostage. You're not yet of the proper age to be released.'

'Haut's going with Hood, whatever that means. He's been looking to hand me off to some other master, or tutor, or whatever title fits. But I won't go. I'm not interested in listening to old men or, even worse, old women, and all their tired, worn-out ideas.'

'You're quick to reject the wisdom of your elders, Korya.'

'And you waste your life away scribbling useless confessions from a suicidal Jaghut too weak-kneed to actually go through with it. In case you haven't been paying attention, sorcery is now among us, wild currents of magic. All you need to do is reach for it.'

'And have you?'

She frowned. 'Haut tells me my aspect awaits elsewhere. It's why he made me a Mahybe.'

'Oh? And what is your, uh, aspect?'

'Kurald Galain. Darkness. The sorcery of Mother Dark herself.'

Ahead, seemingly standing alone, oddly distinct from all the hovels surrounding it, was a stone house with a peaked roof and a squat corner tower. A low wall marked the yard and a gaping gateway the entrance on to the path. 'That doesn't make sense,' said Arathan. 'She doesn't grant anyone the gift of sorcery.'

'Doesn't matter. I'll just take what I need. It's important. Haut explained everything. Blood has been spilled. Hood's wife slain by an Azathanai, corrupting all the sorcery K'rul unleashed. That needs answering, by a purifying form of sorcery, what Haut calls *elemental*. And the magic of Dark is elemental.'

'And Light?'

'The same.'

'So Urusander and his legion have a right to the power they seek. A just cause for this civil war.' When she said nothing, he gestured towards the stone house. 'There it is. An Azath House.'

'Doesn't matter if the cause is just, if the way of achieving it is a crime.'

Arathan grunted. 'Gothos would agree with you. In fact, something of that sentiment is at the core of his argument against civilization. The crimes of progress, of every self-serving rationale for destroying something in the name of creating something new, presumably better. He says a culture's value system is in fact a shell game. It changes in the name of convenience. The stone is under one of the shells, meaning all the others are hollow, and therein lies the hypocrisy of a civilization's pronounced set of values. Even the weight of those values – those stones – changes depending on the whims of the one running the game.' After a moment of silence following his words, he glanced at Korya, to find her staring back intently. 'What?'

'It's easy to find flaws. It's much harder to find solutions.'

'That's because there aren't any. Solutions, I mean. We are imperfect creatures, and the society we create cannot help but reflect those imperfections, or even exaggerate them. The spark of tyranny resides in every one of us. From this, we find tyrannical despots terrorizing entire nations. We are prone to jealousy, and from that, armies invade, lands are stolen and the bodies of victims are stacked like cordwood. We lie to hide our crimes and for this to work, historians need to glide over past atrocities. And so it goes, on and on. In the end, honesty is the enemy of us all. We wear civilization like a proud mask. But it's still a mask.'

'Gothos deserves a kick between the legs,' Korya said, even as she faced the Azath House and set off towards the gateway. Something inside her had abruptly closed up, like the slamming shut of some hidden door.

Arathan saw the sudden flatness come to her eyes, but said nothing, even as he felt a faint pang of something that might be regret. As she approached the Azath House, he followed. 'He'd not disagree with you.'

'That's no consolation.'

'Perhaps not.'

'And this is why I'm done listening to old men. Hope dies to ten thousand small cuts, and these men around us, Arathan, they are most terribly scarred.' She shook her head, her hair, grown long, shimmering upon her shoulders. 'Civilization is all about restraint. That's what laws and rules are for. To check our more venal impulses—'

'Until those laws and rules are twisted around them, becoming a travesty of justice.'

'He's made you old before your time,' Korya said. 'He shouldn't have done that.'

'Flawed and imperfect, even the Lord of Hate.'

'I think I'm going to give up on you, Arathan. Go on, join Hood and Haut and Varandas and all the rest. But it seems to me, of all the enemies you might choose, death is the simplest. So, take your easy way out, and good luck to you.'

As she turned away, Arathan said, 'Wait! What about the Azath House? It's here, you're only steps from the path! Did you come all this way just to turn round again? I thought you wanted to explore it?'

Korya hesitated, and then shrugged. 'Fine, since I'm here.'

She passed through the gateway, on to the flagstoned path. Arathan followed her, remaining a step behind.

The yard to either side of the wending path was a tangled mess of sinkholes and humped mounds. A few small, scraggly trees surmounted the mounds, their branches twisted and bearing only a few of the last season's leaves, wrinkled and black. The path made a sinuous approach to the two stone steps and narrow landing at the foot of a heavy, wooden door.

'That looks solid,' Arathan observed, eyeing the door. 'When did it . . . appear?'

'Gothos said a thousand years ago.'

'That door isn't a thousand years old, Arathan. Maybe a hundred, or even less.'

He shrugged. 'The fittings are iron, blackened but no rust. And that doesn't make sense, either, does it?'

All of the windows fronting the house were shuttered, again with wood, and no light leaked from between the weathered slats.

'No one lives here,' Korya said. 'It feels . . . dead.'

Stepping past her, Arathan walked up to the door. He made a fist and thumped on the thick planks of wood. There was no echo, no reverberation. He might as well have been pounding on a solid wall. Glancing back over a shoulder, he saw Korya still on the path, one hand held palm-up, and in that palm sat the acorn. There was speculation in her study of the yard to one side.

Arathan drew a breath, minded to voice a warning, when with an offhand gesture she tossed the acorn into the yard.

'Oh,' Arathan managed.

Where the acorn had landed amidst yellowed grasses, the earth suddenly heaved, rising and then slumping over, building a mound of steaming black soil.

Behind Arathan the stones of the Azath House groaned. Spinning round, he saw grit trickling like rain down the pitted façade. An instant later Korya joined him, her expression slightly wild.

From the fresh mound in the yard a tree was now growing, branches twisting out from a stunted trunk that visibly thickened. Roots snaked out to grip the mound.

The house groaned again, and Arathan heard a dull click. Turning, he reached for the latch. The door opened, and at a gentle push swung soundlessly inward, revealing a short corridor flanked by alcoves. The light spilling in reached no further.

'The tree is trembling,' Korya said, her voice unsteady and faintly breathless. 'As if it's in pain.'

'What was that acorn?' Arathan asked, even as he edged closer to the door's threshold.

'A Finnest.'

'What's that?'

She licked her lips. 'Lots of things. A place in which to hide your power away, or a piece of your soul. Even a secret you want to keep from yourself.' She hesitated, and then added, 'Sometimes it's a prison.'

'A prison?'

'There was a god inside,' she suddenly said. 'Ancient, forgotten. Someone shed blood in the camp and summoned it. That was a mistake, but Haut – me and Haut – we trapped it.'

'You and Haut, was it?'

'You saw! I had the acorn, not him, right? Yes, the two of us!'

The tree was now as tall as Arathan, but twisted, nightmarish, bleeding sap from swollen fissures in its trunk, its branches shivering incessantly. 'That's an angry god,' he said.

'Doesn't matter. It's not going anywhere.'

'Are you sure? I'd say it was fighting to get out, and whatever is trying to hold it down is in trouble. What I want to know is, what made you throw it into the yard?'

'I don't know. It just felt right.'

One of the larger branches split with a sharp crack. Arathan took Korya by the shoulder and pulled her with him as he crossed the threshold. Once clear he shut the door. The latch settled into place.

The darkness slowly faded.

'Why did you do that?' Korya asked. 'Now we're stuck in here.'

'I doubt it,' he replied. 'See, the lock is a simple one: just lift it clear and the door opens.'

'Fine, but who opened it the first time?'

Haut found Hood at the meagre hearth with its illusionary
fire, the cold flames flickering in the gloom. Squatting down
opposite, he spoke in a low tone. 'We have a problem.'

'I know.'

'We pretty much killed that Azath House, and what's left
has been dying for centuries. Whatever that elder spirit was,
it's a powerful bastard, too powerful for that old yard.'

'Nine of our kin fed that yard,' Hood muttered, his hands
hovering above the flames. 'None made it back out, no matter
what we did to that house.'

'That was long ago, Hood, when it still had some spine.'

'Your thoughts?'

'Summon a Builder.'

Hood bared his tusks in a bitter grin. 'You test my temper,
captain.'

'Then what do you suggest?'

'The Seregahl.'

Haut squinted across at Hood. 'Not company you'd
willingly keep, then.'

'Sheer arrogance has gifted them godly status. They grate.
They pall. They earn endless derision from the other Toblakai,
and fierce enmity from the Thelomen. Worse yet, they have
forgotten the art of bathing.'

'Set them a challenge, will you?'

'The best outcome is they succeed even as they fail. I imagine our nine lost kin will oblige me in welcoming them to the
yard.'

'And the dying house?'

'Summon your Builder if necessary, Haut. I doubt it'll rush
here, eager as a pup.'

Haut continued staring at Hood for a few moments longer,
and then with a sigh he straightened. 'She's a precipitous
child, I'll grant you. Yet—'

'Her instincts were sound.'

'Just so,' Haut said, nodding.

'Send the Seregahl to me, then,' Hood said. 'They deem

themselves worthy of my vanguard? Empty words. I will see them tested.'

'In the Azath yard?'

'In the Azath yard.'

'Hood, you will be the death of us all.'

Hood barked a laugh. 'I will indeed, Haut. Do you now hesitate?'

'I need to find her a minder.'

'No you don't. Arathan will be with her. Together, they will return to Kurald Galain.'

Haut scowled. 'Prophecy now, too?'

'No,' Hood replied, 'I will send them on their way home by a more prosaic pronouncement. My boot to their backsides.'

\*     \*     \*

The nameless leader of the Seregahl clawed through his tangled beard, forcing out twigs and old flecks of food that drifted down on to his chest. 'A voice roars in challenge,' he said in a caustic rumble. 'It aches in the skull. In my skull. In the skulls of my companions. We are not like the other Toblakai. We have come into power. Others of our kind worship us, and rightly so. The Thelomen and Thel Akai fear us—'

There was a snort from just beyond the pallid light of Hood's hearth.

As one, the eleven Seregahl turned at the sound, various visages twisting in various ways. Haut stifled a sigh and then grunted. 'Don't mind her,' he said to the Seregahl leader. 'A curious Thel Akai. Seems in the habit of following you lot around, in case you haven't noticed.'

The leader bared his yellow teeth. 'Oh, we have noticed, captain. Though she'd rather hide like a coward in the gloom.'

The vague, hulking figure in the darkness seemed to shift slightly. 'I but await one of you to wander off,' she replied. 'Then I would challenge that one, and kill him. Instead, you find courage only in your pack. I name you bullies and cowards.'

Haut rubbed at his face and swung round to face the Thel Akai woman. 'Enough, Siltanys Hes Erekol. Choose another time for such challenges. Hood has need of these Seregahl.'

'Yet Hood sits there and says nothing.'

'Nonetheless.'

After a long moment, the Thel Akai named Erekol made a motion that might have been a shrug, and then stepped back into the gloom, and moments later was gone from all sight.

The Seregahl leader was still grinning. 'Many are our challengers. We dispense with each in our own time.'

'Ah,' murmured Hood from where he sat by his fire, 'then it is true, then, what Siltanys Hes Erekol had to say. Unwilling to disassemble this glowering pack so delighting in its strut and raised hackles.'

The leader scowled. 'We are an army. An elite company. We fight as one. Let Erekol collect up more of her kind and then choose the field. We will slay her and every fool with her. But you, Hood, what reason this mocking and insult? Have you not proclaimed us your vanguard? Have you not recognized our ferocity?'

'I have doubts,' Hood replied. 'Many formidable warriors have now joined my . . . legion. Many are worthy of taking the vanguard.'

'Gather them up,' the Seregahl leader growled. 'In sufficient number to stand before me and my kin. This will answer your doubts.'

'At the loss of too many worthy allies,' Hood said, shaking his head. 'Did not Captain Haut speak to you of this ancient enemy? Did you not acknowledge the irritation of its endless roaring in your skulls? I would send you to it, and charge you with silencing the vile creature. Show me your prowess in this manner, Seregahl, and the van is yours.'

The leader grunted, drawing from his back his massive twin-bladed axe. 'This we can do!'

Haut cleared his throat. 'Very well then, my friends. If you will follow me?'

'Lead on, captain!'

\* \* \*

527

When the echoes of the troop's footfalls finally fell away, the Thel Akai woman reappeared, striding up to face Hood with the hearth between them. Her broad, wide-cheeked face was flat and colourless in the reflected light. 'The games you indulge in, Hood.'

'Ah, Erekol, do join me, whilst I explain the lancing of boils.'

'I could do that as easily as some ancient hoary god trapped under a tree. One at a time, as I said.'

Hood studied her for a long moment. 'I know something of your tale. Your . . . reasons. But have you not a surviving son?'

'Left in the care of others.'

'Are you here in the name of vengeance alone, or do you seek to join my legion?'

'Your legion? Your mob of fools, you mean.'

'I have not yet decided on a title.'

She laughed, and then settled into a squat. 'Vengeance,' she said. 'The Seregahl spring their cowardly ambushes, and Thel Akai husbands weep. I'm fed up with their shit, and all those obnoxious proclamations. Thus, I am here to kill your vaunted vanguard, and yet you defy me again and again. What am I to make of that?'

'Where is your son?'

'Aboard a stout ship.'

'In what sea?'

'West. They ply the Furrow Strait, hunting dhenrabi.'

'Near the High King's lands, then.'

She shrugged. 'Thel Akai fear no one.'

'Unwise. The High King has set his protection upon the dhenrabi, and their breeding waters.'

'My son is safe. What matters it to you, Hood?'

'I grieve estrangement, Erekol.'

'I am more than just a mother. I am the chosen huntress of my tribe. And so I am here, hunting.'

'The pack fears you and will never give you the chance to kill its members one by one.'

'They will make a mistake. I goad them.'

528

'They are more likely to come at you in their pack, and so bring you down that way. And accusations of cowardice rarely sting the victors.'

'What do you suggest?'

'Go to the Azath House. That will be a mess, I'm sure. Some Seregahl will be taken. The yard needs them. The house needs their blood, their power.'

'Who resides within?'

'There is no one,' Hood answered. 'None for five hundred years.'

'What fate befell the guardian?'

'We killed him. Yes, a mistake. Precipitous. Regrettable. Should I meet him beyond the Veil of Death, I will apologize.'

'By your hand, then?'

'No. But that is of no matter. The Jaghut may be singular, but we can never deny that we are also one, and responsibility must be shared in all things. As Gothos would tell you, civilization plays its game of convenient evasion. Us. Them. Meaningless borders, arbitrary distinctions. We Jaghut are a people. As a people we must share the full host of our collective crimes. Anything else is a conceit, and a lie.'

Erekol shook her head, even as she straightened. 'I will accept your offer, and make my own ambush, when they least desire it.'

'I wish you luck, Erekol.'

She moved away a step, and then paused and glanced back. 'What vision has found you, and what has it to do with my son?'

'I see him in the High King's shadow. That is not a good place to be.'

'Whence this new gift of prophecy, Hood?'

'I am not certain,' Hood confessed. 'But it may be this. I draw ever closer to death's veil, and its flavour is, I think, timeless. Past, present, future, all one.'

'Death,' she muttered, 'like a people.'

Hood tilted his head, startled by her words, but said nothing as she walked away.

The fire flickered on, colder now, duller, a thing leached of all life. Regarding it, the Jaghut nodded – mostly to himself. Things were coming along nicely, he concluded. He reached out with his hands once more, to steal more of what remained of the fire's heat.

*       *       *

'Unlocked door or not, Korya, there's no one here.'

They stood in a sitting room made cosy by thick rugs, a settee and two chairs that flanked a stone fireplace where embers ebbed like dimming eyes. The air was warm but stale, lit too much by the feeble hearth.

'These rugs,' said Korya, staring down at what was beneath her feet. 'Wild myrid wool, twisted raw, the strands knotted. Dog-Runner, not Jaghut.'

Arathan grunted. 'Didn't know the Dog-Runners wove anything but grasses and reeds.'

'Yes,' she replied, 'you didn't know. But then, you've not been in their camps. You've not sat round their fires, cockles cooking in the ashes, watching the women make stone tools, watching the boys learn the knots and using spindles and combs – the skills they'll need to make the nets and snares they use to trap animals and birds, for when they all begin their year of wandering.'

'A year of wandering? All alone? I like the sound of that.'

She sniffed, at what he wasn't sure, and then walked over to the fireplace. 'Who's been feeding this, I wonder?'

'Korya, we've explored every room. The outer door unlocked by itself, because the house wanted us inside.'

'And why would it do that?' she asked. 'You said the Jaghut couldn't get in. You said they spent centuries trying.'

'To keep us safe, from what you did outside, with that acorn.'

'It was an old god. Forgotten. The Ilnap mages didn't know what they were doing. But why should an Azath House care about us?'

They both turned at a strange shuffling sound from the doorway that led to the main inner corridor. A ghostly figure

530

loomed suddenly in the entranceway. A Dog-Runner, his hair so blond as to be almost colourless, his tawny beard tangled and looking like a tuft of dead grass growing from his chinless jaw. The eye sockets beneath the heavy ridge of his brow were empty pits. A hole had been carved into his broad chest, where his heart should have been. What remained was withered and dry, ribs snapped and jutting from the wound.

'Apparition,' whispered Korya, 'forgive us this intrusion.'

'The dead are unforgiving,' the ghost replied in a thin voice. 'Which is, I suppose, why we are known to be such miserable company. Beg no pardon, plead no indulgence, pray no favour and seek no blessing. Take pleasure in my noticing you, if you must, or let loose a blood-curdling scream. I care neither way.'

Arathan sighed, and then straightened. 'What do you want of us, Dog-Runner?'

'What all old men want, living or dead. An audience for our life's story. Sharp interest we can dull, curiosity we can deplete. An opportunity to dismember your very will to live, if possible. Hearken then to this wisdom, if you would hold to the conceit of being worthy of it.'

Arathan glanced at Korya. 'And you willingly sat around the campfire in company like this?'

She scowled. 'Well, the ones outside aren't dead yet. I'd think dying changes how you think.'

'Or simply exaggerates what was already there.'

'I am now being ignored,' observed the Dog-Runner ghost. 'This, too, is typical. I was once a Bonecaster, a foolish man among chattering women, defenceless against their barbs until respect was earned in the manner they expected. Namely, a man's legendary stubbornness. Although, between you and me, I was more addled than stubborn. What is perceived is rarely the truth, and what is true is only rarely perceived. Between the two, upon which is one best advised to rely? Some delusions, after all, are comforting. While truths, alas, are mostly unpleasant.'

'How came you to this Azath House?' Arathan asked.

'By the front door.'

'Who killed you?'

'Jaghut. In the manner of fatal exploration, as they sought to determine all that was magical within me. Of course, there was nothing magical within me, barring life's spark, which all mortals possess. Said exploration quenched that spark, an outcome I predicted at the top of my lungs to no avail, even as the knife descended. When next you see Jaghut, tell them this from Guardian Cadig Aval: "I told you so." If brave, you may add "idiots" to my message.'

'Oh,' said Arathan, 'I'll do that for you. It would be my pleasure, in fact. Nor do I think Gothos would—'

'Gothos? I've been looking for him, here in the realms of the dead, since he said he was going to kill himself. Yet still he lives? Typical. You can't depend on anyone.'

'He's composing a suicide note.'

'I got there first, as you would have discovered had you accepted my invitation to hear me confess my life's story. For are not all such tales nothing more than suicide notes? A list of deeds, crimes and regrets, loves and still more regrets – in fact an endless litany of regrets, come to think on it. Never mind. It has been some time since I last had anyone else with whom to converse. In the interval, I find that I am a poor audience to my own thoughts. Too much catcalling and derision.'

Arathan stepped closer. 'A moment ago, sir, you spoke of realms of the dead. They're what we're looking for, you see, with Hood and his legion—'

'What now? Is there no refuge left you living won't despoil? I happen to be quite fond of the realms of the dead. None have reason to argue there, or pose or preen. No one is obsessed with saving face, or stung to stupidity by brainless pride. No grudges to hold. Nothing left worth the gleeful gush of spite. Even vengeance proves laughable. Imagine that, friends. Laughable. Ha ha ha.'

'Mother save us,' muttered Korya, turning back to the fire.

'One lost,' the ghost observed smugly. 'And one still to go. Now then, young man, do offer me another mortal conceit I can happily dismantle. There is no end to what I can prove to be pointless in this miserable thing you call your life.'

'Why bother?' Arathan asked the ghost.

Cadig Aval tilted his head. 'Well, you have a point there. Excuse me.' With that, he vanished.

After a moment, Arathan turned to Korya. 'It's said that Azath Houses possess guardians. This Bonecaster was one such guardian, until the Jaghut killed him. But did you hear what he said about realms of the dead? Proof that such places exist! I will speak to Hood about this.'

Korya sneered at him. 'Don't expect that ghost to hold open the gate for you and the rest. Seems the dead prefer their realms to be empty of life.'

'It doesn't matter if we're not welcome, or wanted. This is war, after all.'

'Weren't you listening? The dead have no need to fight, no reason worth fighting for.'

'So we'll give them one.'

'Some woman jangled your jewels and stole your heart. That happens. It's not a good enough reason to abandon the living world. Have you not noticed? Hood's army has raised a standard of grief. But that grief is real, and serious. It's the kind that crushes everything inside. In a way, they're all already dead, or most of them, anyway. Especially Hood. But you, Arathan? Get over it. Get over yourself!'

'And what about Haut, your keeper? Or Varandas? It's not grief that's brought them to Hood, is it?'

'No. Just loyalty. And a sick sense of humour.'

'But you're not laughing.'

She crossed her arms. 'I should have gone with the Jheleck hunters. Learned how to rut like a dog. And roll around on dead things. But I missed my chance. Regrets, like the ghost talked about. Who knows, maybe I'll run into them on my way back to Kurald Galain. Worse things could—'

'Did you hear that?'

The echoes of thunder reached them, and a moment later the walls groaned. The embers in the fireplace flared suddenly. Fierce heat gusted from the hearth, forcing both Korya and

Arathan back a step, and then another. Sweat beaded the walls, and began trickling down.

The ghostly guardian reappeared in the entranceway. 'See what you've done? More company. And me dead. What's worse, no matter what the house thinks, you two won't do as my replacement. Too restless, too eager to see the world. Too hopeful by far to be custodians to a prison.'

Frowning, Arathan approached the Bonecaster ghost. 'A prison? Is that what these Azath Houses are? Then who built them?'

'Now the whole yard's awake. It's all getting ugly. Stay here.' The ghost disappeared again.

Arathan turned to Korya. 'A prison.'

'The Jaghut know that,' Korya replied.

He nodded. 'Yes, I think they do. But . . . the Azathanai? Why worship a prison?'

Shrugging, she moved past him and into the corridor beyond. 'Find one and ask.'

'Where are you going?'

'To the tower, get one of those shuttered windows open, and see what's going on. You coming?'

He followed.

*　　*　　*

Haut watched as the Seregahl leader pulled himself over the low wall of the yard, tattered armour scraping as he rolled clear to thump heavily on the ground. Others were shouting as they clambered in his wake, leaving smears of blood on the stones, while from within the grounds terrible shrieks cut raggedly through the dusty air.

Haut stepped closer to the leader and looked down at the Seregahl's face. Half of the man's beard had been torn away, flensing the skin of his cheek. The look in his eyes was wild, his mouth opening and closing without sound. He had lost his double-bladed axe.

Haut cleared his throat and then said, 'That's the problem with ancient gods, I suppose. Their reluctance to just . . . die.'

Another Seregahl, missing the lower part of his left leg, the ruptured knee joint gushing blood, made a wild cavort of hops before falling seven or eight paces from the wall's gate. Haut watched as the Thel Akai woman walked up to the cursing Toblakai and put the tip of her sword through his neck. The curses ended in a spitting gurgle.

'Get her away from us!' rasped the Seregahl leader, rolling on to his hands and knees. One hand scrabbled at his belt and drew out a knife the size of a shortsword. 'Seregahl! To me!'

The others quickly moved in close around their leader, forming a defensive cordon. Many of them bore wounds from the grasping roots and branches of the frenzied forest of gnarled trees now crowding the house's yard. And by Haut's count, five warriors were missing. The Thel Akai woman stood over the corpse of the man she had just slain, eyeing the troop with an air of vague disappointment.

The tumult in the yard was dying down, although the occasional sharp retort of a snapping branch lingered. Someone was still busy in there. Glancing at the house, he saw that the shutters had been opened on the top level of the squat tower that formed one corner of the building. Two figures were leaning on the sill, their attention fixed on the yard below.

Haut frowned up at them.

'How did they get in?'

He turned to find the Thel Akai woman now at his side, her gaze fixed on Korya and Arathan.

'I've seen the girl,' she continued. 'Tiste make my skin crawl. I don't know why. She wanders your camp, stirring up trouble.'

'What kind of trouble?'

The woman shrugged. 'She mocks them. Hood's followers.'

'The easy disdain of the young,' Haut said, nodding. He paused, and then added, 'I don't know how they got into the Azath House.'

The woman was now regarding the huddle of battered Seregahl. Her lip curled, but she said nothing.

The gate slammed open off to their right and a moment later a figure stumbled into view. Haut drew a sudden breath, and then stepped forward.

A Jaghut, his clothes rotted, his leathers stained with mould. Roots threaded his long, unkempt hair, and soil had mottled the skin of his face and arms. Five hundred years buried beneath the yard had not treated him well. Sighing, Haut drew closer, and then spoke. 'Gethol, your brother will be pleased to see you.'

The Jaghut slowly shifted his gaze, glancing briefly at Haut and then away again. He brushed feebly at the dirt covering him. 'Not dead yet then.'

'He's working on it.'

Gethol spat mud from his mouth, and then coughed and looked over to the Seregahl. 'Five went down,' he said. 'That should do.'

'The house has the old god?'

'Well enough.' Gethol coughed and spat again.

'Ah,' said Haut. 'That is a relief.'

'Where is Cadig Aval?'

'Dead. Apparently.'

'Yet there are living souls in the house. I could feel them.'

Haut shrugged. 'There are, but not for much longer. Will that be a problem?'

'How should I know? No, the house will prevail. This time.'

Returning his attention to the two Tiste in the tower window, Haut waited until he was sure that Korya was looking at him. He waved her down. A moment later both figures pulled back from the window, drawing the shutters closed.

Gethol asked, 'Where is he then?'

'In the Tower of Hate.'

Gothos's brother grunted, and then said, 'Why, it's as though I never left.'

\*      \*      \*

'This fire is dying,' Cred said, leaning closer to study the hissing pumice stones in the bronze bowl. 'Not my magic, not my prowess, but the fire itself.' He straightened and looked around. 'See how the firelight dims everywhere? Something is stealing the heat.'

Brella scowled across at him. 'Then we starve.'

'Or learn to eat things raw, as the Dog-Runners do,' said Stark.

'They cook their food like anyone else,' Brella retorted. She turned her attention to the younger woman. 'A simple walk through the camp would have shown you that. Instead, you cling to ignorant beliefs as if they could redefine the world. I see belligerence settle in your face, so downturned, the frown and the skittish diffidence in your eyes – so like your mother, may the Sea Hoarder give peace to her soul.'

Cred grunted. 'Stark's mother would have defied the very water filling her lungs. Oh, but I admired her for that. In the days before magic, when helplessness haunted us all.' He gestured at the ebbing glow in the brazier before him. 'The ghosts of that time return. And all the driftwood gone from the strand, nothing but grasses in the plain inland. I sit here, facing all that I have lost.'

'I am nothing like my mother,' Stark said to Brella. 'Just as you are nothing like your daughter.'

Grinning, Cred glanced over to see Brella's scowl deepen. 'Not my daughter any more,' she said. 'She casts off the name I gave her. So that she might command us all, and ever from a distance. Captain of a broken army. Captain of beaten refugees, the wreckage of a conquered people. What am I to her? Not her mother.'

'The High King's fleet did for our highborn,' Cred pointed out. 'You and your daughter come closest to anyone who might resurrect a claim to the royal line.'

Brella snorted.

Cred shook his head. 'You held the Living Claim, Brella, and then gave it into my keeping. That is the responsibility of the Ilnap bloodline. By this one ritual, you assert your claim to the Lost Throne. Even your daughter does not deny this.'

' "Captain." '

'She chooses that title because she sees no future awaiting

us. This is why we're here, Brella, vowing to march on death itself. The First Betrayal is the Last Betrayal. So it was prophesied.'

Hissing under her breath, Brella rose. 'I am done with these pointless words. Defeat has become the nectar that sustains us, as would the vile smoke of d'bayang. She leads us on to the path of no return. So be it. But let there be no illusions. We do not lead, only follow. And where this will end, the Living Claim lives no longer.'

'Curse the High King—' began Stark, but Brella turned on her.

'Curse him? Why? We did nothing but raid his coast, loot his merchants and send their ships to the deep. Year after year, season upon season, we grew indolent in our feeding upon the labour of others. Curse him not, Stark. The retribution was just.'

With that, she walked away.

Cred returned his attention to the dying fire. 'The sorcery within me is no weaker for this loss. How is such a thing possible?'

Shrugging, Stark unrolled her bedding and prepared for sleep, even though the day was barely half done. 'Perhaps something feeds on what you offer.'

Cred frowned at the woman, and then nodded. 'Yes, as I said earlier.'

'No, not your magic, Cred. Just the fire, nothing else. Each day we lose more heat – where is the season of thaw? I see the sea flocks flying into the north. Crabs march the shallows, awaiting the next full moon. All around us, the world prepares its time of breeding and renewal. But not here, not in this camp.'

She settled down, drawing up the heavy furs until they covered her entirely.

Fixing his attention once more on the dying fire, Cred considered Stark's words. If indeed the season was turning around them, then they had drifted inward. Stark had the truth of that. Curling down a spoke to settle on the hub, and at the very heart of that hub . . . *Hood.* He straightened. *It has begun.*

538

Varandas squatted opposite Hood. 'What are you doing?'

'I am ending time.'

'No wonder it's taking so long.' Varandas glanced away, seeing the approach of the lone Azathanai who had elected to join this hoary legion. 'One comes,' he said to Hood. 'She has circled for days. Only now are her perambulations revealed as a spiral. Mayhap she will challenge you.'

'I am proof against challenges,' Hood replied.

'Most dullards are. Let reason bludgeon you about the head and then, like a dazed fly, retreat in wobbling flight. The witless are known to defy, with piggy eyes and pressed lips. Making a knuckled fist of their face, they proclaim the stars no more than studs of quartz upon the night sky's velvet cloak, or the beasts of the wild as simple fodder serving our appetites. They carve every asinine opinion in the stone of their obstinacy and take pride in their own stupidity. Why is it that there comes a time in every civilization when the idiots rise to dominate all discourse, with beetled brows and reams of spite? Who are such fools, and how long did they lurk mostly unseen, simply awaiting their day in the benighted light?'

'Are you done, Varandas?' Hood asked.

'The witless have no comprehension of the rhetorical. They misapprehend unanswerable questions, since in their puny worlds of comprehension they possess none. Only answers, solid as lumps of shit, and just as foul.' Varandas looked up then, at the arrival of the Azathanai. He nodded, but her attention was on Hood.

She spoke. 'The dead are marching, Hood. Clever, I suppose. When all wondered how we would march into that realm, instead you bring that realm to us.'

'Spingalle, I did not think you fled too far.'

'I never fled at all,' the Azathanai replied.

'Where, then?'

'The Tower of Hate. Penance.'

Varandas frowned up at her. 'You know, if you truly sought to hide among us Jaghut, you should not have elected the form of a woman of such beauty as to take our breath away.'

She glanced at him. 'Unintended, Varandas. But if my appearance still delights you, I can oblige you in kind.'

'Make me a woman? I think not, and shall remain content with occasional misapprehension. Oh, and if you will indulge me, sidelong admiration of the impostor in our company.'

Jaghut tended towards the lean and bony, but Spingalle had defied that common form, and in the contrast that was her fullness she elicited universal wonder among the Jaghut, men and women both. Varandas studied her for a moment longer, and then with a sigh he returned his attention to Hood. 'She is right. That was clever.'

'Even the witless will shed a spark every now and then,' Hood said. 'Spingalle, I was under the impression that the Tower of Hate was solid.'

'No fault of mine if you believe everything Caladan Brood tells you. But then, you were always a credulous lot, prone to the literal, inured to the figurative. But this molestation of time, Hood, it seems . . . unwise.'

'Wisdom is overrated,' Hood said. 'Now then, Spingalle, will you indeed join us when the day comes?'

'I will. Death is a curiosity. Even, perhaps, a hobby of mine. I confess to some fascination, admittedly lurid. This notion of flesh that passes, soft shells that decay once the spirit has fled, and how such an affliction haunts you all.'

'Us mortals, you mean?' Varandas asked. 'I'll have you know, Azathanai, that those Jaghut who by chance escape premature death invariably welcome an end when at last it arrives. The flesh is a weary vessel, and that which crumbles soon becomes a prison to the soul. Death, accordingly, is a relief. Indeed, an escape.'

She frowned. 'But why confound a soul with the uncertainty of its immortality?'

'Perhaps,' ventured Hood, 'to awaken in us the value of faith.'

'And what value has faith, Hood?'

'Belief exists in order to humble the mundane world of

540

proofs. If mortal flesh is a prison, so too is a world too well known. Within and without, we desire – and perhaps need – a means of escape.'

'An escape you name *faith*. Thank you, Hood. You have enlightened me.'

'Not too much, one hopes,' Varandas said in a growl. 'Lest all wonder die in your lavender eyes.'

'Beauty desires admiration, Varandas, until it tires of it.'

'And does it now pall in your regard, Spingalle?'

'Probably. Besides, too much flattery and the subject begins to doubt its veracity, or at the very least, its worth. And besides, what worth is it, Varandas, to be the object of aesthetic admiration? I but give shape to your imagination.'

'A rare gift,' Varandas replied.

'Not as rare as you think.'

'Your Jaghut guise has soured you, Azathanai. Our misery is infectious.'

'This too is probable. Hood, the Azath House in your abandoned city has won a reprieve. Even the guardian ghost knows invigoration. Still, that was a risky endeavour.'

Hood shrugged where he sat before his cold flames. 'Do me a favour, Spingalle, and spread the word. It will be very soon now.'

'Very well. Varandas, I should never have slept with you.'

'True, as I remain eternally smitten.'

'Somewhat pathetic of you, and therefore decidedly unattractive.'

'Such is the curse of one who loses. But seed this ground between us with hope, and see me flower anew, bearing the sweet scent of delight and anticipation.'

'Varandas, we are about to war with the dead.'

'Yes, well, bad timing is another curse of mine, one not so easily discarded.'

She nodded to them both, and walked away.

Varandas stared after her, and then sighed again. A moment later he said, 'More guests are imminent, Hood. Led by none other than Gothos's brother.'

'Don't be ridic— Ah, well, that was a possibility, wasn't it? What does he want with me, I wonder?'

'A fist to your nose, I should expect.'

Hood grunted. 'Beats a long conversation. In any case, it wasn't really my fault.'

'Yes,' nodded Varandas, 'be sure to tell him that.'

*　*　*

Arathan found himself glancing sidelong at the Thel Akai woman again and again, as she prowled about the low wall enclosing the yard of the Azath House. Her sword was still wet with the blood of a slain Seregahl, and she moved with a grace belying her martial girth. He could not decide if he admired warriors. They had been part of his life for as long as he could remember. As a child he had at first sought to shy away from them, with their clunking weapons and rustling armour. The world never seemed so dangerous as to demand such accoutrements, but that was, of course, naught but the naivety of a child. He had long since learned otherwise.

Korya was arguing with Haut, but they had pulled away, to keep the exchange more or less private. The surviving Seregahl had marched off, limping and battered and, possibly, humbled. Death had a way of divesting the arrogant of their pretences. Even so, he did not expect the humility to last long.

The air was strangely still, yet it seemed to hold an echo of the chaos and carnage that had ripped through the yard not so long ago. The dust hanging in the air was reluctant to settle, or even drift away. If a breath could be held by inanimate nature, then surely it was being held now, and Arathan wondered why.

Snarling something, Korya wheeled from Haut and approached Arathan. 'That's it,' she said. 'Let's go.'

'Go? Where?'

'Anywhere, just away from here!'

They set out, leaving behind Haut, the Thel Akai and a Jaghut woman who now closed in on the captain, carrying in one hand a jug of wine.

542

'And that,' said Arathan as he fell in beside a swiftly striding Korya, 'is what never makes sense.'

'What are you talking about?'

'This dead civilization. This Omtose Phellack, the abandoned city. Look at that Jaghut woman now with your Haut. Sharing that jug. Wine? Where from? Who made it? Have you seen any vineyards?'

'Sanad,' said Korya after glancing back over a shoulder. Her scowl deepened. 'An old lover of his, I think. They're getting drunk together. Again. I don't like Jaghut women.'

'Why?'

'They know too much and say too little.'

'Well, I can see how that might irritate you.'

'Careful, Arathan, I'm not in the mood. Besides, you have no idea what awaits me. You see before you a young woman, a hostage now orphaned, but I am so much more than that.'

'So you keep telling me.'

'You'll see soon enough.'

'I don't see how, but never mind. I don't want that argument again, Korya. There are people I want to find, and they're probably dead. I have things that I need to say to them. Not only that, but I expect there will be many, many warriors beyond the Veil. I want to ask them: was it worth it?'

'Was what worth it?'

'The fighting. The killing.'

'I doubt they'd tell you. But even more, I doubt they'd have anything worth saying. Being dead, they failed, right? You're headed for miserable company, Arathan. Not that they'd welcome you, and not that you'll ever get close anyway. It seems that you are to be my keeper.'

'What?'

'Haut needs to hand me over to someone else. You're of House Dracons, right? Well, you have to deliver me to your father, but in the meantime, I'm now your hostage.'

'You can't be. I won't accept you.'

'Are you not your father's son?'

'Bastard son.'

'But he acknowledged you. You are now of House Dracons.

You have responsibilities. You can't be a child any longer, Arathan.'

'So that's how you all worked it out, is it? I sense Gothos behind this.'

She shrugged. 'I'm your hostage. You have to return me to Kurald Galain, to your father's estate.'

'He doesn't want to see me. He brought me here to keep me away.'

'So take me back and then leave again. What you do after you've discharged your responsibility is up to you.'

'This is . . . underhanded.'

'And don't think we'll be lingering, either. I want to leave. Soon.'

'If you're now my hostage, we'll leave when I decide it, not you.' He thought for a moment, and then frowned. 'I've not done the translating yet—'

'You idiot. You'll never be done with that, because Gothos won't ever stop. I would have thought you'd worked that out by now.'

'But I was just getting to the interesting stuff.'

'What do you mean?'

'Well, it's more or less an autobiography, but his story begins now – or, that is, he began it the day he killed civilization and became the Lord of Hate, and from there it goes back in time, day by day, year by year, decade by decade, century by—'

'Yes, I get it.' She paused, and then said, 'But that's stupid.'

'The point is,' said Arathan, 'it means that there must be an end to it. When at last he finds his earliest memory.'

'So how far back have you managed to transcribe?'

'About six years.'

She stopped, stared at him.

His frown deepened. 'What? What's wrong?'

'How far has he gone back? In his writing?'

'A couple of centuries, I think.'

'And how old is Gothos?'

Arathan shrugged. 'I'm not sure. Two or three, I think.'

'Centuries?'

'Millennia.'

She made a fist as if to strike him, and then subsided. Sighing, she shook her head. 'Gothos's Folly indeed.'

'There are dead people I need to see.'

'See the living ones instead, Arathan. At least they might, on occasion, tell you something worth hearing.' She set off once more, and Arathan followed.

'It would be irresponsible of me,' he said, 'to take you back to a civil war.'

'Oh, just fuck off, will you?' She angled away. 'I'm off to see a man with freckles on his arms.'

# FOURTEEN

---

YEDAN NARAD STOOD FACING THE FOREST WITH HIS back to the grove. The snow upon branches and the ground blackened the boles of the trees, and the crazed scrawl of twigs against the white sky ran like cracks in the face of the world. It was no difficult thing to see the future's end, looming like the breaking of winter.

Each night his dreams tore apart the shrouds of time. He walked a shoreline in a past he had never lived, into a future that was not his. He spoke with queens who called him brother, yet offered him the rotting, skeletal visage of a young woman in the attire of a bride. He felt sweet breath upon his cheek that assaulted his senses like the stain of gangrene.

During each day, as the hunters of the Shake gathered, as the makeshift army of Glyph of the Shore grew, Narad found himself less able to distinguish the real from the imagined, the moment ahead from the moment just past. At times, he would glance up and see the surrounding forest transformed into walls of raging fire, into a ceaseless cascade of silver, mercurial light. From wounds in the air, he saw the lunging bulk of dragons clawing through, the image rushing towards him as if he was, somehow, flying into the face of horror.

In his dreams, they named him warrior. Of his exploits, they spoke words of awe from crowds too formless to comprehend even as he walked through their midst. Somehow, he led them all, sustained by virtues and qualities of command he knew he did not possess. Everything seemed borrowed, perhaps even stolen. The expectations had begun to bleed into the real world, as increasingly he was looked to for guidance. It was only a matter of time before someone – Glyph, or, now, hate-filled Lahanis – exposed him for what he was.

*Narad, lowborn murderer, rapist, who lied to the First Son of Darkness. Why? Because deceit dwells in his heart, and he will duck every hand of justice. Cowardice hides behind his every desire, and just as he fled retribution, so he created for himself false memories, pillaging all he could.*

And yet, it was too late to deny the reality of what was coming. He had promised the Shake to the First Son, but the summons, when it came, would see Lord Anomander – not the Shake – dislodged, made to move in order to achieve the meeting. And in that moment, Narad now knew, he would once more betray the man.

*That shore is an unwelcome one to every stranger. But that shore is what we will call home. When you find us, you will answer our need. Fail to do so, and death will find you here. But even if you give honourable answer, beware your back, for there I will be standing. I am not who you think I am. For all my avowals, there is a weakness in me, a flaw in the core of my being. It will reveal itself. It is only a matter of time.*

'Yedan Narad.'

He turned to see that Glyph had approached him from the swollen camp now crowding the glade. Two steps behind the hunter stood Lahanis, the killer who had once been a child of the Borderswords. She had shown up a week past and now accompanied Glyph wherever he went. Her small hands rested upon the grips of the two long-knives slipped through her belt. Her eyes, fixed upon Narad, told him of her suspicions.

'There are Legion soldiers in the forest,' Glyph said. 'They track someone.'

Narad shrugged. 'A criminal. A deserter.'

'It makes it difficult for us to remain hidden.'

Narad's gaze flicked to Lahanis. 'Then kill the trackers.' At that, he saw her smile.

But Glyph reacted to the suggestion with a troubled frown. 'Yedan Narad. Has the time then come to begin our war of vengeance? A thousand and more have gathered here, but many more have yet to reach us. Though we now claim to be warriors, few of us know the ways of soldiering. We remain hunters. Our habits are ill suited—'

'Was this not what you wanted?' Narad asked him.

He hesitated. 'Each hunting party elects its own leader. In the forest, they seek isolation from other bands. Nothing can be coordinated.'

Lahanis spoke. 'It is simple enough, Glyph, as I have already explained. Call the hunting party a squad, make the leader a sergeant.'

'These are titles and nothing more,' Glyph replied. 'Our habits remain. Yedan Narad, you alone among us understand the soldiering ways. Yet you refuse to guide us.'

'I told you. I never commanded anyone.' *Least of all myself.*

'He's useless,' Lahanis said to Glyph. 'I have said as much. Leave him to his drunken wandering. If you've need of a priest, you have found one, but no priest will ever win anyone a war. I alone possess the knowledge you seek. Grant me command, Glyph, and I will make your people into an army.'

'You, child,' Glyph said, 'have yet to walk the Shore. You remain possessed by hate, and it blinds you to the destiny awaiting us.'

Lahanis sneered in answer to that, and then jabbed a finger at Narad. 'If this man is witness to your destiny, then it has blinded *him*!'

Already uninterested in this conversation, Narad turned away. 'Glyph,' he said wearily, 'consider your habits when you gathered to hunt the herds. Tell me, did each leader battle the next for command?'

'No, Yedan. One was chosen.'

'Upon what basis?'

'Guile, and prowess.'

'Take this to your people, then. The Legion is but a herd.

Dangerous, yes, but even wild beasts can prove dangerous, so that detail should not alarm you. The enemy will behave just as a herd would, but instead of fleeing the sight of you, they will rush towards you. This is the only difference. Have your chosen leaders apply their guile to that.'

'Narad Yedan, I will do as you say. Thank you.'

'You considered that good advice?' Lahanis demanded.

'It speaks to our habits, Bordersword. We were not told we must be remade. The Watch gifts us his wisdom. We understand the way of hunting the great herds.'

'But you will be fighting *here*, in this forest, not upon a plain!'

'Bordersword, often a herd will break apart, with smaller groups fleeing into woodland. We know to anticipate such a thing. The forest poses no obstacle to our understanding the words of the Watch.'

With a frustrated snarl, Lahanis marched away.

Still behind Narad, Glyph sighed, and then moved to stand alongside him. 'She bears too many wounds upon her soul.'

Narad grunted, and said, 'And you do not?'

'She is young.'

'The wounds you speak of are indifferent to that.'

'Our own children were slain. She reminds us of this—'

'More than you realize, Glyph. Had your children lived, they would be just like Lahanis. Think on that.'

The Denier was silent for a time, and then he sighed again. 'Yes. You remind me that there is a difference between the wound survived, and the wound that slays. Only in the first is a new hunger born. We speak of vengeance, but even the loss within us is borrowed. So it is and so it shall remain, for as long as we live.'

'Indulge Lahanis,' Narad said, closing his eyes upon his own pain, his own borrowed wounds. 'Her fire will be needed.'

'I feared as much.' Glyph paused, and then said, 'The Legion soldiers in the forest are thinly scattered. Our hunting bands will know how to deal with them.'

'The habits of the arrow.'

'Just so. Yedan Narad, do you fear the night to come?'

Narad snorted. 'Why should this night be any different?'

'In your dreams, you walk the Shore.'

'I have told you this, yes.'

'Will glory be found there, Yedan?'

Narad knew he should open his eyes, shift his gaze to Glyph, and reveal to the man the raw brutality of an honest reply. Instead, he did not move, barring the sudden trembling of his soul, which he was sure none other could see. 'Glory. Well, if it needs a name . . . we can call it such.'

'What other would you choose?'

*The death of innocence? The loss of hope? Betrayal?* 'As I said, it will suffice.'

'Yedan Narad, upon the day of the war's end, you must lead us. None other will serve. But this day, as we begin the war, you have already served well enough. We see at last the path we must take, to become slayers of men and women.'

'The same habit of hunting, Glyph. Only the prey has changed. I said little of worth.'

After a time, the Denier slipped away. Eyes still closed, Narad stared out upon a raging shoreline, argent with furious fire. He felt the weight of his sword in his hand, hearing but otherwise ignoring its muted peals of glee, while beside him a woman spoke.

*'My prince, our spine is bent unto breaking. Will you not return to us? We need your strength.'*

Narad grimaced. *'How is it that you make a virtue of my refusal of your lives, my refusing your right to them? For that is what you now ask of me. Stand fast, I will shout. Bend we shall, but break they will.'*

*'Sire, you never shout.'*

He waved a hand. *'You know me as a humourless man, and yet you persist. Why dog a beast that never lived?'*

*The woman – a soldier, not a queen – was silent for a time, and then she said, 'I took upon myself a family I never had. A daughter. A son, or was it two? I gave them the delusion they desired. They called me Mother. Until their moments of death, I held to the lie. What compelled me to do such a thing? Even now, while my corpse lies rotting beneath the stones the Andii raised about us, the question haunts me like my own ghost. 'What compels us, Yedan, to so plunder the truth?'*

*He shook his head. 'Nothing less or more than love, I think. Not for the ones you know and have always held close, but for the ones you may never meet. Or for those who, bearing the face of a stranger, stumble into your arms. In that instant, friend, you draw upon the deepest taproot within you. It has no name. It needs no name.'*

*'Then, what do you call it?'*

*He pondered the question for a moment, wondering at her insistence that some things need be named. Then he said, 'Why, call it glory.'*

He opened his eyes and the scene vanished. Once again, before him was the stark contrast of snow and trees, white and black, raised up in front of a fissured sky.

The man he was, in his dreams – the man who was a lover of men – was far wiser than Narad. He spoke with knowledge and forbearance. He spoke like a man at peace with who he was, with who he would ever be. He spoke, too, like a man about to die.

*Oh, my queen, see how I will fail you? He and I, we are brothers in failure, bound as lovers to a singular flaw. And when your day comes, Glyph, your final day of the war, he will lead you, not I. Or so I will pray. Better him than Narad, who will, I fear, take the coward's path.*

In this winter, all thoughts of redemption seemed as frozen and hidden as the ground beneath its mantle of snow.

＊　　＊　　＊

Glyph watched the other packs slipping away from the camp, and then turned to the four hunters gathered behind him. 'We must clear the forest of these invaders. Iron not flint for your arrows. Today, I am not interested in seeing them suffer. Quickly done, a return to winter's silence.'

Lahanis stood among the small group. She alone carried no bow, no quiver of arrows. He would rather she stayed behind, as he had little faith in her woodlore. Borderswords were not trained in forests. Their world had been open land and denuded hills, the tundra of the north. They had often fought from horseback.

But now the Borderswords were no more. Slaughtered in a battle with Houseblades. Lahanis was the only survivor to have joined his people. He would rather she hadn't. The smooth, round face before him was too young for the ferocity in her eyes. Her weapons invited the kind of death that was delivered with an embrace. Not for her the distance of an arrow or a lance. She would fight and don the blood of those she killed, and this red dress was one she yearned to wear.

She frightened him.

But then, so too did Narad, his first brother since his rebirth. The visions plaguing the Watch, as much as Narad had told him, seemed to promise conflagration and endless slaughter. It was as if Glyph had somehow stumbled into an unexpected destiny, making for his people a role none sought, and it was the Watch who would guide them into it.

*But I cannot know. Does he share my love for my people? He would see us used by the First Son. But we owe nothing to the black-skinned Andii, and less to the Liosan, who now wear the guise of bloodless corpses.*

A hunter spoke, 'We are ready, lord.'

*And this! Lord!* They had given him a title, Lord of the False Dawn. Glyph did not understand it. He saw no significance in any dawn, false or otherwise. Nor could he determine who had first fashioned for him that honorific. It seemed to have sprung up from the frozen ground, or perhaps drifted down with the flakes of snow. He did not like it, but as with Narad, the Watch, there was no fighting this tide. Something now grasped them both, and its hands were cold and unyielding. 'Very well. Lahanis, we must travel in silence, with not a single misstep. These Legion soldiers are their scouts, their trackers.'

'I know,' she replied. 'We must be as shadows.'

'You have stained your skin. That is good.'

She frowned. 'I have done nothing.' She raised a hand,

squinting at it. Her skin was the hue of ash. Blinking, she looked across to Glyph. 'You are the same. But I saw you smearing ash upon your faces when first I came among you. I considered doing the same, but then forgot. We are stained, but not by our doing.'

Shaken, Glyph glanced over to where Narad stood, still facing out into the forest. 'I thought him made ill by his visions.'

'We are Deniers.' Lahanis claimed the title as if she had been born to it.

The other hunters were muttering, their expressions troubled.

It was startling that no one else had even taken notice. Glyph could think of nothing to say, no answer to give them, or Lahanis.

'It was on this day,' said Neerak, the first hunter to have spoken to him. His eyes were wide. 'By the spring, lord, yesterday, I saw my own reflection, where we keep the ice clear. Pale, but not as pale as the Liosan. Pale, in the way that I have always been. But see my hands now, my forearms – has a plague come among us?'

*A plague.*

'We chose neither,' Lahanis said. 'We defy the Andii. We defy the Liosan. We have made ourselves apart.'

'But on this day?' Neerak demanded, spinning to face her. 'Why? What has changed?'

Glyph answered. 'I spoke with the Watch. I asked him, do we begin our war today?'

'He told us to kill the scouts,' Lahanis said. 'The war indeed begins. Glyph, he is a priest. I care not what title you give him, but he walks more than one world. Today, by his blessing, we become an army.'

He stared into her eyes, and saw in their eager light the promise of fire and destruction.

*The Last Fish, who now walks, seeking an old enemy. The lake lies almost forgotten, the leagues uncountable between it and where he now stands. The water, he recalls now, was clear. Nothing in it to blind him to his future, a future awash in tears. From water he left, to water he must go. I end where I began.* 'The war claims us now,' he said. He collected up his bow. 'By the blessing of the Watch, we are made into slayers of men and women. Come, then. This forest is our home. Time to defend it.'

Pulling up the cloth that masked his face beneath his eyes, he set out, his pack close behind him.

They moved quickly, upon old trails, hunched down beneath tangles of overgrowth canopying the animal tracks. Theirs was a run that devoured leagues. It flowed swiftly but made little sound, the snow taking their footfalls, the shadows of branches and boles scattering their own shadows as they raced onward. The secret of subterfuge was to move as if one belonged, to fight against nothing, bending and dipping, shifting where needed.

It was near dusk when Glyph, still in the lead, caught sight ahead of figures, three in all, drawn together as if in consultation. Their bulks betrayed their presence, along with the glint of iron buckles, an inverted strip of hide, and plumes of breath from unguarded mouths as they spoke in whispers. When one caught the fluid approach of Glyph and his hunters, he cried out and drew out his sword.

Glyph's arrow sank into his right eye, dropping him instantly.

Two more arrows followed, hissing past Glyph.

Both surviving scouts went down.

The hunters reached the bodies, flowed over them like water, pausing only to cut free arrows. Lahanis pushed close to make certain the scouts no longer lived, but Glyph knew that was unnecessary. All three were dead before they struck the snowy ground. He continued on, shaking the gore from his arrow. The shaft was splintered, the iron point bent where it had struck the inside of the man's skull. Still padding through the forest, Glyph worked loose the point and slipped it into a pouch at his belt, to be hammered straight later. He then snapped the shaft just below the fletching, and pocketed the end as well, before flinging away what remained.

They rushed on, as the dusk slowly closed around them.

*It was as before. My first time, when they sat about a fire and laughed and flirted with the woman in their company. Nothing of them reached the place inside me. Nothing to invite sympathy, nothing to blunt my cold, sharp need for their deaths.*

*Slayers of children. If the blood not upon their own hands, then upon the uniform. They claimed the standard and wore upon their shoulders the banner that belonged to butchers. I felt nothing killing them. I felt nothing sending a flint arrow into the gut of the last one. I felt nothing chasing him down.*

*This must be how soldiers think. It could not be otherwise, for what kind of person murders a child? Defenceless elders? Hearth-wives and hearth-husbands?*

*What kind of person?*

*Why, the one I am become.*

*Do I mock myself now, if I say that I will hunt the uniform, slay the uniform? That the uniform is my enemy, mere cuts and hues of cloth and leather, a lifeless thing of belts, buckles and wool? Or is this my only path, my only hope to remain sane?*

*This, then, must be war. And what begins without must also begin within.*

It was well, he reflected as he rushed on into the night, that he was reborn, for surely his old self must be dead by now, fatally wounded by grief and horror.

*The lake water was once clear, but now, oh now, now it runs red.*

*Yedan Narad, I see what haunts you. For you, and all that you see of what awaits us, my chest now aches.*

Behind him, close, Lahanis said in a hiss, 'Wound the next one, lord. My knives thirst.'

And he nodded. For it was best if they all drank.

Like stained water, they flowed dark through the forest, while above them the sky groped towards night. They travelled a shadow world.

It was a night for killing, and kill they did.

*          *          *

Higher Grace Sheccanto was propped up in her bed, like a corpse bound to the headrest. Pillows were stuffed against her sides to keep her upright, and her head had a habit of dipping, even when she was speaking, until such time as her chin reached her breastbone and her words became incomprehensible. A young acolyte sat upon the bed, close by, ready to help the old woman lift her head once more. Despite this diligence, the words Sheccanto said made little sense.

Warlock Resh sat leaning forward, forearms upon his thighs, in an effort to hear – and understand – the Higher Grace. Finarra Stone stood a few paces back, having already surrendered the task. This, she well understood, would be her last audience with Sheccanto. The Shake might well remain hale in body, but the crown upon the head was broken, if not entirely lost.

None knew what afflicted the old woman. By years alone, she should still be stalwart and sharp of mind, with sufficient power to temper her husband and his increasingly bizarre pronouncements. *Have they both spent years hunched over a forge? This is the iron curse, the stealer of memory, sower of confusion. Something has poisoned them both. Am I witness to the cruellest of assassinations?*

From the terrible, wretched news that had finally penetrated the monastery, her suspicions needed to shake off few chains in pursuit of imagined conspiracies, ones where civility was the first victim. This could well be Hunn Raal's work, aspired to genius. Far better than simply murdering Sheccanto and Skelenal, if one could paralyse the Shake with months, if not years, of ineffective rule.

No far reach for the poisoner of an entire legion, the murderer of Lord Ilgast Rend and the slayer of the Wardens of Glimmer Fate. He had been an unprepossessing man, she recalled, arrogant to be sure, but in the way of many soldiers, for whom that arrogance was a brittle façade hiding a wounded soul. She could forgive that bravado. He had also been a drunkard, the kind for whom the pretence of sobriety was a game, eliciting a smile upon his fleshy features – as if the man believed he was fooling everyone around him, when in truth he himself was the only fool, though even then, a knowing fool. Drunkards such as Hunn Raal had a way of eating themselves from the inside out, and alcohol simply served to dull the pain of his endless chewing. She had expected from him a simple continuation of his degradation, his body hollowed out, his skull filled with terrors, a trembling, stumbling descent into death.

Instead, it seemed that evil itself had manifested in the man, lending him preternatural energy even as it scoured him clean of compassion. He was, she now believed, capable of anything.

*Did he poison them? Has he agents here among the Shake? Spies? Assassins? Would not their loyalty bleach their skin? Look around – we here are unchanged, although, now that I consider it, the amber hue of our skin seems to have lost its gleam, as if dust now settles upon us all.*

*Are we transformed here, or simply revealing our sense of loss? What else is surrendered, when faith dies?*

'The sands will burn,' said Sheccanto, her eyes fixed and staring at a vista none other could see. Those eyes were sunk deep in shadowed sockets, surrounded by withered skin the colour of the winter sky. 'Someone drags me by an ankle, but my flesh is cold. Lifeless. The pain – the pain comes to those who must witness. Ignominy. The fires of outrage. I wonder . . . I wonder. Only the dead see the clarity of war. They chose to dishonour me, but my body cares not. Only the Watch understands. But he can do nothing. Nothing.'

Finarra shifted weight. The old woman wandered unknown landscapes in her mind. Every word she uttered took her farther away. *By an ankle? You will not live that long, Higher Grace. Already they prepare your crypt, beneath this very floor. None shall drag you from it.*

'By royal blood we were born,' Sheccanto said. 'It is well to take the title of queen or king. But the day holds meaning, for what plays across its passage? I will tell you. I will tell you . . .' Her head dipped again, and this time her eyes closed, and she began drawing the rattling breaths of sleep.

Slowly, Warlock Resh leaned back in his chair. He raised his scarred hands to his face.

Finarra cleared her throat. 'I believe Caplo Dreem still awaits us in the compound, warlock. If we are to do this today, it must be soon.'

After a moment, the burly man shook himself and rose to his feet. His attention fixed once more upon the Higher Grace, he said, 'Captain—'

'That rank no longer applies,' Finarra cut in.

'There will be survivors. Must be survivors. They will need you.'

'They have Calat Hustain.'

'And he will not find you a blessing to his grief?'

Bitterness opened within her like a wound. 'Warlock, the war is lost. Urusander has won. Kharkanas will open its gates to him. We Wardens, well, we were never relevant. We patrolled the Vitr. More to the point,' she continued, 'we were the ones who brought T'riss into our realm. Let us judge our demise a just reward for our carelessness.'

He turned from his study of Sheccanto and gazed at her. 'Will you not return to Calat Hustain?'

'I see no point,' Finarra replied. 'The Vitr remains. It will not subside or cease its assault. Calat will begin again. But I will not.'

'We do not resent your presence,' Resh said. 'But you must understand. Caplo is not as he once was. My friend is now unknown to me. He says he will accompany me to Kharkanas, to the Terondai, and, perhaps, to an audience with Mother Dark.' He hesitated, and then said, 'I fear such a meeting.'

'Then refuse him,' she replied. 'The Terondai can wait. You have other concerns.'

'Skelenal would summon all the brothers and sisters,' Resh said. 'He says we must prepare for war. But we have no cause to defend, no reason to fight beyond the pathos of vengeance.' He shook his head. 'The children are dead. The forests have burned. If we possessed any authority over the Deniers, it is now abrogated. We did not defend them. Indeed, we did nothing.'

The arguments were old. Finarra had heard them too many times. 'And this is the way of things, warlock, the means by which evil thrives, and every terrible deed is justified. The dead are already dead, the fires have long since burned out, and the blood now hides beneath rich soil. Each act, if unanswered, unchallenged, breeds the next, and when it is all done, evil stands triumphant.'

'Can you not see that we are weakened?' Resh demanded, wringing his hands as he stood before her. 'Why fight for the Andii, when by Mother Dark's hand our god was slain? The transformations upon either side now set us apart. We are neither, and yet we are nothing.'

She looked away, vaguely disgusted. Her frustration was growing talons and the urge to strike out grew day by day. 'Caplo Dreem may well attempt to kill Mother Dark. And this time, the First Son is not there to stand in your friend's way.'

'There is Draconus.'

She shot him a searching look. 'Not for long, I should think.'

'At the very end, Mother Dark may defy Urusander. She may refuse everything they demand of her. She is a goddess, after all. How do you envisage the power behind that ascension? Is she now stripped of her will? Her independence? Is she helpless, her mind deafened by an endless roar of prayer, beseeching desire, wishes unending?'

Finarra Stone's eyes narrowed. 'You believe your faith emasculated your own god, don't you? You made your god unable to defend itself. Made it helpless.'

'Faith belongs to the mortal mind,' said Resh, 'but one look in the mirror will tell you that it is a lamb in the care of the wolf.'

'And now you are flayed by guilt, left crushed by your own recriminations? I did not think self-pity could be made sacred, but it seems that you have managed it easily enough, warlock, and would make indulgent weeping its libation. And what is to be your sacrifice? Why, only yourself, of course.'

He snorted. 'Speaks the woman who tramples upon her

559

own rank. Who tells me that Calat Hustain has no more need for her.'

After a moment, Finarra offered a wry shrug. 'Then we find comfort in our company.'

Resh looked away. He sighed. 'I have no leash to bind Caplo Dreem. Must I deliver another crime into the presence of Mother Dark?'

'He is your friend, not mine.'

'Was. Now, I am not so sure.' He met her eyes. 'Do you seek to guard against his treachery? Will you draw your blade to defend Mother Dark?'

'Against a dozen beasts? Death will come swiftly.'

'Then why refuse my desire to send you away?'

'I will travel to Kharkanas, warlock, in your company or alone.'

'What do you seek there?'

She said nothing. The truth was, she had no answer to his question, but she felt bound to the fate of the Shake now, like a leaf joining a mass of detritus, impelled by the gathering of its own weight as it swung into the current. But what waited downstream remained unknown. Resh sought a purpose for his brothers and sisters, and believed that he would find knowledge in his study of the Terondai.

And what of Caplo Dreem, blood-tainted and, these days, almost emptied of words? A feral promise glimmered in his eyes. He was now a man quick to bare his teeth. Only a fool would not fear what he had become.

'The sorcery,' said Resh, cutting into her thoughts, 'now pours like blood from a fatal wound. If we are not careful, captain, Kurald Galain will drown in its flood.'

'Then use it, warlock. Use it up if you can.'

'A dangerous invitation.'

'Are you a child, then?' she snapped. 'Unmindful of constraint?'

'A child?' He seemed to consider the suggestion, indifferent to the challenge in her tone. 'Yes, I believe. All of us now. Children. Crowded into a small room, and upon the floor in its centre, a chest filled with knives.'

Suddenly chilled, Finarra Stone turned away, gathering up her gloves and cape from the bench near the door. 'Will you just stand there? Am I to be Caplo's only escort, then?'

They were startled by a sudden racking cough from Sheccanto. The nurse, sitting almost forgotten beside the bed, lunged forward to catch the old woman before she fell. Rocked by the jostling of the nurse, Sheccanto said, 'The royal blood is thinned, but I taste it still. The Watch withers in his solitude, a prince dreaming of his sister. She will know the sword in her hand, and she will rise at the day's end, and so be known as Twilight. Neither monk nor nun, but one of the blood. The Shake must have a queen. Upon the shore . . . a queen.' Her eyes widened and she stiffened in the nurse's arms. 'Oh bless me! My children do not deserve that!'

She slumped back, head lolling. 'Let the Vitr take it,' she mumbled. 'Silver fire . . . the flesh from the bones . . .'

Resh advanced towards her. 'Higher Grace, do you speak prophecy?'

She lifted her head with sudden strength and met the warlock's eyes. 'Prophecy? Fuck prophecy. Immortal shadow, I see the reasons. He is forever restless. You'll know him by that habit.' Then her seamed face stretched into a tortured smile. 'Oh, clever boy. I give him that.'

'Higher Grace?'

'When the First Son comes to you, answer his need. Die for the love you have never known, and never will. Die to save what you will never see. Die in the name of children not yet born. Die for the cause not your own. Go, lover of men, go. Nine assassins await you.' Then she pulled an arm loose from the nurse's grip and pointed at Finarra Stone. 'She knows the sword in her hand. Warlock! Kneel to Twilight. Kneel to your queen.' An instant later, Sheccanto slumped back once more, eyes closing.

Resh leaned closer.

The nurse shook her head. 'Sleep, warlock, that is all.'

Reeling, Resh pulled away. He faced Finarra with fevered eyes.

'It means nothing,' Finarra said. 'Pay her words no heed.

561

Come, the day is nearing its end. We must set out now, or wait until the morning.'

When she quitted the bedchamber, Resh followed. He said nothing in her wake, but Finarra's mind was filled with the look he had given her, its raw need, its terrible thirst.

*Monks and nuns, witches and warlocks, sisters and brothers. All titles for those who would believe. But I am not one with any such need. Not one to run from shrine to shrine, altar to altar, desperate for communion. Higher Grace, your mind is truly gone if you see anything in me.*

Out in the compound, the winter's chill was fierce as the day died. Seeing them appear, Caplo swung on to his horse. He was swathed in dark furs, as if to mock himself. He fixed his feral gaze upon Finarra, and then Resh. 'You've not forbidden her?' he asked. 'This is our journey, warlock. The two of us, in the name of the Shake.'

Reaching his horse, Resh paused to study his old friend for a moment, and then he said, 'Your words are a comfort, Caplo, if you still count yourself among us.'

Caplo Dreem frowned. 'Of course. Why would I do otherwise?'

Resh mounted his horse and gathered up the reins. 'She rides with us now. As you say, Caplo, in the name of the Shake.'

'Warlock,' Finarra warned.

But he simply shrugged. 'Twilight is upon us, I see. All to the good.' He kicked his horse into motion, swinging the beast round towards the gate.

Cursing under her breath, Finarra mounted up and followed Resh and Caplo. They would ride through the night. She looked with envy upon the dark furs riding Caplo's back. Already she was cold.

\*　　\*　　\*

In the wake of the snowstorm, the air had slowly surrendered its bitter chill. Riding winds from the southeast brought burgeoning warmth, softening the sculpted dunes of snow until the faces they showed to the sunlit sky seemed pocked

562

with rot, and the old track upon which Kagamandra Tulas rode blackened with mud and pools of water.

That he trailed other travellers in this season was clear, and while some rode horses, most were on foot, leading burdened mules. Thus far, he had not yet come across any makeshift graves, and for that he was thankful. Since parting ways with Calat Hustain and his Wardens, Kagamandra had met no one. He had not expected to. Winter was mercurial, like a cat hiding its claws, and this spell of warmth meant little. The season would hold for months yet.

He had been gaining on the refugees – if that was what they were – but without haste or any sense of urgency. He had no reason to welcome company, or take upon himself the burdens or needs of anyone else. In any case, he was himself half starved, his horse little better. His father's estate, now his own, was a cold inheritance. He could not even be certain it was still occupied. In his absence, his staff, most of whom had served his father, might well have yielded to the vicissitudes of neglect or, perhaps more likely, ennui. It was entirely possible that he rode to an abandoned ruin. No refugee would find succour there.

The way ahead haunted him with its familiarity. As a youth he had often ridden far from the estate, fleeing the shadow of sire and siblings, seeking solitude in denuded hills, dried lake beds and sweeps of withered prairie. These were the half-formed urges of youth, groping in ignorance, not yet comprehending that the solitude he sought already existed, buried deep in his own mind. Every jarring sense of being different, every fear of exclusion, every instant of estrangement from his laughing brothers and their companions, these were the things setting him apart, pushing him into a world solely his own.

If in his imagination he sought to visualize that empty world, which circled round him at a crawling pace, he saw what now surrounded him, as his horse plodded through slush and mud, with the sky overhead a soft white, and the wind smelling of sodden grass. In that respect, he was already home.

For that reason and others, he felt no urgency to end this journey. If he could twist this trail into a vast loop through the wilderness of the south, he would have no cause for complaint.

But necessities posed their own demand. His horse was dying under him, and the hollowness in his gut had given way to a deep lassitude that had spread through his entire body, broken only by the ache in his joints, flaring up like fire whenever he straightened in his saddle.

His father had been right, he now reflected, to have seen so little in him.

*Sharenas Ankhadu, why do you appear again and again in my thoughts? What is it you speak, with such expressions of derision? I see your lips move, but no sound finds me. I conjure you before me, to give a proper guise to my messenger – who must attend to me in cruel honesty, in the name of worth – but I remain deaf to your words.*

She would, he suspected, mock his self-pity. She would castigate his lethargy. She would, with brittle exasperation, demand his obeisance to his betrothed, and call upon his honour in the name of Faror Hend. *Find her!* she would say.

But there was no one to find. His betrothed was a promise, nothing more. Such things broke with a single careless word, a lone gesture hinting of dismissal. Standing before Faror Hend, Kagamandra would remain mute, his limbs frozen in place. He would think only of the hurts he could not help but deliver, in the absence of anything one might call love.

The track lifted towards a rise, and upon reaching the top, Kagamandra saw in the shallow valley beyond those he had been following. The party had moved to one side of the trail, clearing a space of snow in which to camp. A roped corral to one side also revealed yellowed grass, where three horses and four mules now cropped the dead stalks.

As Kagamandra drew nearer, he was surprised to see, among those now rising from dung fires to greet him, men and women wearing the uniform of the Wardens.

He continued on until he reached the camp and then reined in as two Wardens, a woman and a man, strode up.

The woman was the first to speak. 'My name is Savarro. I was once a sergeant. If you track us at Hunn Raal's bidding, tell him our war with him is done. Tell him,' she added, 'it never existed, but for the ambitions of Lord Ilgast Rend. Above all, tell him to leave us alone. The Wardens are no more.'

Kagamandra leaned on the horn of his saddle. 'Where do you ride, Savarro?'

'This concerns him? Away. What more does he need?'

'Upon this track, Savarro, lies an estate. Perhaps it offers – in your mind – a company of Houseblades who might welcome you in its ranks.'

The man shifted at Savarro's side and then said to her, 'Does he speak true, sergeant? Do we journey to a highborn's estate?'

Behind the two, the others were now gathering, intent on the exchange.

Savarro shrugged. 'I had no thought of us joining the ranks, Ristand. But our food is almost gone. The animals need shelter. The warm spell will not last much longer. The bitterest month of winter is soon upon us.' She waved a hand. 'The estate might take us in as guests.'

'Guests! They'll see us coming and lock the gates! Look at us, no better than marauders.' Ristand was a big man, shaggy and broad-faced, and if not for the black hue of his skin he would have revealed a flushed countenance, wind-burned and filled with temper. 'You said you had for us a destination – but you said nothing about a highborn's shit-smeared estate! Sweet bung-hole, Savarro!'

'Will you ever cease your complaints, Ristand?' She faced Kagamandra again. 'The lord isn't even in residence. Lost his wife years ago. No children. We're as likely to find the place abandoned as anything else, and if so it'll serve us fine to wait out the season.'

'What of forage and food?' Ristand demanded.

Her head snapped round again as she glared at her companion. 'Maybe they took everything when they left, maybe they didn't. At the very least, it's shelter!'

'And what if there's Houseblades and all the rest? What then?'

'Then,' Savarro said as if speaking to a child, 'we ask kindly, Ristand. Meaning, a league from the gates, we bind and gag you. Sling your flea-bitten carcass over a saddle. That at least will give us a chance at some hospitality!' She swung back to Kagamandra. 'Now, leave us be, will you?'

Kagamandra studied her for a long moment, and then he lifted his gaze past her, to the score or so Wardens now gathered on the track. He saw children among them, and servants, cooks and maids. 'You have come from the season's fort, sergeant?'

'We went there first, yes,' she replied. 'To take the news, and bring with us whoever wanted to come.'

'Yet you and these others – you were at the battle?'

'Late to it. Too late to make a difference. We were patrolling Glimmer Fate. Meaning we never drew blades against the Legion.'

Kagamandra was silent, but then gathered his reins and said, 'Make room on the trail. Sergeant, I am not here at Hunn Raal's bidding. You speak of a battle I know nothing about. You say Ilgast Rend commanded the Wardens? Then this is his problem.'

'He's dead.'

'Dead?'

'Hunn Raal executed him,' Savarro said. 'Why do you know nothing of this? From where have you come?'

'I spoke to Commander Calat Hustain,' Kagamandra said, seeing how this now caught their attention. 'He was riding back to the fort, with news, one presumes, of events at the Vitr. But of that I can only surmise, as he was not forthcoming on the matter. He had wounded and dead in his company. I would think he has already arrived, only to find his base abandoned, and no answer as to why.'

'Not true,' Savarro said, confusion now clouding her features. 'A few chose to remain behind.'

'Ah. Well, then, lest you desire Calat Hustain to deem you deserters, hadn't you better return to the fort?'

Voices rose then, arguments erupting. Pushing his mount forward, Kagamandra rode through the press. Once clear, he coaxed his horse into a slow trot, and before too long the shouting began to fade into his wake.

*Houseblades. Do I even have Houseblades?*

\*     \*     \*

The winter fort of the Wardens bore a planked walkway along the length of the walls, accommodating patrols that, to Bursa's mind, had never served much purpose, and even less so now. He stood at his post, feeling a fool, his gaze fixed upon the black wall of the Glimmer Fate's high grasses, or, rather, upon the battered gap in its otherwise unbroken line, and the dragon that occupied it. Motionless as a massive boulder, with scales that, at this distance, looked no different from iron plates of armour, the creature appeared to be slumbering.

Snow covered its spine. Ice sheathed its folded wings, with long icicles, now dripping in the unseasonal warmth, depending from their ridges. The dragon had preceded the troop's arrival by four days, according to old Becker Flatt, the retired Bordersword who had elected to remain when the survivors of the battle reached the fort with their terrible news. The man was in the habit of telling everyone that he had nowhere else to go, and the half-dozen others who had stayed no doubt felt the same. In any case, the dragon had been discovered the morning after the storm. Lying in a gap made by its own massive body, its eyes shuttered, conjured up into a sculpted nightmare, waiting like a promise.

Enough reason to flee this cursed place, as far as Bursa was concerned. When he had heard of the desertion of the battle's survivors, he had not shared the outrage of the others. *I would have done the same. I still might.*

The Vitr's slow assault upon the lands of Kurald Galain now held for him all the urgency of death by old age. Nothing could stop it, after all, and its mysteries tasted stale. The Wardens were finished. The world felt bloodless, the future an empty expanse devoid of purpose.

Beside him, Spinnock Durav leaned on the slumped bales that made up the fort's wall. Like Bursa, he too stared at the dragon upon the edge of the grassline. 'Seventy paces,' he said. 'More or less. Well, there are no caves anywhere nearby, are there? If the beast must hibernate . . .'

Scowling, Bursa said nothing for a moment. It still astonished him, this new hatred he fostered for the young man at his side. Unreasoning as it was, he relished its intensity. Envy was wasted unless it could do damage. 'It bears wounds,' he said. 'The demon does not hibernate. It simply recovers.'

'Ah, well. No one has studied it as you have done, sir.'

'You consider mine an unwise obsession?' Bursa asked. 'Do you imagine these flimsy walls of grass can defend us from that beast? It could kill us all, at any moment. Yet you and the rest – still we stay here. Yes, I study the creature, and be thankful that someone does. What we unleashed from the Vitr will haunt the Tiste, and perhaps see Kurald Galain laid to waste.'

Spinnock was studying him in an odd, disquieting smanner. 'We released nothing, sir.'

'A blunt denial,' Bursa snapped, 'soaked through with hope, but the facts will see it wrung dry. Indeed, it was you and Faror Hend and Finarra Stone. All of this, begun by your fumbling.' After a moment, he shook his head. 'But you, Durav, you simply followed. In truth, you are innocent enough.'

'Your words surprise me,' Spinnock said.

'She asked me to guard you well, but that was in the world now dead. Where we are now, well, we are mere days from each going our own way. I have no desire to be your escort as you return to your family holdings. I have no desire to fall into your Houseblades, and start saluting you. Your noble blood earns nothing from me. I trust I am understood.'

'She? Who?'

'The women all lust after you, Durav. Something you're used to, I suppose. They all yearn to protect you. When I look upon your future, I see you still a child, forever a child. Such is the fate of men like you.'

Smiling, Spinnock Durav offered up a half-hearted salute, and then moved away, resuming his patrol of the walls.

Those weak of mind hurried into old habits, finding solace in their familiarity. *Walk the walls, Warden. Guard the fort. Such is your task.* None of it mattered any more, and it took a quicker mind than Spinnock Durav's to comprehend that everything had changed, that whatever had existed before was now irrelevant.

*I must ride from here. Perhaps tonight. Leave Calat Hustain to his grief. Clearly it has broken him. He still speaks of us as a company. All this talk of rebuilding, of rebirth. There is nothing left. See that dragon, Calat Hustain? This is our new future, as meat for its jaws, our flensed skulls to roll and jostle in its gut.*

*Nine of them.*

*They hunt me in my dreams, and this whispers to me of my fate. I run, in my arms the wealth of Kurald Galain. The crown, the sceptre, the coins tumbling from between my fingers. Then the shadow sweeps over me—*

Growling under his breath, Bursa shook himself to dispel the visions. He would leave tonight. It was not desertion. Like Spinnock Durav, Calat Hustain remained blind to the truths of this new, terrible world. He would find Savarro, Ristand and the others. Old Becker Flatt had said that there had been other survivors, other ragtag groups stumbling in, but they had elected to ride to the Hust Legion. They suffered from the fires of fury, and sought vengeance against Urusander's Legion. Having fled their first battle, they now saw themselves as soldiers. They vowed that they would meet the enemy again, upon another field, and give answer with sword and lance.

*Idiots. No, Savarro had the right of it. Ride out, disappear into the mists. We were misfits. So we began, and into that miserable solitude we now return.*

*Calat Hustain, you gave command of the Wardens to Lord Ilgast Rend. That was your first crime, and it remains unforgivable. Why you haven't already taken your own life baffles me. Must someone do it for you?*

*I would, if I cared. But I don't. Better, I think, that you live, and so suffer guilt, year upon year, until its rot takes you from the inside out.*

A short time later Spinnock Durav returned from his circuit, now approaching Bursa from the other side of the walkway. 'There will be more snow tonight,' he said.

Bursa grunted.

Hearing sounds from the compound behind and below, both men turned to see Commander Calat Hustain emerging from the longhouse. Old Becker shambled at his side, struggling as he attempted to shrug into his armour, his sword-belt trailing from one hand.

'Now what?' Bursa asked under his breath.

'Spinnock Durav!' the commander called. 'Attend to me. Bursa, remain upon the wall.'

*Aye, he'll take the handsome one.* He watched Spinnock clamber down the rope ladder, displaying nauseating agility.

'Bursa.'

'Commander?'

'Observe well, should matters turn awry.'

*What new madness now afflicts you, Hustain?*

Once Spinnock joined them, they continued on to the gate, and moments later reappeared in the clearing, making directly for the slumbering dragon.

Bursa's mouth dried. His heart started a fierce hammering in his chest. He thought to cry out, voice his warning. He thought to shriek his sanity down to them – all this, even as he struggled against the impulse to flee. *They're welcome to die. It matters not to me. Finarra, your precious boy followed Calat Hustain. There was nothing I could do to prevent it. The commander ordered me to remain at my post. I could do naught but witness. I wish, oh, captain, how I wish I could say that he died bravely . . .*

The three Tiste had taken no more than a dozen paces when the dragon's eyes opened and the creature lifted its head, the serpentine neck twisting as the beast fixed lambent eyes upon the intruders.

Impossibly, it then spoke, with a voice that filled Bursa's skull.

'*We will not return. Refuse us this freedom and we shall set aside our hate. We shall find our frenzy, and so awaken to this world Tiamatha. Upon this dread deed, all manner of dismay and disappointment will follow.*'

Commander Calat Hustain said, 'Eleint. You misconstrue our purpose. We do not challenge your presence, nor your claim to freedom.'

'*This pleases me. What breed of creatures are you?*'

'We are Tiste Andii, of Kurald Galain.'

'*I see some advantage in your form. Less effort to fill your stomach. The bliss of modest shelter. A certain elegance in your crawl upon the ground.*'

'You emerged from the Vitr—'

'*Vitr! What giant ogre throwing stones has been whispering in your ear? Or, perhaps, some meddling Azathanai?*' The dragon lifted its head higher and seemed to sniff the air. '*The Queen of Dreams haunts one of you. Poor bastard. But then, she failed the first time, yes?*'

'I do not understand,' Calat Hustain said. 'What can you tell us about the Vitr? How can we stop its advance?'

'*It advances upon this realm?*'

'It does. Slowly, but yes.'

'*There must be . . . a leak.*' The creature suddenly blurred, air swirling about it, lifting snow from the ground.

Squinting, Bursa saw the dragon shrink, its form losing its original shape. The spinning snow settled, revealing a naked Tiste woman where the creature had been.

She strode towards Calat, Spinnock and old Becker Flatt.

She spoke out loud now. 'You wear furs for warmth. Give me some. Also, I hunger. And suffer thirst.' Then she pointed up to Bursa. 'The Queen of Dreams sees me through his eyes. I care not. Horrid woman! Vile Azathanai! We threw your sister out. One of my kin then ate you – too bad he couldn't keep you down!' Returning her attention to Calat, she said, 'Take me in. These things' – she indicated her full breasts – 'are turning into blocks of ice.'

Gallant as ever, Spinnock removed his cloak and advanced. 'Milady,' he said. 'This will keep you warm until we reach the longhouse.'

Bursa saw her eyeing him, an appraisal he had seen before whenever a woman came face to face with Spinnock Durav.

'Lovely,' the woman said, taking the cloak and flinging it over one shoulder. 'And . . . lovely.'

Calat Hustain said, 'Welcome. I am Commander Calat Hustain of the Wardens of Glimmer Fate. Do you have a name?'

'Of course I have a name. Who doesn't?' She was still staring at Spinnock Durav, and then she smiled and stepped close to the young man. 'My kind greet gallantry with a kiss,' she said.

'Indeed?' Spinnock replied, and though Bursa could not see his face, the sergeant well knew that charming smile with which Durav answered her. 'Snout to snout as it were?'

'Never. You surmise truly. I just made that up. Still, do humour me.'

'At the very least,' Spinnock said, 'before I offer up this kiss, tell us your name.'

'Telorast.'

Spinnock Durav stepped back and bowed to her. 'Spinnock Durav. Calat you have met, and our companion is a veteran of the Wardens, Becker Flatt. And upon the wall behind us is Bursa.'

Telorast glanced back up at Bursa. 'Sweet dreams, Bursa?'

He shook his head.

*Dragons are not bad enough, it seems. Now they must wield uncanny magic. And tell me I am possessed.*

She then took her kiss from Spinnock Durav, pressing her body against him as she did so.

Calat Hustain stood to one side. Bursa delighted in the man's discomfort. *Yes, he does this, commander. You should have known better.* After a moment, while Telorast continued to squirm against Spinnock Durav – even as the man now sought to prise her arms from around his neck – Calat swung round and shouted, 'Open the gate! We're coming in!'

*You forgot to add, 'The dragon will be joining us for the evening meal.' Commander, you will rue this gesture. Do I flee tonight? Or remain to satisfy my curiosity? One can hope she loses herself, and devours Durav in a single bite.*

*Finarra, poor Spinnock Durav. The tale I have to tell you conjures a less than pretty scene . . .*

*       *       *

The gate was pushed open, stuttering upon ridges of ice, until further movement was blocked by a heap of crusted snow. The opening it made was barely enough to emit the fur-wrapped figure that stumbled out to greet Kagamandra Tulas. Straightening, the figure squinted up at the lord, and then leaned back in through the gap. 'Trout! Get that shovel – no, the one with the handle, fool. Be quick about it!' Leaning back, the woman faced Kagamandra again. She dipped her head and said, 'Milord, welcome home.'

'Braphen, is that you?'

'Yes, milord. 'Tis Braphen, acting castellan here at Howls. Milord, your arrival was unexpected. No advance rider reached us, alas, to announce your imminent return. I must confess to a laxity in the upkeep, within the main house, that is. Sealed against the winter, sir, and the like.' She ducked her head a second time. 'I submit my resignation, milord, for having failed you.'

'Braphen,' said Kagamandra, dismounting, 'you've grown into a woman. You mentioned Trout? He remains, then. Good. I'm not interested in your resignation. There was no advance messenger. Castellan now? That will do.'

While he spoke, Trout appeared with a battered shovel in his cloth-wrapped hands. Seeing Kagamandra, the old veteran nodded, and then turned his head to one side, and spat into the snow. 'Sir,' he said, and then he bent to the task of clearing the snow that blocked the gate.

Castellan Braphen met her lord's gaze, and shrugged. 'He insisted I make him a captain, milord, or he'd leave. Same for Nassaras, and Igur Lout. Three captains, milord, to command the Houseblades.'

'That many? Well. How many Houseblades do I have, then?'

Braphen blinked, and then wiped her dripping nose with one forearm. 'Well, that's it, milord. Just the captains. The rest left when the orphans arrived. Headed west, I think. Sought to join Lady Hish Tulla's Houseblades, on account of her being related to you and all.'

'Hish Tulla is related to me?'

'She isn't, milord? The family names being so similar, people thought . . . well. Oh.'

Trout had managed to work the gate open by now, following a frenzy of flinging wet snow, and Kagamandra led his horse into the compound beyond. The animal shied as it passed beneath the lintel stone and Kagamandra had to fight the beast to bring it in.

'Abyss below,' he hissed, startled by his mount's sudden terror, 'what ails you?'

Braphen joined him, seeking to calm the animal. 'It's the orphans, milord.'

'What orphans?'

'Them as were gifted into your care, milord, by Lord Silchas Ruin and Captain Scara Bandaris. Hostages, actually.'

Kagamandra said nothing. Trout arrived to take the reins, and led the frightened horse towards the stables.

'I know, milord,' said Braphen, now tugging the gate shut once more. 'Trout's gotten even uglier. We're all agreed on that. Can't say how, or what's changed, but I wager your shock finds reason in his sorry visage. Alas, milord, it's not a shock easily worn off.'

'Silchas Ruin, you said. And Scara Bandaris? From whence come these hostages? More to the point, why give this estate a new name? And what manner of name is Howls?'

Braphen studied him for a moment, wiping her nose once more. 'You've not returned to take the charge of them, milord?'

'No. I know nothing about any hostages. Braphen, my patience is – no, lead me inside. I've need of a meal. Tell me there are winter stores to suffice.'

'Oh yes, milord. Plenty. We built us a new cold cellar, back near the old cistern, and it's stocked full of carcasses.'

'Near the cistern?'

'The *old* one, I said, milord. I mean, the one we found when we started digging. Well, when Trout started digging. So we decided to stop digging. Trout did, rather. The new cellar is beside it, milord, dug into clean dirt. For the carcasses. A big cellar, sir, obviously. It's not easy fitting fifty carcasses in anywhere.'

'Fifty carcasses?'

They had begun walking towards the main house. Kagamandra studied it with growing unease, as echoes of his father seemed to remain, ghostly, like stains upon the grey stones. The building looked smaller, ill fitting his memories.

'For the hostages, mostly, milord.'

'Excuse me, what is for the hostages, Braphen?'

'The meat, milord. Goats and steers and mutton.'

They ascended the ice-sheathed steps. Braphen edged ahead to open the door. 'Milord, welcome back.'

Three strides through, in the cloakroom, a grimy child stood as if awaiting them. He stared up at Kagamandra without expression. He was dressed in a tattered deerskin tunic, his lower legs bare and his feet stained black by ash and the greasy stone tiles.

'Ah, one of my hostages? Very well.' Kagamandra approached the child and reached out a hand to rest it upon the thin shoulder.

The boy bared his teeth and growled.

Kagamandra snatched his hand back.

'Jhelarkan hostages, milord,' said Braphen. 'This one is named Gear.'

'Silchas Ruin and Scara, you said?'

'Yes, milord.'

'I imagine neither has visited since delivering the hostages.'

'No, milord.'

'How many carcasses remain in that cellar?'

'About two-thirds, milord.'

'So there's room for, say, two more?'

Braphen frowned. 'Milord?'

'Never mind. Do we have a cook, or do we all eat raw meat now?'

'Igur Lout commands the kitchen these days, milord. You will find the hearth in the eating hall well lit, as it's where he passes the nights, mostly. With the orphans sleeping during the days for the most part, it's safer that way.' She drew off her heavier furs now, and the contrast of her comfortable excess with Kagamandra's own gaunt frame was startling. She interrupted his comparison by wiping her nose again. 'I will inform Igur to prepare you a meal, milord.'

'Yes, thank you, Braphen.'

Behind them, as Braphen set off for the kitchen, Trout arrived. Seeing Gear, he pointed a finger and said, 'That's the lord's own horse in the stables, you understand? Keep your claws and fangs off it!'

Gear spun and ran off down a corridor.

Trout glared at Kagamandra. 'Sir, I'm taking captain's pay, just like the rest of us still here. Barring the castellan, of course. On account of the hostages.'

'Understood, Trout. Now, join me in the dining room.'

Trout hesitated, and then nodded. 'Sir.' He followed as Kagamandra made his way towards the central chamber.

'And shed that miserable attitude of yours, will you? We're old friends, you may recall. We fought side by side. We've seen the worst the world can offer.'

'Shed, sir? Can't be done. This miserable attitude is all I've got. Nothing underneath. Just something naked and ugly, and all the uglier for being naked. I've not changed at all, sir. And you, well, you look more like you than you ever did before. So yes, let's have us a drink or two, sir. We can catch up. Shouldn't take long. Igur's not a bad cook, sir.'

'And where is Nassaras?'

'Don't know, don't care, and don't dare ask, sir. She's taken a liking to the hostages, you see.'

'Ah. Tell me, how many hostages did they send us?'

Reaching the long dining table, Trout edged forward to

sweep clutter and old foodstuffs from the surface, and then dragged out a chair for himself and sat.

Kagamandra moved to the high-backed chair at the table's head. He saw that it was sheathed in dust. He sat and looked expectantly at Trout, until the man cleared his throat and said, 'There were twenty-five to start, sir. Got maybe twenty left.'

'*What?* We've lost hostages?'

Trout scowled, reaching up to pull at the folds of wrinkled flesh on his cheeks, plucking them away from the bones underneath as if he sought to peel off his own face. It was an old habit, Kagamandra recalled, and probably responsible for the man's flaccid mien. 'Might look like that, but it wasn't none of our doing. The imps like fighting each other. The weakest ones died first. Those that are left are the nasty ones, and I reckon it's not over. Nassaras thinks it's to do with keeping them penned up. They're wild, you see. Some of them are still known to sleep outside, huddled under furs – sometimes the kind that're worn, sometimes their own.'

'They veer into their wolf forms?'

'They ain't got much control of that, sir. Not yet. Too young, I wager, and with no elders to teach them anything, who knows what'll come of this.' His dark, red-rimmed eyes flicked to Kagamandra. 'We beat 'em on the field of battle, sir. Demanded terms of surrender and made them kneel with heads bowed. Hostages, we said. Insisted, even.'

Sighing, Kagamandra nodded. 'No doubt it sounded reasonable in principle.'

Braphen reappeared and behind her walked Igur Lout carrying a battered silver tray on which rested a meal of mostly meat.

'Milord!' Igur said. 'You look awful. I've seen stuff spat up by one of the orphans with more life in it. Here. Eat. Braph, get that decanter of wine over there, and some mugs. It's a puking reunion, by the Abyss! The old company – or what's left of it. But the captain's back – the real captain, I mean, not money-grubbing feckers like Trout here.' The squat, wide man set the tray down in front of Kagamandra and then sat opposite Trout. Eyes on the ugly man, he raised a hand and made a strange corkscrewing motion with his index finger, grinning. 'Goes in one way and out the other, hey?'

Trout said, 'If the rest of us didn't hate cooking, Lout, I'd gut you right here, right now, begging the lord's pardon.'

'I see that little has changed,' Kagamandra said. 'Igur, that joke was old before I ever made captain in the Legion.'

'It's the only one he has,' Trout said, 'which ably under-scores his pathetic state.'

'This meat – is it horse?'

Igur nodded. 'Last one, sir. What we could scavenge off it. Had to beat the orphans back and half of them veered and slathered in gore. That was the day the rest of the Houseblades quit, the shit-smeared cowards. I trust, sir, you're already planning your revenge on Scara.'

Braphen finished pouring out the wine and turned to depart the room, before Kagamandra gestured and said, 'Sit down, castellan. Join us.'

'It's not fitting, sir. I expect they've got complaints about me and the like. In any case, I need to see that your bed-room's made ready.'

'Sit down. My room can wait.'

Igur leaned forward. 'Milord, I told you the first time we rode back in through yon gate, and I'll tell you now. Your father was a fuckwit. We buried him and shed not a tear, except in relief. Even his own staff spat on his shadow and they're long gone besides. It's all yours now, sir, and rightly so. I hear you got a wife coming. Good. Let's hope she has spirit, enough to break the legs on your bed.' He reached out and collected a goblet of wine, and added, 'Your health, milord.' He drank, and leaned back.

There was a long moment of silence, until Trout pointed a finger at Igur and said, 'And this is why no one likes you, Lout, excepting when you cook for us. You got all the delicacy of a pig on a place mat.'

Distant thumping drew everyone's attention. Braphen rose. 'Someone's at the gate, milord.'

'Ah,' said Kagamandra, 'that would be Sergeant Savarro

and her deserters. Igur, best return to the kitchen and begin preparations to feed our guests. They might number a score or more.'

Cursing under her breath, Braphen made for the gate.

Igur rose, collected up the decanter of wine. 'Sir,' he said, 'they might change their mind.'

At that moment, a chorus of howls erupted from somewhere on the estate grounds.

Kagamandra glanced down at the supper he had but just started, and then he stood. 'Well, yes. A warning does seem appropriate, under the circumstances. But I doubt they will change their minds, since they have nowhere else to go.'

'They got horses, sir?'

'And mules, Igur.'

Trout groaned and climbed upright. 'I'll see 'em stabled and all, sir, and I'll take the first watch, too.'

By the time Kagamandra reached the gate, Savarro, Ristand and a half-dozen other Wardens were already crowding Braphen, who stood blocking their way in with one shoulder leaning against the door. Upon seeing Kagamandra, Sergeant Savarro's eyes brightened, and then an expression of dread crossed her features.

Braphen glanced back. 'Milord, they are proving most insistent.'

'Step back, castellan.'

'Milord, it's the discourtesy I am objecting to. They are in no position to insist.'

'Agreed, Braphen. But we will give them the compound at the very least, and the stable for their animals. Sergeant Savarro, kindly hold your people back, will you? The situation here is not as simple as it seems. On second thoughts, have them gather here, this side of the gate, while the two of us renew our acquaintance.'

Braphen retreated to permit the troop to spill into the compound. Kagamandra saw that there had been no split from the ranks, despite the news of Calat Hustain's return. Some of the tension in the air had reached the children, and most were bawling. The mules and horses baulked at the threshold and required some effort to bring them inside. Gesturing to Savarro, Kagamandra moved a dozen paces away from the jostling mob.

She and Ristand joined him, the huge man scowling and casting glares at Braphen.

'Lord, forgive me,' began Savarro. 'You didn't identify yourself earlier—'

'No need for apologies, sergeant. I was in no position to enlighten you on the condition of this estate. Now, it seems that the argument I left behind has been settled, although not in the way I would have expected.'

'We voted, milord, and went with the majority. Continue on. The Vitr's bitter curse on Calat Hustain. We saw too many friends dead on that hillside.'

'That castellan giving us grief,' said Ristand, scowling. 'What kind of welcome is that? It's cold. The sun is going down. The night is going to be frigid. My feet ache and I'm hungry. I told you, Savarro, it's a new age, an age where no one cares to help anyone else. Kurald Galain becomes a realm of refugees. That's no way to live.'

'Will you shut your mouth for once, Ristand?'

'Why should I?' He waved towards Kagamandra. 'Even this estate's lord tried talking us out of coming here. Why else tell us about Hustain's return to the fort? Hunn Raal has the right of it – you fight for kin and the rest can go to the Abyss!'

Kagamandra cleared his throat, and then said, 'You are welcome to stay, Wardens. But my invitation must be qualified—'

'What's that mean?' Ristand's head whipped round to his sergeant. 'What's he mean by that?'

'I mean,' Kagamandra resumed, 'that we have Jhelarkan hostages here. Children. They are as near to feral as wolves. Your horses and mules are not safe, although we will endeavour to set a guard upon the stables.'

'Jhelarkan?' Ristand tugged at his snarled beard. 'See, Savarro? What did I tell you? Qualified. He invites us into a nest of shapeshifting wolves! More horses to keep 'em fed and not eyeing us with hungry eyes! I should have voted against you.'

'But you argued the most for coming here, Ristand!'

'Because this lord here didn't tell me the truth!'

'He didn't know!'

'He does now!'

'Ristand, get out of my face before I cut you into little strips! See to the animals, and arrange us a watch for them, two on guard at all times.'

'They're hostages, sergeant! We can't harm them even if they're chewing off our feet!'

'Just beat them back. Flat of the blades. Milord, how many Jhelarkan hostages are here?'

'Twenty.'

'*Twenty?*' Ristand shrieked.

His cry elicited howls from the main house, rising gleefully into the crepuscular air. Hearing them, Ristand swore under his breath and drew his sword. 'I rescind my vote,' he snapped. 'You hear me, sergeant? I vote the other way. That makes it a majority. I'm not getting my feet chewed off.'

'Ristand! Just go and arrange the guard postings, will you? The vote's done with. We're here now. Besides, I was only humouring all of you, about that majority stuff. I'm sergeant, highest rank left among us. It's my decision.'

'Cock curdling liar! Tit bag whore! I knew it!'

'Go, you're embarrassing us all.'

Ristand snarled and set off back to the others waiting by the gate.

Wiping at her brow, Savarro drew a deep breath and let it out slowly. 'Apologies, milord. Husbands, what can you do?'

\*     \*     \*

Four trackers were on her trail, two of them moving up alongside her. Sharenas Ankhadu caught glimpses of them through the crazed lattice of leafless branches and twigs to either side. The remaining pair had drawn up behind her on the track.

She was exhausted, and the day's light would not fade in time to make any difference in her attempts to evade these hunters. Before dusk's arrival she knew that blades would clash, shattering the silence of the frozen forest.

It would be an ignominious end, filled with bitter frustration and fraught with pathos. *A proper scene, highlighting the sheer indecency of civil war. Soldiers I fought alongside – now we close with murder in our eyes, weapons unsheathed.*

*Where, in all this, was the life I wanted? The victory of peace whispered so many promises. Kagamandra, we should have fled. Together, into the west, the lands of the Azathanai, or even the Dog-Runners. We should have damned the legacy of peace – you with your promised wife you did not love, me with a future empty of passion. Peace should have won us more. It should have won us a softening of all that was harsh and hard within us, an easing of the ferocity we all saw as necessary weapons in war.*

*Instead, too many of us turned fierce eyes upon these plain trappings, these quiet chambers. Too many of us still gripped bared iron, even as we walked into realms of peace, filled with the hope of living peaceful lives.*

*We were contemptuous of such lives, such living. It was beneath us warriors, us harbingers of blood and death. We could see in their eyes – in the eyes of loved ones, estranged friends, husbands and wives – that they knew nothing. Nothing of what truly mattered, what truly counted. They were shallow, ignorant of depravity's depths. We saw them as fools, and then, as our souls hardened in our self-made isolation, we saw them as victims, no different from enemies upon the field of battle.*

*To us, they were blind to the ongoing war – the one we still fought, the one that left our souls wounded, bleeding, and then scarred. The one that cried out to us, demanding a lashing out, an eruption of violence. If only to break this brittle illusion of peace, which we knew to distrust.*

*But I dreamed of being among them, away from the killing and the terror. I dreamed of peace in every instant of war in which I lived.*

*Why, then, could I not find it? Why did it all seem so weak, so thin, so hopelessly shallow? So . . . false?*

The trackers moving parallel to her had begun converging, while those in her wake had drawn close enough for her to hear their thudding footfalls. Desperate, Sharenas looked for somewhere to make her stand – the bole of an old tree, the root-wall of a toppled giant – but there was nothing like that nearby. She was among young dogwoods, elm thickets and young birch. No fire had rushed through any of this, and the leaf-mould was thick beneath the melting snow.

The soldier on her left voiced a strangled cry. Snapping a glance in that direction, she searched for the man, but could no longer see him.

At that instant, the two behind her rushed forward, even as the third scout swung in to flank her.

Mouth dry, sword-grip feeling greasy in her gloved hand, Sharenas spun round to face her attackers.

Both were women, and known to her, but now hatred twisted their features, and the blood was bright in their eyes.

There was no conversation, no pause in their attack.

Blades lashed out. She caught one, deflecting it, while side-stepping to evade the other. At that moment, the third hunter reached her, lunging with his sword.

The tip pierced the rounded flesh of her right hip, slicing it open to the bone. As the cut muscles and tendons parted, she felt them roll up beneath her skin, and her right leg simply gave way beneath her.

A blade struck her helm, dislodging it. Stunned, Sharenas fell on to her side. A savage blow against her sword knocked the weapon from her hand.

Disbelieving, she looked up into the face of one of the women, who now stood above her, bringing her sword around to push through Sharenas's throat.

The woman paused, confusion clouding her face.

An arrow's iron point was protruding from her neck. Blood was rushing down from the ragged tear its passage had made. The life in the woman's eyes retreated, and then she dropped to her knees atop Sharenas.

Pushing the sagging body off, Sharenas dug in the heel of

her one working leg and attempted to scrabble back. The other woman, she saw, was lying a few paces away, her midriff opened wide and its bundle of intestines tumbled out, steaming. Above her body crouched a grey-skinned girl. She held in her red hands long narrow knives, both slick with gore. Twisting round, Sharenas saw the third scout, lying facedown with the shafts of two arrows jutting from his back.

The girl advanced on Sharenas. 'Plenty hunting you,' she said. 'Too many for just a deserter. No matter. You wear the wrong uniform.'

Another voice spoke. 'No, Lahanis. Leave her.'

The girl scowled. 'Why?'

'She is bleeding out anyway, and the cut is too deep to mend. She is already dead. We gave you one.'

'One is not enough.'

'Come, we have cleared this part of the forest, but there are others. They will camp. Light fires. We have a night of killing ahead of us, Lahanis, enough to ease your thirst.'

The scene was dulling before Sharenas's eyes, a grey too flat to be the arrival of dusk. She had one hand pressed against the gash in her hip, and the blood was pumping from the wound in hot waves. Her right leg was lifeless, a weight pinning her to the cold ground. The ache in her skull, and in the muscles and tendons on the left side of her neck, left her gasping, each breath frighteningly shallow.

She heard them move off after recovering their arrows and stripping the bodies.

Some time passed, but it was difficult to know how much. The dimness surrounding her felt disconnected from the sun's vague departure. It was closer, crawling towards her from all sides, as if promising a warm embrace.

*Kagamandra. Look at me now. I hold a hand to the place of my death, seeking to staunch the leak. The blood feels thick now. Thick as clay. It must be the cold.*

*And I feel an ache in my leg. I imagine I can curl my toes, scuff with the heel. Here, on this edge, I rebuild my broken form, as if preparing for what will come. No longer broken, but whole again. Ready to walk into the darkness.*

*And yet . . . Kagamandra. Still I lie here, longing for you with every essence of my being. What holds me to life, if not desire? What vaster power exists? With it, I swear, I feel I can defy the inevitable. Weapon and shield, companion and ally, enough to make the world back away, enough to surmount the highest walls and cross the deepest chasms. Desire, you stand in place of a lover's arms, and make your embrace such dark comfort.*

She heard her own sigh, startling in its clarity, its harsh rattle. Beneath her cold-numbed hand, the gash felt strange, drawn together, the skin puckered and tender. The bunched fists of the rolled-up tendons and muscles no longer burned against her hip bone, as if with her hand she had simply pushed them back into place.

*But that is not possible.*

Disbelieving, Sharenas found the strength to sit up. Her right leg throbbed with the kind of ache that bespoke deep outrage, and yet it lived. Beneath her the spilled blood had mixed with dirty snow and then leaf-mould and mud. It felt hot to the touch and the steam rising from it did not slacken.

The greyness surrounded her still, palpable like an unseen presence. In her head she heard vague whispers, muttering and, now and then, a faint, distant cry. Blinking, Sharenas looked round. This part of the trail was slightly wider than usual, but otherwise unremarkable. She shared the space with three corpses. The spilled entrails, she saw, were frosted over.

*How – how long?*

Groaning, she pushed herself to her feet, stood tottering for a moment before she caught the glint of her fallen sword. She hobbled a step, crouched to retrieve the weapon, and straightened once more.

*Now what?*

The scouts had been stripped of food packs and water flasks, but tightly bound bedrolls and cooking gear remained, all secured to prevent noise when the scouts tracked her. Sharenas realized that she was desperately hungry, and

585

fighting a thirst so fierce she eyed the black spatters of blood on the ground at her feet.

The greyness urged her to feast, revealing its own hunger, bestial and primitive. Sharenas studied the corpse of the woman nearest her, listening to the chorus of faint voices susurrating through her head.

*Are you spirits? Did I summon you? Or was it this impossible sorcery – which I never knew I possessed – that drew you into my company? Do you, perhaps, remember what it was to be consumed with desire? Because that alone sustained me. Kagamandra, I have made the memory of you into my lover. Loyal ghost, I feel still your fiery embrace.*

*But this new hunger, this is a simpler thing. A need both raw and cold. I have lost too much blood. I must restore myself.*

The chattering spirits crowded her, and like a soul dispossessed of physical form, she watched her own body, as it dragged the corpse of the woman to one side of the trail, and then set about cutting strips of red meat from one of the thighs.

Once this was done, she set about making a fire.

*What now?*

*Now this.*

# FIFTEEN

'I HAVE LIVED,' SAID LORD HUST HENARALD, 'IN A world of smoke.' He sat on a stone bench in the chill garden, amidst leafless thickets and snow-capped boulders. Overhead the sky was thick with a grey blending of snowflakes and ash. Someone, perhaps a servant, had settled a thick robe on the lord, rough wool dyed burgundy, and it was draped unclasped across his shoulders like a mantle of old blood.

Galar Baras sat opposite. To his left was the low curving wall of the fountain. The mechanical pump had long ceased to function and the thick ice on the water was streaked and smeared with dead algae. Old layers of soot darkened the snow upon the ground.

'It blinds the fools who dwell in its midst,' Henarald continued, his vein-roped hands red with cold as he picked through a small heap of slag that rested in a pile upon the encircling stone wall. Occasionally, he brought one piece closer to his face for careful examination, eyes narrowing, before returning it to the heap. In the time that Galar had been in audience with the lord, a number of pieces of the ragged waste material had been examined more than once. 'It stings, awakens tears, but leaves nothing seen to give comfort.'

'Milord,' Galar Baras ventured, not for the first time, 'the armour you have sent us. The blades as well. Something now afflicts them—'

'In smoke we dwell, shrouding us in the weariest of days. Do you see this ash? The last of the charcoal. Soon will come to us the stench of poor coal, and the iron will be brittle, red and short. It's the sulphur, you see.' He selected another piece of slag and peered at it. 'We beat order into the world and make a song of smoke, but such music is too harsh, or not harsh enough, for the soul is never as strong as it believes itself, nor ever as weak as it fears. We are, in all, middling creatures, eager to bedeck our lives in trappings of grandeur. Self-importance. But still the smoke remains, blinding us, and what tears find our cheeks are but wet signifiers of irritation, damp whispers of discomfort. The air soon takes them away, to make each face a blank page.' He set the rough piece of slag back down. 'And now, this is all I see, here through the smoke. Faces like blank pages. I know none of them, yet imagine that I should. The confusion frightens me. I am stalked by what I once knew and haunted by the man I once was. You cannot know how that feels.'

'Milord, what has happened to the Hust iron?'

Something flickered in Henarald's blue eyes, like pale sunlight upon a blade. 'Born of smoke – I never imagined how it would feel, this imprisonment. Is it any wonder we cry? Wrapped in flesh, drawn down, muscle to match the fuller's peen, bent and swaged, the patina writ like poetry, yearning for a voice that might be music, only to yield nothing but cries of anguish. Iron is a prison, my friend, and escape is impossible when you are the bars.'

'I never believed them alive, milord. In all my years, wielding this sword at my side, I told myself that I heard nothing living in its voice. Others swore otherwise. Many winced upon releasing the blade from its scabbard. They marched into battle with visages of dread. For one man, a fine soldier, that voice became his own cry of terror—'

Henarald waved dismissively. 'Terror lives a brief span. When there is no possible escape, madness proves a quick and sure refuge.' An odd smile twisted the old man's gaunt features. 'Iron and flesh alike.'

'Milord—'

'The forges are dying. The age of the Hust ends. We burned our way into a world of ash. Could you even imagine, my friend, how it felt? The day I walked a forest of stumps and holes, of ravaged ground, roots clawing the sky, and saw upon all sides the ledger of my enterprise, my sordid fever? Did I think the new vistas promised escape? Did I set my gaze upon distant hills, verdant with nature, and but lick my lips?' He shuddered suddenly, and the wool slipped down to reveal the bones of his shoulders prominent beneath thin skin. The man was naked beneath the robe. 'I might have. I might have. Mother bless me, but I might have.'

The madness of iron was a difficult, terrible thing to witness. Galar Baras looked away, chilled by the stone bench, the frigid, flake-filled air, this mocking knot of garden. After a moment he rose, stepped close to his lord, and returned the robe to its place upon Henarald's shoulders. He saw the tears running down upon the man's spalled cheeks, freezing white and glistening in the deep wrinkles.

'Industry, milord. The demands of progress. These are forces the tide of which we cannot withstand. There is no single man or woman to blame. The crime, if such a thing could be said to exist, is our nature, and our nature we cannot deny, nor defeat.'

Henarald looked up with watery eyes. 'You believe this thing, Galar Baras?' he asked in a hoarse whisper.

'I do, milord. If not the Hust bloodline upon the anvil, then another, or yet another. The Jaghut alone displayed the proper courage, to refuse their own natures, to turn their backs upon progress, but even then, milord, their final congress was one of destruction and abandonment.'

'The Jaghut? The Jaghut, yes. They unravelled the iron, released the screams. So she told me, when she sat here with me, beside the fountain, and touched my brow.'

'Milord? Who?'

He frowned. 'The Azathanai, named by the Tiste Andii.

What was that name? Yes, now I remember. T'riss, born of the Vitr. She sat with me, as I wept in the wake of my gift to Lord Anomander. Upon a night when I could hear the breaking of my soul.'

'She came here?'

His expression drained into something lifeless, spun so far inward that he seemed a corpse. His next words fell flat, devoid of inflection. 'The realms are bound. Beaten and twisted. They tremble to the pressure and yearn to burst apart. Wrapped and folded, wrapped and folded, quenched in the fires of chaos. Within the Hust iron, my friend, Mother bless me, I imprisoned a thousand realms. A thousand and more.' He paused, eyes slightly widening as they remained fixed upon the slag heap. 'She showed me, with her horse of grass, her woven cloak, her russet sword. Magic resists imprisonment – and yet, I worked unknowing, blissfully uncomprehending of my crimes. The forges are dying, as they must, and the world will end, as it must.' He reached up, set a trembling finger upon his brow. 'Here, with a single caress, she gave me leave. And now here I dwell, in this place. This quick and sure refuge.' Suddenly smiling, Henarald reached down to select another piece of slag. He studied it intently. 'We deem this waste. Why? It has all the shout of stone, freed of the weight of iron, smelling only of usage. Waste? No more than a corpse, and it takes a cold soul to deem that detritus.'

'Milord, I beg you – tell me more of the Hust iron, and these realms of which you speak.'

Henarald blinked. 'Realms?' His face twisted. 'You fool! Here I speak of the beauty that is waste, the beauty that is usefulness exhausted. I speak of the freedom in each piece of slag, in each bone upon the field. See how this one curls? Is that not the most perfect smile? It revels in its escape. Beyond our grasp now, don't you understand? Like the ashes rising from the last chimneys, or the wretched sulphur in the coal. Like the barren hillsides, or the mined-out pits. Our industry promises immortality, and yet behold, the only immortal creation it achieves is the wasteland!' He leaned over, plunging his hands into the heap of slag. 'Listen! Bury me in a

590

mound of this treasure, Galar Baras. A barrow constructed of my legacy, piece by piece. Imbue the gesture with ritual, and each one of you select a single fragment. Build the mound by procession, suitably solemn. I would my bones join the pointless concert of freedom. Pronounce me useless and so bless my remains with everlasting peace.'

Shaken, Galar Baras stepped back. He bowed to Henarald – the gesture unseen by the lord, who now sought to embrace the pile of slag with both arms, slipping down to his knees upon the frozen ground beside the fountain's wall – and then departed the garden.

*When such a man loses his way, we are all left feeling lost. We flee, and yet carry with us something of the infection, jarred into imbalance, reeling in our own minds like a drunkard.*

He found himself in a broad corridor, a grand causeway with niches upon each wall, in which stood mundane objects fashioned from metal. They marked a progression, from copper and tin to bronze and iron, from cast to wrought, poured to drawn and folded, an evolution of metallurgy, as if inviting the notion of advancement with the ease of taking a step, and then another, and another. The intention, he well understood, was one of triumph, of wild energies tamed, subjugated. And yet, he now realized, not one object on display revealed the discarded leavings of its making: more than just slag and tailings, but also the bitter taste of the smoke from its forging, the stench of burned hair and flesh, the dusty surrender of wood and sap, streams and rivers fouled, the countless lives altered, for good or ill, by industry's manic zeal.

Despondent, he walked slowly down the corridor until he came to the last niche, which was empty. This vacant space announced the birth of Hust iron. The tale of that absence was one he'd always thought both unlikely and perverse. No object made of that metal, it was said, welcomed the stripping away of function, of value and labour, the reduction to a curiosity, an offering solely for display. The tale was well known of the moment when a Hust sword, bared, was set in the niche. Its howl was heard throughout the estate, and it had been unceasing, deafening. Until recently, Galar Baras had thought the story apocryphal.

Now, he halted opposite the empty niche and stared into the poignant absence.

It had been midday, snow wet upon the ground, when at last the officers of the Hust Legion were fully assembled at the wagons. Amid the sharp unease there was a current of anticipation among the prisoners. If freedom had a cost, and if that charge was the cruel gift of Hust weapons and armour, then this was the moment of consummation, and bound to the notion of freedom there was power. Men and women who had lived in cages, they were the starved before the feast.

Among the officers, only two held back, visibly reluctant to join the others. The woman Rance, who had drowned her own babe, stood beside Wareth. Her wringing hands were so red Galar thought them scalded, and her face was ashen with dread. As for Wareth, well, Galar Baras understood the man's sickly visage, his slumped shoulders and the animal panic flitting about in his gaze as the tarps were drawn back from the nearest wagon.

Captain Castegan had taken a malicious pleasure in finding Wareth's old sword among the wrapped weapons on the bed. Its hide sheath had been marked to distinguish it from the others, with a series of runes branded into the leather. They were the marks of a weaponsmith when, upon completing and then testing a blade's will, it was found to be flawed. In this instance, of course, it was not the iron at fault, but its wielder.

With a half-smile, Castegan clearly intended to make a ceremony of delivering the sword to Wareth. Furious, Galar Baras set out, marshalling hard words for the old man. But to Castegan's surprise Wareth stepped forward and, before the captain could embellish the moment further, plucked the wrapped sword from the veteran's hands. He then stripped away the hide to reveal the naked blade.

Galar Baras saw the weapon jolt in Wareth's grip, as if

seeking to twist round to cut its owner, but Wareth steadied the sword, the muscles of his wrist bunching with the effort. And from the man came a wry smile that he held with bitter disdain as he met Castegan's eyes. 'Thank you, captain,' he said.

'It wants your blood.'

'Enough, Castegan,' warned Galar Baras as he drew nearer.

The moment had been seen by the others. There had been gasps upon witnessing the will of the sword, and some of the anticipation among the prisoners drained away.

Even then, Galar could not be certain that the sword's sudden twist had not belonged to some wayward, suicidal impulse from Wareth himself. But, after a moment's contemplation, that seemed unlikely. After all, in addition to wilful stupidity, suicide also took courage.

'Best sheathe it soon, lieutenant,' Castegan said. 'You wouldn't want an accident.'

The sword had begun moaning, and that in turn woke the other weapons still on the wagon, raising a mournful dirge.

Quickly returning to the wagon, Castegan gestured to Seltin Ryggandas. Expression bleak, the quartermaster directed one of his aides to begin distributing the arms.

The first prisoner to step forward to accept a sword was the blacksmith, Curl.

Another wagon had been brought up, this one stacked with standard scabbards of wood, bronze and leather, and after taking a Hust sword into his hands Curl was directed towards that one. The man unwrapped the blade as he made his way to the second wagon. When the cover fell away, he halted as if struck. His sword had begun laughing. Quickly the laughter rose into a manic cackle.

In shock, Curl flung the weapon to the ground.

The sword shrieked its glee, shivering on the half-frozen mud.

'*Pick it up!*'

Galar Baras was not sure who had shouted that command, but Curl reached down and collected up the weapon. He seemed to struggle to hold on to it as he hurried over to the second wagon. Accepting a scabbard he quickly slammed the weapon home. Its terrible laughter was muted, but only by the scabbard itself.

*Something is wrong. I have never heard—*

Wareth moved up beside Galar Baras and said, 'They have been driven mad, sir.'

'That is ridiculous, Wareth. They are not sentient. There is nothing living within that iron.'

'You still hold to that, sir?'

Galar Baras made no reply, stung by the disbelief in Wareth's tone.

'The others have lost their lust for power,' Wareth then observed of the prisoners, who had all drawn back from the wagons. 'And these are the officers, since you insist on calling them that. How will it be when we equip everyone else in this camp? Granted, more than a few will join in the laughter, being utterly mad already. But most, sir, well, they just made mistakes in their lives. And were busy paying for them.'

'Wareth, make Rebble the next one.'

'Commander, I doubt I can make Rebble do anything he's not of a mind to do.'

'Just convey my order.'

Nodding, Wareth walked over to the tall, bearded man. They began arguing in low tones.

Galar glanced over at Rance. 'You after Rebble,' he said.

'I tried telling Wareth,' she said in a brittle voice. 'I don't like blood. My . . . my first night of womanhood wasn't . . . not a good memory, that is. Sir. I don't want to be here. I can't be a soldier, sir.'

'It's that, or the corps of cutters.'

'But that would be—'

'I'm sure it would,' Galar snapped.

At last, Rebble moved, but instead of making his way to the weapons, he strode to the wagon bearing the scabbards. Collecting one, he faced the other wagon. Then, with an oath, he approached. Reaching the aide he snatched the wrapped sword from the woman's hands. Tearing the hide away he raised the suddenly shrieking blade before his own face, and snarled, 'Save it for the fucking enemy!'

The sword's scream intensified, and from the wagon the moaning sharpened, rising in pitch, and then broke into gleeful laughter.

The prisoners were all backing away. Galar could see, beyond his officers, a crowd gathering from the main camp. The air was taut now, on the very edge of panic.

Rebble sheathed the sword with shaking hands.

Galar could feel the situation slipping away. Even the weapons hanging at the sides of the few remaining regulars were crying out within their scabbards. His own sword's voice reached him, frenetic and fractured.

Wareth returned to his side. 'Commander, we're making a mistake here.'

Galar turned to Rance. 'Get in that line.'

'Yes sir.'

They watched her walk unsteadily towards the wagon bearing the scabbards.

The regulars beyond the thin cordon of guards were crowding closer, strangely mute.

Wareth tried again. 'Sir—'

'I am not aware of any viable option,' Galar said in a low voice.

'I have always believed that they were alive. But . . . somehow, they seemed to be . . . I don't know. Controlled. Chained. Now, sir, they are indeed insane. What will bearing these weapons, and then the armour, do to us?'

Galar Baras hesitated, and then said, 'The day after the Poisoning, Wareth, the iron howled – I was there for that. Its cry haunts me still. Those of us present . . . I think it drove us all slightly mad, and some of us . . . well, not just slightly.'

'It's said,' Wareth muttered, edging closer, 'that the world is rotten with sorcery now. Is it possible that the magic has somehow infected the iron?'

'I don't know.'

Rebble seemed to have regained his composure, although

his expression was fierce as he cajoled the other officers forward to the wagons.

'Rebble was a good choice, sir. For this, you needed a man with no imagination.'

'And you, Wareth?'

The man shook his head, glanced down at the bared blade still in his hand. 'Too much, sir. Far too much.'

'Still, your old weapon has little to say.'

'For now, sir, so it seems.'

Yet, for all Rebble's threats and bluster, the officers resisted. The quartermaster collected another of his aides and directed him to begin scabbarding the swords. The blades were then brought over, one by one, into the tight knot of officers. Galar watched Rance accept a weapon, gripping it awkwardly, her hands so red he wondered if she had washed them in blood.

Cursing, Rebble walked over. 'Commander, this won't work.'

'It will have to,' Galar replied.

'We've not even got to the armour yet – you can't put that shit into a scabbard, can you? And almost nobody from the old Hust's worn it yet, either. Wasn't it delivered the day after the Poisoning?'

'Get back to the others, Rebble,' Galar said. 'Show some spine.'

'Spine?' Rebble's sudden smile was bright and dangerous. 'Oh, I've plenty of that, sir. Too much, maybe. But it ain't the bending kind. You break it and I'm useless. But until then it'll take a lot of weight, sir, and it knows how to push back.'

'Your point, Rebble?'

'Just that, sir. You want me back there, fine. But I'm no merchant. If you want me to sell something I'll make a pitch, only I pitch with my fists, sir.'

'Just pull Curl to your side, and Rance, and each new one to take a weapon. Line them up, Rebble.'

Still smiling, Rebble saluted and returned to the clutch of officers.

'You should have spoken up, Wareth. You have a way with Rebble.'

Wareth grunted. 'Hardly. I just make certain that every order I give him is for something he'd do anyway. That man chose to save my life in the mining camp, but I can't tell you his reason for doing so. He still binds me straight every night.' He shook his head. 'This is how it is among us. Our crimes we hold like shields. Some are solid and strong, but others are flimsy and weak. Some are little more than illusions, or whispers.' He nodded at the officers. 'As with Listar, there. His mystery protects him, though who can say for how much longer. In any case, sir, those shields are more than just things to protect us. They're also what we hide behind.'

Rebble had managed to order the others into a rough line. They had belted their weapons, but even scabbarded the swords at their hips and the others remaining on the wagon's bed still cried out, a cacophony as shrill as gulls upon a battlefield. A mass of regular prisoners had begun pushing closer. Galar saw more than one guard being shoved backwards. Their hands were on the grips of their blades. *They won't hold.*

'They want to see for themselves,' Wareth said. 'They want to know what's coming.'

At that moment, two riders walked their horses into the gap behind the thin line of guards. Recognizing them, Galar Baras felt a tremor of shock.

The two men were having a conversation, loud enough to cut through the clamour of the weapons.

'Hark, old friend, do you hear something amiss?'

'Crows will chatter,' the other replied. 'Why, I once held a blade that did nothing but complain. Eager to cut, but chafing in the misery of peace.'

'What fate that weapon, Prazek?'

'Seduced by rust, in the manner of retired soldiers, sagging prostitutes and decrepit bards with wavering voices. All things end in their time, Dathenar.'

'But swords that chortle in the midst of mayhem, Prazek, surely that is untoward?'

'Promises to the enemy,' Prazek replied, halting his mount and leaning on his saddle horn as he surveyed the prisoners.

'I've a mind to take such a blade and, indeed, to wear both the armour and its dreadful avowal. Someone must speak for the madness of civil war, after all, and if such a war is to have a voice, then these weapons will suit.'

Dathenar reined in and slipped down from his horse. He adjusted his heavy gauntlets. 'Uncanny amusement is to make a song of our sad state of affairs? Well suited indeed. You there! Ready for me a fine weapon!' He strode easily towards the wagon. 'Let it be one that shrieks on my behalf! Let it crow in the manner of . . . of . . .'

'Crows,' suggested Prazek.

'Of crows! Bleak and black above battles just done, outraged by bounty, furious with excess. Trapped between glee and grief, between the empty belly and salvation. Such weapons surely know how to survive, enough to crown the sky with midnight hues. Promises, you say, Prazek? Imagine the quavering knees among the enemy, there in their trembling line – why, the justice of their cause, as they might see it, shrinks like a sac of nuts in ice water. While we stand before them, hands upon engorged grips, swords climbing from slick scabbards—'

'Dathenar! You filade the charming gender of half these soldiers here! What of the round-faced and sweet-eyed, the buxom and the ample, the curved icons of aesthetic perfection?'

Dathenar accepted a sword and scabbard. He drew the weapon with a flourish. It screamed. 'What is this? Am I so ugly as to elicit terror?'

'Not your visage, friend. Perhaps your breath.'

'Impossible! I speak with rose petals upon my tongue. It's a habit of discourse. But, if I understand you, Prazek, you spoke of women.'

'My weakness, yes.'

'It is surely their strength that makes you weak.'

'That, and the unmanning fear of mystery.'

'Then, for a woman here to take hold of such a sword, pommel glistening and iron stiff with anticipation, why, would she not prove far more fearless than any man at her side? Will not the blade shiver in deafening horror at her willingness to see it tested?'

'Tested and tried, blunted and nicked, made limp if such a thing were possible. I now see your point, Dathenar.'

'There are points and then there are points. I am now eager for loud armour, if only to invite a clash of opinions.'

'Elegance was ever your suit, Dathenar. By fine tailoring and cloth's perfect cut, by colours in subtle complement and boots of profound polish, you are ever the envy of others.'

'Grace is an acquisition, Prazek, though it demands a mindful application. Only by practice am I born to it, as natural as the coiled and perfumed curls upon my head.'

'And when your helm howls, Dathenar? How will you answer?'

'With a smile, friend, as befits my supreme confidence. You, quartermaster! Is it not time for an unveiling of armour? Your officers need timely garb, with your clerks no doubt eager to allot names to kit, in even rows to prove salient organization, and scrolls coded by the colour of their wax, or some such thing. Look at me, sir! Do I not stand as if naked here?'

Standing close beside Galar Baras, Wareth muttered a disbelieving curse. 'Commander? Who are these fools?'

Smiling, Galar Baras shook his head. 'An unexpected blessing, Wareth. But even so, I did not expect Lord Anomander to be so . . . generous.'

'Sir?'

'The two finest officers from his Houseblades, Wareth. Lieutenants Prazek and Dathenar.'

Two of Seltin's assistants had appeared, carrying between them a hide-wrapped bundle. They reached Dathenar and set it down at his feet.

'Well, unwrap it now, will you, good sirs?'

The prisoners crowded still closer, although this time something had changed. No longer threatening. Urged forward instead by curiosity, and something of the pleasure that might attend the performance of mummers or jesters.

Prazek remained on his horse, and suddenly Galar

understood the value of that, as the man abruptly straightened. 'Soldiers of the Hust Legion! Your wise commander has given me leave to address this momentous moment! Did I truly say "momentous moment"? Why, indeed I did, since we are about to witness a moment so important it demands twice saying.'

'I missed that,' Dathenar called as he watched the unfolding of the hide. 'Pray say it again.'

''Tis overfamiliarity, Dathenar,' Prazek said in a growl, 'that makes you careless in my company.'

'No doubt. Now then, Prazek, in keeping with your moment of momentous import, do call to me our own precious squad, which we found upon the road on our way here. The commander would see what we have made of such misanthropic gallywags.'

'Why, we have made nothing of them yet.'

Dathenar frowned. 'No time like the present, which, if you think on it, could not be truer, with the past done with and the future forever undiscovered. Call them to me, Prazek. They may not be officers, either in material or comportment, but in answering the former we mayhap invite the latter. Failing that, we simply kill them all.'

Prazek swung his mount round and gestured. 'Be not shy, my pretties. Do recall, it was slothfulness on the road that proved your doing in the midst of your quicker comrades' undoing. Dulled of wit and spark, you but stood unnerved while the blood, guts, limbs and heads of your fellow deserters flung about as if of their own accord. Come now, reveal the mercy of your officers in that we permitted your return, and let it be a sundry lesson of fate to everyone else, should one or two be eyeing the empty plains beyond the camp.'

The ragtag deserters shuffled into view.

Seltin caught Galar's eye and the commander answered with a swift nod.

Dathenar now raised up a hauberk of heavy chain. 'Abyss below! We shall be adorned in the impervious! Thus weighted, no such line will ever take a back step! Why, link by link, we best our enemy – and see here, the vambraces! What so amuses them, I wonder? No matter – see if they laugh when I inadvertently sit on them. And the greaves, bracing enough to fend off whatever might seek to bark my shin, be it pup or grovelling servant. And what are these? Scales to drape my shoulders, a coif for head and neck, and at last, the helm! Oh, hollow-voiced one, I would fill your space with bold thoughts – yours if not mine! Now, who will dress me?' He swung round, squinted at the oversized squad of deserters, and then pointed at a woman. 'You are comely enough. Shall we make a game of it?'

Sudden laughter from the crowd of prisoners. And upon that rustle of sound, the manic mirth of the weapons fell away, leaving behind a silence that drew gasps from many.

Dathenar frowned. 'As I suspected, Prazek! For all this performance, Hust iron is without humour. Or any natural delight in the softness of a caressing touch, the chance meeting of shy gazes, a brush of hips – ah, still my sword that I hold – some things aver public witness, for now, at least.'

Prazek stood in his stirrups to face the crowd. 'Leer if you will at this graven and solemn scene of disrobement followed by . . . er, robement. Your attention is most welcome, and hopefully enlightening for the virgins among you.'

Wheeling from renewed laughter, and a few lewd shouts, Prazek kicked his horse forward into a loping, lazy trot, reining in before Galar Baras. The lieutenant dismounted and saluted. 'Commander, by command of Lord Silchas Ruin, we are now at your disposal.'

'Silchas? Not your lord's?'

'Just so, sir, as Lord Anomander has not yet returned to Kharkanas. Captain Kellaras sends his regards.'

'You found some deserters upon the trail, lieutenant?'

Prazek frowned. 'A wayward patrol, I'm sure, sir. Returned to the fold as you see, barring a few malcontents.'

'You are welcome to their care, lieutenant.'

'We shall adopt them indeed, sir. But between us, I would wager none fit as officers. Still, glory is possible in any corner. We will retain a measure of misplaced optimism suitable to the fate awaiting us all.' Prazek then stepped closer. 'Sir, all is amiss in Kharkanas. Lord Urusander will not wait until the season's turn, or so it is believed. He will bring blood's fire to winter, but few will find comfort in its bask.'

Galar Baras nodded, and then turned to Wareth. 'Inform the quartermaster that there is no further need to wait. Distribute weapons and armour to the regulars.'

He saw a flash of uncertainty in Wareth's expression, but then the man nodded and walked off.

Bedecked in the unusually robust armour of Hust iron, Dathenar approached. 'See me, sir, in jangling array. Six with linked arms could make a wall, twenty in a circle a bailey. We will attend to the field like legged keeps. I feel assembled into a fortress, with myriad taunts from the battlements of my shoulders and nape, and upon the helm's brim, why, such mocking derision as to infuriate the enemy.'

'Heavy kitting,' Galar Baras agreed. 'It was in Lord Henarald's mind to see a new kind of soldier, stolid and steadfast. The Hust Legion has a history of holding a line, and often it was will alone that blunted the foe's desire. But now, with armour such as this, we will add iron to our spines.'

'Well said, sir. I trust Prazek has informed you of our elevation.'

Galar Baras smiled with little humour. 'I wondered at what insubordination led you here.'

'A bridge left unguarded was the first of our crimes,' Dathenar replied. 'But worse than that, we malingered too long in the Citadel, lured into cups until we sloshed with careless aplomb. Fools that we were, to so offend the white crow with our indolence. We judge this just, and will endeavour, sir, to avoid all future disapprobation.'

'By this,' Prazek added, 'he means we will serve with all the distinction nature has accorded us, and more besides.'

'Pushed past nature, aye,' Dathenar said, nodding. 'Into arcane constructs of obscure logic, yielding to us the perfect symbol with swords that crow and armour eager with contempt. See how well it fits, sir. One day the Hust Legion will be asked to stand against the impossible. I foresee this legion breaking hearts, sir.'

Galar Baras felt his gaze slide away from Dathenar's bright, challenging regard. He looked upon the mob now gathering to receive weapons and armour. 'Lieutenants, I leave the two of you in command. I must ride to Hust Forge. If it is at all possible, I will reawaken Toras Redone to our need for her. At the very least, I wonder if she has even heard of the fall of the Wardens. If not, best I be the one to bring her the news.'

'You delight in heavy burdens, sir.'

Dathenar's observation had come in a casual tone, but the truth of it cut Galar Baras, so that he stood for a moment, bereft of words, with something roaring in his skull. Shaking himself free of the paralysis, he turned away from the two lieutenants, and then paused and glanced back. 'Welcome to the Hust Legion. Look to Wareth to inform you of any details with respect to the prisoners. Oh, and there is a killer in our midst, revisiting, perhaps, old hurts. Wareth will give you the details.'

'Intrigue and mystery, sir, keep us young.'

Galar Baras eyed Dathenar, with his now placid expression, and then Prazek, who stood smiling like a man about to dance. 'Again, you are both most welcome.'

An empty niche in a corridor, from which echoes still seemed to drift out, rebounding from some other place, but with weariness and overtones of loss. As the recollection of that day slowly faded from his mind, Galar Baras turned away from the niche and resumed his walk. Earlier in the day, before his eventual audience with Lord Henarald, he had walked the work yard, shocked by the fading energy of cooling blast furnaces, tall chimneys all but one yielding no column of smoke, an air of exhaustion heavy in the bitter winter air.

Behind the dozen bricked furnaces with their flanking bellows, there had been a row of wagons, sagging with coal left unattended. He had seen in all this the truth of what Henarald would soon tell him: the forges were dying. The charcoal was gone, the new seams of coal rotten. The age of weapons was itself coming to an end, in the manner that would surprise only a fool. *War, this artless collapse that sees every forged blade worked to its sole purpose. How is it, then, that in the perfection of the form, and in its equally perfect application, we bring upon ourselves nothing but chaos and destruction? Am I alone in seeing the irony of this? Industry, you unfold in the machinations of our minds, so sweetly reasoned that we believe you both inevitable and righteous. But see what you build. No, step around the monuments, around every glorious edifice. Walk here, to this place of tailings and slag.*

*Henarald was right. The only freedom left the world belongs to what we discard, the pointless wastage we so quickly sweep away. See the birds dance on the heaps, thinking every glistening twinkle the betrayal of an insect's wings. But to feed there is to die, and the hunt's lure rewards with nothing but starvation.*

He had walked the yards, and now, as he drew closer to the inner wing of the keep, where Toras Redone had either retreated or been locked away from the sight of others, he listened for the distant roar of the forges, but heard nothing.

*Industry, your artistry was an illusion. Your offer of permanence was a lie. You are nothing more than the maw we built, and then fed until both we and the world sank down in exhaustion, and in the failing of your fires, your never-satisfied hunger, we turn not upon you, but upon each other.*

*The Jaghut alone dared face you and name you the demon in their midst. Us? Why, we will die at your feet as if you were an altar, and hold with our last breath to the belief in your sanctity, even as the rust seizes your soul, and the last drop of blood falls from ours.*

As with so many other things, Galar Baras realized, the seeds of civilization's death were sown in its birth. But the Jaghut had proved that progress was not inevitable, that the fates could be defied, broken, utterly discarded.

He reached the door, studied its black bronze, its rivets and stained wood. Beyond it, alas, was his love. No matter her condition, he knew that he would fall to his knees upon seeing her, if not in body then in his soul. *We do well to curse love. That makes us so abject, so eager to surrender. She need only meet my eye to know that I am hers, to do with as she pleases. Where then is my courage?*

He hesitated.

*Toras Redone, I bring sad news. The Wardens have been destroyed in battle. But Calat Hustain survives, and is blameless in the fate of his people. Or can that be said? Did he not give his command to Ilgast Rend? Was he not precipitous in setting out to the Vitr in such a time as this? The news is sad indeed, and you will choose which – the end of the Wardens, or that your husband still lives.*

He could imagine himself, standing before her, unbowed by her sordid presence. Speaking his mind, flensing all decorum from the raw hungers and needs that plagued both him and her. *But no, I can hardly be certain of her, can I? She was drunk the night she made me her plaything. It left embers between us, fanned by flattery and chance gazes locked a moment too long. For all her games, her memory of that night might be blurred, stripped of all detail.*

*In her appetites she was ever blind, taking all within her reach.*

*I may walk in to find her recalling neither me nor herself. Grief and horror and recrimination, and jugs of wine. There may be nothing left of Toras Redone. Denied her chance to die with her soldiers, denied again upon the morning that followed, by my own hand—*

*Oh, she should recall that, I would think. In a flare of hate, she will recall my staying hand.*

Courage retreated before love. A brave man would have let her drink deep the poison.

*Sad tidings, my love. He lives. You live. And so do I.*

*The Hust Legion? Well, the iron lives, too. You'll know its voice by the laughter, the black chatter of crows feasting upon the dead. Listen, then, to war's cold welcome.*

He reached out, closed his hand upon the door's heavy iron ring. It was time to look upon what was left of his love.

*     *     *

'In times of war, privileges of rank are won in blood. Or so,' Prazek added, 'we make it known.' He reached out to add another chip of dung to the fire. A small hearth, set well away from the others of the camp. Faror Hend had seen it from a distance while walking the perimeter, ensuring that the pickets were in place, and that two of every three soldiers on guard were, in fact, facing inward, upon the camp. For all that, there had been no desertions since the distribution of the Hust weapons and armour. None, indeed, since lieutenants – now captains – Prazek and Dathenar assumed temporary command of the Hust Legion.

Curious, Faror Hend had made her way to the flickering flames out upon the plain, fifty paces beyond the pickets, to find the two officers from Lord Anomander's Houseblades attending a private fire ringed by stones that had been collected from a nearby cairn. Upon seeing her hesitant approach, and even as she had begun turning away, Dathenar had spoken an invitation to join them. And now she sat opposite the two men, feeling out of place.

Gallan had once called them his soldier poets, and after half a week in their company, official and otherwise, she well understood the honorific. But theirs was a wit too sharp for her, and even to witness it was to feel one's own mind as something too blunt, likely to stumble should it seek to keep pace with the two men. Still, it proved a modest wound, given how entertaining they often were.

But this was a night for sober reflection, at least thus far, and what eloquence was loosed sounded wry, almost bitter at times. More to the point, it was heavy with exhaustion, and Faror had come to comprehend the sheer effort of aplomb. In the watery light of the fire, the faces before her were drawn, haggard, revealing all that they were wont to hide from others. This particular window's view humbled her.

'Private fires,' said Dathenar, nodding in answer to Prazek's earlier assertion. 'We tend them as would any common soldier or peasant, and by any starry measure above we are just as unnoticed in the eyes of the firmament. Rank, my friend, is an impostor.'

'It is the dung in my hand that belies my artless grace, Dathenar. Clumsy and feckless of gesture, I long for an able servant to make these flames dance as is proper. Perhaps it is the cold, or the too brief interim of desiccation afforded this chip, but I feel no heat from this fire. A cold serpent entwines my bones this night, and not even the fair face of Faror Hend can defeat this hearth's woeful dearth.'

Dathenar grunted. 'With a fire tended between us and her, my friend, we dare not reach through the heat, though we might – in most private and complimentary fashion – yearn for her softer warmth as a place beyond what burns.'

'Sirs,' said Faror Hend after a moment, 'it seems my presence is an imposition—'

'Not at all! Prazek?'

'Anything but! Faror Hend, by the flame's soft glow, your lovely visage blesses the night. If we falter, it is from beauty's reflection, so poorly do we hide our longing. I see you surrounded in darkness, like the mien of a moon that looks upon a sun we cannot see. As Dathenar noted, you are well beyond our reach, humbling our regard.'

'Forgive us,' Dathenar murmured.

'If I am reduced to a view, sirs, then best I keep quiet, to better serve your elevation of my worth.'

'Ah, Prazek, see how she stings? In our appreciation we are unmanned.'

Faror Hend sighed. 'Commanding this legion is surely a burden. But you are not entirely alone, sirs. And more help may be on the way, when Galar Baras returns with Toras Redone.'

'Will she ride Galar Baras home, I wonder?'

Faror Hend blinked at Prazek, startled by his question. 'It is said her spirit is broken, and no surprise at that. Hunn Raal was clever in his infamy. But then, he did offer her the poisoned wine. Was that a gesture of mercy, do you think?'

Prazek eyed her for a moment, and then shrugged. 'Rank is the issue here, alas. There are times when it is the spine of an army that carries its commander, but these are rare moments. Propriety insists that it is the commander who must bear the army's burden, roughly measured by its will, its heart and its resolve.'

Dathenar added, 'But a legion of prisoners, well . . . we must find our spine, I think. No armour intended for mortals can sustain flesh weakened by a damaged spirit. No weapon can lend its wielder the ferocity of its purpose. We are fitted in the trappings, but they are not enough.'

Faror Hend shook her head. 'You two have done well. You must know that. Better, in some ways, than Galar Baras. You weave seduction with your words and manner. You invite in us a confidence we cannot muster on our own.'

Prazek grunted. 'Fourteen dead men, each and all slayers of women and children. Someone is confident enough, it seems.'

'I fear Wareth is not working too hard on finding the murderer,' Faror Hend said. 'Although, that said, he worries on Listar's behalf. Oddly, that man still lives, even though he refuses added protection.'

'There is a clue there, I should think,' Dathenar observed.

'Some feel the accusations are suspect,' she replied. 'Those against Listar, I mean. Sergeant Rance looks upon him and shakes her head, saying he is no killer. I am inclined to believe her.'

'Women see nothing in him, then.'

'Nothing to suggest he has blood on his hands, no.'

'Then the murderer,' concluded Dathenar, 'agrees with you. A woman wields the knife.'

Faror Hend nodded. 'That is generally accepted, sir.'

'Wareth drags his feet.'

'Perhaps he hopes the situation will simply go away,' Faror suggested. 'That at some point, the killer will be satisfied that enough justice has been served.'

'You sound doubtful.'

'I cannot say, Dathenar. Justice, I would think, acquires strength upon its deliverance, enough to sustain the zeal.'

'She speaks of momentum,' Prazek murmured, poking at

the fire with a flimsy stick. 'The unseen current. Will without mind. An army can find it as easily as can a mob. We must hope for Toras Redone's resurrection. We must hope that the Hust Legion will find sure guidance to whatever fate awaits it.'

'And much of that responsibility,' Faror said, sighing, 'falls to us officers as well. Before you two arrived, well, Galar Baras did not have many from which to choose. Wareth, Rance, Rebble, Curl – you've met them now, and the others. Even Castegan—'

'Castegan,' Prazek interrupted, making the name a growl. 'We know his cut, Faror Hend. Leave that man to us.'

'Though as yet unknown, sir, I already regret his fate. I surely would not want both or either of you to set upon me your sanction.'

'Opprobrium will do for that man,' Dathenar said, waving the stick in a dismissive gesture. 'He is lonely and grieves, yet twists both into spite for the survivors, of whom he is the first and foremost. We will turn him about.'

'Or slap him silly,' Prazek said.

'Rance,' said Dathenar after a moment, looking up at Faror. 'She is the quiet one with the wounded hands, yes?'

'She heats a brimming cauldron every morning,' said Faror. 'Nigh unto boiling. Then, behind her tent, stripped down to the waist, she plunges her hands into the scalding water. She scrubs them raw with pumice and lye.' After some hesitation, during which neither man spoke, she continued. 'She has no memory of drowning her newborn babe. But her hands remind her. The pain reminds her too, I suppose. She answers what she never felt, and cannot recall, with rituals of hurt. Sirs, I beg you, this is not to be challenged. It may be that she cannot command a company, but that she holds herself together at all is, to me, remarkable.'

'I knew few details,' Dathenar said in a low voice, 'but I sensed well something unbreakable within her. Faror Hend, we would burden her further.'

'Sirs—'

'This legion wears and wields madness,' Prazek said. 'It

609

will need its own spine. Neither Hust's history, nor its fame, nor even its infamy, will suffice this rebirth. The weapons and armour laugh, but the timbre of that voice betrays helplessness. So, we cannot look even to the fever of magic iron.'

'We have prisoners,' Dathenar said, his gaze hard upon her. 'This is our lot. Up from pits and holes carved down through rock and earth. Up from where we put them. No outside authority will reach them, for their habits long ago rejected that authority. There is a vast difference between kneeling and being forced to kneel. Galar Baras was right in plunging into their midst. Now it falls to us to take their stock, to see what we can use.'

'But Rance's inner torment?'

'We will be cruel, yes.'

'She does not scrub her hands raw out of some manic need to cleanse unseen stains, Dathenar. If either of you think the symbol so crass as that—'

'No, Faror, we heard you well enough.'

Prazek nodded. 'A ritual intended to awaken pain, because the pain keeps her here, keeps her conscious. Keeps her alive.'

'Nothing of that can belong to the Legion, sirs.'

In answer, Prazek drew his new sword. The reflected flames licked down its length with a lurid red tongue. A dull muttering sound rose from the blade, breaking then into a low, dreadful laugh. 'This attends us all, Faror Hend. Every edge, however, promises pain, yes? Prisoners – by the title alone we see their plight. All was taken from them. For each, some past incident has been made into a shrine of hurts, betrayals, losses and sour violence. Like penitents they can but circle this unholy moment, whipping their backs to keep it alive. They will speak of forgetting what they have done. Some will even claim to have done so. Others will protect their shrine, believing it a place of righteous justice, thus absolving themselves of all responsibility. But all this – all these pronouncements, these evasions, these pathetic defiances – they are helpless and hopeless. Each man, each woman, up from the pit, is burdened with what they must live with.'

Dathenar added, 'Loss of freedom delivers its own pain. This is an army that ritually scalds itself every dawn. The soldiers fill their days with talk of freedom – some even seek to run away – but now, at last, they begin to see. There will be no freedom, neither here nor there – out beyond the camp-fires, beyond the pickets. No freedom at all, Faror Hend.'

'We must make of the Hust Legion,' said Prazek, sheathing the weapon once more, 'a promise. To each prisoner, each soldier. Wake with pain? March with pain? Eat with it? Sleep with it? Breathe it with every breath drawn in, every breath loosed? Oh yes, my friends. And here is the Hust Legion, an answer to you all.'

'The Hust Legion builds the fire in the crisp light of the sun's rise,' said Dathenar. 'Sets the cauldron upon the coals, and calls the soldiers into line. Hands into the scalding water, thus beginning the pain of a new day.'

'We will make this legion their home,' Prazek said. 'A familiar temple to house their familiar, personal, shrines of pain. The iron now laughs, in proof of its imprisonment, its helplessness. When we are done with our soldiers, we shall make the iron weep.'

Faror Hend stared at the two men, their harsh visages lit in flames. *Abyss below, I face two monsters . . . and find myself blessing their every word.*

\*     \*     \*

Tent walls made for flimsy barriers, and through the entirety of Wareth's short career as a soldier of the Hust Legion he had felt neither safe nor protected by them. The waxed canvas even failed in disguising an occupant's presence come the night, with oil lamps or lanterns painting silhouettes upon the walls. When, as he prepared for sleep, the scratching came upon the front flap, followed a moment later by the tap of a knife pommel on the ridge pole, he considered for a long moment the prospect of not responding. Yet there had been no hiding his presence, and to pretend otherwise seemed both puerile and petty.

Grunting an invitation, he sat upon the cot to await yet another messenger with still more bad news, as it seemed the litany was unending, and when enough people were gathered anywhere the train of news never paused. It was no wonder that most officers stumbled between exhaustion and incompetence, as each fed the other. That history recounted the tales of battles gone awry, filled with appalling errors in judgement, a cascade of fatal decisions and the pointless slaughter of hundreds, if not thousands of misled soldiers, no longer surprised Wareth.

Logistics could gnaw like termites through the base of a tree—

Sergeant Rance stepped through the tent entrance.

'What now?' Wareth asked.

She flinched at his tone, and half turned as if to leave again – and in that instant Wareth comprehended that nothing official had brought her into his company. Silently cursing, he raised a staying hand and said, 'No, wait. Do come in, Rance. Take that bench there – someone delivered it for reasons unknown to me. Perhaps the seating of guests? That seems reasonable.'

'It's nothing, sir,' she said. 'I saw the light, and motion, and wondered at your being awake this late.'

'Well,' he said, watching her tentatively settle on to the bench, 'there is some good timing in all this, Rance. I found myself drawn short by a thought. Tell me, what do you know about the habits of termites? I recall seeing mounds – nay, towers – in the drylands to the south, constructed of mud. But here in Kurald Galain we mostly know of them as delivering ruination to wood. I have in my mind an image of a large tree riven through by the insects – did I see some such thing as a child? I must have.'

She studied him with an odd expression, and then said, 'I recall a house that collapsed, in the village where I lived. The beams were found to have been eaten through from the inside. Their cores were dust. Or so I heard, sir. I do remember seeing the wreckage. It had more or less fallen in from each side. The weight of the roof timbers, I suppose.'

'Logistics,' Wareth said. 'The line of messengers, busy messengers, with busy words. Even as this army sleeps, problems spread like some plague – or an infestation.'

'It's been three nights since the last murder.'

'We're all armed now, Rance. I'd imagine that those men fearing retribution for past crimes have taken to sleeping in their armour. More to the point, a sword left out of its scabbard will betray the arrival of a stranger.'

'It will?'

Wareth nodded. 'I suppose I should have explained that, but I imagine that the soldiers will make their own discoveries. Indeed, for all I know, the armour will do the same. A Hust camp needs no watchdogs, no geese. A Hust soldier standing on guard cannot be sneaked up on if he or she keeps a blade bared. But now, why, the armour could well suffice.' He paused, and then cocked his head. 'Hardly a sound defence against intrigue or treachery, however. Nothing in Henarald's iron can sniff out poisoned wine, after all.'

'They said it was a curse,' Rance said.

'What was?'

'The termite infestation, sir. A curse upon the family, and the father in particular. Careless with his cock.'

'Excuse me?'

'The rooster in his yard, sir. It used to escape, terrorizing the younger children.'

'Ah. Well then, was there something specific you wished to discuss?'

She glanced away, and then shrugged. 'I am to report to Captain Prazek and Captain Dathenar on the morrow, immediately following the seventh bell.'

'You are?'

She nodded, and then frowned. 'You knew nothing of it? Oh. Then I wonder what they might want of me.' A moment later she straightened her back, and then slowly slumped – though whether in defeat or relief, Wareth could not tell. 'I am to be dismissed. That's it. Well, I'm surprised it took this long.'

'Rance, I'm not aware of anything like that. They would have spoken to me first, I assure you. No, they have some other purpose for wishing to speak to you. And, to be honest, I'm glad you've told me. I will accompany you tomorrow.'

'Sir, there's no reason—'

'I selected you, remember? In fact, you are my responsibility.' Still something uncertain flickered in her gaze. Wareth considered for a moment, and then he said, 'A coward upon the field of battle is driven by an overwhelming need to survive, to escape from all threat, all risk. But upon the day to day matters away from that field of battle, a coward can well display virtues, such as loyalty. And on occasion, both fortitude and integrity might rear their pale heads into day's light. Said virtues might even assemble all at once, in a single moment.' He offered her a wry smile. 'I am too easily painted in a single hue, Rance.'

'I know that,' she replied. 'In that single colour you can hide other things about you. Few will see. Few will bother. Even the title itself – coward – can be used to hide behind, if you're clever enough.'

He shrugged. 'I'm not, alas.'

She snorted. 'And here I thought you lied well, as cowards should be able to do.'

'Titles have that way, Rance. Coward. Murderer.' Seeing her blanch, he shook his head and added, 'You misunderstand. I can claim both, you see. On the day we were freed, I killed a man with a shovel—'

'I know.'

He blinked. 'You know of that?'

'Every woman does, sir. The men were about to attack them – the cats of your pit so roughly awoken, pushed out into the morning light. You broke open the first bastard's skull, dropped him dead, and that stopped the others long enough for you to send Rebble to the sheds. Gave the cats time to arm themselves. You saved lives that day, sir. Stopped rapes.'

Wareth looked away. 'It wasn't quite like that,' he said. 'I just didn't think it all through, that's all. Never liked the one I killed either.'

She shrugged. 'Real cowards always think it through, all the way through, sir.'

'Not if they see their chance at getting rid of a tormentor, which I did. I simply forgot about his friends.'

'Well,' she said, 'now at last I see the fear in you, sir. You're frightened by the thought that you did the right thing, a brave thing. It doesn't fit with who you think you are.'

'If not for Rebble and Listar, I would have run,' Wareth said. 'Don't let that tale live on in the camp, not among the cats, Rance. It wasn't the way you've just told it.'

'You first, and then Rebble and then Listar, sir. Us cats set you apart, sir. The three of you. You didn't know it – not until now, I suppose – but you had the cats of your pit with you from that moment. Now, every pit's cats know it, and they're with you, too.'

'You're heading for disappointment, Rance. Warn them. Warn them all.'

'We know you're clever, sir.'

'How? How do you know that?'

She studied him for a long moment, and then offered him a most peculiar and baffling smile, before rising to her feet. 'I just thought I should let you know, sir, about them wanting to see me tomorrow. You see, I know they're clever, far too clever, I suppose. Like you, only not like you. They see no value in wasting time. In any case, sir, you now have some time to think on finding a new sergeant to replace me. That's what I was here to say, sir.'

He watched her leave the tent. *What was all that? They're not dismissing her. They wouldn't do it that way. They have something else in mind. I'll find out when she does, in the morning.*

*In the meantime, why didn't I swing that conversation back to the careless cock?*

This was what came of being exhausted. A dulled wit was blind to nuance, even the hint of possible innuendo, when it offered that narrow trail between empty charm and crass invitation. But then, how many years had it been since he'd last played such games? And what of Rance? *Dreams of intimacy might feel deadly to a woman who took love into her hands, then drowned it. Abyss take me, these are venal thoughts. That I dare imagine her and me together – that I dare upend the world's rightful order, to believe that either of us deserves such a thing.*

*Murderer and coward upon the one hand, child-slayer upon the other. Not for them tender moments, nor soft laughter, nor sweet pleasures. Not for them anything like love, or the wanting of happiness, and how deep the outrage, should they seek contentment.*

*No, these are the privileges of the innocent.*

*For surely they must be innocent, to desire for themselves such privileges, and then claim them as their right.*

*But for us who are guilty, the desire itself is a crime. That we should dare such things for ourselves, for whatever wrecked remnant is left in our lives.*

*Forget Rance. Forget anything playful. Eschew every soft thought, Wareth. Not for you and not for her. Not, indeed, for the new Hust Legion.*

*The weapons and armour can laugh for us, since they exist without guilt, and know nothing of blame.*

His gaze strayed across to where his scabbarded sword hung from a peg in the centre pole. *Barring you, of course. You know me too well. You delight in our reunion, if only to anticipate and then witness my final fall. How you will delight in orchestrating your vengeance. I know it is coming, old friend. And for all that I betrayed in you, why, I welcome it.*

It was time to douse the lamps, and make of these walls something opaque and impenetrable. If there was one trait he did not share with other cowards, it was his utter absence of fear when in darkness. He knew it well as a state in which he could hide, silent, unseen.

*Yet Mother Dark would strip that from us. Give us eyes to pierce any gloom. Many may consider that a blessing, an end to the fear of what cannot be seen, what cannot be known. Is it only fear that makes us pray for answers? What do we lose by not knowing? Not understanding?*

Lamps doused, he sat on the cot, wishing that he were blind inside and out. *Bless me with darkness if you must, but*

*make it the blessing of not seeing. Do that, Mother Dark,
and I will serve you. There are times, as you must well know,
when ignorance is no enemy.*

*     *     *

Galar Baras found Toras Redone standing near a shuttered
window, shrouded in gloom. The window was one of the tall,
narrow ones that looked out upon the forges. Its copper
shutters were old and pitted, the edges of each slat rippled
and uneven, and the faint glow coming through was the blue
of a moonless night. He could see, by those liquid ribbons
painted upon her, that she was naked.

Inactivity had softened her form. There was nothing visible
of the hardness that came with a life of soldiering. Rolls of
flesh sagged over the points of her hips, burying them deep.
The drink had bulged her belly, which in turn emphasized the
arch of her back beneath rounded shoulders. She stood in
profile, curled, her breasts pushed out and resting upon the
fat below them. The faint blue rows of light tracked her form
like an arcane script, its style both melodic and drunken.

She had cut her hair short, which paradoxically made her
head and face seem more feminine. After a long moment, she
turned her gaze to him. 'Galar Baras. Like the rising sun you
were. Swift to touch on my intent, swifter still in striking the
darkness from my hand. I recall falling to my knees. I recall
eating bitter soil. You'd think it sweet, wouldn't you? Wine
and earth, or, rather, wine and dust. Whatever the poison, it
must have been tasteless. Anyway, I cannot for the life of me
determine what it was I found so bitter, so cruelly tart upon
my tongue.'

'Commander,' said Galar Baras, 'could we return to that
morning, and had I truly comprehended what had happened,
well, I might have hesitated . . . long enough.'

In swinging round to face him, the rows of blue script
flowed as if painted on a silk curtain stirred awake by a
draught. 'I doubt that,' she said.

'Will you now return to us, commander? We have need
of you.'

617

'How will he see me now, do you think?' She slowly raised heavy arms. 'Not the woman he married, to be sure. The thing is, and I see it well in your eyes, you look upon all of this and imagine it soft as pillows. What you've yet to experience, lover, is the weight of it. Too solid to be a pillow, I assure you.' She then reached out as if to accept his hand. 'Come, let me show you.'

'Toras—'

'Ah! Is this the truth of it then? You imagine disgust in my husband's face, and it twists you away from desire. Even the kiss of temptation proves suddenly sour. And what of wickedness? Did we not both delight in that? No longer, I see. Now you would stand before me, an officer with a duty to decorum, shouting your propriety with every crisp salute.' Her hand beckoned him again. 'Come along, lover, let's dispel your fantasies and then we'll be done with it, and you can beg again for my return to the Legion. Do this, Galar Baras, and I will reconsider my future.'

She was sober, or at least as sober as he might ever expect her to be. Grief, he supposed, had muted her habit of grand gestures. Or perhaps it was simply that there was more of her, the weight adding sloth to her practised indolence.

None of this should have attracted him. None of this should have awakened his hunger for her.

Seeing something in his gaze, or hearing the change in his breathing, Toras Redone smiled slyly. 'At last, lover. Come to me. It is dissolution you long to caress. Others might deem that, well, sordid, but you and I, we understand each other.'

He stepped forward, and then his hands were upon her cool skin. 'Toras,' he said, 'I came here to speak to you of Lord Henarald.'

'Cast him from your mind, Galar. He's found his own dissolution.' She brushed her lips against his, pressing more of her body against him. 'If he hasn't already, he will talk to you about smoke, and things left to waste.'

'Yes.'

'Him and us, Galar, we but worship different aspects of the same grisly god. The end of things will lure us, until in our lust we make an end of our world. It's nothing but variations in scale. This . . . dissolution.'

He wanted to pull away from her. Instead, he drew her tighter into his arms.

She laughed. 'Oh, Galar, how I've missed you.'

She had ever been, he reminded himself, good with lies. That all that she had said before her last statement had been true, he did not doubt. But Toras Redone's world was a private one, with room only for herself. She would take visitors, provided they understood well enough to expect only what she offered.

So he mulled on the lie, even as his body fell into the motions of long held desires. She had indeed been honest, he discovered, in how she had described her new shape, and what in his mind had been soft as pillows now proved impediments to reaching her at all, in any place where pleasure might be found. Curiously, even this challenge proved alluring.

Later, Galar Baras found himself wondering which man he was: the one he both saw in himself and showed to virtually everyone else, or the man she made him into, with such knowing in her eyes, such recognition in her low laughter, that he felt himself reduced to . . . *to a faint script, scrawled across her skin, riding every undulation and curve, every fold.*

*The night writes me upon her, in a language only she can understand. I stagger away, all meaning undone, all sense stripped away. Where, in this wretched love, is my reason?*

He would return her to the Legion. The officers and soldiers would see him as a man of formidable powers, if not an unassailable will. And only in the occasional glance she would send his way would he be reminded of their hidden language, there upon its sweet vellum of stretched skin, unseen by anyone else.

*Which man is the truth of me?*

To that question, he had no answer.

*　　*　　*

As if even metal lips could somehow be soft, the Hust armour muttered like mouths pressed against flesh. But this was a

619

cruel seduction. From the vambraces, from the chain and scale and greaves, came a sound like rain threading through trees, cold streams upon a forest floor, a chorus of whispering. With the helm fixed upon his head, Wareth listened to the faint imprecations and felt an uncanny chill ripple through him. There was something almost suffocating in the weight, with its cloying murmurs, as if he was in the embrace of a woman he did not desire.

Stepping out from his tent, he found himself facing Rebble. He too was armoured, and from the tangle of his wild beard there was the white flash of a rueful grin.

'Like wearing your fears, isn't it, Wareth?' He then rapped knuckles against the scabbarded sword at his hip. 'And this thing. Abyss take me but she's eager for my temper.'

'She?'

He shrugged. 'As close as I'll get, I suppose, to having a wife. Beautiful in hand until she cuts.'

Shaking his head, Wareth said, 'I must attend a meeting with the captains.'

Rebble's small eyes narrowed. 'You'll shadow Rance, then? Well, it was only a matter of time.'

'What was?'

He glanced away, shrugged again. 'For me, it's out to the pickets. I need the walk, need to get used to all this weight. It's the helm I hate the most – I got enough voices in my fucking skull.'

'Find Listar for your patrol, Rebble.'

Rebble cocked his head. 'For a coward, you've uncommon loyalty, Wareth. Makes you hard to figure. I'm not complaining, sir. Maybe the opposite, in fact. It's something that gets noticed.'

'Enough of that, Rebble. You'd be better off listening to your armour, and sword. There's a battle coming, but it won't be me in the front ranks. Remember that. Galar knows enough to keep me as far from the fighting as he can. But you, and Listar – and all the other officers and squad leaders – you're heading into something else. My loyalty won't put me at your side when that time comes.'

There was a momentary glint of something ugly in Rebble's eyes, and then he smiled. 'No one's planning on your statue, sir. Not even a painted portrait, or a fucking bust or something. You're Wareth, and we all remember that.'

Wareth nodded. 'It's well that you do.'

'In any case,' Rebble continued, 'I looked for Listar but could not find him. But I'll make another round, look in on his tent and whatnot. He should turn up.'

Wareth watched Rebble walk away. Soldiers were mustering for the breakfast bell. There was little conversation, and not everyone had emerged from tents wearing their armour, although a belted sword adorned every soldier in sight. Had it been as simple as that? Weapons to make these men and women into soldiers?

Setting out, Wareth rolled his shoulders against the permanent ache in his lower back. The heavy chain surcoat wasn't helping matters, and the round-cornered plates of his shoulder-guards sat like tiles upon a slanted roof, pulling at the muscles of his neck.

He was used to the eyes tracking him as he walked through the camp. Contempt needed no words. The scabbard holding his sword was the same one Castegan had given him, and he found a perverse satisfaction in wearing that brand. He could see little of worth in Rance's words the night before. The cats needed someone better. His actions upon that day of liberation had, in all likelihood, been a last spasm of decency, undermined in the next breath by unpalatable truths.

The memory of the shovel crushing Ganz's skull was an echo that never quite left him, and in that manner, it persisted in the way of all things venal. *He never saw it coming. No, Ganz was filling up with lust, charging the violence of his strength against women who could not match it. He'd shown the same against me. A thousand small slights to make my confession a weighty tome of reasons, justifications.*

*But the truth was, I saw my chance and took it.*

*He never saw it coming. That's why I struck when I did. Old Wareth the coward, well, he's no fool. An easy mistake to make, one supposes. But fear only paralyses in the possibilities, and on that day it lagged a step. The man was dead before my terror could even wake. Did I know that at the time? Did I, as Rance and the other cats might believe, act before the coward in me had a chance to stop me?*

It was questionable, at least in his own mind, whether the distinction was in any way significant.

He approached the command tent. One of the guards, a regular, offered him a sneer, but said nothing when he passed by and entered the tent.

'Lieutenant Wareth! Join our morning repast, will you?'

The speaker was Captain Prazek. Wareth had halted a stride into the chamber upon seeing the two captains at a table, breaking their fast with Rance. The woman sat stiffly, the food upon the plate before her untouched. A pewter cup filled with mulled wine was in her red hands, held close against her stomach, the steam rising to her face like a veil of smoke. The look she cast him was blank.

Dathenar had leaned to one side to drag another chair to the table opposite Rance, with the two captains positioned at either end.

Wareth remained standing. 'My apologies, sirs. But your guest is one of my officers. I feel that I should be present if some issue of discipline is involved.'

'Honourable sentiment, lieutenant,' Dathenar said, while around a mouthful of food Prazek grunted agreement. 'Now, do join us. We shall hope, by virtue of imitation and the pressure to conform, that the witnessing of taking food to mouth will incite in our guest the same inclination, thus putting us all at ease.'

'She is perhaps wiser than we think,' Prazek observed after making a scene of swallowing. 'This sausage mocks the pretence. But,' he added, spearing another piece, 'I am assured that it lodges in the pit of the belly, and remains silent, if not unobtrusive, until the moment of its rebirth into the world.'

'Hardly an image to encourage our appetites, Prazek,' said Dathenar. 'Unless you know more of the cook's supply than do we.'

The chair awaiting Wareth was too elaborate for common

camp gear, possessing curved armrests. 'Perhaps,' he said as he pushed himself down into the seat, which proved uncomfortably narrow, 'we could discuss the reason for summoning Sergeant Rance.'

Prazek wagged the speared piece of sausage in the air. 'But I assure you, lieutenant, that issue, despite its inherent complexities, is one in which a sated belly is advised. After all, we must find a means to twist crime into crusade—'

'Vengeance into virtue—'

'Obsession into ritual.' Prazek frowned at the meat, and then slipped it into his mouth. He chewed.

Wareth looked from one man to the other. 'I do not understand,' he said.

Rance cleared her throat and then spoke. 'It's to do with the murders, sir. The investigation in which it seemed you had lost interest. It is why I visited you last night, to give you the chance to act before the captains did.' She frowned across at him. 'I was certain that you had found the killer, but for some reason you chose not to end things.'

Wareth studied her. 'I gave up because it made no sense.'

She glanced away.

*Abyss take me, I've been a fool.* 'How did you move the bodies, Rance? And what of your fear of the sight of blood?'

'I can't tell you, sir, about any of it, because I do not remember the murders. I simply awaken in my tent, with blood on my hands. I find my knife unsheathed, but thoroughly cleansed.' She hesitated. 'I scrubbed off what I could. I thought that it was that habit that finally betrayed me.'

But Wareth shook his head. 'It seems we misread that obsession,' he said, 'and set upon it a much earlier crime.'

'It began there, yes, but even then, sir, there was simple necessity. I don't like the sight of blood. I hate the feel of it even more.' Straightening in her seat, she set the tankard down. 'It would be better, sir, if you were the one to arrest me.'

Wareth sighed. 'You leave me little choice, but what should also be apparent to the captains here is the extent of my incompetence.'

'I am not alone,' Rance said. 'In this body you see, I am not the sole occupant. There is someone else – we've never met. She walks when I sleep, and in her freedom she murders . . . people. Child of my own womb, men who have killed women – these are only lists. Categories. Satisfied with one, she will move to another. A new list. You need to kill me, sir.'

Sick with dread, heavy with something like disappointment – if such a bland word could be used – Wareth shook his head, as if he could deny this entire morning. He faced Prazek. 'I understand now, sir, why you stepped around me for this.'

Prazek's brows lifted. 'Do you?'

'I – I like Rance.'

'The woman you know, you mean,' corrected Dathenar.

'Well, yes. Of the other, I know only the corpses she leaves in her wake – and even then, the details do not make sense.'

'The other,' said Dathenar, 'is a mage.'

'Excuse me?'

'A wielder of sorcery,' Prazek said. 'A natural adept. That said, she is somewhat feral. She uses what she needs to clean up her mess. But the knife work, why, that is most mundane, wouldn't you say?'

'She exists,' said Rance, 'in a world without remorse. That, sirs, should be reason enough to see her executed. But I fear she will defend herself, and if she is as the captain says – a mage – then you must act now, while she sleeps.'

Dathenar grunted. 'Two within you, sergeant, and between them, the one demanding punishment is the innocent one.'

'Yet this body is the only one we possess, sir. Kill me, and the other one dies as well.'

'The death of two for the crimes of one? 'Tis skewed scales no matter how they tilt.'

Rance made a sound of exasperation, but there was something brittle in her eyes now. 'Then what will you do to me?'

'The mage,' said Dathenar, 'we deem useful.'

'*What?*'

'If awakened to its companion, who, it seems, possesses conscience—'

'No.' She sat forward. 'No. It is bad enough to know what you've done, but to remember it as well – *no.*'

In that instant, Wareth understood her. How sweeter would it be to recall nothing of Ganz's crumpled skull? The weight of the shovel in his hands, the snap of reverberation along the wooden handle, the sound of the man's breaking neck? *Take up the shovel. Blink. Stand looking down upon his body. As if I but stepped over the moment, blessed to see only the aftermath.*

*Rance, the woman hiding in you took hold of your baby and drowned it. You remember nothing. The mage is not without conscience, not without mercy, all too desperate to protect her twin. I can almost hear her: 'Not for you, my love. I will protect you, as only I can. Sleep, dear sister, and dream of nothing.'* 'Sirs,' said Wareth. 'She is right. If you have some plan of somehow merging the two within Rance . . . please, don't.'

'Lieutenant,' said Dathenar, though he held his gaze fixed upon Rance, 'you see but one side of this – the Rance now sitting before us. She, in turn, knows only this world as well. And yet what of the one hiding behind her eyes? The one cursed to darkness, and horror?'

With his knife, Prazek tapped the side of the pewter plate before him. 'While they continue to avoid one another, each circling the truth of the other, a single question remains, and upon that question balances the future of Rance.' He waved the knife. 'Perhaps yes, there is a kind of mercy, at least insofar as sits the woman before us at this moment. And perhaps indeed, we are driven – out of that most honourable mercy – to spare her.'

'If not for that one question,' Dathenar said. 'They must be made to meet. Only in that moment, and all that follows, is forgiveness possible. One for the other, and back again.'

'More to the point,' Prazek added, 'there is no one else capable of telling the mage to stop the killing.'

Rance was trembling, shaking her head in refusal, yet she seemed unable to speak.

Dathenar sighed. 'We cannot execute an innocent woman.'

'Justice must not be seen to stumble,' said Prazek. 'Not

here, not now. The test before us will measure our own worth.'

'The ritual must be attended by all—'

'Ritual?' Wareth stared at Dathenar. 'What ritual?'

'We sent a rider last night,' Prazek said. 'Southwest, to the Dog-Runners.'

'Why?'

'We seek a Bonecaster,' Dathenar said. 'It will be understood,' he added, 'that a demon possesses Rance, one that needs to be exorcized. But this ritual – and comprehend well what I mean here, both of you – will speak in answer not just to Rance, but to the prisoners – every prisoner – and, indeed, to the Hust Legion itself.'

'The demons need exposing,' said Prazek. 'Dragged into the day, as it were.'

'And then extirpated.'

Wareth stared at the two men. 'Dog-Runners? Sirs, we are soldiers in the service of Mother Dark. You would invite a witch of the Dog-Runners? We are the Hust Legion!'

'Indeed,' said Dathenar. 'And as it stands, lieutenant, we are also, to not put too fine a point on it, royally fucked.'

'We believe,' added Prazek, 'that Galar Baras will return with Commander Toras Redone. What of *her* demons, lieutenant?'

'But our goddess—'

Prazek leaned forward, his eyes suddenly hard. 'A ritual, sir, to make the iron howl. Until we turn about this imbalance of power, until we stand as masters over our own blades, over the links sheathing us, we are nothing. The crimes crowding us are vast, countless, of such myriad details as to paralyse us all. This legion, and all within it, needs purging.' He nodded, not without sympathy, towards Rance. 'And she will lead us. Face to face with what she was, and is. A child-slayer.'

Faror Hend remained at a distance, but within sight of the tent entrance, and watched as Rance emerged. The woman seemed almost too weak to remain upright, and when Wareth appeared, moving quickly to take her weight, she pushed him away and stumbled into an alley, where she fell to her knees and was sick.

Prazek and Dathenar had sent Listar away in the depth of the night just past. Upon one horse, with two more trailing, the man had set out on to the plain.

There were many rituals in the world, private and public, honest and false. At some point, in each and every one, some kind of transformation was invited in the participant, to be embraced with belief. And, at that same instant, those who were there to observe were in turn invited into participation, and with it, that selfsame belief.

She understood all of that. A mirror was held up, one purporting a truth that could be hitherto believed hidden, unseen, or simply unrecognized. And a single step was invited, from one reflection into the other. In this step, she knew, an entire world could change. Irrevocably.

Listar, haunted man, wearing his accusation as if it truly fitted him, rode to find a witch, or a shaman – a Bonecaster of the Dog-Runners, a people unlike the Tiste, a people brushing shoulders with something wild and primitive.

*Rituals. Spirits of earth and sky, of water and blood. Headdresses of antler and horn, furs of the hunter and hide of the hunted. This shall be the Legion's own mirror.*

*Mother Dark, where are you in all of this?*

The morning was bright and cold. Upon the camp, along every pathway and track, smoke hung in wreaths low over the frozen ground, as the Legion wakened to the new day.

# SIXTEEN

---

'IT IS OUR CURSE, ONCE WE ARE PAST CHILDHOOD, TO look upon innocence through a veil of sorrow.'

Standing beside Lord Anomander as they gazed out across the landscape, Ivis grunted. 'Milord, it's only what we've lost that makes innocence sting so.'

Their breaths plumed, quickly whipped away in the building north wind. The day's eerie gloom was deepening.

After a moment, Anomander shook his head. 'I would hold, my friend, that what you describe is but one side of the matter, and indeed one that looks only inward, as if the borders of your life enclose everything to be valued, while what lies beyond is of no worth whatsoever.'

'Perhaps I misunderstood, milord.'

'Consider this, Ivis. The sorrow belongs also to our sense of what awaits that child. The harsh lessons, the wounds taken and felt but not yet understood, the losses and the failures – those the child is destined to make, and those made by others. The battering of belief, and the loss of faith, which begins with oneself and then comes, in a relentless storm, from loved ones – parents, tutors or guardians. By such wounding is innocence lost.'

Thinking on his own childhood, Ivis grunted.

Anomander sighed, and then said, 'Sympathy is not a weakness, Ivis. To grieve for the loss of innocence is to remind yourself that yours is not the only life in this world.'

Before them, from this height of the tower, the forest to the north was a matt, greyish dun, its canopy of twigs and branches like a rumpled carpet of thorns. Bruised clouds were smeared across the sky above the trees, the hue of iron. The icy spit in the wind stung the face. Snow was coming.

'There is no other path possible,' Ivis said after a time. 'We are hardened to the ways of living, and of life itself. These things cannot be avoided, milord. In any case, from what we've heard, young Wreneck has already had more than his share of suffering.'

'And yet, has he once uttered a question about any of it, Ivis? Has he ever voiced in wonder why things are as they are?'

'Not that I have heard,' Ivis confessed, scratching at his beard and feeling icy crystals tangled in the whiskers. 'In that way, milord, perhaps he is older than his years.'

'Must it fall to the child to ask questions no adult dare ask?'

'Possibly. If so, then the lad has missed his chance, and now thinks nothing of all that. He's decided what he must do, and the vengeance he has avowed is anything but childlike. Some fated aspect of his nature has set him upon the path. He does not question it.' Ivis paused, considering, and then he shrugged. 'Perhaps he is something of a simpleton.'

'It is truly a cynical world, Ivis, when we see stupidity and innocence as the same thing.'

'Civil war makes cynics of us all, milord.'

'Does it now?' Anomander shifted slightly from where he leaned on the merlon, eyeing Ivis for a moment. 'This hunger for change,' he said. 'It sets for itself a future in which every desire is appeased, each one won by sword, or blood, or an enemy brought to its knees. And at that instant, Ivis, so brightly painted in triumph, does the world freeze? Does time itself cease, nothing crawling on; not a single moment following in its usual tumble? But what world offers this impossibility? Only the one begat in a mind, and then raised in chains, never to be set free. The fashioning of nostalgia, my friend, imprisons us.'

'Milord, did we not fight for our homeland? You, me, Draconus and all the others? Did we not fight to throw back invaders? Did we not win our freedom?'

'We did. All those things we did, Ivis. Yet, has time stood still? From that moment of victory? Do you still see us all standing triumphant and flushed, as if trapped in one of Kadaspala's paintings? Victory belongs on canvas, not in the real world. No, here, we move on. Urusander and his soldiers stumble from the field, to find tavern corners and bleak mornings. The nobles? Back to their estates, to frown at children grown into strangers, and wives or husbands with love gone cold.' He shook his head again, turning back to the vista beyond the estate walls. 'Still the echo chases us, and so we dream of making the moment eternal.'

'I have heard, milord, that you refused Kadaspala's request. For a portrait. And now, alas, it is too late.'

'Too late? Why is that?'

'Why, milord, because he is now blind.'

'I would trust his hand more now than when he had eyes to see, Ivis. Yes, I believe I would accept his request. He is at last free to paint what he will, with no argument from the world beyond.'

'I doubt he will approach you, milord.'

'Agreed, but for reasons of which you may not be aware.'

'Milord?'

'He blames me, Ivis. For the rape and murder of his sister. For the death of his father.'

'He is mad with grief.'

'We tarried,' Anomander said. 'In no hurry to reach the place of the wedding.'

Ivis watched as Anomander reached down with one hand to rest it upon the pommel of the sword at his hip. 'Had I named it Grief, perhaps ... but in this, why, I stand with young Wreneck. Vengeance, I said, avowed with a child's bright eyes, so sure, so unerring with fiery conviction. Since that day, Ivis, I cannot but wonder, have I made a mistake?'

'You seek Andarist, milord. You seek your brother, to make it right.'

'We will speak, yes. But what words will be exchanged? I do not know. By all rights, I should turn back now, to Kharkanas. If my brother will hold to his sense of betrayal, let him continue. Are there not greater matters at hand than one man's grief?'

'Or another's vengeance?' Even as he spoke, Ivis cursed himself for a fool.

But, surprisingly, Anomander replied with a bitter laugh and then said, 'Well spoken, Ivis. I admitted to fear, did I not? But it is the fear that drives me in pursuit of Andarist. The fear of unknown words, not yet spoken, which I now race to answer . . . as if every moment of silence between us pulls another stone from the bridge one of us must cross.'

'So, in your courage, milord, you are the one taking the steps.'

'Is that courage now, Ivis?'

'It is, sir. All too often cowardice wears the habit of wounded pride.'

Anomander was silent for some time, and then said, 'There was a priest. I met him upon the road. As it turned out, we were both upon the same pilgrimage.' He paused. 'The estate house my brother built is now a shrine. As if horror and blood had the power to sanctify.'

'I believe it to be so, milord,' said Ivis, his gaze dropping to study the barrows edging the killing field.

'I saw something,' Anomander resumed. 'When the priest appeared upon the threshold of the house, blood started from his hands, from wounds that opened fresh, though he took no blade to them. Blood is answered with blood. It seems that faith will be written in what we lose, my friend.'

Uneasy, Ivis shivered. 'I grieve for that priest, milord. Surely, he would rather bless with something other than his own blood.'

'I am beset by dreams – nightmares – of that meeting. I confess, Ivis, that in my visions I come to the certitude that the wounds upon that man's hands, with their tears of blood,

631

are the eyes of a god. Or goddess. The priest raises them between us, his hands, the wounds, and my stare – which I cannot break – fixes upon those crimson eyes. What they leak arrives like a promise. In these dreams, I flee as would a soul broken.'

'A place not holy then, milord, but cursed.'

Anomander shrugged. 'We come upon circles of stones, the ancient holy sites of the Dog-Runners, and proclaim them cursed. What future beings, I wonder, will find the ruins of our own sacred sites, and name them the same?' The breath hissed from him. 'I am cold to these notions of faith, Ivis. I cannot but distrust the ease of our proclamations, so ephemeral their arrival, so facile their dismissal. Look at the war now upon us. Look to the fate of the Deniers. Look now to the birth of the Liosan. Faith stalks our land like a reaper of souls.'

At last, Anomander's thoughts had brought Ivis to the place he desired. 'Milord, I have heard nothing from Lord Draconus. He responds to not a single missive. In such absence, I must be bold. Upon the day of battle, milord, I will lead the Houseblades of Draconus to you, and submit to your command.'

Anomander said nothing. His gaze held upon the lowering clouds in the north, even as the first flakes of snow spun down to join the sleet.

'Milord—'

'Lord Draconus will return, Ivis. I am done with this pointless hunt. If Andarist and I are to become estranged, then I will bear the wound. I intend to leave for Kharkanas in the next day or so. Grief may well dress itself in the hair shirt of wounded pride, but vengeance matches its indulgence.'

'Milord,' said Ivis, 'it would be better if you did not. Return to Kharkanas, I mean. Leave Draconus to . . . to the place he has chosen for himself. I cannot explain this seduction of darkness, except that it is, somehow, the essence of his gift to the woman he loves. His decision seems beyond sanction, does it not? As well, there are the nobles to consider – your allies upon the field of battle.'

'They will fight for me, Ivis.'

'If Lord Draconus—'

'They will fight for me,' Anomander insisted.

'And if they do not?'

'Then they will learn to rue their failing.'

The threat chilled Ivis. He studied the heavy clouds weaving their wind-tangled skeins of snow and sleet. In the kitchen below, dinner was being prepared, a feast to honour their unexpected guests. In the main hall, the Azathanai, Caladan Brood, sat like a half-tamed bear in the only chair that could take his bulk – Lord Draconus's own. The surgeon, Prok, had taken to sitting with the High Mason.

In her private chambers, Lady Sandalath lavished attention upon Wreneck, as if he could stand in place of her own son – the son no one was permitted to acknowledge. The boy was mostly recovered from his ordeals, but he wore solemnity with the natural grace of a veteran of too many wars, and already he had begun to chafe under her obsessive ministrations. It was well enough that Wreneck had been a friend of Sandalath's son, but years spanned the two children, with Wreneck the elder, and nothing in his life thus far belonged to a pampered nobleborn child. Ivis saw his strained patience when in the lady's company.

Elsewhere in the keep, house-guards patrolled the corridors, walked the rooms and hallways, stamped up and down tower stairs.

'Milord,' ventured Ivis. 'You said you would speak with your Azathanai companion, regarding the daughters of Draconus.'

Grunting, Anomander nodded. 'I shall, this evening, Ivis. He is not entirely unaware of something amiss in this keep. For myself, even the mention of sorcery makes me uneasy. That said, they are the children of Draconus, and as to his relationship with them, you know better than do I. How would he respond to such horrors?'

'As of yet, milord, he has made no response at all.'

'You cannot be sure of his seeming indifference,' Anomander replied. 'It is quite possible that no messages or reports have reached him.'

'Milord? But I dispatched urgent—'

'All such missives are set just beyond the door to the Chamber of Night, upon a low table the servants can barely see. Has it yet occurred to Draconus that messages await his attention? Possibly not. So again, I ask: how would he respond to the news of one of his daughters dying at the hands of the remaining two? Or the slaughter of his servants in the keep?'

Ivis hesitated. 'Milord, I have pondered such questions unto exhaustion, and am no closer to any sure reply. He took away his bastard son, Arathan, into the west lands. A natural boy of seventeen at the time. Eighteen now. But his daughters . . . they remained children. Their younger half-brother had grown past them all. It is uncanny, sir.'

'Did he hold them close?'

'The daughters?' Ivis thought about the notion, and then eventually shook his head. 'He tolerated them. The names he gave the three tells its own tale, I wager. Envy, Spite and Malice. Malice was the one murdered and then burned in a bread oven.'

Anomander blinked. 'Such details still shock me, my friend.'

'Not a night easily forgotten,' Ivis said. 'We could have smoked them out long ago, milord, if not for our fear of the sorcery they possess.'

'Perhaps, with Caladan Brood in our company, now might be the time, Ivis.'

'But you are both soon to leave us, milord. Can mere shackles hold them?'

'No matter what,' Anomander said, 'we will not leave you helpless. That said, I have no notion of the extent of Brood's own power. He proved adept enough in lifting and moving heavy stones, and has spoken of the earth's own magic, as would a man familiar with it. Does he possess anything beyond such things? As to that, I am as curious as anyone might be. We will discuss the matter this evening.'

'I thank you, milord.'

'In this, Ivis, I am but the bridge. It will be Caladan Brood upon the other side. My modest charge is to invite you across it.'

'Even so, milord, I am grateful.'

'The evening draws upon us, friend,' said Anomander. 'Shall we quit this tower top?'

'My chilled bones would indeed welcome some heat, milord.'

*    *    *

Too much of Lady Sandalath reminded Wreneck of his own mother. Whilst she was being dressed for the dinner, he had slipped out of her chambers and now wandered the corridors of the keep. At intervals he came upon pairs of guards bearing lanterns and gripping shortswords. They eyed him warily, and more than one had admonished him for being unattended.

They saw him as still a child. He might have told them otherwise. He might even have reminded them that it was children they now guarded against, children who so frightened them that they walked through rooms and down passageways with drawn weapons, starting at shadows. The old ways of thinking, the ones that pushed children into childlike things, were now gone. The truth of that was obvious to Wreneck. Whatever was coming in this new world, it would divide people into the ones being hurt and the ones doing the hurting, and he was done with being hurt. Age made no difference. Age had nothing to do with it.

The voices in his head, which spoke most clearly in the moments before sleep, still came to him in his waking moments, but muted, murmuring words he often could not make out. He could not be sure, but they all seemed afraid, and at times he was startled by some internal cry, a warning no one else heard, as if they saw dangers unseen by anyone else.

He found it difficult to believe that they were as they said they were. Dying gods. Such beings, dying or not, had no interest in Wreneck, the stable boy, who had done nothing worth much in his whole life, and who thought of the future

635

as a single moment, a spear's point jabbing down, punching through skin, sliding into meat and whatever else the skin protected. A spear taking a life away, and in his mind his list of names, each one fading before his eyes with each thrust of the spear, each in turn, one by one, until the list was gone, and all that was left to him was empty.

This was his only future, and when it ended, when his task was done, there would be nothing but a vague, blurry world of his life spent with Jinia. But even there, something whispered of oblivion, inviting him into a world of imagination, like an island surrounded by the Abyss.

*Abyss.* That was a word he'd heard spoken as a curse and as a prayer, as if two faces hid in the darkness, and who knew which one groping hands might find?

He could have told the guards about his thoughts, to show that they weren't thoughts anyone would expect from a child. But something held him back. He was beginning to suspect that being seen as a child was in itself a kind of disguise, one that he might be able to use, come the night when he did murder.

Perhaps the dying gods had warned him against revealing too much, but he was not convinced of that – in any case, he'd told Lady Sandalath nothing of his plans, and he was certain that the First Son and the Azathanai would both remain silent on the matter. He had no choice but to show himself to her as only a child, a friend of Orfantal who, with her and with Wreneck himself, was all that remained of House Drukorlat. Jinia was another, of course, but she too had become Wreneck's secret, his way of protecting her from anyone and everyone.

It was complicated, and troubling, and the lady's need to hold him close, so tight that sometimes he could barely draw a breath, just made him uncomfortable. He had no desire to stay in this keep.

He reached a portal that opened on to the landing of a spiral staircase. The light spilling in from the oil lamps set in the niches in the corridor behind him did not reach far, and by the first turn of the stone steps Wreneck found himself in darkness. He continued upward.

Towers interested him. He had never been higher than a single level above the ground, and that had been in Lady Nerys's estate, and the house had been burning down around him and Jinia. Climbing trees had shown him how everything changed when seen from any height, but often the thick canopies of other trees blocked most of his view downward. From atop a tower, he believed, there would be nothing to impede his view.

Everything below, when he reached that height, would be familiar, and yet each thing would be transformed in his eyes, becoming something new. This notion seemed to displease the dying gods in his head.

At the level just below the top floor of the tower, he came to a landing and found himself facing a blackwood door. Beads of water ran down its furrowed face. The pool at its base had spread out over the flagstone landing, cold enough to form slush here and there, and thin, crackling layers of ice. Standing before the door, he could feel waves of cold coming from it.

Eyes on the heavy latch, Wreneck stepped forward.

'*Don't!*'

He spun round.

A small girl was crouched on the stairs above the landing, wearing little more than rags. Her thin, smudged face was pale but not white. This told Wreneck that she belonged to neither Mother Dark nor Lord Urusander. She was, in that respect, the same as him. 'You're one of the daughters,' he said. 'The ones who killed people.'

'Send them away.'

'Who?'

'The spirits. The ghosts. The ones swarming around you. Send them away and then we can talk.'

'They're all hunting you,' Wreneck said. 'Everyone here in the keep. They say you killed your sister, the youngest one.'

'No. Yes.'

'You burned her in an oven.'

'She was already dead. Dead but not knowing it. The oven.

That was us being merciful. We're not the same as the rest of you. We're not even Tiste. What's your name?'

'Wreneck.'

'Send the spirits away, Wreneck.'

'I can't. I don't know how. They can't do anything. They're dying.'

'Dying, but not dead yet.'

'They're scared right now.'

The girl smiled. 'Because of me?'

'No.' He gestured. 'The door, and what's behind it, I think.'

The smile vanished. 'Father's secret room. You can't open it. It's locked. Sealed. Warded by magic. If you touch that latch, you'll die.'

'What's a Finnest?'

'A what?'

'Finnest. The dying gods keep screaming about a Finnest.'

'Don't know. Never heard of it. Do you have anything to eat?'

'No. Which sister are you?'

'Envy.'

'Where's the other one?'

Envy shrugged. 'She tried strangling me with my hair. I fought her off. I beat her good. That was this morning. She crawled away and I've not seen her since.'

'You two don't like each other.'

Envy held out her hand, palm-up. A lurid red glow appeared, floating above it. 'We're coming into our power. If I wanted to, I could become a woman. Right here. I could grow up right in front of your eyes.' The glow now sent out a tendril, curling like a serpent as it entwined her hand and then snaked up her wrist. 'Or I could make myself look just like . . . what's her name again? Oh, like Jinia.'

Wreneck said nothing.

Envy stretched out her other hand, and another serpent of fire appeared to match the first one. 'I can reach into your mind, Wreneck. I can, if I want, pull things out and crush them. Your love for her. I could kill it.' Her arms lifted, and the tendrils of flame acquired snake-heads, jaws opening to reveal fangs that glittered like diamonds. 'My bite is venomous. With it, I can make you my slave. Or make you love me more than you ever loved Jinia.'

'Why would you do that? I'm just a boy.'

'A boy blessed by old gods – you might think they're dying. They might even tell you that. But maybe they're not dying at all, Wreneck. Maybe you're keeping them well fed, with your dreams of blood and vengeance. The older things are, the hungrier and thirstier they get.'

'The only thing hungry and thirsty here is you, Envy.'

'I told you. I'm older than I look.' The serpents sank back beneath the skin of her arms and she beckoned. 'Forget Jinia. I'm much better, Wreneck. With my help, we can banish those old spirits. Back into the black earth. Give yourself to me and I'll keep you for ever, and as for those soldiers who hurt you and raped Jinia, well, with me at your side, Wreneck, we'll show them such agony as to shatter their souls.'

'I'd rather use my spear.'

'You won't get close to them.'

'Lord Anomander will help me.'

'That pompous fool? He's frightened of sorcery. I once thought he might be worthy of me, but he isn't. Sorcery, Wreneck. A new world is coming, and there will be beings in it with such power as to topple mountains—'

'Why?'

She frowned. 'Why what?'

'Why topple mountains?'

'Because we can! To show our power!'

'Why do you have to do something just because you can? Why do you have to show your power if you already have it anyway? Aren't you even more powerful when you don't bother toppling mountains, when you don't bother showing off?'

Envy scowled at him. 'Those old gods are feeding on you,' she said. 'Give yourself to me, Wreneck, and together we'll turn on them. We'll feed on them instead. We'll devour them

639

and take their power. With sorcery you can get to those soldiers, no matter where they're hiding. More to the point, Wreneck, they won't be able to hide at all.' She rose and moved down a step. 'We could go straight to them. We could leave tonight with none to stop us.'

'I need my spear—'

'I'll make you a new one.'

'I don't want a new one.'

Her small hands curled into fists. 'Are you going to mess up everything I'm promising you on account of a damned spear?'

'Anyway,' said Wreneck, 'Ivis said Lord Anomander was going to talk to the Azathanai about catching you and your sister.'

Envy's eyes narrowed. 'I've told you too much.'

The serpents of flame reappeared. Writhing, they shot out from her hands, the snake-jaws stretching wide.

Something roiled up in front of Wreneck, luminous and billowing. The twin snakes sank their fangs into it, and Wreneck was rocked back as a scream arced through his skull. He felt the death of the old god like a fist to his chest. All breath knocked from his lungs, he fell against the black-wood door.

Something upon the other side of that door hammered into it, rattling the frame and spilling wet grit from the ceiling. The impact jolted Wreneck and he sagged, stunned and helpless.

Envy struck again, the snakes lashing out.

Another god intervened, took the wounds, and died in agony.

Laughing, Envy stepped down on to the landing. 'I'll kill them all, Wreneck! Unless you surrender to me!'

Dimly, Wreneck saw a flash of motion on the stairs behind Envy, and then that form launched itself through the air, landing upon Envy's back. Arms wrapped tight about her neck, dirty fingers raking red furrows across the girl's chest, neck and face.

Shrieking, Envy twisted round, as the weight of the other

girl, wrapped about her by the neck, dragged them both to the floor.

The other girl howled manic laughter as she clawed at Envy. 'You can't have him! You'll never have him!'

*Oh, this must be Spite.*

He pulled himself towards the edge of the landing, ignoring the hammering fists upon the door behind him, ignoring the two sisters tearing at each other with snarls and lashing nails. Bruising his elbows and knees, he slid awkwardly down the steps.

Keening, the remaining gods closed in around him.

'*Warn the Azathanai, child! Warn the High Mason! These two, these two . . . these two . . .*'

The words faded, as if the entire chorus of voices uttering them had been pushed off a cliff's ledge. Wreneck felt very tired. He was lying upon another landing, half in and half out of the dull light from the corridor beyond. The sounds of fighting and thumping fists echoed down the stone steps still, and he found it hard to believe that no one else in the keep could hear.

He shivered in the icy draught that flowed above the tiled floor of the corridor. From somewhere outside, he could hear the wind, gusting and punching at shutters, beating against stone walls.

A winter storm was upon them.

And the dinner bell was sounding, low, like distant thunder.

Wreneck closed his eyes, and let darkness take him.

\*      \*      \*

'The lad's taken to wandering,' said Yalad. 'Hunger will draw him to the table before too long.'

They sat at the dining table with the others from the household staff, along with the Azathanai, awaiting Lord Anomander, Ivis and Wreneck.

Sandalath frowned at the gate sergeant. 'You describe him as if he was a dog.'

Yalad's soft smile faltered. 'My apologies, milady. I meant

no disrespect. But Lord Anomander found him half starved, and the boy is not yet fully recovered.'

'He has known too little comfort in his life,' she replied. 'I must accept some responsibility for that. I should have stood against my mother, in whom grief fed cruelty. She struck at Wreneck because he was the most helpless among us.' She shook her head. 'There is much to mend here.'

Seated opposite Yalad, Surgeon Prok collected up his goblet. 'Flesh heals quickly when compared to the spirit. Milady, for the child you will need patience. Perhaps indeed your mother was too free with her whip, but that may prove less damaging, in the long run, than simple neglect. The lad has no reason to trust, and no precedent in which to place any faith in the notion itself.'

'He need not fear me,' Sandalath said, her tone hardening. 'I feel castigated by you, Surgeon Prok, for the boldness of my love.'

Prok blinked at her. 'You can love a stone, but do not expect it to love you back. Milady, that child has guarded eyes. His wounds now bear scars, and those scars dull all feeling. You may see that as a flaw, but I assure you, just as the body will protect what was damaged, so too will the soul.' He swallowed down a mouthful of wine, meeting her glare with a calm expression. 'All too often, in seeking to heal, we reopen wounds. Never a good idea, in my experience.'

'The fact remains,' Sandalath said, 'I don't know where he has gone, and the dinner bell has sounded.'

At that moment, Lord Anomander and Ivis arrived in the dining hall.

Relieved, Sandalath said to Ivis, 'Young Wreneck is nowhere to be found, good sir. Both your gate sergeant and the surgeon here believe that I worry without reason, whilst the High Mason and the others say nothing at all. I am made to feel foolish.'

Caladan Brood spoke. 'Thus far, I have made no effort to quest through the stones of this keep.'

Anomander grunted, and asked, 'Why the reluctance?'

The Azathanai made no reply.

Ivis swung to Yalad. 'Gather a squad and inform the patrols – find the lad.'

'Yes sir,' Yalad replied, rising from his chair. 'Milady, again, my apologies.'

'We shall assist,' Prok said. 'Madame Sorca? Bidishan?'

In moments the others, along with Setyl and Venth Direll, had departed the chamber, leaving Sandalath alone with Ivis and their two guests.

'He shall be found, milady,' Lord Anomander said, drawing out a chair and settling into it. 'High Mason, you would not explain your reluctance earlier. Will you do so now?'

Caladan Brood hesitated, and then shrugged. 'These daughters – the blood of their mother runs fierce within them. Since our arrival, I have felt them explore their power. This is a crowded keep, Anomander, and by that I do not mean those of flesh and blood as we find around us. Something else dwells here, and it knows I have come, and likes it not. Regarding Wreneck, however . . .' He hesitated, and then shrugged. 'He has acquired formidable protectors.'

'All this mysticism tires me,' Anomander said in a growl, reaching for a goblet. 'This sorcery proves to be an insidious art, inviting the worst in us.'

Though Ivis said nothing, Sandalath – who had been watching him – saw in his expression something sickly. 'Master Ivis, are you unwell?'

The man seemed to flinch at the question. He combed thick fingers through his greying beard, and then spoke. 'This sorcery seems in step with our natural unravelling of decorum and decency,' he said, eyeing Caladan Brood. 'The forest is restless with earth spirits. I have seen with my own eyes the spilling of sacrificial blood, only it was no mortal doing the bleeding. High Mason, I am told your powers belong to the earth. What can you tell me of a goddess suspended above the ground on a bed of wooden spikes? Impaled through her body, even her skull, yet she lives, and speaks . . .'

With the others, Sandalath stared at Ivis. The scene the

man described horrified her, and upon his visage, now laid bare, was something both haunted and suffering.

After a long moment of silence, Lord Anomander spoke. 'Ivis, where did you find this . . . goddess?'

Ivis started. 'Milord? In the forest, a glade.'

'Does she remain there?'

'I do not know. I confess, I have not the courage to return.'

'And she spoke to you? What did she say?'

Frowning, Ivis glanced away. 'That we shall fail in all that we do. The world changes and there will be no peace in what comes. What will be born anew will be as a babe atop a heap of corpses. A living crown,' he concluded in a hoarse rasp, 'upon dead glory.'

With a muffled oath, Anomander rose to his feet. 'Enough of this nonsense. You did not imagine this, Ivis? She is out there? I will speak with this goddess – I will defy these prophecies of failure and death.' He drew his cloak about him. 'Failing that,' he added with a half-snarl, 'I will end her torment.'

'I sought the same, milord,' Ivis said. 'She mocked me for it. Remove the spikes and she will indeed die. To live, she must suffer, a goddess of the earth.' He looked again to Caladan Brood. 'As the earth suffers in turn.' Facing Anomander once more, he said, 'Milord, the Tiste are as talons carving through the flesh of the world. Every ragged furrow is a victory won. Every savaged span of flesh maps our progress – but it's all for naught. When we kill what we stand on, it all ends, and whatever destiny we believed in for our kind is revealed as worthless.'

By the time he was done, Ivis was trembling. He took hold of the wine jug and drank from its curled lip, spilling on to his shirt.

Lord Anomander stood as if frozen in place. Then he swung to face the Azathanai. 'What advice, High Mason, or has your tongue died in your mouth?'

The Azathanai's attention seemed to be fixed on the table-top before him. 'One in pain longs to share the suffering,' he said. 'Even a goddess. She has made artistry of despair and delights in an audience. Anomander, she will have nothing worthwhile to say to you. Indeed, she will deceive where she can. In any case, she is not real.'

Ivis scowled. 'I saw her—'

'You walked into a dream, Master Ivis, but not one of your own making. There are places, in the wilderness, when the visions of the Sleeping Goddess become manifest. Most often, they are caught from the corner of the eye, a flash, something blurred or hinted at. If violence attends her dreaming, however, they can sustain themselves, even unto an exchange of words.' He rolled his shoulders in an odd shrug. 'But most often, they appear as beasts. Hounds, or demonic cats with red eyes—'

'An impaled goddess?'

'Hers is an uneasy sleep, Master Ivis. In any case, none here can deny the wounding done to the earth in these Tiste lands. The assault has been savage and sustained, and the wilderness dies. Here, in this place, the Sleeping God does indeed bleed from wounds. Every wooden spike marks a triumph of progress.' He lifted his gaze to Anomander. 'Would you now undo all that has been achieved in the name of civilization?'

Anomander's eyes flattened as he studied the Azathanai. 'Should I walk out from this keep on this night, I have that power? Should I find this goddess? Speak the truth now, Brood, if you would earn my respect.'

The High Mason's broad face seemed to stretch as the Azathanai bared his teeth, revealing long canines. 'Arrogance does not intimidate me, Rake, as you well know by now. Presumption, even less so. Upon my answer hangs all respect? But what if the answer displeases you? What manner of friendship do you seek?'

'Then quest through the stones of this keep, and tell us what dwells here,' Anomander said. 'Between us,' he added in a bitter tone, 'only one of us has been free with admissions of weakness and flaw. Or shall I assume you perfect?'

Caladan Brood slowly closed his eyes. 'Then I shall say it plain. Unleash me upon this keep, and few shall survive the night. If I awaken my power, I will be a lodestone to the daughters of Draconus, and to the host of forgotten gods protecting young Wreneck, and to whatever other entity hides here. Sorcery will feed upon sorcery. Come the dawn, this estate and most of the lands of Lord Draconus could well be a scorched ruin.'

'Now who mocks with bravado?'

At that, Caladan Brood rose. 'You'll sting me awake, Anomander? So be it then.'

*　　*　　*

'He's mine!'

Sleepily, Wreneck opened his eyes. The back of his head ached and something made the hair sticky in that place, where it rested upon cold flagstones. Blinking, he stared up at a low ceiling of black stone slick with mould. Both shoulders were pressed against gritty walls, as if he'd been thrown into a sarcophagus. He struggled to sit up, only to be roughly pushed back by a naked heel slamming into his chest.

'Stay there, fool!'

Envy moved into a crouch above him, her knees on his chest. 'Say nothing,' she continued in a harsh whisper. 'We're between the walls. People might hear us. If they do, we'll have to kill you.'

'They're nowhere close,' hissed another voice, from somewhere behind Wreneck. 'That was the muster bell we heard. Everybody's rushed down to the main hall. Listen – not a sound now. But I heard the main doors slam.'

'That was the demon pounding on the door,' Envy replied.

'No it wasn't.'

'You're bleeding from your ears, Spite, on account of me bashing your skull. It's no wonder you're hearing things.'

'It was the main doors. I don't think anyone's left in the house.'

'They wouldn't do that. Why would they do that? We've got a hostage!'

'He's nothing. Worthless.'

646

'If he was yours, Spite, you wouldn't be saying that. But he's mine. My slave. My first one, and you can't have him. I'm ahead of you now and that's what you hate the most, isn't it?'

'I'll kill him before I let you take him as your slave!'

'Too late!'

Envy scrambled upright to stand on Wreneck's chest. She weighed almost nothing. Suddenly angry, Wreneck reached up and grasped Envy's ankles. He lifted and then pushed her up and over his head. Her shriek was cut short as she collided with her sister. The two fell to fighting again.

Rolling on to his side and then on to his stomach, Wreneck drew his hands and knees under him and pushed himself upright, twisting round to watch the sisters beating at each other with fists and knees.

The girls suddenly ceased their thrashing. Both glared up at him.

'Kill him now,' said Spite. 'If you don't, I will.'

'No you won't. He's mine.'

'Just kill him, Envy!'

'Fine, I will, then.'

At that instant, it seemed that the entire house lurched to one side. Groaning, the stones of the walls spat out grit and dust. Howling filled Wreneck's skull and he clutched the sides of his head.

Spite's eyes were suddenly wide. 'What was that?'

Wreneck forced words past his clenched jaw. 'The Azathanai,' he said, finally making out the inchoate screaming of the dying gods. 'The High Mason, who built this house. And made the Sealed Chamber, though he didn't know what Draconus wanted it for. Someone's been feeding what's been trapped inside that room. Feeding it with bad thoughts, making it stronger. But now the wards are collapsing, and it's trying to get out.'

Spite loosed a terrified squeal, pulling away from Envy. 'We have to get out of here!'

She fled up the narrow passage. A moment later, with a final glare back at Wreneck, Envy followed her.

The roar of voices dropped off, leaving only moaning echoes draining like water through Wreneck's thoughts. Nauseous, one shoulder rubbing against the stone wall, he set off in the direction opposite that taken by the sisters.

The Azathanai was the only person in the house barring Wreneck, Envy and Spite. Everyone else was gone. The dying gods began muttering again, urging him onward. He reached a junction in the passageway and saw thin lines of light on the wall opposite. A moment's fumbling in the gloom found the latch. With a click the door opened, grating on stone ball-joints, revealing a room beyond that Wreneck was unfamiliar with. He stumbled in, letting the door swing back.

Still dazed, he looked round. A low, long table dominated the centre of the chamber, hewn from a single block of wood, with gutters carved down the length of its long sides. Small buckets hung from hooks at the corners. Along one wall were a half-dozen rows of pegs, from which depended small iron tools – small-bladed knives, gouges, wood-handled saws, clamps and awls.

The air smelled of something bitter.

A faint shriek sounded, but it seemed far away, so he decided to ignore it. He crossed the room until he stood before the tools. He selected one of the small knives. The blade was surprisingly sharp, and Wreneck wondered what this room was for, with the strange table and its buckets.

A proper door opened out on to a corridor. It told him little – he was not even sure what floor he was on. Choosing a direction at random, he set off, the dying gods gibbering in his head.

*　　*　　*

They were gathered in the barracks. The alarms had roused the Houseblades and Ivis was pleased to find them mostly dressed and properly kitted when he led his group into the main dining hall, and now the hearth blazed with fresh wood and the bitter cold was being driven back.

Lord Anomander remained near the door, as if still of a mind to set out into the fangs of the storm, seeking his audience with the impaled goddess. Sandalath, accompanied by Yalad and Surgeon Prok, had taken a chair closer to the hearth. Ivis eyed the trio as he was joined by his lieutenant.

'Orders, sir?'

'What? No. Yes. Have your soldiers preparing kits – enough to support us should we need to evacuate the grounds.'

'Sir? Are we under attack?'

'Unknown,' Ivis replied. 'Possibly. I know, it's a beastly storm out there, but we can find shelter in the wood if need be. Go on, Marak. Food, water, winter clothes, blankets, tents and cookware.' Without awaiting a reply, he walked over to the hearth.

'Milady, Caladan Brood will find Wreneck. You can be sure of that.'

'What makes you so certain?' Sandalath asked. 'He forced us out into the cold, Ivis. He warned us against destruction – my child is in there! I do not trust these Azathanai. Their hearts are cold, their eyes like stone. Oh, where is Lord Draconus? This is all his fault!'

Yalad stood. 'Master Ivis, I would like to volunteer to return to the main house. It may be that the High Mason has his hands full with those two witches. Wreneck could well find himself trapped between warring magicks – who will consider the worth of such a small life?'

Ivis twisted round, saw that Anomander was now watching them.

After a moment, the lord strode over. 'Sand,' he said, moving to crouch opposite and taking one of her hands in both of his. 'There is indeed something cruel in this new age of sorcery. But I have travelled with Brood for some time now. When we first found Wreneck, the lad was near death. It was Caladan who prepared a reviving broth for the child. Not the act of a heartless man.'

Sandalath leaned forward. 'Milord, you know my trust in you is absolute. If you assure me, then I must be satisfied.'

Yalad said, 'Master Ivis—'

'Attend to Lady Sandalath, gate sergeant.'

'Yes sir.'

Thunder shook the building, eliciting shouts of surprise. Anomander moved quickly back to the door that faced on to the parade ground. A sudden flash of actinic light lanced through the shutters, followed by a second eruption that sent shards of stone hailing down on the barracks roof. Soldiers cursed, reaching for their weapons.

'Lieutenant Marak! Take four squads to the stables and start saddling the horses – Horse Master Venth, prepare to take the mounts out to the summer drill-ground. If we have to, we'll see them sheltered in amongst the trees.'

Ivis watched as the Houseblades steadied themselves, with Marak moving among them, and then he joined Anomander at the door. 'Milord, your friend did not exaggerate, did he?'

The First Son had pushed open the door, enough to look out. Snow spun in around him with something like anger, as if the wind itself was outraged. 'An outer wall has buckled,' he said quietly. 'The roof above it simply exploded. But now . . . nothing.'

'Milord—'

Anomander punched a fist against the wooden frame of the door. 'Abyss take this sorcery, Ivis! I feel helpless against such powers. What city can stand against such a thing? What throne is safe, when the air itself can be made to burn? Is this what Urusander will deliver to the battlefield?'

'If he does, milord, then we must answer in kind.'

'And who among us can?'

Ivis had no answer. He could see, in the courtyard beyond, a scatter of broken stone and shattered roof tiles on the snow. To the right of the main entrance, the wall was no longer vertical. Massive stones now bulged outward. *The guest ante-chamber.* Where the low peaked roof had been was now a gaping space, jutting roof beams lifting splintered fists into the spinning snow.

'That tower, there, Ivis, to the left—'

Ivis shifted his gaze, and then blinked. Steam or smoke was pouring from its sides, through countless fissures between the stones, but there was no hint of flames or any other source of light. He shook his head. 'That tower, milord . . . there is a chamber there, a locked door. All are forbidden to enter.'

Anomander half drew his sword, and then let it slide home again. 'Does my courage falter here, Ivis?'

'Milord, wisdom alone keeps you here. When you can do nothing against such forces, what point in sacrificing your life?'

Anomander barked a bitter laugh. 'Ah, yes, this wise lesson here. If you would hold your enemy at bay, trapped into helplessness, chained to what cannot be known, only feared . . . why, I begin to comprehend a tactical value to sorcery, beyond its actual manifestation. The question remains, alas: how does one answer it? How does one defeat it? Pray, Ivis, offer me a soldier's answer.'

'How have we ever answered such impossible risks, milord? We march forward, under whatever hail awaits us. We bare teeth at the enemy, even as they damn us for our temerity. A true soldier, milord, will never bow to sorcery – this I now believe.'

Anomander grunted. 'I can almost hear Scara Bandaris, in his manner of laughing when nothing works. I remember, the day we faced the last Jhelarkan horde . . . "War?" he cried. "Why, another name for shit, my friends. So now, keep your heads above the flood and swim for your fucking lives!"'

'Then, milord,' said Ivis, 'if you'll step to one side and give me leave, I have a boy to find.'

The gaze of the First Son was suddenly bright, even as he moved aside. 'Do not tarry overlong, my friend, lest you force me to come and get you.'

'*My* charges, you and them, milord. *My* responsibility.'

Another detonation shook the grounds, another sudden flash, this time from the east tower. The squat structure wavered, tottered like a drunk on a bridge. Shutters fell away from the narrow windows.

'Milord, I beg you, do not come after me. If I do not return, take command of the Houseblades.'

'Best hurry, Ivis. This night seems fraught with grand gestures. I will watch. I will abide, as only a humbled man can.'

Nodding, and without a glance back at Sandalath, Ivis set out across the snow-sculpted, shard-studded compound.

*     *     *

Envy limped up the dust-filled corridor. She'd hurt the bastard, but there were lessons still to be learned. Standing there, admiring the effects of her ambush, had been a mistake. His retaliation had the feel of a back-handed swing – though he stood across the dining chamber, ten or more paces distant. The power that had struck her had been shocking in its breadth, its vicious might. Perhaps more surprising, however, was that she had survived being flung through a solid stone wall to land amidst rubble in the antechamber. Stunned, staring upward, she had only vaguely comprehended the imminent collapse of the roof – which would surely have buried her. A savage pulse of power had sent the roof up and out. Sudden cold flooded in. Shivering, she had crawled out from the wreckage, one knee throbbing and barely able to take her weight.

The Azathanai had set off after Spite.

*You think you finished me? You didn't. I'm not one to be ignored, fool, as you shall discover!*

She edged along the corridor, with fires dancing along her limbs to keep her warm.

*Father's poor house, all ruined. See what neglect gets you?*

An eruption of sorcery shook the house again, like a god's fist, and Envy gasped at her sister's sudden, terrible shriek.

A moment later, Spite skidded into the corridor ahead. One arm had been shattered, with splinters of bone jutting from torn flesh halfway between elbow and shoulder. The wrist and hand were both twisted round too far, the thumb now on the outside and the palm facing forward. In icy fascination, Envy stared at the mangled limb as Spite staggered towards her.

'Help me!'

Behind Spite, the Azathanai stepped into view.

Envy lashed out with raging fire, snaking round Spite to engulf the Azathanai.

652

He was knocked into the wall behind him, but only momentarily. Rolling his shoulders, he leaned forward and pushed through the coruscating magic that now roiled to fill the corridor.

Spite reached Envy, slipped past, and kept running.

Something tore Envy's serpents of fire into shreds. Squealing, the girl backed away as the Azathanai advanced.

\*     \*     \*

Sword in hand, Ivis stepped through the doorway. Beyond the cloakroom alcove, the main hall beckoned him forward. At first he saw no movement in the large chamber, although the flames from the hearth threw writhing shadows everywhere, as if a fever had taken the fire.

A moment later, he saw the boy. Wreneck was kneeling before the hearth, feeding wood into it with a strange, mechanical rhythm. Burning wood was piled high, spilling out over the stone surround.

'Wreneck!'

The boy did not turn, nor give any other indication that he heard his name being called.

Ivis approached, uncanny chills riding his spine.

In the fire's frantic flames, he saw something like a face. A woman's, round and soft, with eyes promising everlasting warmth. Ivis felt his legs moving, bringing him closer to the hearth. He barely heard the sword fall from his hand.

*She . . . she is beautiful . . .*

He was beside the boy now, feeling the fierce heat against his face, seductive as a lingering kiss. He saw her hands, reaching out to beckon him still closer.

*'Ivis. I know you. From Raskan's blessed memories, I know you. Feel the terrible sorcery surrounding us? Seething through this cursed house? It invites, yes? Sweet as a caress. Look to the boy. He wants to join me, but he has protectors – they resist, though we are kin. I tell them, my womb can hold them all. Them, the child, you. I can keep you safe from the little creatures – oh, Draconus, look what we made here! Surely, lover, we can take some ragged pride, but mind the edges!*

'*I can keep you all safe. Come now, Ivis. Did you not dream of fire? For this keep? For the girls, prison bars of flame. Cages of cracked stone, rubble, blackened beams, and upon it all – when at last the fury cools – a blessed shroud of snow. Let them dig their way out – it will take months, if not years.*

'*Come now, feed the fire, and for that gift I will repay you in turn. My sweetest kiss, my swallowing lips, my red all.*'

Burning logs had toppled out from the hearth, rolling across the thick rugs. One came to rest against the legs of a chair, with small tongues of flame licking upward.

Ivis knelt beside the boy. Together, side by side, they pushed more wood on to the raging mound.

*Warm.* Ivis smiled. *Winter dies here. Here and now.*

*Winter dies.*

Surrounding them, the flames laughed.

*          *          *

Sandalath rocked, her arms drawn in, wrapped about her body. *My boy. I've lost my boy.* She had seen Ivis leave the barracks, had seen something like a parting between the master-at-arms and Lord Anomander. She had watched the Houseblades preparing, gathering gear as if they were all about to flee. The First Son's promises seemed to be crumbling in her mind. *My son is in there. Yalad mocked my concern – and now look at us.*

'Milady . . .'

Frowning, Sandalath fought to focus on the face opposite her. 'Surgeon Prok. What is it? What has happened?'

'The keep has caught fire,' he said. 'I feel I should prepare you. It is not the flames we must worry over – not too much, that is. The smoke is what kills more often than not.'

'Fire?'

'In the main hall, milady. The front entrance is blocked – none will come through it. That said, there are other exits. The annexe behind the kitchen, for example. Wreneck knows it, I'm sure.'

654

'The house is burning?'

'Ivis is a brave man.'

She looked to Lord Anomander again, but the First Son had not moved. He stood framed in the doorway, snow swirling in around him. 'He will do something,' she said. 'He always protected me.'

Yalad had been drawn away by one of the Houseblades. The horses were in a frenzy outside the stables. Then there came shouts and Surgeon Prok rose. 'Forgive me, milady. The horse master has been injured.'

She watched him hurry away, and found herself alone. Gathering up her cloak, she rose and walked through the press of Houseblades with their kits crowding the dining tables, their quick and sure movements as they buckled straps and checked bindings, their closed-in faces as they concentrated on keeping fear at bay. It was all understandable and all very professional.

She was at the barracks kitchen door when Lord Anomander turned and raised his voice. 'We are leaving the compound now – every outbuilding is at risk from those flames, including this one. Finish up what you're doing – we are now out of time for anything more. Assemble at the gate, and be quick about it!'

It was well that the First Son had taken command, with Ivis now gone.

*There are other ways out. And in.*

Sandalath walked into the kitchen, moved down its length to the side door that opened out on to the refuse pit. As she stepped into the night, the howling wind swept in to embrace her, shocking in its intensity. Skirting the pit, she moved along the outer wall towards the main house. Into the shadows between a storehouse and the wall, and then out again, with the servants' door now directly opposite.

It was unlocked, though she had to pull hard as snow had drifted up against it. Heat and smoke gusted into her face, biting at her eyes.

*I used the servants' door to sneak away from Mother, to find Galdan in the fields beyond. He liked his wine, did*

*Galdan, so I'd bring him a stoppered jar, from the cellar. For afterwards.*

*Along this corridor, then. Mother hears nothing.*

*I've come for my son, finally. This time, no one will take him away.*

She moved beneath the smoke, which roiled along the arched ceiling of the corridor and then began tumbling down as she went deeper into the building. But things were strangely unfamiliar. A doorway she had expected wasn't where it should have been, and here, when the passage should have swung right, it now swung left.

*Ivis. You must have undressed me. In the carriage. I was so hot. Faint. Your hands were upon my body, but I don't remember that. I wish I did.*

She stumbled against stone steps, bruising a shin and then a knee as she fell against the hard edges. Smoke was pouring past her, rushing upward. She heard a scream, and then a piercing howl from somewhere above. *Orfantal?*

Sandalath climbed upward.

\*     \*     \*

Caladan Brood stepped into the main chamber. Before him, filling most of the room, was a figure wrought in flames, its belly massive, swollen and stretched as it rested heavily upon the flagstones. In its burgeoning, it had pushed the dining table against one wall, while simply crushing most of the chairs. Above this belly, still huge and yet disproportionately small compared to what lay below, was a woman's upper torso, heavy breasts, rounded shoulders, a fat-layered neck beneath a round face. The eyes were black coals amidst the fire, fixing now upon the High Mason.

'I felt you, brother.'

'Olar Ethil, do you have them?'

She nodded, her expression satiated. 'I do. Safe.'

'Will you yield them, when this night is done?'

'Do you ask it of me?'

'I do.'

'For you then, Brood, yes, I will yield them. But what of you? Are you proof to these mundane fires?'

'For a time,' he replied. 'Enough. Your daughters hide.'

'You hurt them badly.'

'And if I finish it?'

Olar Ethil laughed. 'Draconus cannot hate you more than he already does.'

'And you?'

She shrugged. 'I am here, am I not? Protecting these two mortals.'

'From your daughters? Or from the fire you so eagerly unleashed?'

'Both.' She waved a languid hand, the motion making a roar. 'You built well. Too good a home for the likes of me.'

'Your vengeance, then, for his having rejected you. That, Olar Ethil, is petty.'

'Beware the scorned woman.'

'Then why save Ivis and the boy?'

The woman was silent for a time, eyes narrowed to slits as she studied Caladan Brood. 'Not the path I chose.'

'The Finnest in the tower?'

Slowly, she nodded. 'Do you wish to know more?'

'Is it my business?'

'No, I think not, brother. I've done little thus far. Made use of a weak mind, too fragile for this or any world. No. This is between Draconus and me.'

'I did not know you parted with such vehemence.'

'We didn't. Until his servants betrayed me. I gave of myself. I made a gift. I took into myself a tortured soul, and brought it peace. For this blessing, that soul's companions delivered terrible pain.' She paused, and then waved the hand a second time. 'Look about you, Caladan. See how even your gift to Draconus has been twisted. Those who would stand near him – each and all will end up suffering.'

Caladan Brood tilted his head as he regarded her. 'You have cursed him.'

'He curses himself!' The scream was an eruption of flames,

transforming the chamber into an inferno. She then laughed. 'Best leave now, brother!'

'And your daughters?'

'I will drive them out – is that not enough? Leave their fate to their father – he deserves no less!'

Nodding, Caladan Brood strode into the flames, making for the front doors. The fire sought to devour him, only to flinch back on all sides. This demanded some effort on the High Mason's part. With each step he took, the flagstones cracked beneath him.

*     *     *

The flames curled strangely as they edged round the corner ahead. Envy slowed her painful steps. *Those are not mine. But not real either. This is another kind of sorcery. I feel it, like a well-fount – reeking of my essence, but far worse.* She stared as the fire twisted upon itself, formed a face in ceaseless motion, as if every expression was nothing more than a mask beneath which raged some undeniable heat. *Truths. What the skin hides.*

A woman's face, now smiling, now speaking. 'Oh, look at you. Naughty girls – you gave me Malice, but not the living child, whom I would have protected. No, the undecided child. Held between life and death by your father's protective spells. Of course, he sought only to keep you free of the risk of death, knowing well the wildness of your spirits.' Her smile broadened. 'As ever, he meant well. What parent does not dread outliving their children? But then you broke her neck.'

'Not me! It was Spite!'

'There are two chambers to the heart, child, and so you were named in answer to your twin sister. Meaning, you two are in truth one, bitterly divided in the hopes of weakening your power. But poor Malice, who came after, what was left to her? Denied a place, denied a home . . . what other name could attend such a child?'

'It was an accident, Mother! An accident!'

The flames spun closer, the face swelling to crowd the corridor. 'I have your sister, Envy. Caladan broke her badly.

He might well have killed her, had I not sent him away. He might well have killed you both, and by that laid waste to your father's lands. How many would have died? Too many, child. You two are not worth their lives.'

Envy sank down on to her knees. 'Help me, Mother. I've been bad.'

'You are of my blood,' Olar Ethil said. 'And for that reason alone, I will spare you the wrath of the Finnest. But my, how you and Spite have poisoned it! She will see Draconus. How unfortunate, because the thing inside that husk bears little resemblance to your father. Still, what comes of this fated meeting will shatter the world.'

'Save us! We'll be good – you'll see!'

The massive face tilted slightly. 'Good? Well, let's say you'll have plenty of time to ponder such promises. For now, daughter, let's make for you and your sister a most displeasing tomb.'

Envy shrieked as the floor gave way beneath her, and then from above descended a mass of shattered rubble and splintered wood, as the house began its tortured collapse.

*She's burying us! Mother, you bitch!*

\*       \*       \*

Sandalath was thrown against a wall as the tower rocked around her. Steam swirled hot through pockets of bitter cold, and water streamed down the stone steps. Wreneck was waiting for her – just a little further. He sat huddled, curled up. She could see him in her mind. Moaning under her breath, she righted herself and continued upward.

*I remember this tower. I remember a door. I didn't like it, that door.*

*We went up to the top, to watch the battle. Such a terrible day. So many lives lost, their souls torn loose, spilling out, riding cries of pain into the air – how it swirled around us!*

*Orfantal – no, Wreneck – no – I don't know. I can't think!*

She hesitated, and then stumbled upward, as if a fist was

pushing her, driving into her back. She heard the echo of cackling laughter.

*I was never strong. Mother told me so. She had to take care of everything. All the mistakes I made. Galdan, our games. The child that came of that – I didn't know it worked that way. If they'd told me, I wouldn't have done any of that. But then it was too late, and Mother had to fix things, again, to make it right.*

*All the lies, the stories. She told me I couldn't be a mother, not to Orfantal. You can't be allowed to love a mistake. You can't be the one to nurture it, watch it grow into something you can't control. Every child is a hostage. Every child is to be sent away, until the face fades from the mind. This, Mother said, is the only freedom left to me.*

She reached the landing, where the water was gushing out from the rents in the massive blackwood door. The stones were glowing as if trapped in a furnace, revealing that the water was black as ink. *Dorssan Ryl. It was the lord's gift to Mother Dark, the way it changed. Draconus turned it into liquid night, into the blackness between the stars.*

*See how it pours!*

*Orfantal. I am coming. Nothing to fear, not any more.*

*I didn't mean to burn the stables down, but I was angry. At Mother. I was so angry! But oh, how those horses screamed.*

She could hear them again, as if the flames carried their voices in triumph, lifting them into the night amidst all the sparks and smoke. She saw poor Wreneck, so young, all covered in soot and scorch marks, his hair crisp and crumbling, his eyes filling with tears as he fought against Jinia's grip, as he tried to run back into the stables to save the horses.

And how Orfantal stood off to one side, still in his nightclothes, staring at Wreneck with one small fist pressed up against his mouth.

*Shush, Wreneck. It's too late for them. Too late for everyone.*

And Mother spinning round to glare at the stable boy. '*This was your fault, wretch! Listen to those screams, child!*

*You killed them all!'* And then she marched forward, raising her cane. And the blows rained down, upon Wreneck's head, and Jinia's forearms and shoulders, and all Sandalath could do was stand, frozen, helpless, hearing the cane striking flesh and bone, staring at Orfantal who watched it all but understood nothing.

*Hush, my son. The screams are only in your head. It's done with, now. Just the flames and their eager roar.*

She reached the door. The latch was loose and almost fell away from the wood panel, and the door swung easily.

'Lord Draconus! I knew you would return! It was the Azathanai, setting fire to the stables – can't you hear the horses screaming? Oh, please, stop it now – stop all of this—'

He reached for her, lifted her from her feet – she'd not known him to be so tall, big as a giant. But hostages were always young. It was being young that made them precious, so Lord Anomander told her, laughing as he wheeled her through the air, and how she squealed her delight, safe for ever in his strong hands.

But now she hung suspended in the air, in a chamber with its stone walls gouged deep on all sides, as if clawed by a trapped beast. With more rents crisscrossing the wooden floorboards, with the ceiling beams looking chewed, shredded.

She felt something like a fist curl in her belly, low down, and it grew. Back arching, Sandalath gasped as her clothes stretched, as she swelled, skin tightening. *Galdan! Look what we did! I didn't know! Mother is furious with me! She says it's a snake – a snake inside me, and it's growing!*

Fluids spilled from between her legs. She saw Draconus, looming before her, his face twisted in something like helpless frustration. She felt one of his hands reaching down, reaching in, and dragging the baby out.

She watched as he lifted the thing between them, and saw immediately that it was lifeless, a slick, red doll with flopping limbs. Snarling, he flung it away.

Another fist made a knot in her belly, began growing.

Another dead child. A bellow of fury from Draconus as he threw it to one side.

She lost count. Stillborn after stillborn. Mind glazed with shock, eyes unable to close or even blink, with not a single breath drawn, she watched as the scene played out again and again. There was no pain, no sense of anything beyond the swelling, the terrible release, and then his howling anger.

Until everything changed.

A child's cry, small fists waving about, feet kicking.

*Mother, I didn't mean it. I swear. I didn't know.*

Draconus pulled her close, pushed the wailing creature into her arms.

She looked up into the man's eyes, but those eyes, she saw now, did not belong to a man. They were as black and depthless as the waters of Dorssan Ryl. When he opened his mouth, as if attempting to speak, the inky waters poured from it. Anguish twisted the face. Releasing her to drop to the ravaged wooden floor, where she almost lost her balance, the figure staggered back, as if in horror.

Sudden vehemence flooded Sandalath, and the voice that came from her was not her own. 'This child, Draconus, has taken the best of you. This child is made pure. All the love you harboured, that you so callously hoarded, and meted out with such reluctance – it now resides in this babe, given to a mother too broken to love her back.

'Oh, Draconus, how do you like me now?

'Tell this to Mother Dark, when next you see her. She is neither the first nor the last, but nothing you covet and nothing you need will be found in her arms. I have wounded you, Draconus. Will she be content with what's left of you? I doubt it.

'My fire lives on, but it is a lonely flame. May you kiss the same cold lips. May you yearn for what you can never have, and find no warmth in this or any other world.

'Your soldiers burned me! In hate, they hurt me! All of your careless games, Draconus, now return to you! Come back to this Finnest, see what I have done!'

Sandalath felt the presence flee her. The tiny girl in her

arms, dripping with birth fluids, was plucking at her sodden blouse, hungry for what the cloth hid.

Revulsion rippled through her, but some instinct made her yield to the babe's need. She fumbled at the clasps, pulled her blouse apart, and let the girl suckle.

Draconus was gone – she didn't recall seeing him leave – and now, impossibly, the morning sun was pushing through the warped slats of the shutters. She could smell bitter, acrid smoke.

As the child drank eagerly, she staggered, body aching, over to the window, reaching out to tug back the shutters.

The smouldering ruin of the house surrounded the tower, the fire-cracked stones heaped up around the base. Flames had caught the barracks, but there the fire had but scorched one corner, where the stones had sunk down into a pit now filled with frozen meltwater. From beyond the outer wall, in the direction of the training field, a dozen or more columns of white smoke rose straight up, the only motion in this frozen daybreak.

She listened to the child's deep breaths even as the mouth drew on the nipple. Already the babe felt heavier, bulkier. Its skin was onyx, its black hair fine and long. The eyes were large and strangely elongated, luminous as they stared upward, past Sandalath's face, seemingly focused on the empty morning sky. Something in that small, round face reminded Sandalath of her mother.

*You'll get what you need, but nothing more.*

Turning about, she set out for the stairs.

*       *       *

Ivis sat huddled in blankets as close to the stone-ringed cookfire as he could manage, yet still shivers trembled through him.

He recalled little. Standing upon the threshold to the main chamber, and then . . . awakening out beyond the wall, his hands shredded and torn and full of slivers.

Yalad told him that he had walked out from the raging flames, with Wreneck in his arms. But not even his clothes were singed, and the boy was also miraculously untouched. Still, there had been horror and grief in the camp when it was discovered that Lady Sandalath was missing. Yalad had clawed at his face, as the weight of a dead hostage crashed down upon him – the man given the responsibility for her safety.

The storm had moved on in the night, and now there was no wind to stir the icy air. The household of Lord Draconus, and all the Houseblades, were now homeless.

Ivis frowned at the small flickering flames of the cookfire, as if some part of him was waiting to see something in those bright, dancing tongues. *Lord Anomander, how am I to take this? You challenged the Azathanai, upon a matter of respect. See the cost of that, milord. A house in ruin, a hostage lost to the flames. Two daughters? Well . . . there is that, I suppose.*

*Pride will undo us all, I fear.*

If he cared to, he could lift his gaze from the flames, look across the camp to where stood Lord Anomander, with Caladan Brood at his side. Their guests, bearers of unbearable gifts. It was said of the High Mason, in the night just past, that he stood to witness the collapse of the edifice built by his own hands, and how he had then spoken of the lintelstone above the gate, with its secret words carved into it, and how he had muttered, as if to himself, of a bitter truth in such a hopeful sentiment.

What this meant, Ivis could not guess.

If he looked the other way, to the figure crouching at the next campfire, he would see young Wreneck, whose eyes were now closed but only on the inside, revealing a regard like blank glass. Upon emerging from the burning estate, the boy had been quiescent in Ivis's arms, at least until he heard the terrified horses, upon which he had thrashed as if fevered, kicking and pushing until Ivis had no choice but to release him.

It had been Yalad who then grasped Wreneck, even as the boy lunged back towards the flames of the house, screaming his need to save the horses – even though the beasts were already being driven through the gate behind them.

*Well. This winter's seen its share of madness. We can agree on that, can we not?*

He was slow to react to the cries of alarm, and then amazement, and then the sudden descent of shocked silence, but at last, as each detail registered in his mind, assembling into a progression, he looked up.

A crowd, led by Yalad, had rushed across the field, only to halt halfway. Upon the far side, climbing weakly from the ditch, was Lady Sandalath. At first, Ivis thought her wearing a crimson skirt – one that he did not know she possessed – but then he saw how it was a stain, spilled out from between her legs. And he saw that she carried a small shape, pressed against her bared chest.

He thought it a doll, until he saw a tiny hand curling tight into a fist.

As Yalad and the others backed away, as Lord Anomander and the High Mason moved towards her only to stop again after but a few strides, as Ivis himself rose to watch as Sandalath drew closer – the crowd parting before her – and approached him, only one man stepped into her path.

'Milady,' said Surgeon Prok, tilting his head. 'I must attend to you, I'm afraid. To you both, in fact.'

She halted before the surgeon, and said, 'If you insist.'

He stepped closer. 'May I see the child, milady?'

'A girl,' she said.

'I'd wager . . . four, perhaps five weeks old, but that—'

'She is mine,' cut in Sandalath, her tone oddly without inflection. 'The one that lived. Her name,' she added, 'is Korlat.'

'Milady—'

'She is filled with love,' Sandalath continued, 'but not mine.' She then pulled the babe away from her breast and held it out to Prok.

Only then did the surgeon falter, and the look upon his face, as he turned to meet Ivis's gaze, was a crumpled ruin of grief.

As no one moved, as no one spoke, as all stared at Sandalath who offered the babe with outstretched arms, a small figure moved past Ivis and edged around Surgeon Prok.

'Can I hold her, milady?' Wreneck asked, and without awaiting a reply he accepted the babe, drawing his own blanket up around the naked child. 'Orfantal has a sister,' he said, 'and she's big!' He reached down with one finger, which the babe suddenly grasped.

Smiling, Wreneck turned to Ivis. 'Master, she's a strong one.'

Wretched, anguished beyond words, Ivis found himself staring at them both, through a veil of sorrow.

# BOOK THREE

*The Gratitude of Chains*

# SEVENTEEN

CAPTAIN HALLYD BAHANN COULD WELL RECALL HIS season of terror as a child, when a pack of wild dogs, driven out of the forest by wolves, had invaded the village. The creatures knew no fear. Three villagers, two women and an old man, had been pulled down, torn apart outside their own homes. When a dozen adults gathered weapons and set out to kill the beasts, the dogs vanished into the hills. A hunt was organized, but though the well-armed, mounted party scoured the broken crags, ravines and draws, they found few signs and spent three fruitless days of searching before returning home.

A week later, two children vanished while playing in a yard, leaving behind tatters of gory clothing and blood-splashed wooden toys.

The village was young, the homes new and the ground of the farms surrounding it only recently broken. The pocket forest skirting the shallow river that curled round the raised oxbow upon which the village had been built still held enough trees to be considered wild. Hallyd Bahann's father had set out the morning after the children had disappeared, riding north. That night, alone with his cloying mother, who'd made fear a way of life, Hallyd had shivered with dread, unwittingly drinking in his mother's terror. He could still remember that night, mapped like a brand on his soul.

His father returned the next day, with company. At his side trotted a fur-clad savage, pock-scarred and covered in matted hair. The stranger smelled foul. He ate raw meat and slept through the afternoon in filth of his own making, near the back door of the house. With the sun setting, he rose, and Hallyd recalled watching the man lope out into the gloom.

The stranger returned three days later, dragging a mass of boiled skulls on a rope. There had been, it turned out, twenty-six dogs in the feral pack. In payment, he was given a cask of cider, which he drank while sitting on the ground in the front yard. The liquor made him vicious, growling when anyone drew near – as word went out, and curious villagers came by to look at the skulls, and at the Jheleck who had collected them – but eventually the cask was empty, and the hunter passed out.

He was gone when Hallyd woke the next morning, though the dog skulls remained, heaped into a pyramid. Hallyd's father cursed upon discovering that the Jheleck had stolen the empty cask.

To this day, the dogs gave shape – flitting and deadly – to Hallyd Bahann's fears, and in his nightmares he often saw their bared fangs, and imagined in their eyes something remorseless, untamable.

The scout was huddled before him, shivering, wrapped in furs. A soldier of the Legion, reduced to this pitiful state.

'We were on her trail. We were closing in. Then everything changed – the night came alive. Arrows, sir, they attacked us with arrows, as if we were wild beasts! Deniers. I was in a squad, me and four others. I alone escaped. There were hundreds, captain, moving in packs – those wretched, stinking forest-grubbers – and we thought we'd killed them all!'

Weary, disgusted, Hallyd waved the soldier away. Two of his guards closed in, dragged the man out of the tent. Nothing disappointed him more than seeing a soldier reduced by terror. *You ran, you fool, abandoning your squad-mates. You ran, when you should have stood your ground, when you should have fought.* Even so, at least now he knew what awaited them behind the treeline to the west. The hunt for Sharenas was now incidental. It seemed that they were far from done with the Deniers.

*Arrows. The coward's way. Well, that should not surprise anyone.*

*Wicker shields. But where will we find what we need to make them?*

'Lieutenant Esk!'

The tent flap was tugged aside and a tall, willowy woman entered, armour clanking. 'Captain?'

'You commanded the south flank yesterday, yes? Did you draw within sight of Manaleth?'

'Yes sir.'

'What flag rode the high winds?'

'Neither the lord nor the lady was present in the keep, sir.'

'You are certain of that?'

'Yes sir.'

Hallyd Bahann rose, grunting at a twinge in his lower back. He'd never much liked riding. 'It's the worst of winter – what's driven the highborn out from their keep, I wonder?'

Lieutenant Esk had no suggestions.

'Assemble twenty of our best, lieutenant, for some night work. We're taking that keep, by stealth if at all possible.'

'Sir?'

'We need to resupply, lieutenant. Do you imagine the castellan would be generous to the enemy?'

'No sir.'

Seeing her hesitate, he said, 'Go on, out with it.'

'Thus far, sir, we have not overtly drawn noble blood—'

'Lord Andarist would beg to differ.'

'But no such accusation has been formally levelled, has it, sir?'

'You have something to suggest?'

She nodded. 'Sir, the word's out, from the surviving scouts who reached us. The Deniers are now organized, and since that is so, then it follows that someone is doing the organizing. It would be a stretch to imagine the forest-grubbers managing that on their own. I understand the Shake monasteries have proclaimed themselves neutral, but they do share the same faith, sir.'

'Go on. I am intrigued.'

'Yannis and Yedan monasteries, sir. If stealth can win us entry into Manalle's keep, then why not the monasteries? In terms of resupply, we could do no better, and besides, we would be effectively removing the Shake from the field, and thereby not have to rely on their promises of neutrality. Besides, how much faith can we place in goodwill, sir, in the midst of civil war?'

'An attack, justified by the charge that their agents have turned their forest-dwelling followers into an army?'

'As I said, sir, someone is organizing the forest-grubbers. Who else would have reason to do so? And more to the point, who else could claim the authority?'

'The priestly warriors of the Shake, lieutenant, are formidable. It won't be like facing the Wardens.'

'Stealth, sir, as you said. A night attack, an opened gate. If we catch them unawares.'

Hallyd considered. There was merit to this. What a coup it would be! Hunn Raal would have no choice, then, but to acknowledge Hallyd Bahann as second only to Raal himself. The annihilation of the Shake was tactically sound. Esk was right – it would be foolish to trust in that official pronouncement of neutrality.

*We could loot the temples, strip their stores, their weapons. We could cut out the heart of their pathetic cult. But most of all, we will be ending the old line of regal blood, thereby eliminating any complications for the future. No possible rivals to the thrones, not with Sheccanto and Skelenal dead.*

'Inform your fellow officers, Esk, we ride southeast, to Yannis.'

'Yes sir.'

'Oh, and how many scouts made it back?'

'Eleven thus far, sir.'

'Execute them on charges of cowardice and abandoning their comrades. Cowardice is rot and I'll not see it fester in my ranks.'

'Yes sir.'

For years, Hallyd had believed that the lone Jheleck had killed with his own hands all those wild dogs, only to overhear, one day, an offhand comment from his father. The savage had simply poisoned the animals with tainted meat. The lesson shifted in Hallyd's mind, then, from notions of appalling prowess and physical might to the elegance of cold expedience. *And for that, the fool got paid in cider and a single cask. Even the cunning can be witless. In that man's place, I would have demanded ten horses, or more.*

'*How big a fool was that hunter, son?*' his father had asked when they'd discussed it. '*Poison. I could have done the same to the cider.*'

'*Why didn't you?*'

'*No point. Either way, it's a fouled cask.*'

Hallyd Bahann began dressing in his armour. *Fouled cask. Yes. When I return, Hunn Raal, I'll see your forced smile, feel your brittle clasp of congratulations upon my shoulder, and see you struggle to keep your footing firm.*

*But fear not, when all is said and done, and we've ridden through the gates of the Citadel, trailing our collection of skulls, you and I will share a drink. But then, I could never match you cup for cup, so I'll take instead some mulled wine, and leave to you the cask.*

*We'll toast your cunning and mine, and then take measure of the wits between them.*

He paused, thinking about the drunken fool, sweaty and clumsy as he struggled to pleasure Tathe Lorat. Indeed, by the time he returned, she would have unmanned him utterly.

*We'll make of him our fool, and when he is finished, why, we'll turn upon Urusander himself. Old man, you had your glory, but those days are long past, now. Father Light is but a title, and one that, I wager, can be worn by any of us.*

*Ah, my friends, the days ahead will be adventurous.*

*       *       *

Wearing cloaks of unbleached fleece, Master-at-arms Gelas Storco and Sergeant Threadbare lay well concealed upon the ridge, amidst ash-grey ribs of snow, exposed granite and withered grass. The sergeant held a seeing tube to one eye. It was said to be Jaghut in origin, and had been in the possession of Greater House Manaleth for more than two centuries. Threadbare, leader of the company of scouts and trackers, had explained the inner workings of the brass and blackwood tube, but talk of mirrors and polished lenses made little sense to Gelas.

No matter. That it could see farther than the naked eye was all that mattered. The master-at-arms shifted slightly, as the cold of the ground seeped up through his garments. 'Well?'

'I wager three hundred,' Threadbare replied, her breath a stream of white. 'They're definitely doubling back.'

'So, not the forest after all, and more important, not us either.'

'So it seems, sir. Inviting the question, where now? Have they tucked tail?'

Gelas Storco grunted. 'Tell me again what that fool said.'

Three nights past, before the appearance of Hallyd Bahann's company, a half-dead Legion scout had arrived at the keep gate. He had been fevered and wounded. Threadbare had found the stubs of two hunting arrows in the man's back. Skilled at healing, she had worked on him through the night, cutting out the flint heads, but too much blood had been lost, and what remained was now poisoned by infection. The scout had died even as dawn broke the eastern horizon.

Threadbare lowered the eye-piece, rolled on to her side to face him. 'Thousands in the forest, hunting Legion soldiers, chasing them down, shooting them with arrows.'

'But Hunn Raal's soldiers swept that forest, killing everyone. We saw the fires, breathed the damned smoke. Abyss below, we heard the screams.'

'I've given that some thought, sir.'

He grimaced. 'I'm sure you have. You're always giving thought to things, Threadbare. It's why I keep you close, so I don't have to.'

'Yes sir. Well, the Legion invaded the forest at the season's

674

turn. The Deniers have the strange habit of dividing up their activities. Women gather and harvest, staying close to the camps, keeping an eye on the children along with the elders.'

'What do the men do, then? Sit around picking their arses?'

'I said it was strange, sir. When they're not picking their arses, the men go off on hunts. Off in search of the herds when the migrations are under way.'

'What migrations? More to the point, what herds?'

'It was a traditional thing. To my mind, sir, it's as much an excuse to get away from domestic life as anything else.'

'You mean, the men have fun sleeping on cold ground, cooking wretched meals all on their own, and otherwise making pigs of themselves?'

'Well, sir, they *are* ignorant savages.'

'You think the Legion missed the hunters, but now the hunters have returned, only to find their wives and children slaughtered.'

'If so, sir, then that forest over there is a realm consumed by rage.'

'So Bahann indeed tucked tail and is on his way back to Neret Sorr.'

She shook her head. 'I don't think so, sir. It's more likely they thought that war done with, only to now realize that it's barely begun. But who commands the forest savages?'

'No one, that's why they're savages.'

'And their faith?'

Gelas scowled. 'Ah.' He wagged a finger at her. 'See, I'm cleverer than you think. Bahann's going to attack the monasteries.'

'I was thinking just the same, sir.'

His gaze narrowed on her. So innocent and pretty. 'What am I good at, sergeant?'

'Sir?'

'Describe my talents, as you see them.'

'Well, sir. You conduct a reign of terror over your Houseblades, but you're fair about it, in that you don't count favourites. So, even while we all hate you, it's a disciplined

675

hate, and when you issue orders, we obey. And why wouldn't we? You'll be at the forefront of any nasty work, because you're nastier than all the rest of us, on account of you being angry all the time—'

'You can shut your mouth now, Threadbare.'

'Yes sir.'

'Since you know all that, sergeant, you needn't bother with all that ghee you're lathering my way. Yes, I figured it out. Good for me. But now we're looking at a new problem, aren't we?'

'With our lady gone, it's down to you, sir, to decide whether we warn the monasteries or not.'

Gelas nodded. He shifted again. 'This snow's not melting under me at all, dammit.'

'That's not snow, sir, it's bedrock.'

'Ah, that explains it then. Where was I? Right. Decisions.'

'Urusander's Legion is the enemy, sir. And Bahann's out from under Raal's wing, with but three hundred soldiers. If we warn Yannis and Yedan, how many warriors can they muster? Five hundred? Six? Are they good fighters?'

'They're utter pigs, Threadbare, and no, I'd not want to mess with them.'

'Just so. The question then is, sir, is there any tactical value to seeing Bahann and his three hundred cut to pieces, while at the same time forcing the monasteries to relinquish their neutrality and side with us? Big losses for Raal, big gains for the highborn and Mother Dark.'

He studied her. 'You're saying it's obvious, aren't you?'

'Sir?'

He pointed at the eye-piece in her hands. 'Tell me again how that works.'

'There is a mirror and three lenses perfectly fitted—'

'Shut your mouth, Threadbare.'

'Yes sir.'

He slithered back from the ridge, rose and brushed snow from his thighs. 'Back to the keep. We need to send out a rider.'

'To warn the monasteries, sir?' She remained lying on her

bed of yellow grasses, not even cold though her cheeks glowed, with clear eyes that reminded him how many decades it had been since he'd last caught the regard of anything as young and as beautiful as this woman.

'I trust you all understand,' he said to her, 'that the hate is entirely mutual.'

'Of course, sir.'

'But having said that, I'd step into a blade's path for every damned one of you.'

'That too, sir, is mutual.'

He grunted. It would have to do.

*    *    *

After a night of freezing rain, the battlements of Vanut Keep glistened, the ice capturing the morning sunlight in sparks that flared and dripped. But already water had begun flowing down the sheathed stone flanks of the solid walls and squat towers, until it seemed as if the walls were melting.

Word had come of three riders on the road below, bound, presumably, for Kharkanas. Lady Degalla, already mounted and in position at the head of the train, alongside Lady Manalle, now beckoned closer the sergeant of the tower's watch. 'Do they bear a standard, Mivik?'

The young Houseblade shook his head.

Manalle said, 'Then they're not mine, Degalla. Besides, if Gelas had need of delivering an urgent message, he'd send one, not three, and that one would be Threadbare.'

Degalla's husband, who along with Manalle's spouse would be riding behind his wife, barked a laugh. 'That is an odd name, milady.'

'She arrived with it,' Manalle replied. 'A child of Wardens, I believe, but before they ever acquired that title. The first discoverers of the Vitr did not immediately formalize their obsession, Jureg. In any case, it's Threadbare who carries the important news.'

Manalle was ever pleased to display the breadth of her learning, which was only occasionally onerous. Her other habit, alas, was to run away with her monologue, quickly leading the conversation astray. Most of the time, Degalla was content to suffer Manalle's entirely subconscious need to be the centre of everyone's attention – *as if her looks weren't enough for that* – and she was relieved that her husband had simply smiled and nodded and bitten back his serpent's tongue that could, if he so chose, drip with acerbic venom.

Degalla cleared her throat. Toleration of guests was deemed a virtue. 'Now that it has been determined that the riders below are not delivering a message from Manaleth, perhaps we should determine who is upon the road below. Jureg, do accompany me. Lady Manalle, please remain in the care of my Houseblades for the moment, as the safety of my guests must ever remain uppermost in my mind.'

With that, she nudged her horse forward, Jureg falling in beside her, and they rode clear of the gate and on to the winding cobbled track leading down to the road below.

Winter traffic was rare in the best of times, and apart from an unexpected visit from Captain Sharenas over a month past, the tower watch had seen no one riding either from or to Kharkanas since the first snows. Footprints had been noted on occasion, as refugees crossed the road in the dead of night, seeking whatever sanctuary they could find in the forest to the north, but the coming and going of Deniers was of little interest to Degalla.

The three riders below had either heard or seen their approach from the keep's steep track, and were now drawn up, awaiting them.

'Two nights,' Jureg said, 'and I'm of a mind to flee to Urusander to kiss his sword.'

'Oh, she's not that bad,' Degalla said. 'The overly schooled are always at risk of becoming insufferable.'

'Her armour of knowledge is proof against my keenest jibes,' Jureg replied sourly.

'Indeed, you can only crush such a creature with knowledge superior to her own. Or the sweeter cut that is common sense. However, should a theory be easily shredded by an utterance of the obvious, then you'll have made a lifelong enemy. Be warned of that, husband.'

They had slowed their mounts, as the cobbles were slick, the slope treacherous. 'Hedeg Lesser wears the smile of the punch-drunk,' Jureg observed. 'I wager she describes the origin of every carnal position, and finds heat not in the act, but in the deluge of words beneath which she drowns all spontaneity. In her husband's eyes there is the dulled despair of the defeated: a victim of explanations.'

'Have you only pity for Hedeg, then?'

'He stirs to life in her absence, but it takes work. I've yet to decide the effort's worth.'

'Well, we will share their company for some days yet, in our yielding to Hish Tulla's invitation.'

The track levelled out momentarily, and then swung round into the final descent, and at this point they found themselves close enough to discern the three riders in detail.

'Ah,' murmured Degalla.

Her husband said nothing.

Close to the keep's gate, Lady Manalle and her husband, Hedeg Lesser, had edged their mounts some distance from the Vanut Houseblades, sufficient for the pair to speak without being overheard.

Below, their hosts picked their way down the slick track.

'I swear,' muttered Manalle, 'if I must witness yet one more exchange of knowing looks between those two, I will weather the curse of murder, guest-named or not. Worse, I may well descend into torture, out of sheer malice.'

Her husband tugged at his close-trimmed, greying beard. 'Careful, beloved. That's not a curse thinned by blood or years. Would you truly consign our family to everlasting condemnation?'

'I am tempted. It is the selfish pleasure that most easily forgets consequence.'

'Then there is her venal brother to consider. Lord Vanut would delight in a blood feud.'

'Wretched family,' muttered Manalle.

Her husband nodded in commiseration, and then asked, 'Who are those riders, do you think? Emissaries from Urusander?'

'I doubt that. Such would bear a standard, bold and diffident as befits both their vulnerability and their arrogance.' She glanced over and was pleased to see her husband's appreciative smile. There had been no accident in the inversion of her last statement. Diffident arrogance and bold vulnerability – what sweeter descriptive for emissaries of the Legion, coming among the highborn with belligerent promises of peace and preening threat? 'Perhaps,' she ventured, 'survivors from the Wardens.' A moment later she shook her head. 'I still cannot fathom Ilgast Rend's stupidity.'

'If word of the slaughter at Andarist's estate had reached him, Manalle, might you not forgive him his outrage?'

'Then let him beat fists against a tree. Not waste thousands of lives in a futile gesture. He made us all seem precipitous, enslaved by base needs. Never mind Urusander – none of this is his game – it is Hunn Raal's, and Hunn Raal is a clever man.'

'When sober.'

'His every stumble invites you to underestimate him, husband.'

'She should have included us in the ride down,' Hedeg said. 'It was a deliberate snub.'

Manalle shrugged. 'We would have done the same at the gates of Manaleth.'

'To mark our irritation, yes. But what cause has she to be irritated with us? We are ever courteous, even as Degalla mocks your superior intelligence, while Jureg clumsily gropes for secrets in his witless conversations with me.'

'Be at ease, husband. We prove their betters with patience.'

Hedeg said nothing. They had begun their exchange voicing positions opposite its conclusion: for all his wife's brilliance, she was ever at risk of lending fangs to her contempt. The time for feuds was not now. *But as she has counselled, patience. Once these lowborn thugs are dispensed with, then, Lady Degalla, my wife will face you with drawn blade, for all the slights we list here.*

'I never much liked Hish Tulla,' said Manalle.

*Of course not. Even more beautiful than you, and better with any weapon you'd care to name. Of course you hate her, beloved. Tutors can teach nothing about envy, beyond their own, and those rivalries and petty feuds give proof of their own failure in managing it.* His wife was indeed brilliant, but this did little to constrain the swirl of base emotions churning beneath that genius. Erudition offered the illusion of objectivity, as befitted learned opinion, but the venal thing beneath had the face of a spoiled child.

*Ah, wife, if you but guessed at the generosity of my love for you . . .*

Degalla raised a gauntleted hand in greeting. 'Emissaries of the Shake,' she said, ignoring for the moment the peculiar presence of a Warden. 'You ride to Kharkanas? Are we to find significance in that?'

The warlock – she thought he might be named Resh, though her memory was uncertain – shrugged at her questions. 'Lady Degalla. Jureg Thaw. I see, among the retinue at the gate, two standards. You have been hosting Lady Manalle and Hedeg Lesser. It's curious to see the highborn out in this bleak season.'

Jureg spoke. 'Warlock Resh, you have found yourself a survivor from the Wardens. But the Shake are hardly known for their largesse, much less sympathy. Is she a prisoner?'

The third figure was covered in a hood of black wolf fur, the skin draped over his habit, but something in his posture led Degalla to suspect who it was who had elected to remain hidden from them. She recalled hearing of an incident, outside the door to the Chamber of Night. Smiling at the hooded figure, she said, 'I am told Lord Anomander displayed forbearance upon the threshold to Mother Dark's holy sanctuary. But surely it is known that he no longer resides in the Citadel, leaving such matters to Silchas Ruin.'

Resh tilted his shaggy head. 'What matters are you referring to, milady?'

'Why, the protection of Mother Dark, of course. I would not think the approach unguarded. Nor should you.'

But her words elicited nothing from the hooded man slumped on his horse. Perhaps, she considered, she had been wrong. An instant later she amended her position. It was, she felt certain, Caplo Dreem within those shadows.

'Shall we be sharing the road, milady?' Resh asked.

'For a time,' she replied.

Her husband cleared his throat. 'There are rumours – signs – that Deniers remain in the forest, and have grown belligerent.'

'If so, we've not heard about it,' the warlock replied. 'In any case, what need have we to fear our followers?'

'Your followers?' Jureg frowned. 'And how did you heed their pleas for help this summer past?'

'We made what offers of refuge we could.'

'For the children, yes, as surety to your future. But I understand that few lived long enough to ever reach your monastery gates.'

'Are these matters of some concern among the highborn, Jureg? If so, why?'

'Neutrality will avail you nothing,' her husband replied. 'You are ruled by an old woman and an even older man. Inaction and fear of change plague their every moment, and that infirmity seems to have infected the rest of you. Should Lord Urusander win this war, warlock, do you truly imagine that he will leave you alone? Or, rather, will Hunn Raal leave you alone? Will the new High Priestess of Light? Yours is a misplaced faith, by any measure.'

The Warden snorted. 'This is pathetic. There is nothing here worth hiding. Ladies Degalla and Manalle are setting out with their husbands and a retinue of servants and guards. Presumably, one of the highborn has called for a meeting – that it's taken this long is the only reason for being coy. I'd be just as embarrassed under the circumstances. As for us, why, Warlock Resh wishes to examine the nature of the Terondai. Sorcery now seethes through Kurald Galain – is this a consequence of Lord Draconus's gift? Or was the Azathanai, T'riss, the source? Is it not wise to determine the source of this magic before indulging in it?'

After a long moment, Degalla shook her head. 'And your perusal of a pattern on a floor requires the presence of an assassin? No, Warden, but I'll grant you your innocence, and conclude that you have been deceived by your companions.'

At that, Caplo Dreem finally lifted his head, drawing back his hood. He smiled at Degalla. 'I can hear them,' he said.

'Excuse me?'

'Hedeg and Manalle. They speak quietly, but are beneath the arch of the gatehouse, sending down sufficient echo. I can hear their every word.'

Degalla twisted round, stared up at her distant guests, and the steep, long climb to where they sat astride their horses. 'Impossible,' she said.

'What are they saying?' Jureg asked.

Caplo's strange eyes remained fixed on Degalla. 'They revel in their contempt for you, milady. More, there is a smell about Hedeg, hinting of some future violence, with you the victim. It is likened to a licking of the lips, a sudden heat of pleasure beneath the skin of the face, a darkening gleam in the pools of the eye. Indulging in anticipation is a sensual repast for those two. They have long shared a fiery bed of vindictive lust, and the coals run deep.'

Jureg shot Degalla a glance. 'Manalle believes herself superior with the blade.'

'Fear not,' Caplo replied. 'Her intelligence is a fortress no doubt can vanquish, but in the matter of crossing swords, it will prove her undoing. It is not the keenest wit that guides a weapon master's hand, but the easy surrender to instinct, and the faith such a thing demands. Manalle cannot relinquish control, and this will one day kill her.'

'Be silent, assassin,' snapped Degalla, but she eyed Caplo in consternation. There was something uncanny about the man, something wild and barely constrained. 'You presume beyond all reason.'

'Perhaps I do,' he said, offering her a feral smile.

Resh stirred. 'Milady?'

'Warlock?'

'We have reason to believe that Lord Urusander will not

683

wait until winter's end. Even now, his legion prepares to march.'

It seemed that the presumption was far from done. 'And you offer us this for what purpose?'

'You have little time, milady. If Lord Anomander has left the Citadel, then he has abrogated his responsibility. It might be wise to elect for yourselves a new warlord.' He paused, and then waved a hand. 'To be honest, seen from the outside, does Anomander truly reflect your cause? I would think the man rages and may well be consumed by the need for vengeance, in his brother's name.'

'You are free with your advice, warlock. Whom then do you propose?'

'Why, the one who would lose the most, milady, is surely the one who would fight the hardest.'

After a moment, Jureg spat.

Degalla stared at Resh in disbelief.

'But then,' Resh continued in a drawl, 'Draconus is not well liked among the highborn, is he? Despite his fame as a commander and his prowess on the field of battle. Despite the zeal with which he would apply himself to the cause of maintaining things as they are. Despite his incorruptible nature. Alas, the poor man's crime is being loved by your goddess—'

'If loved then she would have married him!'

'Oh? And that would sit well with you?'

Degalla said nothing.

His voice a rasp, Jureg said, 'I trust you are eager to be on your way. Give our regards to the painted floor, warlock.'

Receiving the dismissal with indifference, the three set off once more, and soon vanished round a bend in the track.

'He was baiting you—'

'I know what he was doing!'

'Something about the assassin . . .'

'Never mind him,' she said.

'Wife?'

'The woman, the Warden.'

'What of her?'

'Perhaps it was but a trick of the light, but for an instant there, I could swear she was wearing a circlet of gold. A crown.'

'I saw nothing like that.'

After a long moment, Degalla shook her head. 'Of course not. You are right.'

'Still,' Jureg said in a low murmur, 'I cannot but wonder . . .'

'What now, husband?'

'If Caplo could indeed hear Manalle and Hedeg, from so far away . . . perhaps we must assume he has heard us just now, as well.'

She glared at him.

\*     \*     \*

'Why did you speak so of Draconus?' Finarra Stone demanded, once they were well beyond the two highborn.

Resh shrugged. 'They irritated me.'

'So you sent a viper into their snug bed. Does being petty please you?'

'Sometimes,' he admitted.

Caplo surprised her by speaking. 'I was once a man with few doubts, Warden. Until the day I looked into Father Skelenal's eyes, and saw in them a truth I could not countenance. Our god has been slain, but in the time before that death – in the decade upon decade of service and worship – that old man was a monster in our midst. We knew it, and yet we did nothing. In his eyes, Warden, I saw us all reflected, and liked it not.'

'I am not aware of anything monstrous,' Finarra said, 'but then, why would I be? Yours is a secretive temple.'

'Secretive, yes. Curious, isn't it, how that habit so quickly devours propriety, decency, integrity, and indeed love. Beware any congress, Warden, that indulges in secrecy – you can be certain that it does not have your interests in mind, nor will it accord you the proper respect as befits the innocent, or, as they might label you, the ignorant. The secretive mind starts at every shadow, for it has peopled its world with suspicion.'

'You describe a poisonous pit, Caplo, one in which I have no desire to dwell.'

'Such a congress assembles a world in which assassins are necessary,' Caplo said. 'Such a congress may speak and act in the name of justice, but in justice it does not believe. Its only faith lies in efficacy, and the illusion of control it offers.'

'In your world, then,' said Finarra, 'hope is fruitless.'

'Not at all, Warden. That fruit is well fermented, and given freely to the uninitiated, until drunks stagger down every street, sleep in every alley. Hope is the wine, forgetfulness the reward. We will pour it down your throats from the moment of your birth, until the instant of your blessed death.'

'You propose an end to secrecy, Caplo Dreem?'

'I have the eyes to pierce every shadow. The ears to track every footfall. I have the claws to carve out the hidden-away, huddling in their hidden places. But imagine, Warden, my bitter gift, and its grisly promise. Exposure. Revelation. The insipid laid bare, the liars dragged out into day's light, all the venal creatures who so thrive with their secrets.'

Warlock Resh sighed, loudly. 'He goes on like this, Finarra Stone. Promises of . . . something cataclysmic.'

She grunted. 'I've seen the same promise countless times, warlock, in the eyes of the fort's mouser.'

There was a pause, and then Resh laughed.

Scowling, Caplo made much of drawing his hood back up, once more hiding his face.

*    *    *

There had been a child filled with laughter, and though she possessed her name, Lahanis recalled little of that strange – and strangely frail – creature who had dwelt so blissfully among the Borderswords. It was a memory that dwelt in summer meadows, or racing beneath the shadows of massive trees, with insects buzzing in and out of startling sunlight, and the sound of a warm wind through leaves. Boys had chased her, but she was quicker than any of them, cleverer besides. Though young, perhaps impossibly so, she had made a game of their desires, and found it easy to mock their confusion, their troubled urges for something more. The awakening of mysteries must have haunted her as well, she suspected, but she had no recollection of that. Every scene pulled from the past found that laughing child at the centre of a web, in command of everything, but understanding nothing.

The girl, with her piping laughter, belonged in a world of delusion, not yet spun dangerous, not yet tangled and treacherous. The seasons fought wars in her memory, but each time, echoed by the shrill peal of the girl's voice, summer emerged triumphant, filling the world left behind with scented air on soft breezes and stubborn flowers disdainful of spring's bright but brief glory.

Laughter was lost now, and Lahanis could think of it only as a child's toy, dropped on to the ground, forgotten amidst the tufts of yellowed grasses that rose unevenly above the snow like broken baskets. Summer too was dead, its death-cry fading on cold winds, its funeral made into its own season of leaves falling like ashes. And the child who had known both laughter and summer, who had dwelt in that lively, colour-splashed world, well, somewhere her bones hid beneath the glittering skin and lifeless muscle of ice and snow.

This new child belonged to winter, finding her voice in the rasp of knife-blades against a whetstone, drawn to the momentary heat of spilled blood and cut-open bodies, last breaths slipping out in thin white streams, and all the stains that fear and pain made in scuffed snow.

She cared little for Glyph and his reasons for this new war. She was indifferent to the bitter grief of the hunters, and their anguish at discovering that no amount of murder could fill the emptiness inside them. For Lahanis, it was enough that killing was taking place; enough that summer's green forest was transformed into winter's hunting ground, and she was free of the webs of the past.

For all that, and her habit of avoiding the priest with the scarred face, she had felt the man's attention drawn to her, like threads sent out to ensnare her, and this made Lahanis

uneasy. There were many kinds of hunting, she now understood, and one of them was *intent*, born of focus or even
obsession. It bore the face of a boy grown past his confusion,
with the lure of mystery beckoning, where all games vanished
and suddenly everything was in earnest. Even the laughing
Lahanis, in those lying summers, had known enough to be
wary of such boys among the pack pursuing her.

But she did not think the priest desired her in that way. There
was something broken in his study of her, something too weak
to be calculating. Still, a part of him circled her in the camp, and
again and again a glance would find their eyes meeting.

When he rose in the depth of night, with the air cold enough
to bite the lungs, and walked out beyond the clearing, to
stand beneath skeletal trees blackened with soot, Lahanis
edged out from under her furs, her knives in her hands.

Priests did not belong in war. They had a way of reminding
killers that their living was a crime, an abomination, that the
world created by blood and fury was itself an act of madness.
And though the priest might bless, though the priest might
proclaim for his or her own side a certain righteousness
beneath the eyes of their god, surely such claims crumbled to
war's incessant blows. Before the flickering knife, every face
was the same, and every death delivered was another knot on
the tally string. Knotted strings that grew into ropes and
ropes into chains. Every tally a crime, every crime yet one
more step away from any god.

Slipping past sleeping forms, the hunters huddled beneath
furs, fast breaths riding unpleasant dreams, limbs twitching,
or faces upturned in the promise of death's simple semblance,
she was silent as she crept up behind the man, drawing to
within a few quick steps, her blades ready.

Then he spoke. 'It wasn't long ago, Lahanis, when someone cut away my mask.' He turned slightly, only enough to
make out her form on the edge of his vision. 'He used fists to
make his point. What point was he making, you wonder? I
have long pondered that question. Night after night.'

She said nothing, lowering her knives to hide them as best
she could.

After a moment, he resumed. 'I was misusing a boy, because he was highborn. Mocking his innocence, in tones that promised some cruel future. Orfantal – that was the boy's name. He deserved none of it. So, when I'd gone too far, the man entrusted with the care of the boy beat me unconscious.'

Still she made no response, wondering why he was telling her such things. The faces of those she killed were just a jumble of features meaning nothing, each one a thing of surfaces. The mask he dared speak of, and claim as his own, was the only one that mattered to her. What could he know of her mind?

Narad then continued. 'But wouldn't a single punch have been enough? Even a kick to my head, across that gap between us. The man was a veteran of the wars. He knew all about explosive violence, and he knew just how thin was that thread of civility holding him back, him and his kind. A few careless words from me, to a five-year-old boy, and the thread snapped.'

She could not move now, not even had she desired to finish what had been in her mind, here beneath the crooked branches and strewn stars. Narad's words had reached through to something inside, tearing it free and shaking it so that it rattled. And before she could reconsider, she said, 'That's why, Yedan Narad.'

She saw him tilt his head. 'What do you mean?'

'A five-year-old child.'

'What of it? I knew I was being cruel—'

'It's not what children are for,' she said, a weakness coming upon her. She suddenly felt ill. 'The boy,' she continued, 'was still in his summer. Not even seeing the mysteries. He was just alive, Yedan Narad, simple as a dog.'

'I never laid a hand on the boy.'

'Yes. And he was too young to understand your words. But that veteran wasn't, was he?'

There was silence, until Narad sighed haltingly, and his voice was thick as he said, 'Do such children still dwell within us, Lahanis? Do they simply wait, finally wise, finally smart enough to comprehend their old wounds? Until some witless fool jabs it all awake, and the boy inside fills the man he became, and one punch isn't enough, isn't even close to being enough.'

*The boy inside. The girl inside, with her laughter and her summer.*

Lahanis had thought the girl dead, countless versions of her huddled in all those broken baskets littering the past. *The girl inside fills the woman she has become.*

*I saw them murder my mother, my aunts, my brothers and cousins. There, at summer's end.*

*But that laughing girl, she has knives now, and tally strings, and she runs anew, through another forest, leafless and burned.*

'I doubt it gave him much comfort,' Narad said.

*You would be wrong.*

He finally swung fully round to face her, and saw the knives in her hands. His brows lifted and he looked up to meet her eyes, before offering up an apologetic smile. 'I was about to tell you something.'

'Speak, then.'

'The Legion will not ignore what we have done. They will come for us, and there will be a battle.'

'Only one?'

'If we are unlucky.'

'And if we're not? Not . . . unlucky?'

'Well, yes, that is it, isn't it. By fortune we would plant a single, bloodied tree, from which we would seed an entire forest.'

The image pleased her. 'A new home for the Deniers.'

'Indeed? Would *you* be pleased to live in it?'

She shrugged to hide a momentary dismay at the bleakness of the promise. 'Enough battles to end the war. Isn't that how it works, Yedan Narad?'

He looked away. 'I hope to meet Orfantal again, one day, to offer him my apology.'

'He won't even remember the slight.'

'No?'

'No. If he remembers anything, Yedan Narad, it will be the veteran's fists and boots, beating you unconscious. He'll remember that.'

'Ah . . . that is . . . unfortunate.'

'The dog cowers at harsh words, but flinches at a kick. Of the two, only one of them will turn a dog bad.'

'He struck me, not the boy,' Narad growled, as if that made a difference.

She turned about, sheathing her weapons, and took a step before pausing to glance back over her shoulder. 'Do not look at me any more.'

'Lahanis?'

'You can't save me. There's nothing to save. Nothing to bless.'

He said nothing as she walked away. Returning to her now chilled furs, she curled up beneath them and fought against the shivers of cold shuddering through her.

Priests still did not belong to war, but she'd begun to understand their presence in every army's camp. *It is not the day of fighting that needs blessing, but the night without peace that follows it.*

Her wedding dress was rotting, but the smell of her violation was fresh, wafting over Narad as she appeared beside him. He had turned about, when he was certain that Lahanis had lost her desire to murder him, and once more he faced the forest.

She stood close, their arms almost brushing. 'Someone wore the crown today,' she said.

'What crown?'

'While another must be turned away, and so be made to fail. The royal blood must be thinned, prince.'

He shook his head. Obscure statements were irritating enough, but her insistence upon unearned and unwelcome titles was infuriating. He no longer stared out into a forest. Somewhere, in between blinks, the world was transformed. Before him, riding the coruscating waves of the silver sea, was the carcass of a dragon, rolling up on to the strand, then turgidly flopping as the waves receded. A trail of blood and gore climbed the white sands from the scaled body, wavering drunkenly, ending where Narad stood, punctuated by the point of his resting sword. He was breathing hard, oily sweat cooling on his red-streaked skin.

'Her name was Latal Menas.'

'Who?'

'The dragon, my prince. She was all grief and rage. The path led her here, into our realm. Or, perhaps, through it. When Tiamath last sembled, when the conflagration awakened and all that they kept apart was now one, the Suzerain took the life of Latal's mate. It was the death of Habalt Galanas, prince, that has precipitated this.'

He felt his jaw bunching, molars grinding, stirring to life the familiar ache in his neck muscles. 'This? Nothing has precipitated this, my queen. A breach. Opportunity. Expedience.'

Her laugh was soft, but brief. 'Yedan. You've a gift for brevity, and simple lines, sharp as that which divides sea from shore. Habalt Galanas was host to the proper blood. Proper to the Suzerain's need. Darkness indivisible, until that blood spilled out. The kin should have known. Never trust an Azathanai.'

'I felt that killer's return—'

'Not you, my prince.'

'No?'

'And even then, it was your spirit that trembled at his return, long after your sister knelt at the side of your corpse, speaking words you could no longer hear.'

'But . . . not me.'

'Not you, not yet.'

He passed a stained hand over his eyes, seeking to dismiss the scene before him. 'Grief and rage, you said? It seems I am cursed to stand in the way of such things.'

'Even Tiamath has weaknesses,' she said. 'The host can be sundered by the killing of but one. The thing is, how do you choose which one? Each sembling alters the flaw. You must ask yourself, how did Draconus know which one?'

He snorted. 'Simple. As you said, darkness indivisible. He knew his own. Had Galanas's death not shattered the sembling, he would have died beneath the fury of Tiamath, and none of this would have come to be.'

She sighed. 'Must we ever blame Draconus?'

Shrugging, recovered from his ordeal, Narad shook dragon blood from the blade of his sword.

'Careful,' she admonished, 'lest some of that blood find its way into you. I'd not see you consumed by a stranger's rage, a stranger's grief, and memories not your own.'

'No fear of that,' he muttered in reply. 'I've no room left inside.'

Her etiolated hand rested lightly upon his shoulder, and with the contact her voice changed. 'My brother, there is so much I would say to you, if only I could. Your worship unnerved me. I well understood, if but dismissively, your odd aversion to capturing me on canvas. But it so sweetened my vanity—'

'My queen, I am not that brother.'

'You are not? Then tell me, please, where is Cryl? How he longed for a depth to me that simply did not exist! His love was a girthed thing, cast upon my shallow self, but how terribly the delusion strained his faith, his belief!'

Narad turned at last to face her, and saw clearly, for perhaps the first time, the young woman in her wedding dress, who was no queen, no high priestess, desired by many yet blessed by none. Her face was past its mask of pain, past the mask of shock that followed, past its last guise of life leaving. Her eyes looked out from a place only the dead knew, but the loss and confusion in them somehow reached across the gulf. Narad raised a hand, brushed her cold cheek. 'I was a lover of men,' he said. 'But in my last days, I told no one how visions of you tormented me. How I stepped from one time into another, the only constant this perfect shoreline – oh, and the blood.'

'Then,' she said, 'are we both lost?'

'Yes. Until it plays out. Only then will our spirits know peace.'

'How long?' she asked. 'How long shall we have to wait, before our suffering ends?'

Narad hefted his sword. 'See – the storm awakens again. Not long, I should think, my queen. Not long at all.' But even as he said it, he knew it for a lie. But he would hold to his false assurances, for her sake.

Behind him as he stepped forward, she asked, 'Yedan, who killed Draconus? Who chained him within a sword of his own making? I do not understand.'

He paused, did not turn round. 'Yes. There is that. It is odd,' he admitted. 'Who killed Draconus? The same man who frees him. Lord Anomander, First Son of Darkness.'

'Another one,' she hissed, 'whom my brother would not paint. Tell me, my prince, how you know all this?'

Shapes were massing behind the veil of the fiery wall. 'I have an answer, but it makes no sense.' He hesitated, and then glanced back at her. 'You say the crown has been worn?'

She nodded, already fading from his vision.

'Who? When will I meet her?'

But she was gone.

Facing the shore again, his gaze flicked down to the carcass of the dragon he had just killed. *Latal Menas. I feel your blood in my body, the heat of all you knew and all you felt. But against my guilt, you are less than a whisper. Still, how did you know what you knew?*

*In your language, Eleint, Menas is one name for Shadow. The name you seemed eager to attach to this narrow strand, this Emurlahn of ours. Your voice comes from the half-seen, in the place neither here, nor there, and in the gloom – as if barely sketched by a ragged, dry brush – I saw a throne . . .*

Another blink, and before him was the forest, sullen in its winter white and black as the sky to the east began to pale. He was shivering, joints stiff with cold, his feet numbed inside their straw-packed leather boots. Upon hearing someone approach, he turned to find Glyph.

'Yedan Narad, you have lingered beyond the Watch. Your visions leave you raw. Come, a fire is being lit.'

He studied the Denier. 'We are being used.'

Glyph managed a half-shrug. 'We have made vengeance a god.'

'A simple answer, but I doubt it.'

'Then who, Yedan Narad?'

'Something in need of a refuge, I think. Against what is to come. And it would spend our lives, Glyph, to defend its secret.'

For the first time, Glyph seemed uncertain. He glanced away, and then back again. 'You promised us to Lord Anomander.'

'No. He too is an unwitting player.'

Glyph's breath streamed in the cold air. In . . . out . . . in again. 'I would rather have my god of vengeance.'

Narad nodded. 'Easily fed, never appeased. I see worshippers beyond counting, a faith too stubborn to die, too foolish for wisdom. But if I am to be its high priest, be warned. My thirst for vengeance seeks no other face but my own.'

'Once the others are dead.'

'Once they are dead, yes.'

'Yedan Narad, I will find you on that day.'

'And will you do what needs doing?'

'Yes.'

'Good,' Narad replied. 'I am relieved to hear that.'

'Will you join us in breaking fast, Yedan Narad?'

Gaze shifting to the campfire now lit just behind Glyph, Narad saw Lahanis, wrapped in her furs, moving close to take some of the warmth. 'I will,' he said. 'Thank you.'

\*     \*     \*

Sergeant Threadbare was halfway to Yannis monastery when her mount slipped on ice hidden beneath a thin smear of snow. The horse struck in a heavy splintering of leg bones and a shriek of pain. In her efforts to throw herself clear of the beast, Threadbare landed awkwardly against a slope studded with boulders, shattering her shoulder and snapping one clavicle.

The damage seemed to have opened a passage deep into

her body for the cold, and she sat against the slope with agony riding every harsh breath, watching the horse thrash and kick on the slick trail that was now stained with mud, shit and a few spatters of blood. The animal's nostrils were flared, its ears flattened and its eyes bulging. She would have to take a blade to its throat, and be quick to ease her remorse with notions of mercy. But it was proving very difficult to move.

*Halfway. Whose cruel game is this?* There was no chance of reaching the Shake in time, no chance of warning them against the incipient attack. Indeed, she was not even sure that she would have the strength to make it back to Manaleth.

The trail had led her alongside a low range of hills, a serrated line upon her right as she rode east. Now, that same rough spine was at her back, and the level plain stretching out before her was whiter than the sky above it. Another storm was on its way.

The horse's gusting breaths stirred her awake – she had been dozing, falling into something formless but strangely warm. Blinking, she studied the beast. It was no longer fighting, simply lying on its side, chest heaving with each breath – but now the exhalations came in a spray of frothy blood.

*Ribs. Punctured lung.*

She pulled free her sword, worked her way down on to the level track. Using the weapon for support, its tip driven into the thick ice, she forced herself upright. With most of the snow melted or swept away, she could now see the full reach of the ice – and it made no sense. The track was actually slightly humped where the horse had slipped and fallen, and yet upon either side the snow was thin upon gravel-studded mud.

It wasn't easy to bring a four-legged animal down. The sweep of ice stretched longer and reached wider than a horse's stance, even at a slow trot.

'Do you delight in its suffering?'

Threadbare swung round, lifting her blade, but both efforts left her gasping in pain.

A woman stood before her, fair-skinned, golden-haired. She was thin, almost gaunt, as if trapped in a body eternally lost in adolescence. Dressed in linen and wearing boots that seemed woven from grass, she stood as if indifferent to the cold.

As the stranger was unarmed, Threadbare turned back to her mount. She readied her sword as she looked for the throbbing jugular in the animal's neck. But a hand settled on her uninjured shoulder, and the woman's voice rode a warm breath that caressed her jaw. 'It was a question in truth. But now I see, you would end its ordeal.'

'I'm hurt,' Threadbare said. 'I won't be able to make a deep cut. It needs to be right.'

'Yes. I see that. Shall I help?'

'I'm not giving you my blade.'

'No. Of course not.' The woman's hand slid away, and then she stepped round, placing herself between Threadbare and the dying beast. Lowering herself into a crouch, she rested a hand upon the horse's neck. For a moment, it seemed as if the animal lost all colour, until even its sorrel coat looked grey, and then the illusion was gone. And, Threadbare now saw, the horse no longer drew breath, and its eyes were closed.

'How did you do that?'

The stranger straightened. 'I learned much regarding mercy,' she said, now smiling, 'from a Warden friend. Did my act please you?'

'Does it matter? It's done. I was riding east.'

'Yes.'

'I need to deliver a message.'

'But now your message will be too late. Besides, you are injured, and a storm is coming, which will add to your suffering.'

Threadbare stepped back. 'If you would end mine as you did the horse's, then I'd rather you didn't.'

The woman tilted her head. 'If the horse could speak, would it have said the same?'

'It was dying.'

'So are you.'

'Not if I can find shelter, here in these hills. Somewhere to wait out the worst of the storm.'

'I am making use of a cave,' the woman said. 'It is not far. Will you join me?'

'I don't see much choice. Yes. But first, can you help me remove my kit from the saddle?'

Together, they collected Threadbare's gear. The horse still steamed with heat, and once, when Threadbare inadvertently brushed the beast's flank, she saw again, in a momentary flash, a hide made colourless. Snatching her hand back, she blinked. 'Did you see—'

'See what?'

'Nothing. Would you be so kind as to carry this?'

The woman collected the bedroll.

'Lead on,' Threadbare said.

Smiling again, the woman set out, up the steep hillside. Stepping carefully, hunched protectively around her injuries, Threadbare followed. 'You've not told me your name,' she said.

'Nor have you told me yours.'

'Sergeant Threadbare. You mentioned a friend. A Warden. I know – knew – many of them. Who was this friend of yours?'

They skirted the summit and edged down into a defile. 'Her name was Faror Hend.'

Threadbare said nothing for a few strides, and then she sighed. 'It may be that she is dead.'

'No. She lives.'

'You've seen her, then? Since the battle?'

'She lives.'

'You are the one named T'riss, aren't you? The Azathanai.'

They traversed a twisted track flanked by sheer walls of raw limestone. After fifteen or so wending paces, the path suddenly opened out into a hollow, the level floor of which was crowded with shards of stone, many pieces of which seemed to bear mortar. A broad but low cave-mouth interrupted one of the high walls.

Threadbare studied the scene with narrow eyes. 'That was sealed,' she said. 'It's a crypt, isn't it?'

T'riss faced the cave, one finger pressed to her lips. 'A crypt? Why, yes, I suppose it was. Hence the corpse interred within.'

'Dog-Runner?'

She glanced across at Threadbare, fine brows lifting. 'Dog-Runner. Robust, are they not? Broad and strong, thick-boned, a heavy, projecting face, with ever so mild eyes of blue or grey?' She shook her head. 'No, not a Dog-Runner.'

Threadbare had begun shivering. 'I need to get inside. I need to build a fire.'

'There is one already built. A crack leading up takes the smoke, not that there is much smoke. The bones were very old, I think, to burn so readily.'

'Azathanai,' Threadbare said in a mutter, 'you move awkwardly in this world of ours.'

Inside the shelter of the cave, just beyond a sharp bend, Threadbare found the hearth that T'riss had made, and saw a thigh bone threaded with cracked white, black and the orange gleam of fierce heat, resting athwart the ring of stones. The thigh bone, Threadbare saw, was as thick as her upper arm, and nearly of a length to match that of her shoulder to her fingertips.

'No,' she said as T'riss came in behind her, 'not a Dog-Runner.'

Upon the track left behind, the carcass of the horse shimmered again, bleaching every hue, and a moment later the animal coughed, and then scrambled unsteadily upright, upon legs suddenly hale. The blood flecking its nostrils was already frozen, and no new blood rode the even breaths the beast now took as it stood, momentarily shivering, ears flicking and head turning as it searched for its rider.

But the woman was gone, and the saddle had been removed, left lying on the trail. Even the bit had been drawn from the horse's mouth.

It could smell snow on the wind.

Sudden thoughts of its warm stable, back in the safe confines of Manaleth Keep, urged the beast into motion. A steady canter, upon a path firm and certain, the purchase of every hoof unquestioned, would take it home before dusk.

*     *     *

With the wind howling, it was no wonder that it took some time before her pounding against the door elicited a response. A shutter opened, a face pressing into the gap to squint at her.

'In the name of mercy,' she shouted, 'I seek sanctuary!'

The eyes studied her – the ratty wolf furs she'd wrapped about herself, the rags making bulky mittens covering her hands, the ice-studded woollen cloth covering the lower half of her face. Then the gaze shifted past her, searching to either side.

'I'm alone! Alone, and frozen near to death!'

The face withdrew, and then she heard heavy latches being drawn. A moment later the door swung inward. Hunched against the wind, she slipped through.

Within the gatehouse, one monk stood before a second, inner door, while another now pushed shut the outer door.

Brushing clumsily at the shards of ice crusting her cloak, she said, 'My hands have lost all feeling.'

'Winter welcomes no one,' the first monk said, setting the latches once more. 'You are foolish to travel.'

'My horse slipped, broke a leg.'

'You are pale,' said the second monk, even as he thumped on the inner door, which opened in answer. In the courtyard beyond stood a child swathed in woollen robes, holding a lantern, its light fighting feebly against the night.

'Frostbitten, I'd wager,' she replied, shuffling into the gap of the second doorway, where she paused to squint at the second monk.

'Too even in tone for—' began the man.

The knife-point pushed through the rags wrapped about Lieutenant Esk's hand, driving up beneath the monk's chin. As the man toppled back into the arms of his fellow, Esk reached out with her other hand, and a second knife hammered into the side of the child's head. Releasing her grip on that weapon, she leapt to close with the first monk, thrusting with the knife, filling his left eye socket with cold iron, burying it to the hilt.

Letting go of that weapon as well, Esk hurried to the outer door and pulled up the latches. She leaned against the portal until it swung free.

Crouched amidst swirling snow just beyond waited her soldiers. At her gesture, they hurried in to crowd the gatehouse.

'Take that boy's body – drag it in here. Scuff up that snow, and see the lantern brought inside – no, no need to light it again. Across the courtyard is the main house. You, Pryll, stay here with Corporal Paralandas. When the first squads arrive, send them to the east building – that's the barracks – in case they manage to break out. Sergeant Telra, take your three to the barracks. Bar the doors and be liberal with the oil, especially round the windows. Set it all alight as soon as you're ready. Rathadas, you and Billat are with me – to the main house. All right, then, let's go about our work – I'm freezing my tits off out here.'

No alarm was raised as Esk and her soldiers set out across the compound. Somewhere on the track west of the monastery, her commander would be leading the remaining troops. Should the warrior monks sequestered in the barracks awaken in time to force their way past the barricaded doors, Esk's few squads would have a fight on their hands, but so long as they could hold the main gate until Bahann's advance squads arrived, all would be well.

The best outcome, of course, would be Hallyd Bahann arriving to the chorus of screams from the burning barracks.

In the meantime, she had Higher Grace Sheccanto to hunt down. The woman was rumoured to be ill, bedridden. With Rathadas and Billat behind her, Esk opened the main building's door and edged inside. Heat gusted round her, scented with the evening meal. Wicks had been turned down in the few lanterns left lit, and the three soldiers padded quietly into the main hall.

Near the hearth was a pair of high-backed, padded chairs, and a figure was seated in one of them, his head tilted to one side, his eyes closed. Muffled beneath furs that someone had settled over him, only his head and his right hand were visible, the wrinkled skin grey-hued and slack in sleep.

Esk approached him, drawing her sword.

She drove the blade deep into the man's neck, stepping up in the same instant to close her hand over his mouth. She watched his eyes open as the blade slid its way through his neck, and as the point erupted from the other side it made a sluice for a welter of blood. As he died, the man met the lieutenant's gaze, but without comprehension. His last breath eased out from his nostrils, painting Esk's left hand in red. Now, the eyes looked at nothing.

Pulling her sword free, she stepped back, looked round, and then whispered, 'A high room, somewhere the heat rises. Central, away from any outer walls. Billat, take the lead on the stairs.' But as she moved away, Rathadas reached out to stay her. He had drawn close to examine the dead man in the chair, and now with his other hand he held up the arm that had been hidden beneath the furs.

'Lieutenant!' he hissed.

Even as he spoke, she saw the signet ring, and then the faded swirl of tattoos spiralling up the thin, pallid wrist.

'You just murdered Skelenal!'

Esk scowled. 'What's he doing here? Well, saves us a march down to Yedan monastery, doesn't it?'

'Royal blood—'

'Be quiet, damn you. Do you actually think Hallyd Bahann was going to let them live?'

Rathadas stepped back.

Esk eyed both men, gauging the shock on their faces. 'What the fuck did you expect to happen, you fools? This is a civil war. How crowded do you want the steps to the throne? We're here, clearing the path. Skelenal's dead. Now it's time to see his wife join him.'

By her measure, the barracks should have been fired by now, but thus far the storm's wild gale was sweeping away all other sounds from outside. Despite this, someone in the main building would see the lurid glow of the flames before too long.

'We have to move. Billat, you're point on the stairs. Rathadas, cover my back. Let's get going.'

They were reluctant, as if dragging free of treacle, but Esk bit back on her frustration, her growing fury. Soldiers followed orders. This was unquestioned, beyond challenging. The Legion obeyed, making for a simpler, sweeter world. There was no need to fret about the royal blood staining her left hand, or its grislier counterpart still dripping from her sword. Skelenal was no king. He had elected to become a priest, to join an order worshipping a now dead god. In her mind, he'd simply made a bad cast of the bones, making his eventual murder if not inevitable, then likely.

Billat reached the top of the stairs, then suddenly withdrew, back down a step. A hand gesture froze both Esk and Rathadas. He edged down another step and leaned close to whisper in Esk's ear.

'Two guards, at hall's end. Either side of a large door.'

Some careless indulgence, she concluded, had left Skelenal alone in the main chamber, an old man asleep in a chair by the hearth. But here, before what had to be Sheccanto's private chamber, diligence remained. Frowning, Esk brought her sword down, tugging her wolfskin cloak over to hide the weapon, and then, indicating with a nod that her soldiers remain where they were, she climbed past them both and stepped out into the corridor.

At the far door, both warrior monks rose from the wooden chairs upon which they had been sitting.

Smiling, Esk approached. 'I was told that the Higher Grace would receive me, no matter how late my arrival. Friends, I have important word from Lord Urusander.'

The monk to the right of the door took two steps forward. There was a short-handled throwing axe tucked into his belt, but in his left hand he held a heavy knife with an angled blade. 'Of course,' he said. 'Come ahead. She will be pleased to see you.'

With her gaze fixed on the monk who was speaking, Esk

barely registered the blur of motion from the other man. With ten paces between her and the nearer monk, Esk felt a heavy blow to her left shoulder, of such force as to half spin her round. Looking down, she saw an axe, its blade buried deep in her shoulder.

Shocked, suddenly confused, she felt her back thud against a wall.

The nearer monk was rushing towards her now.

*Ah, shit. Fooled no one.*

Motion from the stairs revealed both Rathadas and Billat charging forward, their swords drawn.

The monk reached her first. She had raised her sword, thrusting its point towards the man, waiting for his heavy knife to move as he sought to sweep aside her blade – but he would miss, as she disengaged his attempted beat. Or so it should have been.

Instead, the monk threw the knife underhand with barely three paces between them.

Another heavy blow punched under her right arm, and she saw her sword leap from her grip, clattering against the wall before falling to the floor. The thrown knife had slipped between ribs, the massive, crooked blade sliding into her right lung. Sagging, slumping down the wall, Esk gagged as her mouth filled with blood.

*Bodyguards. Of course they're good. It started out too easily, down at the gatehouse.*

As the monk swept past her to engage with Rathadas and Billat, he ran the thin blade of a parrying knife across her throat.

A sting, sudden warmth, and then nothing.

Seeing the monk casually slice open the lieutenant's throat, Rathadas cursed and charged to close with the bastard.

His sword had the advantage of reach, as the monk facing him was readying a short-handled, single-bladed axe in his right hand, and a thin parrying knife in his left. His expression, as he watched Rathadas approach, was calm.

'She came to parley!' Billat shouted from behind Rathadas.

'She came to die,' the monk replied.

Rathadas bellowed as he attacked, slashing crossways to either cut or force away the monk's two out-thrust hands. Instead, he cut through nothing but air. Recovering, he brought the blade back up, point angled to take the monk from low should the man seek to close – but something obstructed it, swept it out to the side. The parrying knife tapped his temple, making a sound like a nail driven through the side of a clay pot.

As the sound echoed, Rathadas stepped back, shaking his head. He was having trouble seeing. He then realized that he did not know where he was, or what the strange man now stepping past him had done to him. He stood, uncomprehending, as a second stranger reached him. Frowning, Rathadas watched the man swing a heavy knife casually towards him. Vaguely alarmed, he tried raising an arm to block the knife – which looked sharp and might hurt him – but his arm would not answer, or perhaps it was simply too slow. The knife edge sawed through his neck, cutting muscle, gristle and bone.

The world tilted crazily as Rathadas watched the floor rising to meet him.

Billat screamed when he saw Rathadas's head roll forward, toppling from the man's still upright body. A moment later, the lead monk reached the soldier. Cursing that they'd not been permitted to carry their shields, Billat backed away, his sword thrust out, its point dancing to keep his distance from the advancing monk. A shield would have made all the difference. He'd not have needed to worry about that second weapon, and behind a shield he could have charged the man, blocking the axe even if it was thrown at him, and then his sword would have done its work quickly.

He nodded to himself, only then realizing that he was sitting down, almost opposite the staircase. Sweat stung his eyes, making it difficult to understand what his hands were doing, there in his lap, repeatedly moving in a way something

705

like shovelling, as they sought to push his intestines back into his body. It wasn't working.

A shield. And a sword. Things would have turned out differently if he'd had those. He wouldn't be sitting here on the floor.

Blinking back on a world that now stung, he saw his hands give up, and the guts roll out. He recalled trying to dig a latrine once, in sandy clay, and how the side walls kept caving in, until that damned pit was fifteen fucking paces across, and his comrades – all laughing – had had to throw him a rope so he could climb up the sloping sides. They'd known about the sand, of course. It was a rite of passage, being made into a fool, but how it had burned, how it had stung.

Humiliation. What a last thing to remember.

*       *       *

The heat from the fire engulfing the barracks forced Sergeant Telra and her soldiers back towards the entrance to the main building, where she decided they would await the reappearance of the lieutenant, once the ugly work inside was done with.

The shrieks from inside the barracks were gone now. No one had made it outside, meaning that she and her comrades had yet to bless their swords this night. Often, war forgot about being all about fighting, and instead became a sordid exercise in destruction, in flames and burned bodies stepped over, as if the aftermath had a way of creeping unseen over the present. In some ways, of course, that was a relief, but one could be left with the sense of having missed out on everything.

The heat and the flames, the billowing black smoke rising only to tumble over beneath the ceiling of white clouds, all reminded her of the last time she'd set fire to a building. That one had been an estate, empty but for a horrid old woman. Something of a debacle, to be honest. She'd exceeded her orders. Well, truth was, she'd been drunk.

Motion from the gatehouse drew her attention and she turned to see the first of Bahann's advance squads arriving.

706

Lieutenant Uskan was in the lead, sword in one hand and shield drawn round and set. Telra bit back a sneer. The man's excessive caution hinted at cowardice, as far as she was concerned. Stepping forward, she said, 'Sir. Lieutenant Esk is still in the main building. We got the company unawares – not a single man made it out of the barracks.'

'How long?' he demanded.

She frowned at his flushed face beneath the helm's rim. 'Sir?'

'How long has she been in there, sergeant?'

'Well, now that you mention it, some time's passed.'

'Stay here,' he ordered, gesturing his squads to follow him. He brushed past Telra and entered the main building, his soldiers trooping after him.

Stepping back to join her three comrades, Telra watched for a moment, and then shrugged. 'Well, leave 'em to it, I say. We did our bit.'

None of her soldiers replied.

She looked across at them. 'Got a problem with any of this?'

The three men shook their heads.

It was then that the first screams erupted from the main house.

\*       \*       \*

Dawn was paling the sky when Captain Hallyd Bahann at last stepped into the compound of Yannis monastery. He halted upon seeing Sergeant Telra directing her soldiers on the laying out of bodies. Legion bodies.

Scowling, he marched up to Telra. 'Sergeant, where's Lieutenant Esk?'

'Dead, sir. Uskan's inside. He's badly wounded. He went in there with eighteen soldiers, sir, came out with three still standing. It was Sheccanto's bodyguards, sir.'

'Abyss take me, how many did she have?'

'Two, sir.'

Hallyd Bahann found himself unable to muster a reply to that. He swung round to scan the corpses that had been lined up in three rows on the ground. The men and women looked chopped to pieces. Most bore multiple wounds. Smoke drifted over them like ethereal veils. The heat from the burned-down barracks had melted all the snow in the compound, leaving the bodies in puddles of sooty water now stained red.

He turned to Telra. 'And you didn't go in to help them?'

'Sir? Lieutenant Esk ordered us to guard the gatehouse. That was the last order she gave us.'

'Very well,' Bahann said after a moment.

'Oh, and sir?'

'Yes?'

'We got them both, sir. Sheccanto and Skelenal.'

'Skelenal? Well, then some good's come of this mess after all.' He turned and strode into the main building.

Lieutenant Uskan was seated in a plush chair near the hearth in the main hall. The chair opposite him held a corpse, which Uskan seemed to be studying intently, as if they'd been sharing a conversation just now interrupted. From the waist down the lieutenant was soaked in blood.

Hallyd Bahann cursed under his breath. 'Uskan,' he said.

The veteran glanced over with glassy eyes. 'Sir. Building secured.'

'How much of that blood on you is yours?'

'All of it, sir. I won't see the sun's rise.'

'Tell me those bodyguards are dead.'

Uskan bared his teeth in a smile. 'They are, but as you can see, it wasn't easy. It's a damned good thing, sir, that the rest of those monks went up in flames.'

'Who killed Sheccanto? Was it you, Uskan?'

'No. Truth is, sir, no one killed her. She was dead when my soldiers finally broke down the door to her room. Cutter Hisk says the body's long past stiff, too.'

'Meaning?'

Uskan laughed. 'Meaning, sir, she probably died yesterday afternoon.'

'You find that amusing, do you, lieutenant?'

Uskan leaned his head to one side and spat blood. 'Those poor monks were defending a corpse. They killed eighteen soldiers. And all of it was for nothing. Amusing, sir? No. Fucking hilarious.' He paused, a frown settling on his pale brow. 'Did I say eighteen? Wrong. Make that . . . nineteen . . .'

Hallyd Bahann glared at him, until he realized that Uskan couldn't see anything, because the man was dead.

The commander stepped back, eyed the two corpses facing each other in their plush chairs.

Telra appeared at his side. 'Sir, we should collect his body—'

'No,' Bahann replied. 'Leave him where he is. For all we know, he and that old man are swapping stories right now. Move our other dead back into the hall. We're going to burn it all down.'

'We have prisoners, sir—'

'Prisoners?'

'Servants. Children, mostly.'

'Find them a wagon. Send them down to Yedan monastery.'

'We're not going to attack it, sir?'

'No. They've lost both their leaders and that monastery is now full of widows. Let them grieve.'

'And us, sir?'

With some effort, Hallyd Bahann dragged his gaze away from the two corpses in their chairs. He eyed Telra. 'We're heading into the forest. We've dealt with the Shake. Now we'll deal with the Deniers.'

'Yes sir.'

'I'm field promoting you to lieutenant.'

'Thank you, sir.'

After a moment, he shook his head. 'Uskan never really seemed to be the kind of soldier to die in battle. Not like this.'

Telra shrugged. 'Perhaps, sir, he got careless.'

Bahann squinted at her, wondering, but her face was expressionless, and stayed that way.

# EIGHTEEN

---

THERE HAD BEEN AN AGE, PERHAPS A CENTURY BACK, when artists had turned their talents to working in stone and bronze. As if stung by the prodigious masterpieces raised up by the Azathanai, and in particular the High Mason Caladan Brood, these Tiste artists had pursued techniques to match, if not surpass, the efforts of their neighbours. In the pursuit of realism, and then the conjuration of natural forms elevated into a kind of aesthetic perfection, the use of plaster casting – upon living, breathing models – had been perfected. The art form had burgeoned in a spectacular, albeit brief, flurry of statuary that saw works proliferating throughout the public spaces of Kharkanas, and in the gardens, grand halls and courtyards of the nobility.

But any civilization that saw art as a kind of cultural competition was, to Rise Herat's mind, well down the road to disillusion, and the collapse of statuary as a form of artistic expression came on the day that a Tiste merchant returned from the lands of the Azathanai, transporting in her train a new work by some unknown Azathanai sculptor.

If the Azathanai had been paying attention to the Tiste sculptors, they had been unmoved. The idealization of the Tiste form, the body transformed into marble or bronze and thereby stripped of its mortality, was a kind of conceit, possibly defiant, probably diffident. The work that had been brought into Kharkanas was massive, wrought in rough bronze. It bore sharp, jagged edges. It writhed with panic and fury. Upon a broad, flat pedestal, a dozen hounds surrounded a single hound, and that beast, in the centre of the storm, was dying. Its companions tore into its flanks, sank fangs into its hide, pulling, stretching, tearing.

Gallan told the tale of a score or so of Kharkanas's finest sculptors, all gathering in the private courtyard where stood the Azathanai bronze. Some had railed, filling the air with spiteful condemnation, or voicing their sniffing contempt for the raw hand that had sculpted this monstrosity. A few others had fallen silent, their gazes fixed upon the work. Only one, a master artist considered by most to be the finest sculptor in Kurald Galain, had wept.

Among the Tiste, art had given shape to an ideal. But stone never betrayed. Bronze could not deceive. The ideal, made to kneel to political assertions of superiority, had, almost overnight, descended into mockery.

'By this,' Gallan had said, 'perfection is made mortal once again. By this, our conceit dulls.'

The Azathanai bronze, deemed offensive, had been removed from public display. Eventually, it had found its way into a crypt beneath the Citadel, a broad, low-ceilinged room, now home to scores of other works, that Gallan had named the Tarnished Chamber.

The historian had set three lanterns down, casting sharp light upon three sides of the Azathanai bronze, which some-one had rather uninspiringly called 'The Savaging of the Hound'. He had then circled the work, studying it from vary-ing heights and angles. He had made a window with his hands to block out all but the details. He had drawn close to smell the metal and its patina of greasy dust, and had set fingertips against the verdigris where it coated the beasts like mange.

Despite the steady, unwavering light, the animals seemed to blur with motion, spinning round their snarling victim. He had read from some treatise that, if seen from above, it was clear that the circling hounds actually formed an inward spiral of flesh and rending canines; and the scholar had gone on to suggest – to a subsequent chorus of disbelief – that the animal in the centre, by virtue of its own writhing, twisted form, was itself spiralling inward. The man's final outrage was to wonder if the sculpture depicted, not many beasts, but one: an animal destroying itself, turning round and round and ever inward into a vortex of self-annihilation.

For the historian, the only appalling thing about the scholar's interpretation was its plausibility. After all, had the artist not sought to convey a hidden meaning with this scene, the beast in the centre of this violent storm would have been a stag, perhaps, or a bull.

Though he heard the door to the chamber squeal with motion, Rise Herat did not turn round until the newcomer spoke.

'Here, historian? In the name of Dark, why?'

Rise Herat shrugged. 'It is private enough.'

Cedorpul grunted. 'The only spies in the Citadel are our own.'

'Yes, curious, that. After all, isn't the purpose of spying the protection of our own people? Have we descended into insouciance so far, priest, as to claim, with a straight face, that we are protecting our people from themselves?'

The round-faced man pursed his lips, and then waved dismissively.

Rise Herat smiled. '"*Oh deadly language, how so you offend me!*"'

Scowling, Cedorpul said, 'Remind me not of that wretched man, our court coward, our sneering seneschal of high mages! His elevation was shortlived. I will stand in his stead.'

The historian turned back to 'The Savaging of the Hound'. 'Do you recall this, priest?'

'Before my time. It is ghastly. No wonder it hides here. Only in darkness could you now bless this. Douse the lights – we've no need of them.'

'It is Azathanai.'

'Is it now? Well, then yes, I can see why you'd be curious.'

'All the others in here, however, are Tiste.'

712

Cedorpul waved dismissively. 'Every fad fades in time, historian. If you would be the purveyor of hoary frenzies from before the age of modern enlightenment, then make a study of this chamber. Line the statues into a library of stone and mouldy bronze. Drag up a desk, light a candle, and pen your treatise.'

'And what treatise would that be, priest?'

Cedorpul shrugged, glancing around. 'The past is a litany of naïve expectations.'

'But at last, we are now much wiser.'

'Just so.'

'Well, there are indeed some, even other scholars, who find comfort in the belief that past ages in history can be seen as phases of our childhood, thus absolving them of knowing any better, and thus absolving us, in the present, of any lingering sense that maybe, once, long ago, life was better than it is now.'

'Is this the reason for summoning me? I'd rather a rough draught on a tattered scroll set upon my desk, where I can get to it a few decades from now, when at last I have the time.'

'Yes, I'm sure,' Rise Herat replied, still studying the Azathanai bronze. 'But things are not better, are they?' He turned, waved a hand in a broad sweep. 'See here, in our Tarnished Chamber, our surrendered ideals. Such childish optimism!'

Cedorpul began turning away. 'If that is all—'

'Speak to me of sorcery.'

The priest paused, twisted to regard him. 'What do you wish to know?'

'The reach of your power. Your control over it.'

'And in this, you are taking an academic interest?'

'No. In this, I work at the bidding of the High Priestess.'

A faint shadow seemed to crease Cedorpul's cherubic features, as if showing, in an unguarded instant, his old man's face belonging to some distant future. 'She has cause to doubt me now?'

'Perhaps it is our newfound need, priest, to protect us from ourselves. Cast me in the cloak of a spy. Familiar ground to ease your discomfort.'

'As court seneschal, I will not embarrass her.'

'Then you claim to some prowess.'

'I claim sufficient confidence.'

'I think, Cedorpul, that both prowess and confidence have swept away the young, cheerful man that I once knew.'

'Is there more you would ask me?'

'Who is your enemy?'

'My enemy?'

'If you are gathering power – those streams of sorcery – against whom will you unleash it?'

'I am a servant of Mother Dark.'

'That kind of servant she has not asked for, Cedorpul.'

The priest suddenly bared his teeth. 'Ah, yes, I recall now. Your mysterious audience with Mother Dark, in the company of Lanear and that Azathanai. But the details of that meeting? Why, none of you deigned to inform me, or anyone else for that matter. I hear that you earned Lord Silchas Ruin's ire, and even this did not sway you. Thus, a well of secret knowing that you can draw from at will, as it suits your moment of need.'

'You already know enough. She refused Lord Anomander's desire to march on Urusander. She commanded him to keep sheathed his sword.'

'Am I to be commanded to do nothing as well? If so, then let her speak such words to me.'

'And if I told you that we did not speak with Mother Dark? That our journey ended abruptly, and that we were guided out from that realm by Lord Draconus?'

'Then you further undermine your authority to advise me on her behalf.'

A surge of anger silenced Rise Herat. He turned back to study the Azathanai bronze, breathing deeply as he mastered his emotions. 'Authority? Oh how we all strain to see into the darkness, pleading for its heavy but sure hand. Settled well upon one shoulder, guiding us on to the true path.'

'I will be the seneschal,' said Cedorpul. 'I will be the authority when it comes to the collective sorcerous capabilities of the Citadel, of the Tiste Andii.'

'And whose authority supersedes your own?'

'Mother Dark's, of course. I but await her guidance—'

'Knowing that it will not come. Cedorpul, am I witness to a usurpation of power?'

'When Lord Anomander returns to Kharkanas, historian, I will announce to him that I stand at his side, and that it is the express wish of the seneschal that he draw his blade. That he fight in the name of Mother Dark. And upon the field of battle, why, there I will stand, with my cadre, to lend magic to his might.'

Rise Herat focused anew on 'The Savaging of the Hound'. He could almost hear its howls. *Not many, but one. And no end to this violence but death's sure promise. That merchant. She said that she'd paid nothing for it. That the unknown sculptor among the Azathanai offered it as a gift to the Tiste.*

*Ideals are like a bitch hound. What she spawns might prove vicious. What she spawns might, in time, turn upon her. Is this what this work announces? No, but I will read into it what I choose, and by that choice, the language of art can never die. All it takes is a little effort.*

*But then, whenever has that exhortation convinced anyone?*

After a long moment, Cedorpul said, 'Report back to the High Priestess. Ensure that she understands.'

'Of course.'

He listened to the man walk away, the echoes of his footfalls filling the unlit spaces between marble and bronze.

Chambers that came to house forgotten works of art, Rise Herat reflected, were little more than repositories of sorrow, and all the more heartbreaking if this was where innocence was lost. He decided that he would not return.

＊　　＊　　＊

The door had been left ajar and the boy had followed the dog into the room, surprising Emral Lanear where she sat behind veils of smoke, the huge filigreed bowl of the water-pipe on the table at her side, heavy and gravid with its sly promise.

Lids low, playing the mouthpiece across her lips, she observed her unexpected guests.

The dog collected a small pillow that had slipped down from a divan. With the pillow clamped possessively in its mouth, the animal spun round, dropping down and holding its head close to the polished floor, its eyes bright and fixed on the boy.

He edged forward.

Claws clattering, the dog bolted, dodging first to one side and then to the other, deftly evading the boy's reach, and then the animal was past, out through the door with its prize.

Hissing in frustration, the boy tensed as if to set off in pursuit, but after a moment his shoulders dropped, and he straightened.

'The dog chooses the game,' Lanear said.

The boy glanced over, and then shrugged. 'I like playing, too. Only he's so fast.'

'You are the hostage Orfantal.'

'I know I'm supposed to be with a tutor. But Cedorpul decided he won't teach me any more.'

'Oh? Why is that? Were you unmindful? Rude?'

Orfantal nodded. 'He was showing me a conj . . . conjuration. Magic, I mean.'

'I know the word, yes,' said Lanear, gesturing with the mouthpiece. 'Do continue.'

'It was making sounds. I didn't like them. So I dispelled it – the conjuration.'

'You dispelled it?'

'It wasn't hard.'

Lanear drew on the mouthpiece, briefly wondering when she had grown so careless with propriety. But the sharpness blossoming in her lungs swept away the moment's disquiet. 'Do you rival his power, then?'

'Oh no. He's not very good.'

She laughed out a cloud of smoke. 'Oh, dear. Careful, Orfantal. Cedorpul is a certain kind of man one finds on occasion. Round of form, soft to the eye, with a childish modesty still held on to, until the gift of his youth assumes the pose of affectation, sufficient to irritate his more mature fellows, even as it seduces weak-minded women. That said, such a man has the capacity for venality and spite.'

'I shouldn't make him angry at me?'

'Yes, as I said. Not wise.'

Orfantal approached, settling down rather close to her knees on a padded footstool she had moved aside earlier in order to give room to her folded legs. The boy's eyes were dark, liquid, and perhaps not as innocent as they should have been. 'Are you a priestess?'

'I am the High Priestess, Orfantal. Emral Lanear.'

'Do you have any children?'

'From my womb? No. But of the realm? Perhaps it could be said, all of the Tiste Andii.'

'Why is it that no one gets to know their mothers?'

'What do you mean?'

His gaze slipped away. 'This is a nice room. The smoke smells like incense. It shows me the currents.'

'What currents? Ah, the draughts—'

'Not those currents. The other ones. The ones of power. Dark. Kurald Galain. What bleeds from that pattern in the floor in the outer room by the front doors.' He lifted a small hand towards the mouthpiece she held, and delicately prised it from her grip. Angling the end upward, he watched as smoke curled free.

She waited for him to try it. She waited for his expression of shock, and then his coughing. She waited, she realized with a faint shock, for some company.

Instead, Lanear's eyes widened as the swirl of smoke thickened, stretched out, making a sinuous dance as it found a serpentine form. The smoke then swung a viper's head towards her, hovering opposite her face. She saw darkness where its eyes should have been, as liquid as Orfantal's own.

'Who,' she asked in a faint gasp, 'who stares at me from those eyes, Orfantal?'

'Just me.'

The snake of smoke then withdrew, as if drawn back through the mouthpiece. In moments it was gone.

Smiling, Orfantal handed the mouthpiece back to her. 'Cedorpul is collecting mages.'

Blinking, she focused on him once again. 'Is he?'

'He wants everyone to work on sorcery that breaks things, or hurts people. He says we need that, because the Liosan have it, and to stop them using it on us, we have to use it on them first.'

Lanear leaned back. She drew again on the pipe, but this time the smoke felt almost solid as it slithered down into her lungs. Startled, she looked down at Orfantal, but the boy was staring at something at the side of the chamber. She sent a stream of white towards the ceiling, and then said, 'Orfantal, what do you think of Cedorpul's reasoning?'

The boy frowned. 'Is that what it is?'

'He anticipates a battle, doesn't he? Between magicks.'

'Gallan says that darkness can only retreat. But then he says that retreating is the only way to win, because sooner or later the light passes, and what flows in behind it? Darkness. Gallan says Light's victory is mortal, but Dark's victory is eternal.'

'I did not think,' ventured Lanear as she studied this strange young boy, 'Gallan had much time for children.'

'No, but he liked my pet.'

'Your dog?'

Orfantal rose. 'No, not Ribs. My other pet. Ribs isn't mine, but maybe,' he added, moving towards a side door – the one he had been looking at earlier, 'I'm his.'

He opened the door, and she saw now the dog, Ribs, lying as if about to pounce in the side passage, the pillow still in its mouth.

Orfantal rushed forward.

Spinning round, Ribs fled up the passage.

The boy followed, his bare feet light upon the floor, as if borne on feathers.

She heard the chase, dwindling away, until all was silent once more.

718

*Careful, boy. Now you're playing Gallan's game.*

Rustleaf offered none of the escape that came with d'bayang. Instead, it but enlivened the brain. For this moment's repast, she'd chosen wrongly. And the loss of . . . company . . . left her feeling bereft.

*       *       *

Endest Silann set out from the Citadel, in search of decency. Crossing the two bridges, he made his way into the city, where the cold had drawn most people indoors. The snow had retreated to places less travelled, up against walls and in alleys where the white smears were dusted with grey soot. He moved between high estate walls, passing barred gates of iron and wood. Where the street ascended the bank, away from the river and above the floodplain, the estates burgeoned in size, and many of the long walls bore niches in which stood old statues, the marble figures painted in lifelike colours, with oversized eyes in each face offering a dispassionate regard to the cloaked man shuffling past.

In more ways than he deemed healthy, Endest preferred their blank stares over the intensity that plagued him in the Citadel. Followers stalked him now, fixing upon his every gesture with febrile attention, leaning into his every word, his every passing comment. He had met the need for a prophet with denial, and, when that failed, with silence. But this did little more than intensify their regard, crowding with imagined significance all that he did.

Any catalogue of mortal deeds could only assemble a list of flaws. Perfection belonged to the dead, where in the act of passing from what the senses could observe to what the memory reinvented, any fool could ascend into legend. But Endest Silann was not yet dead, not yet freed from mortal constraints. Sooner or later, prophets returned to their god, only to slip beyond and away, sliding their cold flesh into apocrypha – holy texts and blessed scrolls – and this was an impatient passage for the would-be witnesses waiting in the wings. He felt that he was already outliving his usefulness, and those who would pontificate and interpret his life would rather that life ended soon, if only to get him out of the way.

He walked towards the Winter Market grounds, and thirty paces behind him, as they had done since the Citadel, a score or more priests tracked him. They would do better with Cedorpul, but for all the manifestations of magic his old friend now commanded, there was nothing sacred in curious games with smoke and shadows, and even darkness made to flow like blood left no trail on the stones.

That gift, it seemed, belonged to Endest Silann alone.

His hands were wrapped in gauze that needed changing a dozen times a day. Mother Dark's eyes saw through red tears and blotted linen, or, as was increasingly the case, they saw nothing at all, as he had taken to sliding his hands into the thick sleeves of his woollen robe, a habit the other priests now copied.

Behind him, in the Citadel, a plague had come, a kind of fever. *In a body with nothing to do, the mind will dance.* But that was the least of it. Some dances mapped steps into madness, with ferocious momentum. He was weary of the spies, the small groups huddled whispering in corners, the strange glances and guarded expressions. Even more tiring, beneath all that he was witness to roiled an undercurrent of fear, and that was difficult to swim against.

The future was a place of uncertain promise in the best of times, where hope and optimism warred with doubt and despair, and there were those who fought such battles in the streets, or in the home, with the enemy no longer the shadow in one's own soul, but someone else – a neighbour, a wife or a husband, a liege or a peasant. *Doubt is the enemy. Despair a weakness, and hope becomes not something to strive for, but a virtue eager to draw blood from every sceptic.*

*'Turn me away from the unsightly!'* the optimists cry. *'Yield this dream to joy, to revelry and laughter. Enough confabulation and noise to drown the distant cries of the suffering, to blind me to the world's woes! What care I for tragedies not of my own making? Such things are beyond my control, anyway, and indeed beyond my ability to change.'*

In many ways, Endest had no argument with such views. The heart's capacity was finite. So people explained, again and again, to justify all that had grown cold and lifeless within them. If imagination had no limits, surely the soul did.

*And yet, what thing of certain limit can in turn create something limitless? This seems a breaking of some fundamental law. The unbound from the bound, the infinite from the finite. How can such things be?*

Eyes in his hands, to make witness to all that he did. He had set out in search of decency, and now, striding into the Winter Market, his own eyes watering to the sudden heat beneath the cloth roof, the redolent odours of myriad people, foodstuffs and animals. The first thing his gaze found was a wall of tiny wooden cages, stacked high, each cage home to a songbird.

There was no song in their voices. Instead, a cacophony of terrible stress and fear assailed him. As if of their own accord, his hands slid out from his sleeves.

A young man sat on a stool in front of the cages, grease on his lips and his fingers as he ate from a skewer of meat and vegetables. Seeing Endest Silann, he nodded. 'Half to the temple, for the young women, but I was not expecting you for weeks yet.' He indicated the cages behind him with a tilt of his head. 'They save their songs for spring. Who would want these shrieks, hey?'

Endest Silann felt her then, his goddess, stealing into him, suddenly attentive, curious. 'Where are they from?' he asked.

The man shrugged. 'The countryside, and to the south. Caught in fine nets during their migrations.' He then made a face. 'Getting fewer every year, though.'

'And this is your living?'

The man shrugged. 'It serves me well enough, priest.'

Endest's followers had arrived by now, and others were drawing close, as if tasting something new in the air.

'You make a living from the imprisonment of wild creatures.'

The man suddenly scowled, and stood up, tossing the skewer to the ground and wiping at his hands. 'Not just me. Trappers, too. But it is not my coin that buys them, is it? If not for your own temple, priest, I might be a different man from the one you see here.'

'And where is your own cage? The one in your skull.'

The scowl grew dark, menacing.

'The one,' Endest continued, 'that traps your conscience?'

'Look to your own for that!'

Other merchants and hawkers pushed closer now.

Endest held out his hands, watching as the bandages sagged, unfurled sodden to dangle and then slip down on to his wrists. He felt the blood welling, trickling down his palms.

The mongers before him backed away.

'If only,' Endest Silann said, 'you gave her reason to fight.' He glanced back over a shoulder and met the eyes of the nearest acolyte. 'Take these cages back to the Citadel. All of them.' Facing the hawker, he shook his head. 'This is your last day here. You will be paid for these birds, but no more, and never again. In the name of Mother Dark, the capturing and selling of wild creatures is now forbidden.'

Voices rose in outrage.

The hawker bared his teeth. 'Will you send soldiers after me, then? Because I will defy you—'

'No, you will not. I understand you, sir, the pleasure you take from what you do, you hoarder of all you can never feel, or hope to feel.'

'Mother Dark has no power – we all know as much! And your soldiers – Urusander will deal with them soon enough!'

'You don't understand,' said Endest Silann, and as he said this, he realized that Mother Dark did not understand either. 'I set out today, into this city, looking for decency. But I could not find it. It was all hidden away, behind walls, perhaps, withdrawn into intimate moments and the like.' He shook his head. 'In any case, I was mistaken in my search. The decency I was seeking was not the kind a mortal can see, but only feel.'

A figure had pushed through the belligerent crowd facing Endest Silann, and the priest saw sorcery curling round it.

The seller of songbirds saw the newcomer and smiled. 'Cryba! Have you heard? I am condemned by my finest customer! Forbidden from selling ever again these wretched creatures! Why, if not for these eager followers of his, I would kill every bird here just to spite him!'

Cryba nodded a warning at Endest. 'Get out of here, fool. This is commerce, not faith. Different laws here, different codes.'

'No doubt,' said Endest Silann. 'Yield your magic, sir. I have found my own power, in the name of decency. You would be unwise to challenge it.'

The man sighed and shook his head. 'So be it.' He flung out his right hand. An arc of actinic light erupted, stabbed into Endest Silann's chest.

He felt it tear through him, racing along his limbs, swirling in his chest, and then vanishing inward as if swallowed by a whirlpool.

Cryba stared in disbelief.

'Why, sir, did you think anger, aggression and pride would have any power over decency?'

Cryba raised both hands—

The hundreds of cages sprang open. The birds rushed out in a whirling mass and converged on Cryba, whose scream was quickly muffled beneath swarming wings.

The acolytes behind Endest Silann had one and all fallen to their knees. The crowd before him had retreated before the raging tumult of freed creatures, each bird an affront to their belief in mastery. The seller of songbirds was huddled on the ground, arms hiding his face.

Moments later, the flock swirled out from beneath the canvas awning, winging up into the sky above the city. Endest felt them leave, racing southward – bright sparks of joy.

Where Cryba had been there was now nothing, not even a scrap of clothing.

The hawker lifted his head. 'Where's Cryba?'

'Given another chance,' Endest replied. 'An unexpected

gift. It seems that my sorcery, such as it is, hides unanticipated depths of forgiveness. They carry his soul now, I believe. Well, tatters of it, perhaps.'

'Murdered!'

'To be honest,' Endest said, 'I am most surprised that they did not kill you instead.'

Staggering, the seller of songbirds – his skin suddenly seeming more grey than black – turned and fled, deeper into the maze of tunnels beneath the awnings.

Endest Silann glanced back at his followers. 'What you will make of this,' he said to the still kneeling figures, 'is of no consequence. The sorcery within reach defies your compass, and mine. It may well usher forth from the Citadel's Terondai, or rise from the earth itself. It may ride the currents of winter's breath, or swirl beneath the ice on the river. Perhaps it bridges the stars themselves, and straddles the chasm between the living and the dead.' He shrugged. 'It arrives bereft of flavour, as open to abuse as to uses guided by moral considerations. It arrives raw as clay from a pit. Awaiting the grit of our imperfections, the throwing hands and the spinning wheel, the glaze of our conceit and the rage of the kilns. Today, I do not act in the name of Mother Dark. I act in the name of decency.' He paused again, and then said, 'So, rise you all, and attend to me. I have only begun.'

Endest Silann swung round to face the bowels of the Winter Market, with its masses, and all the private needs, the hidden fears and worries, the stresses of livings barely maintained, seemed to rise in ferment before him. And through this heady mix, he saw as well the pain of captivity, belonging to animals destined for slaughter; even the tubers, lying naked and arrayed for the taking, exuded a faint yearning for sweet earth.

*Cages for our lives. Just another prison of necessity, wildly walled with every justification imaginable – these bars truncating what we believe to be possible. So many traps of thought.*

*Mother Dark, is this not what we all ask of you? Where is your promise of relief? For the joys we cling to are but islands*

*in a sea of torment, and every moment of contentment is
becalmed peace, edged with exhaustion.*

*Watch then, Mother Dark, as I deliver a day of release.*

He felt her recoil.

But not retreat, and her gaze remained, and saw all there
was to see, as he set forth, reaching out with his power to
deliver the blessing of peace, from which none escaped. His
followers wailed in his wake, while before him hardened men
and women – with their wary but hungry faces, their knife-
sharp eyes and their scars of toil – flinched before falling to
their knees, before covering their visages as every struggle,
every inner turmoil, was, for a short time, eased. For many,
Endest saw as he moved down the aisles, such release loosed
tears – not of sorrow, nor even of something like happiness,
but of simple relief.

He moved among them like a drug, delivering a gift of the
insensate, delivering to each person, in their turn, the benison
of inner silence.

Tethered goats, hens in crates, tiny Eleint in their tall, net-
walled prisons. Bats scrambling against the insides of wooden
boxes, hares bound by one ankle – tearing the ligaments in
their own legs as they bolted again and again, flinging themselves into the air – bawling myrid, tender dog pups, yet more
songbirds, and squealing monkeys from the south – Endest
Silann opened every door, severed every tether, and then,
whispering *home*, sent the creatures away. *Home to your
mothers. To your flocks, your herds, your forests or jungles.
Home, in the name of some simpler justice, some simpler
promise.*

Figures loomed before him, charging in fury, only to halt
as their rage vanished, as his blessing devoured them and
made of each wounded soul a small thing that could, if one
so chose, be cupped in loving hands.

Even death was open to refusal, as he came upon long
tables crowded with dead fish that suddenly began flapping,
gills working, eyes shining. And with a gesture he sent them
away. *Go then, to your rivers and lakes. Today, the world
returns to an untouched state. Today, I freeze all of time, and*

*free you all to linger in the instant, this thing between breaths. This mote of peace.*

Mother Dark watched as he strode through the chaos, as he unravelled the market, stole away food, denied to all the press of hunger. She watched, because she could do nothing else, for her eyes were inside wounds in his hands, and wounds did not blink.

Sorcery proved a thief of many things. Endest Silann found himself standing facing the centre of a square. Behind him was a portal that led back into the Winter Market, and from that canvas-lined throat drifted wailing and grief, only now dwindling as the day's muted light hastened its surrender to dusk.

In the square before him crouched a dragon so vast and so close as to make his mind reel. Its scales were crimson edged in ochre or gold, deepening to bronze beneath its jaw and down the length of its throat. Black talons had punched deep into the cobbled ground. Its wings were folded behind humped shoulders, and the creature had lowered its massive, wedge-shaped head, fixing gold, lambent eyes upon the priest.

The dragon spoke into his mind with a woman's voice. *'Are you returned to us, mortal?'*

He struggled to find his voice. Looking down, he saw that he held his hands upturned, the palms with their weeping wounds facing the dragon. She was witness. She was present.

*'You gave her the same peace, mortal. The same curse, and, with all those behind you, she now suffers its loss.'* The huge head tilted slightly. *'But this did not occur to you, did it? The gift's . . . other side. In your wake, mortal, a thousand Tiste now lie stricken with despair. I was drawn here – your effulgence was a beacon, your sorcery a terrible flowering in a dark, and dangerous, forest.*

*'You were lost in it, mortal. You would not have stopped. You would have taken the entire city, and indeed, perhaps your entire land.'*

'What if I had?' Endest voiced the question quietly, in no way defiant, but honest with wonder and horror.

726

'*Your gift of peace, mortal, was not what you imagined it to be. Their moment of bliss was not bliss. An end to life's torment has but one name and that name is death. An end to torment and, alas, also an end to joy, and love, and the sweet taste of being.*'

'It was not death! I brought creatures back!'

'*In surfeit of power, there is the instinct to redress the imbalance. For each instant of death that you delivered, mortal, you reawakened a life. But the sorcery seduces, yes? Beware its assurances. Too often in magic, the blessing proves a curse.*'

Struck silent, numbed by the implications of the dragon's hard words, Endest Silann stared into the creature's eyes. After a long moment, he said, 'Then I thank you, Eleint. But still I wonder, why did you bother?'

'*I am made curious by acts of love, no matter the path they take – after all, in such a state, you are blind, and can but stumble unwittingly. You Tiste interest me. Raw, unbridled, as if Draconean blood lingered in your own.*

'*If indeed it does,*' the dragon continued, slowly spreading its wings, '*then your civil war is no surprise.*'

'Wait!' cried Endest Silann. 'Is this all you will give us? Where do you go? What is your name?'

'*Questions! I will not travel far, but do not look to me for succour. Love is but a flavour, no more and no less enticing than bitter anguish, or sour regret. Still, it . . . entices.*' The dragon's wings were now fully spread, belling to unfelt winds, and the claws plucked free of their grip upon the cobbled expanse, as if they alone had been holding the creature bound to the earth. '*I yield to you, Endest Silann – whose heart is too vast, whose soul begins to comprehend its own infinite capacity – my love. This time, to stay your ecstasy, I set finger to your lips. Next time, it may fall to you to offer me the same.*

'*I am named Silanah. Should you choose to seek me out, find me before passion's gate, where I am known to abide. Curious and . . . as ever . . . enticed.*'

The dragon rose effortlessly, and the air buffeting the priest with each snap of the enormous wings was thick with sorcery, sharp as spice on the tongue.

He would have fallen to his knees, but somehow Mother Dark prevented the gesture. Instead, he stood facing skyward, watching the dragon vanish into the low clouds as his crowd of followers rushed to join him, their questions a deafening chorus he ignored. Limbs shaking, he closed his eyes. Blood streamed from his hands, as Mother Dark wept within him, like a woman with a broken heart.

*　　*　　*

There was little mercy in the dusk, as the last light failed to hide the huge reptilian creature rising from the heart of Kharkanas. As one, the three travellers reined in, their mounts suddenly tossing heads and stamping on the frozen track.

Finarra Stone reached for her sword, then let her hand retreat back to the reins.

Winging southward, the dragon vanished into the heavy clouds.

Beside her, Caplo Dreem softly snorted. 'Your sword, captain? As futile gestures go . . .'

'And by the scent clinging to you,' Warlock Resh retorted in her defence, 'you were an instant away from scattering into the wilds of the wood upon either side of us. Grant the captain a more gentle regard, Caplo, lest you reveal the need to elevate yourself at the expense of others.'

'Quickly stung, old friend. I meant nothing cruel by it.'

'Naught but the intimation of your superiority, you mean.'

The assassin shrugged. 'This ween is without pride, warlock. In any case, the beast is gone. Shall we resume this journey and so undertake our unremarked arrival in the Wise City?'

They set out once more, the horses nervous and reluctant.

'I would think guards attend the city's gate, assassin,' said Finarra. 'Thus, we will not escape remark, and word will precede us to the Citadel by way of signal from the tower.'

Caplo shrugged. 'Even my tilt into modesty cannot go unchallenged.'

'We are frayed,' said Resh in a low growl. 'Witness to a dragon rising from Kharkanas.'

'Enough to humble us, yes?' Caplo asked.

Finarra sighed. 'Then forgive my pedantry, assassin.'

'I anticipate we will be but an afterthought, given the events in the city on this day, but as you say, captain, the Citadel will indeed prepare for us.'

'If I knew what either of you intended,' Finarra said, 'I'd be rather less fraught. We are to enter the Citadel, and stand before a painted pattern upon a floor. Is that all? A few moments of frowning regard, as if we were invited to peruse a portrait of uncertain talent.'

'Uncertain talent, captain, or uncertain of our ability to comprehend said talent?'

'What value discussing that distinction?'

'Only to pass the time, captain.'

'I would rather know your intentions. You and Resh both.'

'Nothing untoward, I'm sure,' answered Caplo in a murmur. 'If the pattern tells a tale, we would read it. If it presents a conundrum, we shall ponder it. If a riddle, we shall play in it.'

'And if it offers you nothing?'

'Then we shall take upon ourselves the pose of fools.'

'Speak for yourself,' said Resh. 'I intend to step into that Terondai's pattern, to see the path it offers and, if I can, to take it.'

'What if you're not welcome?' Finarra asked him.

Resh smiled across at her, a flash of white teeth in dark beard. 'I shall have a sword-wielder at my side.'

She stared. 'You expect me to accompany you? Into some unknown magical realm?' She shook her head. 'I don't know what appals me more, your assumption, or your faith that my sword can defend you.'

'I am not as inclined,' said Caplo, 'to risk such a journey. But if you ask it of me, friend, I will guard your other flank.'

She turned on the assassin. 'Then what do you seek, Caplo Dreem? You had such bold words earlier, as I recall.'

'I cannot answer you, captain,' Caplo replied. 'You see bravado, but I assure you, I am lost.'

The admission sharpened her regard, but the assassin's face remained hidden within his coarse woollen hood. Glancing across at Resh, she noted his frown. 'Warlock, is it not time for the Shake to choose? Your god is dead. You assert your neutrality and the truth of your desire makes grey your very skin. But even if you will not kneel to Mother Dark, surely Lord Urusander has named you and your kind an enemy of the realm – should the Liosan win this war, there will be no place for the Shake.'

Caplo snorted. 'Let Urusander face the monks in battle if he will.'

'Then why not assemble them and ally with Lord Anomander and the Andii?'

'And place ourselves in the shadow of the highborn?' Caplo retorted. 'What blessings have they ever given us? Tell me of the Houseblades who rode out from the keeps to help defend the Deniers of the forest! No, they were content enough with that slaughter—'

'As were you and your monks!'

'To our shame,' Resh confessed. 'We are bound to the commands given us by the Higher Graces. Nor does it seem likely that they will change their minds, even should Anomander come calling at Yannis.'

Finarra cursed under her breath. *All fools. No greater betrayer of reason than wanton pride!*

Ahead waited the city's main gate. A single guard stood to one side of the open passageway.

Resh edged his mount slightly forward as they reached the entrance. He leaned over the saddle horn as if in anticipation of the guard's accosting them, or at the very least enquiring as to their intent, but the young man simply waved them through.

Finarra Stone drew breath, preparing a tongue-lashing, but Caplo reached out to grip her arm just beneath the shoulder. A warning squeeze held her mute until they filed into the passage, past the guard, and then the assassin released his hold on her.

The hooded face turned her way. 'I doubt he had occasion to challenge the dragon's arrival, captain. To ready a spear, or reach for a belted sword.' He lifted a hand in a dismissive gesture. 'Events can make us all small, humbled into ourselves. Besides, two of us are priests, come to a city of priests and priestesses. And, lastly, our skins are not white.'

'It is the laxity that so offended me,' she said, angling her mount to ensure that he could not reach her a second time. There had been something uncanny in his touch even through the coarse fabric of her uniform.

They rode out on to the concourse. Dusk was deepening to night, and everywhere lanterns were being extinguished, inviting darkness into the city. From one of the Citadel towers, a bell tolled sonorously, dull and slow, as if announcing a dirge.

Resh grunted. 'At last, some ritual attends this faith.'

The streets before them were mostly empty. Finarra wondered if some kind of exodus had already started. Perhaps Urusander's Legion was already on the way. She knew too little of the present state of affairs, and the ignorance she had once welcomed now stung her. 'Let us waste no time in this,' she said, 'and ride straight to the Citadel. If anything, the day's end should have enlivened the Terondai.'

'An astute observation,' Resh said.

A short time later they reached the first guard post upon the north shore of the Dorssan Ryl, and once again were waved onward on to the bridge. Upon the other side, the Citadel's massive doors stood ajar, and from within there was a commotion, and the hint of many people gathered.

'Something has occurred,' Caplo observed. 'Priests and priestesses mill within—'

'Do they attend the Terondai?' Resh demanded.

'No,' the assassin replied. 'A fallen comrade, I think.'

The three newcomers dismounted at the arched entrance, left the reins of the horses to hang untethered. There was no one to collect them.

With growing unease, Finarra followed Resh and Caplo through the portico and emerged into the main chamber.

731

Though no torches flared and not a single lantern remained lit, she found she could easily pierce the gloom. As Caplo had described, a score or more priests were gathered in a circle around one of their own – a man lying prone, splashed in blood. Priestesses moved about the periphery of this rough circle, agitated and frightened. Few took notice of the new arrivals.

Warlock Resh stepped forward. 'Make way,' he said. 'If none among you has the skill to heal, I will see to the wounded man—'

'There is nothing to heal,' said one priest, but he and the others moved apart nonetheless, and Resh reached the figure. Crouching, he stared down for a time, saying nothing.

Finarra moved up behind him. 'His hands are pierced,' she said. 'The wounds do not close.'

Resh grunted.

The same priest who'd spoken earlier now said, 'None of this is for you – any of you. This is Endest Silann, chosen among all the priests. Mother Dark has blessed him, raised him above the rest of us. He has just performed a miracle. We were witness to dead creatures returned to life. To hundreds of citizens kneeling before him.' The man hesitated, and Finarra saw something wild and loose in his gaze. 'He banished a dragon.'

'Banished?' Caplo snorted.

'The priest is right,' Resh said, straightening. 'I cannot heal these wounds. Sorcery bleeds from them.' He shook his head, passing one hand before his eyes as if making an obscure sacred gesture. 'Our reasoned and rightful world is askew.'

The warlock's last words rippled through Finarra, their passage leaving her chilled, trembling.

'I once worshipped both reason and right,' Caplo said. 'Until I was made witness to their frailty. Now, neither yields faith worthy of the name. Leave them their moment, my brother. I see the Terondai before us, unattended, a scrawl of godly graffiti. Let us peruse it.'

Nodding, Resh pulled back, out of the crowd that now struck Finarra as somehow sordid. *Miracles demand a price, it seems. There is nothing more bloodless than a gathering of gawkers.* She followed Resh and Caplo.

Moments later they stood before the Terondai, the magical gift of Lord Draconus to his beloved Mother Dark.

Carved in black upon dulled, grey flagstones, the vast pattern gleamed as if wet. Something about it confounded Finarra, as if the meaning of the design – even unto its precise lines – eluded her. She was frightened by a sudden yearning to step upon it, to place herself in the centre.

'I can make nothing of this,' Resh said. 'Not while I stand outside it.' He glanced across at Finarra. 'Captain, will you attend me?'

'Yes,' she replied, but the word came out dry, fragile.

Caplo hissed out a breath. 'It warns me away,' he said. 'Not for me, this wretched power. Forgive me, brother. I cannot join you.'

Resh nodded as if unsurprised.

'What will you do?' Finarra asked the assassin.

'I will take the mundane path to this power,' he replied, drawing his furs closer. 'I will walk to the Chamber of Night.'

Her brows lifted. 'You seek an audience with Mother Dark?'

'No. With Lord Draconus.'

'To what end?'

He gestured a long-fingered hand at the Terondai. 'This was not made by a Tiste. I will find his scent. I will pierce the veil of his eyes, and look upon his soul. Such gifts are untoward, as is he who bequeathed it.' He faced them both and drew back his hood, revealing feral eyes. 'I have a suspicion.'

'And if it proves accurate?' Resh asked. 'What then, my friend?'

'There is a truth here, well disguised. I mean to tear it loose. I mean to reveal the game. Only then will we know the stance we must take.'

'You will decide this for the Shake?' Resh asked in soft tones.

Caplo Dreem smiled with tender sorrow. 'Ah, friend, it seems a worthy sacrifice.'

Finarra's breath caught. She glanced back at the priests and priestesses, but none paid them any attention. The man on the floor had begun stirring. She looked back at the assassin. 'You expect to die, Caplo?'

He shrugged.

It seemed that there was nothing more to say. Facing the Terondai once more, Resh gathered himself, and then strode on to the pattern. Finarra followed an instant later.

They stood then, close to the centre, studying the strange scars beneath their feet.

A faint wind brushed her face, smelling of dust. She lifted her gaze and gasped.

The Grand Hall was gone. Instead, they occupied a flag-stoned clearing, surrounded by tall trees, beneath a sky dull as stained pewter. 'Warlock . . .'

Resh was now studying the forest encircling them. His sigh was uneven. 'I did not think we would be invited.'

'What makes you so certain that we were?'

He shot her a glance, and then frowned.

'Is it not more probable,' she persisted, 'that we have slipped through? Had we been blessed by Light, we would have been blunted, perhaps even destroyed. But, in turn, we are not her children. Not any more. Evading commitment, even the realm finds itself undecided about us.'

'An interesting possibility,' he admitted after a moment.

'Something in our nature has placed us between worlds,' she continued. 'I wonder . . . is this even Dark?'

'It must be. The Terondai is aspected.'

'Aspected?'

'Magic comes in many flavours,' he replied. 'The Terondai is a gate, a portal. It can take us nowhere but into the heart of its power, and that power is Dark.'

'Then . . . where is she?'

'Imagine a realm virtually without limit, captain.'

'I see little value in a gate that leaves people lost, unable to

734

take their bearings.' She gestured. 'Where is her precious Chamber of Night?'

'Upon our own world,' Resh said, 'there may be but one gate, one egress. But what if there are infinite worlds? What if the Terondai leads to countless other gates, each affixed to its own world?'

'Then we are truly lost, warlock.'

'But is Mother Dark?'

She scowled. 'Is this the source of her power? Is this how Draconus made her into a goddess?'

'I don't know. Possibly.'

'Have you learned what you needed to, Resh? Can we now attempt to return to our world? Assuming that is even possible. I am sorely unbalanced by this.'

He studied her in the gloom. 'Is each aspect of sorcery truly closed from all the others? Does that even make sense? What if those aspects of magic are themselves realms of a sort? Should there not be more gates? Gates that pass between them? From Dark to Light, perhaps, or into Denul, even? If so, then who fashioned these portals? And what of Draconus, who had the power to create such a gate in the Citadel itself? Whence came such knowledge?'

She shook her head, knowing that he expected no answers from her.

'Captain,' Resh continued, 'where is the gate for the Shake?'

'*What?*'

'Or perhaps it does not yet exist. Perhaps it will fall to me to conjure it into being. Or indeed, to both of us.'

'Me? Better you had brought Caplo! I am a stranger to such magicks!'

'We are far from done here,' Resh said. 'We have taken but the first step on this journey. It falls to us, Finarra Stone, to find the gate of our aspect.'

'Our aspect? We don't have an aspect!'

'I believe that we do. Neither extreme suits us, only that which dwells between the two.' He shrugged. 'Name it Shadow . . . to match the cast of our skin, yes?'

'And you believe we will find our new gate from here? From Dark?'

He shrugged. 'Or from Light. Does it matter which? Both realms bear edges. Borderlands. Places of transition. We must simply find such a place and claim it as our own.'

'And how will you create this gate?'

'I have no idea.'

'We are not returning to the Citadel, are we?'

'I think not, captain.'

'Our camp gear and food remains with our horses – will you have us consume ether for sustenance?'

He eyed her with an odd, inquisitive expression. 'Perhaps,' he replied, 'faith will provide.'

*       *       *

The morning air had been damp and cloying on the day that Captain Kellaras parted company with both Gripp Galas and Hish Tulla, just north of Kharkanas. Flakes of snow drifted down and the night's fall had settled upon the rutted track, filling the deep imprints left by horses and oxen, and to Kellaras it seemed as if the world struggled to erase what had been, seeking a cleaner promise for what was to come.

The delusion was momentary. War was coming, he reminded himself as he checked the girth-straps of his horse. Impatient and heartless, it would crawl across the season, out from its familiar nest of thaw and heat, and in his mind's eye he saw a vision of frozen corpses and lurid gashes of red, arrayed upon the white ground. *Whatever was pure soon leaves. Even eyes can soil a scene.*

When he turned he found Gripp Galas seated astride his horse. Behind the man, already some distance down the western track of the crossroads, Hish Tulla rode on. Whatever parting she had shared with her husband had been brief and quiet. Kellaras cleared his throat. 'I would still rather you permitted me to accompany you, Gripp.'

'Pelk is the only company I require,' the old man replied. The shrug he then offered was apologetic. 'I will see her off to Kharkanas as soon as we are done.'

Kellaras glanced at Pelk, but her expression was closed where she sat astride her mount. The night just past had been one of fierce, if virtually silent, lovemaking. The woman to whom he had given his heart had a way of disappearing in front of his eyes. 'If that is her wish,' he said.

Gripp smiled. 'Pelk?'

'It is,' she replied, twisting in her saddle to squint at the north track awaiting her and Galas. 'If the captain will be found there.'

Kellaras shook his head in wonder. 'I shall, unless our forces have been assembled upon a field of battle.'

'If that should be the case,' Gripp Galas said, his smile falling away, 'then our efforts will have been in vain.'

'Best hurry then,' Kellaras said.

Nodding, Gripp had collected up the reins. With Pelk at his side, he rode on to the north track, plunging into the scorched forest. Kellaras had waited until he lost sight of them before swinging his mount southward.

It was now a week later. Kellaras haunted the Citadel, watching the rise of new rituals appearing among the priesthood, the processions at dusk and midnight, while at dawn the robed figures knelt with heads bowed, as if greeting with sorrow the unseen sun. He had witnessed the solemn snuffing of candles, the guttering of lanterns left to burn out the last of the oil. He had seen High Priestess Emral Lanear overseeing the daily obeisance and prostrations with glassy eyes.

And in the midst of all this, a growing paranoia suffused the Citadel, until the old royal keep acquired the habiliments of a prison. It was pathetic, as far as Kellaras was concerned. Particularly when faith was so simply and undeniably announced by a stain upon the skin. The endless spying could not even skirt the notion of potential blasphemies among the believers. Instead, it was raw in its politics, a secular jostling of power and influence around an indifferent centre. And through it all there was the reek of impending panic.

But today, word had come of a miracle in the city's Winter Market, an unofficial procession led by Endest Silann – whose hands were purported to bleed without surcease. And then, providing proof to the tales told by surviving Wardens, a dragon had descended upon a square in the city, only to be sent away by the selfsame prophet of darkness.

Kellaras wished he was drunk, if only to weaken whatever credence such tales were worth. Instead, in answer to a summons, he stood in the ancestral family chamber of the Purake waiting for Silchas Ruin to take notice of his arrival. The white-skinned warrior was at a table, leaning over a large, ornately illustrated vellum map, one detailed enough to note elevations, with scrawled observations pertaining to ease of passage among various trails and tracks. The work was Kadaspala's, devised in the wake of the wars against the Forulkan and the Jhelarkan, a belated gift the value of which had been questionable, at least until this moment.

Finally, Silchas Ruin stepped back, and slumped into a high-backed chair. He eyed Kellaras for a moment before speaking. 'A dragon to mock our walls. A season to mock our rest. Have you seen Grizzin Farl?'

'No, milord, not for many days.'

Sighing, Silchas gestured at the map. 'We will meet the Legion at the Valley of Tarns. It is shallow and broad, the old riverbed wide and not too stony. There are defiles to the east of it, the tangled wreckage of a burned forest to the west. Tell me, do you think Lord Urusander will oblige us?'

'He is reputed to be confident, milord.' Kellaras hesitated, and then added, 'The valley is known to him, since it is where he first mustered the Legion, before marching south to meet the Forulkan.'

'Will he appreciate the irony?'

'I do not know him well enough to answer you, milord.'

'Hunn Raal will delight in it,' Silchas Ruin predicted. 'I have received a missive from Captain Prazek—'

'*Captain*, milord?'

'Field promotion, one presumes. The Hust Legion will soon depart the training grounds.'

'Prazek judges them ready, then?'

'Of course not! Don't be foolish, Kellaras. No,' Silchas rose, suddenly impatient, 'we have simply run out of time.'

A bell rang in the outer room.

With a flash of irritation twisting his features, Silchas snapped, 'Enter!'

The Houseblade who stepped into the chamber saluted both men and said, 'Lord Silchas, there has been an ... occurrence, at the Terondai. A monk of the Shake and a Warden were seen to be taken.'

'Taken where?'

'Milord, they strode on to the pattern, and then simply vanished. Another monk is even now approaching the Chamber of Night—'

'Unchallenged?'

The young woman before them blinked. 'The High Priestess dismissed the guards upon the approach some time ago, milord. It seems ... there is nothing to defend.'

'This monk,' said Kellaras. 'Is he known?'

'No sir. Hooded to hide his face. But the one who vanished in the Terondai was Warlock Resh.'

There was a moment when none moved, and then Silchas reached for his sword-belt. 'Both of you, ready weapons and attend me.'

The three set out in haste.

*Caplo Dreem. Sheccanto's favourite assassin. And this time, Anomander does not stand in his path.*

\*      \*      \*

A single Houseblade had followed Caplo Dreem, accosting him at the entrance to the corridor leading to the Chamber of Night's door. Irritated and mostly unmindful, the assassin left the man's corpse sprawled across the cracked flagstones and continued on until he faced the sweating blackwood barrier. The polished wood was now crowded with carved runes that framed illustrated panels. Caplo paused, frowning at the images for a moment. *Scenes of gift giving. That one must be Draconus, and that faintest of outlines ... Mother Dark. Or what's left of her. Odd, isn't it, how it is the goddess who receives gifts? What shall we make of him who bears them?*

739

But such ponderings were but distractions. A wild fever burned in Caplo Dreem, the hunger to unfold, one into many, as if snapping the chains of his own flesh and bone. He bared his teeth in anticipation, and then kicked against the door to the Chamber of Night.

The strength within him was startling even to his own eyes. The blow proved savage enough to splinter the wood, sending cracks through the delicate carvings. The ancient iron hinges broke with popping sounds, and a second kick sent the portal toppling with a heavy crash upon the threshold.

Bitter cold assailed Caplo and he voiced an animal snarl in answer. *Take me then, Old Blood. We have known restraint for too long.*

He blurred, burgeoned, and with visceral jolts veered into a dozen lithe, feline forms, each one black as the surrounding darkness. In his wake he left the tatters of his clothing, his worn boots, the leather belts and straps bearing his knives, and the hood and heavy wolf fur cloak, all heaped into a disordered pile.

The earth beneath his many padded feet was frozen clay, slick and unyielding. From twelve pairs of eyes, he studied the way ahead – the stunted, leafless trees rising from the plain, the wayward lines of boulders marking out mysterious patterns upon the vague slopes a short distance before him, and off to the right – those many eyes narrowed – the skeletal frame of a wheeled wagon. Even incomplete, it was massive, almost beyond comprehension. To look upon it was to reel with the jarring impossibility of its scale – and he felt his ears flattening with instinctive fear.

A man stood near one enormous wooden wheel. He had turned upon Caplo's arrival.

*I see you, Draconus! And yet . . . yet –*

Spreading out, the panthers edged forward, tails twitching, twelve pairs of eyes fixing upon the man who now slowly approached. The promise of violence flared within Caplo. *Old Blood, why did I deny you for so long?*

'You Shake are a presumptuous lot, aren't you?'

*He is weak. Weaker than I expected. As if some part*

*of his soul is missing. Even more pleasing, he is unarmed.*

Draconus shook his head. 'D'ivers now, as well. The Shake consort with forces they do not understand. Not just the cursed legacy of desperate Eresal eludes that understanding, but so too the one you would now challenge.'

As Caplo drew closer, he saw chains strewn upon the ground, the rough links stretching back towards the wagon, vanishing beneath its vast bed. Scores, perhaps hundreds, they made a web upon the frozen clay, the heavy shackles at their ends gaping and glistening with frost. Seeing them, Caplo felt faint unease rippling through his dozen bodies.

'You mean to kill her, Caplo Dreem? You will fail. She is well beyond your reach.'

Caplo focused his thoughts, sent them out towards Draconus. *'Do you hear me, lord?'*

Draconus grunted. 'I've listened since the moment of your arrival, D'ivers. My weakness, my incompleteness . . . these hands' – he lifted them – 'you deem less than weapons.'

*'I care nothing for her. The power here is yours and yours alone.'*

'Not any more. Such was my gift to the woman I love.'

*'And who are you to give it?'*

Draconus shrugged. 'Here, I am named the Suzerain of Night.'

*'The Tiste House of Dracons is a deceit. Old scents, known to the Old Blood within me. You are an Azathanai.'*

Reaching down, Draconus collected up a length of chain. 'If it's me you want, assassin, come along then. You can collect your coin from Urusander later – or is it Hunn Raal? I would not imagine Sheccanto or even Skelenal have given this deed their blessing.'

*'Now you speak plain, Draconus. No highborn poetry to ride your last breaths.'*

The Azathanai shrugged. 'I can't be bothered.'

The twelve panthers now surrounded Draconus, giving Caplo a view of the huge man from every angle. Somehow, this did not confuse him, and the flood of senses was a delicious roar in his mind, rising like flames.

The Old Blood was not interested in subtlety. Caplo attacked at once, from all sides. Twelve panthers, converging upon a single enemy.

The chain lashed out, wrapping tight upon a leaping form, and Draconus yanked it close even as the remaining beasts slammed into him. Caplo felt his many fangs sink deep into the man's flesh. He felt his claws score deep furrows upon the muscles of the Azathanai's broad back – down to scrape along ribs and shoulder blades. More talons plunged into the man's stomach. The muscles there clenched suddenly to trap those claws, defying every effort at evisceration, but Caplo held on. Jaws from another beast ground tight around the back of Draconus's thick neck, seeking the windpipe.

Through all of this, somehow the Azathanai remained standing. The panther he had snared with the chain came within reach of his hands, and, releasing the chain, Draconus drove thumbs deep into the beast's throat. Blood sprayed and the cat screamed.

Caplo felt its sudden death in a wave of agony.

Flinging the carcass away, Draconus reached round to tear loose the animal clinging to his back and neck, and the Azathanai's strength was appalling. Unmindful of his own torn flesh, he pulled the writhing breast around, and then broke its spine with a savage twist of his wrists.

Caplo howled.

Fangs and claws tore flesh to shreds, ripped through muscles, yet still Draconus remained upright, his wide-legged stance unyielding.

A third panther – the one with its foreclaws sunk deep into the Azathanai's gut – died beneath the skull-shattering blow of a single fist.

Caplo released his sense of all but one cat – leaving them to fight on by instinct – and flung his strength into that single creature, which had locked its jaws about the man's left thigh, and now, writhing and spinning round with a surge of unnatural strength, he toppled Draconus. The remaining panthers closed in to finish him.

Another died, neck broken, its head suddenly loose in the grip of the man's hands.

But the panthers savaged the writhing, kicking, blood-soaked figure.

Caplo shrieked when a lone hand stabbed into the gut of the beast he rode, and in a welter of blood and fluids his guts were pulled out from their cavity. The assassin fled the dying cat, found another.

But Draconus found that one immediately, rolling to pin it beneath him, even as he began punching, each blow of his fist shattering ribs, flensing the lungs beneath them.

The death of so many beasts broke something in Caplo. Howling, he tore himself free of the Azathanai. The six surviving panthers reeled in retreat, flanks heaving, ears flat, fangs bared. They halted a half-dozen paces from the prone man.

Who then laughed from where he lay on his back. 'Come, let us finish it.'

*'Why won't you die!'*

'I should have,' Draconus replied, shifting on to his side to spit out a gout of blood. 'Or you *would* have, since I summoned my Finnest.' He coughed, spat again. 'But it seems to have gone astray . . .' He groaned and pushed himself to his hands and knees. Blood poured from his wounds, making thick puddles beneath him. 'And that's not good.' He glanced over with dull red eyes. 'Still, I'll leave one of you. For the chains. Though I doubt you'd deem them a mercy.'

Hissing, Caplo backed away.

'You all thought me unmindful,' Draconus said. 'An impediment to your newfound powers. You, Syntara, Raal, even my beloved. But things have been unleashed. Indeed,' he paused to cough again, 'it's all becoming something of a mess.' He waved one hand back towards the massive wagon. 'But I'm working on it. Take some faith in that. Tell your Higher Graces this: I will see it all through, and by that alone, you will one day find a throne awaiting you.'

*'We have no need of a throne! We have no realm to rule!'*

Draconus showed red-stained teeth in a cruel grin. 'Heed

your fucking leopard instincts, Caplo, and find some patience. Restraint, even. I'm working as fast as I can.'

Caplo crouched his forms low, studied the ravaged Azathanai. *'You promise us a realm?'*

'And a throne. Do they seem gifts? Remind yourself of that the day you need to defend them both.'

*'Where will we find these . . . gifts?'*

Draconus grunted a bitter laugh. 'Not in your precious monasteries.' He pushed himself to his feet, stood tottering, his dripping hands held out slightly for balance. 'You have a choice here. Leave, and seek those already upon the shore. Or try me again. But should you prevail against me, ruin will haunt you all – with my blessing.' And he offered Caplo another crimson smile, this one faintly sad.

The six panthers turned to depart.

Behind them, Draconus raised his voice. 'That way, Caplo? Are you sure?'

Snarling, the assassin padded to the gate. Moments before passing through the shattered doorway, he sembled into his Tiste form, and then staggered to the massive wounds upon his naked body.

*I should have thought of that.*

Gasping, blinded by pain, he stumbled through the portal.

\*     \*     \*

Since seeing High Priestess Emral Lanear, Orfantal had struggled with an overwhelming desire to curl into her lap. She seemed a mother of bad habits, and this intrigued him. He was not interested in making sense of it – thinking too much about things hadn't done him much good, thus far. There was something clean and pure in his sense of the guardian wolves he had on occasion conjured into being, and what he could feel of their minds told him that there were creatures in the world – in all the worlds – that lived simpler lives. He wanted to emulate such ways of living.

And so he haunted her, keeping his eyes hidden within the wreaths of smoke drifting around her as she sat, unmoving apart from the steady rise and fall of the water-pipe's mouth-piece in one hand and the swell and ebb of her chest. So many things were possible now. He could drift unseen through the Citadel, wandering its corridors, sliding beneath doors and into chambers that had once been forbidden him. His body, small as it was, could of course achieve none of this. So he had left it behind, in the cell where he slept, with Ribs lying against the door.

He rode the currents of Kurald Galain, but for all their enticements, from the fascinating patterns and sly invitations of the Terondai to the red tears of Mother Dark's eyes – unable to look away in the palms of the priest, Endest Silann – Orfantal found himself drawn back to the High Priestess, who still sat alone in her chamber, gaze heavy upon the slightly open door, as if awaiting someone.

But for the moment, none in the Citadel had thought to seek her out, despite the two strangers who had unlocked the pattern of passage in the Terondai – one of its many wondrous gifts – and disappeared from sight. The discovery of a murdered guard in the corridor leading to the Chamber of Night had sent alarm winging among the Houseblades and their officers, only to somehow deftly avoid – by choice or chance – the many acolytes of the priesthood.

She sat unknowing, then, her right leg folded over the left, like a queen upon a throne.

Distant agitations in the sorcerous darkness brushed Orfantal's awareness, and a moment's focus made out, in his mind's eye, the figures of Silchas Ruin, Captain Kellaras, and a woman Houseblade, hurrying towards the Chamber of Night.

Orfantal hesitated. Seeing too much made things complicated all over again. His spirit, wandering in this way, possessed no voice, and what it heard was thin and muted, as if every sound came through walls. He could draw as close as he liked to Emral Lanear, but make nothing known of his presence.

That was probably just as well. Some things had a way of frightening people. Even so, he groped for a means of warning her that things were happening, and that blood had been spilled outside the Chamber of Night.

So intent was his focus upon her now, he was caught unawares by the sudden arrival of Endest Silann.

But she looked up and seemed to sag in her throne. 'If only we could all find someone else to carry our anguish,' she said.

The priest, looking ashen and drained, tilted his head slightly. 'Or send it out and away in white streams of smoke.'

'If she regrets her lack of success,' Lanear replied, 'at last we find common ground.'

'There has been violence in the Chamber of Night.'

The High Priestess drew hard on the mouthpiece, then spoke with held breath. 'The realm beyond those doors is a fraught place.'

'A Shake assassin reached that realm.'

She let out a slow, lengthy sigh of smoke. 'Caplo Dreem returned, then. To finish whatever he intended the first time.'

'You seem unconcerned.'

'Was she?'

'Lord Draconus defeated the assassin. Apparently. Terribly wounded and naked, Caplo re-emerged, too weak to resist arrest by Lord Silchas Ruin. A few words were exchanged before the assassin fell unconscious. There is talk of summary execution. And a pronouncement of war upon the Shake.'

'Tell me of her concern.'

Silann's gaze fell. 'I cannot. But Lord Draconus did not escape unharmed from the encounter. She attends him with . . . solicitude.'

'Where is Cedorpul?'

'High Priestess, I unleashed magic in the city. I sought to bless the citizens of Kharkanas, in ways she might desire – if only she would tell us. Instead . . .' His voice caught then, and it was a moment before he could continue. 'Anger proves a poor fuel for forgiveness.'

'Cedorpul?'

'It fell to an Eleint, descending from the sky, to halt my . . . my largesse.'

'All on this day?' Abruptly, Lanear laughed, only to stifle the sound. 'Forgive me, Endest. I was, for some time here, musing on the span of a single bowl's pleasure. The world is a place of many rooms indeed, but in this one, I knew the luxury of peace.' She slowly set the mouthpiece down on to its silver tray. 'Where, I ask a third time, is Cedorpul?'

'I am informed, High Priestess, that with grievous outrage and indignation, Cedorpul has set out upon the trail of Warlock Resh and the Warden officer who accompanied him through the Gate of Darkness.'

'Alone?'

'So I understand. I knew a fever following my audience with the dragon. All I can report is what I was subsequently told.'

'A fever. Yours or hers?'

He shrugged.

'Will you lead me to where Silchas Ruin has taken the assassin?'

'Of course, High Priestess. But one other matter awaits us.'

'And that is?'

'The child upon your lap,' Endest replied.

Startled, Orfantal fled the chamber.

＊　　＊　　＊

Kellaras had not participated in the rough handling of Caplo Dreem. Instead, he and the other Houseblade had but followed Silchas Ruin as the lord dragged the unconscious assassin by one ankle down stairs and along corridors, to a wing of the old palace where waited scores of empty cells. For all Ruin's outrage, the traverse had seemed cruel, but cruelty was gathering in this last remaining brother.

Selecting a cell, Silchas pulled Caplo inside, and then ordered the Houseblade to affix shackles to the man's ankles and wrists. This action stirred Caplo to consciousness and he blinked up at the young woman, watching as the thick iron rings clicked shut one by one. His dark eyes tracked her retreat when she was done.

Silchas Ruin faced the prisoner, and made to speak, but Caplo lifted a hand with a weak gesture that rattled the links, and said, 'My apologies, milord, for the slain guard. Impatience is a twitching blade and no thought slowed my hand. For what it is worth, it is the only crime for which I accept your purview.'

Silchas grunted. 'An assault upon the sacred precincts of Mother Dark?'

'She claims less of it than you think.'

'And Draconus?'

Caplo glanced away. 'A hard man to kill. Did I not say as much before passing out? My mumbled . . . confession. Let it not be said I shied from the truth.'

'He will not demand your head, assassin?'

'I doubt it.'

'Why not?'

'He's busy.'

Silchas scowled, crossing his arms. After a moment, he cast Kellaras a beleaguered look. 'Step forward, captain, I beg you. Convince me against persisting in wasting everyone's time. Better yet, separate this man's head from the rest of him.'

'Forgive me, milord, but I don't understand any of this. Have the Shake declared war? Is this man here at Sheccanto's behest? True, a god died, but the blame for that must surely belong to the Azathanai, T'riss.' Kellaras eyed the prisoner. 'Caplo Dreem, who sent you?'

'No one.'

Kellaras mused on that reply, and found no falsity in it. 'Where did Warlock Resh go, when he and that Warden vanished at the Terondai?'

'I don't know.'

'Then neither had knowledge of your intentions?'

Caplo grinned, moving to sit up with his back against the wall. 'I had a suspicion. They knew that much.'

'A suspicion? Regarding what?'

'Oddly enough, though I found the truth of it, I find myself subsequently reluctant to pronounce it. I have,' he added, closing his eyes as he rested his head against the wall, 'made revision.'

'Please explain what that means,' Kellaras said.

'I was in error. Not every truth is a crime. Though,' he blinked open his eyes and smiled up at Kellaras, 'too many of them are. Still, not this time. Foolish me, but then, ignorance is a poor excuse for anything, and I'll not hide behind it.'

'Do you expect to live, Caplo Dreem?'

The man shrugged, and then winced at his wounds.

Silchas Ruin growled under his breath. 'A slain Houseblade of House Purake. Confound the rest, but this crime stands unchallenged.'

'With regret.'

The lord settled one white hand upon his grip of the sword at his side. Iron began sliding from the scabbard, then halted at a sound from the doorway behind them.

'Belay that, lord,' said Emral Lanear, stepping into the now crowded cell. Kellaras saw the priest, Endest Silann, edge in behind her, his hands devoid of cloth or bandage, the wounds dripping freely to paint his fingers. His face belonged to that of an aged man.

'House Purake claims the right of punishment,' Silchas Ruin said to the High Priestess.

'No doubt,' she replied, eyeing Caplo Dreem. 'But I would question him first.'

'You waste your time,' Silchas replied. 'He is all riddles.'

'I have no interest in Mother Dark,' said Caplo Dreem to Lanear. 'I have never represented a threat to her.'

'And yet, you trespass.'

'My argument was with Lord Draconus. We had it out, and now we are done with each other.'

'With at least one corpse in your wake,' she pointed out.

'Release him,' said Endest Silann.

All turned to face the priest. The command seemed to have momentarily left Silchas Ruin speechless. Emral Lanear glanced back at her companion. 'By your command, Endest?'

'No,' he replied.

'She makes her wishes known to you? You had led me to believe that Mother Dark's attendance upon you yielded nothing of her will. Has that changed?'

'Draconus is wounded, and this angers her,' Endest replied. 'Nonetheless, Caplo Dreem is to be banished from Kharkanas. That is all.'

'What of justice for the House of Purake?' Silchas Ruin demanded. 'Is that not a virtue to be defended by our goddess? We, who are sworn to her service? Will she deny us this as well?'

No response came from Endest Silann. He turned to leave, and Kellaras distinctly heard the priest mutter, 'Come along now, boy, this was not for you.'

Even the High Priestess seemed at a loss. 'Lord Silchas, I am sorry,' she said.

He glared at her, and then made a sharp gesture with one hand. 'No matter.' He shot her a look and added, 'How does it sit with you, High Priestess? Being . . . superfluous?'

Her expression tightened, but she said nothing.

'Oh, Kellaras,' sighed Silchas Ruin, 'free the man.'

\*     \*     \*

Rise Herat stood in the unlit corridor, staring at a tapestry. The absence of light proved no obstacle to his study of the dragons woven into the scene. He had been atop the tower when the Eleint sank down from the heavy clouds in a spiralling descent that took it into the heart of Kharkanas. It was well, he reflected yet again, that he was not a believer in omens.

*Still, even I must lend credence to the notion of harbingers. We are in difficult times to be sure, but our disputes seem petty in the face of such powers loose once again in the world. There are forces at work far beyond our frail borders.*

*But anger and fear make an enemy of humility, and of all the emotions within reach of a desperate mind, they loom closest.*

*If only desperation was not a plague among mortals. If only our lives were not spent rushing from one breach to the next.*

There had been word of Endest Silann's blessing of peace in the Winter Market, and the anguish left in its wake. But how many now denied the simple truth of that aftermath, its rattling lesson of despair? *Peace haunts us like a dream, an echo half forgotten, but still whispering its perfect promise.*

The ancient tapestry offered no lies, no inventions of the imagination. The dragons depicted were accurate. In the scene seven of the creatures whirled above a burning city. There was no attribution to this work of art – even the age that spawned it was lost to memory, and nothing of the city itself was recognizable. *Nothing but the river running through it, black as a fissure in bedrock.*

If Kharkanas rested upon ruins, they'd yet to be revealed. Only the temple at the heart of the Citadel hinted of a world now vanished.

Then again, the city trapped by thread and dye was burning, dying within a firestorm. In such a storm, even the rocks would shatter, crumbling to dust.

*Omens are for fools, but every truth of the future resides in the present, if only we have the will to see.*

After a time, he realized that he was no longer alone. Turning, he frowned at the figure standing a step behind him. 'Grizzin Farl, for all your girth, you move in silence.'

The Azathanai sighed. 'Humble apologies, historian.'

'I was thinking of you.'

'Indeed?'

'Vast forces at work, making a mockery of our conceits. Was this all begun by the woman we call T'riss? Or, as I suspect, should we look to Lord Draconus? Or you, perhaps, with your curious presence here, or, rather, your *persistence*?'

'You would blame others for your ills?'

'A feeble deflection, Azathanai. The realm of Eternal Night, or whatever it's called, is too vast for us Tiste Andii to call home. And do not offend me by suggesting that Mother Dark

751

lays claim to it. She is but an interloper. For all we know, she wanders as one lost, or even in fear, cowering at her Consort's side.'

'Neither, I should think,' Grizzin Farl replied.

'Dragons,' said Rise Herat, turning back to look upon the tapestry once more. 'Will we see more of them? Do they gather like vultures spying a wounded creature? Do they but await our inevitable death?'

Grizzin Farl scratched through his beard, his eyes glittering from some unseen light. 'Now you describe a deceit in truth, historian. The fate of Kurald Galain barely registers with creatures such as the Eleint, and what they feed upon is nothing so crass as flesh and bone. Though, it must be said, they will indulge from time to time. It is important, Rise Herat, that you understand something of their nature.'

'Oh? Please, continue.'

Ignoring the ironic invitation, Grizzin Farl stepped up beside the historian and squinted at the tapestry. 'Inclined to scavenging,' he said. 'Less the hunter, then, than the opportunist. They dislike, even fear, each other's company—'

'This depiction suggests the opposite.'

'No, it doesn't.'

'Explain.'

'They become a Storm, sir. A Storm of Dragons, and that is a terrible thing. No single Eleint can resist, once a certain threshold is crossed. Gather enough of the beasts – create a big enough Storm – and they merge. They become one beast, possessing many heads, many limbs, but a single, undeniable identity. Such a Storm has a name among the Azathanai. Tiamatha. Goddess of destruction. *Tiam* among the Thel Akai. The Fever Queen.' He paused, and then nodded at the tapestry. 'Here, merely a Storm. Ill chance that it should gather above a city, but you well see its annihilating force.'

'The fire – that is *incidental*?'

Grizzin Farl shrugged. 'Something drew them all there. There is that, I suppose.'

'Something? What thing, Azathanai?'

'Unknown. Perhaps . . . a wounded gate?'

'Abyss take you, Farl! How can a gate be wounded?'

'Careless usage, I imagine. That, or some form of elemental opposition.'

*Elemental opposition?* 'Such as Light upon Dark?'

'Not necessarily, historian. Forgive me if my careless words have alarmed you. You now fear some kind of violence to attend the union of Mother Dark and Father Light, but that is far from incumbent.'

'I fear the violence *leading* to that union!'

A flicker of sorrow softened the huge man's features. 'Yes, the necessity for a delicate balance awaits you. I see that now. But still, be at ease. Dragons have indeed returned to the world, but they are scattered and would remain so, given the choice. The Storm is an unpleasant manifestation even for the Eleint trapped within it.'

'Never mind that – what of the gate? What of this damned marriage?'

'If neither resists, all will be well.'

'And if one proves . . . reluctant?'

'The mere recognition of necessity lends one wisdom, don't you think? Enough to ease the pain of such reluctance.' He paused, and then added, 'At last, something manifest to give breadth to your prayers?'

'Why, yes,' Rise Herat snapped. 'How thoughtful of you.'

'Does this tapestry possess a name, by any chance?'

'Threaded upon the back. "The Last Day".'

'Ah. Nothing else, then?'

'No. I would think,' Rise bitterly added, 'nothing more was necessary.'

*       *       *

He felt her touch upon his shoulder, and then she spoke. '*You heal quickly, my love.*'

'I was once beset in a like manner,' Draconus said. 'Back then, it was hounds.' He hesitated, feeling her essence closing gently around him. 'Hounds are cleverer than panthers. The assassin was new to his curse. He left too much to their instincts. Cats hunt in the manner of pinning or binding

753

their prey, clinging tight, jaws about the windpipe, until the prey suffocates. But hounds . . . well, as I said. They are cleverer.'

'*Yet you survived both.*'

He said nothing for a long moment, and then sighed heavily. 'My love, what would you have me do?'

Mother Dark's embrace was all-consuming, impossibly tender, and in utterly engulfing him she took away the world: the forest and standing stones, the unfinished wagon and its chains, the pools of blood upon the ground. '*Beloved, my heart is for you. As it was, as it is, and as it shall ever be.*'

He nodded. 'As you will, then.'

'*You tremble. Does my touch hurt you?*'

'No.'

'*Then . . . what?*'

He was thinking of the D'ivers hounds, all those centuries past. Assailing him from all sides. Even with the fullness of his power, they had nearly torn him apart. 'Nothing of import,' he said after a moment. 'Just memories.'

'*Let not the past haunt you, my love. In that realm, we are all ghosts.*'

'As you say.'

She kept the world away for some time, and he was content with that.

˷   *   *   *

'They don't look much like wolves,' Sergeant Savarro said to her husband.

The huge man tugged at his beard. 'Surprised they ain't ate up those little ones we brought along.'

Savarro grunted. 'No. Seems they like other children just fine. Playing with 'em like they was pups or something.'

Veered into their canine forms, a dozen Jhelarkan hostages tumbled with the children of the refugee families from the Warden's fort. The new snowfall in the compound was all churned up by their antics, and high-pitched squeals and shouts joined the chorus of mock growls. The scene was appallingly bucolic.

'It ain't so bad,' Savarro continued.

'You're trying too hard,' Ristand said, grimacing. 'You should've let me change my vote. We should've stayed a night or two and then got us out of here. They now call this place *Howls* for a fucking good reason. The mules are so scared they stopped eating.'

She sighed. 'That's what makes me so sick of you, you know that? You keep changing what happened to suit what you're thinking right now. Fucking men.'

'I ain't changed nothing! You're just remembering it wrong, like a typical woman.'

'I've seen you eyeing that Nassaras.'

'Not that again!'

'Go on then! Drag her into the barn, tear her clothes off and rut like a damned hare. A *fat* damned hare! Slap your paws on her big tits. Bite at her neck. Make her groan as you try crawling up inside her—'

'Abyss take us, woman, let's go!'

Together they rose and hurried back into the keep.

Just inside the entrance, Lord Kagamandra had to quickly step to one side to let the two Wardens past. He paused, watching them rush through the dining hall, and then thump quickly up the stairs.

Trout stepped into view from near the hearth. 'Not again,' he muttered.

Kagamandra opened the front door and glanced outside, then shut it again and returned to the dining hall. 'No blood,' he said. 'I mistook those screams.'

'Numbers went down fast,' Trout said, shifting where he stood, absently pulling at his stubbly cheeks hard enough to expose the red rims below his dark eyes. 'Might be they ain't feeling so crowded any more. It's been days since we last stumbled on to a chewed-up carcass.'

'The blind one still survives, and that's surprising,' Kagamandra said musingly, as he moved to sit down at the table.

'More wine, milord?'

'It's not even noon.'

'Aye. More wine?'

Kagamandra eyed the ugly captain. 'You'd see my mind dulled, made witless, to take the sting from my plans for vengeance. Since when did the fates of Scara Bandaris and Silchas Ruin concern you?'

'It ain't them, milord. It's you. You just got here, and all you been talking about is leaving again. With Silchas in Kharkanas, no doubt, and Scara probably riding with Urusander, you'd end up stuck between two Abyss-damned armies. It's a simple fact, sir, that they needed to send the hostages somewhere. Remote, out of the way, peaceful even.'

'Thank you, Trout. You always had a way of reining me in.'

'Sarcasm ill fits you, milord. Besides, conscience has an ugly face, most times.' And he smiled to make even more ghastly his visage.

'Still,' Kagamandra said, 'if a war is in the offing, what are we doing here?'

Trout pulled a chair close and slumped down in it. He squinted at the flames of the hearth. From somewhere in the kitchen, there was a shout and pots clanged as Igur Lout's new assistants once more got underfoot. 'Aye,' Trout said. 'Braphen said as much, too. It's that damned itch, isn't it? Takes us all. Riding out, fuck the winter and all that. Just riding out, back into war.'

'Feeling old, Trout?' Kagamandra asked quietly.

'We all are, is my bet, sir. And still . . .' He shook his head, half his face twisting into a grin as he glanced at Kagamandra. 'We could do some damage, hey? I was never much for Urusander's bleatings, and Hunn Raal's a pig and I don't expect that's changed any. But I wonder, sir, what happens when you find yourself facing Scara Bandaris across that field? Will the pranks continue when it's life and death on the bloody line?'

'The notion has occurred to me,' Kagamandra replied. 'I cannot say what clout Scara possesses among the high command in the Legion. If I am able, I will speak to him and attempt to dissuade him. This civil war is a bitter legacy of our past triumphs.'

'Scara's would be a lone voice,' Trout said.

'No. There is another. Captain Sharenas.'

Trout's gaze narrowed on his lord, and then he nodded, returning his attention to the hearth. 'Need more wood,' he said, grunting as he rose. 'Cold in the bones won't do, if we're to ride.'

Kagamandra smiled at his old friend.

Trout paused. 'What of the Wardens?'

'I'll put it to them, but to be honest, Trout, I think the fight's out of this bunch.'

'You begin to speak like a soldier again, milord. I've missed that. I'll get some wood.'

Kagamandra watched the man depart.

From almost directly above came a rhythmic thumping, while clanging and Lout's ongoing harangue continued in the kitchen. Outside, children and beasts frolicked in the snow.

He rubbed at his face. *Ah, Sharenas. I cannot stay in one place, it seems. Snapping jaws upon my flanks, I am inclined to bolt.*

*My betrothed? I cannot say. Together and apart, we travel lost to each other, as the fates demand.*

*This keep seems paltry and small. Not a place she could call home, and I'll not insult her with the offer.*

A child outside attempted a howl, and moments later the hostages gave answer.

Shivering, Kagamandra looked to the ebbing fire, but found little heat there. Trout had best hurry with that wood.

# NINETEEN

'RESTITUTION,' SAID VATHA URUSANDER, 'SEEMS SUCH a simple concept. A past wrong made right, even should generations span the injustice. Even if questions of personal culpability no longer obtain, there are the spoils of the crime to consider.'

Renarr slid her gaze from her adoptive father where he stood by the window, over to young Sheltatha Lore, who had a way of making adolescence itself a triumph. Long limbs draped upon the divan, her slim torso slightly curled in feline grace – as if she but awaited the sculptor and the chisel, the unblinking eye finding its myriad obsessions. *'Art,'* Gallan once said, *'is the sweet language of obsession.'* Renarr thought that she'd begun to comprehend the poet's assertion, as she idly gave herself the artist's eye when looking upon her not-so-innocent charge.

In the meantime, Urusander continued. 'A concept may seem simple, until its careful consideration unveils unending complications. How does one measure such spoils when cause and effect settle one upon the other in endless repetition, like sediments in stone? Raise up that first cause like a spire – the years after will see it weathered to a stub, its solidity reduced to grains, its height levelled amidst the heaps of its own detritus. Even then, how does one assign a value to all that was gained, over all that was potentially lost? Is innocence worth more than knowing? Is freedom worth more than seeming necessity? What of privilege and greed? And power and force? Are they a match in coin, or weight of gold, to destitution and loss? Helplessness and impotence?'

Plucking at some thread or lint, Sheltatha Lore sighed. 'Dear me, milord, surely you comprehend that restitution holds a thousand meanings, ten thousand – numbers unending, in fact.' One supple arm reached out and down to collect up the goblet of wine, which she brought to her lips. A careless mouthful, and then, 'What about the victim indifferent to gold? Contemptuous of coin? Or the one whose beliefs reject vengeance? What of the Denier in the forest who can only weep for the loss of trees and the deaths of loved ones? How many wagons filled with loot will satisfy him or her? How many newly planted trees, or rebuilt huts? How many monuments to honour their dead? Restitution,' she said, after another mouthful of wine, 'may live in the present, promising a just future, but it dwells in the sordid past. The word itself ignores the lesson of its necessity, and so will breed its own generations. But at the last, milord, the only restitution won in the final bargain will be that of the wild's return, to all that civilization destroyed and enslaved. Restitution is not found in the words of compensation, guilt, and wretched bargaining. It is found in the silence of healing, and that silence only comes when the criminals and their ilk, their very civilization, are gone.'

Urusander turned, with something like delight in his eyes. 'A sound argument, Sheltatha Lore. I will give your words some thought.' He turned to Renarr. 'She is your student? You have many talents indeed, Renarr, to awaken such a lively mind.'

Sheltatha snorted. 'This lively mind, milord, was forged in neglect and abuse, long before I crossed paths with Renarr. Isn't that always the way? Isolation hones the inner voice, the unspoken dialogue between the selves – and surely there are many selves within each of us. Some uglier than others.'

There was something of the challenge in Sheltatha's tone.

'I see little that is ugly in you,' Urusander said quietly.

'Youth is the soul's disguise, milord. It serves, until it is used up. For now, sir, you are seduced by what you see. What if I told you that a vicious, venal demon hides within me? A thing of scars remembering every wound?'

'Then, perhaps,' said Urusander, turning once more to the window, 'I would welcome you to our company.'

Sighing, Renarr settled back in her chair. 'Your soldiers don't want restitution, Father. What they lost can't be returned to them. No, they want wealth, and land. They want to carve up the holdings of the nobles. They want titles. And see how, for all their simple greed, they are now painted white, as if their every squalid want has been blessed. Is it any wonder they grow bold?'

'I am subjected to their demands daily, Renarr,' Urusander replied. 'If this not be a burden I accept, then someone else surely will.'

'Hunn Raal,' said Sheltatha Lore, leaning over to refill her goblet. 'Now there's an ugly man.'

'The Legion readies to march,' Urusander said, eyes still on whatever had caught his attention through the window. 'Hallyd Bahann's delay in returning will no longer hold us back.'

Renarr studied her adoptive father for a moment, and then said, 'Not by your command? Not in answer to your will? Will you simply be pulled along, swept up in this flood of self-serving indignation?'

'You advise I defy the wishes of my soldiers?'

'I advise nothing,' she replied.

'No,' murmured Sheltatha Lore, 'she's much too subtle to do that.'

'In the early morning,' Urusander said, 'I can look down upon the pickets. The camp's guards, standing so still in the whiteness. As if carved from marble. I stand here, a sculptor of these creations, the maker of an army of stone. Three thousand stone hearts in three thousand stone breasts. And I tremble – as I have always done, when I am about to give the command to march, to find battle, to see my creations shattered, broken.' He lifted a hand and settled it against the cold lead pane. 'This is a dreadful truth: much as I would like to imagine an army of such perfection that it need never draw a blade, need never deliver death and have death delivered unto it, I recognize the brutal truth. Each and every soldier out there has had his or her flesh hacked away, everything soft – all gone. Leaving nothing but stone, cold and hard. Intent on feeling nothing. Existing only in order to destroy.'

There was silence in the chamber, until Sheltatha stretched on the divan and spoke in a loose tone. 'More likely the nobles will surrender, milord. There'll be no battle. Simply show the sword and the will behind it, and your enemies will kneel.'

'If they do,' Urusander replied, 'they will leave the field with their Houseblades intact. We but delay the clash.' He faced the chamber, eyed both women. 'This is what Hunn Raal does not understand. Nor the High Priestess. The marriage wins us nothing but an uneasy delay. Which of the noble families will be the first to yield a portion of its land?' He waved a hand. 'The two thrones are meaningless. These conjoined hands, dark and light, cannot win us peace.'

Sheltatha slowly sat up, her eyes bright on Urusander. 'You mean to betray them. Your own soldiers.'

'I wanted peace. All I ever wanted.'

'Hunn Raal will see you dead. High Priestess Syntara will hand him the dagger, with every blessing of Light she can conjure.'

'We march to battle,' Urusander said to her, voice suddenly cold. 'We will force the nobles to fight us. We will shatter the Houseblades, and leave the highborn with no choice but to negotiate. And then there will be restitution.'

'All to keep Hunn Raal from your back.'

'I will see peace forged.'

'Hunn Raal—'

'Is an outlaw and a murderer. I will hand him over to the Hust Legion, with my blessing.'

Sheltatha smirked. 'Your first gesture of reconciliation.'

Looking between the two, Renarr could not decide which one dismayed her the most. After a moment, she shut down such emotions, mentally turned away from them both. None of this mattered. None of this was relevant. *The winter loses its grip upon the Legion. The camp whores, men and women alike, gasp at the sudden rush of coins, the eager tumble of bodies. By this, they know. They understand. We are to march. Cut a heated path through the season. There is excitement riding the lust, because lust comes in so many flavours. Time to taste them all.*

*None of it concerns me. Not any more.*

*My adoptive father has come to his sense of duty. He will take the hand of Mother Dark. This is not so vast a deviation for Vatha Urusander. He was always one to embrace sacrifice, to set aside his own wants and needs. Indeed, he yearns for such moments, such gestures. They are what he would use to set him apart from the rest of us.*

*Noble acts, like the spreading of a peacock's tail. Nothing for himself, and everything for those who witness. After all, let it not be misunderstood. It is his very reluctance that spawns the virtue, and by the virtue's power, he will force upon this realm all the justice it can stomach.*

*But even then, he will defy the most egregious demands from his soldiers, and so they will see him as a betrayer. This too will stand as a sacrifice. This too will taste of virtue.*

*But none of it matters.*

*Soon, I will stand with Urusander, in the Citadel. I will see him made a husband once more. I will see the marriage done. I will see the beginning of his overtures. The first gestures at reconciliation, restitution, the sure path to some kind of justice – the kind none like, but all can live with.*

*The dust will begin settling. There will be relief. Elation. The storm has passed. It'll not turn now.*

She rose. 'I will take my leave, milord. Sheltatha's lessons are done for this day.'

But Urusander was at the window once again, and only now did Renarr hear the clamour of the Legion breaking camp. To Renarr's announcement, he simply nodded, and then, as if in afterthought, he added, 'Preparations will take some time. We march on the morrow, or perhaps the day after.'

'Heady times,' said Sheltatha Lore in a low voice, smiling down at the wine in her goblet. Raising her voice, she said, 'Milord, I beg you, on the day of your justice, spare not my mother.'

When Urusander made no reply, Renarr quickly left the chamber.

\*　　\*　　\*

'A procession will be necessary,' said High Priestess Syntara from where she stood near the altar. 'A lighting of sacred torches, perhaps, to burnish the dawn. I will lead. With awakened Light suffusing my person, bright as the sun, and yet purer. We must make the dawn our first blessing, each and every day, even while on the march.'

Seated on a stone bench, Sagander studied the woman from beneath heavy lids. Pomp to cow the masses was all very well, but this woman's vanity was too transparent. She lacked subtlety. 'I was speaking of Sheltatha Lore,' he said. 'In the keeping of a whore is not acceptable. A whore but makes other whores, even should they be children. The habits of the adult seduce, and against such things no child can resist.'

'From my understanding,' Syntara said, 'Tathe Lorat's daughter was never a child. I told you, she is too damaged for my temple. It is a wonder that my blessing of white still remains upon such soiled flesh.'

*You were one of Emral Lanear's temple whores, woman – what of* your *soiled flesh?* Of course, he dared not point out such details, lest they sully this woman's desperate reinventions. *Besides, reinventions are necessary, enough to knock history into some semblance of destiny, when it is all said and done.*

*I will pen the new truths of all this. The eyes and the hand of a witness, here within the inner sanctum of a newly forged realm. Sagander will be a name revered for ages to come.*

'Besides,' Syntara continued, 'your obsession over that child is unseemly.'

'Baseless lies!'

The High Priestess shrugged. 'It hardly matters. Tathe

763

Lorat was free in gifting her daughter, and cared little about the nightly unveiling of horrors. If Sheltatha Lore's lessons with you involved the art of sucking your cock, what of it?'

Sagander's hands curled into white-knuckled fists where they rested on his lap. 'I sought her salvation,' he whispered.

Syntara smiled down at him. 'Many are the paths to salvation. Or did she remain . . . unconvinced?'

'You bait me.'

'I offer you any child in my temple, historian.'

He glared at her. 'High Priestess, I was a tutor. An honourable profession that I never – not once – sullied by what you suggest. Indeed, I find your invitation reprehensible.'

She studied him for a moment longer. 'Good. The fewer of your weaknesses they can exploit, the better.'

*The ones* they *would exploit, or you?*

'The army prepares,' he said, made uneasy by her steady regard. 'But Hunn Raal hides in his tent, refusing all messengers.'

'The Mortal Sword has no time for such mundane trivialities,' Syntara said, moving to circle the altar and the makeshift throne positioned on the dais behind the altar-stone. Torches blazed in the chamber, with candelabras set on every available niche and flat surface. Every shadow had been banished, every dollop of darkness expunged. The throne awaited a dressing of gilt, and it seemed that this one, at least, would remain here in the temple.

'I am surprised you have elected to join us,' Sagander said.

'The High Priestesses must meet. We must both attend the sacred wedding.'

'Leaving this temple virtually empty.'

She paused with one hand on the back of the throne. 'There is no risk, Sagander. What concerns you so?'

He began reaching down to the leg that was not there, but caught himself in time. 'I will need a cart, and attendants.'

'No doubt,' she said.

'Do you believe there will be a battle?'

'Consider the blood spilled as a necessary sacrifice. Indeed, as a source of power. Does that bother you, historian? I should think you'd be pleased.'

'War never pleased me, High Priestess. It is crass, an admission of failure. It is, alas, the triumph of stupid minds.' He eyed her. 'Yet now, you hint that Liosan is a thirsty faith.'

'There is something raw in its power, yes,' she replied. 'But on a field of battle, Sagander, men and women will die. Are we to waste such spillage? Are we to deem it useless?'

Sagander gestured. 'You have one altar. Is that not enough?'

'Is not every battlefield sanctified? Are there not countless sacrifices made upon that holy ground?'

'Gods of war are barbaric creations, High Priestess. To consort with them must be beneath us.'

'They will gather nonetheless.'

'Then see them defied! Banished!'

Syntara laughed. 'You're an old man indeed, historian. Some things are inevitable. But like you, I expect this war to be short. A single day, a single battle. Besides,' she added, 'Lord Draconus will be among the victims on that day. Insofar as necessary sacrifices go, he stands alone.'

'I should think Mother Dark would refuse to hand him over,' Sagander said, shifting on the bench where he sat, his back to the bare stone wall. 'Much less see him slain.'

Syntara blinked languidly as she studied Sagander once more. 'That has been anticipated.'

He squinted up at her. *Damn that wretched glow!* 'What do you mean?'

'Draconus will not leave the battlefield. Or, rather, he will. Laid out cold upon a bier.'

'Would that he fell by my hand,' Sagander said, with a rough sigh, his hands once again curling into tight fists.

Syntara smiled. 'By all means, historian, wade out into the charge of battle, and meet him with a blade. By hatred alone you should blaze with impenetrable armour. Fired with righteous zeal, how could your sword not swing sure and true? How could it not cleave asunder all who would stand in your way?'

His gaze fell from her. 'I wage war with words,' he said.

'Yet it seems you fight every battle in its aftermath, historian, to accommodate a mind insufficiently quickened to repartee. Why, even that whore Renarr can disarm you with a flick of her wit.'

He flinched, and then scowled at the tiled floor. 'That manner of cunning is a shallow thing, forged in a society of eager malice.'

'School, you mean.'

'Just so,' he said, irritated by Syntara's ebullience. *She gloats. This makes her ugly, despite the penumbra of light, despite the natural beauty of her face, the burnishing of eternal youth offered by this infernal magic.* A faith that blinded one to natural flaws made perfection a false conceit, one defying too careful an examination. It must eschew complexity, promising simplicity in its stead. He suspected it would prove popular indeed.

'I give you leave to spit upon his corpse,' Syntara said. 'If such a thing pleases you.'

'That is one procession I will gladly join,' he replied.

*          *          *

The day was nearing its end and from the keep's tower came faint wailing as the priestesses announced the dying of Light with ritual grief. Captain Infayen Menand supposed it a proper gesture, even if the voices sounded strained and false. But this was as much effort as she was prepared to make in contemplating the myriad complexities of faith, since her attention was fixed upon the distant figure of Hunn Raal, as the Mortal Sword made his solitary way down into the town of Neret Sorr.

Beside her stood Tathe Lorat, while behind them both, soldiers worked into the dusk, preparing for the march. The air was bitter cold with a wind sweeping down from the plains of the north, and it was likely that they would ride that wind all the way to the gates of Kharkanas.

'Frozen ground,' she said. 'Solid underfoot, until the hot blood turns it all to mud.'

766

'The glow of white fades,' Tathe Lorat replied, 'with every doubt stirring awake in the mind. I yearn to discover a sorcery for myself, if only to lend the illusion of loyalty.'

'So do we all,' Infayen said with a grunt. 'I dislike a faith that knows the mind.'

'Then we are little different,' Tathe replied. 'Hunn Raal—'

'Is dangerous,' cut in Infayen. 'When he's not spilling his cock into the fire, that is.'

'I felt his ire, Infayen. I felt its capriciousness. Careless, deadly. He could have broken every bone in my body, all for the crime of insolence.'

'And the man less a captain with every day that passes.'

'My appetites never weakened discipline.'

Infayen glanced across at her. 'It was well known that you played no favourites, Tathe Lorat. If you could make it wet or hard, you'd have it to bed.'

'When I have title, and wealth, I will take a score or more lovers. I'll fuck every Houseblade I hire. To ensure their absolute loyalty.'

'That's one way, I suppose. What of your husband?'

'What of him? The man can't even track down a lone renegade captain. He'll return here to Neret Sorr, tail between his scrawny legs, only to find us long gone. No, what we must win for ourselves will have to be by my hand, not his, and that's a debt from which he'll never recover.'

'Your esteem is a miserly thing, Tathe Lorat.'

'I've not your hero's blood, Infayen, to give clout to my claims.'

Infayen watched as Hunn Raal slipped from sight, down between ramshackle buildings. 'He's not making for the keep.'

'No.'

'Some other task commands him.'

'Hunn Raal will grant us no favours in the court, Infayen.'

'No, he will turn on us all.'

'We need to consider our . . . options.'

'That is your need, Tathe Lorat, not mine. The Infayen line finds a grave in every battle. That said, perhaps you would take my daughter under your care when that time comes.'

'You trust me in this? I will see her sullied. The light of her young eyes dulled with use. Children are like dolls, and this woman here at your side plays rough.'

Infayen turned and smiled at her. 'You've not met my daughter yet, have you?'

Tathe Lorat shrugged. 'Have you met mine?'

'Menandore is no fool.'

'Nor is Sheltatha Lorat, I assure you.'

Infayen frowned. 'And yet . . .'

Shrugging, Tathe Lorat drew her heavy cloak about her shoulders and turned back to the camp. 'Break them young, and all that they make of themselves afterwards lies thinly over the scars.'

Infayen swung round and joined the other captain as they walked back into the army's encampment. She sighed. 'Some mothers should never be mothers at all.'

'I expect both our daughters would agree with you, Infayen Menand.'

*　　*　　*

The master blacksmith of Urusander's Legion was a squat, broad, scar-faced man of middle years. He stood with his back to his forge, limned in its fiery glow, his small eyes narrowed on Hunn Raal. 'Now what?'

The Mortal Sword of Light glared at the smith. 'Maybe it's not big enough,' he said.

'Big enough for what?'

'Legion discipline seems to have failed your manners, Bilikk.'

'The commander sent me to work in Gurren's stead. I'm as much the town's smith as the Legion's. Besides,' he added, 'word is you don't take the title of captain no more. Mortal Sword? What the fuck is that? Ain't no Legion rank I ever heard of. You lookin' for worshippers now? Fuck that on a stick.'

There was a sound from the door to Gurren's old house and Witch Hale emerged, drawing a tattered shawl about her narrow shoulders. 'Hunn Raal,' she said, making the name a sneer. 'What you're calling for here isn't Legion work. Heard you went and stood in a fire. Burned half your clothes off, but left you uncharred. That's ugly magic, Raal. You want to stay away from the flame bitch, she's got appetites you don't want to know.' She cocked her head, regarding Hunn Raal. 'Or maybe it's too late. It is, isn't it?'

'You were not invited, witch,' Hunn Raal said. 'Don't test my patience. Go.'

'Me and Bilikk got history between us now,' Hale replied. 'Where he goes, I go.'

'This is Liosan business.'

'And we all got stained, didn't we? Only, when your mind decides it's not sure, why, the glow fades.' She lifted an arm, letting the loose sleeve slip down, revealing her scrawny, ashen wrist. ''Tis strange purity that washes off, don't you think?'

'The stains of your sins hardly surprise me, witch. Your magic's a sordid thing. Unwelcome on this sanctified ground, and do not think for a moment that all of Neret Sorr isn't sanctified, in the name of Tiste Liosan.'

'I feel it,' she said. 'But I don't fear it. Neither does the flame bitch.'

'You think you can stand against me?'

'I don't care about you, Raal. It's Bilikk I mean to guard this night.'

'And I need him – do you think I would not protect him?'

'Once his use is past, no. You won't give him a second thought.'

He studied her, curious. 'What do you think is about to happen here, witch?'

'What did she offer you?'

This night was not going as planned. *Build me a fire*, she'd said. *I will guide you to the First Forge. A sceptre must be made. And a crown . . . or did she say that could wait? She'd made me drunk on her. Not wine, not ale, but her strong grip on my damned cock.*

*A goddess of some sort. A demon of the fire. Flame bitch? That will do, I suppose.*

*Fucked up my memory, to be certain. Sceptre, crown . . . throne?*

'You are addled,' Hale said. 'Already lost in the unnatural heat of Bilikk's forge – see how nothing burns away? How the flames grow even unfed? She's coming—'

The forge behind Bilikk suddenly erupted. A tongue of fire arced out like a whip, striking Witch Hale, who shrieked as she was flung back through the doorway of the house, landing crumpled on the wooden floor, where her body began burning like resinous wood. In moments the floor and then one wall of the house were alight.

Stunned, terrified, Hunn Raal sought to back away.

Impossibly fast, the entire house was wreathed in flames. From the second level came screams.

*His apprentices.*

Fires now rose along the low walls of the smithy, encircling Raal and Bilikk. The stacks of charcoal raged, the buckets of water boiled and spat, the woodshed vanished inside an incandescent maelstrom.

Their clothes burned, and yet neither man was harmed, even as the heat engulfed them, and the air itself was devoured by the torrent of flames.

She spoke then. '*This will do. Two young lives in the rooms above. Cousins to a slain man, both of them filled with grief. I have purged their torment, taken away the feel of poor Millick's fists. Now that was a senseless thing, wasn't it? But all ashes now, all bedded in peace.*

'*And the witch! Delightful sacrifice!*'

Bilikk cried out something then, but his words were lost in the roar of the conflagration surrounding them.

Tentacles of flames snared the smith, dragging him screaming into the forge, where he vanished inside the white fire.

'*Come along then, Hunn Raal. I was summoned to the fashioning of one sceptre, and now another. I attend*

770

*the flames. I feed the First Forge all that it needs. The blood in my womb, the lust we ignite between us, the seed you and your kind all spill into me. Step forward, it is time. We await you.'*

He was helpless against her invitation. Suddenly without need to draw breath, his skin untouched by the heat and flames, Hunn Raal strode forward.

Where the smith's forge had been there was now only white incandescence, and yet, at its core, there waited something like a gateway, framed in flickering flames.

The Mortal Sword stepped through.

The world beyond was a thing of ashes and blasted earth, the sky blindingly white.

She spoke in his head, her being filling him, like folds of flesh closing about his soul in a mockery of an embrace. *'Love remains at the heart of this, Hunn Raal. It is shapeless to begin with, a thing of sensations. Warmth, comfort, safety. So it resides in the newborn child, fanned to life by the one who bore it. This bond takes time, but once made, it is unbreakable, and to challenge it is to awaken fire.'*

'You are a goddess of the hearth,' Hunn Raal said. Raging flames marred the horizon, as if they had come upon an island in a sea of fire. The ash filling the air drifted on sullen currents. 'You devour, and behind your warmth there is the promise of pain.' He saw Bilikk, kneeling a short distance ahead. Just beyond the blacksmith the ground lifted into a rough cone, and from its ragged mouth smoke rose in sinuous coils, shimmering amidst intense heat. 'Goddess,' Hunn Raal continued, 'you know nothing of love.'

*'Every gift of warmth awakens memory of the womb, Mortal Sword. But the child within you drowned in wine long ago. Shall I raise up its tiny corpse? Here, look upon what you have killed.'*

He saw before him the body of a small child. For a moment he thought it sheathed in blood, and then he realized the fluid dripping from its limbs, running lazy tracks down its round face, was not blood, but wine. He staggered back a step. 'Go to the Abyss!'

771

'*I can return it to life, Hunn Raal. This dead child within you. Dead and deadened. Stained beyond all innocence.*'

As he stared in horror, the creature opened its eyes, revealing the perfect blue of the newborn. 'Stop this! Why do you torment me? This speaks not of love, you cursed bitch!'

'*Oh, we are all mothers to what spawns inside us, for us to nurture or neglect, to love or cast away, to comfort or abuse, feed or starve. To worship as life, or sacrifice with death. No soul exists, Hunn Raal, that does not kneel before a private altar, blessing in one hand and a dagger in the other. What choice do you make for your life? Do you mark each morning with gratitude, or death?*

'*That dagger can be many things,*' she continued remorselessly. '*It serves as the tool of slaying, and no matter how blunt the edge, it draws blood each and every time. Blink sleepy eyes open, Hunn Raal, and reach for the goblet – to numb every cut you make upon your own soul.*'

'No more, I beg you—'

'*Who will bless your beloved altar? That question is asked again and again, day upon day, year upon year. A lifetime of that one question. Set that gift of blessing outside the borders of your flesh, or claim it as your own – the choice matters not.*

'*But should you curse instead of blessing, Hunn Raal, ah, that is entirely of your own making. And so wounding yourself, you make a habit of wounding others. A life's habit.*

'*And yet,*' she added in vicious contempt, '*your Urusander dares speak of justice. If he would have it, who would be left standing?*'

The child, hovering in the air, flecked with ashes, blinked languidly.

'Send it away,' he whispered.

The conjuration vanished. '*Balance. The blessing and the knife. The time has come, Mortal Sword, to forge us the symbols you will need.*'

As if tugged, Hunn Raal stumbled forward, and moments later found himself standing beside Bilikk. The blacksmith was weeping, but no tears survived the scalding heat.

'*The First Forge. Oh, it manifests in myriad ways. I doubt Draconus found it beneath a sky of white. In his place of finding, it would be dark, with the sky sheathed in impenetrable smoke. Only the glow from the forge's eager mouth to guide him. Hunn Raal, have you brought what I asked?*'

The Mortal Sword reached to the hide-wrapped object he had strapped to his weapon-belt. He loosened the bindings and let the hide fall away, revealing a length of bone, sun-bleached and weathered. 'Dog,' he said. 'Or wolf, if it matters.'

'*One more elegant in its irony than the other, Hunn Raal. The dogs of my children, or their wild brethren. Found on the plain, yes?*'

'Yet another of my commands that left the scouts bemused, but they found what you asked for, goddess. But is this all we are to have? A thigh bone to make the Sceptre of Light? What need for a forge?'

'*Light's essence dwells in fire.*' He sensed her amusement. '*You have recovered your arrogance, Hunn Raal. Your sly superiority – the drunk's first and only game. But you remain utterly ignorant. He kept you all children, and that was a mistake. And in your isolation . . . when at last he offered you all a mother, it was too late.*'

'Enough of your insults. Bilikk waits – guide him in what must be done.'

'*I am not the one to guide your blacksmith,*' she replied. '*Here, the will of the First Forge commands. It chooses whom to use. If you had come alone, your lack of talent, the dearth of your knowledge and skill, would have yielded a poor result. But this one, I imagine, will prove a worthy source.*'

Bilikk had remained kneeling, motionless, his head lowered with his chin on his chest.

Proffering the thigh bone, Hunn Raal said, 'Here, take this.'

But the man made no response.

Tapping his shoulder with one end of the thigh bone elicited nothing. Crouching, Hunn Raal leaned close to peer at Bilikk's face. 'Abyss take us, the fool's dead.'

'*Well, yes. You have need of his skills and experience. I think we are ready—*'

As if he had been punched, Hunn Raal's head snapped back, and in the stunned confusion filling his mind, he was assailed by a sudden rush of memories not his own. Fragments, shredded and momentarily nonsensical, images flashing in his thoughts, igniting behind his eyes – *the village was little more than his extended family. He knew them all, and there was warmth, and any child – every child – was safe. In those years, had he known it, he had lived in a paradise, in a realm where love abounded, and even the common petty rivalries and disputes as might plague any large family proved rare and quick to wither on the vine.*

*There was something there. The commonplace was made somehow sacred. There was no reason for it, nothing he could point to, and dwelling in its midst felt wholly natural, and in those early years he had no sense that the world beyond the village was any different. He – I—*

*How we lived was how we were meant to live. How we lived was, I soon discovered to my horror, what others only aspired to, or dreamed of, or cynically dismissed as impossible.*

*I was a child there, and then an apprentice to Cage, learning the art of the forge. For all the hard tools of the farmers and the coopers and wheelwrights, Cage's greatest love was in the making of toys. From castoffs, from tailings, from whatever he could find. And not simple creations for the village children, either! No, my friends, Cage crafted tiny mechanisms, physical riddles and elaborate jokes that confounded and delighted all.*

*For all his size, he was a gentle man, was Cage. Until the day he left the smithy and walked to the far end of the village, went into the house of Tanner Harok, and there broke the man's neck.*

*Paradise was a living thing, like a tree, and occasionally, among its many roots sunk deep into the rich earth, one root turned foul and infected, and finally rotten.*

*Infidelity. A word I'd not even understood until then. A crime of betrayal. The victim was trust, and its death sent shock through the entire village.*

*Poor Cage. So bitterly perfect in his naming – he'd found his knowing a prison, tormented by what he could not ignore.*

*And then there were two widows, not just the one, and the village was in need of a blacksmith.*

*While I, poor apprentice, not yet ready, not yet recovered, I needed a new village.*

*There are all kinds of betrayals. By the Abyss, that wide-eyed boy who was me learned that fast enough. Fuck one thing and it fucks everything else.*

*The Legion found me and then pressed me into service. There was a war to fight. As if I cared. I remember my first sight of you, Hunn Raal—*

Snarling, Hunn Raal choked off Bilikk's voice – the squalid memories, each one crowding the next as they mapped out the dull lessons of a dull life. He had no interest in such things, but there was new knowledge in his muscles and bones, skill behind his measuring eye, a timbre to his senses. He knew the art of the forge now.

*Stolen talent, stolen skill.*

*It'd be useful to learn how this is done—*

The fire bitch's harsh laughter echoed in his skull. *'Then aspire to godhood, Hunn Raal! But no, not even godhood. Become an elemental force, a disembodied will, a flavour in the air, a stain upon the ground.*

*'The First Forge's gift to you will not last, in any case. Once we leave this realm, the ghost of your blacksmith will flee your wretchedly mortal body. You cannot hold what would not have you. Anything else is possession, and I assure you, Hunn Raal, you would not like possession.'*

'Then we're wasting time here,' Hunn Raal said. 'I have a sceptre to forge.'

*'Then descend into the fires, Mortal Sword. I will await your return.'*

A sudden suspicion took him and he scowled down at the

thigh bone in his hand. 'Dog or wolf. This creation will not belong to Light – not in its entirety.'

'*My reward for this bargain, Hunn Raal. By your blessed Light I will see. A privilege I do not mean to abuse, I assure you.*'

'A detail you'd rather the High Priestess knew nothing about, I take it.'

'*True enough. Only you.*'

'Then I in turn might make use of your . . . sight.'

'*I expect you will. Now go.*'

He glanced over at the kneeling corpse beside him. *Just as well. Saves me killing him later.*

*     *     *

Old things returned to life exuded an air of fragility that no amount of polish, paint or gilt could hide. Resurrection was an illusion, as what returned was never the same as what had gone away, although a careless glance might suggest otherwise. That, or the willing blindness of belief.

Lord Vatha Urusander's armour was brought to him. Freshly oiled, lacquered and bearing new leather straps. The vambraces to sheathe his wrists were newly painted, inlaid with a gold sunburst. A breastplate of white enamelled wood, fringed in gold filigree. A fur-lined cloak of crimson, embroidered with gold thread. Only the weapon-belt and its scabbarded sword remained unadorned.

As he was dressed by his servants, Urusander stood motionless, and upon his lined face there was no emotion. Then he spoke. 'In my mind, I see Kadaspala. Paintbrush between his teeth, three more balanced in one hand. He eyes this regalia with a jaded disposition, and yet nods at its political necessity. He would play that role. Purveyor of legend. The elevation of the banal into myth.'

Renarr, seated in her usual chair, tilted her head and said, 'In such pose, Father, you more invite the artist who works in stone, or bronze.'

'They battle each other for permanence, I'm sure,' Urusander muttered. 'But my thoughts are on Kadaspala.

776

Some thought him an inveterate complainer, a wallower in misery. Some voiced their dismissal of him with careless ease, as if from a position of intellectual superiority, or at least wizened pragmatism. How that always angered me.'

'He was well able to fight his own battles,' Renarr pointed out, watching the servants cinch straps and fasten buckles, fussing over the falling folds of the cloak.

'Against such fools, nothing he could say would shake them from their judgement.'

'No, nothing would,' she agreed. In the compound below, officers of the Legion had gathered, flinging jests and laughter as they readied their mounts or checked weapons. Captain Tathe Lorat had collected her daughter for this, under the wary eye of Infayen Menand, and by all reports Hunn Raal was still missing.

'So it falls to me,' Urusander continued. 'I am disinclined to ignore stupidity, no matter how seemly its garb. Oh, I do not decry the act of judgement itself, or even the notion of righteous opinion. Rather, it is the tone I so despise. No, their dismissal proclaims nothing that is intellectually superior. And the insult behind their judgement fails to hide their venal paucity of wisdom. Every fool eager with an opinion invites the same judgemental weapons wielded against *them*. As in a field of battle, all is fair. Would you not – no, give me that belt, I'll set my own sword, damn you – would you not agree, Renarr?'

'Stunted intellects are rarely stung by such judgement, Father.'

'Then let us drag them into the clearing, into the light. I am no artist. I am simply a soldier. I will call them out and challenge their defence, such as it is.'

'You've not the audience,' Renarr replied.

After a moment, Urusander sighed. 'No. I have not.'

'In any case,' she continued, 'I am less forgiving of the notion that all opinions are equally valid. Some are just plain ignorant.'

Urusander grunted. 'Leave me now,' he said to the servants, and watched as they hurried from the room. He faced Renarr.

'My mind is diminished with age. I lack the verisimilitude of years past. Worse yet, my fires have ebbed. Awaiting me now, Renarr, is the desire to dispense with contemplation. Have done with the musings that so afflict the artist who sees too much, who knows too well, who would defy the rush of base appetites. A battle awaits us. Let us ride to meet it.'

She rose then, collecting her own cloak. 'You have set your mind as well as your sword.'

Urusander paused, and then sighed. 'No matter the outcome, this battle will be my last.'

She studied him, but said nothing.

He stood, still possessing all his airs of command, the grace of competence, while beneath all the gilt, the surficial propriety, something broken hid its swollen face.

*Duty, it seems, is a harsh mistress to this man. We are invited to sympathy.*

*But see him march to the river of blood.*

'Will you ride at my side?' he asked.

'Father, from this moment on, I'll not leave it.'

The swollen face lifted then, revealed itself to her, and she saw it clearly.

*Well, that is no surprise, is it? We hide our own, each and every one of us. Bruised and beaten by injustice.*

And in that child's face, so bloated with tears, she saw hope.

*Oh, how the lessons of betrayal are so quickly forgotten.*

\*      \*      \*

From the high wall of the keep, High Priestess Syntara had looked down upon the curled snake of Urusander's Legion, watching how it seemed to ripple in the dawn. Steam rose from it as if the entire creature had just crawled out from the earth, mixing with the smoke from the town's forge, where a fire had burned the building and its yard to the ground, taking with it at least four people, including the Legion's blacksmith. Townsfolk had fought that fire through the night, finally quenching it just before dawn.

The Legion's tail half encircled the town, but its blunt head was angled facing south. The image remained with her as she led her procession down into the courtyard, cutting through the gathered officers awaiting the arrival of Urusander.

She was not inclined to join them. While the soldiers of the Legion still turned to their commander in all things, the faith and its sacred servants did not bow to that now insufficient military structure. Until Urusander was made Father Light, he was nothing more than the leader of an army.

*This serpent is mine, and we holy servants of Light shall lead the van. With blinding venom, we shall be its fangs. Best Urusander understand this immediately. Best this lesson be delivered to every officer here, and every soldier down below.*

*Their petty lust for wealth and land is too base for the righteousness awaiting us.*

Still Hunn Raal was nowhere to be seen.

*If he'll not be first, surely he'll be last. The Mortal Sword desires a vast audience, presumably. Or, perhaps, he's lying insensate in some alley . . . though I should not hope for such an unlikely ignominy.*

*I will find me a destriant of the faith. I must choose my champion, a worthy foil to our Mortal Sword. Perhaps among the highborn, or in the Citadel itself.*

Passing through the gate in solemn silence, the High Priestess and her flock, one and all brocaded in white, set out down the cobbled track.

\*　　\*　　\*

'The whore has airs,' murmured Tathe Lorat, watching the procession pass. Torches and lanterns, fine flowing robes of bleached and crushed wool threaded in starburst patterns, and skin so pale as to be cadaverous. She grunted. 'See how bloodless we seem.'

Infayen Menand set her hand against her mount's muzzle, letting it breathe in her scent. It had been too long since they had last ridden to battle. The horse was getting on. *She might even fail beneath me. A fitting demise for us both. But she'll taste my eagerness to take down Houseblades – those*

*privileged betrayers so quick to sell their blades to the high-*
*born. She'll answer me one more time.*

'I set little weight to this faith,' Tathe Lorat continued in a low voice. 'Not enough, fortunately, to see this porcelain tarnished. It seems kind to indifference.'

'If Light blesses,' Infayen said, 'it does so indiscriminately. It will touch every scene, from sweet bliss to sweet horror. The scouts make no report of your husband's imminent return. Are you concerned?'

'Indeed I am. Incompetence will win us no favours.'

'And if you had set out to hunt down Sharenas Ankhadu?'

Tathe Lorat bared her teeth. 'Her head would ride my company's standard, and on this morning its rotted visage would be mere tatters of flesh on bone.'

Infayen frowned. 'Hallyd has some capacity for command, Tathe Lorat. You denigrate him for reasons well hidden behind the flag you're now waving. Contempt blinds both ways.'

Tathe Lorat glanced towards her daughter, who stood a short distance away, lithe and relaxed with her back resting against a wall.

Seeing this, Infayen's frown deepened. *Would that Sharenas had found your tent first that night, Tathe Lorat. But no matter. You'll not take your daughter under wing again.*

Infayen was eager for the battle ahead. The first spilling of highborn blood had been by her hand, after all, a detail none could take away from her. *Though my soldiers lost their discipline. The Enes clan fought too well. Blood ran high, especially when Cryl Durav appeared. The rape was a crime too far. Well, even in war there can be regrets.*

*But we'll be laying in rows plenty of highborn corpses before this is done, to give the Enes clan company. Sometimes, privilege needs a serious fucking over, to send the message home. And now, it must be said, outrage serves as a banner for both sides. The fighting will be fierce.*

*I only pray that I can cross blades with Andarist, if not Silchas Ruin. Perhaps even Anomander.* Few could agree on which of the three was best with the sword. But by nature,

Anomander still seemed the most formidable. *If I find him wounded on the field, or exhausted. If I catch him unawares. If he stumbles, slips in bloody mud.*

The details would be lost, in time. The truth would be made simple. *The day the Houseblades of the highborn fell, Infayen Menand slew Lord Anomander Purake on the field of battle, and thus died the First Son of Darkness.*

*It was hardly surprising that the surviving brothers then murdered her. Besides, the Menand bloodline was ever fated . . .*

'Your smile is cold, Infayen Menand.'

She glanced across at Tathe Lorat. 'Where will it take place, do you think?'

'What?'

'The battle, what else?'

'Tarns.'

Infayen nodded. 'Yes. Tarns. Urusander will see to it.'

'They'll not risk damaging Kharkanas itself. The city is, after all, the prize.'

*That city means nothing to me. I'd be just as happy to see it burn.* 'Where Urusander will be made king.'

'Father Light.'

Infayen shrugged. *The only title of interest to me shall be mine. Infayen Menand, Slayer of the First Son of Darkness.* A chance shifting of her gaze caught Sheltatha Lore's eyes fixed upon her. After a long moment, Tathe's daughter smiled.

Infayen's unease was momentary, and quickly forgotten with the arrival of Lord Urusander.

Their commander was not one for speeches, but Infayen felt the sudden rise of excitement and anticipation. It was finally coming to pass. *We march to Kharkanas, and there will be justice.*

*　　*　　*

They had managed only a hundred and fifty wicker shields, so Captain Hallyd Bahann paired up his three hundred soldiers, one to bear the shield and the other to wield weapons.

781

The forest line ahead was patchy, broken up by the vagaries of fire and stumps left by past cutting. The snow on the ground looked dirty, crusted and hard and not yet softened by the morning light.

*The morning light. Such as it is. What goddess is she that invites gloom? That dims her realm, as if we were all on the edge of losing consciousness?*

He was still flush with his triumph at the monastery, though the victory had proved bloodier than anticipated. Sending the children out on to the south track to walk to Yedan panged him somewhat. The winter was reluctant to yield its bitter harvest of cold and snow. But they had been warmly clad, dragging sleds on which provisions had been stored. If they didn't lose the trail, they would already be at the monastery, warm and safe.

*Necessities in war are often cruel. I could hardly take them with us, not with a true battle looming.*

*These cowardly Deniers, with their bows and ambushes – we will have them.*

*And, if our luck holds, we may well find Sharenas Ankhadu among them, drawn into their company by shared crimes. Traitors will flock.*

Lieutenant Arkandas strode up to him and saluted. 'Sir, we have been seen.'

'Good,' Hallyd snapped. 'If necessary, we will drive them to the river's edge.' They would leave the horses behind, guarded by a half-dozen soldiers. He expected a running battle, quickly mired by the uneven ground, the deep snow and the wreckage of the mostly ruined forest.

Old fire set a stench upon the land that even time struggled to expunge – some caustic residue of burned sap, perhaps, or simply the reek that was born of destruction. Violence was a stain upon the earth. *And yet*, Hallyd took note of his white hands as he tugged on his gauntlets, *crimes leave no stain upon the skin, nor mark upon the face. From this we are to take meaning. Absolved, the crimes cease to be. Blessed, the face is made innocent once again.* 'Lieutenant.'

'Sir?'

'Ready the line. We will advance to the trees.'

'Our scouts report many Deniers awaiting us, sir.'

'I should hope so! True, it's a rare courage. Let us take advantage of it, shall we?'

'Yes sir.'

He eyed her. 'You have doubts, Arkandas?'

'That they will contest us? No sir. But I mislike the use of arrows. That said, we shall probably have to rush to close, at which time bows will avail them little against iron blades.'

'Just so,' Hallyd agreed. 'We bloody them until they break, and then we begin the hunt.'

She glanced at him for a moment, and then said, 'Sir, it may well be that Lord Urusander has already led the Legion on to the south road.'

Scowling, Hallyd Bahann nodded. 'Once we are done here, we'll march south.'

'Yes sir. The soldiers will be pleased by that.'

'Will they now? Remind them, lieutenant, that this day will deliver its own pleasures.'

As she moved off to relay his orders, Hallyd drew his sword and gestured to his shield man. 'Stay close and make keen your sight, Sartoril. These bastards have no honour.'

＊　　＊　　＊

From the cover of the forest, Glyph eyed the Legion soldiers as they formed up into a skirmish line, backed by three more lines roughly staggered behind it. Beside him crouched Lahanis, knives ready in her ash-hued hands. Glancing at her, seeing her trembling eagerness, Glyph murmured, 'Patience, I beg you. We must draw them in. Once among the trees, their advance will become uneven. The shields ever more cumbersome. They will think the worst of the threat from arrows is past.'

She hissed in frustration. 'They'll see us retreat. Again. They will call out their contempt. And when the arrows finally fly, they will curse us as cowards.'

'You and the other Butchers will have plenty of wounded

to finish off,' Glyph reminded her. 'Just stay back until few are left to fight.'

'Your priest knows nothing of battle.'

'This is not a battle, Lahanis. It is a hunt. This is driving a herd on to bad ground, and then killing every beast. This is about snags and mires, sinkholes and roots.'

'Sooner or later,' she predicted, 'you Shake must learn how to fight, to stand and not yield a step.'

'We'll need armour and blades for that.' He nodded towards the now advancing Legion lines. 'And today marks our first harvest.'

She tapped his forearm with the flat of one knife-blade. 'When they realize their error, Glyph, they will attempt to withdraw – back out on to the plain. Let me take my Butchers in behind them, to await their retreat.'

'Lahanis—'

'They look to me now to lead them! They have seen the joy of true combat – they *came* to me! Your own hunters! Do not forsake them, Glyph!'

He glanced back. He knew Narad waited somewhere among the trees of the deeper wood. No longer a soldier, no longer one to stand among his hunters, his warriors. No, just as Lord Urusander would not join in battle – unless all else was lost – so too was Narad's value too great to risk. *Witches have found him – now attend him. Shamans name him their prince. They speak of old gods, abandoned by faith, bereft of worshippers, who are less than shadows. And yet, they abide at this world's edge. Like storm-wrack upon a shore.*

*The lost will gather, to build a dream of home. The Watch welcomes them all.*

'Glyph!'

He nodded. 'Very well. But be sure to wait until they are well past, and kill all the wounded who might be retreating.'

'None shall survive,' Lahanis promised, and then she moved off to re-join her score of followers.

*Her Butchers. Among us of the forest, the dressing of meat is a common skill. She takes the name and makes it a horror.*

*Such are the children of war.*

The morning was chilly, but sweat lay slick upon Glyph's palms, and he shifted yet again his grip on the bow. *I walked out of the water, dreaming of death. I left the lake, having wept into the waters the last of my grief. I painted ash on my face to make a mask, but the ash is no longer needed, and the mask has become me.*

*Narad speaks of a battle. But not this battle. He speaks of a war. But not this war. He speaks of a shoreline, but no shoreline we can see.*

*No matter. In the meantime, there is this.*

*      *      *

'Stay the fuck closer, damn you!' Arkandas snarled.

Telra lifted the shield again and caught up to her lieutenant. 'Why don't I just climb into your tunic, sir?'

'Keep an eye out for the first arrows!'

'They're retreating again,' Telra said, cursing as she stumbled into a hole hidden by deep snow. Her breath was harsh, her throat clawed at by the bitter cold air. Grunting, she climbed free and staggered forward.

Arkandas paused to let her catch up. 'They're not running though, are they?'

'No sir. When you're laying a trap like this one, you don't want to get too far ahead of your prey.'

'Do you see Hallyd?'

'No.'

'He needs to sound the recall. We need to close ranks and then begin a withdrawal.'

'Yes sir.'

'I think he was off to our right. Let's angle that way.'

Telra blinked at her lieutenant. 'Because you don't think the fool's done any of that.'

'We'd have heard.'

Offering Arkandas a bright white grin, Telra said nothing.

'He wants to push them right through the entire forest, all the way to the fucking river.'

'Yes, well, I guess he used to be smarter.'

'Watch your mouth, Telra. Now, stay close and let's find the captain.'

Pausing to wave on those soldiers directly behind them, Arkandas led Telra to the right, across the advance. When the arrows did not come, as the soldiers closed on the forest's edge; when the Deniers simply melted back another dozen or so paces, keeping their distance and taking cover behind tree-falls and boles and heaps of snow, Telra knew what was coming. Captain Hallyd Bahann seemed oblivious of the tactic being employed against them. Telra felt a burgeoning of fear and growing dread. Someone had organized the bastards. A mind was at work against them. *And we're walking right into this.*

'Lieutenant—'

'Save your breath, Telra! We'll get to him – see? There he is. We'll—'

The arrow that buried its obsidian point into the side of Arkandas's neck was burning along the last third of its tar-smeared shaft. Impacts thudded against Telra's wicker shield and she shrank down behind it, even as the lieutenant made a faint gurgling sound, before sinking on to her side, lying almost within reach, her boots kicking at the snow as if trying to run.

Flames now sent smoke up from the facing of Telra's shield as still more burning arrows hammered into it. *Fuck.*

Looking down, she met Arkandas's eyes and was startled by the strangely languid blink the lieutenant gave her, before the life behind those eyes flickered, and then went out.

Soldiers were screaming and shouting around her. Flaming arrows flitted like sparks through the gloom. Bearers with their shields aflame flung them away, scrabbling for their swords and the smaller bucklers they carried, and the arrows kept coming, finding flesh.

Backing up, hunched down, she looked to find Hallyd Bahann and saw, amidst the chaos, the captain's shield man, Sartoril, his cloak burning, the shafts of three arrows jutting from his back as he stumbled towards cover.

'Sound the retreat!' Telra shouted. 'Withdraw!'

Someone stumbled against her and she turned to find Corporal Paralandas. 'Telra! Where's the lieutenant?'

'Dead,' Telra replied, pointing six or so paces ahead. 'Where's Farab and Pryll? We've got to get the squad together and pull the fuck out of this mess!'

'Hallyd?'

'Sartoril's done and the captain's nowhere in sight. Probably face-down in the bloody snow.'

Paralandas wiped at the snot glistening on his upper lip. 'Saw thirty or so rushing the enemy. None of them made it twenty paces. Telra, there's easily a thousand of them in front of us!'

'We're cooked,' Telra agreed. 'Follow me – we'll round 'em up as we can.'

'Retreat?'

'Damn right we're retreating!'

Arrows hissed past as the two soldiers, scrabbling and sliding in the snow, began pulling back.

*     *     *

Lahanis crouched down over the dying soldier, stabbing one slick blade into the snow to one side and using the freed hand to reach into the wide gash in the man's throat. Cupping the hot blood, she brought it up to smear it across her face. Licking her lips, she smiled down at the soldier. The wound frothed as he struggled to breathe, but she could see he was drowning. *Slowly, yes? Good. Know your end is coming. Know it in your soul. Look well on your slayer.*

*Sometimes when you chase the girl, she turns on you.*

There had been a rush of retreating soldiers, only a few of them wounded. Someone had finally ordered a withdrawal. Some had pushed through their ambush, but Glyph and his archers had been close on the Legion's heels. Arrows thudded into exposed backs, the sound of their impacts all around her like a sudden hailstorm. She found herself running after soldiers who had flung away their swords and bucklers, pulling off their helms to see better, and she cut down one after

787

another from behind, whilst her fellow Butchers did much the same, many using hatchets and axes, crushing skulls and shattering knees.

On all sides, carnage, as the retreat became a rout, and the rout a slaughter.

Laughing, Lahanis moved away from the drowning man, seeking another victim.

*　　*　　*

Glyph reached for another arrow but found the hide quiver empty. Letting the bow drop, he drew his hunting knife as he began moving from one Legion body to the next, checking for signs of life. Where he found them, his blade extinguished them.

He had never seen so many bodies, had never imagined what it would be like to move through a battlefield, seeing the blood, the excrement, the food-flecked fluids that had spilled out from gutted men and women. He could not have imagined mortal faces capable of finding so many different expressions for death, as if an artist had gone mad in this forest, carving one white visage after another, chiselled from the frozen snow itself, splashed with crimson as if from bleeding hands.

Glyph found himself staggering among the corpses, no longer examining bodies, no longer caring if he saw the faint stream of breath.

The day was getting colder. Shivering, he paused to lean against the bole of a blackened tree. A hunter stood before him, speaking, but Glyph could find no meaning in the words he heard, as if some other language was spoken in this terrible place.

Slowly, however, as if from a vast distance, comprehension returned to him.

'. . . breathes still, war-master. He begs for his life.'

'Who?'

'Their leader,' the hunter replied. 'He names himself Captain Hallyd Bahann. We found him hiding in the hollow of a fallen tree.'

788

'Bind him. Send him back to the Watch. Begin stripping armour and recovering weapons, and arrows.'

'This is a great victory, war-master!'

'Yes.' *Now find that sculptor. Chase him down. Pin him to the ground. Still his red hands. No more of his work on this day. An end to it. No more.* 'Yes. A great victory.'

*       *       *

Narad stood wrapped in furs, watching as they dragged the enemy commander closer. Captain Hallyd Bahann's crotch was stained. Tears muddied his cheeks. He stank with all the animal smells of panic. Dignity, Narad well knew, was hard to come by, especially in battle and all that came afterwards. Survival itself could leave one feeling sullied.

*Better they had killed him. I want nothing to do with this.*

Glyph's hunters, now warriors, were returning to the camp in small groups, burdened with bloodstained leather armour, weapon-belts and helms. Their faces were flushed despite the grey cast of their skin, yet something lifeless hid behind all of that, something scoured out and unlikely to ever return. This deadness accompanied the arriving warriors like a roll of fog across moorland, bleak and miasmic. Narad felt it swirl around him, seeking a way in.

*Now warriors, but this is no elevation of stature or rank, no prize freshly won. This is a descent felt deep in the soul, as if a newfound skill was only now comprehended as a curse. This is competence maligned, pride besmirched. We now walk a levelled world.*

'A ransom will be paid. This I promise!'

Narad frowned at the captain who had been thrown down at his feet. He struggled to make sense of the man's fraught words. 'Ransom? What need have we for coin?'

'I have value! I am an officer of the Legion, damn you.'

*Yes. I recall taking orders from ones such as you, sir. I recall, as well, where that led.* 'Every soldier,' he said, 'holds to a faith. That the ones commanding them are honourable, that necessity is bound to righteousness. This keeps the stains from becoming permanent. Imagine the betrayal, then, when the soldier discovers neither honour nor righteousness in those commanders.'

'Lord Urusander's cause is righteous enough, you fool. Abyss take me,' Hallyd snarled, 'that I should argue morality with a forest-grubbing murderer.'

Narad tilted his head as he studied the man at his feet. 'Was it by Lord Urusander's command that a family at a wedding should be slaughtered? Name for me, sir, the moral justification for that. What of the bride – the poor bride – raped to death upon the hearthstone? Where, I beg you, is the honour to be found in such atrocity?'

'The excesses of that ... event, belong to the captain commanding that company. She exceeded her orders—'

'Infayen Menand, yes. But I am curious – where did the instances of excess begin? The bride's ill usage, or the first sword to leave the scabbard? Some paths acquire a momentum of their own, as I am sure you comprehend. One thing leads inevitably to the next. So, from noble beginnings, to unmitigated horror.'

Hallyd bared his teeth. 'Take it up with Infayen.'

'Perhaps we will.'

Hallyd Bahann's face suddenly twisted. 'They will hunt you down! They will flay the skin from every damned one of you!'

Narad glanced up as three figures approached. A shaman and two witches. They had come down from the northwest, from the lands of House Dracons. *With their bags filled with bones and talons, with teeth and acorns, feathers and beads. With magic like smoke around them. Say nothing more to me of ancient spirits and forgotten gods, and I'll not speak of my memories of your kind screaming inside a burning longhouse.*

The one bearing the antlered headdress now spoke. 'Yedan Narad, we will take him if you like.'

'Take him?' He eyed the three. Their flat visages revealed nothing.

'A clearing,' the shaman continued. 'Filled with sharpened stakes. It is fitting.'

'What are they talking about?' demanded Hallyd Bahann, struggling to shift position, twisting round in an effort to glare up at the shaman.

'They seek to prolong your death, I think,' Narad replied, sighing.

'Torture? Abyss below, have mercy on me. It's not done to soldiers – don't you people understand that? When did the Tiste sink to the level of savages?'

'Oh, we are savages indeed,' Narad said, nodding. 'Not soldiers at all, sir. You should have considered that before you sent your soldiers into the forests to slay the innocent. Before your soldiers raped the helpless. In your world, sir, you called your victims Deniers. What gift of your civil comportment did they so egregiously deny? Never mind. We have now fully embraced your ways, sir.'

'You're a damned deserter! That sword at your belt!'

Narad shrugged. 'But I wonder, sir. What worth this civilization, when savagery thrives within it? When criminals abound in safety behind its walls? And no, I speak not of the Deniers, but of you and your soldiers.'

'No different from you! What company? Tell me!'

'Why, none other than Captain Infayen Menand's.'

Hallyd's eyes narrowed. 'Ah, and do I see a bride's blood on your hands?'

'Yes,' said Narad, 'I think you do.'

'Then—'

'Then yes sir. I followed orders. That was my crime, remains my crime, remains forever my crime.'

'I'll give you Infayen Menand,' Hallyd hissed. 'Free me. I swear I'll lead her here, into ambush.'

'Why is it, captain, that every army kills its deserters? Could it be, perhaps, that such objection by common soldiers in fact threatens the entire façade? That delicate tower of twigs and sticks, of stretched spider-silk and beads of sap, this tottering construct of institutional insanity that makes a cage of every virtue, only to then whisper of *necessity*?'

'Deserters are cowards,' growled Hallyd Bahann.

'Some are, I'm sure,' agreed Narad. 'But others, well, I suspect they simply *object*. And refuse, and deny. They do what anyone who has been betrayed might do, yes? And if so, must we not look at the betrayers?'

'Justify what you've done all you like.'

'I did try just that, sir, without much success. In fact, I could not even get past the reasons, sickly and contemptuous as they proved to be, much less justifications. And that was my discovery, captain. The journey from reasons to justifications should be long and difficult, and indeed, few of us truly deserve the journey's completion. But we know that, don't we? So, we simply . . . cheat.'

As he had been speaking, Narad noted Glyph's arrival, with a blood-drenched Lahanis a step behind him. *Have we lost a single warrior?*

Hallyd struggled anew against his bindings.

'Yedan Narad?'

He looked up at the shaman. 'He is not to die slowly,' he said. 'Neither he nor any other made captive. Slit his throat, as you would any other quarry brought down and at last within your reach. Whatever we possess that we believe sets us apart from the beasts, let us not make it cruel.'

After a long moment, the two witches and the shaman bowed to him, and one of the witches knelt down beside Hallyd Bahann. She grasped his sweaty hair in one fist and pulled his head back. Iron flashed and then blood poured out upon the ground. The captain's wet sigh came from his throat, the only sound he made as he died.

The shaman said, 'We would take his body to the clearing, and the sharpened stakes. For the forest, Watch. For the weeping trees. For the burned ground beneath the snow, and the sleeping roots.'

Narad nodded. 'As you will.'

As the shaman helped the two witches drag away Hallyd Bahann's corpse, Glyph strode up to Narad. 'Some escaped,' he said. 'Made it to the horses.'

'How many?'

Glyph glanced back at Lahanis, who shrugged and said, 'A score, perhaps. Half of them wounded before they could ride away, as we were among them. We have captured most of the horses.' Her smile was stained pink. 'We'll not starve, priest. We'll not,' she added after a moment, 'have to eat our slain.'

Narad turned away at that. Two hunters had found the leavings of a meal in a camp not far off. Someone had made a repast of a dead soldier's thigh. He prayed that someone was not now here in this swollen camp.

In any case, Lahanis was correct. Food was scarce and starvation had gripped their ragged army. It was a poor fate for well-trained horses, but needs must.

'Yedan Narad.'

'Glyph?'

'Your plan worked, but no future commander will be so foolish as to repeat Bahann's stupidity on this day.'

'That is true.'

'Urusander will come for us.'

'Perhaps.'

'Will you have an answer for them?'

'Glyph, the same answer. Always the same answer.'

'Yedan, you have become a war-master in your own right.'

But Narad shook his head. 'No, I have not. But the one who speaks through me, Glyph . . . ah, that one. Cold, a soul unloved. There are some for whom doubt does not weaken, for whom uncertainty only strengthens resolve. I said "cold", did I not? The wrong word. Indeed, there is no word for that man. In my dreams, I become him. In my dreams, he dwells within me.'

'We lost no one,' Glyph said.

Narad closed his eyes. 'Not true.'

'Yedan?'

'Before this battle, we lost everyone.'

After a long moment, Glyph suddenly sobbed. Quickly turning away, he stumbled off.

Left in his wake, Lahanis glared at Narad. 'This is how you celebrate our victory?'

'When there is nothing to celebrate, Lahanis, then my answer must be yes, this is how we are to celebrate our victories.'

She snarled and then swung about, marching off to re-join her Butchers.

Narad stared after her. The loss of children was a terrible thing.

# TWENTY

THE WINDS BATTERED AT THE STONE WALLS OF Tulla keep, sweeping round the turreted cones of the tower roofs that had been raised to fend off the winter, scouring free of snow the walkways, the crenellations and the black pocks of the murder holes in the outer walls and gatehouse. The granite, grey as ice, was cold enough to burn skin.

The keep surmounted a crag of stone, but the jagged outcrops of the surrounding ridge rose higher still, like the stubs of rotted teeth, and there the snow huddled in pockets, ice forming rivers in the cracks and fissures. Sukul Ankhadu so disliked this season, with the cold laying siege to the keep and the wagonloads of firewood dwindling as the months dragged on. More than half the rooms and an entire wing of the main building had been abandoned to the chill, and this did nothing to insulate the remaining rooms where braziers burned continuously, or hearths blazed night and day.

Under the disapproving regard of Castellan Rancept, she had taken to drinking more wine than usual, ill befitting a girl not yet into womanhood, and wandering about wrapped in a fur robe the trailing edge of which had once been white.

Restlessness was a dark force in the soul, riding currents of longing for what could not be found, much less recognized. Rooms shrank, corridors narrowed, and the light from lanterns and oil lamps seemed to withdraw, abandoning the world to shadows and gloom.

She stood now, alone, in an unused fitting room crowded with chests and winter gear stored here on behalf of the keep's guests, of which there were many, with more arriving each day. The floor's thin planks of wood beneath her moccasins were covered by a worn rug, and both warmth and voices from the chamber below drifted up to her.

Lady Hish Tulla's return had been less than delightful. A woman torn from her new husband made for fierce moods and a displeased outlook, and already Sukul longed for the days when she and Rancept had been virtually alone amidst servants, grooms and maids, while the Houseblades kept to their barracks gambling with bones or playing Kef Tanar.

But even Sukul could agree that a meeting of the highborn bloods was long overdue. Her own interest in the matter was increasingly losing its intriguing and delightful irrelevance – that sense of its being a game, a curious realm of machination and ambition – and luring her into the world of adults, where she could dwell beneath notice, unremarked upon and thereby made invisible.

The voices rising from beneath her belonged to a trio of guests. Sukul had met Lord Vanut Degalla and his odious wife Syl Lebanas once before, at some event in the Citadel, although her memory of the details was vague – she had been very young then, too wide-eyed to comprehend much beyond a few names and the faces to which they belonged. Her sister Sharenas had expressed disdain for the pair, although Sukul could not quite recall why. The third guest sharing the small chamber below was Lady Aegis, of House Haran, an outlying estate inclined to isolation. Tall, attractive in a regal fashion, somewhat diminished by the obvious efforts she made to maintain that regal air, Aegis had already set herself in opposition to Hish Tulla, for reasons Sukul did not yet understand.

Moving quietly, she seated herself on a chest, drawing her fur robe closer about her shoulders, and listened.

Syl Lebanas was speaking. 'The fault lies with Anomander,'

she said yet again. 'I think we can all agree on that. It falls to the comportment of Mother Dark's champion to affect the proper unity among the highborn. After all, the face of our enemy is hardly obscure—'

'Oh, enough of that, Syl,' cut in Aegis, her clipped manner of speaking hinting, as always, at impatience and contempt. 'Insist upon simplicity as it seems you must, if only to find false comfort in your mastery of the situation. The truth of this matter . . . far more complicated. Allegiances uncertain. Loyalties suspect. What looms before us is nothing short of a fundamental reordering of power in the realm. As such . . . promises to be vicious.'

'Against which,' Vanut Degalla murmured, 'even you must acknowledge, Aegis, Lord Anomander has failed and continues to fail in placating. Blood will be spilled in the Citadel itself before this is done.'

'Let the two priestesses set talons to each other,' Aegis retorted. 'All this talk of Father Light and Mother Dark. Since when did matters of religion demand . . . unveiling of daggers, much less swords? Before this pogrom – before the atrocity . . . unmitigated slaughter of innocents – we Tiste dwelt well enough in a plurality of faiths.'

Degalla snorted. 'My dear Aegis, and how many Deniers crowded your distant holdings? Scant few, I should think. No, the worm of disaffection was set among us the day Draconus elevated our queen into a goddess. While even you, wife, would see Anomander the instigator of our present disorder. He is not.'

'Even so,' Syl insisted, 'he has indeed failed in meeting the challenge.'

'The failure is not his,' Degalla said.

'I am content enough,' said Aegis, 'seeing him reduced.'

'I am sure.'

'What do you mean by that, Vanut?'

'Sheathe your knives, Aegis. Your refutation on the matter of Andarist's choice of woman to wed lacked subtlety. What future do you imagine? Why, if a schism now exists between Anomander and Andarist, you will surely offer commiseration to ease a certain grief and the pain of bereavement. But no matter. We would see the Legion weakened, but not necessarily destroyed.'

'The challenge,' added Syl Lebanas, 'lies in achieving that.'

'Then you two would side with Hish Tulla,' said Aegis.

Degalla replied, 'The diminishing of power and influence upon both sides would be ideal, Aegis. Anomander feels free to indulge himself in personal matters – not well suited to the commander of Mother Dark's armies. We are all agreed on that, yes?'

'And should he be stripped of such responsibility?'

'Then a more modest sibling might serve in his place.'

'But not,' said Syl, 'that bloodless brother of theirs. If, among the three, there is one to truly fear, it is Silchas Ruin.'

'Why?' demanded Aegis.

Vanut Degalla answered. 'Silchas Ruin does not understand loyalty.'

Aegis snorted. 'Meaning, he cannot be bought. But you think Andarist can?'

'I leave his suborning to your sympathetic hands.'

'Then we are agreed?'

'We will attend the battle, and see how it plays out,' Vanut said.

'Hish will believe us with her, then?'

'She can believe what she likes. In this, we are hardly alone in our unwillingness to commit. My sister agrees entirely with this position, and so too House Manaleth.'

Aegis spoke again, her tone suddenly harsher. 'You know something, Degalla.'

'Let us say, we are confident in matters, to the extent that anything can be predicted. It is, indeed, more a matter of expectation.'

'Enlighten me further.'

'Have faith, Aegis.'

'Faith?'

'Just so,' and Sukul could hear the sly smile in Syl Lebanas's voice. 'Faith.'

'We should return to the dining hall,' Vanut Degalla said. 'My sister will not attend, preferring to leave this night to me. I believe I heard the bell announcing the arrival of yet another highborn.'

Aegis grunted. 'That should be enough to begin things, then.'

'Hish Tulla will decide.'

Syl laughed softly. 'Yes, we can be generous on occasion.'

'When it costs nothing.'

'It pleases me that we do understand one another, Lady Aegis.'

Sukul listened to them leave, waited a few moments, and then rose from the chest. The game of betrayal was indeed a subtle one, when it came to adults and their ways. And yet, a child's glee remained, swirling beneath the surface. Recognizing this came to Sukul as something of a shock. *Boys and girls in the end after all. Here I believed politics to be something lofty, clever and sharp with wit. But it is nothing like that.*

*Desire is venal. Needs give way to hunger, fostering the illusion of starvation – as Gallan has said – and the world becomes a pit of wolves. 'In the cruel game of politics, we are brought low by the child within each of us, until every howl is deafening in its abject stupidity, and none can hear the wails of the suffering.'*

She felt sick to her stomach. In need of another goblet brimming with wine.

*Restlessness, let me dull thy sting.*

\*     \*     \*

Rancept's breathing wheezed noisily in the steamy confines of the kitchen. The cook had driven his cast of helpers into the scullery and from within that side chamber with its vast iron sinks came the clash of pots, plates and cutlery, leaving the castellan and his two informal guests alone at the carving table. Sekarrow wore the livery of a Houseblade of House Drethdenan, although her long fingers and delicate hands were clearly better suited to the four-stringed iltre she idly plucked than to the plain sword at her belt. There was a delicacy about her that most men would find endearing, and her eyes were large and luminous, set within a childlike face. Her brother, Horult Chiv, made for a stark contrast, with his face of sharp angles and his frame robust and stolid, and the hands he rested upon the tabletop were broad, battered and blunt. Horult was captain of the same Houseblades, and also Drethdenan's long-time lover. Such a union could of course produce no heirs, but in all other manner the two men were indeed married and seen as such.

In his long years of life, Rancept had had occasion to reflect on the wondrous variability of love, as might anyone left standing on its periphery, too bent and battered to draw another's eye. He was no sceptic in his observation of tenderness, but the longing in his soul did not incline him to bitterness. Some were destined to walk alone through life, others not. Drethdenan's adoration of Horult Chiv delivered a kind of balm to all who witnessed it.

The nobles were gathering in the dining hall, and while Horult might well have elected to sit beside Lord Drethdenan, as was the right of any spouse, instead he appeared in the company of his sister, joining Rancept where he sat finishing his meal.

Horult Chiv's demeanour suggested some measure of unease, if not frustration, but as Rancept knew neither of these two people well he remained silent, wiping up the last of the stew's gravy with a piece of bread, pausing regularly in his chewing to draw a breath or two.

Finally, Sekarrow dropped her fingers from the strings and settled the instrument into her lap as she leaned back in the chair. Eyeing her brother, she said, 'Caution is not a flaw.'

Horult rapped the tabletop with his knuckles, a sharp sound that made Rancept jump. 'It has its place, I grant you. But not in this matter.'

'He fears what he might lose,' she said.

'So much that what he fears may well come to pass.'

Her thin brows lifted. 'He will lose you?'

Horult started, and then glanced away. 'No. Of course not. We have had disagreements before.'

'You mistake my meaning, brother.'

'In what manner?'

Sighing, Sekarrow looked across to Rancept. 'Castellan, I beg you, indulge my dimwitted sibling with an explanation.'

Grunting, Rancept said, 'Not for me to intrude, unless invited.'

Leaning forward, Horult gestured. 'Consider it done. Tell me, what so dims my wits that I comprehend nothing of my sister's warning?'

'You command his Houseblades, sir. On a field of battle, soldiers die. Officers die.'

The knuckles rapped again, hard enough to momentarily silence the dishwashers in the other room. 'That is . . . selfish. What value this presumption of responsibility when the first threat sees it shy away? I *am* a soldier. That entails risks. We are in a civil war. A pretender seeks to claim a throne.'

'Not entirely accurate,' Sekarrow murmured, returning to tuning her iltre. 'He but seeks a second throne, to stand beside the first, and of the two, at least *his* would be seen. I have heard tell that no vision proves keen enough to pierce the veil of darkness our beloved Mother now wraps about herself. Indeed, some say she is now nothing more than darkness manifest, a thing of absences so profound as to give the illusion of presence.'

'Poets can play games with such notions all they like,' Horult retorted. 'One throne, two thrones, it matters not one whit. I dream of the day when pedantry ceases to be.'

Smiling, Sekarrow said, 'And I dream of the day it is no longer necessary. Precision of language is to be valued. Don't you agree, castellan? How many wars and tragedies might we have avoided if meanings were not only clear, but agreed upon? In fact, I would hazard the suggestion that language lies at the root of all conflict. Misapprehension as the prelude to violence.'

Rancept pushed the plate away and settled back, collecting up his tankard of weak ale. 'The buck dragged down by wolves might disagree.'

'Hah!' snorted Horult Chiv.

But Sekarrow shook her head. 'There is necessity in hunger, of which we do not speak here, castellan. Nothing of hunter or prey, at least not in the simplest sense of their meaning. Instead, we take such natural inclinations and twist them into our more civil state of being. The enemy to our way of thinking becomes the prey, assuming it is too weak to claim any other title, and we the hunter. But such words themselves, "hunter" and "prey", seek a kind of synonymy with nature, when the reality is in fact one of murder.' She brushed at her uniform's leather shoulder-guards. 'Murder is then obscured behind a cascade of words intended to deflect that brutal truth. War, soldiers, battles – the mere vocabulary of our existence, as commonplace as breathing, or eating and drinking. And, of course, as necessary.' She twisted a peg and then strummed the strings, making a discordant clash of notes. 'Uniforms, training, discipline. Honour, duty, courage. Principles, integrity, revenge. To obscure is to empower the lie.'

'And what lie might that be?' Horult demanded.

'Why, that being a soldier excuses us from the murder we commit. Have you ever wondered, dear brother, what lies at the heart of the Legion's demand for justice?'

'Avarice.'

Her brows lifted once more. She turned another peg, strummed again, yielding if anything a more jarring sound. 'Castellan?'

Rancept shrugged. 'As your brother suggests. Land, wealth.'

'To compensate their sacrifice, yes?'

Both men nodded.

'But . . . what sacrifice do they mean?'

Horult threw up his hands. 'Why, the one they made, of course!'

'And that is?'

Her brother scowled.

'Castellan?'

Rancept scratched at his misshapen nose, felt wetness on his fingers and reached for his handkerchief. 'The fighting. The killing. The fallen comrades.'

'Then one must ask at some point, I should think: what compensation should a civil state give to those who murdered in its name?'

'There was more to it than that,' Horult objected. 'They were saving the lives of loved ones, of innocents. They were standing between the helpless and those who wished them harm.'

'And does this act require compensation? More to the point, is not that act, of defence of the weak and the helpless, something that should be expected of *every* able adult? Indeed, are we not describing something we share with every beast and creature of this world? Will not a mother bear defend her cubs? Will not soldier ants die defending their nest and queen?'

'Then, by your very words, sister, war is indeed natural!'

'When was the last time you saw thousands of worker ants line a parade of their victorious soldiers? Or the queen emerge from the bowels of her nest to drape medals and honours upon her brave subjects?'

'Even there,' Horult said, stabbing at her with a finger, 'you trap yourself. Some are born weak and helpless, but others are born to be soldiers. Each finds a place in every society.'

She smiled. 'Workers and soldiers. Queens and kings. Gods and goddesses, all overseeing their fine and finely ordered creation. The worker enslaved to work, the soldier enslaved to the cause of defending and killing. The helpless doomed to remain helpless. The innocent cursed into a lifetime of naivety—'

'And children? What of defending them?'

'Ah yes, the children who must grow up to make more workers and more soldiers.'

'You find your own arguments dragging you into a quagmire, beloved sister.'

She strummed the strings again, making Rancept wince. 'Language keeps us in our place. And, when necessary, puts us in our place. Let's go back to that question of compensation. The poor legion out there, even now marching down upon helpless Kharkanas. Land. Wealth. In answer to the sacrifices made. The castellan speaks of that sacrifice: the killing, the wounds, the friends lost. Name me the number of coins sufficient to compensate for being made into a murderer. How high the stack to match a lopped-off limb, or a lost eye? How broad the stretch of land needed to keep the ghosts of fallen comrades at bay? Show me, I beg you, the coin and the land sufficient to ease a soldier's anguish and loss.'

Slowly, Horult Chiv leaned back.

Sekarrow's smile was soft. 'Brother, the man who loves you fears your wounding. Your death. Against that, land is worthless, coin an insult to the soul. He hesitates, because he sees clearly what he might lose. For love, he will do nothing. And, perhaps, love is the only valid reason for doing nothing.' She shifted her attention to Rancept. 'What think you on that, castellan?'

He wiped again at his nose. 'I would hear you play,' he said.

Snorting again, Horult Chiv stood. 'She can't,' he said, moving off to collect a new jug of ale, and two tankards.

Sekarrow shrugged apologetically. 'No talent.'

'The arguments begin in yonder hall,' said Horult, sitting back down and pouring ale into all three tankards. 'Let us drink, and in silence – such as we can manage here – bemoan the cruel misuse of horsehair, wood and glue.'

Rancept squinted at the siblings, and decided he liked them both. He reached down for his tankard.

*　　*　　*

Families were sordid things, Lady Hish Tulla reflected as she looked upon the uncle she had not seen in decades. The curse of estrangement burned like a brand when its subject made a game of sudden, unexpected appearances, bearing an expression of amusement and expectation, as if past crimes could settle like sand. In the moment of seeing the tall, thin form of Venes Turayd, however, as he brushed snow from his furs just within the entranceway, the storm within her ignited with all the fury of its shocking birth.

An uneasy truce had been achieved in their protracted

804

dance of avoidance in the managing of family lands and interests. Although, upon belated consideration, Hish Tulla realized that this meeting was inevitable. Venes commanded a considerable element of her Houseblades, and she would need them for the battle to come. Her summons had made no provision against his attending.

Berating herself, she stepped forward. 'Venes, have you brought the company?'

'Ensconced nearby, milady. The summer high pasture camp upon the slopes of Istan Rise.' He paused, and then said, 'If not for my many spies, I could have hoped to find you with your new husband at your side. Gripp Galas, who once stood upon one flank of the First Son of Darkness, less a sword than a dagger, I gather. But then, the court of the Citadel was always an insipid, venal place. You reached down far, dear niece, to win Anomander's favour.'

'Oh, Uncle Venes, how it stings you to find yet another man between us. How fares the old wound in this long winter? Do you greet every morning aching deep beneath that scar? I trust it burns you still.'

'As does your perennial regret, milady, that your blade missed what it sought.' He drew off his gauntlets, glancing around. 'The others?'

'In the dining hall. We'll consider you the last and begin immediately.'

His smile was hard and cruel. 'If votes are tallied, I will oppose you.'

'On principle.'

He nodded. 'Just so.'

'I will have your company nonetheless, as is my prerogative.'

'My dogs are now wolves, milady. Consider yourself warned. More to the point,' he added, 'I will twist your every order.'

'Come to my room tonight, Uncle, and I can finish what I started, and to announce my satisfaction I will nail your severed cock above the door.'

He laughed as he tucked the gauntlets into his sword-belt.

'Drunken appetites had their way with me in my youth, but no longer. As for past regrets, I believe I can continue to rely upon your discretion.'

'Oh?'

'If you hadn't been discreet, surely Gripp Galas would have found me by now. Dagger or sword? The former, I should think, as my prowess with the latter has not diminished with the years.'

'Nor his.'

Shrugging, Venes moved past her. 'This house . . . as cold as ever.'

She followed her uncle into the dining hall.

*       *       *

Under the baleful glare of Rancept, Sukul Ankhadu collected a goblet and poured some wine; then, nodding to the castellan's two companions at the kitchen table, she made her way out into the dining hall.

The vast hearth crackled and spat sparks, flames fiercely devouring the split logs of pine. Smaller braziers squatted in the corners and flanked every entranceway leading into the huge chamber. Lamps hung from hooks high on walls and from ceiling rafters, turning the smoky air amber. For an instant Sukul searched among the dozen or so dogs scuffling here and there, seeking Ribs, but then she recalled, with a pang, the animal's loss.

Not dead, thankfully. *The boy, Orfantal. They're in the Citadel now. I would have liked him under my wing, that boy. To learn the art of being unseen. It was not so displeasing, too, his obvious adoration of me. There was so much I could have done with that.*

*And might still. We are sworn to each other, and Orfantal's not one to cast aside such promises. Future alliances will see sweet fruition, when it is us who stalk the halls of power.*

Water-pipes had been set out, adding spice to the bitter woodsmoke and the acrid taint of wine that had been spilled on the table's wooden surface. Sukul sauntered closer, eyes upon a hunting hound that had accompanied Lord Baesk of

House Hellad. The beast looked as old and grey as its master, but its eyes were sharp as they tracked her.

Lady Manalle was speaking, her tone defensive and somewhat despairing. 'Infayen's treachery is a family matter, and we should think no better of her daughter – none of us has seen Menandore since Mother Dark's investiture.'

'Infayen will see you ousted should the Legion triumph,' said Lord Trevok of House Misharn in his cracked voice. The scar on his neck, running from beneath his left ear down to the breastbone, was livid, making a track for the sweat that seemed to plague the man even in the cold. 'Urusander will see us all replaced, by lesser cousins and the like – all those disaffected from our own class who flocked so eagerly to his banner in the wars—'

'Because,' cut in Lady Raelle of House Sengara, 'these waters are far from clear. We must simply accept that this battle will see kin set upon kin. No matter what the outcome, the highborn will lose family members, thus weakening us for generations to come.'

Sukul drew close to the hound, smiled at the slow sweep of its tail.

Vanut Degalla had twisted slightly to regard the woman beside him. 'Your point, Raelle?'

'Is this. If we are to be made weaker, our enemies must be made weaker still. Urusander and his legion must be broken. That means ensuring the death of Hunn Raal, Tathe Lorat and Hallyd Bahann. And Infayen Menand, for that matter.' She leaned her slender frame back, using both hands to sweep away her long hair until it was clear of her shoulders. 'In such congress, dear Manalle, disloyal highborn cease to be family matters.'

Degalla set down the mouthpiece of his water-pipe and moved his hand to rest upon Raelle's forearm. 'My dear, we know how you grieve over the murder of your husband, and this now feeds an obsession to see Hunn Raal dead. In your place, I would feel the same, I assure you. But too much confusion surrounds Ilgast Rend – what he was doing there, how he came to command the Wardens in Calat's absence, or even why he thought to challenge the Legion without any support. Even a commander can die in battle—'

'But he didn't,' Raelle said in a tight voice, eyes half-lidded as she regarded the man's hand on her wrist. 'He didn't die in the fighting. Raal had him beheaded.'

Glancing over at Vanut Degalla's wife, Sukul saw a pallid hue to Syl Lebanas's dark face, her lips pressed into a thin line.

Degalla withdrew his hand, making its departure a caress. He then leaned back, retrieving the mouthpiece. 'I have heard the same rumours, Raelle.'

'Not mere rumours, Vanut. I am telling you what happened. All this wringing of hands over Urusander, when it is Hunn Raal we should be concerned about. It's now said he has come into magic—'

'This talk of sorcery is a distraction,' Trevok said in a rasp. 'Leave Hunn Raal to his conjuries and cantrips. Urusander cannot be allowed to ascend a throne. Lop off the head and the beast dies – Urusander's death will see Hunn Raal driven in flight from Kharkanas, with all his murderous cronies tucking tail and joining him.'

'I think not,' said Drethdenan, his soft voice cutting across the heated words of the others, all of whom now faced him. Clearing his throat, the slight man continued, 'Hunn Raal is of the Issgin line. With Urusander dead, he will advance his own claim. For the throne. Indeed, he might well be delighted to hear of the bloodlust some of us here now hold for Urusander.' Drethdenan offered Lord Trevok a sad smile. 'You, old friend, have never forgiven Urusander's failure to protect your family in the Summer of Raids. Hunn Raal knows this as well as any of us, and no doubt anticipates and perhaps even relies upon such feelings among us. Not just you, Trevok, but also Manalle and Hedeg Lesser, both of whom blame Urusander for Infayen's betrayal of the House.' He waved a hand. 'Whilst Raelle finds herself virtually alone in recognizing Hunn Raal as the real threat here.'

'Hardly,' snapped Manalle. 'Hunn Raal is a seducer of men and women both, with his whispers of indulgence, his sodden smiles and wild promises. Lord Drethdenan sees well the threat posed by Raal.'

'I would hazard,' ventured Hish Tulla from where she sat at the head of the table, 'none of us is so foolish as to ignore Hunn Raal. By the same measure, we must also recognize the threat presented by High Priestess Syntara, who would see Mother Dark's pre-eminence ended. Whosoever believes that two sides in opposition achieve a lasting balance that stands superior to a single, undivided loyalty knows nothing of history.'

Degalla hissed out a thick stream of smoke. 'Lady Hish Tulla, what we seek here is the unity of the highborn. Leave Mother Dark to her own concerns, and with them her precious First Son and House Purake.'

Venes Turayd thumped down his goblet, having just drained it, and said, 'My niece seeks to make a single bowstring of these precious strands here, to send arrows into the heart of more enemies than we dare count. What value our privileged standing when there are few left to kneel before us?'

Hish Tulla sat back, gaze fixed on Vanut Degalla as she elected to ignore her uncle's words. 'Vanut, the matter before us most certainly concerns our position with respect to House Purake and its central role in the defence not just of Mother Dark, but of Kharkanas itself. Urusander will see the highborn reduced, our holdings cut away. Our own blood in his ranks will be elevated into our places at the head of each family.'

'Then where, in this chamber, is House Purake?'

'Where it should be, in the Citadel!'

Vanut smiled without much humour and said, 'Not precisely true, Hish Tulla, as you well know. The First Son? Wandering the forest. Brother Andarist? Hiding in a cave with his grief. No, only Silchas Ruin remains in the Citadel, white-skinned and busy dismantling his brother's officer corps. Who is left to the Houseblades beyond Silchas himself? Kellaras? Indeed, a fine warrior, but he is only one man who now walks with back bruised by Ruin's incessant bullying.' He pulled harshly on his pipe. 'We all have our spies in the Citadel, after all. None of this should come as any surprise.'

'White-skinned?' Hish Tulla said in a deceptively calm tone.

Venes Turayd snorted, reaching for the nearest jug of wine.

Shrugging, Vanut Degalla glanced away. 'At the very least, proof against Mother Dark's blessing. Indeed, one might perhaps question Anomander himself, with his hair of white. Only the third and the least of the brothers, it would seem, remains outwardly pure.' His brows lifted. 'What are we to make of that?'

There was silence for a time, broken only when Baesk stirred in his seat and said, 'The question remains before us. Do we gather to defend Kharkanas, and all that we hold dear, or do we yield to Urusander, Hunn Raal, the High Priestess, and three thousand avaricious soldiers?'

'Too simple,' Vanut murmured. 'There is another option.'

'Oh?'

'Indeed, Baesk, one which you might well embrace, given your two young children and their uncertain futures. We have the choice of . . . biding our time. How long before those avaricious soldiers begin squabbling among themselves? How long before certain alliances are sought, tilting a feud's outcome? Indeed, how long before Hunn Raal petitions for the glorious rebirth of House Issgin?' He suddenly rose and faced Hish Tulla. 'Do not misunderstand me, honoured host. I too believe we must indeed assemble our Houseblades on the day of battle, to attend to the defence of Kharkanas if necessary. No, what I suggest here is that we create a contingent plan. That we establish a place and the time in which to regroup, marshal our resources anew, and begin a much longer, far more subtle campaign.'

'Yield a second throne,' said Aegis, 'only to immediately begin gnawing its frail legs.'

Vanut Degalla shrugged. 'Urusander expects this battle to decide matters. I suggest, should it come to that, we make the peace that follows a bloody one.'

Standing nearby, in the falling off of light between two lamps, Sukul Ankhadu could see the horror slowly descend upon Hish Tulla's features.

Remorselessly, Vanut continued, 'Will any House here refuse to attend the battle?'

No one spoke.

'Will all commit their Houseblades to the fight?' Drethdenan asked, his placid eyes narrow and fixed on Vanut, as if he sought to read what hid behind the man's benign expression. 'And I would think, in this case, silence is no answer.'

Trevok asked, 'Who will command House Purake – Mother Dark's very own Houseblades?'

'Does it matter?' Vanut retorted. 'It is tradition that each of us commands our own, yes? As for matters of disposition upon the field, well, the Valley of Tarns offers few opportunities for complicated tactics. No, such fighting as might come will be straightforward.'

'Lord Anomander will command,' said Hish Tulla.

'With Mother Dark's blessing?' Manalle asked.

'She blesses none of this.'

'Nor the proposed marriage,' added Hedeg Lesser in a growl.

'Leave that issue to one side,' Vanut Degalla said. 'It has no influence on the battle itself – would you not agree, Hish Tulla? If Anomander commands, he will commit to the battle.'

'Of course he will,' said Hish Tulla, her lips strangely pale.

'You sow confusion, Vanut,' said Lady Aegis, her brow furrowed. 'Only to seemingly sweep it all aside.'

Seating himself once more and reaching for his goblet of wine, Vanut sighed and said, 'Many points of contention needed . . . airing.'

Sukul noted Lady Manalle's sudden scowl, and a flash of undisguised hatred in the woman's eyes as they remained fixed upon Vanut Degalla.

*None here could call another friend.*

*And what they would so desperately defend and preserve*

*is both base and crude. Their own positions, the hierarchy of private privilege. They wage their own perpetual war, here among their own kind, and would keep it so – unsullied by newcomers, with all their crass habits and blunt words.*

*It is no wonder Mother Dark blesses none of this.*

She had forgotten the goblet in her hand, and only now did she drink, watching as most of those at the table did much the same, with similar eagerness. *A decision has been reached. Not a consensus, merely the illusion of one. And this is how they play, these people.* The hunting hound settled down at her feet, chin upon the floor.

*I dream of magic in my own hands. I dream of scouring clean the entire world.*

*Vermin abounds, and oh, how I would love to see it crushed. Not a corner in which to hide, not a hole deep enough.*

Draining her goblet, she leaned against the wall and let her eyes fall half closed, imagining conflagrations of some unknown, but eternally promising, future. While, at her feet, the savage hound slept.

*     *     *

'I am going to my favourite room,' said Sandalath Drukorlat, her eyes oddly bright in the gloom of the carriage. 'In a tower, highest in the Citadel.'

Clutching the heavy baby in his arms and seated opposite its mother, Wreneck nodded and smiled. Broken people so often sounded no different from children, leading him to wonder what it was that had broken inside their heads. Rushing back into childhood was like trying to find something simple in the past, he supposed, but then, he was closer to such memories, and there was little back there that seemed simple to him.

'I knew a man with only one arm,' Sandalath continued. 'He left me stones, in a secret place. He left me stones, and he left me a boy. But you knew that, Wreneck. He was named Orfantal, that boy. I pushed him out all wrapped up in a story I didn't want anyone to know about. Much good that did me. It's what women and men do, there in the high grasses.'

Sitting beside Wreneck, the keeper of records, Sorca, cleared her throat and reached for her pipe. 'Memories best kept to yourself, I think, milady, given the present company.' She pulled out a button of compacted rustleaf and crumbled and tamped it into the pipe's blackened bowl.

Outside, the harsh breathing of Houseblades surrounded the rocking, pitching carriage as men and women leaned shoulders to the wheels, pushing it through the deep snow covering the muddy road. The warhorses fought against the ill-fitting yokes, and all the arguments from two nights past, when the oxen were butchered to feed everyone, now returned to Wreneck as he listened to Horse Master Setyl cajoling the affronted mounts with tears in his voice.

'She called me a child when I birthed Orfantal,' Sandalath said to Sorca. 'A child to birth a child.'

'Nonetheless.' Sparks flashed, smoke bloomed, rose, and then streamed out between the shutters of the window.

'Captain Ivis undressed me.'

Sorca coughed. 'Excuse me?'

Wreneck glanced down at the babe's face, snuggled so sweetly in her blanket of fur. So little time had passed, so rare the occasions that her mother offered a tit to appease her hunger, and yet Korlat had gained twice her birth-weight – or so Surgeon Prok had claimed. She was sleeping now, as she often did, her round face black as ink, her hair already thick and long.

'It was so hot,' Sandalath continued. 'His hands upon me . . . so gentle . . .'

'Milady, I implore you, some other subject.'

'There was nothing to be done for it. That needs to be understood by everyone concerned. The room is safe, the only safe place in the world, up the stairs – *slap slap slap* go the bare feet! Up and up to the black door and the brass latch, and then inside! Slip the lock, run to the window! Down and down the eyes fall, to all the people below, to the bridge and that black black *black* water!'

In his arms, Korlat stirred fitfully, and then settled once more.

'Lord Anomander was braver then,' Sandalath then said, in a harsher voice.

Sorca grunted. 'Sorcery can unman the best of them, milady. Was it not the Azathanai who held out a staying hand? You wrongly impugn the First Son.'

'Up into the tower, we'll be safe there, where the flames can't reach us.'

Korlat opened her eyes, looked up into Wreneck's own, and he felt a heat come to his face. Those eyes, so large, so dark, so knowing, left him shaken, as they always did. 'Milady, she's awake. Won't you take her?'

Sandalath's gaze flattened. 'She's not ready yet.'

'Milady?'

'To take sword in hand. To swear to protect him. My son, my only son. I bind her, with chains that can never be broken. Never.'

The fury in her stare made Wreneck look away. Sorca tapped her pipe against the door's wooden frame to loosen what was left in the bowl, then started producing clouds that a wayward gust through the shutters sent over Wreneck.

His head spun, and as Korlat's eyes slipped behind veils of smoke, he saw her suddenly smile.

*　　*　　*

The household staff and the company of Draconean Houseblades made for a desultory and decrepit escort to the Son of Darkness and his Azathanai companion as they slowly worked their way southward on the road to Kharkanas. Captain Ivis struggled against a sense of shame, as if the private matters of him and his kin had been suddenly and cruelly dragged into the light. The lone carriage and its occupants, trailed by two salvaged wagons loaded down with feed and camp gear, had to his eyes the bearing of a refugee train. Horses fought in their traces, the Houseblades cursed and stumbled as they pushed the conveyances through the heavy snow and now mud, and voices spoke – when they spoke at all – with harsh words, bitter and belligerent.

Amidst these foul moods, Ivis found his own plummeting as they trudged on into the deepening gloom. The fire's embrace lingered like a heat beneath the skin, appallingly seductive, frightening in its intensity. *She was an Azathanai, said Caladan Brood. His kin, a sister and mother to the Dog-Runners. Olar Ethil by name. What has she done to me?*

Looking ahead on the road, he squinted at the backs of Lord Anomander and his huge companion. They were speaking, but in tones too low to drift back to the captain. *Milord, we are awash in strangers, and these rising waters are cold. Civil war proves an invitation and we are now infected by the venal wants of outsiders. They take to us with contempt, ruining whatever cause we hold to, only to then impose themselves and their own. Until their flavour pervades. Until our every desire tastes awry, spoiled in the heat.*

*I would spit you out, Olar Ethil. And you, Caladan Brood. I would march into the past and bar the arrival of T'riss and her poisoned gifts. None of you are welcome. And all you gods of the forest, of the stream and the rock, the tree and the sky, begone from us!*

*I'll not see us point fingers elsewhere for the crimes we commit here. And yet, it shall come to pass. I am certain of it. The face of blame is never our own.*

'Captain.'

He glanced over to find Gate Sergeant Yalad now at his side, a figure draped in a scorched cloak, a face still singed from past flames. 'What?'

The young man flinched slightly, then looked away. 'Sir. Do – do you think they're dead?'

Ivis said nothing.

Clearing his throat, Yalad continued, 'The Houseblades fear . . . retribution.'

'They'll not return,' Ivis snapped. 'And even if they did, it was Caladan Brood who attacked them, not you, not me. Even there, what choice did any of us have? They would have seen us all dead.' But even as he spoke, he thought of his own secret desire from months past – to see the

Hold burned down, with both daughters trapped within.

*Abyss take me, she must have touched my soul long before that night. Her fire, lit beneath my notice, where it smouldered on, feeding the worst in me.*

*Have we all been manipulated? This entire civil war? Perhaps indeed the blame lies elsewhere.*

'Sir, I meant retribution from Lord Draconus.'

Ivis started. He scowled. 'Nothing upon you or them, Yalad. Make that plain. I will face Lord Draconus alone. I will take responsibility for what happened.'

'Respectfully, sir, we don't agree with that. None of us.'

'Then you're fools.'

'Sir, what has happened to Lady Sandalath?'

'She was broken.'

'But . . . the other thing? The child—'

Ivis shook his head. 'Enough. We will not speak of that.'

Nodding, Yalad fell back a few steps, leaving Ivis once more alone with his thoughts, which, he realized, proved an unwelcome return. *The child deserves no reprobation. Surely, among all things before us, birth must be deemed innocent. There is no culpability in conception, none that should stain her. Nor, I suspect, the unwelcoming mother.*

*Ah, Sandalath, you have become a most ill-used hostage, your fates arrayed before us in condemnation of our promises to protect you. The blame is mine, as I stood in place of Lord Draconus, and again and again I have failed you.*

*Now comes sorcery with a rapist's cock, the blunt demand denying all mercy. Crown the need, bedecked in raiment, and glory in the release, and all the power it announces with an unwanted child's cry.*

*What spirit, freed of its chains as the flames rose, laid you down upon the stone floor? Caladan Brood shies from all comment. But something fierce with outrage burns in that Azathanai. I would know its face. I would know its name.*

What had happened to Sandalath in Dracons Hold was a far crueller embrace than the one Olar Ethil had given to Ivis. He knew with a certainty that the fire-spirit, the goddess of the Dog-Runners, had taken for herself no active role in

Sandalath's fate. And yet . . . *I felt her glee. And her turning of pain into vengeance invoked crimes I could not discern – perhaps even the crime of Sandalath's fate. There was something old in all this, something full of ancient wounds and past betrayals.*

*We were all sorely used.* And so, with grinding inexorability, his thoughts returned to his sense of helplessness, and his gaze fixed once more upon the broad back of Caladan Brood. *Foolish Azathanai. You meddle among us, and we feel your contempt. But upon the day we have had enough of your torment, you will know the wrath of the Tiste. As did the Jhelarkan and the Forulkan.*

*Lord Anomander, let not these fools seduce you.*

They were in darkness now, swallowed by the immanence of Mother Dark's influence. Blind as indifference, this strange faith. The faint ethereal blue glow of the fallen snow made for a ghostly path, beckoning them into the last stretch of forest before the land opened out to the environs of the Wise City. Two, perhaps three days to the north gate.

Yalad returned. 'Sir, our scouts flanking to east report birds.'

'Birds?'

'Many, many birds.'

'How distant?'

'Perhaps a third of a league, sir. They also say the snow beneath the trees has seen the passage of people.'

'Which way?'

'Every way, sir.'

'Very well, collect a squad and pull out to the side. I will speak to Lord Anomander, and then join you.'

Nodding, Yalad moved off. Picking up his pace, Ivis hurried forward. 'Milord!'

Both Anomander and Caladan halted and turned.

'There has been a killing, Lord Anomander,' Ivis said. 'To the east, third of a league.'

'You wish to investigate?'

'Yes, milord.'

'I will accompany you.'

Ivis hesitated, and then glanced back at the carriage.

'Have the remaining Houseblades prepare camp, captain,' Anomander said, shaking loose his cloak as he adjusted his sword-belt. 'Defensive perimeter and pickets.'

'Yes sir.'

'It may be that companies of the Legion are foraging, or perhaps hunting down yet more Deniers,' said Anomander, frowning at the fire-scorched line of trees verging the eastern side of the track. He hesitated, and then glanced at the Azathanai. 'I would have you remain here, High Mason.'

'As you wish,' Caladan replied with a grunt. 'But the blood upon the ground has frozen, and of the bodies you will find, none remain alive.'

'How long past?' Anomander demanded.

'Days, perhaps.'

'Are we observed?'

'A curious question. In the immediate, no, none look out from yonder wood.'

'And in the other?'

'First Son, if we sense unblinking regard settled upon us, in each of our moments, beginning to end, what then might we do differently?'

Anomander frowned. 'Best we comport ourselves with such an audience in mind, whether it exists or not.'

'Why?'

'I hold that such witnessing does indeed exist, unflinching and beyond the mechanisms of deceit, and that in our eagerness to dissemble, we yield it little respect.'

'And what witness might this be?'

'Nothing other than history, High Mason.'

'You name an indifferent arbiter, subject to maleficence in its wake.'

Anomander made no reply. Gesturing to Ivis, he said, 'Let us find this killing ground, captain.'

They strode back to Yalad and the waiting squad. Weapons were drawn, but through the shroud of gloom the faces arrayed before Ivis were difficult to distinguish, beyond the faint glitter of their eyes. 'Thank you, gate sergeant. Remain here and see to the camp. The Azathanai suggests that we are in no danger, but I will have you diligent nonetheless. Pickets and a perimeter.'

'Yes sir.' Yalad waved a Houseblade forward. 'Gazzan was the scout who spied the birds, sir.'

'Good eyes in this perpetual darkness,' Ivis commented to the young man.

'Heard them first, sir. But it's odd, how they fly with no hearkening to the night.'

After a moment, Lord Anomander said, 'You mean to say, sir, that the creatures behave as if it was still day.'

'As it indeed is, milord. Late afternoon.'

'Perhaps,' ventured Ivis, 'Mother Dark has blessed all life within her realm with this dubious gift.'

At a nod, Gazzan set out, leading them into the forest.

*Eyes upon us, named history or otherwise, can still make a man's skin crawl.* 'Milord.'

'Out with it, captain. I well see your dismay.'

'These Azathanai now among us ... they make me uneasy.'

'It is my suspicion, Ivis,' said Anomander in a low voice, 'that they have always been among us. Unseen for the most part. But in their machinations we are tossed and turned like blindfolded fools.'

The notion rattled Ivis. He combed through his beard, felt ice crystals beneath his fingernails, and then spat to one side. 'I would we turned on them, milord, if what you say is true.'

'You would either way,' Anomander retorted, with some amusement in his tone.

'My lord's keep is in ruin,' Ivis said in a growl. 'An ancient edifice and ancestral home, brought down in a single night. Was there no other means of dealing with the daughters? Fire and smoke, the tumbling of walls, and such a maelstrom of sorcery as to make me sick with fear for the future.'

Anomander sighed. 'Just so, Ivis. Yet, did I not bait him? The fault is mine, captain, and I will make that plain to your lord.'

'You dismiss the threat posed by Envy and Spite.'

'As any sober reflection would lead us to do, Ivis. No matter their power, their minds remained those of children. The sorcery indeed lent claws to their impulses, a lesson we are all obliged to heed, given the child within each of us. But in truth, old friend, I anticipated an emasculation, a reducing of the threat in a manner more civilized than what we were witness to.' He shook his head. 'It was a brutal night, and the shock of it reverberates still.'

'Sorcery, milord, lacks all subtlety.'

'As will any force wielded without restraint. And here, Ivis, you set your knife-point into the heart of my dread. I despise the use of the fist, when a caress would better serve.'

'These Azathanai see it differently, milord.'

'So it seems. And yet T'riss affected a simple touch, and see now its consequences. I have thought,' Anomander added with a bitter laugh, 'my loyalty's abiding would have seen off this silver hue upon my mane, but she would see me set apart, and that I must now live with.'

'There was a spirit, milord, within the fire—'

'Brood spoke of her, yes. Olar Ethil, a matron of the Dog-Runners.'

'An Azathanai.'

'If the title means anything, then yes, an Azathanai.'

'She offered the ecstasy of destruction, milord.'

'As would any creature of flames.'

'And desire,' Ivis added. 'You speak of caresses, but I tell you, I now live with the curse of such a caress.'

Ahead the trees thinned, revealing part of a glade. The grackle and murmur of ravens descended from the bared branches on all sides, whilst black shapes danced on the churned-up, frozen snow between dark huddled forms. The cold air held the stink of bile and faeces.

Drawing closer, silent now, they reached the glade's edge and looked out upon scores of corpses, many stripped down near naked, their flesh frozen black, the wounds and gaping holes pecked open, purple-hued and glistening with frost.

'Their skin misleads,' said Ivis. 'These dead are Liosan.'

'Fleeing Liosan, sir,' Gazzan added. 'Struck from behind as

820

they ran. Axe and spear, and arrows. Broken, sir, in a rout.'

'The Deniers,' someone muttered from the squad, 'have found their teeth.'

'Or the monks have finally ventured out to their flock,' Ivis said. 'And yet . . . arrows. Nothing noble in that.'

Anomander's breath hissed out in a plume that swept ghost-like into the glade. 'The nobility adhered to by the Legion slaughtering peasants in the woods, captain?'

'A crime demanding—'

'A crime, sir? Is this how we are to divide the blood on our hands? One side just, the other an outrage? Best take a blade to ensure the distinction, and cleave to the cause with a sure eye! But I tell you this: history's unbidden gaze shall not be given leave to turn away, not by absolving words or the cynical dip into semantics. Remember what you see here, captain, and leave every excuse upon the ground. A life defending itself has right to any means, be they teeth and nails, or arrows.'

'Then will atrocity be met with atrocity, milord? How swift our descent to the savage!'

Anomander waved a dismissive hand. 'Best be clear-eyed on that truth, sir, and see the descent for what it is.' He faced Ivis with fierceness burning in his eyes. 'We knew war directly, the two of us. In the slaying and the slaughter, savagery was our lover, locked step in step with our relentless advance. Do you deny it?'

'The cause was just—'

'Did that stay your hand, even once?'

'Why would it, milord?'

'Indeed, why would it?' He then turned back to the clearing and its corpses. 'Why would it, when justice serves the savage? Why would it, when the cause justifies the crime? Justifies? *Absolves*, more like. I wonder if the rise of priests among us was for the sole purpose of blessing the killing we would do. Priests, kings, warlords, highborn. And, of course, officers and the iron-clad fist that backs them.' He swung round. 'So bless this field. In the absence of priests, we can leave the gods out of it. Bless it for what it is, Ivis, in a world where killing is no crime.'

Shaken, Ivis backed up a step. 'Milord, you give cause for despair.'

'*I* give it? Abyss below, Ivis. I've but carved words to name what we'd rather not name. If the messenger delivers despairing news, is he the cause of it?'

He moved past Ivis then, on his way back to their camp upon the road. Ivis waved his squad to follow, watched them file silently past, and finally, with a lingering glance back at the glade and its hooded sentinels murmuring among the trees, he took up the rear.

*We are past distinctions. He said as much. The field behind me announces the same. And if, in these shattered woods, a goddess slowly sinks down upon a bed of spikes, to that crime even history is blind.*

\*     \*     \*

It was a delusion to imagine that a wild forest was filled with such bounty as to keep the belly full. Even in the absence of wolves and hunting cats to keep their numbers down, deer and elk could starve in the winter. Sharenas Ankhadu understood, now, the purpose behind the seasonal hunts of the Deniers. Victuals needed collecting, pits needed digging, meats smoked or salted to be buried in caches. In such a realm, bound to the seasons, a single family struggled, and what congress existed between each one was both fraught and tense.

The moans and pangs of an empty stomach found no relief in the sentiments of nobility and dignity. Nothing proud was conferred by the laying bare of raw need. And yet, she now recalled bitterly, she had, in shared company with her kin, often spoken with a kind of voyeuristic nostalgia, longing for simpler days, when purity meant fingers pressed deep into the earth, or the brutal pursuit of some scampering prey, as if her own blood held a memory of past lives, each one a paragon of virtue.

But time played its tricks with such things. The noble face with its mouth stained red, the battered hands with dirt beneath cracked and chipped nails, the worn furs and threadbare tunics, and the blank, solemn gaze so often mistaken for dignity, did not belong to her past, but existed in step with her – among these forest dwellers, and the cast-outs in their caves in the hills.

Delivering slaughter upon them had been a crime almost beyond measure.

*Beloved Kagamandra, I now comprehend the meaning of unconscionable. No bleaching of the skin can cleanse what we have done here.*

*And now, see what we have made them, our suffering kindred of the forest. If nobility hid in their mourning shrouds, the time for grief has passed.*

She moved among corpses. She saw faces she recognized, although death stole away most of what she remembered of them. Most of the arrows had been cut out from the wounds they had made, although here and there a shattered shaft had been left behind, tossed aside once the arrowhead had been retrieved. Beyond the rough, jumbled line of fallen soldiers, there were others who had been caught in flight. Their frantic paths of retreat were plain enough to see.

Hallyd Bahann's company, drawn here by Sharenas herself.

*Here is a lesson, my love, but one I'll not venture to broach. In any case, best look away now, as I become another raven amidst this feast. A flicker of this iron beak, some flesh to dull the pangs. While on the branches, jaded black eyes ponder their new rival.*

Hearing a noise she turned.

Their approach had been quiet, and now they stood less than twenty paces away. Sharenas adjusted the knife in her hand, eyeing the strangers. Then her eyes narrowed.

*Bah, he is anything but a stranger.* 'Gripp Galas,' she said, her voice cracking with disuse. 'Marriage palled, did it? The woman beside you is comely enough, but her instead of Hish Tulla? Age has taken your sight along with your wits.'

'Sharenas Ankhadu?'

'Why doubt who stands before you? Did I not visit your winter nest? Did I not huddle shivering beneath furs in that unheated cell you call a guest room?'

The woman suddenly scowled. 'Once the fire was lit, it warmed up quickly enough.'

Sharenas squinted at her. 'Ah, yes. You, then.' She waved with her knife to the bodies surrounding them. 'Seeking old friends, perhaps?'

'If so,' Gripp Galas said, 'then for a different purpose than you, it would seem.'

'The forest is unfriendly.'

'And, I believe, has been so for some time, Sharenas Ankhadu.'

'I am a deserter. A murderer of fellow officers and more than a few of these soldiers and scouts. They were hunting me.'

'This was a battle, not an ambush,' said the woman.

'Widowers with nothing to lose, but the taste of blood on the tongue invites a recurring thirst.'

'For them, or you?'

Sharenas smiled across at the woman. 'Pelk. Once on Urusander's staff. You never had much to say.'

'Sending soldiers out to fight and die demands little, as you well know, captain.'

'You were a trainer. A weapon master.'

'I did what must be done to make an army, captain,' said Pelk, drawing closer, eyes now scanning the frozen, contorted bodies in the snow. 'Made orphans of you all, and then showed you the teats of the only bitch left, and her name was War.'

The words chilled Sharenas – her first real sense of cold in what seemed weeks. 'I am undecided about you two, so halt your advance, Pelk. Be warned, I am now a sorceress.'

'A piss-poor one,' Pelk snapped. 'You look starved. You're filthy, and you stink.'

'These ones,' said Gripp Galas. 'They were hunting you? Whose company?'

'Hallyd Bahann. If he isn't dead, he should be.' Sharenas paused, and then said, 'I would have butchered them all in their damned tents, but as it was, I got to Esthala and her useless husband. And Serap Issgin. Before running out of time.'

'And who set this task upon you, captain?'

Sharenas studied Pelk's flat face, bemused by her question. 'Urusander.'

'By his command?'

'By his utter uselessness.'

'And these ones?'

'Deniers, Pelk. That much should be obvious.' She grinned at Gripp Galas. 'Precious Legion soldiers, so finely trained and honed by Weapon Master Pelk there, hunted down like animals.'

Gripp Galas said, 'We have food, captain.'

'As do I.'

'Then the choice is yours,' he replied. 'Feast here, or return to civilization.'

Her laugh broke into a cackle and she spread her arms, taking in the battlefield. 'Yes! This civilization! Strip me down, bathe me, dress me, and see to the buckles of my belt and armour, and why, I can march in step with you. Orphan no longer, hey, Pelk?'

'Better that than this, captain. Or have you truly acquired a taste for Tiste flesh?'

'Haven't we all? Oh, I know, my crime here is my lack of subtlety. No, take your bulging bellies and leave me be, both of you. I care not what mission drags you into this forest, and the Deniers won't bother asking, either. Await the greeting arrows, but save your shocked looks for them, not me.'

She crouched, cut free a large piece of frozen meat from a woman's thigh.

From the trees, ravens screamed their outrage.

Gesturing, Gripp Galas led Pelk off to their left, westward. The road was not far in that direction. Perhaps they thought it safer.

*Well, my love, I'll allow them this: if not safer, then certainly more civil in its habit of passage. To and fro, on matters of grave import. Enough self-importance to deflect an arrow's flight? We'll see, I suppose. Darling of mine, I have reached such a noble state, that even dignity tastes like raw meat.*

Satisfied with the cut she now held in her left hand, she set off in the opposite direction.

*     *     *

Gripp's sigh was rough, jagged. 'Have we seen the future, Pelk?'

'Now there's a lesson,' she replied as they wound among the blackened boles of the trees.

'Which is?'

'Future's face, sir, is no different from the past's face. Savagery is fangs upon its own tail, and no escape is possible. We are encircled, with no way out.'

'Surely,' Gripp replied, 'civilization can offer us something more.'

She shook her head. 'Peace is a drawn breath; war the roar of its release.'

'I have had a thought,' said Gripp Galas after a time of crunching footsteps through brittle snow. 'It may be that even Andarist will not tarry in his isolation.'

She seemed to chew on this, before saying, 'We seek his brother, sir, and will urge him to join us in returning to the estate. Now you suspect that Andarist will not be there?'

'Just so . . . a feeling.'

Pelk was silent again for a dozen or so strides, and then she said, 'Where, then, are we to guide Lord Anomander?'

'Into the current, perhaps.'

'And where will this flood take us?'

Gripp Galas sighed. 'Kharkanas. And a field of battle.'

It was well past dusk when they neared the road, only to see firelight ahead. Raising a hand, Gripp Galas studied the distant camp.

Pelk grunted softly. 'Carriage and wagons. Many soldiers.'

'Houseblades, I think,' Gripp replied.

They approached. Another dozen strides, and from nearby cover two figures rose before them, levelling spears. Gripp spoke. 'Just the two of us. Your livery is Dracons – is Captain Ivis with you?'

The Houseblades were both women. They moved further apart. One spoke. 'You've not the look of Deniers. Advance and identify yourselves.'

'Gripp Galas, and with me is the gate sergeant of House Tulla, Pelk. I am known to your captain—'

'You are known to me,' the other woman said, lowering her spear and stepping closer. 'I fought at Fant Reach.'

Gripp nodded. With Pelk at his side, he moved forward.

Escorted by the Houseblade who had fought at Fant Reach, they continued on into the camp straddling the road. It was clear to Gripp that the entire company of Dracons Houseblades was here, meaning the keep was abandoned, and the supplies in the wagons, along with the carriage, indicated that the household accompanied the troops. The implications left him uneasy.

'Sir,' said Pelk, pointing to figures standing near one fire. 'Our search is at an end.'

Now Gripp Galas saw his old master, in the company of Captain Ivis and a huge, broad figure cloaked in furs. The firelight played upon all three in a game of glinting metal and burnished leather. From somewhere near the carriage, a baby was crying.

Lord Anomander's gaze fixed upon Gripp as he approached.

'Gripp? Why have you come among us?'

'Milord, I have come in search of you.'

Frowning, Anomander glanced across at either Ivis or the other man – Gripp could not be sure which – and then the First Son of Darkness stepped out of the firelight. 'Walk with me, old friend.' They moved away from the fire, and Pelk stepped forward to greet Captain Ivis.

Anomander continued, 'I feel the heat upon me already fade. South, then, upon the road. Beyond this civil shell, perhaps we'll find the familiar stars above us. Sufficient to recall nights long past.'

'Milord, forgive me—'

'Yes,' Anomander cut in, an edge to his tone, 'forgiveness jostles to the fore, demanding dispensation, as it ever does.

You are not with your wife. You are not withdrawn to that sanctuary of love, so high-walled as to be secure from all travails.'

'We were well retired, milord, wintered and sedate. But our isolation proved far from complete. Emissaries from Lord Urusander. Your own Captain Kellaras. And, milord, one other.'

'And which of these sent you to me, so unmindful of past gifts?'

'Kellaras, milord, in his desperation, came with news from Kharkanas. Captain Sharenas Ankhadu, with warnings of the Legion's impending march. And the other . . .' Gripp hesitated, and then said, 'Milord, Andarist came to us, seeking the privacy of our remote estate.'

Anomander was silent. They walked the frozen slush of the road. Already the lights from the camp's fires were well behind them, and what heat might have lingered from those flames was long gone from both men.

After a time, Gripp spoke again. 'Your brother Silchas sent Prazek and Dathenar to the Hust Legion, in aid of Galar Baras, although I am certain that Commander Toras Redone will finally relent, and will resume command in time for the Legion's march to Kharkanas. In any case, we can presume they have already begun that march. Your own Houseblades await you in the Citadel.'

Anomander raised a hand then, forestalling Gripp. 'I am well enough informed,' he said, 'of matters pertaining to Kharkanas.'

'Of Prazek and Dathenar, Silchas had your blessing, milord?'

'My brother's mind is his own. In my absence, he is free to judge on matters of necessity.'

'And Andarist? Milord, did you know he had found us?'

'Not as such, Gripp, but then, who took him into her arms in his bleakest moment? Hish Tulla . . . ah, Gripp Galas, what have you done in leaving her side?'

'You are needed, milord. Unless we would see uncontested Urusander's occupation of Kharkanas.'

'The blade is denied me, Gripp, by Mother Dark herself.'

'Milord? Then you will surrender?'

Anomander's steps slowed, and he tilted his head back, studying the span of stars in the sky above. 'Captain Ivis begs me to assume command of his Houseblades. His own lord is less than a ghost, yet one whose shadow seems to haunt every one of us. Urusander's triumph will see Draconus deposed, perhaps even outlawed. At the very least, a self-imposed banishment.'

'You seek to deliver Ivis to his master, milord? Unto seeing Dracons Keep utterly abandoned?'

'Draconus is a friend,' Anomander replied.

'My wife fears his allegiance.'

'She fears the treachery of her highborn kin.'

'Just so, milord.'

'Tell me, Gripp Galas, do you think, should I request it of him, Lord Draconus would hold his forces in reserve?'

Gripp Galas looked away, south down the road. There was frost in the air itself, glittering like the falling dust of shattered stars. On this night, cold as it now was, he could well imagine the sky cracking with all the sound of thunder, until the darkness descended, a storm to take the world. 'I'd not jar that man's pride.'

Anomander was silent, still studying the stars.

Gripp Galas cleared his throat. 'Milord, how is it you know of Kharkanas? Unless you but recently returned there—'

'The High Mason knows the trembles of the frozen earth beneath our feet. More to the point, he is close to Grizzin Farl. These Azathanai walk their own roads of sorcery, it seems. In any case, each question I think to ask is in turn answered.'

'Yet . . . not the one concerning Andarist?'

Anomander seemed to grimace. 'A question I chose not to ask.'

*But . . . why?*

'Gripp Galas, your refutation of my gift to you breaks my heart. But even in this, how can I not see my own wounded pride? The faces of both friend and enemy, it seems, offer us a mirror to our own, each in its time, each in its place. Should we not acknowledge these similarities of accord, and so find humility against our righteousness? How many wars must we fight before we ever draw a blade? The answer, I now think, is beyond count.'

'Mother Dark would not see her lover torn from her arms, milord.'

'No, I would think not, Gripp Galas.'

'Then, shall we stand in Urusander's way?'

'Gripp Galas, where is your wife?'

'At her western keep, milord, where she gathers the high-born. She vows they will stand with you. And with the Hust Legion—'

'Hold little faith in the Hust,' Anomander said. 'Convicts have no reason for loyalty. Were I among them, I would frame a curse for the moment of our need, and for every howl of my sword I would show defiance, until the iron itself shatters. No, old friend, if they are to have an instant, united in their congress, it shall burn with such refusal as to sear our souls.'

'Then, milord, we face a grave battle.'

They stood, unspeaking. Overhead, the stars cast down their unblinking regard.

'Dracons Keep is a burned ruin,' Anomander said. 'Destroyed by magic, at my invitation. Gripp, has this new-found sorcery touched you?'

'No, milord, and I am thankful for that.'

'I fear I must one day search it out and claim it for myself. Yet another shield, another skin of armour.'

'But not yet.'

Anomander shrugged. 'Neither propensity nor proclivity finds me, alas.'

'One would think, milord, as a benison befitting the First Son of Darkness, some sorcerous power would be incumbent.'

'When the title proves less a gift than a curse, I am well relieved that nothing attends it.'

'How will we face it? On the field of battle, when Hunn Raal unleashes his magical arts?'

Anomander glanced across at him. 'An Azathanai accompanies me. In singular purpose, bound by vow, he has yet to reward me or my patience.'

A suspicion whispered through Gripp Galas then, and he frowned. 'What befell Dracons Keep?'

Anomander drew breath as if to make retort, only to instead return his gaze to the stars, and release a long, weary sigh. 'Then I will see my first invitation to him as yet another weight of burden upon the High Mason, and his efforts that followed. That said, he did indeed warn me: his magic is anything but subtle, when unleashed in fullest fury.'

'For that reason alone, milord, I am glad to know nothing of the taint.'

'Forbearance mitigates the Azathanai, and with good reason, as you say. But then, by my cajoling, I saw his power awakened.' He paused, and then continued, 'If such a thing is within Hunn Raal's reach, then I fear that in the meeting of our two armies we shall fall like wheat before the scythe.'

'Yet the Azathanai chooses to stand at your side, milord. Bound by vow, you said.'

'He offers me an end to this civil war.'

'By wise words, milord, or wilful destruction?'

'It is my thought that he is undecided.'

The chill of the night had reached Gripp's bones now. Shivering, he drew his cloak tighter about his shoulders. 'You keep him within sword's reach, then.'

'Gripp Galas, you shall not attend this battle.'

'Milord—'

'Must I command you again?'

'My wife will be there, commanding her Houseblades.'

'Convince her otherwise.'

At a loss for words, Gripp said nothing.

'Her uncle is a fine commander,' Anomander said. 'Take her away, Gripp. Take both of you away.'

'She would never forgive you,' Gripp whispered. *Nor would I.* After a moment, while Anomander remained silent, Gripp cursed himself for a fool. *Of course he knows that. And accepts the bargain, to see us live.*

Neither speaking, both men turned about, to retrace their way back to the camp.

✻    ✻    ✻

Pelk watched the Azathanai move away, presumably heading for his bedrolls. She glanced at Ivis a moment, before crouching to hold her hands closer to the fire.

'You chose not to return to the Legion,' Ivis observed after a moment.

'So it seems,' she replied.

'Spared yourself this pogrom against the Deniers.'

'I did.'

'The Deniers have begun to fight back.'

She nodded.

'Pelk.'

'It's done with, Ivis. It was a fine season, with misery on all sides, while our private island gave us refuge. Any storm can sweep the sand away. As it did to our blessed idyll. I have no regrets.'

He slowly settled on to a felled tree trunk that had been dragged close to the hearth, positioning himself upon her left. 'I do,' he said in a low voice. 'That I ever turned away. That I was foolish enough to think it meant little. A time away from the fighting and the madness. Those damned Forulkan blathering on about justice, even as they bled out on the ground. When I left you, I left something of me behind.' He hesitated, and then said, 'When I went back to find it . . .' He shook his head. 'A loss that can never be recovered, never redressed.'

Pelk studied him, and then said, 'Broken heart, Ivis. Heal it might, but the scar remains, and what you miss most is how it was before it broke, when that heart was whole. So, yes, you can't get that back.'

'Then you went and almost died.'

'I got careless. Wounded people do.'

Ivis put his hands up to his face.

She thought to reach out to him, a touch, offering him the gentle weight of her hand on his shoulder. Instead, she edged both hands closer to the flickering flames and the harsh heat. 'Best forget all of that,' she said. 'It was a long time ago. You weren't the only fool, you know.'

He looked up with reddened eyes. 'And now?'

'I've found another.'

'Ah.'

'Kellaras.'

'Yes . . . a good man. Honourable.'

'You?'

'No. No one. Well . . . no. I always look higher than my station. It's my own private dance with inevitable disappointment. Someone beyond reach remains forever pure, unsullied. There is that, at least.'

She levelled her gaze on him. 'You stupid fucking fool, Ivis.'

He pulled back as if she'd struck him across the face.

Pelk went on, 'I ended up in the service of Lady Hish Tulla. I saw her reach down to Gripp Galas, if you must think of it that way. Bloodlines and rank and station and whatnot. All rubbish. If you find someone who fills your heart, fills in all the cracks and stops all the leaking, to the Abyss with station, Ivis. But you see, I understand you all too well. It's your excuse for doing nothing.'

'I can't. She's a hostage in my care!'

'For how much longer? Or, if you can't wait, then resign your commission with House Dracons.'

He studied her with bleak eyes.

Shrugging, she rummaged in her pack and drew out a flask. 'In the meantime, old lover, let's drink against the night and remember other nights from long ago, when we had nothing and everything, when we knew it all but didn't know a fucking thing. Let's drink, Ivis, to the sunken islands of our youth.'

He grimaced, and then reached for the flask. His mouth twisted in a mocking grin. 'I see, looming before us, the shoals of past regrets.'

'Not me. I regret nothing. Not even not dying.'

'I hurt you that bad?'

'As bad as I did you, I wager, though I'm only seeing that now.'

'You thought me indifferent?'

'I thought you a man.'

'I – oh, Abyss take me, Pelk.'

'Drink up.'

He raised the flask. 'To fools,' he said.

She watched him drink, and then took the flask back and lifted it. 'To every fool who felt like dying, but didn't.'

At that, she saw his smile transformed, revealing the love still alive in it, and for the first time in decades, she felt at peace. *Just as I always said, the heart's never in the place you think it is. But for all that, it's good at waiting, when waiting is all there is.*

\*　　\*　　\*

'I have been pondering,' said Surgeon Prok, 'on the nature of sustenance as it relates to the newborn.'

Wreneck squinted across at the man, his face of sharp angles lit by the firelight, the gauntness of his drawn cheeks, and thought of carvings he had seen in the woods, upon the boles of trees. It was a habit among the Deniers to make faces in trees, often upon the verges of forests, close to the cleared land and planted fields. His mother had told him it was to frighten away strangers, and to warn them against cutting down any more trees. But Wreneck had never been frightened by those visages. And he didn't think they were warnings. He saw in them nothing but pain.

'Any midwife would speak plain enough,' Prok continued, his attention seemingly fixed upon Sorca while he avoided the eyes of Lady Sandalath, who held her swaddled babe but otherwise paid the child no attention, her eyes fixed instead upon the flames in the firepit. 'Mother's milk above all else, of course. And coddling, and caressing. A child left unhandled withers in the spirit and often dies. Or, later in life, falls into a habit of needs beyond relief, as of a thirst impossible to quench.'

'I hold her,' Wreneck said. 'And stroke her hair.'

834

Prok nodded. 'But it is the mother's touch, young Wreneck, that gives the greatest sustenance.' He hesitated, and then reached for some wood to add to the fire. Sparks lifted into the night. 'Lacking these natural things, what other sustenance is possible for a newborn? One would answer: none. This and only this.'

'Take her into *your* arms, Prok!' snapped Sandalath. 'Then you will find no starveling feeble in its cries!'

'No need, milady. A healer's eyes make the first examination, even before a hand reaches out. Thus, we must broach the mystery. There are unnatural forces here—'

Sorca snorted. 'Now there's a stunning diagnosis.'

Grimacing, Prok continued. 'Not just in the conception – we must assume, lacking as we are in any details – but also in the child herself.'

'She has but one purpose,' Sandalath said. 'To protect her brother. She cannot do this yet. She knows this. She hastens herself.'

'I doubt there is a will behind—'

'But there is, Prok. Mine!'

'You feed her something unseen, then, milady?'

Sandalath's face was glowing in the reflected flames as she studied the fire, and at Prok's strange question a curious smile drifted to her lips. 'Mother would have understood. We make them what we need them to be.'

'You speak of words delivered in years to come, milady.'

'I speak of my will, sir. I speak of need as power, which clearly you do not comprehend.'

'Need . . . as power.' Prok frowned into the flames. 'Indeed, your words confound me. The very notion of need hints at weakness, milady. Where in it do you find power?'

'Mother took him away from me. She sent him to Kharkanas. That was wrong. It was wrong, too, to send me to House Dracons, to make me a hostage again.'

'Then I'd question the worth of her advice on matters of parenting.'

'I will find Orfantal. I will make it the way I want it to be. No one can stop me. Not even Korlat.'

The conversation left Wreneck troubled, but he could find no reason for what he was feeling. Something burned fierce in Lady Sandalath, but he wasn't sure it was love, or tenderness. He wasn't sure if it was a good thing at all.

'The child is growing too fast,' said Prok. 'In unnatural manner. Sorcery feeds Korlat, a most alarming conclusion. Is she but the first such progeny?'

'A demon gave her the child,' said Sorca. 'You posit an unlikely trend.'

'Milady,' Prok persisted, addressing Sandalath, 'life itself is a burden. Your daughter has her own needs. The brother you would have her protect will not see it as you do. Indeed, he will likely cast a protective eye upon Korlat.'

'He will not. He is the one who matters. The one I chose.'

'Was Korlat given leave to choose you, milady? Or the manner of her conception? The seed of her father? How many burdens must she be made to bear?'

'Only one. She will be my son's guardian.'

Wreneck thought of the time in the carriage, when he held the baby and looked down into that perfect face with its shining eyes. He saw no burdens there. *No, they're what the rest of us bring, if we're to people her world. My mother's fear of the forest, her fear of being alone, her fear of me dying somewhere with her never knowing. Even her fear of Jinia, and me marrying her and us moving away. We bring those things. Those fears.*

*And like Sandalath said, those fears are needs, and together they have power.*

*But I turned away. I did what I had to do. I took on a different burden. The one about disappointing people. Needs can pull, or they can push.*

*I'll find Orfantal. I'll explain things. I'll make him promise to turn away from his mother. Away from her, and straight to Korlat. Be a brother, I'll say. The older brother. Take her hand, and don't let your mother ever pull you two apart.*

*I'll do all that. In the Citadel. And then I'll go and look for the bad soldiers. I'll kill them, and then I'll go home, to Jinia.*

*I'll take away Mother's burdens – not all of them, just the ones I can do something about.*

'You all seem to forget,' Sandalath said. 'That demon. He chose me. Not you, Sorca, or any other woman. Me.'

So low were Prok's words that Wreneck alone heard them: 'Abyss take me . . .'

*       *       *

Sukul Ankhadu found Rancept in an antechamber near the servants' corridor. He had laid out his scale shirt, his greaves and vambraces and his helm, which still bore its bent nose-guard. The weapons were set in a row on the floor: a mace, a shortsword, and a dagger that was more a spike than anything else. A round shield of a style not used in a generation, a buckler, and a hatchet completed his array of equipment.

His breathing was loud and wet as he crouched, inspecting buckles and straps.

Leaning against one wall, Sukul studied the man. 'You're abandoning me,' she said. 'Who will be left? Only Skild because of his game leg, and the maids.'

'Skild will continue your schooling,' Rancept replied.

'And what schooling did you have?'

'Scant.'

'Precisely. I learn more sniffling underfoot at the meetings than I have from years of Skild's lessons.'

He was silent for a time, examining the leather wrap of the mace's handle. And then he said, 'It takes a superior mind to achieve cynicism, and I don't mean superior in a good way.'

'Then how do you mean it?'

'Convinced of its own genius, levitating upon the hot air of its own convictions, many of which are delusional.'

Grunting, Sukul sipped from the goblet she now carried with her everywhere. 'The counter to all that, castellan, invariably cites a sense of realism in defence of a cynical outlook.'

'Cynicism is the voice of ill-concealed despair, milady. The reality the cynic hides behind is one of his or her own making. Convenient, wouldn't you say?'

'I liked you better when all you did was mumble.'

'And I you when the glow of your cheeks was youth's blessing.'

'Back to that again, is it? Tell me, did that woman, Sekarrow, ever play that musical instrument – what was it called? That iltre?'

'Thankfully, no.' He slowly, awkwardly straightened, reaching for the small of his back.

'I argued for your staying, Rancept. You're too old for battle. But Lady Hish Tulla said it was your decision to make. I disagree. It was hers. It remains hers. I will speak to her again.'

'I would rather you didn't, milady,' Rancept replied, collecting his quilted shirt and working his way into it, his breaths harsh and loud.

'They will use sorcery.'

'I expect so, yes.'

'Your armour won't help any of you against that, will it?'

'Probably not.'

'You're going to die.'

'I will do my best to avoid that, milady. Is it not time for your lessons? Go and lighten Skild's mood for a change.'

She set her goblet down on a ledge. 'Here, that needs tying up the back.'

'Summon a maid.'

'No, I'm here and I'll do it.' He crouched down again and she moved up behind his broad, misshapen back. She tugged at the drawstrings, then released them suddenly and flung herself against him, arms wrapping tight. 'Don't go,' she pleaded, eyes filling with tears.

He touched one of her hands, the gesture tentative. 'Milady – Sukul, all will be well. I promise this.'

'You can't!'

'I will return.'

'You don't know that – I'm not a child! The Houseblades cannot stand long against Urusander's Legion!'

'We have the Hust—'

'*No one has the Hust!*'

'Milady. Something you've not considered. Something, it seems, that no one has considered.'

'What?'

'The Hust blades. The Hust armour. Against sorcery, what answer will they give?'

He now slowly, tenderly, prised loose her grip around his neck, and then straightened and swung round to face her. His blunt hands settled on her shoulders.

Through tears, she looked up at him. 'What – what do you mean?'

'I know only a little of Hust iron, milady, but what I do know is the anger within those swords, and now, perhaps, that armour. It is my belief that the Tiste have possessed sorcery for some time now, much longer than most would believe. There is something elemental in those weapons, in that iron.'

She stepped back, slipping free of his hands and shaking her head. 'Their rightful owners are all dead, Rancept. Now criminals carry them!'

'Indeed, and what will come of that?'

'Your faith is misplaced.'

He shrugged. 'Milady, I served my own time in the mining pits – a criminal, as you say.'

*What?*

His smile was a terrible thing to witness. 'Think you this bent frame was the one I was born with? I was a lead rock-biter. Five years in the tunnels.'

'What did you do?'

'I was a thief.'

'Does Lady Hish Tulla know this?'

'Of course.'

'Yet . . . she made you castellan!'

'Not at first,' he said. 'I needed to earn her trust, of course. Well, her mother's trust, come to that. It was all long ago.'

'I don't want you to go.'

He nodded. 'I know.'

'I want to say how much I hate you right now.'

'Aye.'

'But it's the opposite of hate.'

'I suppose it is, milady.'

'Don't get killed.'

'I won't. Now, can you tie those strings? But not too tightly. My muscles swell with swinging that mace.'

He turned again and crouched down. She looked at his broad back, the massive bulges of strange muscles, so uneven, like knots on a tree trunk. 'Rancept,' she asked as she stepped forward, 'how old were you, when you were in the mines?'

'Eleven. Left when I was sixteen.'

'A lead rock-biter – is that what it was called? You were made that at eleven?'

'No. Had to earn that, too. But I was a big lad even then.'

'What did you steal?'

'Food.'

'Rancept.' She pulled at the strings, tied a knot.

'Milady.'

'Ours is a cruel civilization, isn't it?'

'No crueller than most.'

She thought about that and then frowned. 'That sounds . . . cynical.'

He said nothing.

They worked together in silence, getting Rancept readied for war. Through it all, Sukul Ankhadu waged a war of her own, against the despair that threatened to overwhelm her.

But when at last they were done, he reached to rest a finger against her cheek. 'I think of you, milady, not as a hostage, but as a daughter. I know, I am presumptuous.'

Unable to speak, she shook her head, and felt, in a rush of emotion, the despair swept away, as if before a flood.

# TWENTY-ONE

'THE WAYS OF TISTE CONFUSE,' SAID HATARAS RAZE, slipping free of the heavy bhederin furs as the sun's light clawed through the high clouds, leaving her naked from the hips upward.

Fighting his incessant chill, Listar looked away. He was leading all three horses, as the two Bonecasters refused to ride the animals, although they examined them often, running their red-painted hands across the sleek hides. It was, Listar had come to realize, a habit of theirs, this endless touching, caressing, palms resting firm upon flesh. Most nights, the two Dog-Runner women were busy doing that with each other. Even more disconcerting, they seemed indifferent to the cold.

In response to Hataras's observation, Listar shrugged. 'Crimes must be punished, Bonecaster.'

'All that work,' said the younger of the two women, Vastala Trembler. 'Build fire in winter. Against the stone. Then cold water. Stone cracks, tools can be made.'

'But you see these weapons I wear, Vastala? They are iron. The rock must be broken and then melted. I do not know the intricacies. I just hauled the rubble up from the pits.'

'As punishment,' said Hataras.

'Yes.'

'For iron, which all Tiste use.'

'Yes.'

'And find pleasure in.'

He sighed. 'It's just our way, Bonecaster. As yours are different from ours.'

Vastala Trembler had bundled up all her skins and furs, and was carrying them on one shoulder. She wore hide moccasins and nothing else, barring an obsidian knife bound to a leather thong around her neck. 'The Ay get restless.'

Listar frowned, looked about for the huge wolves, but the rolling plain with its windswept drifts of old snow seemed empty of life. As if to give credence to their name, the Dog-Runners had company wherever they travelled. Twice since departing the encampment, Listar had seen a half-dozen of the enormous beasts paralleling them in the distance. But the last time had been three or four days past. He'd thought them gone. 'What has made them restless?' *And more to the point, how do you even know?*

'They wonder,' Vastala replied, 'when it's time to eat horse. As do we.'

'We're not starving, are we?'

'Fresh meat better.' She lifted one red hand and made a strange, elaborate gesture.

A step behind her, Hataras laughed. 'Then take him, fool.'

'Punished Man,' said Vastala, moving up alongside him. 'Would you like to lie with me tonight? It is privilege. Bonecasters can have anyone.'

'I will take him night after,' Hataras said. 'Too much waiting. He thinks us ugly, but in dark he will feel our beauty.'

'I've not told you my crime,' Listar said, edging away from Vastala. 'You'll want nothing to do with me. I had a mate. I killed her.'

'No you didn't,' Vastala retorted, drawing close again.

'You know nothing of it!'

'You have never taken a life.'

A snort from behind them, and then, 'Insects. Lice. Gnats.'

Vastala glared back at Hataras. 'A Tiste life, then. You know this. Nothing stains him.'

'Mice, spiders, fish.'

In a flash, Vastala spun and launched herself at Hataras. Both went down scratching and snarling, biting and kicking.

Listar halted, the horses nervously gathering up around him. He squinted northward, waiting for the scrap to work through to its exhausted, sex-filled conclusion. It was not the first fight between these women. He could not recall what had set them at each other the first time, but he had stared at them, alarmed, and then bemused, as the vicious grappling soon found nipples and the tangled thatch between their legs, and before too long the struggling grew rhythmic, with moans and gasps instead of snarls, and he had looked away then, his face burning.

These were the women he was escorting to the Hust Legion, the women who were meant to give shape to a ritual of some kind of absolution. Beyond the unlikelihood of success, Listar was troubled by such notions of forgiveness. Some things did not deserve what captains Prazek and Dathenar sought.

He knew Rance had been the killer in the camp. He had awaited her knife, and would have welcomed it. Instead, she had danced around him, until the anticipation left holes burning in his gut. And then he had been sent away, out into the wild plains of the south, as if there'd been no thought of his fleeing, running away from all that he was.

The women were now coupling, in the way that women did when together, each with her face in the other's crotch. At least, he assumed that was a typical position, although he could not be certain. A few other times, fingers had been involved.

They would be at this for some time. Sighing, he looked away, drew off his satchel and crouched down, unclasping the flap. *Hands upon horseflesh. A judgement of meat. No wonder they run with dogs, not horses.* He drew out the makings of a meal and set to preparing it. 'We are not far from the camp,' he said.

As he expected, neither woman replied.

'We're not eating the horses. You two were supposed to ride with me, to deliver us quickly to the Hust camp. We are short of time.'

Hataras lifted her head, licked her lips and then said, 'A ritual of cleansing, yes. Stains taken away. You ride, we run.'

Vastala rolled over and sat up. 'The Ay now hunt. Mother will provide.'

Studying the two of them as they recovered, their flushed faces and glowing cheeks, the wetness of sex on their sloping, almost non-existent chins, he said, 'This Mother you speak of, the one you cry out to when . . . when doing what you just did. She is your goddess?'

Both women laughed. Hataras climbed to her feet. 'Womb of fire, the promise that devours.'

'Child Spitter. Swollen Spring.'

'Guardian of the Dreamer. False Mother.'

'Deadly when spurned,' Vastala said. 'We appease to keep her claws sheathed. She is masked, is Mother, but the face of blood-kin is a lie. Azathanai.'

'Azathanai,' echoed Hataras, nodding. 'She keeps the Dreamer asleep. The longer the sleep, the weaker we become. Soon, Dog-Runners will be no more. One dream ends. Another begins.'

'Mother whispers of immortality,' said Vastala, making a face. 'A path out from the dream. Let her sleep, she says.'

'We do not fear Mother,' added Hataras, walking over to run a hand along a horse's flank. 'We fear only the Jaghut.'

Listar frowned. 'The Jaghut? Why?'

'They play with us. Like Azathanai, only more clumsy. They think us innocent—'

'Children,' Vastala cut in.

'But look into our eyes, Punished Man. See our knowing.'

'The Dreamer birthed us and we are content. Our lives are short.'

'But fullest.'

'We struggle to eat and stay warm.'

'But love is never a stranger.' Hataras stepped away from

the horse and approached Listar. 'Punished Man, will you wait with others? Or we give you ritual now? We end torment in soul.'

'How, Bonecaster? How will you do such a thing, to any of us?'

Vastala settled down beside him. 'Many dreams are forgotten upon awakening, yes?'

He glanced away from her appallingly open expression. 'But not memories,' he said. 'They just rise up, like the sun. Each morning, after a moment's bliss, they return. Like ghosts. Demons. They return, Vastala, with all the fangs and claws of the truth. We awaken to what's real, what was and can't be taken back.'

She reached out with a tanned, blunted hand and touched his cheek. 'There is no real, Punished Man. Only dreams.'

'It feels otherwise.'

'There is fear in awakening,' she replied, 'even when the dream displeases. In the voice in your head, even as it cries out, begs to wake up, another voice warns you. You awaken to a world unknown. This is cause for fear.'

'We need our guilt, Vastala Trembler. Without it, all conscience dies. Is that what you would do to me? To us? Take away our conscience? Our guilt?'

'No,' answered Hataras, who now crouched opposite him, her eyes bright and wet. 'There is another path.'

'What is it?'

'Only what must be felt, in the heart of the ritual. Shall we ease you now?'

He shook his head and swiftly began packing up the leavings of his meal. 'No. I am a Hust soldier now. I will stand with my comrades.'

'Your fear speaks.'

He paused. 'Fear? More like terror.'

'If you are made to surrender the lie of your crime of murder,' said Vastala, 'you will face the crime of your innocence.'

'For which,' Hataras said, 'you feel greater guilt than could any bloodied blade in your hand.'

'She killed herself,' Listar whispered, 'out of spite. She arranged it to make it seem her death was by my hand.' Shivers rippled through him, and he sank back down, bringing his hands to his face. 'I don't know what I did to earn that . . . but it must have been something. Something.' *Abyss below, something . . .*

Their hands were upon him now, surprisingly soft and warm. They left heat wherever they touched.

'Punished Man,' said Hataras, 'there was nothing.'

'You can't know that!'

'Her ghost is chained. You drag it behind you. You have always done.'

'This was what she wanted,' said Vastala. 'At first.'

'It was madness, Punished Man. Her madness. A spirit broken, a dream lost in the mists.'

'We will wait,' said Vastala. 'But for her, we cannot.'

'Her dream is a nightmare, Punished Man. She begs like a child. She wants to go home.'

'But no home waits for her. The hut where you lived – with all its rooms – still screams with her crime. To send her there is to send her to a prison, a pit, the very fate of your punishment – but an eternal one.'

'No,' he begged. 'Don't do that to her. I tell you – she had a reason! There must have been – something I did, or didn't do!'

'Be at ease, Punished Man,' said Hataras. 'We will make her a new home. A place of rest. Peace.'

'And love.'

'You will feel her from there. Feel her anew. Her ghost will touch you again, but with tender hands. As the dead owe to the living, no matter their state. The dead owe it, Punished Man, to salve your grief, and to take from you the grief you feel for yourself.'

He wept, while their hands slipped from him, and their voices fell into a cadence, making sounds that seemed less than words, yet truer somehow, as if they spoke the language of the souls.

After a time he thought he heard her then. His wife. The

sounds of weeping to answer his own. He felt their shared grief washing back and forth, cool and impossibly bittersweet. The madness of long ago, the endless torment of uncertainty each time he stepped into a room where she waited, the dread of what might come the instant he looked into her wild, panicked eyes.

If there was magic in the world worthy of its power, this was surely it.

*I must tell everyone. There is another kind of sorcery. Awake in the world, awake in our souls.*

And her words on that last day, before he set out to place an order with Galast the cooper, for the casks they would need at the estate. '*I have a surprise for you, beloved husband, for your return. Proof of my feelings for you. You will taste my love, Listar, when you come home. You will taste it, in ways unimagined. See how my love blesses you.*'

And so he had, returning home filled with a new hope, and yet something trembled beneath the surface of his thoughts, a visceral fear. Hope, he now knew, was a vicious beast. Every thought a delusion, every imagined scene perfect in its resolution and yet utterly false; and when he found her, with the braided cord about her neck that she must have slipped over the bedroom door's latch – in a house emptied of servants, who each later swore that they had been sent away by Listar's express command – and when he comprehended the power of the will that kept tightening the cord while she sat against the door, only then did he understand the blessing of her love for him.

Illness, a mind bent, a soul broken, wherein every cruel impulse had slipped its leash. He knew now the horror behind her eyes, the fleeing child within who had nowhere to run.

He lowered his hands, wiped at his eyes, and looked to the two Bonecasters kneeling opposite him. So many undeserved gifts.

*But the Dream will fade. The Dog-Runners will die out.*

*Abyss take us, that loss is beyond all recompense.*

Something left him then. He did not know what it was, could not know, but its departure was like a sob, a relinquishing of unbearable pain. And in its absence, there was . . . nothing.

Faintly, as he sank to the ground, he heard one of the Bonecasters speak. 'She makes the home ready. For her husband, for the day he joins her.'

'It is well,' the other replied. 'But still, they make ugly huts.'

'Let him sleep now – no, stop that, Vastala, leave his lovely black cock alone.'

'This is my payment. I will have his seed.'

'He does not give it freely.'

'No, but I take it freely.'

'You are such a slut, Vastala.'

'We can keep him asleep. You can have him after me, when this cock recovers.'

'He may be asleep, but it surely is awake. Don't empty him, Vastala. I want my share. Don't be greedy.'

'I'm always greedy.'

'Too greedy, then.'

He heard his wife laughing as a heavy, brawny pair of legs straddled him, as he was pushed inside, and a body began moving rhythmically against him.

'It is dark enough,' said someone, 'when you keep your eyes closed.'

This was, Listar decided, the strangest dream, but one for which he had no complaint.

\*     \*     \*

Commander Toras Redone had been riding beside him in silence since they'd broken camp that morning. By the day's end they would reach the Hust encampment. Galar Baras studied the track ahead as it slipped between denuded, pock-marked hills, bending round slopes of tailings, the scoured flats where furnaces had once stood, along with sheds and ditches, all lining the old road to either side.

The day was cool, but he could feel the weather turning, as if a new season was rushing upon them. Word had come on the day they had left Henarald's estate: Urusander's Legion had departed Neret Sorr. They had begun their march on Kharkanas.

He listened to the horses' hoofs strike the frozen ground, at times sharp as the strike of a ballpeen against raw rock. The sword at his hip murmured incessantly.

'If you think I hate them, you would be wrong.'

Startled, he glanced across at her. She wore a heavy cloak of sable, the hood drawn up to hide her profile, and sat slumped heavily in the saddle. 'Sir?'

She smiled. 'Ah, back to the honorifics, then? No more thought of the sweat between us, as we grapple every night beneath the furs? Our breaths shared, out from me and into you, out from you and into me, our taste as one – could two people hold each other tighter? Oh, for a sorcery to merge our flesh. If I could, I would swallow you, Galar Baras, my body a mouth, my arms a forked tongue to wrap about you, to pull you in.'

'I beg you, sir, no more of that.' *Your words torment me.*

'This day too bright? All things in stark detail, a focus so sharp as to cut the mind? No matter, come the night I will fold you in, yet again, like a lost child. I was speaking of Urusander's Legion. And Hunn Raal, whom I should despise, but do not.'

He thought about that, and then shrugged. 'He is truly of the Issgin line, sir, a betrayer, a poisoner – if not hate, then what?'

'Yes, the Issgin line. Possessing a well-matched claim to the throne, only to lose the bloody struggle. By virtue of failure, they are now condemned, tarred, vilified as the quintessential villains. Do not let our perpetual reinvention of the past deceive you, captain.'

He shrugged. 'Then is this pity that you feel?'

'Consider well my warning. We can make no claim to righteous vengeance. These prisoners now wearing the Hust, they have no anger to mine, no ruinous rubble to crush down with fury. You may well seek to bleed down upon them all, and so stain them alike, but such a desire will fail, captain.'

He said nothing to that, as she had touched upon his own

fear. There was no cause for this new Hust Legion. *In manner, they are mercenaries who have already been paid, with all the suspect loyalty such an error in judgement entails.*

'Hunn Raal and his ilk seek stature and wealth,' said Toras Redone. 'A redistribution of power. The highborn of the Greater and Lesser Houses deem the table crowded enough. So, we now have a war.'

'There is also the matter of Urusander, and the High Priestess Syntara—'

'Temple squabbles, and worse yet, captain, some hoary remnant of misplaced notions on monarchy, when our queen has long since left us to become a goddess, making the whole debate a charade. But let them elevate Urusander into godhood, a Father Light for Mother Dark. Do you see the assumption yet?'

'I'm afraid I do not, sir.'

'It is this atavistic absurdity, this clinging to kings and queens who must be bound in matrimony, as the putative parents of Kurald Galain. Captain, listen to this drunken whore here, when she tells you that there can be a Father Light and a Mother Dark without the former having to jam his cock into the latter's cunt. More to the point, a god and a goddess *need not be married* to rule us. Let her keep her lover. Let him fuck his scrolls. What of it?'

He stared at her, speechless.

She tilted her hood back, showed him her sallow, puffy face. The ebon hue was fading, like a failing of convictions. Her smile was broken. 'But they'll not listen to me, captain. It's gone too far. The highborn will see Draconus taken down. The priestesses will see their victims wed. Hunn Raal will see the power of the nobles broken, and his own lackeys in their place.'

'Sir, Lord Anomander—'

'Is a man. Of honour and integrity. Mother Dark commands him to keep sheathed his sword. He thinks this a denial. A refusal of all that he is. He sees no other path, comprehends nothing of her meaning.'

'Then, by the Abyss, Toras, someone should tell him! No! She should! Mother Dark!'

'She has, from the arms of her lover.'

'Too subtle!'

She laughed. 'Too subtle by far, Galar Baras. Should have left this all to us women with lovers, yes? We are the ones who trampled the barriers, the sacred agreements, snapped the chains constraining our sordid appetites. We see outside the strictures – look at you, Galar Baras. We could ride to the very edge of the Hust camp, only to have me drag you from your saddle and fuck you blind, witnessed by all, and you could not stop me. Could you?'

'There is virtue in being brazen, Toras? What of your husband?'

'Yes, the humiliation of being so publicly cuckolded, and there we lay bare the heart of everything.'

'How?'

She drew her hood up again, reaching down for her flask, from which she drank, long and deeply, before saying, 'Men. It's all about saving face. Every argument, every duel, every battle, every war. You would level a world to keep from being made to look a fool. And so you shall.'

'I will speak to Lord Anomander. Your solution is simple yet elegant. Indeed, as you say, it is wholly natural. Urusander seeks no wife. Mother Dark seeks no husband, yet she has not once spoken against the notion of a god at her side. Lord Anomander will realize this.'

'They'll not let him.'

'Sir?'

'He is trapped. Utterly, irrevocably trapped. Mind you, so is Urusander. Chained and caged. The holders of the keys, darling, are the priestesses, and Hunn Raal. And, of course, the highborn. No,' she said, after another mouthful from the flask, 'there will be a battle. Many people must die – do you not feel it, captain? This clawing thirst?'

'I feel, commander, fates converging, a maelstrom of deaths, all unnecessary, all a terrible waste.'

She grunted. 'Better a whore on the throne. Or behind it.'

Her comment left him bemused, and he said nothing as he pondered its meaning.

They rode out from the knot of hills, and saw before them the Hust encampment. As they lifted their mounts into a canter, and drew closer to the picket line, Galar Baras glanced across at Toras Redone, to see her face turned towards him.

She laughed.

*     *     *

Wareth sat in his tent, staring at the armour lying on a carpet opposite him, the blood hue of the iron links, the overlapped coin-shaped scales protecting the leather straps, the studded rivets sheathing the gauntlets. He looked upon the helm, flared at the neck, with a camail of chain depending from just inside the rim, and the broad cheek-guards flanking the nasal spine. For all the artistry inherent in the design, there were no elaborations, no creative touches, not a single swirl or inset pattern. Like the swords, the armour was plain, purely functional. It promised the utilitarian application of prowess in the midst of violence. There was something both beautiful and terrible in this.

And yet, none of it was for him. The trappings rode him uneasily, no matter how tightly he fit the straps, or cinched the buckles. There needed to be solid flesh beneath the chain, not this shying unease that now seemed to plague him, as if every muscle upon his bent frame had become uncertain. Shivering despite the brazier, he sat with his hands together, fingers knotted.

Cursed weapons and the like belonged in fairy tales, along with magical rings and staves that sprouted fire. In each, a wish was fulfilled only for a price to be paid, the wagers of life reduced to a simplistic morality tale delivered to children. But here, in this world, even sorcery defied the conventions of wishes made real, unearned power suddenly within reach, and none of these gifts settled easily into the reality he had made for himself.

Too many of the prisoners had seen it differently. They now strutted. They laughed with the blades, hummed in time with the keening links of chain. They took to the marching in serried ranks, the wheels in formation, the chorus of weapons drawn in unison. Their crimes dwindled behind them, their punishments – whether felt deserved or otherwise – had been magically transformed.

And yet.

*And yet. It all remains a game to them. They sneer behind the backs of every officer. At night, gathered round their squad fires, they spit sizzling contempt into the flames, telling each other stories of looting, pillage and all the helpless victims to their every desire.*

*We are an army of monsters. Thugs. Mother help us should we ever win a battle.*

Both Prazek and Dathenar had lost something in the days since their arrival, as if their equanimity was under siege by all that they witnessed, and all that they feared was still to come.

Wareth pitied the return of Galar Baras, and the thought of Commander Toras Redone seeing for herself the vicious travesty of her legion filled him with shame.

*I warned them. This was a mistake.* Corruption was inevitable. The Hust Legion should have been left dead, every sword and every hauberk of chain buried with the rotting flesh in the barrows.

Should they prevail against Urusander, should they crush this uprising, the Hust Legion would stand alone, unmatched on the field. It would turn on the highborn and their rich estates. It would turn on Kharkanas itself.

*We will break this world. I warned them, and now it's too late. The beast is made, its thousand limbs shaken loose, its multitude of eyes blinking open, each ablaze with avarice and lust.*

*Not even Prazek and Dathenar can hope to hold these reins. Nor Galar nor Toras Redone. Nor Faror Hend, nor any of us who once lived in the pits. We're rolling to our feet, bristling and bold, and this sneer – still hiding in the shadows – will soon turn to a snarl.*

An unexpected call to muster had sounded. He stared at his armour, and then, with trembling hands, he reached for it.

853

*      *      *

Faror Hend had been standing on the edge of the camp, facing east, when the harsh tone of the bell reached her. She had been waiting for something to appear on the horizon. A mounted figure, gaunt atop a weary horse, a man of grey and black, or perhaps revealing the bleached skin of one blessed by another god. She had thought to remain where she was as that rider approached, as if pinned to the frozen earth, spikes driven through her boots. She wondered at the words they might exchange, when at last he drew up before her.

Less than a legend, yet more than a careless promise of a future to be shared between them. She imagined him drawing closer, revealing ever more detail, a fleshless face, the hard angles of bone beneath stretched skin, his long iron-grey hair hanging limp from a peeling pate. And in the sockets where eyes belonged, only darkness.

*'I've come for what was promised.'*

*She nodded but said nothing as he continued.*

*'Youth was lost to me. I will now have it back.' Raising a skeletal hand. 'Here, to hold.'*

*'Yes, Lord Tulas, I understand. It was all I was ever meant to be, all I was made for. You name my purpose, sir.'*

*'I have no power to steal your youth, nor would I. Rather, I would see you age. This, and this alone, is what I seek.'*

*'Sir, will I never awaken your desire?'*

*'You have already. In my keep there is a throne, elevated to embrace my lifeless presence. There I will sit, to witness the years take you. Such are the appetites of old men. My desire is appeased, my lust, coiled as a serpent, dreams of heat and is content in its torpor.'*

*'Kagamandra Tulas, I will be your wife.'*

*'You will be my regret.'*

*She frowned. 'And this is all? There can be . . . nothing else?'*

*'You speak of children,' he replied.*

*'Yes.'*

*'Have as many as you like. I see you having no shortage of lovers.'*

'I see.'

'You see before you the future's face, Faror Hend.'

She shrugged. 'That visage belongs to all of us, milord. Your death's mask. The decay. The husk. You do not frighten me.'

'I'll never find you,' he said, as he began to fade before her eyes.

'No, we ride soon to a battle. I do not expect to survive it.'

'Then . . . farewell, my darling. Think of me, and all that we could have had . . .'

Blinking, she squinted at the horizon, growing darker with each passing moment. Unbroken the line. No distant rider. Not yet.

Kagamandra Tulas, I impugn you with disservice. I raise you as a spectre of my own creation. This youthful visage that you see hides a welter of evil. Spinnock saw as much, and so he rejected me. If you ride now, Lord Tulas, better you arrive too late.

There was no fighting these despondent notions, these conjurings of an imagination driven to despair. The army at her back terrified her, and she found herself desiring only its annihilation. Even the charms of the captains could not hold this fraying leash for much longer. The swords whispered promises of murder, and their wielders did but lick their lips.

They were condemned, you see. Rejected by us all and cast down into the pits. Sentenced to labour in tunnels of unlit rock, where even thoughts could not escape to the light. Wareth comprehends. Even in Rebble's eyes there is a glint of fear. And thrice since Rance has tried to take her own life. So now she sits in her tent, a guard standing over her, and will not speak.

Castegan has taken to the pipe, lost in his opiate dreams. The entire command structure totters, only moments from utter collapse.

The camp was stirring behind her, in answer to the call to muster. She heard the laughter of swords half-drawn, the rising atonal song of the chain hauberks and the keening cacophony of helms being readied.

*Yes, war will deafen us all. This seems fitting enough, I suppose.*

Sighing, she turned about and made her way into the camp, and to her tent, where awaited both weapon and armour.

*I was a Warden. I did not ask for this.*

*They said others were coming. Refugees from the winter fort. But none have arrived. I remain alone. They were wise to avoid this place, this fate. Would that I could flee and join them now, wherever they may be.*

Instead, she walked to her tent.

\*        \*        \*

Seltin Ryggandas, the quartermaster, had rushed into the command tent with the news. Galar Baras was returning with Commander Toras Redone. After dismissing the man, Prazek collected up his gauntlets and then paused, looking down at Dathenar. His companion was sprawled in the padded chair that seemed more suited to an estate, flanking a fire, with a dog lying asleep at its foot. Where it had come from, none knew.

'Despondent in this surrender of our brief elevation, now we must scan left and right, seeking another bridge to patrol.'

'We yield in the manner of the genuflected,' Dathenar replied. 'Upon hands and knees, posterior raised to take the boot.'

'Boot, or riding crop. 'Tis rumoured she has rough appetites.'

'Then I'll wince in ecstasy.'

'Rise then, my friend, fore and aft, and let us make a stand of our surrender, as befits the discarded.'

Sighing, Dathenar climbed to his feet. 'We hand over a belligerent beast, our knuckles scraped and raw, and must compose our features with earnest innocence.' He collected up his cloak and fastened the clasp high on his left breast. 'Evince no hint of relief, as three thousand pairs of eyes will be fixed upon us, give or take.'

'A one-eyed man among the ranks.'

'A women whose left wanders.'

'While the right impugns.'

'Jaded eye.'

'Jaundiced eye, lowered eye, squinting eye, ego's eye, an I in the eye other than thine own, that we should meet, to gauge the distance between us, these gulfs too treacherous to cross, the self an island among islets, the chain relegated to maps.' Prazek paused, and then sighed. 'An eye to draw the straightest line, or rounded in wondrous regard, unto itself.'

'They shall stare at us,' Dathenar said, nodding.

'The weight of such knowing offends me,' Prazek replied. He paused at the tent's doorway. 'Presumably, Galar Baras has prepared her. Still, these new soldiers know her by name alone, an utterance swaddled in reluctance. A broken woman, no less. How fragile her approach, how timorous her comportment.'

'As you say,' Dathenar agreed. 'Then gird yourself once more, friend, as we place ourselves between the archer and the arrow butt. Paint the placid façade, targeted upon your face—'

'Attain the aplomb, the swaggering ease of confidence.'

'Unruffled the surface of our equanimity.'

'Pellucid the shallows.'

'Impenetrable the depths.'

'We must be moon-drawn, the steady advance of an ocean's familiar broach.'

Dathenar nodded and approached the tent flap. 'Time, then, to lap her boots.'

They exited the tent, looked out upon the companies already forming up in a rising moan of armour and the chittering of scabbarded swords. The sun was nearing zenith, lending a hint of warmth, and where snow lingered on the plain, amidst tangled stretches of yellow grass, it made deflated dunes.

As the ranks assembled to either side of the camp's central parade ground, two riders appeared at the far end.

Side by side, Prazek and Dathenar set out to meet them.

The time for conversation had passed, barring the swords and their almost nervous muttering, and so neither captain spoke as they crossed the ground.

Near the far end, Galar Baras and Toras Redone reined in, and then slowly dismounted in time to greet Prazek and Dathenar, who arrived and saluted the commander.

She was not quite sober as she regarded the two captains, her glassy eyes amused, her expression ironic. 'Anomander's lieutenants. Or, rather, captains now, of the Hust Legion. Silchas Ruin empties his brother's martial treasury.' She drew a deep breath. 'Report, then, on the readiness of these soldiers.'

Dathenar cleared his throat. 'Commander, most welcome. We invite you to inspect the new recruits.'

'Recruits.' She seemed to chew on the word for a moment, and then glanced at Galar Baras. 'Captain, I understand that none of these . . . recruits are in fact volunteers.'

'You could say that,' Galar replied. 'The pits were closed—'

'But their punishment has not ended, with forgiveness bargained and a deal struck. Rather, it's been extended, and in place of hammers and picks, they now wield swords.'

Galar Baras nodded.

She faced Dathenar again. 'Which are you?'

'The other is Prazek, sir. We are less interchangeable than it might at first seem.'

'Spoken true,' Prazek added. 'I am less inclined to the disingenuous.'

'Yet more to pontification,' Dathenar added.

Prazek resumed. 'Are these soldiers ready, you ask, sir?' He scratched at his beard and pondered for a moment, and then said, 'Readiness is a curious notion. Ready for what, precisely? An argument? Assuredly. Betrayal? Possibly. Courage? Of a sort. A battle? Oh, I should think so.'

She studied him for a moment. 'Less disingenuous, you said.'

'I was being—'

'I gathered that,' she snapped. 'Your opinion, Dathenar?'

'Dilemmas regard us upon all sides, commander. Officers culled from the least objectionable among them still reveal a host of flaws. Surviving soldiers of the old legion vacillate between horror and shame. Swords defy their wielders in refusing to duel, leaving them fisticuffs and mundane knives. Armour howls in the night at the scamper of a mouse. These recruits step in time, however, and wheel in a fashion, and close shields, and when we speak of the coming clash, why, something dances in their eyes.'

'Discipline?'

'Poor.'

'Loyalty to the soldier to either side?'

'Unlikely.'

'That said,' Prazek opined, 'they are likely to strike fear in the heart of their enemies.'

'Hust iron will do that.'

'Indeed, sir. But more so the evident inability of their officers to control their soldiers.'

'Then you two have failed.'

'So it seems, sir. Will you now cast us out? Demote us? Send us into the ranks, cowed as curs under boot?'

'Oh, you'd like that, wouldn't you?'

Prazek smiled.

Toras Redone paused and then said, 'Join me, all of you, and let us walk this gauntlet. We will speak more in the command tent, where I can have a drink, and you two can tell me, in your scattered manner, how you plan to fix this.'

'Sir?' Dathenar asked. 'Command of the Hust Legion is now yours, surely. Level your orders upon us, and we will do all that you ask.'

'Level of head, smoothly planed, as it were,' Prazek added.

Toras Redone snorted. 'I command soldiers, not savages. Galar Baras, I should have heeded your warnings. They would have us march in aid of Kharkanas and Mother Dark? Abyss below, I see a weasel in a rabbit's den.'

'Perhaps,' said Dathenar, 'in a supporting role . . .'

She looked at him, but his expression remained unchanged, stolid and serious.

'No,' she said. 'Try as you might, you'll not make me laugh.'

'Yes sir.'

Prazek gestured. 'Commander, would you be so kind as to begin the inspection?'

*　　*　　*

Wareth stood in front of his company. He had watched, from the corner of his eye, the extended conversation between the three captains and their commander. If meant to test the fortitude of this newfound discipline, it would have little effect either way – this was not an instance of soldiery quavering beneath the stentorian, icy regard of superior officers. Rather, it was the gimlet regard of criminals, murderers one and all, fixed brazen and defiant upon those who presumed to command them.

At last, however, Toras Redone set out to walk the arrayed ranks, and where she passed, the Hust iron lifted a high keening, rippling with her passage. Some among the front lines flinched at the sound. Others grinned, and then studied the commander with renewed attention.

She suffered their insolence, each step measured in the manner of someone who knew how to control their inebriation.

Her pace did not change until she came opposite Wareth, where she halted and faced him. 'Ah, my mercy.'

He met her eyes. 'Sir.'

'Something you would say?'

'Yes sir.'

'Out with it, then.'

'Welcome back, sir.'

Oddly, his words seemed to rattle her. After a moment, she said, 'Should I offer the same to you, Wareth?'

'I am unchanged, sir.'

'Well,' she said, 'it seems we have something in common.'

Then she had moved on, and Wareth was left, alone once

more in front of his troops. The sword at his hip was shivering inside the scabbard, as if to mock his cowardice, and behind him someone muttered something that elicited low laughter, until a snarl from Rebble silenced everyone.

*Now you see for yourself, Toras Redone. But then, perhaps you are right for this. I could smell the alcohol fresh on your breath, see the settled wastage in your face bespeaking your determination. Abyss knows, your marriage to Calat Hustain must be a disaster, to have led you to this state.*

*But sometimes not moving is the greatest act of cowardice one can find. Safe in the hole, the cramped walls, the sodden womb of staying right where you are.*

*Galar, she will do, when it comes to leading us all into ruination. Did you know this?*

\*       \*       \*

When the inspection was done and the soldiers had been dismissed, Faror Hend joined the other officers in assembling within the command tent. Present were Wareth, Rance, and the other criminals who had been promoted, along with the quartermaster, Castegan and now Galar Baras. Flanked by Prazek and Dathenar, Commander Toras Redone had been invited to sit in the worn but plush chair, into which she sank, cradling a jug of wine.

'Is this everyone? Good. I haven't got much to say. None of us asked for this.' She paused to drink down two quick mouthfuls. 'I trust you hold no delusions about me. The legion I once commanded is gone. In its place, a nightmare waiting to happen. Criminals?' She gestured lazily at Wareth and the others. 'I speak plain, but none of you are officers, barring the titles you've been given.' Her gaze levelled on Wareth. 'Abyss take us, we have a coward in our midst – oh, he holds the proper pose, but it seems that is all any of us has. A pose. Will that be enough to disabuse Hunn Raal's ambitions? Enough to make Urusander's Legion recoil? I doubt it. Mother help Lord Anomander. Mother help Kharkanas.'

There was silence, and then, reluctantly, Faror Hend cleared her throat and said, 'Commander.'

Toras Redone settled her bleary eyes upon her. 'Oh yes, the lost Warden. You have something to say?'

'Yes sir. What the fuck is this?'

Toras Redone blinked.

'If we're only here to pity ourselves, we could have gone back to our tents and done it there, as we've pretty much been doing ever since we got here. Shall we all get drunk with you now, sir? Not yet acquired our quota of wallowing?'

'This one,' said Toras Redone, 'has spine. No wonder she seems so out of place.'

'Fine,' she replied. 'I'm happy to leave at your convenience.'

'Commander,' said Dathenar, 'the officers assembled here have done exceptionally well under the circumstances.'

Toras Redone affected an exaggerated frown. 'You chastise me, Dathenar?'

'I am dismayed by your quick dismissal. The state of this legion was, until your arrival, the responsibility of myself and Prazek. Castigate us as it please you, but as to the matter of those officers under us, ignorance is an unworthy display.'

Toras Redone snorted. 'And on the field of battle, who among you here can rally his or her soldiers? A buckling company? A handful of squads holding the centre of a line? Who here can make a fist of every command? Dathenar, you and Prazek cannot be everywhere. Nor can Galar Baras.' She pointed a finger at Rance. 'You, sergeant. Tell me, who among your soldiers will follow you?'

'None, sir,' Rance replied. 'They follow no one.'

Castegan spoke up. 'Commander, I did warn Galar Baras against this madness. True, it was all by command of Silchas Ruin, but Galar could have refused it, and done so with his honour intact. Silchas is *not* Anomander, after all.'

Toras Redone slid her gaze across to him. 'Ah, dear old Castegan. I imagine your optimism overwhelmed all and sundry. Galar Baras maintained his honour by following orders. Whatever misgivings he held he kept to himself. But I have been warned – a new sorcery afflicts the Hust iron.' She drank again, three long swallows, and then settled back further in the chair. 'They judge us,' she said in a low tone. 'Each sword. And that dreadful armour. Judgement. Condemnation. Iron has no respect for flesh. It never did. But these blades, they now *thirst*.' Abruptly, she shook herself. 'Prazek, prepare this legion to march. We leave tomorrow. Pray Lord Anomander finds his way home. Failing that, Silchas Ruin can take command of what he has wrought.'

Faror Hend said, 'Then I will take my leave—'

'No you won't,' cut in Toras Redone. 'You, I want at my side, if only to prop me up.'

'Find someone else.'

'None but you, lieutenant. Now, all but Galar Baras and Prazek and Dathenar, out. You have work to do. Warden, see that my wagon is well stocked.'

Faror Hend stared down at the commander for a moment longer, then saluted and departed the tent.

Outside, she found a few of the others milling. Wareth met her eyes and smiled. 'Well played, Faror.'

'We waited for this? Abyss take us.'

'As it will,' Wareth replied, glancing across at Rance, and then at the two guards standing nearby, waiting to escort the woman back to her tent. After a moment, he offered Faror Hend a smile. 'We assemble. Face the enemy. Give the orders, and then see what happens.'

'She was unduly harsh on you,' Faror said.

Wareth shrugged. 'Not unexpected. Her mercy was never meant to absolve me, nor mitigate her contempt. We were fighting a war, after all.'

Rance spoke to Wareth. 'You must tell her. About me.'

'I leave that to Prazek and Dathenar.'

'The commander will decide the right thing to do,' Rance said. 'I welcome the end to this.'

Frowning, Wareth said, 'Has it not occurred to you, Rance, that there may not be time . . . to deal with you? She wants us on the march tomorrow—'

'What?' Rance's face filled with dismay.

Faror Hend grunted and then shook her head. 'Expect two more days, at least, before we are ready.'

'Still,' said Wareth, 'too little time.'

Faror Hend stepped close to Rance. 'An end to things . . . well, yes, Rance, I can see how you might long for that. But what if dying doesn't end anything?'

At that, Rance recoiled. After a moment, in which terror twisted her face, she spun round and rushed away. Her two guards were startled by her haste, and hurried to catch up.

'You seeded a cruel thought, Faror Hend.'

'My patience is fraying. In any case, in this mood I should speak with no one else for the rest of this day. After all,' she added bitterly, 'I have to see a wagon stocked with wine.'

'She never liked Castegan,' Wareth said. 'Sobriety makes for a cautious soul. She was never one for being cautious.'

Faror Hend studied Wareth for a moment, and then, shrugging, she set off.

*　　*　　*

Galar Baras watched his commander – his lover – getting drunk. Prazek had taken a seat at the map table, where he seemed to be studying the supply report Seltin Ryggandas had left there before departing. Dathenar paced near the tent flap, as if silently debating something, a frown marring his brow.

'I should have left this to you, Galar,' Toras Redone said, her words thick and low. 'But that cell made me bored. You'd think I'd welcome such solitude, just me and my . . . wine. And now, well, look at us. If the corpses had been raised up, by swords refusing death itself, I would have led them. Vengeance was a fire I could have stoked, fury a storm I would have ridden. We would have caught Hunn Raal unawares, and descended upon Neret Sorr. An army of undead, silent but for their screaming weapons, to deliver righteous slaughter.' She lifted the jug, sloshed it to gauge how much was left, and then drained it. When done, she let the jug fall to the floor beside the chair, loosed a heavy sigh, and continued, 'But the dead don't care. Neither lust nor vengeance stirs their motionless limbs. No indignant rage flashes in their lifeless eyes. I walked among them, and with each body I stepped over, I felt something more taken away from me. Some . . . essence. Dathenar, bring me another jug – there, against the back wall. Excellent, a man who knows to follow orders. We'll need that.'

Prazek looked over from where he sat by the table. 'And so each death surrenders its name, choosing but one, whispered again and again, from countless pale lips. And that name is Loss, and to utter it is to feel it. Diminished, death by death, this essence of what we once were.'

Dathenar stood near her, watching as she tugged free the jug's stopper. Then he said, 'Fallen friends cease to ask how you fare, cease to answer in kind. They may retreat from your thoughts, but never quite far enough. If in our minds we walk as one among many, in the midst of families knotted by blood and by choice, and witness, as years pass, the crowd grow ever smaller, then we come to comprehend – as we must – a day when we walk alone, abandoned by all.'

'Or contemplate another kind of abandonment,' Prazek said, nodding, 'when it is we who must leave the others. A last step comes to us all. Regret and sorrow will ride the final breaths of each of us, moments of pity perhaps for those who must remain, those who must take another step, and then another, trailed by none but ghosts.'

'They were my friends,' said Toras Redone in a ragged whisper. 'One and all. My family.'

'You are not entirely alone,' Galar Baras pointed out.

She smiled, but her eyes remained fixed on the dry earthen floor. 'I walk no reasonable path. The fewer that remain, the more easily we find ourselves lost.' She drank again. 'But this womb is red and sweet. It bears the colour of blood, but is quick to lose its warmth. It enlivens the mind, in the instant before it dulls every thought. It licks the cunt, only to take all feeling away. For all that, I am eager for the insensibility, so easily mistaken for lust.'

'Yet you berated Wareth for his cowardice,' said Dathenar.

She scowled. 'No wonder Silchas sent you packing.'

Prazek spoke. 'We have stood guard upon many a bridge,

Dathenar and me. Lofty our presumption of stout diligence, our capacity to fend either approach.'

'But the river runs past,' Dathenar said, 'with mocking indifference. Such is the fate of those who guard the civil, this span of bold traverse upon which peasants and kings will walk, each in their time. Stand in vigil, even as the stone and mortar rots beneath our boots. You would share pity before death's distant bell? Be on with it then, commander. The river's surface ripples with black and silver, a commingling of despair and hope.'

'And what lies beneath that surface, alas, is anything but clear.'

Galar Baras stared at the two men, one to the other, and then back again as each spoke. Their voices possessed a cadence. Their words carried him frail as a leaf upon a stream. Glancing down, he saw desolation in his lover's eyes.

'Pity,' she finally said, as if tasting the word yet again. 'It suffices. But I keep my tears in a jug. You'll see me astride my mount on the day of battle. I will not shy from that fate.'

'We have spoken nothing of fate,' Prazek said.

'By its utterance the word invites,' Dathenar observed.

'Surrender,' said Prazek, 'by another name.'

'Yet it awaits, a promise to the future, in which all power is yielded. To swim or drown beneath a reckless sky.'

'I'll order the advance when such is required of me,' said Toras Redone. But her red eyes were glazed, her lips wet. 'You three will command a thousand each. You will array your eight cohorts into a flattened wedge and march to close. I expect we'll hold a flank—'

'I will advise Lord Anomander that we take the centre,' said Prazek.

She lifted her gaze with an effort, studied him. 'Why?'

'Should our side prevail, sir, it may be necessary for our flanking allies to turn on us.'

Toras Redone let her head tilt forward again, until she was peering at the jug on her lap, or her hands that held it as if it was a baby. 'Now there is a fate unanticipated – forgive me my addled mind. Of course we take the centre, as we will be the wild beast with blood in its mouth. Cut-throats and thugs, sadists and murderers, our iron shrieking its own thirst. None of you can rein that in, can you?'

'It's not likely,' said Dathenar, resuming his pacing.

'Would that Hunn Raal returned to us,' she then said, 'with yet more wagons loaded with fatal casks. We could make husks of the armour, again, and take every hand from every sword. And,' she lifted the jug and kissed its broad mouth, 'begin anew.'

Galar Baras wanted to weep. Instead, he said, 'Some other discarded or neglected segment of the population . . . but none comes to mind, alas.'

Prazek rose as if bidden by some unseen signal from his friend, who moved to draw back the tent flap, and as he stepped into the dull light beyond he said, 'Well, there're always children, though the armour might need refitting.'

The two men departed.

Toras Redone coughed, and then asked, 'Did I dismiss them?'

*In every way imaginable, sir.* 'I would depart too, sir, to oversee the preparations of my cohorts.'

'Yes,' she said, 'as I am too far gone to even fuck right now.'

*Without your will or your leave, Toras, there is nothing I could find to make love to. It may seem a fragile agreement, with you sodden most of the time, but I will hold to it nonetheless.*

He waited a moment longer, if she would speak again, but then saw that her eyes had closed, her breaths now slow and deep.

*The commander cannot see you now, as she communes with her jug of tears, with not a drop spilled to the world.*

*       *       *

'The ways of the Tiste,' muttered Hataras Raze, her level blue gaze fixed upon the encampment ahead. 'They scurry like ants upon a kicked nest. Each one a child to the world.'

'Soldiers the worst,' said Vastala Trembler, who now

walked holding Listar's left hand, while he gripped the lead for the horses with his right. The feel of her warm palm against his own was strangely miraculous, a gift undeserved, and he still did not know what to make of it. Earlier in the day, it had been Hataras walking close at his side, her fingers brushing his forearm on occasion, or resting on his hip. There seemed to be few barriers in the sensibilities of the Dog-Runners.

His eyes were not as sharp as theirs and it was a few moments before he made out the bustle of activity in the camp ahead. 'They're preparing to march,' he said. 'We're just in time.' He glanced at Vastala. 'What did you mean, soldiers were the worst?'

'Our children play the hunt. To learn the ways. But once the first blood is on their hands, they stop play. They meet the eyes of the hunt as adults, not children.'

'Cruel necessity,' said Hataras, nodding. 'To give thanks to the spirit of the slain beast seeks to silence the terrible guilt within the hunter.'

Listar nodded. 'I have heard of such practices. Among the Deniers.'

Vastala grunted. 'Such gratitude is real,' she said, 'but if the hunter remains a child inside, the guilt is false. Only a hunter who is grown to an adult inside can understand the burden of such guilt. And knows that no animal spirit is appeased by its slayer's gratitude.'

Hataras stepped ahead to twist round and study Listar as they walked. 'A wolf drags you down, Punished Man, and begins to feed on you before your last breath. Its tail wags in gratitude. Tell me, are you appeased? Do you forgive with your last breath? Do you now see,' she continued, 'the delusion of the hunter?'

'But soldiers—'

Vastala's hand tightened its grip. 'Soldiers! They blunt their guilt for every life taken. Their souls bear desperate shields, deflecting every threat away from themselves and towards their leader, king, queen, god or goddess. The one who demands of them the spilling of blood. In defence. Or conquest. Or punishment.'

'Or disbelief,' added Hataras. 'Death to the faithless for the misguided Deniers.'

'Children inside,' Vastala said dismissively. 'Guilt a lie. Wrongness made righteous. Lies to the self, lies to all others, lies to the god worshipped, lies to the children to come. Soldiers play, in the name of goddess or god, king or queen. In the name of generations to come. In the name of all but the true name.'

Hataras gestured ahead. 'The child self. Cruel without necessity. Cruelty that tastes of pleasure. Such exists among hunters whom we have failed. Such exists among soldiers.'

They were drawing closer. Listar prised his hand loose from Vastala's grip, felt the cold bite of its absence. 'And criminals,' he muttered under his breath.

'So,' said Hataras, 'to the ritual. Dog-Runners do not abide adults who stay children inside. We force truths upon them. To draw aside the veil, this is what we will do.'

'I told you of the woman, Rance.'

'Yes, Punished Man. We will examine her.'

'Be warned,' interjected Vastala, 'some things we cannot heal. Some things need to be cut away. Sometimes the one lives, sometimes it dies.'

'Our captains wish you to begin with her,' said Listar. 'And they wish your ritual to be witnessed by all in the camp.'

Vastala smiled. 'We are to perform. Good. Dog-Runners not shy.'

'Indeed,' Listar replied, recalling the night just past.

Vastala drew close to him again and peered into his face, and then she nodded. 'Hataras, you spoke true. Our children will bear the tilt of his eyes. Our children will carry within them the promise of a life beyond the fate of the Dog-Runners. So. It is an even exchange.'

The notion that he had planted the seeds of children in these two women made Listar flinch. He forced his thoughts away, telling himself that such things could not yet be known, and that their words of payment – for the ritual to come – could not be weighed in flesh and blood.

Ahead, soldiers stationed at the pickets had seen them, and

while one set off to deliver the news, others began gathering from the camp, drawn out to the defensive line by curiosity, or, perhaps, boredom.

'I think,' said Listar, 'the secret's out.'

'No Azathanai hide in yonder camp,' said Hataras. 'Good. They are obsessed with secrets.'

Listar frowned at her. 'You can sense their presence?'

Both women nodded. 'We have learned this talent,' said Vastala.

'By tasting the fires of the hearth, the breath of smoke.'

'By lapping the valley between Mother's legs.'

'Tellanas,' Hataras said, nodding again. 'Sorcery is the snake eating its own tail. It looks upon itself and in looking it devours, and in devouring, it grows. So the magic attends an endless feast. Our goddess Mother is trapped in a circle of herself. But we Bonecasters, we dance.'

For all their bluntness, these two women often confounded Listar. He had no understanding of this magic of which they spoke. To him, the Azathanai were half-legendary figures, not quite obscure enough for him to disbelieve in their existence, yet vague enough in details to lend him scepticism regarding their exploits. They straddled a line of veracity, and until tales of the one named T'riss, and her curses uttered in the Citadel of Kharkanas, reached Listar, he had given little thought to the Azathanai. *Builders. Gift givers.*

*And, it now seems, meddlers.*

'If they would be gods,' he now said, as the guards ahead waved them forward, 'why not reveal such? Why hide their power?'

'Worship is vulnerability,' replied Hataras. 'See how we dance around Mother? We are her weakness, even as she is ours.'

'Worse yet,' added Vastala, 'they too are children inside. Players of games.'

Listar squinted, seeing Wareth and Rebble now, the two men pushing their way through the small crowd awaiting them. *It is strange, to call these two my friends. And yet, they are. The coward and the bully. But I wonder, how much courage does it take to live with your fear? And how vast is Rebble's heart, to cast so kind an eye upon those of us who are weak? We too readily judge and then dismiss.*

*But I think it is not Rance who should fear most what is to come. It is Wareth.*

*       *       *

'Listar looks different,' said Rebble, tugging at his fingers to make the knuckles pop. 'Younger.'

Wareth nodded. *Or, perhaps, no longer so old.* 'Then they may have worked on him already,' he said.

Rebble grunted. 'By how they hover around him, I'd say there was truth in your words, Wareth. Worked on him, hah.'

'I meant the ritual.'

'I meant sex.'

'Yes, well. I suppose word's already reached Prazek and Dathenar, but why don't you make sure, and see that Rance is escorted into the centre of the parade ground. That's how they want this to proceed.'

'Assuming those witches will do as asked.' Rebble paused. 'Whatever that is, and damned if I have a clue.'

'Nor I, to be honest. As for these Bonecasters agreeing to it, well, they're here, aren't they?'

Grunting, Rebble stepped forward. 'Listar! Welcome back! Bring 'em in to the middle of the parade ground.' Then he turned about, grinned enigmatically at Wareth, and set off back into the camp.

Wareth studied the two Dog-Runners. For all their blunt, stolid forms, there was a sensuality about them, and in their manner of moving, and their gestures, he wondered if they were sisters. *Still, they seem young to be powerful witches.*

Listar handed the reins of the trailing horses to a nearby soldier and then walked up to Wareth. For a moment, it seemed that the man contemplated closing with an embrace, but at the last instant he halted, and nodded awkwardly. 'Lieutenant.' He glanced to one of the Bonecasters who now moved past him to stare up into Wareth's eyes. 'Ah, this is

871

Hataras Raze. And here, Vastala Trembler. Bonecasters of the Logros clan of the Dog-Runners.'

Hataras reached out and rested one thick, calloused forefinger against Wareth's chest. 'This one, the coward?'

'So he calls himself,' Listar replied.

She pushed Wareth back a step with that stiff finger, and then, moving past, said, 'Bah. We are all cowards, until we are not. Now, where is the tormented woman?'

'Take your pick,' a feminine voice offered from the crowd.

Hataras grinned. 'Good!'

Another woman spoke, 'You here to kill all the men?'

Vastala replied, 'In a way, yes!'

Listar scowled, and then turned to Vastala. 'Please, no more of Dog-Runner humour. Come along, we're to head to the centre of the camp.'

'Have the soldiers encircle us there,' Hataras said, continuing on.

'I think that is the plan,' Listar replied, his gaze now searching Wareth with some confusion.

But Wareth was unable to respond. *We are all cowards, until we are not.* The words thundered through him, as did the easy dismissal with which she had uttered them. He wanted to turn, to set off after Hataras Raze, to demand more from her. *Do you offer me hope? A rebirth? If cowardice only before now, then when and how its end? What side of me still hides? Where, in myself, have I not already crawled, or cowered, or searched?*

*Do not offer me such words! Do not leave me with them, damn you!*

The crowd had parted, and closed in again to form an informal escort as the Bonecasters made their way into the camp, Listar lingering between them and Wareth.

'Sir?'

'C-can they do this, Listar?'

After a long moment, Listar nodded, and said, 'Mother help us all.'

\*   \*   \*

872

Galar Baras scowled at Prazek, and then Dathenar. 'You are both addled,' he said. The three of them stood just outside the command tent. A moment later he waved away the soldier who'd delivered the news of Listar's return. Stepping close to Prazek, he said, 'This is madness. We are Tiste Andii. Children of Mother Dark. To bring in foreign witches—'

'Children we may be,' Prazek cut in, 'but of the Hust, not Mother Dark.'

'Be not deceived by the cast of the skin,' Dathenar added. 'That was a summary blessing. The Hust iron now claims these men and women, and it bridles with newborn power. Sorcery and witchery, a dance of the unknown, yet we would face it. We would grasp it. We would make it our own.'

Galar Baras shook his head. 'The commander will not sanction this.'

'Our commander lies insensate to the world,' Prazek retorted.

'A singular proclamation,' said Dathenar, 'to embrace all manner of leader and politician. Waters made opaque by unsecured belief and misapprehension, to which dear Toras Redone has splashed a sampling of sour wine. We meet her inebriation with indifference, deeming it irrelevant to the failures implicit among all who would rule us.'

'Mother Dark,' said Prazek, scratching at his beard, 'made no distinction in her blessing, and now leaves the skin to will its hue, as befits each man's and each woman's mercurial moods. This is a wavering faith, a host of questions devoid of stipulation.'

'The Hust Legion,' said Dathenar, 'requires more than that. Manic blades and moaning armour will not suffice. The shared residue of pits and picks, shackles and groaning carts, of crimes snared and punishments binding, all prove insufficient to our need.'

Galar could now see a knot of figures entering the parade square, while from all sides, soldiers had abandoned their preparations for the march and were drawing closer in a rough, jostling ring. Swords bickered in scabbards. Chain and scales muttered incessantly. Dark faces remained expressionless.

Overhead, the sky was pale and dull, a formless white stretched across the heavens. A hint of warmth rode the soft winds from the south. The day seemed to slump, heavy feet rooted to the still frozen ground. Sounds were dying away, one by one, like unfinished thoughts.

He watched as the two Dog-Runner witches emerged from an unbidden divide among the soldiers, heading towards Rebble who now stood with Sergeant Rance at his side. The bearded man was gripping Rance's left arm. Frowning, Galar Baras swung to Prazek. 'Is that woman to be their sacrifice? I cannot permit—'

'No blood will be spilled,' Prazek said.

'How do you know?'

'Not the Dog-Runner way,' Dathenar said. 'Join us, Galar Baras. Stand in your commander's stead. You need neither condone nor bless. We shall witness, and in witnessing, partake. Alas, what finds us on this day may well fail in penetrating our commander's present state of unconsciousness.'

'Unfortunate,' muttered Prazek, 'that the one who, perhaps, needs healing the most, has inadvertently excused herself. But then, who could have predicted the timing of this?'

'Sergeant Rance,' said Dathenar to Galar Baras, 'has been killing men in the camp. And yet the woman you see yonder is in fact innocent, though the blood stains her hands.'

'What riddle is this?'

'Another hides within her, Galar Baras. One adept with sorcery, and yet consumed by the madness of murder.'

'What will these witches do to her?'

'We don't know.'

Galar Baras stared at Dathenar, and then at Prazek. 'And our soldiers are to witness all this as well? Have they not suffered enough scenes of punishment and retribution? And to now be reminded once again on the very day before we march? Gentlemen, you will see this legion torn apart!'

'Possibly,' Prazek conceded. 'The manner in which we gamble defines the stakes. Win or lose, it shall be absolute.'

874

The two witches reached Rance, who at the last moment pulled back and would have fled if not for Rebble's sudden, somewhat harsh intercession, as he wrapped both arms about her. Rance struggled in his grip, and then sagged as if in a faint, slipping down to the ground.

'No,' said Galar Baras, moving forward. 'This is wrong.'

One of the witches knelt beside Rance, who now hung by one arm in Rebble's grasp, her hair covering her face, as motionless as if death had taken her.

As Galar Baras drew closer, Rebble looked over and met the captain's eyes. 'She's fled,' he said. 'Not away. Inside.'

'Rebble, let her go.'

He released his grip and her arm flopped down.

The witch who knelt beside Rance now held up a staying hand. 'No closer, Lover of Death.'

The title halted Galar Baras in his tracks. He was unable to speak. From the ring of soldiers surrounding the parade ground, there was now utter silence. Not a sword cackled. The chain and scale had ceased their desultory murmur. Something had come into the air, potent and febrile.

The other witch began dancing with slow steps, her naked form swaying above her broad hips. 'Watch me!' she cried. 'All of you! I am Vastala Trembler, Bonecaster of the Logros! Watch me, and I will open your eyes!'

*　　*　　*

Faror Hend pushed through the ring of silent soldiers, her eyes fixed on the prone form of Rance. Fear shortened her breath. There was nothing fair in this. Even Rebble, who had now taken two steps back from where the Bonecaster knelt over Rance, was making a mute appeal to Galar Baras who also stood nearby.

But the witch who had been dancing in a circle around Rance now began stretching her steps into an outward spiral, and some unseen power emanated from her, visibly pushing away both Rebble and Galar Baras. As Faror Hend drew nearer, she felt a pressure building against her, resisting each step. After a moment she halted, panting. The dancing woman seemed to be trembling, shivering, her form blurring as if seen through thick glass.

Rance suddenly cried out, her shriek answered by three thousand Hust swords with a fierce metallic shout. Staggering back, Faror Hend saw soldiers collapsing in the line, one after another, while others struggled, fighting against something – and now she could feel it, a slithering sensation beneath her armour, as if snakes had been loosed here. Yet, wherever she frantically reached, she felt nothing.

*They are beneath my skin!* She fell to her knees, desperately pulling at the straps and buckles.

*　　*　　*

An inexplicable rage filled Wareth as he pushed against the overwhelming pressure that rolled in waves from the centre of the parade ground. Whatever sorcery this was, it seeped through the armour as if it was little more than cheesecloth. It raced across his skin, and then burrowed beneath it, rushing into muscles and then bones. He was roaring his fury but could hear nothing but the deafening rush of that terrible power.

He could feel his blood thinning to water in his veins, while something else flooded through him, thick and viscous. It seemed to burn through his rage and his terror, whispering secrets he could feel but not hear.

But Rance was thrashing on the ground, her agony and torment plain to see, and he would not stop as he clawed his way towards her. The Bonecaster kneeling at her side had reached into Rance's abdomen, as if plunging her hands through flesh, and there was blood on her forearms, clear fluids stretching like webs down from her elbows.

No woman could survive such wounds. He found he was reaching for his sword, but the blade would not pull free of the scabbard. It was howling, as if matching Rance's pain, and yet helpless, its pealing voice shrill with frustration.

He fought his way closer, was now less than ten paces from the dancing witch, whom he could barely see as she slipped past his field of vision, her arms seeming to spin.

*No one should die like that—*
An eruption took his mind, swept away every thought. Amidst the chaos, he felt a revelation, opening like a poisonous flower. He stared into its core and, inexorably, felt his sanity torn apart by what he saw.

*  *  *

Whatever gifts the Bonecasters had bestowed upon Listar sustained him through the ordeal of the ritual. On his knees at the edge of the clearing, he witnessed the collapse of everyone. The weapons and armour fell silent, as if struck mute by their uselessness in the face of this foreign sorcery. He saw officers fall. He saw the Bonecaster Hataras lift something small and bloody from Rance, quickly wrapping its still form in a hide. He saw Vastala cease her dance, shedding her trembling like a skin, whereupon she fell to her knees and vomited on to the frozen ground.

Listar staggered to his feet. He made his way towards them, his eyes on the body of Rance. There had been blood, but now there was none. She was unmarked, her eyes shut, and as he came closer he saw the steady rise and fall of her chest.

'Punished Man,' said Hataras, her voice raw and her eyes red. 'She had a twin, dead in her mother's womb. A short life starved and wanting, struggling and failing.' She waved a hand. 'But it had power that not even death could still.'

Not quite understanding, Listar reached Rance. He studied the woman. 'She will live?'

'The other wanted a child. She found one. Gave it death to be with her. A night of drowning, to begin many other nights. Death and blood on the hands. Blood on the sorcery itself.'

Vastala stumbled closer, wiping at her face. 'A tormented sea,' she said, 'yet I drank deep. I drank it dry, leaving bones and rocks and shells. Leaving all that drowns in light and air. What remains in them is a gift of dust.'

Listar knelt beside Rance.

Hataras moved closer, settled a hand upon his shoulder and leaned close. 'Punished Man. You need to understand.'

He shook his head. 'I don't.'

'No soul is truly alone. It only seems so, when it is the last left standing in a field of war. And that war is waged within each of us. Her twin – that shrunken, blackened corpse in the womb – it fed on every thought murdered upon awakening, or snuffed out in its sleep, where hopes unfold into dreams and dreams become nightmares. It devoured the rendered remains of stillborn ideas, sudden wants, of avarice and betrayal. Imagination, Punished Man, can be a most wicked realm.'

Vastala spoke. 'I took from them everything. I have left them nowhere to hide.' She paused, looked around. 'I have made this army into a terrible thing. These soldiers. They will not hesitate. They will march into Mother's fire if it is asked of them. They will fight all who face them. And they will die, one by one, no different from any other soldier. No different, and yet, *utterly* different.' She pulled Hataras to her feet. 'My love, we must flee. They will rise soon, in silence. They will blink. They will not meet the eyes of friend or rival. The cursed iron flinches from their touch. These soldiers, beloved, are an abomination.'

'This is what you gave us?' Listar demanded. 'This is not what was asked of you! We sought a blessing!'

Vastala bared her teeth. 'Oh, they are blessed, Punished Man. But think on this, what comes to a mortal soul, when it finds that truth is unwelcome?' She faced Hataras again. 'What fate the witch within the orphaned twin?'

Hataras shrugged. 'Her possessor lies dead, its flesh gone, but the husk of its soul remains. This one,' and she nodded at Rance, 'must learn to reach into it, to find the sorcery residing there.'

'Ugly magic,' said Vastala.

'Yes,' Hataras agreed. 'Ugly magic.'

Listar remained beside Rance. Looking around, he saw the army fallen, as if slain where they stood. *It must have been like this when Hunn Raal poisoned them all.*

The Bonecasters had already departed the clearing. He felt the absence of their touch as a sharp ache somewhere deep inside. *So easy their abandonment of me. No, I do not understand Dog-Runner ways.*

Then his gaze caught movement, and he turned to see a woman stepping out from the command tent. She stood, swaying slightly, looking out upon the thousands of motionless soldiers, lying in poses no different from death, and the weapons remained silent. The only sound Listar could hear was the soft wind, carrying with it the last of the afternoon's warmth.

*Abyss take me, that must be Toras Redone.*

Listar climbed to his feet. He made his way towards her. When she saw him she flinched and took a step back. 'No more ghosts,' she said.

'They are alive,' Listar replied, slowing his steps. 'All of them. It is not what it seems.'

Her lips curled in a wretched smile. 'Nor am I.'

'There were Bonecasters among us,' Listar said. 'A ritual.'

She studied him with red-rimmed eyes, from a face bleak and desolate. 'And what did this ritual achieve, beyond the collapse of my soldiers?'

He hesitated, and then said, 'Sir, forgive me. I do not know.'

# BOOK FOUR

_The Most Honourable Man_

# TWENTY-TWO

THE SEA FADED INTO MISTS BEHIND THEM, AND BELOW a vast rolling plain appeared. Skillen Droe tilted the cant of his wings and began descending. The landing was rougher than K'rul had expected and he tumbled from his companion's clutches, coming to a stop against the edge of a ring of stones mostly hidden by yellow grasses.

'*There is the dust of a settlement ahead,*' Skillen Droe said, folding his wings. '*I am of no mind to invite arrows and curses, and besides, I weary of flight.*'

Groaning, K'rul sat up. 'We return to our world,' he said, looking around. 'We are in the lands of the Jheleck.' He paused and eyed Skillen Droe. 'I suppose they don't like you either. I can't recall if you've mentioned them already.'

'*It is not in my nature to offend people. Endeavouring to do well invariably yields unexpected consequences.*'

'And the Jheleck?'

Skillen Droe shrugged his sharp-angled shoulders. '*Taking offence is all too often the retreat of a petty mind.*'

'Passive aggression, is what you mean,' said K'rul, pushing himself to his feet. 'The act of taking offence becomes a weapon, and its wielder feels empowered by the false indignation. That said, I doubt this is what afflicted the Jhelarkan.' He tottered for a moment before recovering his balance. 'My legs are half asleep and my skull is empty of blood. I am in need of a meal, I think, but the walk will do some good. An encampment, you say?'

*'A gathering, and some excitement. K'rul, we have met too many fellow Azathanai. Such encounters leave me despondent.'*

They set out, at K'rul's slow, halting pace. 'We are afflicted with the stature of gods without the incumbent sense of responsibility. Our endless wandering is in fact an eternal flight from worshippers, no different from a father fleeing his wife and children.'

*'And between the man's legs, the opportunity to repeat the whole mess. With another woman, in another place. K'rul, you impugn my good deeds.'*

'It's all down to actually acknowledging the need to grow up, something so many men have trouble with. A weathered visage and a loose child behind it. A door slammed in the face of every potential lesson, the rapid thump of footsteps off into the night.'

*'An entire people can succumb to this same crime,'* observed Skillen Droe. *'Irresponsible flight redefined as progress.'*

'Yes, the delusion of godhood belongs to us all, mortal and immortal alike. Can we say, with any certainty, whether some other god exists, a being beyond all of us, and we to it as children to a parent?'

*'Orphaned, then, for no hand clasps our own, no mother or father guides us. In our abandonment, K'rul, we but flail, lost and unknowing.'*

They had been spotted. A dozen or so veered Jhelarkan now paced them on the plain, black and shaggy and loping as if moments from closing in for the kill.

'I dare say,' ventured K'rul, 'we would twist from that hand's grip at the first opportunity, even unto denying its very existence. You see, Skillen Droe, the dilemma of our wilfulness?'

*'I see that children will delude themselves into the guise of grown adults, aping adult concerns, whilst their child selves crouch amidst the basest of emotions, the jealousies and spites, the blind wants and desperate needs, few of which can*

*ever be appeased without the shedding of blood, or the rendering of pain. Children ever delight in the suffering of others, particularly when delivered by their own hand. Does it not fall to ones such as us, K'rul, to set a moral standard?'*

'And how did that fare among these K'Chain Che'Malle of yours?' K'rul asked. 'Your moral guidance yields you the form of a winged assassin.'

*'Yes, well. Sometimes the notion of right and wrong is best delivered in a welter of furious slaughter.'*

'As the child within you lashes out.'

*'K'rul, I recall, at last, how often conversation with you becomes infuriating.'*

'I speak only to encourage humility, something we Azathanai woefully lack. For this reason, Skillen Droe, did I open my veins and let the blood of power flow into the world.'

*'A child encouraging other children. I see chaos in the offing.'*

K'rul grunted. 'It's always in the offing, old friend.'

Four of the giant wolves pulled away from the pack and approached, tails lowered and ears flattened.

*'We are not welcome,'* said Skillen Droe, unfolding his wings once more.

'Patience,' K'rul replied, holding up his bloodless hands.

The wolves halted a few paces away, and the lead one sembled, rising on its hind legs as blurring took its form. The wolf fur rolled back to become a heavy cloak, and from the confused uncertainty of the creature's transformation a woman's face appeared, followed by the rest of her mostly naked body. She was whipcord lean, her belly flat and her breasts small. Startling blue eyes looked out from a heart-shaped face, framed in a mane of black hair.

'More strangers,' she said. 'Despoiling sacred ground.'

'Our apologies,' K'rul said. 'We saw no cairns.'

'Because you don't know what to look for. We are done with cairns, as the Tiste looters destroyed all that they found. Now, we sanctify the earth with blood and piss. With splintered bones. All who despoil holy ground are slain.'

K'rul sighed and turned to Skillen Droe. 'It seems we will have to fly after all.'

*'No. As I said, I am weary. Though I do not desire it, I will kill these rude creatures if necessary. Ask this woman what afflicts the camp beyond? There is an Azathanai there. I can feel it. I believe the Jhelarkan celebrate the return of their ancient benefactor.'*

'Only you would call celebration an affliction.' K'rul turned back to the woman. 'My companion and I regret our trespass. We are but travelling through, seeking the shores of the Vitr. Even so, if Farander Tarag is in the camp beyond, we would pay our respects to our Azathanai kin.'

The woman scowled. 'Farander Tarag has severed all ties to the Azathanai. Divided in perpetuity, they now embrace the wild, and join us in the ancient glory of the beasts. They will not greet you as kin. Begone, both of you.'

K'rul grunted in surprise. 'A D'ivers ritual? Farander has reached back far indeed.'

Skillen Droe clacked his serrated jaws to signal something, perhaps contempt. *'Farander Tarag always was something of a narcissist. This does not surprise me and nor should it surprise you, K'rul. Who else could suffer Farander's company but Farander? Oh, and these blunt-browed creatures. The wild yields little of value to the mind capable of imagining beyond the horizon. The Jheleck are now benighted, sealing their fate.'*

K'rul sighed. To the woman, he said, 'Very well. Alas, my companion is too weary to fly, and so we can do nothing but walk. You cannot kill us, so enough of that nonsense. But be assured we will give wide berth to your encampment.'

The woman snarled, and then veered into her wolf form. Re-joining her kin, she wheeled with them and loped off to return to the pack.

K'rul glared at Skillen Droe. 'Were your words only for me, Skillen?'

*'Of course not. What value a threat unheard?'*

'I see now how your poor manners invite discord.'

'*Your observation baffles me. I was nothing but polite, insofar as such a thing is possible when contemplating murder. Was my regret not palpable?*'

'No, not really.' Shaking his head, K'rul set off again, this time angling westward to take them clear of the encampment. Skillen Droe strode at his side, wings folded once more.

'*The Tiste will know trouble should they attempt to invade Jheleck lands again. Of course, the ferocity of the wild knows little cunning, beyond what nature provides. In the hunt there is necessity. In defence of the defenceless, or of oneself harried into a corner, there is desperation. Neither feeds the vagaries of war.*' He clacked his jaws again. '*Their retreat shall be endless, I predict, across every realm, age upon age. The wild can do nothing but die.*'

'Nonsense. Civilization is ephemeral. Domestication of beasts removes their ability to survive without constant attention. Enslavement and breeding of plants weakens them against pest and blight. Imprisoning water invites disease, and, at the last, the breaking of the soil exhausts its capacity to renew itself. Gothos might well be the Lord of Hate, but nothing of what he said was wrong.'

'*And so your argument is that, eventually, the wild will return.*'

'Yes.'

'*Yet, in unleashing sorcery upon all the realms, K'rul, you offer a weapon to defy the wild, in ways not yet imagined.*'

K'rul glanced to the right, squinting at the dust-laden encampment and its swarming figures. 'It may seem that way, yes, at first. But in the absence of magic, what else might civilization beat into weapons against the wild?'

Skillen Droe was silent for a long moment, and then he said, '*The K'Chain Che'Malle enslaved natural laws. They transformed their world with the tools of technology.*'

'Indeed, and how have they fared?'

'*Their war against nature is complete. Now they twist the very blood in their children, to make forms new and deadly.*'

'And sent you packing.'

'*A crude and displeasing description of my leaving them to their own devices. In creating birds, they bent to the task of constructing cages for them. I chose to not linger, and if my departure proved somewhat tumultuous and discombobulating, it was no fault of mine. Indeed, had I not lost my sky-keep, I would have retired within its inviting confines, there to contemplate the peace of solitude.*'

'For most,' said K'rul, 'solitude invites angst.'

The pack still paced them to the east. The day's modest warmth was fast fading and here and there, in hollows, patches of wind-sculpted, dirty snow were visible. The season's turn this far north was still months away.

'*Angst. I have never understood that,*' Skillen Droe said.

'For many, contemplation is like small, sharp teeth chewing from the inside out. We're in the habit of swallowing down our demons, and then deceiving ourselves by believing they die in dissolution. Instead, they delight in their hidden refuge, and feed day and night.'

'*I know nothing of such demons.*'

'Give us distractions to craze the eye, deafen the ear, and dull the mind, and we can survive a lifetime of despair. For all your efforts, among one people after another, Skillen Droe, I fear that you have failed in listening to any of them. In future, focus on the artists, to best discern the honest cry of the lost.'

'*It is well known that a civilization intent on self-destruction will disempower its artists,*' said Skillen Droe. '*I witness this again and again. You misunderstand my purpose, K'rul. I am not a saviour.*'

'Then why do you find yourself hiding in civilizations of the mortals?'

'*I get bored, K'rul.*'

'Bored with yourself?'

'*Bored with everything, and everyone. I search for something I cannot name. A beacon, perhaps, in the darkness of perpetual ignorance. A spark of defiance among the wilfully obtuse. This endless drone irritates me, the frenzied flurry of busyness for little purpose beyond perpetuating a dissatisfying life. The constructs of the intellect are delusional, and so I become the fist of unreason. The gods, I say, care nothing for machines. Care nothing for the lies of habit, nothing for the tyranny of how things were always done and therefore must always be. The gods are deaf to excuses, rationalizations, justifications. Instead, they listen in the silence beyond the machines for the whispered opening of a single heart.'*

K'rul had halted during this speech. He studied his companion, this towering, reptilian assassin, slayer of dragons, who had uprooted mountains and lifted them into the sky. 'You speak of love,' he said. 'This is your beacon, your spark of defiance.'

*'The K'Chain Che'Malle look into the night sky and build for it laws and principles, as if the act of definition suffices, serving as justification prior to invasion, conquest and exploitation. Should they ever succeed, they will infect the heavens with the same wars, the same venal desires and hungers, the same witless adherence to those laws and principles by which they shackle all they see, and all they claim to know. Tell me, K'rul, when you look up into this coming night, what do you see?'*

'What I see matters less than what I feel.'

*'And what do you feel?'*

'I feel . . . wonder.'

Skillen Droe nodded. *'Just so. And wonder, my friend, is the intellect's most feared foe. Its path is love, and love is the language of humility. The rational mind would stand over it with a bloodstained sword, and in the empty bleakness of its eyes you will see its triumph.'* The assassin shook his head and fanned wide his wings. *'This I have learned, among the K'Chain Che'Malle. This, K'rul, is why I stand at your side. The magic you offer – oh, they will seek to cage it, in laws and principles, in rules and squalid structure. But we both know that they will fail, for their minds are trapped in cages of their own making, and all that lies beyond will remain forever unknown, and unknowable, to them. And this they cannot abide.'*

'They will fail,' K'rul agreed, 'because *I* am unknowable.'

'*Yes. And your gesture, K'rul, was an act of love, yielding unending wonder. What you have done will infuriate the world.*'

K'rul shrugged. 'That will . . . suffice.'

They resumed their journey.

*     *     *

A broad, flat stone, ten paces across, squatted above the tide-line, at the very edge of the caustic miasma that drifted from the Vitr. Long before the unnatural sea's birth, in the age when the Builders were content working with raw rock, earth and trees, this massive stone had been worked into an altar, its surface roughly flattened by antler picks, with the spiralling grooves left to the elements to soften through seasons of rain, snow, heat and cold.

But none of this had prepared the altar for the acidic bite of the Vitr's roiling breath. The patterns upon its surface were mostly gone, and the grooves that remained were brittle to the touch. Just as faith died with a people's death, so too this obelisk and the worship it embodied.

The Thel Akai, Kanyn Thrall, crouched upon the flat surface, leaning on his short-handled, double-bladed axe. The weapon had once belonged to a Thelomen chieftain. Its forger had pronounced it cursed, unsurprisingly, after Thrall had killed the chief in single combat. Such trophies could only be claimed with a touch of irony, an acknowledgement that edges cut both ways. Kanyn Thrall had smiled when he discarded his broken spear, its famed point blunted and barely recognizable beneath a welter of gore, and collected up the cursed axe.

Some weapons possessed only a single moment of triumph within them. Clearly, the axe he now held was biding its time.

With that thought foremost in his mind, lingering in an idle way, he tilted his head slightly as he regarded the dragon drawn up upon the Vitr's strand, directly opposite him and interceding itself between him and the hovering, crackling gate of Starvald Demelain. The gate had been born, in rupturing fury, far to the south, where it had spilled out a broken storm of dragons, but it had since migrated here, sung close by his mistress's siren call, and day after day she strengthened the anchors now holding the gate in place.

Songs like the silky strands of a spider, a web very nearly complete. All that remained, he reminded himself, was some sorry bastard's soul torn loose and stuffed into the gaping wound that was Starvald Demelain. *A soul to seal the maw, and pray it's a mighty soul, a stubborn soul, a soul made to suffer.*

*Not mine, then.*

The dragon had clearly split away from the broken storm – as, he suspected, had most of the others – and circled round, possibly to flee back through the gate. But then, what was stopping it?

*Not me. Not my mistress. Not our guest, still half starved, still entirely lost. No, this dragon seems determined to stand in my stead. But I need no help guarding this gate.*

*And still it refuses to speak.*

He reached one hand up to rub at his face, shocked yet again at the deep lines that furrowed it. Shifting slightly – even a Thel Akai born to crouch and squat could know aches in the posture, eventually – he turned his gaze back over his right shoulder, to where the Second Temple stood in tilted disregard amidst lifeless sand dunes. *Second Temple. So she calls it, with that mocking smile. 'While you, Kanyn Thrall, you claim the first one. That flat stone, that eroded failure soon to dissolve beneath the waters of the Vitr. Not that my abode will last much longer, of course. Still, I am optimistic. Its Chamber of Dreaming remains empty, but still, on late nights, I enter it, listening for her whisper.'*

*Foolish woman. Your lover drowned, and you'll not again lie with your queen. Just as I will never again lie with my king, since no two men can ever shit out an heir. This is how things are, Ardata. Let's make use of our guest's soul, swollen as it is with self-pity, and stopper the gate shut, and then let us leave, seeking some other worthy cause.*

He couldn't see her. Somewhere inside the Second Temple, he surmised, drifting from empty room to empty room, fingers making patterns in the air that lingered like floating webs in her wake.

Come the night she'd take his cock, the lesser pleasure being the only pleasure, and he'd take her wet hole, for much the same reason. It was, all things considered, comical.

*A Thel Akai tale to be sure, a long joke's sudden punchline. I see the host rocking back in delighted laughter, enough to drown the sting to be sure. Though my king's eyes would look on, veiled behind the fixed smile. Old men should never linger.*

The guest, however, was there, seated upon a toppled column below the shattered steps, whetstone motionless in one hand, sword-blade resting across his thighs. He was staring out at the Vitr, his mouth somewhat open, somewhat hanging. A man not yet old enough to take stock of his orifices, snapping them shut to all worlds but the intimate one. *No, instead he gawks, and gawps. He works at something and then that mouth hinges open, to show the heavy drama of his deed. Pant pant pant, each breath almost but not quite silent. Irritating as all the hells Ardata claims to have survived. Whatever 'hells' are.*

He had stumbled into them some time back, this stranger, this guest. Walking, he told them, from a dead horse – the fool had carried the saddle to prove it – up from the south, a dying wanderer, or perhaps a refugee, or even a criminal. *Choose the title you like, just add 'dying' to it and that'll do.*

Kanyn was of no mind to lend aid. His days of offering salvation were far behind him. But the Mistress had insisted, and it was only much later that the Thel Akai warrior had divined her unspoken motivation.

He eyed the swollen, swirling wound that was the gate of Starvald Demelain. Extraordinary that a single soul could seal it shut. *But not mine. Not hers, either.*

The dragon was staring at him, as it had been staring at him ever since he took his station opposite it, the very morning of its confounding arrival. As far as staring contests went, not even a Thel Akai could match a dragon's baleful, unblinking regard. Instead, Kanyn would periodically meet those reptilian eyes and offer up a twisted expression, slowly shutting one eye while screwing up the other, perhaps, or dangling his tongue, or sending its glistening tip upward to touch his own nose. A finger to savage the itch in one ear, another to explore the caverns of his nose. A sudden farting sound, or coughing out a hidden handful of dirt and dust. Occasionally, he'd reach to his own genitals, as if about to begin playing with himself.

But that never went further. Besides the indignity of such a thing, the damned dragon's eyes never even narrowed.

He contemplated walking up to it and pissing on its snout. 'What would you say to that?' he called out suddenly. 'Bladder's full, after all. Give a man who needs to piss a target and he's happy. Shall we make me happy?'

The guest had looked over, and now he slipped down from the column and walked towards Kanyn Thrall. 'Thel Akai, why do you bother?'

Kanyn squinted. 'Already feigning banal uninterest in our winged interloper? That did not take long. I wonder, is that the secret gift of those low in intelligence, that makes them so well armoured against amazement? The cynic's shallow wit, yes? I almost admire you. No, honestly. What bliss would I know had I half the wit! Tell me, at least, that you ate the horse.'

The guest halted. 'Served me too well, sir, for such ignominy!'

'So you hollowed your stomach instead. Horses are as quick to serve a master when dead as when living, you fool. That's what blind servitude is all about.'

'There are other kinds of service, Thel Akai.'

'Such as?'

The man drew himself up slightly and Kanyn groaned inwardly, bracing himself for another grave pronouncement. 'I left my brave mount where it fell, and in so doing, I served the honour I held for it.'

'You honoured it by wasting it? Ah, I see. Naturally. Why didn't I think of that? Now kindly strut back to that column, will you? You're sucking up all the hot air.'

'I do not know why you dislike me so.'

'That's right,' Kanyn replied, looking back to the dragon and settling once more, 'you don't.'

'Should I take offence?'

'Why not? I daily leave a heap of it in that latrine pit behind the temple. Help yourself.'

After a moment, the guest turned away, and Kanyn heard the soft clack of the man's mouth finally closing. *Ah, see that? He's learning.* He studied the dragon again. Not beasts he was familiar with. This was the first one he had ever seen. Wheeling down from the skies of legend, fierce and massive, unknowable and – to anyone other than a Thel Akai – frightening.

But the Old Goddess had spewed out enough contempt on the matter of dragons, raising her huge fists before her to tell her children of skulls crushed flat, blood spraying from slitted nostrils, and all the rest. Tales to stain all wonder from her brood, a soaking of disdain.

Even so, it was a formidable beast.

*'Finally!'*

The voice hissed deafeningly inside Kanyn Thrall's head, startling him so much that he bit his own tongue. Cursing, he spat red and then straightened, hefting the axe into both hands. 'Finally what, lizard?'

*'Old Goddess, is it? That would be Kilmandaros. Some Azathanai are too stupid to be gods, unless, of course, they breed even stupider children. In which case, why, paradise beckons!'*

'You speak in my head with the voice of a woman. What name do you claim?'

The dragon lifted her snout, and then stretched her jaws wide in the manner of a yawning cat. A mangled knot of wet armour was lodged between two jagged molars. The jaws closed again, with a faint squeal. *'Are you worthy of knowing my name? The bitch of spiders calls you Kanyn Thrall.*

*Thus, you have nothing to give me in return. I only bargain, Thel Akai. Gifts are for fools.'*

'I can give you something in return, dragon. My axe blade between your eyes. A name, if you please, to etch on to the iron, alongside the many others I have slain.'

*'Others? Other dragons? I think not, and let us be clear here, Kanyn Thrall, your other victories have all the bravado of rats crunched underfoot. I make breakfast of mortal heroes and shit out pitted iron at day's end. I make morsels of Tiste champions, snacks of Thel Akai hunters, paltry meals of Jhelarkan, Dog-Runners, Thelomen and Jheck.'*

Kanyn Thrall tilted his head back and laughed. 'You've been listening in! Enough to harvest the names of many of those who dwell in this realm! But we well know the path of your passage, from the gate's first manifestation on the south shore of the Vitr to here, and now. If you found a snack or two on the way, unsurprising. But champions and heroes? Thel Akai and Thelomen? You, dragon, are full of shit.'

After a long moment, the dragon subsided. *'Disrespect is ill advised.'*

'A threat to make me quake! Do try another!'

*'I could take you in my talons, Kanyn Thrall of the Thel Akai, and stretch your soul across the wound.'*

'Come close and you will rue it.'

*'Look into my eyes, Kanyn Thrall. In them you may see . . . a warning.'*

'I see nothing but witless—' In the last moment, he caught the reflection in those massive, reptilian orbs. Bellowing, he wheeled, but not in time, as a second dragon, skimming low over the Second Temple, lunged upon him, snapping down its talons to close about the Thel Akai.

The creature flung Kanyn Thrall into the air, and crooked wings lifting like sails to buffet the air, caught him a second time, talons punching through his scale armour to bite into his flesh. The axe spun away.

Kanyn was thrown to the ground, the impact breaking his right leg beneath the knee. He howled in pain, rolling on to his side, glaring down at the two glistening, snapped ends of the bones jutting through the skin.

The second dragon landed with a heavy thump beside the huge stone, its tail flicking from side to side. *'Curdle, my love! I've told you about taunting Thel Akai!'*

A new voice spoke from behind Kanyn. 'And I told your lover about injuring my companions.'

The new dragon twisted its head round. *'Ardata! Speaking of lovers, where is yours? She was a reluctant soul to be sure. Resisting the snare we made for her. Mayhap she escaped, but into what? Why, the Vitr, and that is a most forgetful sea! No matter, enough of us made use of her.'*

Swathed in animal skins so old that patches of hair were missing, Ardata sedately approached with all the grace of an empress, until she stood over Kanyn Thrall. Glancing down, she frowned. 'That's an evil break. Lie still. We'll have to deal with it and the rest of your wounds in a mundane way, since I've yet to explore this Denul Warren.' Her thin face bore the deep lines of all who chose to dwell too close to the Vitr, although she had assured him that such details quickly faded with distance. *'Youth is restored, my friend,'* she had told him, *'although your old man complaints are another matter.'*

*Funny woman, ha ha.* The Thel Akai studied her plain-featured face through the haze of pain, even as she spoke once more to the second dragon.

'Telorast, you and Curdle were banished once from this realm. Do not expect to linger long this time around, either. You are still the biting fleas on the hide of this world.'

*'Hear that, love? The dog is of a mind to scratch. Are we frightened?'*

*'Where have you been?'* Curdle demanded.

*'South of the Vitr, beyond the stubborn plain. I visited a modest fort, occupied by quaking Tiste, now as black as that plain's grasses. Most curious.'*

*'The Suzerain.'*

*'No doubt. In any case, I chose a sweet form to entice*

*them and so learned much. Light is born anew, Curdle, and the Tiste are divided between it and Dark. There is civil war. Isn't that quaint?'*

Curdle rose slightly, arching her spine as her wings unfolded. *'And the Grey Shore?'*

*'An uglier birth in the offing, beloved. Still in its throes.'*

*'It will be ours!'*

*'Shhh! The spiders are listening!'*

Ardata turned as the Tiste guest joined them. The man held his sword, eyeing the dragons. 'Put your blade away,' she said to him. 'Feed the brazier within the temple. Set two of my thin blades into the flames. Then, fetch water from the well and find something we can use to make splints. Is any of that beyond you?'

The young Tiste scowled. 'No.'

'Go, then. We will join you shortly.' She swung back to the dragons. 'Your ambitions overreach, again.' She paused, and her voice hardened as she added, 'You misused the Queen of Dreams, and that I will not forget.'

*'A threat?'* Telorast laughed, the hissing mirth filling Kanyn's skull. *'Feed us another Thel Akai, then.'* A moment later she sembled into the body of a Tiste woman, onyx-skinned, radiant, and naked. 'Look at me, Curdle! There are pleasures to be found in this modest morsel! Match me in kind, so that we may clasp hands and beam most becomingly! In that smug way of couples no matter what the world. Come, let us preen!'

Curdle blurred as well, drawing inward to coalesce into another Tiste woman, this one taller than her lover, heavier-boned.

'You're somewhat fat,' Telorast observed, pouting.

Curdle smiled. 'I like it. More weight to throw around. In a crowd of Tiste, others will step from my path. Is that civil war over yet?'

Telorast shrugged. 'White-skinned and black-skinned, at odds. Armies on the march, blah blah.'

'Nothing worth our attention, then.'

'Oh, we should draw close when the clash comes. The

black-skinned army bears odd weapons. Tiste iron quenched in Vitr.'

At that, Ardata stepped back, her breath hissing. Even Curdle flinched.

'Madness!' Curdle cried, reaching up to bury her hands in her thick black hair. Frowning suddenly, she began running her fingers through that hair. 'Oh, I like this, though.'

'A worthy mane indeed,' Telorast observed, sidling closer to her lover.

Ardata hissed again, in frustration, and then said, 'Telorast! About those weapons—'

'Oh, never mind. They're not killing dragons, are they?'

Kanyn Thrall settled his head back. The pain was building in waves, as if his broken leg now rested on the brazier the damned guest kept feeding, a wild grin on the fool's face. Blood sizzled and melted fat popped and hissed on the embers. Eyes closed, he grimaced.

A moment later Ardata's cool hand settled on his brow. 'Sleep now, friend. I can at least give you that.'

And so the world went away for a time.

         ✻      ✻      ✻

Two uneventful days had passed since the Jhelarkan encampment. K'rul stood with Skillen Droe on a natural berm on which tufts of dead grasses made rows of tangled, brittle humps. The two Azathanai looked out over the pellucid, silvered sea of the Vitr as the sun died at their backs.

'This leaks from somewhere,' K'rul said after a time. 'A fissure, some wellspring, a broken gate. It doesn't bode well.'

'*When the Builders take notice they will do something about it.*'

K'rul grunted. 'Builders. They confound me.'

'*They answer to no one. They rarely speak at all. They are guided by forces too old for words. Too old, perhaps, for language itself. I see in them elemental nature, a knotting of implacable laws and principles beyond challenge. They are what all life struggles against, made manifest and so eternally unknowable.*'

'Living symbols? Animated metaphors?' K'rul made a face. 'I think not, unless termites and ants also serve your description. I believe the Builders to be essentially mindless.'

*'Then we do not disagree.'*

'You concern yourself with meaning. I suggest that they are without meaning.' He nodded at the Vitr. 'No different from this chaotic brew. Forces of nature indeed, but also possessing the same absence of will. Nature destroys and nature builds. Build up, tear down, begin again.'

*'They are the makers of worlds then.'*

'Worlds are born from the cinders of dead stars, Skillen Droe. No fire burns true. Something is always left behind.' He glanced at his companion. 'Or are you without such uninvited visions? The violent births, realm upon realm, age after age?'

Skillen Droe shrugged his sharp, angled shoulders. *'I know them, yet deem them nothing more than our own birth memories, the eruption of light, the shock of cold air, the sudden comprehension of our innate helplessness. We enter the world unprepared and, if we will indeed prove to be mortal, we stumble to its end, also unprepared.'*

'And the Builders?'

*'The forces of nature will take note of us, on occasion, as if we were no more than flies buzzing before the face. Mortality is but a brief iteration, an enunciation of the ineffable; worthy of an instant's wonder, until the after-image dims and fades before the eye, and then, aptly, forgotten.'* Skillen Droe spread his wings. *'This air is foul. But you were right.'*

'About what?'

*'Dragons have passed this way. You said that one or two would be drawn back to the gate. And the gate has indeed wandered and now awaits us to the north. And yes, Ardata remains.'* He turned to eye K'rul. *'Just as you said. Tell me, does this ever-flowing blood of yours lend you a new sensitivity? Does your awareness now encompass this entire realm? In loosing your blood, K'rul, have you perhaps deceived us all, and now make claim to unimagined power*

and influence? You create a new realm with this magic. It seeps out and stains all within reach, and that reach spreads. And who stands at its heart? Why, only modest K'rul, dripping generosity. So, I must ask: have you usurped us?'

K'rul scratched at the stubble of his beard. 'Oh, I suppose so, Skillen Droe. But temper your indignation, my friend, for the one who stands at the heart stands there in weakness, not strength.' He grimaced. 'I am not Ardata, with her webs and hunger. The centre of my empire, such as it is, demands no sacrifice. I am that sacrifice.'

'To worship is to lap at your blood, then, where it drips from the dais.'

'Errastas and Sechul Lath discovered a more brutal way of feeding on blood, couched in the language of violence and death. Their path opposes mine, but that makes it no less powerful. Indeed, perhaps, given its seductive qualities appealing to the worst in us, it shall overpower me in time.' He paused, and then sighed. 'I do fear that, and yet, what moves I make against them, I cannot do alone.'

'Me, your ignorant, naïve ally.'

'And dragons.'

'And Ardata?'

'I don't know, to be honest. I am curious, of course. What holds her there, upon the shores of the Vitr, beneath the gate of Starvald Demelain? Is it simply the loss of the Queen of Dreams? Or is there something else, something more? A web, after all, can be more than just a trap. It can also be a means of holding everything together, keeping it from tearing itself apart.'

'You ascribe to her motives far too much generosity of spirit, K'rul. She is Azathanai, no different from you or me in our manner of disguising secret purpose, hidden motivations, beneath our laudable gestures.' A long-fingered, talon-clad hand waved languidly. 'Like this one, and your unseen Empire of Weakness. I do not comprehend you, K'rul. What ruler seeks to rule an empire by asking for the empathy of its citizens?'

'And if empathy – and compassion – are that empire's only source of strength?'

'Then, my friend, you and it are doomed.'

K'rul considered that. 'Errastas's path is a dead end.'

'Errastas's path places no value in where it ends, dead or otherwise.'

'Yes, you may have a point there.'

'I will help you, but only so far, K'rul. I have no interest in attending your eventual demise. But for what we must do, here and now, Ardata will be essential. And she does not like me.'

'I will speak on your behalf, Skillen Droe, and seek from her . . .' he smiled, 'a little empathy.'

They turned away from the Vitr then, and set out, angling somewhat inland from the sea's caustic bite, and continued walking northward.

It was in K'rul's mind that Ardata would counter his request with one of her own. He wondered if Skillen Droe understood that. *But it is the dragons who will decide, and what could be more troubling than to elect dragons as the arbiters of what is just?*

Night was settling upon the world, the first stars burning awake overhead. They continued on, both knowing without need for conversation that their walk would not end until they reached Starvald Demelain.

*          *          *

He had helped Ardata set the Thel Akai's broken bones, both of them as thick around as his wrists. Looking down upon them, as he pulled on Thrall's massive foot whilst she guided the bones back beneath the ruptured skin, he had never felt so insignificant. Against a warrior such as this, he was no more than a child, and for all the sting of his sword, Kanyn Thrall could simply sweep him aside, dismissing him as if beneath notice.

It was an ugly feeling, this humility. The deeds of his past, which had seemed vast and weighty, were little more than the small measures of a small life. When she set to tending the punctures in the Thel Akai's torso, he had gone outside once more, to retrieve Kanyn Thrall's beloved axe.

901

Ignoring the two Tiste women – who were anything but – he made his way down to the strand of the Vitr. In the short time that the axe had been lying on the dead sand, the bitter fumes had mottled the iron, stealing its proud polish. He grunted lifting the weapon from the ground, and staggered more than once as he made his way back up the berm.

The temple's scattered ruins, the tumbled blocks and toppled columns, had the battered appearance of some past violence, as if the resident god or goddess had ended faith in a frenzy of rage. He had found rotted bones here and there, lending weight to his notions. Faith and slaughter all too often settled into a deadly embrace. He had fled Kurald Galain on the cusp of such a war, and had no regrets about that part of his leaving. But that flight had not prevented the transformation of his skin. Initially white as snow, he was now sun-burnished a radiant gold. What had at first appalled him now appealed, though he did find himself looking, with considerable admiration, upon the onyx perfection of Telorast and Curdle.

Leaning the axe against a broken block of limestone, he hesitated, and then settled down on the stone to watch the last of the light drain from the world.

Moments later the two women joined him, each taking a seat, one on either side, both close enough to brush arms and thighs.

'Bold young warrior,' murmured Telorast. 'Tell me you like them nimble. She'd batter you bruised and senseless, while I, on the other hand, display more modest curves, but no less enticing, yes?'

'I thought you two were lovers.'

'Lovers, sisters, mother and daughter, these attributions are meaningless. Details from the past, and the past is dead. In this moment, there are only women and men. Mere proximity invites potential. Isn't that right, Curdle?'

'We're always right, that's true. How could it ever be otherwise? But this Tiste warrior here, he thinks highly of himself.'

'Or once he did,' Telorast observed, 'but, alas, no more.

Oh, Kurald Galain! How it delights in the vista of its own navel! Puckered horizons and root long since past drawing sustenance. But here you are, Tiste warrior, painted in Light, godly in youth, with nothing but clouds in your golden eyes.'

'Blame Ardata,' hissed Curdle. 'She won't use him in the proper way!'

'She has a Thel Akai's cock to play with, my love. Think on that.'

'The prowess of Azathanai knows no bounds,' Curdle said, nodding. 'She must veer to fit him. Diabolical genius, but easily spoiled.'

'Quickly bored.'

'All sensitivity blunted. And now, Telorast, you went and nearly killed that giant cock!'

'You didn't want him in the first place!'

'Didn't I? Well, that's true, I didn't. But now that he's useless, I've changed my mind!'

'He'd split you in two, Curdle, even as bloated and big-boned as you've made yourself.'

'I see plenty of flab on you, Telorast!'

'Not flab. Roundness. There's a difference. I don't wobble when I walk. I sway.'

When he made to rise, both women reached out and pulled him back down.

'We're not done with you, warrior,' Curdle said. 'I've been watching you, you know. The blessing of Light is upon you. It defies the Vitr. That's useful.'

'Stop that,' Telorast said. 'You're just confusing him.'

'Confusion is good. It'll make him more pliable. Warrior, at the least give me your name.'

'Osserc, son of Lord Vatha Urusander, who is commander of the Legion.'

'Son, lord, commander – shields to deflect, shields behind which to hide. Let us bring you out into the sunlight, Osserc.'

'Enough of that, Curdle. Tell him something useful instead.' Telorast rested a hand on his thigh. 'A secret we can share.

Just to show how generous we are. Tell him about the Grey Shore.'

Curdle flinched, and then leaned forward to glare at Telorast. 'Are you mad? Our plans are perfect this time! Once we claim the throne, this Light-blessed creature will be our enemy!'

'Liosan. Their name for Light, Curdle. Besides, this fool here isn't going anywhere. Haven't you worked that out yet? I just got here and I worked that out. Is the Vitr rotting your brain, sister? Is that it? Been here too long lusting after that Thel Akai?'

'We were making eyes at each other. It was delightful! My brain hasn't rotted. I'm not the one suggesting we blab about the Grey Shore.'

'They'll find another name for it,' said Telorast. 'They do things like that. We're *Eleint*, remember?'

'Someone really should kill the Suzerain.'

'Agreed. This time, we'll see it done. Find the right sword, point it his way, and see his black blood spray!'

'I'm bored,' said Curdle. 'Fuck this warrior, my love. I want to watch.'

'Do you?'

'I said I did, didn't I?'

'The last time we did that the poor bastard got ripped to pieces.'

'Not by *my* claws, Telorast!'

'Well, it's exciting when you watch!'

Curdle patted Osserc's shoulder. 'Don't worry about anything like that happening, warrior. We were dragons then, and that's different.'

Osserc cleared his throat, and said, 'I have taken a vow of celibacy. Therefore I must decline the invitation. My apologies, uh, to you both.'

'That vow needs breaking,' Telorast said in a growl.

He saw, with some relief, that Ardata had emerged from the temple. She strode closer. 'Leave off him, you two. I but tolerate your presence here and you'd do well to bear that in mind.'

'She scuttles out from the ruin, Telorast! The web trembles as our power challenges it! See the terrible strain on her face?'

'That would be the Vitr,' said Telorast. 'But that in itself is telling, isn't it? Even the Azathanai are not immune.'

'The Vitr will eat holes in this realm, Ardata,' said Curdle, leaning forward slightly and settling a soft hand on Osserc's thigh. 'Do you comprehend this? Holes, gnawed through. Starvald Demelain was only the first.' The hand squeezed. 'There is sorcery flooding this world. There will be pressure. Wounds will burst open. The Vitr is the Great Devourer, the Hunger Never Appeased—'

'Ooh, I like that one,' Telorast said in a murmur, her own hand stealing over his other thigh to sidle into his crotch.

Osserc drew a sharp breath as he felt his cock answer to the light touch.

Ardata crossed her arms, but it seemed her attention was fixed solely upon Curdle. 'Tell me more,' she said.

'Do we bargain now?' Curdle smiled, her own hand stealing down, and when it found Telorast's hand already there, fingers curling alongside his cock, it tried to pull away its rival.

Groaning, he pushed himself to his feet and quickly stepped clear of both women. Wheeling round, he glared down at two suddenly pouting faces. 'I am past being a thing to be used,' he said in a snarl.

'That's all right,' said Telorast, 'you'll come back to it, eventually.'

Curdle nodded. 'It's in his nature. You saw that too, my love? My, we're clever, aren't we?' She turned her attention back to Ardata. 'Well?'

'What do you wish?'

'Oh, this man here for one,' Curdle replied. 'But also, a thing for the future. When the Grey Shore rises, and the way in is unopposed, you will ensnare Kilmandaros. Oh, not for ever, of course. Even you couldn't manage that. But for a time.'

Telorast added, 'Enough for my sister and me to fly to the heart unopposed, and to claim what awaits us there.'

Ardata scowled. 'The Throne of Shadow.'

'It belongs to us!' Telorast shrieked.

After a moment, Ardata shrugged. 'You spoke of holes.'

'Wounds, gates, one for each aspect of sorcery,' said Curdle. 'The Vitr's hunger for power is endless. It will make a space within itself for each aspect. Caverns, tunnels.'

'Whence came this Vitr, Curdle?'

'Starvald Demelain has always . . . leaked,' Curdle replied. 'In our home realm, we have sailed over silver seas, nested upon rotting crags jutting from the chaos. We have rushed above its wild torrent in the times when it has thundered through other realms—'

'All realms,' whispered Telorast. 'Even the Suzerain's.'

'Then the Queen of Dreams—'

'Swallowed by one such wound,' Telorast replied, leaning back. 'A modest one, a fissure leaking out from this very gate here, from Starvald Demelain. We who patrolled from the other side took note, and rode the sudden rush. Out! Out into this new world, hah!'

'And her fate?' Ardata asked in a cold tone.

Telorast glanced at Curdle, who shrugged but said nothing. Sighing, Telorast continued, 'The Vitr steals memories – or, rather, it blinds the mind to the memories it holds. Made witless, one is reborn, and must make a new life.'

'Where is she then?'

Telorast smiled. 'You need to extend your web far, Ardata, to feel her telltale tremble. But it is my thought that the strange Azathanai who found herself among the Tiste, who held within her the gate of Light, of Liosan, and then flung it from herself as if discarding a burdensome cloak, why, that might well have once been your Queen of Dreams.'

Ardata stared at Telorast for a long moment before saying, 'When was this?'

Curdle giggled. 'Silly woman – look to the Tiste who came upon you and your Thel Akai lover! So brightly burnished by the indifferent gift of Light! How long was the journey? There is your answer.'

'But recall, Ardata,' chimed in Telorast, 'she remembers you not.'

'Your love has lost its tether,' Curdle said, giggling again. 'Poor Ardata.'

When Ardata started to turn away, Curdle jumped up. 'A moment, Azathanai! We made a bargain!'

Osserc saw Ardata glance at him, and then she shrugged. 'I own him not.'

'But you do! A dying man resurrected!'

'Oh, very well. Take him then, but leave him alive.'

'Of course,' Telorast said, smirking. 'We apprehend your need for him.'

Curdle now turned to Osserc and smiled. 'Your time is short, mortal. Reach now for all that may give you pleasure. There is no sweeter intensity than your final days.'

Frowning, Osserc took a step towards Ardata. 'What is she talking about? What have you planned for me, Ardata?'

'We need a soul,' she replied. 'To seal the gate.'

'A soul? Mine?'

Her eyes were level. 'It is a worthy end, Osserc. One other thing to consider: it is not permanent – nothing is. Sooner or later, you will be spat out, to find yourself unchanged from the day of your imprisonment. Ages might well have past. You may find yourself standing on a world you do not even recognize, an entire realm to explore. More than that, Son of Liosan, you will possess power such as you would never have known before. Even within the maw of a gate and in the midst of agony, power is exchanged.'

He stared at her in disbelief. 'Agony? To be spat out from centuries of that – I would be a madman!' He looked quickly to Curdle and Telorast, and then back to Ardata. 'Find another! Use Kanyn Thrall!'

She slowly shook her head. 'I value him more than I do you, Tiste. Besides, Curdle spoke true. I own your life, for it was I who returned it to you.' She turned to Curdle and Telorast. 'Eleint, give him pleasure, enough delights to sustain him for a time. But be quick about it – I have a lover to find.'

There were three Jhelarkan. They had veered two days past, loping to keep pace as Scabandari pushed his exhausted horse onward, northward, well away from the caustic fumes of the Vitr Sea to the east.

At midday of this third day, his horse stumbled, and in an instant the three shaggy, black-furred giant wolves closed in. Even as his mount righted itself, he brought his lance around to meet the leap of the wolf on his right. The point drove into the beast's chest with a ripping, snapping sound, the heavy iron blade breaking ribs as it sank deep.

The impact yanked the lance's shaft from his grip, but the leather butt on the saddle held – long enough to pull the entire saddle on to the horse's flank, taking the warrior with it. He heard the shaft splinter beneath the bowing weight of the dying wolf.

In that time, a second wolf closed its massive jaws around the left hindquarter of the horse, using its own weight to drag the animal down. The third and last Jheleck hunter lunged under the horse's neck, snapping up to tear open the beast's throat. Screaming, the horse collapsed beneath the onslaught.

Scabandari threw himself clear of his toppling, thrashing mount, his ears filling with its mortal screams. Rolling, he regained his feet, dragging free his sword even as the third wolf spun round to launch itself at him.

His backhand swing caught the creature on its right shoulder, enough to push its momentum to one side – the jaws snapped empty air a hand's breadth from his face, hot blood and warm spit spraying against his right cheek. Stepping further round, he plunged the sword's point behind the Jheleck's shoulder blade, pushing hard to reach the heart.

Coughing, the Jheleck fell on to its side, the motion nearly pulling the sword from Scabandari's grip. Regaining his hold – frantically unaware of where the last wolf was – he tugged the weapon free and staggered back.

Growling, the last wolf crouched over the dead horse.

The Tiste cursed under his breath. 'Content with that, are you? Well, I'm not.' He advanced.

The wolf held its ground until the last moment, only to suddenly wheel and dart away, ten or twelve long strides, before spinning round again.

Cursing a second time, Scabandari approached his dead mount. With one eye on the circling wolf, he retrieved what he could of his supplies, including the last two water-skins strapped to the saddle. Neither had burst with the animal's fall – the one source of satisfaction in this whole travail thus far.

Finally, with the skins over one shoulder, his bedroll, blanket and the remnants of dried foodstuffs in a pack slung over the other shoulder, he slowly backed away, sword held at the ready.

When he had moved some distance from the kill-site, he saw the wolf close in to feed on the horse carcass.

A true wolf would linger here for days, gorging itself on meat. But this Jheleck would desire vengeance for the slaying of its two kin. It would resume tracking him before too long. The next attack, the warrior guessed, would come at night.

He trudged on, ever northward. The trail he had been following was more or less gone, but it had been unrelenting in its northerly push, and so he felt confident that he remained on Osserc's heels.

Close to dusk, he came upon Osserc's dead horse, untouched by scavengers and only now bloating in the chill, dry winter air. Wayward winds from the east brought with them the biting acid of the Vitr – the shoreline had drawn closer here.

He made a cursory examination of the carcass. Osserc had taken no meat from the beast, which seemed an odd oversight, but he had collected up the saddle and tack, which was downright bizarre. Shaking his head, he continued on.

As the sun's southerly light faded, he heard a howl in his wake.

'Stupid pup. Even with your jaws on my throat, I'll eviscerate you. It's an exchange neither of us will win. By this, we proclaim our superior intelligence! Well, come along then, let us meet in the night, and between us raise yet another monument to foolishness.' He paused in his steps, considering his words, and then nodded to himself. 'Such delight resides in stating the obvious! As if mere words could tilt the world, sway it from its inevitable path. But then, what are we but the narrators of time's senseless plunge ahead, with us pilgrims ever eager to raise banners wherever we make a stand. Yes, see me work the knife into this frozen earth . . .' His words fell away as he saw, upon a rise ahead, two figures walking side by side, their backs to him.

One had the look of an old man.

The other was twice his companion's height, serpent-tailed and leather-winged, a projecting, blunt snout making itself visible as the creature looked to left and to right in time with its slightly splayed strides.

Scabandari slowed his steps.

The wolf howled behind him, closer now. Close enough, as it turned out, for the two strangers to hear it, for they both halted and swung round.

Sighing, he resumed his march. The strangers waited for him to catch up.

The pale old man was the first to speak when Scabandari arrived. 'You confound us,' he said. 'Where's your saddle? I would have thought it majestically valuable, tooled by an artisan, or, perhaps, of leather supple enough to eat – rather than gamy horseflesh, one presumes.'

'Wrong Tiste.'

'Ah.' The old man nodded. 'Then . . . you pursue one before you?'

'Not pursuit as such. More like . . . retrieval, as of a wayward child who has wandered off, unmindful of whatever modest responsibilities he might possess.' He struggled to keep his eyes on the old man. The reptilian demon at the stranger's side was repeatedly yawning, fangs clacking.

'Well,' the old man said, 'children are like that. Now, as for the Soletaken on your trail . . .'

'They wanted my horse. Two fell when I objected. The last one – the most witless of the three, I would imagine, but thus far the luckiest, now contemplates revenge.'

'Not any more,' the old man said, 'as this faint breeze wanders south, and the Jheleck catches scent of Skillen Droe. You are safe enough, and since it seems that we walk the same path, you are welcome to accompany us.'

'If it is not an imposition,' Scabandari said.

'Oh no,' the old man said with a wan smile. 'I would welcome proper conversation.'

'Ah. Then your pet does not speak?'

The giant creature now swung its elongated head to the old man and seemed to stare down at him for a long moment, before suddenly snapping open its wings and, with a beating of the cold air, lifting from the ground.

'Skillen,' said the old man, 'concurs with your assessment. The surviving wolf is indeed appallingly stupid. He will chase it off. Failing that, he will rip it to pieces.'

'Oh, I plead some mercy in that regard,' Scabandari replied, even as the reptile rose higher into the air above them. 'The herds are gone, after all. All hunters must hunt, all eaters of meat must eat meat.'

'Generous of you,' the old man said, with an expression filled with approval. 'Skillen hears you and will consider your plea. It is sufficient, you will be relieved to know, to offset that insult about his being my pet.'

'My apologies for misapprehending, sir.'

'I am K'rul. My companion and I are Azathanai. And you, Tiste?'

He bowed. 'Scabandari, once of Urusander's Legion, but now I suppose I must be considered a deserter.'

'Yes, that explains your abandonment of Light's blessing. It seems, Scabandari, that you march to the Grey Shore.'

He was unsure of the meaning of that. 'I seek to retrieve Urusander's son, Osserc.'

K'rul shrugged. 'That may be as it may be, Scabandari, but your soul finds its own path.'

'I know nothing of this Grey Shore.'

'Nor should you, since it is yet to arrive.'

911

Scabandari frowned, and then smiled. 'I think I shall enjoy our conversations, K'rul.'

'Then we shall be as two men dying of thirst finding the same wellspring bubbling up from the rock. Too long have I battled my companion's infernal obduracy.'

'He speaks, then?'

'Somewhat.'

Scabandari tilted his head in silent query.

'With the empathy of a serpent and the largesse of a calculating bird of prey, Skillen Droe strains the value of converse.'

Scabandari nodded. 'I have heard that Azathanai prefer solitude, by and large, but I shall not enquire as to the exigency that has brought two together, for such an arduous journey.'

K'rul's smile faded. 'No,' he said, 'best not. Ah, here returns my winged companion, with only a modest tuft of black hide in his talons.'

Scabandari nodded again. 'I thought I heard a distant yelp.'

'That Jheleck brave will dine well on his story.'

'He was a she,' the Tiste replied. 'But, as you say, K'rul. Tell me if you will, what lies ahead?'

'Well, if this Osserc survived the walk, we shall no doubt find him. Beyond that, it is hard to know for certain. Excepting one thing.'

'And that is?'

'We will have a conversation or two with a dragon, and if you can imagine my frustration with Skillen Droe, it is nothing compared to what I anticipate. Now, we are three again,' he added as Skillen Droe landed nearby with a heavy thump. 'And the place we all seek is not far now.'

＊　　　＊　　　＊

'My apologies, Ardata,' said Kanyn Thrall. The agony from his shattered leg rose in waves, and the puncture wounds in his chest ached with every strained breath he managed. 'I failed you.'

912

She stood looking down on him. 'Are you chilled? You shiver and tremble. Has fever come upon you?'

'I believe so,' he replied. 'Your ministrations may have failed as well. I hear voices. Women arguing and moaning in pleasure – this seems a strange union to me.'

'They abuse Osserc,' Ardata replied distractedly.

He frowned up at her, even as he drew the furs tighter about himself. 'Who?'

'The dragons have assumed Tiste forms. They are Soletaken, it seems, and possess, I now suspect, ancient blood of the First Tiste. It explains their singular obsession with thrones, and power.'

'Your thoughts are elsewhere, Ardata. I weary you—'

'Oh, shut up, Kanyn Thrall. Self-pity is most unattractive. Yes, my mind is on other things. Specifically, should I endeavour to kill two dragons? Osserc's soul will seal the gate, and then I must leave here, journeying south. I fear those bitches will simply pluck him free the moment I depart. The only reason they might not is fear of yet more Draconic rivals in this realm. Do you see my dilemma?'

He studied her, jaws clenching as another wave of agony rippled through him. 'My failing compounds it, then, and that, Ardata, is simple fact, not self-pity.'

She crouched down beside him and set a cool hand upon his forehead. 'You are afire, Thel Akai. Against this I can do nothing.'

'Then leave me here and be on your way, Ardata.'

'My wife has returned from the Vitr,' she said. 'Her memory is lost. I must find her. I must return her to me.'

He nodded.

After another moment, Ardata straightened. 'It is a curious mercy,' she said, 'that I must now drag Osserc from the clutches of two insatiable women.'

'Given what awaits him, yes, most curious.'

'Fare well, Kanyn Thrall.'

'And you, Ardata.'

Even after she left the dusty chamber, he felt her presence. His fever had hatched a thousand spider eggs beneath his skin, and the creatures now swarmed. *Let us not call this love, then. But still, woman, it seems your touch is eternal. Ah, bless me.*

*     *     *

They heard the shrieking before they came within sight of the ruined temple. Scabandari glanced at K'rul. 'Is this expected? Are we about to come upon some dread sacrifice to a long-dead god?'

Ahead, wild firelight flared and flickered, limning in light the ragged lines of the temple. Above this, something vast and ominous hovered in the air, dull and throbbing crimson.

In answer to Scabandari's questions, K'rul sighed. 'She hesitates. Not because her victim shrieks his terror at the fate awaiting him, but because she senses me and Skillen Droe.'

In that moment two huge winged shapes lifted into the air, rising up to flank the suspended wound.

Skillen Droe clacked his jaws and opened his own wings, but K'rul turned to his companion, one hand lifting. 'A moment, assassin, if you please. Yes, they scented you, and know you for who you are.'

If the demonic reptile made reply, Scabandari could not hear it, but he saw K'rul shrug.

They continued on, approaching the temple grounds. Scabandari stared up at the dragons. Skillen Droe was not as large as they, and yet he sensed their fear and alarm. K'rul had named the creature *assassin*, after all. *Yes, I can see that. In the southlands of the Forkassail there dwells a wasp that preys on spiders the size of my hand. Size means less than the venom of the sting, and I think now that Skillen Droe is a most venomous foe.* 'K'rul, you spoke of conversation with dragons, not battle.'

'I did.'

'Yet you bring this . . . companion.'

'Yes. I need those dragons to listen to me.'

'They are more likely to flee!'

K'rul gestured again at Skillen Droe, as if dismissing a silent complaint. 'No, that is not likely, Scabandari. Dragons have little comprehension of retreat. They tend to stand and fight, even when death is inevitable. A sound measure of their arrogance.'

'More sound the measure of their stupidity!'

'Yes, that too.'

Something in that shrieking voice gnawed at Scabandari, and when it abruptly stopped he involuntarily quickened his pace. Reaching the first of the toppled columns, he saw before him a large bonfire. Beside it was a tall woman, her hair fiery red, her skin the hue of alabaster. At her feet was a huddled, weeping form.

Scabandari flinched as Skillen Droe sailed past him to land heavily close to the woman.

Breathing hard, K'rul came up behind Scabandari. 'Ah,' he said, 'unfortunate.'

'That man at her feet,' said Scabandari, 'is the man I came to find.'

'I surmised as much. Alas, my friend, his soul is destined to seal the gate of Starvald Demelain.'

Baring his teeth, Scabandari drew his sword. 'I think not.'

'You cannot stand against this,' K'rul said. 'If the gate is not sealed, more Eleint shall come, not by the score, but by the thousands. This realm shall be destroyed in their senseless fury, for those dragons will war one upon the other. And should the Storm of the Mother manifest—'

'Enough dire prophecy,' Scabandari snapped. 'That is the only son of Lord Urusander. His father needs him, if only to be reminded of the world to come. But more than that, Kurald Galain needs him.' He moved forward, directly towards the red-haired woman, who had at last turned to face the newcomers. Something avid in her gaze made him stop in his tracks.

She offered him little more than a flicker of attention before unveiling a glare at K'rul. 'You! Ah, now I see. This sorcery is your doing. Idiot. How does it defy me?'

'You are Azathanai,' K'rul replied. 'My blood is not for you.'

915

'You have interrupted me,' she said then, with a momentary glance directed at Skillen Droe. 'And you! I told you I never wanted to see you again!'

The look the reptilian assassin sent back at K'rul seemed somehow plaintive.

K'rul shook his head and then spoke again to the woman. 'Ardata, tell the dragons to return. Skillen Droe is not here to shed blood. We have bargains to make, with you all.'

'Bargains?' Ardata's smile was not particularly pleasant. 'Oh, those two will enjoy that.'

Scabandari pointed the tip of his sword at Ardata. 'Osserc is under my protection,' he said. 'Find another sacrifice.'

The woman scowled, and then shrugged before stepping back. 'It seems our options have expanded. Come ahead then and wipe his nose, but should I decide that indeed Osserc remains the best choice, I will kill you to get to him, if necessary.' She gestured down at the huddled form. 'Is he worth that?'

Osserc looked up suddenly, eyes wide and red. They fixed upon Scabandari and he shrieked, 'Take him instead!'

The dragons no longer hovered, though Scabandari could not recall seeing them depart, but now two Tiste women emerged from the gloom.

'Look, Curdle, another warrior! One for each of us!'

K'rul cleared his throat. The sound was modest and yet it drew everyone's attention. 'We face a quandary to be sure,' he said. 'Ardata, neither Osserc nor Scabandari here is suitable for sealing Starvald Demelain.'

'What do you mean?'

'I mean that the surviving Tiste of this world all carry the blood of the Eleint. It is the chaos at the core of their souls. If you send Osserc's soul into the gate, he will seal nothing. Indeed, he will act as a clarion call to your kin. The same for Scabandari.'

Ardata whirled on the two Tiste women. 'And did you know this?' she demanded.

The one named Curdle shrugged. 'Possibly.'

'Possibly not,' the other added.

'Then you bargained falsely!'

Curdle's brows lifted and she turned to her companion. 'Did we, Telorast? I can't recall.'

'You asked for the pup and . . . what else? Oh yes, that thing about Kilmandaros. That was all of it, I'm sure, Curdle. So, no, we did not bargain falsely.'

'Just as I thought,' Curdle replied. She turned to Ardata. 'The decision to use Osserc was yours, Ardata. It had nothing to do with us. But I might have hinted, being naturally generous, at the risk of *aspected* gates.'

'She failed in taking the hint,' Telorast observed, with a look of stern reproach at Ardata. 'The Azathanai think themselves so clever.'

'Eleint,' said K'rul, 'Skillen Droe is here seeking redemption. He has offered, in just this moment, to seal the gate with his soul.'

Scabandari caught faint motion from the entrance to the temple, and he turned to see a huge figure hobbling into the firelight. He backed up to stand before Osserc, who still knelt, and risked a glance down. 'Milord? I think it is time to return home, do you not agree?'

Wiping at his face, Osserc nodded. 'I have been . . . Scabandari, I have been sorely abused.'

'Indeed, milord.' A moment later, Scabandari's attention was drawn back to the two Tiste women, both of whom now strode closer.

'Most generous,' Curdle said in a faintly awed whisper. 'The Slaughterer of Dragons seeks redemption. Did not honour die long ago? It seems not. Well then, on behalf of my kin, living and slain, I accept your offer, Skillen Droe. Seal Starvald Demelain.'

'There is a catch,' K'rul said.

Both women snapped their attention to him. 'Ah, hear this, Curdle?' crooned Telorast. 'It could never be so easy, could it?'

'I have need of you two,' said K'rul. 'In fact, I have need of all the Eleint who have come into this realm.'

'What manner of need?' Curdle demanded.

'Guardianship.'

There was a long pause, and then Telorast hissed. 'The Gates of Sorcery!'

'My Warrens, yes. In return, you can feed upon your chosen aspect.'

'Warrens,' said Telorast. 'Well named, Azathanai.'

'But you are not to resist those mortals who would draw upon my sorcery,' added K'rul.

'Then against whom do we guard?'

'Azathanai, for one. Your fellow Eleint, for another.'

Ardata suddenly cut in, 'These two will defy you, K'rul. They seek the Throne of Shadow, upon the rise of the Grey Shore. It is their singular obsession.'

K'rul shrugged. 'They need only convey my offer to their kin. What will come of the Grey Shore is not yet known.' He returned his attention upon the Tiste women. 'Well?'

Curdle scowled. 'It seems too generous. All in the manner of gifts. Where is the loss for us? The sacrifice? K'rul is devious, the most devious of all the Azathanai. I am suspicious.'

'I am indeed being overly generous,' K'rul replied. 'And this is my reason: another Azathanai seeks to usurp my Warrens, to corrupt them utterly. Should he succeed, even the Eleint of this realm will suffer a harsh fate. Control over the gates of my Warrens is essential, and so I turn to the only beings capable of becoming guardians – indeed, wards – of my sorcery.'

'Now he flatters us,' Telorast said.

'He asks only that we voice the offer to our kin,' Curdle pointed out. 'You and me, love, we yield nothing.'

'True.'

K'rul shrugged. 'The only thing you two yield is your choice of Warrens. In fact, given your obsession, it seems that you will surrender them entirely in favour of a throne that may never appear. That of course is your choice.'

Telorast turned to her companion. 'I see no reason to remain here, Curdle. Do you?'

'None at all!' Curdle replied. 'K'rul, we accept your bargain! Where then are these unclaimed gates?'

'Here and there. Follow the scent of magic and you will find them.'

Scabandari gasped as the two Tiste women seemed to blur, vanishing inside twin burgeoning clouds that moments later manifested as a pair of dragons. Wings hammering the air, scattering sparks from the bonfire, they lunged upward into the darkness.

In their sudden absence, no one spoke.

Then Scabandari gestured with his sword. 'Who is this giant?'

As attention fixed upon the huge stranger, the man straightened, leaning against a column. 'I am Kanyn Thrall. Fever has taken me and I shall soon be dead. Yet within, I feel the power of my soul. Sufficient, I should think, for one last service to you, Ardata—'

He got no further, as Skillen Droe leapt forward, wings wide, one clawed hand reaching out to grasp him. The bones of the wings seemed to crackle as the assassin carried Kanyn Thrall upward.

Ardata shrieked.

The winged assassin plunged into the maw of the gate of Starvald Demelain. Both vanished. An instant later, so too did the gate itself, like an iris closing until swallowed by the night.

Uncomprehending, Scabandari stared first at K'rul, and then at Ardata. 'What just happened?' he asked.

'The gate is sealed,' replied K'rul.

Ardata turned on him. 'Deceit! You planned this!'

'Don't be a fool!' snapped K'rul. 'We knew nothing about that Thel Akai!'

'And Skillen?'

'Has a mind of his own. And really, should that surprise either of us, Ardata?'

'Then – he has gone into the Draconean realm? Has he lost his mind! They will tear him to pieces!'

'Well, they tried that last time, didn't they?'

Ardata turned on Scabandari. 'Look what you've done, Tiste!'

919

'I merely pointed at the man, milady!'

Snarling, Ardata made to march off, towards the temple, but K'rul stepped into her path. 'A moment,' he begged. 'I need your help.'

Her look of stunned incredulity was almost comical to Scabandari's eyes, and yet she halted.

'The gates of my Warrens, Ardata, the ones the dragons will now seek out.'

'What of them?'

A brief look of intense frustration twisted K'rul's face. 'What value guardians, Ardata,' he said in a painfully slow voice, 'if they can leave whenever they please?'

She crossed her arms. 'Go on.'

'I need your talent . . . with webs. Or, in this case, chains.'

'You . . . devious . . . bastard. Anything else you would ask of me?'

'Yes. You need to sew up the carcass of a dragon upon the south shore of the Vitr Sea.'

'Why?'

'I need it.'

'Why?'

'It once belonged to Korabas, forever shunned by her kin, because she is—'

'The Devourer of Magic. Abyss below, K'rul! But . . . a carcass?'

He rubbed at his face. 'Yes, well. It's complicated, but someone is at this very moment about to complete a ritual, opening a gate into the Warren of Death.'

'Take note, K'rul, of my extraordinary self-control in that I am not at this moment strangling you.'

'My faith in you is, as ever, well founded.'

'And in return for all this?'

'Your lover escaped the Vitr in the belly of Korabas, Ardata. She walked into the halls of Kharkanas, and took upon herself the Tiste name T'riss. Ardata, my power manifests across this entire realm. She may well seek to hide herself from other Azathanai, but from me that is not possible. Accordingly, when we are done, I will take you to her.'

'A Warren of Death? You are truly mad, K'rul. Who rules it?'

He smiled. 'As of yet, no one. Do we have a deal?'

'Yes, although I am sure I will come to regret it. Every gate a snare, then? I admit, that part pleases me.'

'I thought it might.'

They walked into the temple.

Scabandari returned now to Osserc, who had regained something of himself and now stood near the dying embers of the bonfire. 'Milord, we have a fraught journey ahead of us.'

'We'll not survive it. Not without horses.'

'I will make a request of K'rul, then.'

Osserc spat into the embers. 'Bargain with the Azathanai and they will own your life, Scara. No, we will find another way, and if we die upon the trail, so be it. I have this night won nothing but the truth of my own pathetic soul. My friend, I stand here, shamed before you.'

Glancing away, Scabandari found himself studying the pallid gleam of the distant Vitr Sea. 'We have the trail ahead, then, to forge in you a new soul.'

Osserc's abrupt laugh was harsh, filled with self-contempt. 'You have little to work with, I'm afraid.'

'Regret is a worthy temper,' Scabandari said. 'It shall be where we begin.'

'Your faith may prove misplaced, Scara.'

He smiled. 'I am hardly immune to lessons still to learn, Osserc. Very well then, let us test the measure of each other, and the day we stand before the Wise City, open ourselves one more time to the other, and see all there is to be seen.'

After a long moment, Osserc nodded. 'In a back chamber of the temple there are supplies. Water and food. I've not seen the Azathanai eat, or drink for other than simple pleasure.'

'Then we'll take what we can carry, and be on our way.'

'Scara, it's the middle of the night and I'm exhausted!'

'As am I, but damned if I'll camp in their company. Who knows what new need they might find for us?'

# TWENTY-THREE

'SHALL WE FIND AMOROUS BLISS ONLY AMONG THE dead?' Lasa Rook asked. 'Rolling among the flopping limbs so cadaverous and cold, our heat of passion a thing stolen by insensate flesh, to be wasted in the manner of the sun's heat on a stone?' The Thel Akai raised her ample arms. 'The day's death is but prelude, Hanako of the Scars, a reminder repeated all too often – each night, in fact, as if our souls needed such ominous stirring!' Her gaze, settling upon him where he sat by the ring of rocks that encircled their modest cookfire, turned suddenly sly. 'I see your flitting regard, eager cub, upon these breasts of mine, and the lure of my cocked hip with its inviting swell. Death's threshold awaits us, closer now. On the morrow we shall see for ourselves this modest encampment of the desolate and the despondent, and if you'd an audience to our inaugural rutting, why, a more embittered mob you could not find.'

Sighing, Hanako glanced across to where Erelan Kreed crouched, his unending mutter of words rising and falling to unknown passions, a mélange of languages most of which were utterly foreign to both Hanako and Lasa Rook. He had awakened two nights past, fretful and distracted. Erelan Kreed was, as the Jaghut Raest had predicted, now a stranger, a warrior lost to hidden worlds and memories not his own.

Kreed was turned away from them and the fire, his broad

922

back like a wall blocking the light from his hooded eyes, his tortured face. He rhythmically worked one hand through his beard, pausing every now and then to loose a low, chilling laugh.

'Never mind him,' said Lasa Rook. 'I grow irritated at your lack of attention, Hanako of the Scars. Must I peel away all constraint?' She began untying the strings of her shirt. 'So readily exposed in mute invitation' – the shirt slipped from her shoulders to fall to the ground – 'these swollen needs, the appurtenances of sensual appetites—'

'Lady of the Fire, Lasa! Your husbands—'

'My husbands! Mouldering in the rock-pile! Torn limb from limb from limb! Decayed of countenance, never more to weakly smile or flinch or cringe! From crow-picked tongues, never again a mewled whimper or pathetic beseechment! Ah, the empty echo in my ears! And you, bold young warrior! See how I lick my lips – no, not those lips, fool – and come closer, before death sweeps down upon us with all the senseless weight of boulders and gritty dust!'

Hanako clutched the sides of his head. 'Enough! What glory is there in such ready surrender?' As soon as the words left him, he bit down, but too late.

Lasa Rook's gasp trailed away, leaving nothing but silence, although as he glared at the fire he heard her collecting up her shirt. Then she spoke. 'This path of mine proves in error, then. Oh, my foolish ways now turn about to let loose the most vicious snarl. The pup at bay, cock limp and awaiting the tree, modest claws readied for scratching the earth, a scent piddled here, a proud strut there. Foolish Lasa Rook, were you blind? This one seeks to do the seducing! Not for him the come hither! No! As the Lord of Temper told you plain as day, this one requires the conquest!'

Hanako moaned and said nothing.

The laugh that came from Erelan Kreed at that moment was appalling in its cruelty, and then the warrior spoke to them both for the first time since consciousness returned. 'My sister hunts me. There is no refuge. We must traverse the night, children of Kilmandaros. The bitch wants my seed and will take it from this Thel Akai corpse if necessary. Into the timeless realm for us, then, and best we be quick about it.'

Straightening, Hanako took a step towards Erelan Kreed. 'Who speaks with your tongue, Erelan?'

'Blood is memory, child. Need is immortal. Above all, vengeance never dies, never fades and never grows cold. In my heart there burns refusal, a fire nothing can quench. Refusal and defiance, such wildness in these two sentiments, such pure ... *horror.*' He bared his teeth at them. 'Only among the Jaghut will she hesitate.'

When it was clear that he would say nothing more, Hanako turned to Lasa Rook, met her flat, sober eyes. 'I believe,' he said, 'we should hurry.'

She tilted her head back to regard him with level eyes. 'To you, Hanako of the Scars, I am now closed. Sting at my in-difference, see me turn away again and again. A wall around me I shall raise, even in the realm of the dead, with corpses stacked high. I am the widow's trap, forever closed, forever sealed away—'

'Lasa Rook, I was speaking of resuming our journey.'

'—and your hunger for me shall grow, a poison in your soul—'

*'There is a dragon hunting us!'*

She blinked. 'I heard him,' she said in a low tone. 'His sister wants his seed. How peculiar! What sister would ever desire a brother's seed? Lifelong proximity alone would incite such levels of revulsion as to spew out a veritable ocean of disgust and derision! Why, if I think of my own brothers in such light, all that lives within me curdles and puckers, a flinching retreat so sour I feel the need to spit.' She looked over at Erelan Kreed. 'On your feet then, bold warrior, drag-on-blooded. Lasa Rook and Hanako of the Scars shall stand in defence of your dignity!'

'Lasa, a dragon!'

She waved dismissively. 'They die too, pup, as we well know.'

'Let us simply hasten, Lasa Rook,' Hanako said, collecting up his gear. 'Into the protection of the Jaghut.'

'I shall lead,' she pronounced. 'You may watch me from behind, Hanako, pining for all that you shall never possess. Draw not too near, either! I have claws and fangs at the ready!' She set out then, and a moment later Erelan Kreed straightened and fell in behind her.

Hanako looked down at the fire. It took only a few moments to stamp out its flames, and then he set off after them.

Twenty paces in, Lasa Rook glanced back over her shoulder and winked. 'Alas, the truth wins free! I shall crumble at your first touch, young pup!'

Hanako hesitated, and then with a half-snarl he threw down his pack. 'All right,' he said. 'Erelan Kreed, do go on and mayhap the dragon will find us first, if only to feed. We will catch up with you anon.'

Brows lifting, Lasa Rook walked back towards Hanako. 'Truly? Oh, now I am come over all shy!'

He stared at her, wanting to scream.

*       *       *

Korya Delath found Haut gathered with a dozen or so of his compatriots, Varandas, Senad and Burrugast among them. The Jaghut had been laughing but their amusement fell away, quickly hidden like a private thing, when she strode among them.

Seeing her, Haut straightened. He muttered something low to the Jaghut woman, Senad, and then gestured. 'Mahybe, we must talk. There are tasks awaiting you—'

'Why should any of that matter to you, Haut?' Korya asked, her glare shifting to encompass all the Jaghut present. 'You're all about to die. What do the dead care for the woes of the living?' She pointed at her old master. 'You once told me that there were things we were going to do. The two of us, to answer for the Azathanai's murder of Hood's wife. What has come of that?'

Haut's expression twisted slightly, and it seemed to Korya that he almost ducked to unseen blows. Seated beside him, Senad laughed low and knowingly, meeting Korya's cold regard with weary amusement.

Burrugast growled under his breath and then said, 'So much to atone, so little time.'

Snorting, Varandas moved to Haut's side and settled a hand on the captain's shoulder. 'Out of the mouth of babes, a veritable torrent of nonsense. Grief is a fist, but to hold it too long is to feel all strength drain from it. So brutally aged by loss and despair, you would shake it still, with palsied fury. Drag her aside, friend, and make quick and clean the cut.'

Korya fixed her attention on Varandas, studied his lean, scarred face. 'You tell yourselves that I don't understand. But I do. You're all giving up. Clothe it in silks if you like, or, more accurately, a jester's mocking attire. It doesn't matter.'

Varandas's nod was solemn. 'Well enough, Korya. I am a fool but not a blind one. We are indeed a legion of despair, and here we stand with a gaping chasm between us and you. Age is a siege you have not yet experienced. Your bones remain strong, your foundations not yet undermined. The towers of belief you have raised in yourself still stand tall and proud. Certainty's armour remains untarnished, undented.'

Burrugast added, 'Haut spoke from a place of wounding. It was but the last of many.'

After a long moment, Haut sighed and then gestured for Korya to follow him.

They walked to the encampment's edge, looked out eastward over the deep night's level plain, where the stars pricked the darkness with a strange, dull light. The moon had crept into the sky just before sunset and though half the night had passed, still it clung to the horizon, swollen and the hue of copper.

'What is happening?' she whispered. 'The stars . . .'

'In the last days of life,' Haut said, 'there comes to the dying soul a single, long night. For most, it passes locked in step with the world, and come the dawn, the sleeping face is preternaturally still. Rarely does such a night impose itself on others. It is a private thing, a stretched expanse, a realm of dying wind and laboured breath.' He faced her in sorrow. 'Hood has invoked the Long Night, to open to our souls the passage into death. Now, this night, the stars do not sparkle, the moon does not rise. Tell me, when did you last draw breath? Blink? Whence the next beat of your heart?'

She stared at him in growing horror. 'The gate has opened.'

'Yes. How long shall this night be? None knows, perhaps not even Hood.'

'This is monstrous . . .'

Haut rubbed at his lined face, looking old and worn out. 'He has stopped time. Stolen life's necessary rush, the rolling needs that burn with defiance. In all realms, life wills itself into being, plunging ever forward in the name of order, out-racing the chaos of dissolution.'

She shook her head, half in disbelief, half in terror. 'But . . . how vast is this . . . this end of time?'

'For now, the encampment,' Haut replied. 'But there are ripples, unseen by us mortals, and they spread far and wide. Stirring, agitating, awakening. I would imagine,' he mused, 'the dead themselves now hearken to this challenge.' He settled a hand on the old sword at his belt. 'It seems we shall have our war after all.'

'All this, Haut? For the grief of one slain woman?' She stepped back from him, and then faced the plains once more. Stared at the motionless, lifeless night sky. *He speaks true. No breath to draw barring those needed for words. My heart . . . I hear nothing, not even the swish of blood in the veins.* 'Hood used the magic,' she suddenly announced. 'All that the one you name K'rul has given to the world. He's taken it all inside.'

'Stilled every fire,' Haut said. 'Nothing burns. The exhalation of heat, the very vigour of life, all stopped. As within, so without. But then, is this not what death is? Stepping out from time's incessant flow? Slipping from sight?' He sighed, and then shrugged. 'We are in the Long Night, we who choose to follow him. But you, Korya, here you do not belong.'

'And I'm to knock Arathan unconscious and drag him away from here?'

'Gothos holds at bay Hood's . . . imposition. He creates a

refuge, signified by his Folly, his unending tome, his eternal narrative. To defy the death of time, he would tell a story.'

'His story.'

'It may be his,' Haut agreed. 'Indeed, it may be precisely what he says it is. A suicide note, a confessional to failure. And yet, do you see this subtle defiance? While the tale continues, there can be no surrender to despair.'

'No,' she snapped, 'of course not. The lord has his hate, after all.'

'Burning hot as the sun, yes.'

'Does his hate include Hood?'

'Hood? Abyss take me, no. He loves the man as only a brother can.'

'Yet, a brother not.'

Haut shrugged. 'And now Gethol, returned from something worse than death. A prison we all thought was eternal. Sometimes the deeds of the past, Korya, lead to a place where no words are possible. And yet, does not the love remain? Thus, the three of them, one the spark of hate, one the sigh of grief, and one – well, one stands between the two.'

'Will Gethol join Hood, then?'

'I would think not, but all of that is between them. When I spoke of Gothos's refuge, I meant to say that Arathan is protected.'

'What of me?'

'You are a Mahybe, Korya, a vessel formed to contain. By this alone, death cannot reach you.'

She grunted. 'Oh, you've made me immortal, have you?' When he said nothing, she slowly turned from the dead night sky above the plain. 'Haut?'

'Hold on to your potential,' he said, 'for as long as you can. There's enough room inside you for a dozen lifetimes, maybe more. That's down to your resilience and your cleverness.'

'To what end?'

'One day, the Azathanai Errastas will seek domination over the sorcery now suffusing this realm. And he will make it a thing of spilled blood, and should he succeed, magic will prove the cruellest gift of all.'

'You would set me against an Azathanai?'

Haut offered her a wry smile. 'Already I pity him.'

'What took so long?' Lasa Rook moaned plaintively, pulling sweaty strands of blonde hair from her face. 'Look upon the beasts, O Lord of Duration, and see how the quick and the fierce suffices. By the tumbled rock-pile, Hanako, you have worn me out!'

He sat up, blinking, his twin hearts only now slowing their savage syncopation. He squinted into the north.

Lasa Rook continued, 'Was it worth the wait? Does my bruised flower answer? No. Instead, the mumble below continues, tremors of the flesh and the spirit trembling like a startled fawn in the night. Oh, dear pup, you have dragged the moon to the ground! You have spun the stars with such abandon as to shatter the wheel! The body reels, the earth shudders. Now look upon me in the days to come and see the knowing glint in my eye, the sly knowledge of our terrible secret—'

'Not so secret,' Hanako said.

She sat up, her hair full of twigs and grass blades, and twisted round. 'Hanako! We are attended by three hoary ghosts! Aaii! They stagger in the manner of revenants, with crumpled visages and eyes withered like dusty dates!'

'Your husbands,' Hanako said, 'drawn to us, no doubt, by your shrieks.' He lumbered to his feet. 'Apologies dry upon my tongue. Shame and remorse chill my hearts, and in the face of righteous challenge, I shall raise no blade to defend myself.'

'Oh,' Lasa Rook said, squinting. 'They are not dead then?'

'No, only exhausted, it seems. Worn out by this deadly pursuit, and now here, their worst fears realized.'

She climbed to her feet, still naked, and brushed the dust from her arms, and then her breasts. 'You have licked off all my sweet scents, Hanako. This puts me at a disadvantage. Say nothing. Leave this to me. They are my husbands, after all.'

929

Groaning under his breath, Hanako swung round to the south. The night sky above that horizon looked peculiar. 'You promised that we would defend Erelan Kreed, and yet here we are. My lust, Lasa Rook, has broken our vow. Now he walks alone. For all we know, the dragon has already found him.'

'Oh, enough of that nonsense, Hanako! See these dejected, broken men, my pets all bedraggled and forlorn. Are these the faces lighting with love and delight? Halt the world, my husbands have found me! Caught naked and lathered, flushed and sated beyond all measure! By my crime I have belittled them all! What recompense is possible? What price forgiveness?'

The three men drew closer and then stopped with a dozen paces between them and Lasa Rook, who stood facing them, brazen and tall.

After a long, tense moment, the eldest of them pointed at Hanako though his gaze remained fixed on his wife. His mouth worked soundlessly for a time, and then, in a strangled voice, he said, 'You never once slashed any of *us* to bloody ribbons!'

Lasa Rook shot a look at Hanako, her brows raised. 'Oh,' she said as she turned back to her husbands, 'that.' She shrugged. 'Many are the beasts lying in the grasses, each a habit unto itself. Some will ambush. Others yawn and doze till comes the night, when all manner of savagery is unleashed. Yet others flick their tails, watchful and opportunistic. I am a woman of appetites and curiosity, Garelko.'

'But . . . another husband? How many do you need?' Garelko pulled at his thin hair. 'Oh, it's never enough with you, Lasa Rook! No, you need to hunt down the finest warrior of all the mountain tribes! Slayer of more Thelomen than any of us can count!' He pointed a shaking finger at Hanako. 'And . . . you! You!'

'Oh, be quiet – and you, Tathenal, not a word! Same for you, Ravast! I thought you all dead! Dragon-slain! Devoured, digested, shat out!' Hands now on her hips, she shook her head and continued in a lower tone, 'I grew doubtful of the three of you. How deep your love for me? In our home, ah, I caught a sniff of complacency.'

'Complacency?'

'Yes, Garelko! Was it mere contentment? Or love's sordid decay? A challenge was needed. So I set out, on the slithery tail of a Jaghut's raging grief. Would my husbands dare follow? Would they even notice my absence?'

Garelko pointed again at Hanako. 'And this one? Was he too a test?'

'Oh, who knows what set him on this trail. Such a young brave already weary of mundane challenges! But against that which cannot be defeated, ah, now there is a fate worthy of legend! Or,' she added with a sigh, 'some such thing.'

'We heard your screams!' Ravast suddenly blurted.

'As you were meant to, were you indeed still alive – and what surer siren could I devise to bring you running?' She waved a careless hand back towards Hanako. 'Oh, he was fun I'll grant you, a beast indeed, to now challenge your inventiveness in all the years of delight still to come!'

'You'll not stay with him?' Garelko asked. 'You'll not claim him as another husband?'

'Three are chore enough,' she replied. 'Besides, heed his destination! Do I seem a woman tired of life? Still, was not this journey an exciting one?'

Sourly, Tathenal said, 'Dams have broken, wife, and now unseen rivers of wild thought devour the ground beneath us all. None are as we once were. Not even you. I see in Hanako's eyes a renewed resolve. He will indeed march with that dread legion, and I will walk at his side. We have new enemies within each of us now, challenges to our sense of who we truly are, and these, my love, must be answered.'

When Tathenal moved forward to take his position at Hanako's side, Lasa Rook's eyes followed with raw dismay.

'Oh my,' she breathed. And her gaze snapped back round when Ravast spoke.

'Beloved wife,' the young warrior said, 'I will take the measure of this grieving Jaghut, and upon the threshold of a choice that cannot be unmade, only then will I decide my path.'

Garelko's expression was suddenly ravaged. 'Now, Lasa Rook,' he said in a broken rasp, 'see what you have done?'

'Oh I see,' she retorted, crossing her arms. 'Clever punishment! Listen well, the three of you! I will accompany you to the Jaghut's silly camp, where you can well contemplate joining the ragged mob that has fallen for his madness! But I shall not cross the threshold, even if you would all leave me a widow in truth! I am young still and the villages are bursting with handsome men, some of whom are even useful!' She paused, and then resumed, 'So contemplate well my lively future, husbands, and of troubled waters beneath the ground, consider most soberly their paltry gifts. From beyond the Harrowed Gate, husbands, you might well hear my lustful cries challenge the world itself!'

When she swung round to face Hanako, he saw the fierceness of her gaze, and was shaken. Turning to Tathenal, he said, 'Go back with her, sir. The three of you, drag this woman home, bound and gagged if you must.'

'The pup rejects me? After one tussle in the grass?'

He frowned at her. 'You misunderstand, Lasa Rook. I am come to love you, but you burn too hot for me, and this fire in you is the raging glory of *life*, not death. Should you march down to the Jaghut . . . I fear a moment of fury, and a choice that cannot be unmade. Not for one such as you the realm of death, and so I beg you – I beg you all – go home.' He swung his gaze south. 'If I hurry, I will catch Erelan Kreed, and so guard his flank.'

Lasa Rook hissed, 'You're not actually contemplating joining those fools, are you? Was this not simply a lark? A cheerful cavort in the manner of spectators witnessing a mummery of absurdity? Hanako of the Scars, you are too young for the rock-pile!'

He shook his head. 'I have my reasons, Lasa Rook, and they shall remain mine, forever unspoken, yet no less indurate. And now there is Erelan Kreed, whom I will not abandon. What glory is found in turning aside? What truth can be revealed unless one indeed walks through the gate? No, I will find what I seek.'

She now glared at the four of them. 'You . . . you *men*!'

When Hanako set out, the others fell in behind him. He heard a sharp low cry from Garelko and turned to see Lasa Rook gripping his right ear as she hissed, 'Convince these idiots, old man, or you'll rue your failure!'

'I'll try! I swear it!'

Setting his gaze southward again, Hanako hurried on. 'Forgive me my pace,' he called out. 'Find your own to suit – it matters not.'

'What do you mean, Hanako?' Tathenal asked.

In reply, Hanako pointed ahead. 'See the sky? There, my friends, the world holds its breath.'

He heard their soft exclamations and low muttering, as yet another argument erupted between Lasa Rook and her husbands.

Hanako was glad of the lovemaking. That had been a fire in need of dousing. Now his mind felt clear, his resolve harsh and bold with new resilience.

*Death, I will face you at last. Unblinking, I will face that which all who are said to be heroic must face. And I will have my answer.*

*But I am no fool. Lord of the Rock-Piles, I'll not deny you. Each time, you win in the end. Indeed, you never lose. And so I will ask you, O Lord of Death, what worth the victory . . . in such a crooked game?*

\*　　\*　　\*

Gethol's mottled face bore an expression of old pain and suffering that Arathan suspected was permanent. Five centuries buried beneath the earth, bound in roots, must have taken such a toll that he wondered how the Jaghut remained sane. *Assuming sanity was ever there in the first place. These are Jaghut, after all.*

Gethol was staring at Arathan with a strangely remote contemplation, as if in studying the young black-skinned Tiste Andii, he was in fact looking through to something else.

The uncanny regard unnerved Arathan, but he was not prepared to reveal that to this brother of Gothos. He stared back.

After the passage of some time, Gothos glanced up from his desk and said, 'Is this really necessary?'

Gethol frowned and then, with a shrug, he looked away. 'This charge of yours. This bastard son of Draconus.'

'Yes, what of him?'

'Yes,' Arathan added, 'what of me?'

Grunting, Gethol said, 'Some things are better left unsaid, I suppose.'

Gothos set his stylus down. 'I imagine you said very little for a rather long time, Gethol.'

'This is true.'

'All those useless words.'

'Spake the writer leaning over his tome.'

'If I presume in error, brother, do enlighten me.'

Gethol lifted a gnarled hand and eyed it speculatively. 'My talons need trimming. Still, I am thankful I possessed them, although I expect the Seregahl I dragged into my place might venture a different opinion.'

'Were your eyes open?' Gothos asked.

'No, of course not. That would sting, and besides, there is very little to see. Consider the interred, the buried man, be he in sandy soil or sodden peat. Note the closed eyes, the peaceful expression, the firm set of the mouth.'

'Like that, then.'

'No,' Gethol replied, 'nothing like that. Most buried people are dead, after all. Death seems to insist upon a solemn mien. Then again, in choosing an eternal expression, I imagine peaceful is preferable to, say, the rictus of terror.'

'And yours, brother?'

'Oh, I would suggest . . . disappointment?'

Gothos sighed and rubbed at his face with ink-stained fingers. 'We all volunteered, Gethol. It was just ill-luck that—'

'My fateful misstep, yes. It was, perhaps, more a case of my unexpected downturn in fortune. One does not rise in the morning, say, considering ending the day in black soil and bound by the roots of a tree, or, for that matter, being imprisoned for five centuries.'

'Yes, that does seem unlikely,' Gothos replied. 'Still, the contemplation of what the fates hold in store must surely accompany each morning's greeting.'

'You always were the one obsessed with solemn contemplation, brother, not me.'

'I deem it a measure of intellect.'

'A failure I am proud to acknowledge,' Gethol replied, baring his blackened tusks.

'Hence the misstep.'

The grin fell away.

'It is invariably those lacking in intellect,' Gothos expounded, 'who unceasingly rue their misfortune. The curse of the witless is to beat one's head against the obstinate wall of how things really are, rather than what they insist upon their being. Thud, thud, thud. I envisage indeed an expression of dull disappointment, year upon year, century upon century.'

'I blame Hood,' Gethol growled.

'Of course you do.'

The brothers nodded in unison, and then fell silent.

Arathan leaned back in his chair, looking at each one in turn. He crossed his arms. 'You two are ridiculous,' he said. 'I believe the time has come to take my leave of you. Gothos, my gratitude for your . . . forbearance. The food, drink and the work you had me do. While I gather you and Haut have decided on where I am to go now, I humbly point out that I am of an age to make my own decisions. And I will now walk to Hood's side, there to await the opening of the gate.'

'Alas,' Gothos said, 'we cannot permit that. You made yourself a gift to me, after all, on behalf of your father. I don't recall relinquishing my possession of that gift. Gethol?'

Gethol returned to eyeing Arathan speculatively. 'I have only just arrived, but you've made no mention of anything like that.'

'Just so. As for Haut, Arathan, bear in mind that young

935

Korya Delath, who must now return to Kurald Galain, will be without a protector.'

'So find someone else,' Arathan snapped. 'Why not Gethol here? It's not as though he has anything to do.'

'Curiously,' mused Gethol, 'I am of a mind to do just that. Accompany you and Korya, that is.'

'Then she has an escort and you two don't need me tagging along! Besides, Father sent me here to be beyond the reach of his rivals in the court of the Citadel.'

Gothos cleared his throat. 'Yes, about that.'

'You have heard something?' Arathan sat forward. 'How? You've never left this damned chamber!'

'Perturbations in the ether,' Gothos said, frowning.

'Perturbations in the what?'

The frown deepened at Arathan's incredulity.

Gethol snorted.

Sighing, Gothos said, 'A Forulkan traveller arrived in Hood's camp yesterday. A delightfully dour female named Doubt. She spoke of events to the east.'

'What kind of events?'

'Oh, let me not imply that they have already occurred. Rather, a path has been set upon that has but one destination.' He blew out his breath. 'In keeping with my unassailable observations on the inherent self-destructiveness of civilization—'

'Not again,' Gethol groaned as he climbed to his feet. 'Now at last we come to the reason why I dived beneath that tree in the house's yard – the only escape left to me. I believe I will pay one last visit to Hood, if only to partake in the joy of stinging awake his shame.' He eyed Arathan. 'You may join me there, assuming you survive the imminent monologue.' He strode from the chamber.

'Milord,' said Arathan to Gothos, 'spare me the lecture, if you please. I would know the details of what has happened, or is about to happen.'

'Well, that is just it, young Arathan. By the time you and Korya return to Kurald Galain, the smoke will have cleared as it were. The dust settled, the mass burial trenches filled in, and so on and so forth. From this it is probably safe to assume the ousting of your father. Indeed, I would be surprised to find him anywhere in that realm.'

'Then, what will I be returning to?'

'Ashes and ruin,' Gothos replied, with a satisfied smile.

*　　*　　*

'I advise against this,' Korya said, studying the Azath House with its freshly mangled, sapling-crowded yard. 'The guardian is a ghost, and a miserable one at that. Truly, Ifayle, nothing of wisdom will come from that thing.'

'And yet,' said the Dog-Runner, 'he was once of my kind.'

She sighed. 'Yes, as I told you.'

'Then I would speak with him.'

'The house may not let us in. It's stronger now . . . more potent. Can you not feel it?'

He glanced at her with his startling blue eyes. 'I am not a Bonecaster. My sensitivities lie elsewhere.' His attention sharpened on her. 'Mahybe. Vessel. Yes, I see that you share something with this house.'

'What?'

'A similarity of purpose, perhaps.' Abruptly he turned about to stare northward with narrowed intent. 'My grieving kin are on the move.'

'How – how do you know that?'

Shrugging, he said, 'It is near time, isn't it?'

Korya hesitated, unable to meet his gaze when at last he faced her again.

'Ah,' he said softly, 'you wanted to get me away.'

'Where they're going is not for you,' she said. 'Now, will you speak with Cadig Aval or not? We've come all this way, after all.'

When she walked through the yard's gate and on to the winding pathway, Ifayle followed.

'You have a devious mind, Korya Delath. But you mis-apprehended. I am but an escort, a keeper of sorts. My mother forbade me to enter the realm of death.'

'When did she do that?'

'Not long ago. Her pronouncement upset me, but I understand. Grief cannot be borrowed. And yet, with her soon gone from me, it seems that I will come to know my own grief. It is, I think, like a flower passed from one to the next, generation upon generation. A solemn hue, a poignant scent that stings the eyes.'

They stood before the door. Korya nodded and said, 'It seemed too easy, persuading you to come with me.'

'Mother knew you for a sly one,' Ifayle said, with a sad smile. 'We have made our parting. I do not expect to see her again.'

'Come with me,' she suddenly offered, her breath catching as the notion took hold in her mind. 'Come with us, me and Arathan, to Kurald Galain!'

He frowned. 'And what awaits me there?'

'No idea. Does it matter?'

'My people—'

'Will still be there, whenever you decide it's time to go home.' *If you decide to go home at all, that is*, she silently added. *After all, with you along, fair Ifayle, I can take my time deciding.*

'I have seen this Arathan,' Ifayle said musingly, 'but we have not spoken. Indeed, it seems he deliberately avoids me.'

'Haut says he is to be my protector,' Korya said, 'but to be honest, it's probably the other way round. He's led a sheltered life, has seen and experienced little. I see little future for Arathan, to be honest. It may be that our family will have to take him in.' She sighed. 'Your company on the journey, Ifayle, would be most welcome. Indeed, a relief.'

'I will consider it,' he said after a moment.

Heart thudding, Korya quickly nodded, and then reached for the door's handle.

It opened to her.

'He knows we're here,' she whispered.

'Good,' Ifayle replied, stepping past her and entering the Azath House.

She followed.

As before, the narrow alcove was dimly lit by some

unknown source of light, the air cool and dry. The stone wall opposite glistened with something like frost, and an instant later the apparition of the long-dead Bonecaster stepped out from the roughly cut wall.

Before it, Ifayle bowed. 'Ancient one, I am Ifayle, of the—'

The voice that cut him off was dry and weary. 'Some tribe, yes, from some plain, or forest, or crag, or perhaps a shore-line, a cave set high above the crashing waves. Where one year blends seamlessly into the next, the sun rising each morning like a new breath, settling each night like a hint of death.' The ghost of Cadig Aval waved an ethereal hand. 'From this, to that. Will it ever end? The food is plentiful, the hunt dangerous but fruitful and, of course, exciting. Strangers pass in the distance, revealing new ways of living, but what matter any of that? Still, the winters grow colder, the winds from the north harsher. There are times of hunger, when the animals do not come, or the sea retreats and the bounteous tidal pools disappear. And those strangers, well, more and more of them appear. It seems they breed like maggots. In the meantime, distant kin fall silent, and you sense their absence. Many have left the mortal earth, never to return. A few others now walk among the strangers, who shock the world with mercy. Blood thins. They lose the ways of the earth and the threads of the Sleeping Goddess. They lose the power to see the magic in the hearth-fires. Everything dwindles. You rise one morning and look at your cave, your precious home, and see only its poverty, its exhaustion, and the pale, dirty faces of the few children left to you shatter your heart, because the end is nigh. And then—'

'Oh for crying out loud!' Korya snapped. 'Why don't you just give him the knife to slash open his own throat!'

Cadig Aval fell silent.

Turning to Ifayle, Korya said, 'I tried to warn you. He has nothing of worth to say to the living.'

'Not true,' the guardian said. 'To my mortal kin here, I will speak words of dread import. Ifayle, son of whomever, from this tribe or that, dweller of cave or forest or plain, the fate I described will never come to you. The Dog-Runners shall not

939

vanish from the world. When the tyrants come among you, the Strangers in Hiding, look to the dreaming of the Sleeping Goddess. Within, a secret hides.'

When he paused, Ifayle tilted his head. 'Ancient one?'

Korya crossed her arms. 'He's just making the most of the moment,' she said. 'After all, he'll have scant few of these.'

Cadig Aval said, 'Sadly, the truth of your words, Tiste maiden, is like a knife-thrust into my soul. Then again, I already weary of discourse, and long for the interminable silence of my unending solitude. Thus, the secret. Ifayle, at the core of a dream there is something that cannot be broken. Indeed, it is deathless. Reach into this core, Dog-Runner, to seek the makings of a ritual. Call as well upon Olar Ethil, seeking the spark of Telas – the Eternal Flame – to enliven what remains of you.' This time, the ghost's pause was much briefer. 'But be warned. The deathless gift of the Sleeping Goddess's dream will end your own dreams. The future loses all relevance and so is made powerless. In escaping death, you must all die, sustained by naught but the spark of Telas.'

Something trembled through Korya and she shivered. 'Ifayle,' she said in a low whisper, 'none of that sounds good.'

'No,' Cadig Aval said to her, 'you are correct, Tiste. A terrible fate awaits Ifayle and his people.'

'Besides,' she said, 'I don't believe in prophecy.'

'You are wise,' the guardian replied. 'Blame Hood. Time has ceased. Past, present and future are, here and in this frozen instant, all one. Those of us of sufficient power can make use of this, reaching far with our vision. Oh, and it helps being dead, too.'

Ifayle bowed before the guardian. 'I will remember your words, ancient one.'

'Stop that. I'm not that ancient, you know. Not really. Not in the vast scheme of things. As old as a world? The lifeline of a star? Understand: we exist for the sole purpose of being witness to existence. This and this alone is our collective contribution to all that has been created. We serve to bring existence into being. Without eyes to see, nothing exists.'

'Then indeed we have purpose,' said Ifayle.

Cadig Aval shrugged. 'Assuming all that exists has purpose, an assumption of which I remain unconvinced.'

'What do you need to be convinced?' Korya demanded.

'Persuasion.'

'From whom?'

'Yes, that is the frustrating part, isn't it?'

With a faint snarl, Korya took Ifayle by the hand, pulling him back towards the door. 'We're leaving now.'

'Well,' said Cadig Aval behind them, 'it was fun while it lasted. Perhaps,' the ghost added, 'that is all the purpose required.'

Outside, on the pathway once more, Ifayle asked, 'Where are we going now?'

'To collect Arathan, of course,' she answered, pulling him along. 'We need to get away from here – away from this gate of death. Can't you feel this stopping of time reaching for us? It crawls under my skin, trying to burrow deeper. We stay too long, Ifayle, it will indeed kill us.'

'And where shall we find Arathan?'

'With Gothos, I expect.'

'I think,' Ifayle said after a time, 'we need a better reason to exist.'

She considered his words, seeking an argument against his assertion, but could not find one.

*　　*　　*

Fourteen Jaghut gathered round Hood, Haut among them, waiting. At last and with a sigh, Hood withdrew his hands from the pale flames – none of which flickered, the thin tongues motionless, suspended above the embers – and looked up. After a moment he nodded. 'It begins.'

'Well that sounds portentous,' Varandas offered as he adjusted his loincloth. 'As if summoned by solemn gravity, his vanguard now surrounds their fearless and fearful leader. Hood, grief-shrouded, eye-hollowed, revenant of sorrow. Does he now rise to his feet as his mournful army draws close on all sides? Breaths are held with expectation—'

'No,' cut in Burrugast. 'Just held. Your words, Varandas, are more gravid than grave. In any case, it is poor form to speak of graves—'

'But of graven visages,' interjected Gathras, 'why, we are legion. Does the dirge now commence, O shrouded hollow Hood? We are the eye of the frozen world, and lo, it does not blink. Let us remember this moment—'

'I see no likelihood of forgetting,' Haut interrupted.

Gathras cast a cool look upon him and then nodded. 'As you say, captain. What does it mean, however, that you hold rank in an army that never was?'

'Potential is to be valued in all things,' Burrugast pointed out.

'To my sorrow,' added Senad. 'Of lovers I have had plenty. 'Twas Haut's domination of all suitors that earned him his rank. For behold, the army was mine, and while all were fine troopers, only the captain was – and remains – the captain.'

Grunting sourly, Gathras said, 'I'd wondered and now you give answer. The wonder drains away like piss on a pile of stones and yet one more bright colour fades with the knowing. Someone point the way into oblivion. I lean upon the threshold, as eager as any despairing woman or man.'

'Despairing of eagerness in anything,' said Burrugast, 'I will follow, with dragging steps.'

Haut glanced over a shoulder. 'Let death earn the dragged steps, Burrugast. Look, a last tangle of despondent travellers. Toblakai, Thel Akai, Thelomen? They all look the same to me, to be honest.'

'Subtle observation was ever your failing, Haut,' said Senad. 'Were it otherwise, you would have achieved much higher rank.'

'Would that be warlord, Senad, or lovelord?'

'Varandas, flailing you began this conversation and flailing you end it.'

Hood rose in time to greet Gethol, who now pushed into view between Senad and Burrugast.

'I have come to say goodbye, Hood,' Gethol announced. He paused, and then said, 'An army such as this I have never seen, and hope never to again. Why would you imagine that these "soldiers" would fight against what they all seek in the first place? Death will impose peace and embrace all who come into its arms.'

'Perhaps Gethol has something there,' Gathras observed. 'After all, five centuries staring into death's leering face might well have earned an inkling or two.'

'Denied all else, inklings were his only sustenance,' Haut pointed out, frowning at Gethol who still stood facing Hood. 'Dare I say it under the circumstances, but time is wasting.'

Varandas was the first to laugh. In moments the others followed. Alas, only the Jaghut found their humour alive and well. Above it all, Burrugast raised his voice. 'Remember your promise, Hood! You will lead us to the very face of the hoary spectre, the Lord of Rock-Piles, the Red Shroud, Gatherer of Skulls, and whatever other absurd title we devise!' He raised his arms, spread them wide. 'And we shall demand then . . . an answer!'

A Thel Akai woman, blonde-haired, who had been among the last of the stragglers, now shouted, 'An answer to what, you tusked oaf?'

Arms still raised, Burrugast spun round to face her. 'Oh, that,' he said. 'Well, we have plenty of time to come up with one or two questions, don't we?'

The Thel Akai woman now turned on the rest of her party. 'Do you hear this? Not for Lasa Rook a host of pathetic entreaties! Now, dear husbands, can we finally go home?'

As if in reply, the youngest of the Thel Akai warriors stepped away from his fellows. 'Heed your wife,' he said to the others.

One of the husbands snarled. 'We've been heeding her all the way here, Hanako Cuckolder! Now it is up to her to follow us or not! Into death's realm I say! Husbands, are you with me?'

The other two Thel Akai both nodded, though fear was writ plain on their faces.

'Tathenal, are you mad?' Lasa Rook was near tears, her face reddening. 'It was just a game!'

943

'But this isn't!' Tathenal retorted.

Haut saw Hood say something to Gethol, who nodded and walked away, out from the press surrounding Hood and his frozen fire.

And in that moment, he knew the time had indeed arrived. Eyes filling with tears, he looked to Hood. *Goodbye, Korya Delathe. Until we meet again, as indeed we shall. Let this moment end. But no ending will find—*

*       *       *

'Arathan!'

Drawing his cloak tighter against the chill outside Gothos's tower, he turned to see Korya approaching with a Dog-Runner youth half a step behind her.

The night seemed impossibly dark, but a wind had risen, sweeping in from the sea to the west. The acrid bite of salt flats rode each gust. 'Ah,' said Arathan, 'this must be the one with the blue eyes and freckles on his arms.'

Scowling, Korya said, 'He is named Ifayle.'

The Dog-Runner bowed, and then smiled. 'Arathan, son of Draconus, I have heard much of you.'

'He's coming with us,' Korya pronounced.

'Yet another protector,' Arathan replied, 'making my presence even more irrelevant.' He turned from them both. 'I am going with Hood. Not even Gothos can stop me.'

'Arathan—'

Waving dismissively behind him, he set out for the camp, the wind slapping at his back, and now he tasted salty rain on its swirling breath. Looking for the moon, he found it gone from the sky, and only a thin swath of stars was visible, above the east horizon, as clouds massed above him.

A miserable dawn was in the offing, though the paling of the east was still a bell or so away.

Emerging from the ragged edge of the abandoned city, he looked out upon the vast camp, its huddled hide tents and makeshift shelters, its scattering of cookfires dying now in the depths of the night. For once, it seemed the turning weather had driven everyone into their hovels, for he saw no one.

944

He continued on, seeking the singular, isolated pale star that was Hood's strange fire. There would be Jaghut gathered round that, no matter how foul the weather. And yet, as he drew nearer, he saw no one but a lone standing figure, his back to Arathan.

*Hood?*

Hearing his approach, the figure turned.

There were streaks upon Gethol's seamed, hollowed cheeks. Seeing Arathan, he said, 'They are gone.'

*What?* 'No, they can't be!'

'You were never meant for this, Arathan. Gothos has relinquished you to my care. I will guard you home,' he said, and then with a nod behind Arathan, 'and these two, as well.'

Turning, Arathan saw that Korya and Ifayle had followed. He advanced on her. 'You knew!'

'I felt them leave, if that's what you mean.'

'Leave? Leave where? They left . . . everything!'

She shrugged. 'No point taking it with them, I suppose.'

Now Ifayle was weeping as well, but this did nothing to soften Arathan's hard anger, his sense of betrayal.

'They stepped outside time, Arathan,' said Korya. 'Omtose Phellack always favoured . . .' She paused, searching for the right words.

Clearing his throat, Gethol said, 'The lure of stasis, Korya Delath. Very perceptive of you. One day, perhaps, you will see what Jaghut can do with ice.'

Helpless, Arathan looked around, and then raised his hands. 'So that's it? Abandoned again? What of my own desires? Oh, never mind those, Arathan! Just go where you're told!'

'The path you take in Kurald Galain,' said Gethol, 'belongs entirely to you. But let me make this plain enough. Gothos is done with you. He returns his gift.'

'But Father won't be there, will he?'

'You wish to find him?'

Arathan hesitated and then scowled. 'Not particularly.'

'It is near dawn,' resumed Gethol. 'I will gather provisions. It is my thought that we depart this day.'

'I can't even say goodbye to him?' Arathan asked.

'I believe you already have, Arathan. In any case, the Lord of Hate now revels in his renewed solitude. Would you dampen his joy?'

'He never revels.'

'A manner of speech,' Gethol said, shrugging apologetically. He turned to the others. 'And a Dog-Runner, it seems. What fun. Shall we all meet at dawn then? At the city's old east gate? The twin stumps, that is. The ones flanking what used to be a road. Oh, never mind. Come to the city's edge; I'll find you.'

Arathan watched Gethol walk away. Avoiding Korya's steady gaze, he turned to find the ashes of Hood's hearth. The first thin blades of grass were growing from it, their bright green colour awaiting birth in the sun's rise.

'They're dead, Arathan,' Korya said behind him. 'Or as good as. Whoever you wanted to find there, beyond those gates, well, she'll still be there, no matter how long it takes you to finally join her.'

He shot her a glance, and then shook his head. 'It's not – you don't understand. Never mind.' He pulled his cloak tighter and glared at the sky. 'So where in the Abyss has the spring gone, anyway?'

# TWENTY-FOUR

T HE VALLEY OF TARNS WAS BROAD IN ITS BASIN, A span three hundred paces across and twice as long. Its ends were marked by narrow gorges, carved out by fast waters long vanished. Upon the north ridge the land behind the crest formed a gentle slope studded here and there with saplings that had been planted a half-dozen years past. None had fared well and what remained of them would pose little obstacle to the enemy's command of that side.

Closer to hand, the south slope was steeper, rocky, untreed. But the crest line where the three Andii had halted their horses was broad and even. Slumped in his saddle, Rise Herat watched Silchas Ruin survey the impending field of battle. In bearing Lord Anomander's brother epitomized all the virtues necessary in a commander. Straight and regal in comportment, severe in expression, he and his white horse could well have surmounted a pedestal, a mounted figure rendered in bronze or marble – *indeed, marble, white as snow, white as the skin of our enemy. A triumphal statue, ambivalent in what it celebrates. Even the side upon which it resides is ambiguous. But let us invite this enigmatic hesitation and leave it for posterity.* 'Sir, Lord Urusander will delight in this site.'

Silchas glanced at him, as if irritated by the interruption to his contemplation. 'As do we, historian. See the faint track of the old stream upon that level floor? It divides the valley as would a heartline. Upon that gauge we will measure this battle's tide.' He paused, and then said, 'Describe this well, sir. Was this not the legendary first camp of the Tiste? Down from the ash-filled sky, our first nest?'

'Our exhausted refuge,' Herat said, nodding.

'And did we not feed from the flesh of dead dragons? Perhaps, historian, if there is any truth to such legends, those brittle burned bones remain beneath the earth and snow.'

*To be soon joined by countless others. Already, I see the pyre we must make. Our refuge befouled, our nest unravelled.* 'I would think, commander, on the day of battle we will hear the weeping of ghosts upon the wind.'

Silchas Ruin studied him for a moment, and then nodded. 'Send your arrow again, historian, when next you face Vatha Urusander. It is fitting, I think, that we both bear that wound.'

High Priestess Emral Lanear cleared her throat as she edged her mount between the two men. 'You are too generous in meting out blame, commander, to so inflict the Andii, when the cause of this rests with the Liosan.'

'Blame? High Priestess, forgive me for misunderstanding the historian. I thought we referred to grief, not blame. In that, surely, we must share?'

'I doubt Hunn Raal would agree,' Lanear replied, the lines of her face stark in the pale morning light.

'Nor,' added Rise Herat – against the suddenly bitter taste in his mouth – 'Lord Draconus.'

Silchas frowned. 'Draconus?'

All too aware of Lanear's level gaze upon him, Herat shrugged and said, 'Repository of the highborn's ire, obstacle to a peaceful union of the Andii with the Liosan, his refusal to engage with anyone has, as much as anything else, incited this civil war.'

'I would not think of it that way,' said Silchas Ruin uncertainly.

'A cruel assessment, historian,' opined Lanear, 'and yet, sadly accurate.'

'Lord Draconus is an honourable man,' said the white-skinned commander. 'He well comprehends the precariousness of his position. In his stead, I wager I would do much the same as he, under these trying circumstances.'

'Indeed?' the High Priestess said in some surprise. Then she nodded. 'Ah, I understand. His appearance on the field . . . here, would prove disastrous. For us. While Hunn Raal would delight in it. If not for the opportunity to slay the Consort, then for the very real possibility of seeing the Houseblades of the highborn abandon the field.'

Herat cleared his throat, and then said, 'Well stated, High Priestess. But we can be certain that Lord Draconus understands this dilemma. That, as you say, his sense of honour will win out over his stung pride, and so he will make no appearance, but will remain with Mother Dark.'

'If not pride to see him unleashed, then the desire for vengeance,' Lanear added, to Herat's mind unnecessarily. He could see the agitation and uncertainty in Ruin's expression. He could see, plainly enough, the doubts he and Lanear had sowed.

'Pride is the enemy,' Herat announced. 'Had Lord Draconus stepped aside – had he chosen to surrender his position as Consort to Mother Dark, well, how vastly different would be this day, and those to come.'

'And now,' said Lanear with a sigh, 'it is too late.'

Silchas Ruin said nothing for a time. He remained upright on the saddle, his red eyes seeming to scan the valley floor below. His horse dipped its head, stamped occasionally at the frozen ground. *The statue contemplates, as all statues must. Their moment now trapped in eternity, their eternity not quite as long as they thought it would be. Stony eyes fixed well upon a crumbling future.* 'Perhaps it isn't,' he finally said.

It was a struggle to keep his attention on the commander, rather than casting a triumphant look to Emral Lanear. The historian's breath was suddenly tight in his chest. 'Milord?'

'Too late,' Silchas Ruin explained. 'I shall go to the Chamber of Night. I shall demand to see Lord Draconus. I shall appeal to his honour.'

'An honourable man,' Lanear said slowly, as if searching for words, 'would not abide the spilling of so much blood in his name.'

*And what of Mother Dark? What of her love, wrapped like chains about Lord Draconus? Consort or husband – the distinction means so much less than so many would have it. It has become the weapon, a thousand hands upon the grip. She holds him close to ease the pain in her heart. The pain of a realm bent upon self-destruction. The pain of her children torn apart, of Light bleeding into the Dark, rich as blood, thin as tears.*

*I'll not write of this. I'll not record our venal manipulations. Centuries from now, my ilk will ponder this day and the silence embracing it. They'll devise theories, they'll plumb the nadir world of motivations and all the fears we keep hidden. They will even defend Silchas Ruin, whilst others condemn him.*

*Go now, commander, poke the serpent in its lair. Lord Draconus does not flee, because she does not permit him the luxury. This is not his pride at work, but hers. Pride and love, the power of the former grants sanctity upon the latter. We venture now, commander, into a place where none of us belong.*

He stared down at the heartline of the valley.

*For we have made a woman's love our field of battle, and now will see her lover dragged forth in sacrifice.*

*No, I will not write of this.*

Silchas Ruin gathered up his reins. Then he hesitated. 'I am a warrior,' he said. 'I do not shy from necessity. If we are to fight Vatha Urusander and his legion, then I will lead us into that battle.'

'None doubt your virtue,' said Lanear.

They waited.

'And yet,' said Silchas, 'if peace can be won, here on the cusp of slaughter, by the will of a single man . . .'

'Appeal to his honour,' said Lanear. 'Lord Draconus is an honourable man.'

'The will,' said Herat, 'not of one man, commander, but of

two men. Such a thing will be remembered, and celebrated.'

Silchas scowled, and Herat wondered if he'd pushed too far, or indeed, if he had erred in his judgement of the man's vanity. 'In this,' Silchas then said in a growl, 'I am but the messenger of his conscience. When the echoes of my horse's hoofs have passed, little else will linger.' He faced the historian with a stern visage. 'I trust that is understood.'

Rise Herat nodded.

All three turned then at the sound of approaching horses. A pair of riders, coming up from the track that led back to Kharkanas. Cedorpul and Endest Silann.

Lanear spoke. 'Best ride on, milord. These priests of mine are my business, not yours.'

'Cedorpul promises sorcery,' Silchas said.

'At a battle we may well avoid, milord.'

Silchas Ruin swung his mount around. He would pass the two priests on the narrow track, but Herat was certain that few, if any, words would be exchanged. 'I ride to the Chamber of Night,' the commander announced. 'But that business, as you say, High Priestess, is not theirs to debate. Blunt them. Confound them if you must, but ensure my path remains clear.'

'I shall do as you say, milord,' said Lanear.

Silchas Ruin set off, gathering his horse into a quick canter.

Rise Herat glanced back at the valley. 'We have done with it, then,' he said in a low voice.

'Dispense with that tone,' Lanear snapped. 'Condemnation avails us nothing. We cannot predict what words may pass between him and Draconus. What comes is now out of our hands, historian.'

But he shook his head. 'And does that smoke suffice, High Priestess, to fill your body and blind you to guilt? If so, I'm of a mind to join you next time you imbibe. We can wallow in opaque insensibility, and deem all that races past us scant distraction. Let the clouds find our veins, swell the chambers of our hearts, and whisper sweet promises of oblivion.'

951

If she intended a retort, she bit back on the words with the arrival of Cedorpul and Endest Silann.

'High Priestess!' cried Cedorpul as he reined in. 'I was dismissed with but a single word! Have we not a battle to discuss? To where does he ride?'

'Take no offence,' Lanear replied. 'There is time still. Our commander attends to many things. Tell me, have you brought word of the Hust Legion?'

Cedorpul frowned, and then shook his head. 'Nothing from the south, and it is indeed worrisome. We cannot hope to defeat the Liosan with only the Houseblades defending us.'

'Then what manner of plans did you think to discuss?' Rise Herat asked him.

'My sorcery, of course! It finds shape.'

'Shape?'

'I have mastered malice, historian. I will be ready to face Hunn Raal.'

Herat turned to Endest Silann. The man was gaunt, aged, harried. Herat suspected that he had not come here of his own will. The priest's hands were tightly bound in strips of linen, stained red in blooms and edged in pallid gold. He wore coarse wool to fend off the cold, but his head was bare. 'Endest Silann, do you bring Mother Dark's blessing to this newfound magic of Cedorpul's?'

'It has the flavour of darkness,' the man replied, not meeting the historian's eyes.

'Bestowed by her, then?'

After a moment, he shook his head.

'Myriad are her aspects,' Cedorpul said, his round cheeks fiery red, his face that of a glutted child. 'Many forces lie beneath or beyond her notice. I have drawn from such, ensuring not to stir her equanimity.'

Endest glanced across at Cedorpul, as if unimpressed with this explanation, but voiced no opinion.

Lanear cleared her throat, something she did often of late, and then said, 'Your journey was wasted, alas, and has proved trying for Endest Silann. Your gestures are riddled with haste,

952

Cedorpul, leaving me concerned. One would think eagerness anathema to the control of magic—'

'One would if speaking from a place of utter ignorance!'

'Mind your manners, sir!' said Herat.

Cedorpul turned on him with a sneer. 'And you comprehend even less, historian. Your pondering ways are in for a shock. Indeed, the entire world is due its rude awakening.'

'Then do ring the discordant bell, priest,' replied Herat wearily, 'and delight in our fleeing its clamour.'

Teeth bared, Cedorpul pulled his mount around and kicked savagely at its flanks. The startled beast leapt forward, hoofs biting at the frozen road.

'Pray it throws him,' muttered Endest Silann as they watched Cedorpul ride away. 'Swift be night's sudden setting, to defy his newfound dawn. Pray his neck breaks, to leave lolling his interrupted ambition. Pray his limp body rolls beneath indifferent hoofs, to give lie to nature's horror at what he contemplates.'

'A potent curse,' Rise Herat said, chilled by the dry venom of the man's tone.

Endest Silann shrugged. 'Nothing potent resides in my words, historian. Like yours, my breath sings useless warnings, bestirring a fistful of air, all too quickly swept away. What we have to say wins us less perturbation than a sparrow's leap from a twig.'

Rise Herat could find little with which to disagree in that assessment.

But Emral Lanear spoke, 'You may be surprised, then, priest. Words alone have ushered in civil war, after all, and our fates now reside in the words soon to be spoken, either here or in the Citadel.'

Offering up a second shrug, Endest Silann said nothing. Then he nudged his horse to the crest, and once there he halted the beast and let drop the reins. He began unfolding the strips of cloth binding his hands.

'What are you doing?' Lanear demanded.

'I am showing her the field of battle,' Endest answered without turning.

'Why?'

'To see winter's end, High Priestess. The unsullied snow of the basin. The empty slopes, the unoccupied ridges. The muted blessing of a simple breeze. The world delivers its own gifts.' He held up and out his hands, from which blood now dripped. 'It is our common flaw to make the wondrous familiar, and the familiar a thing bound in the tangled wire of contempt.'

'You would torture her,' accused Lanear.

Endest slowly lowered his hands. 'Her?' he asked.

They watched him wrap up his hands once more. It was more difficult now, with all the blood that had streamed down from the wounds. Herat was thankful that the priest had not turned those crimson eyes upon him. *She would see too much. My goddess, witness to my guilt.*

Lanear looked up the track. 'If Cedorpul should catch up with Silchas Ruin . . .'

'Pray,' said Rise Herat, 'he cuts him down for his temerity.'

At that, Endest Silann twisted in his saddle to regard the historian. Then he nodded. 'I see.'

'Do you?' Herat asked.

'Yes. You will lay her out on the altar of her love, and make a knife of your unwelcome cock.' He raised his hands again, now bound, now blind. 'She will never forgive him.'

'Better him than thousands,' Lanear said, but her onyx skin was ashen.

Endest faced her, and then bowed. 'Alas, High Priestess, for all your machinations, he won't be the only man to fall. Her will is not to be scorned.'

The warning chilled Rise Herat, while Lanear looked away to make plain her dismissal. 'Endest Silann,' she said, sighing again. 'Your name is cursed in the city's markets. Your misguided blessings summoned a dragon. And people went hungry for a time. The very faith of Mother Dark sustained damage in the eyes of the commonfolk, and her blessing has been seen to fade among more than a few of them. You have made yourself an unwelcome prophet, and accordingly, I know not what to do with you, barring a diminishment of your rank in the priesthood.' She fixed her gaze upon him. 'You are an acolyte once more, sir. With a difficult path to redemption awaiting you. Indeed, it may prove impossible for a mortal man to achieve.'

If she sought to sting, his sudden laugh crushed that hope. He bowed again. 'As you will, High Priestess. Then, by your leave, I will return to the Wise City, seeking the glimmer of its namesake.'

'Do not expect to be welcome to council,' she said in a hiss.

He smiled. 'But I never have been, High Priestess. Still, I take your meaning and will abide by it. I embark on a welcome return to being forgotten and, indeed, beneath notice.' Fumbling at the reins, he managed to pull his horse back on to the track, where he set off at a slow trot.

Neither the historian nor the High Priestess spoke for a time, and yet neither seemed eager to begin the return journey. Finally, Lanear said, 'If Cedorpul proves his power, he will be most useful in opposing Syntara and Hunn Raal.'

'Then you had best mend that bridge and be the first to cross,' Herat said.

'I shall bribe him with privilege.'

The historian nodded. 'Among tactics, nothing else proves as successful. Feed his vanity, make costly his ire.'

'Such efforts would fail with Endest Silann.'

'Yes.'

'He remains dangerous.'

'Indeed. While Mother Dark continues to make use of him.'

'I will think on what to do about that,' she said, drawing out a clay pipe and a pouch: rustleaf mixed with something else.

'He kept her attention away from us.'

'What of it?'

'He knew, even then. What she might see.' Then he shook his head. 'Look at us, hiding from our goddess, and relieved by her continued ignorance. As prophet, Endest Silann walked among the commonfolk. He opened his hands so that she could not turn away, could not blink. You think by this act did he condemn the faithless, the misguided, the banal selfishness of each person who suffered that regard. But I think, now, the one he sought to condemn was her.'

To that she had no reply. He watched her tamping the herb into the bowl. She then tipped in some embers from a silver and enamel box that was now part of her regular attire, tied to her sash by a leather string. *We are creatures of ritual and habit, repeating patterns of comfort. Alas, too often we also repeat patterns of disaster. As every historian cannot help but comprehend. From the minuscule and mundane to the monumental and the profound, we draw and redraw the same maps, enough to make a book, enough to make a life.*

Smoke plumed on the breeze.

*Clouds inside and out. Obscure me from myself, that I might imagine my demeanour noble, my stance statuesque. Yes, I will have some of that.*

\*       \*       \*

Endest Silann found Cedorpul on the road, leading his horse by the reins. As he slowed his mount to a walk and drew up alongside the priest, Cedorpul cast him a dark glare. 'Damned beast threw a shoe. I had hoped to catch Silchas Ruin.'

'You hope for many things,' Endest said.

'You were of little use back there. I once knew you as a friend. Now, I know not what you are.'

'Apparently, an acolyte once more. Punished for my walk in the market. And now, it seems, distrusted. But I wonder, is it me the High Priestess would see excluded from council, or Mother Dark?'

Cedorpul kicked at a stone on the path, watched it roll into the shallow ditch. 'Elemental Night. It did not take me long to find it. She does not command that realm, Endest. I assure you of that. It is vast. There are rivers, pools of power, of which she knows nothing.' He glanced up at Endest. 'What do you make of it? Is our goddess an impostor?'

'If she does not rule that realm, Cedorpul, then who does?'

'I wish I knew. Perhaps,' he added, 'the throne remains unclaimed.'

'Ambition unbridled, Cedorpul, can make ugly even the most benign and placid visage.'

The man scowled, and then spat. 'I am a wizard now. The world bends to my will.'

'In a small way, to be sure.'

'Do you mock me?'

Endest Silann shook his head. 'I advise caution, knowing it will be unheeded. You say there are sources of power within the realm of night, many of them unclaimed. You are right.'

Cedorpul's small eyes narrowed. 'What do you know? What has she told you?'

'She tells me nothing.'

'You have always been too coy for my liking, Endest Silann.'

Endest could make out the walls of Kharkanas ahead, a grim black line rising from the horizon. The horses' slow walk on the frozen road made a solemn beat. 'Wizardry, magery, sorcery, alchemy, thaumaturgy. Myriad arts, each one wondrous in what it can create, and wholly destructive in what it means.'

'Explain that.'

Endest Silann smiled. 'You sound like Silchas Ruin. Simplify, reduce, divide and decide. Very well. This power you now possess, it is a way of circumvention. It slips to one side of mundane reality. It draws on unseen energies to twist nature. It imposes a flawed will upon the shape of the world, upon its laws, its rules and its propensities. It is, in short, a cheat.'

Cedorpul was silent for a few steps, and then he nodded. 'I will allow all of that. Go on.'

'One cheats to escape the rules, howsoever those rules are expressed. A winter wind casting a chill upon your bones? A simple cantrip warms you through and through. That, or the mere expedient of donning a cloak. You choose the former as it requires less effort. You choose out of convenience.' He paused, and then continued. 'A thousand enemies marching

957

upon you. Draw your sword and prepare for a day of brutal fighting. Or, with a wave of one hand, incinerate them all. As you see, each time, we fall upon the side of convenience. But how cold, how cruel, is that measure of worth? Consider again that line of soldiers. Consider each of their lives, wagered there on the field, and consider as well a day's hard battle, the wounded, the many slain, the wills bent and then broken. Consider, most of all, the survivors. Each one blessing his or her fortune. Each one returning home, at last, to drop the bundled armour and weapon-belts to the floor, to then embrace a weeping loved one, with, perhaps, children gathering round, their eyes alight with the joy only a child can feel.' Squinting, he could now make out the Citadel's bulky towers. 'But wave the hand. Much simpler, much quicker, and call it mercy, against all the suffering and pain. Deliver death sudden and absolute, and to walk a field of ashes invites an easy dismissal – far easier indeed than to stumble across a field of corpses, hounded by the chorus of the dying.'

'A wave of the hand,' Cedorpul said in a growl. 'Hunn Raal will delight in that simple gesture.'

'And will you match him with destruction of your own? Why not, then, set the two of you upon the other, alone on the field, our champions of magic, there to duel to the death?'

'In that, our function is no different from that of armies, is it?'

Endest nodded. 'True. But with armies, a higher body count, a more profoundly disturbing cost for those who fight, and for those who did not fight. We are all damaged by war. Even those who command. Those who insisted upon the necessity whilst remaining safe in their keeps and palaces. Even they pay a price, though few of that ilk have the courage to admit it.'

'You reach for abstraction again, Silann, as is your predilection. Now is the time to be pragmatic. Even you must see that. But we are astray in this dialogue. You spoke of mysteries gleaned.'

958

'Only this, then. I have my own cheats, Cedorpul. But they are without malice. Their strength, such as I understand it, lies in sustainment. Protection. Defence.'

'Then you will attend the battle?'

'Yes.'

'Can you defend us against Hunn Raal?'

'I believe that I can.'

'Abyss take them, then! We shall win this war!'

'Understand, Cedorpul, just as Hunn Raal's sorcery can be negated, so too can yours.'

'If so, then we're back to swords and shields!'

Endest Silann nodded. 'Yes. Most . . . inconvenient. But I see, upon both sides, no matter the outcome, a host of thankful husbands and wives, a multitude of delighted children. I see tears of joy and relief, and a welling of such love as to sear the sky above us.'

Cedorpul halted then, dropping the reins to bring his hands up to his face, and all at once he was weeping.

Endest Silann reined in his horse and clumsily dismounted. He strode up to his old friend and took him into an embrace. 'Understand me,' he whispered as the man in his arms sobbed, 'I have confidence. But not certainty. I may be able to blunt him only, to save some, but not others. And so I beg you, brother, wring the malice from your power. Twist until the last venal drop falls away. Defend us. That and no more. Be the wall against the fury. Hate finds an easy path with this sorcery. We have reason to fear this new world of ours.'

Face pressed into Endest Silann's shoulder, Cedorpul managed a nod.

They stood thus, in the dim afternoon light, while the two horses wandered down to crop the brittle grasses at the road's edge.

*       *       *

Kellaras stood, girded for war. Around him the Houseblades of Lord Anomander's company were readying their gear, the arms room crowded with silent men and women while

959

the metal and leather murmured its wholly natural discord, blessedly senseless, yet no less ominous.

Word had come. Urusander's Legion was but half a day away.

The Houseblades of other highborn families were arriving in Kharkanas, most of them taking up temporary residence in the city's open squares and rounds, or in the walled compounds surrounding the many private estates.

In his youth, Kellaras had commanded his own fear, on the days leading up to a battle, and in the battle itself. Indeed, he had found a kind of joy in the simplicity of fighting, as if some arguments could only be waged when the last word was spoken, its echo long fading away, and all uncertainty could cleave to the edge of a sword. But rumours had reached them all of sorceries awaiting this clash, against which no shield or armour could defend. Surrounding him now, these Houseblades readied themselves, and their silence was thick with dread. *That each of us should be now made obsolete, as useless as sticks against iron blades. Shall we line up only to be cut down from afar? Will Hunn Raal dispense with all honour, even as he calls the rally in that virtue's name? Can one man kill us all?*

A house steward entered the chamber and approached Kellaras. 'Sir, Lord Silchas Ruin is returning to the Citadel.'

'Alone?'

'It seems so, sir.'

Kellaras adjusted his sword-belt, recalling the last time he met Silchas in a hallway of the Citadel while wearing his armour. The man's fury had been fierce. *'Its display whispers of panic.'* This time, alas, he did not expect a reprimand. It seemed long ago, now. A thousand excuses uttered with each step they took, now lying discarded in their wake. *Time, chewing up the future and spitting out the past. And each moment, trapped in its eternal and instantaneous present, stands helpless and aghast.*

*Silchas arrives alone. Historian, you dare not return to see all this? Then stand at a distance. We will be your players in this narrative, anonymous as pawns. Oh, do at the very least summarize us as the multitudes. Assign us our ancillary roles, and leave to us, if you will, the shadows.*

*Pelk, how I miss you now.*

He followed the steward into the main chamber, with its vast inky Terondai on the floor and motes of dull dust drifting in the air. He could hear the outer gates being thrown open, their clank and squeal muted by the hall's thick wooden doors. Silchas Ruin was moments from arriving. *Fitted to bursting with commands, you come like a flung torch, scattering shadows everywhere with every lash of your flame.*

*Rise Herat, why this shying? You rode out with him, after all. Are you now too full to witness any more of this? Our leader returns alone to the Citadel, and would stand as an island in this calamitous storm. We are all on history's churning tide, historian, and in the end – when every blazing torch has guttered out – we walk in shadow, we of the multitude, anonymous in our victimhood, and yet so very necessary.*

*Now do heed me, historian. Enough bodies in the flow will raise any river beyond its banks. And against this flood, none will be left standing.*

The doors swung open and Silchas Ruin strode into the chamber. Eyes alighting on Kellaras, the lord nodded and without pausing his march, said, 'With me, captain,' and then was past.

Kellaras fell in behind the tall, white-skinned warrior. The pace was merciless, the man bristling as he strode down the corridor, heading for – Kellaras now knew – the Chamber of Night. He felt somewhat humiliated hastening in the man's wake, as if tugged along on a leash. Every step was a surrender, a relinquishing of his own will. It made something inside him – grim as a thwarted child, hands closed into fists – yearn to lash out. This was, he realized with a faint shock, *true*, in all the countless venues of life, the endless tumble of scenes where wills clashed, where hackles lifted and fangs flashed from beneath stretched lips. *The cowering dog is the one most likely to bite, isn't it? They take us at this moment, these unwavering men and women who presume to rule over us, and but point us in the direction of a weaker victim. This is their game, knowing or not, and as ever the assumption is that we'll never turn on our masters – so long as an enemy remains within reach of our blunted, frustrated fury.*

*And what, then, did the soldiers of Urusander's Legion discover, when the last enemy retreated over the horizon? Nowhere left for that angry child within. The game had ended, the leaders told them to go home.*

*But see us now, see how we make scenes inviting that old humiliation. And see how we rush to that rage, so familiar, so simple. This child within us never grows up. And, Abyss take me, it doesn't want to.*

Along the narrow corridor with its cracked, uneven floor. Reaching the recently repaired door of warped blackwood, Silchas Ruin set his hand upon the latch, and then paused to look at Kellaras. 'Stay close to me, captain.'

Kellaras nodded, the gesture deepening his humiliation, his thoughts in a turmoil of something edging towards self-hatred. *This, Mother forgive me, is the curse of the one who salutes. One wolf leads the pack, the rest of us expose our throats.*

Silchas Ruin opened the door and strode into the Chamber of Night. Kellaras followed.

No preternatural gifts of sight could conquer the darkness within. Even the faint gloom from the doorway fell off only a few steps beyond the threshold.

'Close the door,' said Silchas Ruin.

Kellaras pulled it shut behind him, the new latch making no sound.

Now, his eyes might as well be closed. His remaining senses quested, and then contracted, reducing his world to the slow beat of his heart, the rasp of his breath, the feel of lifeless air against his skin.

Silchas Ruin spoke, startling him. 'Lord Draconus! The time has come!'

The echoes fell away.

'Urusander's Legion approaches the Valley of Tarns! Tell me, Draconus, where are your Houseblades? Pray you surrender them to my command. Pray you understand the necessity of your absence on the day of battle.'

Silence answered him.

Kellaras heard Silchas Ruin shifting his stance – the soft click of a ring against the pommel of a sword, the scuff of boot heels on the gritty clay. 'She does not understand,' he said. 'We must speak, Draconus, as one man to another.'

A moment later, Lord Draconus emerged, ethereal and limned in fragmented silver light, as if parts of him reflected something unseen, too cold to be born of flame, too brittle to belong to moonlight. 'Silchas,' he said with a smile softening his features.

'Draconus. Thank you for acceding to my request.' Silchas Ruin paused, and then said, 'Even here, sir, you must sense the closing of this noose – we are moments from strangling our own realm, moments from seeing the death of far too many Tiste. They *will* see another throne, Draconus. They *will* see a Father Light at the side of Mother Dark.'

Draconus seemed to lose interest halfway through Ruin's warning, his gaze shifting away, glancing briefly over Kellaras before continuing on, as if something off to the right had caught his attention. 'You said that she does not understand,' he said when Silchas had finished.

'This is a matter of a man's honour.'

Draconus looked back, brows lifting.

'None will accept you, sir,' Silchas said. 'Even should she marry you, you will ever remain a Consort in the eyes of the highborn. Among Urusander's Legion, you will be the man who humiliated Lord Urusander, at the very gates of Kharkanas. The followers of Liosan will see you as the thief of their Throne of Light. The High Priestess—'

'And all this,' Draconus interjected, 'arrayed against the simple gift of love.'

Silchas Ruin was silent for a moment. 'Honour, sir, stands before all else. Should it fail you, the gift you speak of will falter. Poisoned, corrupted by weakness—'

'Weakness?'

'Love, sir, is surely that.'

'It has never touched you, then, Silchas Ruin.'

'Am I the one holding the realm hostage to it?' Silchas seemed to struggle for a few breaths, and then he said, 'I said we must speak, you and me. Please hear my words, Draconus. Her love for you is undeniable – not even your enemies question it. How could they? She defies everyone for you – her children, each one estranged, abandoned by her closed heart. This is obstinacy. It is plunging the realm into destruction—'

'It is simply love, Silchas.'

'Then why will she not marry you?'

Draconus barked a bitter laugh. 'That choice was never given us—'

'You should have done it nonetheless. They would have swallowed it down, eventually. Had you done so, there would be no civil war. Even the birth of the Liosan—'

'No,' Draconus cut in. 'Not that.'

'What do you mean?'

'Father Light was a title born the moment she took hers. The Azathanai T'riss, who came from the Vitr, did not create it. She but sanctified it. More to the point,' he added, 'the Liosan are necessary, and not just them.'

'Then this civil war belongs to Mother Dark?'

His face hardened. 'Oh, you mort—' He halted, and then in a calmer voice said, 'No. It belongs to all of you. To every face in the battle line, every soul with a command upon his or her lips. It belongs to the ones who turned away when they shouldn't have, who chose expediency over decency, who make their reality a cold winter, too hard and too harsh for sentimental fools. It belongs to the ones without imagination, without courage—'

'Courage? You who hide in this – this *nothing* – you dare challenge our bravery?'

'Do you claim to be a brave man, Silchas Ruin?'

'I know what I am!'

'Then . . . lay down your sword.'

'Surrender?'

'You call it that?'

'They will take the city! They will raise a second throne! And you, Consort, will be cast out!'

'These,' said Draconus wearily, 'are not revelations.'

Silchas Ruin shook his head. 'None will sympathize with your plight, Draconus. Not after this. Not after so much blood has already been spilled.'

'Ah, you lay that at my feet as well?'

'They will hunt you down—'

'And in so doing,' cut in Kellaras, his voice pushing between the two men, 'break Mother Dark's heart.'

The words silenced both Draconus and Silchas Ruin, the latter of whom turned helplessly to Kellaras.

'So,' said Draconus to Silchas after a long moment, 'what would you have me do?'

'Does she listen now, Lord Draconus?'

He shook his head. 'This is our world here, old friend.' Then he added, with a slight tilt of his head as he regarded Silchas, 'I see the hand still upon your sword. None, then, shall surrender.'

'We cannot,' snapped Silchas Ruin. 'We lose too much. We lose it all.'

Draconus slowly nodded, looking thoughtful and then, with narrowing eyes, curious. He waited.

Silchas Ruin hesitated.

Tears filled Kellaras's eyes, but he could not look away. *No, Silchas, don't do this.*

'The honourable thing, Lord Draconus, is to step aside.'

'I already have, Silchas, or do you imagine I volunteered this role of Consort?'

'Then . . . *step again.*'

'Ah, I see. It seems, after all, that at least one man must surrender.'

'It is—'

'The honourable thing,' Draconus finished, nodding, and then looking away once more.

*She'll not forgive you, Draconus. Do not agree to this. I understand you. I have found the love of which you speak, the love that holds and has held you for all this time. Silchas would make honour its enemy, its slayer.* He drew breath to speak.

But Draconus said, 'You spoke of my Houseblades.'

'As I rode in, sir, their standards were sighted from the north tower. They are upon the forest road, in column.'

'Ah.'

'My brother Anomander is with them.'

Kellaras started, facing Silchas Ruin.

'Yet,' said Draconus, 'you still claim command.'

'You well know his dilemma,' Silchas said harshly. 'She forbids him unsheathing his sword!'

'It is your belief then, sir, that he will not break that covenant?'

'He is the First Son of Darkness!'

A faint, sad smile creased the hard features of the Consort, and still he kept his gaze averted. 'As you say. I imagine you know your brother's mind in this. Very well. But I will have my Houseblades.' He swung his head and fixed Silchas with a lifeless stare. 'In my exile.'

The heartbreak burgeoning in Kellaras's chest was fierce enough to steal his breath.

Silchas Ruin had the decency to bow. Or, perhaps, it was unintentional irony. If anything else, Kellaras would never forgive him. 'Lord Draconus, will you accompany us, then?'

'In a moment. The door is directly behind you. Await me in the corridor beyond.'

'You will make your farewell to her?'

The question seemed to strike Draconus like a slap across the face. What had been lifeless in his eyes suddenly flared, if for but an instant. 'Silchas,' he said in a low voice, 'have you lost your mind?'

As the commander hovered, as if uncomprehending of the wound he had driven into Draconus, Kellaras stepped forward and took Silchas by one arm. 'Now, sir.'

He very nearly dragged Silchas back to the door. Fumbling, he somehow found the latch. The doorway spilled in a bloom of light that hurt his eyes, and then he pulled Silchas through.

966

At the last moment, before he closed the door once more, Kellaras looked back at Draconus.

The Consort stood watching, a man bereft of love, who had just felt the cold kiss of honour upon his lips. The only man present who understood courage.

It was a sight Kellaras would never forget.

When they were gone, Draconus gestured wearily with one hand, and a moment later Grizzin Farl appeared from the darkness.

The Azathanai stepped close and laid a hand upon the Consort's shoulder. 'Forgive me, Draconus. I could not protect your love.'

'You never could. Nor, it seems, can I.'

'I did not know,' sighed Grizzin, 'that love could die so many deaths.'

Draconus grunted. 'It has enemies beyond count, my friend. Beyond count.'

'Why is that, I wonder?'

'To those never touched by it, it is a weakness. To those in its bittersweet embrace, it lives a life besieged.'

'A weakness? Surely a judgement born of envy. As to the siege of which you speak . . .' Grizzin sighed again and shook his head. 'What profundity can I find? After all, I fled my wife.'

'Is your love stretched?'

Grizzin seemed to consider the notion for a moment, and then said, 'Alas, not in the least. As for hers . . . I wager she could throw a pot across half a continent as easily as spanning a room.'

'Well,' Draconus said with a smile, 'I have on occasion seen you duck at the slightest sound.'

'Aye, her love is hard as iron.'

Neither man spoke for a few moments longer, and then Draconus moved forward, towards the door.

Grizzin turned but took no step to follow. 'Draconus?'

The Consort seemed to flinch, but then he glanced back. 'Yes?'

'Where will you go?'

'Far enough, I suppose, to hear its snap.'

Grizzin turned away quickly, to hide the sudden emotion that threatened to crumple his features. He blinked at the darkness. And heard the door open and then close. Only when alone did he whisper, 'Forgive me.'

Then he set off to find her. There would be no stretching this love, nothing made so taut as to snap. The words he would bring to Mother Dark were a knife's cut. He was, after all, the Protector of Nothing.

* * *

When citizens take to the streets of a city, driven there by something agitated and ineffable, a strange fever descends upon them in the course of their restive milling. As if it was a contagion carried on sullen currents of air – too vague and wayward to be a breeze or wind – this thief of reason longed for violence. There were times when a people collectively stumbled, staggering beyond the borders of the civil commons, out into light or plunging darkness, out into screams in the night or the blistering kiss of fire. At other times, this sidestep was something else, less obvious and far more profound. A revelation, breaking the fever with sudden cool air upon the brow and the last of the chills falling away, the sweat drying, a new day begun. A revelation, alas, that delivered a crushing truth to all who discovered it.

*We of the multitudes, we of the civil commons, we are the flesh and blood of an enslaved body. This sidestep carried us into the path of an executioner's axe, and the head is no longer our master. It rolls unanchored, the echoes of the severing cut making it rock to and fro, at least for a time. Motion some might mistake for life. Flickering eyelids and eyes that could have flashed with intelligence, but the glitter is now no more than reflected light. The mouth hangs open, lips slack, the cheeks flaccid and sagging towards the floor.*

*Once enslaved, we wander without purpose, and yet a rage burns within us. This, we tell each other, was not our game. It was theirs. This, we cry to the gathering crowd, is our final argument with helplessness.*

*An end! An end to it all!*

But mobs are stupid. Venal leaders rise like weeds between the cobblestones. They cut each other down, with nails and teeth. They carve out pathetic empires in a tenement building, or upon a corner where streets conjoin. Some rise up from the sewers. Others plunge into them. Bullies find crowns and slouch sated on cheap thrones. The dream of freedom is devoured one bloody bite at a time, and before too long a new head enslaves the body, and quiescence returns.

Until the next fever.

*Surely,* thought Rise Herat as he and Emral Lanear rode towards the open gates of Kharkanas, moments from pressing into the crowd, *surely, there must be another way. An end to the cycle thus described. That sidestep belongs to a people beaten senseless by the careless onslaught of injustice. For there to be any change – any change at all – it seems the revolution must never end. Instead, it must roil like a storm feeding itself, on the very edge of calamity and loss of all control, tottering imbalanced but never quite falling. With none to rule, all must rule, and for all to rule, they must first rule themselves. With none to guard the virtues of a just society, each must embody those virtues of justice. But this demands yet more – ah, Abyss take me, I have indeed lost my mind.*

*My very own fever burns in my skull, that of hope and optimism. With love, even, like Endest Silann's dragon, ever circling overhead.*

*The severed head on the floorboards is still making faces, still twitching. That glitter in the eyes is indeed the flicker of intelligence, dimming to be sure – as the armies prepare to meet – but alas, this remnant is without reason.*

*We man ramparts with nothing at our backs. We face a future that has no face but our own, older and no more the wiser. This weariness comes with the tide, rides in the current, and no eddy offers secure respite.*

What had Silchas Ruin done? What had he said to Lord

Draconus? Assuming the Consort deigned to meet the man. *And what of these crowds, the faces now turning to regard us? Strangers. But even that word, 'stranger', arose from a time of kin-hearths and a half-dozen huts marking the very limits of a people, a realm, a temporary nest in the seasonal rounds – when we lived in nature and nature lived in us and no other divide existed beyond what was known and what was unknown.*

*Strangers. We've bred and multiplied into the isolation of anonymity, too many to count, no point in trying. Let my eyes glaze over these unfamiliar faces before me. The alternative is too ghastly, should I see in each visage my own longing for something better, and for somewhere else, a place in which we all belonged. A place without strangers, a civilization of friends and family.*

But the notion mocked him as soon as his mind uttered it. Civilization entrenched the old words, like 'stranger', replete with all the anachronistic fears that had spawned them in the first place. *Different ways of doing things, forever jarring us with confusion – and when confusion takes us, every primitive thought returns, weak as an ape's whimper, savage as a wolf's snarl. We return to our fears. Why? Because the world wants to eat us.*

His snort of bitter amusement was louder than he'd intended, drawing Lanear's attention even as they drew up to the gateway.

'Irony,' she said to him, 'is a cheap pleasure.'

\*     \*     \*

The low outer wall of Kharkanas had been raised long ago to defend against spears and the belligerent press of savages. It was born in a time when warfare was simpler, a clash of mere flesh and peacock displays, where warriors stood as heroes who knew their legends were coming. Originally, Ivis saw as he rode at the head of the column, alongside Lord Anomander, Gripp Galas and Pelk, the wall had been little more than a berm, a mounded, sloped embankment of soil and rocks. The trench of its excavation had made the moat surrounding it, but the steep sides were long gone, and the dressed stone now surmounting the bank had the appearance of a row of discoloured, uneven teeth.

*The city might as well be an upturned skull, the bowl soon to take our clattering selves, like so many errant thoughts.* 'Milord,' he said to Anomander, 'it is my thought to halt the Houseblades here, to encamp beyond the city's walls. I would think the streets crowded enough.'

The First Son of Darkness seemed to consider the suggestion for a moment, and then he nodded. 'Settle the household staff as well, then, until such time as I can make arrangements.'

'Or Lord Draconus makes a reappearance,' Ivis said.

'That would be ideal,' Anomander replied. 'I see many standards upon the walls. It is clear that the highborn have gathered their forces.'

Gripp Galas cleared his throat and said, 'Lady Hish Tulla can be persuasive.'

When Anomander reined in, the others followed suit, and the column halted on the road. The First Son of Darkness said, 'Captain, should the opportunity arise, I will speak to Draconus. I am to blame for the loss of his keep.' He hesitated a moment, and then added, 'The daughters are not dead. So I am informed.' He glanced at Caladan Brood – whose attention seemed fixed upon the city ahead – and continued, 'Resolutions prove bloody, even unto the breaking of stone. What will others make of the rubble left in our wake? I fear a toppling of these flimsy walls. I fear fire and smoke dressing the buildings within. I fear for the lives of the Tiste.'

'Milord,' interjected Gripp Galas, 'you would drag to your feet a host of ills, few of which belong there.'

'The First Son of Darkness,' said Anomander. 'Is this title an empty one? Is the honour a conceit of the one who bears it? What of responsibilities, old friend? Too easily does title invite indolence, or worse, the cynicism that comes from moral compromise. Advisers will urge necessity, expedience, the pragmatic surrender that settles like a callus upon the soul.' He looked to Gripp Galas, and Ivis could see the indecision in the Son of Darkness. 'Is my hide so hardened now? I see the future newly fated, a momentum fierce as a spring flood.'

Gripp Galas's expression flattened. 'Milord, she refused you any choice. She still does. Even as Urusander's Legion descends upon us. What would we have you do?'

'Now that is the question,' Anomander replied with a nod. 'And yet, consider this. I am denied drawing my weapon, but what has this prohibition yielded? Does Urusander honour my constraint? Does Hunn Raal yield to Mother Dark's plea for peace? Does the Liosan High Priestess counsel a gesture in kind? And what of the Deniers, victims honed into slayers, enemy now to all who would dare their forest home? No, Gripp, denied one choice, there remained many others, a hundred paths to reconciliation, and none taken.'

Ivis spoke, finding his own voice harsh and jarring, 'Then meet Lord Urusander on the field, milord. Keep your sword sheathed and ask the same of him.'

'Hunn Raal will defy you both,' Gripp Galas said in a harsh tone. 'He wants this. I suspect the High Priestess does as well. They will see the black waters of Dorssan Ryl turn red, to announce their ascension.'

'But downstream of the city, surely,' Anomander said in a mutter, once more facing Kharkanas. Crowds were assembling, lining the sides of the Forest Track Road where it plunged like an arrow to the city's heart. Faces were fixed upon the Son of Darkness and his ambiguous retinue. Others among the citizenry had climbed the bank to appear on the wall.

Ivis turned about and nodded Gate Sergeant Yalad forward. 'Prepare a camp, among the trees. See to the needs of our hostage and the household staff – it may be we have one last night to spend under the cold stars.'

'Yes sir. Captain?'

'What?'

'The Houseblades, sir. They're ready for this fight.'

*Abyss knows, so am I.* 'Temper their zeal, Yalad. We serve the wishes of Lord Draconus.'

'Yes sir. But . . . should he remain absent . . .'

'We will deal with that when the time comes. Go on now, gate sergeant.'

When Ivis returned his attention to Anomander, Caladan Brood was speaking.

'. . . on the day I am needed, Anomander Rake.'

'And until then?'

Brood gestured to the forest. 'This close to the city . . . there are many wounds in the earth. I will heal what I can.'

'Why?'

The question seemed to surprise the Azathanai, and then he shrugged and said, 'Anomander, ours remains a strained friendship. For all that we have travelled together, we know little of each other. Our minds, the paths our thoughts take. Yet you continue to intrigue me. I know your question was not meant to convey your indifference to such wounding. Rather, you but reveal a hint of your growing despair.'

'You offered me peace.'

'Peace, yes, but no peaceful path was promised.'

'If I stand aside, sword not drawn, will you seek to convince me that none of the blood to be spilled will stain my hands? I should hope not. If I choose peace for myself, Brood, stolid as a stone in a stream, will I not make the currents part? How minor this perturbation – my paltry will? Or will the stream divide, split asunder, to seek different seas?'

Caladan Brood cocked his head. 'Does it matter? Does what you choose make any difference?'

'This is what I am asking you, Azathanai.' Anomander waved back at the forest edge. 'Does your healing?'

Brood considered for a moment. 'I appease the ego. The goodness that comes of it is incidental to a dying forest, a fatally wounded earth. Nothing talks back to me. Nothing voices its gratitude. Though I would have it otherwise, if only to make myself feel—'

'Better?'

'Useful.'

The distinction seemed to have some impact on Anomander, for he flinched. 'Off you go, then, until you are . . . needed.'

With a faint bow, Caladan Brood swung round and made

his way towards the spindly treeline where even now the Houseblades were preparing camp.

At that moment, two riders emerged from the city, horses cantering up the Forest Track Road. Eyes narrowing, Ivis identified Lord Silchas Ruin – astride a white mount – and an officer of Anomander's own Houseblades.

Now, there would be words. The notion – its obviousness – struck him as nonetheless ominous. *This is the madness of it all. Mundane conversations, fragments of meaning and dubious import. All the things left unsaid. If we could assemble our words, merge those inside and out, we would be startled to find that we speak but a tenth of what we think. And yet, each of us presumes to expect that the other understands – indeed, hears both the spoken and the unspoken.*

*Mad presumption!*

'Milord?'

'Ivis?'

'Pray you free the words, let them tumble, with not one left unspoken.'

Anomander's gaze narrowed as he studied Ivis. 'My brother approaches, along with my captain, Kellaras.'

'Just so,' Ivis replied, nodding. He saw Gripp Galas studying him. Pelk, too. He wondered what they saw, what they thought they saw. He wondered at his own log-jam of unuttered words, and his reluctance to kick it loose.

*My own courage in this matter fails me. Yet I ask of it him. Lord Anomander, you are the First Son of Darkness. The time has come to show it. I beg you, sir, make us all braver than we are.*

\*     \*     \*

Wreneck climbed down from the carriage, almost slipping on the ice coating the slatted step. He turned about quickly and drew his small knife, to begin hacking away the sheath of ice. 'Beware, milady,' he called up as Sandalath prepared to dismount, her bundled daughter crooked in one arm.

'I see, child,' she said, evincing once more the new haughtiness that had come to her.

974

Wreneck chipped away, eager to finish and turn about – eager to set his eyes at last upon the great city of Wise Kharkanas. But that glory would have to wait. The last flat sheet of white ice broke free, slipped away. 'There, milady,' he said, returning the knife to his belt and reaching up to offer her his arm.

She took it delicately, and then settled much of her weight upon it, making Wreneck come near to staggering as he adjusted his footing. A moment later she stood beside him, her gaze bright upon the city behind him. 'Ah, I can see my tower. The Citadel beckons. I wonder, is Orfantal at a window? Can he see his mother at last? I am sure that he can – I feel his gaze upon me, his wonder at what I carry. My present to him.'

Korlat looked three years old now, though she voiced no sounds, sought nothing that might be words in that mysterious language of babies. Yet her eyes never rested, and even now she peered out from the folded blanket, like a thing feeding on all that it saw.

Surgeon Prok stood nearby, watching both the mother and the daughter. He had resumed drinking wine, growing drunker the closer they had come to Kharkanas, and the journey's end. A clay jug hung loosely from his right hand, and he was swaying slightly. 'Milady, the child needs to walk.'

Frowning, Sandalath glanced across at the man, and it seemed a moment before she recognized him. 'She walks already,' she replied. 'In realms not seen by you. Realms you cannot even imagine. Her spirit explores the night, the place of all endings, the place moments from rebirth. She walks in the world that exists before the first breath is drawn, and the one that comes when the last breath falls away. They are one and the same. Did you know that? A single world.' Sandalath straightened, adjusting her cradling arm, and smiled at Prok. 'She will be ready.'

Wreneck now looked to the city. He saw its low wall, the crowds lining it. He saw the wide street awaiting them, the broad double gate with its massive blackwood doors swung open and tied in place. He saw more people than he'd thought existed, and all were facing him. *They see Lord Anomander. They wonder at his hesitation.*

*But now comes the white-skinned brother with the eyes of blood – that must be him. He looks . . . terrifying.*

Retrieving his spear and his small bundle of possessions from a side-rack on the carriage, Wreneck moved forward. He wanted to be close enough to hear the brothers greet one another. He wanted to know when the battle would start, so he could take up his spear and be ready for it. He saw Captain Ivis approaching. 'Sir? When do we ride into the city? I must visit the Citadel and speak to Orfantal. It is important.'

Distracted, Ivis moved past, but then said, 'Tomorrow, perhaps.'

Wreneck stared after the man, and saw now that the Houseblades were making up an encampment.

*No, I cannot wait that long. I need to talk to Orfantal before his mother does. I need to explain things.*

Wreneck continued forward, in time to arrive close to Lord Anomander even as Silchas Ruin and another man reined in.

To one side, Gripp Galas turned to Pelk and Wreneck heard him say, 'Lady Hish Tulla is in the city. Find her, Pelk—'

'In a moment,' Pelk replied, her gaze fixed on the man beside Silchas Ruin, and Wreneck saw that he studied her in return.

As Pelk moved forward, the man dismounted, and an instant later they were in each other's arms.

All this before either brother had spoken, and both lords now looked on, startled perhaps, while Pelk and the man embraced.

From where Wreneck stood, he saw the man's eyes shut, his lips moving as he whispered to her, and she held him all the tighter.

Silchas Ruin broke the moment. 'Brother, did you find Andarist?'

'I have set that aside, Silchas,' replied Anomander. 'The sword at my hip retains its name, forged in the heat of my outrage. And yet, had I imagined our Mother's staying hand,

I might have set Vengeance upon the blade of my dagger instead. Of all the myriad scenes in the tumult of possibility awaiting us, I would not shy from striking from darkness and shadow. A blow between the shoulder blades no longer seems so crass.'

Anomander's words drew round all who stood near enough to hear them. When Pelk and Kellaras pulled apart, Pelk stepped back and then, with a nod towards Gripp Galas, set off for the city gate. Wreneck watched her go with an ache in his chest. *Jinia sent me away, because of all the broken things inside her. But one day I will return to her, and my love will mend every broken thing inside both of us. Even the stables that caught fire, which is when everything awful first began. Milady said that I was to blame. Maybe she was right. Maybe it was my fault after all. I can't remember. Could be I killed all those horses. I need to fix that hurt – because it still hurts, if I was the one who did it, and if it wasn't Sandalath who met her man there and the lantern they'd lit so they could see each other getting drunk on the wine he'd brought with his one arm. If it wasn't that after all, but me, spying on them and watching what they did when they put their hips together and moved like dancing on the straw, and the horses shuffled and nickered and the lantern light was steady, but the straw stalks were pushed up against the lantern by their feet, up against the hot glaze. I should have seen that, instead of watching them.*

*It began there, all the hurts. Began with the screams of dying horses, and two shadowy figures running out before the flames got them, and there was Lady Nerys with her cane and she shrieked at me since I was standing right there, watching the fire and listening to the horses, and those blows came down and they hurt so bad but then I got hit on the head and things went numb and strange and that's why I don't remember anything any more about that night.*

*Except what I maybe made up. Her and that one-armed man.*

*But it was you who cared for me after that, Jinia. And I didn't forget. I can't forget. And that's why I'll fix everything. Soon. I just need to kill some people first.*

'A dagger from the shadows. You describe betrayal, my brother.'

'Array before me all manner of obstacles, vengeance finds its own path.'

With a grunt, Gripp Galas said, 'Just ask Hunn Raal. About betrayal. See how he weighs it in his own mind, Lord Silchas. If need be, I will be the hand and the knife both—'

At that Anomander swung to face his old friend. 'No. I forbid it, Gripp Galas. Too often have you struck in my stead. Your time as my quiet justice is done. Have we not spoken? Return to your wife. I am past all need for you.'

The harsh words seemed to batter at Gripp Galas, and all the fire of his own rage died in his old man's eyes. With a single bow, he turned away and walked, unsteadily to Wreneck's eyes, towards Kharkanas, trailing in Pelk's wake.

'We await word on the disposition of the Hust Legion,' Silchas said to Anomander.

The First Son spoke to Kellaras. 'Captain, are our Houseblades assembled?'

'Yes, milord. And the highborn have indeed answered the call. The Greater Houses are all here.'

Silchas Ruin made to speak then, but his brother spoke first. 'Silchas, I thank you for all that you have done. I know you were reluctant, and yet you indulged me in my efforts to reconcile with Andarist.' He hesitated, and then continued. 'It may be that the blood of family, so quick to turn sour on the tongue, had misguided me. In the name of one family, I neglected the other. We three brothers matter less than the Tiste Andii – is this not the burden of command?'

Silchas Ruin's voice was flat. 'There have been developments, Anomander. Of those, in a moment. What do you now intend?'

'I must defy our Mother, in the name of her sons and daughters. Silchas, I will draw my sword. I will take command.'

Silchas was silent for a long moment, and then he nodded. 'I thank you for that, brother. Give me command of our

Houseblades and I will be more than content. Of the more grave demands awaiting us, I leave them to you.'

Anomander sighed and nodded. 'And these developments?'

Silchas made a gesture for patience before turning to Kellaras. 'Captain, return to our company. I will be inspecting them shortly.'

Kellaras glanced at Anomander, who remained expressionless, and then the captain saluted Lord Silchas Ruin, wheeled his horse, and set off.

To Wreneck's eyes, the world seemed to acquire a glow, as of golden light trembling on water. He could smell the old gods of the forest, closing in, crowding around him. But they said nothing, as if they were, one and all, holding their breath.

Silchas Ruin resumed. 'We have sorcery at our disposal. The priest, Cedorpul, who will stand against Hunn Raal. By this, we may indeed negate the threat of magic. Accordingly, we return to the privilege of mere flesh and the will behind it. To the blade, brother, the clash that drowns all words.'

Wreneck studied Silchas Ruin, wondering what the lord had been wanting to say, instead of what he did say. It was strange to him, as the moment passed unremarked, that Anomander had not seen what he had seen. And, of those figures lining the berm, now numbering thousands, he saw how many of them looked peculiar, almost ghostly. He had no idea so many people lived in Kharkanas. But then, as he watched, he saw yet more appearing, rising from the earth of the berm.

*The gods of the forest are back. But they don't speak in my head. They but show me what no one else here can see.*

*The Tiste are attending. From every age. Since the very beginning. Come to witness.*

*Why?*

'Very well,' Anomander said. 'Now, shall we ride to the Citadel?'

Wreneck's gaze was drawn away from the ghostly multitude, so crowding the living that many stood half inside mortal bodies. A flicker of colour had caught his eye: a flag rising above the highest tower of the Citadel. He pointed and said, 'Milords! What is that?'

Both men lifted their heads.

'That, young Wreneck,' said Anomander, 'announces the approach of the Hust Legion.'

'We must send a rider to them,' said Silchas Ruin, his tone suddenly bridling with pleasure. 'They can march directly to the south flats on the edge of the Valley of Tarns.'

'The place of battle. Yes, we will do that.'

'Brother, would you ride with me to the place of battle? There are details to discuss regarding our disposition. Urusander is barely half a day away, after all, and indeed, should he seek haste, we could well greet the dusk with the clamour of iron.'

Anomander seemed momentarily disconcerted. His gaze shifted back to the Citadel. 'It was my thought that I meet with Mother Dark and her Consort. If only to explain my defiance of her will in this matter. Lord Draconus will understand, perhaps, before she does. I would seek his alliance.'

'Draconus knows enough to stay away from the battle,' said Silchas.

That drew Anomander's attention. 'You have spoken to him? There have been tragedies I must share with him, for which I am responsible—'

'Brother,' said Silchas levelly, 'Draconus prepares to flee.'

Hurt and confusion marred Lord Anomander's face. And, whispered a dull voice in Wreneck's head, *disappointment.*

'Ivis and his company,' said Silchas, 'are at your disposal. Perhaps, brother, Ivis should ride with us to Tarns?'

Anomander passed a hand over his eyes, and then nodded. 'That would delight him.'

'Allow me to deliver the invitation,' Silchas said, gathering up his reins, then kicking his mount forward, passing Anomander and then Wreneck, who now moved up to just slightly ahead of the Son of Darkness.

'Milord, I must go to the Citadel.'

'Indeed?'

'To speak to someone.'

Anomander said, 'Proceed in my name, and at the palace gate deliver the news that I ride with my brother to Tarns, and, depending on Urusander's patience, I may or may not return to the Citadel before the battle.' He studied Wreneck for a moment, and then removed a thin silver torc from his left arm. 'This bears my sigil, but even this may prove a dubious escort – the city is crowded and its mood is pensive. Hide my gift, Wreneck, whilst you traverse the streets.'

Wreneck moved up to take the torc.

'You wouldn't rather wait for hostage Sandalath and the others?'

'No sir. I want to go now.'

'I envy your vision, so clear of eye, so sharp in its desire.'

Wreneck glanced over at the ghosts massed along the berm, and then back to where Ivis had settled the camp, and there he saw many other ghosts, as many as the trees in the forest, or perhaps more. 'Milord,' he said, 'I don't always see what I desire. Sometimes, what I see, I don't understand at all.'

'You have left childhood behind, then. Should you mourn its passing in the years to come, remember this day.'

*I will, whether I want to or not.* 'Thank you, milord, for saving my life. When I'm done at the Citadel, I'll go to Tarns, too, with my spear in hand, and I'll fight beside you.'

His vow was meant to please the lord, and yet Anomander's face seemed to fold in on itself, as if retreating from the promise of grief instead of glory. Wreneck straightened. 'You have your vengeance, milord, and I have mine.'

'Then,' the man said, 'how is it possible for me to deny you? Until then, Wreneck.'

Nodding, Wreneck bowed, and then he leaned the spear over one shoulder and stepped on to the cobbled road leading into Kharkanas.

The ghosts watched him, but like all the gathered spirits and gods, they too remained silent.

*Maybe that's what death is. The place you find yourself when there's nothing left to say.*

'Envy has many teeth,' said Prazek as he rode alongside Dathenar, near the head of the train. 'For men such as you and myself, for whom love can deliver the promise of downy cheeks, soft lips and the sweetest nest of delight; or, through the opposite door, a bristled chin and manly tenderness . . . such as it is.' He paused to mull, and then resumed, 'Is it any wonder others look on and feel the gnaw and nip of outrage? Envy, say I, Dathenar.'

'I am minded, friend Prazek, of the many artful expostulations of love, by decidedly lesser poets and bards of our age, and ages past. Shall I plumb this wretched trench? Ah, know you this one? "Love is a dog rolling on a dead fish." '

'Strapala of the South Fork. Guess this one: "I wallow in my love, and you the heart of a sow . . ." '

'Vask, dead now a hundred years!'

'And still mired in mediocrity, no blow to his fame, no mar to his name, no challenge to all that is lame—'

'Barring what you peddle, Prazek.'

'I yield the floor, step lightly over the chalk defining my place, and call an end to toeing the line.'

'Consider this one, then. So heartbroken this poet he spent four years and a hundred bottles of ink defending his suicide, only to break his neck upon a bar of soap—'

'Lye to die, dead by suds, quick to the slick and slip away no time for a quip.'

' "Forsaken this love, my tongue doth probe, to touch – but touch! – the excretion of the snail's slime, and now all atingle at exquisite poison, my heart dances like a rat on a griddle, but still she stands with but a faint smile 'pon her sweet lips, tending the fire and tending, tending, and tending the fire!" '

'There is a delicacy to that anguish, urging me to admiration.'

'His talent was all accidental. And yet, not.'

'Stumbling panged into genius – this does seem a rare talent. By nature of suffering, indulged with passion, to make something sticky of excess, and yet the lure of honey in the flower's budding mouth, drawing one in, and, as he might say, in.'

'And in,' Dathenar added, nodding. 'Have I confounded you?'

'No, a moment longer. I am on fertile ground and must only sharpen the plough. Was it Liftera?'

'Of the Isle? No. Her railing was ever too sour to do aught but crush the petals in desperate grip.'

'Teroth?'

'That alley cur? You insult the name of the accidental suicide. One more effort and then I must proclaim my triumph.'

'Still it echoes oh so familiar . . .'

'Well it might.'

Before them, the city's south wall – dismantled here and there, slumping elsewhere – drew closer, the buildings beyond it dark as smoke-stained stone. The gates were open and unattended. Not even a guard was visible.

'Four years of wallowing?'

''Til the soap upon the tiles.'

'Such an ironic death should have made him famous.'

'His body of work put paid to that.'

'Quoth me another line or three!'

' "Too dark this dawn! Too bright this sunset! Too gloomy this day, too starlit this wretched night!" '

'Too miserable this fool who sees nothing good in anything.'

'He was suicidal, as I said. Four years the span of his career, as he unleashed all that was within him, broken of heart, blind to the insipid self and all its false confessions – broken of heart, said I? Empty of heart, too obsessed with the trappings of rejection to focus upon the object itself. She said no and before her breath left the word he was off, epic visions filling his head, the ordeal stretched out like a welcoming lover. Hark well the willing martyr and make jaded your eye upon his thrashing agony – this is a game played out to its gory end, with an audience evermost in mind.'

'In the offing a bronze, I should think. Or a painting, broader than high, a swept vista—'

'Done, and done, too, the bronze.'

'What? Varanaxa? Gallan's mocked hero? But that man was an invention! A fiction! Gallan's public snipe at his fawners!'

'I posited no distinctions.'

Prazek sniffed. 'The broken heart of a poet gets pumped dry fortnightly.'

'From a healthy one, nothing worthwhile bleeds. So some would claim. But it is these appetites of which we should steer well wide, yet not canted too cynical. Instead, invite a curiosity as to the self-made victim and his self-wounded self. What urge spurs the cut? What hunger invites the bite upon one's own flesh? This is death turned inward, the maw and the wound made one, like lovers.'

'Varanaxa,' sighed Prazek. 'For that epic farce, Gallan was vilified.'

'He cares not.'

'More to the fury of his enemies, that!'

'And herein hangs a lesson, should we dare pluck it.'

Prazek squinted ahead, to the train's foremost riders: Commander Toras Redone and at her side Captain Faror Hend. 'Suicidal indifference?'

Dathenar shrugged, and then said, 'I am wary.'

Galar Baras had ridden back along the column, driven to distraction no doubt by three thousand soldiers marching in silence. There were no stragglers, few conversations, the weapons and armour mute. The sound of the Hust Legion was a dull drum roll that brooked no pause, a slow thunder drawing ever closer to Kharkanas.

The thaw that had been whispered on the south wind the past few days was now dying away, and the snow crunched beneath boot and hoof, a growing bite to the air as the morning lengthened.

'That confounded ritual,' said Dathenar in a frustrated growl. 'I awakened on thin ice. But which way to crawl? No shoreline beckons with high tufts of yellow grass and the stalks of reeds. To shift a hair's breadth is to hear the ice creaking beneath me. My eyes strain to read this placid, windswept mirror – is it clouds that promise more solid blooms? The grey sky warning of treacherous patches? Do I lie upon my back, or face-down? Still, through it all, something writhes in my gut, my friend, in anticipation of blood.'

Prazek shook himself. 'What has changed? Nothing. Everything. The ritual tattooed a mystery upon our souls. Blessing or curse? We remain blind to the pattern. And yet, as you say, there is anticipation.'

Dathenar gestured at the unoccupied walls ahead. 'See the fanfare awaiting us? Bitter indifference castigates us, Prazek.'

'No matter, friend. Was I not speaking of love?'

'You were, the heart under siege. Though I cannot fathom your reason for this sudden crisis.'

'Criminals,' Prazek said. 'No punishment allows for the tender caress, the meeting of hands in soft clasp, the hesitations that linger, the confessions that release.' He paused. 'A stillborn twin, now the repository of sorcery, and she who would mine it left broken and filled with self-loathing. So Wareth would take her into his arms. Yet he too allows himself no worth, indeed, no right. Can I not wonder, friend, at those who hold that love is a privilege?'

Dathenar grunted. 'Every god of the past claimed it a benison. A reward. By its fullness are our mortal deeds measured. Doled out like heavenly coins, as among the Forulkan.'

'Indeed, and consider that. How can this currency so define itself? Value rises in scarcity of love, plummets in surfeit? The gods played at arbiters, yet demanded love's purest gold in coin. Who then to measure *their* worth? I challenge the right of this, Dathenar.'

'And so you may, but to what end?'

'Dispense with contingency in the giving of love. Shall I push Rance into Wareth's arms? Shall I insist upon their right to love?'

'You distract yourself,' Dathenar replied. 'The Dog-Runner witches did something to us – all of us barring our commander, that is – and now she leads a legion that knows not itself, yet shows disinclination to introspection. While she in turn . . . ah, no matter.'

Prazek glanced across at his friend. 'I distract and you despair. Pray that Toras Redone decides.'

'Upon what?'

'Life, and love. For surely the former is an expression of the latter that gives reason for the former.'

'Easy for you to say.'

'Dathenar, did the Bonecasters cleanse our souls?'

Up ahead, the commander and Faror Hend reached the gate and rode without pause into the city.

'No,' Dathenar replied. 'They but reordered its myriad possessions.'

'For what purpose?'

Dathenar shrugged.

Prazek let loose a low growl. 'And so . . . anticipation dogs us all.'

Shifting in his saddle, Dathenar glanced back at the column. The soldiers wore their armour. Their hands rested upon the pommels of the swords. Their kit bags were slung over one shoulder, their shields upon their backs. They wore their helms, leaving every face in shadow.

When Faror Hend returned from the gateway and signalled a halt, the Hust Legion's incessant thunder ceased its heavy rumble for the first time that day. The silence that fell into its wake sent shivers through Dathenar.

Faror Hend reined in before them. 'We're to wheel right and skirt the city,' she said. 'We march to the Valley of Tarns. Urusander's Legion draws nigh.'

'This very day?' Prazek asked.

'Have the soldiers drop their kits and leave the baggage train here,' she said, her face blank.

Both men swung their mounts around. They could see Galar Baras cantering towards them. Prazek waved a signaller forward. 'Envy has many teeth,' he muttered as the signaller rode closer. 'Enough to spawn a civil war.'

Dathenar nodded.

From the Hust weapons and armour, down the entire length of the column, the iron began to moan.

✳    ✳    ✳

Wareth moved to the ditch at the road's side, leaned over, and spewed out the morning's breakfast. Behind him, not a single soldier called out in derision or amusement. Not a single man or woman voiced disgust. Wiping at his mouth, and then-spitting out the last of the bile, he straightened and turned round.

He was being ignored. The faces beneath the helms were fixed upon the new flag being raised by the signaller. Upon receipt, the squad sergeants called out the commands to ready to wheel and then drop kits. Shields were shifted higher on the shoulder, swords brought round to the point of the hip. Chain links hissed like waves on sand, and then the Hust iron began its song. Pensive, a dirge, perhaps, or something trapped by unseen forces, unspoken wills – the eerie song swept through Wareth like a chill. Shivering, he looked on, as Rebble brought the company around, with the lead elements already descending from the road.

He looked for Rance but could not see her. She had been avoiding him, and he well knew why. Attentions from a coward could not be welcome, especially for a soul as wounded as hers. Her determination to live was weak enough without his dubious presence. He was, after all, a visible affront, for her demons were not ones from which she could flee. *But then, neither are mine. If only she could see that.*

'Wareth.'

Blinking, he turned to find Listar at his side. He studied the man's narrow face. 'What is wrong, Listar?'

'What is wrong? Abyss take me, Wareth, *everything.* Everything's wrong! Look at them! The ritual—'

'Which you brought to us, Listar,' Wareth said. 'And not even you know what has been done to us.' He gestured. 'None of us do.'

'And yet . . .'

Nodding, Wareth sighed. 'And yet.'

987

There was no joy in the song of the Hust iron. Wareth shook his head. 'Listen to that,' he said. 'What do you make of it?'

Listar rubbed at his face. He mumbled something Wareth could not hear.

'What?'

'The iron, Wareth, is filled with dread. The swords do not grieve for those they would slay, but for those wielding them.' He paused, and then glanced at Wareth. 'She defied your wish, and Galar Baras's too. Here you are, ordered to lead us into battle. It seems she is indifferent to your fate, and by extension, to all of us under your command.'

Wareth could not argue against any of that. 'Do not look to me, Listar.'

'We won't. We'll follow Rebble. Just be certain of one thing, Wareth. Voice no orders. Issue no commands. If you bolt, we'll not follow you.'

Wareth thought back to a few moments ago, when terror emptied his gut. 'I am unmade,' he said. 'If they look my way at all, they see right through me.'

'We'll not burden you with our hope, if that is what you mean.'

The words should have stung. Instead, he felt relieved.

The column was re-forming, and they watched as Toras Redone and her retinue cantered from the city's gate to take position as the Legion's vanguard once more.

Horse hoofs thumped in the snow-laden grasses as Galar Baras rode up, reining in beside Wareth. The captain's face was flushed with the cold. 'Wareth!'

'Sir.'

'Your company is under my command, along with the seventh, the ninth and the third. We are to present the right flank.'

Wareth nodded.

'Rebble will lead them down into the valley.'

'We are to fight on this day?'

'If Urusander seeks it.'

'Dusk chases him,' said Listar.

'It chases us all, Listar,' Galar replied, gathering up the reins once more.

*     *     *

Commander Toras Redone rolled unsteadily in her saddle, righted herself with an effort. Her face was slack, her eyes muddy red. A moment later, as Faror Hend drew up alongside her, the commander smiled. 'Had I known today would be the day . . .'

'You would have done what?'

Toras Redone's smile broadened. 'Level your tone, darling. And punctuate your query with a "sir", if you please. Why, I would have rationed the wine, of course. It begins to sour in my belly, as voluminous as I have made it. Plenty of room left, it seems, for anxious thoughts.'

Faror Hend rose in her stirrups, twisted round and checked back on the column. Then she settled once more. 'Your anxiety not sufficiently dulled? Sir? Not yet drowned? Thrashing still in that dark nectar?'

'You are too sober a conscience, Faror Hend.'

'You need not concern yourself with that much longer, sir, as my words are running down. Soon, my silence will give you its final cry.'

'You surrender too easily,' Toras Redone replied. 'Will you yield your life as cheaply in the battle to come? Are you not betrothed to a war hero? Why are you not at his side? Perchance, he awaits us at the Valley of Tarns, or is that consideration the cause for your despondency?'

Faror Hend bit back a cruel retort, and said, 'Kagamandra Tulas may well be there, the hero in search of yet another war.'

'Against you, I wager he has no defence,' Toras Redone said. And, as if she had somehow caught a hint of Faror's unspoken retort, she continued, 'He chooses the lesser trial, then. I well understand him, you know. Calat Hustain was always too bright a light for my dulled eyes, too upright in his virtues, too untested his forgiveness – no matter how egregious my crime. He weakened my knees, and to stand at his side was to tremble in the shadow of his piety. Is it any wonder I reached for a lover?'

'Galar Baras deserves better.'

Toras Redone did not respond for a moment, and then she said, 'I meant wine, of course. But she's a generous whore, I find, quick to yield my flesh to someone else's pleasures.'

Faror Hend closed her eyes briefly, willing a bit between the teeth of her fury.

Beside her, the commander laughed. 'This war is such a travesty. So crude in its cruelty, so obvious in its tragedy. Look instead to a life in times of peace, to see the subtler – and yet still brutal – battles of the soul. Day upon day, night after night. The soldier longs for the simplicity of war, making a coward of every sword-wielder. Peace, my dear, is the bloodiest affair of all.'

'I weigh things differently, sir.'

'Do you? I think not. Instead of finding your husband to be, you rode to the Hust Legion. Instead of claiming an estate and giving it the shape of your heart, you perch here like a crow on my shoulder, quick to judge but oh so slow to cast inward that unflinching regard.' She waved a hand. 'But I welcome your spite nonetheless. You are my barbed shield, Faror Hend. I draw you ever closer to feel the sting of the spikes, here on my chest, pricking the skin above my heart, and I but await the first crush of battle to see me home.'

'You'll make no descent into the press, sir,' Faror Hend said. 'I'll not let you.'

'Indeed, and why such mercy?'

'Because,' she snapped, 'it is the very opposite of mercy.'

Toras Redone seemed to reel in her saddle, pulling herself upright with severe effort. Her face was suddenly set, the smile long gone, her gaze fixing forward now, to what awaited them all.

*       *       *

Once across the inner bridge, Kellaras dismounted close to the Citadel's gatehouse and, handing the reins over to a steward, made his way into the keep. Its severe façade rose before him as he traversed the compound. *It has not the look of a temple, but a fortress. And is it not odd, all things considered, how so often one demands the other.* That faith needed defending suddenly struck him awry, the very notion jarring his thoughts, and it seemed that he tottered on the edge of a revelation. After a moment he righted himself, picking up his pace as he reached the broad flight of steps.

*Philosophers can't have been blind to any of this – my startling realizations stumble in well-trodden troughs of discourse, no doubt. No faith worthy of itself needs defending. Indeed, there can be no such thing as an external threat to faith – barring that of genocide. And even there, killing the flesh impugns not the faith held within it.*

*No, the sordid truth is this. Faith's only enemy exists in the mind that calls it home. The only forces that can destroy faith are those the believer wields against him or herself.*

He reached the doorway, saw the door left open – swung wide, in fact – and strode into the keep.

*A believer whose face twists, who points an accusing finger at a disbeliever, who then draws a blade with blood in his mind – that believer pronounces a lie, for his doubts are his own, and were he truly honest before his god, he would voice them. No number of corpses imaginable for this believer to stride over can quell the threat – the potency – of self-doubt.*

*A true believer, indeed, need never draw a weapon, need never rise in argument, or howl in fury, or make fists, or roll in a mob to crush some helpless, innocent enemy. A true believer needs none of those things. How much of the world insists on living this lie?*

Blinking, he found himself standing at the entrance of a side corridor, the one leading to the chamber where Lord Draconus waited. Vaguely, he recalled hearing words spoken near the Terondai, a conversation perhaps, and a question thrown towards him. Frowning, Kellaras turned, in time to see Cedorpul and Endest Silann approaching him.

'This war,' Kellaras said, forestalling them, 'is unnecessary.'

Both priests halted at his words, and then Cedorpul snorted and shook his head. 'Dear captain, we all know that.'

'We fight because we have lost faith.'

'Yes,' said Cedorpul, his round face grave.

'Fighting,' Kellaras continued remorselessly, 'is proof of our lost faith. And now people will die in payment for our own private failings. This is not a civil war. Not a religious war.' He paused, helplessly. 'I don't know what it is.'

Endest Silann stepped forward. 'Captain, take care of your loved ones.' He lifted his hands with their sodden, crimson bandages. 'It is our folly to see a hole at the centre of our world, one of empty darkness, a manifestation of absence.'

'But it is not empty,' whispered Kellaras. 'Is it?'

Endest Silann glanced back at Cedorpul for an instant, and then, facing Kellaras once more, he shook his head. 'No sir. It is not. She has filled it, to the brim. It is swollen with her gift.'

Behind him, tears were falling freely down Cedorpul's cheeks.

Kellaras brought his hands to his face, as Pelk's visage filled his mind. 'Her gift,' he said.

'Draconus was the proof of it,' Endest said, 'if only we'd the courage to see. All of this,' and he gestured with his bloody hands, 'is filled with love. Yet see what rears up to stand in its way. See our innumerable objections to this simple, most profound gift.' His smile was broken. 'This is a war of fools, captain. Like every war before this, and every war to come. And yet, as proof of our failings, as proof of our weakness, and every petty distraction we so willingly embrace, it is, alas, no more than what we deserve.'

Kellaras backed away from the two men. 'I await Lord Anomander and Silchas Ruin,' he said.

Cedorpul grunted. 'Too late for that. They ride to the Valley of Tarns.'

The words stilled the torment in Kellaras's mind, and then horror rose in its wake. 'What? Surely Lord Anomander would have—'

Endest Silann interrupted him. 'Lord Anomander has been away. He relies upon his brother's judgement.'

Kellaras looked to each man in turn, and back again, still uncomprehending despite the dread he felt, still lost by this turn of events. 'Lord Draconus waits,' he said.

This was a day of revelations, a cruel cacophony of simple words plainly stated. He saw the flush leave Cedorpul's face. He saw Endest Silann flinch, and then come close to staggering before regaining his balance. Kellaras turned to the corridor behind him. 'Here,' he said, and started walking.

Neither man followed.

*The war of fools. And the greatest folly of all, it is now clear to me, is to dream of peace. Faith, with all your promise, and all your betrayal . . . must I see you as the enemy of hope?*

He reached the door and hesitated. Beyond it sat a man bereft of love, a man now profoundly vulnerable to betrayal. And once more, it would be delivered with banal declaration. The world had tilted in Kellaras's mind. He saw voices, a torrent of words that had done their work, now slowly withdrawing, retreating from what was coming. And by the time this was done, the voices would be without words, reduced to piteous cries.

*All to begin again. Born only to die. See what we have made of the time between the two.*

Behind him, a priest wept, while another bled. Kellaras reached for the latch.

*    *    *

Wreneck knew he had nothing to fear as he hurried through the crowds in the street. Ghosts closed tight around him, and it seemed that they blinded most people to the young man slipping between them, rushing fast as his legs could carry him. They made for him a path in ways Wreneck had no hope of understanding.

The shaft of the spear rested heavily across his right shoulder. He held the weapon tilted high, to keep the leather-wrapped iron head away from others. The silver torc that

Lord Anomander had given him was tucked under his coat. Among the ghosts he saw warriors, long dead, still bearing their fatal wounds. It was all he could do to avoid their faces, their steady gazes fixed so solemnly upon him. For all he knew, his father was among them.

Something was wrong. He understood that much. The dead of the Tiste belonged somewhere else, a world hidden away from mortals. They had no reason for being here. And yet, he now wondered, perhaps they were always present, and it was only his newfound curse that he could see what others could not. It was possible that such crowds always existed, thousands upon thousands, wherever living Tiste dwelt, drawn like moths, hovering and swarming around what they had lost.

They had nothing to say, or perhaps they could not be heard, which made them nothing more than eyes, trapped in the faint memories of bodies. The thought that death was a prison horrified Wreneck, and he felt his own mind now tracking other, even crueller thoughts. *I seek vengeance. I want to hurt the people that hurt Jinia and me. I want to send their souls into this empty ghost-realm. I want them to just stand there, mute, seeing but never able to touch. I want them to suffer.*

He had never thought himself evil, but now he wasn't so sure. Vengeance seemed such a pure notion, a taking away from those who'd done the same. Evening things out, death for death, pain for pain, loss for loss.

Even Lord Anomander believed in vengeance.

But now . . . what kind of satisfaction would it bring? How was it that even grown-up men and women talked about vengeance, as if it had the power to fix things? *But it doesn't fix much, does it. Yes, the killers and rapists are dead, so they won't ever do it again. There's that, isn't there. Pushing them off the cliff of life, down into the Abyss.*

*But they don't go there. They go nowhere. They join every other ghost. They could as easily have died in their sleep, a thousand years old, surrounded by loved ones. It makes no difference, not to them.*

*But does it make a difference to me? This killing, this justice? I guess . . . once they're dead, justice stops mattering to them. So it belongs to the living. It doesn't belong to any waiting god, because the gods aren't waiting for those souls. Worse yet, the gods in that realm are themselves dead, no different from anyone else.*

*Justice belongs to the living.*

He imagined driving his spear into the bodies of the soldiers who'd hurt Jinia. Imagined their faces twisting in agony, their bowels spilling out, their boots kicking at the ground. He saw them looking up at him, at his face, at his eyes, with confusion, and all the questions they couldn't ask. But he'd tell them why they were dying. He'd do that, because that was important if justice was to be served. *'This is why you're now dying. I did this, because of what you did.'*

He found himself crossing the outer bridge, and then the second, inner one. No one barred his path. He strode under the arch of the open gateway, into the compound, where scores of Houseblades were mounting up, their horses steaming and the hot smell of dung heavy in the air. Even here, ghosts abounded, the dead come to watch, watch and wait. He slipped through the jostling chaos, reached the keep's entrance, up the steps and then inside.

The ghost of a giant wolf was lying at the foot in the stairs beyond the vast hall, its eyes now fixing on Wreneck as he drew closer. Impulsively, Wreneck said, 'Take me to Orfantal.'

The beast rose, began climbing the steps. Wreneck followed.

'You're one of his,' he said. 'I don't know how I know that, but you are. You died a long time ago, but he brought you back, to keep watch on things. You're dangerous, but not to the living.' And now he realized that he had not seen any ghosts within the keep itself. 'You drive them off. Orfantal sees them, too. He sees them and doesn't like it.'

The boy was not the boy Wreneck remembered. The Citadel, with its massive walls and hallways, its rituals and worship, had changed Orfantal.

'I think,' he said now to Orfantal – as if the boy could hear through the ears of the ghost wolf – 'you're going to frighten your mother.'

*     *     *

Venes Turayd's expression was wry and almost contemptuous as he regarded Pelk. She had entered the estate's courtyard, pushing through the readying Houseblades and making for the building entrance when Venes, seeing her, had stepped into her path. Now he blocked her way, his knowing smile showing its edges. 'Why, Weapon Mistress Pelk, all done folding bed sheets and sweeping out rooms?'

'Move aside, milord,' Pelk replied. 'I must speak to Lady Hish Tulla.'

'She's too busy fretting. But if you have relevant news, I will hear it.'

'Yes, I'm sure you will, but not from me.' When she rested her gloved hand upon the pommel of her sword, his smile broadened.

'My wolves surround you, mistress, but even in their absence, I do not fear your skill.'

She cocked her head. 'What a foolish statement, milord. Any sword-wielder, no matter how talented, should know, and understand, fear. Without it, you are likely to get yourself killed, even by an enemy less skilled than you. I cannot think who trained you, sir, but clearly it wasn't me.'

Their conversation had drawn a few of Turayd's wolves closer. The chill air of the courtyard was rank with men's sweat, and the Houseblades edged in to crowd her.

Sighing, Pelk said, 'Call off your pups, milord. Playing at bullies demeans them, assuming such a thing is possible. If, on the other hand, each one is brave enough to face me alone, why, I invite it. I have folded enough bed linen, and swept enough corners, and my mood now inclines to killing. And so, do oblige me by holding your ground, sir. If I am to hang for spilling noble blood, I will delight in making you the first to fall.'

There was a commotion behind her, and a moment later

996

someone voiced a shout of pain and staggered to one side. Gripp Galas now moved up beside Pelk, his shortsword drawn and its tip bloody. 'Apologies, milord,' he said to Venes Turayd. 'Hard to draw in this press, and yet I was of a mind to check the edge of the blade, the battle being nigh and all. Now, sir, my wife is within? Excellent.' Hooking an arm around Pelk, he moved forward, forcing Venes to step aside. 'But please,' Gripp added as they made for the door, 'do maintain your vigil, since we do not wish to be disturbed.'

They entered the building, where Gripp paused to sheathe the sword. 'Pelk,' he said in a low voice as the door closed behind them, 'my wife's uncle is an unpleasant man, but murdering him on the steps of the estate would have been unwise.'

She bared her teeth. 'Gripp Galas, I have lost all faith in wisdom. As for my reasons, best you not know them all.' She paused, and seemed to shiver, as if deliberately shrugging off her bloodlust. 'One day I will indeed kill him, sir. Best you know that now, and be certain to not stand in my way.'

Gripp's gaze narrowed on her for a moment, and then he said, 'His thugs would have cut you down.'

'Too late to make a difference.'

'Captain Kellaras would disagree.'

Pelk frowned. 'I keep forgetting.'

'You forget your love?'

'No. I forget that someone else – anyone else – cares about me.'

He studied her for a long moment, and then took her arm again. 'Let us find your lady, shall we?'

Hish Tulla was in the large room adjoining the master bedroom, attended by servants helping her don her armour. Upon seeing Gripp and Pelk enter, the brooding storm-clouds of her visage suddenly cleared and she let out a heavy sigh. 'I had begun to wonder,' she said.

Gripp Galas spoke even as Pelk drew breath to begin her report. 'Beloved, we are forbidden the field.'

'What?'

'Lord Anomander forbids us this battle. It seems your uncle will lead your Houseblades after all.'

'I will defy him—'

'And so wound him.'

'He wounds us!'

Gripp Galas nodded. 'Yes. He does. He took offence at my return – more than even I expected. I am driven away, an unwanted cur.' He paused, and then suddenly smiled. 'There is a certain freedom to this.'

Hish Tulla's eyes held on her husband for a moment longer, and then shifted to Pelk. 'My husband's loyalty lies slain, before the battle's even begun. What have you to say to me?'

'I nearly killed your uncle, milady. Prevented only by your husband's intercession.'

'Anything else?'

'Lord Anomander has taken command of the Draconus Houseblades. Lastly, by signal flags above the Citadel, the Hust Legion even now makes for the Valley of Tarns. It is time to assemble and ride from the city.'

'Lord Anomander takes command? Not Silchas Ruin?'

Pelk shrugged. 'If he has not already announced it, he will, milady. The First Son of Darkness will defy Mother Dark.'

At that Gripp Galas turned, shock written deep in the lines of his face.

Pelk continued. 'If Lord Anomander refuses you both, it is because he wants you to live. No, he needs you to live. There will be sorcery. The slaughter awaiting us may be absolute.'

'What of our honour?' demanded Hish Tulla.

Pelk scowled. 'In this new war of magic, milady, honour cannot exist. Respect dies with the distance, the very remoteness of murder. Battle becomes a chore, but one swiftly concluded, and only the ravens will dance.' She set her hand again upon the pommel of her weapon. 'All my skill, all that I gave my life to teaching – my very vow to see my students survive – is now meaningless. If death can strike without discrimination, then truly we are fallen. I see a future in which spirit dies, and if this day is to be my last, I will not regret it too much.' She glanced at Gripp Galas. 'I expect

Kellaras to join me in the dust of death, so think not to chide me again, Gripp Galas.'

Neither Gripp nor Hish Tulla had anything to say to that.

Pelk nodded. 'Now, by your leave, I will return to your uncle, and inform him of his command.'

'See that they fight,' Hish Tulla said, but her tone was empty, hollowed out. 'You are his second in command. Make certain that he understands that.'

'I will, milady, and should he betray, I will cut him down in the instant.'

'I doubt,' said Hish Tulla as she gestured her servants closer again – this time to begin removing her armour – 'Venes Turayd holds any delusions about your resolve, Pelk.' She turned her head to her husband. 'What say you, beloved? Shall we ride to my western keep?'

Gripp frowned at her. 'You will surrender all responsibility?'

'He loves us too dearly, does he not? We shall depart, bearing the cuts of our freedom.' She shrugged. 'Our trail will be obvious enough, by the blood we drip. Pelk, keep Rancept close.'

'Of course, milady, if such a thing is possible—'

'I said keep him close, Pelk. There is sorcery in that man, far older than anything Hunn Raal might use.'

'Rancept?'

'He is Shake, Pelk. A Denier, if you must use the term. But more than that, he once dwelt among the Dog-Runners. He is the child of a different mother. Hold him to your side, Pelk, for I would see you again.'

Pelk bowed.

Hish Tulla said to her husband, 'You did as Kellaras asked. You returned Lord Anomander to his senses. He commands you no longer.'

'Yes, beloved.'

'Never again.'

He nodded.

Pelk departed the chamber, feeling strangely elated, almost content. Whatever came of this day, love would survive. She understood Lord Anomander, and the offence he had taken at Gripp's return. In this one instance, honour had lost the battle, and simple decency would prevail.

She approached the outer door, eager to both delight and irritate Venes Turayd. Then they would set out for the Valley of Tarns, leading the Houseblades of House Tulla, and she would ride behind Venes and, at her side, old bent Rancept, his breaths as harsh as those of the horse he straddled.

Kellaras would live or he would die. No different from Pelk herself. *And you, Ivis, you old fool. Find your new love if you can when all this is done. We're past every regret, and the past has lost all its claws, all its teeth, and can hurt us no more.*

Now, time had come to face the dying day. She kicked open the door.

# TWENTY-FIVE

LTHOUGH IT LEFT HIM WITH CONFUSED EMOTIONS tugging him this way and that, the idea pursued Orfantal, and no matter where his mind raced, the idea swept up around him the instant he paused. Children should be able to choose their own mothers. Of course such a thing was impossible. And yet, was it not even worse that mothers could not choose their children? He knew enough about being unwanted and unwelcome. He knew even more about being a disappointment.

The mother he sought, could he so choose, would have the strength to look him in the eye, and to see and not fear who he was. There would be a reserve about her, a kind of selfishness, perhaps, that in itself would give him enough room to grow into his own world, making his own choices about how to live.

Gripp Galas would have laughed at the notion. The child, he would say, needs guidance. The child, he would insist, was not ready to understand the world, not ready to make a place in it. And these things were probably true, but a balance was needed nonetheless. Until his arrival in the Citadel, Orfantal had been smothered beneath his mother's needs. He had been weighted down with the fears and dreads of his grandmother. Of his father there was only absence, a vast realm of ignorance in which Orfantal could raise heroes standing beneath bold standards, and that suited him well enough.

Heroic death appealed to him like nothing else, when he imagined his future life, when at last he clawed free of his mother and her shrinking world.

He'd sensed his mother's arrival. His powers had grown, and now the city and its outskirts trembled as if sheathed in his own skin. The black river, with its crisp shelves of ice along the banks, felt like his own heartline, rich with the tireless flow of blood, too swift to freeze solid, too fierce to be turned aside. He felt his mother and her uncertain steps. He shivered to the sudden presence of the First Son of Darkness, whose spirit was like a mailed fist; and the stranger beside him, in the moments before retreating back into the forest – that man held in his heart all the resolve of a wounded world, of nature steeling itself against a storm of its own making.

Orfantal was still a child, and yet in the space given to him, since his arrival at the Citadel, he had soaked in the dubious wisdom of ancient stone walls, of floors laid out in ritual, of magicks swirling down every passage, murmuring the memories of old gods. He had prodded awake sleeping spirits, and each one had given him new words, new thoughts, new ways of seeing. But, for all that, his mind remained as it had always been, quick to absorb all the new things given him, and as quick to find itself wandering lost in confusion, knowing he was not yet able to understand it all. Knowing that such gifts, these blessings of stone and old gods, were meant for someone older, wiser – someone who understood enough to be afraid.

He saw the boy Wreneck, his old friend who'd stopped being his friend, rushing into the keep. It was startling to find that Wreneck could see the wolf ghost he'd left there, near the Terondai, and Orfantal was not yet sure if he was pleased by that, or alarmed.

Wreneck looked much older than Orfantal remembered, scarred and sure-eyed, like a warrior or a hunter. He carried a spear, and no one he passed in the corridors challenged him. Orfantal did not know if he should be frightened as Wreneck followed the ghost ever deeper into the Citadel, and ever closer to where he now hid.

But all these details were shoved to the wayside upon the return of Emral Lanear, the mother he would have chosen for himself. He longed to curl up in her lap again, not just in spirit, but with his own body, its solid limbs and the weight of his head resting on her breast.

Everywhere there was the talk of war, of the battle to come. Everywhere in the Citadel, and in the city beyond, there was a miasma of fear and uncertainty. People were in motion, restless and at times scurrying, as if their labours could reshape the future. And how their hands worked! He watched pots being scrubbed, stacked and dried, and then hung on hooks in neat rows. He watched clothes being folded, floors being swept, cords of wood perfectly stacked. Axe-edges honed, blades polished. Everywhere his mind looked, he saw a frenzy of order taking hold of men and women.

Panic was the enemy, the mundane necessities of living a ritual of control, and as control was torn away – out beyond the walls, out beyond the city itself, those busy hands at the ends of those arms – they all retreated to what was in reach. That and nothing more.

*And this is us. This is the Tiste.*

*And, the ghosts tell me, this is how a civilization falls.*

He would curl into her lap, as she sat in her chair, tendrils of smoke rising about them. In a chamber well guarded by his ghostly wolves. Children only ever had one place of retreat.

*My real mother is skin over wounds. She hurts everywhere inside, and she wants to bring it to me. She has a new child, a thing of sorcery, a thing of terrible power. I see the Eleint in the baby's eyes, the father's ancient power.*

*If Mother keeps her close, that toddling thing, she will poison it. She will make a monster.*

Wreneck was coming closer. He would reach this room in only a few moments. Orfantal blinked, withdrawing his vision, his multitude of strange senses that quested everywhere like unseen draughts. He glanced down at Ribs, watched the dog dreaming in a cascade of twitches. Easier to make the beast sleep than to see it ever fleeing.

If he had the words, he would tell Emral Lanear so many

things. If he had the words, he would say this: *Mother Emral Lanear, I feel your clouded mind, and all the guilt you refuse to think about. I feel your grief at beauty lost, there in the mirror. And I would tell you otherwise, how your beauty is something no mirror could capture.*

*Mother of Darkness cannot be seen, so you stand in her stead. Her true representative. Even you do not understand that. Just like the goddess, you are the mother of us all. And that space surrounding you, that vast space, it is your gift of freedom. To your children.*

*But it seems we've made it a place for killing.*

But no such words came to him, except in the echo of someone else's voice. There were times – and he heard this in a whisper – when the poet took liberties, to sweep aside the confusion in service of clarity. To make things plain.

Some indulgences must be borne. For others, patience was wearing thin.

The door opened. Wreneck stepped warily into the chamber. 'Orfantal?'

Orfantal uncurled from Lanear's chair. 'She's back,' he said. 'She's coming here, I think.'

'What? Who?'

'The High Priestess. Hello, Wreneck.'

'I've come to warn you.'

'Yes, my mother. And her new child.'

'Korlat. She's named Korlat.'

'Ah.'

'Orfantal, what's happened to you?'

'I escaped,' he replied. 'Only now I'm going to be dragged back, and not even the High Priestess can help me. I mean, she won't, because it isn't her place and anyway she doesn't understand. Mother's here. She's on her way.'

'She wants Korlat to protect you.'

Orfantal laughed. At the sound, Ribs awoke, lifted his head to study Orfantal, and then looked to Wreneck. Wagging his tail, he rose and approached the boy.

Frowning, Wreneck patted the dog's head. 'I like this one the best,' he said. 'The ghosts scare me a bit.'

'What's that spear for?'

'For the ones who attacked us, who burned down the estate and killed Lady Nerys and hurt Jinia. They're in Urusander's Legion.'

'You'd better hurry,' Orfantal said, unsurprised at any of the news Wreneck delivered, unsurprised and, he realized, unaffected. Perhaps he'd heard it all before. He couldn't remember. The Citadel's wise stone filled his head, but the wisdom was lost, confused, wandering the corridors.

'I will. But I needed to warn you first. About your mother.'

Orfantal held out a hand to forestall Wreneck's explaining any further. 'Yes. Don't worry, I see her. All of her. Thank you. Wreneck, were you my friend once?'

The boy's eyes widened, and he nodded.

'Are we still friends?'

'I am,' Wreneck replied. 'To you, I mean.'

'I think you're a hero now, Wreneck. Remember how we played? All those battles? The last two to fall, you and me. Remember that?'

'It isn't like that, though,' Wreneck said. 'It's about not being strong enough, or fast enough. It's about enemies with empty eyes, stabbing you with their sword. It's about you lying there, bleeding and hurting, while soldiers make an innocent girl bleed between the legs, and there's nothing you can do, because you weren't good enough to stop them.'

'The heroes always die,' whispered Orfantal.

'I've got people to kill,' Wreneck said, backing towards the door.

'And I've got to be a big brother, just like you were once, to me.'

'Be good to her?'

'I will, Wreneck.'

'Better than I was to you.'

Orfantal smiled. 'Look at us now. We're all grown up.'

*      *      *

Lord Draconus was sitting in the dark, motionless in a high-backed chair near the unlit hearth. The air was cold, lifeless, yet the chamber felt suffocating as Kellaras stepped inside and closed the door behind him. 'Milord.'

It may have been that Draconus had been asleep, for he now started and straightened slightly. 'Captain.'

'I was to come here, milord, to tell you of your impending audience with Lord Anomander.'

'Yes. I will speak to him. There is much to discuss.'

'Instead,' Kellaras resumed, 'I must inform you that Anomander has ridden out with Silchas Ruin, to the Valley of Tarns. Urusander's Legion draws close. There will be a battle before the sun has set.'

Draconus was motionless, and he said nothing for a long moment, and then he rose from the chair. 'Where are my Houseblades?'

'They ride to the battle, milord.'

'This was not what was agreed.'

Kellaras said nothing.

'Who has taken command of them, captain?'

'Lord Anomander has chosen to set aside Mother Dark's prohibition. He commands the forces of the Tiste Andii.'

'And the highborn?'

'They too assemble for the battle, milord. All are in attendance, with their Houseblades. Also, the Hust Legion returns to us, not as it once was, but nonetheless . . .'

Draconus moved past the captain, swinging open the door. When he set out down the corridor, Kellaras followed.

*A damned pup again, rushing to someone else's pace. Would I could take any door, to either side of this passage, and simply step out of this mess. Find myself in an empty room, a place of silence, big enough to swallow the echoes of my raging mind.* Instead, he said, 'Milord, will you ride after them?'

'I will have what is mine,' Draconus said.

'In the Chamber of Night, milord, you acceded to Silchas Ruin's request—'

'He has deceived me, and I will know if his brother was part of that.'

'Sir, your presence—'

Reaching the door leading into the hall, Draconus halted and turned to Kellaras. 'Anomander understands honour. At least, he once did.'

'He will yield to you your Houseblades, milord. I am certain of it.'

'And see us withdraw from this farce?'

Kellaras nodded. 'So I believe of my master, milord.'

Draconus bared his teeth. 'If only to keep the loyalty of the highborn.'

'Sir, will you make him choose?'

Draconus swung round again and moments later they were crossing the hall, the Consort indifferent to the Terondai beneath his boots.

They were not alone in the vast chamber. The High Priestess and the historian stood nearby, still in their outdoor garb, halted now by the abrupt appearance of Draconus. Kellaras saw in both faces a sudden, misplaced unease, and he wondered at that, even as both bowed to the Consort.

'Milord,' said Emral Lanear. 'Does Mother Dark stir at last? Will she advise me on what must be done next?'

Draconus strode past her without replying.

Kellaras saw the shock on Lanear's drawn face, followed swiftly by indignation. Beside her, the historian smiled without much humour, and rested a hand on the woman's shoulder.

'High Priestess, is it not clear? He rides to the Valley now.'

She spun to face him, but said nothing – and then Kellaras too was past, stepping swiftly to catch up to Draconus.

*This farce spills out. It mocks its way through the Citadel, dancing down the corridors. Soon, it will howl.*

Once outside, they headed for the stables, Kellaras trailing Draconus like a man on a leash.

\*     \*     \*

The streets were clear when the companies of Houseblades set out, each from their highborn's respective holding in the city. Most were on foot, ordered into a slow jog as they headed first eastward and then, once beyond the outer gates, on to the northeast road, where company upon company linked up to form a column.

At the very head and forming a vanguard rode the high-born themselves. Vanut Degalla, Venes Turayd, Aegis, Manalle, Baesk, Drethdenan, Trevok and Raelle. Immediately behind them, also mounted, the masters- and mistresses-at-arms, along with a score of lesser officers, aides, signallers and message-bearers.

Riding a massive, broad-backed horse, Rancept found himself in the company of Captain Horult Chiv and Sekarrow. In their martial accoutrements, the night in the kitchen at Tulla Keep seemed long ago and impossibly far away.

Sekarrow, her iltre stored inside a leather case strapped to her saddle, her gloved hands resting on the horn, reins loosely wrapped about them, leaned companionably close to the castellan and said, 'Has Lady Hish preceded us, then?'

The jostling from the trotting horse sent stabs of pain through Rancept's bent frame, forcing his breath out in sharp gasps. It was a moment before he managed to speak. 'She leaves this to her uncle.'

Sekarrow uttered a surprised grunt, and said, 'That seems . . . unlikely. Something must have happened—'

'Yes, something did.'

Riding up on to Rancept's other side, Horult Chiv rapped his gauntleted knuckles against the wooden scabbard of his sword. 'Castellan, know this: my lord Drethdenan is resolved. If it comes to calling out cowards, he will not hesitate!'

Rancept nodded, although he was far from convinced. It seemed that Horult elevated his beloved far beyond the opinions most might hold of the man's fortitude. That said, Rancept hoped the captain was right.

Venes Turayd was not a man to be trusted, not on this day. Pelk, riding at Turayd's side, had made clear her opinion in this matter, conveyed with a simple glance instead of words. Rancept had been already resolved to follow orders, as expected, until such time as a command threatened his honour, at which moment he would do what needed doing.

He'd lived long enough to find the weight of a crime – even one of murder – a burden he would willingly carry. There was little that could be done to him that would not, in truth, prove a salvation. His bones ached incessantly. Drawing breath was like drinking draughts of pain, without surcease. He'd seen enough of life to know he wouldn't miss it much. His only regret was the grief his death would level upon those who cared for him.

Venes Turayd was a man inclined to abuse the honour of others, as if needing to despoil what he himself lacked. But he would not have Rancept's last surviving virtue, and in the moment of its challenge the castellan would give answer. And Pelk would guard his back.

Deep in his twisted body, he knew that betrayal was coming.

The heavy, long-handled axe at his hip was a comforting weight. The armour wrapped tight about his shoulders clattered as he rocked in the saddle. The surrounding gloom did little to diminish the acuity of his eyes as he looked out upon stubbled fields, and, glancing back over his sloped shoulder, upon the ranks of Houseblades, each House bearing its proud standard.

*Sleeping Goddess, hear my prayer. Your earth will drink deep this day. Nothing will change this. But this surface here, these shallow thoughts and quick deceits, they are where I will find myself. Grant me a clear path, and I will leave you the severed head of Venes Turayd, raper of children, betrayer of the Sons and Daughters of Mother Dark.*

*Today is our day of accounting. Sleeping Goddess, walk with me and dream of death.*

*Sukul Ankhadu, forgive me.*

'One day,' said Sekarrow, 'I will learn to play the damned thing.'

Her brother snorted. 'But not today.'

'No, I suppose not,' she replied. 'I am told, however, it makes a sorrowful sound.'

'Not today,' Horult Chiv repeated in a growl.

'No, not today.'

The afternoon was drawing to a close. They were late readying horses, and Endest Silann stood watching as Cedorpul harangued the grooms. In a few moments, the two of them would set out again, upon the track they had but just traversed, well in the wake of the Houseblades and the Hust Legion. Should they then return to Kharkanas, one more time, everything would have changed.

His hands were cold, but not numb. This was something that made his blood into ice, and that ice burned as it leaked out from the wounds in his palms. He thought, idly, that it might be an indication of Mother Dark's fury.

Moments earlier they had seen Lord Draconus and Captain Kellaras ride out, their horses' hoofs hammering the stones of the courtyard and then the bridge, the sound discordant, as if some madman was working an anvil. Haste and anger, hurts ill disguised. Iron and stone made for bitter music.

*The pilgrim makes a path. But no longer is he followed. Miracles pall in the disapproval of authority, and what was once a gift is now suspect. And so, yet again, we crush the blossom in our hand, lift our gaze from the tumbling petals, and ask the world, 'Where, then, is this beauty you promised?'*

But beauty could be a terrible thing, a force to cut the eye and leave wounded the witness. Even perfection, if such a thing could be said to exist, could arrive like an affront. Endest Silann lifted his gaze to the sky, studied its fierce contradiction of afternoon light and enervating gloom, and wondered if, on this day, dragons would take to the air, with eyes eager to feast on the slaughter below.

*There is this, you see. They are drawn to sorcery. Reasons unknown, my knowledge itself a mystery. I know what I know, but know not how I know it.*

Cedorpul shouted him over to where he waited with the two now saddled horses. Nodding, Endest Silann joined him, and a short time later they rode out across the first bridge, leaving the looming hulk of the Citadel in their wake.

With renewed energy, Cedorpul grinned across at him.

'Today, my friend, we shall see the power of magic! The power to withstand, to defy, to refuse!'

'We will do what we can,' Endest replied.

'We shall prevail,' Cedorpul said, his face flushed. 'I feel it in my heart.'

'We need only hold.'

'Sorcery will see an end to armies and battles,' Cedorpul said. 'Perhaps even an end to war itself. Together, the two of us, we can lead our realm into a new era of peace. Mark my words.'

The sound of the hoofs beneath them was a cacophony, rattling Endest Silann's thoughts, and he could think of no reply to Cedorpul's assertions. They rode on at a quick canter, the road before them strangely empty this close to the city, though the air itself seemed turgid. If there were refugees fleeing Kharkanas, they were on the south road, although in truth Endest did not believe the city's inhabitants were fleeing. *Mother Dark, your children have nowhere to go.*

Even if Urusander's Legion proved victorious, the notion of his soldiers looting Kharkanas was too heinous to consider. *No, this will be decided in the Valley of Tarns. Nothing else is required. The Wise City will survive this.*

'We will drive this Liosan from our world!' Cedorpul said. 'What say you?'

Endest Silann nodded, but could manage nothing more. His hands wept with the anguish of a goddess, and yet the tears of blood burned, making him think of rage.

\*　　\*　　\*

All the soldiers were gone. Wreneck hurried through a city emptied of almost everyone except ghosts, and they too had begun a march, eastward, in a silent progression of damaged and diseased figures. He saw children with bloated faces, bruised by the pillows that had stilled their last breath. Others, much younger than Wreneck himself, bore broken limbs, from beatings, he imagined, as he recalled the cane coming down upon his own body, and all this made him rush through the city of Kharkanas, barely seeing the magnificent buildings on either side of the street. He drew his spear around so that he could find strength in its solid shaft of dark wood, gripping it with both hands. As if, with this weapon, he could fend off his own memories.

There were so many ghosts who had been hurt somehow. He wondered at that, fighting a chill that burgeoned from somewhere deep inside him. He wondered at all the broken people, and all their secret histories, and at how none seemed able to hide their hurts now that they were dead. Yet none wept. They walked, instead, with eyes like dusty stones plucked from a dry riverbed. They were too pathetic to frighten him, too hopeless to make him think he could in any way help them.

The world was a big place, bigger than he'd ever imagined. And it was old, too, impossibly old. The dead never went away, he knew now, and they crowded him, moving in a noiseless mass, spilling out through the gate in the outer wall, and on to the road. He didn't want to be seeing any of this, and he wondered at the curse that now afflicted him. *I must have done something wrong. All those times I failed. All the times I proved too weak, and because of my weakness people got hurt. This is where it comes from. It must be. I was never good enough.*

His breaths harsh, he ran through the ghosts, striving to win free of them all, to find a clear space on the track. A few turned to follow him with their dull eyes. One or two reached out as if to take hold of him, but he evaded their grasp even though he knew their efforts were useless – their flailing hands simply slipped through him, no different from the last of the bodies he pushed through as he finally outraced them and found himself alone on the cobbled road.

Some distance ahead, he saw another lone figure, tall, dressed in heavy robes, hobbling like a man with broken feet. It did not take long before Wreneck caught up and came alongside the man.

A narrow, deeply lined face, an iron-grey beard snarled and seemingly stained with rust. Seeing Wreneck, the old man smiled. 'Late to the battle, soldier! As am I, as am I.

Shall we hasten? I have no Houseblades. They must have left without me – no, wait, that's not right. My Houseblades bear the swords I forged, my armour, too. I made them into a legion. I left them somewhere. I'll remember where, I'm sure, sooner or later. Ah!' He took a few quick steps forward, leaned down to collect a rock, and showed it to Wreneck. 'Slag,' he said, his face twitching. 'You find it everywhere. Our legacy – my son's wife, you know her? When they were but betrothed, I happened upon her in a room and saw that she had a small blade in one hand, and she was using it to cut the insides of her thighs. She was hurting herself, you see. I could make no sense of it. Can you?'

Wreneck wanted to hurry on, leave the strange old man behind. Instead, he shrugged. 'She was trying to feel something. Anything.'

'But she was loved. We all loved her. Surely she understood that.'

Wreneck glanced back to the mass of ghosts on the road behind them. 'She didn't believe you. You loved her because you didn't really know her. That's what she believed, I mean. You didn't know her so whoever you loved wasn't her, it was someone else, someone who just looked like her. But she knew better.' *Jinia, wait for me. Don't do anything to hurt yourself. And please, please, don't let me see you among these ghosts.*

The old man still held out the ragged piece of slag, and now he closed his fingers about it, tight enough to break skin and draw blood. It ran down the edge of his palm, down to stain his cuff. He offered Wreneck a ghastly smile. 'Every pit we carved into the earth. Every hill we tore down. Every tree we burned, the wastelands of poison we left behind. It's the same, young soldier, exactly the same. Wounding ourselves. And, as you say, wounding ourselves because we're not who we think we are. We're far less than that.' He grunted. 'I used to play in the murdered places, with my toys, my painted heroes of lead and pewter.' He reached round and drew out a heavy leather satchel he had been carrying hidden beneath his cloak. 'I brought them along, you see, because we're going to have a battle.'

'It'll be a real battle, sir, and I need to get there in time, so we have to hurry—'

'You take one side and I'll take the other. I have ones painted in green livery, others in blue. Upon either side of the ditch here, we line them up, you see?' He reached out and grasped Wreneck's arm, pulling him to the side of the road. 'I'm green and you're blue,' he said, his eyes bright as he spilled out what was in the satchel.

Wreneck looked down on the battered toy soldiers, a hundred or more. He watched as the old man deftly separated the two colours, pushing the blue-painted ones up against Wreneck's worn boots.

'But we need rules for this,' the old man continued as he collected up the green soldiers and made his way across the snow-filled ditch and seated himself on the far bank. 'Fronting strength, flanking weakness. Adds and subtracts. The attrition of unrelieved pressure – I have dice for this, knucklebones in fact. Not Tiste, of course. Forulkan. I'll explain the adds and subtracts once our troops engage. Quickly now, line yours up, there along the valley's crest!'

'Sir, the real battle—'

'You will obey your lord!'

Wreneck flinched at the shouted command, and then he set the spear down to one side and knelt on the edge of the road. 'Yes, milord.'

The first of the ghosts reached them, passing along on the road, paying no attention whatsoever to the two figures off to one side.

The old man licked his purple lips and began speaking in a quick, almost breathless tone. 'I have my Hust Legion. See? I told you I would find them, and here they are!' He gestured down at his green-painted toys. 'Superb soldiers one and all. Can you hear their swords? Bitter prisons, making the iron howl. They have bonuses against pressure. But you, Urusander, you have bonuses for ferocity, for all that your soldiers learned fighting the Jheleck. You see how it balances out? We are well suited in opposition, yes? My legion can hold its ground.

1014

Yours can attack like no other. Our strengths lock horns, as it should be.'

Wreneck paused in lining his soldiers up along the edge of the ditch. He thought back to all the mock battles he'd played with young Orfantal, and tried to recall what Orfantal had said about strategies and tactics and other things Wreneck didn't really understand. But just like Orfantal, this old lord had a fever for war. Wreneck frowned. 'But, milord, if our strengths lock horns, then more soldiers die. I should trick you into attacking me, and then withdraw once you're down in the valley, and then come in on your flanks. I should make you turn to defend and then get you to attack, over and over again. That way, I can still use my strength even as I turn yours into a weakness.'

The lord stared across at him, and then giggled. 'Yes! Of course! Of course! But you see, nobody's supposed to win. We both get bloodied and then we both withdraw. Better yet, we turn on our commanders and, why, we cut their heads off! We throw down our weapons! Throw away our armour! We tell the bastards to go fuck themselves and then we go home! Hah!' He half slid down on to the ditch's slope. 'Now, it's time to advance! To war! The standards are raised! This is the secret joke, you see. When we all agree on insanity . . . it's still insane!'

Wreneck watched the old man laugh, watched the face redden, the watery eyes bulging. He wondered at the joke, not quite sure of it, and then he wondered if that joke might end up killing the lord, as the tears ran down the old man's lined cheeks, as the laughter grew more helpless, and finally as, hysterical, the breaths growing harder and harder to draw, the man choked and gagged, clutching his chest.

The ghosts marched past, pebble-eyes fixed on nothing.

Upon each side of the ditch, a few of the tiny soldiers toppled in the wind as the wet mud gave way beneath them.

Gasping, the lord righted himself and wiped at his eyes. 'Now,' he said in a rasp, 'it begins with magic, or so I'm told. Powerful spells, but the first and most powerful one no one even sees. It's the sorcery of war itself, the ritual words flung back and forth, everyone moving into place – there, set those up again, it's not yet time for them to fall. But they've all agreed. There's no choice. You have to agree on that first, you have to weave it, a web that snares everyone. No choice, no choice, must be done, draw the sword. There's no choice, we agree on that. We have to agree on that, to begin with. No choice, oh dear, no choice, oh, how sad, how regrettable. No choice. Keep saying it and it comes true, do you understand? No choice!' He sighed, leaned back to study his troops. 'Split into three. The centre will advance first. The wings will stretch and form the horns – this is simple tactics, you understand. Nothing subtle or clever on this day. But wait! Before all that, the mages must duel!'

Wreneck looked back to the road, watching the dead filing past. There were many soldiers among them.

'What do the mages do?' he asked the lord.

The old man frowned. 'I don't know. Let me think. Magic. There must be a structure to it, lest it serve nefarious purposes. It cannot simply be a force no one understands. Not a metaphor, then, nothing like a poet's meat. People make use of it, after all, don't they?'

'Milord, I don't understand.'

'Sorcery! If this then not that, if that then not this! Chart the cause and effect, mutter and write notes and pretend that such things impose limits and rules, abeyances and prohibitions, all these contingencies to milk the brain with an inventor's delight – pah! The poet's meat is a better way of seeing it. Metaphor. Meat to be wrung until the blood drips. Meat to invite thoughts of rendering, something hacked away from some unseen body, a giant's corpse lying unseen in the forest, or among the hills, or amidst storm-clouds in the sky. The flesh in one hand, dripping with heat, the butcher's take on the world, where all invites the cleaver and knife, where all must perforce be lifeless to take the cut, the cold, empty chop! Yet look! The flesh cut away bleeds still, and there is heat, and something pulses – the twitch of wounded nerves.' He paused to regain his breath, and then pointed across at Wreneck. 'The poet knows it's alive. The butcher believes it

1016

dead. Thus, the gift upon one side and upon the other the taker of that gift, the sorceror, the butcher, the blind, clumsy bastard.'

The lord shifted to study his rows of soldiers, and then reached down and lifted one free. 'Here he is. The poet recoils. All those tales of childhood, the magicks and the witches and wizards, the cursed gems and sacred swords – magic, my young friend, belongs to twin goddesses' – and he smiled – 'I see them still. Name this first one Wonder, and she leads you by the hand into unlikely realms. Your delight is her reward! Now, the other, why, let's call her Warning. The other side to every magical gift, to every strange world. The poet knows all this, or the poet should, at any rate. Wonder and Warning, what other detail does one need in the comprehension of magic?'

Wreneck shrugged, and then, when that did not seem enough, he shook his head.

'We use what we don't understand,' the lord explained, scowling. 'It's a simple message, a simple metaphor. We use what we don't understand. To invent rules and make charts and lists is to forget the meaning of the metaphor. Such a mind is locked into its rational cage, a most limited realm, a realm of self-delusion and presumption, a narcissistic stance, and the rules and logic only serve to reflect the brilliance of the one using them, as if, indeed, that is the singular purpose of the entire pointless exercise!' He wagged a finger at Wreneck. 'The poet cocks a leg and pisses on them all! It's meat and the meat bleeds, and the blood is warm and the blood fills the cup of the hand and to use it is to kill it and to kill it is a crime.' He set down the soldier he'd collected, positioned further down the bank of the ditch. 'My idiot champion of ignorance. Now you – wait, what is your name?'

'Wreneck.'

'Now, good Wreneck, select your champion.'

Wreneck picked up one of his soldiers and moved to place it opposite the lord's lone figure. 'Like this, milord?'

The old man frowned. 'I must add another.'

'Two against one?'

'No matter. One of mine is going to die.'

'How do we fight with magic, milord?'

'Why, I'll roll the bones, of course.'

'Then how do you know one of yours is going to die?'

'Because magic demands meat, Wreneck. Blood in the hand, fading heat, something broken, something dying, a crime unforgivable.'

Wreneck looked down at all the soldiers. 'Milord, are we gods?'

The old man snorted. 'Less than that, less than who we are, in fact. Toy soldiers and dolls, puppets and deeds writ small, we're the venal manipulators of the unpleasant. With secret purpose, we lay waste to lives we ourselves have invented. With hopeless despair, we hammer home lessons no one pays any attention to.' He laughed again, a bitter, caustic sound. 'All a waste, my young friend, all a waste.'

The old man began weeping then, and after a time, Wreneck reached down to the lord's second mage, and tipped the figure over until it was flat upon the ground.

＊　　　＊　　　＊

'Soon,' said Lord Vatha Urusander as they rode towards the valley, 'the thaw will come. There is a will to water, never as wayward as it might seem. It finds certain paths in its hunt for the lowest land, for the places where it can rest. When the flood takes the streams, the streams flow into the river, and the flood rises yet higher. It spills out and finds refuge in hollows and sinkholes, in pits and trenches. When I was a child, the thaw was the season I loved the best. Those pools of cold, cold water – water beetles would appear in them, from where I knew not, and yet their glory would be brief, as the pools slowly dried up.'

Renarr rode at Urusander's side. They were not part of the Legion's vanguard. Well ahead, Hunn Raal and his captains commanded the army's bristling point, and behind them trundled the heavy carriage bearing High Priestess Syntara, Sagander the one-legged scholar, and young Sheltatha Lore.

Riding alongside the carriage was Infayen Menand. Renarr and the commander had only each other for company, with the first company of soldiers marching a dozen paces behind.

'I had a clay jar,' Urusander resumed. 'I spent my days capturing the beetles, and then releasing them into the streams. Nothing mattered more to me than saving their small lives. Unlike those bugs, you see, I knew what was coming. This incurred in me a responsibility, young as I was, and from that an obligation. I could not stand to one side, yielding to cruel nature.'

'The water beetles,' said Renarr, 'probably bred in the mud left behind by the pools, and there the eggs remained until the next season of flood.'

Urusander was silent for a time then.

Renarr twisted slightly round to observe the soldiers marching behind them. After the midday's break, they had donned their armour and readied their weapons. Scouts had reported the enemy massing on the south side of the valley. It seemed that no one was much interested in delaying the battle. The following dawn offered no gift of light – not this close to Kharkanas. And yet it seemed precipitous nonetheless, at least to Renarr's mind. The soldiers would be weary after the day's march, after all.

'Did I kill in my misplaced mercy?' Urusander suddenly asked.

'You were a child, as you say. At that age, we are easy playing at gods and goddesses. Carve a trough at the pool's edge, watch it drain away. Stir up the silts and mud, scattering whatever had been hidden there. We become fickle chance to the life that knows nothing of us. The life we victimize, the life buckling to our misguided will.' She paused, and then shrugged. 'The thaw offers up a world of pools. Year after year. All that you altered eventually returned to what it had been before. You but passed through, hastening as always into an older body, older interests, older desires.'

'You speak with the voice of a crone, Renarr, not a woman half my age. In your company, I am belittled. How then was this wisdom of yours earned? In the whores' tent? I should think not.'

*Perhaps, Urusander, beneath the eager weight of your son. Now there was a self-proclaimed god, far past the age when he should have abandoned the conceit. He settled his body on mine, pushed himself inside to my small cry of pain, and looked into my eyes seeking the twin reflections of his own face. Just as every woman he takes finds herself gazing up into his frantically searching eyes. A boy desperate to find the man he should have been. And no amount of thrusting cock can grant him that one benediction.*

*To your son, Urusander, every woman is a whore.*

'You confuse age with wisdom,' she said. 'The whores' tent was my temple. I paid in years for the blessing of moments. While the men and women who used me bled out worthless coin, and thought themselves absolved of the bargain's sad and sordid truth. Consider, sir, the abject failure that is sex without love. The act denigrates both flesh and soul, and all the gasps and moans that cut through the night cannot replace what was so willingly surrendered.'

'And what, Renarr, did you and your men and women surrender?'

'Why, dignity, I should imagine.'

'Just that?'

'No. If intimacy is a virtue.'

'And is it?'

She turned her head away from his regard, as if hearing a strange sound to one side, and this was sufficient to hide her unbidden and unwelcome smile. 'A fragile one, of course. Too fragile, perhaps, for this world.' The smile lingered, a thing of unbearable pain and grief, and then faded. A moment later and she was able to look ahead once more, offering the man at her side an untroubled profile.

'You confound me, Renarr.'

'There is an unexpected gift to my years of unrelieved education. But you know it as well. See us here, two dispassionate orphans. Uprooted before a flood of foreign ideas, unexpected discoveries and terrible realizations. Your eternal hunt for justice, sir, but circles a host of simple truths. We are all believers in justice as applied to others, but never to ourselves. And this is how we make virtue a weapon, and delight in seeing it make people bleed.'

'The imposition of law is civilization's only recourse, Renarr.'

'And in its inevitable exceptions lies civilization's downfall.' She shook her head. 'But we have argued this before, and again I say to you, make every law subservient to dignity. By that rule and that rule alone, sir. Dignity to and for each and every citizen, each and every enslaved beast of burden, each and every animal led to slaughter – we cannot deny our needs, but in serving those needs, we need not lose sight of the tragedy of those who in turn serve us with their lives.'

'The people are never so enlightened, Renarr, as to comprehend such a thing.'

'A judgement inviting your contempt.'

'Perhaps. But sometimes, contempt is all many of them deserve.'

Renarr nodded, her gaze on the army's vanguard. 'Yes. Too many gods and goddesses in this world, this world and every other.'

'I am a figurehead,' said Lord Urusander.

She felt no need to respond to that. Some things were too obvious for words.

'I fear Hunn Raal,' he added.

'So do we all.'

\*       \*       \*

Sagander fidgeted, his watery gaze darting again and again to the leg that was not there. He licked his lips, sipping constantly from a flask of water he carried in a pocket on the inside of his robe. The carriage rocked its occupants, sliding at times on slick ice covering one or two cobbles, crunching down with a jolt that rattled the shutters and made the dozen bright lanterns swing wildly on their hooks. Each jarring motion made the old man wince.

From beneath veiled lids, High Priestess Syntara watched

the self-proclaimed official historian of the Liosan. Here in this sanctified temple on wheels, she could read his innermost thoughts and with idle ease she plundered them. Each one was bright with outrage and venom, swirling madly around a vortex of betrayal, for betrayal was at the core of everything for poor Sagander. He blamed Lord Draconus. He blamed now dead Borderswords. He blamed Draconus's bastard son Arathan. But she saw for herself the blow he sent to Arathan's head, the boy reeling in his saddle, stunned into witlessness. She saw Arathan's horse attack, saw its hoofs stabbing savagely down, heard the snapping of bones.

No one else was to blame for the loss of that leg – no one but Sagander himself, and of course that was something he could not – could never – admit. It was pathetic, the raving accusations of an ego blind to its own lies. And the manner in which a thousand exculpatory words could drown out a simple truth was something that made her thoughtful, as they drew ever nearer to the Valley of Tarns.

They were fast approaching the time when the shout of words would give way to the shout of swords. She would finally discover the extent of Hunn Raal's sorcerous power, and that was the source of some trepidation. No matter how certain her own faith and no matter the vast reach of her own magic, the Mortal Sword of Liosan posed a threat, and with this recognition she discovered a new irony, in that the only obstacle blocking Hunn Raal's true ambitions was Lord Vatha Urusander.

*Our reluctant Father Light, who already moves like a puppet, confounded by a tangle of strings. Still, a throne waits for him, and once Urusander is seated in it, Hunn Raal can reach no higher.*

Her secret missives with Emral Lanear made it clear that both High Priestesses understood the politics of what was coming. *This very evening I shall ride into Kharkanas, and in the company of Urusander's Legion shall cross the bridges and claim the Citadel. And I shall be met by Emral Lanear, and before all we will embrace like old friends.*

*And in the Chamber of Night, Mother Dark will have to*

*acknowledge us. She will have to face us, and accede to the inevitable.*

'This battle shall be glorious,' said Sagander suddenly, startling both Syntara and a dozing Sheltatha Lore. Tathe Lorat's daughter had been injured while on the march, when a slipping horse inadvertently stepped down on her foot, breaking bones. She now sat directly opposite Sagander, her bandaged foot occupying the space where his missing leg would have been, and Syntara knew well that the pose was not accidental.

*Venal child. I am of a mind to give her to Emral Lanear, as she'd make a fine temple whore. Her and her new tutor, Renarr. Such women are worthy of contempt and little else. But they have a value nonetheless, as things to be used.*

'I shall witness,' Sagander went on. 'And record, as befits a proper historian.'

'There may be no battle,' said Syntara.

Sagander frowned, then took another sip from the flask and licked his lips. 'Winter's dry air is a curse,' he muttered, and then shook his head. 'High Priestess, of course they will fight. Their backs are to the wall – hah, the city's wall, in fact.'

'The highborn still hold their lands and their wealth,' Syntara pointed out. 'To gamble all that upon a single field . . . no, they are not all fools, historian. They'll not make it so easy to dislodge them from their privilege. I would hazard,' she concluded, 'they will choose to bide their time. Once we crowd in, and days turn into months, they will begin sowing discord.'

'The Legion's loyalty—'

'Ends when the Legion is dissolved,' she said. 'Once that happens, avarice and acquisitiveness will burgeon. Friends will fall out.'

'We need only pronounce an expansion of our borders,' Sagander said. 'This will ensure there is enough land to go round.'

Sheltatha Lore snorted. 'Historian, look at a map before speaking so foolishly. Our borders are rough things for a

1023

reason. We are surrounded by poor land, once home to wild herds that are no more. Wherever settlers tried to break the soil, they failed. To the north are the Jheleck, already pushed as far as they can go – if we renew that war, sir, we will be facing a most desperate enemy and it will be a fight to the death with no quarter possible. But oh, that's right, we won't have our legion any more, will we? The east belongs to the Vitr's foul influence, while the Forulkan are to the south. West? Ah, but you know that path well enough, yes?'

Sagander's frown was now a scowl. 'Do not presume to know more than your betters, child. I am well aware of our geographical limits. The push must be south and west. As you say, I do know, firsthand now, the land of the Azathanai, and I tell you: they have yielded it. And to the south, well, the Forulkan are defeated. They live in fear of us.' He waved a hand. 'The fighting that may come of that we can leave to the Hust Legion.'

'Yes, of course.' Sheltatha smiled. 'And it will be most informative, I should think, watching them today, these embittered prisoners and cast-offs.'

'In any case,' Sagander said, 'we need only clear the forests to find more arable land.'

'And the fate of the Deniers?'

'You have not been paying attention,' Sagander snapped. 'Most of the women and children have been slaughtered. No, their time is done, and like so many other forest creatures, they will fade away.'

'And you admit no pity for them, historian?'

'Pity? A waste of effort.'

'Yet not,' Sheltatha said, 'when it comes to your own infirmity.'

Sagander glared at her.

'Be silent, Sheltatha,' said Syntara with a weary sigh. 'We all have our appointed roles, after all, to occupy our thoughts. Look to yourself instead, and the destiny soon to find you.' She smiled across at the young woman. 'I see you already spreading your legs in a temple cell – shall we make you a gift to Mother Dark?'

'Well, Syntara, who knows? I'll see if your old cell is still there, shall I? Though I imagine the sheets will need a thorough washing, with a nice flat rock to beat out the worst of the stains, if such a thing is even possible.'

In cold fury, Syntara lashed out, a sorcerous eruption of raw power meant to strike Sheltatha in the face. Instead, it was somehow shunted aside, slamming into the carriage door's shutters. Splintered wood exploded within the confines, slivers striking both Sagander and Syntara. Crying out, the High Priestess reached up to her face and felt splinters jutting out from her cheeks. Uncomprehending, she pulled her hands away and stared at the fresh blood covering them.

Sagander, in the meantime, was clutching at his throat, where a large shard of wood jutted out, and blood pumped in fast spurts, spilling down into his lap. Syntara frowned across at the historian. That was too much blood, and there was horror in the man's eyes.

Unscathed, Sheltatha stared at Sagander too, expressionless, watching as the man choked, and then drowned in a welter of red.

The carriage had rocked to a halt moments after the flare of magic, the horses screaming in shrill fear. Now the battered door was yanked from its weakened hinges, and Infayen Menand leaned in. Her flat eyes scanned the wreckage within, and then, as Sagander sagged down in his seat, she reached out and dragged the historian outside.

Syntara saw the woman drop the old man's body to the cobbled road, glance down at it briefly as others quickly gathered round, and then lean back into the carriage, her gaze fixing on the High Priestess.

'Not blinded? Lucky you. But really, unleashing magic inside a carriage? What possessed you to display such stupidity, High Priestess?'

When Syntara struggled for an answer – still shocked by the blood on her hands, the wet trickles upon her cheeks – Sheltatha Lore said, 'Captain, I think I'd prefer to ride my horse, painful as that might be.'

Infayen blinked at the young woman. 'While you are untouched. Curious.'

'Her temper missed its mark. Now, will you lend me an arm, captain?'

With another glance at Syntara, and then a shrug, Infayen reached up to help Sheltatha climb out of the carriage.

Leaving Syntara alone with her wounds, and the soaked cushion seat opposite her, which still dripped.

In near hysteria, the High Priestess screamed for her servants.

*     *     *

Renarr remained on her horse while Lord Urusander dismounted to crouch down beside the dead historian. From her vantage point, she could see Hunn Raal riding back from the vanguard.

A half-dozen priestesses had crowded into the carriage, from which Syntara's harsh voice still rang out its shock and fury. Captain Infayen Menand was helping Sheltatha Lore to a waiting horse, but the limping woman seemed otherwise unharmed and free of blood-spatter, and nothing of her comportment evinced the horror of what had just happened within the carriage.

Renarr's eyes narrowed on her student for a moment longer, and then Hunn Raal reined in alongside Infayen. Low words were exchanged, before the Mortal Sword dismounted and moved to where Urusander was now straightening above Sagander's corpse.

'Commander, the High Priestess?'

Urusander frowned. 'A few cuts, I am told. Nothing more.'

'To her face, one presumes,' Hunn Raal said, something in his tone hinting at amusement. 'I have sent for a Denul healer – it wouldn't do to have such beauty permanently marred, would it now? Especially on this auspicious day.'

Urusander seemed to study Hunn Raal before saying, 'Auspicious, captain? Poor Sagander here marks the first tragic, meaningless death on this day, but not, unfortunately, the last.'

'Blood is always the price,' Hunn Raal said, shrugging. 'For anything worthwhile, that is. Come now, commander, are we not soldiers? And who better would know the truth of what I say?'

'Sorcery claims its first victim,' Urusander said, 'but, presumably, not the intended one. Heed the lesson, captain. Control is but an illusion – sorcery is indifferent to how it is used.'

'An expert now, commander?' Hunn Raal asked with a smile.

'No, just clear-eyed. Not eager to surrender my reason, my ability to think. Of course, Raal, you've had decades of practice in dulling your wits.' Dismissing the man, Urusander swung round and returned to his horse. With his back to Hunn Raal, he saw nothing of the Mortal Sword's momentary glare, before the easy smile reappeared.

Renarr's attention now fixed upon Sagander. The blood looked black in the weak gloom, like a strange beard covering the man's chin and neck. His eyes were still open, but now only partly so, the lids settling halfway down. She thought of all the fires that had burned behind those eyes only moments ago. *Defiant in every surrender, as befits an ageing man. For the right ones, a laudable resolve, sufficient to earn respect and dignity. For one such as Sagander, alas, far too infused with envy and self-pity. No matter – all is dull now, every flame quenched.*

*A man of accidents, was Sagander. Our historian is dead, but make of that no ill omen. He just failed at luck. And that is a failure awaiting us all, sooner or later.*

Urusander mounted his horse and settled into the saddle. 'Blood in the temple,' he said. 'Inauspicious.'

She glanced at him. 'The High Priestess wields a dull knife.'

'Your meaning?'

'Expect nothing subtle. Not in this magic so harshly blessed by Light.'

'Abyss take us,' Urusander said in a low voice, 'I will stop this battle.'

Renarr shook her head. 'And if you should die, by design or' – and she gestured down at Sagander's body, which soldiers were now lifting from the road – 'mischance, who will step forward to claim the throne? Who will reach, in your stead, for Mother Dark's hand?'

Urusander said nothing, but he watched as Hunn Raal rode back towards the vanguard.

'Warn her,' Renarr said. 'Warn her about the Issgin bloodline. Proclaim your heir as soon as you can and leave no doubt.'

Urusander flinched. 'My son is nowhere to be found. And if he was here at my side . . . ah, still I would hesitate.'

'An absent heir is in fact ideal, is it not?'

He stared at her, for a moment uncomprehending. She looked away, to wait it out.

The horns sounded, and it was time to resume the march. Sagander's body now sprawled in careless repose by the roadside. The first of the crows that had been tracking the Legion landed in the muddy field close by, heads cocking as they regarded the waiting feast. Their time would be short, as the army's train included grave-diggers, near the back of the column.

It didn't take much courage for the first crow to hop closer, but what followed Renarr did not see, for she had already ridden past. *Ah, now, a life dismissed. As easy as that.*

Shortly after, even as the rim of the valley opened out ahead of them, Lord Urusander said, 'As you said, Renarr, as you said.'

She wondered why she bothered.

\*       \*       \*

Tathe Lorat could feel the heat of her fury, like a fever beneath the skin. A score of survivors from her husband's company had finally caught up with the Legion, bearing news of the disaster. The fool was dead, his soldiers slaughtered in the manner of beasts. The Deniers of the forest had won a great victory, but she knew it would be short-lived.

*We officers of the Legion are to be given land, holdings.*

*Where else but in the forests? We will cut down every tree
and leave the Deniers nowhere to hide. We'll ride them down
as if they were no more than rabid curs. I'll see them skinned,
their hides tanned, and make banners for my Houseblades.*

*Still . . . to be honest, he wasn't much of a husband. Slow
of wit, a man who delighted in the thought of my spreading
my legs for other men – well, there are worse flaws than that,
I suppose. Once I settled into it. Once I gave up the notion
of driving him into outrage. Once I understood that I couldn't
hurt him, no matter how hard I tried.*

*Betrayal loses its heat with an indifferent, uncaring victim.
He smiled the first time I announced that I'd taken to another
man's bed. That smile stung – oh, how it stung! After that, it
got easier, but something was gone from it. The excitement
of deceit, of forbidden lusts, all of that went away. Until all
I had left was the novelty.*

*He thought to give me to Hunn Raal. If Raal had invited
me to his bed I would have done it, with a knife hidden in my
sleeve. I would have slit the drunk's throat, and now we'd be
free of him and his sorcery, free of this new tyranny.*

*Lord Anomander, I'll not dissuade you should you reach
Hunn Raal. I'll not defend the bastard. Mother Dark, hear
my prayer though my skin is white, though I am Liosan!
Grant your First Son the power to defy Hunn Raal's magic.
Do this, and I will reject the Light. I will return to you. This
I promise.*

Infayen Menand rode up alongside her. 'A misplay of
magic,' she said. 'That one-legged scholar is dead.'

Tathe Lorat grunted but said nothing.

'It's on the wind,' Infayen said. 'Violence, bittersweet. Can
you not feel it, Tathe?'

'No.'

'Ah, the tragic news of your husband's death has left you
wounded.'

'I have no time to grieve,' she replied, scowling. 'My
husband's death has made me ill. Violence? This wind smells
of mud and little else. Oh, do not give me that shining gaze,
Infayen Menand, I know well the grisly glory you seek for

yourself. You enjoy killing, and that is not something I can abide.'

'And yet, can you not hear the mocking laughter of the Deniers?'

'I hear that well enough, but they shall have to wait for my vengeance. And should I make it one of horror, they have earned it. I may yield to satisfaction, once I am done, but no gleam shall light my eyes.'

'War is simple,' Infayen Menand said. 'This is why I love it so. Free yourself of all restraint in what is to come, Tathe Lorat.'

'I will keep my head, thank you. We have grievances with the highborn and today they will be made to answer for them. They are one and all servants of Mother Dark, and she is to blame for this day. Her and none other. Those we face in this battle do not deserve to die.'

Infayen shook her head. 'But die they will. This is not the time for pity, or mercy. With such notions clouding your head, you will be killed in the valley below.'

'I will defend myself but no more than that,' Tathe said, startled by her own decision. 'You are too quick to cast away your respect for those about to face us. Lord Anomander, Draconus, Silchas Ruin. Have you forgotten how they fought at our side? Is it so easy for you to find hate for those who were once your friends? Be assured, I will bear that in mind.'

Infayen Menand laughed. 'You were never my friend, Tathe Lorat. I've no time for sluts.'

Tathe Lorat smiled. 'I have often wondered at that.'

'At what?'

'You and your kind, so quick to judge.'

'What "kind" would that be?'

'Fish-cold, frightened of love and quick to point a finger, when what you truly feel is envy, at my freedom, my willingness and all the pleasures I embrace.'

'As you pushed your daughter into a man's arms.'

'Oh, is that what is bothering you? Do not be deceived by Sheltatha and her airs of sophistication. She begged me

1030

the first time, and after that, there was no stopping her.'

'I do not believe you.'

*Well enough, but Infayen, did you really think I would tell you the truth of what lies between me and my daughter? As you point out, we're not friends.* 'Think what you like, then.'

They reached the valley, the cohorts spilling out from the old road and forming up along the crest, and for the first time Tathe Lorat saw the enemy arrayed upon the opposite side. The highborn were there, with all their Houseblades. She didn't think she had quite believed that would happen. And there, holding the centre, the Hust Legion. Her gaze narrowed on those solid ranks. *Are they drugged? Prisoners, criminals, they should be agitated, nervous, terrified. They should be rioting even now.* Instead, the ranks were motionless, the only movement coming from the three standards raised above the companies, where the faint wind rippled the dark cloth.

Infayen said, 'The wind moans its promise of—'

'You fool!' Tathe Lorat snapped. 'That's not the wind moaning. It's the Hust swords – look, they're drawn!'

          \*     \*     \*

The soft keening filled the air, as if iron could know pain, and pain could rise and twist like threads, weaving a tapestry to trap this moment, binding every soul of the Hust Legion. Wareth stood motionless, feeling himself circling an emptiness inside, wondering if the absence within him announced an end to things, a fate, his future wiped clean. *A future without me, without Wareth of the Pits, the coward, the fool. Just a name now, uttered by the survivors, at least in passing, and soon to be forgotten.*

*Like so many others.*

It was no wonder the Hust iron mourned, for surely that was what this sound was, all these voices making the noise that precedes a sob, and he waited for that wrung-out cry with trembling limbs, his hands feeling drained of blood, his legs watery beneath him.

He wore his helmet now, as did his fellow soldiers of the

Hust. The hinged cheek-guards were locked in place, shutting out most of the world to left and right, barring a curved gap at eye-level that Wareth found far too narrow for his liking. The keening of the iron filled his ears, but there was a coldness to this intimacy, as if it whispered like a lover who promised nothing but grief.

His fear circled the emptiness, terrified of slipping and plunging into that unknown. Yet the panic he felt was somehow constrained, trapped in its mad circling. There was nowhere to run to, no 'away' in the midst of this press of bodies. He had believed that he would escape this fate, remaining among the commanders in their place at some high vantage point, well away from the actual fighting. Instead, Toras Redone had seen through him, her sodden gaze too knowing, her recollection of him uncanny in its detail. *What source her omniscience? How so easily her striking home, and that smile! She knew too well my mind, this drunken goddess. Who now cups my soul in one hand, rolls me to the fore, no less and no more than just another piece in this dread game.*

He imagined himself now, a skein of tangled threads at the mercy of the artist, woven in fate, just one more life made immortal in this panoply of stupidity. He saw his likeness upon a greasy wall, almost lost in some wick-addled corridor, a thing to pass in life's bright-spark scurry, while his own colours dulled to candlesmoke and dust, and the knotted threads of his eyes faded to the senseless march of decades, and then centuries.

*What manner the ritual of those Bonecaster witches? What truth now caps my soul, set down by their infernal dance? I see it blank. I circle it in terror, fearing my fall, my steps round and round in furious haste, tottering, slipping, catching, wheeling and reeling – oh, gods!*

As the iron wept, the prisoners stood unmoving and made no sound, not a mutter, not a sigh. While, upon the other side of the valley, Urusander's Legion shook out to form solid ranks. Bleached faces in the distance, iron polished almost white, now the hue of bone in the faltering light.

*Wareth of the Pit, oh yes, he fell that day. 'Tis said the artist caught him, there in that front line of the Hust Legion. Toras Redone promised the coward a quick death. There was mercy in that, don't you think?*

*Prazek and Dathenar? Why, they held the flanking companies. But in that moment – so I'm told – even they said nothing. The poet soldiers were struck silent, muted by the iron's grief. And that sound! From the helm, piercing the skull to run riot in the brain – that was no battle cry! That was no promise of glorious victory. The Dog-Runner witches cursed them one and all, those poor fools of the Hust!*

'But you don't know,' he whispered. 'You weren't there. The witches promised us truth, and we were on the edge of it. Here, in this moment. We all felt it. We all trembled before it. And the iron? This dread keening? Why, it is the sound of knowing.'

*The Hust iron grieves, and it grieves for us.*

He looked across at the enemy ranks, and felt pity.

*   *   *

Renarr rode with Lord Urusander to where Hunn Raal and the other captains now gathered, positioned centrally as the Legion assembled in ordered ranks along the ridgeline to either side. She reined in a few moments before Urusander and watched him continue on, pushing his horse forward until he reached the very edge, where he stared across at the enemy.

'They mean to make a fight of this,' Hunn Raal said, his voice carrying. 'Or so they would have us believe. I for one am unconvinced.'

Renarr saw Urusander glance at Hunn Raal, but he said nothing and a moment later returned his attention to the ranks lining the far side of the valley.

'I see Lord Anomander's standard!' said Infayen Menand, half rising in her stirrups. 'He defies Mother Dark! Mortal Sword, I beg that you allow my company to face him!'

Hunn Raal laughed. 'As you wish, captain. Ride to your

cohort, then. Inspire them with a bold speech. Promise them glory and loot. Go on, Infayen, lift yet again the honour of the Menand bloodline.'

She studied him quizzically, as if uncertain of his tone, but then wheeled her horse round and set off.

Still smiling, Hunn Raal raised a flask to his lips and drank down three quick mouthfuls. 'Lord Urusander,' he said, 'glad you could join us. Under normal circumstances, I would of course yield to your genius for tactics and whatnot. Alas, this will not be a battle for clever manoeuvres. Even your legendary cunning, commander, will but flail in what is to come.'

'You remain determined to bring sorcery to this battle, Hunn Raal?'

'I do, Lord Urusander. We are past a *civil* war. Now, two faiths are about to collide. Which camp of the faithful has prepared best for this? Let's find out, shall we?'

'And if your magic is answered in kind, captain?'

Hunn Raal shrugged. 'Make your faith a wall against which the enemy will scrabble, desperate for purchase, eager for a breach. The strength of your belief is proof against such things.' He twisted in his saddle to regard Urusander. 'Do you doubt me, sir?'

'And will the confession of doubt see my corpse laid out in the field below?'

Hunn Raal shrugged. 'I do not anticipate you riding down into the press, sir. If you do, no assurances are possible.'

'And the failing shall be mine.'

'Make your faith a wall.'

Urusander said nothing for a moment, as if considering all that hid behind Hunn Raal's words, and then he seemed to cast away all that troubled him. 'Walls may shield you, but they blind you as well, Hunn Raal. Will you make faith synonymous with ignorance? If so, I shall with great interest observe this battle, and, to your satisfaction, I shall do so from here.'

Hunn Raal's laugh was easy, almost careless. He gestured and a number of his own guards edged their mounts forward, moving until they in effect surrounded Urusander. 'I acknowledge your courage, sir. Contrary to your promise, it has occurred to me that you might be of a mind to ride down into the valley, not with your soldiers, but alone, to parley with Lord Anomander. Seeking a path to peace, an end to this battle before it is even begun.'

Urusander made no immediate reply, and then he shrugged. 'I see now that peace is no longer a possibility.'

'Not here. Not yet. Peace, sir, will but delay the inevitable. We are here in strength. A year from now, with each captain off building estates and breaking new land, we become vulnerable. We need this battle. We need this victory, and we need to make it an overwhelming one. Only then will true peace be possible. More to the point,' he added, 'we need you on a throne beside Mother Dark.'

'So I am to yield command of my legion to you, Hunn Raal?'

'For your safety, sir, I will stand in your stead.'

A golden glow was building around the group of officers, and Renarr saw the approach of High Priestess Syntara, the refulgent light spilling out from her. Flanked by priestesses bearing bright lanterns on poles, she walked slowly, and soldiers parted for her, some fighting suddenly skittish horses. Unmindful of the jostling, Syntara strode up close to Hunn Raal, and then past him, taking position beside Urusander.

'Father Light,' she said. 'I will remain at your side here. I will be your shield against all sorcery.'

'She should be able to manage that well enough,' Hunn Raal said, nodding. He gathered his reins. 'Now, this miserable day falters. The time has come. Captains, to your cohorts.' Nudging his mount forward, he guided his horse to the crest. He then dismounted and set off, alone, down the gentle slope.

Upon the opposite side of the valley, Renarr could make out two figures, both on foot and both working their way down a short distance before separating and taking position directly below the two gaps in the army's three distinct divisions.

It seemed a strange way to begin a battle. In her mind's eye a memory suddenly returned, and she saw a bloodied girl chasing a boy with a stone; saw her catch up, saw her swing the stone down with both hands, crushing the boy's skull.

Where were the whores now? Rising on her stirrups, she looked until she found them, a ragged row well off to the right. Collecting her reins, she headed for them.

*Leave it to the whores to find the best vantage point.*

She had vowed to remain at Lord Urusander's side, but such a thing was not possible at the moment. *No matter, he will be safe enough where he is. Syntara will see to that.*

She was halfway to where the camp-followers were gathered when the first wave of magic ignited the dusk.

*　　*　　*

The horse's broad back creaked beneath her, shedding dust and seeds that whispered down through the woven grasses of its body. Sergeant Threadbare cursed under her breath, fighting against a shudder. Golems of twisted grass and roots, of twigs and branches – the horse was dead as the winter, and yet its limbs moved, its long head dipped, and the track beneath its bundled hoofs slid past as they rode towards the Valley of Tarns.

Beside her, T'riss was clad once more in her strange armour of woven reeds and grass. Hardly proof against the chill, but the Azathanai woman seemed unaffected by such things. Her long blonde hair hadn't seen a comb in a long while, leaving it knotted, ratty and wild, lending her an air of quiet madness, and Threadbare had come to believe that the unkempt halo of hair mimicked the scattered thoughts of the woman herself.

The cave that had been their refuge was far behind them now, as Threadbare's impatience finally succeeded in wearing down the Azathanai's distracted indifference. They had fallen into a kind of rapport on this journey. Threadbare found most of it nonsensical, but she had gleaned enough to feel a growing urgency, as if something terrible was about to happen.

'Tell me again,' she said, resuming her assault upon her

companion's obfuscation, 'what is so important about the Valley of Tarns?'

'The spirits whisper the name,' T'riss replied.

'Yes, so you keep saying.'

'And you know where it is. So we ride there.'

'Right.' Threadbare considered for a moment, and then said, 'You see, it's like this, Azathanai. I don't argue against the idea that ghosts exist. That is, I've never seen one. But even so, some places where people died badly, well, they stink of it, no matter how long ago it all was. It's not a stink you smell with your nose. It's some other kind of stink. And it seeps straight in and makes you feel awful. In any case, these spirits you keep listening to – are they ghosts?'

'Your words make them cringe. The world wears down. What once were mountains are now hills. Rivers change their paths. Cliff-sides crumble, forests rise and then disappear again. There are different kinds of life, and some of them move too slowly for you to even see. Unless you've been away, returning only to discover that nothing is as it once was.'

'How fascinating,' Threadbare replied. 'This thing about ghosts and spirits, though. You see, I'm of a mind to think that ghosts have nothing useful to say, nothing good, nothing pleasing. I figure that, mostly, they're miserable things, trapped halfway between one place and the other. I wouldn't follow any advice from that quarter, is what I'm saying.'

'Coming back,' the woman riding beside her said, 'foments a crisis. Has everything truly changed? Those rivers, the forests and the worn-down crags? Or is it just the world of the one who returns that has changed? The world inside her, that is. And so an argument begins, between the soul and this rock, or that hill, those trees. This sorcerous night, so powerful in shrouding the day. Anger builds, frustration mounts. Denial becomes a fever, and that fever begins to rage.'

The day was drawing to a close. Somewhere to the south was the rumble of thunder, a strange thing for the season. Threadbare caught the occasional flash of lurid light, flickering through the heavy clouds that grew darker by the moment.

'What do the spirits care about the Valley of Tarns? What's happening there?'

'They speak of an old man in a ditch. A boy is with him, and toy soldiers fight on the floor of the ditch. The old man casts the die. Soldiers fall. A most ferocious battle, and in the boy's mind he can see it all, every detail. He can hear the screams of the wounded and the dying. He can see the faces filled with fear, or pain, or grief. But the old man crows with every victory, even as tears track down his lined cheeks.'

'The spirits told you all this?'

'They watch. It is all they can do. But events far away have stirred them awake. Now they walk the earth, helpless. The time for their own war is yet to come.'

The first stinging spatter of sleet bit at Threadbare's face. Ahead, the clouds were unleashing their slivers of frozen rain in slanted columns that marched across the land. She pointed to the south. 'Azathanai, is any of this natural? That thunder and lightning – is that happening at the valley?'

T'riss reined in suddenly, forcing Threadbare to pull hard on the braided reins of her own golem, swinging it round to face the Azathanai in time to see the woman twist in the woven saddle, tilting her face upward . . .

. . . as three dragons burst from the heavy cloud cover behind them, low enough for both Threadbare and her companion to feel the roiling wall of air buffet them an instant before the enormous creatures sailed overhead.

Turning, Threadbare's gaze followed the dragons as they sailed southward into the storm. Her mouth was dry, her chest tight. She shot T'riss a wild, frantic look. 'What in the Abyss are we riding into?'

'Do you hear laughing?' the Azathanai asked, her brows lifting. 'The dead are laughing even as they weep. Why is that, I wonder?'

'You wonder? You fucking wonder? What is all this, damn you?'

T'riss shrugged. 'Oh, Light and Dark never liked each other. Worse than Sky and Earth. But, as must be obvious to anyone who cares to consider such matters, Life and Death rule us all. Unless, of course, Death forgets itself. I fear that has occurred. Death had forgotten itself. The ghosts are here and still here, because they can't find the gate.' She shook her head, as if exasperated. 'What a mess.'

'*What's happening at the Valley of Tarns?*'

'A battle. A battle is happening. The one everyone expected, but few wanted. Or so they claimed. But the truth is, blood-lust is a plague, and it has found your people. Oh well.'

Swearing, Threadbare yanked her mount around and, eyes narrowing to slits, glared into the sleet and the roiling clouds of the south. Driving her heels into the flanks of the golem snapped twigs and branches, but the creature surged forward, and in moments reached a gallop.

A short time later T'riss caught up with her, and swung a bright face to Threadbare. 'I had no idea they could go so fast!' she shouted, and then yelped with laughter.

'Get away from me, you lying witch!'

Surprise flashed in the Azathanai's face. 'I never lied, my dear, I but confused. There is a difference, you know!'

'Why, damn you?'

'Well, to keep you alive, I suppose. I like you, Threadbare. I like you a lot.'

*Abyss below, she's fallen for me! Stupid woman!*

T'riss angled her horse closer, until almost within reach, and said, 'But I admit to wondering, with not a little trepidation.'

'What?' Threadbare snapped.

'Those Eleint, of course. Worse than vultures, those things.'

*What?* 'They weren't summoned?'

'Summoned? Dear me, I certainly hope not!'

'Then what the fuck do they want? A field of corpses to feed on?'

'Not corpses, Threadbare. Magic. They feed on magic. Alas, there's far too much of it about, these days.'

'And whose fault is that?'

T'riss blinked. 'Why, mine, I suppose.'

'I should kill you!'

'Oh, don't think that – you break my heart! Besides, if it all gets out of control, you'll want me there.'

Threadbare glared ahead to the storm-wracked clouds, the incessant flash of lightning, and the now endless drum roll of thunder. *If it gets out of control?*

'Either way,' T'riss continued, 'let us hope that no more dragons come to the fray.'

'Meaning you can handle three of them?'

'Of course not, but if others come, there will be a storm like none other, and that wouldn't be good. No, never mind, my dear. Rather, let's think more pleasant thoughts, shall we?'

'Oh I am, T'riss. Believe me, I am!'

'Your expression breaks my heart!'

*     *     *

His body filled with agony, bruised and battered bloody, Endest Silann crawled towards the motionless form of Cedorpul. Steam rose from the deep furrows gouged into the slope of the valley side. Overhead the sky convulsed, the black clouds splitting apart to flashes of blinding light. The darkness itself was rent with strange slashes, through which the afternoon's setting sun cut without obstruction. Whatever sorcery had been cast upon the land by Mother Dark was now wounded.

The distance between them seemed vast, as if Endest had set upon himself the task of crawling across an entire world. The pain rolled through him in waves, still echoing the barrage of assaults he had just weathered. Upon the opposite slope, Hunn Raal was down on one knee, head hanging. He had flung wave upon wave of Light-filled, coruscating magic, tumbling it down the slope, tearing up the ground as it crossed the valley's basin, until it rolled up the slope in a surge to hammer into the two priests.

But they had held.

*Until now.*

The armies lining the crest upon either side had yet to move. Endest wondered what they had just witnessed. The sorcery, when at last it struck him, had at times lifted him from the ground, until he hung in the air, tendrils of actinic light tearing at him as an enraged child would savage a rag doll.

But for all that, nothing slipped past. Dark and Light swirled in deadly embrace, spiralling skyward to convulse in the clouds overhead. Flung back to the earth, Endest Silann had fought on, and a hundred paces to the west, Cedorpul had done the same.

Until the latest waves had crashed into them. Endest Silann had heard Cedorpul's scream, the sound like an iron blade scoring slate. He had caught flashes, amidst his own torment of defence, of Cedorpul's suspended body spraying out horrifying volumes of blood, and when at last he fell back to the ground he was limp, broken.

Still, Endest crawled towards his old friend, watched by thousands.

He could excuse it. Shock was a terrible force. Horror stole all strength from flesh and mind. Nothing was left. Every choice seemed impossible. The world had just tilted, and every soul upon it struggled to regain balance.

*This is the death of innocence. The child's world is gone. Torn to pieces. What follows? None can say. But see me here, squirming like a broken-backed snake. See me here, in your stead, my friends. Such power as you witnessed has brought us low. Every one of us.*

His grasping hands leaked thick, sluggish blood. His palms pressed down upon the broken, steaming mud and stones. He blinded her with every reach, but even that no longer mattered. Endest felt himself to be dying, and a dying man should be left alone.

*'My lords, we have failed you. Soldiers of the Hust, Houseblades, we have failed you. Forgive us.*

*'But no! Disregard this self-pity. We fail from a crisis of faith. Violent defence revealed the truth of that, just as Hunn Raal impugns the glory of Light. Ah, such weak vessels . . .'*

He crawled onward, as strange shadows swept over him. Head twisting, he peered up at the heavy clouds, squinted as he saw massive dark shapes wheeling through them. *My love, are you there? Turn away now, please. Do not look down.*

*Simple truths are often the hardest ones to bear. Dying alone is the only real way of dying, after all. The most personal act, the most private battle. Leave me to it, and if my strength holds I will reach my friend's side. I ask for nothing more. I seek no other solace.*

*Death punctuates this pilgrim's path. He should have known that all along.*

\*　　\*　　\*

'Dissension among the commanders!' cried the ancient lord, his knees now stained with mud, his hands strangely blue with the cold. He'd placed a number of the lead soldiers in a circle behind the ranks. 'Dismay has stolen the First Son's heart. Others hold him back – he would rush down to that dying man, the only one left. Sleet and fierce winds buffet them! Winter freezes their tears! He strains, fearless against the terrible sorcery!'

Wreneck stared down at the small figures to either side of the ditch. The advance had involved scant few of the soldiers, as the lord had insisted that champions must magically duel first. In the midst of frantic rolls of the knucklebones and triumphant cries from the old man, the sky lowered, and frozen rain began to pummel them. Shivering and miserable, Wreneck sat hunched beneath the torrent. Again and again he glanced to where he'd set down the spear, watched the ice growing upon its iron point, water trickling across the wooden shaft. In the meantime, the old man continued his tale.

'Here then,' he said in a ragged voice, 'is where the heart breaks. Old standards are raised. Honour, loyalty. Even . . . ah, that is most sorrowful, is it not? To lift high this last virtue, to utter its lonely name, and in its sweet shadow, ah, Wreneck, I see soldiers toppling by the score.' He fell back on to the slope of the ditch and stared up into the blackened sky, the sleet slashing at his weathered face. 'Shall we hear their words, then? They stand, almost alone. They face each other, and all that once bound them now unravels. And yet, such decorum! Such ... *dignity.*' He reached up filthy hands to claw at his face.

Wreneck studied the soldiers, and saw now that the old man had moved his 'dying' champion to the side of his fallen comrade; whilst upon Wreneck's own side of the ditch, his lone champion remained standing, ankle-deep in the mud. *Do I push him down too? Are we done with these ones, then?*

The thunder was gone, the last of the lightning had flashed and now sunset and gloom fought a silent war in the sky. The column of ghosts continued on, too many to even comprehend, but heads turned to watch them as they passed.

'One day,' the old lord muttered as he eyed Wreneck, 'you will become a man – no, make no spurious claim. You may wear the accoutrements. You may wield that artless spear and play at the dead-hearted, and make dull coins of your eyes, but these masks you don are too fresh. Your face is yet to settle into the mould it would so bravely display.'

Wreneck lifted his head, frowned across at the man as he continued.

'Cast in fire-hardened clay, an empty space defined, simply awaiting all that is malleable. By this means we pour our children into adulthood. Alas, too many of us prove unskilled in the shaping of that mould. Or careless, or so bound up in our own torments that all we make becomes twisted in its own right, a perfect reflection of our malformed selves.' He waved weakly down at the soldiers. 'Yielding this.'

'The world,' said Wreneck, 'needs soldiers. Things were done. People were ruined. A soldier gives answer. A soldier makes right.'

'You describe an honourable pose.'

'Yes, milord. Honour. That must be at the heart of a soldier, or a guard, or a city watch. You keep honour inside and it becomes what you defend – not just your own, but everyone else's too.'

'Then I must ask you, Wreneck of Abara Delack, does honour wear a uniform? Do describe it, boy.' He waved at the lead soldiers. 'Blue or green? Does honour wear a skin's hue? Black or white? Blue or grey? What if it wears all of them? Or none? What if no uniform can make such a claim for the one wearing it? It's naught but cloth, leather and iron, after all. It protects one and all and cares nothing for virtue.' He sat up suddenly and leaned forward, his eyes bright. 'Now imagine a new kind of armour, my young friend. One that *does* care. Armour of such power that it changes the wearer. A mould to challenge the set ways of the grown man and woman, a mould that forces their bodies, and the souls cowering within them, to find a new truth!'

Wreneck rubbed at his face, feeling his cheeks stinging with heat. 'Gripp Galas told me that Lord Anomander's Houseblades is a company that demands the highest virtues of its members. So the uniform *does* have a virtue.'

The lord made a face and settled back. 'Until it's lost. Iron is hard but words are soft. You can squeeze words, all those spoken virtues, into any mad and maddening mould. You can make honour drip blood. You can make honesty the destroyer of lives. You can make conscience a weapon of fear and hate. No, young Wreneck, I speak of an unyielding truth – look here, see my Hust Legion! I have discovered something, about my swords and my armour. The reason for their screams, their howls. It's not pleasure. Not bloodlust. No glee in the midst of slaughter. It's none of those things.'

'Then what is it?'

The lord's face suddenly crumpled, folded in on itself with grief. He fell back as a sob took him.

Wreneck stared down at the lead soldiers. He knew about the Hust Legion. He knew about swords that were said to be cursed. And now there was armour, too. He glanced back at the spear lying on the ground, the shaft and point now crusted with frozen rain.

He wanted to be away from this old man and all his tears and confusing words. Soldiers were needed, for when things went bad. For when people needed protecting. *Blue or green? Is the only difference the side they're on? What happens when soldiers stop protecting people? When they start protecting other things? And what if those things are awful, or cruel or selfish? What happens to honour then?*

'Dignity,' the old lord muttered again, as he began to weep in earnest.

'Milord?'

A frail hand waved carelessly, 'Advance your cohorts, child, and see us break like chaff before the breeze.'

'But milord, nothing has changed!'

He drew a deep, shuddering breath, and then shook his head. 'Everything has changed, my young friend. The game drips blood. Upon my side, priests buckle beneath the weight of their doubts. The goddess has no face – her darkness swallows all. Upon your side, the light blinds. We wage a war against our own irrelevance, which is what gives it such a nasty edge. Do lead your troops down into the valley. We can ignore the dragons for now.'

*Dragons?* 'Milord, tell me more about the First Son. Why does he argue with his companions? I don't understand.'

The old man wiped at his face, smearing it with mud. 'He is made to feel useless, with that sword he would draw. He is witness to a priest's death, torn apart by Kurald Liosan's indifference. He sees how power ignores the righteous; how it can be grasped by anyone – a blade in the night, a gesture that kills. His soul quakes, young Wreneck, and now the Consort arrives, and anger swirls, but dignity holds. Do you comprehend the cost of that?'

Wreneck shook his head. 'I don't understand dignity, milord. I don't know what it means, or what it looks like.'

The lord's red-rimmed eyes narrowed on Wreneck, and then the old man grunted. 'I see it well enough,' he said in a mutter.

After a moment, Wreneck began moving his soldiers down into the ditch's uneven base. Runnels of rain pooled in pockets here and there, where the frozen sleet gathered to build crystals, raised up like tiny castles. He knocked down many of these icy forts as he arranged the toys into something resembling a line.

'We'll see the mud red,' the lord said. 'Bodies will make

their own rain, crimson and hot. Cowards and heroes get lost in the mix . . .' He began moving his soldiers down to meet the enemy. 'Meanwhile, the highborn curse one another and then withdraw, exposing my flank on that side. They deem themselves clever, you see. Unlike the Hust, they hold to the privilege of choosing. If hearts break among them, they fail in turning this tide, this wash back into the sea of the future. Gone, Wreneck. I lie exposed. No matter, the Consort will take his Houseblades and ride to meet you. That clash proves a shock, for no other soldier is as well trained, or as fierce behind their lord.'

The old man leaned closer to Wreneck, his own eyes suddenly fierce. 'He had no choice, you see. You have to see that, don't you? Tell me that you understand. He had no choice! Nor did the First Son! They are of a kind, mirrors of honour.' He leaned back and set two soldiers on the ridge and made them face each other. 'Here, like this. Remember what you see here, Wreneck. No sculpture will render them in this pose. No painter will stroke their likeness on this day. Not paint, I say, nor marble nor bronze. Not thread, not song. No poem to capture this moment. Nothing, my friend, nothing but you and me. Their eyes meet and they accept the other, and now they ride down into battle, to reconcile themselves with failure.' His voice caught in another ragged sob and he wiped viciously at his tears.

'Will you cast the bones, milord?'

'What? No. No need. Cowards and heroes, the wise and the fools, the red mud takes them all. No matter. I once came upon a hare caught in a snare. It fought that trap. It sought to leap away, again and again – and when I knelt there beside it, I saw how its efforts had stripped the skin from its ankle, down to the very bone. And looking into its eyes, I saw something. A truth. Anguish, my friend, is not exclusive to people. Anguish is a language known to, and shared by, all things that live. Battle strips away everything until only anguish remains – even the triumphant cry betrays the echo of what is lost. Relief comes in tears to match any sorrow. The living bemoan their luck, the dying curse theirs. To survive is to stagger away in disbelief, and see before you a life spent in flight from this moment, the memory of this day and others like it. You run, my friend. Every veteran runs, on and on, to their dying day.' He flattened both hands over his eyes, clawing at his brow. 'Oh my, who dares face the tragedy of this? The survivors who must live with this . . . this *loss*.'

Wreneck watched as the lord, pulling his hands away from his face, began toppling his soldiers, slowly, one by one. Without the cast of the die, without a single triumphant cry. And now Wreneck too was weeping, though he was not sure why.

'Build your estates,' the lord mumbled. 'Clear the land. Plant your crops. Let loose your herds. Into your cherished rooms bring the finest furniture, the most beautiful tapestries. Thick rugs upon the floor, wood for the hearth, the squeal of playing children and mouths to the tit. Poets and minstrels to visit, feasts to invite, wealth to display. While in the dead of night, before ebbing flames, you sit alone, fleeing behind your eyes. Fleeing, and fleeing, for ever and for ever more.' He sent another soldier falling into the mud. 'Pity the victors, Wreneck. In winning, they lost everything. In killing, they surrendered their own lives. In all that they won, they murdered love, the only thing worth fighting for.'

'I fight for love,' Wreneck whispered. 'I mean to, for Jinia, who they hurt.'

The lord blinked at him, his face grave. 'Leave your spear,' he said. 'Run to her. Give back to her whatever she lost.'

'But – how?'

'Vengeance shrinks the heart, Wreneck. It is not a worthy path.'

Wreneck wiped away his tears, studied the toppled soldiers in the ditch.

'It's done,' the lord whispered. 'Strike the flag. Draconus has fled, his Houseblades cut down to the last. He weeps in rage, and darkness devours him. The Hust – my beloved Hust – almost half gone. A coward came to the fore, seeing the exposed flank and imminent slaughter. He rallied his fellow convicts and, with extraordinary fortitude, he led them into a withdrawal. Many who would have died now live thanks to him. Toras Redone – ah, my sweet Toras – I cannot say her fate. I dare not. The poet soldiers live still – the First Son will be pleased to discover that, I'm sure. They fought well, as expected, and now, unhorsed by battle, they walk with their fellow Hust. Weapons sheathed, the iron silent, they lick their wounds and look upon one another – it was the ritual, you see. That terrible ritual. It took away the virtues – every one of them. Honour, integrity, loyalty, duty – flung them away! Not one soldier among them can find comfort in the lies they would tell themselves. Those so very necessary lies, the ones that keep a man or a woman sane. My poor Hust!'

'I don't understand,' said Wreneck.

'Each soldier now faces the truth, inside and out . . .'

'Milord? What truth?'

'Only this: for all that they have done, there is no excuse. None. Justification sloughs off each and every deed. Nothing holds, nothing hides. Deceit is impossible. They have taken lives! Not just in this battle, but in all the battles they ever fought – the ones that sent them to the mines, the ones that wounded so many, the ones that made so many people – loved ones – suffer for what they'd done! This is why the iron mourned, you see. It knew what was coming.' He leaned forward once more, his eyes wide. 'Take a man or a woman, strip away all the lies they tell themselves, until they stand naked unto themselves, their souls utterly exposed. Then, make them *soldiers*. Tell them to kill. Do you see? No armour can defend them. No sword can be other than what it is – a length of sharpened iron that steals lives. Now,' he added in a hoarse whisper, 'see them walk from the field of battle. See their faces, there beneath the helms. See their eyes. I tell you, Wreneck, you cannot imagine the anguish writ there. You cannot. Nor can I. And yet, and yet *I see it. I see it!*'

They sat in silence for a time, unmoving, although it seemed that waves of pain struck the old man, making his face twist. Wreneck looked away from the distress. He scanned the lead soldiers lying in the ditch. In his mind he heard the wails of the wounded and the dying. He saw soldiers reel from the field, and just as the lord had described, there was something shattered in their eyes. While elsewhere others shouted in brittle triumph, as if each was somehow trapped into doing something they thought they were supposed to do. That pleasure. The satisfaction.

But the old man had spoken of relief. The wonder of it, and the quivering disbelief, to have survived by luck what took down so many. He remembered his own failure, yet again, lying on the ground outside the estate, curling up round the wounds in his body.

The sad thing was, he now knew, the dying still had things to do, things to say. The dying still had faces they wanted to look upon one more time. Pleasures they wanted to reach for, holding tight. The dying longed for all the embraces that would never find them, and theirs was a world of sorrow.

He thought he could hear the grieving swords of the Hust, the moaning helms and keening hauberks. They crowded each and every soldier of the Hust as they filed from the valley, in lines ragged and broken, with many helping their injured comrades. The iron gave voice to exhaustion, and all the things lost on this day.

For a moment, his will to go on faltered. When adults stumbled this badly, what was the point in looking up to them?

'Wreneck.'

He looked over at the old lord, and saw how one side of the man's face sagged, as if being pulled down by unseen hands. Even the utterance of his name had come out muddy, muffled. 'Milord? What's wrong with your face?'

'Mask. Broken. Listen.'

'Milord?'

The old man was slipping to one side, his right arm limp. 'Go then. If you must. Go. To your battle. Tell them.'

'Tell who? What?'

'My Hust. Tell them. I'm sorry.'

'Tell them you're sorry? Sorry about what?' Wreneck moved over to collect the spear. The shaft and its crusted sheath of ice bit into his palm, but as he tightened his grip, the ice melted.

The lord lurched to one side, closer to his line of lead soldiers. He struggled, face straining, to drag his left arm – the one that still worked – closer to the toys. And then, with one careless sweep of his forearm, he knocked the rest of them down. He settled on to his side then, head on his arm as if ready to sleep. When he opened his eyes, the left one was red, leaking. 'Sorry,' he said in a whisper. 'All done. All done.'

He fell asleep.

Wreneck hesitated, and then set down the spear once more. He crossed the ditch, pulling off his own waxed cloak – the one given to him by Lord Anomander himself – and settling it over the lord.

The wind clawed through the weave of his tunic. Shivering, he retrieved the spear and then stiffly regained the side of the road, joining the mass of ghosts still marching along it.

By keeping to the road's verge, he was able to avoid passing through too many of them, and once he quickened his pace, the cold went away.

# TWENTY-SIX

A S THE FIRST FLASHES OF SORCERY LIT THE EASTERN sky, the historian Rise Herat fled the tower's roof. Boots on the spiralling steps downward, taken at speed, a dizzying descent. Once upon the main level of the Citadel he traversed little-used passages and corridors, encountering no one, and then resumed his descent, until he found himself in the cavernous hall crowded with the failed sculptures of the past, the heaps of rolled-up, rotting tapestries, the forgotten portraits. Ignoring the bronze monstrosity of the snarling hounds – that had so haunted him the last time he had been here – he made his way to the stacked tapestries.

Some mindful cleric had tagged each roll, and in faded script had written the title and what was known of each piece, along with an index number of some sort. If the Citadel's archives held any master list, Herat knew nothing of it. Kneeling, he worked his way through the leather tags dangling from the ends of the rolls, squinting at the embossed script where the ink had faded to almost nothing. At last he found the one he sought.

It was a struggle pulling the tapestry from the stack, and his efforts sent many rolls sliding and spilling out to unravel upon the floor. The dust stung his eyes, made his nose run. He felt more than saw moths fluttering about, brushing his skin when he dragged the tapestry clear. Finding a stretch of unobstructed floor, Herat unrolled his prize.

Lanterns were no longer necessary. Darkness failed in hiding a thing. *More's the pity.* He stood and stared down at the vast scene stitched into the fabric. *'The Battle of The Storm in the Founding Age', artist unknown.* He had last seen it more than thirty years ago, though he could barely recall the context. Perhaps it had been found in a storage cupboard, during one of the many refurbishings of rooms that had occurred as the Citadel's population burgeoned with acolytes, priests and priestesses. Or upon a wall in some long-sealed chamber that had been reopened. The details hardly mattered, the title even less.

*What battle? What storm? What Age of Founding?*

He studied the swarm of figures upon the blasted landscape, the scores of flying dragons shredding the dark clouds hanging low over the battlefield. His eyes narrowed on the flanking hilltops, where stood the rival commanders of the two armies locked together between them. From one such figure, tall and martial, something like a stain, or scorching, marred the weave, blackening the air surrounding the man.

He'd thought it nothing more than damage, the bloom of rotting mould, perhaps, or where a torch had been held too close to the hanging. But now he saw, as he looked more closely, that the very threads were black.

*It's him. Draconus. The helm hides his face, but the manner of his stance betrays him. That, and the darkness, like smoke. I saw it today, as he strode across the Terondai.*

*Abyss below, what have we done?*

A voice spoke behind him. 'I sought you upon the tower.'

Herat closed his eyes, not yet turning to face her. 'Yet you tracked me here.'

'Your journey was reported,' Emral Lanear replied. 'This is my temple, after all.'

'Yes,' the historian replied, eyes opening again, gaze returning once more to the tapestry laid out on the floor before him. 'There is honour,' he said, 'and then there is stupidity.'

'What do you mean?'

Still he would not turn to face her. 'If in the course of our lives, we find ourselves in the same place, again and again . . . what lesson is not being heeded? What wilful idiocy obtains, proof against any self-examination, any reflection or contemplation? How is it, High Priestess, that a single man or woman's life can so bitterly match the history of an entire people?'

After a long moment, she moved up to stand beside him. Her attention fixed upon the tapestry.

'Draconus,' said Herat, 'has done this before. See him? That wreath of darkness he wears like a cloak – or wings. See the woman at his side? Who was she, I wonder? What forgotten ancestor embraced his gifts, only to vanish from all memory?'

'That is no more than a stain,' she said. 'Your imagination—'

'Is beggared by truth,' he said sharply. 'Blind yourself if you must. At last, I begin to understand.'

'What? What is there to understand, historian? We have done what was needed.'

'No, I think we have failed.'

'What do you mean?'

'We saw Draconus, Kellaras on his heels. They were setting out for the Valley of Tarns.'

'Yes, so that Draconus can retrieve his Houseblades.'

'But he won't,' Herat said. 'He can't. Don't you see? This is *his* battle. It's been *his* war, from the very start. We just didn't realize it.'

'You are speaking nonsense,' Lanear snapped. 'Liosan is to blame. And Urusander's Legion. Hunn Raal—'

'Failure finds myriad details, High Priestess, each one like a trap. Each one can snare you into believing the moment was unique. And so you are deceived into focusing on the details instead of the failure itself. In this manner,' he added, 'failures breed unchecked, unchallenged, and more often than not, unrecognized in what they all share.'

'Which is?'

He shrugged. 'The face in the mirror.' He heard her breath

catch, but continued remorselessly. 'This is a squalid revelation, High Priestess. Nor are we alone in our . . . errors in judgement. Draconus and the ways of love . . . it is my thought that, time and again, his ways of love become ways of war. Call him a fool – it's easily enough done. But even then, Emral, spare the man a moment of pity.'

'He was to be our only sacrifice, Herat. We set Silchas upon him, and what was done was only what was necessary.' She gestured dismissively at the tapestry. 'This signifies nothing, a web for your fears and overwrought imagination.' Stepping away, she said, 'I will leave you to struggle in its strands. I must resume my preparations for the arrival of my Liosan counterpart.'

He saw no point in responding, and simply listened to her dwindling footfalls.

*Ah, Draconus. You poor, misguided man. All that power, all those years – how many thousands? And still you stumble, your arms laden with gifts, your words forever lifeless in their entreaties.*

*Perhaps you Azathanai were too few, more an extended family than strangers inviting fascination. Perhaps, in your collective knowing, you all knew one another too well. Or perhaps, Draconus, your failure was and is a personal one, written deep in your bones and blood, in that heart too generous, too bloated with all it would give, and far too intent on the giving to receive anything in return. To make generosity into a weapon . . . ah, you understand nothing, nothing at all, do you?*

*Consider your friends, good sir, so few in number, so wary in their regard. Few could match your largesse. Of them all, only Anomander could stand as your equal, and even then, an equal measure quaintly discounting your secrets. Still, I wonder if he suspects . . .*

Herat could almost see them, there upon the ridge overlooking the Valley of Tarns. How, he wondered, would that fateful exchange play out? Terse in the manner of men for whom deeds and gestures mattered more than any words. A meeting of gazes, a recognition of intentions, and then, at the last, the simple nod bespeaking the tragic cost of all to come.

*Shall I write of that encounter? Am I not the historian, the caged witness behind the bars, flinching at the mad world beyond?*

*I see sleet slanting down from a glowering sky, a washed-out winter's afternoon, with only a hint of the coming storm. I see Lord Anomander turn from his steady contemplation of the distant enemy ranks – or perhaps, in the wake of dread magic, he wheels, his face twisted in grief—*

*No, let us hook ourselves upon the meat of this battle before the flesh cools. To dangle and spin in wayward regard. See Draconus, dismounting from a blown horse. With Captain Kellaras behind him, colours muted in such a way as to flatten him against the background, our lone witness bound in threads. Few others are present, none with the temerity to draw closer, to hear the two men speak. Only the captain, a face of black threads bleached by the passing centuries. His name will be forgotten, his role beneath mention.*

*Like the armies about to clash, he and they are but foot-notes, reduced to a sentence or two, or some rhythmic oration of set phrases to lay out the battle, the time of fever, stumbling to the knees, vanishing thereafter.*

*But he watches as the two men greet one another. They are friends, after all, and there is much for each man to recognize when looking upon the other. The future will fail in knowing this. A battle for a woman's affections, yes, that's summary simple enough – after all, what value motivations? It is the deed that is important. A lover upon one side, an adopted son upon the other.*

*And yet, nothing they say speaks of that. Indeed, I know enough to claim that such notions do not occur to them at all. Not at this time, not at any other.*

'Consort.'

'Lord Anomander,' Draconus replies, tilting his head in deference. The gesture is minimal, and yet for all that, Anomander's brows lift. The respect they have known for *one another has ever precluded such formal gestures. Anomander is indifferent to his noble blood. Draconus knows that, and knows as well that this is no mere affect-ation on the part of the First Son of Darkness. Nor is Anomander inclined to disparage privilege. The man simply dismisses the entire charade. For this reason, these two men are friends.*

*But now, here, something has changed.*

*'I see, milord,' Draconus continues, 'that my Houseblades are positioned upon your east flank. I see Ivis at the ready, wearing the mask of war.'*

*But Anomander knows nothing of the Consort's return to the world, or what bargains, if any, were made between him and Silchas Ruin. 'Indeed, Draconus. They present a most powerful fist, as Urusander's Legion is about to discover. And the gap between them and the Hust Legion is held by Silchas Ruin and my Houseblades.'*

*At that, Draconus turns, his gaze now fixing upon the far western flank, where foment now stirs the highborn command. His face tightens, but only for a moment, as his attention returns to Anomander. 'Milord, your brother came to me, as this day's commander.'*

*Anomander's gaze grows more acute now. 'I have drawn my sword,' he replies. 'I have taken my rightful place.'*

*'Then it follows, milord, that I must take mine.'*

*There is silence then, between these two men.*

*Is this how it was? As simple as that? The Consort rides to take command of his Houseblades, hard upon Anomander's eastern flank. The gathered nobles burst apart in mock fury. Stung by the offence, the western flank dissolves. Companies wheel, withdraw, march away in high dudgeon. And all at once, the outcome of the battle is no longer in doubt.*

Rise Herat turned away from the tapestry. He lifted his head, as would a drowning man breaking the surface, and looked round. Bronze and marble statuary surrounded him, the hues a sharp contrast. Great leaders, heroic soldiers, even a few scholars and figures of state. There was no order to the press, and as Herat studied them, he heard in his mind the rising clamour of battle. Amidst the flattened shadows of the chamber, his imagination woke to life every statue, as weapons were drawn, as the killing commenced.

He drew a sharp breath, silencing the tumult, freezing every figure in its tracks.

*Unless the sorcery was unleashed. Yet negated, made useless as Light locked jaws with Dark. Any other possibility obviates the necessity of any portentous moment. Anomander, Draconus, Kellaras, all of them shattered by infernal magic. And Hunn Raal strides across a field made into a charnel house. Even the victorious legion is silent, aghast at the carnage.*

*No. Instead, let us set sorcery aside. Every weapon will be met, by sword or shield. Fear and defiance, failure and triumph, the miserable dance is all played out. But even that is yet to come. Return us to Draconus and Anomander. The priests have answered Hunn Raal. Nothing has changed.*

'I despise sorcery,' the First Son says in a faint, brittle tone. 'Is this what awaits us? Will Hunn Raal and his kind make mockery of battle?'

Lord Draconus glances across at Kellaras, his expression unreadable. He walks to Anomander's side, and Kellaras edges his mount closer to the two men.

The two lords face the valley, where sleet is gathering in ribbons of dull white across the ravaged basin. Here and there, steam or smoke still rises from ruptured earth.

Draconus speaks. 'Will you deny me, friend? Have we not fought side by side before?'

Anomander seems to tremble a moment, before turning to the Consort. 'You seek my leave, Draconus? To what end?'

'If you command me to withdraw, I shall. But understand me, Anomander. I will have Ivis and my Houseblades.'

'You would break his heart, then.'

Draconus turns, slightly, to squint at Ivis in the distance where he remains at the head of his mounted company – and the captain's gaze is fixed upon his lord, as if but awaiting the summons. 'I see it. The fever has taken him. I should not be surprised at that.'

*Anomander nods. 'Urusander's Legion prepares to advance.' He studies the enemy ranks, and then asks a most fateful question. 'How fares Mother Dark?'*

*Draconus seems to flinch at Anomander's simple question. 'She refuses my presence. I fear she knows my mind, and what lies between us is now wounded.'*

*'Fatally so?'*

*'I cannot say. Would you have it so?'*

*Anomander shakes his head. 'No, never that, Draconus.'*

*A few moments pass, while both armies hesitate, while the sky loses its will and the sleet falls away to nothing, and a strange, exhausted silence takes hold of the dusk. Then Draconus says, 'I can make it right.'*

*Something passes over Anomander's face, as if he has just weathered a slap, but he slowly nods and then says, 'Draconus, I must name this love, this courage of yours.'*

*'I shall make it right,' Draconus says again.*

*'Take command of your flank, then, sir. Ivis and Silchas Ruin await you.'*

*'I shall lead my Houseblades,' Draconus says. 'Your own I leave to your brother, of course.'*

*'As you wish.'*

*'Anomander?'*

*'Yes?'*

*'We shall not yield.'*

*'No, Draconus, I expect not.'*

*'She will see that, won't she?'*

*Anomander makes no reply.*

*Draconus passes a hand over his face, and then adds, 'There is the matter of your brother, Silchas Ruin.'*

*'Draconus?'*

*'I rode here, friend, wondering if you had commandeered my Houseblades. If you had simply taken them from me.'*

*'Ah, I see. And if I had?'*

*'I will speak to Ivis on the matter. Anomander, I chose to believe otherwise.'*

*'Thank you,' Anomander replies.*

*'Your brother—'*

'*Later, perhaps,*' *Anomander says in a tone of peculiar finality.*

*Draconus studies his friend for a moment longer, his expression flattening with something like resignation, and then he turns to where his lathered horse still stands. He mounts up, and then rides out to the left flank to take command of Ivis and his Houseblades.*

Rise Herat blinked, and then wiped at his eyes. It was the briefest of pauses, and now the sounds of battle resumed, the jarring discord of blackened bronze and bleached marble, the statues trapped in their hopeless war. *Mere flesh betrays the armour and raging swords of the Hust. Prisoners, criminals, dying in the name of a civilization that has cast them out. Too ill fitted to thrive, and now they die by the score.*

*Ivis falls, fighting for his lord. Silchas Ruin rages, weeping as his sword flails at all who would draw near. Lord Anomander stands soaked in blood. He has carved a space around him, and sees at last the inevitable end to this carnage. He strides from the field, climbs the mud-streaked slope. Upon the ridge the standard of the Tiste Andii appears before him. He reaches the youth who stands holding it upright. Gently takes the tall, wavering pole from the boy's hand—*

*And Draconus? Nowhere to be seen. His body will never be found.*

*It is no easy thing to kill an Azathanai.*

Herat brought his hands to his eyes, plunging the terrible scene into blessed darkness. *And we have done this. Emral and I . . . Abyss take us.*

The standard tilted, and then swept down.

*Done. All done.*

With a cry, he staggered through the chamber, colliding with statuary, his eyes still covered by his damning hands. He fell more than once, scrambling frantically back to his feet. Disoriented, bruised and bleeding, he set off again, only to find himself lost among the towering figures.

They crowded him. With hands smeared in his own blood, they reached for him. Shrieking, he lunged and staggered about.

The chamber echoed his cries, until a thousand voices wailed in pain and grief.

All in the name of one man.

*        *        *

'She will see you now.'

High Priestess Emral Lanear flicked her gaze upward to see the Azathanai, Grizzin Farl, standing in the doorway. She lifted the mouthpiece to her lips and drew in another mouthful of smoke. She filled her lungs, feeling the familiar bite, the shock dulled to faint pleasure. Frowning at the huge, bearded man, she shook her head. 'I'm sorry, sir. Who will see me now?'

Almost shyly, Grizzin Farl edged into the room. 'Mother Dark. Your goddess.' After a moment, he shrugged and said, 'The wounded heart contracts, like the closing of a fist. She will see you now, and you in turn will see her. Out from the darkness, a manifestation of flesh, blood and, perhaps, tears.'

Lanear sent out a stream of smoke, and then snorted. 'A little late for that.'

'Such things do not pass swiftly, High Priestess, even for a goddess.'

After a moment, Lanear set the mouthpiece down and then rose from her chair. 'Has word come from Tarns?'

'Not yet.'

Seeing him hesitate, she cocked her head. 'Go on. No doubt, you have ways of . . . seeing things.'

He sighed. 'Lord Anomander has struck the standard. The battle is over. Triumphant, the Liosan now approach the city. Many have died. That said,' he added, 'it could have been worse.'

She sat back down, all strength leaving her legs, and reached a trembling hand to retrieve the mouthpiece. 'And . . . Draconus?'

'Gone.'

'Not dead?'

Grizzin Farl glanced away. 'Gone, I think, is a better word.'

1060

'Mother Dark knows this?'

'She has known this for some time, yes.'

Lanear smoked, studying the Azathanai through a veil of curling white. 'And now, she will see her High Priestess.'

'Yes.'

'Why?'

'I would think,' he ventured, 'preparations must be made. A wedding, yes?'

After a moment, she stood again, gathering her robes about her. 'Lead on, Azathanai.'

The journey did not take long. They exchanged no further words, and a short time later they stood before the door to the Chamber of Night.

\*　　\*　　\*

Surgeon Prok leaned against the sill of the window and used the palm of his right hand to melt the ice upon the thin, bubbled glass. 'The tower's flag has settled,' he said after a moment. 'Defeat. Surrender. Occupation. But then,' he added as he straightened and turned to Sorca, 'they are foreigners in habit only, and soon that too shall fade. I see an admixture ahead, and cannot but wonder at what spawn such union will yield.' He lifted up his flask and drank another mouthful of spirit.

Sorca looked around, moved to a plush chair and sat heavily. 'Beware the torch, lest your breath catch fire.'

'If my words are fire, it's a modest flame.'

She took out an iron pick and began cleaning her pipe.

Prok glanced at the door, through which Lady Sandalath and her daughter had departed but moments ago, on their way to that fateful meeting with her son. He had heard that two hostages dwelt in the Citadel, one a girl made mostly feral by neglect. Orfantal was the other. Sandalath's bastard child. 'I am fair drunk,' he admitted with a nod. 'Yet, what numb relief is offered proves a mockery to feeling. My heart still breaks, but no sharp crack issues forth. Rather, I faintly hear a dull sob. Such is the dubious gift of drink.'

'You know the signal of the flags for certain, Prok?'

He nodded. 'For my crimes. Somewhere to the east, the standard has been tilted. The defenders of Mother Dark have been broken.' He shrugged. 'Victory and defeat. Both states are frozen in time. The moment is flushed, and yet the bloom quickly fades.'

'You have seen too many battles,' Sorca observed.

'Yes I have, but I assure you, one is too many.'

She sparked alight her pipe. 'So, now. A wedding.'

Prok nodded. 'A celebration too solemn, too false. I see husband and wife standing inside a circle of sword-points. Shall they now smile? Clasp hands? Will the thrones indeed sit side by side? A royal chamber one half painted in light, the other drenched in darkness? Drink fails my powers of imagination, as ever, which I deem a blessing.'

'Is your curiosity as dull?'

'Not dull, just cold and lifeless. And you?'

'It will be awkward,' she said after a moment's contemplation. 'Fitful. Uneasy witnesses will struggle for words, strain to conjure the necessary smiles and congratulations. The ceremony strives but fails in the end. I for one am pleased to avoid invitation.'

He smiled at her with little humour. 'Us commonfolk will be spared the ordeal, although I imagine some public display will be in the offing. These symbols are necessary, if only to ease our anxiety.'

'Lady Sandalath's mind is broken,' said Sorca, squinting at the bowl of her pipe.

'There is a steep toll to trauma,' Prok replied. 'Her mind must distance itself, find a place of retreat. Possibly,' he mused, 'a childhood memory, some refuge.'

'She speaks like no child, surgeon.'

'No, I suppose not. Something has twisted in her soul.'

'Do you fear for the child?'

He shot her a glance. 'Which one?'

Sorca looked away, said nothing as she smoked. Then, abruptly, she spoke again, though her tone was laconic. 'How fares the ledger, I wonder?'

'Excuse me? What ledger?'

She made a face. 'Who died, I mean. Lord Anomander? Captain Ivis? What of Lord Draconus himself?' When he made no answer, she continued. 'I like the gate sergeant, Yalad. So very earnest, don't you think? And considerate, of the lady, and the girl-child. I hope he still lives.'

'It falls to that, doesn't it? Details of administration now, with you clerks and list-makers venturing out from the shadowy alcoves. Who gets what, who pays, who gets paid. Missives sent out to families in the countryside, regretful in tone, yet urging an everlasting pride in the ones who sacrificed their lives defending . . . whatever.'

She studied him through the smoke. 'You dislike my kind, don't you?'

He shrugged. 'The need for organization demands attention, once the dust settles, or, in this case, once the blood sinks into the mud. Do I dislike the clerks, so crucial to civilization's vitality?' He let out a breath. 'Probably. Scratching styluses instead of familiar faces, columns and lists instead of dreams and desires. Life's sacred wonder, reduced to notations. What do we give up, Sorca, with this need to organize, categorize, summarize?'

'Granted,' she said, 'mine is a soulless task, a task demanding soullessness, a task ensuring a soul's surrender. You cannot imagine, Surgeon Prok, the soul's slow death, in the repetitive twitching of a hand.'

Prok studied her for a long moment, and then he stepped close, reached down, and took her hand. She lifted her gaze to him, and managed a broken smile.

*     *     *

'Hello, Mother,' said Orfantal, rising from the bench. 'This is her? My sister.'

Sandalath stood near the door, holding the hand of the small girl with the raven-black hair and luminous eyes. Her eyes remained fixed upon her son, wondering what it was about him that frightened her. The steadiness of his solemn gaze seemed to drain all certainty from her, and she felt a burgeoning desire to abase herself before him, seeking forgiveness.

He strode forward then, smiling at Korlat. 'I'm Orfantal,' he said to her. 'Your brother. I'm here to take care of you.' He glanced up at Sandalath. 'Isn't that right, Mother?'

She shook her head. Waking nightmares had begun plaguing her. Something was stirring inside, all cruel edges and stinging rebuke, as if some part of her now hovered overhead, whispering down a host of unpleasant truths. '*You weren't good enough for any of them. The children he dragged from you, one failure after another. He pushed them through—*' She shook her head a second time. *He was a god*, she now replied to her other self. *He chose me. Me!*

'Mother?'

Sandalath nodded. 'No. She will protect you, not the other way round. Even if it takes her life, Orfantal, she will protect my perfect, beautiful child.' She paused. 'I may not always be there, you see. I may have to go away again.' She pulled her hand free of Korlat's grip, and it proved easier to do than expected. 'Take her now,' she said to Orfantal. 'I am going to my room.'

'Your room?'

'I have lived in the Citadel before, you know!' Her harsh retort made both children flinch, and Korlat hurried to Orfantal, and he took his sister into his arms and lifted her, anchoring her on one hip.

Sandalath saw Korlat's small, pudgy arms wrap themselves tight about her son's neck. 'Yes,' she said. 'That's better. I never planned on you, Orfantal. It was all a mistake. But now I see. There was a reason, after all, a reason for you. You count, but she doesn't.'

'I love her already,' said Orfantal.

'She'll grow past you—'

'I know,' he said.

'And she will protect you for ever.'

'Soon,' he said, 'I will be as her younger brother. There is the blood of an Azathanai in her.'

'No. A god.'

He tilted his head.

'A god, Orfantal! One who expects things from you, just as

I do. This god – you must understand this – this god has no patience. He despises weakness. If we're weak, he'll hurt us. Tell me you understand!'

'I understand.'

'Good.' Sandalath returned to the door. 'I have a safe place, a place for hiding. I'm going there, and locking the door.'

'Yes. Goodbye, Mother.'

She halted, glanced back at him. 'When everything burns, come and find me. In the tower.'

He nodded again. Satisfied, despite the tremble of panic behind her thoughts, she left the chamber. In the corridor she stood motionless for a moment. *The Citadel. I'm home.* Smiling, she set off for the tower, and her secret room.

*    *    *

It was the duty of one who failed in protecting anything to linger, kneeling in the ashes, and give some thought, once so much has been lost, to what little remains. Grizzin Farl was well experienced with this modest compensation. After all, if one could draw breath, then all was not lost. If one could find some remnant of hope, then the pain of grief was but transitory, and what burdens awaited settling would find shoulders capable of sustaining them.

But few of these platitudes did much to lessen the pain of acute loss, and all too often they could be raised up as barriers to feeling anything. At the very least, he reminded himself, Azathanai had not clashed in the Valley of Tarns, although it had been close. Nor had the dragons manifested into a storm of chaos, content merely to witness from the swirling clouds overhead. The magic unleashed on the field of battle had been modest, all things considered, but even this revelation had its price. A man was dead, after all.

'Have you nothing to say to me?' Emral Lanear asked him as they hesitated before the door to the Chamber of Night.

'What do you wish me to say?'

'You have been in her presence, Azathanai. Is she . . . is she reconciled to what must be?'

Grizzin Farl frowned. 'She . . . acknowledges the necessity.

1065

Under-stands the value of the symbol, that is. Liosan exists now. The Tiste fall upon Light or upon Dark. The manner in which the two manage to co-exist, here in one place, remains to be seen.'

'This was a civil war,' Lanear snapped. 'No one invited a new religion to the mess! But there, perhaps I am wrong. Your sister brought this Liosan – tell me, Grizzin Farl, how far you Azathanai intend on taking this?'

'Taking what?'

'Your manipulation of the Tiste. Or shall you now step back, denying the blood on your hands?'

'Denial is a waste of time, High Priestess. And, alas, there is no stepping back. Indeed, it is the very opposite. We are drawn.'

She blinked. 'And who is responsible for that?'

He looked away, found himself studying the blackwood door before them, this beaded barrier still to be breached. 'Not "who" as such, High Priestess. More like . . . *what.*'

'Very well, then *what* is responsible for your sudden interest in us?'

'We are poor at the finer emotions. An unveiling of all that is vulnerable in a mortal heart draws us in the manner of moths to a flame. Perhaps we seek some incidental warming of the soul. Or our curiosity is rather more clinical. Perhaps you but awaken forgotten appetites. Our natures are not unified, High Priestess. Each Azathanai is unique.' He shrugged. 'We have come to witness the breaking of a heart.'

He weathered the growing horror in her eyes, offering no defence.

A moment later, with a sudden gesture, she opened the door and strode into the Chamber of Night.

The Throne of Darkness awaited them, and the woman seated on it was expressionless, her eyes clear and cold as they fixed upon Emral Lanear.

The High Priestess knelt, head bowing. 'Mother,' she whispered.

'Stand. Face me.' Her voice was flat.

Emral Lanear straightened.

Mother Dark continued, 'Grizzin Farl, leave us now.'

'As you wish. High Priestess, I will await you in the corridor.' He turned and departed, closing the door behind him.

'Mother, Lord Anomander—'

'Is not of your concern,' the goddess interrupted. 'You shall place two high-backed chairs in the old throne room. I believe the raised dais is broad enough to accommodate them. One shall be of blackwood, the other bonewood. On the outside of the white chair you will set an embrasure. On the outside of my chair, an empty brazier, blackened inside and out. Also upon the outside of each chair, affix a scabbard for a sceptre. Coordinate these details with High Priestess Syntara. Lord Urusander and I will take upon ourselves the authority of this union, in the name of the realm. You and Syntara will attend as witnesses. For the ceremony itself, none other shall be present. A formal announcement afterwards will constitute the only public acknowledgement of the marriage. Three days of feasting will follow. Each and every Greater or Lesser House will give freely of its largesse.'

Emral Lanear listened to these instructions, delivered with an utter absence of warmth, and looked upon a face devoid of emotion. It was better than she had expected. 'Lord Urusander leads his legion to the city, Mother. How soon do you wish this private ceremony?'

'As soon as possible. Inform Lord Anomander that the highborn must convene. It is expected that Lord Urusander will wish to advance reparations on behalf of his soldiers, although it is likely that he will delegate in that regard. The Greater Houses must yield land, wealth and labour, but these are matters of administration and, one presumes, bargaining. Bring no details to my attention – I have little interest in how the carcass is apportioned.'

'And in matters of faith, Mother?'

The goddess seemed to flinch at the question. 'I offered you all an empty vessel, or so you imagined it. I was witness, then, to your varied ways of filling it. Yet what was hidden within, which none of you chose to see, is now displaced, and now, perhaps, must be considered dead.' She raised a thin hand. 'Are you eager for a list of prohibitions? For prescribed positions and holy ordinances? Am I to tell you the way to live your life? Am I to lock doors, draw close shutters? Am I to guide you like children, with all the maternal needs of a mother upon whose tit you will all feed, until your dying day? What words do you wish from me, Emral Lanear? A list of all the deeds that will earn the slap of my hand, or my eternal condemnation? What crimes are acceptable in the eyes of your goddess? Whose murder is justified by your faith in me? Whose suffering shall be considered righteously earned, by virtue of what you judge a failing of faith, or indeed sacrilege? Describe to me the apostate, the infidel, the blasphemer – for surely such accusations come not from me, but from you, High Priestess, you and all who will follow you, in your appointed role of speaking for me, deciding for me, acting in my name, and justifying all that you would do in your worship of your goddess.'

'From faith,' replied Emral Lanear, 'do we not seek guidance?'

'Guidance, or the organized assembly and reification of all the prejudices you collectively hold dear?'

'You would not speak to us!'

'I grew to fear the power of words – their power, and their powerlessness. No matter how profound or perceptive, no matter how deafening their truth, they are helpless to defend themselves. I could have given you a list. I could have stated, in the simplest terms, that *this* is how I want you to behave, and *this* must be the nature of your belief, and your service, and your sacrifice. But how long, I wonder, before that list twisted in interpretation? How long before deviation yielded condemnation, torture, death?' She slowly leaned forward. 'How long, before my simple rules to a proper life become a call to war? To the slaughter of unbelievers? How long, Emral Lanear, before you begin killing *in my name*?'

'Then what do you want of us?' Lanear demanded.

'You could have stopped thinking like children who need

to be told what's right and what's wrong. You damned well know what's right and what's wrong. It's pretty simple, really. It's all about harm. It's about hurting, and not just physical, either. You want a statement for your faith in me? You wish me to offer you the words you claim to need, the rules by which you are to live your lives? Very well, but I should warn you, every deity worthy of worship will offer you the same prescription. Here it is, then. Don't hurt other people. In fact, don't hurt anything capable of suffering. Don't hurt the world you live in, either, or its myriad creatures. If gods and goddesses are to have any purpose at all, let us be the ones you must face for the crimes of your life. Let us be the answer to every unfeeling, callous, cruel act you committed, every hateful word you uttered, and every spiteful wound you delivered.'

'At last!' cried Emral Lanear.

'You didn't need me for that rule.'

'No, Mother, we didn't. We don't. But now, at least, we have you to tell us that doing the right thing is actually *worth* something. Abyss knows, this mortal world rarely rewards such generosity of spirit!'

'Doesn't it? Well, if you believe that wealth and power are rewards, then yes, you would be right. Alas, they're not.'

'But those who have neither will suffer, often at the hands of those who do.'

'Alas, the wealthiest among us are also the most childish of us, in their acquisitiveness, their selfishness, their stubborn denial of the obvious truth that it is better to share than to hoard, for hoarding breeds resentment, and resentment will, in the end, get you killed. The face of the one sitting atop a hoard is a child's face, obstinate and stubborn. Is it any wonder such people would twist and distort any and every faith that preaches love?'

'Love?'

Mother Dark was silent for a long moment, and then she leaned back. 'Oh, Emral Lanear. Even when I but showed it, when I refused to give it a word, see how quickly it was poisoned by all who looked upon it. None of you could abide it, could you? It is yet to occur to any of you, I think, that in naming you all children, I was not being complimentary.'

'Then I deem you presumptuous.'

'As you will. As you will.'

'So, Mother, is that all? Our realm is now divided in its faith. You can expect Syntara to have taken her religion into that place of prescription and prohibition. She will have made her list, her rules.'

'Father Light shall prove more than just a title,' Mother Dark replied. 'As Syntara shall soon discover. I know Vatha Urusander. I admire him, and respect him. Syntara's present freedom shall not last. If I can give Urusander very little, I will at least awaken him to his newfound power. Beyond that, let there be justice.'

The promise chilled the heart of Emral Lanear.

\*     \*     \*

Heavy with mud and spattered gore, Captain Kellaras turned his head, blinking blood from his eyes as he scanned the heaps of dead and dying men and women. He could see where Ivis had gone down, ringed in the corpses of those who'd fought at his side, and those Legion soldiers who had surrounded them. Perhaps Draconus was among them, yet one more cold body leaking into the mud. But he doubted it. There had been strange blooms of impenetrable darkness, stains in the air. There had been a hoarse cry, filled with grief and rage, dwindling as if the one voicing that cry had retreated, fleeing, or had been somehow devoured by the darkness itself.

His dulled gaze now caught the scene he had been searching for. Lord Anomander, alone, stood watching the slow approach of Lord Urusander flanked by a dozen guards. The standard had been toppled, with nothing left but bitter formalities. *Alone at the last. Not even Caladan Brood remaining. Or did you send him away, milord? Yes, I think you would have.*

Kellaras sheathed his sword, its notched edge catching as he slid it into the scabbard, a thick welling of congealed blood rising up to gather below the hilt. Among Anomander's

Houseblades, but a handful remained. Of the Houseblades of House Dracons, he saw none standing.

*Ah, Ivis. I did not see you fall, forced to turn away at the last moment. The wonder of your charge finds glory in its failure – we can look to little else, we of the Andii, when seeking solace from this day.* Draconus and Ivis had led their forces deep into the enemy facing them. Their company had killed easily twice its number, and even the frantic flanking attacks from Urusander's mounted cavalry had done little to slow its advance.

In the end, alas, they were too few, even when joined by Anomander's own Houseblades.

*Ivis, did your lord abandon you at the end? I fear he did.*

Kellaras wiped the grime from his stinging eyes, no longer interested in seeing the official surrender, no longer wanting to witness his lord's humiliation. *The First Son deserves better than this. I shall look into the eyes of the highborn and await their flinch. But this is scant satisfaction.*

What seemed a lifetime ago, he and the Consort had ridden hard upon the road, with a terrible storm breaking over the Valley of Tarns. At the first pounding of thunder, Draconus had cursed, low and heartfelt.

*Neither lightning nor thunder. Magic. Unleashed.* Kellaras had expected to come upon a scene of unnatural slaughter. Instead, they had arrived in time to see the last desperate defence of two priests. Light and Dark entwined like serpents, jaws locked upon the other above the valley's floor. The final detonation that tore them apart sent both priests and even Hunn Raal to the ground.

But it was Hunn Raal who first regained himself.

Kellaras was not entirely certain who the surviving priest was. The man was covered in mud and streaming blood; his clothes were scorched and shredded. The path he made in his belly-crawl to his companion left a smear like the track of a slug. And the other priest . . . *Cedorpul. None other. And now, that cheerful young man is dead. He must be. No one could survive that assault.*

Where he and Draconus had drawn up their horses, Lord

Anomander stood ringed in a rough circle of aides, messengers and standard-bearers. Yet these Andii maintained a distance, as if Anomander stood alone upon an island.

Draconus and Kellaras halted. The ground was muddy, their mounts uncertain of their footing. Overhead the sky still convulsed in a miasma of sickly clouds through which shadows flitted.

Eyes fixed upon the valley below, Anomander shook his head. 'I must go down to that priest—'

'Leave him for the moment, friend,' Draconus said, dismounting. 'Your guards are correct. If Hunn Raal sees you draw within range, he will strike at you with what he has left. On another day, I could have swatted him down. Instead, I am weakened here. Incomplete, if you will.'

Turning, Anomander studied the Consort, and then tilted his head. 'Incomplete? No matter. Here you are.'

'You have taken command. What would you have me do, friend?'

'Do you censure me in her name, Consort?'

'No. It is said you have named your sword Vengeance. How sure is your rectitude, Anomander? I would think, thus named, the blade will demand from you a purity of purpose. Of course,' he added with a faint shrug, 'you will need to surrender everything else.'

'Will I? Draconus, have our vows gained veracity in this new, sorcerous age?'

'I should think so, yes.'

'Vengeance,' Anomander said in a musing tone, his eyes narrowing upon the enemy forces opposite.

'I have pondered,' resumed Draconus, 'the notion of a righteous blade. Not as would Lord Henarald and his Hust iron. I would value no opinion from my chosen weapon, merely a certain efficacy. Justice, should such a notion exist, must lie in the hand wielding the blade.'

'And how would you name your new sword?' Anomander asked.

'There is something inherently chaotic in any weapon. Do you see this?'

'If it lacks moral spine, then, yes, I see this well enough.'

Kellaras listened to these two men, their nonsensical, seemingly irrelevant discussion so at odds with the moment, with the ever-growing pressure of two armies about to clash. He wondered, for the first time, if both men were utterly mad.

'Then,' Draconus asked, 'will you this day draw your sword in its name? More to the point, *can you*? I spoke of what must be surrendered, lest your weapon fail you.'

'Friend,' said Anomander, 'your presence here is divisive.'

'I know.'

'We will lose the highborn. We will, in turn, lose this battle.'

'Will you send me away then, Anomander?'

'I mean to fight for you, Draconus.'

'Yes, I see that.'

'But, if you will leave here . . . take your Houseblades.'

'How can I?' Draconus demanded. 'And how can you, who would stand in my place here, invite such a thing of me?'

Anomander replied, 'I state what is possible, with no blame in attendance.'

'Your brother, I think, has little understanding of you,' observed Draconus. 'Nor, it seems, of me.'

'My brother?'

'It does not matter. We are here, and neither intends to yield. You would fight in my name. I, therefore, shall fight in yours.'

They stood in silence then. Until, after a time, Draconus stirred. 'I will join Ivis now.'

'Fare you well, Draconus.'

Climbing astride his horse, Draconus hesitated, and then said, 'And you, Anomander.' He rode off to join his Houseblades.

The First Son fixed his attention once more on Urusander's Legion. Soldiers had descended to help a staggering Hunn Raal make his way up the slope. 'Kellaras.'

Startled, Kellaras dismounted and joined Anomander. 'Milord.'

'What did my brother do?'

'He spoke to Draconus.'

'And?'

'He convinced him to flee.'

'Flee?'

'Draconus agreed. He understood the necessity, milord. But he would take his Houseblades into exile with him.'

'Only to discover that they rode with me.'

'Yes, milord.'

'So, he would flee.'

'In the name of love, milord, yes.'

'To force upon him that choice, Kellaras, was unconscionable.'

'Sir, we were desperate.'

Anomander turned sharply to Kellaras. 'You were party to this? You added your weight to my brother's entreaty?'

'Milord, I was witness. That, and nothing more. Your brother has little interest in my counsel.'

'Yet . . . ah, I see. Silchas led me here, after all.' He studied Kellaras for a moment longer, and then faced the valley once more. 'Very well.'

*Very well? That and nothing more?* 'Milord? Shall I return to Lord Silchas Ruin? What message shall I convey to him?'

Anomander now faced the left flank, watching as Draconus reined in close to Silchas. Once there, an argument began, but they were too distant, their voices too low, for anything to be heard. Despite that, Kellaras could see Ruin's shock and then dismay. An instant later, Anomander's brother was on his horse and riding fast – not towards Anomander, but angling behind the assembled ranks. He was, Kellaras realized, riding for the highborn.

*He'll not get there in time. They have seen Draconus. They have seen what has happened.*

'No message,' Anomander replied. 'Join my Houseblades, captain. You will be needed to act in my brother's stead.'

'Yes, milord.'

'Oh, and Kellaras.'

'Milord?'

'Place yourself and my Houseblades under the command of Lord Draconus.'

'Sir?'

'My friend is here in the name of love, captain. In the absence of anything else, is that not a worthy cause? No, let us take his side.'

Kellaras glanced to the far right flank. 'Milord, the highborn will not be so sentimental—'

'Sentimental, am I? Is love so paltry a thing, to be plucked and dropped to the ground at the first breath of contempt? Man or woman, disparaging love is a crime of the soul, for which the future will turn away its face.'

'I doubt they fear such a fate, milord.'

'They will learn to, captain. This I swear.'

Sensing a new presence, Kellaras twisted round and saw, a few paces behind them, the Azathanai, Caladan Brood. The huge figure was motionless, his expression revealing nothing. Following his gaze, Anomander grunted and said, 'I have begun to wonder where you were, Caladan.'

The Azathanai made to speak, but then lifted his face to the sky. A moment later he scowled. 'Lord Anomander,' he said, as if exasperated, 'there will be no more magic from the enemy on this day.'

'Indeed?' Anomander snapped. 'Then should I walk down now, to that brave priest below—'

'Send soldiers down to collect him.'

'Their lives are of less worth?'

'No. But you will be needed here, for the battle is about to begin.'

'Do you vouch for their safety?'

'In collecting the poor priest? Yes. In the battle to come, alas, no such thing is possible.'

'No,' Anomander replied. 'I imagine not. Unless, of course, you choose to awaken what is within you, as you did at Dracons Keep.'

'Milord, shall I slaughter your enemy then?'

'Can you?'

Caladan Brood nodded.

'And kill thousands. You would take that burden?'

Baring his teeth, Caladan Brood said, 'It would not be mine, would it?'

Kellaras sat frozen in place, unable to pull away from the conversation. On the far right flank, the mass of Houseblade companies had begun tearing apart, and among the highborn nobles there was chaos – into which Silchas Ruin now rode.

In answer to Caladan Brood's question, Anomander said, 'No, I suppose not.'

The Azathanai glanced again at the heavy clouds overhead. 'But I would advise you decide on the instant, First Son.'

'A single word from me can win this battle, and with it, the entire war.'

'It can,' Caladan replied.

'Returning Draconus to his love's side. Ending this incursion of Liosan into our realm. Saving even the precious possessions of the highborn.'

'Just so.'

A half-dozen soldiers set out, hurrying down to where the priests were now lying side by side, one dead and the other perhaps only moments from joining him.

'Am I a coward,' Anomander asked, 'to abjure from giving you leave to slaughter my enemy? If I refuse you, Azathanai . . .'

'You will lose this battle, milord, and many of your Tiste Andii will die. In place of that, sir, I offer you naught but Liosan dead. But as I said, time is short. Wait too long, and I will be matched.'

'By Hunn Raal?'

'No. He is still too clumsy with the power of Elemental Light. Another comes, and she is not far.'

Anomander seemed nonplussed.

Suddenly stiffening, Kellaras said, 'Forgive me, sirs. Azathanai, do you speak of one of your own?'

Caladan Brood sighed, and then nodded. 'She whom you have named T'riss. Content only with balance, I'm afraid. A sentiment plaguing many of my kin.'

'But not you,' said Anomander.

The Azathanai shrugged. 'You wanted peace, First Son.'

'My answer to all that I fear. My response to all that threatens me. Caladan Brood, you would see me become a tyrant in the name of purity, in the name of a peace that is maintained at any cost.'

'Yes, milord.'

'Azathanai, I must refuse you.'

'I understand—'

'Do you? I name that presumption, sir. This war belongs to the Tiste. Absolve none of us. Nor, indeed, is such absolution yours to give.' He cast Kellaras a glare. 'Ride on, captain, this instant!'

'Milord.' Kellaras gathered up his reins. Moments later he was riding for the left flank, and his mind was a storm of chaos. *You decry sentiment, Anomander? You damned fool, by what other name have you just surrendered certain victory?*

Ahead, he saw Lord Draconus, and at his side, Ivis. Both men were now positioned in front of their Houseblades, and it was clear that they would lead the charge.

*Not a coward's thought, not there, with those two fools. Abyss below. Sentiment!*

*Win her back, will you, Draconus? With this dusk and its suffocating madness? I fear not, sir, oh, Mother save us, I fear not.*

*     *     *

And now, an eternity later, the battle was done, and still the night held back, a drawn breath suspended in the firmament. Kellaras remained standing in the midst of the battlefield. Figures moved here and there, lending what aid they could to those fallen who still lived. Here, at last, it mattered not the uniform worn, as every piteous cry proclaimed no colours, and even the skin, cloven white or black, was made one in the mud.

Someone approached from his left, and Kellaras slowly turned, to see Silchas Ruin. He felt his own spine stiffening as he straightened, concealing the fury he felt behind his soldier's mask, his survivor's insensate mien. 'Milord,' he said.

'He struck the standard?'

Kellaras nodded. 'And now makes formal surrender.'

Silchas Ruin was wounded, blood thick upon his left shoulder. 'It was the highborn, Kellaras. Our betrayers. Mother Dark's own children of the blood. Did you see the Hust, captain? Did you see how they held? I'd not thought it possible. Convicts. Murderers. Truly that iron is its own sorcery.' He stood, now watching his brother in the distance. 'He struck the standard,' he said again.

'Milord, you are wounded—'

'This? Infayen Menand. She attacked while I was engaged with two others, sought to come upon me from behind, but I caught the motion.'

'Her fate?'

Silchas shrugged. 'She was a Menand.' He was silent for a moment, and then he asked, 'Captain, the Hust Legion – was their retreat by Redone's command?'

'I do not know, milord. Only that nearly a thousand of them lie dead, having not retreated a single step.' He hesitated, and then said, 'If indeed it was Commander Toras Redone who ordered the flag, she did the right thing.'

Silchas Ruin's stained face twitched in a cold half-grin as he studied Kellaras. 'Ah, captain, the world's torment knows ease with your opinion voiced.'

'I would think not, sir. Indeed,' he added, his voice hardening, 'on this day, we are the makers of this world's torment. The only ease granted now is named death.'

'And surrender,' Silchas Ruin said, his moment of contempt past. His eyes narrowed on the distant scene. 'Ah, now Hunn Raal comes to the fore. Spent, and yet even at this distance I see the smear of his smile.'

'Yes,' said Kellaras – though not bothering to follow Ruin's hard gaze. 'It seems there is to be a marriage.'

Silchas Ruin nodded, and then spat red into the mud at his feet. 'Sound the bells, Wise Kharkanas. Retrieve your refugees to line the streets. Roll out the crimson bandages to make suitable bunting and streamers. Lay out the weapons to make the aisle for our king and queen. Something notched and stained underfoot – was not iron our first glory, captain? The very birth of the Tiste, if the legends are to be believed.' He waved a hand more red than white. 'As suits the moment.'

'Milord, I saw a dragon. Overhead. In the storm-clouds.'

'I did not.'

Kellaras frowned, only to realize that he had nothing more to say.

'Captain.'

'Milord?'

'My brother still stands alone. Are you not of his Houseblades? Take your surviving company and join him.'

*And what of you, his brother?* 'Yes sir.' Kellaras turned to gather his Houseblades. As they drew up around him, he saw Silchas Ruin wander off, westward, as if he would now walk to Kharkanas. Kellaras then glanced to the southeast, in time to see the last of the Hust Legion reach the crest. The sound of its iron, faint yet clear, rode the icy tears of the wind.

*     *     *

They reached the road, the valley behind them. Prazek drew off his gore-spattered gauntlets and dropped them to the ground. 'Well,' he said around a cut lip already scabbed black, 'that was a sorry day.'

Dathenar slowly hunched over, still struggling to regain his breath from a mace-blow that had driven him from his feet. '"Sorry", is it? No, friend, set sorrow aside. Disband this beleaguered company of regrets. I see no blessing in their sordid attendance.'

'They line the road like refugees,' Prazek said, spitting.

'And would seek the shelter of rationalization, as befits their desperate need. But these are modest roofs, and the crowds jostle beneath each one, as would a family of fools breeding out of their house, too many bodies and not enough rooms. Shall we build additions? Extend this paltry roof? Bah, let's just breed some more.'

'And to this you say?'

Dathenar shrugged. 'Why, I say, fuck you in your fuckery. But we are right, friend. Regrets breed regrets, a spawn unceasing in humping zeal. At the last, we are less than animals. For all our claim to nature's graces, we are absent dignity.'

Prazek considered his friend's words for a moment. Then he glanced around, at the figures shuffling past. 'See this current,' he said in a low mutter, 'and here I am, snagged, tugged and frayed.' Abruptly he sat down on the cold, wet ground.

After a moment, Dathenar did the same.

'I have often wondered,' mused Prazek, 'at the mind of certain of our fellows, those for whom the hunt incites a flush of zeal, the eyes bright as a child's. I have seen the arrow strike true. Some noble creature in a glade, head lifted in alarm, only to crumple to the iron bite. By your confession, friend, I see now what is slain. Dignity is the natural stance of beasts. Their innate essence, which, perhaps, the hunters in their moral paucity envy, and so grow vicious. To slay out of spite, ah, Dathenar, the years are stripped away.'

Dathenar sighed. 'Behold the child revealed, flushed and bright, posing beside the kill. If we war against nature, why, we war against dignity itself. Our sordid dominion makes ascension a lie. The truth is, we *descend*, with all the dignity of a disease.'

Prazek wiped at his face, wincing at his torn lip. 'Salvage me some hope, I beg you.'

Dathenar reached across to settle a hand on his friend's shoulder. 'Well,' he said, 'there is this.'

*     *     *

Wareth remained at Rebble's side, holding the man's weight as best he could as they clambered up the last few paces to reach the crest. The moment they arrived, Rebble reached up and gripped Wareth's arm, just above the elbow, and tugged hard.

'In the name of our Mother, Wareth, set me down.'

Together, they settled to the ground, Wareth being as gentle as he could with his friend. Rebble settled on to his back, eyes filled with pain as he stared skyward. 'I make it thirty-seven,' he said.

Wareth looked down, saw the blood still streaming from the sword-wound in Rebble's chest. But the man wasn't coughing blood – there was that mercy, at least. 'Thirty-seven?'

Rebble lifted a trembling hand. 'Doubt I can make it,' he said, 'but I'll give it a try.'

Wareth wiped at his face. 'You're not making any sense,' he said.

'Tell me, Wareth, did I see true? Toras Redone kneeling beside a body? Was it Faror Hend who fell?'

*To earn such grief? Such wails and tearing at hair?* 'No, Rebble. Galar Baras.'

'Ah. Then. I see.'

'She drew a knife and would have cut her own throat. Faror Hend prevented her, twisted the weapon free. In her face there was vengeance and satisfaction, as she glared down at the broken woman. Rebble, such things shake me.'

Others of the broken legion were settling here and there. Wareth saw drawn faces, expressions taut with the pain of wounds. But even then, something seemed to be missing.

'Crack the knuckles,' Rebble said.

'What?'

'One for every life I took, every fucked up stupidity I went and did. I make it four, for today. Not sure they all died, though. I'm thinking they didn't. I'm hoping they didn't. Anyway,' he smiled up at the heavy clouds, 'thirty-seven. Rebble's idiot toll.' He paused then, and shifted his gaze slightly, enough to meet Wareth's eyes. 'Them Bonecasters . . . quite the gift they gave us . . .'

Baffled, Wareth said, 'I still don't know what it was.'

'Truly?'

Wareth nodded.

Rebble laughed, and then winced.

'What gift, Rebble? What did that ritual do?'

'No more lies. That's all. No lying to anyone else. But mostly, no lying to yourself.'

Frowning, Wareth shook his head. 'I've never lied to myself.'

Rebble studied him for a moment, and then said, 'So, you never even noticed.'

'No. I suppose not.'

Rebble brought his hands together over his belly. He began cracking his knuckles.

'I need to know,' Wareth said. 'Why did you protect me? Back in the pit? Why did you bother?'

'Why did I bother?'

'Being my friend.'

Knuckles cracked. 'I don't know,' Rebble replied, and then he smiled. 'I guess you had an honest face.'

Wareth settled back on to his haunches. He saw now that everyone among the Hust had halted their march, gathering in silent clumps. *No lies, is that what is missing here? In these faces? These raw stares into the distance?*

Listar still lived, but he didn't know about Rance. So many of the other officers drawn up from the prisoner ranks were dead. They'd come to the fore in the Legion's desperate withdrawal, holding back the enemy and giving up their lives to do so.

Wareth's throat was still raw from his frantic shouting. And yet, impossibly, the Hust had responded to his desperate commands, and when Prazek and then Dathenar curled their companies around, folding them into the retreat, the Hust Legion's day of battle was done. Through it all, Toras Redone was nowhere to be seen, until the very end.

He listened to his friend cracking his knuckles until the sound of bones popping stopped.

Rebble never managed all thirty-seven, and, as simply as that, his only friend was gone.

He edged closer, to lift Rebble's head and rest it on his thighs. He groomed the man's beard with his fingers, pulling at the knots,and studied the peaceful repose of the face, knowing that he would never again see it animate, that hard grin, the sly flick of the gaze, and the raging temper that hung like a storm-cloud behind everything.

*Rebble, my friend. You weren't any more than what you were. I treasured you. How I treasured you.*

Someone moved to halt at his side and Wareth looked up into Listar's face. 'He's gone, Listar.'

'Just the two of us, then,' Listar replied.

'Two?'

'Who stood between them and the Cats.' Listar paused and then said, 'The coward and the man who wanted to die. The honourable one – why, as you say, now he's dead.'

Wareth considered the man's words, and their harsh, blunt tone. 'No lies,' he said.

'I couldn't do it, Wareth. I couldn't kill anyone. All I did was defend.'

'So it was with most of them, Listar. I saw it, on all sides. That's how I knew that we would never win. Wouldn't yield either. Just stand there, dying. I saw it, Listar, though I didn't understand it. Not until Rebble explained. The ritual—'

'Yes, my beloved gift to you all.'

'You were sent.'

'I was sent. But what did I ask for? From them? Has anyone even asked me that? They said we needed something to absolve us, to cleanse us, to sweep away the curse of our crimes.'

Wareth stroked Rebble's cooling brow. 'Is that not what you asked, Listar?'

'No. Not quite.'

'Then . . . what?'

'I wanted us – all of us – to accept who we were. To face our crimes, our cruel pasts, our vicious thoughts. If we're to feel, Wareth – I told the Bonecasters – if we're to *feel*, then do not let us hide, or run from those feelings. Do not let us pretend.'

Wareth lifted his gaze, squinted up at Listar.

'You still don't get it,' Listar said. 'You're not the only coward. Not even close. This Hust Legion, all these convicts. Wareth, most of them are cowards. Those men we faced down in the pit, the ones eager to get at the women. Was it just lust? No. Rapists are many things, but mostly they're cowards, the kind that has to feed on victims. It's a different kind of cowardice from yours, Wareth, but it's still cowardice. Why did they all hate you? Because you were the sole coward not in hiding.' The man paused then, looking away. 'Look at them, Wareth. Blessed by my gift. Seeing them, I think that Rebble's the lucky one.'

With that, Listar stumbled away.

Wareth stared after him. *No lies. Well, that's no proof against being stupid.*

*Shit, I forgot to ask him about Rance.*

*   *   *

'Priest.'

Endest Silann looked up, saw a woman in the livery of a Houseblade. His attention proved brief, as inevitably he resumed staring at his hands where they rested on his thighs.

'Are you fit to stand?' the woman asked.

'What do you want?'

'We need a burial place consecrated.'

He thought to laugh at that, glancing briefly at the valley floor below, with its hundreds of corpses, its dead and dying horses.

'Not there, priest. But it's not far. We're building a cairn for just one man.'

Endest held up his hands. 'Tell me,' he said, 'what do you see?'

'Old blood.'

'Anything else?'

'What else would there be to see?'

He nodded. 'Just so. Her eyes are gone. Not even a scar remains. She's left me.'

A few moments passed. 'Ah, you were that one, then. From the market. The one who spoke with a dragon. More to the point, you were one of the priests who stood against Hunn Raal. Now I wonder, why is no one attending you?'

1084

'I sent them away.'

She stepped forward and hooked a hand under his left arm, lifting him to his feet. 'You did damned well, priest. Gave us a chance. We just didn't take it.'

He couldn't make much sense of this woman, or what she truly wanted from him, but he let her guide him up the track. They passed through the exhausted soldiers of the Hust, but the sight of so many broken men and women was too much, and Endest dropped his gaze, studied the snow and sleet-crusted mud and stone at his feet.

After ascending a short slope they left the track, and the woman drew him over to where a huge old man was busy piling the last of the stones to a cairn. This man's breaths were harsh, and when he glanced over at them, Endest saw why. He had lost most of his nose. But the injury was old. He wore the same livery as the woman.

All around them, on this faint summit, horse hoofs had stamped deep into the mud, and nearby waited three horses, one bearing a filigreed saddle.

The woman spoke to the other man. 'They gave up, then?'

'They didn't like it, Pelk. Didn't like it at all. But it seemed they didn't want to cross me.'

'No one wants to cross you, Rancept.'

She finally halted Endest close to the cairn. 'In there,' she said.

'Who?'

'Lord Venes Turayd.'

'The lord is dead?'

The woman glanced at her companion, who wiped at his weeping nose and then shrugged. She then turned back to Endest Silann and said, 'I should think so, by now.'

*       *       *

Faror Hend found Prazek and Dathenar sitting on the muddy road. Both men still wore their chain hauberks, but their helms and gauntlets were on the ground beside them, and from the scabbarded swords sounded a low, incessant mutter.

Her own blade was silent. Drawing off her helm, she felt the blessed cold wind on her brow, and the low moan of the iron that had filled her head was suddenly gone. 'I made them take her away,' she said. 'Under guard. Galar Baras died from a broken neck, when his wounded horse threw him. She wanted to fight, you know. She wanted to throw herself into the fray, so that someone could kill her. I would have welcomed that, and indeed, I would have joined her. Instead, she was too drunk to stand.'

Dathenar nodded. 'We are vulnerable, one and all, Faror Hend, to the madness of our desires. So much of the longing in our lives is revealed as a longing for death. These guises are myriad, but none are available to us now, nor for our lives to come.'

'Absent the sweet and lustful lies,' added Prazek, 'the future appears bleak.'

'Too eager with the wagging finger, the iteration of old warnings renewed one more time. All our secrets lead us to grief.' Dathenar grunted and then slowly climbed to his feet. 'I am soaked through.' His eyes shifted and he half turned to the west. 'They must be drawing near the city by now.'

Faror Hend felt like weeping, for what she knew not. There was no lack of reasons; rather, there was a vicious crowd of them, so many before her she was unable to choose among them. *Betrothed. Kagamandra Tulas, hear my confession. I cannot love a hero, cannot love an honourable man, cannot give myself to him as one should. I have nothing to match your worth, and should I try, I will die. It may take centuries before my flesh catches up, but it will, eventually. The soul is weak. It can wilt to a chilled breath. But the husk abides, with few hints to the hollowness it hides.*

'We should gather the Legion,' said Prazek, rising to join Dathenar. 'Midnight draws near, I should think. We must march to our train, to the wagons.'

'Prazek,' said Dathenar, turning to face his friend. 'We abandoned the bridge. A step taken, one to either side, and into the benighted waters we did plunge.'

'It's said none ever rise again from the Dorssan Ryl.'

'I feel the same, friend.'

Faror Hend looked to the south, and saw there a small group of riders. They were still distant, but the man in the lead looked tall, sitting straight in the saddle, with a mane of grey hair.

*Of course.* 'I will leave you to it, then,' she said to Prazek and Dathenar.

'Faror Hend?'

'You spoke of a bleak future. I go to meet mine.'

*         *         *

Unaccompanied, Lord Anomander, First Son of Darkness, sat on his horse, gaze fixed on the valley below. He merely tilted his head for an instant in Kellaras's direction as the captain rode up to halt beside him.

'Milord, your brother has set out for Kharkanas. He is walking. We should be able to catch him.'

Anomander seemed momentarily confused. 'Kharkanas?'

'Milord, there will be a wedding. The details of peace.'

'The details of peace,' Anomander repeated. 'But Kellaras, there is no peace within me.'

Kellaras said nothing.

Then his lord continued, 'No, leave them to it. I will ride to my brother, to Andarist. I will yield vengeance.' He turned then, giving Kellaras his full attention. 'Her name is Pelk, yes? Perhaps, will she be returning there as well?'

'I do not know, milord. It is possible. Do you wish me to accompany you?'

Anomander smiled. 'I would welcome your company, Kellaras.'

Nodding, the captain collected the reins. 'Now, milord?'

'Yes. Now.'

Side by side, they set out, into the north.

*         *         *

Wreneck took little notice of the two riders who came down into the valley from the northeast. Instead, he continued walking among the corpses of the fallen Legion soldiers. The ground under them was torn and savaged, as if it had been chewed. He used his spear as if it was a staff in order to keep his balance as he stepped over bodies, crouching down every now and then to study lifeless faces.

Pain and death made them hard to recognize, and even the memories to which he clung were now blurred in his mind's eye.

He was cold, and the night was strangely grey, as if trapped inside a cloud of ash that refused to settle. The dying horses had finally gone quiet. Crows came down like night's tattered flags, and they too had nothing to complain about, yielding a silence to the field that seemed almost suffocating.

One frozen visage drew his attention and he made his way over to stand above it, looking down. *Is this one of them? He might be. I have seen him before. Yes, this is one of them. Someone got to him first. But it doesn't matter who got here first. It only matters who comes last.*

*I said I would avenge Jinia, and now here I am.*

He brought the spear around and tilted the iron point down, edging it forward until it rested on the breast of the dead man.

*I will stab deep. That's all I need to do. His ghost is here. Close. I can't see them any more, but I know they're here. They have nowhere else to go.*

*Stab deep. Push the blade in, slicing through the leather, the wool, the skin. This is what vengeance means. What I'm doing right here.*

Hearing a sound he glanced up. Two women sat astride horses made of knotted grasses and twigs. They sat in silence, watching him from a dozen paces away.

He didn't know either of them. They didn't match the faces he was looking for. Wreneck returned his attention to the dead man. He leaned on the spear, but the leather armour would not give. *It needs a thrust.* He drew the weapon back, and then poked it against the body.

'He's not bothered,' said one of the women. 'Go ahead, if you must. But abusing a corpse is unseemly, don't you think?'

*Unseemly?* Wreneck looked around at all the dead bodies. Shaking his head, he poked a second time. The leather armour was tough. He leaned closer then, to find what had killed the man. He saw a nick in the corpse's throat, where blood had sprayed and then poured out on to the ground. It didn't seem like much, but no other wounds were visible.

He prodded a third time, hard against the chest, and then stepped back. He turned to the two women. 'It's all right now,' he said. 'I'm done avenging what they did to her. I'm going home now.'

The woman who had spoken earlier now leaned forward on her saddle. 'And I, sir, am your witness. She is avenged.'

'What's your name?' Wreneck asked. 'I need to know, since you've witnessed and everything.'

'Threadbare.'

The golden-haired woman beside Threadbare said, 'And I am T'riss.' She smiled. 'Your witnesses.'

Satisfied, Wreneck nodded. Home was a long way away and he had a lot of walking to do. He would salvage a cloak from one of these bodies, with maybe a second one for a blanket.

*Jinia, it's done. I feel better. I hope you will, too.*

*Sometimes it takes being a child to do what's right.*

*　　*　　*

'What was all that about?' T'riss asked. 'You send children into war now, Tiste?'

'His blade was clean,' Threadbare replied. She raised her gaze skyward. 'They're gone, right? Not still winging around up there in the gloom and clouds?'

'Gone, for now.'

Threadbare sighed, gathering up the braided reins. 'I think I prefer it this way,' she said.

'Prefer what?'

'Coming too late to fight. Missing the whole fucking mess. I've seen enough of it, T'riss. Look around here. All these sad corpses. It's a stupid argument that ends up with someone dead and the others looking guilty behind all that satisfaction.' She looked over at T'riss. 'I am riding to Kharkanas, to find my people. What about you?'

'There is a forest,' T'riss replied, 'where waits another Azathanai. I think I need to see him.'

'What for?'

'He will know of me. Who I once was.'

'That makes a difference?'

'What do you mean?'

Threadbare shrugged. 'Whoever you were isn't who you are now. Sounds to me you're heading for confusion and probably misery. Maybe some secrets should stay secrets. That ever occurred to you?'

T'riss smiled. 'All the time. The thing is, we almost clashed. Here, in the Valley of Tarns. Had I come in time. Had he awakened his power. The dragons would have . . . enjoyed that.' She paused, and then shrugged. 'But something happened. Someone, I think, held him back. Someone pretty much saved the world. I'm curious, aren't you? About this Tiste who refused my Azathanai brother?'

Threadbare studied T'riss for a time, and then sighed. 'Where is this forest, then?'

'Just outside the city.'

'So, it seems we ride together for a little while longer.'

'Yes. Is that not delightful?'

Threadbare saw the boy nearing the northern ridge of the valley. 'That vengeance of his,' she said. 'He did it right, I think.'

'The dead weep for him.'

'They do? In pity?'

'No,' T'riss replied. 'In envy.'

Threadbare kicked her mount forward. 'Fucking ghosts,' she muttered. *I'm of a mind to join them.*

＊　　＊　　＊

Renarr followed Lord Vatha Urusander into the old throne room. Within the spacious chamber, lightness and darkness waged a belaboured contest, too sombre to be a battle, too desultory to be a war. This was a sullen acceptance, as of two powers recognizing the other's necessity. Definition, Urusander might say, by opposition.

Candles and a brazier illuminated one of the two thrones that had been set up side by side on the dais. Its wood was white, polished pearlescent, and over the arms gold-threaded silks had been draped. The other throne seemed to emanate negation, making it difficult to discern, as if some lifeless mote stained the eye.

Mother Dark had been seated on that throne, though upon Urusander's entrance into the chamber she now stood. At the foot of the dais and flanking the approach waited the two High Priestesses, both turning to face Father Light. Syntara was resplendent in her sunburst vestments, her brocade glittering and her braided hair looking like ropes of gold wire. Heavy white makeup disguised the fresh cuts on her face.

High Priestess Emral Lanear – whom Renarr had never seen before – wore a black robe, untouched by ornamentation. Her onyx face looked distraught, with deep lines bracketing her mouth. She was older than Syntara, her features almost too plain in the absence of paint and colour. A woman, concluded Renarr with a mental smile, inviting darkness.

This moment, Renarr understood, belonged to the surface. Nothing here announced depth or solidity. The ceremony would be in the manner of all ceremonies: momentary and ephemeral. A sudden focus, filled with intent, which would ring hollow for ever afterwards.

She thought it fitting.

As Urusander paused a few paces in front of her, Renarr moved off to the right, towards the flanking row of braziers suspended from three-legged iron stands. The warmth was welcome but would soon become oppressive. She found herself drawing closer to where Hunn Raal stood.

The man's faint smirk was just as welcoming as the heat from the glowing embers: a thing of familiarity, a wry reminder of the occasion's falsity. Mockery attended the moment, and in this respect Hunn Raal belonged to this scene. He had recovered from the sorcerous battle, if one chose to ignore the ruptured pads of the palms of his hands, the gaping, bloodless fissures streaking his fingers. That, and the incessant low tremble that the destriant fought with sips from his flask. Still, he stood in the manner of a man wholly satisfied.

She considered this scene, caught as it was on the cusp of dawn, when night and day fell into their eternal, exhausted battle, against the backdrop of a bleeding sky, and wondered how it would be seen in posterity. *Necessity's bared teeth, transformed into smiles of joy in the centuries to come. That vast span of wilful forgetfulness we call history.* Looking round the chamber, she saw but one other witness who might be asking the same questions. *Rise Herat. The historian. I once attended one of his lectures. A night of self-hatred, I recall, uttered in the lifeless tones of an anatomist lecturing surgeons. Only, the body on the slab was his own. He was past even enjoying the pain he inflicted on himself.*

*When the historian's love of history dies . . . alas, there is nowhere to go, no place to which one might flee and then hide.*

*Unless one chooses to live a life insensate.* She glanced again at Hunn Raal, and saw how the man and the historian more or less faced one another, and as she noted this Vatha Urusander stepped forward, moving in between the two men as he approached the dais, and the woman who would become his wife.

He halted at the halfway point when Mother Dark suddenly spoke. 'A moment, if you will, Lord Urusander.'

The man tilted his head, and then shrugged. 'As much time as you need,' he replied.

She seemed to consider that invitation for a breath or two, and then resumed. 'This will be suitably written, as befits such an occasion. Two wounded halves . . . conjoined. The High Priestesses will speak, each on behalf of her . . . her aspect. And what is conjoined will be, one expects, *healed*.' She paused, studying each person present, and then continued with an air of impatience. 'The elaboration can await its writing. What we are witness to here is a bargain sealed in blood. Many have died to see our hands joined, Vatha Urusander, and I am in no mood to celebrate.'

Renarr saw Syntara's flash of anger, but then Urusander was speaking.

'Mother Dark. On behalf of my soldiers, I once petitioned the highborn – and you – in the name of justice.' He waved dismissively. 'This was not a challenge to my faith in you.'

'No,' she said, 'that challenge came from elsewhere. Tell me then, will you now deny the title of Father Light?'

'It seems that I cannot.'

'No,' she agreed. 'It seems that you cannot.'

'But this was not what I asked for.'

'Nor is this my answer to your request for justice.'

'Then, Mother Dark, we are understood?'

'We are, Vatha, as best we can be.'

He nodded then, and Renarr saw how the tension left his body.

'Rise Herat,' said Mother Dark.

The historian took a single step forward. 'Mother Dark?'

'Our priestesses here will reconvene with you. Take a side chamber. Together, the three of you should be able to invent an appropriate retelling of this fated and fateful union. Concoct, if you will, a marriage to celebrate.'

'Then, Mother, there is to be no ceremony here?'

Ignoring the question, Mother Dark's attention shifted then, fixed upon Renarr. 'I do not know you,' she said. 'Only that you appeared a step behind Vatha Urusander. But this detail alone suffices. Will you voice a vow to never speak of what has taken place here?'

'I eagerly await the official version, Mother Dark,' Renarr replied. 'And shall speak of no other. Why, already I see the gilt bright upon my memories of this glorious ceremony.'

Mother Dark's lips creased slightly in what might have been a suppressed smile. 'Do you so vow?'

'I do,' Renarr said, nodding.

Vatha Urusander said, 'Mother Dark, Renarr is my adopted daughter.'

'In title? What of your son?'

'My son shall inherit as much of what I possess as he may desire. Renarr has refused all symbols of recognition, beyond my old man's harmless affectation in naming her my daughter.'

'She indulges you.'

'Just so,' Urusander answered.

Mother Dark's gaze shifted now to Hunn Raal. 'You name yourself the Mortal Sword of Light, and I see in your belt a sceptre fashioned of Elemental Light. When were you planning on placing that sceptre into the hands of its rightful possessor?'

Hunn Raal's smirk tightened slightly, and then, with an easy shrug, he drew the sceptre from his belt and approached Urusander. 'Milord,' he said. 'Father Light. This sceptre was forged in your name, for this day, and for all the days of your rule to follow.'

When he held it out, Vatha Urusander took it and immediately returned his attention to Mother Dark.

His smirk returning, Hunn Raal bowed and stepped back.

'Husband,' said Mother Dark. 'Will you now join me here, and take your throne?'

Urusander hesitated, and then said, 'Wife, I am unused to the ways of rule, much less faith.'

'Rule is but a flavour, a scent in the air, Urusander. Little different from your habits of command in your legion. I have found that it is best maintained by selective silence.'

'I have found it so, as well,' Urusander replied. 'Although, on occasion, those under my command begin to presume too much. I have, thus far, been reluctant to effect . . . discipline. Such acts must be unequivocal and perfectly timed.'

'Then you understand the nature of rule as well as I do. It is, as you say, a shame when the ones being ruled lose sight of the example we would set. Now, as to faith, well, seek no guidance from me, Urusander, for I have surely failed in that test. I expect, however, our priestesses will find the days and nights ahead to be busy ones, as they fulfil, with zeal, the fullest transcription of their responsibilities, and all the observances they deem sacred in our names.'

'I share your confidence,' Urusander replied. 'And in the end, I am certain that we will be told the manner of worship to be expected and, presumably, demanded from our believers.'

'Probably,' Mother Dark agreed. 'We can but eagerly await such delineations, and the time when you and I need not worry over our missteps born of ignorance.'

After a moment, Urusander resumed his approach to the dais. Mounting it, he paused in front of his throne and then, seeing the slotted scabbard awaiting the sceptre, settled the object into its place. Turning, he faced Mother Dark.

When she held out her right hand, he raised his, bringing it up beneath hers. Their hands clasped briefly before parting once more.

Facing the chamber, Mother Dark and Father Light stood for a moment, as if posing for posterity, before both sat down on their thrones.

'That's it,' muttered Hunn Raal beside Renarr. 'Done.'

She turned to him. 'Recall his assertion,' she observed.

'His what?'

'He names Osserc his heir, Hunn Raal. We have witnessed, and so it is, as you say, done.'

Something dark flitted across his expression, then was gone, his smile returning. 'Ah, the boy. Yes indeed. Well, he was the pup in my shadow, and should he ever return . . .' Shrugging, Hunn Raal turned away.

Closer to the thrones, both High Priestesses were speaking with their deities, quietly, for the moment at least.

Swinging round to follow Hunn Raal, Renarr found herself facing the historian.

'I would know more about you,' he said to her. 'For the official version.'

'Invent what you need,' Renarr replied.

'I would rather not misrepresent you.'

'You would have me the detritus to cling to, amidst the flood of lies?'

'Something like that.'

'Perhaps later, historian,' she said as she reached the door 'I will give you all that you need, and more.'

* * *

Renarr did her best, then, to walk away from all of it. Vatha Urusander had been given a series of opulent rooms, as if anticipating a delay in the consummation of his marriage to Mother Dark, and it was in these rooms that she found her momentary refuge.

Witnessing the battle had left her drained. The sorcery had been shocking, appalling. It had been unfortunate that Hunn Raal had not only survived but prevailed, inasmuch as he had been the last one left standing.

In the company of the men and women who sold their bodies, and the near-feral pack of children swarming the ridge, Renarr had watched the sordid consequences of the failed magicks as soldiers clashed in the valley below. She had tried to imagine her mother down there, in the press, commanding her company in the slaying of fellow Tiste. But that proved difficult. Something about it did not – could not – fit, and it was some time before she realized that her mother would never have participated in such a travesty.

Military honour was bound to service. The virtue of honour could not stand alone, could not stand for itself. Service sustained honour, when nothing else could. Tearing it away from all that gave it meaning reduced the soldier to a thug, a bully. She had, with that realization, stepped back, her attention shifting to all the children gathered now along the crest to watch the killing below.

They were a neglected, contrary lot. Weak and brutal, small but hardened, broken but sharp-edged. And like any broken thing, they existed in the realm of the discarded. When they looked up, they saw women eager to lift their skirts and men exposing ornate painted codpieces. They saw other men and women walking the camps, swords belted at their hips, coarse in humour and coldly practical in their needs.

*Lessons on a pragmatic life. Whatever we do as adults, we*

*make in our children more of what we are. Is there no end to this? Scholars speak of progress, but I fear now that they are mistaken. This is not progress that we see, it is elaboration. Nothing of the old ways ever goes away, it just hides beneath modernity's confusion.*

No, her mother would have refused the charade. She would, indeed, have forced Urusander to act. In the name of honour. In the name of the soldier.

Renarr found herself the sole occupant of Urusander's intended quarters, with not even a servant present. She wandered through the rooms, stirring the ashes of her regret. *A single ember remains, and surely it shall burn me, and my name, for ever more. But some things we do not choose. Some things are chosen for us.*

She heard the outer door open and then shut. Returning to the main room she saw Vatha Urusander. He seemed startled to see her, but only momentarily. He smiled. 'I am glad to find you here, Renarr.'

'Is she done with your company already?'

'It has been a long time since we last slept. There are storms in our heads, and storms between us. Of the latter, I see a calm ahead. Of the former . . .' He shrugged, and walked towards the window overlooking the broad sward behind the Citadel.

'Will you deal with Hunn Raal?' she asked, drawing closer to him.

His back was broad, but it now belonged to an ageing man. There was sadness in this detail.

'Deal with him? I had ambitions there, didn't I? He names himself my Mortal Sword. This should make plain who serves whom.'

'And does it?' She hesitated a few steps behind him, watching as he leaned forward close to the windowpane and looked down.

'A keep's refuse,' he muttered. 'How it backs the wall, below the chutes. I wonder, do we build houses simply to keep the garbage out? It should be buried.'

'It buries itself,' Renarr replied. 'Eventually.'

'Hunn Raal deems himself immune. Perhaps he is right in that. Leave him to Syntara. He's her problem, not mine. Mother Dark has the right of it. We step back, saying little. The condition of our people is for them to decide. I considered setting forth my laws, my foundations upon which a just society could rise. But how soon before my words are twisted? My premises twisted and suborned? How soon before we, in our mortal natures, corrupt such laws, each time in answer to a wholly self-serving need?'

'Have we seen the last of honourable men and women, Vatha Urusander?'

He straightened once more, but did not turn to face her. 'The brutes are in ascension, Renarr. Against that, reason has no chance. You think the blood has ended? I fear it is only beginning.'

'Then, sir, nothing has been solved.'

'I am not the man to solve this,' Urusander said. 'But,' he added after a moment, 'you knew as much, didn't you?'

'Yes.'

'What of my son?'

'His judgement was in error.'

'Error?'

'A young man bereft of responsibility will yearn for it,' she replied. 'A young man will see the virtues of duty and honour as shining things, harsh and not subject to compromise. From such a position, he may well make mistakes, but they remain well meant.'

Still he would not face her. 'Something in you is broken.'

'Something in me is broken.'

'My son killed the man you loved. He . . . misapprehended the situation.'

'Yes.'

'Yet, it seems, you have forgiven him.'

'I wish,' she said, 'you had killed Hunn Raal. I wish you would stand behind your sense of justice.'

He grunted. 'No exceptions, no compromises. Had I done what was right, each and every time . . .'

'Instead, you did nothing, and now here you stand, Vatha Urusander. Father Light.'

'Yes, my blinding gift.' He was silent for a time, and then he said, 'Have you seen it yet?'

'What?'

'My portrait. In the corridor on the approach to these chambers. Kadaspala did well, I think.'

'I am afraid I did not notice it,' Renarr said. 'I give little regard to art, especially the compromised kind.'

'Ah, then, are all portraits a compromise? In his sour moments, I think Kadaspala would agree with you.' He leaned both hands on the windowsill. 'Well,' he said, 'it seems that I am not to be forgiven.'

'Only your son.'

She saw him nod, and then he sighed and said, 'Tell them, will you, of the likeness. So deftly, so honestly captured by that blind man's hand.'

'He was not blind when he painted you, I think.'

'Wasn't he? No, demonstrably not, as far as that goes.'

'Vatha Urusander,' said Renarr, 'there will be justice.'

She saw him nod again, in the instant before her knife sank deep beneath his left shoulder blade, stilling the beat of his heart. Unblinking, she stepped back, leaving the dagger in his back. He tilted forward, forehead striking the leaded window, before his legs gave out and he fell to the floor at her feet.

Looking down, she saw the smile on his face. Peaceful, content, lifeless.

*　　*　　*

*Nothing ends. There is matter and there is energy, and some believe these two the only things in existence. But a third exists. It infuses both matter and energy, and yet also stands alone. Let us call it potential. Only in the realm of potential can we act, to effect changes upon all existence. Indeed, it is the realm in which we live, we living things, in our stubborn battle with success and failure.*

*Yet the truth remains. Of the two, success and failure, only one ends the game.*

*Now, poet, I see the shock writ deep upon your lined face, and yet it must be clear to you, even in this moment of despair, that love was at the heart of this tale, and now we must once more settle back and take breath, steadying ourselves for what is still to come.*

*The warriors wallow in what they will, in all that they make of the world, which is little more than destruction and suffering. Recall the child with the stone, on her knees in the grass, a boy's crushed face beneath her? Such is the glory of the belligerent.*

*Revel in it, if you're of the mind to.*

*What comes next, my friend, is entirely another kind of glory.*

*What is the secret of sorcery? It is potential. Now then, on the dawn of magic's burgeoning, let us see what they make of it.*

STEVEN ERIKSON'S

# THE MALAZAN BOOK OF THE FALLEN

*The genre-defining epic series*

'Homeric in scope and vision . . . a story that never
fails to thrill and entertain . . . a saga that lives up
to its name, both intellectually and in its dramatic,
visually rich and lavish storytelling'
SFSITE

### GARDENS OF THE MOON
Bled dry by interminable warfare, infighting and
confrontations with Anomander Rake and his Tiste
Andii, the Malazan Empire simmers with discontent.
Sinister forces gather as the gods themselves
prepare to play their hand . . .

### DEADHOUSE GATES
In the Holy Desert Raraku, a long prophesied uprising
has begun and an untried commander battles to save
the lives of thirty thousand refugees. War and betrayal,
intrigue and roiling magic collide as destinies
are shaped and legends born . . .

## MEMORIES OF ICE
The ravaged continent of Genabackis has given birth
to a terrifying new empire: the Pannion Domin. But
something more malign threatens this world. The
Warrens are poisoned and rumours abound that the
Crippled God is unchained and intent on revenge . . .

## HOUSE OF CHAINS
In Northern Genabackis, a raiding party of tribal
warriors descends from the mountains into the
southern lands. For one among them – Karsa Orlong –
it is the beginning of an extraordinary destiny . . .

## MIDNIGHT TIDES
After decades of internecine warfare, the tribes of
the Tiste Edur have united under the Warlock King.
But ancient forces are awakening and the impending
struggle is but a pale reflection of a far more
profound, primal battle . . .

## THE BONEHUNTERS
The prospect of laying siege to the ancient fortress
of Y'Ghatan makes the Malaz 14th army uneasy,
however this is but a sideshow. The Crippled God
has been granted a place in the pantheon – a schism
threatens and mortal blood will be spilled . . .

## REAPER'S GALE
The Letherii Empire is in turmoil. And the Edur fleet
draws ever closer. Warriors, gods and wanderers
converge. Soon there will be a reckoning – and
it will be on an unimaginable scale . . .

## TOLL THE HOUNDS
The Lord of Death stands at the beginning of a conspiracy that will shake the cosmos, but at its end there waits another. For Anomander Rake, Son of Darkness, has come to right an ancient and terrible wrong . . .

## DUST OF DREAMS
On Letherii, the exiled Malazan army prepares to march into the Wastelands to fight for an unknown cause against an enemy it has never seen. As others gather to confront their destinies, they all face a dread power that none can comprehend . . .

## THE CRIPPLED GOD
The Bonehunters are marching to an unknown fate; in Kurald Galain, they await the coming of the dread Tiste Liosan; the Forkrul Assail wish to cleanse the world; the Elder Gods, too, are seeking to return. And to do so, they will free a force of utter devastation from her eternal prison . . .

'Nobody does it better than Erikson . . . the best fantasy series around'
*SFFWORLD*